Tarzan's Quest

Tarzan of the Apes has heard only rumours of the Kavuru – a race of strange white savages. But when they steal the daughter of Muviro, chief of the Waziri, the Lord of the Jungle sets out in search of their legend-shrouded village on a mission of rescue – or, if need be, of revenge. He can not know that his trail runs close to that of a strange group of survivors of a crashed plane – including his beloved mate, Jane – who struggle for survival against the terrors of Africa and an even worse danger within their own party …

Tarzen the Magnificent

Tarzan encounters a lost race with uncanny mental powers, after which he revisits the lost cities of Cathne and Athne, and does battle in an arena with some of the jungle's most savage beasts …

Tarzan and the Forbidden City

Tarzan cared little for the fate of adventurer Brian Gregory, drawn to the legendary city of Ashair by the rumour of the Father of Diamonds, the world's hugest gem. But to the ape-man the tie of friendship is unbreakable, and Paul d'Arnot's pleas move him to agree to guide the expedition Gregory's father and sister have organized for his rescue. An expedition that will lead them to remote Ashair … as prisoners of its priests, doomed to die in loathsome rites.

Tarzan and the Foreign Legion

When the American bomber crashes in the jungles of enemy-held Sumatra, the survivors face the perils of a completely unknown world … and the RAF colonel who has flown with them as observer seems to compound their danger by going mad – stripping to a loincloth and throwing away his weapons except for his knife. But for Colonel John Clayton, Lord Greystoke, the hazards of wild beasts and a remorseless enemy are a familiar and joyously accepted challenge – a chance to return to his true identity of Tarzan of the Apes.

Tarzan and the Madman

When a young man – strong and bronzed and dressed only in a loin-cloth –
calls himself 'Tarzan', causes chaos and confusion among the jungle peoples,
only the true Lord of the Jungle can set things right – and salvage his rapidly-
tarnishing reputation.

Tarzan and the Castaways

Stranded on an uncharted Pacific island, Tarzan is forced to take command
of an ill-sorted party to insure their safety from a band of mutineers led by a
madman – a lost colony of Mayans, avid for potential victims for their barbarous human sacrifices, only adding to the danger. But the Lord of the
Jungle has unexpected allies, for cast away with his band is a shipment of
African animals unknown to the island, striking terror in the hearts of
Mayans and mutineers alike – but old friends and familiar antagonists to the
man brought up among them: Tarzan of the Apes.

Also by Edgar Rice Burroughs

Tarzan
1. Tarzan of the Apes (1912)
2. The Return of Tarzan (1913)
3. The Beasts of Tarzan (1914)
4. The Son of Tarzan (1914)
5. Tarzan and the Jewels of Opar (1916)
6. Jungle Tales of Tarzan (1916, 1917)
7. Tarzan the Untamed (1919, 1921)
8. Tarzan the Terrible (1921)
9. Tarzan and the Golden Lion (1922, 1923)
10. Tarzan and the Ant Men (1924)
11. Tarzan, Lord of the Jungle (1927, 1928)
12. Tarzan and the Lost Empire (1928)
13. Tarzan at the Earth's Core (1929)
14. Tarzan the Invincible (1930-1)
15. Tarzan Triumphant (1931)
16. Tarzan and the City of Gold (1932)
17. Tarzan and the Lion Man (1933, 1934)
18. Tarzan and the Leopard Men (1935)
19. Tarzan's Quest (1935, 1936)
20. Tarzan the Magnificent (1936, 1937)
21. Tarzan and the Forbidden City (1938)
22. Tarzan and the Foreign Legion (1947)
23. Tarzan and the Madman (1964)
24. Tarzan and the Castaways (1965)
25. Tarzan and the Valley of Gold (1965) (authorized sequel by Fritz Leiber)

Martian Tales*
1. A Princess of Mars (1917) (aka Under The Moons Of Mars, 1912)
2. The Gods of Mars (1918)
3. The Warlord of Mars (1919)
4. Thuvia, Maid of Mars (1920)
5. The Chessmen of Mars (1922)
6. The Master Mind of Mars (1927)
7. A Fighting Man of Mars (1930)
8. Swords of Mars (1934)
9. Synthetic Men of Mars (1938)
10. Llana of Gathol (1948)
11. John Carter of Mars (1941)

Pellucidar
1. At the Earth's Core (1914)
2. Pellucidar (1923)
3. Tanar of Pellucidar (1928)
4. Back to the Stone Age (1937)
5. Land of Terror (1944)
6. Savage Pellucidar (1963)

Venus
1. Pirates of Venus (1934)
2. Lost on Venus (1935)
3. Carson of Venus (1939)
4. Escape on Venus (1946)
5. The Wizard of Venus (1970)

The Land That Time Forgot
1. The Land That Time Forgot (1918)
2. The People That Time Forgot (1918)
3. Out of Time's Abyss (1918)

Other Science Fiction
The Moon Maid (1926) (aka The Moon Men)
Beyond the Farthest Star (1941)
The Lost Continent (1916)
The Monster Men (1929)
The Resurrection of Jimber-Jaw (1937)

The Mucker
1. The Mucker (1914)
2. The Return of the Mucker (1916)
3. The Oakdale Affair (1917)

Jungle Adventure Novels
The Man-Eater (1915)
The Cave Girl (1925)
The Eternal Lover (1925) (aka The Eternal Savage)
Jungle Girl (1932) (aka Land of the Hidden Men)
The Lad and the Lion (1938)

* Not available as SF Gateway eBooks

Tarzan's Quest and Other Tales

SF GATEWAY OMNIBUS

TARZAN'S QUEST
TARZAN THE MAGNIFICENT
TARZAN AND THE FORBIDDEN CITY
TARZAN AND THE FOREIGN LEGION
TARZAN AND THE MADMAN
TARZAN AND THE CASTAWAYS

Edgar Rice Burroughs

GOLLANCZ
LONDON

First published in Great Britain in 2014 by Gollancz
An imprint of the Orion Publishing Group
Orion House, 5 Upper St Martin's Lane, London WC2H 9EA
An Hachette UK Company

A CIP catalogue record for this book is
available from the British Library

ISBN 978 0 575 12919 1

1 3 5 7 9 10 8 6 4 2

Typeset by Jouve (UK), Milton Keynes

Printed and bounded by CPI Group (UK) Ltd, Croydon, CR0 4YY

The Orion Publishing Group's policy is to use papers
that are natural, renewable and recyclable products and
made from wood grown in sustainable forests. The logging
and manufacturing processes are expected to conform to
the environmental regulations of the country of origin.

www.orionbooks.co.uk
www.gollancz.co.uk

CONTENTS

ENTER THE SF GATEWAY ...

Towards the end of 2011, in conjunction with the celebration of fifty years of coherent, continuous science fiction and fantasy publishing, Gollancz launched the SF Gateway.

Over a decade after launching the landmark SF Masterworks series, we realised that the realities of commercial publishing are such that even the Masterworks could only ever scratch the surface of an author's career. Vast troves of classic SF and fantasy were almost certainly destined never again to see print. Until very recently, this meant that anyone interested in reading any of those books would have been confined to scouring second-hand bookshops. The advent of digital publishing changed that paradigm forever.

Embracing the future even as we honour the past, Gollancz launched the SF Gateway with a view to utilising the technology that now exists to make available, for the first time, the entire backlists of an incredibly wide range of classic and modern SF and fantasy authors. Our plan, at its simplest, was – and still is! – to use this technology to build on the success of the SF and Fantasy Masterworks series and to go even further.

The SF Gateway was designed to be the new home of classic science fiction and fantasy – the most comprehensive electronic library of classic SFF titles ever assembled. The programme has been extremely well received and we've been very happy with the results. So happy, in fact, that we've decided to complete the circle and return a selection of our titles to print, in these omnibus editions.

We hope you enjoy this selection. And we hope that you'll want to explore more of the classic SF and fantasy we have available. These are wonderful books you're holding in your hand, but you'll find much, much more ... through the SF Gateway.

www.sfgateway.com

INTRODUCTION

from The Encyclopedia of Science Fiction

Edgar Rice Burroughs (1875–1950) was a US writer whose early life was marked by numerous false starts and failures – at the time he began to write, at the age of 36, he was a pencil-sharpener salesman – but it would seem that the impulse to create the psychically charged Science-Fantasy dream-worlds that became his trademark territory was deep-set and powerful. Once he began to write, with a great rush of built-up energy, within two years he had initiated three of his four most important series. He never stopped.

Certainly the first of his published works has ever since its first appearance served as a successful escape from mid-life burdens and frustrations. *A Princess of Mars* (1917), which was originally published February–July 1912 in *All-Story* as 'Under the Moons of Mars' as by Norman Bean, opens the long Barsoom sequence of novels set on Mars (Barsoom). (Many of Burroughs's novels appeared first in magazines; we are giving only first book publications here).The long array of Barsoom tales established that planet as a venue for dream-like and interminable Planetary Romance sagas in which sf and fantasy protocols mixed indiscriminately as an enabling pretext and human men were preternaturally strong, due to the manly intensity of their native Earth gravity. *The Gods of Mars* (1918) and *The Warlord of Mars* (1919) further recount the exploits of John Carter as he variously befriends and battles various green, yellow and black Martians without the law, and wins the hand of the red-skinned (and oviparous) princess Dejah Thoris. The standard of storytelling and invention is high in the Barsoom books, *Chessmen* and *Swords* being particularly fine; but it has always been difficult for some critics to accept the Planetary Romance as being, in any cognitive sense, sf. Although Carter's adventures take place on another planet, he incontrovertibly travels there by magical means, and Barsoom itself is inconsistent and scientifically implausible to modern eyes. It is clear, however, that Burroughs's immense popularity has nothing to do with conventional sf virtues, for it depends on storylines and venues as malleable as dreams, exotic and dangerous and unending.

The long Tarzan saga came next (see below), occupying much of his time before the creation of his third major series. The Pellucidar novels based on the Hollow-Earth theory of John Cleves Symmes, began with *At the Earth's Core* (1922) and continued in *Pellucidar* (1923), *Tanar of Pellucidar* (1930),

Tarzan at the Earth's Core (1930) – a notable 'overlap' volume – *Back to the Stone Age* (1937), *Land of Terror* (1944) and *Savage Pellucidar* (1963). Pellucidar is perhaps the best of Burroughs's locales – a world without time where Dinosaurs and beast-men roam circularly forever – and is a perfect setting for bloodthirsty romantic adventure. The first of the series was filmed disappointingly as At the Earth's Core (*1976*).

His fourth series, the Venus sequence – created much later in Burroughs's career – concerns the exploits of spaceman Carson Napier on Venus, and consists of *Pirates of Venus* (1934), *Lost on Venus* (1935), *Carson of Venus* (1939) and *Escape on Venus* (1946). These books are not as stirring and vivid as the Barsoom series. A posthumous story, 'The Wizard of Venus', was published in *Tales of Three Planets* (1964) and subsequently as the title story of a separate paperback, *The Wizard of Venus* (1970). Two of the stories from *Tales of Three Planets*, 'Beyond the Farthest Star' (January 1942 *Blue Book*) and the posthumous 'Tangor Returns' (in *Tales of Three Planets* 1964), form the opening of a fifth series which Burroughs abandoned. They are of particular sf interest because they are his only tales with an interstellar setting. The two stories were subsequently republished as a paperback entitled *Beyond the Farthest Star* (1965).

Of Burroughs's non-series tales, perhaps the finest is *The Land that Time Forgot* (1924; revised in three volumes under the original magazine titles: *The Land that Time Forgot* 1962, *The People that Time Forgot* 1962 and *Out of Time's Abyss* 1962), set in the lost world of Caspak near the South Pole, and cunningly presenting in literal form – for animals here metamorphose through evolutionary stages – the dictum that ontogeny recapitulates phylogeny. The book was loosely adapted into two films, *The Land That Time Forgot* (*1975*) and *The People That Time Forgot* (*1977*). Also of interest is *The Moon Maid* (1926), which describes a civilization in the hollow interior of the Moon and a future Invasion of the Earth.

Among Burroughs's other books, those which can be claimed as sf include: *The Eternal Lover* (1925), a prehistoric adventure involving Time Travel featuring a character, Barney Custer, who reappears in the Ruritanian *The Mad King* (1926); *The Monster Men* (1929), a reworking of the Frankenstein theme, which should not be confused with *The Man without a Soul* (1922), which is not fantasy or sf; *The Cave Girl* (1925), another prehistoric romance; *Jungle Girl* (1932), about a lost civilization in Cambodia; and *Beyond Thirty* (1956), a story set in the twenty-second century after the collapse of European civilization.

It cannot be claimed that Burroughs's works aim at literary polish, or that their merits are intellectual. His lovers and his critics agree on this. Nevertheless, because of their efficient narrative style, and because Burroughs had a genius for highly-energized literalizations of dream-worlds, they have endured. Tarzan is a figure with the iconic density of Sherlock Holmes or Dracula. His 'rediscovery' during the 1960s was an astonishing publishing phenomenon, with the majority of his books being reprinted regularly. He had never been forgotten, however. Burroughs has probably had more imitators than any other sf writer, ranging from Otis Adelbert Kline in the 1930s to Kenneth Bulmer (writing as Alan Burt Akers) in the 1970s, with homages from much later writers like Terry Bisson in *Voyage to the Red Planet* (1990) and Hitoshi Yoshioka in *Nangun Kihei Taii John Carter* ['Southern Cavalry Captain John Carter'] (2005). Serious sf writers who owe a debt to Burroughs include Leigh Brackett, Ray Bradbury, Michael Moorcock and, above all, Philip José Farmer, whose Lord Grandrith and Ancient Opar novels are among the most enjoyable of latter-day Burroughs-inflected romances. Burroughs was posthumously inducted into the Science Fiction Hall of Fame in 2003. It was clear he belonged there.

The massive Tarzan saga, which begins with *Tarzan of the Apes and Other Tales* (Gollancz centenary omnibus, 2012), is just as much sf (or non-sf) as the Barsoom series. Though clearly influenced by H Rider Haggard, Burroughs did not attempt to imitate one of that writer's prime virtues: Haggard's effort to embed his tales in a vision of history, even though (to modern eyes) his work seems almost dementedly dated, certainly in its imperialist assumptions about race. Allan Quatermain's Africa, even though it is romantically exaggerated, can distress modern readers; but Tarzan's Africa is a Never Never Land, and must accepted as being no more governed by the reality principle than Barsoom. *Tarzan of the Apes* (1914), the story of an English aristocrat's son raised in the jungle by 'great apes' (of a non-existent species) as a kind of feral child or Noble Savage, was immensely popular from the beginning, and Burroughs continued producing sequels to the end of his career. In most of them Tarzan has unashamedly fantastic adventures, some of which – discovering lost cities and live Dinosaurs, being reduced to 18 in (46 cm) in height, visiting the Earth's core – marvellously evoke the conventions of Pulp sf. Burroughs did not perhaps entirely grasp the iconic power of his aristocrat/barbarian Lord in *Tarzan of the Apes* itself – which continues with *The Return of Tarzan* (1915), *The Beasts of Tarzan* (1916), *The Son of Tarzan* (1917) and *Tarzan and the Jewels of Opar* (1918), all relatively uninspired. *Jungle Tales of Tarzan* (1919) gains creative fire through its clever reminders of Rudyard Kipling's two *Jungle Books* (1894, 1895); and in 'Tarzan's First Love' (September 1916 *Blue Book*) Burroughs invokes Apes-as-Human material otherwise left tacit: which is to say Tarzan falls in love with an ape.

The final volume of this series of Tarzan omnibuses, *Tarzan's Quest and Other Tales*, contains *Tarzan's Quest* (1936), *Tarzan and the Forbidden City* (1938), *Tarzan the Magnificent* (1939) and *Tarzan and the Foreign Legion*

(1947), *Tarzan and the Madman* (1964) and *Tarzan and the Castaways* (1965). Tarzan embarks on quest after quest, into constantly varying territories, most spectacularly perhaps in *Tarzan and the Forbidden City*, where his discoveries convey a sense of wonder that remains fresh today. He is a figure as deep in our dreams as Sherlock Holmes. We may be 'wiser' now; we may know that Africa never contained his like, nor perhaps should we wish it had. But we will never stop dreaming of Eden, we will never stop loving stories whose heroes are both powerful and guiltless. Tarzan welcomes you home again.

For a more detailed version of the above, see Edgar Rice Burroughs' author entry in *The Encyclopedia of Science Fiction*: http://sf-encyclopedia.com/entry/burroughs_edgar_rice

Some terms above are capitalised when they would not normally be so rendered; this indicates that the terms represent discrete entries in *The Encyclopedia of Science Fiction*.

TARZAN'S QUEST

1

The Princess Sborov

'My dear Jane, you know everyone.'

'Not quite, Hazel; but one sees everyone in the Savoy.'

'Who is that woman at the second table to our right? – the one who spoke so cordially. There is something very familiar about her – I'm sure I've seen her before.'

'You probably have. Don't you remember Kitty Krause?'

'O-oh, yes; now I recall her. But she went with an older crowd.'

'Yes, she's a full generation ahead of us; but Kitty'd like to forget that and have everyone else forget it.'

'Let's see – she married Peters, the cotton King, didn't she?'

'Yes, and when he died he left her so many millions she didn't have enough fingers to count 'em on; so the poor woman will never know how rich she is.'

'Is that her son with her?'

'Son, my dear! That's her new husband.'

'Husband? Why, she's old enough to—'

'Yes, of course; but you see he's a prince, and Kitty always was – er – well, ambitious.'

'Yes, I recall now – something of a climber; but she climbed pretty high, even in aristocratic old Baltimore, with those Peters millions.'

'But she's an awfully good soul, Hazel. I'm really very fond of her. There isn't anything she wouldn't do for a friend, and underneath that one silly complex of hers is a heart of gold.'

'And kind to her mother! If anyone ever says *I'm* good-hearted, I'll—'

'S-sh, Hazel; she's coming over.'

The older woman, followed by her husband, swooped down upon them. 'My darling Jane,' she cried, 'I'm so glad to see you.'

'And I'm glad to see you, Kitty. You remember Hazel Strong, don't you?'

'Oh, not of *the* Strongs of Baltimore! Oh, my dear! I mean I'm just – how perfectly wonder – I must present my husband, Prince Sborov. Alexis, my very, very dearest friends, Lady Greystoke and Miss Strong.'

'Lady Tennington now, Kitty,' corrected Jane.

'Oh, my dear, how perfectly wonderful! Lady Greystoke and Lady Tennington, Alexis, dear.'

'Charmed,' murmured the young man. His lips smiled; but the murky light in his deep eyes was appraising, questioning, as they brooded upon the lovely face of Jane, Lady Greystoke.

'Won't you join us?' invited the latter. 'Please sit down. You know it's been ages, Kitty, since we had a good visit.'

'Oh, how perfectly won – oh, I'd love to – I mean it seems – thank you, Alexis dear – now you sit over there.'

'Why, Kitty, it must be a year since I have heard anything of you, except what I have read in the newspapers,' said Jane.

'At that, you might be very well informed as to our goings and comings,' remarked Sborov, a little ironically.

'Yes, indeed – I mean – we have a whole book filled with newspaper clippings – some of them were horrid.'

'But you kept them all,' remarked the prince.

'Oh, well,' cried Princess Sborov, 'I mean – I suppose one must pay for fame and position; but these newspaper people can be so terribly horrid.'

'But what have you been doing?' inquired Jane. 'Have you been back home again? I'm sure you haven't been in London for a year.'

'No, we spent the whole year on the continent. We had a perfectly wonderful time, didn't we, Alexis dear? You see it was last spring in Paris that we met; and dear, dear Alexis just swept me off my feet. He wouldn't take no for an answer, would you, darling?'

'How could I, my sweet?'

'There, you see, isn't he won – and then we were married, and we've been traveling ever since.'

'And now, I suppose, you are going to settle down?' asked Jane.

'Oh, my dear, no. You never could guess what we're planning on now – we are going to Africa!'

'Africa! How interesting,' commented Hazel. 'Africa! What memories it conjures.'

'You have been to Africa, Lady Tennington?' inquired the prince.

'Right in the heart of it – cannibals, lions, elephants – everything.'

'Oh, how perfectly wonder – I mean how thrilling – and I know that Jane knows all there is to know about Africa.'

'Not quite all, Kitty.' '

'But enough,' interposed Hazel.

'I'm going down myself, shortly,' said Jane. 'You see,' she added, turning to Prince Sborov, 'Lord Greystoke spends a great deal of time in Africa. I am planning on joining him there. I have already booked my passage.'

'Oh, how perfectly wonderful,' exclaimed the princess. 'I mean, we can all go together.'

'That is a splendid idea, my dear,' said the prince, his face brightening.

'It would be lovely,' said Jane, 'but you see, I am going into the interior, and I am sure that you—'

'Oh, my dear, so are we.'

'But, Kitty, you don't know what you're talking about. You wouldn't like it at all. No comforts, no luxuries; dirt, insects, smelly natives, and all kinds of wild beasts.'

'Oh, but my dear, we are – I mean, we really are. Shall I tell Lady Greystoke our secret, darling?'

The prince shrugged. 'Why not? She could have little more than a passing interest.'

'Well, maybe someday she will. We all grow old, you know, my dear.'

'It seems incredible to think –' murmured Alexis half to himself.

'What did you say, darling?' interrupted his wife.

'I was just going to say that Lady Greystoke might think the story incredible.'

'Now you must tell me,' said Jane. 'You have my curiosity aroused.'

'Yes, indeed, do tell us,' urged Hazel.

'Well, my dears, you see it was like this. We have been doing a great deal of flying the past year, and it's perfectly wonderful. We just love it, and so I bought an aeroplane in Paris last week. We flew to London in it; but what I was going to tell you is about our pilot. He is an American, and he has had the most amazing experiences.'

'I think he is what you call a rackster in America,' said Alexis.

'You mean a gangster, my dear,' corrected the princess.

'Or a racketeer,' suggested Hazel.

'Whatever he is, I do not like him,' said Alexis.

'But, my dear, you have to admit that he is a good pilot. I mean that he is perfectly wonder – and he has been to Africa and had the most frightful experiences.

'The last time he was there, he got track of a witch-doctor who possesses the secret of an amazing formula for renewing youth and inducing longevity. He met a man who knows where the old fellow lives way in the interior; but neither of them had money enough to organize an expedition to go in search of him. He says that this will make people as young as they wish to be and keep them that way forever. Oh, isn't it wonderful?'

'I think the fellow is a scoundrel,' said Alexis. 'He has induced my wife to finance this expedition; and when he gets us down there in the interior, he will probably slit our throats and steal our jewelry.'

'Oh, my darling, I am sure you are quite wrong. Brown is the last word in loyalty.'

'He may be all of that, but still I don't see why you want to drag me to Africa – the bugs, the dirt; and I do not like lions.'

Jane laughed. 'Really, you might spend a year in Africa without seeing a lion; and you will get used to the bugs and the dirt.'

Prince Sborov grimaced. 'I prefer the Savoy,' he said.

'You will go with us, dear, won't you?' insisted Kitty.

'Well,' hesitated Jane, 'I really don't know. In the first place, I don't know where you are going.'

'We are going to fly direct to Nairobi and outfit there; and, my dear, to get any place in Africa, you *have* to go to Nairobi first.'

Jane smiled. 'Well, it happens that that is where I intend going anyway. Lord Greystoke is to meet me there.'

'Then it's all settled. Oh, isn't it wonderful?'

'You almost make me want to go,' said Hazel.

'Well, my dear, we would be delighted to have you,' exclaimed Princess Sborov. 'You see, I have a six-passenger cabin plane. There are four of us, and the pilot and my maid will make six.'

'How about my man?' asked the prince.

'Oh, my dear, you won't need a man in Africa. You will have a little colored boy who will do your washing and cooking and carry your gun. I read about it time and time again in African stories.'

'Of course,' said Hazel, 'it's awfully sweet of you; but I really couldn't go. It's out of the question. Bunny and I are sailing for America Saturday.'

'But *you'll* come with us, Jane dear?'

'Why, I'd like to, Kitty, if I can get ready in time. When do you start?'

'We were planning on going next week; but, of course, I mean – if—'

'Why, yes, I think I can make it all right.'

'Then it's settled, my dear. How perfectly won – we'll take off from the Croydon Airdrome next Wednesday.'

'I'll cable Lord Greystoke today; and Friday I am giving a farewell dinner for Lord and Lady Tennington, and you and Prince Sborov must be there.'

2

Sound Above the Storm

The Lord of the Jungle rose from a crude, leaf-covered platform constructed in the crotch of two branches of a mighty patriarch of the jungle. He stretched luxuriously. The slanting rays of the morning sun mottled his bronze body through the leafy canopy that stretched interminably above him.

Little Nkima stirred and awoke. With a scream, he leaped to the shoulder of the ape-man and encircled his neck with his hairy arms.

'Sheeta!' screamed the monkey. 'He was about to spring on little Nkima.'

The ape-man smiled. 'Nkima has been seeing things in his sleep,' he said.

The monkey looked about him among the branches of the trees and down at the ground below. Then, seeing that no danger threatened, he commenced to dance and chatter; but presently the ape-man silenced him and listened.

'Sheeta comes,' he said. 'He is coming upwind toward us. We cannot smell him but if Manu had the ears of Tarzan, he could hear him.'

The monkey cocked an ear downwind and listened. 'Little Nkima hears him,' he said. 'He comes slowly.' Presently the sinuous, tawny body of the panther forced its way through the brush and came into view below them.

'Sheeta is not hunting,' said Tarzan. 'He has fed and he is not hungry.' And thus reassured, Nkima commenced to hurl invectives at the savage beast below them. The great cat paused and looked up, and when he saw Tarzan and Nkima he bared his fangs in an angry snarl. But he started on again, for he had no business with them.

Feeling secure in the protection of Tarzan, little Nkima waxed belligerent, as he always did under similar circumstances when the possibility of danger seemed remote. He hurled at his hereditary enemy every jungle epithet that he could put his tongue to, but as these seemed to make no impression upon Sheeta he leaped from Tarzan's shoulder to a trailing vine that bore a soft, ill-smelling fruit, and gathering one of these he hurled it at the panther.

By accident, his aim proved true; and the missile struck Sheeta on the back of the head.

With an angry snarl, the beast wheeled about and started toward the tree that harbored his annoyer. Screaming with terror, little Nkima fled upwards to the safety of the smaller branches that would not bear the weight of the great cat.

The ape-man grinned up after the fleeing monkey and then glanced down at the angry panther. A low, growling 'Kreeg-ah' rumbled from his throat, and the other beast below returned an answering growl. Then it turned and slunk away into the jungle, rumbling in its throat.

The ape-man was returning leisurely from an excursion into a remote district of the great forest, far from his own haunts.

He had heard strange rumors, and he had gone to investigate them. From deep in the interior, on the borders of a tractless waste that few men had entered and from which some had never returned alive, had come a strange and mysterious story since so long before the memory of living man that the facts had become interwoven with the legends and the folklore of the tribes inhabiting this borderland to such an extent that they had come to be accepted as something inevitable and inescapable; but recently the disappearance of young girls had increased to an alarming extent and had occurred in tribes far removed from the mysterious country.

But when Tarzan investigated and sought to solve the mystery, he was balked by the fear and superstition of the natives. So fearful were they of the malign, mysterious power that snatched their young girls from them, that they would give Tarzan no information or assist him in any way to aid them; and so, disgusted, he had left them to their fate.

After all, why should the ape-man concern himself? Life to the jungle-bred is a commodity of little value. It is given and taken casually as a matter of course. One loves or kills as naturally as one sleeps or dreams. Yet the mystery of the thing intrigued him.

Young girls, always between the ages of fourteen and twenty, vanished as into thin air. No trace of them ever was seen again. Their fate remained an unsolved mystery.

But by now Tarzan had relegated the matter to the background of his thoughts, for his active mind could not long concern itself with a problem that did not closely concern him and which at any event seemed impossible of solution.

He swung easily through the trees, his alert senses conscious of all that transpired within their range. Since Sheeta had passed upwind, he had known by the decreasing volume of the great cat's spoor that the distance between them was constantly increasing – proof that Sheeta was not stalking him. From far away, muted by the distance, sounded the roar of Numa, the lion; and deeper in the forest Tantor, the elephant, trumpeted.

The morning air, the sounds and smells of his beloved jungle, filled the ape-man with exhilaration. Had he been the creature of another environment, he might have whistled or sung or whooped aloud like a cowboy in sheer exuberance of spirit; but the jungle-bred are not thus. They veil their emotions; and they move noiselessly always, for thus do they extend the span of their precarious lives.

Scampering sometimes at his side, sometimes far above him, little Nkima travelled many times the distance of his Master, wasting much energy; as, safe in the protection of his benefactor, he insulted all living things that came his way.

But presently he saw his Master stop and sniff the air and listen, and then little Nkima dropped silently to a great bronzed shoulder.

'Men,' said Tarzan.

The little monkey sniffed the air. 'Nkima smells nothing,' he said.

'Neither does Tarzan,' replied the ape-man, 'but he hears them. What is wrong with the ears of little Nkima? Are they growing old?'

'Now Nkima hears them. Tarmangani?' he asked.

'No,' replied Tarzan, 'Tarmangani make different sounds – the squeaking of leather, the rattle of too much equipment. These are Gomangani; they move softly.'

'We shall kill them,' said Nkima.

The ape-man smiled. 'It is well for the peace of the jungle that you have not the strength of Bolgani, the gorilla; but perhaps if you had, you would not be so bloodthirsty.'

'Ugh, Bolgani,' sneered Nkima, contemptuously. 'He hides in the thickets and runs away at the first sound that he hears.'

The ape-man changed his direction to the right and made a great circle through the trees until presently he reached a point where Usha, the wind, could carry the scent spoor of the strangers to him.

'Gomangani,' he said.

'Many Gomangani,' exclaimed Nkima, excitedly. 'They are as the leaves upon the trees. Let us go away. They will kill little Nkima and eat him.'

'There are not so many,' replied Tarzan, 'no more than the fingers upon my two hands, a hunting party, perhaps. We will go closer.'

Moving up on the blacks from behind, the ape-man rapidly closed up the distance between them. The scent spoor grew stronger in his nostrils.

'They are friends,' he said. 'They are Waziri.'

The two jungle creatures moved on in silence then, until they overhauled a file of black warriors who moved silently along the jungle trail. Then Tarzan spoke to them in their own tongue.

'Muviro,' he said, 'what brings my children so far from their own country?'

The blacks halted and wheeled about, gazing up into the trees from which the voice had seemed to come. They saw nothing, but they knew the voice.

'Oh, Bwana, it is well that you have come,' said Muviro. 'Your children need you.'

Tarzan dropped to the trail among them. 'Has harm befallen any of my people?' he asked, as the blacks clustered about him.

'Buira, my daughter, has disappeared,' said Muviro. 'She went alone toward the river, and that is the last that was ever seen of her.'

'Perhaps Gimla, the crocodile—' Tarzan commenced to suggest.

'No, it was not Gimla. There were other women at the river. Buira never reached the river. We have heard stories, Bwana, that fill us with terror for our girls. There is evil, there is mystery in it, Bwana. We have heard of the Kavuru. Perhaps it is they; we go to search for them.'

'Their country lies far away,' said Tarzan. 'I have just come from a place that is supposed to be near it, but the people there are all cowards. They were afraid to tell me where I might find the Kavuru, even though their girls have been stolen by these people for so long that no man can remember when it began.'

'Muviro will find them,' said the black, doggedly. 'Buira was a good daughter. She was not as other girls. I will find those who stole her, and kill them.'

'And Tarzan of the Apes will help you,' said the ape-man. 'Have you found the trail of the thieves?'

'There is no trail,' replied Muviro. 'That is why we know it was the Kavuru; they leave no trail.'

'Many of us think that they are demons,' said another warrior.

'Men or demons, I shall find them and kill them,' replied Muviro.

'From all that I could learn,' said Tarzan, 'these Bukena live nearest to the Kavuru. They have lost the most girls. That is the reason it is thought that they live nearest to the Kavuru, but they would not help me. They were afraid. However, we will go first to the kraals of the Bukena. I can travel faster; so I will go ahead. In four marches, perhaps three if nothing detains you, you should be there. In the meantime, it may be that Tarzan will have learned more.'

'Now that the Big Bwana is with me, my mind is happy again,' said Muviro, 'for I know that Buira will be found and returned to me, and that those who took her will be punished.'

Tarzan glanced up at the skies and sniffed the air. 'A bad storm is coming, Muviro,' he said. 'It is coming from where Kudu, the sun, beds down at night; you will have to trek directly into it, and it will hold you back.'

'But it will not stop us, Bwana.'

'No,' replied Tarzan. 'It takes more than Usha, the wind, and Ara, the lightning, to stop the Waziri.'

'Already Usha is drawing his veil of clouds across the face of Kudu, hiding him from his people.'

Torn and ragged clouds scudded across the sky; and in the distance, far to the West, thunder reverberated. The ape-man remained with his head thrown back, watching the impressive spectacle of the gathering storm.

'It will be a bad storm,' he said, musingly. 'See how frightened the clouds are. Like a great herd of buffaloes, they stampede in terror, fearful of the roars of the thunder god that pursues them.'

The wind now was whipping the topmost branches of the trees. The thunder grew nearer and increased in violence. As the clouds sank thicker across the sky, gloomy darkness settled upon the jungle. Lightning flashed. Thunder crashed terrifically, and then the rain fell. It came in solid sheets, bending the trees beneath its weight; and over all Usha screamed like a lost soul.

The eleven men squatted with shoulders hunched against the beating rain, waiting for the first fury of the storm to spend itself.

For half an hour they sat there, and still the storm raged unabated. Suddenly the ape-man cocked an attentive ear upward, and a moment later several of the blacks raised their eyes to the heavens.

'What is it, Bwana?' asked one, fearfully. 'What is it in the sky that moans and whines?'

'It sounds very much like an aeroplane,' replied Tarzan, 'but what an aeroplane would be doing here, I cannot understand.'

3

Out of Gas

Prince Alexis poked his head into the pilot's compartment. His face, overcast with a greenish pallor, reflected apprehension, if not actual fright. 'Are we in any danger, Brown?' he shouted above the roar of the exhaust and the blast of the propeller. 'Do you think you can get us out of here?'

'For God's sake, shut up,' snapped the pilot. 'Ain't I got troubles enough without you asking fool questions every five minutes?'

The man in the seat beside the pilot looked horrified. 'S-s-sh,' he cautioned. 'You shouldn't speak to his 'ighness like that, my man. It's most disrespectful.'

'Nuts,' snapped Brown.

The prince staggered back to his seat in the cabin. He almost succeeded in registering offended dignity when a current of air tossed the ship at the moment and threw him off his balance, so that it was a very angry prince who lurched awkwardly into his seat.

'Fasten your safety belt, darling,' admonished his princess. 'We are apt to turn over at any minute. I mean, really, did you ever see anything so terribly rough? Oh, I wish we had never come.'

'So do I,' growled Alexis. 'I didn't want to come in the first place; and if I ever get my feet on the ground again, the first thing I am going to do is fire that impudent boor.'

'I think, under the circumstances,' said Jane, 'that we really ought to overlook any idiosyncrasy of manner that he may manifest. He's got all the responsibility. He must be under a terrific nervous strain; and, regardless of everything else, I think you will have to admit that so far he has proved himself a splendid pilot.'

'Annette, my smelling salts, please,' cried Princess Sborov, in a weak voice; 'I am sure I'm going to faint. I certainly am.'

'Sapristi, what a trip!' exclaimed Sborov. 'If it were not for you, dear lady,

I should go crazy. You seem to be the only one in the party with any poise. Are you not afraid?'

'Yes, of course I am afraid. We have been flying around in this storm for what seems an eternity, but getting excited about it won't do us any good.'

'But how can you help being excited? How could anyone help being excited?'

'Look at Tibbs,' said Jane. 'He's not excited. He's as cool as a cucumber.'

'Bah!' exclaimed Sborov. 'Tibbs is not human. I do not like these English valets – no heart, no feeling.'

'Really, my dear,' expostulated the princess, 'I think he is perfect – a regular gentleman's gentleman.'

A vivid flash of lightning shot the dark clouds that enveloped them. Thunder roared and crashed. The ship lurched drunkenly onto one wing and nosed suddenly down. Annette screamed; the Princess Sborov swooned. The plane spun once before Brown could pull her out of it. He righted her with an effort.

'Wh-ew!' he exclaimed.

'My word,' said Tibbs.

Princess Sborov was slumped in her chair. Her smelling salts had fallen to the floor. Her hat was over one eye; her hair dishevelled. Alexis made no move to come to her aid.

'You had better look after the princess, Annette,' said Jane. 'I think she needs attention.'

There was no answer. Jane turned to see why the girl had not responded. Annette had fainted.

Jane shook her head. 'Tibbs,' she called. 'Come back here and look after the princess and Annette. I'm coming up to sit with Brown.'

Gingerly Tibbs made his way into the cabin, and Jane took the seat beside the pilot.

'That last was a bad one,' she said. 'I really thought we were through. You handled the ship marvellously, Brown.'

'Thanks,' he said. 'It would be easier if they were all like you. The rest of them get in my hair. Although,' he added, 'Tibbs ain't so bad. I guess he's too dumb to be scared.'

'You are having real trouble with the ship, aren't you, Brown?' she asked.

'Yes,' he said. 'I didn't want to tell the others. They'd have gone nutty. We've got too much of a load. I told the old lady so before we took off; but she was set on bringing everything but the kitchen sink, and now I can't get no elevation. That's the reason I can't get up above this storm, just wallowing around here in this muck without any idea where we are or which way we're going; and there's mountains in Africa, Miss, some damned high mountains.'

'Yes, I know that,' replied Jane. 'But you must have some idea where we are; you have a compass, and you know your air speed.'

'Yes,' he said, 'I got a compass; and I know my air speed; but there's another thing that the rest of 'em better not know. The compass has gone haywire.'

'You mean—?'

'I mean we're just flying blind in this pea soup without a compass.'

'Not so good; is it, Brown?'

'I'll say it's not.'

'What are we going to do about it?'

'If we could get at the baggage compartment, we could throw all the junk out,' he replied; 'but we can't, and there you are.'

'And in the meantime we may crash into a mountain at any moment, is that it?'

'Yes, Miss,' he replied, 'or run out of gas and have to come down, which will probably be just as bad as hitting a mountain.'

'There's no other way out?' she asked. Her voice was level, her eyes unafraid.

'Well, I've got a little plan I'd like to work,' he said, and turned to her with a grin.

'What is it, Brown?'

'Well, we can't get at the junk to throw it overboard; but the prince must weigh about a hundred and fifty pounds. That would help some.'

Jane turned her head away to hide a smile, but evidently he saw it.

'I thought you'd like the idea,' he said.

'We shouldn't joke about such a thing, Brown,' she reprimanded.

'I guess we can't help it,' he said. 'We both got that American sense of humor.'

'Is the petrol – gas really very low, Brown?' she asked.

'Look,' he indicated the gauge on the dash. 'We're good for about an hour at the outside.'

'And no parachutes.'

'Nary a chute. Most people don't bother with them on a cabin job.'

She shook her head. 'It does look bad, doesn't it? But we'd better not tell the others how really bad it is. There is nothing they can do to help themselves.'

'Not a thing,' he said, with a wry smile, 'unless they want to pray.'

'I think they've been doing that already.'

'What are you going to do – just cruise around until the gas is gone?'

'No, of course not. If I don't find a hole in this mess in half an hour, I'm going to nose down easy and try to get under it. There'll be nothing to it, if we ain't over mountains. That's all I'm afraid of. Then I may find a place where I can get her down, but I'm hoping for a hole. I'd like to look down first.'

'Jane! Jane!' It was a plaintive wail from the cabin. 'Oh, my dear, where are we? I mean are we all dead?'

Jane looked back. Tibbs had recovered the lost smelling salts and had successfully applied first-aid to the princess. Annette had come to and was sobbing hysterically. The prince sat tense and ashen-faced, beads of perspiration standing upon his forehead. He was quite evidently in a blue funk. He caught Jane's eye.

'Is there any hope?' he asked. 'Has Brown said anything?'

'We'll be all right if he can find an opening in the clouds,' she replied. 'That is what he is looking for.'

'If we'd had a decent pilot, we'd never have gotten into this,' grumbled the prince. 'As I told you, Kitty, you should have hired a good French pilot. These Americans don't know anything about flying; and into the bargain you don't know anything about this fellow, Brown.'

'I guess that guy never heard of the Wright Brothers or Lindbergh,' grumbled Brown.

'Don't mind what he says,' said Jane. 'We are all under a terrific nervous strain, and not exactly accountable for what we say or do.'

'It doesn't seem to be bothering you much, Miss,' said Brown.

'Well, it's just the way we happen to be,' she said, 'and we can't help that either. Just because I succeed in hiding it, doesn't mean that I am not frightened to death.'

'You're sure a good sport,' said Brown. 'You've got guts, and so I don't mind telling you that I don't feel like no little schoolgirl going to her first picnic. I can think of lots of things I'd rather do than crash in the middle of Africa.'

'What did he say?' demanded Sborov. 'We are going to crash? Look what you have gotten me into, you old fool,' he cried, angrily, turning upon his wife, 'you and your rejuvenation and your perpetual youth. Sapristi! You've had your face lifted so many times now that you could be arrested for indecent exposure.'

The Princess Sborov gasped. 'Why, Alexis!' she exclaimed. Then she burst into tears.

'Oh, why did I ever come?' wailed Annette. 'I did not wish to come. I am afraid. I do not want to die. Oh, mon Dieu, save me! Save me!'

'Here, madam, try the smelling salts again,' said Tibbs.

'Nice party,' remarked Brown. 'Perhaps they think I'm enjoying it.'

'In great danger, we think mostly of ourselves,' said Jane.

'I suppose so. I'm thinking mostly of myself right now; but I'm thinking of you and Annette and Tibbs, too. You're worth saving. As far as the other two are concerned, I'd like to chuck 'em overboard; but I think I read somewhere that there was a law against that.'

'Yes, I believe there is,' smiled Jane. 'But, really, Brown, do you know I have an idea that you are going to get us out of this all right?'

'That's the first encouragement I've had,' he replied. 'And I'm sure going to try to get us out of this. It all depends upon what's underneath this mess. If there's any ceiling at all, we'll have a chance; and that's what I'm hoping for.'

'I'm praying for it.'

'I'm going to start down now, Miss. I'll just ease her down slowly.'

'At a hundred and fifty miles an hour.'

'Well, we won't lose elevation that fast.'

The ship struck a down current and dropped a hundred feet, careening wildly. The screams of the Princess Sborov and Annette, the maid, mingled with the curses of Alexis.

Jane gasped. 'Well, we went down pretty fast that time,' she said.

'But when she drops like that, you can be sure you're not on the ground, anyway. The air has to have some place to go. It can't get through the earth; so they never carry you all the way down.'

For tense minutes the two sat in silence. Then suddenly Jane voiced a quick exclamation. 'Look, Brown,' she cried, 'trees! We're below it.'

'Yes,' he said, 'and with five hundred feet to spare but—'

She looked at him questioningly. 'We're not much better off, are we? How much gas have you left?'

'Oh, maybe fifteen or twenty minutes, and I don't need to tell you – well, it doesn't look so hot.'

'Nothing but forest,' she said; 'there's not a place to land anywhere.'

'We may find an opening, and believe me it won't have to be a Croydon either.'

'And if you don't find an opening?'

He shrugged. 'We'll just have to set down in the tree tops,' he said. 'The chances are pretty fair that we won't all be killed, Miss.' He turned and looked back in the cabin. 'Tibbs, get into a seat and fasten your safety belt. Put your wraps and pillows in front of your faces. I am going to make a forced landing in a few minutes. I will tell you when. If you pad your faces, you may not get hurt at all.'

Nobody made any reply. The princess moaned, and Annette sobbed.

'There's a terrific wind, isn't there?' said Jane. 'Look at those tree tops bend.'

'Yes,' he said, 'and in a way that may help us. The wind will cut down our ground speed a lot; and if I can hook the tail skid into those trees, we may land on them easy-like and hang there.'

'You know those tree tops may be a couple of hundred feet from the ground, or even more?'

'Yes,' he said, 'I suppose they may, but I don't think we'll go through them;

they look too dense. And if I set her down easy, the wings and fuselage will catch and hold her. I think we've got a chance.'

The ship skimmed on a few hundred feet above the swaying forest top for several minutes. There was no sign of a clearing; no break in those wildly tossing waves of green.

'We're out of gas now, Miss,' said Brown, and mechanically he cut the switch. Then he turned back once more to the cabin. 'Hold everything,' he said; 'I'm going to bring her down.'

4

In the Kraal of Udalo

The ship settled toward the madly tossing sea of green foliage below. Blinding rain drove in sheets against the windows of the cabin. Vivid lightning shot the gloom beneath the dark, glowering clouds. Thunder crashed. Straight into the teeth of the gale, Brown nosed down. The force of the wind held the ship until it seemed to hover above the tree tops as the pilot leveled off just above them; and as the ship settled, he brought the tail down sharply. There was a crash of splintering wood, the ripping of torn fabric as the ship nosed down into the swaying, slashing branches. And above the noise of the storm and the crashing of the ship were the screams and curses of the terrified passengers in the cabin.

But at last it was over. With a final ripping, tearing jolt, the ship came to rest.

Then, for a tense and terrible moment, silence.

Brown turned to the girl at his side. 'Are you hurt, Miss?' he asked.

'I don't think so,' she said; 'just dazed. It was terrible, wasn't it?'

He turned then and glanced back into the cabin. The four passengers were hanging in their safety belts in various stages of collapse. 'All right back there?' he demanded. 'How about you, Annette?' There was a note of greater concern in Brown's voice.

'Oh, mon Dieu!' moaned the French girl. 'I am already dead.'

The Princess Sborov groaned. 'Oh, how horrible! Why doesn't someone do something for me? Why doesn't someone help me? Annette! Alexis! Where are you? I am dying. Where are my smelling salts?'

'It would serve you right,' growled Alexis, 'dragging me off on a crazy adventure like this. It's a wonder we weren't all killed. If we'd had a French pilot, this would never have happened.'

'Don't be so stupid,' snapped Jane. 'Brown handled the ship magnificently.'

Alexis turned upon Tibbs. 'Why don't you do something, you idiot? You English and Americans are all alike – stupid, dumb. I wanted a French valet in the first place.'

'Yes, Sir,' said Tibbs. 'I am very sorry that you didn't get one, Sir.'

'Well, shut up and do something.'

'What shall I do, Sir?'

'Sapristi! How should I know? But do something.'

'I am sorry, Sir, but I am not a mountain goat nor a monkey. If I unfasten this seat belt, I shall simply land on your head, Sir.'

'Wait a minute,' called Jane. 'I'll see what can be done.' And she unfastened her belt and climbed up into the cabin.

The ship had come to rest at an angle of about 45 degrees with the nose down, but Jane easily made her way into the cabin; and Brown followed close behind her. She went first to the Princess Sborov.

'Are you really seriously hurt, Kitty?' she asked.

'I am torn in two; I know that all my ribs are broken.'

'You got us into this, Brown,' snapped Alexis. 'Now get us out of it.'

'Listen,' said the American, 'you may be better off in than out, for when we get on the ground I ain't pilot no more. I ain't responsible then, and I won't be taking any of your lip.'

'Did you hear that, Kitty?' demanded Alexis. 'Would you sit there and let a servant talk to me like that? If you don't discharge him, I will.'

Brown snorted. 'Don't make me laugh. You didn't hire me, you little runt; and you ain't going to fire me.'

'Don't be impudent, my man,' cried Alexis, his voice trembling. 'You forget who I am.'

'No, I don't forget who you are; you ain't nothing. In the country you come from, half the cab drivers are princes.'

'Come, come,' snapped Jane. 'Stop bickering. We must find out if anyone is really injured.'

'Get me out of here,' wailed Princess Sborov. 'I can't stand it any longer.'

'It would be foolish to try to get out now,' said Jane. 'Just look at that storm. We shall be safer and much more comfortable here in the ship while the storm lasts.'

'Oh, we'll never get down from here. We are way up in the tops of the trees,' wailed Annette.

'Don't worry none, sister,' said Brown, reassuringly. 'We'll find a way to get down from here when the storm lets up. The ship's lodged tight; she won't fall no farther; so we might as well sit tight like Lady Greystoke says and wait for it to quit raining and blowing.'

Tibbs strained his eyes upwards through the window at his side. 'It doesn't seem to be clearing any, if I may say so,' he remarked.

'These equatorial storms oftentimes end as suddenly as they commence,' said Jane. 'It may be all over, and the sun out, within half an hour. I've seen it happen a hundred times.'

'Oh, it won't ever stop raining; I know it won't,' wailed the princess, 'and I don't see how we are ever going to get down from here if it does. This is terrible. I mean I wish I'd never come.'

'Crying about it now, Kitty, won't do any good,' said Jane. 'The thing to do is try to make ourselves comfortable and then make the best of it until the storm lets up and we can get down. Here, Brown, get a couple of those seat cushions and put them down here on the floor in front of the princess' chair. Then we'll unfasten her seat belt and she can turn around and sit on the floor with her back against the pilot's compartment.'

'Let me help, Milady,' said Tibbs, as he unfastened his belt and slid forward.

'The rest of you had better do the same thing,' said Brown. 'Unfasten your belts and sit on the floor with your backs against the seat in front of you.'

With some difficulty and much sobbing on her part, the Princess Sborov was finally arranged in a more comfortable position; and the others, following Brown's suggestion, disposed themselves as best they could for the wait, long or short, until the storm should subside.

Tarzan and the Waziri hunched in what meager protection they could find until the storm should abate; for, in its fury, it was a force against which it were foolish for man to pit himself unless the need were great.

For a while Tarzan had heard the roar of the ship's motor, even above the storm. It had been evident to him that the ship was circling, and then gradually the sound had diminished and quickly faded into nothingness.

'Bwana,' said Muviro, 'were there men up there above the storm?'

'Yes, at least one,' replied the ape-man, 'above it or in it. In either event, I should not care to be in his place. The forest stretches many marches in all directions. If he were looking for a place to land, I do not know where he would find it.'

'It is well to be on the ground,' said Muviro. 'I do not think that the gods intended that men should fly like birds. If they had, they would have given them wings.'

Little Nkima cuddled close to his Master. He was drenched and cold and miserable. The world looked very black to Nkima, and there was no future. He was quite sure that it would always be dark, but he was not resigned to his fate. He was merely too crushed and unhappy to complain. But presently it commenced to get lighter. The wind passed on with a last, dismal wail. The sun burst forth, and the crushed jungle arose once more to its full life.

The ape-man arose and shook himself, like a great lion. 'I shall start now for Ukena,' he said, 'and talk with the Bukena. This time, perhaps, they will tell me where the Kavuru dwell.'

'There are ways of making them talk,' said Muviro.

'Yes,' said Tarzan, 'there are ways.'

'And we will follow on to Ukena,' said Muviro.

'If you do not find me there, you will know that I am searching for the Kavuru and Buira. If I need you, I will send Nkima back to guide you to me.'

Without further words, without useless goodbyes and Godspeeds, Tarzan swung into the dripping trees and disappeared toward the West.

Strange stories had come from the Bukena, and filtered by word of mouth through a hundred tribes to Uziri, the land of the Waziri. They were tales of the Kavuru, tales of a savage, mysterious people, whom no man saw, or seeing, lived to tell. They were demons with horns and tails. Or again, they were a race of men without heads. But the most common report was that they were a race of savage whites, who had reverted to barbarism and went naked in their hidden fastness. One story had it that they were all women, and another that they were all men. But Tarzan knew the distortion that was the fruit of many tongues, and gave little heed to things he heard; only the things that he had seen with his own eyes was he sure of.

He knew that many tribes stole women, but oftentimes these women were seen again. Yet the women that the Kavuru stole were not, and so he was willing to admit that there was some tribe dwelling in a remote fastness that specialized in the stealing of young girls. But many of the other stories he heard, he did not believe.

For instance, there was the fable of the longevity and perpetual youth of the Kavuru. That, Tarzan did not believe, although he knew that there were many strange and unbelievable happenings in the depths of the Dark Continent.

It was a long trek, even for Tarzan, back to the country of the Bukena. The forest was soggy and dripping; the jungle steamed. But of such things and their attendant discomfort, the ape-man took small note. From birth he had become inured to discomfort, for the jungle is not a comfortable place. Cold, heat, danger were as natural to him as warmth and comfort and safety are to you. As you take the one, he took the other, as a matter of course. Even in infancy, he had never whined because he was uncomfortable, nor did he ever complain. If he could better conditions, he did so; if he could not, he ignored them.

Just before dark, Tarzan made a kill; and the fresh meat warmed him and gave him new life, but that night he slept cold and uncomfortable in the dank and soggy forest.

Before dawn he was astir again, eating once more of his kill. Then he swung off swiftly upon his journey, until the good red blood flowed hot through his veins, bringing warmth and a sense of wellbeing.

But Nkima was miserable. He had wanted to go home, and now he was going back into a strange country that he did not like. He scolded and fretted a great deal; but when the sun came out and warmed him, he felt better; and then he scampered through the trees, looking for whom he might insult.

On the morning of the third day, Tarzan came to the kraal of Udalo, chief of the Bukena.

The sight of the tall, bronzed white, with the little monkey perched upon his shoulder, striding through the gate into the village, brought a horde of blacks jabbering and chattering about him. He was no stranger to them, for he had been there a short time before; and so they were not afraid of him. They were a little awed, however, for tales of the mighty ape-man had reached them even over the great distance that separated Ukena from the land of the Waziri.

Paying no more attention to them than he would have to a herd of wilde-beest, Tarzan strode straight to the hut of Udalo, the chief, where he found the old man squatting beneath the shade of a tree, talking with some of the elders of the tribe.

Udalo had been watching the approach of the ape-man along the village street. He did not seem overly pleased to see him.

'We thought the Big Bwana had gone away, and that he would not return,' said the chief; 'but now he is back. Why?'

'He has come to make talk with Udalo.'

'He has made talk with Udalo before. Udalo has told him all that he knows.'

'This time Udalo is going to tell him more. He is going to tell him where lies the country of the Kavuru.'

The old man fidgeted. 'Udalo does not know.'

'Udalo does not talk true words. He has lived here all his life. The young girls of his tribe have been stolen by the Kavuru. Everyone knows that. Udalo is not such a fool that he does not know where these young girls are taken. He is afraid of what the Kavuru will do to him, if he leads people to their kraal. But he need not be afraid; the Kavuru need not know how Tarzan finds them.'

'Why do you want to go to the kraal of the Kavuru? They are bad people.'

'I will tell you,' said Tarzan. 'Buira, the daughter of Muviro, the hereditary chief of the Waziri, has disappeared. Muviro thinks that the Kavuru took her; that is why Tarzan, who is war chief of the Waziri, must find the kraal of the Kavuru.'

'I do not know where it is,' insisted Udalo, sullenly.

As they talked, warriors had been approaching from all parts of the village, until now Tarzan and the chief had been surrounded by scowling, silent spear-men.

Udalo appeared ill at ease; his eyes shifted restlessly. The whole atmosphere seemed surcharged with suspicion and danger. Even little Nkima sensed it; he trembled as he clung tightly to Tarzan.

'What is the meaning of this, Udalo?' demanded the ape-man, indicating the surrounding warriors, with a nod. 'I came in peace, to talk to you as a brother.'

Udalo cleared his throat nervously. 'Since you were here and went away, there has been much talk. Our people remembered the stories they had heard about the Kavuru. It is said that they are white men who go naked, even as you. We do not know anything about you; you are a stranger. Many of my people think that you are a Kavuru, that you have come to spy upon us and select young girls to steal from us.'

'That is foolish talk, Udalo,' said Tarzan.

'My people do not think it is foolish talk,' growled the chief. 'You have come to the kraal of Udalo once too often.' He rose slowly to his feet. 'You shall not steal any more of our young girls.' And with that, he slapped his palms sharply together; and instantly the surrounding warriors leaped upon the ape-man.

5

'The Lion Is Coming!'

'I can't stand it any longer,' said the princess. 'I mean this cramped position is killing me, and it is cold in here; I am nearly frozen.'

'What right have you got to whine?' growled Alexis. 'You got us into this, you and your aviator.' He spat the last word out contemptuously.

'Listen, Prince,' said Jane, 'you and the rest of us can thank Brown's cool head and efficiency for the fact that we are alive and uninjured. It is little short of a miracle that none of us is hurt. I'll venture to say that there's not one pilot in a thousand who could set this ship down as he did.'

'I beg your pardon,' said Tibbs, 'if I may say so, it has stopped raining.'

'And there's the sun,' cried Annette, excitedly.

Making her way to the door, Jane opened it and looked down. 'We are only fifty feet from the ground,' she said, 'but we may have a little difficulty getting down – that is, some of us may.'

'What in the world are you doing, my dear?' demanded the princess, as Jane commenced to take off her shoes and stockings.

'I am going to have a look around. I want to see if I can get at the baggage compartment. We are going to need some of the stuff in there. I'm afraid we are going to find it mighty uncomfortable on the ground; it may be cold in here, but it will be cold and wet both, down there.'

'We might make a fire, madam, if I might be so bold as to suggest it,' offered Tibbs.

'Everything is rather wet and soggy, but perhaps we can manage it. It's too bad we haven't gasoline left. That would help a lot.'

'There'll be some in the sump in the bottom of the tank,' said Brown.

'But why are you taking off your shoes and stockings?' asked the princess.

'It's the only safe way to climb around in trees, Kitty.'

'But my dear, I mean – after all, you don't intend to climb around in that tree?'

'Precisely, and that is what you will have to do, too, if you ever want to get down from here.'

'Oh, but my dear, I couldn't. I positively couldn't do it.'

'We'll help you when the time comes, and see that you don't fall; and while I am looking around, Brown, I wish you and Tibbs would remove all the safety belts and fasten them together into one long strap. It may be necessary to lower the princess to the ground, and a strap will come in handy in getting the luggage down safely.'

'You better let me go out and look around, Miss,' said Brown; 'you might fall.'

Jane smiled. 'I am used to it, Brown,' she said. 'You'd probably be in far more danger than I.' And then she stepped out onto the crumpled wing and leaped lightly to a nearby branch.

'Great scott, look out, Miss, you'll fall!' shouted Brown.

'Be careful, madam! You'll kill yourself.' Tibbs almost showed emotion.

'My dear, I mean, come back,' wailed the princess.

Annette screamed and covered her eyes with her palms.

'My dear lady, come back! For my sake, come back!' begged Alexis.

But Jane paid no attention to them, as she took two short steps along the branch that brought her within reach of the baggage compartment. It was not locked, and she quickly opened the door.

'Wh-ew!' she exclaimed. 'What a mess. There's a broken branch rammed right up through here. It's a good thing for us it didn't come through the cabin.'

'Is everything ruined?' asked Alexis.

'Oh, my no, some of the things must be damaged, but I imagine we can salvage nearly everything; and one of the first things I want to salvage is a pair of shorts. Skirts are bad enough at any time, but in a tree-top they are a calamity. What luck! Here is my bag right in front. I won't be but a jiffy, and after I've changed I'll be able to accomplish something.'

She opened her bag and selected two or three garments. Then she swung lightly to a lower branch and disappeared from their view beneath the ship.

'Say!' exclaimed Brown, admiringly. 'She's as much at home in the trees as a monkey. I never saw anything like it.'

Alexis clambered to a point from which he could look out of the door. Brown and Tibbs were removing the safety belts and fastening them together.

Alexis looked down and shuddered. 'It must be a hundred feet to the ground,' he said. 'I don't see how we are ever going to make it; and those branches are wet and slippery.'

'Take off your shoes and stockings like she did,' advised Brown.

'I'm no monkey.'

'No?'

'If I might venture to suggest it, Sir, we could fasten the strap around you and lower you.'

'It will hold a thousand pounds,' said Brown; 'it's tested for that. It'll sure hold you, but you'd better leave your title behind; that's the heaviest part of you.'

'I've stood about enough of your impertinence, fellow,' snapped Alexis. 'Another word like that from you and I'll— I'll—'

'You'll what?' demanded Brown. '– you and who else?'

'I wish you two would quit quarrelling,' said the princess. 'I mean, aren't things bad enough as they are without that?'

'My dear, I do not quarrel with servants,' said Alexis, haughtily.

'In the first place,' said Brown, 'I ain't no servant; and in the second place, you'd better not quarrel if you know what's good for you. There's nothing I'd like better than an excuse to smack you on the beezer.'

'If you ever dare lay hands on me, I'll—'

'What? Fire me again?' exclaimed Brown. 'Now I'll just naturally have to paste you one to learn you your place; then maybe you'll remember that you ain't nothing but a worm, and that if you had a title a block long you'd still be a worm.'

'Don't you dare strike me,' cried the prince, shrinking back.

'What is the meaning of all this?' Jane stepped lightly into the doorway of the cabin. 'I thought I told you two to stop quarrelling. Now before we go any further, I want to tell you something. We're stranded here, the Lord only knows where; there may not be a white man within hundreds of miles; we shall have to depend solely upon our own resources. Quarrelling and bickering among ourselves won't get us anywhere; it will just make our plight all the worse. One of us has got to take charge. It should be a man, and the only man here having any jungle experience, insofar as I know, or who is capable of commanding, is Brown. But there's too much friction between him and the prince; so Brown is out of the question.'

'I will take full charge,' said Alexis.

'The heck you will!' exclaimed Brown.

'My rank entitles me to the post,' insisted Alexis, haughtily.

'You said it,' jibed Brown. 'You're rank all right.'

'No, Alexis, you're out, too,' said Jane. 'We've got to have someone whom all will obey.'

'That just leaves Tibbs, then,' said Brown. 'Tibbs will suit me all right.'

'Oh, dear me, no,' cried Tibbs. 'Really, if you'll permit me, I couldn't think of assuming so much authority. I – I – well, you know, I haven't been accustomed to it, madam.' He turned piteously to Jane. 'But you, madam, I am sure that we would all be extraordinarily proud to have you for our leader.'

'That is what I was going to suggest,' said Jane. 'I know the jungle better than any of you, and I am sure there isn't anyone else we could all agree on.'

'But it's our expedition,' objected Alexis. 'We paid for everything; we own the ship and all the supplies; I am the one who should command. Isn't that right, my dear?' He turned to his wife.

'Oh, really, my dear, I mean. I don't know. Since you said those horrid things to me, I am crushed. My world has collapsed around my ears.'

'Well,' said Brown, 'there's no use chewing the fat any more about that. Lady Greystoke is boss from now on, and if there's anybody that don't like it, I'll attend to them.'

The Princess Sborov was slumped dejectedly on the floor of the ship, her handkerchief pressed to her eyes. 'It doesn't make any difference to me,' she said; 'I don't care what happens now. I don't care if I die; I hope I do.' As she finished, she glanced up, presumably to note the effect of her words upon her listeners, and for the first time since Jane had returned to the ship she saw her. 'Oh, my dear,' she exclaimed, 'what a cute outfit. I mean, it's perfectly ducky.'

'Thanks,' said Jane, 'I'm glad you like it; it's practical, at least.' She was wearing shorts, and a leather jacket. Her legs and feet were bare. A figured red scarf, wrapped once around her head, confined her hair and served the purposes of a hat.

'But, my dear, won't you freeze to death?' demanded the princess.

'Well,' laughed Jane, 'I won't exactly freeze to death, but I shall probably be cold lots of times – one gets used to being either too hot or too cold in the jungle. Now I am going down to look around for a suitable camping place, and you'd all better pray that there's one close by. While I am gone, Brown, you and Tibbs lower the luggage to the ground. Alexis, you go below and receive it; there's got to be someone there to unfasten the strap each time.'

'Let Annette do it,' growled Alexis. 'What do you suppose we've got servants for?'

'Each of us has got to do his share, Alexis,' said Jane, quietly, 'and there are certain things, the heavier and more dangerous work, that will naturally fall to the men. There are no servants and no Masters among us now. The sooner we all realize that, the better off and the happier we are going to be.'

Alexis approached the door of the ship gingerly and looked down. 'Let Brown go down,' he said; 'I'll help Tibbs lower the baggage to him.' Then he glanced in the direction of the baggage compartment. 'How could anyone get out there on that branch,' he said, 'and do anything? He'd fall and break his neck.'

'Ah, can the chatter and go on down, as Lady Greystoke told you to,' said Brown. 'Say the word, Miss, and I'll toss him down.'

'No you won't; you don't dare touch me.'

'Then get on over the edge and start down.'

'I can't; I'd fall.'

'Put the strap around him, Brown,' said Jane, 'and you and Tibbs lower him to the ground. I'm going along now.' And with that, she jumped lightly to a nearby branch and swung down through the leafy foliage toward the ground below.

She breathed the odors of the steaming jungle with a keen delight. The restrictions of ordered society, the veneer of civilization, fell away, leaving her free; and she sensed this new freedom with a joy that she had not felt since she had left the jungle to return to London.

Everything about her reminded her of Tarzan. She looked about her, listening intently. It seemed inevitable that at the next moment she would see a bronzed giant swing down through the foliage to clasp her in his arms; and then, with a sigh and a rueful smile, she shook her head, knowing full well that Tarzan was probably hundreds of miles away, ignorant both of her whereabouts and her plight. It was possible that he might not even yet have received her cable, telling him that she was flying to Nairobi. When he did receive it and she did not come, how would he know where to search for her? They had flown blind for so long that even Brown had no idea how far off their course they had been, nor even the approximate location of their landing place. It seemed quite hopeless that they should expect outside help. Their only hope lay within themselves.

Whatever their situation, she and Brown she felt might reasonably expect to pull through; that is, if they had been alone. But how about the others? Tibbs, she thought, might have possibilities of resourcefulness and endurance. She had her doubts about Alexis. Men of his stamp were oftentimes almost as helpless as women. Annette was young and strong, but temperamentally unfitted for the grim realities of the jungle against which they would have to pit themselves. Her efficiency and even her strength would be lessened by the constant terror in which she would exist. As for Kitty, Jane mentally threw up her hands – hopeless, absolutely hopeless, in the face of any hardship, emergency, or danger. Yes, she felt that she and Brown could pull through; but could they pull the others through? It went without saying that they would not desert them.

Her mind partially occupied with these thoughts, she moved through the lower terrace of the jungle, for so thickly was the ground overgrown with underbrush that she had kept to the lower branches of the trees to make her progress easier.

She did not go far in one direction, because she realized the difficulty of transporting their supplies for any great distance through the heavy undergrowth.

Circling, she sought for an open space, however small, in which they might build a temporary camp; but the jungle appeared to become wilder and less penetrable.

She had completed half the circle, and was on the side of the ship opposite that from which she had descended, when she came unexpectedly upon a game trail.

Immediately her spirits rose, for now they were assured of comparatively easy going and the certainty, almost, that eventually they would find natives.

Before returning to the ship, she followed the trail a short distance, when suddenly she came upon a small stream and, beside it, an opening in the underbrush, perhaps an acre in extent.

Elated, she turned back toward the ship, following the trail to ascertain how close it ran to the point from which the baggage must be transported.

As she turned, she heard a slight rustling in the undergrowth behind her, a sound which her trained ears detected quickly and almost identified. Yet she was not sure.

Nevertheless, she increased her gait, taking quick glances ahead and upward that she might always have an avenue of escape located in the event of sudden necessity.

The sound continued, a little behind her and paralleling the trail along which she moved.

She could hear Brown and Alexis quarrelling with one another and bickering over the handling of the baggage. Alexis was on the ground, and he seemed very close. Of course, she might be mistaken. The thing that she heard might not be what she feared it was; but perhaps it would be as well to warn Alexis before it was too late, and so she called to him.

'What is it?' he demanded, sullenly.

'You had better climb a tree, Alexis. I think a lion is following me. He is very close.'

'I can't climb a tree,' shouted Alexis. 'I can't move through this undergrowth. Help! Brown, help! Do something, somebody!'

'Lower the strap to him and pull him up,' shouted Jane. 'It may not be a lion; and he may not bother us if it is, but we'd better be on the safe side.'

'Hurry up with that strap, you fool,' shrieked Alexis.

'There ain't no hurry,' Brown replied, tantalizingly; 'at least, I ain't in no hurry.'

'If you let that lion get me, it'll be murder.'

'Oh, I guess he can stand it,' replied Brown.

'Hurry up and lower that strap, you murderer.'

'Ain't I lowering it, as fast as I can?'

'Oh, I can hear him now; he's right on top of me; he'll get me.'

'That is me you hear, Alexis,' said Jane, reassuringly.

'Well, what if he does get you?' demanded Brown. 'Ain't a lion got to eat? In California they feed them animals that ain't no good; so what are you crabbing about?'

'Hurry now, Brown,' cried Jane. 'The lion is coming, and he's coming fast.'

6

The Ballot of Death

As the Bukena warriors closed in upon him, Tarzan stood with folded arms, ignoring them. He was surrounded by many spears; and he knew that at this instant, if he sought to escape or give battle, a dozen spear points would transfix him instantly.

His one hope lay in gaining time, and he felt that he could accomplish this best by feigning indifference.

'Kill the Kavuru!' shouted a woman in rear of the warriors. 'They stole my daughter.'

'And mine,' screamed another.

'Kill him! Kill him!' urged others of the savage throng.

A very old man, who had been squatting beside Udalo, leaped to his feet. 'No! No!' he screamed. 'Do not kill him. If he be a Kavuru, his people will come and punish us. They will kill many of us and take all of our girls.'

Instantly the blacks commenced arguing among themselves. Some insisted upon killing him, others wanted to take him prisoner, while others thought that he should be released to mollify the Kavuru.

As they jabbered, the spearmen in the front rank relaxed their vigilance. Some of them turned around and sought to expound their views to those behind them, and in this circumstance Tarzan thought he saw his chance to escape. With the speed of Ara, the lightning, and the strength of Gorgo, the buffalo, he leaped upon a nearby warrior and holding him as a shield in front of him, charged through the human ring that surrounded him, turning constantly so that no weapon could be directed against him without endangering the life of the black.

So quickly had he acted that the blacks were taken entirely off their guard; and he had won almost to the clear, where he might have made a quick run for the village gate, when something struck him heavily on the back of the head.

When he regained consciousness, he found himself in the dark interior of an evil-smelling hut, his wrists and ankles securely bound.

With the return of consciousness came recollection of what had transpired; and the ape-man could not restrain a slow smile, for it was evident to him that the faction that had been afraid to kill him was more powerful than that which would have taken his life. Once again luck was with him.

For the time being, therefore, he was safe; and so he was certain of escape; for he was so constituted that while life remained in him, he could not conceive a permanent captivity; nor could anything for long shake his confidence in his ability to extricate himself from any predicament that might overtake him; for was he not Tarzan of the Apes, Lord of the Jungle?

Presently he commenced to test the bonds that secured his wrists and ankles. They were very strong and there were a great many strands, and soon he saw that it would be hopeless to attempt to liberate himself. There was nothing to do, therefore, but wait.

Unlike an ordinary man, he did not waste time wondering what his fate would be. Instead, he composed himself as comfortably as he could and fell asleep.

And while he slept, a council of warriors plotted in the council house with Udalo, the chief. It was they who were wondering what Tarzan's fate should be.

The old man who had first warned them against killing their prisoner was still his staunchest defender. He was Gupingu, the witch-doctor. He prophesied that dire calamity would befall them if they harmed this man who, he assured them, was a Kavuru. But there were others who spoke quite as insistently for death.

'If he is a Kavuru,' said one of these, 'his people will come and punish us as soon as they find that we have attacked him and made him prisoner. If we kill him, he cannot go back to them and tell them; and the chances are that they will never know what became of him.'

'Those are true words,' said another; 'a dead Kavuru is better than a live one.'

Then Udalo spoke. 'It is not for one man to decide,' he said. 'The talk of many men is better than the talk of one.'

On the ground beside him were two bowls. One contained kernels of corn and the other small, round pebbles. He passed one of these bowls to the warrior upon his right and one to him upon his left. 'Let each warrior take a kernel of corn and a pebble – just one of each, not more,' he said.

They passed the bowls from hand to hand about the circle; and each warrior took a kernel of corn and a pebble; and when the bowls were returned to Udalo, he set them down beside him and picked up a gourd with a small neck.

'We will pass this gourd around the circle,' he said, 'and each man shall speak either with a kernel of corn or with a pebble for the life or the death of the stranger. If you wish him to live, put a kernel of corn in the gourd; if you wish him to die, put a pebble.'

In silence, the gourd was passed around the grim circle as savage eyes followed it from the tense, painted faces of the warriors.

The dropping of the fateful ballots into the hollow gourd sounded distinctly in every part of the large council-house. At last the gourd completed the circle and came back to Udalo.

There were fully a hundred warriors in the circle; and Udalo could not count to a hundred, but he had an equally certain way of determining the outcome of the voting even though he was unable to determine how many votes were cast upon each side.

He emptied the contents of the gourd upon the ground in front of him. Then with one hand, he picked up a grain of corn and, simultaneously, with the other, a pebble, and placed each in its respective bowl; and this he continued to do as long as there were kernels of corn and pebbles to match one another. But this was not for long, for he soon ran out of corn; and even then there were seventy-five or eighty pebbles left, showing that only a few had voted to spare the life of the ape-man.

Udalo looked up and around the table. 'The stranger dies,' he said. A savage, sinister shout rose from the assembled warriors.

'Let us go and kill him now,' said one, 'before the Kavuru can come and find him among us.'

'No,' said Udalo, 'tomorrow night he dies. Thus will the women have time to prepare a feast. Tomorrow night we shall eat and drink and dance, while we torture the Kavuru. Let him suffer as he has made us suffer when he stole our children.'

A roar of approval and satisfaction greeted this suggestion.

The council was over. The warriors had returned to their huts. Fires were banked. Silence had fallen upon the village of the Bukena. Even the usually yapping curs were silent. The kraal was wrapped in slumber.

From a hut near the chief's, a figure crept silently into the night. It paused in the shadow of the hut from which it had emerged and looked fearfully about.

Nothing stirred, and silently as a ghostly shadow the figure crept along the village streets.

Tarzan had been awakened by the savage cries from the council-house; and he had lain sleepless for some time because of the discomfort of his bonds, but presently he dozed again.

He was not yet fully asleep when something awakened him – a sound that you or I, with our dull ears, might not have heard – the sound of naked feet creeping slowly and stealthily toward the hut where he lay.

Tarzan rolled over so that he could see the entrance to the hut, and presently it was filled by a shadowy form. Someone was entering. Was it the executioner coming to destroy him?

7

The Merry Company

The lion broke through the underbrush into the trail a short distance behind Jane. It was then that she called her warning to Alexis.

At sight of Jane, the lion bared his fangs and growled. Then he came toward her at a trot, and as he did so the girl leaped for an overhanging branch. As she caught it, the lion charged. He leaped for her, and his raking talons barely missed her bare foot as she drew herself safely out of his reach. With a hideous growl, he turned and leaped again.

The prince was only a short distance away, but he was hidden by the dense underbrush beneath the ship. The angry growl sounded very close; the man was paralyzed with terror.

From her position on the branch of the tree, Jane could see him. 'You'd better get out of there, Alexis,' she said, 'but don't make any noise. If he hears you, he'll come for you; he's terribly sore about something – must have missed his kill last night.'

Alexis tried to speak, but no sound came from his throat. He just stood there trembling, an ashen pallor on his face.

Jane could not see Brown, but she knew that he was directly above Alexis. 'Brown,' she called, 'drop the end of the strap to the prince. Fasten it around your body underneath your arms, Alexis; and Brown and Tibbs will pull you up. I'll try and keep Numa's attention riveted on me.'

The lion was pacing back and forth beneath the tree, glaring hungrily up at the girl.

Jane broke off a small, dead branch and threw it at the beast. It struck him in the face; and, with a roar, he leaped again for the branch on which Jane stood.

In the meantime, Brown lowered the end of the strap quickly to Alexis. 'Hurry up; fasten it around you,' he said. 'For Pete's sake, what's the matter with you? Get a move on.' But Alexis just stood there trembling, his teeth chattering, and his knees knocking together.

'Alexis, snap out of it,' cried Jane. 'You've got to get that belt fastened around you before the lion discovers you. Don't you understand? It's a matter of life and death with you.'

'You poor sap,' yelled Brown. 'Get a move on.'

With trembling hands, Alexis reached for the belt, and at the same time he seemed to find his voice and commenced to scream lustily for help.

'Keep still,' warned Jane. 'The lion hears you; he is looking in your direction now.'

'Hurry up, you dumb cluck,' shouted Brown.

The lion was tearing through the underbrush, searching for the author of these new sounds. Jane threw another branch at him, but it did not distract his attention. He only growled and started cautiously into the brush.

With fumbling fingers, Alexis was tying the belt about his body.

'Hoist away, Brown,' cried Jane; 'the lion is coming!'

Brown and Tibbs pulled away lustily, and Alexis rose out of the underbrush.

The lion came steadily on. At last he was directly beneath the terrified man. Alexis, looking down straight into the cruel eyes of the carnivore, voiced a scream of horror.

Slowly, a few inches at a time, Brown and Tibbs were raising Alexis out of harm's way; but still he was perilously close to the great beast. Then the lion rared up to its full height and struck at him. A raking talon touched the heel of the man's shoe; and, with a final scream, Alexis fainted.

Brown and Tibbs redoubled their efforts. The lion dropped back to the ground, gathered himself and sprang. Again he missed, but only by inches; and before he could spring again, Alexis was safely out of his reach.

The two men hoisted the limp body of Sborov to the ship, and with considerable difficulty dragged him into the cabin.

At sight of him, the princess commenced to scream. 'He's dead! he's dead! Oh, my darling, and your Kitty was so cross to her Allie.'

'For Pete's sake, shut up,' snapped Brown. 'My nerves are about shot, and anyway the sap isn't dead; he's just scared stiff.'

'Brown, how dare you speak to me like that!' cried the princess. 'Oh, it's terrible; nobody knows what I'm suffering. I mean, no one understands me; everyone is against me.'

'Lord,' cried Brown, 'a little more of this and we'll all be nuts.'

'Excuse me, madam, but he seems to be coming to,' said Tibbs; 'I think he'll be all right in a minute, mam.'

'Do something, Annette,' cried the princess. 'What are you sitting there for – just like a bump on a log? I mean, where are the smelling salts? Get some water. Oh, isn't it terrible? Oh, darling, Allie, speak to your Kitty.'

Alexis opened his eyes and looked about him. Then he closed them and shuddered. 'I thought he had me,' he said, in a trembling whisper.

'No such luck,' said Brown.

'It was a very close call, Sir, if I may make so bold as to say so, Sir,' said Tibbs.

Jane stepped into the cabin doorway. 'All right?' she asked. 'From the noise you were making, Kitty, I thought something dreadful had happened.'

'The Lord only knows what would happen if something really should happen,' said Brown, disgustedly. 'I'm getting fed up on all this screaming and bellyaching. I never had no royalty in my hair before, but I sure got 'em now.'

Jane shook her head. 'Be patient, Brown,' she said. 'Remember this is all new to them, and naturally anyway their nerves are on edge after all that we have passed through.'

'Well, ain't the rest of us got nerves, Miss? Ain't we got a right to be upset, too? But you don't hear none of us bawling around like them. I suppose being royal gives 'em the right to be nuisances.'

'Never mind, now,' said Jane; 'you're getting as bad as the others, Brown. The thing that I am interested in just now is what we are going to do about that lion. He may hang around here for hours; and as long as he does, we're just blocked. He's in a nasty mood, and it won't be safe to go down there until we know that he has cleared out. The best thing for us to do is to kill him, as he may hang around this neighborhood waiting for a chance to get some of us. He's an old fellow; and because of that, he may be a man-eater. They get that way when they are too old to bag their regular prey.'

'A man-eater!' The Princess Sborov shuddered. 'How horrible. I mean, how terribly horrible.'

'I think we can get rid of him,' said Jane. 'You brought rifles, of course, Alexis?'

'Oh, yes, indeed, two of them – high-powered rifles – they'd stop an elephant.'

'Good,' said Jane, 'where are they?'

'They're in the baggage compartment, Miss; I'll get them,' said Brown.

'And bring some ammunition, too,' said Jane.

'Who's going down there to shoot the horrid thing?' demanded the princess.

'I, of course,' said Jane.

'But, my dear,' cried the princess, 'I mean, you just couldn't.'

Brown returned with a rifle. 'I couldn't find no ammunition, Miss,' he said. 'Where is it packed, Sborov?'

'Eh, what?' demanded the prince.

'The ammunition,' snapped Brown.

'Oh, ammunition?'

'Yes, ammunition, you—'

The prince cleared his throat. 'Well, you see, I – ah.'

'You mean you didn't bring any ammunition?' demanded Brown. 'Well, of all the—'

'Never mind,' said Jane. 'If there's no ammunition, there's no ammunition, and grousing about it isn't going to get us any.'

'If I may be permitted, I think I can be of assistance, Milady,' said Tibbs, not without some show of pride.

'How is that, Tibbs?' asked Jane.

'I have a firearm in my bag, Milady. I will kill the beast.'

'That's fine, Tibbs,' said Jane; 'please go and get it.'

As Tibbs was moving toward the doorway, he suddenly stopped. A flush slowly mantled his face; he appeared most uncomfortable.

'What's the matter, Tibbs?' asked Jane.

'I – I had forgotten, Milady,' he stammered, 'but my bag has already been lowered down there with the bloomin' lion.'

Jane could not repress a laugh. 'This is becoming a comedy of errors,' she cried, '– rifles without ammunition, and our only firearm in possession of the enemy.'

'Oh, my dear, what are we going to do?' demanded the princess.

'There's nothing to do until that brute goes away. It's almost too late now anyway to try to make camp; we'll simply have to make the best of it up here for the night.'

And so it was that a most unhappy and uncomfortable party shivered and grumbled through the long, dark night – a night made hideous by the roars of hunting lions and the shrill screams of stricken beasts. But at last day broke with that uncanny suddenness that is a phenomenon of equatorial regions.

The moment that it was light enough Jane was out reconnoitering. The lion was gone; and a survey of the surrounding country in the immediate vicinity of the ship, from the lower branches of the trees, revealed no sign of him or any other danger.

'I think we can go down now and start making camp,' she said, after she had returned to the ship. 'Is most of the baggage down, Brown?'

'All but a few pieces, Miss,' he replied.

'Well, get it down as rapidly as possible; and then we'll cut an opening to the trail; it is only a few yards.'

'All right, Miss,' said Brown. 'Come on, Your Majesty, we'll lower you down to unhook the stuff at the other end.'

'You won't lower me down,' said Alexis. 'I wouldn't go down there alone again for all the baggage in the world.'

Brown looked at the man with disgust that he made no effort to conceal. 'All right,' he said, 'you stay up here and help Tibbs; I'll go down and unfasten the stuff when you lower it to me.'

'If you think I'm going to balance out there on that limb and unload the baggage compartment, you're mistaken,' said the prince. 'It's absolutely out of the question; I get very dizzy in high places, and I should most certainly fall.'

'Well, what are you going to do?' demanded Brown; 'sit around here while the rest of us wait on you?'

'That's what you servants were hired for,' said Alexis.

'Oh, yeah? Well—'

'I'll go down below,' said Jane. 'Brown, you and Tibbs lower the stuff to me. Now let's get busy,' and with that she turned and dropped down through the trees to the ground below.

With a grunt of disgust, Brown climbed out on the limb that led to the baggage compartment, followed by Tibbs; and the two soon lowered away the remainder of the luggage.

'Now lower your passengers,' called Jane, after Brown had told her that there was no more baggage. 'Alexis, you come first.'

'Come on, Your Majesty,' said Brown; 'you're going first.'

'I told you that I wouldn't go down there alone,' said the prince. 'Lower the others.'

'All right, Your Majesty, but if you don't go now, you'll either climb down yourself or stay here till Hell freezes over, for all I care. Come ahead, Annette; I guess you're the one to go first, and then we'll lower the old lady.'

'Brown, how dare you refer to me so disrespectfully?' It was the voice of the Princess Sborov coming from the interior of the cabin.

'There's nothing wrong with her ears,' said Brown, with a grin.

'I'm terribly afraid, Mr Brown,' said Annette.

'You needn't be, little one,' he replied; 'we'll see that nothing happens to you. Come on, sit down in the doorway and I'll put this belt around you.'

'You won't drop me?'

'Not a chance, my dear. I might drop royalty, but not you.'

She flashed him a quick smile. 'You are so very nice, Mr Brown,' she said.

'You just finding that out? Well, come on, sister; climb out on this branch here. I'll help you. Steady – now sit down. Ready, Tibbs?'

'Ready, Sir,' replied Tibbs.

'All right. Now down you go.'

Annette clutched her rosary, closed her eyes, and started praying, but before she realized it she had touched the ground and Jane was helping to remove the belt from about her.

'Now, princess,' called Brown.

'Oh, I can't move,' cried the princess. 'I'm paralyzed. I mean, I really am.'

Brown turned to Sborov. 'Go in there, mister, and fork your old lady out,' he snapped. 'We ain't got no time to fool around. Tell her if she don't come pronto, we'll leave you both up here.'

'You unspeakable ruffian,' sputtered the prince.

'Shut up, and go on and do what I tell you to,' growled the pilot.

Sborov turned back to his wife and helped her to the door of the cabin, but one glance down was enough for her. She screamed and shrank back.

'Hurry up, hurry up, hurry up,' said Brown.

'I can't. I mean, I just can't, Brown.'

Brown made his way to the cabin. He carried the end of a long strap with him. 'Come on,' he said, 'let me get this around you.'

'But I can't do it, I tell you. I mean, I shall die of fright.'

'You won't die of nothing; half-witted people live forever.'

'That will be enough out of you, Brown. I have endured all of your insults that I am going to.' The princess bridled and attempted to look very dignified, in which, in her dishevelled condition, she failed miserably.

Brown had stooped and fastened the belt about her.

'Ready, Tibbs?' he asked.

'Yes, Sir. All ready, Sir,' replied the valet.

'Come on then, princess. Here, you, give me a lift. Shove on her from behind.'

Brown pulled from in front, and Alexis pushed from behind, and the Princess Sborov shrieked and clawed at everything in sight in an attempt to get a hold that they could not break.

'What's the matter up there?' demanded Jane. 'Is anyone hurt?'

'No,' replied Brown. 'We're just moving the better half of the royal family. Now listen, princess, we're doing this for your own good. If you stays up here alone, you starves to death.'

'Yes, go on, Kitty. You're delaying things,' said Alexis.

'A lot you'd care if I were killed, Alexis. I suppose you'd be glad if I were dead – it's all that will you got me to make. I was a big fool to do it; but, believe me, I mean, just as soon as I find writing materials, I'm going to change it, after what you said to me and what you called me. I'll cut you off without a cent, Alexis, without a cent.'

The eyes of Prince Sborov closed to two ugly slits. His brow contracted in a frown, but he made no reply.

Brown took the princess' hands and held them away from the chair to which she had been clinging. 'There ain't no use, princess,' he said, a little less harshly this time, for he saw that the woman was genuinely terrified. 'Tibbs and I'll see that you don't get hurt none. We'll lower you easy, and Lady Grey-stoke and Annette are down there to help you. Just get hold of yourself and show a little spunk for a minute and it will be over.'

'Oh, I shall die, I know I shall die.'

Brown and Alexis lifted her out of the cabin onto the branch that passed close to the doorway. Slowly they eased her off it and then lowered her care-fully to the ground.

'Well, Tibbs,' said Brown, 'I guess you're next. Do you want to be lowered, or will you climb down?'

'I shall climb down,' replied Tibbs. 'You and I can go together and perhaps help one another.'

'Hey, how about me?' demanded Sborov.

'You climb, too, you louse, or you can stay up here,' replied Brown, 'and I don't mean maybe!'

8

Ydeni, the Kavuru

Framed in the small doorway of the hut and silhouetted against the lesser darkness beyond, Tarzan saw the figure of his stealthy nocturnal visitor and knew that it was a man.

Helpless in his bonds, the Lord of the Jungle could only wait, for he could not defend himself. And though he chafed at the thought of giving up his life without an opportunity to defend it, he was still unmoved and unafraid.

The figure crept closer, groping in the darkness, when suddenly Tarzan spoke. 'Who are you?' he demanded.

The creature sought to silence him with a sibilant hiss. 'Not so loud,' he cautioned. 'I am Gupingu, the witch-doctor.'

'What do you want?'

'I have come to set you free. Go back to your people, Kavuru, and tell them that Gupingu saved you from death. Tell them that because of this, they must not harm Gupingu or take his daughters from him.'

Darkness hid the faint smile with which Tarzan received this charge. 'You are a wise man, Gupingu,' he said; 'now cut my bonds.'

'One thing more,' said Gupingu.

'What is that?'

'You must promise never to tell Udalo, or any of my people, that I freed you.'

'They will never know from me,' replied the ape-man, 'if you will tell me where your people think we Kavuru live.'

'You live to the North, beyond a barren country, by a high mountain that stands alone in the center of a plain,' explained Gupingu.

'Do your people know the trail to the Kavuru country?'

'I know it,' replied the witch-doctor, 'but I promise not to lead anyone there.'

'That is well – if you know.'

'I do know,' insisted Gupingu.

'Tell me how you would reach this trail; then I shall know whether you know or not.'

'To the North of our kraal, leading to the North, is an old elephant trail. It winds much, but it leads always toward the country of the Kavuru. Much bamboo grows on the slopes of the mountain beside your village, and there the elephants have gone for years to feed on the young shoots.'

The witch-doctor came closer and felt for the bonds around Tarzan's ankles. 'After I have freed you,' he said, 'wait here until I have had time to return to my hut; then go silently to the gates of the village; there you will find a platform just inside the palisade from which the warriors shoot their arrows over the top when enemies attack us. From there you can easily climb over the top of the palisade, and drop to the ground on the outside.'

'Where are my weapons?' demanded Tarzan.

'They are in the hut of Udalo, but you cannot get them. A warrior sleeps just inside the doorway; you would awaken him if you tried to enter.'

'Cut my bonds,' said the ape-man.

With his knife, Gupingu severed the thongs about the prisoner's ankles and wrists. 'Wait now, until I have reached my hut,' he said, and turning, crawled silently through the doorway.

The ape-man stood up and shook himself. He rubbed his wrists and then his ankles to restore circulation. As he waited for Gupingu to reach his hut, he considered the possibility of regaining his weapons.

Presently, dropping to his knees, he crawled from the hut; and when he stood erect again upon the outside, he drew a deep breath. It was good to be free. On silent feet he moved down the village street. Other than in silence, he sought no concealment for he knew that even if he were discovered they could not take him again before he could reach the palisade and scale it.

As he approached the chief's hut, he paused. The temptation was very great; for it takes time and labor to produce weapons, and there were his own only a few paces from him.

He saw a faint light illuminating the interior of the hut – a very faint light from the embers of a dying fire. He approached the entrance, which was much larger than those of the other huts, and just inside and across the threshold he saw the figure of a sleeping warrior.

Tarzan stooped and looked into the interior. His quick, keen eyes, accustomed to darkness, discovered much more than might yours or mine; and one of the first things that they discovered were his weapons lying near the fire beyond the body of the warrior.

The throat of the sleeping man lay bare and fully exposed. It would have been the work of but a moment for the steel-thewed fingers of the ape-man to have throttled life from that unconscious figure. Tarzan considered the possibilities of this plan, but he discarded it for two reasons. One was that he never chose to kill wantonly; and the other, and probably the dominating reason, was that he was sure that the man would struggle even if he could not cry out and that his struggles would awaken the sleepers inside the hut, an event which would preclude the possibility of Tarzan retrieving his weapons. So he decided upon another and even more dangerous plan.

Stooping and moving cautiously, he stepped over the body of the warrior. He made no sound, and the two steps took him to his weapons.

First of all, he retrieved his precious knife, which he slipped into the sheath at his hip; then he adjusted the quiver of arrows behind his right shoulder and looped his rope across his left. Gathering his short spear and bow in one hand, he turned again toward the entrance, after a hasty glance around the interior of the hut to assure himself that its occupants were all asleep.

At that instant, the warrior rolled over and opened his eyes. At the sight of a man standing between himself and the fire, he sat up. In the gloom of the interior, it was impossible for him to know that this was an enemy, and the natural assumption was that one of the inmates of the hut was moving about in the night. Yet the figure did not seem familiar, and the warrior was puzzled.

'Who's that?' he demanded. 'What's the matter?'

Tarzan took a step nearer the man. 'Silence,' he whispered. 'One sound and you die; I am the Kavuru.'

The black's lower jaw dropped; his eyes went wide. Even in the semi-darkness, Tarzan could see him tremble.

'Go outside,' directed the ape-man, 'and I will not harm you; and go quietly.'

Shaking like a leaf, the warrior did as he was bid; and Tarzan followed him. He made the warrior accompany him to the gates and open them; then he passed out of the village of Udalo into the black jungle night. A moment later he heard the shouts of the warrior as he aroused the village, but Tarzan knew that there would be no pursuit. They would not dare follow a Kavuru into the night.

For an hour Tarzan followed the trail toward the North in accordance with Gupingu's directions. All about him were the noises of the jungle night – stealthy movements in the underbrush, the sound of padded feet, the coughing grunts of a nearby lion, the roar of a distant one; but his sensitive ears and nostrils told him where danger lurked; so that he was always alert to avoid it.

He was moving upwind, and presently he caught the scent of a lion that had not fed – a hunting lion, a hungry lion; and Tarzan took to the trees. A short search revealed a comfortable resting place, and here he lay up for the remainder of the night. Wondering what had become of Nkima, whom he had not seen since he was captured, he fell asleep, soothed by the familiar jungle sounds.

With the coming of dawn, he moved on again toward the North; and back in the village of Udalo, little Nkima cowered among the branches of the tree above the chief's hut.

He was a most unhappy little monkey, a very frightened little monkey. During the night the blacks had run from their huts shouting and jabbering. That had awakened Nkima, but he had not known the cause of it; he did not know that it meant that his Master had escaped from the village. He thought he was still lying in the hut where he had seen the Bukena take him.

When Nkima awoke again, dawn was dispelling the darkness. Below him, the village streets were deserted. He heard no sound of life from any hut. He looked down upon that one to which they had dragged his Master; and, summoning all his courage, he dropped quickly to the ground and scampered along the village street to the entrance to this hut.

A woman, coming from her hut to start her cooking fire, saw the little monkey and tried to catch him; but he escaped her and, racing across the village, scaled the palisade.

Not daring to enter the village again, and terrified at the thought of being alone in this strange country, Nkima fled through the jungle in the direction of home. And so Nkima went his way not knowing that his Master had escaped.

All day Tarzan made his way North along the winding elephant trail. It was not until late in the afternoon that he was able to make a kill; and then after feeding he lay up once more for the night.

In the afternoon of the second day the nature of the country changed. The jungle became more open and there were park-like places where there was little or no underbrush and the trees grew farther apart. It was a country entirely new to Tarzan, and as such whetted his imagination and aroused within him the instinct of exploration which had always been a powerful factor in affecting his destiny; for he had that intelligent inquisitiveness which set him above the other beasts of the jungle.

As he moved silently along his way, constantly on the alert, a vagrant breeze carried to his nostrils a strange scent that brought him to a halt. For a moment he stood in statuesque pose, every faculty alert.

Tarzan was puzzled. The scent was that of a Tarmangani, and yet there was a difference. It was an odor entirely new to him; and then, mingling with it, but fainter, came the familiar scent spoor of Numa, the lion.

Those two in proximity often meant trouble, and while Tarzan was not particularly interested in saving the man from the lion, or the lion from the man, whichever was hunting the other, natural curiosity prompted him to investigate.

The trees ahead of him grew sufficiently close together so that he could move through their branches; and this he elected to do, since always it gave him an advantage to come from above upon those he sought, especially where, in the case of men, they would not be expecting him.

The perception of the eyes of man is normally in a horizontal plane, while those of the cat family, with their vertical pupils, detect things above them far more quickly than would a man. Perhaps this is because for ages the cat family has hunted its prey in trees, and even though the lion no longer does so, he still has the eyes of his smaller progenitors.

As Tarzan swung in the direction of the strange scent spoor, he was aware that the odor of the lion was becoming stronger much more rapidly than the other scent, a fact which convinced him that the lion was approaching the man, though whether by accident or intent he could not of course determine; but the fact that the lion scent was that of a hungry lion, led him to believe that the beast was stalking the man.

Any beast with a full belly gives off a different odor from one that is empty; and as an empty stomach is always a hungry one, and as hungry lions are hunting lions, to Tarzan's mind it was a foregone conclusion that the man was the quarry and the lion the hunter.

Tarzan came in sight of the man first, and the initial glimpse brought the Lord of the Jungle to a sudden stop.

Here, indeed, was a white man, but how different from any white man that Tarzan had seen before! The fellow was clothed only in a loincloth that appeared to be made of gorilla hide. His ankles and wrists and arms were loaded with bracelets; a many-stranded necklace of human teeth fell across his breast. A slender cylinder of bone or ivory ran transversely through the pierced septum of his nose; his ears were ornamented with heavy rings. Except for a mane of hair from his forehead to the nape of his neck, his skull was shaved; and in this mane were fastened gay feathers which floated above a face hideously painted; and yet, with all these earmarks of the savage Negro, the man was undoubtedly white, even though his skin was bronzed by much exposure to the weather.

He was sitting on the ground with his back against a tree, eating something from a skin bag fastened to the string that supported his loincloth, and it was apparent that he was absolutely unaware of the proximity of the lion.

Cautiously, silently, Tarzan moved nearer until he was in the tree directly above the unconscious man. As he examined him more closely, he recalled the many fables concerning the Kavuru, and especially the one which described them as white savages.

This stranger, then, might be a Kavuru. It seemed reasonable to assume that he was, but further speculation on this subject was interrupted by a low snarl a short distance away.

Instantly the savage white was on his feet. In one hand he grasped a heavy spear, in the other a crude knife.

The lion burst from the underbrush at full charge. He was so close that the man had no chance to seek safety in the tree above him. All that he could do, he did. Swiftly his spear hand flew back, and in the next lightning move he launched the heavy weapon.

Perhaps the suddenness of this unexpected attack had momentarily unnerved him, for he made a clean miss; and simultaneously Tarzan leaped for the carnivore from a branch above the two.

He struck the lion at the shoulder diagonally from above just as he reared upon his hind legs to seize his victim. The impact of the ape-man's body toppled the lion upon its side. With a frightful roar, it regained its feet but not before the ape-man had locked his powerful legs around the small of its body and encircled its massive throat with one great arm.

As the two beasts fought, the white savage stood an awestruck witness to the strange duel. He heard the growls and roars of the man mingle with those of the lion. He saw them roll upon the ground together as lashing talons sought to reach the bronzed hide of the man-thing; and then he saw the knife hand rise and fall; and each time it drove the blade deep into the side of the King of beasts, until at last the roaring ceased and the tawny body collapsed in the final spasm of death.

The ape-man leaped erect. He placed a foot upon the carcass of his foe and raising his face to the sky voiced the kill-cry of the victorious bull ape.

At that weird and hideous call, the white savage shrank back and clutched the hilt of his knife more tightly.

As the last weird note died away in the distance, Tarzan turned and faced the creature whose life he had saved.

The two stood appraising each other in silence for a moment; then the savage spoke. 'Who are you?' he demanded, in the same dialect that the Bukena used.

'I am Tarzan of the Apes,' replied the ape-man. 'And you?'

'I am Ydeni, the Kavuru.'

Tarzan experienced that sense of satisfaction which one feels when events bear out his judgment. This was, indeed, a bit of good fortune, for now he would at least know what sort of people the Kavuru were. Perhaps this fellow would even guide him to the country he sought.

'But why did you kill the lion?' asked Ydeni.

'If I had not, he would have killed you.'

'Why should you care if he killed me? Am I not a stranger?'

The ape-man shrugged. 'Perhaps it was because you are a white man,' he said.

Ydeni shook his head. 'I do not understand you. I've never seen anyone like you before. You are not a black; you are not a Kavuru. What are you?'

'I am Tarzan,' replied the ape-man. 'I am looking for the village of the Kavuru; now you can take me there. I wish to speak with your chief.'

Ydeni scowled and shook his head. 'No one comes to the village of the Kavuru,' he said, 'other than those who come there to die. Because you have saved my life, I will not take you there, nor will I kill you now, as I should. Go your way, Tarzan, and see that it does not lead you to the village of the Kavuru.'

9
Sheeta, the Leopard

With the aeroplane party safely deposited on the ground, Brown cut a narrow path to the trail, using a small hand axe that fortunately had been included in the heterogeneous and generally quite useless impedimenta that the Prince and Princess Sborov had thought essential to the success of their expedition.

Tibbs had offered to help cut trail, but a lifetime of valeting had not fitted him for anything so practical as wielding a hand axe. He meant well, but he could hit nothing that he aimed at; and for fear that he might commit mayhem or suicide, Brown took the implement from him.

Sborov did not offer to help; and Brown ignored him entirely, knowing that he would prove less efficient, if possible, than Tibbs. But when it came to transporting the baggage, the pilot insisted that the prince do his share.

'You may be the scion of a long line of cab drivers,' he said, 'but you are going to work or get a punch on the nose.'

Sborov grumbled, but he worked.

After the luggage had been transported to the little clearing beside the stream that Jane had found, she directed the building of a boma and some rude shelters.

In this, the brunt of the work fell on Brown and Jane, though Annette and Tibbs assisted to the best of their ability. No one expected Kitty Sborov to do anything but moan, and she didn't. Alexis was assigned to the building of the boma after someone else had cut the brush – a job that was far beyond either his physical or mental attainments.

'I can't see how guys like him ever live to grow up,' grumbled Brown, 'nor what good they are after they do grow up. I never seen such a total loss before in my life.'

Jane laughed. 'He dances divinely, Brown,' she said.

'I'll bet he does,' replied the pilot. 'Damned gigolo, bringing along just a dinky little hand axe and rifles without any ammunition.' He spat the words out disgustedly. 'And look at all this here junk. Maybe there's something in it; we ought to take an inventory and see what we got.'

'That's not a bad idea,' said Jane. 'Oh, by the way, Tibbs, where's that gun of yours? We really should have it handy.'

'Yes, Milady, right away,' said Tibbs. 'I never travel without it; one can never tell when one is going to need it, and especially in Africa with all these lions and things.'

He located his bag, rummaged through it, and finally located his weapon, which he withdrew gingerly and exhibited not without considerable pride, holding it up where all might see it.

'There she is, Milady,' he said, 'and rather a beauty I fancy, too.'

Jane's heart sank as she looked at the little single shot .22 short pistol that Tibbs dangled before her so proudly.

Brown burst into a loud laugh. 'Say,' he said, 'if the Germans had known you had that, there wouldn't have been no World War.'

'Beg pardon, Mr Brown,' said Tibbs, stiffly; 'it is really a very fine weapon. The man I got it from said so himself. It stood me back seven bob, Sir.'

'Let me see it,' said Brown. Taking the pistol he opened the breech. ''Tain't loaded,' he said, 'and it wouldn't be no good if it was.'

'Bless me, no!' exclaimed Tibbs; 'I wouldn't think of carrying a loaded weapon, Sir; it's too dangerous. One never knows when it might go off.'

'Well,' said Jane, 'it may come in handy shooting small game. Got plenty of ammunition for it?'

'Well – er – Milady,' stammered Tibbs, 'you see I've always been intending to buy ammunition for it, but I never got around to it.'

Brown looked at the Englishman in pitying astonishment. 'Well, I'll be—'

Jane sat down on an upended suitcase and burst into laughter. 'Forgive me, Tibbs, but really it's too funny,' she cried.

'I'll tell you what we'll do,' said Brown. 'We'll put Tibbs on guard tonight and if he sees a lion he can throw that thing at him. It ain't any good for nothing else.'

'I don't see how you can laugh, Jane,' said Kitty. 'Suppose a lion should come. Tibbs, you should have brought ammunition. It is very careless of you.'

'It doesn't make any difference, Kitty, for as far as a lion is concerned, that pistol is just as effective empty as it would be loaded.'

'I know we are all going to be killed,' moaned Kitty. 'I wish I were back in the ship; it's much safer there.'

'Don't worry,' said Jane; 'the boma will be some protection, and we will keep a fire going all night. Most beasts are afraid of a fire; they won't come near one.'

Late in the afternoon, a shelter had been completed with two compartments, one for the women and one for the men. It was a very crude affair, but it provided some shelter from the elements and it induced a feeling of security far greater than it warranted, for it is a fact that if we can hide in something, however flimsy, we feel much safer than we do in the open.

While the shelters and boma were being built, Jane busied herself with another activity. Kitty had been watching her for some time, and finally her curiosity got the best of her.

'What in the world are you doing, dear?' she asked, as she watched Jane shaping a small branch with the hand axe.

'I am making weapons – a bow and arrows, and a spear.'

'Oh, how perfectly wonder – I mean, isn't it ducky? It's just like you, my dear, to think of archery; it will help us to pass the time away.'

'What I am making will help us obtain food and defend ourselves,' replied Jane.

'Oh, of course!' exclaimed Kitty; 'how perfectly silly of me, but when I think of archery I always think of little arrows sticking in the straw target. They are so colorful, my dear – I mean, the way they are painted. I recall such beautiful pictures of young people in sport clothes, of green turfs, and sunshine against a background of lovely trees. But who do you suppose ever thought of using bows and arrows to hunt game? I'm sure it must be original with you, my dear; but it's very clever of you, if you can hit anything.'

Toward the middle of the afternoon Jane had completed a very crude bow and half a dozen arrows, the tips of which she had fire-hardened.

Her work completed, she stood up and surveyed the camp. 'You are getting along splendidly,' she said. 'I'm going out to see what I can rustle for supper. Have you a knife, Brown? I may need one.'

'But, my dear, I mean you're not going out there alone?' cried Kitty.

'Sure she's not,' said Brown. 'I'll go along with you, Miss.'

'I'm afraid,' said Jane, with a smile, 'that where I am going, you couldn't follow. Here, let me have your knife.'

'I reckon I can go anywhere you can go, Miss,' said Brown, grinning.

'Let me have the knife,' said Jane. 'Why it's a nice big one! I always did like to see a man carrying a man-sized knife.'

'Well, if we are ready,' said Brown, 'let's start.'

Jane shook her head. 'I told you, you couldn't follow me,' she said.

'Want to lay a little bet on that?'

'Sure,' said Jane. 'I'll bet you a pound sterling against this knife that you can't keep up with me for a hundred yards.'

'I'll just take you up on that, Miss,' said Brown; 'let's get going.'

'Come ahead, then,' said Jane. And with that, she ran lightly across the clearing, leaped for a low hanging branch and swinging herself into the trees was out of sight in an instant.

Brown ran after her, seeking to catch a glimpse of her from the ground, but he was soon floundering in heavy undergrowth.

It didn't take him long to realize that he was beaten, and rather crestfallen he returned to the camp.

'Gracious!' exclaimed the princess. 'Did you ever see anything like it? It was perfectly wonderful. I mean, it really was; but I am so afraid something will happen to her out there alone. Alexis, you should not have permitted it.'

'I thought Brown was going with her,' said Alexis. 'If I had known that he was afraid, I would have gone myself.'

Brown eyed Alexis with contempt too deep for words as he returned to his work on the shelter.

'I should think anyone would be afraid to go out there,' said Annette, who was helping Brown thatch the roof with large leaves. 'Lady Greystoke must be so very brave.'

'She's sure got guts,' said Brown; 'and did you see the way she took to them trees? Just like a monkey.'

'Just as though she had lived in them all her life,' said Annette.

'Do you really think she can kill anything with her bow and arrows?' asked Tibbs; 'they look so – er – ah inadequate, if I may make so bold as to say so.'

'Say,' said Brown, 'she's not the kind that would go out there if she didn't know what she was doing. I thought all the time, until just before we crashed, that she was another one of them silly society dames that had never had anything in her noodle heavier than champagne bubbles; but believe me I take my hat off to her now; and you can believe me, when I take orders from a dame she's got to be some dame.'

'Lady Greystoke is a very remarkable woman,' said Alexis, 'and a very beautiful one. Kindly remember also, Brown, that she is a lady, a member of the English nobility, my man; I resent the lack of deference you show by referring to her as a dame, and saying that she has guts. I know you Americans are notoriously ill-bred, but there is a limit to what I can stand from you.'

'Yeah?' inquired Brown; 'and what are you going to do about it, you damned pansy?'

'Alexis, you forget yourself,' said the princess. 'You should not stoop to quarrel with an employee.'

'You're darned tootin', lady,' said Brown. 'He better not stoop to quarrel with this bozo; I'm just laying for an excuse to push in his mush.'

Annette laid a hand upon Brown's arm. 'Please, Mr Brown,' she said, 'do not quarrel. Is it not bad enough as it is, that we should make it worse by always quarreling among ourselves?'

Brown turned and looked at her quizzically; then he covered her little hand with his. 'I guess you're right, girlie, at that. I'll lay off him, if he'll lay off me.' He closed his hand on hers. 'I guess you and me's going to hit it off O.K. kid.'

'Hit what off, Mr Brown?'

'I mean, we're going to be pals!' he exclaimed.

'Pals? What are they?'

'Buddies – friends. I thought you savvied English.'

'Oh, friends; yes, I understand that. I should like to be friends with Mr Brown. Annette likes to be friends with everyone.'

'That's all right, baby, but don't be too promiscuous, for I have a feeling that I'm going to like you a lot.'

The French girl cast her eyes down coquettishly. 'I think, Mr Brown, we had better get along with our work, or we shall have only half a roof over our heads tonight.'

'O.K. kiddo, but we'll talk about this friendship business later – there ought to be a full moon tonight.'

After she left the camp, Jane moved rapidly and silently through the trees paralleling the little stream which she tried to keep in view while she searched for a place where the signs indicated the beasts were accustomed to come to drink.

A light breeze was blowing in her face, bringing faintly various scent spoors to her nostrils, which, while not as sensitive as those of her mate, were nevertheless far more sensitive than those of an ordinary civilized person. Jane had learned long ago that senses may be developed by training, and she had let no opportunity pass to train hers to the fullest of her ability.

Now, very faintly, she caught the suggestion of a scent that set her nerves to tingling with that thrill which only the huntsman knows. Quarry lay ahead.

The girl moved even more cautiously than before; scarcely a leaf stirred to her passage, and presently she saw ahead that which she sought – a small, harnessed antelope, a bush buck, which was moving daintily along the trail just ahead of her.

Jane increased her speed; but now more than ever it was imperative that she move silently, for the little animal below her was nervous and constantly alert. At the slightest unusual sound, it would be gone like a flash.

Presently she came within range, but there was always intervening foliage that might deflect her arrow.

Patience is the most important asset of the jungle hunter, and patience she had learned from Tarzan and from her own experiences.

Now the antelope halted suddenly in its tracks and turned its head to the left; at the same instant Jane was aware of a movement in the underbrush in that direction. She saw that she could wait no longer; already something had startled her quarry. There was a small opening in the foliage between her and the antelope. Like lightning, she drew her bow; the string snapped with a whang and the shaft buried itself deep in the body of the antelope behind its left shoulder. It leaped high into the air and fell dead.

Jane had reason to suspect that something else was stalking the antelope; but she could see nothing of it, and the turn in the trail had resulted in a crosswind that would carry the scent of the creature away from her.

She knew that it was a risky thing to do; but she was hungry, and she was aware that all her companions were hungry; they must have food, for a cursory examination of the baggage had revealed the fact that besides some sandwiches which had already been eaten, their stock of provisions consisted of a few chocolate bars, six bottles of cognac and two of cointreau.

Trusting to luck and pinning her faith in her speed, Jane dropped lightly to the trail and ran quickly to the fallen animal.

She worked rapidly, as Tarzan had taught her to work. Slitting its throat to let it bleed, she quickly eviscerated it to reduce the weight; and as she worked, she heard again those stealthy sounds in the underbrush not far distant along the back trail.

Her work completed, she closed the knife and slipped it into her pocket; then she raised the carcass of the little antelope to her shoulder. As she did so, an angry growl shattered the silence of the jungle; and Sheeta, the leopard, stepped into the trail twenty paces from her.

Instantly Jane saw that it would be impossible to escape with her kill, and resentment flared high in her bosom at the thought of relinquishing her prey to the savage cat.

She felt reasonably sure that she could save herself by taking to the trees and leaving the carcass of the antelope to Sheeta, but a sudden anger against the injustice of this contretemps impelled her to stand her ground and caused her to do a very foolish thing.

Dropping the antelope, she strung her bow and pulling it back to the full limit of her strength she drove an arrow straight at the breast of Sheeta.

As it struck, the beast voiced a horrifying scream of pain and rage; then it charged.

To those in the camp, the cry sounded almost human.

'Sapristi! What was that?' cried Alexis.

'Mon Dieu, it was a woman's scream!' exclaimed Annette.

'Lady Greystoke!' said Brown, horrified.

'Oh, Alexis, Alexis! Annette!' cried the princess; 'My smelling salts, quick; I am going to faint.'

Brown seized the puny hand axe and started in the direction of the sound.

'Oh, where are you going?' cried Kitty. 'Don't leave me, don't leave me.'

'Shut up, you old fool,' snapped Brown. 'Lady Greystoke must be in trouble. I am going to find out.'

Tibbs pulled his empty pistol from his pocket. 'I'll go with you, Mr Brown,' he said; 'we can't let anything happen to Milady.'

10

Abduction

When Ydeni refused to lead him to the village of the Kavuru, Tarzan was neither surprised nor disappointed. He knew men and especially savage men and the numerous taboos that govern their individual and tribal lives. He would have preferred to have gone to the chief of the Kavuru with one of his own people whom Tarzan had befriended; but if this were impossible, he was at least no worse off than he had been before he had met Ydeni. And he was confident that no matter how brutal or savage the man might be, he was probably not without a spark of gratitude for the service Tarzan had rendered him.

'If I came as a friend,' said Tarzan, 'surely there could be no harm in that.'

'The Kavuru have no friends,' replied Ydeni. 'You must not come.'

The ape-man shrugged. 'Then I shall come as an enemy.'

'You will be killed. You saved my life; I do not wish you to be killed, but I could not prevent it; it is the law of the Kavuru.'

'Then you kill the girls that you steal?' demanded the ape-man.

'Who says that the Kavuru steal girls?'

'It is well known among all people. Why do you do it? Have you not enough women of your own?'

'There are no Kavuru women,' replied Ydeni. 'The rains have come and gone as many times as there are fingers and toes upon four men since there was a Kavuru woman – since the last one gave her life that the men of the Kavuru might live.'

'Eighty years since there have been women among you?' demanded the ape-man. 'That is impossible, Ydeni, for you are still a young man, and you must have had a mother; but perhaps she was not a Kavuru?'

'My mother was a Kavuru, but she died long before the last woman. But I have told you too much already, stranger. The ways of the Kavuru are not as the ways of lesser people, and they are not for the ears of lesser people. To speak of them is taboo. Go your way now, and I will go mine.'

Convinced that he could get no more information from Ydeni, Tarzan took to the trees; and a moment later was lost to the sight of the Kavuru. Purposely he had gone toward the west so that Ydeni would be deceived into thinking that he was not on the right trail toward the Kavuru country. However, he did not go far in that direction; but quickly doubled back toward the spot where he had left the white savage; for he was determined that if Ydeni would not lead him willingly to his village, he should do so unknowingly.

When Tarzan had returned to the spot where he killed the lion, the Kavuru was no longer there; and assuming that he had gone toward the North, his pursuer set off in that direction.

After pursuing a Northerly course for a short time, Tarzan realized that there were no indications that his quarry had come this way.

Quickly he started a great circle in order to pick up the scent spoor.

For an hour he ranged through forest and open glade before, at last, Usha, the wind, carried to his nostrils the scent spoor of Ydeni; and when at last he came upon the object of his search Tarzan was perplexed, for the Kavuru was moving due South.

Tarzan reasoned that Ydeni might be doing this to throw him off the trail, or perchance he had misinformed him as to the location of the Kavuru village; but he was sure now that if he clung tenaciously to the trail, Ydeni would eventually lead him to his goal.

Back over the long trail he had come since he had escaped from the village of Udalo, the chief, Tarzan dogged the footsteps of his quarry; yet never once was Ydeni aware that he was being followed, though oftentimes he was plainly visible to the ape-man.

Tarzan found it interesting to study this strange creature whose very existence was tinged with mystery. He noted the weapons and the ornaments of Ydeni and saw that they differed from any that he had ever seen before. He was particularly interested in the slender fibre rope that was wrapped many times around the Kavuru's waist; for of all the savages in the jungle, as far as Tarzan knew, he alone used a rope as a weapon. He wondered just how Ydeni would use it.

Late one afternoon, when Tarzan knew they must be approaching the village of the Bukena, he was surprised to see Ydeni take to the trees, through which he moved with considerable agility and speed, though in no respect to compare with those of the Lord of the Jungle.

He moved with the utmost wariness, stopping often to listen intently. Presently he uncoiled the rope from about his waist, and Tarzan saw there was a running noose in one end of it.

Now Tarzan heard voices ahead of them; they came faintly as from a great distance. It was evident that the Kavuru heard them, too, for he slightly changed his direction to bear more in that from which the voices came.

Tarzan was keenly interested. The attitude of the man in front of him was that of the keen hunter, stalking his prey. He felt that one mystery was about to be cleared up.

In a short time, the Kavuru came to the edge of a clearing and halted. Below him, working in the small fields, were a number of women. Ydeni looked them over; presently he espied a girl of about fifteen and made his way to another tree nearer her.

Tarzan followed, watching intently every move of the Kavuru. He heard him voice a strange call, so low that it must barely have reached the ears of the girl. For a moment she paid no attention to it; and then presently she turned and looked with dull, uncomprehending eyes toward the jungle. The sharpened stick with which she had been cultivating the maize dropped from her limp hand.

Ydeni continued to voice that weird, insistent call. The girl took a few steps in the direction of the jungle; then she paused; and Tarzan could almost sense the struggle that was going on within her breast to overcome the mysterious urge that was drawing her away from the other women; but Ydeni's voice was insistent and compelling, and at last she again moved listlessly toward him. She moved as one in a trance, with staring eyes fixed on Ydeni.

Now the Kavuru retreated slowly deeper into the forest, calling, always calling to the helpless girl that followed.

Tarzan watched; nor did he make any effort to interfere. To him, the life of the black girl was no more than the life of an antelope or that of any other beast of the jungle. To Tarzan, all were beasts, including himself, and none with any rights greater than another, except that which he might win by strength or cunning or ferocity.

Much more important than the life of the black girl was the possibility of fathoming the mystery that had always surrounded the disappearance of girls supposed to have been taken by the Kavuru.

Ydeni lured the girl deeper into the forest, halting at last upon a broad limb.

Slowly the girl approached. It was evident that she was not the Master of her own will. The weird, monotonous droning chant of the Kavuru seemed to have numbed all her faculties.

At last, she came directly beneath the tree and the branch where Ydeni crouched. Then the man dropped his noose about her.

She made no outcry, no protest, as he tightened it and drew her slowly up toward him; nor ever once did the chant cease.

Removing the rope from about her, he threw her limp body across one of his broad shoulders and turning, started back in the direction from which he had come.

Tarzan had watched the abduction of the girl with keen interest, for it explained the seeming mystery of the disappearance of so many other young girls during past times. He could readily understand the effect that these mysterious disappearances would have upon the superstitious minds of the natives; yet it was all very simple except the strange, hypnotic power of the Kavuru. That was not at all clear to him.

He wondered how the natives had come to connect these disappearances with the Kavuru, and the only reasonable explanation seemed to be that in times past some exceptionally tenacious relatives had prosecuted their search until they had come by accident upon the abductor and his prey and so learned the identity of the former without ascertaining the method he had used to achieve his ends.

Feeling no responsibility in the matter, Tarzan was not moved by any impulse to rescue the girl, his only concern now being to follow Ydeni back to the village of the Kavuru, where he was confident he would find Muviro's daughter, Buira, if she still lived.

Ydeni kept to the trees for hours, until he must have been reasonably certain that he had passed beyond the point where possible pursuers would be likely to search, since they had no trail to follow. Then he came to the ground; but he still carried the girl, who lay across his shoulder as one dead.

On and on he plodded, apparently tireless; and in the trees just behind him followed Tarzan of the Apes.

It was very late in the afternoon when the Kavuru halted. He carried the girl into a tree then, and tied her securely to a branch with the same rope that had snared her. Leaving her, he departed; and Tarzan followed him.

Ydeni was merely searching for food; and when he found some edible fruits and nuts, he returned with them to the girl.

The hypnosis which had held her in its spell for so long was now relinquishing its hold upon her, and as Ydeni approached her she looked at him with startled eyes and shrank away when he touched her.

Releasing her bonds, he carried her to the ground and offered her food.

By this time, full consciousness had returned; and it was evident that the girl was aware of her plight and the identity of her abductor, for an expression of utter horror distorted her features; and then she burst into tears.

'Shut up,' snapped Ydeni. 'I have not hurt you. If you give me no trouble, I shall not hurt you.'

'You are a Kavuru,' she gasped in horror-laden tones. 'Take me back to my father; you promised him that you would not harm any member of his family.'

Ydeni looked at the girl in surprise. 'I promised your father?' he demanded. 'I never saw your father; I have never spoken to one of your men.'

'You did. You promised him when he liberated you from the hut in which Udalo had you bound. Udalo would have killed you; my father, Gupingu, the witch-doctor, saved you. Because of that you made the promise.'

This recital made no impression upon Ydeni, but it did upon the grim and silent watcher in the trees above. So this was the daughter of Gupingu. Apparently Fate was a capricious wench with a strange sense of humor.

Knowledge of the identity of the girl gave a new complexion to the affair. Tarzan felt that by accepting his freedom at the hands of Gupingu he had given the witch-doctor passive assurance that his daughters would be safe from the Kavuru. It was a moral obligation that the Lord of the Jungle could not ignore; but if he took the girl from Ydeni and returned her to her people, he would be unable to follow the Kavuru to his village. However, with a shrug he accepted the responsibility that honor seemed to lay upon him.

Now he devoted himself to a consideration of ways and means. He could, of course, go down and take the girl by force, for it never occurred to him that any creature, least of all man, might be able to prevent him from having his way; but this plan he scarcely considered before discarding it. He did not wish Ydeni to know that it was he who took the girl from him, since he realized the possibility of Ydeni being useful to him in the event that he reached the village of the Kavuru, for after all he had saved the man's life; and that was something that only the lowest of beasts might forget.

He waited therefore to see what disposal Ydeni would make of the girl for the night, for he had it in mind now to take her by stealth; and if that failed, the likelihood of Ydeni recognizing him would be greatly lessened after dark;

and so he waited, patient as any other beast of prey that watches for the propitious moment to attack.

Seeing that she would be unable to move the Kavuru by her pleas, the girl had lapsed into silence. Her brooding eyes glowered sullenly at her captor. Fear and hate were reflected in them.

Darkness was approaching rapidly when the Kavuru seized the girl and threw her roughly to the ground. She fought like a young lioness, but Ydeni was powerful and soon overcame her. Then he deftly bound her hands behind her back and trussed her legs so tightly that she could scarcely move them. Terrified, she lay trembling.

'Now,' he said, when he had finished, 'you cannot run away. Ydeni can sleep; you had better sleep; we have a long march tomorrow, and Ydeni will not carry you.'

The girl made no reply. The man threw himself upon the ground near her. A silent figure moved stealthily closer in the trees above them. It was very dark and very quiet. Only the roar of a distant lion, coming faintly to their ears, gave evidence of life in the jungle.

Tarzan waited patiently. By the man's regular breathing, he knew that Ydeni slept; but his slumber was not yet deep enough to satisfy the ape-man.

A half hour passed, and then an hour. Ydeni was sleeping very soundly now, but the girl had not yet slept. That was well; it was what Tarzan wished for.

He bent low from the branch where he lay and spoke to the girl in a low whisper. 'Do not cry out,' he said. 'I am coming down to take you back to your people.'

Very gently he lowered himself to the ground. Even the girl beside whom he stood did not know that he had descended from the trees. He stooped over her with a sibilant caution on his lips.

The girl was afraid; but she was more afraid of the Kavuru, and so she made no outcry as Tarzan raised her to his shoulder and carried her silently along the jungle trail until he could take to the trees with less likelihood of arousing Ydeni.

At a safe distance from the sleeping man he paused and cut the girl's bonds.

'Who are you?' she whispered.

'I am the man that Udalo would have killed and that your father set free,' replied the ape-man.

She shrank back. 'Then you are a Kavuru, too,' she said.

'I am no Kavuru. I told them that, but they would not believe me. I am Tarzan of the Apes, chief of the Waziri, whose country lies many marches toward the rising sun.'

'You are a Kavuru,' she insisted; 'my father said so.'

'I am not, but what difference does it make if I take you back to your father?'

'How do I know that you will take me back?' she demanded. 'Perhaps you are lying to me.'

'If you'd rather,' said the ape-man, 'I will set you free now; but what will you do here alone in the jungle? A lion or a leopard will surely find you; and even if one did not you might never find your way back to your village, because you do not know in what direction the Kavuru carried you while you were unconscious.'

'I will go with you,' said the girl.

11

'Seventy Million Dollars'

Brown and Tibbs followed the game trail in the direction of the uncanny scream that had startled the camp. 'Milady!' shouted Tibbs. 'Milady, where are you? What has happened?'

Brown quickly forged ahead of Tibbs, who had not run a hundred feet in ten years. 'Yes, Miss!' he bellowed, 'where are you?'

'Here, follow the trail,' came back the answer in clear, unshaken tones. 'I'm all right; don't get excited.'

Presently Brown came in sight of her. She was withdrawing the last of three arrows from the carcass of a leopard, and just beyond her lay the eviscerated carcass of an antelope.

'What the – what's all this?' demanded Brown.

'I just killed this bush-buck,' explained Jane, 'and Sheeta here tried to take it away from me.'

'You killed him?' demanded Brown. 'You killed him with your arrows?'

'Well, I didn't bite him to death, Brown,' laughed the girl.

'Was it him or you that let out that yell?'

'That was Sheeta. He was charging; and when my first arrow struck him, he didn't seem to like it at all.'

'And one arrow settled him?' asked the pilot.

'I let him have two more. I don't know which one stopped him. All three went into his heart.'

Brown wiped the perspiration from his forehead. 'By golly,' he said, 'I've got to take my hat off to you, Miss.'

'Well, you can put it back on, Brown, and pack that antelope back to camp. I'll like that a whole lot better.'

Tibbs had come up and was standing in wide-eyed astonishment gazing at the dead leopard. 'If I may make so bold, Milady, I might say that it's most extraordinary. I would never have believed it, Milady, upon my honor, I wouldn't. I never thought those little arrows would kill anything bigger than a bird.'

'You'd be surprised, Tibbs,' said Jane.

'I am, Milady.'

'Do we take the cat back to camp, too?' asked Brown.

'No,' replied Jane. 'Saving the pelt is too much of a job; and, besides that, Princess Sborov would probably collapse with fright at sight of it.'

The pilot picked up the carcass of the antelope, and together the three returned to camp.

Annette was standing wide-eyed, awaiting them. She breathed a sigh of relief when she saw that all three had returned safely.

'Oh,' she cried, 'you really got something to eat. I am so hungry.'

'Where are the prince and princess?' demanded Jane.

Annette snickered, and pointed toward the shelter. 'As soon as Brown and Tibbs left, they ran in there and hid,' she whispered.

Almost immediately the prince appeared. He was very white, and he was also very angry. 'You men had no right running off and leaving this camp unguarded,' he snapped. 'There's no telling what might have happened. Hereafter, see that both of you are never absent at the same time.'

'Oh, Lord, give me strength,' groaned Brown. 'I am long suffering, but I can't stand much more of this bozo.'

'What's that?' demanded Alexis.

'I was just going to say that if you ever shoot off your yap in that tone of voice to me again, I'm going to make a King out of you.'

'What?' demanded Alexis, suspiciously.

'I'm going to crown you.'

'I suppose that is another weird Americanism,' sneered the prince; 'but whatever it is, coming from you, I know it is insulting.'

'And how!' exclaimed Brown.

'Instead of standing around here quarreling,' said Jane, 'let's get busy. Brown, will you and Tibbs build a fire, please. Alexis, you can cut up the antelope. Cut five or six good-sized steaks, and then Annette can cook them. Do you know how to grill them over an open fire, Annette?'

'No, Madame, but I can learn, if you'll just show me once.'

The princess emerged from the shelter. 'Oh, my dear, whatever have you there?' she demanded. 'Oh, take it away; it's all covered with blood.'

'That's your supper, Kitty,' said Jane.

'Eat that thing? Oh, don't; I shall be ill. Take it away and bury it.'

'Well, here's your chance to reduce, lady,' said Brown, 'because if you don't eat that, you ain't going to eat nothing.'

'How dare you, Brown, intimate that you would even think of keeping food away from me?' demanded the princess.

'I ain't going to keep no food away from you. I'm just trying to tell you that there ain't no food except this. If you won't eat this, you don't eat, that's all.'

'Oh, I never could bring myself – really, my dear, how it smells.'

Less than an hour later, the princess was tearing away at an antelope steak like a famished wolf. 'How perfectly thrilling,' she took time out to remark. 'I mean, isn't it just like camping out?'

'Quite similar,' said Jane, drily.

'Terrible,' said Alexis; 'this steak is much too rare. Hereafter, Annette, see that mine are quite well done.'

'You take what you get, playboy, and like it,' said Brown. 'And hereafter don't use that tone of voice in speaking to Annette or anyone else in this bunch.'

Tibbs was very much embarrassed. He always was when what he considered a member of the lower classes showed lack of proper deference to one of what he liked to call the aristocracy. 'If I may make so bold as to inquire, Milady,' he said, addressing Jane in an effort to divert the conversation into another channel, 'might I ask how we are going to get out of here and back to civilization?'

'I've been thinking a lot about that myself, Tibbs,' replied Jane. 'You see, if we were all in good physical condition, we might follow this stream down to a larger river when eventually we would be sure to come to a native village where we could get food and employ guides and carriers to take us on to some settlement where there are Europeans; or, failing in that, we could at least hire runners to carry a message out for us.'

'I think that is a splendid idea, Milady; I 'ope we start soon.'

'I doubt that we could all stand the hardships of a long trek,' said Jane.

'I suppose you mean me, my dear,' said the princess, 'but really I am very fond of walking. I remember I used to walk a mile every morning. That was before dear Mr Peters passed on. He insisted upon my doing it; he was such an athletic man himself. He played golf every Wednesday afternoon. But after he went, I gave it up; it hurt my feet so.'

'We could build a litter,' suggested Alexis. 'I have seen pictures of them in the cinema. Brown and Tibbs could carry the princess.'

'Yeah?' demanded Brown, 'and who'd carry you?'

'Oh, I think that would be just wonderful, I mean, I think that would solve every problem!' exclaimed Kitty. 'We could build the litter large enough for two and then we could both ride.'

'Why not a four-passenger job?' demanded Brown; 'and then Tibbs and I could carry you all.'

'Oh, no,' exclaimed the princess. 'I'm afraid that would be much too heavy a load for you.'

'The fellow is attempting to be facetious, my dear,' said Alexis; 'but certainly there is no reason why they could not carry you.'

'Except only one,' said Brown.

'And pray, what is that?' asked Kitty. 'I mean, I see no reason why you and Tibbs should not carry me.'

'It's absolutely out of the question, Kitty,' said Jane, with some asperity. 'You simply don't know what you're talking about. Two men could not carry anyone through this jungle; and no matter what you may think, you wouldn't last an hour if you tried to walk.'

'Oh, but my dear Jane, what am I going to do – stay here forever?'

'One or two of us will have to go out and look for help; the others will remain here in camp. That is the only way.'

'Who's going?' asked Brown, 'me and Tibbs?'

Jane shook her head. 'I'm afraid Tibbs couldn't make the grade,' she said; 'he's never had any experience in anything of this sort, and anyway he'd be very much more useful in camp. I thought you and I should go. We know something about Africa, and how to take care of ourselves in the jungle.'

'I don't know about that,' said Brown. 'I don't see how both of us can go and leave these people. They are the most helpless bunch of yaps I've ever seen.'

The Sborovs showed their resentment of Brown's blunt appraisal, but they said nothing. Tibbs appeared shocked, but Annette turned away to hide a smile.

'I'll tell you what we'll do,' continued the pilot. 'You stay here and take care of these people and run the camp. I'll go out and look for help.'

'I wouldn't trust him, Jane,' said Alexis. 'If he once got away, he'd never come back; he'd leave us here to die.'

'Nonsense,' snapped Jane. 'Brown is perfectly right in saying that both of us should not leave you. None of you is experienced; you couldn't find food; you couldn't protect yourselves. No; one of us will have to stay; and as I can travel faster through the jungle than any of you, I shall go out and look for help.'

There were several protesting voices raised against this program. Alexis sat regarding the girl through half-closed lids; he seemed to be appraising her; the expression in his eyes was not pleasant. Presently he spoke.

'You shouldn't go alone, Jane,' he said. 'You're right in saying that I couldn't be of much help around the camp. I'll go with you; you should have someone to protect you.'

Brown laughed, a very rude and annoying laugh. The princess looked shocked and startled.

'Why, Alexis,' she cried, 'I am surprised that you would even suggest such an impossible thing. Think of Jane's reputation.'

It was now Jane's turn to laugh. 'My dear Kitty,' she cried, 'don't be ridiculous. Of course, I don't intend to let Alexis go with me, but not for the reason that you suggest. When one's life is at stake, one may ride roughshod over conventions.'

'Naturally,' agreed the prince.

'Well,' said the princess, definitely, 'Alexis may go; but if he goes, I go with him.'

'That's right,' said Alexis, 'you got us into this mess; and now you're trying to put obstacles in the way of our getting ourselves out of it. If it were not for you, we could all leave together; and as for that, if it hadn't been for you and your American pilot, we wouldn't be in this fix now.'

'Oh, Alexis,' sobbed the princess, 'how can you be so cruel to me? You don't love me any more.'

He shot a contemptuous glance at her, and turned and walked away. There was an uncomfortable silence that was finally broken by Jane.

'I shall leave in the morning,' she said, 'very early. Do you think, Brown, that you could provide food for these people while I am away?'

'I reckon I can if they're light eaters and ain't particular what they eat,' he replied, with a grin.

'Do you know which plants and fruits are edible and which are unsafe?' she asked.

'I know enough of the safe ones to get by on,' he said, 'and I'll leave the others alone.'

'That's right; be very careful about what you eat and drink.'

Brown grinned. 'We won't have much to be careful about.'

In the growing coolness of the jungle night, the warmth of the beastfire was pleasant; and most of the party remained around it, only Alexis, moody and sullen, holding aloof. He stood in the opening of the men's shelter, glowering at the figures illuminated by the fire. His dark eyes rested upon his wife, who sat with her back toward him; and his expression at this time that he was free from observation was marked with loathing. The thoughts that were passing through his petty brain were not lovely thoughts. In the outer rim of the light from the fire, he looked what he was, a small, cheap grafter who had suddenly become sinister and dangerous.

And then his eyes moved on to Jane and his expression changed. He licked his full, weak lips – lips that were flabby and repulsive.

His gaze wandered again to his wife. 'If it were not for you,' he thought – 'seventy million dollars – I wish I were out of here – that fellow, Brown; I'd like to kill him – Annette's not so bad looking – seventy million dollars – Paris, Nice, Monte Carlo – the old fool – Jane is beautiful – I suppose the old fool will live forever – dead, dead, dead – seventy million dollars.'

Over by the fire, Jane was arranging for the guarding of the camp by night. 'I think three four-hour shifts will be long enough,' she said. 'It's just a matter of keeping the fire going. If any animals come around, you'll be able to see their eyes shining in the dark. If they come too close, light a brand and throw it at them. They are all afraid of fire.'

'Oh, my dear, do I have to do that?' cried Kitty. 'I never could, really, I mean, do I have to sit out here alone at night?'

'No, my dear,' said Jane, 'you'll be excused from guard duty. How about you, Annette? Do you think you could do it?'

'I can do my share, Madame,' said the girl, 'whatever the others do.'

'Atta girl,' said Brown.

'If I may make so bold as to suggest it, Milady,' said Tibbs, deferentially, 'I rather think the three men should stand guard. It's no job for a lady.'

'I think Tibbs is perfectly right,' said the princess. 'And I really think that Alexis should not stand guard; he's a very susceptible person to colds; and night air always affects him; and now I think that I shall go to bed. Annette, come and help me.'

'You'd better turn in, too, Miss,' said Brown. 'If you're going to start out early in the morning, you'll need all the sleep you can get.'

Jane rose. 'Perhaps you're right,' she said. 'Goodnight.'

When she had gone, Brown glanced at his watch. 'It's nine o'clock now, Tibbs. Suppose you stand guard until midnight, then wake me, and I'll take it until three. After that, his nibs, the grand Duke, can watch until morning.'

'Really, Mr Brown, if you mean the prince, I rather fawncy he won't be caring to stand guard.'

'Well, he's going to,' said Brown, 'and he's going to like it.'

Tibbs sighed. 'If it weren't for the princess,' he said, 'we wouldn't have to stay here at all. I don't fawncy staying here and just waiting. I'm sure something terrible will happen to us if Lady Greystoke leaves us. She's the only one that can do anything.'

'Yes,' said Brown, 'the old girl is a damned nuisance. You might bump her off, Tibbs.' Brown grinned, rose, and stretched. 'I'll be turning in, Tibbsy. Wake me at midnight.'

Sborov was sitting in the entrance of the shelter which was only a few steps from the fire and as Brown entered, he spoke to him. 'I couldn't help but overhear your conversation with Tibbs,' he said. 'I am perfectly willing to do my share. Call me at three, and I will stand guard. I'm going to bed now. I am a very sound sleeper, and you may have difficulty in waking me.'

The change in the man's tone and attitude so surprised Brown that for once he had no reply to make. He merely grunted as he passed on into the shelter. Sborov followed and lay down, and in a few moments Brown was fast asleep.

It seemed to him when Tibbs woke him at midnight that he had not slept at all.

He had been on guard but a few minutes when Annette joined him. She came and sat down beside him.

'What the Dickens are you doing up this time of the morning, girlie?' he demanded.

'Something awoke me about half an hour ago,' she said, 'and I haven't been able to get back to sleep. I don't know what it could have been, but I awoke with a start; and I had a feeling that there was someone crawling around inside the hut. You know, it's really very dark in there after the curtain is hung up in front of the door.'

12

Murder In the Night

'Maybe it was Lady Greystoke you heard moving around in the hut,' suggested Brown.

'No,' said Annette, 'I could hear her breathing. She was sound asleep.'

'Then it must have been the old girl.'

'It was not she, either. After I woke up, I heard her sort of groaning in her sleep and snoring I guess it was, but she stopped right away.'

'Then I guess you must have been dreaming, girlie,' said Brown.

'Perhaps I was,' said the girl; 'but some unusual sound must have awakened me, for I sleep very soundly; and I was sure that I heard someone afterward.'

'Perhaps you had better go back and go to sleep again now,' he suggested.

'Really, Mr Brown, I couldn't. I am so wide awake; and then I – I felt funny in there, as though – oh, I don't know.' She lowered her voice to a whisper. 'It was as though there were something terrible in there, something that frightened me. You don't mind my staying out here with you, do you, Mr Brown?'

'I'll say I don't, girlie. You and Lady Greystoke are about the only human beings in the bunch. The rest of 'em are nuts.'

'You do not like them, Mr Brown?'

'Oh, the old girl's harmless; she's just a nuisance; and Tibbsy means well, I guess; but when it comes to doing anything more than pressing somebody's pants, he just ain't all there.'

'And the other one?' inquired Annette. 'I think you do not like him so much.'

'Him? He's the last zero after the decimal point.'

'No, I do not like him, either, Mr Brown. I am afraid of him.'

'Afraid of him? What you got to be afraid of him about?'

'In London he say things to me a man should not say to a nice girl.'

'Well, the dirty so and so,' growled Brown. 'If he ever makes any cracks at you again, honey, let me know. Say, I'd spill him all over the ground and then wipe him up with himself.'

'You would protect me, Mr Brown?' She raised her dark eyes to his, questioningly.

'And how!'

The girl sighed. 'You are so beeg and strong.'

'You know,' said Brown, 'I like you a lot, girlie.'

'I am glad. I think I like you, too.'

Brown was silent for a moment. 'If we ever get out of here,' he said, presently, and then stopped.

'Yes?' she inquired. 'If we ever get out of here, what?'

He fidgeted uneasily, and threw another piece of wood on the fire. 'I was just thinking,' he said, lamely.

'What were you thinking?'

'I was just thinking that maybe you and me – that maybe—'

'Yes?' she breathed, encouragingly.

'Say, you don't have to call me Mr Brown.'

'What shall I call you?'

'My best friends call me Chi.'

'What a funny name; I never hear a name like that before. What does it mean? It is not really your name?'

'It's short for the name of the town where I come from – Chicago,' he explained.

'Oh,' she laughed, 'then you spell it C-h-i and not S-h-y. I think maybe you should spell it the last way.'

'I ain't never been accused of being shy before,' he said, 'but I guess you're right. When I try to say things to you, my tongue runs out on me.'

'What funny expressions you use. You Americans are all so funny.'

'Oh, I don't know,' he said; 'it's the foreigners that seem funny to me.'

'Am I funny?'

'Well, you got some funny little ways with you, but when you pull them, they're cute.'

'You think so? I am glad that you do, Mr Brown.'

'Chi.'

'Chi. Have you another name? Maybe that would be easier to say.'

'Yep. My real name's Neal.'

'That's a nice name.'

'So's Annette. I'm crazy about Annette.'

'You like the name?'

'Yes, and the girl, too – I like the girl a lot.' He reached over and took her hand and drew her toward him.

'No, you must not do that,' she said sharply, and pulled away; and then suddenly she cried out, 'oh, look, look,' and pointed.

Brown looked up in the direction that she indicated. Blazing against the dark background of the forest were two yellow-green points of flame.

Annette moved quickly toward him and pressed against his side. 'What is it?' she whispered in a frightened voice.

'Don't be scared, honey; it's only looking at us. That won't hurt us none.'

'What is it?' she demanded.

'I've seen cow's eyes shine like that in the dark,' he said; 'it might be a cow.'

'But you know it's not a cow. There are no cows in the jungle. You just say that so that I will not be frightened.'

'Well, now that you mention it, maybe there ain't no cows in the jungle; but whatever it is, I'm going to frighten it away.' He stooped over and gathered a stick from the fire; one end of it was blazing. Then he stood up and hurled it at the burning eyes.

There was a shower of sparks, an angry growl, and the eyes disappeared.

'That fixed him,' he said. 'See how easy it was?'

'Oh, you are so very brave, Neal.'

He sat down beside her; and this time, he boldly put an arm about her.

She sighed and snuggled closer to him. 'A nice girl should not do this,' she said, 'but it make me feel so safe.'

'You never was less safe in your life, girlie,' said Brown.

'You think the eyes will come back?' she asked, with a shudder.

'I was not thinking about eyes, girlie.'

'Oh.'

It was long after three o'clock before Brown thought to awaken Sborov. When the prince came into the firelight, he was nervous and ill at ease.

'Did you see or hear anything during the night?' he asked.

'Something came up and looked at us,' said Brown; 'but I threw some fire at it, and it beat it.'

'Everything all right in camp?' he asked.

'Sure,' said Brown, 'everything's O.K.'

'I slept so soundly that anything might have happened,' said the prince. 'I never knew a thing from the time I lay down until you awakened me.'

'Well, I guess I'll go tear off a few yards myself,' said the pilot, 'and you better go back in and try to get some sleep, girlie.'

They walked together the few paces to the shelter. She shuddered a little. 'I hate to go back in there,' she said. 'I do not understand why, but I just dread it.'

'Don't be silly,' he said. 'There ain't nothing going to hurt you. That dream got your nanny.'

'I do not know what is my nanny,' she replied, 'and I am not so certain it was a dream.'

'Well, you run along like a good girl; and I'll sleep with one eye open. If you hear anything, call me.'

It was daylight when Brown was awakened by a piercing scream from the adjoining shelter.

'My word!' exclaimed Tibbs. 'What was that?' But Brown was already on his feet and running to the women's quarters. He saw Sborov standing by the fire, ashen-grey in the morning light. His lower jaw drooped loosely; his eyes were staring, fixed upon the hut in which the women slept.

Brown collided with Annette, who was running from the hut as he started to enter.

'Oh, Neal,' she cried, 'it was no dream. Something horrible happened in there last night.'

He brushed past her and went into the hut. Jane was standing in horrified silence, gazing down at the Princess Sborov.

'God!' exclaimed Brown.

Kitty Sborov was dead, her skull split wide.

'How horrible,' breathed Jane. 'Who could have done this thing?'

Tibbs joined them. He remained silent and unmoved in the face of this gruesome discovery, always the perfect servant.

'Where is the prince?' asked Jane.

'He was on guard,' said Brown. 'He was standing there by the fire when I came in.'

'Somebody will have to tell him,' she said.

'I reckon it won't be no news to him,' said Brown.

Jane looked up at him quickly. 'Oh, he couldn't!' she cried.

'Well, who could, then?' demanded the pilot.

'If you wish, Milady,' suggested Tibbs, 'I will inform his 'ighness.'

'Very well, Tibbs.'

The man stepped out into the open. The prince was still standing gazing at the hut; but when he saw Tibbs coming toward him, he gathered himself together.

'What's the matter in there?' he asked. 'What was Annette screaming about?'

'Something has happened to her 'ighness – she's – she's dead.'

'What? – Who? – It can't be possible. She was quite all right when she went to bed last night.'

'She has been murdered, your 'ighness,' said Tibbs, 'oh, so 'orribly!'

'Murdered!' He still stood where he was, making no move to approach the hut. He watched Jane and Brown emerge and come toward him.

'It is horrible, Alexis,' said Jane. 'I can't imagine who could have done it, nor why.'

'I know who did it,' he said, excitedly. 'I know who did it and I know why.'

'What do you mean?' demanded Jane.

Alexis pointed a trembling finger at Brown. 'Last night I heard that man tell Tibbs to kill her. One of them must have done it, and I don't believe that it was Tibbs.'

'Prince Sborov, I don't believe that it was either one of them,' said Jane.

'Ask Tibbs if he didn't tell him to kill her,' cried Sborov.

Jane looked questioningly at Tibbs.

'Well, Milady, Mr Brown did suggest that I "bump her off"; but it was only by way of being a joke, Milady.'

'How was she killed?' asked the prince.

Jane looked puzzled. 'Why – why, it must have been with the hatchet. Where is the hatchet?'

'Find the hatchet, and you'll have the murderer,' said Sborov.

'But suppose he threw it away?' asked Jane.

'He couldn't have thrown it away. I've been on guard here since three o'clock, and nobody entered your part of the shelter after Annette went in after I came on guard. Whoever did it, probably hid it.'

'It happened before you went on guard,' said Annette. 'It happened before Mr Brown went on guard. It was that that awakened me; I know it now; and when I thought she was moaning in her sleep and snoring, she was really dying – it was the death rattle. Oh, how horrible!'

'Just when was that, Annette?' asked Jane.

'It was while Tibbs was on guard and about half an hour before Mr Brown went on. I couldn't get back to sleep, and I went out and joined him. I sat up with him until he awoke the prince.'

Jane turned to Tibbs. 'Was Mr Brown asleep when you went in to wake him at midnight?' she asked.

'Yes, Milady,' replied Tibbs.

'How do you know?'

'Well, I could tell by his breathing for one thing; and then I had difficulty in arousing him.'

'He might have feigned that,' said Sborov

'Was the prince asleep when you went in there, Tibbs, to awaken Brown?'

'He seemed to be sound asleep, Milady. I carried a burning brand in for a torch. I could see them quite distinctly.'

'He was asleep, and I was pretendin' to be, I suppose,' said Brown.

'Find the hatchet,' said Sborov.

'Well, suppose *you* find it,' retorted Brown. 'I don't know where it is.'

'Tibbs says that both of you were asleep. That leaves Tibbs and Annette and me under suspicion,' said Jane.

'There ain't no sense to that way of figuring,' said Brown. 'We all know that you and Annette didn't have nothin' to do with it; so you two are out. I know damned well that I didn't do it, and I'm just about as sure that Tibbs didn't; so that puts it up to the only one in the bunch that would profit by the old woman's death.'

'You'd profit as much as any of us,' pointed out Sborov, sullenly. 'You knew that your life was at stake, that if you didn't get out of here very soon you might never get out. You knew and you said that my wife was all that made it impossible for us to start together tomorrow. I can see your whole line of reasoning, my man. You felt that the princess could never get out of here, anyway; and so you just hurried matters along by killing her yourself.'

'All right, Sherlock Holmes, you've got it all figured out, haven't you? But what are you going to do about it?'

'Find the hatchet,' repeated Sborov.

'All right,' said Jane. 'You men go in the women's part of the shelter and search, and Annette and I will search your part.'

Sborov followed Jane to the door of the men's hut. 'I cannot go in there where she is,' he said, 'I want to remember her as she was when I last saw her – alive.'

Jane nodded. 'Help us search here, then,' she said.

There was really no place to search except among the litter of grasses that the men had used as beds.

Jane searched the pile upon which Alexis had slept, while Alexis took Tibbs' and Annette poked around in those belonging to Brown. Presently the girl's hand came into contact with something cold and hard. She stiffened as her fingers touched it, as though by intuition she knew what it was. With a shudder she withdrew her hand. For a moment she remained very quiet and tense. She was thinking rapidly. Then she arose to her feet. 'There is nothing here,' she said.

Sborov glanced up at her quickly. 'There is nothing here, either,' said Jane.

'I can find nothing in Tibbs' bed,' said Alexis; 'but perhaps, Annette, you did not search Brown's bed carefully enough. Let me see.'

She took a step toward him as though to prevent the search. 'What is the use?' she said. 'It is not there; it's just a waste of time to look again.'

'Nevertheless, I shall look,' said Alexis.

Sborov stooped and slipped his hand in among the grasses. He did not have to search long. 'Here it is,' he said. 'I don't see how you could have missed it, Annette,' he added, with a sneer. 'You must have had your own reasons.'

He withdrew the hatchet from among the grasses and held it up to their view. The head was smeared with blood.

'Are you satisfied now, Jane?' demanded the prince.

'I can't believe it of Brown,' she said.

'But you could have believed it of me?'

'Frankly, Alexis, yes.'

'Well, you've got plenty of proof now as to who did it. What are you going to do about it? The fellow ought to be destroyed.'

'Who ought to be destroyed?' demanded Brown. He and Tibbs were standing in the doorway.

'The hatchet was found in your bed, Brown,' said Jane. 'The prince has it; as you can see, it is covered with blood.'

'Oh, so you planted that thing in my bed, did you, you lousy little runt? Trying to frame me, eh?'

'I do not understand your talk,' said Alexis. 'I only know what I heard you say last night and what I found in your bed. Tibbs has already corroborated my report of what you said, and Lady Greystoke and Annette saw me find the hatchet in here right where you had hidden it.'

Brown looked from one to another with a questioning expression in his eyes. Could it be that these people believed that he had done this thing? He realized that what slender evidence was at hand pointed to him.

'Well,' he said, 'don't get it into your heads that you're going to hang me.'

13

Treachery

The little band of Waziri warriors under Muviro had moved steadily westward since their encounter with Tarzan. The ten moved silently along a winding jungle trail; there was no song nor laughter; and when they spoke, which was seldom, their tones were low, for they were in a country strange to them, with the temper of whose people they were not familiar. They moved warily, every sense alert.

Some time during this day they hoped to contact the Bukena, the people who lived nearest to the Kavuru; and here they hoped to have word of Tarzan of the Apes.

Presently, above the subdued noises of the jungle, they heard the excited chattering of a monkey above them; and a moment later a familiar little figure swung downward through the trees.

'It is Nkima,' said Muviro. 'The Big Bwana must be near.'

Little Nkima jabbered with excitement. He leaped to the shoulder of Muviro and jumped up and down, screaming and chattering. He leaped to the ground and ran ahead very fast, jabbering excitedly in his high, little voice, as he continually looked back at them. He would run ahead until a bend in the trail threatened to hide them from his view; then he would run back and tug at Muviro's legs before starting off again at great speed.

'Something is wrong,' said one of the warriors to Muviro. 'Little Nkima is trying to tell us.'

'He wants us to hurry,' said Muviro; 'perhaps something has happened to the Big Bwana.' Then he broke into a trot, his fellows following close behind; but still Nkima ran ahead always urging them to greater speed.

Members of a warrior clan that is trained from childhood in feats of endurance, the Waziri could maintain for hour after hour a pace that would soon exhaust an ordinary man.

Their smooth, ebony bodies glistening with sweat, their broad chests rising and falling to their unhurried breathing, their supple muscles rolling easily, they presented a splendid picture of primitive savagery, to which a note of barbaric color was added by anklets and armlets of strange design, their weapons, their shields, and the flowing white plumes that surmounted their heads.

Here, indeed, were men, the very sight of whom would have instilled respect, and perhaps fear, in the hearts of any strange tribesmen who might see them.

And thus it was, when breaking from the jungle into a clearing, little Nkima still in the lead, they burst upon the view of a score of women working in the fields before the village of Udalo, chief of the Bukena.

With terrified cries of warning, the women fled for the village gate.

Bukena warriors inside the kraal seized their weapons and ran to meet their women; and as the rearmost of the latter entered the village, the warriors made haste to close the gate behind them; and as some attended the gate, others manned the barbette inside the palisade over the top of which they could loose their arrows upon an enemy.

At the sight of the village and the fleeing women, Muviro had halted his warriors. He saw the hostile attitude of the Bukena, but he attributed it to the fact that they did not know whether he came in peace or war.

Nkima was very much excited. He waved his hands and jabbered loudly; he was trying so hard to make them understand that his Master was a captive in the village. It was always a mystery to Nkima that these Gomangani could not understand him. It seemed that no one could understand him except his cousins, brothers, and sisters, and his beloved Tarzan. Everyone else must be very stupid.

Muviro left his companions at a short distance from the village and advanced slowly toward the palisade, making the sign of peace that the villagers might know that they did not come with hostile intent.

Udalo, the chief, standing upon the barbette, looked down upon the approaching warrior and his companions. He knew that these were indeed fighting men; and while there were only ten of them he was glad to see the peace sign, for there might be many others back in the forest and this only an advance guard.

As Muviro halted at the foot of the palisade and looked up, Udalo addressed him.

'Who are you? What do you want?' he demanded.

'I am Muviro, chief of the Waziri. We have come here to meet our big chief, Tarzan of the Apes, or to get word of him. Has he been here?'

Gupingu, the witch-doctor, was standing beside Udalo. Searing his heart was the memory of a secret he dared tell no one – the secret of the release of Tarzan upon his promise that the Kavuru would not steal the daughters of Gupingu; and yet almost immediately Naika, his favorite daughter, had been stolen.

Gupingu was confident now that not only was Tarzan a Kavuru, but that it was he who had come back to steal Naika. Resentment and hatred burned in the breast of Gupingu. He recalled that Tarzan had said that he was a Waziri; and, assembling all the facts as he knew them, he conjectured that the Waziri were either the vassals or the allies of the Kavuru.

'Do not trust them, Udalo,' he said to the chief; 'they are the people of the Kavuru who escaped us. He has sent them back here to be revenged.'

Scowling down upon Muviro, Udalo thought quickly.

He would like to be revenged upon the Kavuru but he feared reprisals; and, too, he did not know but what there might be a large body of them back in the forest. The truth or falsity of this he must ascertain before he could make any definite plans.

Annoyed because he had received no answer, Muviro spoke again, this time impatiently. 'We come in peace,' he said, 'to ask a question. Is Tarzan, our Master, here?'

'There,' whispered Gupingu to Udalo, 'he admits that the Kavuru is his Master.'

'He is not here,' said Udalo; 'we know nothing of him, and I do not know that you come in peace.'

'You are not speaking true words,' said Muviro. 'Little Nkima, the monkey, is Tarzan's friend. He brought us here, and he would not have done so had Tarzan not been here.'

'I did not say that Tarzan had not been here,' retorted Udalo; 'I say that he is not here, and that I know nothing of him. I do not know where he went after he left here.'

'If—'

'We do not fear ten men,' said Udalo, 'the ten may enter the village; then we may talk. If you come in peace, you will do this; if you do not do it, Udalo will know that you have come to make war. As you can see, he has many warriors. We are not afraid of you, but we do not want war.'

'We have come in peace,' replied Muviro, 'but warriors do not lay aside their weapons. If you have so many brave warriors, why should you fear ten men?'

'We do not fear ten men,' said Udalo; 'the ten may enter and bring their weapons, but the rest of your warriors must not approach the village.'

'There are no others with us,' said Muviro. 'We are alone.'

This was the information that Udalo wished. 'You may come in,' he said; 'I will order the gates opened.' Then he turned and whispered to Gupingu.

Murviro signalled for his men to approach. The gates swung open, and they entered the village of the Bukena.

Udalo and Gupingu had left the barbette and gone together toward the chief's hut. They were whispering volubly with many gesticulations, Gupingu explaining, Udalo assenting and giving orders. At the chiefs hut they separated, Udalo remaining to await the coming of the visitors, while Gupingu hastened to his own hut.

As the Waziri entered the village street, they were surrounded by warriors and conducted to the hut of the chief, where Udalo awaited them.

Here commenced one of those long palavers so dear to the hearts of African natives. With endless circumlocution they iterated and reiterated, and in the end nothing had been said by Udalo other than that Tarzan was not in his village and that he knew nothing whatsoever about him; nor did he know anything concerning the Kavuru or the location of their village, none of which Muviro believed.

And while the palaver progressed, Gupingu was busy in his hut grinding herbs and boiling them in water to extract their juices. He constantly muttered and mumbled to himself, but it is doubtful that he was chanting an incantation over the mess that he was brewing and for the same reason that he did not lay out amulets before him or make passes over the brew with magic sticks or the tail of a zebra – he had no audience.

While the Bukena warriors and their visitors palavered and Gupingu concocted his brew, the women were busy preparing a feast at the orders of Udalo; and in the trees beyond the clearing, a little monkey waited, whimpering and desolated – waited for the release of his Master whom he thought to be still confined in a hut in the village.

At last Gupingu left his hut, carrying his brew in a small gourd, and made his way directly to the women who were preparing the native beer for the feast.

The women were already filling the gourds that would be passed around

among the warriors. Gupingu went to the one who was filling the large ceremonial gourd that would be passed first to the chief and then to the visitors.
They held a whispered conversation and then Gupingu walked away, leaving
behind him the small gourd containing his brew. He approached the palaver
from the rear of the Waziri, and catching Udalo's eye he nodded. Then the
chief clapped his hands and ordered the feast served.

The women came, bringing food and drink; and in the lead was one carrying the ceremonial gourd of native beer.

Udalo took it from her and in silence raised it to his lips. His throat moved,
as in the act of swallowing; but none of the liquor passed his lips; then he
passed it to Muviro, who took a long drink and handed the gourd to the Waziri
next beside him; and so it passed among them all, but when the last of the ten
had drunk, the woman was waiting to take the gourd, though it was not yet
empty, and the other women brought other gourds of beer to the Bukena warriors; nor did Muviro nor any of his companions suspect that anything was
wrong, for had they not seen Udalo drink from the same gourd as they?

Now food was brought, but Muviro did not partake of it. He was looking,
strange and glassy-eyed, at his fellow Waziri. What had gone wrong with his
eyes? Everything was blurred. He saw his men sitting there with stony stares,
their bodies weaving drunkenly; then Muviro, the chief of the Waziri, staggered to his feet. He seized his long knife and drew it from his loincloth.
'Kill!' he cried. 'We have been poisoned.' Then he lurched and fell.

Several of the remaining Waziri tried to rise; but the brew of Gupingu
worked quickly and well; and though the Bukena warriors had leaped to
their feet at a word from Udalo, following Muviro's command to his followers, their ready spears were not needed, as one by one the Waziri collapsed
upon the ground.

The Bukena gazed in astonishment upon this strange sight, for only Udalo
and one woman knew what Gupingu had done.

The witch-doctor leaped among the fallen Waziri and beat his chest.

'The medicine of Gupingu is strong,' he said. 'It lays low the enemies of the
Bukena; even the great Kavuru it lays low.'

'Kill!' shouted a woman, and others took up the refrain. 'Kill! Kill! Kill!'

'No,' said Udalo. 'Bind them securely so that they cannot escape and put
them in the hut where the other Kavuru was confined. I shall send runners
to the other villages of the Bukena; and when the moon is full on the second
night, we shall dance and feast and eat the hearts of our enemies.'

Shouts of approval met this announcement, as warriors fell to the work of
binding the prisoners and carrying them to the hut where Tarzan had been
confined.

In a tree at the edge of the jungle, a little monkey sat gazing disconsolately
at the gates of the village. He brightened momentarily when he saw some

warriors emerge; lithe young men these, who started off at a brisk gait in different directions; but they were not his beloved Waziri, and he sank again into despondency.

It was many hours before the Waziri recovered from the effects of the narcotic. After they commenced to regain consciousness it was some little time before they could realize their plight. Their heads ached and they were very sick. When they tried to move, they discovered that they were fast bound.

'I knew,' said Muviro, after they were able to talk among themselves, 'that the chief lied to me. I should have been more careful. I should not have drunk his beer or allowed you to.'

'I saw him drink it, and so I thought it was safe,' said another.

'He only pretended to drink it,' said Muviro. 'This Udalo is a very bad man.'

'What do you think he will do with us?'

'I do not think,' said Muviro; 'I know.'

'And what do you know?'

'I have heard about these Bukena. I have heard that while they are not cannibals, they do eat the hearts of their enemies, thinking that this will make them brave, for they are great cowards.'

'They will eat our hearts?'

'Yes.'

'When?'

'That we may not know until we are led out; but if we see that they are preparing for a great feast, we shall know that our end is near.'

'And we must lie here and be slaughtered like goats?'

'If one of us can loosen his bonds, we may die as Waziri should – fighting,' replied Muviro.

'If only the Big Bwana could know,' said a young man; 'he would save us.'

'I think perhaps that the Big Bwana is already dead,' said Muviro. 'I think that Udalo has killed him, and eaten his heart; and if that is so, I am ready to die, too; for I do not care to live if the Big Bwana be dead.'

'Nor I,' said another. 'I am so sick and my head hurts so, that I shall be glad to die.'

Night came, but no one approached the hut to bring them water or food. They were very miserable, and Muviro was chagrined to think that he had been led into such a trap. He was ashamed of himself, and he felt that only death could atone for his great fault.

Miserable as they were, however, there was one even more miserable – a little monkey that shivered and trembled in a tree beyond the clearing that surrounded the village of Udalo, the Bukena. He heard the roar of Numa, the lion, and the cry of Sheeta, the leopard; and he climbed as high as he dared and hung there shivering and trembling waiting for the thing that he knew was about to leap upon him and devour him. For such was the life of little Nkima.

14

Nkima Forgets

Naika, the daughter of Gupingu, the witch-doctor, accompanied her new captor because the only alternative was to be left alone in the jungle, a prey not only to wild beasts but to the numerous demons that infest the grim forest. At first, she momentarily expected the worst; but as time went on and no harm befell her, she gained confidence in the tall, bronzed warrior who accompanied her. Eventually all fear of him vanished.

But if she were no longer afraid of Tarzan, she was far from being without fear; for the jungle night was very black and she conjured in that Stygian gloom all manner of horrifying creatures lying in wait to spring upon her. She could not understand how he travelled so surely through the darkness, and she marvelled at his great courage.

She knew that few men are so brave, and therefore it occurred to her that he must be a demon.

Here, indeed, was an adventure, one that she, Naika, could boast about as long as she lived; for had she not travelled at night through the jungle with a demon? She should have liked to ask him point-blank, but of course there was always the danger of offending a demon. Perhaps if she questioned him adroitly, he might accidentally reveal the truth.

It took quite a little willpower to screw up her courage to the point where she might ask him any question at all; but finally she succeeded. 'What country are you from?' she asked.

'I am from the land of the Waziri.'

'What sort of men are they?'

'They are black men.'

'But you are white.'

'Yes,' he replied, 'but many years ago, when I was much younger, I was adopted into the tribe.'

'Have you ever met a demon?' she asked.

'No, there are no such things.'

'Then you are not a demon?'

'I am Tarzan of the Apes.'

'Then you are not a Kavuru?'

'I told you I am from the land of the Waziri. When you are back among your people, tell them that Tarzan of the Apes is not a Kavuru. Tell them also that he rescued you from the Kavuru, and that they must always be friends with Tarzan and the Waziri.'

'I will tell them,' said Naika; and, after a moment, 'I am very tired.'

'We will stop here the rest of the night,' said the ape-man.

Picking her up, he carried her high among the trees until she was very much afraid; and when he set her down upon a branch she clung frantically to the bole of the tree.

Here the moon was filtering through the foliage, and it was much less dark than on the ground. In this semi-light, Tarzan cut branches and built a platform upon which Naika could lie during the night.

In the early morning, Tarzan gathered food for himself and the girl; and after they had eaten, they resumed their journey toward the village of the Bukena.

Feeling that she was approaching her home, and with all her fears dissipated, Naika's spirits rose. She laughed and chatted happily; and so at last they came to the edge of the clearing that encircles the village of the Bukena.

'You are safe now, Naika,' said the ape-man. 'Return to your people and tell them that Tarzan of the Apes is not their enemy.' Then he turned and disappeared into the forest, but not before a pair of sharp little eyes had seen him; and as Naika ran shouting toward the gates of the village, little Nkima swung through the trees screaming at the top of his voice, as he pursued his Lord and Master into the forest.

The diminutive monkey soon overtook the ape-man, and with a final ecstatic yelp leaped to one of his broad shoulders.

Tarzan reached up and took the little fellow in his hand. 'So Nkima is back again,' he said; 'Sheeta did not get him.'

'Nkima is not afraid of Sheeta,' boasted the monkey. 'Sheeta came into the trees hunting for little Nkima; crouching, he crept; he came close. Little Nkima took a stick and beat Sheeta on the head. Sheeta was afraid, and ran away.'

'Yes,' said Tarzan, 'little Nkima is very brave.'

Thus encouraged, the monkey became enthusiastic and still more imaginative. 'Then came the Gomangani, many Gomangani; they were going to kill little Nkima and eat him. Little Nkima took two sticks and beat them on the head. They were afraid; they ran away.'

'Yes,' said Tarzan, 'everyone is afraid of little Nkima.'

Nkima stood up in the palm of Tarzan's hand and beat his chest. He grimaced, showing his teeth, and looked very fierce. 'Everyone is afraid of Nkima,' he said.

Back along the trail to the North, in search of the village of the Kavuru went Tarzan and Nkima; and in the village of the Bukena Naika was the center of an admiring and curious throng.

She told her story well, omitting nothing, adding considerable embroidery; it was a good story and it held her listeners spell-bound. She told it many times, for the blacks like repetition; and always she stressed the fact that Tarzan had saved her, that he was the friend of the Bukena and that they must never harm Tarzan or the Waziri; and at that time she did not know that ten Waziri lay bound in a nearby hut waiting for the orgy that would spell their doom.

The Bukena warriors looked at one another and at Udalo, their chief. Udalo was slightly disconcerted; his runners had long since reached their destinations, and by this time the inhabitants of several villages must be on their way toward his kraal. Udalo did not know what to do about it.

Gupingu was troubled, too. He realized now that the giant white, whom he had liberated, had not stolen his daughter as he had thought, but had rescued her and returned her to him. Udalo looked at him questioningly, but Gupingu did not know what to say.

At last the chief spoke, for he saw the question in the eyes of his warriors. 'You said, Naika, that you thought this Tarzan of the Apes was a demon; you said that he was fearless in the dark, and that he did things that no man could do; you said also that he went through the trees even more easily than the Kavuru. All these things we believe, but we could not believe them if we knew that he were a man like ourselves. He must therefore be a demon. None but a demon could have escaped from his bonds and left the village as easily as he did.'

'If he were a demon, why did he save me from the Kavuru and return me to the village?' demanded Naika.

'The ways of demons are strange,' said Udalo. 'I think that he wanted to make our fears dead, so that he could come safely into our village and harm us as he pleases. No, I am sure that he is a demon and a Kavuru, and that the prisoners we have taken are Kavuru. We shall not let them escape; they might come back and kill us, and furthermore the Bukena are coming from every village to dance and feast and eat the hearts of our enemies.'

Thus did the highest court of the Bukena uphold itself and place its final seal upon the death warrant of Muviro and his warriors.

Through the brooding forest, moving Northward, went the Lord of the Jungle, ignorant of the impending fate of his people; and on his shoulder rode Nkima, his little mind fully occupied with his boasting and the present.

Short is the memory of Manu, the monkey. Great is his egotism and his selfishness. Little Nkima had not meant to forget the Waziri; they were his friends and he loved them.

But being wholly occupied with thoughts of himself and with relief at being safe again in the arms of his Master, the plight of the Waziri had been crowded into the background of his consciousness. Eventually he would think of them again, but perhaps only after it was too late to be of any benefit to them.

And so the afternoon was half gone, and Nkima was happy, and Tarzan was satisfied; for once again he was on the trail of the Kavuru, concerning whom his curiosity had been intrigued by his brief contact with Ydeni and the suggestion of mystery that Kavuru's few words had lent to the manners and customs of this strange and savage tribe.

Tarzan had not forgotten the Waziri; but his mind was at rest concerning them for he felt that now, because of his rescue of Naika, they would be welcomed in the village of Udalo and directed on their way toward the Kavuru country.

The ape-man seldom spoke unless that which he had to say warranted expression. Ordinarily he kept his thoughts to himself, especially in the presence of men; but he often relaxed with little Nkima and with Tantor, the elephant, for of such were the friendships of his childhood; and deep-rooted within him was the sense of their loyalty and sympathy.

Thus it happened that while he was thinking of the Waziri, he spoke of them to Nkima. 'Muviro must be close to the village of the Bukena,' he said; 'so he and his warriors will not be far behind us when we reach the village of the Kavuru. Then little Nkima will have many good friends to defend him from Sheeta, the leopard, and from Histah, the snake, and from all the Gomangani who would catch and devour him.'

For a moment Nkima was silent. He was gathering his thoughts and his memory. Then suddenly he began to leap up and down upon Tarzan's shoulder and screech in his ear.

'What is the matter with you, Nkima?' demanded the ape-man. 'Are your brains chasing one another around in your head? Stop screaming in my ear.'

'Tarzan, the Waziri! The Waziri!' cried the little monkey.

Tarzan looked quickly around. 'What of them?' he demanded. 'They are not here.'

'They are there,' cried Nkima. 'They are back there in the village of the Gomangani. Their feet and their hands are wrapped with cord; they lie in the hut where Tarzan lay. The Gomangani will kill them and eat them.'

Tarzan halted in his tracks. 'What are you saying, Nkima?' he demanded, and then as best he could in the simple language that is common to the greater apes, and the lesser apes, and the little monkeys, and to their cousin Tongani, the baboon, and to their friend Tarzan, he narrated all that he had witnessed since he had met the Waziri in the forest.

The ape-man turned about then, and started back toward the village of the Bukena. He did not ask Nkima why he had not told him this before because he knew full well; nor did he scold the little monkey, nor reproach him, for he knew that it would do no good. Little Nkima would always be a monkey; he was born that way; and he would never have the mind of a man, even though in many other respects he was more admirable than man.

The sun had not been long down when Tarzan came to the village. From a tall tree at the edge of the clearing, he looked down at the scene beyond the palisade. He saw that there were many people there, many more than there had been before; and he guessed that they were gathered for a feast. But his knowledge of the customs of the blacks told him that it would not be this night. Doubtless they were awaiting others that would come upon the morrow; perhaps then the feast would be held, and he guessed that the Waziri were being saved for sacrifice at that time.

When boldness is necessary, the ape-man acts boldly. No spirit of bravado animates him; and when no emergency confronts him, his acts reflect only the caution and stealth of the wild beasts who, impelled by instinct, avoid all unnecessary risks and dangers.

Tonight he reasoned that if the Waziri were already dead he could accomplish nothing by boldly entering the kraal of the Bukena; if they were still alive there was little likelihood that they would be harmed before the following night; but if he were wrong, and this night were the night set for their destruction, he would know it in ample time; for they would be brought out into the open where they would be tortured and killed for the edification of the assembled Bukena. Then he would have to do something about it; in the meantime, he would go closer where he could see and hear what transpired in the village.

'Tarzan goes into the village,' he whispered to Nkima. 'If Nkima comes, he will make no noise. Does Nkima understand?'

'No noise, no talk,' repeated the monkey.

Moving quietly through the trees, Tarzan circled the village; and close beside him, silent as he, moved little Nkima.

At last the two came opposite the rear of the kraal. That part of the village seemed dark and deserted, for all were congregated in the wide street before the hut of Udalo, the chief.

Tarzan dropped to the ground and moved toward the palisade. When a few paces from it, he sprang swiftly forward, leaped into the air, and ran up the barrier with all the agility of little Nkima, who followed close behind him. Then the two dropped silently into the shadows among the huts in the rear of the village.

Creeping stealthily, noiseless as the shadow of a shadow, the two crept toward the hut of the chief. Separated biologically by countless ages, one a little monkey, the other a peer of England, yet there was little difference in the way they passed through the night and swung nimbly into the tree that overshadowed Udalo's hut.

As Tarzan looked down at close range upon the dancing, shouting blacks, he realized that they had been partaking too freely of their native beer; and he knew that under such circumstances anything might happen.

A big black, half drunk, was haranguing Udalo. The man was evidently a sub-chief from another village.

'Bring out the Kavuru,' he said; 'let us have a look at them; we'll give them a taste of what they are going to get tomorrow night.'

'The others are not here,' said Udalo; 'we should wait for the rest of the tribe.'

'Bring them out,' demanded another; 'we have not seen them; we want to see the Kavuru who steal our girls.'

'Bring them out,' shrieked a woman. 'They stole my daughter, let me burn out their eyes with a red-hot coal, that they may suffer as I have suffered.'

Then Tarzan heard the voice of a child. 'Do not harm the Waziri,' she said; 'they are the friends of Tarzan, and Tarzan is a friend of the Bukena. He saved me from the Kavuru and brought me back to my village.'

'You cannot trust the Kavuru or a demon,' said Udalo. He turned to some of his warriors. 'Bring the prisoners,' he said, 'but see that they are not killed tonight.'

Already Tarzan of the Apes was on the ground behind the hut of the chief. Here was an emergency. Every danger, every risk, must be faced without hesitation, boldly, after the manner of the Lord of the Jungle.

He moved quickly to the hut where he had been confined; and as he stooped and entered it, his sensitive nostrils told him that the Waziri were there.

'Silence,' he whispered; 'it is I, Tarzan. They are coming for you. I will cut your bonds. We will fall upon the warriors who come and take their weapons from them; bind and gag them; let them make no noise. Then bring them where Tarzan leads, to the rear of the chief's hut.'

He worked quickly as he talked; and when the three warriors came to fetch the prisoners, all of them were free and waiting, waiting in silence in the darkness.

15

A Bit of Cloth

'Don't get it into your heads that you are going to hang me.' There was a challenge in Brown's tone that sounded to Jane like the defiance of a guilty man; and yet she could not believe that it was he who had killed the Princess Sborov.

'We shall hang no one,' she said. 'We cannot take the law into our own hands; we must all be equally under suspicion until a properly constituted court of law determines our guilt or innocence. There is but one thing to do; we must try to reach the nearest established civilized authority, tell our story, and let the law take its course.'

'I quite agree with you, Milady,' said Tibbs.

'Well, I don't,' grumbled Alexis; 'it wouldn't be safe to travel through this lonely country with a murderer who might easily kill all of us and thus dispose of all the witnesses who could testify against him.'

'And what do you suggest?' asked Jane.

'That we leave the murderer here, make our way to the nearest post, report the affair, and leave it to the authorities to apprehend the guilty man and arrest him.'

Jane shook her head. 'But we don't know who the murderer is; in the eyes of the law, we are all equally suspects. No, the only proper thing to do is to find a magistrate or a commissioner, tell our story and request an investigation.'

'Not for me,' said Brown. 'I wouldn't have a chance in one of these foreign ports. There ain't anybody in Europe got any use for an American anyway, but they sure knuckle down to titles. What chance would an American without money have against a prince with millions? Nix, Miss, there ain't nobody goin' to railroad my neck into a noose!'

'You see, Jane,' said Alexis, 'he practically admits his guilt. An innocent man would not be afraid to stand trial.'

'Listen, Miss,' said Brown, turning appealingly to Jane, 'I ain't never bumped anyone off yet; but if you don't want another killing around here, make that fool shut up and keep shut up.'

'Then you refuse to come with us, Brown?' demanded Jane. 'I think you are very foolish.'

'I may be foolish, Miss; but I ain't taking no chances with no foreign court. An English court might be all right, but we are not in English territory. No, I came out here with these people in the hopes I could get hold of that formula for perpetual youth. That would be worth millions back home; and now that I am here, I am going ahead and try to find it. I don't know how, but I am going to try.'

'There are so few of us,' said Jane, 'and we are so poorly armed that we really ought to stick together, at least until we contact some friendly natives.'

'I didn't plan on leaving you cold, Miss,' said the pilot. 'I'll stick until you and Annette are safe.'

'I was sure you would, Brown; and now that that's settled, we've something else to do – a very unpleasant duty. The princess must be buried. I guess you men will have to dig the grave.'

The only implement they had with which to dig was the hatchet that had been used to kill the princess; and thus a task, sufficiently gruesome in itself, was rendered incalculably more so.

While one of the men loosened the earth with the hatchet, the other two scooped it out with their hands; and while the men were thus occupied, Jane and Annette prepared the body for burial as best they might by wrapping it in articles of the victim's clothing taken from her baggage.

Annette wept continually; but Jane, even though she felt the loss infinitely more than the little French maid could have, remained dry-eyed. She had work to do, a duty to perform; and she could not permit her personal sorrow to interfere.

When all was in readiness and the body lowered into the grave, Jane recited as much of the burial service as she could recall, while the others stood about with bowed heads, the men uncovered.

'I think,' said Jane, when it was all over and the grave filled, 'that we had better break camp immediately; no one will want to remain here.'

'Have you any plan?' asked Alexis. 'Do you know where we are going?'

'There are only two things we can do,' said Jane. 'One is to follow this trail toward the west, and the other is to follow it toward the east. The toss of a coin could decide that as intelligently as any of us. Not knowing where we are, it is impossible to know in which direction lies the nearest friendly village. Personally, I should prefer going toward the east because there lies the country with which I am familiar, the country where I have many friends among the natives.'

'Then we go to the east,' said Brown. 'You're boss; what you say goes.'

'I doubt the wisdom of your decision, Jane,' said Alexis. 'The Belgian Congo must lie to the west, if we are not already in it, which I believe; and in that event, we shall strike civilization sooner by going in that direction.'

'It's all guesswork at best, Alexis,' said Jane. 'It really doesn't make much difference which way we go. Let's leave it to a vote. How about you, Tibbs?'

'I – ahem – I beg pardon, Milady, I shall cast my lot with the majority.'

'You're a lot of help,' said Brown.

'And you, Annette?' asked Jane.

'Oh, if you and Mr Brown wish to go to the east, I wish to go to the east also.'

'That's settled,' said Jane; 'we go to the east then.'

'I still object,' demurred Alexis. 'As the financial head of the expedition, the one who has paid and must pay all the bills, I believe that some consideration should be shown my wishes.'

'Alexis,' said Jane, 'you make it very difficult. Like the rest, you will have to follow my orders, or when there is a question, accept the will of the majority. As for financing the expedition, each of us has the necessary wherewithal if we care to use it, and it's not money; it's cooperation and loyalty, courage and endurance.'

Alexis had been watching her closely as she spoke, and suddenly his whole attitude changed. 'I am sorry, Jane,' he said, 'I spoke thoughtlessly. You must understand that I am terribly upset by what has happened. I have lost my dear wife, and I am heart-broken.'

Brown turned away disgustedly and held his nose with a thumb and forefinger.

'All right, Alexis,' said Jane. 'Now let's gather up what necessities we can carry and get going.'

'How about breakfast?' demanded Brown.

'Oh, I had forgotten all about breakfast,' said Jane. 'Well, it will have to be bush-buck again.'

'I don't believe I can eat a mouthful,' said Annette to Brown.

'Oh, yes you can, girlie,' replied the pilot; 'you gotta eat whether you want it or not. We've probably got a lot of hard days ahead of us and we got to keep up our strength.'

'I'll try,' she said, 'for you.'

He squeezed her arm. 'And say,' he said, 'you don't believe I done it, do you?'

'No, Mr Brown, I do not believe it.'

'Aw, can the mister, girlie.'

'All right – Neal, but I do not see how he could have done it; I do not see how a man could kill his wife. She was such a nice lady.'

'Yeah, she was sort of nuts, but she was all right at that. She was a whole lot better than him. As a matter of fact, the old dame killed herself.'

'What do you mean? How could she kill herself so horribly with a hatchet?'

'Well, she done it all right; she done it when she told him she was going to change her will.'

'Oh! What a terrible man.'

'I've known of fellows that was bumped off for less than what this guy will get,' said Brown. 'Back in the land of the free and the home of the brave, you can get it done to almost any guy for a hundred smackers.'

'One hundred smackers? What is a smacker? My English, she is not so good.'

'I've noticed that, kiddo, but don't worry; I'll learn you.'

'Now I must cook the meat for our breakfast,' said Annette, 'if you will cut off a few slices for me from the hind quarters.'

'Sure.' He felt in his pockets. 'Where's my knife? Oh, yes, I remember,' and he turned to Jane. 'Say, Miss,' he called, 'let me have my knife if you are through with it.'

'You haven't any knife,' laughed Jane, 'but I'll loan you mine.'

Brown rubbed his chin. 'That's right; I did lose, didn't I?'

While Annette was cooking the antelope, the others busied themselves selecting such things as they thought they would need and could carry on the march. Tibbs was busy repacking suitcases under the direction of Alexis. Jane gathered her weapons together and then fastened a small hand-bag to the belt that supported her shorts. It was such a bag as a woman uses to carry her money, keys, lipstick, and such odds and ends. Other than this and her weapons, Jane selected nothing more than what she wore.

Brown, who was wearing aviator's boots, chose to take along an extra pair of shoes and several pairs of socks. He also crammed the contents of a carton of cigarettes into various pockets and inside his shirt. These things, with a supply of matches, and the fateful hand-axe, constituted his entire equipment. He knew the bitterness of heavy packs.

As Annette grilled the meat over the coals, her eyes were attracted by something at the edge of the fire, among the cooling ashes. It was a bit of burned fabric to which three buttons remained attached. With a piece of stick, she turned it over. As it had been lying flat on the ground near the edge of the fire, the underneath portion of the fabric was not burned; the color and pattern remained.

A look of recognition entered her eyes; then they half closed in brooding, speculative contemplation of her find.

Brown wandered over toward the fire. 'I'll finish the meat,' he said; 'you go and gather together what you are going to take.'

'I don't know what to take,' said the girl. 'I can't carry very much.'

'Take whatever you need, girlie,' he said; 'I'll help you carry the stuff. Take extra shoes if you have them and plenty of stockings and a warm wrap. Unless I'm mistaken, we are going to need a lot of shoes and stockings, especially you. Them things you are wearing was never meant to walk in nohow.'

'I have two pair of low-heeled shoes,' said the girl.

'Then throw them things away and take the low-heeled ones.'

'All right,' she said; 'I'll go and get my things together. While I am gone, you might like to look at this,' and she touched the piece of burned fabric with the stick she was holding.

Brown picked the thing up and looked at it; then he whistled as he raised his eyes to the person of Prince Alexis Sborov. Annette walked away to make up her bundle. Tibbs was still busy packing. Jane was seated on a rotting log, deep in thought. Brown was whistling; he seemed very much pleased about something. Presently he looked up at the others.

'Come and get it,' he called.

'Beg pardon,' said Tibbs, 'come and get what?'

'Chuck,' explained Brown.

'"Chuck"!' sneered Sborov.

Jane rose. 'I guess we eat,' she said, 'and after all, I am hungry. I didn't think I should be.'

They all gathered around the fire where Brown had laid strips of cooked meat on a little bed of clean twigs close beside the coals.

'Come ahead folks; pitch in,' said Brown.

'Tibbs,' said Alexis, 'you may fetch me a piece not too rare nor too well done – about medium.'

Brown looked up in undisguised disgust. He jabbed a stick into a piece of meat and tossed it at Alexis. 'Here, Napoleon,' he said, 'we are sorry we ain't got no gold platters; but the keeper of the imperial pantry ran out on us and no one else ain't got no key.'

Alexis gave Brown a venomous look, but he picked up the sorry-looking piece of meat and took a bite of it.

'This is terrible,' he said; 'it's burned on the outside and raw on the inside. My stomach will never be able to stand such cooking as this. I shall not eat it.'

'Well, ain't that just too bad!' said Brown. 'Let's all cry.'

'You better eat it, Alexis,' said Jane. 'You'll get awfully hungry before night.'

'Tibbs will prepare my food hereafter,' said Alexis haughtily. 'I shall eat apart.'

'That will suit me,' Brown assured him, 'and the farther apart, the better.'

'Come, come,' said Jane, 'don't start that all over again; we've had enough of it.'

'O.K. Miss,' assented Brown; 'but there is something I'd like to ask the grand Duke. I notice that he's changed his coat. That was a mighty nice coat he was wearing last night, and I thought if he wasn't going to use it no more, I'd like to buy it from him – that is, if nothing ain't happened to it.'

Alexis looked up quickly, his face paling. 'I do not sell my old clothes,' he said. 'When I am through with it, I'll give it to you.'

'That's mighty nice of you,' said Brown. 'May I see it now? I'd like to find out if it fits me.'

'Not now, my man; it's packed with my other things.'

'All of it?' demanded Brown.

'All of it? What do you mean? Of course it's all packed.'

'Well, here's one piece you forgot, Mister,' and Brown held up the charred remnant of the sleeve with the three buttons still remaining on it.

Sborov's face took on a ghastly hue; his eyes stared wildly at the bit of cloth, but almost as quickly he regained his self-possession.

'Some more American humor?' he asked. 'That thing doesn't belong to me.'

'It looks a powerful like the coat you was wearing last night,' said Brown. 'Annette thinks so, too; but Tibbs ought to know; he's your valet. Ever see this before, Tibbs?'

The valet coughed. 'I – er—'

'Come over and take a good look at it,' said Brown.

Tibbs approached and examined the piece of fabric carefully, turning it over and wiping the ashes from the buttons.

'When did you see that last, Tibbs?' demanded Brown.

'I – really—' He glanced apprehensively at Sborov.

'You're a liar, Tibbs,' shouted the prince. 'I never had a coat like that; I never saw it before. It's not mine, I tell you.'

'Tibbs didn't say nothing,' Brown reminded him; 'he ain't opened his trap except to say "I – er." He never said it was off your coat; but you're going to, ain't you, Tibbs?'

'It looks very much like it, Sir,' replied the Englishman. 'Of course, I couldn't exactly take oath to it, seeing as how it's so badly burned.'

Brown turned his gaze upon Alexis. 'The blood must have spattered some when you hit her.'

'Don't!' screamed Alexis; 'my God! Don't. I never touched her, I tell you.'

'Tell it to the judge,' said Brown. 'You'd better hang on to that evidence, Annette,' he added; 'the judge might like to know about that, too.'

Alexis had quickly gained control of himself. 'It was my coat,' he said; 'someone stole it out of my luggage; it's what you call in America a frame.'

'Let's leave this whole terrible matter to the courts,' said Jane; 'it's not for us to try to decide, and constantly harping on it only makes our situation all the more bitter.'

Brown nodded. 'I guess you're right, Miss, as usual.'

'Very well, then. If you have all finished eating, we'll start. I've left a note stuck up in the shelter telling about our accident and the direction we are taking, and giving the names of all in the party, just on the chance, the very remote chance, that someone might pass this way someday – some white hunter who could take our message out in case we never get out ourselves. Are you all ready?'

'All ready,' said Alexis. 'Tibbs, my luggage.'

Tibbs walked over to where his small handbag, a large Gladstone, and two suitcases were stacked.

'Where's your luggage, Jane?' asked Alexis. 'Brown could carry that.'

'I'm carrying my own,' replied Jane, 'what little I'm taking.'

'But you haven't any,' said the prince.

'I am carrying all that I am going to take. We are not travelling deluxe.'

They were all standing silently watching Tibbs trying to gather up the four pieces of baggage so that he could carry them.

'Beg pardon, Sir,' he said, 'but if I may make so bold as to say so, I don't think that I can carry them all.'

'Well, let Annette carry that small bag of yours, then. You certainly ought to be able to manage three pieces. I've seen porters carry twice that much.'

'Not across Africa,' said Jane.

'Well,' said Alexis, 'I've only brought along what I actually need; I've left nearly all of my stuff behind. Tibbs will have to manage somehow. If Brown were the right sort he'd help him.'

Only by the exercise of all his willpower had Brown remained silent; but now he exploded. 'Listen, mister,' he said, 'I ain't going to carry none of your stuff, and neither is Annette, and if Tibbs does, he's a damned fool.'

'I fancy I rather agree with you, Mr Brown,' said Tibbs, and dropped all three of the pieces of baggage.

'What?' demanded Alexis. 'You refuse to carry my luggage? Why, you impudent upstart, I'll—'

'No you won't, Sir,' said Tibbs; 'I know just what you are going to say, Sir, if I may make so bold as to say so; but it won't be necessary, Sir.' He drew himself up haughtily. 'I am giving notice, Sir; I am leaving your employ now, immediately.'

'Lady Greystoke,' said Alexis, with great dignity, 'you have assumed command here. I demand that you compel these people to carry my luggage.'

'Nonsense,' said Jane. 'Take an extra pair of shoes and some socks and whatever else you can carry, and come along. We can't waste any more time here.'

And thus the unhappy party started upon the trail toward the east. They had had but two guesses; and they had guessed wrong, but fortunately they could not know the dangers and the terrors that lay ahead of them on the trail toward the east.

16

The Message

The three Bukena warriors crept into the hut where Tarzan and the ten Waziri warriors lay waiting for them in silence.

As the last of the three entered, Tarzan leaped upon him. Powerful fingers closed about the fellow's throat; and simultaneously the other two were dragged down by Muviro and a couple of his warriors. There was no outcry; there was only the subdued sound of the shuffling feet of struggling men, and that for but a moment.

Quickly the three were bound and gagged; then the Waziri, headed by Tarzan, carried them to the tree beside the chiefs hut, where a corner of the

84

latter concealed them from the sight of the drunken natives assembled in the street in front.

Shouldering one of the warriors, Tarzan swarmed up into the tree; then after he had deposited his burden safely where it would not fall, the Waziri handed the other two up to him.

Taking his victims up into the denser foliage where they would not be visible from the ground, Tarzan laid them side by side across the huge branch that projected out over the negroes assembled below.

Tarzan ran his rope through the bonds that encircled the ankles of one of the prisoners. Then he removed the gag from the fellow's mouth and lowered him, head foremost, toward the ground; but before the fellow's head broke through the foliage and came in sight of those below, Tarzan voiced the warning cry of the bull ape. Instantly the dancing stopped; the natives looked around them in evident terror; the sound was very close; it seemed right beside them, but as yet they had been unable to locate it.

Silence followed; and then the head of one of their fellows broke through the foliage above them, and slowly his body descended.

The blacks were already on the verge of panic, for this was a mysterious, supernatural occurrence for which they could find no explanation in their past experience; yet they hesitated, perhaps fascinated and momentarily incapable of movement.

The deep voice rang out above them. 'I am Tarzan of the Apes. Let those beware who would harm Tarzan or his Waziri. Open the gates and let my people go in peace, or many of you shall die by the hand of Tarzan.'

The victim hanging head downward found his tongue. 'Open the gates,' he screamed. 'Let them go before they kill me.'

Still the blacks hesitated.

'The time is short,' said Tarzan, and then he started to drag the warrior back up into the tree again.

'Do you promise that none of us will be harmed if we open the gates?' demanded Udalo.

'None will be harmed if you open the gates and let us go in peace, returning their weapons to my Waziri.'

'It shall be done,' said Udalo. 'Fetch the weapons of the Waziri; open the gates; let them go, and may they never return.'

Tarzan drew the warrior back up into the tree and laid him beside his fellows.

'Keep still,' he warned them, 'and I shall kill none of you.' Then he dropped to the ground and joined the Waziri.

Fearlessly they walked around the end of the hut; and the blacks gave way fearfully, opening a path before them. Some little boys ran timidly forward with their weapons, for the warriors had not dared to do so. The gates were opened, and Tarzan led his Waziri toward them.

'Where are my three warriors?' demanded Udalo. 'You have not kept your word.'

'You will find your three warriors alive in the tree above your hut,' replied the ape-man. He halted and turned toward the chief. 'And now, Udalo, when strangers come to your kraal, treat them well, and especially Tarzan and the Waziri.' A moment later the black jungle night beyond the palisade had swallowed them.

Little Naika, the daughter of Gupingu, the witch-doctor danced up and down and clapped her hands. 'It is he!' she cried. 'It is the white warrior who saved me. I am glad that he and his Waziri got away before we killed them. I told you not to do it.'

'Shut up,' cried Udalo, 'and go to your hut. I never want to hear that white man spoken of again.'

'I thought that it was the end,' said Muviro, as they crossed the clearing toward the forest.

'Thanks to Nkima's bad memory, it came very near being the end,' replied the ape-man. Then he voiced a strange, weird note; and an answer came from the blackness of the jungle trees.

'He is still there,' said the ape-man to Muviro.

'Hurry, hurry,' cried the monkey. 'Little Nkima is fighting with Sheeta, the panther; he is beating him on the head with a stick; he is pounding him on the nose. Sheeta is very frightened.'

Tarzan grinned and walked on slowly through the forest, and when he came under the first tree, the little monkey dropped down upon his shoulder. 'Where is Sheeta?' demanded Tarzan.

'Little Nkima beat him so hard on the face that he ran away.'

'Little Nkima is very brave,' said the ape-man.

'Yes,' replied the monkey, 'little Nkima is a mighty fighter, a mighty hunter.'

The following day, Tarzan and the Waziri moved slowly toward the North, resting often, for the latter were still suffering from the effects of the drug that had been administered to them by Gupingu, the witch-doctor. Finally, when Tarzan realized their condition more fully, he ordered a halt; and the party went into camp upon the banks of a river.

As time had never been a matter of consequence to the ape-man, delays, except in cases of immediate emergency, gave him no concern. He could wait there for one day, or two days, or as long as was necessary while his warriors recuperated; nor would he leave them while they needed someone to hunt for them. He made them rest therefore while he foraged for food.

The day after they had left the village of Udalo, a lone warrior trotted into the clearing and approached the gates of the kraal. The white plume of the Waziri waved above his head; and in his hand he carried a split stick, in the end of which an envelope was inserted.

When warriors met him at the gates, he asked to see the chief; and they took him to Udalo, but not without misgivings; for he bore a marked resemblance to the ten prisoners who had escaped them.

Udalo eyed the warrior sullenly. 'Who are you?' he demanded, 'and what do you want in the village of Udalo?'

'I am a Waziri,' replied the man. 'I bear a message for the Big Bwana, Tarzan. The sun has risen many times since he left his country to come here in search of the Kavuru. I have followed to bring this message to him. Have you seen him?'

'He has been here, but he has gone,' said Udalo, sullenly.

'When did he go, and in which direction?' asked the messenger.

'He went away yesterday with ten Waziri warriors. They took the trail toward the North. You will follow him?'

'Yes.'

'I will give you food before you go, and when you find Tarzan tell him that Udalo treated you well.' The fear of the Lord of the Jungle was in the heart of Udalo, the chief.

It was mid-day of the following day. The Waziri lay resting in their camp beside the river. Tarzan squatted at the base of a tree fashioning arrows for his quiver. Little Nkima perched upon one of his shoulders, busily occupied by that age-old simian pastime of searching for fleas upon his belly. He was vastly contented.

Presently the ape-man raised his head and looked toward the South where the trail debauched upon the clearing where they were encamped.

'Someone comes,' he said.

The Waziri stirred themselves. Some of them seized their weapons and started to rise, but Tarzan reassured them.

'There is no danger,' he said; 'there is only one. He comes boldly, and not by stealth.'

'Who could it be?' asked Muviro. 'We have seen no one in all this lonely country since we left the Bukena village.'

The ape-man shrugged. 'We shall have to wait,' he said, 'until our eyes tell us, for he is downwind from us.'

Little Nkima, noting the listening attitudes of the others, abandoned the pursuit of a singularly notable specimen and following the example of the Waziri, stared intently toward the South.

'Something comes?' he asked Tarzan.

'Yes.'

Little Nkima slipped quickly down behind Tarzan's back, and peered anxiously across his left shoulder. 'Something is coming to eat little Nkima?' he demanded.

He glanced up into the tree behind him, gauging the distance to the lowest branch, and debated in his little mind the wisdom of discretion. However, feeling reasonably safe in his present sanctuary, he stood his ground; and a moment later a lone warrior trotted into the clearing. At sight of the party encamped there, he voiced his pleasure in a series of savage whoops; and the Waziri returned his greeting in kind, for he was the runner bearing a message for Tarzan.

As he came forward with the message in the split stick to deliver it to Tarzan, little Nkima evinced great interest and as the message was handed to his Master he seized the stick and commenced to scold and jabber when Tarzan took the envelope from it.

The ape-man removed the message and dropped the envelope to the ground, whereupon little Nkima sprang upon it and occupied himself in a futile endeavor to make it remain upright on the end of the stick as the messenger had carried it.

The Waziri were looking expectantly at Tarzan as he read the message, for messages delivered in the depths of the forest were rare indeed.

As he read, Tarzan's brow clouded; and when he had finished he turned to Muviro.

'There is bad news, Bwana?' asked the black.

'The mem-sahib left London for Nairobi in an aeroplane,' he said; 'that was just before the big storm. You remember, Muviro, that after the storm broke we heard an aeroplane circling above?'

'Yes, Bwana.'

'We thought then that it was in great danger. Perhaps that was the ship in which the mem-sahib rode.'

'It went away,' Muviro reminded him, 'and we did not hear it again. Perhaps it went on to Nairobi.'

'Perhaps,' said the ape-man, 'but it was a very bad storm and the pilot was lost. Either that, or he was in trouble and looking for a landing place; otherwise he would not have been circling as he was.'

For some time Tarzan sat in thought, and then the silence was broken by Muviro. 'You will go back at once to Nairobi, Bwana?' he asked.

'What good would it do?' asked the ape-man. 'If they reached Nairobi, she is safe; if they did not, where might I search? In an hour an aeroplane might fly as far as one could travel on the ground in a day; perhaps, if they had trouble, it flew for many hours after we heard it before it came down; and if the pilot were lost, there is no telling in what direction it went. The chances are that I should never find it; even if I did, it would be too late. Then, too, it may as easily be that it came down in the direction we are going as in any other direction.'

'Then we may continue to search for my daughter, Buira?' asked Muviro.

'Yes,' said Tarzan. 'As soon as you are rested and well again, we shall go on toward the country of the Kavuru.'

Little Nkima was becoming more and more excited and irritable. Notwithstanding all his efforts, the envelope would not remain upright upon the end of the stick. He chattered and scolded, but it availed him nothing; and then Tarzan noticed him, and taking the stick from him spread the slit end open and inserted the envelope.

Nkima watched him intently, his head cocked upon one side. Tarzan repeated the operation several times, and then he handed the envelope and the stick to Nkima.

An adept in mimicry, the monkey re-enacted all that he had watched Tarzan do; and after a few trials succeeded in inserting the envelope into the end of the stick.

His achievement filled him with enthusiasm and pride. Jabbering excitedly, he leaped from Waziri to Waziri until all had examined the marvel that little Nkima had wrought; nor did his excitement soon subside, and in the exuberance of his spirits he went racing through the trees clinging tightly to the stick that bore the envelope in its end.

Tarzan and the Waziri laughed at his antics.

'Little Nkima is proud because he has learned a new trick,' said one.

'He thinks now he is a great witch-doctor among the monkeys,' said Muviro.

'It is like many of the useless things that man learns,' said Tarzan. 'It will never do him nor anyone else any good; but if it makes him happy, that is enough.'

For three days more the Waziri rested, and then Muviro said that they were ready to continue on toward the North.

In the meantime, Tarzan had dispatched the runner back to Nairobi with a message for Jane and also one to the authorities there, asking them to make a search for the ship in the event that it had not already arrived.

Little Nkima was still intrigued by his new accomplishment. He would sit for an hour at a time taking the envelope out of the stick and putting it back in, and he never permitted it out of his possession. Wherever he went, he carried the stick and the envelope with him.

Having been several days in this camp, and having seen no danger, Nkima, always restless, had formed the habit of wandering farther and farther away. He found some other little monkeys of his own species with whom he tried to make friends; but in this he succeeded only partially; the males bared their teeth and chattered at him, scolding; and sometimes when he came too close, they chased him away. But handicapped though he was by his stick and his envelope, he always succeeded in eluding them; for Nkima was an adept in escaping danger.

But there was one who did not bare her teeth and scold. However, it was difficult for Nkima to find her when there was not an old male hanging around; and old males can be very disagreeable.

This last day in camp, however, he was more successful; he discovered her some little distance from her fellows.

The young lady was coy; she did not repulse him but she led Nkima a merry chase through the trees. It was all in fun; and they were enjoying it greatly, for she was not really trying to escape from Nkima, nor was he seriously intent upon capturing her, for he knew that eventually she would stop and let him come close.

And so, thoughtless of time or direction or distance, they swung through the trees, a little lady monkey and Nkima with his stick and his envelope.

They had had a glorious time and thoroughly understood one another when the little lady finally came to rest upon a broad branch. That they might permanently cement this friendship, each was soon searching for what he might find upon the head of the other, and certainly that is almost the last word in intimacy – the final proof of trust and confidence and friendship.

They were very happy, and only once did a shadow momentarily becloud this bliss. That was when the young lady sought to snatch the stick and envelope from Nkima. He bared his teeth in a terrible grimace, and gave her a resounding box on one of her shell-like ears. She lowered her head sheepishly then and cuddled closer to him, and it was plain to see that she liked this dominant male and his cave-man tactics.

What a day for little Nkima! They hunted for fruit and nuts; they ate together; they scampered through the trees; they sat enfolded in each other's arms; and little Nkima was entirely unaware that Tarzan and the Waziri had broken camp and started North again. Perhaps if he had known, it would have made no difference at the moment for the alchemy of love works strange metamorphoses in the minds of its victims.

To their consternation, while they were still far away, night overtook them; and they were afraid to return through the menacing darkness of the glowering forest. They were afraid; but they were happy, and when the moon rose it looked down upon two little monkeys clutched tightly in each other's arms. Above their heads rose a little stick bearing an envelope in its split end.

17

The Snake

It was with feelings of relief that the five left the scene of the tragedy that had cast a pall of gloom and horror over them; and while the future held out little of encouragement to them, the very fact of being on the move raised their spirits to some extent.

Brown had insisted upon marching at the head of the little column, and Jane had acceded to his request. Annette stayed as close to Brown as she could. Jane brought up the rear and Alexis walked with her. Tibbs plodded along behind Annette.

Either because he tired more quickly than the others, or because he wanted to get out of earshot of those whom he considered servants and beneath him, Alexis lagged.

'We shouldn't fall so far behind the others,' said Jane. 'We must not become separated. You will have to walk a little faster, Alexis.' Her tone was just a little impatient.

'I thought it would be nice for us to be alone together, Jane,' he said. 'You see, you and I have nothing in common with those others; and it must be as much of a relief to you as to me to have the companionship of one of your own class.'

'You will have to get over that,' said Jane; 'there are no class distinctions here.'

'I am afraid you do not like me, dear lady.'

'You have been very annoying at times, Alexis.'

'I have been terribly upset,' he replied, 'and most of all by you.'

'By me? What have I done?'

'It is not that you have done anything; it is just that you are you. Can't you understand, Jane? Haven't you noticed?'

'Noticed what?'

'From the first, you attracted me strangely. There seemed to be no hope, though, and I was desperately blue; but now I am free, Jane.' He seized her hand. 'Oh, Jane, can't you like me a little?'

She jerked her hand from his. 'You fool!' she exclaimed.

His eyes narrowed menacingly. 'You are going to regret that,' he said. 'I tell you I'm in love with you, madly in love. I'm desperate, and I won't stand idly by and see an illiterate aeroplane pilot get the woman I want.'

'Just what do you mean by that?' The girl's eyes and voice were level and cold.

'It's too obvious to need explanation. Anyone can see that you are in love with Brown.'

'Alexis, did you ever hear a man referred to as an unspeakable cad? I have; but until this minute I never knew what it meant. I never could have conceived the sort of man it describes until now. Move on now. Get away from me. Get up there with Tibbs.'

Instantly his manner changed. 'Oh, Jane,' he pleaded, 'please don't send me away. I don't know why I ever said that; I was just mad with jealousy. Can't you understand that it is because I love you so? Can't you understand and forgive me?'

She made no reply but started ahead, increasing her gait to overtake the others.

'Wait!' he exclaimed, huskily. 'You've got to listen to me. I'm not going to give you up.' He seized her by the arm and pulled her toward him, endeavoring to throw his arms about her. Then she struck him; and, jumping back, levelled her spear to hold him off.

For a moment they stood there facing one another in silence; and in that moment she saw something in his eyes, in the expression on his face, that made her fear him for the first time. She knew then how really dangerous he was, and it was no longer difficult for her to believe that he had murdered his wife.

'Go up there now as I told you,' she said, 'or I will kill you. There is no law here but the law of the jungle.'

Perhaps he, too, read something in her narrowed lids and icy tone, for he did as she bid, and went on ahead of her in silence.

By mid-afternoon, Tibbs and Alexis and Annette were almost exhausted; and when the party reached a favorable spot, Jane called a halt.

The trail by which they had come had followed the meanderings of the stream upon which they had been camped, and thus the water problem had been solved for them.

'What now, Miss?' demanded Brown. 'Hadn't we better rustle some grub?'

'Yes,' she replied. 'I'll go out and see what I can bring in.'

'I'm going to have a look-see myself,' said Brown. 'We can go in different directions and maybe one of us will find something.'

'All right. You go on up the trail, and I'll take to the trees and follow the river. I may run across a drinking hole.' She turned to the others. 'And while we are gone, the rest of you can be building a boma and gathering firewood. All right, Brown, let's get going.'

The three that remained in camp seemed physically unable to drag themselves to their feet, but Alexis was resourceful.

'Tibbs,' he said, 'go out and gather material for the boma and get some firewood.'

Motivated by years of servile obedience, the Englishman rose painfully to his feet and started away.

'I'll help you, Tibbs,' said Annette, and started to rise.

Alexis laid a restraining hand on her arm. 'Wait,' he said, 'I want to talk with you.'

'But we must help Tibbs.'

'He can do very nicely by himself. You wait here.'

'What do you want, Prince Sborov? I've got to go and help Tibbs.'

'Listen, my dear,' said Alexis, 'how would you like to have a hundred thousand francs?'

The girl shrugged. 'Who would not like to have a hundred thousand francs?' she demanded.

'Very well, you can earn them – and very easily.'

'And how?' Her tone was skeptical.

'You have something that I wish. I will pay you one hundred thousand francs for it; you know what it is.'

'You mean the burned sleeve of your coat, Prince Alexis?'

'You won't let them frame me, Annette? You won't let them send me to the guillotine for something I didn't do, when everybody in this party hates me; they will all lie about me, and when they bring that piece of burned cloth into court, I shall be convicted in spite of my innocence. Give it to me. No one need ever know; you can say that you lost it, and as soon as we get back to civilization I will give you one hundred thousand francs.'

The girl shook her head. 'No, I could not do that. It may be all that will save Mr Brown.'

'You are wasting your time on Brown,' he said, nastily. 'You think he loves you, but he doesn't. Don't be fooled.'

The girl flushed. 'I have not said that he loves me.'

'Well, you think so; and he's trying to make you think so; but if you knew what I know, you wouldn't be so anxious to save his worthless head.'

'I do not know what you mean. I do not care to talk about it any more. I will not give you the piece of cloth.'

'Well, I'll tell you what I mean, you little fool,' snapped Alexis. 'Brown's in love with Lady Greystoke, and she's in love with him. What do you suppose they've gone off into the jungle for? Why, to meet each other, of course.'

'I do not believe it,' said Annette. 'I will not listen to any more.'

She started to rise; and as she did so, he leaped to his feet and seized her.

'Give me that piece of cloth,' he demanded, in a hoarse whisper. The fingers of his right hand encircled her throat. 'Give it to me or I'll kill you, you little fool.'

Quick as a cat, and with surprising strength, she tore herself away from him and screamed.

'Help, Tibbs! Help!' she cried.

The Englishman had not gone far, and he came running back.

'If you tell on me,' cried Sborov in a low whisper, 'I'll kill you. I'll kill you as I killed her.'

Annette looked into his eyes, as Jane had, and was frightened.

'What's wrong, Sir?' demanded Tibbs, as he approached them.

'It wasn't anything,' said Alexis, with a laugh. 'Annette thought she saw a snake.'

'I did see a snake,' she said.

'Well, it's all right now, Tibbs,' said Alexis; 'you can go back to your work.'

'I shall need a little help, Sir,' said the Englishman. 'I cannot do it all alone.'

'I'll come with you, Tibbs,' said Annette.

Alexis followed them. He walked very close to Annette and whispered, 'Remember, if you tell them.'

'I don't fancy having a snake around the camp,' said Tibbs, 'the nasty beggers. I don't like 'em.'

'Neither do I,' said Annette, 'but I won't be afraid when Mr Brown comes back. If a snake tries to harm me then, he will kill it.' She did not look at Tibbs as she spoke, although she seemed to be addressing him, but at Alexis.

'I think I would not tell the others about the snake,' said Sborov; 'it might frighten Lady Greystoke.'

'My word, Sir, I don't believe she's afraid of anything, Sir.'

'Nevertheless, see that you don't mention it,' cautioned Alexis.

'Why, here's Mr Brown now,' cried Tibbs. 'He's running. Something must have happened.'

'What's wrong?' demanded Brown. 'I heard someone scream. Was that you, Annette?'

'Annette saw a snake,' said Alexis. 'Did you not, Annette?'

'Where is it?' asked Brown. 'Did you kill it?'

'No,' replied the girl, 'I had nothing with which to kill it; but if it frightens me again, you will kill it.'

'You bet your life I will, girlie. Where is it now?'

'It got away,' said Alexis.

Annette looked straight into his eyes. 'Next time it will not get away,' she said.

Brown's pockets were bulging with fruit which he took out and laid on the ground.

'I hope this ain't poison,' he said. 'I had a heck of a time getting it. Lady Greystoke will know whether or not we can eat it.'

'Here she comes now,' said Annette.

'What luck, Jane?' asked Alexis.

'Not so good,' she replied, 'just a little fruit. I didn't see any game.' Her eyes fell on the fruit that Brown had gathered. 'Oh, you found the same thing,' she said. 'Well, it won't taste very good, but it's safe and it's food. I thought I heard a scream a few moments ago. Did any of you hear it?'

'It was Annette,' said Brown; 'she seen a snake.'

Jane laughed. 'Oh, before Annette gets out of Africa, she'll be used to snakes.'

'Not this one,' said the girl.

A puzzled expression crossed Brown's face. He started to speak, and then, evidently thinking better of it, remained silent.

Not much had been accomplished toward the building of the boma and collecting the firewood; so Jane and Brown lent a hand in the work which moved much more rapidly with the aid of the hand-axe.

It was dark before the work was completed, and then they felt that they could take their ease around the fire that Jane had built.

Jane showed them how they might make the fruit that constituted their sole food supply more palatable by roasting it on the end of a stick. So hungry were they that even Sborov ate without complaining; and as they ate, a pair of eyes watched them from behind the concealing foliage of a nearby tree.

Brown had insisted that the three men assume the duty of guarding the camp; and though Jane and Annette insisted upon doing their share, the pilot was firm in respect to this matter and would not be moved.

'Two hours on and four off won't hurt nobody,' he insisted, 'and you girls are going to need all the sleep you can get if you're going to keep up with us.'

The statement made Jane smile, for she knew that she could endure more than any of them, not excepting Brown; but she appreciated the spirit that animated him; and knowing how jealous men are of their protective prerogative she bowed to his will rather than offend him.

The three men matched coins to determine the order in which they should stand guard.

'I wish you'd let me be a sentry,' said Annette.

'No, that ain't no work for a girl,' said Brown.

'Oh, please, Neal, just once,' she begged. 'Oh, please.'

'Nothing doing.'

'Oh, just one little hour. You are on from two to four, Neal. Wake me at four and let me stand guard until five. Then I will wake the prince. It will be almost morning, anyway.'

'Let her do it, if she wants to,' said Jane.

'All right,' said Brown, 'but it ain't goin' to be the regular thing.'

All were stretched out around the fire, apparently sleeping, when Tibbs woke Brown for his first tour of duty at eight o'clock.

Tibbs was so exhausted that he was asleep almost as soon as he lay down. Then Annette raised on one elbow and looked around. A moment later she came over and sat down beside Brown.

'You better get back to bed, kid,' he said.

'I just wanted to talk with you for a minute, Neal,' she said.

'What's on your mind, girlie.'

She was silent for a moment. 'Oh, nothing in particular,' she replied. 'I like to be alone with you; that is all.'

He put an arm about her and pressed her closer, and thus they sat in silence for a moment before Brown spoke again.

'You know, I've been thinking a lot about that snake business, Annette,' he said. 'It sounded sort of fishy to me. You sure you wasn't stringin' me?'

'Stringing? I don't know what stringing is.'

'Well, skip it. I seen funny looks pass between you and the grand Duke when you was handing me that line about snakes. On the level now, kiddo, give me the low-down.'

'The low-down?'

'The facts – truth. What was it all about?'

'I am so afraid of him, Neal. Promise me that you won't tell him that I told you. I think of what he did to her; he would do the same to me; he said so.'

'What? He said he'd kill you?'

'If I told.'

'If you told what?'

'That he had tried to take that piece of coat sleeve away from me.'

'That was when you screamed?' he asked.

'Yes.'

'I'll get him for that,' said Brown.

'Please don't say anything about it; please promise me,' she begged. 'Only don't leave me alone with him again.'

'All right, then,' he promised; 'but if he ever makes another break like that, I'll sure get him. You needn't be afraid of him.'

'I am not afraid when you are with me. I do not know what I should do if it were not for you.'

'You like me a little, kid?'

'I like you a great deal, Neal.'

He pressed her closer to him. 'I guess I like you a lot, too – more than I ever liked anyone else.'

She nestled closer to him. 'Tell me how much that is,' she whispered.

'I'm not much good at saying things like that. I – I – well, you know what I mean.'

'I want to hear you say it.'

He cleared his throat. 'Well – I love you, kid.'

'And you don't love Lady Greystoke?'

'Eh? What!' he exclaimed. 'What put that into your head?'

'He said so; he said that you loved her, and that she loved you.'

'The dirty rat! Imagine that dame, the wife of an English viscount, falling for me. That is to laugh.'

'But you might – what you call it – fall for her.'

'Not on your life, kid; not while I've got you.'

She put her arms around his neck and drew him down toward her. 'I love you, Neal,' she murmured, before their lips met.

They felt that they had the night and the world to themselves, but that was because they were not aware of the silent watcher in the tree above them. She sat with him until he awoke Sborov.

The camp was sleeping soundly when Tibbs finished his tour of duty at two in the morning and called Brown again.

At four Brown hesitated to awaken Annette, but he had given his word that she might stand guard for an hour; so he shook her gently.

'It's four o'clock and all's well,' he whispered. Then he kissed her ear. 'And now it's better.'

She raised herself to an elbow, laughing. 'Now you lie down and sleep,' she said, 'and I'll stand guard.'

'I'll sit along with you for a while,' he said.

'No, that was not in the bargain,' she insisted. 'I want to watch alone. I shall feel very important. Go on, and go to sleep.'

Then quiet fell upon the camp – a quiet that was unbroken until Jane awoke after daylight. She sat up and looked about her. No one was on guard. Alexis, who should have been, was fast asleep.

'Come on, sleepy heads,' she cried; 'it's time to get up.'

Brown sat up sleepily and looked around. He saw Alexis just awakening.

'I thought the grand Duke was on guard,' said Brown. 'Did you take his place?'

'There wasn't anyone on guard when I woke up,' said Jane, and then she noticed. 'Where is Annette?'

Brown sprang to his feet. 'Annette!' he cried. There was no answer. Annette was gone.

18

A Bit of Paper

When morning broke, Nkima, had he been a man, would have said that he had not slept a wink all night; but that was because when he was awake he was so worried and frightened that the time had dragged interminably. During the night, he regretted that he had not stayed with Tarzan and determined to return to the camp the first thing in the morning; but when morning came, dispelling the gloom with brilliant sunshine, his little monkey mind forgot its good resolution and concerned itself only with the moment and his new playmate.

Off they went, racing through the jungle, swinging from limb to limb, scampering high aloft, dropping again to lower levels.

Nkima was very happy. The sun was shining. It would always shine. He could not vision that another night of cold and dread was coming quickly.

Farther and farther toward the west they scampered, farther and farther away from camp; and in one hand Nkima clutched the little stick with the split end, topped by the soiled and crumpled envelope. Through all the playing and the love-making and the long night, little Nkima had clung to his sole treasure.

The little she, who was Nkima's playmate, was mischievous. She was also covetous. For long had she looked upon the stick and the envelope with envy, but she had been cuffed once for trying to take them; so she was wary, yet the more she saw them, the more she wished them.

Nkima was running along a branch holding the envelope on high. The little she was following in his wake when she saw her chance – just ahead, a limb beneath which Nkima would have to pass. Quickly she sprang upward and raced ahead along this limb; and, as Nkima passed beneath her, she reached down and seized the envelope. She was disappointed because she did not get the stick, too; but even a part of this wonderful thing was better than nothing.

Having achieved her design, she scampered on ahead as fast as she could go. Nkima witnessed the theft, and his heart was filled with righteous anger and indignation. He pursued her, but fear lent her a new speed.

On they raced; but the little she always seemed to have the advantage, for she steadily outdistanced Nkima until she was lost to his sight; and then his indignation and sorrow at the loss of his treasure was submerged in a fear that he had lost the little she also.

But he had not. He came upon her perched innocently in a high-flung crotch, contentedly eating a piece of fruit. As Nkima approached her, he looked for the envelope. It was gone. He wanted to pound her, but he also wanted to hug her; so he compromised by hugging her.

He asked for his bit of paper. Of course, he had no name for it; but he made her understand. It seemed that she had become frightened and thrown it away.

Nkima went back a little way to look for it, but he became interested in some fuzzy caterpillars that he passed on the way; and when he had eaten all that he could find, he had temporarily forgotten the paper.

A little river flowed beneath them. Rivers always intrigued Nkima. He liked to follow them; so he followed this one.

Presently he espied something that brought him to a sudden stop. In a small, natural clearing on the bank of the river was a flimsy man-made hut.

Nkima thought that there must be Gomangani around; and he was wary, but he was also very curious. He watched and listened. The place seemed deserted. Finally he mustered sufficient courage to drop to the ground and investigate.

Followed by the little she, he crept toward the entrance to the hut. Cautiously he peeked around a corner of the door frame and peered within. There was no one there. Nkima entered. Luggage and clothing were strewn about the floor. He looked things over, seeking what he might appropriate. Then his eyes fell upon a piece of paper fastened to the wall with a sliver of wood. With a yelp of delight, Nkima leaped for it. Then he scampered out of the hut with his prize, raced across the clearing, and swarmed up to the topmost branches of a giant tree. Behind him came the little she.

By the time Nkima had succeeded in inserting the piece of paper in the notch at the end of the stick, his interest in the other things that he had seen in the hut had, monkey-like, waned.

Now he recalled the tall warrior who had brought the piece of paper in the end of the stick to Tarzan. Nkima decided that he would do likewise. He felt very important and was only sorry that he did not have a white plume to wave above his head.

Holding to this single idea for an unusually long time, Nkima raced back in the direction of the camp where he had left Tarzan and the Waziri.

It was late in the afternoon when he got there, and his little heart leaped into his throat when he discovered that his friends were gone.

He was very sad and a little frightened, although it was not yet dark; but when his lady friend came and sat close beside him, he felt better.

Unfortunately, this respite from despair was all too brief. The little band of monkeys to which his playmate belonged came trooping through the trees. They saw Nkima and the shameless young creature who had run away with him.

Jabbering, chattering, scolding, several of the males of the clan came swinging through the trees toward Nkima and his light-of-love. For a moment, just a fleeting moment, Nkima had visions of standing his ground and doing battle; but the leading male was an old fellow, very large and strong. His fangs were bared in a most disconcerting manner; and he voiced terrifying threats that made Nkima's heart quail, so that on second thought he determined to go elsewhere and go quickly; but his lady friend clung to him tightly, hampering his movements, for she, too, was frightened. Perhaps she did not want to lose Nkima who, after all, had a way with him.

The terrifying old monkey was approaching rapidly, and then Nkima did a most ungallant thing; he struggled to free himself from the lady's embrace, and when she only clung more tightly he tore at her arms to disengage himself, and then struck her in the face until she finally released him.

By now, Nkima was screaming in terror. The little she was screaming, and so were all the other monkeys. Bedlam reigned in the jungle; and to the accompaniment of this din of rage and terror, little Nkima broke away and fled; but through it all he had clung to his stick with its fluttering bit of paper, and now toward the North he bore it away like a banner, but scarcely triumphantly.

Some of the males pursued him for a short distance; but when terror impelled little Nkima only a bird on the wing might hope to overtake him; and so his pursuers soon gave up the chase.

For some time thereafter, Nkima did not reduce his speed; he continued to flee, screaming at the top of his voice.

It was only after he had almost reached the point of exhaustion that he slowed down and looked back, listening. In his mind's eye was the picture of the snarling visage of the old male; but he was nowhere to be seen, nor was there any sound of pursuit; so little Nkima took heart and his courage commenced to return. He even swaggered a little as though he were returning triumphant from a well-earned victory. Had he had a wife, he would have gone home to her and bragged of his exploits; there are men like that; so who may censure little Nkima who was only a monkey.

Presently he found the trail of Tarzan and the Waziri. He knew that they had been travelling North, and so he came down and sniffed the earth in the game trail that they had been following. Clear in his nostrils was the scent spoor of his friends. This heartened him, and he hurried on again.

Little Nkima moved through the trees many times faster than a man on foot. His fear of the coming jungle night held him to his purpose, so that he did not stop along the way to chase butterflies and birds.

That night he perched high among the smaller branches where Sheeta, the panther, cannot go.

19

Hate and Lust

The discovery that Annette was missing from the camp momentarily stunned the remaining members of the ill-fated expedition.

'What could possibly have become of her?' demanded Jane. 'I know that she wouldn't just have wandered off into the jungle. She was too much afraid of it.'

Brown advanced slowly upon Sborov. There was murder in his heart and it was reflected in his eyes. 'You know where she is, you rat,' he said. 'Tell me what you've done with her.'

Sborov fell back, instinctively raising his hands in defense. 'I know nothing about her,' he said; 'I was asleep.'

'You lie,' said Brown, still advancing.

'Keep away from me,' cried Sborov; 'don't let him get me, Jane; he'll kill me.'

'You're right I'm going to kill you,' growled Brown. It was then that Sborov turned and ran.

Brown sprang forward. In a dozen steps he had overtaken the terrified man and seized him by the shoulder. Screaming, Sborov wheeled to fight with all the mad ferocity of the cornered rat fighting for its life. He pounded and scratched and bit, but the American bore him to the ground and closed his fingers upon his throat.

'Where is she?' demanded the American. 'Where is she, you—'

'I don't know,' gasped Sborov. 'As God is my judge, I don't know.'

'If you don't know, you might as well be killed anyway, for you ain't no good for anything then nohow.'

Brown's fingers tightened upon the throat of the terrified Sborov, who still struggled and fought furiously to free himself.

All that it takes so long to tell happened in the span of a few brief seconds.

Nor during this time was Jane idle. The instant that she realized the gravity of the situation and that Brown was really intent upon destroying Sborov, she seized her spear and ran toward them.

'Stop it, Brown,' she commanded. 'Let the prince up.'

'Not 'til I've given him what's coming to him,' cried the pilot; 'and he's going to get it, even if I hang for it.'

Jane placed the point of her spear beneath Brown's left shoulder-blade and pushed until he felt the sharp point against his flesh.

'Drop him, Brown,' demanded Jane; 'or I'll run this spear straight through your heart.'

'What do you want to kill me for, Miss?' demanded Brown. 'You need me.'

'I don't want to kill you, Brown,' she said; 'but that fact won't do you any good unless you obey my command and remember that I am leader of this expedition. You are doing a foolish thing, Brown; you haven't any evidence to uphold your judgment. Remember, we haven't made the slightest investigation. We should do that first to determine the direction in which Annette left camp, and whether she left alone or was accompanied by another. We can also tell by examining the spoor if she went willingly or was taken by force.'

Slowly Brown's fingers relaxed upon the throat of the struggling, gasping prince; then he released him and rose slowly to his feet.

'I guess you're right, Miss,' he said; 'you're always right; but poor little Annette – what she told me yesterday about that rat made me see red.'

'What did she tell you?' asked Jane.

'He waylaid her yesterday and tried to take that piece of coat sleeve away from her, and then he threatened to kill her if she told. It wasn't no snake that made her scream yesterday, Miss, leastways not an honest-to-God respectable make; it was him. She was terribly afraid of him, Miss.'

Alexis was gasping his breath back slowly. He was trembling from head to foot from terror.

'Is this true, Alexis?' demanded Jane.

'No,' he gasped. 'I just asked her for the coat sleeve so that I could see if it was really mine, and she commenced to scream just to get me in trouble. She did it just for spite.'

'Well,' said Jane, 'we're not accomplishing anything this way. The rest of you stay where you are while I look for some kind of tracks. If we all wander around looking for them, we'll obliterate any that there may be.'

She started to circle the camp slowly, examining the ground carefully. 'Here they are,' she said presently; 'she walked out this way, and she went alone.'

Jane walked slowly for a few yards, following the footprints of the missing girl; then she stopped. 'They end here,' she said, 'right under this tree. There is no indication of a struggle, no sign that she was forced. As a matter of fact, she walked very slowly. There are no other footprints near hers. It is all very strange.'

Jane stood for a moment, looking first at the footprints that ended so mysteriously and then up into the branches of the tree above. Suddenly she sprang upward, seized a branch and drew herself up into the tree.

Brown came running forward and stood beneath her. 'Have you found anything, Miss?' he asked.

'There's only one explanation,' she replied. 'People do not vanish into thin air. Annette walked from the camp to the spot where her footprints ended beneath this tree; she did not return to the camp. There is only one place that she could have gone, and that is up here where I am.'

'But she couldn't have jumped up there the way you did,' protested Brown. 'She just couldn't have done it.'

'She didn't jump,' said Jane. 'Her tracks would have shown it, if she had jumped. She was lifted up.'

'Lifted up! My God, Miss, by what?' Brown's voice was trembling with emotion.

'It might have been a snake. Miss, if you'll pardon me for suggesting it,' said Tibbs; 'it could have reached down and wound itself around her and pulled her up into the tree.'

'She would have screamed,' said Brown; 'we'd have heard her.'

'Snakes charm their victims so that they are helpless,' said Tibbs.

'That is all poppycock, Tibbs,' said Jane, impatiently. 'I don't believe snakes do anything of the sort, and it wasn't a snake that got her anyway. There has been a man up here. He has been in this tree for a long time, or if not a man some sort of a man-like creature.'

'How can you tell that?' demanded Brown.

'I can see where he squatted on this big branch,' she replied. 'The bark is scuffed a little, for he must have remained in the same position for a long time; and then in a line between where his eyes would have been and the camp, some small twigs have been cut away with a knife, giving a less obstructed view of the camp. Whatever it was, sat here for a long time watching us.'

Sborov and Tibbs had approached and were standing nearby. 'I told you I had nothing to do with it,' said the former.

'I can't figure it out,' said Brown; 'I just can't figure it out. If she had been frightened, she would have screamed for help and some of us would have heard her.'

'I don't know,' said Tibbs, 'but I saw something like it once before, Sir. His Grace had a castle on the east coast up in Lincoln. It was a most lonely place, overlooking the North Sea. We only went there once a year for about six weeks; but that was enough, and what happened there the last time was why I gave notice. I couldn't stand the place any longer. Her Grace, the Duchess, was murdered there one night, and that was 'arrowing enough; but what 'appened three days later was, to my way of thinking, even worse.

'Her Grace had a maid she was very fond of, and three nights after the duchess was murdered, the maid disappeared. She just vanished into thin air, as it were, Sir. There was never a trace found of her from then until now, and the country folk round said that Her Grace had come back for her – that it had 'appened before in the Castle of the Duke of Doningham – so I was thinking—'

'For Pete's sake, shut up!' cried Brown. 'You'll have us all nuts.'

'Horrible,' muttered Alexis.

'Well, whatever it was, it wasn't a ghost,' said Jane. She dropped to the ground beside Brown and laid a hand on his arm. 'I'm sorry, Brown,' she said; 'I know you were very fond of her, but I don't believe that there is anything we can do, except to try to reach some outpost of civilization and report the matter. Then a search will be made.'

'It will be too late then,' said Brown. 'I reckon it's too late now. She was so little and delicate. She couldn't have stood very much. She probably is dead by this time.' He stopped speaking and turned away. 'Perhaps she's better off dead,' he added.

In silence the four ate of what little they had to eat, and then set out once more on their seemingly hopeless journey.

There were few attempts at conversation. The four seemed stunned by the series of calamities that had overtaken them. Suspicion, fear, and distrust dogged their footsteps; and beside them stalked the shadow of the nameless menace that had snatched Annette away.

Brown suffered more than the others, so much so that his mind was numb even to his hatred of Alexis. So completely did he ignore him that it was as though the man did not exist.

Jane walked at the rear of the column. Her tread was firm and light; but Alexis, who was directly in front of her, was footsore and weary. He was, however, no worse off than Tibbs for whose soft muscles continued exercise was little better than torture.

'Jane,' said Sborov, after they had walked a long way in silence, 'haven't you any idea what it was took Annette away?'

Jane shook her head. 'All I know is that I don't believe in ghosts, and that no animal could have done it; therefore it must have been a man, but what sort of man, I have no idea. Whatever it was must have been as agile as a monkey, and for that reason I cannot bring myself to believe that it was a member of any native tribe – they are, as a rule, far from being excellent climbers; and I never heard of one who travelled through the trees as this – creature must have to reach our camp and depart again with Annette without leaving any spoor on the ground.'

'But you are willing to believe now, that it was not I?' queried Sborov.

'There is no reason to believe that you did it,' replied Jane.

'Then why not give me the benefit of the doubt in the other matter. You must know that I couldn't have killed Kitty.'

'What does it matter what I think?' asked Jane. 'That is a matter for the court to decide.'

'Your opinion matters a lot to me, Jane. You have no idea how much.'

She looked at him shortly. 'I have no desire to know.'

The note of finality in her tone was lost on Sborov. 'But I want you to know,' he persisted. 'I've never known anyone like you; I'm mad about you, Jane. You must have seen it.'

The girl shook her head impatiently. 'That will be about enough of that, Alexis,' she said. 'Our situation is sufficiently difficult without your making it any worse.'

'Does it make it any worse for you to know that someone is with you who loves you very much?' he demanded. 'Oh, Jane,' he cried, 'I could make you very happy.' Then he seized her arm and tried to draw her to him.

Once again she wrenched herself free; once again she struck him heavily in the face with her open palm. Instantly his expression changed. His face became contorted with rage.

'I'll get you for this, you little—'

'You'll do what?' demanded a man's voice angrily.

The two looked up. Brown was striding toward them, followed by Tibbs. The hand-axe swung at the pilot's side in his right hand. Sborov cowered and backed away.

'I'm going to finish you now, once and for all,' said Brown.

Jane stepped between the two men. 'No, Brown,' she said, 'we can't take the law into our own hands, as much as we'd like to.'

'But you're not safe as long as he's alive; none of us is.'

'I can take care of myself,' replied Jane; 'and if I can, I guess the rest of you can.'

Brown hesitated, but finally he acquiesed. 'Very well,' he said, 'I can wait.' There seemed a world of meaning in those few words, nor was it lost on Sborov.

That night they camped again near the little river whose winding the trail followed.

The instant that they stopped, Sborov and Tibbs threw themselves upon the ground thoroughly exhausted.

'If I may say so, Milady,' said the latter, 'I fancy I couldn't carry on for another half hour if my life depended upon it. Tomorrow you had better go on without me; I'm afraid I can't keep up, ma'am; and I'm only delaying the rest of you.'

'You're doing splendidly, Tibbs,' said Jane, encouragingly. 'I know it's hard on you now; but you'll be surprised how quickly your muscles will toughen as they get accustomed to the work, and then you'll be able to keep up with any of us.'

'I 'ope so, Milady, but the way I feel now I don't believe I'll be able to go on.'

'Don't worry, Tibbsy, we'll stick by you,' said Brown, reassuringly.

'It's mighty good of you, Mr Brown, but—'

'But nothing,' said Brown. 'We could get along with one less member in this outfit,' and as he spoke, he stared straight at Sborov, 'but it ain't you, Tibbsy.'

'Now,' said Jane, 'I'm going out to look for meat. I want you men to promise me that you will not quarrel while I'm gone. We have already had too much bloodshed and disaster.'

'Tibbsy don't never fight with no one,' said Brown, 'and I won't be here; so you won't have to worry.'

'You won't be here?' demanded Jane. 'Where are you going?'

'I'm going with you, Miss.'

'But you can't. I can't hunt with you along.'

'Then you won't do no hunting,' said Brown, 'because I'm going with you. You may be boss, but there's one thing you ain't going to do no more.'

'What is that?' asked the girl.

'You ain't going off alone by yourself, again, after what happened to Annette.'

'If I may say so, Milady, I think Mr Brown is quite right. We can't take any chances with you, Milady.'

Jane shrugged. 'Perhaps you're right,' she said, 'from your point of view, but really I'm much better able to take care of myself in the jungle than any of you.'

'That ain't neither here nor there,' said Brown. 'You just ain't going into the jungle alone, and that's that.'

'All right,' said Jane, with a laugh. 'I suppose I'll have to give in. Come ahead then, Brown; we'll see what we can find.'

Tibbs and Alexis watched them depart, and then the former turned to the prince. 'Beg pardon, Sir,' he said, 'but hadn't we better start building a boma and gathering firewood?'

'Yes, you had,' said Alexis; 'and you'd better hurry up about it as it will soon be dark.'

'You're not going to help me, Sir?' demanded Tibbs.

'Certainly not, my man. I'm far too tired.'

'And 'ow about me, Sir? I'm tired, too.' Tibbs was surprised at his own temerity.

'You've no business to be tired. I'm not paying you to be tired. I'm paying you to work. Come, get busy; and don't be impudent. You seem to be forgetting yourself, Tibbs.'

'If I may make so bold as to say so, your 'ighness, if you're not careful, I shall.'

'What do you mean, you impertinent puppy?' demanded Alexis.

Tibbs sat down on the ground and leaned his back against the tree. 'I mean, Sir, that if you don't help and do your share there won't be any boma and there won't be any firewood when Lady Greystoke and Brown come back to the camp. I daresay they'll both be very angry, especially Brown. If I were you, Sir, I wouldn't antagonize him any more. I suspect that he does not like you; and out here in the jungle Sir, where there ain't no laws nor no Bobbies, he wouldn't need much more of an excuse to kill you.'

For a minute or two Alexis sat in silent thought; then he rose painfully and slowly. 'Come on, my man,' he said, 'and I'll give you a hand with the boma.'

It was almost sunset when Jane and Brown returned with a small antelope, slices of which Tibbs was soon grilling before a cooking fire, while the others sat silently waiting.

There was little conversation as they ate their slender meal. It was an ill-assorted company, with little in common among them other than the grim disasters which had befallen them and which made such depressing conversation that they were taboo as though by a tacit understanding. The girl and Brown each found the other the most congenial member of the party; and what little talk there was passed between these two; but very soon even they were silent; and presently all slept, except Tibbs who had the first watch.

The long night wore on to the accompaniment of savage, jungle sound, usually remote but sometimes so close as to arouse the sleepers – stealthy sounds, weird sounds, fierce and savage sounds, sometimes whispering, sometimes thundering, died softly, dying into nothingness, or reverberated through the jungle until the earth trembled.

Each in his turn, the men stood guard. At four in the morning, Tibbs, completing his second tour, awoke Alexis who was to follow him.

Shivering in the chill of early morning, Sborov piled more wood upon the fire. Then he stood with his back toward it gazing out into the night.

Just beyond the farthest reaches of the firelight rose a black, impenetrable wall of darkness – a mysterious world filled with nameless terrors; when a tongue of flame leaped higher in the air than its fellows its light glanced momentarily from the bole of a tree or from a cluster of leaves giving the impression of movement out there beyond the rim of his little world.

There were noises, too, sounds that he could not interpret. His fear and his imagination put strange interpretation upon the things that he saw and heard. A moaning woman floated at the border line of reality. He could swear that he saw her.

Sborov recalled the ghost of the murdered woman that came back for her maid, and cursed Tibbs. A beast screamed and Sborov shuddered.

He turned away from the forest and sought to concentrate his mind upon other things. His eyes wandered over the figures of his sleeping comrades. They fell upon the hand-axe lying close beside Brown. Sborov breathed an imprecation and tore his gaze away. It fell on Jane and rested there. How beautiful she was. Why did she spurn him? He had always had luck with women. He fascinated them, and he knew it. He could not understand why

Jane repulsed him; and so he blamed Brown, whom he hated, assuring himself that the fellow had talked against him and embittered Jane's mind.

His eyes wandered back to Brown and the hand-axe. How he hated the man and feared him. The fellow would kill him. He had threatened him more than once.

Alexis felt that if the man were dead, his own life would be safer and – there would be no one to stand between him and Jane.

He rose and walked nervously to and fro. Every once in a while he shot a glance at Brown and the axe.

He walked closer to Tibbs and listened. Yes, the fellow was already asleep, sound asleep. He must have been asleep almost at the instant he touched the ground. Jane was asleep, too, and so was Brown. Sborov assured himself of both of these facts.

If Brown were only dead! The thought repeated itself monotonously, drumming on his tired brain. If Brown were only dead! Presently Alexis Sborov seemed galvanized by a sudden determination. He moved directly, though stealthily, toward the sleeping Brown. He paused beside him and kneeled upon one knee. Listening intently, he remained there silent, motionless; then cautiously one hand crept out toward the axe.

Brown moved and turned in his sleep, and Sborov froze with terror; then the pilot resumed the regular breathing of sleep. Sborov reached out and seized the axe handle. His mad eyes glued upon the forehead of the sleeping man, he raised the weapon aloft to strike.

20

Nkima Plays a Game

Tarzan and the Waziri moved on in search of the village of the Kavuru. It was yet early in the morning; the dawn mists still defied the efforts of a low-swinging sun to dispel them. The spirits of the searchers were low, for they were many long marches from their homeland; and with each passing day a sense of the futility of their quest had been increasingly impressed upon them, for not once since they started had they seen any sign or clue to suggest that they were on the right track; only vague rumors based upon tribal legend had suggested the fate of Buira, the daughter of Muviro.

Several of the warriors felt that they were chasing a myth; and only great courage and loyalty kept them, uncomplaining, on the trail.

It was true that Tarzan had met Ydeni, the Kavuru, and that he had rescued Naika, the daughter of Gupingu, and heard her story; yet these things had occurred at such a remote distance from the land of the Waziri that even Muviro was commencing to doubt that it had been a Kavuru who had been responsible for the disappearance of Buira, for why should these strange men go so far afield when they could find young girls much closer to their mysterious village.

But upon this chill and misty morning, it was not the Waziri alone who were depressed and discouraged. Upon the trail behind them, a damp and bedraggled little monkey swung through the trees. In one hand he carried a stick in the end of which fluttered a bit of paper; that he still clung to it was a miracle, for Nkima was not particularly tenacious of purpose. Perhaps it had become a fixed idea, for the stick was often an encumbrance to him; yet it never occurred to him to discard it.

There was however another thought that was forming in his mind – it was the thought that he was very far from his own country, that he had lost Tarzan and could never find him again, and that he was very much afraid. It made him wish to turn around and start for home. He was almost upon the verge of turning about, when he recollected the grimacing visage of the disagreeable old male whom Nkima was certain thirsted for his life-blood somewhere upon the back trail; and then there were Sheeta, and Histah, the snake, and the bad Gomangani. All these lay behind him; and until he encountered some of their like upon the trail he was following, his little mind so functioned that he could not anticipate their presence there – what little Nkima did not know did not bother him. And so he continued on his way into a land that seemed free from inhospitable monkeys and bloodthirsty beasts and men.

As the ascending sun warmed him, his spirits rose; and after he had discovered and robbed a bird's nest, sucking the eggs, he felt equal to any adventure.

Then came the crowning moment of happiness. In the trail ahead of him, he saw a file of ten ebon warriors led by the giant white man who was his god. With a loud scream of joy that attracted the attention of the men below him, Nkima fairly flew through the trees to drop upon one of Tarzan's broad shoulders.

'Where has Nkima been?' asked the ape-man. 'Tarzan thought that at last Sheeta had caught him.'

'Little Nkima has been fighting with all the Manus in the forest,' replied the monkey. 'They tried to stop little Nkima from coming through their trees, but he scratched them and bit them and hit them with a stick; then he chased them into the country where Kudu, the sun, lies down at night. That is where little Nkima has been; that is what he has been doing; that is why he has been away from Tarzan.'

The ape-man smiled. 'Little Nkima is very brave,' he said, as he stroked the little head nestled in the hollow of his neck.

Tarzan noticed that Nkima still carried the message stick, and was surprised that his little friend should have been constant to one idea for so long a time; and then he noticed that the paper in the end of the stick was not the same as that which Nkima had taken away with him. The ape-man's curiosity was aroused.

'What is that in the end of your stick, Nkima?' he asked. 'Where did you get it? It is not the thing that Tarzan gave you. Let me see it.' And he reached for it.

Now Nkima had forgotten just why he had clung to the stick. He had forgotten that he had been mimicking the Waziri warrior who had carried the message to Tarzan. Also, he was very happy and wanted to play; so when Tarzan tried to take the paper from the end of the stick, Nkima saw therein a challenge and an invitation to a new game; and so he leaped nimbly from Tarzan's shoulder and scampered away, waving the stick with its bit of fluttering paper above him.

The ape-man called to him to come back, but Nkima's thoughts were wholly centered upon play; and he only climbed the higher, grimacing and chattering in great good humor, as he challenged the ape-man to catch him.

Perhaps if Tarzan had guessed the message that fluttered from the end of the cleft stick and all that it meant to him and one dear to him he would not have laughed so lightly and let Nkima go his way unrebuked, but he did not know. Upon such trivial things may hinge the lives and happiness of men.

Seeing that Tarzan did not pursue him, nor even pay any further attention to him, Nkima soon lost interest in the game and started to descend again to his Master. But once more Fate intervened, this time in the form of a fledgling bird trying its wings for the first time in short, uncertain flights.

Little Nkima espied it, and forthwith forgot all else in the excitement of the chase. When the bird rested upon a twig he crept toward it; but when he would have seized it it flew away just eluding his grasp. Again and again was this repeated, and as long as the bird remained in sight the excitement of the chase held Nkima enthralled.

Farther and farther North he followed the fledgling, bearing with him the message that would have meant so much to Tarzan of the Apes; but at length, in a flight much longer sustained than any it had previously attained, the bird disappeared; and that was the last that Nkima saw of it.

For no good reason he had pursued it, for thus his little monkey mind functioned. He had wasted his time, he had missed an opportunity to accomplish something worth while; and he had nothing to show for his pains. But then we have seen men do likewise. We have all chased chimeras.

For some time Nkima continued on toward the North, impelled by the rapidly fading vestiges of the urge that had been driving him; but presently he noticed the paper in the end of the stick that he had been carrying mechanically because he had been carrying it for so long. This recalled Tarzan to his mind and the fact that he was again alone in a strange land. He decided to return to the ape-man and the Waziri, but even as the determination was forming he heard something to the North of him that aroused his curiosity, demanding investigation. It was the voice of a human being.

Now, by nature Nkima is curious; and in addition Tarzan has trained him to investigate unusual occurrences; so it was not at all strange that he swung on through the trees in the direction of the voice that had attracted his attention, for the moment wholly absorbed in this new interest.

From a lofty height he at last looked down upon the objects of his interest, two Tarmangani, a he and a she. And when Nkima saw the he-Tarmangani he was glad that he was perching safely out of reach, for here was indeed a terrifying Tarmangani. Nkima had never before seen a white man like this one. He had seen the Gomangani, the black men, thus arrayed, but never a white man.

The fellow was large and powerful, with a fierce, evil face, the ferocity of which was surely not lessened by the straight piece of bone or ivory six or eight inches long that pierced the septum of his nose, nor by the feathers in his head dress, nor the paint on his face, the rings in his ears, and the necklace of human teeth lying against his massive chest.

Nkima noted all these things and more – the loincloth of gorilla skin, the armlets, wristlets, and anklets, the fibre rope wound many times about the waist, the dagger, and the spear.

This was indeed a Tarmangani to avoid. He filled little Nkima with fear, but not so his companion. She was of a far different mold – small, dainty, and with no indications of barbaric ornamentation. Had Nkima been accustomed to making intelligent deductions from his perceptions he would have guessed immediately that the she was not of the same tribe, perhaps not of the same race as the man; but he could not have guessed that she was a French girl named Annette. No more could he know that the man was her captor, nor that he was a Kavuru. The mind of Nkima had its limitations.

However, his curiosity was once more aroused. For this reason and another, he followed them. The other reason presupposes imagination, a characteristic that little Nkima possessed, as must all creatures that know how to play; for play is often make-believe, and make-believe requires imagination of no mean order.

So now little Nkima pretended that he was stalking the two Tarmangani; he pretended that they were afraid of him and that presently he would leap upon them and destroy them. It was great fun for Nkima of whom almost nothing in the whole jungle was afraid, little Nkima who could destroy so few creatures in his teeming world, from whom nothing more important than a fledgling bird might seek to escape. It gave him a fleeting sense of superiority. There are men like that. Often one sees them strutting, clothed in a shred of tenuous, evanescent authority, play-acting at importance.

Pursuing this exciting game, he lost all sense of time, of which, at best, he had little or no conception. Presently night would come; and then he would know that time had passed, but while it was passing he gave it no thought.

The afternoon waned. The quarry passed out of the forest into an open plain at the foot of a tall mountain. The distance from the forest to the mountain was not great. Nkima could see across the plain, cut with little ravines, cluttered with huge boulders, to a village that lay at the foot of a perpendicular cliff.

A little river wound down toward the forest from the village, as though it rose in the village itself and flowed out beneath the gates of the lofty palisade. These things Nkima saw. He also saw the two he had been stalking cross the plain toward the village, but he did not follow them. After all a game is a game; there is no use carrying one too far.

He saw the gates open to admit the couple. He saw them close behind them. Then, for the first time, he realized that night was falling; and suddenly he became very lonely and afraid.

He thought of Tarzan and the safety of that bronzed shoulder; then he turned and scampered through the trees back into the South, clutching the forked stick tightly in his little fist, whimpering as he went.

21

Only Two Left

Tibbs awoke suddenly out of a sound sleep, and as he opened his eyes he saw Sborov with upraised hatchet kneeling above Brown. With a cry of warning, he leaped to his feet. Sborov hesitated an instant and looked quickly toward Tibbs. It was that momentary hesitation that saved Brown's life.

Tibbs' cry awakened him, and almost instinctively he recoiled and rolled to one side; perhaps it was a natural reaction to the note of warning and the terror in the voice of the Englishman.

Sborov struck, but the sharp blade missed Brown by a fraction of an inch and was buried in the earth where his head had lain but a brief instant before.

At Tibbs' cry Jane leaped to her feet, fully awake on the instant. Sborov, on one knee, reached his feet before Brown, and clinging to the hatchet fled into the jungle.

Brown started in pursuit, but Jane called him back. 'Don't follow him,' she said. 'What's the use? We are well rid of him; he won't dare come back now. If you followed him, he might lie in wait for you and kill you. We can't spare any more; we are all too few now.'

Brown turned back. 'I hate to let him get away with anything like that. But I suppose you're right. He could hide and get me in that mess of trees and undergrowth before I knew what it was all about.' He shook his head ruefully. 'But I still hate to let him go; he ought to get what's coming to him.'

'He will – out there alone,' prophesied Jane.

'Hi 'opes 'e does before hever Hi lays eyes on 'im again, the bounder, if you'll pardon me, Milady.'

'I think you're quite right, Tibbs; we all feel the same about the man. But now we are only three – though he never was much good to us.'

'"Much good"!' exploded Brown. 'Migawd, Miss, he wasn't *no* good. He never done a thing except make trouble. If I don't never see the sight of him again that will be twenty years too soon.'

'Prince!' There was a world of contempt and irony in the American's tones. 'If they was all like him I don't wonder they been kickin' 'em out.'

Jane smiled. 'There have been some pretty good ones, Brown; and there still are. Princes like Sborov are not really princes at all – it is often just a courtesy title, as meaningless as a colonelcy in Kentucky. They don't rate very high in their own countries.'

Brown grinned. 'They sure are the fair haired boys in America, though. It was that title the poor old lady fell for, and look what it cost her. American women are fools, the way they go for titles.'

Jane smiled good naturedly. 'I'm an American, you know, Brown.'

The pilot flushed. 'Heck, no, Miss, I didn't know it. I'm sorry.'

'You needn't be, because you're right about some American women – the climbers. It's not as bad as it used to be; but Americans still buy titles, and they don't often get very much for their money beside the titles. Oftentimes even the titles are as spurious as their owners.

'I recall reading a book written a number of years ago by a French count who had married a daughter of one of America's richest railroad families. He made fun of his wife's people, their poor taste, their love of money. Yet nothing that they were accused of could have been in such rotten taste as this book, nor was their love of money any greater than his by his own admission; for he bragged of having sold his title for their money. In the same breath he spoke of the honor of his house and his ancient lineage. He and his kind are sickening.

'I grow more and more to agree with my husband's appraisal of beasts and men – he prefers the beasts.'

Brown shook his head dubiously. 'I ain't got much use for men, myself,' he admitted; 'leastwise some men, but if your husband was in our fix I reckon he'd be doggone glad to get out of this jungle back where there were plenty of men and no beasts.'

'You don't know my husband.'

'Well, perhaps he'd rather be here than in good old Chi; but I wouldn't.'

'Then we'd better start getting out,' suggested Jane. 'There's nothing to keep us here any longer.'

'Quite right, Milady, if you'll pardon my saying so,' agreed Tibbs.

'I'm for hopping off right away,' said Brown. 'Perhaps – well, perhaps—'

'Perhaps what?' asked Jane.

'I was just thinking of Annette. I know there ain't no chance of running across her, but I can't help hoping.'

'We're all hoping, Brown. That's about all we can do, I'm afraid.' Jane laid a sympathetic hand on the man's arm.

As the three set out once more upon the trail toward the east, a pair of eyes watched them from the foliage of a nearby tree, sinister, unblinking eyes that appraised the two men casually but were most often centered upon Jane.

Brown took the lead, setting a pace that would not be too hard on Tibbs; he had learned that whatever pace he set, the girl was equal to it; perhaps even more. He often wondered at her strength, endurance, and nerve. She was not at all the sort of person that he had imagined a titled English woman would be. He had always thought of women of her class as pampered, help-less creatures. It seemed strange to him now that he should look up to one as a trusted, dependable leader; that is, it seemed strange when he gave the mat-ter any thought; otherwise, it appeared perfectly natural. He had never followed a man in whom he had greater confidence, or for whom he had more respect, than this slender, beautiful lady of quality.

Behind Brown came Tibbs. The night's rest had refreshed him. His mus-cles were already becoming inured to the hardships of the trail. He swung along this morning like a veteran.

'Hit's a grand day, Milady,' he remarked, 'if you don't mind my saying so. I feels as 'ow things was goin' to be a little bit of all right, you know, from now on.'

'I hope so, Tibbs. Perhaps the worst is over. If we only knew just where we were, it would make things so much easier. We may be headed straight for some friendly village where we can get guides, or we may be headed into a wilderness. That is what troubles me most. If we only *knew*.'

'The Duke of Doningham used to say that what we don't know won't never harm us, Milady.'

'It won't do us any good, either,' laughed Jane.

'But maybe 'e wasn't ever lost in Africa,' suggested Tibbs. 'Hi never 'ad no idea Africa was such a large place.'

'It covers quite a lot of territory, Tibbs. It's no place to be lost.'

'Hi'd 'ate to be lost in it all alone, Milady – like 'is 'ighness. My word, Milady, but 'e must be frightened back there all alone – nothin' only his thoughts to keep 'im company.'

'And such terrible thoughts, Tibbs. I shudder to think what they must be; but I'm not worrying about him – it's poor little Annette.'

Tibbs was silent. He too was thinking of Annette.

Gliding silently through the trees behind them followed a tireless stalker. Seldom now were those cruel eyes allowed to wander from the slender figure of the girl swinging along behind the two men.

As the hours passed, Tibbs commenced to tire again. He lagged a little and dropped farther behind Brown. He no longer sought to converse with Jane. He was too tired to talk. The last couple of times that he had glanced back to see if the girl were coming he had stumbled because his muscles were so weary and his feet seemed so heavy; so he gave it up, and set his mind wholly upon plodding steadily ahead.

He thought that Brown would never stop. What was the man made of, anyway – iron? His legs and feet seemed to be mechanical things that must go on and on, forever. They no longer seemed a part of him. Yet he realized that he had done better today, that he had tired less quickly than on previous days. That was something; but – sitting down would be Heaven. Would Brown never stop?

But at last Brown did stop. 'This looks like as good a place as any to stop for the night,' he said. 'Tired, Tibbsy?'

The Englishman staggered up and threw himself to the ground. 'Tired!' he echoed. 'Mr Brown, there ain't no word in the whole bloomin' Hoxford Hinglish Dictionary that's as tired as Hi am.'

Brown laughed. 'Well, I don't feel so chipper myself,' he admitted. 'I'll bet the lady's the freshest one of all. Say, where is she?'

Tibbs looked back along the trail. 'She was right behind me the last time I looked. Doubtless she'll be along in a second.'

'She shouldn't get so far behind,' grumbled Brown. It was evident that he was becoming apprehensive. Then he called aloud. 'Hi, there! Lady Greystoke!'

There was no answering call. The two men stared expectantly along the trail. Tibbs rose wearily to his feet. Brown called again. There was only silence. Brown looked at Tibbs. There was an expression on the American's face that Tibbs had never seen there before. It was fear; but it was not fear for himself.

At a run Brown started along the back trail. Tibbs staggered after him.

Occasionally Brown would stop and call the missing girl's name aloud, but there was never any answer. They kept on until darkness overtook them.

Tibbs was exhausted; he could go no farther. Brown, too, was almost at the limit of his powers. They threw themselves to the ground.

'It ain't no use,' said Brown wearily. 'She's gone – just like Annette – and I think in the same way. Why didn't she let me kill him? Why didn't I kill him anyway? I knew I should of.'

'You think it was the prince?'

'Sure it was, the dirty— Oh, what's the use? It's all my fault for lettin' a woman tell me what to do. She's a grand woman, but women are all alike when it comes to a job like that; they're too soft hearted. I ought to of killed him when I first wanted to. We'd of had Lady Greystoke and Annette both with us now if I had.'

'Hit ain't your fault, Mr Brown,' said Tibbs soothingly. 'You only done what any man would 'ave done. We hall of us promised to hobey Lady Greystoke, hand she told you not to kill 'im. Though, if you'll pardon my saying so, Hi think the blighter ought to have been killed long ago.'

The rumble of a lion's roar echoed through the darkening forest awakening the men to the dangers of the coming night. Brown groaned.

'If I only knew where they were! If I just knew they was alive. If he hasn't killed 'em; just think of 'em back there somewheres in the dark with only that – that pansy to look after 'em.' The gloom of Brown's mood was reflected in his voice.

'You don't really think 'e'd kill Lady Greystoke, do you?' demanded Tibbs, horrified. It was quite one thing to kill a lady's maid, but another, an unthinkable thing, to kill a titled lady. Tibbs' viewpoint on such matters was largely a matter of heredity (his people had been serving people as far back as any of them knew) and training and habit of thought. His snobbishness was the snobbishness of the serving class, ingrained and ineradicable.

'No, I don't think he'd kill her, unless she resisted him; and there ain't no question about that. But he did have good reason to want to kill poor little Annette. If it was him that got her, she's dead all right. God, if I could only lay my hands on him! What say we back-track tomorrow and keep on huntin' 'til we find him. We may never find them, but it would be some satisfaction to find him. What do you say, Tibbsy? I'll let you help me kill him.'

'Hi've never been one that believed in bloodshed, Mr Brown; but Hi do say, hand Hi'm not ashamed of hit, that hif 'e killed Lady Greystoke and Annette Hi'd like nothing better than to do 'im in all by my bloomin' self; but, Mr Brown, Hi don't think we ought to turn back. Hi think we should carry on just like Milady told us to, hand get 'elp to come back 'ere hand search for them – someone that knows the country.'

'I suppose you're right, Tibbsy. We couldn't find the Empire State building if it was wandering around in this man's jungle, let alone a couple of girls.'

A lion roared again, nearer this time.

'I reckon we'd better climb a tree, Tibbsy, and wait for daylight. It don't look like sleepin' on the ground was goin' to be very healthy.'

'My father always said it was most un'ealthy. 'E got rheumatism something terrible sleeping on the ground in the Crimea.'

'Then let's climb,' said Brown. 'I don't want to get rheumatism.'

22

Stalked by Numa

Nkima spent a night of terror. Sheeta, the leopard, prowled on the ground, climbed through the trees. Nkima clung to the loftiest branch that would support his weight and shivered from cold and terror throughout the long night. But at last day dawned, and with the first lessening of the terrifying darkness he swung off through the trees in search of Tarzan and the Waziri. And still he clung to the little cleft stick with the bit of paper fluttering from its tip.

He had not gone far when he heard the voices of men. His little heart beat wildly as he sped in the direction of the sound. So anxious was he to find Tarzan that he had no place in his mind for any doubt that the voices he heard might be those of others than his friends.

Nor were they.

Chattering and screaming, Nkima dropped plummetlike from high branches to alight upon the shoulder of his friend. One arm encircled Tarzan's neck, and from the little clenched paw the cleft stick brought the fluttering bit of paper directly in front of the ape-man's eyes. He saw writing upon it, handwriting that even in a brief glance he recognized. Yet he could not believe. It was incredible, preposterous to even imagine that little Nkima bore a message penned by Jane. The remarkable similarity between this handwriting and hers could be nothing more than a fantastic coincidence.

Before Nkima could again escape him Tarzan slipped the message from the stick; and, while the monkey chattered and scolded, scanned it hurriedly. The Waziri, watching him, saw sudden concern mirrored in his expression.

'Where did you get this, Nkima?' demanded the ape-man. 'Who gave it to you?'

Nkima stopped scolding and scratched his head. Where did he get it? He could not recall. Many things had happened since then. His memory was a long, dim corridor; and this event a tiny thing at the far end.

'Something is wrong, Bwana?' asked Muviro. 'Nkima has brought you bad news?'

'It is a message from Lady Greystoke. She and a party of friends were forced down in an aeroplane. They are lost somewhere without provisions or weapons.'

He turned his attention again to Nkima. 'Who gave you this?' he demanded. 'Was it a she? – a Tarmangani?'

Slowly Nkima was recollecting. 'It was not a Tarmangani,' he said.

'A Gomangani?'

'It was not a Gomangani.'

'Who did give it to you, then?'

Now Nkima recalled. 'No one gave it to Nkima. Nkima found it in a wala.'

'What does he say, Bwana?' asked Muviro; for Nkima had spoken in the language of his people, which only Tarzan, among men, understands.

'He says he found it in a "nest",' explained the Lord of the Jungle. 'That might mean a house, or a hut, or a shelter, the lair of a wild beast, or the nest of a bird. I will find out.'

'Nkima, what built the nest in which you found this?'

'Tarmangani. The Gomangani do not build a wala like it.'

'Where is it? Try to recall. You must take me to it. Where was it?'

Nkima waved a paw loosely in the general direction of the West.

'You will take Tarzan to this nest,' said the ape-man.

Instantly Nkima was all excitement. He felt quite important. He hopped to the ground and pulled on Tarzan's leg.

'Come with Nkima,' he begged.

'Lead your warriors toward the North until you find the village of the Kavuru,' Tarzan directed Muviro. 'If they are unfriendly, and you cannot enter their village to recover Buira, wait for me there. If you find her and take her away, leave some sign that will tell me so. You understand?'

'Yes, Bwana.'

'Then Nkima and I go to search for Lady Greystoke.'

It was not by a direct route that Nkima led Tarzan toward the shelter in which he had found the message, but a circuitous one that retraced his wanderings. Each of his mischances and adventures of the preceding days was a landmark on the back trail, and thus slowly he found his way back toward the shelter.

At one point he told Tarzan he had seen a strange Tarmangani with a she-Tarmangani; and Tarzan was almost convinced that it might have been Jane, the captive of a Kavuru. He was tempted to give up the search for the shelter where the message had been found and attempt to trail the man and the woman; but Nkima could not tell him in which direction they had gone, the spoor had disappeared, and his judgment told him that the place to start his search for Jane was at some point at which he might be positive she had been.

It required infinite patience to endure the vagaries of Nkima's memory and his inability to hold for long to a fixed continuity of thought; but most beasts are patient, and in this respect Tarzan was like his fellows of the jungle. His reward came eventually when Nkima proudly led him down through the trees to the camp that the marooned fliers had made – the camp where Nkima had found the note.

Here Tarzan found indisputable evidence that Jane had indeed been a member of the ill-starred company, and plain before him lay the trail that they had taken toward the east. No longer was he dependent upon Nkima, and with renewed hope he swung off into the unknown country that had swallowed his mate.

Retribution is seldom swift or well directed, yet perhaps in his terror Prince Alexis Sborov was tasting the immediate fruits of his misdeeds through a punishment scarcely less drastic than death itself; for Sborov was an arrant coward, and he was suffering as only a coward might as he trembled alone in the menacing silence of the mysterious jungle.

And he was torn between two terrors, one of which almost cancelled the other. He was afraid of the denizens of the jungle and the thought of facing a jungle night alone, and it was this fear that almost submerged another – his fear of Brown. But not quite. As much as he longed to return to the companionship of those he had persistently sought to offend or injure, the knowledge that Brown would kill him if he did, exiled him to the torture of his terror-stricken loneliness.

When he had finally been forced to definitely abandon any thought of returning to the others, he determined to follow the plan that he had originally suggested to them, the plan that had been voted down in favor of Jane's suggestion that they search toward the east for friendly tribes; and so he set his face toward the west in the hope that he might stumble upon a white settlement in the Belgian Congo.

One ordeal that he dreaded lay ahead of him on this route, for in retracing his steps he must pass the grave of his murdered wife. He had no regrets for his deed; but his superstitious mind was terror ridden by imaginings induced by Tibbs' story of the murdered Duchess of Doningham, who returned from the grave to carry away her maid.

As Tibbs had, so did Sborov see a parallel in the mysterious disappearance of Annette, a disappearance that he could not account for logically in any other way.

But there was no alternative. He must pass close to the grave and the scene of the murder. Once again he would wield the hand-axe in the fullness of his imagination, and once again the warm blood of his victim would splatter upon his hand and his clothing.

The first night he spent among the branches of a tree, too terrified to sleep. He heard the hunting beasts prowl beneath him. He heard the screams of stricken prey. The earth trembled to the roar of the King of beasts; and there were other sounds, stealthy, mysterious sounds that were even more terrifying because he could not identify them.

But at last the night passed and dawn came to look down upon a haggard, unkempt creature that started at its own shadow, a creature exhausted by fright, by sleeplessness, and by hunger, a very different creature from the Prince Sborov of the Paris boulevards.

His hands and arms, his unshaven face, his matted hair were caked with dirt and dried sweat, cut down his shrunken cheeks by muddy rivulets of tears. His mind was tottering. He talked to himself, and then cautioned himself to silence lest his voice might attract the attention of some beast of prey.

Thus he stumbled on through the day, without food and without water – hopeless victim of his own avarice, a sorry contrast to the proud beasts he feared, a sad commentary upon the theory of evolution.

It was mid-afternoon when the thing that he had dreaded occurred. He was walking a broad and, for a short distance, straight trail. As he had been constantly doing, he glanced behind him. His knees trembled. He thought that he must fall. For a moment he was paralyzed.

For where the trail turned to disappear among the underbrush stood a great lion. He was eyeing Sborov appraisingly. What he was doing abroad at that hour of the day when he should have been lying up waiting for evening and the hunting hours is a matter of his own concern, but there he was. He merely stood and contemplated Sborov.

Presently the man regained control of his muscles. He started to move slowly along the trail. He had heard that if one ran, almost any beast of prey would pursue – and overtake; for man is of the slowest of animals.

As Sborov moved away, the lion moved after him. It came slowly, just keeping pace with the man. It was stalking him. When it was ready to do so, it would charge; and that would be the end.

Sborov knew little of the habits of lions; but he had gleaned this much from yarns spun around the camp fires, to which he had listened, even though he had never been encouraged to take part.

He wondered how long it would be before the lion would rush at him and drag him down. He wanted to run. It was with difficulty that he restrained the impulse. He looked longingly at the trees that he was too weak to climb.

A turn in the trail hid the lion from him, and then Sborov broke into a run. An instant later an angry growl sounded behind him. It seemed very close. The man threw a glance back across his shoulder. The lion was advancing at a trot. Its eyes were blazing, terrible yellow-green eyes that shrivelled the last vestige of his self-control.

Sborov voiced a piercing scream of terror.

23

Captive

Tarzan swung through the trees not far from a jungle trail that led toward the east. Nkima scampered sometimes ahead, sometimes above his Master. He was very brave and truculent, for the sanctuary of a bronzed shoulder was always near.

Usha, the wind, was blowing in Tarzan's face. To his nostrils it brought messages from the jungle ahead. It spoke of Histah, the snake, of Wappi, the antelope, and of Sheeta, the leopard. Faintly from a great distance, it told of water it had passed upon its journey. Thus could Tarzan direct his course and select his campsites far ahead when he passed through country that was unfamiliar to him.

There came also upon the breath of Usha the pungent odor of Numa, the lion; and a moment later Tarzan heard the angry growl of the King of beasts. Almost simultaneously he caught the scent spoor of man, of a lone Tarmangani.

Tarzan could almost picture the scene that was being enacted somewhere along that trail ahead of him, and he increased his speed; for a white man in this particular district might well be a member of the party that Jane had accompanied; he might know where she was or what fate had befallen her. It would not do to let Numa destroy him; at least not until Tarzan had questioned him.

No considerations of humanity prompted Tarzan of the Apes to hasten to the aid of this unknown man, nor would it have been selfish callousness to the suffering of another that would have left him more or less indifferent but for the thought of Jane. He was a jungle animal, a fellow to the lion; and he knew that the lion must eat, even as he must. If it did not feed upon this man, it would feed upon some other living creature whose life was as precious to it as the man's was to him; and in the philosophy of the jungle one life is no more valuable than another, unless it be that of one's self or a friend.

Tarzan knew that the two were not far ahead of him. The odor of Numa told him that the lion was not empty and that therefore he was probably stalking the Tarmangani with no immediate likelihood that he would attack unless provoked.

Then the quiet of the jungle was shattered by a scream of terror, and Tarzan guessed that the lion's short temper had been aroused. Instantly the ape-man swung forward at terrific speed, and so swiftly he sped through the middle terrace of the forest that even little Nkima had difficulty in keeping pace.

Sborov thought that the lion was charging, but it was not. It was merely keeping its prey in sight, but the angry growl of annoyance was a warning against attempted escape and a threat of what the quarry might expect if it forced the King to exert himself unnecessarily at this hour of the day when heat lay heavy and humid upon the jungle and royalty should be taking its siesta.

But Sborov would have been deaf to all warnings now even had he understood them. He was crazed with terror. His one, his only impulse was to escape; and so he ran on, his legs staggering from exhaustion and fear, his heart pounding in his throat, choking the screams that trembled there unborn.

Now indeed did Numa wax wroth. This pitiful thing was trying to escape him, and it was making him trot when he wished only to loaf along the trail at his ease until he was again ready to kill and feed. He would put an end to it; and that, quickly. He voiced another warning roar as he prepared to charge – a roar that half paralyzed the man.

Thinking the end had come, Sborov fell to his knees, turning so that he faced the lion; and as he did so a strange thing happened, a thing so remarkable that it surprised the lion quite as much as it did Sborov. A white man dropped from above into the trail between them.

Sborov had never seen a man such as this, a bronzed giant, almost naked; a handsome giant with grim, stern features; a giant who faced a lion with as little apparent concern as one might reveal in shooing away an alley cat. He just stood there facing the lion and waiting; and the lion stopped in its tracks, eyeing the intruder but with evidently growing displeasure.

As Sborov looked at the man he realized that he was really not of gigantic proportions, yet he conveyed the impression of great size. Perhaps it was the suggestion of power and majesty in his mien that gave him the appearance of towering over other creatures. He stood, perhaps, a couple of inches over six feet; rounded muscles flowed smoothly beneath clear, bronzed skin; his proportions were as perfect for his kind as were those of the great lion he faced. It occurred to Sborov that these two were very much alike, and he began to be as afraid of the man as of the other beast.

They stood thus facing each other for but a moment; then the lion growled, lashing its tail, and took a step forward. The man growled, and Sborov shuddered. Now, indeed, was he terrified. Above them a little monkey danced up and down upon the limb of a tree, chattering and scolding. He loosed upon the lion a vocabulary of rich invective, but to Sborov it was only the silly chattering of a monkey.

The bronzed giant moved slowly forward to meet the lion; from the mighty cavity of his deep chest rolled savage growls. Numa halted. He glanced quickly from side to side. He shook his head and, holding it upon one side, snarled; then he wheeled about and stalked majestically away without a backward glance. The man had outbluffed the lion.

Suddenly the newcomer wheeled upon Sborov. 'Who are you?' he demanded. Had the lion spoken, Sborov would have been little less surprised than he was to hear excellent English fall from lips that had just been voicing the hideous growls of a beast. He was so surprised that he did not reply; then the man repeated the question. This time his tone was peremptory, brooking no delay.

'I am Prince Alexis Sborov.'

'Where are the rest of your party – Lady Greystoke and the others?'

Sborov's eyes went wide. How did this man know about them? Who could he be?

'I don't know. They left me alone to die in the jungle.'

'Who left you alone?'

'Only Lady Greystoke, myself, my valet, and the pilot, Brown were left of the original party when they abandoned me.'

'Why did they abandon you?'

'Brown wanted me to die. He did not want me to reach civilization and accuse him of murder.'

Tarzan scrutinized the man closely. There was nothing about him to arouse the ape-man's admiration or liking. 'Whom did he murder?' he asked.

'He killed my wife, because he thought that she could not keep up with the rest of us and would thus prevent Brown's escape from the jungle. He knew that I would not leave her, and he did not want to lose any of the men – he was afraid to travel alone.'

'Then why did he abandon you?' demanded Tarzan.

Sborov realized the inconsistency of his two statements; but his explanation came quickly, glibly. 'He was in love with Lady Greystoke – they ran off together.'

Tarzan's face darkened, and his fingers moved as though closing upon something – a throat, perhaps. 'Which way did they go?' he asked.

'Along this same trail toward the east,' replied Sborov.

'When?'

'Yesterday, I think, or perhaps the day before. It seems very long that I have been alone in the jungle – I have lost track of time.'

'Where are Tibbs and Annette?'

Again Sborov was astonished. 'Who are you?' he asked. 'How do you know so much about us?'

Tarzan did not reply. He just stood looking at the man. What was he to do with him? He would delay his search for Jane, yet he could not leave him alone to die, as he most assuredly would, because he believed that he was a friend of Jane. In her note she had given no details of the mishaps that had befallen them. She had only enumerated the members of the party, explained that their ship had crashed and that Princess Sborov had died. He naturally assumed that Jane was a guest of the Sborovs and that therefore the man must be her friend.

'What became of Tibbs and Annette?'

'Annette disappeared,' explained the prince. 'We do not know what became of her. She just vanished into thin air. Her footprints led to a point beneath a tree. They stopped there.'

'How long ago was that?'

'I think it was the day before Brown ran away with Lady Greystoke.'

'And Tibbs?'

'Tibbs went with them.'

'Why did he take Tibbs and not you?'

'He was not afraid of Tibbs. He knew that I would protect Lady Greystoke and also bring him to justice if we ever reached civilization.'

Tarzan's level gaze held steadily upon Sborov as he appraised the man. He mistrusted him, but no hint of what was passing in his mind was betrayed by any changing expression of his inscrutable face. He was repelled by Sborov's face, by his manner, by the suggestion of contradiction and inconsistency in several of his statements; yet he realized that in the latter must lie some germ of fact.

At least the fellow had definitely assured him that he was on Jane's trail; and convinced him that the girl Nkima had seen with the Kavuru must have been Annette, as Jane must still have been with Brown and Sborov at the time that Nkima had seen the other woman.

'Come,' he said to the man, 'we shall go and find Lady Greystoke and Brown.'

'Brown will kill me,' said Sborov. 'He has threatened to many times.'

'He will not kill you while I am with you.'

'You do not know him.'

'I do not need to know him,' replied the ape-man; 'I know myself.'

'I am too weak to travel fast,' explained Sborov. 'If you know this country, you had better take me to some village and then go on after Brown yourself. I have not eaten for a long time. I doubt that I could walk another mile, I am so weak from hunger.'

'Stay here,' directed Tarzan. 'I will get food; then we will go on after – Brown.'

Sborov watched the man move off into the forest, a little monkey perched upon one broad shoulder.

24

Down into Darkness

Jane's thoughts had been far away as she swung along the trail behind Tibbs and Brown that afternoon; they had been far to the west where a little, time worn cabin stood near the shore of a landlocked cove on the west coast. There had centered many of the important events and thrilling adventures of her life; there she had met that strange demi-god of the forest whom she had later come to know as Tarzan of the Apes.

Where was he now? Had he received her cablegram? If he had, he was already searching for her. The thought gave her renewed hope. She longed for the sanctuary of those mighty arms, for the peace and safety that his strength and jungle-craft afforded.

As her thoughts re-explored the winding back trail of time her pace slowed and she dropped still farther in the rear of her companions. For the moment they were forgotten; she was alone in the great jungle of her memories.

But she was not alone. Eyes watched her every move; from the foliage of the trees above, they watched her, ever keeping pace with her.

Presently she felt an unaccountable urge to turn back. She wondered why. Was it a woman's intuition directing her for her best good? Was it a beneficent or a malign influence? She could only wonder.

At first this peculiar urge was only a faint suggestion; then it became more pronounced, became a force beyond her power to deny. At last she ceased to wonder or to question. Tibbs and Brown seemed very far away. She thought of calling to them, but she knew that it would be useless. For just an instant longer she hesitated, striving to force her will to drive her along the trail in an effort to overtake them; then she surrendered. A power stronger than she controlled her, and she turned docilely back away from them.

It was as though someone was calling to her in a voice that she could not hear but that she must obey. It offered her nothing, nor did it threaten her. She had neither hope nor fear because of it.

When the noose of the Kavuru dropped about her she felt no surprise, no terror – her sensibilities were numbed. She looked into the savage, painted face of the white man who drew her to a limb beside him and removed the noose from about her. It all seemed perfectly natural, as though it were something that had been foreordained since the beginning of time.

The man lifted her to a shoulder and started off through the trees toward the east away from the trail that ran in a Northeasterly direction at that point. He did not speak, nor did she. It all seemed quite in order.

This state of mind persisted for a matter of an hour or so; then it gradually commenced to fade as she slowly emerged from the state of hypnosis that had deadened her sensibilities. Slowly the horror of her situation dawned upon her. She realized that she was in the clutches of a strange, savage creature that was also a white man. She knew now that she had been hypnotized, the victim of a strange power that turned her will to its own purposes yet left her conscious of all that transpired.

She felt that she must do something about it, but what was there to do? From the ease with which the man carried her, she knew that his strength was abnormal – far beyond any that she could pit against it in an effort to escape. Her only hope lay in evolving some stratagem that would permit her to elude him when he was off guard. This she could never hope to do as long as he carried her.

She wondered where he was taking her and to what fate. If she could only carry on a conversation with him she might discover, but what language would such a creature speak? Well, she could only try.

'Who are you?' she asked in English. 'What are you going to do with me?'

The man grunted and then mumbled in a Bantu dialect with which she was familiar, 'I do not understand.'

Jane experienced a moment of elation that was great by contrast with the hopelessness of her situation when she realized that he spoke a language she was familiar with.

'I understand you,' she said in the same dialect that he had used. 'Now tell me who you are and why you have taken me. I am not an enemy of your people, but if you keep me or harm me my people will come and destroy your village; they will kill many of you.'

'Your people will not come. No one ever comes to the village of the Kavuru. If any did, they would be killed.'

'You call yourselves Kavuru? Where is your village?'

'You will see.'

'What are you going to do with me?'

'I take you to Kavandavanda.'

'Who is Kavandavanda?' she demanded.

'He is Kavandavanda.' The man spoke as though that were sufficient explanation. It was as though one said, 'God is God.'

'What does he want of me? What is he going to do with me? If he wants ransom, if you want ransom, my people will pay much to have me back unharmed.'

'You talk too much,' snapped the Kavuru. 'Shut up.'

For a while Jane was silent; then she tried again, spurred on by the discomfort of the position in which she was being carried.

'Put me down,' she said. 'I can travel through the trees quite as well as you. There is no reason why you should carry me. It will be easier for us both if you let me walk.'

At first the Kavuru appeared to ignore the suggestion; but at last he put her down. 'Do not try to escape,' he warned. 'If you do try to, I may have to kill you. No one must ever escape from a Kavuru.'

Jano stretched her cramped muscles and surveyed her captor. He was indeed a savage appearing specimen; but how much of that was due to his natural countenance and how much to the paint, the nose ornament and the earrings she could not guess. Like many savage or primitive people, his age was undeterminable by his appearance; yet somehow she felt that he was a young man.

'What is your name?' she asked.

'Ogdli,' he replied.

'You are a chief, of course,' she said, hoping to make a favorable impression by flattery.

'I am not a chief,' he replied. 'There is only one chief, and that is Kavandavanda.'

She tried to draw him on into a conversation; but he was short and taciturn at first, finally becoming ugly.

'Shut up, or I will cut your tongue out,' he snapped. 'Kavandavanda does not need your tongue.'

Thereafter, Jane was silent; for there was that about her captor and the tone in which he made the threat that told her it was no idle one.

That night he bound her securely with his rope while he lay down to sleep, and the next morning they were on their way again. At the halt he had gathered some fruit and nuts, and these formed the only breakfast that they had.

In the middle of the forenoon they came suddenly to the end of the forest and looked out across a narrow plain to a lofty mountain at the foot of which Jane thought that she discerned what appeared to be a palisade built close to a perpendicular cliff.

The plain was strewn with large boulders and cut by several washes; so that as they advanced across it toward the mountain the palisade was sometimes in view and sometimes hidden from their sight.

As they approached more closely, Jane saw that the palisade was a massive affair of stone and that it formed three sides of a rectangle the rear wall of which was evidently the face of the mighty cliff that loomed high above them.

A small river followed a winding course across the plain from the very foot of the palisade, as though it were born there; though when she came closer she saw that it flowed from beneath the stone wall through an opening left for that purpose.

Her captor shouted as he approached the palisade, and a moment later one of the two massive gates swung open a little way to admit them. Beyond was a narrow street flanked by small stone houses, the flat roofs of which suggested that this was a country of little rain. They were houses similar in design to those built of stone and adobe by the prehistoric builders of the ancient pueblos of southwestern America.

Savage warriors loitered before tiny doorways or tended cooking fires built in little outdoor ovens. Like Ogdli, they were all young men, their ornaments, apparel, and weapons being almost identical to his.

Some of them gathered around Jane and her captor, examining her and asking questions of Ogdli.

'You and Ydeni have all the luck,' grumbled one. 'He captured a black girl and a white girl all during the full of the moon.'

'The black girl got away from him,' said another.

'Yes, but he went right back into the forest and caught a white girl.'

'He will get no teeth for the black girl.'

'No, but he will get a fine string for the white one; and Ogdli will get another row of teeth – that will make four for Ogdli. Kavandavanda will think well of him.'

'He should,' said Ogdli. 'I am the greatest warrior among the Kavuru.'

A big fellow grunted derisively. 'You have but three rows of teeth,' he taunted. 'I have seven,' and he tapped his chest where it joined his throat.

Jane, listening to this strange conversation, made little of it until this gesture of the speaker called her attention to the necklaces of human teeth about his throat; then she saw that there were seven rows of them and that about Ogdli's neck were three similar strands. She glanced at some of the other warriors. Some had one or two, others had none. These necklaces were evidently a sign of greatness, evidencing the prowess of the individual and his success in capturing women.

Suddenly she became aware of a marked peculiarity of her surroundings – here she was in an isolated village of a war-like people far removed from other villages, a village in which there were many men in the prime of life; yet she had seen neither women nor children.

What could it mean? Did some strange custom require that women and children remain indoors at certain hours or upon certain occasions, or were there no women nor children? If the latter were true, then what became of the women captives of which they boasted? But it could not be true; there must be women and children. But if there were women, why did the men attend the cooking fires? That was no fit work for warriors.

These observations and thoughts passed quickly through Jane's mind as she was led along the narrow street by Ogdli. At an intersection her captor turned into a narrow alley and led her to a low, circular building that lent to her surroundings a still greater similitude to the ancient villages of the pueblos; for this was a windowless structure against which leaned a primitive wooden ladder leading to the roof. If it were not a ceremonial kiva its appearance belied its purpose.

With a grunt, Ogdli motioned her to precede him up the ladder; and when she gained the roof she found still further evidence of kivalike attributes, for here the top of a second ladder protruded from a small, rectangular opening.

Ogdli pointed to it. 'Go down,' he commanded; 'and stay down. Do not try to escape. It will be worse for you if you do try.'

Jane looked down through the aperture. She could see nothing – just a black pit.

'Hurry!' admonished Ogdli.

The girl placed a foot upon a rung of the ladder and started slowly down into the black, mysterious void. She was no coward, but her courage was tested to its utmost as she forced her unwilling feet down that shaky, primitive ladder. Uppermost in her mind was the fact that she had seen no women in the village of the Kavuru. What had been the fate of the captives of which the warriors had boasted? Had they, too, descended this ladder? Had they gone down into this dark abyss never to return?

25

Defeat

Muviro and the Waziri came to the end of the forest. Before them stretched a narrow plain that lay at the foot of a lone mountain.

One of the warriors pointed. 'There is a village built at the foot of that high cliff. I see the palisade.'

Muviro shaded his eyes with his hand. He nodded. 'It must be the village of Kavuru. We have found it at last. Perhaps we shall not find Buira, but we will punish the Kavuru. We will teach them to leave the daughters of the Waziri alone.'

The other warriors assented with savage growls; for they were Waziri, known for ages as mighty warriors. Who might dare encroach upon their rights? Who might steal their women with impunity? None.

Other tribes suffered similar losses. They made big noise with tom-toms and shouting. They danced their war dances. And then, when there was little chance of overtaking their enemy, they set out in pursuit; but always they abandoned the chase before they overhauled the quarry. Not so the Waziri. What they undertook, they pursued relentlessly whether it brought victory or defeat.

'Come!' said Muviro, and led his warriors out upon the plain toward the village of the Kavuru. Suddenly he halted. 'What is that?' he demanded.

The Waziri listened. A low droning sound that at first barely commanded the attention of their ears was growing steadily in volume. The warriors, standing in silence, looked up toward the heavens.

'There it is,' said one, pointing. 'It is a canoe that flies. I saw one pass low over the country of the Waziri. It made the same sound.'

The ship came rapidly into view, flying at an altitude of three or four thousand feet. It passed over the plain and the Waziri; then it banked steeply and turned back. With motor throttled, the ship descended gracefully in wide spirals. At a few hundred feet from the ground the pilot gave it the gun, but still he continued to circle low over the plain. He was searching for a landing place. For two hours he had been searching for one, almost hopelessly.

Lost, and with only a little fuel remaining in his tanks, he welcomed the sight of this open plain and the village with heartfelt thanks. He knew that he couldn't get fuel here, but he could get his position, and at least he was saved from making a forced landing over the forest.

Flying low, he saw the Waziri, white plumed savages evidently coming from the forest; and he saw natives emerging from the village, too. He saw that these were different in a most surprising way, and he dropped lower and circled twice more to make sure.

His companion, in the front cockpit, scribbled a note and handed it back to him; 'What do you make of them? They look white to me.'

'They are white,' wrote the pilot.

Owing to the washes and boulders there were not many safe landing places available on the plain. One of the best, or perhaps it would be truer to say least impossible, was directly in front of the village; another, and perhaps a better one, lay across the plain, near the forest. Muviro and his Waziri stood near the edge of it, a band of primitive savages; and the sight of these and the implications their presence suggested determined the pilot to set his ship down nearer the village and its white inhabitants. Tragic error.

Once again the ship circled the plain, rising to an altitude of a thousand feet; then the pilot cut his motor and glided toward a landing.

Muviro resumed his advance upon the village; and as the way led him and his men down into a deep wash they did not see the actual landing of the ship, but when they again reached higher ground they saw two men climbing from the cockpit of the plane, while advancing from the open gates of the Kavuru village was a swarm of savage, white warriors, whose hostile intent was all too apparent to Muviro.

They were white! No longer was there any doubt in the mind of the Waziri chieftain; now he knew that these were indeed the Kavuru. They were shouting and brandishing their spears as they ran toward the two aviators. Apparently they had not as yet discovered the presence of the Waziri; or, if they had, they ignored them.

Muviro spoke to his men in low tones, and they spread out in a thin line and moved silently forward at a trot. They did not yell and prance as do many native warriors, and because they did not they seemed always to inspire greater fear in the hearts of their enemies. There were only ten of them, yet they charged the savage Kavuru, who outnumbered them ten to one, with all the assurance that they might have been expected to have had the odds been reversed.

The fliers, seeing that the natives were hostile, fell back toward their ship. One of them fired a shot over the heads of the advancing Kavuru; but as it had no deterrent effect, the man fired again; and this time a Kavuru fell. Still the savage white warriors came on.

Now both the fliers opened fire, yet on came the Kavuru. Soon they would be within spear range of their victims. The men glanced behind them as though seeking temporary shelter, but what they saw must have been disheartening – a thin line of black warriors trotting silently toward them from the rear.

They did not know that these would have been friends and allies; so one of them raised his pistol and fired at Muviro. The bullet missed its mark; and the Waziri chieftain sought cover behind a boulder, ordering his men to do likewise; for he knew better than the Kavuru the deadly effectiveness of firearms.

Then he called to the two fliers in English, telling them that the Waziri were friendly; but the harm had already been done – the delay permitted the Kavuru to close in upon the two men before the Waziri could join forces with them to repel the enemy. Perhaps it would have done no good, so greatly did the Kavuru outnumber them all.

With savage yells they bore down upon the fliers, though several of their number dropped before the fire that the two poured into their ranks. Now they were close; but close too were the Waziri, who were moving forward again, now at a run.

Presently the Kavuru spears began to fly. One of the strangers fell with a weapon through his heart. Now a volley of spears leaped from the hands of the Waziri, momentarily checking the advance of the Kavuru, who seemed to fear spears more than they did firearms.

They did not retreat, but merely paused a moment; then they launched another flight of spears; and this time the second flier fell, and with him three Waziri. A moment later the Kavuru and Waziri closed in hand-to-hand struggle.

Now there were but seven of the latter; and though they fought valiantly, they were no match for the hundred Kavuru warriors that overwhelmed them.

Fighting close to the bodies of the slain fliers, Muviro and one of his warriors, Balando, salvaged the pistols and ammunition of the dead men. At close quarters the firearms had a more definite effect on the morale of the Kavuru, stopping them temporarily and permitting Muviro and his remaining warriors to fall back in search of shelter. Now there were but four of them: Muviro, Balando, and two others.

The Waziri chief sought to reach a pile of granite rising spire-like from the plain; and at last he was successful, but now only Balando remained alive to carry on the unequal struggle with him. Together they fell back to the rocky sanctuary Muviro had chosen, and while Muviro held the Kavuru at bay Balando clambered to the summit safely out of effective spear range; then he fired down upon the enemy while Muviro climbed to his side.

Again and again the Kavuru hurled their spears aloft; but the height was too great for any but the most powerful muscles, and even the weapons of these had lost so much speed and momentum by the time they reached the level at which their targets stood that they ceased to constitute a menace. The revolvers and bows of the two Waziri, however, still did effective work – so effective that the Kavuru fell back toward their village; and with the coming of the swift equatorial twilight Muviro saw them definitely give up the attack and file back toward the village gate.

As they passed the grounded ship, Muviro saw that they avoided it and guessed that they were afraid of it as of something supernatural; then night fell, blotting out the scene.

Sorrowfully Muviro and Balando descended from the rock that had afforded them sanctuary. They sought shelter and a place to sleep in the forest, the impenetrable gloom of which seemed no darker than their future. But they made no plans; they were too exhausted, too overcome by grief and disappointment to think clearly.

'If only the Big Bwana would come,' sighed Balando.

'Yes,' agreed Muviro. 'If he had been here, this would not have happened.'

26

Tarzan Stalks Brown

The morning mist floated lazily in the still air, the soul of the dead night clinging reluctantly to earth. A strange hush lay on the jungle, a silence as poignant as a leopard's scream. It awakened Brown. He moved gingerly in the crotch of the tree into which he had wedged himself the evening before. He was stiff and lame and sore. Every muscle ached. He looked up at Tibbs, a couple of feet above him, and grinned. The Englishman was spread-eagled across two parallel branches to which he was clinging tightly in restless slumber.

'He looks like he was goin' to be grilled,' mused the pilot. 'Poor old Tibbsy.' He spoke the last words half aloud.

Tibbs opened his eyes and looked around. For a moment his expression was surprised and troubled; then he discovered Brown below him, and full consciousness returned.

'My word!' he exclaimed with a shake of his head. 'Hi was just drawing 'is Grace's bawth.'

'You even wait on 'em in your sleep, don't you, Tibbsy?'

'Well, you see, Sir, hits been my life, always; and Hi wouldn't hask for a better one – peace and orderliness. Heverything clean and straight; heverything always in its place. Hand not 'ard work, Sir. Hand you're always treated well – that is, by gentlemen. It's been my good fortune to be in the service mostly of gentlemen.'

'Like this Sborov guy?' inquired Brown.

' 'E was not a gentleman.'

'But he was a prince, wasn't he? Don't that make him a gentleman?'

Tibbs scratched his head. 'It should but it doesn't; not always. Hi sometimes think when Hi see a bounder with a title that possibly at some time his
mother may have been indiscreet.'

Brown laughed. 'I guess there must of been a lot of indiscretion in high
places,' he remarked, and then: 'How about pullin' our freight, Tibbsy? We
got a long ways to go on a pair of empty stomachs.'

Wearily the two men plodded on through the jungle. All the forces of nature
and the laws of chance seemed to have combined against them from the first.
Now they were sad, disheartened, almost without hope; yet each tried bravely
to keep up the spirits of the other. It was oftentimes a strain, and occasionally
one of them voiced the morbid doubts and fears that assailed them both.

'Do you believe in black magic, Tibbsy?' asked Brown.

'Hi 'ave seen some strange things hin my life, Sir,' replied the Englishman.

'You know what the old dame come down here to look for, don't you?'

'Yes, something that would renew youth, wasn't it?'

'Yes. I know a lot about that. I knew a lot I didn't tell her. If I had she might
not have come, and I sure wanted her to. I wanted to get that formula. Cripes,
Tibbsy! It would be worth a million back in civilization. But it's well guarded.
A few men have tried to get it. None of 'em was ever heard of again.'

'Well, we ain't trying to get it now. We got troubles enough trying to find
our way out of this jungle to be bothering with any helixir of life. If we just go
along and mind our own business, we'll be all right.'

'I don't know about that. I never took much stock in black magic, but it is
funny all the things that's happened to this expedition ever since it started out.
Just like somebody or something had put a jinx on it. It started right off the bat
with that zero-zero flyin' weather; then come the forced landin'; then the old
dame's murdered; then Annette disappears; now Lady Greystoke's gone.

'Do you realize, Tibbsy, that of the six that took off from Croyden there's
only two of us left? It's just like something was following us, pickin' off one at
a time. It sure gets my goat when I stop to think about it. It's doggone funny,
Tibbsy, that's what it is.'

'Hi see nothing amusing in it, Sir,' objected Tibbs; 'but then Hi've always
'eard that you Americans had a strange sense of humor.'

'The trouble is that you Englishmen don't understand English,' explained
Brown. 'But let's skip it. The question is, which one of us will be next?'

'Don't,' begged Tibbs. 'That's just what Hi've been trying not to think
about.'

Brown turned again and looked back at his companion who was following
along a narrow trail. The American grinned. 'Wasn't Lady Greystoke walkin'
behind when it got her?' he reminded.

*

Tarzan, following the trail toward the east, found Sborov a problem. The man was too exhausted to move faster than a snail's pace, and even so he was compelled to rest often.

Tarzan was anxious to overtake Brown and Tibbs with whom he believed Jane to be. He would kill Brown. The very thought of the man caused the scar across his forehead to burn red – the scar that Bolgani, the gorilla, had given him years ago in that first life and death struggle that had taught the boy Tarzan one of the uses of his dead father's hunting knife and thus set his feet upon the trail that led to the Lordship of the jungle.

Ordinarily the life of a strange Tarmangani would have weighed as nothing as against a delay in his search for Jane; but Alexis had given the impression that he had been Jane's friend and protector, and Tarzan could not desert him to the certain fate that would have claimed such as he alone in the jungle.

So the Lord of the Jungle decided to remain with Sborov until he could turn him over to the chief of some friendly tribe for protection and guidance to the nearest outpost of civilization, or place him in the hands of his own Waziri.

Seemingly imbued with many of the psychic characteristics of the wild beasts among which he had been reared, Tarzan often developed instinctive likes or dislikes for individuals on first contact; and seldom did he find it necessary to alter his decisions.

He had formed such a conviction within a few moments after his meeting with Sborov, a conviction which made it doubly distasteful to him to be in the company of the man and waste time befriending him. He mistrusted and disliked him, but for Jane's sake he would not abandon him. Little Nkima seemed to share his mistrust, for he seldom came near the stranger; and when he did he bared his teeth in a menacing snarl.

Chafing under the delay forced upon him by Sborov's physical condition, which bordered on complete exhaustion, the ape-man at last swung the surprised Sborov to his shoulder and took to the trees with the agility and speed of a small monkey.

Alexis voiced a cry of remonstrance that carried also a note of fear, but he was helpless to escape the situation into which he had been snatched as though by the hand of Fate. Should he succeed in wriggling from that vise-like grasp, it would only lead to injury in the resultant fall to the ground below. So Alexis shut his eyes tight and hoped for the best.

He knew that they were moving rapidly through the trees; the swift passage of foliage and twigs across his body told him that. He remonstrated with the bronzed savage that was carrying him, but he might as well have sought conversation with the Sphinx. At last he gained sufficient courage to open his eyes; then, indeed, did he gasp in horror; for at that very moment Tarzan leaped out into space to catch a trailing liana and swing to another tree upon his arboreal trail. Fifty feet below the eyes of the thoroughly terrified Sborov lay the hard ground. He screamed aloud, and then he found articulate voice.

'Take me down,' he cried. 'Let me walk. You'll kill us both.' Overcome by terror, he struggled to free himself.

'It will be you who will kill us if you don't lie still,' warned the ape-man.

'Then take me down.'

'You are too slow,' replied Tarzan. 'I cannot be held to the pace of Kota, the tortoise, if I am ever to overtake the man you call Brown. If I take you down I shall have to leave you alone here in the jungle. Would you prefer that?'

Sborov was silent. He was trying to weigh the terrors of one plan against those of the other. All that he could think of was that he wished he were back in Paris, which really didn't help at all in this emergency.

Suddenly Tarzan came to an abrupt halt on a broad limb. He was listening intently. Sborov saw him sniffing the air. It reminded him of a hound on a scent trail.

'What do those two men look like?' demanded Tarzan. 'Describe them to me, so that I may know Brown when I see him.'

'Tibbs is a small man with thin hair and a pinched face. He is an Englishman with a slight cockney accent. Brown is a big fellow, an American. I suppose he would be called good looking,' added Sborov, grudgingly.

Tarzan dropped to a trail that they had crossed many times as it wound through the jungle, and set Sborov on the ground.

'Follow this trail,' he directed. 'I am going on ahead.'

'You are going to leave me alone here in the jungle?' demanded Alexis, fearfully.

'I will come back for you,' replied the ape-man. 'You will be safe enough for the short time I shall be gone.'

'But suppose a lion –' commenced Sborov.

'There are no lions about,' interrupted Tarzan. 'There is nothing near that will harm you.'

'How do you know?'

'I know. Do as I tell you and follow the trail.'

'But—' Sborov started to expostulate; then he gasped and sighed resignedly, for he was alone. Tarzan had swung into the trees and disappeared.

The ape-man moved swiftly along the scent spoor that had attracted his attention. His sensitive nostrils told him it was the scent of two white men. He sought in vain to detect the spoor of a woman, but there was none – if the two men were Brown and Tibbs, then Jane was no longer with them.

What had become of her? The man's jaw set grimly. That information he would get from Brown before he killed him.

A human life meant no more to Tarzan of the Apes than that of any other creature. He never took life wantonly, but he could kill a bad man with less compunction than he might feel in taking the life of a bad lion.

Any living thing that harmed his mate or threatened her with harm he could even find a species of grim pleasure in killing, and Sborov had convinced him that Brown meant harm to Jane if he had not already harmed her.

The man's statement that Jane and Brown had run away together had not carried the conviction that the implication might have provoked, so sure was the Lord of the Jungle of the loyalty of his mate. Her intentions and her voluntary acts he never doubted nor questioned.

What were his thoughts as he swung along the trail of the two unsuspecting men? That inscrutable face gave no suggestion of what passed in the savage mind, but they must have been grim and terrible thoughts of revenge.

Rapidly the scent of his quarry grew stronger as the distance that separated them grew shorter.

Now he went more slowly; and, if possible, even more silently. He moved as soundlessly as his own shadow as he came at last in sight of two men trudging wearily along the trail beneath him.

It was they; he could not mistake them – the small Englishman, the big American. He paid little attention to Tibbs, but his eyes never left the figure of the aviator. Stealthily he stalked, as the lion stalks his prey.

He was quite close above them. Easily now at any moment he could launch himself down upon his victim.

Tibbs mopped the streaming perspiration from his forehead and out of his eyes. 'Whew!' he sighed. 'Hit all seems so bloody useless. Hit's like lookin' for a needle in a hay stack. We won't never find her anyway. Let's stop and rest. I'm jolly well done in.'

'I know how you feel, but we got to keep on lookin' though. We might find her. The more I think about it, the less I think Sborov got away with Lady Greystoke.'

'What's made you change your mind?' demanded Tibbs. 'Hi thought you was sure he had.'

'Well, in the first place, she was armed; and she had the guts to defend herself. He ain't got no guts at all.'

'"E 'ad enough to murder his poor wife,' objected Tibbs.

'He sneaked up on her in the dark while she was asleep,' sneered Brown. 'That didn't take no guts.'

'But 'ow about Annette?'

Brown shook his head. 'I don't know. I can't make it out. Of course, there was a good reason for his wanting to kill Annette. She had the evidence against him – she knew too much; and she wasn't armed.

'But what gets me is the way her footprints disappeared, just like she'd dissolved into thin air. If his footprints had been there too, and gone on, I'd have thought he picked her up and carried her into the jungle to finish her; but hers were all alone.'

They had stopped now while Tibbs rested. The ape-man crouched above them, listening. He missed no word, but what effect they had upon him was not revealed by any change of expression.

'But 'e couldn't 'ave picked 'er up and carried her hoff and her not scream,' argued Tibbs. 'That would have woke some of us.'

'She might have been too scared to scream,' explained Brown. 'Annette was awful scared of him.'

'Lady Greystoke wasn't scared of him. Why didn't she call for help?'

'Lady Greystoke wasn't scared of nothing. There was some dame, Tibbs.'

'Hi quite agree with you,' replied the Englishman. 'Lady Greystoke was a most extraordinary person. Hi 'opes as how we find her.'

'Yes, and I hope we find Annette. I can't believe she is dead, somehow.' The note of yearning in the aviator's voice was not lost on the silent listener above.

'You was rather soft on Annette, wasn't you?' said Tibbs, sympathetically.

'Plenty,' admitted Brown, 'and that louse, Sborov, told her I was tryin' to make Lady Greystoke. Hell! Can you picture a English noblewoman falling for me?'

'If you'll pardon my saying so, I can't,' admitted Tibbs, candidly.

'No more can I. She was a swell dame, but Annette was the only girl I ever seen that had me ga-ga. I'd give – well, all I ain't got to know for sure what became of her.'

Softly the ape-man dropped to the trail behind the two men.

'I think I know,' he said.

At the sound of his voice they wheeled suddenly and faced him, surprise written large upon the face of each.

'Who the devil are you and where did you come from?' demanded Brown, while Tibbs stood with his lower lip dropped, staring wide-eyed at the strange figure of the ape-man. 'And what do you think you know?' concluded the American.

'I think I know how your two women disappeared.'

'Say,' exclaimed Brown, 'what are you, anyway? This country's got me nuts – people disappearing and you jumping out of thin air like a spook. Are you a friend or what?'

'Friend,' replied Tarzan.

'What you runnin' around undressed for?' demanded Brown. 'Ain't you got no clothes, or ain't you got no sense?'

'I am Tarzan of the Apes.'

'Yeah? Well, I'm glad to meet you, Tarzan; I'm Napoleon. But spill what you know about Annette – about both the dames. What got 'em? Was it Sborov? But of course you don't know nothin' about Sborov.'

'I know about Sborov,' replied Tarzan. 'I know about the accident that wrecked your plane. I know the Princess Sborov was murdered. I think I know what happened to Lady Greystoke and Annette.'

Brown looked puzzled. 'I don't know how you got hep to all this, but you know plenty. Now tell me what happened to the two dames.'

'The Kavuru got them. You are in Kavuru country.'

'What are Kavuru?' demanded Brown.

'A tribe of savage white men. They make a practice of stealing women, presumably for use in some religious rite.'

'Where do they hang out?'

'I don't know. I was looking for their village when I heard about the accident to your ship. I believe I can find it soon. It lies in a very wild country. The Kavuru have secrets they wish to guard; so no one is allowed to approach their village.'

'What secrets?' inquired Brown.

'They are believed to have discovered some sort of an elixir of life, something that will make old people young again.'

Brown whistled. 'So that's it? They were the people we were looking for.'

'You were looking for the Kavuru?' asked Tarzan, incredulously.

'The old dame was looking for the formula for that elixir stuff,' explained Brown, 'and so am I, now that she is dead – someone has to carry on, you know,' he added rather lamely. 'But say, how did you hear of the accident to the ship? How could you hear about it? We ain't seen or talked to no one.' Suddenly Brown ceased speaking. His face darkened in anger.

'Sborov!' he exclaimed.

The prince, rounding a bend in the trail, halted when he saw Brown. The American started toward him, menacingly, an oath on his lips.

Sborov turned to run. 'Stop him!' he screamed to Tarzan. 'You promised you wouldn't let him harm me.'

The ape-man sprang after Brown and seized him by the arm. 'Stop!' he commanded. 'I promised the man.'

Brown attempted to wrench himself free. 'Let me go, you fool,' he growled. 'Mind your own business.' Then he aimed a heavy blow at Tarzan's jaw with his free hand. The ape-man ducked, and the clenched fist only grazed his cheek. The shadow of a grim smile touched his lips as he lifted the American above his head and shook him; then he tossed him into the thick underbrush that bordered the trail.

'You forgot Waterloo, Napoleon,' he said.

Upon the branch of a tree above, little Nkima danced and chattered; and as Brown was extricating himself with difficulty from the thorny embrace of the bushes, Nkima gathered a ripe and odorous fruit and hurled it at him.

Tibbs looked on in consternation, believing that Brown had made a dangerous enemy in this giant white savage; and when he saw Tarzan step toward the struggling American he anticipated nothing less than death for both of them.

But there was no anger in the breast of the ape-man as he again seized the aviator and lifted him out of the entangling bushes and set him upon his feet in the trail.

'Do not again forget,' he said, quietly, 'that I am Tarzan of the Apes or that when I give an order it is to be obeyed.'

Brown looked the ape-man squarely in the eyes for a moment before he spoke. 'I know when I'm licked,' he said. 'But I still don't savvy why you wouldn't let me kill that louse – he sure has it coming to him.'

'Your quarrels are of no importance,' said the ape-man; 'but it is important to locate Lady Greystoke.'

'And Annette,' added Brown.

'Yes,' agreed Tarzan. 'Also that you three men get back to civilization where you belong. You do not belong in the jungle. The world is full of fools who go places where they do not belong, causing other people worry and trouble.'

'If Hi may make so bold as to say so, Sir, Hi quite agree with you,' ventured Tibbs. 'Hi shall be jolly well pleased to get hout of this bally old jungle.'

'Then don't any of you start killing off the others,' advised Tarzan. 'The more of you there are the better chance you will have of getting out, and three are none too many. Many times you will find it necessary for someone to stand watch at night; so the more there are the easier it will be for all.'

'Not for mine with that prince guy along!' said Brown, emphatically. 'The last time he stood guard he tried to kill me with a hatchet, and he'd have done it if it hadn't been for old Tibbsy. If you say I don't kill him, I don't kill – unless he forces me to it; but I don't travel with him, and that's that.'

'We'll get him back here,' said Tarzan, 'and have a talk with him. I think I can promise you he'll be good. He was in a blue funk when I found him – a lion had been stalking him – and I think he'd promise anything not to be left alone again.'

'Well,' agreed Brown, grudgingly, 'get him back and see what he says.'

Tarzan called Sborov's name aloud several times, but there was no answer.

''E couldn't have gotten so very far,' said Tibbs. ''E must 'ear you, Sir.'

Tarzan shrugged. 'He'll come back when he gets more afraid of the jungle than he is of Brown.'

'Are we going to sit here waiting for him?' asked the American.

'No,' replied Tarzan. 'I am going on to find the Kavuru village. My own people are somewhere to the east. I'll take you to them. Sborov will most certainly follow and catch up with us after we stop for the night. Come.'

27

Madmen and Leopards

As Jane reached the foot of the ladder leading down into the dark interior of the kivalike structure in the village of the Kavuru her ears caught a faint sound as of someone or something moving at no great distance from her.

Instantly she froze to silent immobility, listening. She thought that she heard the sound of breathing. Dim light from the opening above relieved the darkness immediately about her, and she knew that she must be revealed to whatever was in the room with her. Then a voice spoke, spoke in English with a familiar accent.

'Oh, madame! It is you? They got you, too?'

'Annette! You are here? Then it was not the prince who took you away?'

'No, madame. It was a terrible white man who held me powerless by some black magic. I could not cry out for help. I could not resist. I simply went to him, and he took me up into the trees and carried me away.'

'One of them took me in the same way, Annette. They possess a hypnotic power beyond anything that I had ever dreamed might be possible. Have they harmed you, Annette?'

'I have only been terribly frightened,' replied the girl, 'because I don't know what they intend to do with me.'

Jane's eyes had become accustomed to the gloom of the dark chamber. Now she could discern more of the details of the interior. She saw a circular room with a litter of dry grasses and leaves on the hard dirt floor. Against one wall Annette was sitting on a little pallet of these same leaves and grasses that she had evidently scraped together. There was no one else, nothing else, in the room.

'What do you suppose they are going to do with us?' asked Jane. 'Haven't they given you any clew at all?'

'None, madame, absolutely none. Nor you? They have told you nothing?'

'The man who captured me was named Ogdli. He told me that much and that he was taking me to someone called Kavandavanda, who, I gathered, is their chief. When I asked more questions he threatened to cut my tongue out, saying that Kavandavanda did not need my tongue. They are most unpleasant people.'

'Ah, madame, that does not describe them – they are terrifying. If only Monsieur Brown was here. You have seen him lately, madame? He is well?'

'Quite well, Annette, in body; but his heart was sick. He was worrying about you.'

'I think he loves me very much, madame.'

'I am sure of it, Annette.'

'And I love him. It is terrible to have this happen now when we might have been so happy. Now we never shall be. I shall never see him again. I have that feeling, madame. It is what you call a – a premonition. I shall die here in this awful village – soon.'

'Nonsense, Annette! You mustn't say such things; you mustn't even think them. What we should be thinking about is escape – and nothing else.'

'Escape? What chance have we, madame?'

'I saw no guard at the entrance to this hole when they brought me in,' explained Jane; 'and if there is none posted at night we can certainly get to the roof. From there on will depend upon what obstacles we find in our way, but it will be worth trying.'

'Whatever you say, madame.'

'Tonight then, Annette.'

'S-sh, madame! Someone is coming.'

Footsteps sounded plainly on the roof above them now, and then the opening through which they had entered was darkened by the form of a man.

'Come up!' he commanded; 'Both of you.'

Jane sighed. 'Our poor little plan,' she bemoaned.

'What difference does it make?' asked Annette. 'It would not have succeeded anyway.'

'We shall have to try something else later,' insisted the other, as she started to ascend the ladder.

'It will fail, too,' prophesied Annette gloomily. 'We shall die here – both of us – tonight, perhaps.'

As they stepped out onto the roof Jane recognized the warrior as the one who had captured her. 'Now what, Ogdli?' she asked. 'Are you going to set us free?'

'Be still,' growled the Kavuru. 'You talk too much. Kavandavanda has sent for you. Do not talk too much to Kavandavanda.'

He took hold of her arm to urge her along – a soft, smooth, sun-tanned arm. Suddenly he stopped and wheeled her about until she faced him. A new fire burned in his eyes. 'I never saw you before,' he said, in a low voice. 'I never saw you before.' It was an almost inaudible whisper.

Jane bared her teeth in a flashing smile. 'Look at my teeth,' she said. 'You will soon be wearing them; then you will have four rows.'

'I do not want your teeth, woman,' growled Ogdli huskily. 'You have cast a spell on me; I, who have foresworn women, am bewitched by a woman.'

Jane thought quickly. The change in the man had come so suddenly, and his infatuation was so apparent that for an instant it only frightened her; then she saw in it possibilities that might be turned to the advantage of herself and Annette.

'Ogdli,' she whispered softly, 'you can help me, and no one need ever know. Hide us until tonight. Tell Kavandavanda that you could not find us, that we must have escaped; then come back after dark and let us out of the village. Tomorrow you can come out to look for us; and perhaps, Ogdli, you will find me – find me waiting for you in the forest.' Her words, her tones, were provocative.

The man shook his head as though to rid his brain of an unwelcome thought; he passed a palm across his eyes as one who would push aside a veil.

'No!' he almost shouted; then he seized her roughly and dragged her along. 'I will take you to Kavandavanda. After that you will bewitch me no more.'

'Why are you afraid of me, Ogdli?' she asked. 'I am only a woman.'

'That is why I am afraid of you. You see no women here. There are none, other than those who are brought for Kavandavanda; and they are here but briefly. I am a priest. We are all priests. Women would contaminate us. We are not allowed to have them. If we were to weaken and succumb to their wiles, we should live in torment forever after death; and if Kavandavanda found it out, we should die quickly and horribly.'

'What is he saying, madame?' asked Annette. 'What are you talking about?'

'It is preposterous, Annette,' replied Jane; 'but Ogdli has developed a sudden infatuation for me. I tried to play upon it in order to tempt him to let us escape – and meet me in the forest tomorrow. It offered hope.'

'Oh, madame! You would not!'

'Of course not; but all is fair in love and war, and this is both. If we ever get into the forest, Annette, it will just be too bad for Ogdli if he can't find us.'

'And what does he say to it?'

'Thumbs down. He is dragging me off to Kavandavanda as fast as he can, so that temptation may be removed from his path.'

'All our hopes are dashed, madame,' said Annette, woefully.

'Not entirely, if I know men,' replied Jane. 'Ogdli will not so easily escape his infatuation. When he thinks he has lost me, it will tear at his vitals; then anything may happen.'

The Kavuru was leading the two girls along the main street toward the rear of the village. Confronting them was a heavy gate across the bottom of a narrow cleft in the cliff that towered ominously above the village.

Ogdli opened the gate and herded them through into the narrow, rocky cleft, beyond which they could see what appeared to be an open valley; but when they reached the far end of the cleft they found themselves in a box canyon entirely surrounded by lofty cliffs.

A small stream of clear water wound down through the canyon and out through the cleft and the village where it was entirely bridged over at the outer gate as well as in the cleft leading into the canyon.

The floor of the canyon appeared extremely fertile, supporting numerous large trees and growing crops. In the small fields Jane saw men laboring beneath the watchful eyes of Kavuru warriors. At first she paid little heed to the workers in the fields, as Ogdli led her and Annette toward a massive pile of buildings standing in the center of the canyon, but presently her attention was attracted to one of the laborers who was irrigating a small patch of kaffir corn.

Suddenly he threw down the crude wooden hoe he was using and stood upon his head in the mud. 'I am a tree,' he screamed in the Bukena dialect, 'and they have planted me upside down. Turn me over, put my roots in the ground, irrigate me, and I will grow to the moon.'

The Kavuru warrior who was guarding the workers in the vicinity stepped up to the man and struck him a sharp blow across the shins with the haft of his spear. 'Get down and go to work,' he growled.

The worker cried out in pain; but he immediately came to his feet, picked up his hoe, and continued to work as though there had been no interruption.

A little farther on another worker, looking up and catching sight of the two white girls, rushed toward them. Before the guard could interfere he was close to Jane. 'I am the King of the world,' he whispered; 'but don't tell them. They would kill me if they knew, but they can't know because I tell everyone not to tell them.'

Ogdli leaped at the fellow and struck him over the head with his spear just as the guard arrived to drag him back to his work.

'They are all bewitched,' explained Ogdli. 'Demons have entered their heads and taken possession of their brains; but it is well to have them around, as they frighten away other evil spirits. We keep them and take care of them. If they die a natural death, the demons die with them; if we were to kill them the demons would escape from their heads and might enter ours. As it is, they can't get out in any other way.'

'And these workers are all madmen?' asked Jane.

'Each has a demon in his head, but that doesn't keep them from working for us. Kavandavanda is very wise; he knows how to use everything and everybody.'

Now they had arrived before closed gates in the wall surrounding the building that they had seen when they first entered the canyon. Two Kavuru warriors stood on guard at the entrance to Kavandavanda's stronghold, but at the approach of Ogdli and his prisoners they opened the gates and admitted them.

Between the outer wall and the buildings was an open space corresponding to the ballium of a medieval castle. In it grew a few large trees, a few clumps of bamboo, and patches of brush and weeds. It was ill-kept and unsightly. The buildings themselves were partially of unbaked brick and partially of bamboo and thatch, a combination which produced a pleasing texture, enhancing the general effect of the low, rambling buildings that seemed to have been put together at different times and according to no predetermined plan, the whole achieving an unstudied disharmony that was most effective.

As they crossed to the entrance to what appeared to be the main building, a leopard rose from a patch of weeds, bared its fangs at them, and slunk away toward a clump of bamboo. Then another and another of the treacherous beasts, disturbed by their passage, moved sinuously out of their path.

Annette, her eyes wide with fright, pressed close to Jane. 'I am so afraid!' she said.

'They're ugly looking brutes,' agreed Jane. 'I wouldn't imagine this to be a very safe place. Perhaps that is why there are no people here.'

'Only the guards at the entrance ahead of us,' said Annette. 'Ask Ogdli if the leopards are dangerous.'

'Very,' replied the Kavuru in reply to the question that Jane put to him.

'Then why are they allowed to run at large?' demanded Jane.

'They do not bother us much in the daytime, partially because they are fairly well fed, partially because only armed men cross this courtyard, and partially because they are, after all, cowardly beasts that prefer to sneak upon their prey in the dark. But it is after dark that they best serve the purpose of Kavandavanda. You may be sure that no one escapes from the temple by night.'

'And that is all that they are kept for?' asked the girl.

'That is not all,' replied Ogdli.

Jane waited for him to continue, but he remained silent.

'What else, then?' she asked.

He gazed at her for a moment before he replied. There was a light in his eyes that appeared strange to Jane, for it seemed to reflect something that was almost compassion. He shook his head. 'I cannot tell,' he said; 'but you will know soon enough another reason that the leopards are here in the outer court.'

They were almost at the entrance when a weird, wailing scream broke the stillness that seemed to brood like an evil thing above the temple of Kavandavanda. The sound seemed to come either from the interior of the mass of buildings or from beyond them – sinister, horrible.

Instantly it was answered by the snarls and growls of leopards that appeared suddenly from amongst the weeds, the brush, or the bamboo and bounded off to disappear around the ends of the buildings.

'Something called to them,' whispered Annette, shuddering.

'Yes,' said Jane, 'something unclean – that was the impression conveyed to me.'

At the entrance there were two more guards to whom Ogdli spoke briefly; then they were admitted. As they passed the portal and came into the interior they heard muffled screams and growls and snarls as of many leopards fighting, and to the accompaniment of this savage chorus the two girls were conducted through the dim rooms and corridors of the temple of Kavandavanda.

Kavandavanda! Who, or what, was he? To what mysterious fate was he summoning them? Such were the questions constantly recurring in the thoughts of the girls. Jane felt that they would soon find answers, and she anticipated only the worst. There seemed to be no hope of escape from whatever fate lay in store for them.

That one hope that had given her strength to carry on through danger-fraught situations many times in the past was denied her now, for she felt that Tarzan must be wholly ignorant of her whereabouts. How could he know where, in the vast expanse of the African wilderness, the ship had crashed? He would be searching for her – she knew that; for he must have long since received her cablegram, but he could never find her – at least, not in time. She must depend wholly upon her own resources, and these were pitifully meager. At present there was only the frail straw of Ogdli's seeming infatuation. This she must nurse. But how? Perhaps when he had delivered her to Kavandavanda he would return to the village and she would never see him again; then even the single straw to which her hope clung in the deluge of dangers that threatened to engulf her would be snatched from her.

'Ogdli,' she said, suddenly, 'do you live here in the temple or back in the village?'

'I live where Kavandavanda commands,' he replied. 'Sometimes in the village, again in the temple.'

'And now! Where do you live now?'

'In the village.'

Jane mused. Ogdli would be of no good to her unless he were in the temple. 'You have lived here all your life, Ogdli?'

'No.'

'How long?'

'I do not remember. Perhaps a hundred rains have come and gone, perhaps two hundred; I have lost count. It makes no difference, for I shall be here forever – unless I am killed. I shall never die otherwise.'

Jane looked at him in astonishment. Was he another maniac? Were they all maniacs in this terrible city? But she determined to humor him.

'Then if you have been here so long,' she said, 'you must be on very friendly terms with Kavandavanda. If you asked him a favor he'd grant it.'

'Perhaps,' he agreed, 'but one must be careful what one asks of Kavandavanda.'

'Ask him if you can remain in the temple,' suggested the girl.

'Why?' demanded Ogdli, suspiciously.

'Because you are my only friend here, and I am afraid without you.'

The man's brows knit into an angry scowl. 'You are trying to bewitch me again,' he growled.

'You have bewitched yourself, Ogdli,' she sighed; 'and you have bewitched me. Do not be angry with me. Neither of us could help it.' Her beautiful eyes looked up at him appealingly, seemingly on the verge of tears.

'Do not look at me like that,' he cried, huskily; and then once more she saw the same look in his eyes that she had noticed before they left the village.

She laid a hand upon his bare arm. 'You will ask him?' she whispered. It was more a statement than a question.

He turned away roughly and continued on in silence, but on Jane's lips was a smile of satisfaction. Intuition told her that she had won. But what would she do with her success? Its implications terrified her. Then she gave a mental shrug. By her wits she must turn the circumstance to her advantage without paying the price – she was every inch a woman.

As they passed through the temple corridors and apartments, Jane saw a number of black men – fat, soft, oily looking fellows that reminded her of the guardians of a sultan's harem. They seemed to personify cruelty, greed, and craft. She instinctively shrank from them if they passed close. These, she assumed, were the servants of Kavandavanda. What then was Kavandavanda like?

She was soon to know.

28

Kavandavanda

An idiot jibbered beneath the gloomy shadows of the forbidding forest. A little monkey swung low from a branch; and the idiot leaped for it, shrieking horribly. From high among the foliage of a nearby tree two appraising eyes watched the idiot. What passed in the brain behind those eyes only the creature and its Maker knew.

The idiot suddenly started to run blindly along a trail. He stumbled and fell. It was evident that he was very weak. He scrambled to his feet and staggered on. Through the branches above, the creature followed, watching, always watching.

The trail debouched upon a little clearing, perhaps an acre in extent. A single tree grew alone near the far side. Beneath the tree sprawled three maned lions; young lions, they were, but in the prime of their strength.

As the idiot stumbled into the clearing one of the lions arose and stared at the intruder, more in curiosity than in disapproval. The idiot saw the lions; and with loud screams, hideous screams, he bore down upon them waving his arms wildly above his head.

Now lions are nervous, temperamental creatures. It is difficult to prophesy just what they will do under any given circumstances.

The others had come to their feet with the first scream of the idiot, and now all three stood watching his approach. For just a moment they stood their ground before such an emergency as had never confronted any of them before, nor, doubtless, ever would again. Then the one who had first risen turned and bounded off into the jungle, his two companions close upon his heels.

The idiot sat down suddenly and commenced to cry. 'They all run away from me,' he muttered. 'They know I am a murderer, and they are afraid of me – *afraid of me! afraid of me!* AFRAID OF ME!' His shrieking voice rose to a final piercing crescendo.

The stalker among the trees dropped to the floor of the clearing and approached the idiot. He came upon him from behind. He was Ydeni, the Kavuru. Stealthily he crept forward. In his hand was a coiled rope.

Ydeni leaped upon the idiot and bore him to the ground. The idiot screamed and struggled, but to no avail. The mighty muscles of the Kavuru held him and deftly bound his wrists together behind his back.

Then Ydeni lifted the man and set him upon his feet. The idiot looked at his captor with wide eyes from which terror quickly faded to be replaced by a vacuous grin.

'I have a friend,' he mumbled. 'At last I have a friend, and I shall not be alone. What is your name, friend? I am Prince Sborov. Do you understand? I am a prince.'

Ydeni did not understand, and if he had he would not have cared. He had been scouting for more girls and he had found an idiot. He knew that Kavandavanda would be pleased; for, while there were never too many girls, there were even fewer idiots; and Kavandavanda liked idiots.

Ydeni examined his captive. He discovered that he was weak and emaciated and that he was unarmed.

Satisfied that the man was harmless, the Kavuru released his wrists; then he fastened the rope securely about Sborov's neck and led him off into the jungle along a secret, hidden path that was a short cut to the village.

His mind broken by terror and privation, the European babbled incessantly as he staggered along behind his captor. Often he stumbled and fell; and always Ydeni had to lift him to his feet, for he was too weak to rise without assistance.

At last the Kavuru found food and halted while Sborov ate; and when they started on again Ydeni assisted him, carrying him much of the way until at last they came to the village of the Kavuru beside the lone mountain in the wilderness.

And in the meantime, Tarzan led Brown and Tibbs along the main trail, a much longer route to the same village; for none of them knew where it was located, and at best could only harbor the hope that this trail led to it.

Sometimes Nkima rode upon Tarzan's shoulder; or, again, swung through the trees above the three men. He, at least, was carefree and happy; Tarzan was concerned over the fate of his mate, Brown was worried about Annette, and Tibbs was always sad on general principles when he was away from London. Being hungry and footsore and weary and terrified by the jungle and its savage life in no way lessened the pall of gloom that enveloped him.

They were not a happy company, but none could tell from Tarzan's manner or expression or any word that fell from his lips the bitterness of the sorrow that he held within his breast. He did not know what fate was reserved for the girl captives of the Kavuru, but his knowledge of the more savage tribes of these remote fastnesses offered but faint hope that he might be in time to rescue her. To avenge her was the best that he could anticipate.

And while his thoughts dwelt upon her, recalling each least detail of their companionship, Jane was being led into a large, central room in the temple of Kavandavanda, King, witch-doctor, and god of the Kavuru.

It was a large, low room, its ceiling supported by columns consisting of the trunks of trees, the surfaces of which, stripped of bark and darkened by antiquity, bore a high polish. Toothless skulls hung in clusters from the capitals of the columns, white against the darkened surfaces of the ceiling and the columns, grinning, leering upon the scene below, watching the silly antics of mortal men through the wisdom of eternity out of sightless eyes.

The gloom of the remoter purlieus of the large chamber was only partially relieved by the sunlight shining through a single opening in the ceiling and flooding a figure seated upon a great throne on a dais carpeted with the skins of leopards.

As her eyes rested for the first time upon the enthroned man, Jane was plainly aware of a mental gasp of astonishment. The picture was striking, barbaric; the man was beautiful.

If this were Kavandavanda, how utterly different was he from any of the various pictures of him her imagination had conceived; and it was Kavandavanda, she knew; it would be none other. Every indolent, contemptuous line of his pose bespoke the autocrat. Here indeed was a King – nay, something more, even, than a King. Jane could not rid herself of the thought that she was looking upon a god.

He sat alone upon the dais except for two leopards, one chained on either side of his great throne chair. Below him, surrounding the dais, were Kavuru warriors; and close at hand the soft, fat slaves such as Jane had seen elsewhere in the temple. Upon the floor, on each side of the dais, a dozen girls reclined upon leopard skins. They were mostly black girls, but there were a number with the lighter skins and the features of the Bedouins.

One of the Bedouin girls and a couple of the blacks were reasonably comely of face and figure, but on the whole they did not appear to have been selected with an eye to pulchritude.

Ogdli led his two charges to within a few yards of the dais; then, as he knelt himself, gruffly ordered them to kneel. Annette did as she was bid; but Jane remained erect, her eyes fearlessly appraising the man upon the throne.

He was a young man, almost naked but for an elaborate loincloth and ornaments. Many rows of human teeth suspended about his neck, covered his chest and fell as low as his loincloth. Armlets, bracelets, and anklets of metal, of wood, and of ivory, completed his barbaric costume. But it was not these things that riveted the girl's attention, but rather the divine face and form of the youth.

At first Jane felt that she had never looked upon a more beautiful countenance. An oval face was surmounted by a wealth of golden hair; below a high, full forehead shone luminous dark eyes that glowed with the fires of keen intelligence. A perfect nose and a short upper lip completed the picture of divine beauty that was marred and warped and ruined by a weak, cruel mouth.

Until she noticed that mouth, hope had leaped high in Jane's breast that here she and Annette might find a benevolent protector rather than the cruel savage they had expected Kavandavanda to be.

The man's eyes were fixed upon her in a steady stare. He, too, was appraising; but what his reaction, his expression did not reveal.

'Kneel!' he commanded suddenly, in imperious tones.

'Why should I kneel?' demanded Jane. 'Why should I kneel to you?'

'I am Kavandavanda.'

'That is no reason why an English woman should kneel to you.'

Two of the fat, black slaves started toward her, looking questioningly at Kavandavanda.

'You refuse to kneel?' asked the youth.

'Most certainly.'

The slaves were still advancing toward her, but they kept one eye on

Kavandavanda. He waved them back. A strange expression twisted his lips. Whether it was from amusement or anger, Jane could not guess.

'It pleases me to discuss the matter,' said the youth; then he commanded Ogdli and Annette to rise. 'You brought in both of these prizes, Ogdli?' he asked.

'No,' replied Ogdli. 'Ydeni brought this one.' He gestured toward Annette. 'I brought the other.'

'You did well. We have never had one like her – she contains the seeds of beauty as well as youth.' Then he turned his eyes upon Jane once more. 'Who are you?' he demanded, 'And what were you doing in the country of the Kavuru?'

'I am Jane Clayton, Lady Greystoke. I was flying from London to Nairobi when our ship was forced down. My companions and I were trying to make our way to the coast when this girl and myself were captured by your warriors. I ask that you release us and give us guides to the nearest friendly village.'

A crooked smile twisted the lips of Kavandavanda. 'So you came in one of those devil birds,' he said. 'Two others came yesterday. Their dead bodies lie beside their devil bird outside the city gates. My people are afraid of the devil bird; they will not go near it. Tell me, will it harm them?'

The girl thought quickly before she replied. Perhaps she might turn their superstitious fear to her advantage. 'They had better keep away from it,' she advised. 'More devil birds will come, and if they find that you have harmed me or my companion they will destroy your village and your people. Send us away in safety, and I will tell them not to bother you.'

'They will not know that you are here,' replied the youth. 'No one knows what happens in the village of the Kavuru or the temple of Kavandavanda.'

'You will not set us free?'

'No. No stranger who enters the gates of the village ever passes out again – and you, least of all, I have had many girls brought to me, but none like you.'

'You have plenty of girls here. What do you want of me?'

His eyes half closed as he regarded her. 'I do not know,' he said in a voice scarce raised above a whisper. 'I thought that I knew, but now I am not sure.' Suddenly he turned his eyes upon Ogdli. 'Take them to the room of the three snakes,' he commanded, 'and guard them there. They cannot escape, but see that they do not try. I don't want anything to happen to this one. Medek will show you the way,' he nodded toward one of the fat blacks standing near the dais.

'What was all the talk about, madame?' asked Annette, as they were being led through the temple by Medek.

Jane told her, briefly.

'The room of the three snakes!' repeated Annette. 'Do you suppose there are snakes in the room?' She shuddered. 'I am afraid of snakes.'

'Look above the doors of the rooms we pass,' suggested Jane. 'I think you will find the answer to your question there. There is a doorway with a boar's head above it. We just passed one with two human skulls over the lintel; and there, on the other side of the corridor, ahead, is one with three leopards' heads. It is evidently their way of designating rooms, just as we number them in our hotels. I imagine it has no other significance.'

Medek led them up a flight of rude stairs and along a corridor on the second floor of the temple and ushered them into a room above the doorway of which were mounted the heads of three snakes. Ogdli entered the room with them. It was a low ceiled room with windows overlooking the courtyard that surrounded the temple.

Annette looked quickly around the apartment. 'I don't see any snakes, madame,' she said, with evident relief.

'Nor much of anything else, Annette. The Kavuru don't waste much thought on furniture.'

'There are two benches, madame, but no table and not a bed.'

'There's the bed over in the corner,' said Jane.

'That's just a pile of filthy skins,' objected the French girl.

'Nevertheless, it's all the bed we'll get, Annette.'

'What are you talking about?' demanded Ogdli. 'Don't think that you can escape. You haven't a chance; so there's no sense in planning anything of the sort.'

'We weren't,' Jane assured him. 'We can't escape unless you'll help us. I was so glad when Kavandavanda said that you were to guard us. You know, you are the only friend we have, Ogdli.'

'Did you see how Kavandavanda looked at you?' the man demanded, suddenly.

'Why no, not particularly,' replied Jane.

'Well, I did; and I've never seen him look that way at a captive before. Neither did I ever know him to permit a person to stand before him without first kneeling. I believe that you have bewitched him, too. Did you like him, woman?'

'Not as well as I like you, Ogdli,' whispered the girl.

'He can't do it!' exclaimed the man. 'He's got to obey the law the same as the rest of us.'

'Do what?' demanded Jane.

'If he tries it, I'll—' A noise in the corridor silenced him, and just in time. The door was swung open by a slave, and as he stood aside the figure of Kavandavanda was revealed behind him.

As he entered the room Ogdli dropped to his knees. Annette followed his example, but Jane remained erect.

'So you won't kneel, eh?' demanded Kavandavanda. 'Well, perhaps that is the reason I like you – one of the reasons. You two may arise. Get out into the corridor, all of you except this one who calls herself Jane. I wish to speak with her alone.'

Ogdli looked Kavandavanda straight in the eyes. 'Yes,' he said; 'yes, high priest of the priests of Kavuru, I go; but I shall be near.'

Kavandavanda flushed momentarily in what seemed anger, but he said nothing as the others passed out into the corridor. When they had gone and the door had been closed, he turned to Jane. 'Sit down,' he said, motioning toward one of the benches; and when she had, he came and sat beside her. For a long time he looked at her before he spoke, his eyes the eyes of a dreamer of dreams. 'You are very beautiful,' he said, at last. 'I have never seen a creature more beautiful. It seems a pity, then; it seems a pity.'

'What seems a pity?' demanded the girl.

'Never mind,' he snapped, brusquely. 'I must have been thinking aloud.' Again, for a space, he was silent, sunk in thought; and then: 'What difference will it make. I may as well tell you. It is seldom that I have an opportunity to talk with anyone intelligent enough to understand; and you will understand – you will appreciate the great service you are to render – if I am strong. But when I look at you, when I look deep into those lovely eyes, I feel weak. No, no! I must not fail; I must not fail the world that is waiting for me.'

'I do not understand what you are talking about,' said the girl.

'No, not now; but you will. Look at me closely. How old do you think I am?'

'In your twenties, perhaps.'

He leaned closer. 'I do not know how old I am. I have lost all track. Perhaps a thousand years; perhaps a few hundred; perhaps much older. Do you believe in God?'

'Yes, most assuredly.'

'Well, don't. There is no such thing – not yet, at least. That has been the trouble with the world. Men have imagined a god instead of seeking god among themselves. They have been led astray by false prophets and charlatans. They have had no leader. God should be a leader, and a leader should be a tangible entity – something men can see and feel and touch. He must be mortal and yet immortal. He may not die. He must be omniscient. All the forces of nature have been seeking throughout all the ages to produce such a god that the world may be ruled justly and mercifully forever, a god who shall control the forces of nature as well as the minds and acts of men.

'Almost such am I, Kavandavanda, high priest of the priests of Kavuru. Already am I deathless; already am I omniscient; already, to some extent, can I direct the minds and acts of men. It is the forces of nature that yet defy me. When I have conquered these, I shall indeed be God.'

'Yes,' agreed Jane, bent upon humoring this madman; 'yes, you shall indeed be God; but remember that mercy is one of the characteristics of godliness. Therefore, be merciful; and set my companion and me free.'

'And have the ignorant barbarians of the outer world swoop down upon us and rob mankind of its sole hope of salvation by destroying me? No!'

'But what purpose can I serve? If you free us, I promise to lead no one here.'

'You can serve the only purpose for which women are fit. Man may only attain godliness alone. Woman weakens and destroys him. Look at me! Look at my priests! You think we are all young men. We are not. A hundred rains have come and gone since the latest neophyte joined our holy order. And how have we attained this deathlessness? Through women. We are all celibates. Our vows of celibacy were sealed in the blood of women; in our own blood will we be punished if we break them. It would be death for a Kavuru priest to succumb to the wiles of a woman.'

Jane shook her head. 'I still do not understand,' she said.

'But you will. Long ago I learned the secret of deathless youth. It lies in an elixir brewed of many things – the pollen of certain plants, the roots of others, the spinal fluid of leopards, and, principally, the glands and blood of women – young women. Now do you understand?'

'Yes.' The girl shuddered.

'Do not recoil from the thought; remember that you will thus become a part of the living god. You will live forever. You will be glorified.'

'But I won't know anything about it; so what good will it do me?'

'I shall know. I shall know that you are a part of me. In that way I shall have you.' He leaned closer to her. 'But I should like to keep you as you are.' His breath was hot upon her cheek. 'And why not? Am I not almost a god? And may not God do as he chooses? Who is there to say him nay?'

He seized her and drew her to him.

29

To What Doom

It was almost dusk when Ydeni led his captive through the village of the Kavuru and to the temple of Kavandavanda. By another trail Tarzan was approaching the clearing before the village. He paused and lifted his head.

'What is it?' asked Brown.

'Is 'is 'ighness coming?' inquired Tibbs.

The ape-man shook his head. 'We are nearing a village. It is the village of the Kavuru; but nearer still are friends – Waziri.'

'How do you know?' demanded Brown.

Tarzan ignored the question, but motioned for silence; then from his lips came softly the call of the quail – three times he voiced it. For a moment, as he stood listening, there was silence; then once, twice, thrice came the answering call.

Tarzan moved forward again followed by his companions, and a moment later Muviro and Balando came running to drop to their knees before him.

Very briefly and in sorrow Muviro told what had happened. Tarzan listened without comment. No emotion of either sorrow or anger was reflected by his expression.

'Then you think it impossible to gain entrance to the village?' he asked.

'We are too few, Bwana,' replied Muviro, sadly.

'But if Buira still lives, she is there,' Tarzan reminded him, 'and your Memsahib and another white girl who belongs to this man.' He gestured toward the American. 'Much that life holds for us three may be behind the gates of that village, and there is the memory of our slain friends. Would you turn back now, Muviro?'

'Muviro follows where Tarzan leads,' replied the black, simply.

'We will go to the edge of the clearing that you speak of, and there we may make our plans. Come.' The ape-man moved silently along the trail, followed by the others.

As they came to the edge of the clearing, he halted. Brown smothered an exclamation of surprise. 'Well! In the name of—Say, do you see what I see? That's a ship.'

'I forgot to tell you,' said Muviro. 'Two men came in a ship and landed. The Kavuru killed them. You can see their bodies lying beside the ship.'

As Tarzan stood at the edge of the forest beyond the village of the Kavuru it was well for his peace of mind that he did not know what was transpiring in the temple of Kavandavanda on the opposite side of the village, for at that very moment the high priest seized Jane and crushed her to him.

Helpless and hopeless, not knowing which way to turn for help, the girl acted upon what appeared an inspiration. Pushing the man's lips from hers, she raised her voice in a single piercing cry: 'Ogdli!'

Instantly the door of the apartment swung open. Kavandavanda released her and sprang to his feet. Ogdli crossed the threshold and halted. The two men stood glaring at one another. Ogdli did not ask why the girl had summoned him. He appeared to know.

Kavandavanda's face and neck burned scarlet for a moment; then went deadly white as he strode past Ogdli and out of the room without a word.

The warrior crossed quickly to the girl. 'He will kill us both, now,' he said. 'We must escape; then you will belong to me.'

'But your vows!' cried Jane, clutching at a straw.

'What are vows to a dead man?' asked Ogdli. 'And I am as good as dead now. I shall go and take you with me. I know a secret passage beneath the courtyard and the village. Thus sometimes goes Kavandavanda to search in the forest for secret flowers and roots. When it is dark, we shall go.'

As Kavandavanda strode through the corridors of his palace, his heart black with rage, he met Ydeni coming with his captive.

'What have you there?' he demanded.

Ydeni dropped to his knees. 'One of those into whose skull a demon has come to dwell. I have brought him to Kavandavanda.'

'Take him away,' growled the high priest, 'and lock him up. I will see him in the morning.'

Ydeni rose and led Sborov on through the temple. He took him to the second floor and shoved him into a dark room. It was the room of the two snakes. Next to it was the room of the three snakes. Then Ydeni shot a bolt on the outside of the door and went away and left his prisoner without food or water.

In the next room Ogdli was planning the escape. He knew he could not carry it out until after the temple slept. 'I will go away now and hide,' he said, 'so that Kavandavanda cannot find me before it is time to go. Later I shall return and get you.'

'You must take Annette, too,' said Jane – 'the other girl. Where is she?'

'In the next room. I put her there when Kavandavanda sent us out of this one.'

'You will take her with us?'

'Perhaps,' he replied; but Jane guessed that he had no intention of doing so.

She very much wished to have Annette along, not alone to give her a chance to escape the clutches of the high priest, but because she felt that two of them together would have a better chance of thwarting the designs of Ogdli once they were in the jungle.

'Do not try to escape while I am gone,' cautioned Ogdli. 'There is only one way besides the secret passage, and that is across the courtyard. To enter the courtyard would mean certain death.' He opened the door and stepped out into the corridor. Jane watched him close the door, and then she heard a bolt moved into place.

In the room of the two snakes Sborov groped around in the darkness. A lesser darkness came from the night outside through the single window overlooking the courtyard. He went to the window and looked out. Then he heard what seemed to be muffled voices coming from an adjoining chamber.

He prowled along the wall until he found a door. He tried it, but it was locked. He continued to fumble with the latch.

In the next room Jane heard him and approached the door after Ogdli left her. The warrior had said that Annette was in the next room; that must be Annette, she thought, trying to return to her.

Jane found that the door was secured by a heavy bolt on her side. She was about to call to Annette when she realized that the girl evidently realized some necessity for silence, else she had called to Jane.

Very cautiously she slipped the bolt a fraction of an inch at a time. Annette was still fumbling with the latch on the opposite side – Jane could hear her.

At last the bolt drew clear and the door swung slowly open. 'Annette!' whispered Jane as a figure, dimly visible in the gloom, came slowly into the room.

'Annette is dead,' said a man's voice. 'Brown killed her. He killed Jane, too. Who are you?'

'Alexis!' cried Jane.

'Who are you?' demanded Sborov.

'I am Jane – Lady Greystoke. Don't you recognize my voice?'

'Yes, but you are dead. Is Kitty with you? My God!' he cried, 'You have brought her back to haunt me. Take her away! Take her away!' His voice rose to a shrill scream.

From the door on the opposite side of the apartment came the sound of running, and then Annette's voice. 'Madame! Madame! What is it? What has happened?'

'Who's that?' demanded Sborov. 'I know – it's Annette. You have all come back to haunt me.'

'Calm yourself, Alexis,' said Jane, soothingly. 'Kitty is not here, and Annette and I are both alive.' As she spoke she crossed the room to the door of the chamber in which the French girl was confined; and, feeling for the bolt, drew it.

'Don't let her in!' screamed Sborov. 'Don't let her in. I'll tear you to pieces if you do, ghost or no ghost.' He started across the room on a run just as the door swung open and Annette rushed in. At the same moment the door leading into the corridor was pushed open; and the black slave, Medek, entered.

'What's going on here?' he demanded. 'Who let that man in here?'

At sight of Annette, Sborov recoiled, screaming. Then he saw Medek in the dim light of the interior. 'Kitty!' he shrieked. 'I won't go with you. Go away!'

Medek started toward him. Sborov turned and fled toward the far end of the room, toward the window looking out upon the courtyard. He paused a moment at the sill and turned wild eyes back toward the shadowy figure pursuing him; then, with a final maniacal scream of terror, he leaped out into the night.

Medek followed him to the window and leaned out; then from his lips broke the same horrid scream that Jane had heard earlier in the day as she was being led from the throne room of Kavandavanda. From below came the moans of Sborov, who must have been badly injured by the fall from the second story window; but presently these were drowned by the snarls and growls of leopards.

The two girls could hear them converging from all parts of the grounds upon the moaning creature lying out there in the night. Presently the sounds of the leopards rose to a hideous din as they fought over the flesh of their prey. For a few moments the screams of their victim mingled with the savage mouthings of the beasts, but soon they ceased.

Medek turned away from the window. 'It is not well to seek escape in that direction,' he said, as he returned to the outer corridor, closing the door behind him.

'How awful, madame,' whimpered Annette.

'Yes,' replied Jane, 'but his sufferings were mercifully brief. Perhaps, after all, it is just as well. His mind is gone. Prince Sborov had become a maniac.'

'What a terrible price he paid. But is it not, perhaps, that he deserved it, madame?'

'Who shall say? But we, too, are paying a terrible price for his greed and his wife's vanity. The thing she sought is here, Annette.'

'What thing, madame? Not the restorer of youth?'

'Yes. Kavandavanda holds the secret, but neither the princess nor any other could have gotten it from him. We should all have met a terrible fate just the same had the entire party succeeded in reaching the village of the Kavuru – the fate that is reserved for you and me.'

'What fate, madame? You frighten me.'

'I do not mean to, but you may as well know the truth. If we do not succeed in escaping we shall be butchered to furnish ingredients for Kavandavanda's devilish potion that keeps the priests of Kavuru always youthful.'

'S-s-sh, madame!' cautioned Annette, fearfully. 'What was that?'

'I don't know. It sounded as though someone in the corridor had tried to scream.'

'Then there was a thud, as though someone had fallen. Did you hear that?'

'Yes – and now someone is trying the door. They are slipping the bolt.'

'Oh, madame! Some new horror.'

The door swung open and a figure stepped into the room. A voice spoke. 'Woman! Are you there?' It was the voice of Ogdli.

'I am here,' said Jane.

'Then come quickly. There is no time to be lost.'

'But how about the slave in the corridor? He will see us go out.'

'The slave is there, but he will not see us. Come!'

'Come, Annette! It is our only chance.'

'The other woman is here?' demanded Ogdli.

'Yes,' replied Jane. 'And if I go, she must go.'

'Very well,' snapped the Kavuru, 'but hurry.'

The two girls followed the man into the corridor. Across the doorway lay the body of Medek. The dead eyes were staring up at them. Ogdli kicked the black face and gave a short laugh. 'He looks, but he does not see.'

The girls shuddered and pressed on behind the warrior. He led them cautiously along dark corridors. At the slightest sound he dragged them into pitch-black rooms along the way until he was sure there was no danger of discovery. Thus, much time was consumed in nerve-wracking suspense.

Ogdli advanced with evident trepidation. It was apparent that now that he had embarked upon this venture he was terrified – the shadow of Kavandavanda's wrath lay heavy upon him.

The night dragged on, spent mostly in hiding, as the trio made their slow way toward the secret entrance to the tunnel that led out into the jungle.

Once more they crept on after a long period of tense waiting and listening in a dark chamber; then Ogdli spoke in a relieved whisper. 'Here we are,' he said. 'Through this doorway. The entrance to the tunnel is in this room. Make no noise.'

He pushed the door open cautiously and entered the chamber, the two girls following closely behind him. Instantly hands reached out of the dark and seized them. Jane heard a scuffling and the sound of running feet; then she was dragged out into the corridor. A light was brought from another apartment – a bit of reed burning in a shallow vessel.

Annette was there, close to her, trembling. They were surrounded by five sturdy warriors. In the light of the sputtering cresset the men looked quickly from one to another.

'Where is Ogdli?' demanded a warrior. Then Jane realized that her would-be abductor had vanished.

'I thought you had him,' replied another. 'I seized one of the girls.'

'I thought I had him,' spoke up a third.

'And so did I,' said a fourth, 'but it was you I had. He must have run for the tunnel. Come, we'll go after him.'

'No,' objected the first warrior. 'It is too late. He has a good start. We could not catch him before he reached the forest.'

'We could not find him there at night,' agreed another. 'It will soon be daylight; then we can go after him.'

'We'll see what Kavandavanda says when we take the women to him,' said the first warrior. 'Bring them along.'

Once again the girls were led through the corridors of the temple, this time to an apartment adjoining the throne room. Two warriors stood before the door. When they saw the girls and were told what had happened, one of them knocked on the door. Presently it was opened by a black slave, sleepily rubbing his eyes.

'Who disturbs Kavandavanda at this hour of the night?' he demanded.

'Tell him we have come with the two white girls. He will understand.'

The black turned back into the apartment, but in a few moments he returned.

'Bring your prisoners in,' he said; 'Kavandavanda will see you.'

They were led through a small antechamber lighted by a crude cresset to a larger apartment similarly illuminated. Here Kavandavanda received them, lying on a bed covered with leopard skins.

His large eyes fixed themselves upon Jane. 'So you thought you could escape?' he asked, a crooked smile twisting his weak lips. 'You were going to run off with Ogdli and be his mate, were you? Where is Ogdli?' he demanded suddenly, as he realized that the man was not with the others.

'He escaped – through the tunnel,' reported a warrior.

'He must have thought Kavandavanda a fool,' sneered the high priest. 'I knew what was in his mind. There are only six men beside myself who know about the tunnel. Ogdli was one of them; the other five are here.' He was addressing Jane. 'I sent these five to wait at the entrance to the tunnel until Ogdli came, for I knew he would come.' He paused and gazed long at Jane; then he turned to the others. 'Take this other one back to the room of the three snakes,' he ordered, 'and see that she does not escape again.' He indicated Annette with a gesture. 'This one I will keep here to question further; there may have been others concerned in the plot. Go!'

Annette cast a despairing look at Jane as she was led from the room, but the other could give her no reassurance nor encouragement. Their position seemed utterly without hope now.

'Goodbye, Annette.' That was all.

'May the good God be with us both, madame,' whispered the French girl as the door was closing behind her.

'So,' said Kavandavanda when the others had left, 'you were going to run off into the jungle with Ogdli and be his mate? He was going to break his vow because of you!'

The shadow of a sneer curled the girl's lip. 'Perhaps Ogdli thought so,' she said.

'But you were going with him,' Kavandavanda insisted.

'As far as the jungle,' replied Jane; 'then I should have found some means to escape him; or, failing that, I should have killed him.'

'Why?' demanded the high priest. 'Have you, too, taken a vow?'

'Yes – a vow of fidelity.'

He leaned toward her eagerly. 'But you could break it – for love; or, if not for love, for a price.'

She shook her head. 'Not for anything.'

'I could break mine. I had thought that I never could, but since I have seen you—' He paused; and then, peremptorily, 'if I, Kavandavanda, am willing to break mine, you can break yours. The price you will receive is one for which any woman might be willing to sell her soul – eternal youth, eternal beauty.' Again he paused as though to permit the magnitude of his offer to impress itself upon her.

But again she shook her head. 'No, it is out of the question.'

'You spurn Kavandavanda?' His cruel mouth imparted some of its cruelty to his eyes. 'Remember that I have the power to destroy you, or to take you without giving anything in return; but I am generous. And do you know why?'

'I cannot imagine.'

'Because I love you. I have never known love before. No living creature has ever affected me as do you. I will keep you here forever; I will make you high priestess; I will keep you young through the ages; I will keep you beautiful. You and I will live forever. We will reach out With my power to rejuvenate mankind, we shall have the world at our feet. We shall be deities – I, a god; you, a goddess. Look.' He turned to a cabinet built into the wall of the apartment. It was grotesquely carved and painted – human figures, mostly of women; grinning skulls, leopards, snakes, and weird symbolic designs composed the decorations. From his loincloth he took a great key, hand wrought, and unlocked the cabinet.

'Look,' he said again. 'Come here and look.'

Jane crossed the room and stood beside him at the cabinet. Within it were a number of boxes and jars. One large box, carved and painted similarly to the outside of the cabinet, Kavandavanda took in his hands.

'You see this?' he asked. 'Look inside.' He raised the lid revealing a quantity of black pellets about the size of peas. 'Do you know what these are?' he demanded.

'I have no idea.'

'These will give eternal youth and beauty to a thousand people. You are free to use them if you say the word. One taken each time that the moon comes full will give you what all mankind has craved since man first trod this earth.' He seized her arm and tried to draw her to him.

With an exclamation of repugnance she sought to pull away, but he held her firmly; then she struck him heavily across the face. Surprised, he relaxed his grasp; and the girl tore herself away and ran from the room. Into the antechamber she ran, seeking to gain the corridor.

With a cry of rage, Kavandavanda pursued her; and just at the doorway leading into the corridor he overtook her. He seized her roughly, tangling his fingers in her hair; and though she fought to extricate herself, he dragged her slowly back toward the inner apartment.

30

'The Dead Men Fly!'

Tarzan and Brown had talked late into the night in an attempt to formulate a feasible plan whereby they might gain entrance to the village of the Kavuru, with the result that the ape-man had finally suggested a mad scheme as the only possible solution of their problem.

Brown shrugged and grinned. 'We could sure get in that way, of course, though it all depends. But how we goin' to get out again?'

'Our problem now,' replied Tarzan, 'is to get in. We shall not have the problem of getting out until later. Perhaps we shall not come out. It really is not necessary that you come in with me if—'

'Skip it,' interrupted Brown. 'Annette's in there. That's enough for me to know. When do we start?'

'We can't do much until just before dawn. You need rest. Lie down. I'll wake you in time.'

Tarzan slept, too – a little way from the others on the edge of the clearing where he had a view of the village. He slept in a low crotch a few feet above the ground; and he slept well, yet he slept lightly, as was his wont. The habitual noises of the jungle did not disturb him; but as the time approached when he must awaken Brown, he himself came suddenly awake, conscious of something unusual that disturbed the monotonous harmony of the forest.

Alert and watchful, he rose silently to his feet, listening. Every faculty, crystal sharp, was attuned to the faint note of discord that had aroused him. What was it?

Swiftly he moved through the trees, for now his sensitive nose had identified the author of the stealthy sound that his ears had detected – a Kavuru.

Presently the ape-man saw the dim figure of a man walking through the forest. He was walking rapidly, almost at a trot; and he was breathing heavily, as one who had been running. Tarzan paused above him for an instant and then dropped upon his shoulders, bearing him to the ground.

The man was powerful; and he fought viciously to escape, but he was wax in the hands of the Lord of the Jungle. The ape-man could have killed him;

but the instant that he had realized that a Kavuru might fall into his hands, he had planned upon taking him alive, feeling that he might turn him to some good account.

Presently he succeeded in binding the fellow's wrists behind him; then he stood him upon his feet. For the first time, his captive looked him in the face. It was still dark, but not so dark that the Kavuru could not recognize the fact that his captor was not one of his own kind. He breathed a sigh of relief.

'Who are you?' he demanded. 'Why did you capture me? You are not going to take me back to Kavandavanda? No, of course not – you are not a Kavuru.'

Tarzan did not know why the man should object to being taken to Kavandavanda. He did not even know who Kavandavanda was, nor where; but he saw an opening, and he took advantage of it.

'If you answer my questions,' he said, 'I will not take you back to Kavandavanda, nor will I harm you. Who are you?'

'I am Ogdli.'

'And you just came from the village?'

'Yes.'

'You do not want to go back there?'

'No. Kavandavanda would kill me.'

'Is Kavandavanda such a mighty warrior that you are afraid of him?'

'It is not that, but he is very powerful. He is high priest of the priests of Kavuru.'

By simple questions Tarzan had learned from the answers Ogdli made enough to give him the lead that he desired to glean further information from his prisoner.

'What did Kavandavanda want of the two white girls that were taken to him?' he demanded.

'At first he would have killed them,' replied Ogdli, willingly, for now he thought that he saw an opportunity to win mercy from this strange giant who was evidently interested in the two girls; 'but,' he continued, 'he suddenly came to desire one of them for a mate. I tried to befriend them. I was leading them out of the village by a secret passage when we were set upon by several warriors. They recaptured the girls, and I barely escaped with my life.'

'So the girls are still alive?'

'Yes; they were a few minutes ago.'

'Are they in any immediate danger?'

'No one can say what Kavandavanda will do. I think they are in no immediate danger, for I am sure that Kavandavanda will take one of them for a mate. Perhaps he already has.'

'Where is this secret passage? Lead me to it. Wait until I get my friends.' He led Ogdli to where the others slept, and aroused them.

'I can show you where the passage is,' explained Ogdli, 'but you cannot enter the temple through it. The doors at either end open only in one direction, toward the forest, for those who do not know their secret; and only Kavandavanda knows that. One may easily pass out of the temple, but it is impossible to return.'

Tarzan questioned Ogdli for several minutes; then he turned to Brown. 'Annette and Lady Greystoke are in the temple,' he explained. 'The temple is in a small canyon behind the village. If we gained access to the village we would still have a battle on our hands to reach the temple. This fellow has told me where I can expect to find the prisoners in the temple; he has also given me other valuable information that may be useful if we succeed in getting to Lady Greystoke and Annette. I believe that he has spoken the truth. He says, further, that one of the women is in grave danger at the moment – I think it is Lady Greystoke, from his description; so there is no time to be lost.' Then he turned to Muviro. 'Hold this man until Brown and I return. If we do not return before dark, you may know that we have failed; then you should return to your own country. Do, then, what you will with this prisoner. Give Brown and me the weapons that you took from the bodies of the fliers. They are of no more use to you, as you have exhausted the ammunition. Brown thinks we may find more in the ship. Come, Brown.'

The two men moved silently out into the clearing, the ape-man in the lead. He bent his steps toward the ship, Brown treading close upon his heels. Neither spoke; their plans had been too well formulated to require speech.

When they came to the ship, Brown immediately crawled into the forward cockpit. He was there for several minutes; then he entered the rear cockpit. While he was thus engaged, Tarzan was busy over the bodies of the slain aviators.

When Brown had completed his examination of the interior of the cockpits, he descended to the ground and opened the baggage compartment; then he joined the ape-man.

'Plenty of ammunition,' he said, and handed Tarzan a full box of cartridges. 'That's about all you can manage – you ain't got no pockets. I've stuffed my pockets full – must weigh a ton.'

'How about petrol?' asked Tarzan.

'Not much more'n a hatful,' replied the American.

'Will it do?'

'Yep, if it don't take too long to get warmed up. Got the chutes?'

Tarzan handed Brown a parachute that he had taken from the body of one of the fliers; the other he adjusted to his own body. They spoke no more. Tarzan climbed into the forward cockpit, Brown into the other.

'Here's hoping,' prayed Brown under his breath as he opened the valve of the air starter. The answering whir of the propeller brought a satisfied smile to his lips; then the ignition caught and the engine roared.

They had waited for dawn, and dawn was breaking as Brown taxied across the rough plain downwind for the take-off. He picked his way among boulders, choosing the best lane that he could find; but he saw that it was going to be a hazardous undertaking at best.

When he reached the limit of the best going, he brought the nose of the ship around into the wind, set the brakes, and opened the throttle wide for a moment. The motor was hitting beautifully.

'Sweet,' muttered the American; then he throttled down to idling speed and shouted ahead to Tarzan, 'If you know any prayers, buddy, you'd better say 'em – all of 'em. We're off!'

Tarzan glanced back, his white teeth gleaming in one of his rare smiles. There was a rush of wind as Brown gave the ship full throttle. It was a perilous take-off, swerving to miss boulders as the ship picked up speed. The tail rose. The ship bumped over the rough ground, tipped drunkenly as one wheel struck a small rock. A low boulder loomed suddenly ahead. It would be impossible to swerve enough to miss it without cracking up. Brown pulled the stick back and held his breath. The ship rose a foot or two from the ground. Brown saw that it was not going to clear the boulder. He could see but a single hope, a slim one; but he seized it instantly. He pushed the stick forward, the wheels struck the ground with a jarring bump, the ship bounced into the air as the stick helped to pull her up just enough to clear the boulder.

She had flying speed by now and continued to rise slowly. It had been a close call; and although the morning air was chill, Brown was wet with perspiration as he climbed in a wide spiral above the forest.

The village of the Kavuru lay below snuggled against the foot of the high escarpment that backed it, but it was not the village in which the two men were interested – it was the box canyon behind it where lay the temple of Kavandavanda of which Ogdli had told them.

Higher and higher rose the graceful plane, watched from the edge of the forest by Muviro, Balando, Tibbs, and Ogdli; and now, awakened by the drone of the motor, by Kavuru warriors congregated in the main street of the village.

'The dead men fly!' whispered a warrior in awed tones, for he thought that the ship was being flown by the two who had brought it down and who had fallen before the attack of the villagers.

The thought, once voiced, took root in the minds of the Kavuru and terrified them.

They saw the ship turn and fly toward the village, and their fear mounted.

'They come for vengeance,' said one.

'If we go into our huts they cannot see us,' suggested another.

That was enough. Instantly the street was deserted, as the Kavuru hid from the vengeance of the dead.

Above the lofty escarpment and the towering cliffs Brown guided the ship. Below them lay the little valley and the temple of Kavandavanda, plainly visible in the light of the new day.

The pilot cut his motor and shouted to Tarzan. 'Not a chance to land there,' he said.

Tarzan nodded. 'Get more elevation, and tell me when.'

Brown opened the throttle and commenced to climb in a great circle. He watched the altimeter. Before they had left the ground he had known the direction of the wind and estimated its force. At two thousand feet he levelled off and circled the rim of the canyon to a point above the cliffs on the windward side.

He cut his motor for an instant and shouted to the ape-man. 'Stand by!'

Tarzan slipped the catch of his safety belt. Brown brought the ship into position again. 'Jump!' he shouted as he brought the ship sharply into a momentary stall.

Tarzan swung onto the lower wing and jumped. An instant later Brown followed him.

31

The Wages of Sin

Kavandavanda's soft, youthful appearance belied his strength. Jane was no match for him, and though she fought every foot of the way, fought like a young tigress, he dragged her back into his inner apartment.

'I ought to kill you, you she devil,' he growled, as he threw her roughly upon the couch; 'but I won't I'll keep you; I'll tame you – and I'll start now.' He came toward her, leering.

Just then a pounding sounded on the outer door of the antechamber; and a voice rose in terror, calling 'Kavandavanda! Kavandavanda! Save us! Save us!'

The high priest wheeled angrily. 'Who dares disturb Kavandavanda?' he demanded. 'Get you gone!'

But instead of going, those at the door flung it open and pressed into the antechamber to the very door of the inner room. There were both slaves and warriors in the party. Their very presence there would have told the high priest that something was amiss even without the evidence of their frightened faces.

Now, indeed, was he impressed. 'What brings you here?' he demanded.

'The dead men fly; they fly above the village and the temple. They have come seeking vengeance.'

'You talk like fools and cowards,' grumbled Kavandavanda. 'Dead men do not fly.'

'But they do fly,' insisted a warrior. 'The two that we killed yesterday are flying again this instant above the village and the temple. Come out, Kavandavanda, and cast a spell upon them, sending them away.'

'I will go and look,' said the high priest. 'Ydeni, bring this girl along. If I leave her out of my sight, she will find some means to escape.'

'She shall not escape me,' said Ydeni; and, seizing Jane by the wrist, he dragged her after the high priest, the warriors, and the slaves into the courtyard of the temple.

The moment that they emerged from the building Jane heard plainly the drone of a ship's motor far above them. Looking up, she saw a biplane circling the canyon.

With fascinated eyes the Kavuru were watching it – with fascinated, frightened eyes. Jane, too, was fascinated. She thought that the ship was searching for a landing place; and she prayed that the pilot might not attempt a landing here, for she knew that whoever was in the ship would meet instant death at the hands of the savage Kavuru.

Then she saw a figure leap from the plane. A gasp of terror rose from the Kavuru. The first figure was followed by a second.

'They come!' cried a warrior. 'Save us, Kavandavanda, from the vengeance of the dead.'

The billowing white chutes opened above the falling figures, checking their speed.

'They have spread their wings,' shrieked a slave. 'Like the vulture, they will swoop down upon us.'

Jane's eyes followed the ship. As the second man jumped, it nosed down, then levelled off by itself, shot across the little canyon, came around in a steep bank, and went into a tail spin almost directly above them.

Brown had opened the throttle wide at the instant that he jumped, for he and Tarzan had planned this very thing, hoping that the ship would crash near enough to the temple to cause a diversion that would enable them to reach the ground before warriors could gather below to receive them on the tips of sharp spears. But they had not anticipated the reality, the fear that gripped the Kavuru at sight of them and the ship.

As they floated gently toward earth, a light wind carried them in the direction of the temple. They saw the crowd gathered in the courtyard looking up at them. They saw the ship diving with wide open throttle at terrific speed. They saw the crowd melt and vanish into the interior of the temple an instant before the plane crashed in the courtyard and burst into flame.

Tarzan touched the ground first and had thrown off the parachute harness by the time Brown was down. A moment later the two men started for the temple at a run.

There was no one to block their way. Even the guards at the outer gate had fled in terror. As they entered the courtyard, a few frightened leopards raced past them. The plane was burning fiercely against the temple wall a hundred feet away.

Tarzan, followed closely by Brown, ran for the main entrance to the building. Even here there was none to dispute their right to enter the sacred precincts.

At a distance they heard the sound of a babel of voices; and, guided by his keen ears, the ape-man hastened along corridors in the direction of these sounds.

In the great throne room of Kavandavanda all the warriors and slaves of the temple were gathered. The high priest, trembling on his throne, was a picture of terror. The girls of the temple, those poor creatures who were awaiting death to give eternal life and youth to the Kavuru, were crouched at one side of the dais, wide-eyed and terrified.

A warrior pushed forward toward the throne. An angry scowl darkened his painted face, made doubly hideous by the ivory skewer that passed through the septum of his nose. Many human teeth lay upon his breast, marks of his prowess as a hunter of girls. He pointed a finger at Kavandavanda.

'Your sins are being visited upon us,' he bellowed. 'You would have broken your vow. We who prevented Ogdli from taking the white girl last night know this. She bewitched him. She bewitched you. It is she who has brought the dead men upon us. Destroy her. Destroy her now with your own hands that we may be saved.'

'Kill her! Kill her!' shrieked a hundred hoarse voices.

'Kill her! Kill her!' shrilled the fat, oily black slaves in their high falsettos.

A couple of warriors seized Jane where she stood among the cowering girls and dragged her to the dais. They raised her roughly and threw her upon it.

Still trembling, Kavandavanda seized her by the hair and dragged her to her knees. From his loincloth he drew a long, crude dagger. As he raised it above the heart of the girl a pistol barked from the doorway of the throne room; and Kavandavanda, high priest of the Kavuru, seized his chest and, with a piercing scream, collapsed beside the girl he would have killed.

Jane's eyes shot toward the doorway. 'Tarzan!' she cried. 'Tarzan of the Apes.'

A hundred pairs of other eyes saw him, too – saw him and Brown advancing fearlessly into the room. A warrior raised his spear against them; and this time Brown's gun spoke, and the fellow dropped in his tracks.

Then Tarzan spoke, spoke to them in their own tongue. 'We have come for our women,' he said. 'Let them come away with us in peace, or many will die. You saw how we came. You know we are not as other men. Do not make us angry.'

As he spoke, he continued to advance. The Kavuru, hesitating to attack, fearful of these strange creatures that flew down from the sky, that had been dead and were alive again, fell back.

Suddenly Brown saw Annette among the other girls beside the dais. He leaped forward, and the warriors fell aside and let him pass. A great emotion choked the words from his throat as he took the girl in his arms.

The ape-man leaped to the side of his mate. 'Come,' he said. 'We must get out of here before they have time to gather their wits.' Then he turned to the girls huddled below. 'Is Buira, the daughter of Muviro, here?' he asked.

A young black girl ran forward. 'The Big Bwana!' she cried. 'At last I am saved.'

'Come quickly,' commanded the ape-man, 'and bring any of the other girls with you who wish to escape.'

There was not one who did not wish to leave, and Tarzan and Brown herded them from the throne room and toward the temple entrance; but they had not gone far when they were met by rolling clouds of smoke and heard the crackling of flames ahead.

'The temple is afire!' cried Annette.

'I guess we're in for it,' growled Brown. 'It caught from the ship. Looks like we're trapped. Does anyone else know a way out?'

'Yes,' said Jane. 'There is a secret passage leading from the temple to the forest. I know where the entrance is. Come this way.' She turned back and they retraced their steps toward the throne room.

Soon they commenced to meet warriors and slaves. These slunk away into side corridors and apartments. Presently they reached the apartments of Kavandavanda. Jane was struck by a sudden thought.

She turned to Brown. 'We all risked our lives,' she said, 'and two of us died in a mad search for the secret of eternal youth. It is in this room. Do you care to take the few seconds it will require to get it?'

'Do I?' exclaimed Brown. 'And how! Lead me to it.'

In the inner room of the high priest's apartments, Jane pointed out the cabinet. 'There is a box in there that contains what you wish, but the key is on the body of Kavandavanda,' she explained.

'I got a key right here,' said Brown; and, drawing his pistol, he fired a shot into the lock that shattered it; then he opened the cabinet.

'There,' said Jane, pointing out the box that contained the pellets.

Brown seized it, and they continued on in search of the tunnel's entrance. But presently Jane paused, hesitant. 'I am afraid we have come too far,' she said. 'I thought I knew just where the tunnel was, but now I am all confused.'

'We must find some way out of the temple,' said Tarzan. 'The fire is spreading rapidly, following closely behind us.'

Smoke was already rolling down upon them in stifling volume. They could hear the ominous roaring of the flames, the crash of falling timbers as portions of the roof fell in, the shouts and screams of the inmates of the temple.

A warrior, choking and half blinded, stumbled into view from the dense smoke that filled the corridor along which they had come. Before the man could gather his faculties, Tarzan seized him.

'Lead us out of here,' he commanded. 'That is the price of your life.'

When the fellow was able to open his eyes he looked at his captor. 'Tarzan of the Apes!' he exclaimed.

'Ydeni,' said the ape-man. 'I did not recognize you at first.'

'And you wish me to lead you out of the temple? You who have slain Kavandavanda, our high priest?'

'Yes,' replied Tarzan.

'If I show you the way through the village you will all be killed. The warriors of Kavuru are recovering from their first fright. They will never let you pass. I could lead you that way and let you be killed; but once you saved my life. Now, I shall give you yours. Follow me.'

He led the party a short distance down a side corridor and turned into a gloomy apartment. Crossing it, he pushed open a door beyond which was utter darkness.

'This tunnel leads out into the forest,' he said. 'Go your way, Tarzan of the Apes, nor return again to the village of the Kavuru.'

Three weeks later a party of six was gathered before a roaring fire in the living room of Tarzan's bungalow far from the savage village of the Kavuru. The Lord of the Jungle was there, and his mate; Brown and Annette sat upon a lion's skin before the hearth, holding hands; Tibbs sat decorously on the edge of a chair in the background. He had not yet become accustomed to sitting on terms of equality with titled personages. Little Nkima, with far greater poise, perched upon the shoulder of a viscount.

'What are we goin' to do with this box of pills?' demanded Brown.

'Whatever you wish,' said Jane. 'You were willing to risk your life to get them. If I recall correctly, I think you said something to the effect that if you had them back in civilization they would make you "lousy" with money. Keep them.'

'No,' replied the American. 'We all risked our lives, and anyway you were the one that really got them. The more I think of it, the less I like my scheme. Most everybody lives too long anyway for the good of the world – most of 'em ought to have died young. Suppose Congress got hold of 'em? – just think of that! Not on your life.

'I'll tell you what we'll do. We'll divide them. There will be five of us that will live forever.'

'And be beautiful always,' added Annette.

'If you will pardon my saying so, Miss,' observed Tibbs with an apologetic cough, 'I should rawther dislike thinking of pressing trousers for so many years; and as for being beautiful – my word! I'd never get a job. Who ever heard of a beautiful valet?'

'Well, we'll divide 'em anyway,' insisted Brown. 'You don't have to take 'em, but be sure you don't sell none of 'em to no cab driver princes. Here, I'll divide 'em into five equal parts.'

'Aren't you forgetting Nkima?' asked Jane, smiling. 'That's right,' said Brown. 'We'll make it six parts. He's sure a lot more use in the world than most people.'

TARZAN THE MAGNIFICENT

Characters and Places

NEUBARI RIVER.
MAFA – an affluent of the Neubari.
THE KAJI – a tribe of warrior women.
LORD AND LADY MOUNTFORD – lost in Africa twenty years ago.
STANLEY WOOD – an American travel writer.
ROBERT VAN EYK – Wood's friend and companion.
SPIKE AND TROLL – white hunters attached to Wood – van Eyk safari.
MAFKA – magician of the Kaji.
CONFALA – Queen of the Kaji.
GONFAL – the great diamond of the Kaji.
ZULI – a tribe of warrior women; enemies of the Kaji.
LORD – an Englishman; captive of the Zuli.
WOORA – magician of the Zuli.
LORRO – Zuli warrior-woman.
THE GREAT EMERALD OF THE ZULI.
KAMUDI – a black man.
MUVIRO – Chief of the Waziri.
BANTANGO – a cannibal tribe.
WARANJI – A Waziri warrior.
TOMOS – Prime Minister of Cathne, City of Gold.
ALEXTAR – King of Cathne.
VALTHOR – Athnean noble.
PHOROS – Dictator of Athne, City of Ivory.
ZYGO – King of Athne.
MENOFRA – wife of Phoros.
DYAUS – Athnean elephant-god.
DAIMON – a demon.
KANDOS – righthand man of Phoros.
GEMBA – a black slave.
HYANK – warrior killed in arena by Tarzan.

I

Out of The Past

Truth is stranger than fiction.

If this tale should seem in part incredible, please bear this axiom in mind. It had its beginning more than twenty years ago, unless one wishes to go further back to the first amœba or even beyond that to the cosmos shattering clash of two forgotten suns; but we shall confine our story, other than by occasional reference, to the stage, the actors, and the business of the present time.

The searing sun rays scorch down upon a shrivelled plain a scant five degrees North of the equator. A man, clothed in torn shirt and trousers upon which dried blood has caked and turned a rusty brown, staggers and falls to lie inert.

A great lion looks down upon the scene from the summit of a distant rocky ledge where a few tenacious bushes cling to give shade to the lair of the King; for this is Africa.

Ska, the vulture, wheels and circles in the blue, sky-writing anticipation far above the body of the fallen man.

Not far to the South, at the edge of the dry plain, another man swings easily toward the North. No sign of fatigue or exhaustion here. The bronze skin glows with health, full muscles glide beneath it. The free gait, the noiseless tread might be those of Sheeta, the panther; but there is no slinking here. It is the carriage of one who knows neither doubt nor fear, of a Lord in his own domain.

He is encumbered by but a single garment, a loincloth of doe-skin. A coil of grass rope is looped over one shoulder, behind the other hangs a quiver of arrows; a scabbarded knife swings at his hip; a bow and a short spear complete his equipment. A shock of black hair falls in disorder above serene, grey eyes, eyes that can reflect the light of a summer sea or the flashing steel of a rapier.

The Lord of the Jungle is abroad.

He is far to the North of his ancient haunts, yet this is no unfamiliar terrain. He has been here many times before. He knows where water may be had for the digging. He knows where the nearest water hole lies, where he can make a kill and fill his belly.

He has come North at the behest of an emperor to investigate a rumour

that a European power is attempting to cause the defection of a native chief
by means of bribery. War and rumours of war are in the air, but of this tale
such things are not a part – we hope. However, we are no prophet. We are
merely a chronicler of events as they transpire. We follow the activities of our
characters to the bitter end, even to war; but we hope for the best. However,
only time can tell.

As Tarzan swung with easy strides out across the plain, no sound escaped
his keen ears; no moving thing, his eyes; no scent, borne upon the soft bosom
of Usha the wind, went unidentified. Far in the distance he saw Numa the
lion standing upon his rocky ledge; he saw Ska the vulture circling above
something that Tarzan could not see. In all that he saw or heard or smelled
he read a story; for to him this savage world was an open book, sometimes a
thrilling, always an interesting narrative of love, of hate, of life, of death.

Where you or I might occasionally pick out a letter or a word, Tarzan of
the Apes grasped the entire text and countless implications that we might
never guess.

Presently, ahead of him, he saw something white shining in the sunlight –
a human skull; and as he came closer his eyes picked out the skeleton of a
man, the bones only slightly disarranged. From among them grew a low desert shrub proclaiming that the skeleton had lain there for a long time.

Tarzan paused to investigate, for to him in his world nothing is too trivial
to pass by without question. He saw that the skeleton was that of a Negro and
that it had lain there for a long time, years probably; which was entirely possible in this hot, dry plain. He could not tell how the man had come to his
death, but he guessed that it might have been from thirst.

Then he saw something lying by the bones of a hand, something half buried by shifting soil; and he stopped and picked it up, drawing it carefully out
of the earth. It was a split stick of hardwood in the split end of which was
wedged a thin parcel of oiled silk.

The silk was stained and brittle and dry. It seemed that it might crumble to
his touch, but that was only the outer layer. As he carefully unwrapped it, he
found the inner layers better preserved. Inside the silk wrapper he found
what he had expected – a letter.

It was written in English in a small, extremely legible hand. Tarzan read it
with interest, interest that was perhaps stimulated by the date at the top of
the sheet. Twenty years had elapsed since that letter had been written. For
twenty years it had lain here beside the skeleton of its bearer in mute testimony to the loneliness of this barren plain.

Tarzan read it:

*To Whom This May Come: I am dispatching this without much hope that it
will even get out of this damnable country, still less that it will reach any white*

man; but if it does, please contact the nearest Resident Commissioner or any other authority that can get help to us quickly.

My wife and I were exploring North of Lake Rudolph. We came too far. It was the old story. Our boys became frightened by rumours of a fierce tribe inhabiting the country in which we were. They deserted us.

Where the Mafa River empties into the Neubari we turned up the gorge of the former as though drawn by some supernatural power, and were captured by the wild women of Kaji, when we reached the plateau. A year later our daughter was born and my wife died – the she-devils of Kaji killed her because she did not bear a son. They want white men. That is why they have not killed me and a dozen other white men captives.

The Kaji country lies on a high plateau above the falls of the Mafa. It is almost inaccessible, but can be reached by following the gorge of the Mafa from the Neubari.

It will require a strong expedition of white men to rescue me and my little daughter, as I doubt that blacks can be induced to enter the country. These Kaji women fight like devils, and they have strange, occult powers of some nature. I have seen things here that – well, things that just can't be but are.

No native tribes will live near this mysterious, ill-omened country; so, little is known of the Kaji; but rumours of their terrifying practices have become part of the folklore of their nearest neighbours, and it is the hushed recital of these that frightens the bearers of any safari that comes within the sphere of their baneful influence.

The white men may never know the cause of it, for the blacks fear to tell them, thinking that the black magic of the Kaji will reach out and destroy them; but the result is always the same – if the safari approaches too close to Kaji, the blacks all desert.

Then that happens which happened to my wife and me – the whites are lured by some mysterious means to the plateau and made prisoners.

Perhaps even a large force might be overcome, for the whites would not be contending against natural forces; but if they succeeded, the reward might be very great. It is the hope of this reward that I hold out against the dangers involved.

The Kaji own an enormous diamond. Where it came from, where it was mined, I have been unable to ascertain; but I suspect that it came from the soil of their own country.

I have seen and handled the Cullinan diamond, which weighed over three thousand carats; and I am certain that the diamond of Kaji weighs fully six thousand. Just what its value may be do not know, but using the value of the Brazilian stone, Star of the South, as a measure, it must be worth close to £2,000,000 – a reward well worth some risk.

It is impossible for me to know whether I shall ever get this letter out of Kaji, *but I have hopes of doing so by bribing one of their black slaves who occasionally leave the plateau to spy in the lowlands.*

God grant this be delivered in time.

Mountford.

Tarzan of the Apes read the letter through twice. Mountford! Almost ever since he could remember, it seemed, the mysterious disappearance of Lord and Lady Mountford had been recalled to the minds of men by rumours that they still lived, until they had become a legend of the wilderness.

No one really believed that they lived, yet at intervals some wanderer from the interior would revive the rumour with more or less circumstantial evidence. He had had the story from the chieftain of a remote tribe, or perhaps from the lips of a dying white man; but there never came any definite clue as to the exact whereabouts of the Mountfords – they had been reported from a score of places all the way from the Sudan to Rhodesia.

And now at last the truth had come, but too late. Lady Mountford had been dead for twenty years, and it was quite improbable that her husband still lived. The child must, of course, have died or been killed by the Kaji. It could scarcely have survived among those savage people through infancy.

To the jungle bred ape-man death was a commonplace phenomenon of existence and far less remarkable than many other manifestations of nature, for it came eventually to all living things; so the possibility of the death of the man and the child induced no reaction of sorrow or regret. It simply meant nothing to him whatsoever. He would deliver the letter to the English authorities at the first opportunity, and that would be all that there would be to it. Or so Tarzan thought. He continued his way, putting the matter from his mind. He was more interested in the manœuvres of Ska the vulture, for they indicated that Ska was circling about some creature not yet dead and which, because of its size or nature, he hesitated to attack.

As Tarzan approached the spot above which Ska wheeled on static wings he saw Numa the lion drop from the ledge upon which he had been standing and move cautiously toward the thing that had aroused the man's curiosity. Though the latter was in plain sight, Numa seemingly ignored his presence; nor did Tarzan alter his course because of the lion. If neither changed his pace or his direction they would meet close to the thing above which Ska hovered.

As the ape-man came nearer the object of his interest he saw the body of a man lying in a little natural depression of the ground – the body of a white man.

To the right of it, a hundred yards away, was Numa. Presently the man stirred. He was not dead. He raised his head and saw the lion; then he struggled to rise, but he was very weak and could only manage to raise himself to one knee. Behind him was Tarzan, whom he did not see.

As the man half rose, the lion growled. It was only a warning in which there was no immediate menace. Tarzan recognised it as such. He knew that Numa had been attracted by curiosity and not by hunger. His belly was full. But the man did not know these things. He thought it was the end, for he was unarmed and helpless; and the great carnivore, the King of beasts, was almost upon him.

Then he heard another low growl behind him and, turning his eyes quickly in that direction, saw an almost naked man coming toward him. For an instant he did not understand, for he saw no other beast; then he heard the growl again and saw that it came from the throat of the bronzed giant approaching him.

Numa heard the growl too and paused. He shook his head and snarled. Tarzan did not pause; he continued on toward the man. There was no sanctuary should the lion attack, no tree to offer the safety of its branches; there were only Tarzan's weapons and his great strength and his skill; but greatest of all was his conviction that Numa would not attack.

The Lord of the Jungle well knew the art of bluff and its value. Suddenly he raised his head and voiced the hideous warning-cry of the bull ape. The man shuddered as he heard the bestial cry issue from the lips of a human being. Numa, with a parting growl, turned and stalked away.

Tarzan came and stood over the man. 'Are you hurt?' he demanded, 'Or weak from hunger and thirst?'

The voice of a beast coming from the lips of this strange white giant had been no more disconcerting to the man than now to hear him speak in English. He did not know whether to be afraid or not. He glanced hurriedly in the direction of the lion and saw it moving off in the direction from which it had come, and he was filled with a new awe of this creature who could frighten the King of beasts from its prey.

'Well,' demanded the ape-man, 'do you understand English?'

'Yes,' replied the other; 'I am an American. I am not hurt. I have been without food for several days. I have had no water today.'

Tarzan stooped and lifted the man to a shoulder. 'We will find water and food,' he said, 'and then you may tell me what you are doing alone in this country.'

II

A Strange Tale

As Tarzan carried the man toward safety, the limp, dead weight of his burden told him that his charge had lost consciousness. Occasionally he mumbled incoherently, but for the greater part of the journey he was as one dead.

When they came at last to water, Tarzan laid the man in the shade of a small tree; and, raising his head and shoulders, forced a few drops of the liquid between his lips. Presently he could take more, and with its revivifying effects he commenced to speak – broken, disjointed, sometimes incoherent snatches of sentences; as one speaks in delirium or when emerging from an anaesthetic.

'She-devil,' he mumbled, '... beautiful ... God! How beautiful.' Then he was silent for a while as Tarzan bathed his face and wrists with the cool water.

Presently he opened his eyes and looked at the ape-man, his brows wrinkled in questioning and puzzlement. 'The diamond!' he demanded. 'Did you get the diamond? Huge ... she must have been sired by Satan ... beautiful – enormous – big as ... what? It can't be ... but I saw it – with my own eyes – eyes! Eyes! ... what eyes! ... But a fiend ... ten million dollars ... all of that ... big ... big as a woman's head.'

'Be quiet,' said the ape-man, 'and rest. I will get food.'

When he returned, the man was sleeping peacefully and night was falling. Tarzan built a fire and prepared a brace of quail and a hare that he had brought down with arrows from his bow. The quail he wrapped in wet clay and laid in the embers; the hare he jointed and grilled on sharpened sticks.

When he had done, he glanced at the man and saw that his eyes were open and upon him. The gaze was quite normal, but the expression was one of puzzlement.

'Who are you?' asked the man. 'What happened? I do not seem to be able to recall.'

'I found you out on the plain – exhausted,' explained Tarzan.

'O-oh!' exclaimed the other. 'You are the – the man the lion ran away from. Now I remember. And you brought me here and got food? – and there is water, too?'

'Yes; you have had some. You can have more now. There is a spring behind you. Are you strong enough to reach it?'

The man turned and saw the water; then he crawled to it. Some of his strength had returned.

'Don't drink too much at once,' cautioned the ape-man.

After the man had drunk he turned again toward Tarzan. 'Who are you?' he asked. 'Why did you save me?'

'You will answer the questions,' said the Lord of the Jungle. 'Who are you? And what are you doing in this country alone? What are you doing here at all?'

The voice was low and deep. It questioned, but it also commanded. The stranger felt that. It was the well modulated, assured voice of a man who was always obeyed. He wondered who this almost naked white giant could be. A regular Tarzan, he thought. When he looked at the man he could almost believe that such a creature existed outside of story and legend and that this was, indeed, he.

'Perhaps you had better eat first,' said the ape-man; 'then you may answer my questions.' He took a ball of hard baked clay from the fire, scraping it out with a stick; then with the hilt of his knife he broke it open, and the baked clay fell away from the body of the quail, taking the feathers with it. He impaled the bird on the stick and handed it to the man. 'It is hot,' he said.

It was, but the half-famished stranger risked burning for an initial morsel. Without seasoning, as it was, no food had ever tasted better. Only its high temperature restrained him from wolfing it. He ate one quail and half the hare before he lay back, at last partially satisfied.

'To answer your questions,' he said, 'my name is Wood. I am a writer – travel stuff. Thus I capitalise my natural worthlessness, which often finds its expression and its excuse in wanderlust. It has afforded me more than a competence; so that I am now able to undertake expeditions requiring more financing than a steamer ticket and a pair of stout boots.

'Because of this relative affluence you found me alone and on the point of death in an untracked wilderness; but though you found me deserted and destitute without even a crust of bread, I have here in my head material for such a travel book as has never been written by modern man. I have seen things of which civilisation does not dream and will not believe; and I have seen, too, the largest diamond in the world. I have held it in my hands. I even had the temerity to believe that I could bring it away with me.

'I have seen the most beautiful woman in the world – and the cruellest; and I even had the temerity to believe that I could bring her away with me, too; for I loved her. I still love her, though I curse her in my sleep, so nearly one are love and hate, the two most powerful and devastating emotions that control man, nations, life – so nearly one that they are separated only by a glance, a gesture, a syllable. I hate her with my mind; I love her with my body and my soul.

'Bear with me if I anticipate. For me she is the beginning and the end – the beginning and the end of everything; but I'll try to be more coherent and more chronological.

'To begin with: have you ever heard of the mysterious disappearance of Lord and Lady Mountford?'

Tarzan nodded. 'Who has not?'

'And the persistent rumours of their survival even now, twenty years after they dropped from the sight and knowledge of civilised man?

'Well, their story held for me such a glamour of romance and mystery that for years I toyed with the idea of organising an expedition that would track down every rumour until it had been proved false or true. I would find Lord and Lady Mountford or I would learn their fate.

'I had a very good friend, a young man of considerable inherited means, who had backed some of my earlier adventures – Robert van Eyk, of the old New York van Eyks. But of course that means nothing to you.'

Tarzan did not comment. He merely listened – no shadow of interest or emotion crossed his face. He was not an easy man in whom to confide, but Stanley Wood was so full of pent emotion that he would have welcomed the insensate ears of a stone Buddha had there been no other ear to listen.

'Well, I gabbled so much about my plans to Bob van Eyk that he got all hepped up himself; and insisted on going along and sharing the expenses; which meant, of course, that we could equip much more elaborately than I had planned to and therefore more certainly ensure the success of our undertaking.

'We spent a whole year in research, both in England and Africa, with the result that we were pretty thoroughly convinced that Lord and Lady Mountford had disappeared from a point on the Neubari River somewhere Northwest of Lake Rudolph. Everything seemed to point to that, although practically everything was based on rumour.

'We got together a peach of a safari and picked up a couple of white hunters who were pretty well familiar with everything African, although they had never been to this particular part of the country.

'Everything went well until we got a little way up the Neubari. The country was sparsely inhabited, and the farther we pushed in the fewer natives we saw. These were wild and fearful. We wouldn't get a thing out of them about what lay ahead, but they talked to our boys. They put the fear o' God into 'em.

'Pretty soon we commenced to have desertions. We tried to get a line on the trouble from those who remained, but they wouldn't tell us a thing. They just froze up – scared stiff – didn't even admit that they were scared at first; but they kept on deserting.

'It got mighty serious. There we were in a country we didn't know the first thing about – a potentially hostile country – with a lot of equipment and provisions and scarcely enough men to carry on with.

'Finally one of the headmen told me what they were scared of. The natives they had talked with had told them that there was a tribe farther up the

Neubari that killed or enslaved every black that came into their territory, a tribe with some mysterious kind of magic that held you – wouldn't let you escape, or, if you did escape, the magic followed you and killed you before you got back to your own country – maybe many marches away. They said you couldn't kill these people because they were not human – they were demons that had taken the form of women.

'Well, when I told Spike and Troll, the white hunters, what the trouble was, they pooh-poohed the whole business, of course. Said it was just an excuse to make us turn back because our carriers didn't like the idea of being so far from their own country and were getting homesick.

'So they got tough with the boys. Whaled hell out of 'em, and drove 'em on like slaves. As Spike said, "Put the fear o' God into 'em," and the next night all the rest of 'em deserted – every last mother's son of 'em.

'When we woke up in the morning there were the four of us, Bob van Eyk, Spike, Troll, and myself, four white men all alone with loads for fifty porters; our personal boys, our gun bearers, our askaris all gone.

'Spike and Troll back-tracked to try to pick up some of the boys to take us out, for we knew we were licked; but they never found a one of them, though they were gone for two days.

'Bob and I were just about to pull out on our own when they got back; for, believe me, if we'd had plenty of it before they left we'd had a double dose while they were away.

'I can't tell you what it was, for we never saw anyone. Maybe we were just plain scared, but I don't think that could have been it. Van Eyk has plenty of nerve, and I have been in lots of tough places – lost and alone among the head hunters of Ecuador, captured in the interior of New Guinea by cannibals, stood up in front of a firing squad during a Central American revolution – the kind of things, you know, that a travel writer gets mixed up in if he's really looking for thrills to write about and hasn't very good sense.

'No, this was different. It was just a *feeling* – *a* haunting sense of being watched by invisible eyes, day and night. And there were noises, too. I can't describe them – they weren't human noises, nor animal either. They were just noises that made your flesh creep and your scalp tingle.

'We had a council of war the night Spike and Troll got back. At first they laughed at us, but pretty soon they commenced to feel and hear things. After that they agreed with us that the best thing to do would be to beat it back.

'We decided to carry nothing but a revolver and rifle apiece, ammunition, and food, abandoning everything else. We were going to start early the following morning.

'When the morning came we ate our breakfasts in silence, shouldered our packs, and without a word started out *up* the Neubari. We didn't even look at one another. I don't know about the rest of them, but I was ashamed to.

'There we were, doing just the opposite of the thing we had decided on – going deeper and deeper into trouble – and not knowing why we were doing it. I tried to exercise my will and force my feet in the opposite direction, but it was no go. A power far greater than my own will directed me. It was terrifying.

'We hadn't gone more than five miles before we came across a man lying in the trail – a white man. His hair and beard were white, but he didn't look so very old – well under fifty, I should have said. He seemed pretty well done in, nothwithstanding the fact that he appeared in good physical condition – no indication of starvation; and he couldn't very well have been suffering from thirst, for the Neubari river was less than fifty yards from where he lay.

'When we stopped beside him, he opened his eyes and looked up at us.

'"Go back!" he whispered. He seemed very weak, and it was obviously an effort for him to speak.

'I had a little flask of brandy that I carried for emergencies, and I made him drink a little. It seemed to revive him some.

'"For God's sake turn back," he said. "There are not enough of you. They'll get you as they got me more than twenty years ago, and you can't get away – you can't escape. After all these years I thought I saw my chance; and I tried it. But you see! They've got me. I'm dying. His power! He sends it after you, and it gets you. Go back and get a big force of white men – blacks won't come into this country. Get a big force and get into the country of the Kaji. If you can kill him you'll be all right. He is the power, he alone."

'"Whom do you mean by 'he'?" I asked.

'"Mafka." he replied.

'"He's the chief?" I asked.

'"No; I wouldn't know what to call him. He's not a chief, and yet he's all-powerful. He's more like a witch-doctor. In the dark ages he'd have been a magician. He does things that no ordinary witch-doctor ever dreamed of doing. He's a devil. Sometimes I have thought that he is *the* Devil. And he is training her – teaching her his hellish powers."

'"Who are you?"

'"I'm Mountford," he replied.

'"Lord Mountford?" I exclaimed.

'He nodded.'

'Did he tell you about the diamond?' asked Tarzan.

Wood looked at the ape-man in surprise. 'How did you know about that?'

'You rambled a little while you were delirious, but I knew about it before. Is it really twice the size of the Cullinan?'

'I never saw the Cullinan, but the Kaji diamond is enormous. It must be worth ten million dollars at least, possibly more. Troll used to work at Kimberly. He said somewhere between ten and fifteen million. Yes, Mountford told us about it; and after that Troll and Spike were keen on getting into this Kaji country, hoping to steal the diamond. Nothing Mountford said could deter them. But after all it made no difference. We couldn't have turned back if we'd wanted to.'

'And Mountford?' asked Tarzan. 'What became of him?'

'He was trying to tell us something about a girl. He rambled a little, and we couldn't quite make out what he was driving at. His last words were, "Save her ... kill Mafka." Then he died.

'We never did find out whom he meant even after we got into the Kaji country. We never saw any woman captive. If they had one they kept her hidden. But then, we never saw Mafka either. He lives in a regular castle that must have been built centuries ago, possibly by the Portuguese, though it may have antedated their excursion into Abyssinia. Van Eyk thought it may have been built during the Crusades, though what the Crusaders were doing in this neck of the woods he couldn't explain. At any rate, the Kaji never built it; though they had done considerable toward restoring and preserving it.

'The diamond is kept in this castle and is guarded along with Mafka and the Queen by Kaji warriors who are constantly on guard at the only entrance.

'The Kaji attribute all their powers and the power of Mafka to the diamond; so naturally they guard it very carefully. For the stone itself they show no particular reverence. They handle it and allow others to handle it as though it were quite an ordinary stone. It is for the Queen that they reserve their reverence.

'I am not certain that I correctly fathomed the connection between the Queen and the diamond; but I think that they consider her the personification of the stone, into whose body has entered the spirit and the flame of the brilliant.

'She is a gorgeous creature, quite the most beautiful woman I have ever seen. I do not hesitate to say that she is the most beautiful woman in the world; but a creature of such radical contradictions as to cast a doubt upon her sanity. One moment she is all womanly compassion and sweetness, the next she is a she-devil. They call her Gonfala, and the diamond Gonfal.

'It was during a moment of her femininity that she helped me to escape; but she must have repented it, for it could have been only Mafka's power that reached out and dragged me down. Only she knew that I had gone; so she must have told him.'

'What became of the other three men?' asked Tarzan.

'They are still prisoners of the Kaji. When Gonfala helped me to escape, I planned to come back with a force of whites large enough to rescue them,' Wood explained.

'Will they be alive?'

'Yes; the Kaji will protect them and marry them. The Kaji are all women.

Originally they were blacks who wished to turn white; so they married only white men. It became a part of their religion. That is why they lure white men to Kaji – and frighten away the blacks.

'This must have been going on for generations, as there is not an unmixed black among them. They range in colour all the way from brown to white. Gonfala is a blonde. Apparently there is not a trace of Negro blood in her veins.

'If a baby is born black it is destroyed, and all male babies are destroyed. They believe that the colour of the skin is inherited from the father.'

'If they kill all the males, where do they get their warriors?'

'The women are the warriors. I have never seen them fight; but from what I heard I imagine they are mighty ferocious. You see, we walked right into their country like long-lost friends, for we didn't want to fight 'em. All two of us wanted was their diamond, Bob van Eyk wanted adventure and I wanted material for another book. If we could make friends, so much the better.

'That was six months ago. Bob has had adventure and I have material for a book, though much good it will ever do me. Spike and Troll haven't the diamond, but they each have seven Kaji wives – all properly married, too, by Gonfala in the presence of the great diamond.

'You see, Gonfala, as Queen, selects the wives for all captured whites; but she herself is not allowed to marry.

'This allotting of the whites is more or less of a racket. The women make offerings to Gonfala, and the ones who make the most valuable offerings get the husbands.

'Well, we saw a lot of Gonfala. She seemed to take a liking to Bob and me, and I sure took a liking to her. Before I knew that she was part black I fell in love with her, and even after I guessed the truth I didn't care.

'She liked to hear about the outside world, and she'd listen to us by the hour. You know how people are. Seeing so much of her and being near her broke down my revulsion for her cruelties; so that I was always mentally making excuses for her. And all the time I kept on loving her more and more, until finally I told her.

'She looked at me for a long time without saying a word. I didn't know whether she was sore or not. If you knew what a big shot the Queen of the Kaji is, you'd realise how presumptuous I was in declaring my love. She's more than a Queen; she's a sort of deity that they worship – all mixed up with their worship of the diamond.

'"Love," she said in a little, low voice. "Love! So that is what it is!"

'Then she straightened up and became suddenly very regal. "Do you know what you have done?" she demanded.

'"I have fallen in love with you," I said. "That is about all I know or care."

'She stamped her foot. "Don't say it," she commanded. "Don't ever say it again. I should have you killed; that is the penalty for daring to aspire to the love of Gonfala. She may not love; she may never marry. Do you not understand that I am a goddess as well as a Queen?"

'"I can't help that," I replied. "And I can't help loving you any more than you *can help loving me!*"

'She gave a little gasp of astonishment and horror. There was a new expression in her eyes; it was not anger; it was fear. I had voiced a suspicion that I had had for some time, and I had hit the nail on the head – Gonfala was in love with me. She hadn't realised it herself until that very moment – she hadn't known what was the matter with her. But now she did, and she was afraid.

'She didn't deny it; but she told me that we would both be killed, and killed horribly, if Mafka suspected the truth. And what she was afraid of was that Mafka would know because of his uncanny powers of magic.

'It was then that she decided to help me escape. To her it seemed the only way to ensure our safety; to me it presented an opportunity to effect the rescue of my friends with the possibility of persuading Gonfala to come away with me if I were successful.

'With her help, I got away. The rest you know.'

III

The Power of Mafka

The ape-man had listened patiently to Stanley Wood's recital. How much he could believe of it, he did not know; for he did not know the man, and he had learned to suspect that every civilised man was a liar and a cheat until he had proved himself otherwise.

Yet he was favourably impressed by the man's personality, and he had something of the wild beast's instinctive knowledge of basic character – if it may be called that. Perhaps it is more an intuitive feeling of trust for some and distrust of others. That it is not infallible, Tarzan well knew; so he was cautious, always. And in that again the beast showed in him.

'And what do you purpose doing now?' he asked.

Wood scratched his head in perplexity. 'To be perfectly frank, I don't know. I am confident that Mafka found out that I had escaped and that it was his magic that followed and brought me down. Perhaps Gonfala told him. She is a Jekyll and Hyde sort of person. In one personality she is all sweetness and tenderness, in another she is a fiend.

'As far as my future actions are concerned. I have a very definite premonition that I am not a free agent.'

'What do you mean?' demanded the ape-man.

'Since it commenced to get dark haven't you felt an invisible presence near us, haven't you sensed unseen eyes upon us, and heard things, and almost seen things? These are the manifestations of Mafka. We are in his power. Where he wills us to go, we'll go; and you can lay to that.'

A shadow of a smile moved the lips of the Lord of the Jungle. 'I have seen and heard and sensed many things since we stopped here, but none of them was Mafka. I have identified them all either through my ears or my nose. There is nothing to fear.'

'You do not know Mafka,' said Wood.

'I know Africa, and I know myself,' replied the ape-man, simply. There was no bravado in his tone, but absolute assurance. It impressed the American.

'You are a regular Tarzan,' he said.

The other shot a quick glance at him, appraising. He saw that the man spoke without knowledge of his identity, and he was satisfied. His mission required that he remain unknown, if possible. Otherwise, he might never gain the information he sought. He had felt safe from recognition, for he was unknown in this district.

'By the way,' continued Wood. 'You have not told me your name. I have seen so many unbelievable things since I came into this country that not even the sight of an evidently highly civilised man wandering almost naked and alone in a wilderness surprised me as much as it otherwise might have. Of course, I don't want to pry into your affairs, but naturally my curiosity is aroused. I wonder who you are and what you are doing here.' He stopped suddenly and looked intently at Tarzan. His eyes registered suspicion and a shadow of fear. 'Say!' he exclaimed. 'Did Mafka send you? Are you one of his – his creatures?'

The ape-man shook his head. 'You are in a most unfortunate situation,' he said. 'If I were not one of Mafka's *creatures*, or if I were, my answer, quite conceivably, might be the same – I should deny it; so why answer you? You will have to find out for yourself, and in the meantime you will have to trust me or distrust me as seems wisest to you.'

Wood grinned. 'I am up against it, ain't I?' He shrugged. 'Well, we're both in the same boat. At least you don't know any more about me than I do about you. I may have been giving you a cock-and-bull story. I admit it must sound fishy. But at least I told you my name. You haven't told me that much about yourself yet. I don't know what to call you.'

'My name is Clayton,' said the ape-man. He might also have said, John Clayton, Lord Greystoke – Tarzan of the Apes; but he didn't.

'I suppose you want to get out of this country,' said Tarzan, 'and get help for your friends.'

'Yes, of course, but there isn't a chance now.'

'Why not?'

'Mafka – Mafka and Gonfala.'

'I can't take you out at present,' said the ape-man, ignoring the implied obstacle. 'You may come along to the Lake Tana country with me if you wish to. You'll get a story there – a story that you must never write. You'll have to give me your word as to that. My only alternative is to leave you here. You will have to decide.'

'I'll come with you,' said Wood, 'but neither of us will ever reach Lake Tana.' He paused and strained his eyes into the lowering dusk of the brief twilight. 'There!' he said in a whisper. 'It's back; it's watching us. Don't you hear it? Can't you feel it?' His voice was tense, his eyes slightly dilated.

'There is nothing,' said Tarzan. 'Your nerves are upset.'

'You mean to tell me you don't hear it – the moaning, the sighing?'

'I hear the wind, and I hear Sheeta the panther a long way off,' replied the ape-man.

'Yes, I hear those, too; but I hear something else. You must be deaf.'

Tarzan smiled. 'Perhaps,' he said. 'But go to sleep; you need rest. Tomorrow you will not hear things.'

'I tell you I hear it. I almost see it. Look! There, among those trees – just a shadow of something that has no substance.'

Tarzan shook his head. 'Try to sleep,' he said. 'I will watch.'

Wood closed his eyes. The presence of this quiet stranger gave him a feeling of security despite his conviction that something weird and horrible hovered there in the darkness – watching, always watching. With the dismal keening still ringing in his ears, he fell asleep.

For a long time Tarzan sat in thought. He heard nothing other than the usual night noises of the wilderness, yet he was sufficiently conversant with the mystery and the magic of black Africa to realise that Wood *had* heard something that he could not hear. The American was intelligent, sane, experienced. He did not seem the type to be carried away by imaginings or hysteria. It was just possible that he was under the spell of hypnotic suggestion – that Mafka could project his powers to great distances. This was rather borne out by the evidence that Tarzan had had presented to him within the past few hours: the death of Mountford's messenger twenty years before, the striking down of Wood within a short distance of the same spot, the death of Mountford for no apparent good reason upon the very threshold of escape.

Mafka's was indeed a sinister power, but it was a power that the ape-man did not fear. All too often had he been the object of the malign necromancy of potent witch-doctors to fear their magic. Like the beasts of the jungle, he was immune. For what reason he did not know. Perhaps it was because he was without fear; perhaps his psychology was more that of the beast than of man.

Dismissing the matter from his mind, he stretched and fell asleep.

The sun was half a hand-breadth above the horizon when Wood awoke. He was alone. The strange white man had disappeared.

Wood was not greatly surprised. There was no reason why this stranger should wait and be burdened by a man he did not know, but he felt that he might at least have waited until he was awake before deserting him and leaving him prey for the first lion or leopard that might chance to pick up his scent.

And then there was Mafka. The thought aroused questions in the mind of the American. Might not this fellow who called himself Clayton be a tool of the magician of the Kaji? The very fact that he denied that he had heard any strange sounds or sensed any unusual presence lent colour to this suspicion. He must have heard; he must have sensed. Then why did he deny it?

But perhaps he was not Mafka's spy. Perhaps he had fallen a victim to the sorcery of the old Devil. How easy it would have been for Mafka to lure him away. Everything seemed easy for Mafka. He could have lured him away to captivity or destruction, leaving Wood to die as Mafka intended – alone by starvation.

Wood had never seen Mafka. To him he should have been no more than a name; yet he was very real. The man even conjured an image of him that was as real and tangible as flesh and blood. He saw him as a very old and hideous black man, bent and wrinkled. He had filed, yellow teeth, and his eyes were close-set and bloodshot.

There! What was that? A noise in the trees! The thing was coming again!

Wood was a brave man, but things like these can get on the nerves of the bravest. It is one thing to face a known danger, another to be constantly haunted by an unseen thing – a horrible, invisible menace that one can't grapple with.

The American leaped to his feet, facing the direction of the rustling among the foliage. 'Come down!' he cried, 'Come down, damn you, and fight like a man!'

From the concealing foliage a figure swung lightly to the ground. It was Tarzan. Across one shoulder he carried the carcass of a small buck.

He looked quickly about. 'What's the matter?' he demanded. 'I don't see anyone.' Then a faint smile touched his lips. 'Hearing things again?' he asked.

Wood grinned foolishly. 'I guess it's sort of got me,' he said.

'Well, forget it for a while,' counselled the ape-man. 'We'll eat presently; then you'll feel better.'

'You killed that buck?' demanded Wood.

Tarzan looked surprised. 'Why, yes.'

'You must have killed it with an arrow. That would take an ordinary man hours – stalk an antelope and get close enough to kill it with an arrow.'

'I didn't use an arrow,' replied the ape-man.

'Then how did you kill him?'

'I killed him with my knife – less danger of losing an arrow.'

'And you brought him back through the trees on your shoulder! Say, that bird Tarzan has nothing on you. How did you ever come to live this way, Clayton? How did you learn to do these things?'

'That is a long story,' said Tarzan. 'Our business now is to grill some of this meat and get on our way.'

After they had eaten, Tarzan told the other to carry some of the meat in his pockets. 'You may need food before I can make another kill,' he said. 'We'll leave the rest for Dango and Ungo.'

'Dango and Ungo? Who are they?'

'The hyena and the jackal.'

'What language is that? I never heard them called that before, and I am a little bit familiar with a number of native dialects.'

'No natives speak that language,' replied the ape-man. 'It is not spoken by men.'

'Who does speak it, then?' demanded Wood; but he got no reply, and he did not insist. There was something mysterious about him, and that in his mien and his manner of speech that discouraged inquisitiveness. Wood wondered if the man were not a little mad. He had heard of white men going primitive, living solitary lives like wild animals; and they were always a little bit demented. Yet his companion seemed sane enough. No, it was not that; yet undeniably the man was different from other men. He reminded Wood of a lion. Yes, that was it – he was the personification of the strength and majesty and the ferocity of the lion. It was controlled ferocity; but it was there – Wood felt it. And that, perhaps, was why he was a little afraid of him.

He followed in silence behind the bronzed white savage back up the valley of the Neubari, and as they drew closer to the country of the Kaji he felt the power of Mafka increasing, drawing him back into the coils of intrigue and sorcery that made life hideous in the land of the women who would be white. He wondered if Clayton felt it too.

They came at length to the junction of the Mafa and the Neubari. It was here, where the smaller stream emptied into the larger, that the trail to the Kaji country followed up the gorge of the Mafa. It was here that they would *have* to turn up the Mafa.

Tarzan was a few yards in advance of Wood. The latter watched him intently as he came to the well-marked forking of the trail to the right leading to the crossing of the Neubari and up the Mafa. Here, regardless of his previous intentions, he would have to turn toward Kaji. The power of Mafka would bend his will to that of the malign magician; but Tarzan did not turn – he continued upon his way, unperturbed, up the Neubari.

Could it be that Mafka was ignorant of their coming? Wood felt a sudden sense of elation. If one of them could pass, they could both pass. There was an excellent chance that they might elude Mafka entirely. If he could only get by – if he could get away somewhere and organise a large expedition, he might return and rescue van Eyk, Spike, and Troll.

But could he get by? He thought of the invisible presence that seemed to have him under constant surveillance. Had that been only the fruit of an overwrought imagination, as Clayton had suggested?

He came then to the forking of the trails. He focused all his power of will upon his determination to follow Clayton up the Neubari – and his feet turned to the right toward the crossing that led up the Mafa.

He called to Clayton, a note of hopelessness in his voice. 'It's no go, old man,' he said. 'I've got to go up the Mafa – Mafka's got me. You go on – if you can.'

Tarzan turned back. 'You really want to go with me?' he asked.

'Of course, but I can't. I tried to pass this damnable trail, but I couldn't. My feet just followed it.'

'Mafka makes strong medicine,' said the ape-man, 'but I think we can beat him.'

'No,' said Wood, 'you can't beat him. No one can.'

'We'll see,' said Tarzan, and lifting Wood from the ground he threw him across a broad shoulder and turned back to the Neubari trail.

'You don't feel it?' demanded Wood. 'You don't feel any urge to go up the Mafa?'

'Only a strong curiosity to see these people – especially Mafka,' replied the ape-man.

'You'd never see him – no one does. They're afraid someone will kill him, and so is he. He's pretty well guarded all the time. If one of us could have killed him, most of the Kaji's power would be gone. We'd all have had a chance to escape. There are about fifty white prisoners there. Some of them have been there a long time. We could have fought our way out, if it hadn't been for Mafka; and some of us would have come through alive.'

But Tarzan did not yield to his curiosity. He moved on toward the North with an easy grace that belied the weight of the burden across his shoulder. He went in silence, his mind occupied by the strange story that the American had told him. How much of it he might believe, he did not know; but he was inclined to credit the American with believing it, thus admitting his own belief in the mysterious force that enslaved the other mentally as well as physically; for the man seemed straightforward and honest, impressing Tarzan with his dependability.

There was one phase of the story that seemed to lack any confirmation – the vaunted fighting ability of the Amazonian Kaji. Wood admitted that he had never seen them fight and that they captured their prisoners by the wiles of Mafka's malign power. How, then, did he know that they were such redoubtable warriors? He put the question to the American. Whom did they fight?

'There is another tribe farther to the East,' explained Wood, 'across the divide beyond the headwaters of the Mafa. They are called Zuli. Once the Kaji and the Zuli were one tribe with two medicine-men, or witch-doctors, or whatever you might call them. One was Mafka, the other was a chap called Woora.

'Jealousy arose between the two, causing a schism. Members of the tribe took sides, and there was a battle. During the fracas, Woora swiped one of the holy fetishes and beat it, telling some of his followers where he was going and to join him when the fight was over. You see, like the people who caused civilised wars, he was not taking part in it personally.

'Well, it seems that this other fetish that he lifts is the complement of the great diamond, the Gonfal, of the Kaji. United, their power is supreme; but separated, that of each is greatly reduced. So the Kaji and the Zuli are often battling, each seeking to obtain possession of the fetish of the other.

'It was the stories of the raids and skirmishes and battles for these prizes, as told me by Gonfala and others of the Kaji, that gave me the hunch that these ladies are pretty mean warriors. Some of the yarns I've heard were sure tall; but the scars of old wounds on most of them sort of bear them out, as do the grisly trophies that hang from the outer walls of Gonfala's palace – the shrivelled heads of women, suspended by their long hair.

'An interesting feature of the story is the description of the fetish of the Zuli – a green stone as large as the Gonfal and as brilliant. It glistens like an emerald; but, holy cats! Think of an emerald weighing six thousand carats! That would be something worth battling for, and they don't know the value of it.'

'Do you?' asked Tarzan.

'Well, no, not exactly – perhaps twenty million dollars at a rough guess.'

'What would that mean to you – luxuries and power? The Kaji probably know little of luxuries; but, from what you have told me, power is everything to them; and they believe that this other fetish would give them unlimited power, just as you think that twenty million dollars would give you happiness.

'Probably you are both wrong; but the fact remains that they know quite as well the value of it as you, and at least it does less harm here than it would out in the world among men who would steal the pennies from the eyes of the dead!'

Wood smiled. This was the longest speech that his strange companion had vouchsafed. It suggested a philosophy of life that might make an uninhabited wilderness preferable to contacts of civilisation in the eyes of this man.

For an hour Tarzan carried the American; then he lowered him to his feet. 'Perhaps you can go it on your own now,' he said.

'I'll try. Come on!'

Tarzan started again along the trail toward the North. Wood hesitated. In his eyes and the strained expression of his face was reflected the stupendous effort of his will. With a groan of anguish he turned and started briskly toward the South.

The ape-man wheeled and hastened after him. Wood glanced back and broke into a run. For an instant Tarzan hesitated. The fellow meant nothing to him; he was a burden. Why not let him go and be relieved of him? Then he recalled the terror in the man's face and realised, also, the challenge that Mafka was hurling at the Lord of the Jungle.

Perhaps it was the latter that motivated him more strongly than aught else when he started in pursuit of the fleeing American.

Mafka's power might be unquestionably great, but it could not lend sufficient speed to the feet of Stanley Wood to permit him to outdistance the ape-man. In a few moments Tarzan overhauled and seized him. Wood struggled weakly to escape at the same time that he was thanking Tarzan for saving him.

'It's awful,' he groaned. 'Don't you suppose I can ever escape from the will of that old devil?'

Tarzan shrugged. 'Perhaps not,' he said. 'I have known ordinary witch-doctors to kill men after a period of many years at distances of hundreds of miles, and this Mafka is evidently no ordinary witch-doctor.'

That night they camped beside the Neubari, and in the morning when the ape-man awoke Stanley Wood had disappeared.

IV

Sentenced to Death

With the realisation that the American had gone there came to Tarzan a fuller realisation of the potency of Mafka's necromancy; for he did not for a moment doubt that it was the influence of the Kaji magician that had forced the desertion of the unwilling Wood.

The ape-man conceded admiration to the cunning and the power that had stolen the man from him, for he had taken particular pains to circumvent just such a possibility. When they had lain down to sleep, Tarzan had fastened one end of his grass rope securely to an ankle of the man he had taken under his protection and the other end to one of his own wrists; but that upon which he had depended most was his own preternatural keenness of sense which ordinarily functioned only a little less actively when he slept than when he was awake.

That Wood had been able to free himself and escape could have been due to no powers of his own; but must have been attributable solely to the supernatural machinations of Mafka, constituting in the eyes of the ape-man a direct challenge to his own prowess.

Perhaps this motivated him in part, but it was also a desire to save the young American from an unknown fate that prompted him to turn back in pursuit.

He did not follow the back trail to the Mafa River, but struck out in a south-easterly direction into the mountainous country that forms an almost impregnable protection for the stronghold of the Kaji.

Deep gorges and precipitous cliffs retarded the progress of the ape-man; so that it was over three days before he reached his objective: a point near the headwaters of the Mafa a full day's march to the east of the City of Kaji.

He had foreseen that Mafka might expect him to follow Wood, which would offer the magician an opportunity to have Tarzan waylaid and destroyed at some point upon the trail where he would be helpless against the onslaught of a well placed detachment of Kaji warrior-women; and so he had elected to come upon Kaji from an unexpected direction and depend upon his animal cunning and his great strength and agility to carry him into the very presence of the malign power the destruction of which appeared to be the only means whereby Wood and his companions might be set at liberty permanently.

But above all, his success depended upon the verity of his conviction that he was immune to the supernatural powers of Mafka; though upon this point there was one thing that troubled him; it seemed to him that Mafka must have known of his befriending of Wood. The very fact that he had taken Wood from him suggested that. Yet this might have been accomplished by means of spies, which the American had specifically stated were employed by the Kaji. There was also the possibility that Mafka's power over his victims was so great that he could read their minds even at great distances and thus see through their eyes the things that they saw; so that while Tarzan had been in the company of the American, Mafka had been as well aware of him and his activities as though he had been present in person; but when Wood was no longer with him, the magician could not exercise his telepathic surveillance over him. This was the premise upon which the ape-man based his strategy.

It was late in the afternoon of the third day after Wood's disappearance that Tarzan paused upon a lofty mountain ridge and surveyed the country about him. In a canyon below and to the South of him raced a turbulent mountain stream. With his eyes he followed its meanderings toward the west where, in the dim and hazy distance, he saw a cleft in the serried range that he knew must be the gorge of the Mafa leading down to its confluence with the Neubari.

He stood, then, near the headwaters of the former stream between the countries of the Kaji and the Zuli.

A west wind blew gently from the lower country toward the summit of the range, carrying to the nostrils of the ape-man evidence of things unseen – of Tongani the baboon, Sheeta the leopard, of the red wolf, and the buffalo; but of the east he had no knowledge except that which his eyes and his ears furnished; and so, facing the west, he was unaware of the eyes that watched him from behind the summit of the ridge above him, eyes that disappeared when the ape-man turned in their direction.

There were a dozen pairs of them, and their owners formed a motley crew of unkempt, savage warriors. Of them, seven were bearded white men and five were blacks. All were similarly garbed in well worn loincloths of the skins of wild beasts. They carried bows and arrows and short, heavy spears; and all the blacks and some of the whites wore barbaric ornaments – necklaces of the teeth of animals and armlets and anklets. Upon their backs were small shields of the hide of the buffalo.

They watched Tarzan as he descended into the gorge of the Mafa and slaked his thirst. They saw him take a piece of meat from his quiver and eat, and every move that he made they watched. Sometimes they spoke together in low whispers that could not carry against the wind to the ears of the ape-man.

One, who seemed to be the leader, spoke most often. He was a white man whose brown hair had greyed at the temples and whose beard was streaked with grey. He was well built, with the hard leanness of the athlete. His forehead and his eyes denoted intelligence. His companions called him Lord.

Tarzan was tired. For three days he had scaled cliffs and crags, descended into abysses, and clambered to lofty summits; and the previous night his rest had been broken by hunting leopards that had caught his scent and stalked him. He had killed one that had attacked him; but others had kept him constantly on the alert, precluding the possibility of continued rest.

The sun was still an hour high when he lay down to sleep behind a bush on the slope above the Mafa. That he was dog-tired must account for that which followed, for ordinarily nothing could have approached without arousing him.

When he did awaken, it was still daylight; and a dozen warriors formed a close circle about him, the points of their spears directed at his unprotected body. He looked up into the savage, unfriendly eyes of a black man; then he glanced quickly around the circle and noted the composition of the group. He did not speak. He saw that he was outnumbered and a captive. Under the circumstances there was nothing that he could say that would serve him any purpose.

His silence and his composure set his captors aback. They had expected him to show fear and excitement. He did neither. He just lay there and appraised them through steady, grey eyes.

'Well, Kaji,' said Lord at last, 'we've got you.'

The truth of the statement was too obvious to require comment; so Tarzan remained silent. He was interested less in what the man said than in the language in which he said it. The fellow appeared definitely Anglo-Saxon, yet he spoke a bastard tongue the base of which was Galla but so intermixed with other tongues that it would have been unintelligible to one less versed in African dialect and European languages than Tarzan. In his brief speech, that could be translated into six English words, he had used as many tongues.

Lord shifted his weight from one foot to the other. 'Well, Kaji,' he said after a brief silence, 'what have you got to say?'

'Nothing,' replied the ape-man.

'Get up!' directed Lord.

Tarzan arose and stretched with the easy indifference of a lion in its own lair.

'Take his weapons,' snapped Lord; and then, half to himself and in English: 'By Jove, but he's a rum 'un.'

Then, indeed, was Tarzan interested. Here was an Englishman. There might be some reason to speak now – to ask questions.

'Who are you?' he demanded. 'What makes you think that I'm a Kaji?'

'For the same reason that you know that we are Zuli,' replied Lord. 'Because there are no other people in these mountains.' Then he turned to one of his fellows. 'Tie his hands behind his back.'

They led him then across the ridge and down the other side of the divide; but it was dark now and Tarzan saw nothing of the country through which they passed. He knew that they followed a well worn trail that often dropped precipitously down the side of a rocky gorge until it reached a gentler descent and wound tortuously as though following the meanderings of the stream that splashed or purled or gurgled at their right.

It was very dark in the gorge; but at length they came out into open, level country; and there it was lighter; though still no landmarks were visible to give the ape-man a suggestion of the terrain of this unfamiliar land.

A dim, flickering light showed far ahead. For half an hour they approached it before its closer aspect explained it. Then Tarzan saw that it was from an open fire burning behind the stockade of a village.

As they approached the gates, Lord hallooed; and when he had identified himself they were admitted, and Tarzan found himself in a village of stone huts thatched with grass. The light from the fire burning in the centre of the main street revealed only a portion of the village, which evidently was of considerable size; the rest was lost in the shadows beyond the limit of the firelight.

Before him, built directly across the principal avenue, loomed a large two-storied stone building. At the village gate were several women garbed and armed similarly to his captors. In the none-too-brilliant light of the fire they appeared to be white women; and there were others, like them, lounging in the doorways of huts or about the fire. Among them were a number of white men; and all of them, but especially the women, evinced considerable interest in Tarzan as Lord led him through the village.

'Ai, Kaji!' they yelled at him. 'You will soon be dead, Kaji.'

'It is too bad he is a Kaji,' shouted one woman, 'He would make a fine husband.'

'Perhaps Woora will give him to you,' bantered another, 'when he gets through with him.'

'He will be no good for a husband then. I do not want lion meat for a husband.'

'I hope Woora feeds him to the lions alive. We have had no good sport since before the last rains.'

'He will not turn this one to the lions. The fellow has too good a head. He looks as though he might have brains, and Woora never wastes good brains on the lions.'

Through this barrage of comment, Lord led his captive to the entrance to the big building that dominated the village. At its portals were a dozen warrior-women, barring entrance. One of them advanced to meet Lord, the point of her spear dropped to the level of the man's abdomen.

Lord halted. 'Tell Woora that we bring a Kaji prisoner,' he said.

The woman turned to one of her warriors. 'Tell Woora that Lord brings a Kaji prisoner,' she directed; then her eyes travelled over the ape-man appraisingly.

'A good specimen, eh?' said Lord. 'What a fine mate he'd make for you, Lorro.'

The woman spat reflectively. 'M-m-m, yes,' she agreed; 'he has good conformation, but he is a little too dark: Now, if one were sure he had nothing but white blood, he'd be well worth fighting for. Do you suppose he's all white? But what's the difference? He's a Kaji, and that's the end of him.'

Since his capture Tarzan had spoken only a few words, and these in the Galla dialect. He had not denied that he was a Kaji for the same reason that he had made no effort to escape: curiosity prompted him to learn more of the Zuli – curiosity and the hope that he might learn something of advantage from these enemies of the Kaji that would aid him in freeing the two Americans and their companions from captivity and releasing them permanently from the malign power of Mafka.

As he waited before the entrance to the palace of Woora he decided that he was rather enjoying the adventure. The frank appraisal of Lorro amused him. The idea of a woman fighting for possession of him appealed to his sense of humour. At the time he did not know exactly what the woman's words connoted, but he made a shrewd guess based on what Wood had told him of the customs of the Kaji.

Indifferently he appraised the woman. She might have been an octoroon, or she might have been a white woman with a coat of tan. Her features were not Negroid. Except for her dark hair she might have passed easily for a Scandinavian. She was a well formed woman of about thirty, clean limbed and with the muscular contours of an athlete rendered graceful by femininity. Her features were good, and by any civilised standards she would have been accounted a handsome woman.

The ape-man's reflections upon the subject were interrupted by the return of the warrior Lorro had sent to advise Woora of Lord's return with a prisoner.

'Lord is to take the Kaji to Woora,' she announced. 'See that the prisoner bears no weapons, that his hands are tied behind him, and that a strong guard accompanies him and Lord – a guard of women.'

With six of her warriors, Lorro escorted Lord and his prisoner into the palace, a palace only by virtue of its being occupied by a ruler – a palace by courtesy, one might say.

They entered a gloomy hall lighted dimly by a burning wick in a shallow pottery dish, a primitive cresset that gave forth more soot than light. Upon either side of the corridor were doorways, across most of which were drawn hangings fashioned from the pelts of animals, mostly buffaloes.

One uncovered doorway revealed a chamber in which a number of warrior-women were congregated. Some lay on low, skin-covered cots; others squatted in a circle upon the floor intent upon some game they were playing. The walls of the room were hung with spears and shields and bows and arrows. It was evidently a guard-room. Just beyond it, the corridor ended before a massive door guarded by two warriors.

It was evident that the guards were expecting the party and had received their instructions, for as they approached the doors were swung open for them to enter.

Tarzan saw before him a large room at the far end of which a figure was seated upon a dais. Two score or more of smoking cressets lighted the interior, revealing walls hung with a strange array of skins, weapons, rugs, silks, calicoes – a veritable museum, Tarzan conjectured, of the loot of many a safari; but by far the most outstanding and impressive feature of the decorations was the frieze of human heads that encircled the chamber – the mummified heads of women, hanging by their long hair, while from the smoke-darkened beams of the ceiling depended a hundred more.

These things the eyes of the ape-man took in in a sweeping glance; then they returned to the dais and the figure upon it. A score of women warriors flanked the dais where the lone figure sat upon a huge throne chair.

At first glance Tarzan saw only an enormous head thatched with scraggy grey hair; and then, below the head, a shrivelled body that was mostly abdomen – a hideously repulsive figure, naked but for a loincloth. The skin of the face and head were drawn like yellow parchment over the bones of the skull – a living death's head in which were set two deep, glowing eyes that smouldered and burned as twin pits of Hell. And Tarzan knew that he was in the presence of Woora.

On a table directly in front of the magician rested an enormous emerald that reflected the lights from the nearer cressets and shot them back in scintillant rays that filled the apartment with their uncanny light.

But it was the man rather than the emerald that interested Tarzan. Woora was no black man, yet it was difficult to determine to what race he might belong. His skin was yellow, yet his features were not those of a Chinese. He might have been almost anything.

For several minutes he sat staring at Tarzan after the latter was halted before the dais. Gradually an expression of puzzlement and frustration overspread his face; then he spoke.

'How is my brother?' he demanded, the words squeaking like a rusty hinge.

The expression on Tarzan's face revealed no emotion, though inwardly he was greatly puzzled by the question.

'I do not know your brother,' he replied.

'What?' demanded Woora. 'You mean to tell me, Kaji, that you do not know that prince of liars, that thief, that murderer, that ingrate, my brother?'

The ape-man shook his head. 'I do not know him,' he repeated, 'and I am no Kaji.'

'What!' screamed Woora, glaring at Lord. 'This is no Kaji? Didn't you tell me you were bringing a Kaji?'

'We captured him near the headwaters of the Mafa, O Woora; and what other kind of man would be there but a Kaji?'

'He is no Kaji, fool,' said Woora. 'I guessed as much the moment I looked into his eyes. He is not as other men. My putrid brother could have no power over this one. You are a fool, Lord; and I have no wish to breed more fools among the Zuli – there are enough already. You will be destroyed. Take his weapons from him, Lorro. He is a prisoner.'

Then he turned to the ape-man. 'What were you doing in the country of the Zuli?' he demanded.

'Searching for one of my people who is lost.'

'You expected to find him here?'

'No, I was not coming here. I was going into the country of the Kaji.'

'You are lying,' snapped Woora. 'You could not come to the headwaters of the Mafa without coming through the country of the Kaji; there is no other way.'

'I came another way,' replied Tarzan.

'No man could cross the mountains and gorges that surround Kaji and Zuli; there is no trail except that up the Mafa River,' insisted Woora.

'I crossed the mountains and the gorges,' said Tarzan.

'I see it all!' exclaimed Woora. 'You are no Kaji; but you are in the service of my loathsome brother, Mafka. He has sent you here to murder me.

'Well,' he laughed mockingly, 'we shall see who is more powerful, Mafka or I. We shall see if he can save his servant from the wrath of Woora. And we'll give him time.' He turned to Lorro. 'Take him away with the other prisoner,' he directed, 'and see that neither of them escapes – especially this one; he is a dangerous man. But he will die even as Lord will.'

V

The Black Panther

Tarzan and Lord were confined in a room on the second floor of the palace of Woora. It was a small room with a single window heavily barred with wooden bars. The door was thick and solid, and secured upon the outside with heavy bars.

When the guard had closed and bolted the door and departed, Tarzan walked to the window and looked out. The moon had risen and the light clouds that had overcast the sky earlier in the night had disappeared.

In the soft glow of the night light, the ape-man saw a walled compound directly beneath the window; and in the shadow of the wall something that was unrecognisable by sight, yet Tarzan knew what it was from the scent that rose to his nostrils. He took hold of the bars and tested them; then he turned back and faced Lord.

'If you had asked me,' he said, 'I should have told you that I was not a Kaji, then you wouldn't have been in this mess.'

Lord shook his head. 'It was only an excuse to kill me,' he said. 'Woora has been waiting for one. He is afraid of me. The men are more important here than they are in the Kaji country. We are allowed to bear arms and be warriors. That is because Woora knows that we cannot escape, as the only route to the outer world lies through the country of the Kaji. They would make slaves of us or kill us.

'Woora has heard that some of the men have banded together for the purpose of escaping. The plan included assassinating Woora and stealing the great emerald, which is supposed to be the source his magic power. With this emerald, which Mafka craves more than anything in the world, we hoped to bribe our way through and out of the Kaji country.

'Woora believes that I am the instigator of the plot, and so he wants to destroy me. Of course, he could do that at any time he wishes, but he is a wily old devil and is trying to hide the fact that he has any suspicions. In this way he hopes to trap all of the plotters eventually, killing them one by one on one pretext or another.'

'How can you know so much of his plans?' demanded the ape-man.

'Even in this land of horror and iniquity there is sometimes love,' replied Lord, 'and there is always lust. A woman close to Woora is honestly in love with one of us. Woora has talked too much to her – that is all. He is supposed to be above temptations of the flesh, but he is not.

'But now everything is spoiled. The others will be afraid. They will stay on until they die.'

'You are an Englishman, aren't you?' asked Tarzan.

Lord nodded. 'Yes,' he said; 'I was an Englishman, but God only knows what I am now. I've been here twenty years – here and in Kaji. The Kaji caught me originally; then the Zuli got me in one of their raids.'

'I thought Woora killed the Kaji he caught,' said the ape-man. 'He was going to have me killed because he thought I was a Kaji, or at least I assumed he was from what I heard after we reached the city.'

'Yes, he kills them all now because we have all the men we need; but in those days there were not enough men. We can only support a limited number of people. There's plenty of meat, for game is plentiful; but fruits and vegetables are scarce. As it is, we breed more than enough to keep up the population – in fact, too many. Most of the babies are killed. Then, too, the women are pretty white. That is what they have been breeding for for God knows how many generations; so there isn't much need for new white blood. It's very rare now that a baby is born with Negroid characteristics, but of course occasionally there is a throwback.'

'Why do they want to be white?' asked Tarzan.

'The Lord only knows. They never see anyone but themselves and never will. The original reason is lost in the past – dead with those who conceived it. Unless, perhaps, Woora and Mafka know. It is said they have been here forever – that they are deathless; but of course that is not true.

'I have a theory about them that is based upon various snatches of information that I have picked up during the past twenty years. They are identical twins who came from Columbia many years ago bringing with them the great emerald, which they probably stole. How they came into possession of the Gonfal of the Kaji, I don't know. Doubtless they murdered someone who was trying to get out of the country with it.

'That they have uncanny occult powers there is no doubt, and the very fact that they believe these dependent upon the great diamond of the Kaji and the emerald of the Zuli may very probably have caused this to be true; so if either Mafka or Woora were deprived of his stone his power would be lost. But killing them would make it surer. We were taking no chances; we were going to kill Woora. But now, as far as I am concerned, the dream is over. I'll go to the lions; you'll be tortured to death.'

'Why the difference?' asked Tarzan.

'I'll furnish sport for Woora in the lion yard, but he won't risk you. They might tear you to pieces, head and all; and Woora wants your brain. I'm sure of that.'

'Why does he want it?'

'You had him guessing; I could see that, and he figures that anyone who can do that must have a pretty good brain; so he wants it.'

'But why?' insisted the ape-man.

'To eat.'

'Oh, I see,' said Tarzan. 'He believes that if one eats the part in which another excels one acquires a measure of this excellence. I have seen it before, often. A warrior eats the heart of a brave enemy to increase his own courage, or the soles of the feet of a swift runner to accelerate his own speed, or the palms of the hands of a clever artisan.'

'It is all rot,' said Lord.

'I do not know,' admitted Tarzan. 'I have lived in Africa all my life, and there are many things that I have learned not to deny simply because I do not understand them. But there is one thing that I guess.'

'What is that?'

'That Woora will not eat my brain; nor will you go to the lions if you care to escape.'

'Escape!' scoffed Lord. 'There is no escape.'

'Perhaps not,' admitted the ape-man. 'I said only that I guessed; I did not say that I knew.'

'How can we escape?' demanded Lord. 'Look at that door; see the bars on that window, and below the window—'

'The panther,' Tarzan concluded for him.

'How did you know a panther was there?' Lord's tone bespoke incredulity.

'The scent of Sheeta is strong,' replied the ape-man. 'I noticed it the instant I came into this room, and when I went to the window I knew that he was in the compound beneath – a male panther.'

Lord shook his head. 'Well, I don't know how you did it; but you're right.'

Tarzan walked to the window and examined the bars and the casing in which they were set.

'Stupid,' he said.

'What is stupid?' asked Lord.

'Whoever designed this. Look.' He seized two of the bars close to the sill and surged backward with all his strength and all his weight. There was a rending of wood as the entire window frame was torn from its seat; then he laid the frame with all its bars upon the floor of the room.

Lord whistled. 'Man!' he exclaimed. 'You're strong as a bull; but don't forget the panther, and the noise'll probably bring the guard.'

'We'll be ready for them,' Tarzan assured him. He had seized the window frame again, and a moment later he had torn it apart. The bars fell from their sockets. Tarzan picked up two of them and handed one to Lord. 'These will make fair weapons,' he said.

They waited in silence for a while, but no guard came. Apparently only the panther had been disturbed. He was growling now; and when they went to the window, they saw him standing in the centre of the compound looking up at them. He was a large beast and coal black.

Tarzan turned to his companion. 'Could you get away if we got outside the city?' he asked. 'Or has Woora the same power to direct the movements of his victims at a distance that Mafka has?'

'There's the rub,' admitted Lord. 'That's the reason we'd planned on killing him.'

'How does he stand with the Zuli? Are they loyal to him?'

'The only hold he has upon them is based on terror. They fear and hate him.'

'The women, too?'

'Yes, every one.'

'What would happen here if he were dead?' asked Tarzan.

'The blacks and whites who are prisoners and slaves would combine with the women in an attempt to fight our way out into the outer world. The black and whites (they are all men) want to get back to their own homes. The women, the true Zuli, have heard so much about the world they have never seen that they want to get out, too. They know from what the whites have told them that they would be rich from the proceeds of the sale of the great emerald; and while they have no first-hand knowledge of money, they have learned enough from the white men here to understand that it will get them everything their hearts desire – especially more white men. Here, each of the whites is married to anywhere from seven to a dozen Zuli women because there are so few of us; so the height of the ambition of every Zuli is to have a husband of her own.'

'Why don't they kill Woora themselves, then?'

'Fear of his supernatural powers. Not only would they not kill him themselves, they would protect his life from others; but when he was once dead, then it would be different.'

'Where is he?' asked Tarzan. 'Where does he sleep?'

'In a room directly behind his throne,' replied Lord. 'But why? Why do you ask? You're not—?'

'I am going to kill him. There is no other way.'

Lord shook his head. 'It can't be done. Man, he is almost as powerful as God and almost as omniscient. But anyway, why are you doing it?'

'One of my countrymen is a prisoner among the Kaji. With the help of the Zuli, I can set him free with all the rest of the Kaji prisoners. I am not so sure that I could do it alone. It would be difficult to get into Mafka's presence. He is more afraid and more careful than Woora.'

'You haven't got into Woora's presence yet, except with your hands tied behind you,' Lord reminded him.

'Is there any way to get into his room except from the throne room?'

'There is a way, but you can't get in. Woora's room has a window looking onto this compound below us. The panther is there to guard Woora as well as to keep prisoners from escaping. You would have to pass through the compound to get to the window.'

'That is not so good,' mused the ape-man. 'I'd have to make too much noise. I'd certainly arouse Woora by breaking the bars at his window.'

'There are no bars there.'

'But the panther! What's to keep him from entering and killing Woora?'

'Woora has even greater power over the panther than he has over us humans. He can control the beast's every act.'

'You are sure there are no bars at the window?' demanded Tarzan.

'Absolutely sure, and the window is always open so that Woora can call the panther to him if he is ever in danger of attack.'

'Excellent! I'll go in by the window.'

'You insist on forgetting the panther.'

'I have not forgotten him. Tell me something of Woora's habits. Who is with him? When does he arise? Where does he eat? When does he first go into the throne room?'

'No one is with him in his sleeping-room, ever. No one, as far as we know, have ever been in it, other than himself. His breakfast is handed in to him through a small opening near the floor on the side of the room opposite the throne room. He gets up shortly after sunrise and eats immediately thereafter. He has a suite of three rooms. What he does there, only the Devil knows. Sometimes he has one of the women warriors come into one of his rooms. They never tell what they see there, or what happens. They are too terrified. What would be perhaps an hour after his breakfast, he comes into the throne room. By this time many of the Zuli have congregated there. Charges are heard, punishments are meted out, the business of the day is attended to. That is, hunting parties and raiding parties are sent out; directions are given for the planting, cultivation, or harvesting of crops. Reports and complaints are listened to by Woora. Then he goes back to his apartments and remains there until the evening meal which he takes in the throne room. That is his day, unless something unforeseen occurs such as the examination of a captive brought in unexpectedly, as you were.'

'Good!' exclaimed the ape-man. 'Everything can be made to conform to my plan.'

'Except the panther,' said Lord.

'Perhaps you are right,' conceded Tarzan; 'we'll see.' He stepped to the window. The panther had quieted down and was lying once more in the shade of the compound wall. Tarzan listened. Presently he turned his companion. 'He is asleep,' he said; then he threw a leg over the sill.

'You are not going down there!' Lord exclaimed.

'Why not? It is the only avenue to Woora, and the panther sleeps.'

'He will not be asleep for long.'

'I do not expect him to be. I only ask him to stay asleep until I am squarely on my feet below there.'

'It is suicide,' said Lord, 'and nothing to be gained by it.'

'Maybe, but let's wait and see.' He threw the other leg over the sill; then he turned upon his belly. In his right hand was one of the heavy bars he had taken from the window. Cautiously, silently, he slipped down until he hung from the sill by one hand.

Lord watched him, breathless. He saw the fingers slip gradually from their hold on the sill; then he looked out. The man had alighted erect and then turned like lightning to face the panther, but the beast had not moved. It still slept.

Tarzan crept toward it, silent as the shadow of Usha the wind. The ape-man had covered half the distance to the panther when the beast awoke; then, before it could gather its wits the man leaped toward it.

In the window above, Lord held his breath. He could not but admire the courage of his fellow prisoner, but he thought him foolhardy. Just then the panther charged.

VI

Trapped

Of all the cats none bears so evil a reputation as the panther. His ferocity is proverbial, his wiliness uncanny, the force and fury of his attack demoniacal. But all these things the ape-man knew and was prepared for. He had weighed his chances with the panther against his chances with Woora, and he had chosen the lesser of two evils first in the belief that thus he might rid himself of both. And now in a few seconds his judgment would be vindicated, or he would be dead.

The black beast charged with all the fury of its kind, and it charged in silence. No growls disturbed the deathly stillness of the night. A serene moon looked down upon the village of the Zuli, and beyond the confines of the compound there was no warning of death.

Lord looked down upon the swift tragedy with something of contempt for the stupidity that would permit a man to throw his life away uselessly, and from another window two deep-set, glowing eyes watched above snarling lips – watched from the window of the room that was Woora's.

Grasping the hardwood rod in both hands, Tarzan swung it above his head in a great circle that started low at his right side, timing it to the fraction of a second so that it met the panther with its full momentum, backed by the strength of the ape-man's giant thews, at the height of the beast's speed.

Full upon the fierce, flat skull it fell before the protracted talons or bared fangs could reach the flesh of the panther's intended prey. There was the sound of splintering wood and bone, the thud of the heavy body upon the hard ground, then silence.

Lord drew in his breath in a quick gasp. Although he had seen the thing with his own eyes, he could scarcely believe. The eyes at Woora's window were filled with a sudden fear – with fear and cunning. They watched intently to see what the next move of the strange prisoner would be.

Tarzan placed a foot upon the carcass of his kill and raised his face to Goro the moon: Just for an instant he stood thus, but no victory cry of the bull ape shocked the silence of the night to warn his enemies that he was abroad. Then he moved in the direction of the window that opened into the room of Woora, the magician; and as he did so, the eyes receded into the darkness of the interior.

The ape-man paused at the open window while his ears and his nostrils searched the dark chamber. His ears heard a faint rustling sound as of the scuffing of sandalled feet upon a floor and the almost silent closing of a door. His nostrils caught clearly the scent of Woora.

Placing a hand upon the sill, Tarzan vaulted silently into the room. He stood in silence, listening, in one hand the splintered remains of the hard-wood rod. He heard no sound, not even the faintest sound of breathing that his ears would have detected had there been another in the room. He concluded, then, that Woora had seen him coming and that the slight noises he had heard had been caused by the magician's departure. Now he must be doubly on his guard.

Lord had told him that there were three rooms in Woora's suite. There was also the throne room adjoining, To which room had the man fled? Had he gone to summon help? This was probable, yet Tarzan heard no sound to indicate that anyone was coming.

The faint moonlight dissipated but slightly the darkness of the room, yet it was enough for the keen eyes of the ape-man as they became accustomed to the gloom. He advanced noiselessly into the apartment, and presently he saw a door in the wall before him and another at his right. The latter, he judged, must lead into the throne room. He approached the other and found the latch.

Noiselessly he pulled the door toward him, keeping partially behind it to shield himself from a surprise blow or a missile. The room was dark as a pocket. He listened intently but heard nothing. His nostrils told him that Woora had been there recently, but his ears assured him that he had gone – probably into the farthest apartment.

He started to retreat to the room he had just quitted – but too late. He knew that Woora had come this way and that he would find him beyond the next door. He felt something beneath his feet that felt like cords laid upon the floor. Instantly he was suspicious – the suspicion of the wild animal that senses a trap.

He started to retreat to the room he had just quitted – but too late. Cords sprang up around him. They pulled at him and tripped him, so that he fell.

Then he felt them closing and tightening about him. He struggled to escape them, but they were everywhere. He was entangled in a mesh of cords.

The door of the third room opened, letting in light. In the doorway stood Woora, a cresset in his hand. His death's head face was contorted in a snarling grin. Behind the magician, Tarzan caught a glimpse of a room that might have been the laboratory of a medieval alchemist but for the grisly array of human heads that depended from the beams of the ceiling.

The apartment was lighted by several cressets, and upon a table in the centre lay the great emerald of the Zuli, radiating its weird and baleful light, so that the entire chamber was filled with a seemingly palpable essence that was, in some way, mysteriously malign.

'You court an earlier and more horrible death than we had planned for you,' squeaked Woora.

The ape-man made no reply. He was examining the trap that had caught him. It was a heavy net of rawhide the mouth of which could be pulled from the floor and closed by a cord that ran through a block depending from a ceiling beam and thence through a hole near the ceiling into the room where Woora had waited to snare his prey. It was plain to Tarzan that this room was devoted solely to the purposes of the net, forming the magician's final protection against an assassin who sought his life.

In this he was only partially right, as previously all of its victims had been invited to his innermost sanctum by the magician and, rendered helpless in the net, easily murdered. Tonight it served a new purpose.

Satisfied with the success of his strategy in luring the stranger to this room, Woora was in a pleasant frame of mind. The fear and the anger had left his eyes. He surveyed the ape-man with interest.

'You intrigue me,' he said. 'I shall keep you here for a while to examine you. Perhaps you will get hungry and thirsty, but one who is shortly to die has no need of food or drink. But you shall watch me eat and drink, and you shall meditate upon the various slow and torturing deaths that man may die. I promise you that I shall select something novel and protracted for you, if only to avenge the killing of my pet – the one creature in all the world that I really loved. You shall die many deaths for that and not a few for seeking to destroy me or steal the great emerald. I do not know which you planned doing, nor do I care. Either warrants the direst punishment of which I can conceive.

'In the meantime I shall show you that Woora can be kind even to an enemy. It is well for you that I am neither cruel nor vindictive. I would save you from unnecessary suffering, from mental anguish induced by the sight of horrible or suggestive objects. Watch me closely.'

As he ceased speaking he stepped into the adjoining room where he busied himself lighting the charcoal in a brazier. It took some time to produce a hot fire; but when this was accomplished, he fetched a long metal rod with a sharpened point and a wooden handle. The point he inserted among the hot coals; then he turned his attention once more to the ape-man.

'The human heads upon the walls of my apartment, the paraphernalia of my profession, the preparations that I must make for your torture and death; the sight of these things would prove most depressing to you and add unnecessarily to your suffering; therefore I am going to burn out your eyes so that you cannot see them!'

And yet the ape-man did not speak. His level gaze remained fixed upon the repulsive figure of the old magician and the weird setting in which he wrought his villainies, all bathed in the unholy green light of the great emerald. What his thoughts were only he knew, but it is safe to assume that they were not of death – not of his own death. Probably they were of escape. He tested the strength of the rawhide net. It gave, but it did not break.

Woora saw him and laughed. 'A bull elephant could not break that,' he said. With his grotesque head cocked upon one side he stared intently at his victim. The laugh died on his lips, leaving a snarl. He was angry because the ape-man showed no fear. He looked to the iron, muttering and mumbling to himself. It had grown hot; the point glowed.

'Take a last look, my guest,' cackled Woora, 'for after a moment you will never again see anything.' He withdrew the iron from the coals and approached his prisoner.

The strands of the net closed snugly about the ape-man, confining his arms; so that though he could move them, he could move them neither quickly nor far. He would have difficulty in defending himself against the glowing point of the iron rod.

Woora came close and raised the red-hot iron to the level of Tarzan's eyes; then he jabbed suddenly at one of them. The victim warded off the searing point from its intended target. Only his hand was burned. Again and again Woora jabbed; but always Tarzan succeeded in saving his eyes, yet at the expense of his hands and forearms.

At his repeated failures to blind his victim, Woora became convulsed with rage. He screamed and cursed as he danced about, foaming at the mouth; then, quite suddenly, he gained control of himself. He carried the iron back to the brazier and inserted it among the coals; then he stepped to another part of the room that was not in line with the doorway, and therefore outside the range of Tarzan's vision. He was gone for but a moment, and when he returned he carried a rope in his hand.

He was chuckling again as he approached Tarzan. 'The iron will be hotter this time,' he said, 'and this time it will reach your eyes.'

He passed the rope around the net and Tarzan and made a slip noose and drew it tight; then he walked around and around the ape-man, binding his hands and his arms with many coils of rope until Tarzan had no use of them for protection.

Now he went to the brazier and withdrew the iron. It glowed strangely red in the weird green light of the chamber. With it, Woora crept slowly toward his victim as though he were trying to prolong the agony of suspense; but Tarzan gave no evidence of fear. He knew that he was helpless, and he awaited the inevitable with stoic indifference.

Suddenly Woora was seized by another spasm of fury. 'You pretend that you are not afraid,' he screamed, 'but I'll make you shriek for mercy yet. First the right eye!' And he came forward again, holding the red point on a level with the ape-man's eyes.

Tarzan heard the door behind him open. He saw Woora shrink back, a new expression of fury writ upon his face; then a man leaped past him carrying a stout wooden bar in his hand. It was Lord.

Woora turned to flee into the next apartment, but Lord overtook him, striking him a glancing blow on the head with the rod. The magician turned then and sought to defend himself with the hot iron. He screamed for mercy and for help; but there was no mercy in Lord's attack, and no help came.

Wielding the rod in both hands, the Englishman struck the iron from Woora's hand, breaking the arm at the wrist; then he swung it again furiously, crashing full on the grotesque skull; and with a splintering and crushing of bone Woora sank to the floor, dead.

Lord turned to Tarzan. 'A close call,' he said.

'Yes, a very close call. I shall not forget it.'

'I saw you kill the panther,' continued Lord. 'My word! I'd never have thought it possible. Then I waited. I didn't know just what to do. Presently I commenced to worry; I knew what a wily old devil Woora was; so I followed you, and it was a good thing that I did.'

While he talked, the Englishman found a knife and cut the bonds and the net that held the ape-man; then the two men examined the contents of the inner room. There was a small furnace in one corner, several retorts and test tubes on a long table, shelves with bottles and vials stored upon them, a small library of occultism, black magic, voodooism. In a little niche, before which stood a chair, there was a crystal sphere. But, dominating all, the centre of everything, was the great emerald.

Lord looked at it, spellbound, fascinated. 'It is worth over two million pounds sterling,' he said, 'and it is ours for the taking! There are still several hours of darkness; and it may be hours more, perhaps days, before anyone discovers that Woora is dead and the emerald gone. They could never overtake us.'

'You forget your friends here,' Tarzan reminded him.

'Any one of them would do the same if he had the chance,' argued Lord.

'They will have their freedom. We have given them that. The emerald should be ours.'

'You have also forgotten the Kaji. How will you pass through their country?'

Lord gestured his disgust. 'There is always something; but you're right – we can't escape except with a large force.'

'There is a question whether you can escape Mafka even then,' said Tarzan. 'I've seen some evidence of his power. By comparison, Woora's didn't amount to much.'

'Well, then, what?'

'I'll go ahead and try to dispose of Mafka,' said Tarzan.

'Good! I'll go with you.'

The ape-man shook his head. 'I must go alone. Mafka's occult powers are such that he can control the actions of his victims even at great distances, but for some reason he has no power over me. He might have over you. That is the reason I must go alone; he might sense the presence of another with me and through him learn my plans – his powers are most uncanny.'

As he ceased speaking, Tarzan picked up the great emerald, and wrapped it in a bit of cloth he had torn from a hanging on the wall.

Lord's eyes narrowed. 'What are you doing that for?' he demanded.

'I'm taking the emerald with me. It will ensure my getting an audience with Mafka.'

Lord gave a short, ugly laugh. 'And you think you can get away with that?' he demanded. 'What do you take me for – a fool?'

Tarzan knew the greed of men. That was one of the reason he liked beasts so well. 'If you try to interfere,' he said, 'I'll know that you are a fool – you saw what I did to the panther and how easily.'

'What do you want with two million pounds? Maybe three million – God alone knows what it's worth. There's plenty for both of us.'

'I don't want any of it,' replied the ape-man. 'I have all the wealth I need. I'm going to use it to get some of my people away from Mafka. When that is done, I won't care what becomes of it.'

He tied two cords to the package holding the emerald. One he looped over his head, the other he tied around his waist holding the package close to his body. He picked up the knife that Lord had laid on the table and stuck it in his own scabbard; then he found a long piece of rope which he coiled and slung across a shoulder.

Lord watched him sullenly. He remembered the panther and knew that he was helpless to prevent the stranger taking the emerald.

'I'm going now,' said Tarzan. 'Wait a day, and then follow with all those who want to get out. No matter whether I'm successful or not you may have to fight your way through the Kaji, but with Mafka out of the way you'll stand a much better chance. If I get through, I'll cache the emerald on the Neubari near the mouth of the Mafa and go on about my business. In about three weeks I shall be back again; then I'll turn the emerald over to the Zuli.'

'To the Zuli!' exclaimed Lord. 'Where do I come in? The emerald belongs to me, and you're trying to cheat me out of it. Is this what I get for saving your life?'

Tarzan shrugged. 'It is none of my business,' he said. 'I do not care who gets the emerald. You told me there was a plan afoot to take it and with the proceeds finance all the Zuli in their desire to go and live in civilisation. I did not know that you planned to betray you comrades.'

Lord's eyes could not meet those of the ape-man, and he flushed as he replied. 'I'll see that they get theirs,' he said, 'but I want to control it. What do they know about business? They'd be cheated out of everything in a month.'

'On the Neubari in three weeks, then,' said the ape-man, as he turned and quit the apartment.

As Tarzan vaulted the sill of the window in the outer room and started across the compound where lay the dead body of the black panther. Lord opened the door leading to the throne room and hastened at a run to the guard-room, his mind busy with a plan based on the belief that the stranger intended to make off with the great emerald and keep it for himself.

VII

Green Magic

The guards in the corridor outside the throne room were so surprised to see anyone coming from the throne room at that time in the night that Lord was past them before they recovered their wits. They pursued him, shouting commands to halt, to the doorway of the guard-room where, by this time, all the women warriors were aroused and leaping to arms.

Lorro was the first to recognise the Englishman. 'What is it, Lord?' she demanded. 'What are you doing here? How did you get out of the cell? What has happened?'

'The great emerald!' cried Lord. 'The Kaji has killed Woora and stolen the great emerald.'

'Killed Woora!' exclaimed half a dozen of the women in unison. 'You mean that Woora is dead?'

'Yes, yes,' replied Lord impatiently. 'But the emerald's stolen. Can't you understand that?'

'Woora is dead!' screamed the women; as with one accord they rushed for the village street to spread the happy tidings.

Out in the night, a short distance beyond the village, Tarzan heard the commotion, followed by the hoarse notes of a primitive trumpet. He recognised the call to arms to which now was added the throbbing of the war drums, and guessed that Lord had spread the alarm and was organising a pursuit.

The ape-man increased his speed, moving unerringly along the trail that he had passed over but once before, and that at night; and behind him came the entire tribe of Zuli warrior women with their white men and their black slaves.

Lord had at last succeeded in impressing on the minds of the Zuli hat the death of Woora was an empty beneficence without possession of one emerald that was to have given them wealth and independence in the outer world; so that it was an angry, bloodthirsty mob that pursued the Lord of the Jungle through the soft African night.

Plain to the ears of the ape-man came the sounds of the pursuit, and he guessed the temper of the pursuers. If they overtook him, he could hope for neither victory nor quarter. There were too many of them for the one, and they were too angry and too savage to accord the other. Only the cunning of the wild beast that environment and training had implanted within him could avail him against such odds.

As he trotted along the winding trail that led up the course of the rivulet toward the divide he became acutely aware of a presence that he could not see. His acute senses told him that he was alone, yet the feeling persisted that he was not alone. Something moved with him, clinging as closely as his shadow. He stopped to listen. The thing seemed so near that he should have heard it breathe, but there was no sound. His keen nostrils sought a clue – there was none.

As he trotted on he sought to reason out the mystery. He even tried to convince himself that he was the victim of a delusion; but Tarzan had never had a delusion – he had only heard that others sometimes had them. And always the presence was with him, haunting him like a ghost.

He smiled. Perhaps that was it – the ghost of Woora. And then, quite suddenly the truth dawned upon him. It was the great emerald!

It seemed impossible, yet it could be nothing else. The mysterious stone had some quality in common with life – an aura that was, perhaps, mesmeric. It was conceivable that it was this very thing that had imparted to Woora the occult powers that had made him so feared, so powerful. This would account in part for the care with which the stone had been guarded.

If this were true, then the same conditions might obtain with the Gonfal, the great diamond of the Kaji. Without it, the power of Mafka would be gone. The ape-man wondered. He also wondered if Mafka's power would be doubled if he possessed both the diamond and the emerald.

How would these stones effect the power of others? Did the mere possession of one of them impart to any mortal such powers as those wielded by Woora and Mafka? The idea intrigued Tarzan. He let his mind play with it for a while as he trotted up toward the divide; then he reached a decision.

Turning abruptly to the right, he left the trail and sought a place of concealment. Presently he found a great boulder at the foot of the canyon wall. Behind it he would be hidden from the view of anyone passing along the trail. Always cautious, he looked about for an avenue of retreat, if one became necessary and saw that he could scale the canyon side easily; then he placed himself behind the boulder and waited.

He heard the Zuli coming up the trail. They were making no effort to conceal their presence. It was evident that they were quite sure that the fugitive could not escape them.

Now the head of the column came into view. It was led by Lord. There were over fifty men, mostly white, and three or four hundred warrior-women. Tarzan concentrated his efforts on the latter.

'Turn back! Turn back!' he willed. 'Go back to the village and stay there.'

The women kept on along the trail, apparently unaffected; yet Tarzan felt the presence of the emerald more strongly than ever. He raised it from his side and tore away the skin in which he had wrapped it. Its polished surface, reflecting the moonlight, gave forth rays that enveloped the ape-man in an unearthly glow.

As his bare hands touched the stone he felt a tingling in his arms, his body, as though a mild electric current were passing through him. He felt a surge of new power – a strange, uncanny power that had never before been his. Again he willed the women to turn back, and now he knew that they would turn, now he knew his own power without question, without a doubt.

The women stopped and turned about.

'What's the matter?' demanded one of the men.

'I am going back,' replied a woman.

'Why?'

'I don't know. I only know that I have to go back. I do not believe that Woora is dead. He is calling me back. He is calling us all back.'

'Nonsense!' exclaimed Lord. 'Woora is dead. I saw him killed. His skull was crushed to a pulp.'

'Nevertheless he is calling us back.'

The women were already starting back along the trail. The men stood undecided.

Presently Lord said in a low tone, 'Let them go,' and they all stood watching until after the women had disappeared beyond a turn in the trail.

'There are over fifty of us,' said Lord then, 'and we do not need the women. There will be fewer to divide with when we get out with the emerald.'

'We haven't got it yet,' another reminded him.

'It is as good as ours if we overtake the Kaji before he gets back to his own village. He's a tough customer, but fifty of us can kill him.'

Tarzan, behind the boulder, heard and smiled – just the shadow of a smile; a grim shadow.

'Come on!' said Lord. 'Let's be going,' but he did not move. No one moved.

'Well, why don't you start?' demanded one of the others.

Lord paled. He looked frightened. 'Why don't you?' he asked.

'I can't,' said the man, 'and neither can you. You know it. It's the power of Woora. The woman was right – he is not dead. God! How we'll be punished!'

'I tell you he is dead,' growled Lord, 'dead as a doornail.'

'Then it's his ghost,' suggested a man. His voice trembled.

'Look!' cried one and pointed.

With one accord they all looked in the direction their companion indicated. One who had been a Catholic crossed himself. Another prayed beneath his breath. Lord cursed.

From behind a large boulder set well back from the trail spread a greenish luminosity, faint, shimmering, sending out tenuous rays of emerald light, challenging the soft brilliance of the moon.

The men stood spellbound, their eyes fixed upon the miracle. Then a man stepped from behind the boulder – a bronzed giant clothed only in a loincloth.

'The Kaji!' exclaimed Lord.

'And the great emerald,' said another. 'Now is our chance.' But no one drew a weapon; no one advanced upon the stranger. They could only wish; their wills could not command disobedience to him who possessed the mysterious power of the emerald.

Tarzan came down to them. He stopped and looked them over appraisingly. 'There are over fifty of you,' he said. 'You will come with me to the village of the Kaji. Some of my people are prisoners there. We will free them; then we will all go out of the Kaji country and go our ways.'

He did not ask them; he told them; for he and they both knew that while he possessed the great emerald he did not have to ask.

'But the emerald,' said Lord; 'you promised to divide that with me.'

'When, a few minutes ago, you planned to kill me,' replied the ape-man, 'you forfeited your right to hold me to that promise. Also, since then, I have discovered the power of the emerald. The stone is dangerous. In the hands of a man such as you, it could do untold harm. When I am through with it, it will go into the Neubari where no man shall ever find it.'

Lord gasped. 'God, man!' he cried. 'You wouldn't do that! You couldn't throw away a fortune of two or three million pounds! No, you're just saying that. You don't want to divide it – that's it. You want to keep it all for yourself.'

Tarzan shrugged. 'Think what you please,' he said; 'it makes no difference. Now you will follow me,' and thus they started once more along the trail that leads across the divide and down into the country of the Kaji.

It was dusk of the following day when, from a slight eminence, Tarzan saw for the first time the city of Kaji and the stronghold of Mafka. It was built at the side of a valley close to the face of a perpendicular limestone cliff. It appeared to be a place considerably larger than the Zuli village from which he had just escaped. He stood gazing at it for a few moments; then he turned to the men grouped behind him.

'We have travelled far and eaten little,' he said. 'Many of you are tired. It will not be well to approach the city until well after dark; therefore we will rest.' He took a spear from one of the men and drew a long line upon the ground with the sharp point. 'You cannot cross this line,' he said, 'not one of you;' then he handed the spear back to its owner, walked a short distance away from the line that he had drawn between them, and lay down. One hand rested upon the gleaming surface of the emerald; thus he slept.

The others, glad of opportunity to rest, lay down immediately; and soon all were asleep. No, not all. Lord remained awake, his fascinated eyes held by the faint radiance of the jewel that conjured in his mind the fleshpots of civilisation its wealth might purchase.

Dusk passed quickly, and night came. The moon had not yet risen, and it was very dark. Only the green luminosity surrounding the ape-man relieved the Stygian blackness. In its weird radiance Lord could see the man he called the Kaji. He watched the hand resting upon the emerald – watched and waited; for Lord knew much of the power of the great stone and the manner in which it was conferred upon its possessor.

He made plans; some he discarded. He waited. Tarzan moved in his sleep; his hand slipped from the face of the emerald; then Lord arose. He gripped his spear firmly and crept cautiously toward the sleeping man. Tarzan had not slept for two days, and he was sunk in the slumber of exhaustion.

At the line Tarzan had drawn upon the ground Lord hesitated a moment; then he stepped across and knew that the power of the emerald had passed from the stranger as his hand had slipped from the stone. For many years Lord had watched Woora, and he knew that always when he would force his will upon another some part of his body was in contact with the emerald; but he breathed a sigh of relief with the confirmation of his hope.

Now he approached the sleeping ape-man, his spear ready in his hand. He came close and stood silently for an instant above the unconscious sleeper; then he stooped and gathered up the emerald.

The plan to kill Tarzan was one of those he had discarded. He feared the man might make an outcry before he died and arouse the others; and this did not fit in with Lord's plan, which was to possess the emerald for himself alone.

Creeping steathily away, Lord disappeared in the night.

VIII

The Leopard Pit

The ape-man awoke with a start. The moon was shining full upon his face. Instantly he knew that he had slept too long. He sensed that something was amiss. He felt for the emerald; and when he did not feel it, he looked for it. It was gone. He leaped to his feet and approached the sleeping men. A quick glance confirmed his first suspicion – Lord was gone!

He considered the men. There were fifty of them. Without the emerald he had no power over them; he could not control them. They would be enemies. He turned away and circled the camp until he picked up the scent spoor of the thief. It was where he had expected to find it – leading down the valley of the Mafa towards the valley of the Neubari.

He did not know how much start Lord had. It might be as much as two hours; but had it been two weeks, it would have been the same. No man could escape the Lord of the Jungle.

Through the night he followed, the scent spoor strong in his nostrils. The trail gave the city of the Kaji a wide berth. The terrain was open and sloped gently, the moon was bright. Tarzan moved swiftly, far more swiftly than Lord.

He had been following the Englishman for perhaps an hour when he discerned far ahead a faint, greenish light. It was moving a little to the right of a direct line; and Tarzan knew that, having passed the city of the Kaji, Lord was swinging back on to the direct trail. By cutting straight across, the ape-man would gain considerable distance. As he did so, he increased his speed, moving swiftly, with long, easy strides.

He was gaining rapidly when suddenly the ground gave way beneath his feet and he was precipitated into a black hole. He fell on loose earth and slender branches that formed a cushion, breaking the fall; so that he was not injured.

When he regained his feet he found that it was difficult to move about among the branches that gave when he stepped on them or entangled his feet if he endeavoured to avoid them. Looking up, he saw the mouth of the pit out of reach above him. He guessed its purpose. It was probably a leopard pit, used by the Kaji to capture the fierce cats alive. And he realised, too, the purpose of the loose earth and branches that had broken his fall; they gave no firm footing from which a leopard could spring to freedom. He looked up again at the pit's rim. It was far above his head. He doubted that a cat could have leaped out of it if there had been no branches on the floor; he was sure that he could not.

There was nothing to do but wait. If this were a new pit, and it looked new, the Kaji would be along within a day or so; then he would be killed or captured. This was about all he had to expect. No leopard would fall in upon him now that the mouth of the pit was no longer concealed by the covering he had broken through.

He thought of Lord and of the harm he could do were he to reach the outside world in possession of the great emerald of the Zuli, but he did not concern himself greatly on account of his failure to overtake the Englishman. What was, was. He had done his best. He never repined; he never worried. He merely awaited the next event in life, composed in the knowledge that whatever it was he would meet it with natural resources beyond those of ordinary men. He was not egotistical; he was merely quite sure of himself.

The night wore on, and he took advantage of it to add to his sleep. His nerves, uncontaminated by dissipation, were not even slightly unstrung by his predicament or by the imminence of capture or death. He slept.

The sun was high in the heavens when he awoke. He listened intently for the sound that had awakened him. It was the sound of footfalls carried to him from a distance through the medium of the earth. They came closer. He heard voices. So, they were coming! They would be surprised when they saw the leopard they had trapped.

They came closer, and he heard them exclaim with satisfaction when they discovered that the covering of the pit had been broken through; then they were at the pit's edge looking down at him. He saw the faces of several warrior women and some men. They were filled with astonishment.

'A fine leopard!' exclaimed one.

'Mafka will be glad to have another recruit.'

'But how did he get here? How could he pass the guards at the entrance to the valley?'

'Let's get him up here. Hey, you! Catch this rope and tie it around under your arms.' A rope was tossed down to him.

'Hold it,' said the ape-man, 'and I'll climb out.' He had long since decided to go into captivity without a struggle – for two reasons. One was that resistance would doubtless mean certain death; the other, that captivity would bring him closer to Mafka, possibly simplify the rescue of Wood and his friends. It did not occur to Tarzan to take into consideration the fact that he might not be able to effect his own escape. He was not wont to consider any proposition from a premise of failure. Perhaps this in itself accounted to some extent for the fact that he seldom failed in what he attempted.

Those above held the rope while the ape-man swarmed up it with the agility of a monkey. When he stood upon solid ground, he was faced with several spear points. There were eight women and four men. All were white. The women were armed; the men carried a heavy net.

The women appraised him boldly. 'Who are you?' demanded one of them.

'A hunter,' replied Tarzan.

'What are you doing here?'

'I was on my way down in search of the Neubari when I fell into your pit.'

'You were going out?'

'Yes.'

'But how did you get in? There is only one entrance to the country of the Kaji, and that is guarded. How did you get past our warriors?'

Tarzan shrugged. 'Evidently I did not come in that way,' he said.

'There is no other way, I tell you,' insisted the warrior.

'But I came in another way. I entered the mountains several marches from here to hunt; that is the reason I came down from the east. I hunted in the back country, coming down from the North. The going was rough. I was looking for an easier way to the Neubari. Now that I am out of the pit, I'll go on my way.'

'Not so fast,' said the woman who had first addressed him and who had done most of the talking since. 'You are coming with us. You are a prisoner.'

'All right,' conceded the ape-man. 'Have it your own way – you are eight spears, and I am only one knife.'

Presently, Tarzan was not even a knife; for they took it away from him. They did not bind his hands behind him, evidencing their contempt for the prowess of men. Some of them marched ahead, some behind Tarzan and the four other men, as they started back toward the city that could be seen in the near distance. At any time the ape-man could have made a break for escape had he wished to, and with the chances greatly in his favour because of his great speed; but it pleased him to go to the city of the Kaji.

His captors talked incessantly among themselves. They discussed other women who were not with them, always disparagingly; they complained of the difficulties they experienced in the dressing of their hair; they compared the cut and fit and quality of the pelts that formed their loincloths; and each of them expatiated upon the merits of some exceptionally rare skin she hoped to acquire in the future.

The four men marching with Tarzan sought to engage him in conversation. One was a Swede, one a Pole, one a German, and one an Englishman.

All spoke the strange tongue of the Kaji – a mixture of many tongues. Tarzan could understand them, but he had difficulty in making them understand him unless he spoke in the native tongue of the one he chanced to be talking to or spoke in French, which he had learned from d'Arnot before he acquired a knowledge of English. The Swede alone understood no French, but he spoke broken English, a language the German understood but not the Pole. Thus a general conversation was rendered difficult. He found it easier to talk to the Englishman, whose French was sketchy, in their common language.

He heard this man addressed as Troll, and recalled that Stanley Wood had told him that this was the name of one of their white hunters. The man was short and stalky, with heavy, stooped shoulders and long arms that gave him a gorillaesque appearance. He was powerfully muscled. Tarzan moved closer to him.

'You were with Wood and van Eyk?' he asked.

The man looked up at Tarzan in surprise. 'You know them?' he asked.

'I know Wood. They recaptured him?'

Troll nodded. 'You can't get away from this damned place. Mafka always drags you back, if he doesn't kill you. Wood nearly got away. A fellow—' He paused. 'Say, are you Clayton?'

'Yes.'

'Wood told me about you. I ought to have known you right away from his description of you.'

'Is he still alive?'

'Yes. Mafka hasn't killed him yet, but he's mighty sore. No one ever came so near escaping before. I guess it made the old duffer shake in his pants – only he don't wear pants. A big expedition of whites could make it hot for him – say a battalion of Tommies. Godamighty! How I'd like to see 'em come marchin' in.'

'How about the Gonfal?' inquired Tarzan. 'Couldn't he stop them, just as he does others, with the power of the great diamond?'

'No one knows, but we think not. Because if he could, why is he so scared of one of us escaping?'

'Do you think Mafka intends to kill Wood?'

'We're pretty sure of it. He's not only sore about his almost getting away, but he's sorer still because Wood has a crush on Gonfala, the Queen; and it looks like Gonfala was sort of soft on Wood. That'd be too bad, too; because she's a Negress.'

'Wood told me she was white.'

'She's whiter than you, but look at these dames here. Ain't they white? They look white, but they all got Negro blood in 'em. But don't never remind 'em of it. You remember Kipling's, "She knifed me one night 'cause I wished she was white"? Well that's it; that's the answer. They want to be white. God only knows why; nobody ever sees 'em but us; and we don't care what colour they are. They could be green as far as I'm concerned. I'm married to six of 'em. They make me do all the work while they sit around an' gabble about hair and loincloths. Godamighty! I hate the sight of hair an' loincloths. When they ain't doin' that they're knockin' hell out o' some dame that ain't there.

'I got an old woman back in England. I thought she was bad. I run away from her, an' look what I go into! Six of 'em.'

Troll kept up a running fire of conversation all the way to the city. He had more troubles than the exchange desk in a department store.

The city of Kaji was walled with blocks of limestone quarried from the cliff against which it was built. The buildings within the enclosure were of limestone also. They were of one and two stories, except the palace of Mafka, which rose against the cliff to a height of four stories.

The palace and the city gave evidence of having been long in the building, some parts of the palace and some of the buildings below it being far more weather-worn than others. There were black men and white and warrior women in the streets. A few children, all girls, played in the sunshine; milch goats were everywhere under foot. These things, and many others the ape-man observed as he was conducted along the main street toward the palace of Mafka.

He heard the women discussing him and appraising him as farmers might discuss a prize bull. One of them remarked that he should bring a good price. But he moved on, apparently totally oblivious of them all.

The interior of the palace reminded him of that of Woora, except that there was more and richer stuff here. Mafka was nearer the source of supply. Here was the loot of many safaris. Tarzan wondered how Woora had obtained anything.

The four men had been dismissed within the city; only the eight women accompanied Tarzan into the palace. They had been halted at the heavily guarded entrance and had waited there while word was carried into the interior; then with a number of the guard as escort, they had been led into the palace.

Down a long corridor to another guarded doorway they proceeded; then they were ushered into a large chamber. At the far end, a figure crouched upon a throne. At sight of him, Tarzan was almost surprised into a show of emotion – it was Woora!

Beside him, on another throne-chair, sat a beautiful girl. Tarzan assumed that this must be Gonfala, the Queen. But Woora! He had seen the man killed before his own eyes. Did magic go as far as this, that it could resurrect the dead?

As he was led forward and halted before the thrones he waited for Woora to recognise him, to show the resentment he must feel because he had been thwarted and the great emerald stolen from him; but the man gave no indication that he had ever seen Tarzan before.

He listened to the report of the leader of the party that had captured the ape-man, but all the time his eyes were upon the prisoner. They seemed to be boring through him, yet there was no sign of recognition When the report had been completed, the magician shook his head impatiently. He appeared baffled and troubled.

'Who are you?' he demanded.

'I am an Englishman. I was hunting.'

'For what?'

'Food.'

While the magician questioned Tarzan he kept a hand upon an immense diamond that rested on a stand beside him. It was the Gonfal, the great diamond of the Kaji, that endowed its possessor with the same mysterious powers that were inherent in the great emerald of the Zuli.

The girl upon the second throne-chair sat silent and sullen, her eyes always on the ape-man. She wore breastplates of virgin gold and a stomacher covered with gold sequins. Her skirt was of the skins of unborn leopards, soft and clinging. Dainty sandals shod her, and upon her upper arms and her wrists and her ankles were many bands of copper and gold. A light crown rested upon her blonde head. She was the symbol of power; but Tarzan knew that the real power lay in the grotesque and hideous figure at her side, clothed only in an old and dirty loincloth.

Finally the man motioned impatiently. 'Take him away,' he commanded.

'Am I not to choose wives for him?' demanded Gonfala. 'The women would pay well for this one.'

'Not yet,' replied her companion. 'There are reasons why I should observe him for a while. It will probably be better to destroy him than give him to the women. Take him away!'

The guard took the ape-man to an upper floor and put him in a large chamber. There they left him alone, bolting the door behind them as they departed. The apartment was absolutely bare except for two benches. Several small windows in the wall overlooking the city gave light and ventilation. In the opposite wall was an enormous fireplace in which, apparently, no fire had ever been built.

Tarzan investigated his prison. He found the windows too high above the ground to offer an avenue of escape without the aid of a rope, and he had no rope. The fireplace was the only other feature of the apartment that might arouse any interest whatsoever. It was unusually large, so deep that it resembled a cave; and when he stepped into it he did not have to stoop. He wondered why such an enormous fireplace should be built and then never used.

Entering it, he looked up the flue, thinking that here he might find a way out if the flue were built in size proportionate to the fire chamber. However, he was doomed to disappointment; not the faintest glimmer of light shone down to indicate an opening that led to the outside.

Could it be possible that the fireplace had been built merely as an architectural adornment to the chamber – that it was false? This seemed highly improbable, since the room had no other embellishment; nor was the fireplace itself of any architectural beauty, being nothing more than an opening in the wall.

What then could its purpose have been? The question intrigued the active imagination of the Lord of the Jungle. It was, of course, possible that there was a flue but that it had been closed; and this would have been the obvious explanation had the fireplace shown any indication of ever having been used. However, it did not; there was not the slightest discoloration of the interior – no fire had ever burned within it.

Tarzan reached upward as far as he could but felt no ceiling; then he ran his fingers up the rear wall of the fire chamber. Just at his fingertips he felt a ledge. Raising himself on his toes, he gripped the ledge firmly with the fingers of both hands; then he raised himself slowly upward. Even when his arms were straight and he had raised himself as far as he could his head touched no ceiling. He inclined his body slowly forward until at length he lay prone upon the ledge. The recess, then, was at least several feet deep.

He drew his legs up and then rose slowly to his feet. He raised a hand above his head, and a foot above he felt the stone of a ceiling – there was plenty of headroom. Laterally, the opening was about three feet wide.

He reached ahead to discover its depth, but his hand touched nothing; then he moved forward slowly a few steps – still nothing. Moving cautiously, he groped his way forward. Soon he was convinced of what he had suspected – he was in a corridor, and the secret of the 'fireplace' was partially revealed. But where did the corridor lead?

It was very dark. He might be on the verge of a pitfall without suspecting it. If there were branching corridors he might become hopelessly lost in a minute or two; so he kept his left hand constantly in contact with the wall on that side; he moved slowly, feeling forward with each foot before he threw his weight upon it, and his right hand was always extended before him.

Thus he moved along for a considerable distance, the corridor turning gradually to the left until he was moving at right angles to his original course. Presently he saw a faint light ahead, coming apparently from the floor of the corridor. When he approached it more closely, he saw that it came from an opening in the floor. He stopped at the brink of the opening and looked down. Some seven feet below he saw stone flagging – it was the floor of a fireplace. Evidently this secret passage led from one false fireplace to another.

He listened intently but could hear nothing other than what might have been very soft breathing – almost too faint a sound to register even upon the keen ears of the ape-man; but his nostrils caught the faint aroma of a woman.

For a moment Tarzan hesitated; then he dropped softly to the floor of the fireplace. He made no sound. Before him lay a chamber of barbarous luxury. At a window in the opposite wall, looking down upon the city, stood a golden-haired girl, her back toward the fireplace.

Tarzan did not have to see her face to know that it was Gonfala.

IX

The End of the Corridor

Noiselessly he stepped into the chamber and moved toward the end of the room, nearer to the doorway. He sought to reach the door before she discovered him. He would rather that she did not know how he gained entrance to the room. A heavy wooden bolt fastened the door from the inside. He reached the door without attracting the girl's attention and laid a hand upon the bolt.

He slipped it back quietly; then he moved away from the door toward the window where the girl still stood absorbed in her daydream. He could see her profile. She no longer looked sullen but, rather, ineffably sad.

The man was quite close to her before she became aware of his presence. She had not heard him. She was just conscious, suddenly, that she was not alone; and she turned slowly from the window. Only a slight widening of the eyes and a little intake of her breath revealed her surprise. She did not scream; she did not exclaim.

'Don't be afraid,' he said; 'I'm not here to harm you.'

'I am not afraid,' she replied; 'I have many warriors within call. But how did you get here?' She glanced at the door and saw that the bolt was not shot. 'I must have forgotten to bolt the door, but I can't understand how you got by the guard. It is still there, isn't it?'

Tarzan did not answer. He stood looking at her, marvelling at the subtle change that had taken place in her since he had seen her in the throne room just a short time before. She was no longer the Queen, but a girl, soft and sweet, appealing.

'Where is Stanley Wood?' he asked.

'What do you know of Stanley Wood?' she demanded.

'I am his friend. Where is he? What are they going to do with him?'

'You are his friend?' she asked, wonderingly, her eyes wide. 'But no, it can make no difference – no matter how many friends he has, nothing can save him.'

'You would like to see him saved?'

'Yes.'

'Then why don't you help me?'

'No, I can't. You don't understand. I am Queen. It is I who must sentence him to death.'

'You helped him escape once,' Tarzan reminded her.

'Hush! Not so loud,' she cautioned. 'Mafka suspects that already. If he knew, I don't know what he would do to him and to me. But I know he suspects. That is the reason I am kept in this room with a heavy guard. He says it is for my protection, but I know better.'

'Where is this Mafka? I'd like to see him.'

'You have seen him. You were just brought before him in the throne room.'

'That was Woora,' objected Tarzan.

She shook her head. 'No. What put that idea in your head? Woora is with the Zuli.'

'So that was Mafka!' said the ape-man, and then he recalled Lord's theory that Mafka and Woora were identical twins. 'But I thought no one was allowed to see Mafka.'

'Stanley Wood told you that,' she said. 'That is what he thought; that is what he was told. Mafka was very ill for a long time. He dared not let it be known. He was afraid someone would take advantage of it to kill him. But he wanted to see you. He wished to see a man who could get into our country and so close to the city as you did without his knowing it. I do not understand it myself, and I could see that he was disturbed when he talked with you. Who are you? What are you? How did you get into my apartment? Have you such powers as Mafka has?'

'Perhaps,' he said. It would do no harm if she thought he possessed such powers. He spoke in a low tone now and watched her closely. 'You'd like to see Stanley Wood escape; you'd like to go with him. Why don't you help me?'

She looked at him eagerly. He could read the longing in her eyes. 'How can I help you?' she asked.

'Help me to see Mafka – alone. Tell me where I can find him.'

She trembled, and the fear that was in her was reflected in her expression.

'Yes,' she said, 'I can tell you. If you—' She paused. Her expression changed; her body stiffened. Her eyes became hard and cold – cruel. Her mouth sagged into the sullen expression it had worn when he had first seen her in the throne room. He recalled Wood's statement that she was sometimes an angel, sometimes a she-devil. The metamorphosis had occurred

226

before his eyes. But what caused it? It was possible, of course, that she suffered from some form of insanity; yet he doubted it. He believed there was some other explanation.

'Well?' he queried. 'You were saying—'

'The guard! The guard!' she cried. 'Help!'

Tarzan sprang to the door and shot the bolt. Gonfala whipped a dagger from her girdle and leaped toward him. Before she could strike, the ape-man seized her wrist and wrenched the weapon from her.

The guard were pounding upon the door and shouting for admittance. The ape-man seized Gonfala by the arm; he held her dagger ready to strike. 'Tell them you are all right,' he whispered. 'Tell them to go away.'

She snarled and tried to bite his hand. Then she screamed louder than ever for help.

On the opposite side of the room from the door where the guard sought entrance was a second door, bolted upon the inside like the other. Toward this the ape-man dragged the screaming Gonfala. Slipping the bolt, he pushed the door open. Beyond it was another chamber upon the opposite side of which he saw a third door. Here was a series of chambers that it might be well to remember.

He pushed Gonfala into the first chamber and closed and bolted the door. The warriors of the guard were battering now in earnest. It was evident that they would soon have the door down and gain entrance to the apartment.

Tarzan crossed to the fireplace and leaped to the mouth of the secret passage just as the door crashed in and the warriors of the guard entered the room. He waited where he was – listening. He could hear Gonfala screaming in the adjoining room and pounding on the door, which was now quickly opened.

'Where is he?' she demanded. 'Have you got him?'

'Who? There is no one here,' replied a member of the guard.

'The man – the prisoner that was brought today.'

'There was no one here,' insisted a warrior.

'Go at once and notify Mafka that he has escaped,' she commanded. 'Some of you go to the room in which he was imprisoned and find out how he got out. Hurry! Don't stand there like idiots. Don't you suppose I know what I saw? I tell you he was here. He took my dagger from me and shoved me into that room. Now go! But some of you stay here. He may come back.'

Tarzan waited to hear no more, but retraced his steps through the passage to the room in which he had been imprisoned. He left Gonfala's dagger on the high ledge inside the fireplace, and had barely seated himself on one of the benches in the room when he heard footsteps in the corridor outside; then the door was swung open and half a dozen warrior women pushed their way in.

They showed their surprise when they saw him sitting quietly in his cell.
'Where have you been?' demanded one.
'Where could I go?' countered the ape-man.
'You were in the apartment of Gonfala, the Queen.'
'But how could I have been?' demanded Tarzan.
'That is what we want to know.'
Tarzan shrugged. 'Someone is crazy,' he said, 'but it is not I. If you think I was there why don't you go ask the Queen.'
The warriors shook their heads. 'What is the use?' demanded one. 'He is here; that is all we have to know. Let Mafka solve the riddle.' Then they left the room.

An hour passed during which Tarzan heard nothing; then the door was opened and a warrior woman ordered him to come out. Escorted by a dozen warriors, he was taken through a long corridor to an apartment on the same floor of the palace. His sense of direction told him that the room was one of the suite which adjoined the Queen's.

Mafka was there. He stood behind a table on which rested something covered with a cloth. Also on the table was the great diamond of Kaji, the Gonfal. Mafka's left hand rested upon it.

The ape-man's keen nostrils scented blood, and his eyes saw that the cloth that covered the object on the table was stained with blood. Whose blood? Something told him that whatever was beneath the bloodstained cloth he had been brought to see.

He stood before the magician, his arms folded across his deep chest, his level, unwavering gaze fixed upon the grotesque figure facing him. For minutes the two stood there is silence, waging a strange battle of minds. Mafka was attempting to plumb that of his prisoner; and Tarzan knew it, but his defence was passive. He was sure that the other could not control him.

Mafka was annoyed. To be frustrated was a new experience. The mind of the man before him was a sealed book. He felt a little bit afraid of him, but curiosity compelled him to see him. It kept him from ordering his destruction. He wished to fathom him; he wished to break the seal. Inside that book was something strange and new. Mafka was determined to learn what it was.

'How did you get to the apartment of the Queen?' he demanded suddenly.
'If I were in the apartment of the Queen, who should know it better than Mafka?' demanded Tarzan. 'If I were there, who should know better than Mafka how I got there?'
The magician appeared discomfited. He shook his head angrily. 'How did you get there?' he demanded.
'How do you know I was there?' countered the ape-man.
'Gonfala saw you.'
'Was she sure that it was I in person, or only a figment of her imagination?

Would it not have been possible for the great Mafka to make her think that I was there when I was not?'

'But I didn't,' growled the magician.

'Perhaps someone else did,' suggested Tarzan. He was positive now that Mafka was ignorant of the existence of the secret passage through which he had gained entrance to the apartment of Gonfala. Possibly this part of the palace belonged to a period that antedated Mafka, but why had no one investigated the fireplaces that were obviously not intended to hold fires? There was one in this very room where Mafka was and doubtless had been many times before. Tarzan wondered if it, too, opened into a corridor and where the corridor led; but he had little time for conjecture, as Mafka shot another question at him.

'Who has that power but Mafka?' demanded the magician superciliously, but there was a suggestion of incertitude in his manner. It was more a challenge to uncertainty than a declaration of fact.

Tarzan did not reply; and Mafka seemed to have forgotten that he had put a question, as he continued to study the ape-man intently. The latter, indifferent, swept the interior of the room with a leisurely glance that missed nothing. Through open doors leading to other apartments he saw a bedchamber and a workshop. The latter was similar to that which he had seen in the palace of Woora. It was obvious that this was the private suite of Mafka.

Suddenly the magician shot another question. 'How did you get to Zuli without without my sentries seeing you?'

'Who said I had been in Zuli?' demanded Tarzan.

'You killed my brother. You stole the great emerald of the Zuli. You were coming here to kill me. You ask who said you had been in Zuli. The same man who told me these other things. This man!' And he snatched the cloth from the thing upon the table.

Glaring at the ape-man with staring eyes was the bloody head of the Englishman, Lord; and beside it was the great emerald of the Zuli.

Mafka watched his prisoner intently to note the reaction to his startling and dramatic climax to the interview, but he reaped scant satisfaction. The expression on Tarzan's face underwent no change.

For a moment there was silence; then Mafka spoke. 'Thus die the enemies of Mafka,' he said. 'Thus will you die and the others who have brought intrigue and discontent to Kaji.' He turned to the captain of the guard. 'Take him away. Place him again in the South chamber with the other troublemakers who are to die with him. It was an evil day that brought them to Kaji.'

Heavily guarded, Tarzan was returned to the room in which he had been confined. From Mafka's instructions to the captain of the guard, he had expected to find other prisoners here on his return; but he was alone. He wondered idly who his future companions were to be, and then he crossed to one of the windows and looked out across the city and the broad valley of the Kaji.

He stood there for a long time trying to formulate some plan by which he might contact Wood and discuss means by which the escape of the American could be assured. He had a plan of his own, but he needed the greater knowledge that Wood possessed of certain matters connected with Mafka and the Kaji before he could feel reasonably certain of its success.

As he stood there pondering the advisability of returning to Gonfala's apartment and seeking again the cooperation that he knew she had been on the point of according him when the sudden Jekyll and Hyde transformation had wrought the amazing change in her, he heard footsteps outside the door of his prison; then the bolt was drawn and the door swung open, and four men were pushed roughly in. Behind them, the door was slammed and bolted.

One of the four men was Stanley Wood. At sight of Tarzan he voiced an exclamation of astonishment. 'Clayton!' he cried. 'Where did you come from? What in the world are you doing here?'

'The same thing that you are – waiting to be killed.'

'How did he get you? I thought you were immune – that he couldn't control you.'

Tarzan explained about the misadventure of the leopard pit; then Wood introduced the other three to him. They were Robert van Eyk, Wood's associate, and Troll and Spike, the two white hunters who had accompanied their safari. Troll he had already met.

'I ain't had a chance to tell Wood about seeing you,' explained Troll. 'This is the first time I've seen him. He was in the cooler, and I was just arrested. I don't even know what for, or what they're goin' to do to me.'

'I can tell you what they plan on doing to you,' said Tarzan. 'We're all to be killed. Mafka just told me. He says you are all troublemakers.'

'He wouldn't have to be a psychoanalyst to figure that out,' remarked van Eyk. 'If we'd had half a break we'd've shown him something in the trouble line, but what you going to do up against a bird like that? He knows what you're thinking before you think it.'

'We wouldn't have been in this mess if it hadn't been for Wood messin' around with that Gonfala dame,' growled Spike. 'I never knew it to fail that you didn't get into trouble with any bunch of heathen if you started mixin' up with their women folk – especially niggers. But a guy's got it comin' to him that plays around with a nigger wench.'

'Shut that dirty trap of yours,' snapped Wood, 'or I'll shut it for you.' He took a quick step toward Spike and swung a vicious right for the other man's jaw. Spike stepped back and van Eyk jumped between them.

'Cut it!' he ordered. 'We got enough grief without fighting among ourselves.'

'You're dead right,' agreed Troll. 'We'll punch the head of the next guy that starts anything like that again.'

'That's all right, too,' said Wood; 'but Spike's got to apologise or I'll kill him for that the first chance I get. He's got to take it back.'

'You'd better apologise, Spike,' advised van Eyk.

The hunter looked sullenly from beneath lowering brows. Troll went over and whispered to him. 'All right,' said Spike, finally; 'I take it back. I didn't mean nothin'.'

Wood nodded. 'Very well,' he said, 'I accept your apology,' and turned and joined Tarzan, who had been standing by a window, a silent spectator of what had transpired.

He stood for a time in silence; then he shook his head dejectedly. 'The trouble is,' he said in low tones, 'I know Spike is right. She must have negro blood in her – they all have; but it doesn't seem to make any difference to me – I'm just plain crazy about her, and that's all there is to it. If you could only see her, you'd understand.'

'I have seen her,' said the ape-man.

'What!' exclaimed Wood. 'You've seen her? When?'

'Shortly after I was brought here,' said Tarzan.

'You mean she came here to see you?'

'She was on the throne with Mafka when I was taken before him,' explained Tarzan.

'Oh, yes; I see. I thought maybe you'd talked with her.'

'I did – afterward, in her apartment. I found a way to get there.'

'What did she say? How was she? I haven't seen her since I got back. I was afraid something had happened to her.'

'Mafka suspects her of helping you to escape. He keeps her locked up under guard.'

'Did she say anything about me?' demanded Wood, eagerly.

'Yes; she wants to help you. At first she was eager and friendly; then, quite abruptly and seemingly with no reason, she became sullen and dangerous, screaming for her guard.'

'Yes, she was like that – sweet and lovely one moment; and the next, a regular she-devil. I never could understand it. Do you suppose she's – well, not quite right mentally?'

The ape-man shook his head. 'No,' he said, 'I don't think that. I believe there is another explanation. But that is neither here nor there now. There is just one matter that should concern us – getting out of here. We don't know when Mafka plans on putting us out of the way nor how. Whatever we are going to do we should do immediately – take him by surprise.'

'How are we going to surprise him – locked up here in a room, under guard?' demanded Wood.

'You'd be surprised,' replied Tarzan, smiling faintly; 'so will Mafka. Tell me, can we count on any help beyond what we can do ourselves – the five of us? How about the other prisoners? Will they join with us?'

'Yes, practically all of them – if they can. But what can any of us do against Mafka? We're beaten before we start. If we could only get hold of the Gonfal! I think that's the source of all his power over us.'

'We might do that too,' said Tarzan.

'Impossible,' said Wood. 'What do you think, Bob?' he asked van Eyk, who had just joined them.

'Not a chance in a million,' replied van Eyk. 'He keeps the old rock in his own apartment at night, or in fact wherever he is the Gonfal is with him. His apartment is always locked and guarded – warriors at the door all the time. No, we never could get it.'

Tarzan turned to Wood. 'I thought you told me once that they seemed very careless of the Gonfal – that you had handled it.'

Wood grinned. 'I thought I had, but since I came back I learned differently. One of the women told me. It seems that Mafka is something of a chemist. He has a regular lab and plays around in it a lot – ordinary chemistry as well as his main line of black magic. Well, he learned how to make phony diamonds; so he makes an imitation of the Gonfal, and that's what I handled. They say he leaves the phony out where it can be seen and hides the real Gonfal at night when he goes to bed; so that if, by any chance, someone was able to get into his room to steal it they'd get the wrong stone. But he has to keep the Gonfal near him just the same, or he'd be more or less helpless against an enemy.'

'The only chance to get it would be to get into Mafka's apartment at night,' said van Eyk, 'and that just can't be done.'

'Do his apartments connect with Gonfala's?' asked Tarzan.

'Yes, but the old boy keeps the door between them locked at night. He isn't taking any chances – not even with Gonfala.'

'I think we can get into Mafka's apartment,' said the ape-man. 'I'm going now to find out.'

'Going!' exclaimed Wood. 'I'd like to know how.'

'Don't let anyone follow me,' cautioned the ape-man. 'I'll be back.'

The two Americans shook their heads sceptically as Tarzan turned away and crossed the room; then they saw him enter the fireplace and disappear.

'Well I'll be damned!' exclaimed van Eyk. 'Who is that guy, anyway?'

'An Englishman named Clayton,' replied Wood. 'At least that's all I know about him, and that came direct from him.'

'If there were such a bird as Tarzan of the Apes, I'd say this was he,' said van Eyk.

'That's what I thought when I first met him. Say, he flits through the trees like a regular Tarzan, kills his meat with a bow and arrow, and packs it back to camp on his shoulder through the trees.'

'And now look what he's done! Up the flue like a – a – well, like something, whatever it is goes up a flue.'

'Smoke,' suggested Wood; 'only he's coming back, and smoke doesn't – except occasionally.'

Tarzan followed the corridor as he had before until he came to the opening into Gonfala's chamber; then he retraced his steps a short distance and felt his way back again with his right hand touching the side of the passageway instead of his left as before; nor was he surprised to discover that the tunnel ran on past the apartment of Gonfala. It was what he had expected – what he had been banking his hopes upon.

Now, past the opening that led to Gonfala's room, he touched the left-hand wall again and, pacing off the distance roughly, came to another opening that he judged would be about opposite the centre of the next apartment, which was one of Mafka's suites. He did not stop here, but went on until he had located three more openings. Here the corridor ended.

He stepped to the edge of the flue and looked down into the fireplace. It was night now, but a faint illumination came from the opening below him. It was a greenish glow, now all too familiar.

He listened. He heard the snores of a heavy sleeper. Was there another in the apartment below, or was the sleeper alone? His sensitive nostrils sought an answer.

With the dagger of Gonfala in one hand, Tarzan dropped lightly to the floor of the fireplace that opened into the room where the sleeper lay.

X

Toward Freedom

Before him was a large chamber with a single door, heavily bolted upon the inside. He who slept there quite evidently slept in fear. It was Mafka. He lay upon a narrow cot. Upon a table at one side rested the Gonfal and the great emerald of the Zuli and beside them a cutlass and a dagger. Similar weapons lay on a table at the other side of the cot. All were within easy reach of the sleeper. A single cresset burned upon one of the tables.

Tarzan crossed noiselessly to the side of the cot and removed the weapons; first upon one side, then the other. Next, he carried the great emerald and the Gonfal to the fireplace and put them upon the ledge at the mouth of the corridor; then he returned to the side of the cot. Mafka slept on, for the ape-man moved as silently as a ghost in the night.

He laid a hand upon the shoulder of the magician and shook him lightly. Mafka awoke with a start.

'Keep still and you will not be harmed.' Tarzan's voice was low, but it was the voice of authority that knew its power.

Mafka looked wildly about the apartment as though searching for help, but there was none.

'What do you want?' His voice trembled. 'Tell me what you want and it is yours, if you will not kill me.'

'I do not kill old men or women or children unless they force me to. As long as my life is safe, yours is.'

'Then why have you come here? What do you want?'

'Nothing that you can give me. What I want, I take.'

He turned Mafka over on his stomach and bound his wrists, his ankles, and his knees with strips torn from the bedding; then he gagged him so that he could not raise an alarm. He also blindfolded him that he might not see how entrance had been gained to his apartment.

These things done, he returned to the corridor and groped his way back to Gonfala's apartment, leaving the two great gems where he had first placed them. He was confident they would never be found by another than himself, so sure was he that these corridors were entirely unknown to the present occupants of the palace.

At the entrance to Gonfala's apartment he listened again, but his senses detected no presence in the room below. As he entered it, a quick glance assured him that it was vacant. A single small cresset lighted it dimly. A door at the far end of the room was ajar. He went to it and pushed it open.

As he did so, Gonfala sat up in her couch near the centre of the room and faced him. 'You have come back! I hoped you would. You have chosen a good time.'

'I thought so – he sleeps.'

'Then you know?'

'I guessed.'

'But why have you come back?'

'Wood and his three friends are prisoners. They are all to be killed.'

'Yes, I know. It is by my orders.' A qualm of pain and self-disgust were registered in her expression.

'You can help them to escape. Will you?'

'It would do no good. He would only drag them back, and their punishment would be even worse than they can expect now. It is hopeless.'

'If Mafka did not interfere would the women obey you?'

'Yes.'

'And if you had the opportunity you would like to escape from Kaji?'

'Yes.'

'Where would you go?'

'To England.'

'Why to England?'

'One who was always good to me, but who is dead now, told me to go to England if ever I escaped. He gave me a letter to take with me.'

'Well, get your letter and get ready. You are going to escape. We will be back for you in a little while – Wood and his friends and I. But you will have to help. You will have to give the necessary orders to the women to let us all pass.'

She shook her head emphatically. 'It will do no good, I tell you. He will get us all.'

'Don't worry about that. Just give me your promise that you will do as I ask.'

'I'll promise, but it will mean death for me as well as for you.'

'Get ready, then; I'll be back with the others in a few minutes.'

He left her room, closing the door after him, and went at once to the corridor. A moment later he dropped into the room where Wood and his companions were imprisoned. It was very dark. He spoke to them in low tones, directing them to follow him. Soon they were all in the corridor.

Tarzan led the way to Mafka's room, the glow from the great gems lighting their way as they approached the end of the corridor.

Spike drew in his breath in astonishment. 'Cripes! The big rock!' he exclaimed.

Troll halted before the radiant stones and gazed at them in fascinated silence for a moment. 'This other – it must be the great emerald of the Zuli. Both of 'em! Lord! They must be worth millions.' He started to touch them, but drew back in terror. He knew the power that lay in them, and feared it.

Tarzan dropped over the ledge into the fireplace then, and the others followed him. As they gathered around Mafka's couch, Wood and his companions were speechless with astonishment when they saw the old magician lying bound and helpless.

'How did you do it?' exclaimed Wood.

'I took the gems away from him first. I think all his power lies in them. If I am right, we can get away from here. If I'm wrong—' The ape-man shrugged.

Van Eyk nodded. 'I think you're right. What are we going to do with this old devil?'

Troll seized one of the cutlasses that lay beside the cot. 'I'll show you what we're going to do with him!'

Tarzan grasped the man's wrist. 'Not so fast. You are taking orders from me.'

'Who said so?'

Tarzan wrenched the weapon from Troll's hand and slapped the man across the side of the face with an open palm. The blow sent him reeling across the room to fall in a heap against the wall.

Troll staggered to his feet, feeling his jaw. 'I'll get you for this.' His voice trembled with rage.

'Shut up and do as you're told.' The ape-man's voice showed no emotion. It was, however, a voice that commanded obedience. Then he turned to Wood. 'You and van Eyk get the gems. Troll and Spike will carry Mafka.'

'Where are we going?' Van Eyk put the question apprehensively. He knew that there was a guard of warrior women in the corridor outside Mafka's suite.

'We are going first to Gonfala's apartments. They adjoin Mafka's.'

'She'll give the alarm, and we'll have the whole bloomin' bunch of 'em on us,' objected Spike.

'Don't worry about Gonfala; just do as I say. However, you may as well take these weapons. Something might happen, of course.'

Wood and van Eyk got the great emerald and the Gonfal from the ledge in the fireplace; then Troll and Spike picked up Mafka, who was trembling in terror; and all followed Tarzan to the door of the apartment. They passed through the adjoining room and the next, coming then to the door leading into Gonfala's suite. Like the other doors, it was barred on the inside. Slipping the bars, the ape-man pushed the door open.

Gonfala was standing in the centre of the room as the party entered. She was clothed as for a journey, with a long robe of leopard skins and heavy sandals. A narrow fillet of beaded doeskin bound her golden hair. At sight of Mafka, bound, gagged, and blindfolded, she gasped and shrank away. Then she saw Wood and ran to him.

He put an arm about her. 'Don't be afraid, Gonfala. We're going to take you away. That is, if you want to come with us.'

'Yes; anywhere – with you. But him! What are you going to do with him?' She pointed at Mafka. 'He'll drag us all back, no matter where we go, and kill us; or he'll kill us there. He kills them all, who escape.'

Spike spat venomously. 'We'd ought to kill him now.'

Van Eyk looked at Tarzan. 'I agree with Spike. Why shouldn't we, when it's his life or ours?'

The ape-man shook his head. 'We don't know the temper of the Kaji women. This man must be something of a deity to them. He represents their power – he *is* their power. Without him, they would be just a tribe of women upon which any other tribe could prey. He means most to us alive, as a hostage.'

Wood nodded. 'I think Clayton's right.'

The discussion was interrupted by a commotion in the outer corridor upon which the apartments of Mafka and Gonfala opened. There was pounding upon the door of Mafka's apartment and loud cries for the magician.

Tarzan turned to Gonfala. 'Call some warrior in authority and see what they want. We'll wait in the next room. Come!' He motioned the others to follow him, and led the way into the adjoining apartment.

Gonfala crossed the room and struck a drum that stood upon the floor near the doorway leading into the corridor. Three times she struck it; then she drew the bolt that secured the door upon the inside. A moment later the door was swung open, and a warrior woman entered the apartment. She bent to one knee before the Queen.

'What is the meaning of the noise in the corridor? Why are they calling Mafka at this hour of the morning?'

'The Zuli are coming, Gonfala. They are coming to make war upon us. They sent a slave to demand the return of their great emerald. There are many of them. We invoke the power of Mafka to make the Zuli weak so that we can kill many of them and drive them away.'

'They have no power. Woora is dead, and we have the great emerald. Tell the warriors that I, Gonfala the Queen, command them to go out and slay the Zuli.'

'The Zuli are already at the gates of the city. Our warriors are afraid, for they have no power from Mafka. Where is Mafka?' Why does he not answer the prayers of the Kaji?'

Gonfala stamped her foot. 'Do as I command. You are not here to ask questions. Go to the gate and defend the city. I, Gonfala, will give my warriors power to defeat the Zuli.'

'Let us see Mafka,' insisted the woman sullenly.

Gonfala reached a quick decision. 'Very well. See that my orders for the defence of the city are obeyed; then come to the throne room, and you shall see Mafka. Bring the captains with you.'

The woman withdrew, and the door was closed. Immediately, Tarzan stepped into the room. 'I overheard. What is your plan?'

'Merely to gain time.'

'Then you didn't intend to have Mafka in the throne room to meet them?'

'No. That would be fatal. If we took him in bound, gagged, and blindfolded they might kill us all. If we gave him his freedom, he would kill us.'

'Nevertheless, I think it a good plan. We'll do it.' A grim smile touched the lips of the ape-man.

'You are mad.'

'Perhaps; but if we try to leave now, we can't get out of Kaji without a fight; and I do not relish fighting women. I think there is another way. Do you know where the imitation Gonfal is kept?'

'Yes.'

'Get it, and bring it here at once. Wrap a skin around it so that no one can see it. Tell no one. Only you and I must know.'

'What are you going to do?'

'Wait and see. Do as I tell you.'

'You forget that I am Queen.' She drew herself up proudly.

'I know only that you are a woman who would like to escape from Kaji with the man she loves.'

Gonfala flushed, but she made no reply. Instead, she quit the room at once, going into the apartments of Mafka.

She was gone but a few moments. When she returned she carried a bundle wrapped in a skin.

Tarzan took it from her. 'We are ready now. Lead the way to the throne room.' He summoned the others from the adjoining apartment; then he turned again to the Queen. 'Is there a private way to the throne room?'

Gonfala nodded. 'This way. Follow me.'

She led them into Mafka's apartments where she opened a small door revealing a flight of steps, and they followed her down these to another door that opened upon the dais where the throne chairs stood.

The throne room was empty. The captains had not yet arrived. At Tarzan's direction, Wood placed the Gonfal on the stand beside the throne; Troll and Spike seated Mafka, still bound, gagged, and blindfolded, in his chair; Gonfala seated herself in the other. Tarzan stood beside the table bearing the Gonfal. The others stood behind the chairs. Van Eyk concealed the great emerald of the Zuli beneath a skin he took from the floor of the dais.

In silence they waited. All but Tarzan were tense with nervousness. Presently they heard approaching footfalls in the corridor leading to the throne room. The doors were swung open, and the captains of the Kaji filed in.

They came with heads bent in reverence for their Queen and the great power of their magician. When they looked up they were close to the dais. At sight of Mafka they gave vent to cries of astonishment and anger. They looked at the strangers on the dais; then their eyes centred upon the Queen.

One of them stepped forward. 'What is the meaning of this, Gonfala?' Her tones were menacing.

It was Tarzan who answered. 'It means that the power of Mafka is gone. All your lives he has held you in the hollow of his hand. He has made you fight for him. He has taken the best fruits of your conquests. He has held you prisoners here. You feared and hated him, but most of all you feared him.'

'He has given us power,' answered the warrior.

'If that power is gone, we are lost.'

'It is not gone, but Mafka no longer wields it.'

'Kill them!' cried one of the captains.

The cry arose from many throats. 'Kill them! Kill them!' With savage yells they pushed forward toward the dais.

Tarzan laid a hand upon the Gonfal. 'Stop! Kneel before your Queen!' His voice was low. In the din of their shouting it probably reached the ears of few if any of the warriors, but as one they stopped and knelt.

Again the ape-man spoke. 'Stand up! Go to the gates and bring in the captains of the Zuli. They will come. The fighting will stop.' The warriors turned and filed out of the chamber.

Tarzan turned toward his companions. 'It worked. I thought it would. Whatever this strange power is, it is inherent in the Gonfal. The great emerald has the same mystic power. In the hands of vicious men it is bad. Perhaps, though, it may be used for good.'

Gonfala was listening intently. The sounds of the battle ceased; then came echoing footfalls in the long corridor leading to the palace entrance. 'They come!' she whispered.

Fifty warrior women entered the throne room of the Queen of the Kaji. Half of them were Kaji and half Zuli. They were a savage company. Many of them were bleeding from wounds. They looked sullenly at one another and at the little company upon the dais.

Tarzan faced them. 'You are free now from the rule of Woora and Mafka. Woora is dead. I shall turn Mafka over to you presently to do with as you wish. His power is gone if you keep the Gonfal from him. We are leaving your country. Gonfala is going with us. As many prisoners and slaves as wish to accompany us may come. When we are safely out we will hand the Gonfal back to one of your warriors, who may accompany us with three companions – no more. It is dawn. We leave at once. Here is Mafka.' He lifted the old magician in his arms and handed him down to the warrior women.

Amidst deathly silence the little company of white men filed out of the throne room with Gonfala, the Queen of the Kaji. Tarzan carried the Gonfal so that all might see it. Van Eyk bore the great emerald of the Zuli concealed beneath a wrapping of skin.

In the main street of the city a little group of black men and white awaited them, summoned by Tarzan through the necromancy of the Gonfal. They were the slaves and prisoners of the Kaji.

'We are leaving this country,' he told them; 'any who wish to may accompany us.'

'Mafka will kill us,' objected one.

Shrill screams issued from the interior of the palace only to be drowned by savage yells of rage and hatred.

'Mafka will never kill again,' said the ape-man.

XI

Treachery

In peace they marched through the country of the Kaji under the protection of Tarzan and the Gonfal. Those who had been prisoners and slaves for years were filled with nervous apprehension. They could not believe this miracle that had seemingly snatched them from the clutches of the old magician who had dominated and terrorised them for so long. Momentarily they expected to be killed or dragged back to certain torture and death; but nothing happened, and they came at last to the valley of the Neubari.

'I'll leave you here,' said Tarzan. 'You will be going South. I go North.' He handed the Gonfal to van Eyk. 'Keep it until morning; then give it to one of these women.' He indicated the three warrior women who had accompanied them from Kaji; then he turned to them. 'Take the stone back; and if any among you can use it, use it for good and not for evil.

'Wood, take the great emerald of the Zuli in trust for Gonfala. I hope it will bring her happiness, but the chances are that it will not. At least, however, she need never want.'

'Where do we come in?' demanded Spike.

The ape-man shook his head. 'You don't; you go out – you go out with your lives. That's a lot more than you could have hoped for a few days ago.'

'You mean to say you're goin' to give the big rock back to the niggers and we don't get no split? It ain't fair. Look what we been through. You can't do it.'

'It's already done.'

Spike turned toward the others. 'Are you fellows goin' to stand for this?' he shouted angrily. 'Them two rocks belongs to all of us. We ought to take 'em back to London and sell 'em and divide up equal.'

'I'm glad enough to get out with my life,' said van Eyk. 'I think Gonfala has a right to one of the stones; the other will be plenty for both the Kaji and the Zuli to carry out their plans to go out into the world. They'll be cheated out of most of it anyway, but they'll get their wish.'

'I think they ought to be divided,' said Troll. 'We ought to get something out of this.'

Some of the white men who had been liberated agreed with him. Others said they only wanted to get home alive and the sooner they saw the last of the two stones the better they'd be satisfied.

'They're evil,' said one of the men. 'They'll bring no good to anyone.'

'I'd take the chance,' growled Spike.

Tarzan regarded him coldly. 'You won't get it. I've told you all what to do; see that you do it. I'll be travelling South again before you get out of the country. I'll know if you've pulled anything crooked. See that you don't.'

Night had fallen. The little band of fugitives, perhaps a hundred strong, were making camp, such as it was, and preparing the food they had brought from Kaji. The blacks, who had been slaves, fell naturally into positions of porters and personal servants to the whites. There had been some slight attempt toward organisation, Wood and van Eyk acting as lieutenants to the man they knew only as Clayton, who had assumed the leadership as naturally as the others had accepted the arrangement.

He stood among them now noting the preparations for the night; then he turned to Wood. 'You and van Eyk will take charge. You will have no trouble unless it be from Spike. Watch him. Three marches to the South you will find friendly villages. After that it will be easy.'

That was all. He turned and was gone into the night. There were no farewells, long-drawn and useless.

'Well,' said van Eyk, 'that was casual enough.'

Wood shrugged. 'He is like that.'

Gonfala strained her eyes out into the darkness. 'He has gone? You think he will not come back?'

'When he finishes whatever business he is on, perhaps. By that time we may be out of the country.'

'I felt so safe when he was with us.' The girl came and stood close to Wood. 'I feel safe with you, too, Stanlee; but him – he seemed a part of Africa.'

The man nodded and put an arm about her. 'We'll take care of you, dear; but I know how you feel. I felt the same way when he was around. I had no sense of responsibility at all, not even for my own welfare. I just took it for granted that he'd look after everything.'

'I often wonder about him,' said van Eyk musingly – 'who he is, where he comes from, what he is doing in Africa. I wonder – I wonder if there could be – if—'

'If what?'

'If there could be a Tarzan.'

Wood laughed. 'You know, the same thought came to me. Of course, there is no such person; but this fellow, Clayton, sure would fill the bill.'

The black boy who was cooking for them called them then to the evening meal. It was not much, and they decided that Spike and Troll would have to do some hunting the following day.

Suddenly Wood laughed – a bit ruefully. 'What with?' he demanded. 'We've got spears and knives. What could any of us kill with those?'

Van Eyk nodded. 'You're right. What are we going to do? We've got to have meat. All the way to those first friendly villages we've got to depend on game. There won't be anything else.'

'If we raise any game, we'll have to send out beaters and chase it toward the spears. We ought to get something that way.'

Van Eyk grinned. 'If we're lucky enough to raise something with *angina pectoris*, the excitement might kill it.'

'Well, they do kill big game with spears,' insisted Wood.

Van Eyk's face brightened. He snapped his fingers. 'I've got it! Bows and arrows! Some of our blacks must be good at making them and using them. Hey Kamudi! Come here!'

One of the black boys arose from the two calloused black heels he had been squatting upon and approached. 'Yes, Bwana – you call?'

'Say, can any of you boys kill game with a bow and arrow?'

Kamudi grinned. 'Yes, Bwana.'

'How about making them? Can any of you make bows and arrows?'

'Yes, Bwana – all can make.'

'Fine! Any of the stuff you use grow around here?' Van Eyk's tones were both eager and apprehensive.

'Down by the river – plenty.'

'Gee! That's bully. When the boys have finished supper take 'em down there and get enough stuff to make bows for every one and lots of arrows. Make a few tonight. If we don't have 'em, we don't eat tomorrow. Sabe?'

'Yes, Bwana – after supper.'

The night was velvet soft. A full moon shone down upon the camp, paling the embers of dying fires where the men had cooked their simple meal. The blacks were busy fashioning crude bows and arrows, roughly hewn but adequate.

The whites were gathered in little groups. A shelter had been fashioned for Gonfala; and before this she and Wood and van Eyk lay upon skins that had been brought from Kaji and talked of the future. Gonfala of the wonders that awaited her in unknown civilisation, for she was going to London. The men spoke of America, of their families, and old friends, who must long ago have given them up as dead.

'With the proceeds from the great emerald of the Zuli you will be a very rich woman, Gonfala.' Wood spoke a little regretfully. 'You will have a beautiful home, wonderful gowns and furs, automobiles, and many servants; and there will be men – oh, lots of men.'

'Why should I have men? I do not want but just one.'

'But they will want you, for yourself and for your money.' The thought seemed to sadden Wood.

'You will have to be very careful,' said van Eyk. 'Some of those chaps will be very fascinating.'

The girl shrugged. 'I am not afraid. Stanlee will take care of me. Won't you, Stanlee?'

'If you'll let me, but—'

'But what?'

'Well, you see you have never known men such as you are going to meet. You may find someone who—' Wood hesitated.

'Someone who what?' she demanded.

'Whom you'll like better than you do me.'

Gonfala laughed. 'I am not worrying.'

'But I am.'

'You needn't.' The girl's eyes swam with the moisture of adulation.

'You are so young and naive and inexperienced. You haven't the slightest idea what you are going to be up against or the types of men there are in the world – especially in the civilised world.'

'Are they as bad as Mafka?'

'In a different way they are worse.'

Van Eyk stood up and stretched. 'I'm going to get some sleep,' he said. 'You two'd better do the same thing. Goodnight.'

They said goodnight to him and watched him go; then the girl turned to Wood. 'I am not afraid,' she said, 'and you must not be. We shall have each other, and as far as I am concerned, no one else in the world counts.'

He took her hand and stroked it. 'I hope you will always feel that way, dear. It is the way I feel – it is the way I always shall.'

'Nothing will ever come between us then.' She turned her palm beneath his and pressed his fingers.

For a little time longer they talked and planned as lovers have from time immemorial; and then he went to lie down at a little distance, and Gonfala to her shelter; but she could not sleep. She was too happy. It seemed to her that she could not waste a moment of that happiness in sleep, lose minutes of rapture that she could not ever recall.

After a moment she got up and went into the night. The camp slept. The moon had dropped into the west, and the girl walked in the dense shadow of the ancient trees against which the camp had been made. She moved slowly and silently in a state of beatific rapture that was engendered not alone by her love but by the hitherto unknown sense of freedom that had come to her with release from the domination of Mafka.

No longer was she subject to the hated seizures of cruelty and vindictiveness that she now realised were no true characteristics of her own but states that had been imposed upon her by the hypnotic powers of the old magician.

She shuddered as she recalled him. Perhaps he was her father, but what of it? What of a father's love and tenderness had he ever given her? She tried to forgive him; she tried to think a kindly thought of him; but no, she could not. She had hated him in life; in death she still hated his memory.

With an effort she shook these depressing recollections from her and sought to centre her thoughts on the happiness that was now hers and that would be through a long future.

Suddenly she became aware of voices near her. 'The bloke's balmy. The nerve of him, givin' the Gonfal back to them niggers. We ort to have it an' the emerald, too. Think of it, Troll – nearly five million pounds! That's wot them two together would have brought in London or Paris.'

'An' he gives the emerald to that damn nigger wench. Wot'll she do with it? That American'll get it. She thinks he's soft on her, thinks he's goin' to marry her; but whoever heard of an American marryin' a nigger. You're right, Spike; it's all wrong. Why—'

The girl did not wait to hear more. She turned and fled silently through the darkness – her dream shattered, her happiness blasted.

Wood awakened early and called Kamudi. 'Wake the boys,' he directed; 'we're making an early start.' Then he called van Eyk, and the two busied themselves directing the preparations for the day's march. 'We'll let Gonfala sleep as long as we can,' he said; 'this may be a hard day.'

Van Eyk was groping around in the dim light of early dawn, feeling through the grasses on which he had made his bed. Suddenly he ripped out an oath.

'What's the matter?' demanded Wood.

'Stan, the Gonfal is gone! It was right under the edge of these skins last night.'

Wood made a hurried search about his own bed; then another, more carefully. When he spoke he seemed stunned, shocked. 'The emerald's gone, too, Bob. Who could have—'

'The Kaji!' Van Eyk's voice rang with conviction.

Together the two men hurried to the part of the camp where the warrior women had bedded down for the night; and there, just rising from the skins upon which they had slept, were the three.

Without preliminaries, explanation, or apology the two men searched the beds where the women had lain.

'What are you looking for?' demanded one of them.

'The Gonfal,' replied van Eyk.

'You have it,' said the woman, 'not we.'

The brief equatorial dawn had given way to the full light of day as Wood and van Eyk completed a search of the camp and realised that Spike and Troll were missing.

Wood looked crestfallen and hopeless. 'We might have guessed it right off,' he said. 'Those two were sore as pups when Clayton gave the Gonfal back to the Kaji and the emerald to Gonfala.'

'What'll we do?' asked van Eyk.

'We'll have to follow them, of course; but that's not what's worrying me right now – it's telling Gonfala. She'd been banking a lot on the sale of the emerald ever since we kept harping on the wonderful things she could buy and what she could do with so much money. Poor kid! Of course, I've got enough for us to live on, and she can have every cent of it. But it won't be quite the same to her, because she wanted so much to be independent and not be a burden to me – as though she ever could be a burden.'

'Well, you've got to tell her; and you might as well get it off your chest now as any time. If we're going after those birds, we want to get started *pronto*.'

'O.K.' He walked to Gonfala's shelter and called her. There was no response. He called again louder; and then again and again, but with no results. Then he entered. Gonfala was not there.

He came out, white and shaken. 'They must have taken her, too, Bob.'

The other shook his head. 'That would have been impossible without disturbing us – if she had tried to arouse us.'

Wood bridled angrily. 'You mean—?'

Van Eyk interrupted and put a hand on the other's shoulder. 'I don't know any more about it than you, Stan. I'm just stating a self-evident fact. You know it as well as I.'

'But the inference.'

'I can't help the inference either. They couldn't have taken Gonfala by force without waking us; therefore either she went with them willingly, or she didn't go with them at all.'

'The latter's out of the question. Gonfala would never run away from me. Why only last night we were planning on the future, after we got married.'

Van Eyk shook his head. 'Have you ever really stopped to think about what that would mean, Stan? What it would mean to you both in the future – in America? I'm thinking just as much of her happiness as yours, old man. I'm thinking of the Hell on earth that would be your lot – hers and yours. You know as well as I what one drop of coloured blood does for a man or woman in the great democracy of the U.S.A. You'd both be ostracised by the blacks as well as the whites. I'm not speaking from any personal prejudice; I'm just stating a fact. It's hard and cruel and terrible, but it still remains a fact.'

Wood nodded in sad acquiescence. There was no anger in his voice as he, replied. 'I know it as well as you, but I'd go through Hell for her. I'd live in Hell for her, and thank God for the opportunity. I love her that much.'

'Then there's nothing more to be said. If you feel that way about it, I'm for you. I'll never mention it again, and if you ever do marry it'll never change me toward either of you.'

'Thanks, old man; I'm sure of it. And now let's get busy and start after them.'

'You still think they took her?'

'I have a theory. They have both the Gonfal and the great emerald of the Zuli. You saw how Clayton used that mysterious power to bend the Kaji and Zuli to his will. They used it to compel Gonfala to accompany them without making any disturbance. You know the experience I had. Mafka dragged me away from Clayton in the same way.'

'I guess you're right. I hadn't thought of that, but why did they want Gonfala?'

Van Eyk looked uncomfortable, and the other noticed it. 'You don't mean—?' he exclaimed.

Van Eyk shrugged helplessly. 'They are men,' he said, 'and not very high types.'

'We've got to find her – we've got to hurry!' Wood was almost frantic.

Some of the blacks picked up the trail of the two men, leading toward the South; and the man hunt was on.

XII

Reunion

Two weeks rolled by. Tarzan was returning from the North with the information he sought. Sometimes he thought of the two Americans and Gonfala and the prisoners he had released from the Kaji and wondered how they fared. There had been enough of them to make their way in safety to the friendly tribes, and after that it would have been very simple to reach the outposts of civilisation. He imagined that they were well on their way by this time with a good safari of trained bearers and ample provisions. He knew that the Americans were amply able to bear the expense even if they were unable to finance themselves on the security of the great emerald of the Zuli.

It was late afternoon as the Lord of the Jungle swung along a game trail at the edge of a forest. A light wind was blowing in his face, waving his black hair. It brought to his nostrils evidence of things unseen that lay ahead. Presently it brought the acrid scent of Numa the lion. It was an old lion, for the odour was stronger than that of a cub or a young lion in its prime.

To Tarzan it was just another lion. He gave it little thought until the wind brought faintly to his nostrils another scent – the scent spoor of a Tarmangani, a she – white woman. This scent came from the same direction as that of Numa. The two, in conjunction, spelled tragedy.

Tarzan took to the trees. Game trails are winding. Through the trees he could move in a straight line, shortening the distance to his destination; and through the trees he could move with incredible swiftness. They had been his natural element since infancy when he had been borne swiftly from danger by his foster mother, Kala the she-ape.

The woman, haggard, unkempt, starving, exhausted, moved slowly and hopelessly along the trail. Her senses were dulled by fatigue and suffering. She heard nothing, yet some inner sense prompted her to turn a backward glance along the trail; then she saw the lion. He was moving softly and slowly after her. When he saw that he was discovered, he bared his fangs and growled.

The woman stopped and faced him. She had not the strength to climb a tree to safety. She knew that flight was useless. She just stood there, wide-eyed and hopeless, waiting for the end. She did not care. She had nothing to live for. She only prayed that death might come with merciful quickness.

When she had stopped, the lion had stopped. He stood glaring at her, his eyes blazing. Suddenly he started toward her at a trot. A few steps and he would charge – that swift, merciless charge of the King of beasts that is the culmination of ferocity.

He seemed to crouch lower, almost flattening himself against the ground; and now a horrid roar burst from his savage throat as he sprang forward!

The woman's eyes went wide, first in horror and then in surprise; for as the lion charged, an almost naked man dropped from an overhanging limb full upon the beast's back. She heard the roars and growls of the man mingling with those of the beast, and she shuddered. She saw a knife flash in the air, once, twice again. Then, with a final hideous roar, the lion slumped to the ground, dead.

The man leaped to his feet. It was then that she recognised him, and a feeling of relief and a sense of security possessed her. They endured for but a moment to be blasted by the hideous victory cry of the bull ape as Tarzan placed a foot upon the carcass of his kill and voiced the weird scream that had echoed so many times through other forests and jungles, deserts and plains.

Then his eyes dropped to the woman. 'Gonfala! What has happened? What are you doing here alone?'

She told him a little – just that she felt that she would bring unhappiness into Wood's life and so had run away. She had come North because she knew that he was going South. She had hoped to find some village where they would take her in; but she had found nothing; and so she had turned back intending to return to the Kaji and the only people that she knew as her own.

'You can't go back there,' Tarzan told her. 'Without Mafka's protection, they would kill you.'

'Yes, I suppose they would; but where else may I go?'

'You are coming with me. Wood will save the emerald for you. You will have all the money you will ever need. You can live then where you wish in safety and comfort.'

It was weeks before the ape-man brought the girl to his home – to the commodious bungalow where his wife welcomed and comforted her. All that time they had sought for word of Wood and van Eyk and their party but had had none. Their total disappearance seemed a mystery to Tarzan, and he planned to set out presently to solve it. Time, however, means little to the ape-man. There were other things to be done, and days passed. Yet time itself was bringing the solution nearer.

Two white men with a small safari trekked through a grim forest – damp, dark, depressing. It seemed endless.

'If ever two people were thoroughly and completely lost, we are they.' Wood had stopped and removed his sun helmet to wipe the perspiration from his forehead.

'We're no more lost than our guides,' van Eyk reminded him.

'If we keep on going east we ought to strike some village where we can get guides.'

All right, let's get going.'

Within half a mile they emerged from the forest at the edge of a wide, rolling plain.

'What a relief!' exclaimed van Eyk. 'A little more of that forest and I'd have gone nuts.'

'Look!' Wood seized his companion by the arm and pointed. 'Men!'

'Looks like a war party. See those plumes? Maybe we'd better lay low.'

'Well, the responsibility is no longer ours. They've seen us. Here they come.'

The two men stood watching a party of a dozen warriors approaching them.

'Gee, they're a good-looking bunch,' commented Wood.

'I hope they're also good.'

The blacks halted a dozen paces from the white men; then one who was evidently their leader approached closer.

'What are the bwanas doing in this country?' he asked in good English. 'Are they hunting?'

'We're lost,' explained Wood. 'We want to get guides to get us out of here.'

'Come,' said the black. 'I take you to the Big Bwana.'

'What's his name?' asked van Eyk. 'Perhaps we know him.'

'He is Tarzan.'

The two whites looked at one another in astonishment.

'You don't mean to tell me there really is a Tarzan?' demanded Wood.

'Who ever tells you there isn't does not speak true words. In an hour you shall see him.'

'What is your name?'

'Muviro, Bwana.'

'Well, lead on, Muviro; we're ready.'

An hour later the two men stood on the broad verandah of a sprawling bungalow waiting the coming of their host.

'Tarzan!' muttered van Eyk. 'It doesn't seem possible. This must be he coming.' They heard footsteps approaching from the interior of the house, and a moment later a man stepped onto the verandah and faced them.

'Clayton!' they both exclaimed in unison.

'I am glad to see you,' said Tarzan. 'I hadn't been able to get any word of you, and I was worried. Where have you been?'

'The night you left, Spike and Troll stole the Gonfal and the great emerald and beat it. They took Gonfala with them. We have been hunting for them. The very first day we lost their trail in some rocky country. We never found it again. Some of our blacks thought they had gone to the South and west. We searched in that direction and got lost ourselves.'

'The Gonfal and the great emerald are both gone? Well, perhaps it is just as well. They would have brought more unhappiness than anything else. Riches usually do!'

'Hang the stones!' exclaimed Wood. 'It is Gonfala I want to find. I don't give a tinker's damn for either of the rocks.'

'I think we shall find her. It is not difficult for me to find anyone in Africa. But now I will have you shown to your rooms. You will find a bath and clean clothes; among them something that will fit you, I'm sure. When you are ready, come to the patio; you will find us there.'

Van Eyk was the first to enter the patio, a flowering paradise around which the house was built. A golden haired girl lay on a reed chaise longue, a copy of the Illustrated London News in her hand. Hearing him, she turned. Her eyes went wide in astonishment.

'Bob!' she gasped as she sprang to her feet.

'Gonfala!'

'Where is he? Is he all right?'

'Yes; he is here. How did you escape from Spike and Troll?'

'Escape from Spike and Troll? I was never with them.'

'You went away alone? Why did you go?'

She told him then what she had overheard Spike and Troll say. 'I knew then that I would spoil Stanlee's life. I knew that he loved me. I never thought that he wanted me just for the emerald. And I loved him. I loved him too much to let him marry me. Perhaps, when he had time to think it over, he was glad that I went away.'

Van Eyk shook his head. 'No, you are very wrong. I spoke to him of the matter; and here is what he said, as nearly as I can recall his words: "I'd go through Hell for her. I'd live in Hell for her, and thank God for the opportunity. That is how much I love her." I think those were about his very words.'

Tears came to the girl's eyes. 'May I see him soon?'

'He'll be out in a minute. Here he comes now. I'll go.'

She looked her thanks.

When Wood came into the patio and saw her, he just stood and looked at her for a moment, devouring her with his eyes. He never said a word or asked a question – just crossed to her and took her in his arms. Their voices were too full of tears of happiness for words.

After a while, when they could speak, each had the other's story. After that they knew that nothing could ever come between them.

In the evening, with the others, they were discussing their plans for the future. Wood said they would be married and go at once to America.

'I must go to London first,' said Gonfala. 'I have a letter to take to the Colonial Office there. You know, I told you about it. Let me get it. I cannot read it. I was never taught to read.'

She went to her room and presently returned with the letter. It was yellow with age. She handed it to Tarzan. 'Please read it aloud,' she said.

Tarzan opened the single sheet and read:

To Whom it May Concern:

   I am giving this letter to my daughter to take to London to identify her if she is ever fortunate enough to escape from the Kaji. They killed her mother shortly after she was born and raised her to be Queen of the Kaji. They call her Gonfala. I have never dared to tell her that she is my daughter, as Mafka has threatened to kill her if she ever learns that he is not her father.

Mountford.

XIII

Cannibals

A low sun pointed long shadows toward the east; the tired day was preparing to lay aside its burdens. Far away, a lion roared. It was the prelude to another African night, majestic as the King of beasts and as savage.

A party of eight men laid down their few belongings and made camp beside a water hole. Two of the men were white. Like their black companions they were armed with bows and arrows and short spears; there was not a fire-arm among them all.

Some of the men carried meat from the last kill, and there were two packages wrapped in skins. Beside their weapons, that was all. It was a poorly equipped safari, if it could be said to have been equipped at all.

The blacks were quiet, speaking in whispers as they cooked the meat for their evening meal. The white men were glum and scowling.

One of them nodded toward the blacks. 'The beggars are scairt stiff.'

The other nodded. 'Cannibal country, and they know it.'

His companion sat scowling down at the two skin wrapped packages for a long period of silence. 'I'm a-scairt myself, Troll,' he said finally. 'Scairt o' these things. I think they's a curse on 'em.'

Troll shrugged. 'I could take a lot o' cursin' for six million pun.'

'Yeh; if we get out alive.'

'I ain't worrit about that. What I'm worrit about is runnin' into that bloke, Clayton. He'll take the rocks away from us.'

'He went North.'

'But he said he was comin' back, an' he said he'd know if we'd pulled anything crooked. I don't like that bloke.'

They lapsed into silence, chewing on the half cooked meat of a tough old boar the blacks had killed the day before. From the forest, a spur of which ran down almost to the water hole, eyes watched them. Again the lion roared.

'The beggar's gettin' closer,' remarked Spike. 'I hopes he ain't no man-eater.'

Troll fidgeted. 'Shut up!' he growled. 'Can't you think of somethin' pleasant for a change?'

'Bein' way out here without no gun'd make any bloke nervous. Look at them damn things!' He kicked his bow and bundle of arrows that lay at his feet. 'I might kill a rabbit with 'em – if I could hit 'im; but I couldn't hit a elephant if he stood still at ten paces – and you know wot kind of a target a lion makes when he charges.'

'Oh, fer cripe's sake, shut up!'

Again they lapsed into silence. The shadow of the forest covered them and stretched out across the plain, for the sun had all but set. Suddenly there was a frightened cry of, 'Bwana! Look!' One of the blacks was pointing toward the forest.

The white men wheeled as they rose to their feet. Coming toward them were a dozen black warriors. Spike stooped to pick up his bow and arrows.

'Lay off!' warned Troll. 'They ain't enough of us – an' anyways they may be friendly.' Spike stood erect again with empty hands. One by one the blacks of their party rose slowly to their feet.

The strangers were approaching cautiously, their weapons ready. They halted a dozen paces from the camp, their grim visaged leader in advance of the others. He surveyed the two white men and their six bearers arrogantly, contemptuously. Troll made the sign of peace.

The leader strode forward followed by his warriors. 'What you do here in the country of the Bantango?' he demanded.

'We look for guides,' replied Troll in the same dialect. 'Big safari behind us – many guns – they come soon; then we go. We wait here they come.'

'You lie,' said the chief. 'My man one he followed you two days; then he come me. No big safari. No guns. You lie.'

'Wot did I tell you?' demanded Spike. 'They's a curse on us – an' look at them filed teeth. You know what them filed teeth mean.'

'I told you it was cannibal country,' observed Troll, lamely.

'Gawdamighty, I'd give both them rocks for a gun,' moaned Spike.

'The rocks!' exclaimed Troll. 'That's it! Wy didn't we think o' that before?'

'Think o' what?'

'The Gonfal. We can use it like old Mafka did, just put a hand on it an' make any bloke do wotever you wants him to do.'

'Blime! That's a idea. Make 'em get out o' here.' He stopped and started to unwrap the Gonfal, the great diamond of the Kaji.

The chief took a step forward. 'What you got?'' he demanded.

'Big medicine,' said Troll. 'You like see?'

The chief nodded. 'Me like, me take.'

The swift equatorial night had fallen. Only the cooking fires of the little camp illuminated the tense scene. From the deep shadows a great lion watched.

Spike undid the thongs that bound the wrappings to the Gonfal, and with trembling hands threw back the skin revealing the great stone shimmering and scintillating in the dancing lights of the cooking fires. The chief recoiled with a short gasp of astonishment. He did not know what the stone was, but its brilliance awed him.

Troll dropped to one knee beside the Gonfal and laid a hand on it. 'Go away!' he said to the chief. 'Lay down your weapons, all of you; and go away!'

The chief and his warriors stood looking at the Gonfal and at Troll. They did not lay down their weapons and they did not go away. As nothing happened, they regained confidence.

'No lay down weapons; no go away,' said the chief. 'We stay. Me take.' He pointed at Gonfal. 'You come our village. You b'long me.'

'You better go away,' insisted Troll. He tried to make his voice sound commanding, but it did not.

'Wot's wrong with the Gonfal?' demanded Spike.

'It won't work.'

'Le'me try it.' Spike stooped and placed a palm on the stone. 'You blokes drop your weapons an' beat it before our big medicine kills you,' he shouted threateningly.

The chief stepped forward and kicked Spike in the face, bowling him over on his back. His warriors rushed in with loud war cries, brandishing their weapons. And then from the outer darkness came a thunderous roar that shook the earth, and a great lion charged into the savage mêlée.

He leaped over the prostrate Spike and brushed past Troll, falling upon the terrified chief and his warriors.

Troll was quick to grasp the opportunity for escape. He gathered up the great diamond, and shouted to Spike and the bearers to follow him and bring the other stone; then he ran for the forest.

A few screams mingled with savage growls rang in their ears for brief moments; then silence.

All night they followed close to the edge of the forest, nor did they stop until they came upon a small stream shortly after daylight. Then they threw themselves upon the ground, exhausted.

As they chewed once more upon the flesh of the old boar their spirits revived, and they spoke for the first time for hours.

'I guess we don't know how to work the rock,' ventured Troll.

'Who says "we"?' demanded Spike. 'I worked it.'

'You?'

'Sure. Didn't I tell 'em they'd get killed if they didn't beat it? And wot happens? The Gonfal calls the old man-eater. You remember that lamp that bloke used to rub – I forget his name – but this works just the same for me. I rubs it and wishes – and there you are!'

'Rats!'

'A'right; didn't I do it?'

'No. That lion was comin' long before you touched the rock. He smelled meat – that was wot brought him, not you and your bloody rock.'

'I'll show you. Here, give it to me.'

Spike took the diamond from Troll, uncovered it, and placed a palm on its gleaming surface. He glowered fixedly at his companion.

'Sit down!' he commanded.

Troll grinned derisively and advised Spike to 'Go to 'ell.' The latter scratched his head in momentary confusion; then he brightened. ''Ere,' he exclaimed; 'I got a better idea.' He scratched a line on the ground with a bit of stick. 'I says now that you can't cross that line – and you can't.'

'Who says I can't?' demanded Troll, stepping across the line.

'I guess maybe there's something I don't understand about this,' admitted Spike. 'That Clayton bloke worked it on the Kaji and the Zuli. You seen him yourself.'

'Gonfala was there,' reminded Troll. 'Maybe that's the answer. Maybe it won't work without her.'

'Maybe,' admitted Spike; 'but the Zuli medicine man done the same work with the emerald, an' he didn't have no Gonfala.'

'Well, try the emerald, then.'

'Le'me have it.'

'I ain't got it.'

'One of the boys must have it.'

'I told you to bring it.'

'One of the boys always carries it,' insisted Spike, turning to the bearers sprawled on the ground. 'Hey, you! W'ich one o' you's got the green rock?' They looked at him blankly; then they looked at one another.

'No got,' said one. 'No bring.'

'Hell!' ejaculated Troll. 'You're a rare un, you are, a-leavin' maybe a three million pun stone back there in the cannibal country!'

XIV

Kidnapped

'Tired?' asked Wood.

Gonfala shook her head. 'Not a bit.'

'You're doing pretty well for a girl who never had to do anything more strenuous than sit on a throne,' laughed van Eyk.

'You'd be surprised. I can probably outrun and outlast either of you. You see, I used to hunt with the Kaji. Mafka insisted on it – lots of exercise. He was a great believer in exercise for every one but Mafka.'

'I'm glad,' said Wood, 'for we've got two long marches between this camp and railhead. I'll be glad when it's over. To tell you the truth, I'm fed up on Africa. I hope I never see it again.'

'I don't blame you, Stanlee; you came near staying here a long time.'

'Yes; eternity is rather a long time.' Wood grimaced. 'It's hard to realise, even now, that we escaped.'

'It's incredible,' agreed Gonfala. 'We're the first persons ever to escape from Mafka; and he'd been there, oh, no one knows how long – the Kaji said always. They believed that he created the world.'

The three were camped at the end of a day's march on their way out toward civilisation. They had a dependable, well equipped safari furnished by Tarzan. The men planned on devoting one day to hunting, as they were in excellent game country; then they would cover the two long marches to railhead. The delay for hunting was Wood's concession to van Eyk, an indefatigable Nimrod, who had obtained permission from the Lord of the Jungle to take out a few trophies for his collection.

As night fell, the light of their beast fire cast dancing shadows through the camp and shone far out into the night, both attracting and repelling the great carnivores upon whose domain they trespassed; for this was lion country. It attracted also other eyes a mile or more to the North.

'I wonder what that might be,' said Spike.

'A fire,' growled Troll; 'what you think it was – a iceberg?'

'Funny, ain't you?'

'Not as funny as a bloke what runs off an leaves three million puns worth o' emerald with a bunch of cannibals.'

'Fer cripe's sake quit chewin' about that; I didn't leave it any more 'n you did. What I mean is, there must be men over by that fire; I wonders who they might be.'

'Natives, perhaps.'

'Or white hunters.'

'What difference does it make?' asked Troll.

'They might put us on the right trail.'

'An' tell that Clayton bloke where we are? You're balmy.'

'How do you know he's around here? Maybe they never even heard of him.'

'He's everywhere. Everybody's heard of him. He said he'd know it if we double-crossed Stanley. After I seen what he done in the Kaji country, I wouldn't put nothin' past him – he omnivirous.'

'Whatever that means.'

'You're igorant.'

'Well just the same, I think we'd oughter find out who made that fire. If they're one thing, we'd better light out of here; if they're the other, we can ask 'em to set us on the right trail.'

'Maybe you said something intelligent at last. It wouldn't do no harm to go have a look-see.'

'That fire may be a long ways off, and—'

'And what?'

'This is lion country.'

'You scared?'

'Sure I'm scared. So are you, unless you're a bigger fool than I think. Nobody but a fool wouldn't be scared in lion country at night without a gun.'

'We'll take a couple of the smokes with us. They say lions like dark meat.'

'All right; let's get goin'.'

Guided by the fire, the four men approached the Wood-van Eyk camp and after reconnoitring made their way to the concealment of a clump of bushes where they could see and not be seen.

'Cripes!' whispered Spike. 'Look who's there!'

'Gonfala!' breathed Troll.

'An' Wood an' van Eyk.'

'T'ell with them! If we only had the girl!'

'Wot do we want of her?'

'You get less brains every minute. Wot do we want of 'er! If we had her we could make the diamond do its stuff just like Mafka did – just like Clayton did. We'd be safe; nothin' nor nobody couldn't hurt us.'

'Well, we ain't got her.'

'Shut up! Listen to wot they're sayin'.'

The voices of the three whites by the campfire came clearly to Troll and Spike. Van Eyk was making plans for the morrow's hunt.

'I really think Gonfala ought to stay in camp and rest; but as long as she insists on coming along, you and she can go together. If there were three men, now, we could spread out farther and cover more ground.'

'I can do whatever a man can do,' insisted Gonfala. 'You can assume that you have three men.'

'But, Gonfala—'

'Don't be foolish, Stanlee. I am not as the women you have known in your civilised countries. From what you have told me, I shall be as helpless and afraid there as they would be here; but here I am not afraid. So I hunt tomorrow as the third man, and now I am going to bed. Goodnight, Stanlee. Goodnight, Bob.'

'Well, I guess that settles it,' remarked Wood, with a wry smile; 'but when I get you back in God's country you'll have to mind me. Goodnight.'

'Perhaps,' said Gonfala.

The chill of night still hung like a vapour below the new sun as the three hunters set out from their camp for the day's sport, and although the hunt had been van Eyk's idea primarily, each of the others was keen to bag a lion. Over their breakfast coffee they had laid wagers as to which would be the lucky one to bring down the first trophy, with the result that not a little friendly rivalry had been engendered. That each might, seemed entirely possible, as the night had been filled with the continual roaring of the great carnivores.

Shortly after leaving camp the three separated, van Eyk keeping straight ahead toward the east, Wood diverging toward the South, and Gonfala to the North; each was accompanied by a gunbearer; and some of the members of the safari followed along after van Eyk and Wood, either believing that one of the men would be more likely to get a lion than would the girl, or, perhaps, feeling safer behind the guns of the men.

From behind an outcropping of rock at the summit of a low hill Northwest of the Wood-van Eyk camp Spike and Troll watched their departure; while below them, concealed from sight, the six men of their safari waited. The two whites watched Gonfala and her gunbearer approaching across the open plain. The direction that she was taking suggested that she would pass a little to the east of them, but that she would then still be in sight of van Eyk and possibly Wood also.

The latter was not at all happy about the arrangements for the day; he did not like the idea of Gonfala going out on her own after a lion with only a gunbearer, but the girl had overridden his every objection. He had insisted, however, upon sending as gunbearer a man of known courage who was also a good shot; and him he had instructed to be always ready with the second rifle in the event that Gonfala got into a tight place and, regardless of custom, to shoot a charging lion himself.

While Gonfala had had little previous experience of firearms prior to a few weeks, it gave him some consolation to reflect that she had, even in that short time, developed into an excellent shot; and in so far as her nerve was concerned he had no cause for anxiety. What he could not have known, of course, was the far greater menace of the two men who watched her from their rocky concealment upon the hilltop.

Gonfala passed the hill beneath the eyes of Spike and Troll and then crossed a low rise that was a continuation of the hill running down into the plain, and from then on she was hidden from the sight of either van Eyk or Wood. The country she now entered was broken by gullies and outcroppings of rock, by low bushes and occasional trees; so that it was comparatively easy for Spike and Troll to follow her without danger of being discovered; and this they did, keeping well to the rear of her and catching only an occasional glimpse of her during the ensuing hour.

Quite unsuspecting the fact that eight men followed upon her trail, Gonfala continued her seemingly fruitless search for a lion, bearing constantly a little to the west because of a range of low hills that lay to the right of her and thus constantly increasing the distance between herself and her two companions. She had about come to the conclusion that the lions had all left the country when she heard, faint and far toward the east, the report of two rifle shots.

'Someone else had the luck,' she said to her gunbearer; 'I guess we came in the wrong direction.'

'No, Memsahib,' he whispered, pointing; 'look! Simba!'

She looked quickly in the direction he indicated; and there among the grasses beneath a tree she saw the head of a lion, the yellow-green eyes gazing unblinkingly at her. The beast was about a hundred yards distant; he was lying down, and as only his head was visible he offered a poor target. A frontal shot, she knew, would only tend to infuriate him and precipitate a charge.

'Pay no attention to him,' she whispered; 'we'll try to get closer and to one side.'

She moved forward then, not directly toward the lion but as though to pass a little to the right of him; and always his eyes followed them, but neither she nor the gunbearer gave any indication that they were aware of his presence. When she had approached to within about fifty yards she stopped and faced him, but he only lay quietly regarding her. But when she took a few steps straight toward him, he bared his great fangs and growled.

Topping a rise behind her, Spike took in the situation at a glance. He motioned to his men to halt, and beckoned Troll to his side. Together they watched the tense scene below them.

'I wish he'd get up,' said Gonfala.

The gunbearer picked up a stone and hurled it at the lion. The result was immediate and electrical. With an angry roar the lion leaped to its feet and charged.

'Shoot, Memsahib!'

Gonfala dropped to one knee and fired. The lion leaped high into the air, its angry roars shattering the silence. It was hit, but it was not stopped; for although it rolled over on its back it was up again in an instant and bearing down on them at terrific speed. Gonfala fired again and missed. Then the gunbearer took aim and pressed the trigger of his gun. There was only a futile click. The cartridge missed fire. The lion was almost upon Gonfala when the gunbearer, unnerved by the failure of his gun, turned and fled. Unwittingly he had saved Gonfala's life, for at sight of the man in flight the lion, already rising over Gonfala, followed a natural instinct that has saved the life of many a hunter and pursued the fleeing man. Gonfala fired again, and again scored a hit; but it did not stop the infuriated beast as it rose upon its hind feet and seized the gunbearer, the great fangs closing upon his head until they met in the centre of his brain.

The girl was aghast as she stood helplessly by while the huge cat mauled its victim for a moment; then it sagged upon the body of the man and died.

'That,' said Troll, 'is wot I calls a bit o' luck. We not only gets the girl, but we gets two guns.'

'And no witness,' added Spike. 'Come on!' He motioned the others to follow him, and started down the declivity toward Gonfala.

She saw them almost immediately and for a moment thought her companions were coming, but presently she recognised them. She knew that they were bad men who had stolen the great diamond and the emerald, but she had no reason to believe that she was in any danger from them.

They came up to her smiling and friendly. 'You sure had a narrow squeak,' said Spike. 'We seen it from the top of that rise, but we couldn't have done nothing to help you even if we'd had guns – we was too far away.'

'What are you doing here?' she asked.

'We was tryin' to find our way to railhead,' explained Spike. 'We been lost fer weeks.'

Troll was recovering the gun and ammunition from the dead gunbearer, and Spike was eyeing the splendid rifle that Gonfala carried.

'We're on our way to railhead,' she explained. 'You can come back to camp with me and go on to railhead with us.'

'Won't that be nice!' exclaimed Spike. 'Say, that's a fine gun you got there. Lemme see it a minute.' Thoughtlessly, she handed the weapon over to him; then she stepped over to the body of the dead gunbearer.

'He's quite dead,' she said. 'It's too bad. Your men can carry him back to camp.'

'We ain't goin' back to your camp,' said Spike.

'Oh,' she exclaimed. 'Well, what am I to do? I can't take him back alone.'

'You ain't goin' back neither.'

'What do you mean?'

'Just wot I says: you ain't going' back to your camp. You're comin' with us.'

'Oh, no I'm not.'

'Listen, Gonfala,' said Spike. 'We don't want no trouble with you. We don't want to hurt you none; so you might as well come along peaceful like. We need you.'

'What for?' Her voice was brave, but her heart sank within her.

'We got the Gonfal, but we can't make it work without you.'

'Work?'

'Yes, work. We're goin' to set ourselves up like Mafka did and be Kings – just as soon as we find a piece o' country we like. We'll live like Kings, too, off the fat of the land. You can be Queen – have everything you want. Maybe, even, I'll marry you.' He grinned.

'The hell you will,' snapped Troll. 'She belongs to me as much as she does to you.'

Gonfala cringed. 'I belong to neither of you. You are both fools. If you take me away, you will be followed and killed; or, at the least, both I and the Gonfal will be taken from you. If you have any sense you will let me go; then you can take the Gonfal to Europe. They tell me that there the money that it would bring would buy you anything that you wanted all the rest of your lives.'

'A fat chance we'd have gettin' rid o' that rock in Europe,' said Troll. 'No, sister, we got it all figgered out. You're comin' with us, an' that's that.'

XV

Clues

Van Eyk dropped his lion with the second shot, and a few minutes later he heard the three shots fired by Gonfala. Wood, having had no luck and attracted by the report of van Eyk's gun, joined him. He was still apprehensive concerning Gonfala's safety; and now that van Eyk had his trophy, he suggested that they send the carcass back to camp while they joined Gonfala. Van Eyk agreed, and they set out in the direction from which they had heard the shots.

They searched for two hours without result, often calling her name and occasionally discharging their rifles; then, more by chance than design, they stumbled upon the little swale where Gonfala had come upon her lion. There it lay upon the body of the dead gunbearer, but Gonfala was nowhere to be seen.

The ground was hard and stony, giving no indication to the untrained eyes of the white men that others beside Gonfal and her gunbearer had been there; so they assumed that, having no one to cut off or carry the head of the lion back to camp, the girl had returned there herself alone; and that, having come from another direction, they had missed her. They were, therefore, not unduly apprehensive until after they reached camp and discovered that she had not returned.

By that time it was late in the afternoon; but Wood insisted upon taking up the search at once, and van Eyk seconded the suggestion. They divided the safari into three sections. Van Eyk and Wood each heading one set out on slightly diverging trails in the general direction that Gonfala had taken in the morning, while the third, under a headman, was ordered to remain in camp, keeping a large fire burning and occasionally discharging a rifle to guide Gonfala if she should return toward camp without meeting either Wood or van Eyk. And all during the night Gonfala and her captors heard the faint report of rifles far to the South.

It was around noon of the following day that, exhausted and disheartened, Wood and van Eyk returned to camp.

'I'm afraid it's no use, old man,' said the latter, sympathetically. 'if she'd been alive she'd have heard our rifles and replied.'

'I can't believe that she's dead,' said Wood; 'I won't believe it!' Van Eyk shook his head. 'I know it's tough, but you've got to face facts and reason. She couldn't be alive in this lion country now.'

'But she had two guns,' insisted Wood. 'You saw that she took the gun and ammunition from the gunbearer after he was killed. If she'd been attacked by a lion, she'd have fired at least once; and we never heard a shot.'

'She might have been taken unaware – stalked after dark and struck down before she knew a lion was near. You've seen 'em charge; you know it's all over in a second if you aren't ready for 'em.'

Wood nodded. 'Yes, I know. I suppose you're right, but I won't give up – not yet.'

'Well, Stan, I've got to get back home. If I thought there was the slightest chance, I'd stay, but I know there's not. You'd better come along and try to forget it as soon as you can. You might never, here; but back home it'll be different.'

'There's no use, Van; you go along. I'm going to stay.'

'But what can you do alone?'

'I won't try to do anything alone. I'm going back and find Tarzan; he'll help me. If anyone can find her or where she was killed it's he.'

Ten days later Wood plodded wearily into the camp that he had not left except in daily fruitless searches for his Gonfala. He had not gone back to enlist Tarzan's aid; but had, instead, sent a long letter to the ape-man by a runner. Every day for ten days he had combed the country for miles around, and each day he had become more convinced that Gonfala was not dead. He had found no trace of a human kill by lions, no shred of clothing, no sign of the two guns or the ammunition that Gonfala had had with her; though he had found plenty of lion kills – zebra, antelope, wildebeest. But he had found something else that gave support to his belief that Gonfala might be alive – the camp of Spike and Troll. It lay only a short distance Northerly from his own camp. Gonfala must have passed close to it the morning that she started out to hunt. What type of men had camped there, he could not know; but he assumed that they were natives; for there were no signs of white men – no empty tins, no discarded scrap of clothing, no indications that a tent had been pitched.

Perhaps, then, Gonfala's fate had been worse than the merciful death the King of beasts would have accorded her. That thought goaded him to desperation, and filled his mind with red imaginings of vengeance. Such were his thoughts as he threw himself upon his cot in hopeless bafflement to reproach himself as he had a thousand thousand times for having permitted Gonfala to hunt alone that day – how long ago it seemed, how many ages of bitter suffering!

A figure darkened the doorway of the tent, and Wood turned to look. Wood sprang to his feet. 'Tarzan! God, I thought you'd never come.'

'I came as soon as I got your letter. You have been searching, of course; what have you found?'

Wood told him of his failure to find any evidence that Gonfala had fallen prey to lions but that he had found a camp in which there had been men recently.

'That is interesting,' commented Tarzan. 'It is too late now to investigate that today; tomorrow I'll have a look at it.'

Early the next morning Wood and the ape-man were at the camp from which Spike and Troll had been attracted by the campfire that had led them to the discovery of the presence of Gonfala. Tarzan examined the ground and the surroundings minutely. His lifetime of experience, his trained powers of observation, his sensitive nostrils revealed facts that were a sealed book to the American. The charred wood in the dead fires, the crushed grasses, the refuse each told him something.

'It was a poor camp,' he said finally. 'Perhaps ten or a dozen men camped here. They had very little food and their packs were few. They did have packs, and that indicates that there were white men – perhaps one, perhaps two; the rest were natives. Their food was poor. That would suggest that they had no firearms, for this is a good game country; so perhaps there were no white men at all. Yet I am sure there were. They had only the meat of an old boar to eat. Some of the bones were split and the marrow extracted. That suggests natives. Other bones were not split, and that suggests white men.'

'How do you know they had packs?' asked Wood, who could see no evidence to suggest anything more than that someone had been there and built fires and eaten food. He could see the discarded bones of their repast.

'If you look carefully you will see where they lay on the ground. It has been ten days at least; and the signs are faint, but they are there. The grasses are pressed down and the marks of the cords that bound the packs are still visible.'

'I see nothing,' admitted Wood after close scrutiny.

Tarzan smiled one of his rare smiles. 'Now we shall see which way they went,' he said. 'The spoor of so many men should be plain.'

They followed toward the North the freshest spoor that led from the camp, only to lose it where a great herd of grazing game had obliterated it; then Tarzan picked it up again beyond. Eventually it led to the spot where the bodies of the gunbearer and the lion had lain.

'Your theory seems to have been correct,' said the ape-man. 'Gonfala, apparently, was captured by this party.'

'That was eleven days ago,' mused Wood despairingly. 'There is no telling where they are now, or what they have done to her. We must lose no time in following.'

'Not we.' replied Tarzan. 'You will return to your camp and start tomorrow for my place. When I have definitely located Gonfala, if I cannot rescue her without help.' (again he smiled) 'I'll send word by a runner, and you can come with an escort of Waziri.'

'But can't I go along with you?' demanded Wood.

'I can travel much faster alone. You will do as I say. That is all.'

And that *was* all. Wood stood watching the magnificent figure of the ape-man until it disappeared beyond a rise in the rolling plain; then he turned dejectedly back toward camp. He knew that Tarzan was right, that a man whose senses were dulled by generations of non-use would prove only a drag on the alert ape-man.

For two days Tarzan followed the trail in a Northerly direction; then an unseasonable rain obliterated it forever. He was now in the country of the Bantangos, a warlike tribe of cannibals and hereditary enemies of his Waziri. He knew that if the captors of Gonfala had come this way it might be because they were themselves Bantangos, and so he determined to investigate thoroughly before searching farther. If they had not been Bantangos, it was very possible that they had been captured by this tribe; for he knew that they were a small and poorly equipped company.

In any event it seemed best to have a look into the village of the chief, to which, unquestionably, important captives would have been taken; but where the village lay, the ape-man did not know. To the east of him a range of low hills stretched way into the North, and to these he made his way. As he ascended them he commenced to glimpse villages to the west and North, and finally from the summit of one of the higher hills he obtained a view of a considerable extent of country containing many villages. The majority of these were mean and small – just a handful of huts surrounded by flimsy palisades of poles.

The valley in which the villages lay was dotted with trees, and on the west abutted upon a forest. It was a scene of peace and loveliness that lent a certain picturesqueness to even the squalid kraals of the Bantangos and belied the savagery and bestiality of the inhabitants. The beauty of the aspect was not lost upon the ape-man, whose appreciation of the loveliness or grandeur of nature, undulled by familiarity, was one of the chiefest sources of his joy of living. In contemplating the death that he knew must come to him as to all living things his keenest regret lay in the fact that he would never again be able to look upon the hills and valleys and forests of his beloved Africa; and so today, as he lay like a great lion low upon the summit of a hill, stalking his prey, he was still sensible of the natural beauties that lay spread before him. Nor was he unmindful of a large village that lay toward the centre of the valley, the largest, by far, of any of the villages. This, he knew, must be the village of the chief of the Bantangos.

The moonless night descended, a black shroud that enveloped the forest, the trees, and the villages, concealing them from the eyes of the watcher; then the Lord of the Jungle arose, stretching himself. So like a lion's were all his movements that one might have expected the roar of the hunting beast to rumble from his great chest. Silently he moved down toward the village of the chief. Little lights showed now about the valley, marking the various villages by their cooking fires. Toward the fires of the largest strode an English Lord, naked but for a G string.

From the hills he was quitting a lion roared. He too was coming down to the villages where the natives had gathered their little flocks within the flimsy enclosures of their kraals. The ape-man stopped and raised his face toward the heavens. From his deep chest rose the savage, answering challenge of the bull-ape. The savages in the villages fell silent, looking questioningly at one another, wide eyed in terror. The warriors seized their weapons, the women huddled their children closer.

'A demon,' whispered one.

'Once before I heard that cry,' said the chief of the Bantangos. 'It is the cry of the devil-god of the Waziri.'

'Why would he come here?' demanded a warrior. 'The rains have come many times since we raided in the country of the Waziri.'

'If it is not he,' said the chief, 'then it is another devil-god.'

'When I was a boy,' said an old man, 'I went once with a raiding party far toward the place where the sun sleeps, to a great forest where the hairy tree-men live. They make a loud cry like that, a cry that stops the heart and turns the skin cold. Perhaps it is one of the hairy tree-men. We were gone a long time. The rains were just over when we left our village; they came again before we returned. I was a great warrior. I killed many warriors on that raid. I ate their hearts; that is what makes me so brave.' No one paid any attention to him, but he rambled on. The others were listening intently for a repetition of the weird cry or for any sound that might presage the approach of an enemy.

Tarzan approached the palisade that surrounded the village of the chief. A tree within the enclosure spread its branches across the top. The ape-man came close and investigated. Through the interstices between the poles that formed the palisade he watched the natives. Gradually their tense nerves relaxed as there was no repetition of the cry that had alarmed them; and they returned to their normal pursuits, the women to their cooking, the men to the immemorial custom of the Lords of creation – to doing nothing.

Tarzan wished to scale the palisade and gain the branches of the tree that spread above him; but he wished to do it without attracting the attention of the Bantangos, and because of the frail construction of the palisade, he knew that that would be impossible during the quiet that prevailed within the village at the supper hour. He must wait. Perhaps the opportunity he sought would present itself later. With the patience of the wild beast that stalks its prey, the ape-man waited. He could, if necessary, wait an hour, a day, a week. Time meant as little to him as it had to the apes that raised him, his contacts with civilisation not having as yet enslaved him to the fetish of time.

Nothing that he could see within the restricted limits of his vision, a section of the village visible between two huts just within the palisade, indicated that the Bantangos held white prisoners; but he knew that if such were the case they might be confined within a hut; and it was this, among other things, that he must know before continuing his search elsewhere.

The evening meal concluded, the blacks lapsed into somnolence. The quiet of the African night was broken only by the occasional roars of the hunting lion, coming closer and closer, a sound so familiar that it aroused the interest of neither the blacks within the village or the watcher without.

An hour passed. The lion ceased his roaring, evidence that he was now approaching his prey and stalking. The blacks stirred with awakening interest with the passing of the phenomenon of digestion and became motivated by the same primitive urge that fills El Morocco and other late spots with dancers after the theatre. A dusky maestro gathered his players with their primitive instruments, and the dancing began. It was the moment for which Tarzan had been awaiting. Amidst the din of the drums and the shouts of the dancers he swarmed to the top of the palisade and swung into the tree above.

From a convenient limb he surveyed he scene below. He could see the Chief's hut now and the chief himself. The old fellow sat upon a stool watching the dancers, but in neither the chief nor the dancers did the ape-man discover a focus for his interest – that was riveted upon something that lay at the chief's feet – the Great Emerald of the Zuli.

There could be no mistake. There could be but one such stone, and its presence here induced a train of deductive reasoning in the alert mind of the ape-man that led to definite conclusions – that Spike and Troll had been in the vicinity and that it was logical to assume that it must have been they who abducted Gonfala. Were they here now, in this village of the Bantangos? Tarzan doubted it; there was nothing to indicate that there were any prisoners in the village, but he must know definitely; so he waited on with the infinite patience that was one of the heritages of his upbringing.

The night wore on; and at last the dancers tired, and the village street was deserted. Sounds of slumber arose from the dark huts, unlovely sounds, fitting bedfellows of unlovely odours. Here and there a child fretted or an infant wailed. Beyond the palisade a lion coughed.

The ape-man dropped silently into the empty street. Like a shadow he passed from hut to hut, his keen nostrils searching out the scents that would tell him, as surely as might his eyes could he have seen within, whether a white prisoner lay there. No one heard him; not even a sleeping cur was disturbed. When he had made the rounds he knew that those be sought were not there, but he must know more. He returned to the chief's hut. On the ground before it, like worthless trash, lay the Great Emerald of the Zuli. Its weird green light cast a soft radiance over the bronzed body of the jungle Lord, tinged the chief's hut palely green, accentuated the blackness of the low entrance way.

The ape-man paused a moment, listening; then he stooped and entered the hut. He listened to the breathing of the inmates. By their breathing he located the women and the children and the one man – that one would be the chief. To his side he stepped and kneeled, stooping low. Steel thewed fingers closed lightly upon the throat of the sleeper. The touch awakened him.

'Make no sound,' whispered the ape-man, 'if you would live.'

'Who are you?' demanded the chief in a whisper. 'What do you want?'

'I am the devil-god,' replied Tarzan. 'Where are the two white men and the white woman?'

'I have seen no white woman,' replied the chief.

'Do not speak lies – I have seen the green stone.'

'The two white men left it behind them when they ran away,' insisted the chief, 'but there was no white woman with them. The sun has risen from his bed as many times as I have fingers on my two hands and toes on one foot since the white men were here.'

'Why did they run away?' demanded the ape-man.

'We were at their camp. A lion came and attacked us; the white men ran away, leaving the green stone behind.'

A woman awoke and sat up. 'Who speaks?' she demanded.

'Tell her to be quiet,' cautioned Tarzan.

'Shut up,' snapped the chief at the woman, 'if you do not wish to die – it is the devil-god!'

The woman stifled a scream and lay down, burying her face in the dirty reeds that formed her bed.

'Which way did the white men go?' asked the ape-man.

'They came from the North. When they ran away they went into the forest to the west. We did not follow them. The lion had killed two of my warriors and mauled others.'

'Were there many in the safari of the white men?'

'Only six, beside themselves. It was a poor safari. They had little food and no guns. They were very poor.' His tone was contemptuous. 'I have told you all I know. I did not harm the white men or their men. Now go away. I know no more.'

'You stole the green stone from them,' accused Tarzan.

'No. They were frightened and ran away, forgetting it; but they took the white stone with them.'

'The white stone?'

'Yes, the white stone. One of them held it in his hands and told us to put down our weapons and go away. He said it was big medicine and that it would kill us if we did not go away; but we stayed, and it did not kill us.'

In the darkness the ape-man smiled. 'Has a white woman passed through your country lately? If you lie to me I shall come back and kill you.'

'I have never seen a white woman,' replied the chief. 'If one had passed through my country I should know it.'

Tarzan slipped from the hut as silently as he had come. As he went, he gathered up the Great Emerald and swung into the tree that overhung the palisade. The chief breathed a choking sigh of relief and broke into a cold sweat.

Strong in the nostrils of the ape-man was the scent of Numa the lion. He knew that the great cat was stalking close to the palisade. He had no quarrel with Numa this night and no wish to tempt a hungry hunting lion; so he made himself comfortable in the tree above the cannibal village to wait until Numa had taken himself elsewhere.

XVI

Tantor

Weary day after weary day Gonfala had trudged North with Spike and Troll. They had made a wide detour to avoid the country of the Bantangos, for although they had both the Gonfal and Gonfala they lacked the courage of their convictions relative to this combination that previously had seemed all-powerful to them.

Gonfala's safety, so far, had lain in the men's jealousy of one another. Neither would leave her alone with the other. Because of her, they had ceased to speak except when absolutely necessary; and each was constantly afraid that the other would murder him. To assure her own safety, the girl watched over the safety of each of the others as though she loved them both.

One of the blacks carried the great diamond, nor did either of the white men attempt to touch it without arousing the savage objections of the other; for now that Gonfala was with them each feared that the other might use the magical power of the stone to destroy him.

Spike was in search of a district which he had passed through on safari several years before.

'It's a regular garden, Miss,' he explained to Gonfala; 'and game! S'elp me, it's lousy with game; and that gentle, from not bein' hunted none, that you can walk right up to 'em an' bat 'em over the head, if you'd a mind to. We could live like Kings and with plenty of servants, too; for the natives is peace-ablelike, and not many of 'em. I mean not too many. We could rule 'em easy what with our havin' the Gonfal and you.'

'I don't know that the Gonfal would do you much good,' said the girl.

'Why not?' demanded Troll.

'You don't know how to use it. One must have certain mental powers to succeed with the Gonfal.'

'Have you got 'em?' asked Spike.

'I could use it unless Mafka desired to prevent me. He could do that, for his mind could control mine. I have never tried to use these powers since Mafka died.'

'But you think you can?' Spike's voice reflected the fear that was in him. He had banked heavily on the power of the Gonfal. All his future plans were dependent upon his being able to control the acts of others through the mysterious powers of the great diamond, and now there was doubt. It haunted him day and night.

'I think so,' replied Gonfala, 'but I shall not use it to help either of you unless I am absolutely assured that neither one of you will harm me.'

'I wouldn't think of hurtin' you, Miss,' Spike assured her.

'Me neither, but you better not trust him,' said Troll.

Spike took a step toward Troll, his fists clenched. 'You dirty crook,' he shouted, 'you're the one needs watchin', but you won't need it much longer. I'm going' to break your neck for you right now.'

Troll jumped back and picked up his rifle. 'Come any closer and I'll let you have it,' he threatened, holding the muzzle of the weapon aimed at Spike's belly.

'You'd better not,' Spike admonished him. 'You may need another gun in some of the country we got to go through. You'd never get through alone with just six niggers.'

'That goes for you, too,' growled Troll.

'Then let's call it quits, and quit our rowin' – it ain't gettin' us nothin'.'

'It won't ever get either one of you me,' said Gonfala, 'and that's what's been the trouble between you. You stole me from my friends, and someday they're going to catch up with you. When they do, it'll be better for you if you haven't harmed me. Stanlee Wood will never give up until he finds me; and when he tells Tarzan I have been stolen, you can rest assured I'll be found and you will be punished.'

'Tarzan!' exclaimed Spike. 'What's Tarzan got to do with it?'

'You know who he is?' demanded Gonfala.

'Sure – everybody's heard of him; but I ain't never seen him. I always thought maybe he was just somethin' somebody made up. What do you know about him? Have you ever seen him?'

'Yes, and so have you.'

'Not us,' said Troll.

'Yes, and so have you.'

'You remember Clayton?' asked the girl.

'Sure, I remember Clayton. That bloke was as good as two – Say! You don't mean—?'

'Yes, I do. Clayton is Tarzan.'

Troll looked worried. Spike scowled; then he shrugged. 'Wot if he is?' he demanded. 'He couldn't never find us – not where we're goin'; and even if he did, wot could he do against the Gonfal? We could do what we pleased with him.'

'Sure,' agreed Troll; 'we could snuff him out like that.' He snapped his fingers.

'Oh, no you couldn't,' said Gonfala.

'An' why couldn't we?'

'Because I wouldn't let you. You can't use the Gonfal without my help, and when Tarzan and Stanlee come I shall help them. You see, with the Gonfal, I can snuff *you* out.'

The two men looked at one another. Presently Spike walked away and called to Troll to accompany him. When he was out of earshot of Gonfala he stopped. 'Listen,' he said; 'that dame's got us to rights. If she ever gets her paws on that rock our lives won't be worth nothin'.'

'Looks like the Gonfal ain't going' to do us much good,' said Troll. 'We can't make it work without her; and if we let her get her hands on it, she'll kill us. Wot are we going to do?'

'In the first place we got to see that she doesn't get to touch it. One of us has got to carry it – she might get the nigger to let her touch it some time when we weren't around. You can carry it if you want to.'

'That's wot I been sayin' for a long time,' Troll reminded him.

'Well, it's different now,' Spike explained. 'Neither one of us can get it to work, an' neither one of us dares let her touch it; so we're safe as long as one of us has it.'

'But wot good is the stone goin' to do us, then?'

'Wait 'til we get up in that country I been tellin' you about. We can make the dame be good then. All we got to do is tell her to work the stone the way we say or we'll croak her. She'll have to do it, too; for where I'm takin' her she couldn't never find her way out after she'd killed us; so it wouldn't do her no good.'

Troll shook his head. 'Maybe she'd kill us anyway, just to get even with us.'

'Well, there ain't nothin' we can do about it now, anyway,' said Spike; 'so let's get goin'. Come on, you niggers! Come on, Gonfala! We're trekkin' – the sun's been up an hour.'

As they broke camp far to the North of him, Tarzan stopped at the edge of the forest that bordered the valley of the Bantangos on the west. He looked about him, carefully taking his bearings; then with the tip of his spear he loosened the earth in the centre of a triangle formed by three trees and with his hands scooped out the earth until he had a hole about a foot deep. Into this he dropped the Great Emerald of the Zuli. When he had refilled the hole and covered it with the fallen leaves and twigs that he had carefully scraped away, no human eye could have detected the hiding place. With his knife he blazed a tree fifteen paces from one of the three trees that formed the triangle. Only Tarzan could ever find the place again. Should he never return, the ransom of a dozen Kings would lie there to the end of time, undiscovered.

Unable to find the trail that the storm had obliterated, the ape-man attempted to deduce from his knowledge of the two men he was now positive were the abductors of Gonfala and from his knowledge of events leading up to the present moment the logical destination for which they were headed.

He knew that they were familiar with the miraculous powers of the Gonfal and that they had been unable to call these powers into being themselves. The chief of the Bantangos had told him of their failure to demonstrate the value of their big medicine. Either by accident or intent they had found Gonfala, and what more natural than that they would assume that with her aid they could command the wonders of the Gonfal? And where would be the best place to utilise these powers? Why, the country of the Kaji, naturally; for there they would be safer from detection than almost anywhere on earth, and there they would find a tribe accustomed to the domination of the stone. There they would find women; and Tarzan felt that if he were any judge of men, that circumstance would have considerable bearing with Troll and

Spike. So Tarzan travelled toward the North on a trail parallel to that taken by Spike and Troll but some distance to the west of it.

For two days Tarzan moved toward the North, and still there was no sign of those whom he sought. He made his kills and ate and slept, and swung on tirelessly through forest or across plains.

As he was passing through a trip of forest along the shoulder of a range of hills thick with bamboo he heard a sound that brought him to halt, listening. It was repeated – the weak trumpeting of an elephant in distress. The ape-man turned aside from the direction he had been travelling and moved cautiously through the bamboo thicket. He was moving downwind; so he made a wide circuit in order to pick up the scent spoor of what lay ahead. There might be something beside an elephant. The caution of the beast aided and abetted the reasoning powers of the man.

Presently the scent of Tantor the elephant told him that he had circled his quarry, and even stronger was the rank odour of Dango the hyena; then harsh and raucous, came the hideous laughing cry of the unclean beast followed by the plaintive help-cry of the elephant. Tantor was in trouble, and the ape-man pushed forward to learn the cause.

Almost as old as Tarzan was the friendship of Tarzan and Tantor. Perhaps he had never seen this elephant before; but still, to Tarzan, he would be Tantor – the name and the friendship belonged to all elephants.

As he came closer, he moved more cautiously – beastlike, always scenting a trap. For those of the jungle, eternal vigilance is the price of life. At last he came close enough so that by parting the bamboo he could see that for which he had been searching. The top of Tantor's back was just visible in an elephant pit. Snapping and growling at the edge of the pit were a pair of hyenas, circling above was Ska the vulture; and from these omens the ape-man knew that Tantor was near death.

Parting the bamboo, Tarzan stepped into the little clearing that the builders of the pit had made, an enlargement of a wide elephant trail. Instantly the hyenas transferred their attention from the elephant to the ape-man, and with bared fangs faced him. But as the man advanced, they retreated snarling. He paid no attention to them; for he knew that ordinarily Dango would not attack any but a helpless man.

As he approached the pit Tantor saw him and trumpeted a feeble warning. The elephant's skin hung loosely on its great frame, evidencing that it had been long without food or water. It had fallen into a pit that must have been dug and then abandoned, either because the tribe that dug it had moved away or because no elephant having fallen into it, they had ceased to visit it.

Tarzan spoke to Tantor in the strange language that he used with the beasts of the jungle. Perhaps Tantor did not understand the words – who may know? – but something, the tone perhaps, carried the idea that the ape-man wished to convey, that he was a friend; but Tantor needed something beside kind words, and so Tarzan set about cutting the bamboo that bore the tenderest shoots and carrying them to the imprisoned beast.

Tantor ate with avidity, the water content of the shoots furnishing at least some of the moisture that his great frame required even more than it required food; then Tarzan set to work with spear and knife and hands upon the seemingly herculean task of excavating a ramp up which Tantor could walk to liberty. It was the work not of an hour but of many hours, and it was not completed until the following day; then, weak and staggering, the great pachyderm climbed slowly from the pit. He was a huge beast, one of the largest old bulls Tarzan had even seen. One tusk, by some peculiar freak of nature, was much darker than the other; and this, with his great size, must have marked him among his fellows as a bull of distinction.

As he came out of the pit, his sensitive trunk passed over the body of the ape-man in what was almost a caress; then, as Tarzan took his way once more toward the North, Tantor turned and moved slowly along the elephant trail toward the east and the nearest water.

Days passed. Stanley Wood, waiting at Tarzan's estate, grew more and more frantic as no news came of the whereabouts of Tarzan. He pleaded with Muviro, headman of the Waziri, to furnish him with an escort and let him set out in search of Gonfala; and at last Muviro yielded to his importunities and sent him away with half a dozen warriors as an escort.

Wood took up the search at the point at which Tarzan had left him, where the clean picked bones of the lion Gonfala had killed lay bleaching in the sun. He knew only that those he sought had started North at that spot. It was a blind and seemingly hopeless search, but it meant action; and anything was preferable to sitting idly, his mind torn by fears and doubts as to the fate of Gonfala.

As they approached the Bantango country, the Waziri, knowing the nature and temper of the inhabitants, counselled making a detour to avoid them; and entirely by chance they selected an easterly route – the route that Spike and Troll had chosen for the same reason. Thus it happened that a week later they received definite proof that they were on the right trail. At a village of friendly blacks they were told that a safari of nine that included two white men and a white girl had stopped overnight with the tribe. The chief had furnished them with guides to the next friendly village to the North.

Wood talked to these men and learned that the chief of the village to which they had guided the safari had also furnished them guides for the next stage of their journey, and for the first time in weeks the young American found hope rekindled in his bosom. He had learned that up to this point Gonfala had been alive and well; and that, from what the villagers had seen, there was no indication that she was being ill-treated.

All the marvellous tracking skill of the Lord of the Jungle had been nullified by a heavy rain, and then chance had set in and sent him upon the wrong trail and Stanley Wood upon the right one.

Through such a trivial vagary of Fate lives were jeopardised and men died.

XVII

Strangers

Spike and Troll were holding palaver with the chief of a Northern tribe. They had come far, guided from village to village by friendly natives. Luck had been with them, but now this good fortune seemed to be at an end. They were trying to persuade the old chief to furnish them with guides to the next village.

'No more villages,' he said. He did not like these white men. He held them in contempt because their safari was small and poor, too poor even to rob. They had nothing but two rifles – and the girl. He had been thinking about her. He was also thinking of a black sultan to the east to whom she might be sold, but he put this thought from him. He did not wish any trouble with the white men. Native soldiers had come to his village once under white officers and punished him for ill-treating the safari of some white hunters. They had come from a great distance just to do that, and the incident had given him vast respect for the power and the long arm of the white man.

'What is North?' asked Spike.

'Mountains,' replied the chief.

'That,' said Spike to Troll, 'is like the country where my valley is. It is surrounded by mountains.' He tried to explain to the chief the valley for which they were searching and the tribe that inhabited it.

A cunning look came into the eyes of the chief. He wished to be rid of these men, and he saw how he might do it. 'I know the valley,' he said. 'Tomorrow I will give you guides.'

'I guess maybe we ain't lucky,' gloated Spike, as he and Troll came from their palaver with the chief and sat down beside Gonfala. The girl did not inquire why; but Spike explained, nevertheless. 'It won't be long now,' he said, 'before we're safe and sound in my valley.'

'You won't be safe,' said Gonfala. 'Tarzan and Stanlee Wood will come soon – very soon now.'

'They won't never find us where we're goin'.'

'The natives will guide them from village to village just as they have guided you,' she reminded him. 'It will be very easy to follow you.'

'Yes,' admitted Spike, 'they can follow us up to where these people will guide us.'

'But there we will stop. They will find you there.'

'We don't stop there,' said Spike. 'I guess I ain't nobody's fool. The valley these people are takin' us to, ain't my valley; but once I get in this here first valley, I can find the other. I passed through it comin' out of my valley. It's about two marches east of where we want to go. When we get to this first valley, we won't need no guides the rest of the way; so, when we leave this here first valley, we'll tell 'em we're goin' to the coast, an' start off to the east; then we'll swing around back way to the North of 'em an' go west to my valley. And there won't nobody never find us.'

'Tarzan and Stanlee Wood will find you.'

'I wisht you'd shut up about this here Tarzan and Stan-lee Wood. I'm sick of hearin' of 'em. It's gettin' on my nerves.'

Troll sat staring at Gonfala through half closed lids. He had not spoken much all day, but he had looked much at Gonfala. Always when she caught his glance he turned his eyes away.

They had been able to sustain themselves this far by killing game and trading the meat to natives for other articles of food, principally vegetables and corn. Tonight they feasted royally and went to their beds early. Gonfala occupied a hut by herself; the two men had another nearby. They had had a hard day's trek, and tired muscles combined with a heavy meal to induce early slumber. Gonfala and Spike were asleep almost as soon as they had stretched themselves on their sleeping mats.

Not so Troll. He remained very much awake – thinking. He listened to the heavy breathing of Spike that denoted that he slept soundly. He listened to the sounds in the village. Gradually they died out – the village slept. Troll thought how easy it would be to kill Spike, but he was afraid of Spike. Even when the man slept, he was afraid of him. That made Troll hate him all the more, but it was not hate alone that made him wish to kill him. Troll had been daydreaming – very pleasant dreams. Spike stood in the way of their fulfilment, yet he could not muster the courage to kill the sleeping man – not yet. 'Later,' he thought.

He crawled to the doorway of the hut and looked out. There was no sign of waking life in the village. The silence was almost oppressive; it extended out into the black void of night beyond the village. As Troll rose to his feet outside the hut he stumbled over a cooking pot; the noise, against the background of silence, seemed terrific. Cursing under his breath, the man stood motionless, listening.

Spike, disturbed but not fully awakened, moved in his sleep and turned over; the first dead slumber of early night was broken. Thereafter he would be more restless and more easily awakened. Troll did not hear him move, and after a moment of listening he tiptoed away. Stealthily he approached the hut in which Gonfala slept.

The girl, restless and wakeful, lay wide-eyed staring out into the lesser darkness framed by the doorway of her hut. She heard footsteps approaching. Would they pass, or were they coming here for her? Weeks of danger, weeks of suspicion, weeks of being constantly on guard had wrought upon her until she sensed menace in the most ordinary occurrences; so now she felt, intuitively, she believed, that someone was coming to her hut. And for what purpose, other than evil, should one come thus stealthily by night?

Raising herself upon her hands, she crouched, waiting. Every muscle tense, she scarcely breathed. Whatever it was, it was coming closer, closer. Suddenly a darker blotch loomed in the low opening that was the doorway. An animal or a man on all fours was creeping in!

'Who are you? What do you want?' It was a muffled scream of terror.

'Shut up! It's me. Don't make no noise. I want to talk to you.'

She recognised the voice, but it did not allay her fears. The man crept closer to her. He was by her side now. She could hear his laboured breathing.

'Go away,' she said. 'We can talk tomorrow.'

'Listen!' he said. 'You don't want to go to that there valley and spend the rest of your life with Spike an' a bunch o' niggers, do you? When he gets us there he'll kill me an' have you all to himself. I knows him – he's that kind of a rat. Be good to me an' I'll take you away. Me an' you'll beat it with the diamond. We'll go to Europe, to Paris.'

'I don't want to go anywhere with you. Go away! Get out of here, before I call Spike.'

'One squawk out of you, an' I'll wring your neck. You're goin' to be good to me whether you want to or not.' He reached out in the darkness and seized her, feeling for her throat.

Before he found it she had time to voice a single scream and cry out once, 'Spike!' Then Troll closed choking fingers upon her throat and bore her down beneath his weight. She struggled and fought, striking him in the face, tearing at the fingers at her throat.

Awakened by the scream, Spike raised upon an elbow. 'Troll!' he called. 'Did you hear anything?' There was no response. 'Troll!' He reached out to the mat where Troll should have been. He was not there. Instantly his suspicions were aroused and, because of his own evil mind, they centred unquestioningly upon the truth.

In a dozen strides he was at Gonfala's hut; and as he scrambled through the doorway, Troll met him with an oath and a snarl. Clinching, the two men rolled upon the floor, biting, gouging, striking, kicking; occasionally a lurid oath or a scream of pain punctuated their heavy breathing. Gonfala crouched at the back of the hut, terrified for fear that one of them would kill the other, removing the only factor of safety she possessed.

They rolled closer to her; and she edged to one side, out of their way. Her new position was nearer the doorway. It suggested the possibility of temporary escape, of which she was quick to take advantage. In the open, she commenced to worry again for fear that one of the men would be killed.

She saw that some of the natives, aroused by the commotion within her hut, had come from theirs. She ran to them, begging them to stop the fight. The chief was there, and he was very angry because he had been disturbed. He ordered several warriors to go and separate the men. They hesitated, but finally approached the hut. As they did so, the sounds of conflict ended; and a moment later Spike crawled into the open and staggered to his feet.

Gonfala feared that the worst had happened. Of the two men, she had feared Spike the more; for while both were equally brutal and devoid of decency, Troll was not as courageous as his fellow. Him she might have circumvented through his cowardice. At least, that she had thought until tonight; now she was not so sure. But she was sure that Spike was always the more dangerous. Her one thought now was to escape him, if only temporarily. Inflamed by his fight, secure in the knowledge that Troll was dead, what might he not do? To a far corner of the village she ran and hid herself between a hut and the palisade. Each moment she expected to hear Spike hunting for her, but her did not come. He did not even know that she had left her hut where he thought he had left her with the dead Troll, and he had gone to his own hut to nurse his wounds.

But Troll was not dead. In the morning Spike found him bloody and dazed squatting in the village street staring at the ground. Much to the former's disgust, Troll was not even badly injured. He looked up as Spike approached.

'Wot happened?' he asked.

Spike looked at him suspiciously for a moment; then his expression turned to puzzlement. 'A bloomin' lorry ran over you,' he said.

' "A bloomin' lorry," ' Troll repeated. 'I never even seen it.'

Gonfala, looking around a corner of the hut behind which she had been hiding, saw the two men and breathed a sigh of relief. Troll was not dead; she was not to be left alone with Spike. She came toward them. Troll glanced up at her.

' 'Ose the dame?' he asked.

Gonfala and Spike looked at one another, and the latter tapped his forehead, 'A bit balmy,' he explained.

'She don't look balmy,' said Troll. 'She looks like my sister – my sister – sister.' He continued to stare at her, dully.

'We better get some grub an' be on our way,' interrupted Spike. He seemed nervous and ill at ease in the presence of Troll. It is one thing to kill a man, quite another to have done this thing to him.

It was a silent, preoccupied trio that moved off behind two guides in a North-easterly direction after the morning meal had been eaten. Spike walked ahead, Troll kept close to Gonfala. He was often looking at her, a puzzled expression in his eyes.

'Wot's your name?' he asked.

Gonfala had a sudden inspiration. Perhaps it was madness to hope that it might succeed, but her straits were desperate. 'Don't tell me you don't remember your sister's name,' she exclaimed.

Troll stared at her, his face expressionless. 'Wot *is* your name?' he asked. 'Everything is sort o' blurrylike in my memory.'

'Gonfala,' she said. 'You remember, don't you – your sister?'

'Gonfala; oh, yes – my sister.'

'I'm glad you're here,' she said; 'for now you won't let anyone harm me, will you?'

'Harm you? They better not try it,' he exclaimed belligerently.

The safari had halted, and they caught up with Spike who was talking with the two guides.

'The beggars won't go no farther,' he explained. 'We ain't made more'n five miles an' they quits us, quits us cold.'

'Why?' asked Gonfala.

'They say the country ahead is taboo. They say they's white men up ahead that'll catch 'em an' make slaves out of 'em an' feed 'em to lions. They've went an' put the fear o' God into our boys, too.'

'Let's turn back,' suggested the girl. 'What's the use anyway, Spike? If you get killed the Gonfal won't do you any good. If you turn around and take me back safely to my friends, I'll do my best to get them to give you the Gonfal and let you go. I give you my word that I will, and I know that Stanlee Wood will do anything that I ask.'

Spike shook his head. 'Nothin' doin'! I'm goin' where I'm goin', an' you're goin' with me.' He bent close and stared boldly into her eyes. 'If I had to give up one or t'other, I'd give up the Gonfal before I would you – but I'm not goin' to give up neither.'

The girl shrugged. 'I've given you your chance,' she said. 'You are a fool not to take it.'

So they pushed on without guides farther and farther into the uncharted wilderness; and each new day Spike was confident that this day he would stumble upon the enchanted valley of his dreams, and each night he prophesied for the morrow.

Troll's mental condition remained unchanged. He thought that Gonfala was his sister, and he showed her what little consideration there was in his gross philosophy of life to accord anyone. The protective instinct of the brutal male was stimulated in her behalf; and for this she was grateful, not to Troll but to fate. Where he had been, where he was going he appeared not to know or to care. He trudged on day after day in dumb silence, asking no question, showing no interest in anything or anyone other than Gonfala. He was obsessed by a belief that she was in danger, and so he constantly carried one of the rifles the better to protect her.

For many days they had been in mountainous country searching for the elusive valley, and at the end of a hard trek they made camp on the shoulder of a mountain beside a little spring of clear water. As night fell the western sky was tinged with the golden red of a dying sunset. Long after the natural phenomenon should have faded into the blackness of the night the red glow persisted.

Gonfala sat staring at it, dreamily fascinated. Spike watched it, too, with growing excitement. The blacks watched it with fear. Troll sat cross-legged, staring at the ground.

Spike sat down beside Gonfala. 'You know wot that is, girlie?' he asked. 'You know it ain't no sunset, don't you?'

'It looks like a fire – a forest fire,' she said.

'It's a fire all right. I ain't never been there, but I've seen that light before. I figure it's from the inside of one of them volcanoes, but I'll tell you wot it means to us – it means we found our valley. When I was in that valley I seen that light to the South at night. All we got to do now is trek along a little west o' North, an' in maybe four or five marches we orter be there; then, girlie, you an' me's goin' to settle down to housekeepin'.'

The girl made no reply. She was no longer afraid; for she knew that Troll would kill Spike if she asked him to; and now she had no reason to fear being alone with Troll, other than the waning possibility that he might regain his memory.

The new day found Spike almost jovial, so jubilant was he at the prospect of soon finding his valley; but his joviality disappeared when he discovered that two of his six men had deserted during the night. He was in a cold sweat until he found that they had not taken the Gonfal with them. After that, he determined, he would sleep with the great stone at his side, taking no more chances. He could do this now without arousing the suspicions of Troll, for Troll had no suspicions. He paid no attention to the Gonfal nor ever mentioned it.

Toward noon a great valley opened before them, the length of which ran in the direction Spike wished to travel; and so they dropped down into it to easy travelling after their long days in the mountains.

The valley was partially forested, the trees growing more profusely along the course of a river that wound down from the upper end of the valley, crossed it diagonally, and disappeared in a cleft in the hills to the west; but considerable areas were open and covered with lush grasses, while on the east side of the valley was a veritable forest of bamboo.

Spike, not knowing if the valley were inhabited; nor, if it were, the nature or temper of its inhabitants, chose to follow the wooded strip that bordered the river, taking advantage of the cover it afforded. Along the river he found a wide elephant trail, and here they were making excellent speed when one of the blacks stopped suddenly, listened intently, and pointed ahead.

'What's the matter?' demanded Spike.

'Men, Bwana – coming,' replied the black.

'I don't hear nothin',' said Spike. 'Do you?' he turned to Gonfala.

She nodded. 'Yes, I hear voices.'

'Then we better get off the trail and hide – at least until we see who they are. Here, all of you! Here's a little trail leadin' off here.'

Spike herded the party off to the left of the main trail along a little winding path through rather heavy underbrush, but they had covered little more than a hundred yards when they came out onto the open plain. Here they stopped at the edge of the wood, waiting and listening. Presently the voices of men came plainly to their ears, constantly closer and closer, until suddenly it dawned on them all that the men they heard were approaching along the little trail through which they had sought to escape.

Spike looked for a place of concealment, but there was none. The thick underbrush was almost impenetrable behind them, while on the other hand the plain stretched away across the valley to the hills upon the west. As a last resort he turned North along the edge of the wood, urging the others to haste until all were running.

Glancing back, Gonfala saw the party that had alarmed them debouching onto the plain. First came a dozen huge negroes, each pair of whom held a lion in leash. Following these were six white men strangely garbed. Even at a distance she could see that their trappings were gorgeous. Behind them following a score or more of other white men. They were similarly dressed but in quieter raiment. They carried spears as well as swords. One of the warriors carried something dangling at his side which, even at a distance, could not have been mistaken for other than it was – a bloody human head.

'They're white men,' Gonfala called to Spike. 'Maybe they'd be friendly.'

'They don't look like it to me,' he replied. 'I ain't takin' no chances after wot I been through gettin' you an' the Gonfal this far.'

'Anyone would be better than you,' said the girl, and stopped.

'Come on, you fool!' he cried; and, coming back, seized her and sought to drag her with him.

'Troll!' she cried. 'Help!'

Troll was ahead of them, but now he turned; and, seeing Spike and the girl scuffling, he ran back. His face was white and distorted with rage. 'Le' go her,' he bellowed. 'Le' go my sister!' Then he was upon Spike; and the two went down, striking, kicking, and biting.

For an instant Gonfala hesitated, undecided. She looked at the two beasts upon the ground, and then she turned in the direction of the strange warriors. No one, she reasoned, could be more of a menace to her than Spike; but she soon saw that the decision had already been made for her – the entire party was moving in their direction. She stood and waited as they approached.

They had covered about half the distance when a warrior in the lead halted and pointed up the valley. For an instant they hesitated; then they turned and started off across the valley at a run, the lions tugging at their leashes and dragging their keepers after them, the warriors keeping in formation behind them.

The girl, wondering at their sudden flight, looked up the valley in the direction in which the warrior had pointed. The sight that met her eyes filled her with amazement. A herd of perhaps a hundred elephants carrying warriors on their backs was moving rapidly down upon them. On the ground at her feet Spike and Troll still bit and gouged and kicked.

XVIII

Ingratitude

Stanley Wood had no difficulty following the trail of Gonfala's abductors to the point at which their guides had deserted them, and from there the trained Waziri trackers carried on until the trail was lost at the edge of a wood where it had been obliterated by the shuffling pads of a herd of elephants. Search as they would they could not pick up the trail again. To Wood, the mystery was complete; he was baffled, disheartened.

Wearily he pushed on up the valley. If only Tarzan were here! He, of all men, could find an answer to the riddle.

'Look, Bwana!' cried one of the Waziri. 'A city!'

Wood looked ahead, amazed; for there lay a city indeed. No native village of thatched huts was this, but a walled city of white, its domes of gold and azure rising above its gleaming wall.

'What city is it?' he asked.

The Waziri shook their heads and looked at one another.

'I do not know, Bwana,' said one. 'I have never been in this country before.'

'Perhaps the Memsahib is there,' suggested a warrior.

'Perhaps,' agreed Wood. 'If the people here are unfriendly they will take us all prisoners,' he mused, half aloud; 'and then no one will know where we are, where Gonfala probably is. We must not all be taken prisoners.'

'No,' agreed Waranji, 'we must not all be taken prisoners.'

'That is a big city,' said Wood; 'there must be many warriors there. If they are unfriendly they could easily take us all or kill us all. Is that not so?'

'We are Waziri,' said Waranji, proudly.

'Yes, I know; and you're great fighters. I know that too; but, holy mackerel! Seven of us can't lick an army, even though six of us are Waziri.'

Waranji shook his head. 'We could try,' he said. 'We are not afraid.'

Wood laid a hand on the ebony shoulder. 'You're great guys, Waranji; and I know you'd walk right plumb into Hell for any friend of the Big Bwana, but I'm not goin' to sacrifice you. If those people are friendly, one man will be as safe as seven; if they're not, seven men won't be any better off than one; so I'm goin' to send you boys home. Tell Muviro we couldn't find Tarzan. Tell him we think we've found where the Memsahib is. We don't know for sure, but it seems reasonable. If you meet Tarzan, or he's back home, he'll know what to do. If you don't see him, Muviro will have to use his own judgment. Now, go along; and good luck to you!'

Waranji shook his head. 'We cannot leave the Bwana alone,' he said. 'Let me send one warrior back with a message; the rest of us will stay with you.'

'No, Waranji. You've heard my orders. Go on back.'

Reluctantly they left him. He watched them until they passed out of sight in the wood; then he turned his steps toward the mysterious city in the distance.

Once again Tarzan of the Apes stood upon the edge of the high plateau at the western rim of the valley of Onthar and looked down upon Cathne, the city of gold. The white houses, the golden domes, the splendid Bridge of Gold that spanned the river before the city's gates gleamed and sparkled in the sunlight. The first time he had looked upon it the day had been dark and gloomy; and he had seen the city as a city of enemies; because then his companion had been Valthor of Athne, the City of Ivory, whose people were hereditary enemies of the Cathneans. But today, ablaze in the sunshine, the city offered him only friendship.

Nemone, the Queen who would have killed him, was dead. Alextar, her brother, had been taken from the dungeon in which she had kept him and been made King by the men who were Tarzan's fast friends – Thudos, Phordos, Gemnon, and the others of the loyal band whom Tarzan knew would welcome him back to Cathne. Tomos, who had ruled under Nemone as her chief advisor, must have been either killed or imprisoned. He would be no longer a menace to the ape-man.

With pleasant anticipation, Tarzan clambered down the steep gully to the floor of the valley and swung off across the Field of the Lions towards the city of gold. Field of the Lions! What memories it conjured! The trip to Xarator, the holy volcano, into whose fiery pit the Kings and Queens of Cathne had cast their enemies since time immemorial; the games in the arena; the wild lions which roved the valley of Onthar, giving it its other name – Field of the Lions. Such were the memories that the name inspired.

Boldly the ape-man crossed the valley until he stood before the Bridge of Gold and the two heroic golden lions that flanked its approach. The guard had been watching his progress across the valley for some time.

'It is Tarzan,' one of them had said while the ape-man was still half a mile away; and when he stopped before the gates they all came and welcomed him.

The captain of the guard, a noble whom Tarzan knew well, escorted him to the palace. 'Alextar will be glad to know that you have returned,' he said. 'Had it not been for you, he might not now be King – or alive. Wait here in this anteroom until I get word to Alextar.'

The room and its furnishings were of a type common in the palaces of the King and nobles of Cathne. The low ceiling was supported by a series of engaged columns, carved doors inlaid in mosaics of gold and ivory gave entry to the corridor and an adjoining apartment, on the stone floor lay some lion skins and several heavy woollen rugs of simple design, mural decorations depicted battle scenes between the lion men of Cathne and the elephant men of Athne, and above the murals was a frieze of mounted heads – lions, leopards, one huge elephant's head, and several human heads – the heads of warriors, beautifully cured and wearing the ivory head ornaments of nobles of Athne – trophies of the chase and of war.

It was a long time before the captain of the guard returned; and when he did, his face was flushed and troubled and twenty warriors accompanied him. 'I am sorry, Tarzan,' he said; 'but I have orders to arrest you.'

The ape-man looked at the twenty spears surrounding him and shrugged. If he were either surprised or hurt, he did not show it. Once again he was the wild beast trapped by his hereditary enemy, man; and he would not give man the satisfaction of even being asked to explain. They took his weapons from him and led him to a room on the second floor of the palace directly above the guardroom. It was a better cell than that he had first occupied in Cathne when he had been incarcerated in a dark hole with Phobeg, the temple guard who had stepped on god's tail and thus merited death; for this room was large and well lighted by two barred windows.

When they had left him and bolted the door, Tarzan walked to one of the windows and looked down upon one of the palace courtyards for a moment; then he went to the bench that stood against one wall and lay down. Seemingly unconscious of danger, or perhaps contemptuous of it, he slept.

It was dark when he was awakened by the opening of the door of his cell. A man bearing a lighted torch stood in the doorway. The ape-man arose as the other entered, closing the door behind him.

'Tarzan!' he exclaimed; and, crossing the room, he placed a hand on the other's shoulder – the Cathnean gesture of greeting, of friendship, and loyalty.

'I am glad to see you, Gemnon,' said the ape-man; 'tell me, are Doria and her father and mother well? And your father, Phordos?'

'They are well, but none too happy. Things here are bad again, as you must have conjectured from the treatment accorded you.'

'I knew that something must be wrong,' admitted the ape-man; 'but what it was, I didn't know – and don't.'

'You soon shall,' said Gemnon. 'Ours is indeed an unhappy country.'

'All countries are unhappy where there are men,' observed the ape-man. 'Men are the stupidest of beasts. But what has happened here? I thought that with the death of Nemone all your troubles were over.'

'So did we, but we were wrong. Alextar has proved to be weak, cowardly, ungrateful. Almost immediately after ascending the throne he fell under the influence of Tomos and his clique; and you know what that means. We are all in disfavour. Tomos is virtually ruler of Cathne, but as yet he has not dared to destroy us. The warriors and the people hate him, and he knows it. If he goes too far they will rise, and that will be the end of Tomos.

'But tell me about yourself. What brings you again to Cathne?'

'It is a very long story,' replied Tarzan. 'In the end a young woman was stolen by two white men. She and the man whom she was to marry were under my protection. I am searching for her. Several days ago I came upon two blacks who had been with the safari of the men who abducted the girl. They described the country in which the safari had been when they deserted. It lay to the south-east of Xarator. That is why I am here. I am going into the country south-east of Xarator in an effort to pick up the trail.'

'I think you will not have to search long,' said Gemnon. 'I believe that I know where your young woman is – not that it will do you or her much good now that you are a prisoner of Tomos. As you must know, he has no love for you.'

'What makes you think that you know where she is?' asked the ape-man.

'Alextar sends me often to the valley of Thenar to raid the Athneans. It is, of course, the work of Tomos, who hopes that I shall be killed. Very recently I was there. The raid was not very successful, as we were too few. Tomos always sends too few, and they are always nobles he fears and would be rid of. We took only one head. On the way out we saw a small party of people who were not Athneans. There were four or five slaves, two white men, and a white woman. The white men were fighting. The woman ran toward us, which made us think she wished to escape the two men she was with. We were going to meet her and take the entire party prisoners when we saw a large body of Athneans coming down the valley on their war elephants. We were too few to engage them; so we ran for the Pass of the Warriors and escaped. I naturally assume that the Athneans captured the young woman and those with her and that she is now in the City of Ivory; but, as I said before, the knowledge won't help you much now – Tomos has you.'

'And what do you think he will do with me? Has he another Phobeg?'

Gemnon laughed. 'I shall never forget how you tossed "the strongest man in Cathne" about and finally threw him bodily into the laps of the audience. Tomos lost his last obol on that fight – another good reason why he has no love for you. No, I don't think he'll pit you against a man this time – probably a lion. It may even be poison or a dagger – they are surer. But what I am here for tonight is to try to save you. The only trouble is, I have no plan. A friend of mine is captain of the guard tonight. That is how I was able to reach you, but if I were to leave your door unbarred and you escaped his life would not be worth an obol. Perhaps you can think of a plan.'

Tarzan shook his head. 'I shall have to know Tomos' plan first. Right now the only plan I have is for you to leave before you get caught in here.'

'Isn't there anything that I can do, after all that you did for me? There must be something.'

'You might leave your dagger with me. It might come in handy. I can hide it under my loincloth.'

They talked for a short time then before Gemnon left, and within a few minutes thereafter Tarzan was asleep. He did not pace his cell, fretting and worrying. His was more the temperament of the wild animal than the man.

XIX
Retribution

The sun is an impartial old devil. He shines with equal brilliance upon the just and the banker, upon the day of a man's wedding, or upon the day of his death. The great African sun, which, after all, is the same sun that shines on Medicine Hat, shone brilliantly on this new day upon which Tarzan was to die. He was to die because Alextar had decreed it – the suggestion had been Tomos'. The sun even shone upon Tomos; but then the sun is ninety-three million miles away, and that is a long way to see what one is shining on.

They came about eleven o'clock in the morning and took Tarzan from his cell. They did not even bother to bring him food or water. What need has a man who is about to die for food or drink? He was very thirsty; and perhaps, if he had asked, the guards would have given him water; for after all they were common soldiers and not a King's favourites, and therefore more inclined to be generous and humane. The ape-man, however, asked for nothing. It was not because he was consciously too proud; his pride was something instinctive – it inhibited even a suggestion that he might ask a favour of an enemy.

When he was brought out of the palace grounds onto the avenue, the sight that met his eyes apprised him of the fate that had been decreed for him. There was the procession of nobles and warriors, the lion drawn chariot of the King, and a single great lion held in leash by eight stalwart blacks. Tarzan had seen all this before, that time that he had been the quarry in the Queen's Hunt. Today he was to be the quarry in the King's Hunt, but today he could expect no such miracle as had saved him from the mighty jaws of Belthar upon that other occasion.

The same crowds of citizens lined the sides of the avenue; and when the procession moved toward the Bridge of Gold and out toward the Field of the Lions, the crowds moved with it. It was a good natured crowd, such as one might see milling toward the gates at a Cub-Giant game or the Army-Navy 'classic.' It was no more bloody minded than those who throng to see Man Mountain Dean and the Honourable Mr Detton or a professional ice hockey game at Madison Square Garden, and who would be so unkind as to suggest that these are looking for trouble and blood? Perish the thought!

They had taken no chances when they brought Tarzan from his cell. Twenty spearmen betokened the respect in which they held him. Now they chained him to Alextar's chariot, and the triumph was under way.

Out upon the Field of the Lions the procession halted, and the long gauntlet of warriors was formed down which the quarry was to be pursued by the lion. The ape-man was unchained, the wagers were being laid as to the point in the gauntlet at which the lion would overtake and drag down its victim, and the hunting lion was being brought up to scent the quarry. Tomos was gloating. Alextar appeared nervous – he was afraid of lions. He would never have gone on a hunt of his own volition. Tarzan watched him. He saw a young man in his late twenties with nervous, roving eyes, a weak chin, and a cruel mouth. There was nothing about him to remind one that he was the brother of the gorgeous Nemone. He looked at Tarzan, but his eyes fell before the steady gaze of the ape-man.

'Hurry!' he snapped querulously. 'We are bored.'

They did hurry, and in their haste it happened. In a fraction of a second the comparatively peaceful scene was transformed to one of panic and chaos.

By accident one of the blacks that held the hunting lion in leash slipped the beast's collar, and with an angry roar the trained killer struck down those nearest him and charged the line of spearmen standing between him and the crowd of spectators. He was met by a dozen spears while the unarmed citizenry fled in panic, trampling the weaker beneath their feet.

The nobles screamed commands. Alextar stood in his chariot, his knees shaking, and begged someone to save him. 'A hundred thousand drachmas to the man who kills the beast!' he cried. 'More! Anything he may ask shall be granted!'

No one seemed to pay any attention to him. All who could were looking after their own safety. As a matter of fact, he was in no danger at the time; for the lion was engaged elsewhere.

The jabbing spears further enraged the maddened carnivore, yet for some reason he did not follow up his attack upon the warriors; instead, he wheeled suddenly and then charged straight for the chariot of the King. Now, indeed, did Alextar have reason to be terrified. He would have run, but his knees gave beneath him so that he sat down upon the seat of his golden vehicle. He looked about helplessly. He was practically alone. Some of his noble guard had run to join in the attack upon the lion. Tomos had fled in the opposite direction. Only the quarry remained.

Alextar saw the man whip a dagger from his loincloth and crouch in the path of the charging lion. He heard savage growls roll from human lips. The lion was upon him. Alextar screamed; but, fascinated, his terror-filled eyes clung to the savage scene before him. He saw the lion rise to make the kill, and then what happened happened so quickly that he could scarcely follow it.

Tarzan stooped and dodged beneath the great forepaws outstretched to seize him; then he closed in and swung to the lion's back, one great arm encircling the shaggy throat. Mingled with the beast's horrid growls were the growls of the man-beast upon his back. Alextar went cold with terror. He tried to run, but he could not. Whether he would or not, he must sit and watch that awful spectacle – he must watch the lion kill the man and then leap upon him. Yet the thing that terrified him most was the growls of the man.

They were rolling upon the ground now in the dust of the Field of the Lions, sometimes the man on top, sometimes the lion; and now and again the dagger of Gemnon flashed in the sunlight, flashed as the blade drove into the side of the frantic beast. The two were ringed now by eager spearmen ready to thrust a point into the heart of the lion, but no chance presented that did not endanger the life of the man. But at last the end came. With a final supreme effort to escape the clutches of the ape-man, the lion collapsed upon the ground. The duel was over.

Tarzan leaped to his feet. For a moment he surveyed the surrounding warriors with the blazing eyes of a beast of prey at bay upon its kill; then he placed a foot upon the carcass of the hunting lion, raised his face to the heavens, and from his great chest rose the challenge of the bull ape.

The warriors shrank away as that weird and hideous cry shattered the brief new silence of the Field of the Lions. Alextar trembled anew. He had feared the lion, but he feared the man more. Had he not had him brought here to be killed by the very lion he had himself dispatched? And he was only a beast. His growls and his terrible cry proved that. What mercy could he expect from a beast? The man would kill him!

'Take him away!' he ordered feebly. 'Take him away!'

'What shall we do with him?' asked a noble.

'Kill him! Kill him! Take him away!' Alextar was almost screaming now.

'But he saved your life,' the noble reminded.

'Huh? What? Oh, well; take him back to his cell. Later I shall know what to do with him. Can't you see I am tired and don't wish to be bothered?' he demanded querulously.

The noble hung his head in shame as he ordered the guard to escort Tarzan back to his cell; and he walked at Tarzan's side, where a noble does not walk except with one of his own caste.

'What you did,' he remarked on the way back to the city, 'deserves better reward than this.'

'I seem to recall hearing him offer anything he wished to the man who killed the lion,' said the ape-man. 'That and a hundred thousand drachmas.'

'Yes, I heard him.'

'He seems to have a short memory.'

'What would you have asked him?'

'Nothing.'

The noble looked at him in surprise. 'You would ask for nothing?'

'Nothing.'

'Is there nothing that you want?'

'Yes; but I wouldn't ask anything of an enemy.'

'I am not your enemy.'

Tarzan looked at the man, and a shadow of a smile lit his grim visage. 'I have had no water since yesterday, nor any food.'

'Well,' remarked the noble, laughing, 'you'll have them both – and without asking for them.'

On their return to the city Tarzan was placed in another cell; this one was on the second floor of a wing of the palace that overlooked the avenue. It was not long before the door was unbolted and a warrior entered with food and water. As he placed them on the end of the bench he looked at Tarzan admiringly.

'I was there and saw you kill the King's hunting lion,' he said. 'It was such a thing as one may see only once in a lifetime. I saw you fight with Phobeg before Nemone, the Queen. That, too, was something to have seen. You spared Phobeg's life when you might have killed him, when all were screaming for the kill. After that he would have died for you.'

'Yes, I know,' replied the ape-man. 'Is Phobeg still alive?'

'Oh, very much; and he is still a temple guard.'

'If you see him, tell him that I wish him well.'

'That I will,' promised the warrior. 'I shall see him soon. Now I must be going.' He came close to Tarzan then, and spoke in a whisper. 'Drink no wine, and whoever comes keep your back to the wall and be prepared to fight.' Then he was gone.

'"Drink no wine,"' mused Tarzan. Wine, he knew, was the medium in which poison was customarily administered in Cathne; and if he kept his back to the wall no one could stab him from behind. Good advice! The advice of a friend who might have overheard something that prompted it. Tarzan knew that he had many friends among the warriors of the City of Gold.

He walked to one of the windows and looked out upon the avenue. He saw a lion striding majestically toward the centre of the city, paying no attention to the pedestrians or being noticed by them. It was one of the many tame lions that roam the streets of Cathne by day. Sometimes they fed upon the corpses thrown out to them, but rarely did they attack a living man.

He saw a small gathering of people upon the opposite side of the avenue. They were talking together earnestly, often glancing toward the palace. Pedestrians stopped to listen and joined the crowd. A warrior came from the palace and stopped and spoke to them; then they looked up at the window where Tarzan stood. The warrior was he who had brought food to Tarzan.

When the crowd recognised the ape-man it commenced to cheer. People were coming from both directions, some of them running. There were many warriors among them. The crowd and the tumult grew. When darkness came torches were brought. A detachment of warriors came from the palace. It was commanded by a noble who sought to disperse the gathering.

Someone yelled, 'Free Tarzan!' and the whole crowd took it up, like a chant. A huge man came, bearing a torch. In its light Tarzan recognised the man as Phobeg the temple guard. He waved his torch at Tarzan, and cried, 'Shame, Alextar! Shame!' and the crowd took that cry up and chanted it in unison.

The noble and the guardsmen sought to quiet and disperse them, and then a fight ensued in which heads were broken and men were slashed with swords and run through with spears. By this time the mob had grown until it filled the avenue. Its temper was nasty, and when once blood was spilled it went berserk. Before it the palace guard was helpless, and those who survived were glad to retreat to the safety of the palace.

Now someone shouted, 'Down with Tomos! Death to Tomos!' and the hoarse voice of the mob seized upon this new slogan. It seemed to stir the men to new action, for now in a body they moved down upon the palace gates.

As they hammered and shoved upon the sturdy portals, a man at the outer fringe of the mob shouted, 'The hunting lions! Alextar has turned his hunting lions upon us! Death to Alextar!'

Tarzan looked down the avenue toward the royal stables; and there, indeed, came fully fifty lions, held in leash by their keepers. Excited by the vast crowd, irritated by the noise, they tugged at their chains, while the night trembled to their thunderous roars; but the crowd, aroused now to demonical madness, was undaunted. Yet what could it do against this show of savage force? It started to fall back, slowly, cursing and growling, shouting defiance, calling for Tarzan's release.

Involuntarily, a low growl came from the chest of the ape-man, a growl of protest that he was helpless to aid those who would befriend him. He tested the bars in the window at which he stood. To his strength and his weight they bent inward a little; then he threw all that he had of both upon a single bar. It bent inward and pulled from its sockets in the frame, the soft iron giving to his giant strength. That was enough! One by one in quick succession the remaining bars were dragged out and thrown upon the floor.

Tarzan leaned from the window and looked down. Below him was an enclosed courtyard. It was empty. A wall screened it from the avenue beyond. He glanced into the avenue, and saw that the crowd was still falling back, the lions advancing. So intent were all upon the lions that no one saw the ape-man slip through the window and drop into the courtyard. Opposite him was a postern gate, barred upon the inside. Through it he stepped into the avenue just in front of the retreating crowd, between it and the lions.

A dozen saw and recognised him at once; and a great shout went up, a shout of defiance with a new note in it – a note of renewed confidence and elation.

Tarzan seized a torch from one of the citizens. 'Bring your torches!' he commanded. 'Torches and spears in the front line!' Then he advanced to meet the lions, and the men with the torches and the spears rushed forward to the front line. All that they had needed was a leader.

All wild animals fear fire. The King of beasts is no exception. The hunting lions of Alextar, King of Cathne, shrank back when blazing torches were pushed into their faces. Their keepers, shouting encouragement, cursing, were helpless. One of the lions, his mane ablaze, turned suddenly to one side, fouling another lion, causing him to wheel in terror and confusion and bolt back toward the stables. In doing so, they crossed the leashes of other lions, became entangled in them, and tore them from the hands of the keepers. The freed lions hesitated only long enough to maul the keepers that chanced to be in their way, and then they too galloped back along the avenue toward the stables.

Emboldened by this success, the torch bearers fell upon the remaining lions, beating them with fire until the beasts were mad with terror; and Tarzan, in the forefront, urged them on. Pandemonium reigned. The hoarse shouts of the mob mingled with the roars of the carnivores and the screams of stricken men. By now the lions were frantic with terror. With leashes entangled, keepers down, manes afire, they could stand no more. Those that had not already broken and run, did so now. The mob was for pursuing, but Tarzan stopped them. With raised hand he quieted them after a moment.

'Let the lions go,' he counselled. 'There is bigger game. I am going after Alextar and Tomos.'

'And I am going with you,' a big voice boomed beside him.

Tarzan turned and looked at the speaker. It was Phobeg, the temple guard.

'Good!' said the ape-man.

'We are going after Alextar and Tomos!' cried Phobeg.

A roar of approval rose from the crowd. 'The gates!' some cried, 'To the gates! To the gates!'

'There is an easier way,' said Tarzan. 'Come!'

They followed him to the postern gate that he knew was unbarred and through it into the palace grounds. Here, Tarzan knew his way well; for he had been here both as a prisoner and a guest of Nemone, the Queen.

Alextar and a few of his nobles were dining. The King was frightened; for not only could he hear the shouts of the mob, but he was kept constantly informed of all that was occurring outside the palace, and knew that the hunting lions he had been certain would disperse the rioters had been turned back and were in flight. He had sent every available fighting man in the palace to the gates when the shouts of the crowd indicated that it was about to storm them, and though assured by his nobles that the mob could not hope to overcome his warriors, even if the gates failed to hold against them, he was still terrified.

'It is your fault, Tomos,' he whined. 'You said to lock the wild man up, and now look what has happened! The people want to dethrone me. They may even kill me. What shall I do? What can I do?'

Tomos was in no better state of nerves than the King, for he had heard the people calling for his death. He cast about for some plan that might save him, and presently he thought of one.

'Send for the wild man,' he said, 'and set him free. Give him money and honours. Send word at once to the gates that you have done this.'

'Yes, yes,' assented Alextar; and, turning to one of his nobles, 'Go at once and fetch the wild man; and you, go to the gates and tell the people what has been done.'

'Later,' said Tomos, 'we can offer him a cup of wine.'

The first noble crossed the room hurriedly and threw open a door leading into a corridor from which he could ascend to the second floor where Tarzan had been imprisoned, but he did not cross the threshold. In dismay he stepped back into the room.

'Here is Tarzan now!' he cried.

Alextar and Tomos and the others sprang to their feet as the opened door let in the murmurings of the crowd that followed the ape-man; then Tarzan stepped into the room, and crowding behind him came Phobeg and the others.

Alextar arose to flee, as did Tomos also; but with a bound Tarzan crossed the room and seized them. No noble drew a sword in defence of the King; like rats fleeing a sinking ship they were ready to desert Alextar. So great was his terror, the man was in a state of collapse. He went to his knees and begged for his life.

'You do not understand,' he cried. 'I had just given orders to release you. I was going to give you money – I will give you money – I will make you a lion-man – I will give you a palace, slaves, everything.'

'You should have thought of all this on the Field of the Lions today; now it is too late. Not that I would have what you offer,' the ape-man added, 'but it might have saved your life temporarily and your throne, too, because then your people would not have grown so angry and disgusted.'

'What are you going to do to me?' demanded the King.

'I am going to do nothing to you,' replied Tarzan. 'What your people do to you is none of my concern, but if they don't make Thudos King they are fools.'

Now Thudos was the first of the nobles, as Tarzan knew; and in his veins flowed better blood from an older line than the King of Cathne could claim.

He was a famous old warrior, loved and respected by the people; and when the crowd in the room heard Tarzan they shouted for Thudos; and those in the corridor carried it back out into the avenue, and the word spread through the city.

Alextar heard, and his face went ashen white. He must have gone quite mad, as his sister before him. He came slowly to his feet and faced Tomos. 'You have done this to me,' he said. 'For years you kept me in prison. You ruined my sister's life – you and M'duze. You have ruined my life, and now you have lost me my throne. But you shall never ruin another life,' and with that he drew his sword so quickly that none could stay him and brought the blade down with all his strength on Tomos' skull, cleaving it to the nose.

As the body slumped to his feet he broke into maniacal laughter, while those in the room stood stunned and silent; then, as quickly as he had done before, he placed the point of his sword at his heart and threw himself forward upon it.

Thus died Alextar, the last of the mad rulers of Cathne.

XX
Athne

The main gate of Athne, the City of Ivory, looks toward the South; for in that direction runs the trail that leads to Cathne, the City of Gold, the stronghold of the hereditary enemies of the Athneans. In that direction ride the warriors and the nobles of Athne seeking women and heads and other loot; from that direction come the raiding parties from Cathne, also seeking women and heads and other loot; so the main gate of Athne is strong and well guarded. It is surmounted by two squat towers in which warriors watch by day and by night.

Before the gate is a great level plain where the elephants are trained and the warriors of Athne drill upon their mighty mounts. It is dusty, and nothing grows there but a sturdy cynodon; and even that survives the trampling pads of the pachyderms only in scattered patches. The fields of the Athneans lie North of the city, and there the slaves labour; so one might approach the city from the South without glimpsing a sign of human life.

It was mid-afternoon. The hot sun beat down upon the watch towers. The warriors, languid with the heat, gamed at dice – those who were not on watch. Presently one of the latter spoke.

'A man comes from the South,' he said.

'How many?' asked one of the players.

'I said *a* man. I see but one.'

'Then we do not have to give the alarm. But who could come alone to Athne? Is it a man from Cathne?'

'There have been deserters come to us before. Perhaps this is one.'

'He is yet too far off to see plainly,' said the warrior who had discovered the stranger, 'but he does not look like a Cathnean. His dress seems strange to me.'

He went to the inner side of the tower then and, leaning over the edge of the parapet, called the captain of the guard. An officer came from the interior of the tower and looked up.

'What is it?' he asked.

'Someone is coming from the South,' explained the warrior.

The officer nodded and mounted the ladder leading to the tower's top. The warriors stopped their game then, and all went to the southern parapet to have a look at the stranger. He was nearer now, and they could see that he wore garments strange to them.

'He is no Cathnean,' said the officer, 'but he is either a fool or a brave man to come thus alone to Athne.'

As Stanley Wood neared the gates of Athne he saw the warriors in the watchtowers observing him, and when he came quite close they challenged him but in a language he could not understand.

'Friend,' he said, and raised his hand in the peace sign.

Presently the gate opened and an officer and several warriors came out. They tried to talk with him, and when they found that neither could understand the other they formed about him and escorted him through the gateway.

He found himself at the end of an avenue lined with low buildings occupied by shops. The warriors who had brought him into the city were white, as were most of the people on the avenue, although there were some negroes. Everyone appeared much interested in him; and he was soon surrounded by a large crowd, all talking at once, pointing, feeling of his clothes and weapons. The latter were soon taken from him by his guard, the officer shouted some commands, and the warriors pushed the people out of the way and started up the avenue with Wood.

He felt very uncomfortable and helpless because of his inability to converse with those about him. There were so many questions he wished to ask. Gonfala might be in this city and yet he might never know it if he could not ask anyone about her who could understand him. He determined that the first thing he must do was to learn the language of these people. He wondered if they would be friendly. The fact that they were white gave him hope.

Who could they be? Their garb, so different from anything modern, gave him no clue. They might have stepped from the pages of ancient history, so archaic were their weapons and their raiment; but he could not place them exactly. Where did they originate, these strange, rather handsome men and women? How and when did they reach this unknown valley in Africa? Could they be descendants of some Atlantean colonists stranded here after the submergence of their continent?

Vain speculations. No matter who they were, they were here; and he was either their prisoner or their guest – the former, he was inclined to believe. One did not usually surround a guest by armed warriors.

As they proceeded along the avenue Wood observed more closely the raiment of his escort and of the people whom they passed. The officer in charge was a handsome, black haired fellow who strode along apparently oblivious of those they passed, yet there was nothing offensive about his manner. If there were social castes here, Wood hazarded a safe guess that this man was of the nobility. The headband that confined his hair supported a carved ivory ornament at the centre of his forehead, an ornament that was shaped like a concave, curved trowel, the point of which projected above the top of the man's head and curved forward. He wore wristlets and anklets of long, flat strips of ivory laid close together and fastened around his limbs by leather thongs that were laced through holes piercing the strips near their tops and bottoms. Sandals of elephant hide encasing his feet were supported by leather thongs fastened to the bottoms of his anklets. On each arm, below the shoulder, was an ivory disc upon which was a carved device; about his neck was a band of smaller ivory discs elaborately carved, and from the lowest of these a strap ran down to a leather habergeon, which was also supported by shoulder straps. Depending from each side of his headband was another ivory disc of large size, above which was a smaller disc, the former covering his ears. Heavy, curved, wedge-shaped pieces of ivory were held, one upon each shoulder, by the same straps that supported his habergeon. He was armed with a dagger and a short sword.

The warriors who accompanied him were similarly garbed, but less elaborately in the matter of carved ivory; and their habergeons and sandals were of coarser leather more roughly fabricated. Upon the back of each was a small shield. The common warriors carried short, heavy spears as well as swords and daggers. From their arms, Wood concluded that what he had first supposed to be ivory ornaments were definitely protective armour.

The American was conducted to a large, walled enclosure in the centre of the city. Here stood the most elaborate buildings he had seen. There was a large central structure and many smaller buildings, the whole set in a park-like garden of considerable beauty which covered an area of several acres.

Just inside the gate was a small building before which lolled a score of warriors. Within, an officer sat at a table; and to him Wood was taken, and here the officer who had brought him evidently made his report. What passed between them Wood could not, of course, understand; but when the first officer left he realised that he had been delivered into the custody of the other.

While similarly garbed, this second officer did not give the impression of birth or breeding that had been so noticeable in the first. He was a burly, uncouth appearing fellow with much less in his appearance to recommend him than many of the common warriors Wood had seen. When left alone with his prisoner he commenced to shout questions at him; and when he found that Wood could not understand him, or he Wood, he pounded on the table angrily.

Finally he summoned warriors to whom he issued instructions, and once again Wood was taken under escort. This time he was led to an enclosure toward the rear of the grounds not far from a quite large one-storied building with the interior of which he was destined to become well acquainted.

He was thrust into an enclosure along the North side of which was an open shed in which were some fifty men. A high fence or stockade formed the remaining three sides of the quadrangle, the outside of which was patrolled by warriors; and Wood realised now that he was definitely a prisoner and far from being either an important or favoured one, as the other inmates of the stockade were for the most part filthy, unkempt fellows, both white and black.

As Wood approached the enclosure every eye was upon him; and he knew that they were commenting upon him; and, from the tone of an occasional laugh, judged that he was the butt of many a rough quip. He sensed antagonism and felt more alone than he would have in solitary confinement; and then he heard his name called by someone in the midst of the assemblage in the shed.

Immediately two men separated themselves from the others and came to meet him. They were Spike and Troll. A wave of anger swept through the American as the implication of their presence here pointed them out as the abductors of Gonfala.

His face must have betrayed his emotions as he advanced toward them; for Spike raised his hand in a gesture of warning.

'Hold on, now,' he cried. 'Gettin' hostile ain't goin' to get us no place. We're in a Hell of a fix here, an' gettin' hostile ain't goin' to help matters none. It'll be better for all of us if we work together.'

'Where's Gonfala?' demanded Wood. 'What have you done with her?'

'They took her away from us the day they captured us,' said Troll. 'We ain't seen her since.'

'We understand she's in the palace,' said Spike. 'They say the big guy here has fell for her. He's got her an' the Gonfal, the dirty bounder.'

'What did you steal her for?' Wood demanded. 'If either one of you harmed her—'

'Harm her!' exclaimed Troll. 'You don't think I'd never let nobody harm my sister, do you?'

Spike winked behind Troll's back and tapped his forehead. 'They ain't nobody harmed her,' he assured Wood, 'unless it was done after they took her away from us. And for why did we bring 'er along with us? We had to 'ave 'er. We couldn't work the Gonfal without 'er.'

'That damned stone!' muttered Wood.

'I think they's a curse on it myself,' agreed Spike. 'It ain't never brought nobody nothin' but bad luck. Look at me and Troll. Wot we got for our pains? We lost the emerald; now we lost the Gonfal, an' all we do is shovel dirt out o' the elephant barns all day an' wait to see w'ich way they's goin' to croak us.'

As they talked they were surrounded by other prisoners prompted by curiosity to inspect the latest recruit. They questioned Wood; but, as he could not understand them nor they he, they directed their questions upon Spike who replied in a strange jargon of African dialects, signs, and the few words of the Athnean language he had picked up. It was a wholly remarkable means of conveying thoughts, but it apparently served its purpose admirably.

As Wood stood there, the object of their interest, he was rapidly considering the attitude he should assume toward Spike and Troll. The men were scoundrels of the first water, and could command only his bitterest enmity. For the wrong that they had done Gonfala it seemed to Wood that they deserved death; yet they were the only men here with whom he could talk, the only ones with whom he had any interests in common. His judgment told him that Spike had been right when he said that they should work together. For the time being, then, he would put aside his just anger against them and throw his lot in with them in the hope that in some way they might be of service to Gonfala.

'They wants to know who you are an' where you comes from,' said Spike; 'an' I told 'em you come from a country a thousand times bigger than Athne an' that you was a juke or somethin', like their officers. They's one of 'em in here with us. See that big bloke over there standin' with his arms folded?' He pointed to a tall, fine looking fellow who had not come forward with the others. 'He's a toff, or I never seen one. He don't never have no truck with these scrubs; but he took a shine to Troll and me, an' is learnin' us his language.'

'I'd like to meet him,' said Wood, for his first interest now was to learn the language of these people into whose hands fate had thrown him.

'Awright, come on over. He ain't a bad bloke. He's wot they calls an elephant man. That's somethin' like bein' a juke at home. They had some sort of a revolution here a few months ago, an' killed off a lot of these here elephant men, wot didn't escape or join the revolutionists. But this bloke wasn't killed. They say it was because he was a good guy an' everybody like him, even the revolutionists. He wouldn't join 'em; so they stuck him in here to do chamber work for the elephants. These here revolutionists is like the gangsters in your country. Anyway, they's a bad lot, always makin' trouble for decent people an' stealin' wot they ain't got brains enough to make for themselves. Well, here we are. Valthor, shake hands with my old friend Stanley Wood.'

Valthor looked puzzled, but he took Wood's outstretched hand.

'Cripes!' exclaimed Spike. 'I'm always forgettin' you don't know no English.' Then he couched the introduction in the bastard language he had picked up.

'Valthor, shake hands with my old friend Stanley Wood.'

'He says he's glad to meetcha,' translated Spike.

'Tell him it's fifty-fifty,' said the American, 'and ask him if he'll help me learn his language.'

When Spike had translated this speech Valthor smiled and nodded, and there immediately began an association that not only developed into a genuine friendship during the ensuing weeks but gave Wood a sufficient knowledge of the Athnean language to permit free intercourse with all with whom he came in contact.

During this time he worked with the other slaves in the great elephant stables of Phoros, the dictator who had usurped the crown of Athne after the revolution. The food was poor and insufficient, the work arduous, and the treatment he received harsh; for the officers who were put in charge of the slaves had been men of the lowest class prior to the revolution and found a vent for many an inhibition when they were given a little authority.

During all this time he heard nothing of the fate of Gonfala, for naturally little news of the palace reached the slaves in the stables. Whether she lived or not, he could not know; and this state of constant uncertainty and anxiety told even more heavily upon him than did the hardships he was forced to undergo.

'If she is beautiful,' Valthor had told him, 'I think you need have no fear for her life. We do not take the lives of beautiful women – even the Erythra would not do that.'

'Who are the Erythra?' asked Wood.

'The men who overthrew the government and placed Phoros on the throne of Zygo, King of Athne.'

'She is very beautiful,' said Wood. 'I wish to God she were not so beautiful.'

'Perhaps it will do her no harm. If I know Menofra, and I think I do, your friend will be safe from the attentions of Phoros at least; and if I know Phoros, he will not let anyone else have her if she is very beautiful. He will always wait and hope – hope that something will happen to Menofra.'

'And who might Menofra be?'

'Above all else she is a she-devil for jealousy, and she is the wife of Phoros.'

This was slight comfort, but it was the best that was vouchsafed Wood. He could only wait and hope. There was little upon which to base a plan of action. Valthor had told him that there might be a counter-revolution to unseat Phoros and return Zygo to the throne; but in the slaves' compound there was little information upon which to base even a conjecture as to when, if ever, this might take place; as there was no means of communication between those confined there and Zygo's sympathisers in the city, while Zygo and most of his loyal nobles and retainers were hiding in the mountains to which they had escaped when revolution overwhelmed the city.

Among other duties that had fallen to the lot of Wood was the exercising of the elephant that was his particular charge. He had been chosen for this work, along with Valthor, Spike, and Troll, because of his greater intelligence than the ordinary run of slaves in the compound. He had learned quickly, and rode almost daily on the plain South of the city under a heavy escort of warriors.

They had returned to the stables one day from the field after the exercise period, which was always early in the morning, and were brushing and washing their huge mounts, when they were ordered to remount and ride out.

On the way to the plain they learned from the accompanying warriors that they were being sent out to capture a wild elephant that had been damaging the fields.

'They say he's a big brute and ugly,' offered one of the warriors, 'and if he's as bad as all that we won't all of us come back.'

'Under Zygo, the nobles rode out to capture wild elephants, not slaves,' said Valthor.

The warrior rode his mount closer to the Athnean noble. 'They are all too drunk to ride,' he said, lowering his voice. 'If they were just a little drunk they might ride. If they were not drunk at all they would not have the nerve. We warriors are sick of them. Most of us would like to ride again under real elephant men like your nobleness.'

'Perhaps you will,' said Valthor, '– if you have the nerve.'

'Hi-yah!' shouted a warrior ahead of them.

'They've sighted him,' Valthor explained to Wood, who was riding at his side.

Presently they too saw the quarry emerging from a bamboo forest at the edge of the plain.

Valthor whistled. 'He's a big brute, and if he's as ugly as they say we should have some real sport. But it's murder to send inexperienced slaves against him. Watch out for yourself, Wood. Just keep out of his way, no matter what the guards tell you to do. Make believe you can't control your elephant. Look at him! He's coming right for us. He's a bad one all right – not a bit afraid of us either by Dyaus.'

'I never saw a larger one,' said Wood.

'Nor I,' admitted Valthor. 'Though I've seen many an elephant in my time. He's got a blemish though – look at that tusk. It's much darker than the other. If it weren't for that he'd make a King's elephant all right.'

'What are we supposed to do?' asked Wood. 'I don't see how we could ever capture that fellow if he didn't want us to.'

'They'll have some females ridden close to him, and try to work him gently toward the city and into the big corral just inside the gate. Look at that, now!'

Up went the big elephant's trunk, and he trumpeted angrily. It was evident that he was about to charge. The officer in command shouted orders to the slaves to ride the females toward him, but the officer did not advance. Like the other three with him, he was an Erythos and not of the noble class. Not having their pride or their code of honour, he could order others into danger while he remained in comparative safety.

Some of the slaves moved forward, but with no great show of enthusiasm; then the great beast charged. He barged right through the line of advancing females, scattering them to right and left, and charged for the bull ridden by the officer in command.

Screaming commands, the officer sought to turn his mount and escape, but the bull he rode was a trained fighting elephant which knew little about running away; besides, his harem of cows was there; and he was not going to relinquish that to any strange bull without a battle; so, torn between his natural inclinations and his habit of obedience to the commands of his rider, he neither faced the oncoming bull nor turned tail toward him; but swung half way around, broadside, in his indecision. And in this position the great stranger struck him with almost the momentum of a locomotive run amok.

Down he went, pitching the officer heavily to the ground; but the fellow was up instantly and running – by far the stupidest thing he could have done; for almost any animal will pursue a thing that flees.

Hoarse screams for help mingled with the trumpeting of the wild bull as the latter bore down upon his fleeing victim. Valthor urged the female he rode into a trot in an effort to head off the charge and distract the bull's attention, and Wood followed behind him; just why, he could not have explained.

Valthor was too late. The bull overtook the terrified man, tossed him three times, and then trampled him into the dust of the plain until he was only a darker spot on the barren ground.

It was then that Valthor and Wood arrived. Wood expected nothing less than a repetition of the scene he had just witnessed with either himself or Valthor as the victim, but nothing of the kind happened.

The Athnean rode his cow quietly close to the great bull, which stood complacently switching its tail, all the madness having apparently passed out of him with the killing of his victim; and Wood, following the example of Valthor, closed in gently on the other side.

All this time Valthor was chanting in a low, sing-song monotone a wordless song used by the elephant men of Athne to soothe the great beasts in moods of nervousness or irritation; and now to the cadence of his chant he added words of instruction to Wood so that the two might work in harmony to bring the wild bull to the city and into the corral.

Between the two cows, which knew their parts well, the bull was guided to captivity; while the officers, the warriors, and the slaves trailed behind, happy and relieved that they had not been called upon to risk their lives.

Valthor already held the respect of his fellow prisoners as well as of the warriors who guarded them, and now Wood took his place as a person of importance among them.

That word of the manner of the capture of the wild elephant had reached the palace Wood had proof the following day when an officer and a detail of warriors came to take him into the presence of Phoros.

'He wishes to see the fellow who helped Valthor capture the rogue,' said the officer.

Valthor leaned close and whispered, 'He has some other reason. He would not send for you just for that.'

XXI

Phoros

Night was creeping stealthily out of its lair in the east, bringing its following of mystery and dark deeds and strange beasts that are not seen by day. Though the sun still coloured the western sky with a fading tinge of red it was already dark and gloomy in the Pass of the Warriors that leads from the valley of Onthar to the valley of Thenar.

In Onthar is Cathne, the City of Gold; in Thenar is Athne, the City of Ivory; in The Pass of the Warriors was Tarzan of the Apes. Alone, he was going to Athne seeking a clue to the whereabouts of Gonfala.

Gemnon had tried to dissuade him from going without an escort; and so had Thudos, whom he had helped to seat upon the throne of Cathne.

'If you are not back within a reasonable time,' Thudos told him, 'I shall send an army to Athne to bring you back.'

'If I am not back in a reasonable time,' suggested the ape-man, 'it may be because I shall be dead.'

'Perhaps,' agreed Thudos, 'but they will not kill you unless they have to. They are always hard pressed to find enough slaves to carry on the work of the city, and they'd never destroy such a fine specimen as you. Like us, they also need men to fight in the arena.'

'You would like that better than scrubbing elephants,' said Gemnon, smiling.

Tarzan shook his head. 'I do not like to fight or to kill, and there are worse things than scrubbing elephants.'

And so he had gone, choosing to travel so that he would not have to cross the valley of Thenar by day, as he wished to approach and reconnoitre Athne unseen. That both valleys, especially Onthar, harboured many wild lions was a hazard he had to accept; but, except for the actual crossing of Thenar, he could take advantage of the protection of forests practically all of the way.

The hazard was great, for the lions of Thenar were not all ordinary lions. Many of them were escaped hunting lions of Cathne which had been often fed with human flesh and trained to hunt men. For generations they had been bred for speed and endurance; so that in all the world there were no such formidable beasts of prey as these.

As night fell, Tarzan heard the roars of the great cats in the valley he had quitted. With every sense alert he passed through The Pass of the Warriors and entered the valley of Thenar. As yet he had heard no lion roar coming from that direction. The wind was in his face. It brought no scent spoor of Numa, but he knew that it was carrying his scent back in the direction of the hunting lions of Cathne.

He increased his speed, for though he had killed many a lion he knew that no living creature could hope to survive an attack by these beasts that often hunted in packs.

He was out now upon the open plain of Thenar. He could still hear the roaring of the lions in Onthar. Suddenly they took on a new note. He knew it well. It told him that they had picked up the trail of some creature and marked, it as their quarry. Was it his trail?

A full moon rose above the mountains ahead of him, lighting the floor of the valley, revealing the dark strip of forest far ahead. The savage voices of the lions grew louder, reverberating in the canyon called The Pass of the Warriors, through which he had just come; then Tarzan knew that the hunting lions of Cathne were on his trail.

You or I could not have counted the lions by their voices; but to Tarzan the distinctive quality or character of each voice was discernible, and thus he knew that five lions were loping relentlessly to the kill. Once more he quickened his pace.

He judged that the lions were about a mile in rear of him, the forest about three miles ahead. If no obstacle intervened he could reach the forest ahead of the lions; but he was crossing an unfamiliar terrain known to him only by the descriptions given him by Gemnon and Thudos, and he knew that there might easily be some peculiarity of the topography of the floor of the valley that would delay him – a deep dry wash with overhanging banks of soft dirt would do it.

On he trotted, his great chest rising and falling regularly, his heartbeats scarcely accelerated by the exertion; but the lions came even more swiftly. He knew from the sound of their voices that they were gaining on him. Knowing them, even as he did, he marvelled at their endurance, so unusual in lions; and was amazed at the results that could be attained by careful breeding. Now, for the first time, he broke into a run; for he knew that the moment they sighted him they would come on much faster than he could run for any great distance. It then would be just a question as to which could maintain the greatest speed for the longest distance.

No washes intervened nor other obstacle, and he came at last to within half a mile of the forest with sufficient distance and time to spare to assure him a reasonable margin of safety; then the unforeseen occurred. From the shadows of the forest a great lion stepped into view before him.

Those who would live long in the jungle must think quickly. Tarzan weighed the entire situation without losing a stride. The forest was his goal; one lion was less of a menace than five, and the one lion was all that stood between him and the forest. With a savage growl he charged the lion.

The beast had started to trot toward him; but now he stopped, hesitant. Would he hold his ground or would he break? Much depended upon whether he was an ordinary wild lion or a trained hunting lion. From the fact that he hesitated instead of carrying through his charge Tarzan guessed that he was the former.

The five lions from Onthar were gaining rapidly now. In the bright moonlight they must have caught sight of their quarry. Their voices proclaimed that. Now they were charging. Had they been wild lions they would have hunted in silence once their prey was marked, but the earth fairly trembled to their roars. Tarzan thought that they wasted too much energy thus, but he knew that they were trained to it so that the huntsmen could follow them even when they were out of sight.

Tarzan saw that the lion facing him was wavering. He was probably surprised at the tactics of the man-thing, at a quarry that charged him; and the roars of the five lions doubtless added to his nervousness. Only fifty yards separated them, and the lion had not made up his mind, when from the chest of the ape-man burst the savage challenge of the bull-ape. It was the last straw – the lion wheeled and bounded back into the forest. A moment later Tarzan swarmed up a friendly tree as five angry lions leaped to seize him.

Finding a comfortable resting place, the ape-man broke off dead branches and threw them at the lions, calling them Dango, Ungo, Horta, and other insulting names, ascribing vile tastes and habits to themselves and their ancestors. A quiet, almost taciturn, man, he was an adept in the use of the jungle billingsgate he had acquired from the great apes among which he had been raised. Perhaps the lions understood him; perhaps they did not. Who knows? Anyhow, they were very angry; and leaped high in air in vain efforts to reach him, which only made them angrier. But Tarzan had no time to waste upon them; and, keeping to the trees, he swung away toward the North and Athne.

He had timed himself to reach the city while it slept, and knew how to approach it from information given him by Gemnon and Thudos who had often visited Athne during the yearly truces when the two cities traded with one another. He passed half way around the city to the North side, which was less well guarded than the South.

Here he faced the greatest danger of discovery, for he must scale the wall in the light of a full moon. He chose a place far from the North gate, and crept toward the city on his belly through the garden stuff growing in the cultivated fields. He stopped often to look and listen, but he saw no sign of life on the city wall.

When he had come to within about a hundred feet of the wall, he arose and ran toward it at top speed, scaling it like a cat until his fingers closed upon the coping; then he drew himself up; and, lying flat, looked down upon the other side. A shed-like building abutted against the wall, and beyond this was a narrow street. Tarzan slipped to the roof of the shed, and a moment later dropped into the street.

Instantly a head was thrust from an open window and a man's voice demanded, 'What are you doing there? Who are you?'

'I am Daimon,' replied Tarzan in a husky whisper. Instantly the head was withdrawn and the window slammed shut. Tarzan, quick witted, had profited by something that Gemnon had told him – that the Athneans believed in a bad spirit that was abroad at night seeking whom it might kill. To Daimon they attributed all unexplained deaths, especially those that occurred at night.

Following the directions he had received, Tarzan moved through the narrow, shadowed streets toward the centre of the city, coming at last to the walled enclosure where the palace stood. He had been told that here he would find guards only at the North and South gates. Other gates, if there were any, were securely fastened and seldom used.

As Tarzan approached the enclosure from the west, he encountered no gate and no guards. The wall was low compared with that which surrounded the city, and so proved no obstacle to the ape-man. Once over the wall he found himself in a garden of trees, shrubs, and flowers, a lovely place of soft, sweet fragrances; but for these he had no senses at the moment – he was searching for other scents than those of flowers.

Winding among small buildings and other gardens he came to a large building that he knew must be the palace; and here, to his surprise, he saw several rooms brilliantly lighted. He had thought that all would be asleep with the exception of the guards.

A number of old trees grew in the garden court that flanked this side of the palace, and in the security of their shadows Tarzan crossed to the building and looked in at one of the windows. Here he saw a large banquet hall down the length of which ran a long table at which a hundred or more men were seated, most of them in various stages of drunkenness.

There was much loud talk and laughter, and a couple of fights were in progress in which no one took any interest except the contestants. The men were, for the most part, coarse, common appearing fellows, not at all like the nobles of Cathne. The man at the head of the table was quite bestial in appearance. He pounded on the table with a great ham of a fist, and bellowed more like a bull than a man.

Slaves were coming and going, bringing more drink and removing empty goblets and dishes. Some of the guests were still eating, but most of them concentrated their energies and their talents upon the principal business of the evening – drinking.

'Didn't I tell you to fetch her?' shouted the large man at the head of the table addressing the assemblage in general.

'Told who to bring what?' inquired another seated farther toward the foot of the table.

'The girl,' shouted the large man.

'What girl, Phoros?'

'THE girl,' replied Phoros drunkenly.

'Oh, THE girl,' said someone.

'Well, why don't you bring her?'

'Bring who?'

'Bring THE girl,' repeated Phoros.

'Who bring her?' asked another.

'You bring her,' ordered Phoros.

The fellow addressed shook his head. 'Not me,' he said. 'Menofra'd have the hide off me.'

'She won't know. She's gone to bed,' Phoros assured him.

'I ain't takin' any chances. Send a slave.'

'You'd better not send anyone,' counselled a man sitting next to Phoros, one who did not seem as drunk as the others. 'Menofra would cut her heart out and yours too.'

'Who's King?' demanded Phoros.

'Ask Menofra,' suggested the other.

'I'm King,' asserted Phoros. He turned to a slave. The fellow happened to be looking in another direction. Phoros threw a heavy goblet at him, which barely missed his head. 'Here, you! Go fetch the girl.'

'What girl, Master?' asked the trembling slave.

'There's only one girl in Athne, you son of a warthog! Go get her!'

The slave hurried from the room. Then there ensued a discussion as to what Menofra would do if she found out. Phoros announced that he was tired of Menofra, and that if she didn't mind her own business he'd take her apart and forget to put her together again. He thought this such a good joke that he laughed immoderately and fell off his bench, but some of the others seemed nervous and looked apprehensively toward the doorway.

Tarzan watched and listened. He felt disgust and shame – shame, because he belonged to the same species as these creatures. Since infancy he had been fellow of the beasts of the forest and the plain, the lower orders; yet he had never seen them sink to the level of man. Most of them had courage and dignity of a sort; seldom did they stoop to buffoonery, with the possible exception of the lesser monkeys, who were most closely allied to man. Had he been impelled to theorise he would doubtless have reversed Darwin's theory of evolution. But his mind was occupied with another thought – who was 'THE girl'? He wondered if she might not be Gonfala, but further speculation was discouraged by the coming of a large, masculine looking woman who strode into the room followed by the slave who had just been dispatched to bring the girl. So this was the girl! Tarzan looked at her in mild astonishment. She had large, red hands, a whiskered mole on her chin, and quite a noticeable moustache. In other respects she was quite as unlovely.

'What's the meaning of this?' she demanded, glaring at Phoros. 'Why did you send for me at this time in the morning, you drunken lout?'

Phoros' jaw dropped; he looked wildly about at his companions as though seeking help; but he got none. Each of those who had not passed out completely was engaged in trying to appear dignified and sober.

'My dear,' explained Phoros ingratiatingly, 'we wanted you to join us and help celebrate.'

'"My dear" nothing!' snapped the woman; then her eyes narrowed. 'Celebrate what?' she demanded.

Phoros looked about him helplessly. Bleary eyed and belching, he looked foolishly at the man sitting next him. 'What were we celebrating, Kandos?'

Kandos fidgeted, and moistened his dry lips with his tongue.

'Don't lie to me!' screamed the woman. 'The truth is that you never intended to send for me.'

'Now, Menofra!' exclaimed Phoros in what was intended to be a soothing tone.

The woman wheeled on the frightened slave behind her. 'Were you told to fetch me?' she demanded.

'Oh, great Queen! I thought he meant you,' whimpered the slave, dropping to his knees.

'What did he say to you?' Menofra's voice was raised almost to a shriek.

'He said, "Go fetch the girl!" and when I asked him what girl, he said, "There's only one girl in Athne, you son of a warthog!"'

Menofra's eyes narrowed menacingly. 'The only girl in Athne, eh? I know who you sent for – it's that yellow haired hussy that was brought in with the two men. You think you been fooling me, don't you? Well, you haven't. You just been waiting for your chance, and tonight you got drunk enough to muster up a little courage. Well, I'll attend to you; and when I get through with you, I'll fix the only girl in Athne. I'll send her to you, if there's anything left of you – I'll send her to you in pieces.' She wheeled on the subdued and frightened company. 'Get out of here, you swine – all of you!' Then she strode to the head of the table and seized Phoros by an ear. 'And you come with me – *King*!' The title bristled with contumely.

XXII

Menofra

Tarzan left the window and walked along the side of the building, looking up at the second floor. There, he surmised, would be the sleeping chambers. In some room above, doubtless, Gonfala was confined. Several vines clambered up the wall. He tested them, trying to find one that might bear his weight; and at last he came to some old ivy that had a stem that was as large around as his arm, a gnarled old plant that clung to the rough wall with a million aerial roots. He tried it with his weight; then, satisfied that it would bear him, he started to ascend toward a window directly above.

Close beside the open window he paused and listened, his sensitive nostrils classifying the odours that came from the chamber. A man slept within. Heavy breathing told him the man was asleep. Its stertorousness and odour told him that the fellow was drunk. Tarzan threw a leg across the sill and stepped into the room. He moved noiselessly, feeling his way through the darkness. He took his time, and gradually his eyes became accustomed to the blackness of the interior. He had the gift, that some men have in common with nocturnal animals, of being able to see in the dark better than other men. Perhaps it had been developed to a higher state of efficiency by necessity. One who can see by night in the jungle has a better chance of survival.

Soon he identified a darker mass on the floor near a side wall as the sleeper. That, however, was not difficult; the man's snores screamed his location. Tarzan crossed to the opposite end of the room and found a door. His fingers searched for lock or bolt and found the latter. It squeaked a little as he drew it back; but he had no fear that it would arouse the man, nor did it. The door opened into a dimly lighted corridor – an arched corridor along which were other doors and the arched openings into other corridors.

Tarzan heard voices. They were raised in angry altercation, and there were sounds of scuffling. The voices were those of Menofra and Phoros. Presently there was a loud scream followed by a thud as of a body falling; then silence. Tarzan waited, listening. He heard a door open farther up the corridor in the direction from which the voices had come; then he stepped back into the room behind him, leaving the door slightly ajar so that he could look out into the corridor. He saw a man step from a doorway and approach along the corridor. It was Phoros. He was staggering a little, and in his right hand he carried a bloody short-sword. His expression was bleary-eyed and vacuous. He passed the door from which Tarzan watched and turned into another corridor; then the ape-man stepped into the passageway and followed him.

When he reached the head of the corridor into which Phoros had turned, Tarzan saw the Athnean fumbling with a key at the lock of a door only a short distance ahead; and he waited until Phoros had unlocked the door and entered the room beyond; then the ape-man followed at a run. He wished to reach the door before Phoros could lock it from within, if such were his intention; but it was not. In fact, in his drunken carelessness, he did not even close the door tightly; and he had little more than entered the room when Tarzan pushed the door open and followed him.

The ape-man had moved with utter silence; so that though he stood just behind Phoros the latter was unaware of his presence. The room was lighted by a single cresset – a wick burning in a shallow vessel half filled with fat. Lying in one corner of the room, bound hand and foot, was Gonfala; in another corner, similarly trussed, was Stanley Wood. They both saw and recognised Tarzan simultaneously, but he raised a finger to his lips to caution them to silence. Phoros stood leering at his two prisoners, his gross body swaying unsteadily.

'So the lovers are still here,' he taunted. 'But why do they stay so far apart?

Here, you stupid fool, watch me; I'll show you how to make love to the girl. She's mine now. Menofra, the old Hell-cat, is dead. Look at this sword! See the blood? That's Menofra's blood. I just killed her.' He pointed the sword at Wood. 'And just as soon as I've shown you how a lover should behave I'm going to kill you.'

He took a step toward Gonfala, and as he did so steel thewed fingers gripped his sword wrist, the weapon was torn from his hand, and he was thrown heavily to the floor.

'Quiet, or I kill,' a low voice whispered.

Phoros looked into the cold grey eyes of an almost naked giant who stood above him with his own sword pointed at his breast. 'Who are you?' he quavered. 'Don't kill me. Tell me what you want. You can have anything if you'll not kill me.'

'I'll take what I want. Don't move.' Tarzan crossed to Wood and cut the bonds that held him. 'Release Gonfala,' he said, 'and when you have done that bind this man and gag him.'

Wood worked quickly. 'How did you get here?' Tarzan asked him.

'I was searching for Gonfala. I followed her trail to this city; then they took me prisoner. Today Phoros sent for me. In some way, probably through some of his people overhearing Spike and Troll, he got the idea that I knew how to work the Gonfal. Spike had been bragging about its powers, but neither he nor Troll had been able to do anything with it. They had also told someone that Gonfala was the goddess of the big stone, and so he brought us together and told us to show him some magic. Our meeting was so sudden and unexpected that we gave ourselves away – it must have been apparent to anyone that we were in love. Anyway, Phoros got it; maybe because he was jealous. He has been trying to make love to Gonfala ever since she was captured, but he was too scared of his wife to go very far with it.'

When Gonfala was liberated Wood trussed up Phoros, and as he was completing the work they heard the sound of shuffling footsteps in the corridor. They all stood, tense and silent, waiting. Would the footsteps pass the door, or was someone coming to this room? Nearer and nearer they came; then they paused outside, as though he who walked was listening. The door was pushed open, revealing a horrible apparition. Gonfala muffled a scream; Wood recoiled; only Tarzan showed no emotion. It was Menofra. A horrible wound gashed her head and one shoulder. She was covered with blood; and reeled with weakness from the loss of it; but she still retained her wits.

Stepping quickly back into the corridor, she closed the door and turned the key that the drunken Phoros had left in the lock; then they heard her crying loudly for the guard.

'We seem to be nicely trapped,' commented Wood.

'But we have a hostage,' Tarzan reminded him.

'What a horrible sight,' said Gonfala, shuddering and nodding in the direction of the corridor. 'How do you suppose it happened?'

The ape-man jerked a thumb in the direction of Phoros. 'He could tell you. I imagine that he's rather glad that we were here with him.'

'What a sweet couple,' said Wood, 'but I imagine there are a lot of married couples who would like to do that to one another if they thought they could get away with it.'

'What a terrible thing to say, Stanlee,' cried Gonfala. 'Do you think that we would be like that?'

'Oh, we're different,' Wood assured her; 'these people are beasts.'

'Not beasts,' Tarzan corrected. 'They are human beings, and they act like human beings.'

'Here comes the guard,' said Wood.

They could hear men approaching at a run along the corridor; they heard their exclamations when they saw Menofra and their excited questioning.

'There is a wild man in there,' Menofra told them. 'He has set the two prisoners free, and they have bound and gagged the King. They may kill him. I don't want them to; I want him for myself. Go in and capture the strangers and bring the King to me.'

Tarzan stood close to the door. 'If you come in without my permission,' he shouted, 'I will kill the King.'

'It looks like you were on a spot, Phoros,' said Wood, 'no matter what happens. If Menofra gets you she'll hand you plenty.' Phoros could make no reply because of the gag.

The warriors and the Queen were arguing in the corridor. They could come to no decision as to what to do. The three prisoners in the room were no better off. Tarzan was puzzled. He told Wood as much.

'I knew an Athnean noble well,' he said, 'and through him I was led to believe that these people were rather noble and chivalrous, not at all like those I have seen here. There was a rumour in Cathne that there had been some change in government here, but the natural assumption was that another faction of the nobility had come into power. If these people are of the nobility, our friend Spike must be at least an archbishop.'

'They are not of the nobility.' said Wood. 'They are from the lowest dregs of society. They overthrew the King and the nobility a few months ago. I guess they are pretty well ruining the country.'

'That accounts for it,' said Tarzan. 'Well, I guess my friend, Valthor, can't help me much.'

'Valthor?' exclaimed Wood. 'Do you know him? Why say, he's the only friend I have here.'

'Where is he? He'll help us,' said Tarzan.

'Not where he is, he won't. He and I were fellow slaves at the elephant stables.'

'Valthor a slave!'

'Yes, and lucky to be that,' Wood assured him. 'They killed off all the other members of the nobility they caught – except a few that joined 'em. The rest escaped into the mountains. Every one liked Valthor so much that they didn't kill him.'

'It is a good thing that I didn't take any chances when I came here,' remarked the ape-man. 'They'd heard these rumours in Cathne; so I came in after dark to investigate before I tried to find Valthor or made myself known.'

There was a rap on the door. 'What do you want?' asked Tarzan.

'Turn the King over to the Queen and we won't harm you,' said a voice.

Phoros commenced to wriggle and squirm on the floor, shaking his head vigorously. Tarzan grinned.

'Wait until we talk it over,' he said; then, to Wood, 'Take the gag out of his mouth.'

As soon as the gag was removed Phoros choked and spluttered before he could articulate an understandable word, so frightened and excited was he. 'Don't let her have me,' he finally managed to say. 'She'll kill me.'

'I think you have it coming to you,' said Wood.

'Maybe we can reach a bargain,' suggested Tarzan.

'Anything, anything you want,' cried Phoros.

'Our freedom and a safe escort to The Pass of the Warriors,' demanded the ape-man.

'It is yours,' promised Phoros.

'And the big diamond,' added Wood.

'And the big diamond,' agreed Phoros.

'How do we know you'll do as you agree?' asked Tarzan.

'You have my word for it,' Phoros assured him.

'I don't think it's worth much. I'd have to have something more.'

'Well, what?'

'We'd want to take you with us and keep you close to me where I could kill you if the bargain were not kept.'

'That too. I agree to everything, only don't let her get her hands on me.'

'There is one more thing,' added Tarzan. 'Valthor's freedom.'

'Granted.'

'And now that you've got all that arranged,' said Wood, 'how in Hell are we going to get out of here with that old virago holding the fort with the guard out there? Have you ever been to a coronation, Tarzan?'

The ape-man shook his head.

'Well, take Phorsie out there, my friend, and you'll see a King crowned.'

'I don't know what you're talking about, but I don't intend taking him out of here until I have some assurance that his promises will be carried out.' He turned to Phoros. 'What can you suggest? Will the guard obey you?'

'I don't know. They're afraid of her. Everybody's afraid of her, and Dyaus knows they have reason.'

'We seem to be getting nowhere with great facility,' commented Wood.

Tarzan crossed to Phoros and removed his bonds. 'Come to the door,' he directed, 'and explain my proposition to your wife.'

Phoros approached the door. 'Listen, dear,' he said ingratiatingly.

'Listen nothing, you beast, you murderer,' she screamed back at him. 'Just let me get my hands on you – that's all I ask.'

'But darling, I was drunk. I didn't mean to do it. Listen to reason. Let me take these people out of the country with an escort of warriors and they won't kill me.'

'Don't "darling" me, you, you—'

'But, my own little Menofra, listen to reason. Send for Kandos, and let us all talk it over.'

'Go in there, you cowards, and drag them out,' Menofra shouted to the guardsmen.

'Stay out there!' screamed Phoros. 'I am King. Those are the King's commands.'

'I'm Queen,' yelled Menofra. 'I tell you to go in and rescue the King.'

'I'm all right,' shouted Phoros. 'I don't want to be rescued.'

'I think,' said the officer of the guard, 'that the best thing to do is summon Kandos. This is no matter for a simple officer of the guard to decide.'

'That's right,' encouraged the King; 'send for Kandos.'

They heard the officer dispatch a warrior to summon Kandos, and they heard the Queen grumbling and scolding and threatening.

Wood stepped to the door. 'Menofra!' he called. 'I have an idea that perhaps you hadn't thought of. Let Phoros accompany us to the border; then when he comes back you'll have him. That will save a lot of trouble for all concerned.'

Phoros looked troubled. He hadn't thought of that either. Menofra did not answer immediately; then she said, 'He might trick me in some way.'

'How can he trick you?' demanded Wood.

'I don't know, but he'd find a way. He has been tricking people all his life.'

'He couldn't. You'd have the army. What could he do?'

'Well, perhaps it's worth thinking about,' admitted the Queen; 'but I don't know that I could wait. I'd like to get my hands on him right now. Did you see what he did to me?'

'Yes. It was terrible,' sympathised Wood.

It was not long before the warrior returned with Kandos. Menofra greeted him with a volley of vituperation as soon as he came in sight, and it was some time before he could quiet her and get the story. Then he led her away where none could overhear, and they whispered together for some time. When they had finished, Kandos approached the door.

'It is all arranged,' he announced. 'The Queen has given her permission. The party will start shortly after sunrise. It is still dark, and the trail is not safe by night. Just as soon as you and the escort have had your breakfasts you may go in peace. Have we your promise that you will not harm the King?'

'You have,' said Tarzan.

'Very well,' said Kandos. 'I am going now to arrange for the escort.'

'And don't forget our breakfasts!' called Wood.

'I most certainly will not,' promised Kandos.

XXIII

Sentenced

Stanley Wood was in high spirits. 'It commences to look as though our troubles were about over,' he said. He laid a hand on Gonfala's tenderly. 'You've been through a lot, but I can promise you that when we get to civilisation you'll be able to understand for the first time in your life what perfect peace and security mean.'

'Yes,' said Tarzan, 'the perfect peace and security of automobile accidents, railroad wrecks, aeroplane crashes, robbers, kidnappers, war, and pestilence.'

Wood laughed. 'But no lions, leopards, buffaloes, wild elephants, snakes, nor tsetse flies, not to mention shiftas and cannibals.'

'I think,' said Gonfala, 'that neither one of you paints a very pretty picture. You make one almost afraid of life. But after all it is not so much peace and security that I want as freedom. You know, all my life I have been a prisoner except for the few short weeks after you took me away from the Kaji and before Spike and Troll got me. Perhaps you can imagine then how much I want freedom, no matter how many dangers I have to take along with it. It seems the most wonderful thing in the world.'

'It is,' said Tarzan.

'Well, love has its points, too,' suggested Wood.

'Yes,' agreed Gonfala, 'but not without freedom.'

'You're going to have them both,' Wood promised.

'With limitations, you'll find, Gonfala,' warned Tarzan with a smile.

'Just now I'm interested in food,' said Gonfala.

'And I think it's coming.' Wood nodded toward the door. Someone was fumbling with the key. Presently the door opened far enough to permit two pots to be shoved inside the room; then it was closed with a bang.

'They are taking no chances,' commented Wood as he crossed the room and carried the two vessels back to his companions. One contained a thick stew; the other water.

'What, no hardware?' inquired Wood.

'Hardware? What is that?' asked Gonfala; 'Something to eat?'

'Something to eat with – forks, spoons. No forks, no spoons, no Emily Post – how embarrassing!'

'Here,' said Tarzan, and handed his hunting knife to Gonfala. They took turns spearing morsels of meat with it and drinking the juice and the water directly from the pots, sharing the food with Phoros.

'Not half bad,' commented Wood. 'What is it, Phoros?'

'Young wether. There is nothing tastier. I am surprised that Menofra did not send us old elephant hide to chew on. Perhaps she is relenting.' Then he shook his head. 'No. Menofra never relents – at least not where I am concerned. That woman is so ornery she thinks indigestion is an indulgence.'

'My!' said Gonfala, drowsily. 'I am so sleepy I can't keep my eyes open.'

'Same here,' said Wood.

Phoros looked at the others and yawned. Tarzan stood up and shook himself.

'You, too?' asked Phoros.

The ape-man nodded. Phoros' lids drooped. 'The old she-devil,' he muttered. 'We've all been drugged – maybe poisoned.'

Tarzan watched his companions fall into a stupor one by one. He tried to fight off the effects of the drug. He wondered if any of them would awaken again; then he sagged to one knee and rolled over on the floor, unconscious.

The room was decorated with barbaric splendour. Mounted heads of animals and men adorned the walls. There were crude murals done in colours that had faded into softness, refined by age. Skins of animals and rugs of wool covered the floor, the benches, and a couch on which Menofra lay, her body raised on one elbow, her bandaged head supported by one huge palm. Four warriors stood by the only door; at Menofra's feet lay Gonfala and Wood, still unconscious; at her side stood Kandos; at the foot of the couch, bound and unconscious, lay Phoros.

'You sent the wild man to the slave pen as I directed?' asked Menofra.

Kandos nodded. 'Yes, Queen; and because he seemed so strong I had him chained to a stanchion.'

'That is well,' said Menofra. 'Even a fool does the right thing occasionally.'

'Thank you, Queen,' said Kandos.

313

'Don't thank me; you make me sick. You are a liar and a cheat and a traitor. Phoros befriended you, yet you turned against him. How much more quickly would you turn against me who has never befriended you and whom you hate! But you won't, because you are a coward; and don't even think of it. If I ever get the idea for a moment that you might be thinking of turning against me I'll have your head hanging on this wall in no time. The man is coming to.'

They looked down at Wood whose eyes were opening slowly and whose arms and legs were moving a little as though experimenting with the possibilities of self-control. He was the first to regain consciousness. He opened his eyes and looked about him. He saw Gonfala lying beside him. Her rising and falling bosom assured him that she lived. He looked up at Kandos and the Queen.

'So this is the way you keep your word?' he accused; then he looked about for Tarzan. 'Where is the other?'

'He is quite safe,' said Kandos. 'The Queen in her mercy has not killed any of you.'

'What are you going to do with us?' demanded Wood.

'The wild man goes to the arena,' replied Menofra. 'You and the girl will not be killed immediately – not until you have served my purpose.'

'And what is that?'

'You shall know presently. Kandos, send for a priest; Phoros will soon awaken.'

Gonfala opened her eyes and sat up. 'What has happened?' she asked. 'Where are we?'

'We are still prisoners,' Wood told her. 'These people have double-crossed us.'

'Civilisation seems very far away,' she said and tears came to her eyes.

He took her hand. 'You must be brave, dear.'

'I am tired of being brave; I have been brave for so long. I should like so much to cry, Stanlee.'

Now Phoros regained consciousness, and looked first at one and then at another. When his eyes fell on Menofra he winced.

'Ah, the rat has awakened,' said the Queen.

'You have rescued me, my dear!' said Phoros.

'You may call it that, if you wish,' said Menofra coldly; 'but I should call it by another name, as you will later.'

'Now, my darling, let us forget the past – let bygones be bygones. Kandos, remove my bonds. How does it look to see the King trussed up like this?'

'It looks all right to me,' Menofra assured him, 'but how would you like to be trussed up? It could be done with red hot chains, you know. In fact, it has been done. It's not a bad idea; I am glad you suggested it.'

'But, Menofra, my dear wife, you wouldn't do that to me?'

'Oh, you think not? But you would try to kill me with your sword so that you could take this wench here to wife. Well, I'm not going to have you trussed up with red hot chains – not yet. First I am going to remove temptation from your path without removing the object of your temptation. I am going to let you see what you might have enjoyed.'

There was a rap on the door, and one of the warriors said, 'The priest is here.'

'Let him in,' ordered Menofra.

Wood had helped Gonfala to her feet, and the two were seated on a bench, mystified listeners to Menofra's cryptic speech. When the priest had entered the room and bowed before the Queen she pointed to them.

'Marry these two,' she commanded.

Wood and Gonfala looked at one another in astonishment. 'There's a catch in this somewhere,' said the former. 'The old termagant's not doing this because she loves us, but I'm not looking any gift horse in the mouth.'

'It's what we've been waiting and hoping for,' said Gonfala, 'but I wish it could have happened under different conditions. There is something sinister in this. I don't believe that any good thought could come out of that woman's mind.'

The marriage ceremony was extremely simple, but very impressive. It laid upon the couple the strictest obligations of fidelity and condemned to death and damned through eternity whomever might cause either to be unfaithful to the other.

During the ceremony Menofra wore a sardonic smile, while Phoros had difficulty in hiding his chagrin and anger. When it was concluded, the Queen turned to her mate. 'You know the laws of our people,' she said. 'King or commoner, whoever comes between these two must die. You know that, don't you, Phoros? You know you've lost her, don't you – forever? You would try to kill me, would you? Well, I'm going to let you live – I'm going to let you live with this wench; but watch your step, Phoros; for I'll be watching you.' She turned to the guard. 'Now take them away. Take this man to the slave pen, and see that nothing happens to him and take Phoros and the wench to the room next to mine; and lock them in.'

When Tarzan regained consciousness he found himself chained to a stanchion in a stockaded compound, an iron collar around his neck. He was quite alone; but pallets of musty grass, odd bits of dirty clothing, cooking utensils, and the remains of cooking fires, still smouldering, disclosed the fact that the shed and the yard was the abode of others; and he conjectured correctly that he had been imprisoned in a slave pen.

The position of the sun told him that he had been under the influence of the drug for about an hour. The effects were passing off rapidly, leaving only a dull headache and a feeling of chagrin that he had been so easily duped. He was concerned about the fate of Wood and Gonfala, and was at a loss to understand why he had been separated from them. His active mind was occupied with this problem and that of escape when the gate of the compound opened and Wood was brought in by an escort of warriors who merely shoved the American through the gateway and departed after relocking the gate.

Wood crossed the compound to Tarzan. 'I wondered what they had done with you,' he said. 'I was afraid they might have killed you.' Then he told the ape-man what Menofra had decreed for Gonfala. 'It is monstrous, Tarzan; the woman is a beast. What are we to do?'

Tarzan tapped the iron collar that encircled his neck. 'There is not much that I can do,' he said ruefully.

'Why do you suppose they've chained you up and not me?' asked Wood.

'They must have some special form of entertainment in view for me,' suggested the ape-man with a faint smile.

The remainder of the day passed in desultory conversation, principally a monologue; as Tarzan was not given to garrulity. Wood talked to keep from thinking about Gonfala's situation, but he was not very successful. Late in the afternoon the slaves were returned to the compound, and immediately crowded around Tarzan. One of them pushed his way to the front when he caught a glimpse of the prisoner.

'Tarzan!' he exclaimed. 'It is really you?'

'I am afraid it is, Valthor,' replied the ape-man.

'And you are back, I see,' said Valthor to Wood. 'I did not expect to see you again. What happened?'

Wood told him the whole story of their misadventure, and Valthor looked grave. 'Your friend, Gonfala, may be safe as long as Menofra lives; but she may not live long. Kandos will see to that if he is not too big a coward; then, with Menofra out of the way, Phoros will again come to power. When he does, he will destroy you. After that there would not be much hope for Gonfala. The situation is serious, and I can see no way out unless the King and his party were to return and recapture the city. I believe they could do it now, for practically all of the citizens and most of the warriors are sick of Phoros and the rest of the Erythra.'

A tall black came close to Tarzan. 'You do not remember me, Master?' he asked.

'Why, yes; of course I do,' replied the ape-man. 'You're Gemba. You were a slave in the house of Thudos at Cathne. How long have you been here?'

'Many moons, Master. I was taken in a raid. The work is hard, and often these new Masters are cruel. I wish that I were back in Cathne.'

'You would fare well there now, Gemba. Your old Master is King of Cathne.

I think that if he knew Tarzan was a prisoner here, he would come and make war on Athne.'

'And I think that if he did,' said Valthor, 'an army from Cathne would be welcome here for the first time in history; but there is no chance that he will come, for there is no way in which he may learn that Tarzan is here.'

'If I could get this collar off my neck,' said the ape-man, 'I could soon get out of this slave pen and the city and bring Thudos with his army. He would come for me to save my friends.'

'But you can't get it off,' said Wood.

'You are right,' agreed Tarzan; 'it is idle talk.'

For several days nothing occurred to break the monotony of existence in the slave pen of the King of Athne. No word reached them from the palace of what was transpiring there; no inkling came of the fate that was in store for them. Valthor had told Tarzan that the latter was probably being saved for the arena on account of his appearance of great strength, but when there would be games again he did not know. The new Masters of Athne had changed everything, deriding all that had been sacred to custom and the old regime. There was even talk of changing the name of Athne to The City of Phoros. All that prevented was the insistence of the Queen that it be renamed The City of Menofra.

Every morning the slaves were taken to work, and all day long Tarzan remained alone, chained like a wild animal. Imprisonment of any nature galled The Lord of the Jungle; to be chained was torture. Yet he gave no sign of the mental suffering he was enduring. To watch him, one might have thought that he was content. Seething beneath that calm exterior was a raging sea of anger.

One afternoon the slaves were returned to the pen earlier than usual. The guards that herded them in were unusually rough with them, and there were several officers not ordinarily present. They followed the slaves into the pen and counted them, checking off their names on a scroll carried by one of the officers; then they questioned them; and from the questions Tarzan gathered that there had been a concerted attempt on the part of a number of slaves to escape, during which a guard had been killed. During the excitement of the mêlée several slaves had escaped into the bamboo forest that grew close upon the eastern boundary of the cultivated fields of Athne. The check revealed that three were missing. Were they ever recaptured, they would be tortured and killed.

The officers and warriors were extremely brutal in their handling of the slaves as they questioned them, trying to force confessions from them that they might ascertain just how far-reaching the plot had been and which slaves were the ring-leaders. After they left the pen the slaves were in a turmoil of restlessness and discontent. The air was surcharged with the static electricity of repressed rebellion that the slightest spark would have ignited, but Valthor counselled them to patience.

'You will only subject yourselves to torture and death,' he told them. 'We are only a handful of unarmed slaves. What can we do against the armed warriors of the Erythra? Wait. As sure as Dyaus is in heaven some change must come. There is as much discontent outside the slave pen as within it; and one day Zygo, our King, will come out of the mountains were he is hiding and set us free.'

'But some of us are slaves no matter who is King,' said one. 'I am. It would make no difference whether Zygo or Phoros were King – I should still be a slave.'

'No,' said Valthor. 'I can promise you all that when Zygo comes into power again you will all be set free. I give you my word that it will be done.'

'Well,' said one, 'I might not believe another, but all know that what the noble Valthor says he will do he will do.'

It was almost dark now, and the cooking fires were alight, and the slaves were cooking their poor meals in little pots. Jerked elephant meat constituted the larger part of their diet; to this was added a very coarse variety of turnip. From the two the men made a stew. Sometimes those who worked in the fields varied this diet with other vegetables they had been able to steal from the fields and smuggle into the pen.

'This stew,' remarked Wood, 'should be full of vitamins; it has everything else including elephant hair and pebbles. The elephant hair and the pebbles might be forgiven, but turnips! In the economy of mundane happiness there is no place for the turnip.'

'I take it that you don't like turnips,' said Valthor.

Since Tarzan had been brought to the slave pen, Troll and Spike had kept to themselves. Spike was very much afraid of the ape-man; and he had managed to impart this fear to Troll, although the latter had forgotten that there was any reason to fear him. Spike was worried for fear that, in the event they were liberated, Tarzan would find some way to keep the great diamond from him. This did not trouble Troll, who had forgotten all about the diamond. The only thing that Troll remembered clearly was that Gonfala was his sister and that he had lost her. This worried him a great deal, and he talked about it continually. Spike encouraged him in the delusion and never referred to the diamond, although it was constantly the subject of his thoughts and plannings. His principal hope of retrieving it lay in the possibility that the rightful King of Athne would regain his throne, treat him as a guest instead of a prisoner, and return the Gonfal to him; and he knew from conversations he had had with other prisoners that the return of Zygo was just between a possibility and a probability.

As the slaves were eating their evening meal and discussing the escape of their three fellows an officer entered the compound with a detail of warriors, one of whom carried an iron collar and chain. Approaching the shed, the officer called Valthor.

'I am here,' said the noble, rising.

'I have a present for you, aristocrat,' announced the officer, who until the revolution had been a groom in the elephant stables of Zygo.

'So I see,' replied Valthor, glancing at the collar and chain, 'and one which it must give a stable-boy much pleasure to bring me.'

The officer flushed angrily. 'Be careful, or I'll teach you some manners,' he growled. 'You are the stable-boy now, and I am the aristocrat.'

Valthor shook his head. 'No, stable-boy, you are wrong. You will always be a stable-boy at heart, and way down deep inside you you know it. That is what makes you angry. That is what makes you hate me, or think that you hate me; you really hate yourself, because you know that you will always be a stable-boy no matter what Phoros tells you you are. He has done many strange things since he drove out the King, but he cannot make a lion out of a jackal's tail.'

'Enough of this,' snapped the officer. 'Here you, snap the collar about his neck and chain him to the stanchion beside the wild man.'

'Why has Phoros thus honoured me?' inquired Valthor.

'It was not Phoros; it was Menofra. She is ruling now.'

'Ah, I see,' said the noble. 'Her psychology of hate for my class is more deeply rooted than yours, for it springs from filthy soil. Your vocation was at least honourable. Menofra was a woman of the street before Phoros married her.'

'Well, have your say while you can, aristocrat,' said the officer, tauntingly, 'for tomorrow you and the wild man die in the arena, trampled and gored by a rogue elephant.'

XXIV

Death

The other slaves were furious because of the sentence imposed upon Valthor, who was to die, the officer had told them before he left, in punishment for the outbreak that had resulted in the death of an Erythros warrior and the escape of three slaves and as a warning to the others. Valthor had been chosen ostensibly because he had been charged with fomenting rebellion among the slaves, but really because he was popular among them and an aristocrat.

Wood was horrified by the knowledge that Tarzan was to die, Tarzan and Valthor, both of whom were his friends. It seemed to him absolutely inconceivable that the mighty heart of the Lord of the Jungle should be stilled forever, that that perfect body be broken and trampled in the dust of an arena to satisfy the bloodlust of ignorant barbarians.

'There must be something that we can do,' he said: 'there's got to be. Couldn't we break these chains?'

Tarzan shook his head. 'I have examined mine carefully,' he said, 'and tested it. If it were cast iron, we might break a link; but it is malleable and would only bend. If we had a chisel – but we haven't. No, there is nothing to do but wait.'

'But they are going to kill you, Tarzan! Don't you understand? They are going to kill you.'

The ape-man permitted himself the shadow of a smile. 'There is nothing unique in that,' he said. 'Many people have died; many people are dying; many people will die – even you, my friend.'

'Tarzan is right,' said Valthor. 'We must all die; what matters is how we die. If we meet death courageously, as befits warriors, there will be no regrets. For myself, I am glad that an elephant is going to kill me; for I am an elephant-man. You know what that means, Tarzan; for you have been to Cathne where the lion-men are the nobles; and you know with what pride they bear the title. It is the same here, except that the nobles are the elephant-men. As they breed lions, we breed elephants; their god, Thoos, is a lion; our Dyaus is an elephant. The nobles who escaped the Erythros revolution took him into the mountains with them, for the Erythra, who have no god, would have killed him.'

'If I were to have my choice of the manner in which I were to die,' said Tarzan, 'I should prefer the lion to the elephant. For one thing, the lion kills quickly; but my real reason is that the elephant has always been my friend; my very best friend, perhaps; and I do not like to think that a friend must kill me.'

'This one will not be your friend, Tarzan,' Valthor reminded him.

'No, I know it; but I was not thinking of him as an individual,' explained Tarzan. 'And now, as, with all our talk, we have arrived nowhere, I am going to sleep.'

The morning of their death dawned like any other morning. Neither spoke of what was impending. With Wood they cooked their breakfasts, and they talked, and Valthor laughed, and occasionally Tarzan smiled one of his rare smiles. Wood was the most nervous. When the time came for the slaves to be taken to their work he came to say goodbye to the ape-man.

Tarzan laid a hand upon his shoulder 'I do not like to say goodbye, my friend,' he said.

If Wood had known how rare was the use by Tarzan of that term 'my friend' he would have been honoured. He thought of many animals as friends, but few men. He liked Wood, his intelligence, his courage, his cleanness.

'Have you no message you would like to send to – to—' Wood hesitated.

Tarzan shook his head. 'Thank you, no,' he said. 'She will know, as she always has.'

Wood turned and walked away, following the other slaves out of the stockade. He stumbled over the threshold, and swore under his breath as he drew a palm across his eyes.

It was afternoon before they came for Tarzan and Valthor, half a hundred warriors and several officers, all in their best trappings, their freshly burnished arms shining in the sun.

In front of the palace a procession was forming. There were many elephants richly caparisoned and bearing howdahs in which rode the new-made nobility of Athne. All the howdahs were open except one elaborate pavilion. In this sat Menofra alone. When Valthor saw her he laughed aloud. Tarzan turned and looked at him questioningly.

'Look at her!' exclaimed the noble. 'She could not be more self-conscious if she were naked. In fact that would not bother her so much. The poor thing is trying to look the Queen. Note the haughty mien, and the crown! Dyaus! She is wearing the crown to the arena – and wearing it backwards. It is worth dying to see.'

Valthor had not attempted to lower his voice. In fact it seemed that he raised it a little. His laughter had attracted attention to him, so that many listened and heard his words. They even reached the ears of Menofra. That was apparent to all who could see her for her face turned fiery red; and she took the crown off and placed it on the seat beside her. She was so furious that she trembled; and when she gave the command to march, as she immediately did, her voice shook with rage.

With the hundred elephants in single file, the many warriors on foot, the banners and pennons, the procession was colourful; but it lacked that something that would have made its magnificence impressive. There was nothing real about its assumed majesty, and the entire pageant was coloured by the spuriousness of its principal actors. This was the impression that it made upon the Lord of the Jungle walking in chains behind the elephant of Menofra.

The procession followed the main avenue to the South gate through lines of silent citizens. There was no cheering, no applause. There were whispered comments as Valthor and Tarzan passed; and it was plain to see that the sympathies of the people were with Valthor, though they dared not express them openly. Tarzan was a stranger to them; their only interest in him lay in the fact that he might serve to give them a few minutes of thrills and entertainment in the arena.

Passing through the gate, the column turned toward the east, coming at last to the arena, which lay directly east of the city. Just outside the main gate, through which the procession entered the arena, Tarzan and Valthor were led from the line of march and taken to a smaller gate which led through a high palisade of small logs into a paddock between two sections of a grandstand. The inner end of the paddock was formed by a palisade of small logs; and was similar to the outer end, having a small gate opening onto the arena. The ape-man could not but notice the flimsy construction of the two palisades and idly wondered if the entire arena were as poorly built.

In the compound there were a number of armed guards; and presently other prisoners were brought, men whom Tarzan had not before seen. They had been brought from the city behind the elephants of lesser dignitaries who had ridden in the rear of Menofra. Several of these prisoners, who spoke to Valthor, were evidently men of distinction.

'We are about the last of the aristocracy who did not escape or go over to the Erythra,' Valthor explained to Tarzan. 'Phoros and Menofra think that by killing off all their enemies they will have no opposition and nothing more to fear; but as a matter of fact they are only making more enemies, for the middle classes were naturally more in sympathy with the aristocracy than with the scum which constitutes the Erythra.'

About four feet from the top of the inner palisade was a horizontal beam supporting the ends of braces that held the palisade upright, and upon this beam the prisoners were allowed to stand and witness what took place in the arena until it was their turn to enter. When Tarzan and Valthor took their places on the beam the royal pageant had just completed a circuit of the arena, and Menofra was clumsily descending from the howdah of her elephant to enter the royal loge. The grandstands were about half filled, and crowds were still pouring through the tunnels. There was little noise other than the shuffling of sandalled feet and the occasional trumpeting of an elephant. It did not seem to Tarzan a happy, carefree throng out to enjoy a holiday; but rather a sullen mob suppressed by fear. A laugh would have been as startling as a scream.

The first encounter was between two men; one a huge Erythros warrior armed with sword and spear; the other a former noble whose only weapon was a dagger. It was an execution, not a duel – an execution preceded by torture. The audience watched it, for the most part, in silence. There were a few shouts of encouragement from the loges of the officials and the new nobility.

Valthor and Tarzan watched with disgust. 'I think he could have killed that big fellow,' said the ape-man. 'I saw how he might be easily handled. It is too bad that the other did not think of it.'

'You think you could kill Hyark?' demanded a guard standing next to Tarzan.

'Why not?' asked the ape-man. 'He is clumsy and stupid; most of all he is a coward.'

'Hyark a coward? That is a good one. There are few braver among the Erythra.'

'I can believe that,' said Tarzan, and Valthor laughed.

Hyark was strutting to and fro before the royal box receiving the applause of Menofra and her entourage, slaves were dragging out the mutilated corpse of his victim, and an officer was approaching the paddock to summon forth the next combatants.

The guard called to him, 'Here is one who thinks he can kill Hyark.'

The officer looked up. 'Which one thinks that?' he demanded.

The guard jerked a thumb toward Tarzan. 'This wild man here. Perhaps Menofra would like to see such an encounter. It should prove amusing.'

'Yes,' said the officer, 'I should like to see it myself. Maybe after the next combat. I'll ask her.'

The next prisoner to be taken into the arena was an old man. He was given a dagger to defend himself; then a lion was loosed upon him.

'That is a very old lion,' said Tarzan to Valthor. 'Most of his teeth are gone. He is weak from mange and hunger.'

'But he will kill the man,' said Valthor.

'Yes, he will kill the man; he is still a powerful brute.'

'I suppose you think you could kill him, too,' jeered the guard.

'Probably,' assented the ape-man.

The guard thought this very funny, and laughed uproariously.

The lion made short work of the old man, giving him, at least, a merciful death; then the officer came, after they had driven the lion back into his cage with many spears, and said that Menofra had given assent to the fight between Hyark and the wild man.

'She has promised to make Hyark a captain for killing two men in one afternoon,' said the officer.

'This one says he can kill the lion, too,' screamed the guard, rocking with laughter.

'But Hyark is going to kill your wild man now; so we will never know if he could kill the lion,' said the officer, pretending to be deeply grieved.

'I will fight them both at once,' said Tarzan; 'that is if Hyark is not afraid to go into the arena with a lion.'

'That would be something to see,' said the officer. 'I will go at once and speak to Menofra.'

'Why did you say that, Tarzan?' asked Valthor.

'Didn't I tell you that I'd rather be killed by a lion than an elephant?'

Valthor shook his head. 'Perhaps you are right. At least it will be over sooner. This waiting is getting on my nerves.'

Very soon the officer returned. 'It is arranged,' he said.

'What did Hyark think of it?' asked Valthor.

'I think he did not like the idea at all. He said he just recalled that his wife was very ill, and asked Menofra to give someone else the honour of killing the wild man.'

'And what did Menofra say?'

'She said that if Hyark didn't get into the arena and kill the wild man she would kill Hyark.'

'Menofra has a grand sense of humour,' remarked Valthor.

Tarzan dropped to the ground and was taken into the arena, where the iron collar was removed from about his neck and he was handed a dagger. He walked toward the royal box below which Hyark was standing. Hyark came running to meet him, hoping to dispatch him quickly and get out of the arena before the lion could be loosed. The men at the lion's cage were having some difficulty in raising the door. The lion, nervous and excited from his last encounter, was roaring and growling as he struck at the bars trying to reach the men working about him.

Hyark held his spear in front of him. He hoped to thrust it through Tarzan the moment that he came within reach of him. There would be no playing with his victim in this encounter, his sole idea being to get it over and get out of the arena.

Tarzan advanced slightly crouched. He had stuck the dagger into the cord that supported his loincloth. The fact that he came on with bare hands puzzled the crowd and confused Hyark, who had long since regretted that he had accepted the challenge so boastfully. He was not afraid of the man, of course; but the two of them! What if the man avoided being killed until the lion was upon them? The lion might as readily leap upon Hyark as upon the other. It was this that added to Hyark's confusion.

They were close now. With an oath, Hyark lunged his spear point at the naked breast of his antagonist; then Tarzan did just what he had planned to do, knowing as he did his own agility and strength. He seized the haft of the spear and wrenched the weapon from Hyark's grasp, hurling it to the ground behind him; then Hyark reached for his sword; but he was too slow. The ape-man was upon him; steel thewed fingers seized him and swung him around.

A great shout went up from the crowd – the lion was loosed!

Grasping Hyark by the collar of his jerkin and his sword belt, the ape-man held him helpless despite his struggles. For the first time the crowd became really vocal. They laughed, jeering at Hyark; they screamed warnings at the wild man, shouting that the lion was coming; but Tarzan knew that already.

From the corner of an eye he was watching the carnivore as it came down the length of the arena at a trot. He could get a better estimate of the beast now as it came closer. It was a small lion, old and pitifully emaciated. Evidently it had been starved a long time to make it ravenous. Tarzan's anger rose against those who had been responsible for this cruelty, and because of it there was borne in his mind a plan to avenge the lion.

As the lion approached, Tarzan went to meet it, pushing the frantic Hyark ahead of him; and just before the beast launched its lethal charge, the ape-man gave Hyark a tremendous shove directly toward the great cat; and then Hyark did precisely what Tarzan had anticipated he would do – he turned quickly to one side and broke into a run. Tarzan stood still – not a muscle moved. He was directly in the path of the lion, but the latter did not hesitate even an instant; it turned and pursued the fleeing Hyark, the screaming, terrified Hyark.

'The brave Hyark will have to run much faster if he hopes to get his captaincy,' said Valthor to the guard. 'He would have been better off had he stood still; the lion was sure to pursue him if he ran. Had he stepped to one side and stood still, the lion might have continued his charge straight for Tarzan. At least he would have had a chance then, but he certainly cannot outrun a lion.'

Just in front of the loge of Menofra the lion overtook Hyark, and the screaming man went down beneath the mangy body to a mercifully quick end. Before his final struggles had ended the starving beast commenced to devour him.

Tarzan came up the arena toward the royal loge and the feeding lion. On the way he picked up Hyark's discarded spear and crept silently onto the lion from the rear; nor did the lion, occupied with his greedy feeding, see the approaching man. The crowd sat tense and silent, marvelling, perhaps, at the courage of this naked wild man. Closer and closer to the lion crept Tarzan; and still the lion fed upon the carcass of Hyark, unconscious of the ape-man's presence. Directly behind the carnivore Tarzan laid the spear upon the ground. He had brought it only as a measure of safety in the event his plan miscarried. Then, with the swiftness and agility of Sheeta the panther, he leaped astride the feeding cat and grasped it by the mane and the loose hide upon its back, lifting it bodily from its kill and at the same time swinging around and whirling the beast with him, roaring and striking, but futilely. It was the lightning quickness of his act that made it possible – that and his great strength – as, with one superhuman effort, he flung the beast into the royal loge; then, without a single backward glance, he turned and walked back toward the prisoners' paddock.

The lion's body struck Menofra and knocked her from her chair; but the lion, frightened now and bewildered, thought for the moment only of escape; and leaped to an adjoining loge. Here he lashed out with his taloned paws to right and left among the screaming nobility. From one loge to another he leaped, leaving a trail of screaming victims, until he chanced upon a tunnel, into which he darted and galloped to freedom beyond the amphitheatre.

The stands were in an uproar as the populace cheered Tarzan as he entered the paddock and took his place again beside Valthor on the crossbeam. The guard who had ridiculed him looked at him now in awe, while the other prisoners praised and congratulated him.

'Menofra should give you a wreath and a title,' said Valthor, 'for you have given her and the people such entertainment as they have never seen before in this arena.'

Tarzan looked across at the royal loge and saw Menofra standing in it apparently unhurt. 'The lion missed a golden opportunity,' he said; 'and as for the wreath and the title, I do not deserve them; for it was the lion, not Menofra or the people, that I was trying to entertain.'

When the stands had quieted down and the wounded been removed, the officer in charge returned to the paddock. 'You were a fool,' he said to Tarzan, 'to throw the lion into Menofra's loge. If you hadn't done that, I believe she would have given you your liberty; but now she has ordered that you be destroyed at once. You and Valthor go in next. You will take your places in the centre of the arena immediately.'

'I wish,' said Valthor, 'that you might have had a better reception in The City of Ivory. I wish that you might have known my own people and they you. That you should have come here to die is tragic, but the fates were against you.'

'Well, my friend,' said Tarzan, 'at least we have seen one another again; and – we are not dead yet.'

'We shall be presently.'

'I think that perhaps you are right,' agreed the ape-man.

'Well, here we are. Have you any plan?'

'None,' replied Tarzan. 'I know that I cannot throw an elephant into Menofra's loge.'

'Not this one,' said Valthor. 'I know him. I helped capture him. He is a devil and huge. He hates men. They have been saving him for this, and they will probably kill him afterward – he is too dangerous.'

'They are opening the elephant paddock,' said Tarzan. 'Here he comes!'

A great elephant charged, trumpeting, through the opened gates. At first he did not appear to notice the two men in the centre of the arena, and trotted around close to the stands as though searching for an avenue of escape; then quite suddenly he wheeled toward the centre and trotted toward the two men.

Tarzan had noted his great size and the one tusk darker than the other, and on the screen of memory was pictured another scene and another day – hyeñas at the edge of a pit, snapping at a huge elephant with one dark tusk, while above circled Ska the vulture.

The elephant's trunk was raised, he was trumpeting as he came toward them; and then Tarzan stepped quickly forward and raised a hand with the palm toward the beast.

'Dan-do, Tantor!' he commanded. 'Tarzan yo.'

The great beast hesitated; then he stopped. Tarzan walked toward him, motioning Valthor to follow directly behind him, and stopped with one hand upon the trunk that was now lowered and feeling exploratively over the ape-man's body.

'Nala Tarzan!' commanded the ape-man. 'Nala Tarmangani!' and he pulled Valthor to his side.

The elephant raised his trunk and trumpeted loudly; then he gathered first one and then the other in its folds and lifted them to his head. For a moment he stood swaying to and fro as Tarzan spoke to him in low tones; then, trumpeting again, he started off at a trot around the arena while the spectators sat in stunned amazement. The great beast had completed half the oval and was opposite the prisoners' paddock when Tarzan gave a quick command. The elephant wheeled sharply to the left and crossed the arena while Tarzan urged him on with words of encouragement in that strange mother of languages that the great apes use and the lesser apes and the little monkeys and that is understood in proportion to their intelligence by many another beast of the forest and the plain.

With lowered head the mighty bull crashed into the flimsy palisade at the inner end of the paddock, flattening it to the ground; then the outer palisade fell before him; and he carried Tarzan and Valthor out onto the plain toward freedom.

As they passed the main gate of the amphitheatre and headed South they saw the first contingent of their pursuers issuing from the arena and clambering to the howdahs of the waiting elephants, and before they had covered half a mile the pursuit was in full cry behind them.

While their own mount was making good time some of the pursuing elephants were gaining on him.

'Racing elephants,' commented Valthor.

'They are carrying heavy loads,' observed the ape-man: 'five and six warriors beside a heavy howdah.'

Valthor nodded. 'If we can keep ahead of them for half an hour we've a good chance to get away.' Then he turned from the pursuers and looked ahead. 'Mother of Dyaus!' he exclaimed. 'We're caught between a wild bull and a hungry lion – the Cathneans are coming, and they're coming for war. This is no ordinary raid. Look at them!'

Tarzan turned and saw a body of men that approximated an army coming across the plain toward them, and in the van were the fierce war lions of Cathne. He looked back. Closing in rapidly upon them were the war elephants of Athne.

XXV

Battle

'I think we yet have a chance to escape them both,' said Valthor. 'Turn him toward the east. Zygo and his loyal followers are there in the mountains.'

'We do not have to run away from our friends,' replied Tarzan.

'I hope they recognise you as a friend before they loose their war lions. They are trained to leap to the backs of elephants and kill the men riding there.'

'Then we'll approach them on foot,' said the ape-man.

'And be caught by the Erythra,' added Valthor.

'We shall have to take a chance; but wait! Let's try something.' He spoke to the bull, and the animal came to a stop and wheeled about; then Tarzan leaped to the ground, motioning Valthor to follow him. He spoke a few words into the ear of the elephant, and stepped aside. Up went the great trunk, forward the huge ears; as the mighty beast started back to meet the oncoming elephants.

'I think he'll hold them up long enough for us to reach the Cathnean line before they can overtake us,' said Tarzan.

The two men turned then and started toward the advancing horde of warriors – toward ranks of gleaming spears and golden helmets and the lions of war on golden chains. Suddenly a warrior left the ranks and ran forward to meet them; and when he was closer, Tarzan saw that he was an officer. It was Gemnon.

'I recognised you at once,' he cried to the ape-man. 'We were coming to rescue you.'

'How did you know that I was in trouble?' demanded Tarzan.

'Gemba told us. He was a prisoner with you in the slave pen; but he escaped, and came straight to Thudos with word that you were to be killed.'

'Two of my friends are still prisoners in Athne,' said Tarzan, 'and now that you have caught many of the warriors of Phoros out here on the plain in a disorganised condition—'

'Yes,' said Gemnon; 'Thudos realised his advantage, and we shall attack at once as soon as we get back to the lines.'

Valthor and Gemnon had met before, when Valthor was a prisoner in Cathne. Thudos the King welcomed them both, for Gemba had told him of the Erythra; and naturally his sympathies were with the aristocracy of Athne.

'If Thoos is with us today,' he said, 'we shall put Zygo back upon his throne.' Then, to an aide, 'Loose the lions of war!'

The great bull with the dark tusk had met the first of the war elephants of Athne head on with such a terrific impact that all the warriors were hurled from the howdah and the war elephant thrown to the ground; then he charged the next and overthrew it, whereat the others scattered to avoid him; and a moment later the war lions of Cathne were among them. They did not attack the elephants, but leaped to the howdahs and mauled the warriors. Two or three lions would attack a single elephant at a time, and at least two of them succeeded ordinarily in reaching the howdah.

The commander of the Erythros forces sought to rally his men and form a line to repel the advance of the Cathneans; and while he was seeking to accomplish this, the Cathnean foot warriors were upon them, adding to the rout that the great bull had started and the lions almost completed.

The Erythros warriors hurled spears at their foes and sought to trample them beneath the feet of their mounts. The Cathneans' first aim was to kill the mahouts and stampede the elephants, and while some warriors were attempting this, others pressed close to the elephants in an endeavour to cut the girths with their sharp daggers, precipitating the howdahs and their occupants to the ground.

The shouts of the warriors, the trumpeting of the elephants, the roars of the lions, and the screams of the wounded produced an indescribable bedlam that added to the confusion of the scene and seemed to raise the bloodlust of the participants to demonic proportions.

While a portion of his forces was engaging the Erythra on the plain before the city, Thudos manœuvred the remainder to a position between the battle and the city, cutting off the Erythra retreat; and with this and the killing of their commander the Athneans lost heart and scattered in all directions, leaving the city to the mercy of the enemy.

Thudos led his victorious troops into Athne, and with him marched Tarzan and Valthor. They liberated Wood and the other prisoners in the slave pen, including Spike and Troll; and then, at Wood's urgent pleading, marched to the palace in search of Gonfala. They met with slight resistance, the palace guard soon fleeing from the superior numbers that confronted them.

Tarzan and Wood, led by a palace slave, hurried to the apartment where Gonfala was confined. The door, fastened by a bolt on the outside, was quickly opened; and the two men entered to see Gonfala standing above the body of Phoros, a dagger in her hand.

At sight of Wood, she rushed forward and threw herself into his arms. 'Word just reached him that Menofra is dead,' she said, 'and I had to kill him.'

Wood pressed her to him. 'Poor child,' he whispered, 'what you must have suffered! But your troubles are over now. The Erythra have fallen, and we are among friends.'

After the fall of Athne, events moved rapidly. Zygo was summoned from the mountains and restored to his throne by his hereditary enemies, the Cathneans.

'Now you can live in peace,' said Tarzan.

'Peace!' shouted Thudos and Zygo almost simultaneously. 'Who would care to live always in peace?'

'I replace Zygo on the throne,' explained Thudos; 'so that we Cathneans may continue to have foes worthy of our arms. No peace for us, eh, Zygo?'

'Never, my friend!' replied the King of Athne.

For a week Tarzan and the other Europeans remained in Athne; then they set off toward the South, taking Spike and Troll and the great diamond with them. A short march from Athne they met Muviro with a hundred warriors coming to search for their beloved Bwana, and thus escorted they returned to the ape-man's own country.

Here Tarzan let Spike and Troll leave for the coast on the promise that neither would return to Africa.

As they were leaving, Spike cast sorrowful glances at the great diamond. 'We'd orter get somethin' out o' that,' he said. 'After all, we went through a lot o' hell on account of it.'

'Very well,' said Tarzan, 'take it with you.'

Wood and Gonfala looked at the ape-man in astonishment, but said nothing until after Troll and Spike had departed; then they asked why he had given the great diamond to two such villains.

A slow smile torched the ape-man's lips. 'It was not the Gonfal,' he said. 'I have that at home. It was the imitation that Mafka kept to show and to protect the real Gonfal. And something else that may interest you. I found the great emerald of the Zuli and buried it in the Bantango country. Someday we'll go and get that, too. You and Gonfala should be well equipped with wealth when you return to civilisation – you should have enough to get you into a great deal of trouble and keep you there all the rest of your lives.'

TARZAN AND THE FORBIDDEN CITY

I

The rainy season was over; and forest and jungle were a riot of lush green starred with myriad tropical blooms, alive with the gorgeous colouring and raucous voices of countless birds, scolding, loving, hunting, escaping; alive with chattering monkeys and buzzing insects which all seemed to be busily engaged in doing things in circles and getting nowhere, much after the fashion of their unhappy cousins who dwell in unlovely jungles of brick and marble and cement.

As much a part of the primitive scene as the trees themselves was the Lord of the Jungle, lolling at his ease on the back of Tantor, the elephant, lazing in the mottled sunlight of the noonday jungle. Apparently oblivious to all his surroundings was the ape-man, yet his every sense was alert to all that passed about him; and his hearing and his sense of smell reached out far beyond the visible scene. It was to the latter that Usha, the wind, bore a warning to his sensitive nostrils – latter the scent spoor of an approaching Gomangani. Instantly Tarzan was galvanised into alert watchfulness. He did not seek to conceal himself nor escape, for he knew that only one black man was approaching. Had there been more, he would have taken to the trees and watched their approach from the concealment of the foliage of some mighty patriarch of the forest, for it as only by eternal vigilance that a denizen of the jungle survives the constant threat of the greatest of all killers – man.

Tarzan seldom thought of himself as a man. From infancy he had been raised by beasts among beasts, and he had been almost full grown before he had seen a man. Subconsciously, he classed them with Numa, the lion, and Sheeta the panther; with Bolgani, the gorilla, and Histah, the snake, and such other blood enemies as his environment afforded.

Crouching upon the great back of Tantor, ready for any eventuality, Tarzan watched the trail along which the black man was approaching. Already Tantor was becoming restless, for he, too, had caught the scent spoor of the man; but Tarzan quieted him with a word and the huge bull, obedient, stood motionless. Presently the appeared at a turn in the trail, and Tarzan relaxed. The black discovered the ape-man almost simultaneously, and stopped; then he ran forward and dropped to his knees in front of the Lord of the Jungle.

'Greetings, Big Bwana!' he cried.

'Greetings, Ogabi!' replied the ape-man. 'Why is Ogabi here? Why is he not in his own country tending his cattle?'

'Ogabi looks for the Big Bwana,' answered the black.

'Why?' demanded Tarzan.

'Ogabi has joined white bwana's safari. Ogabi, askari. White Bwana Gregory send Ogabi find Tarzan.'

'I don't know any white Bwana Gregory,' objected the ape-man. 'Why did he send you to find me?'

'White Bwana send Ogabi bring Tarzan. Must see Tarzan.'

'Where?' asked Tarzan.

'Big village. Loango,' explained Ogabi.

Tarzan shook his head. 'No,' he said; 'Tarzan no go.'

'Bwana Gregory say Tarzan must,' insisted Ogabi. 'Some Bwana lost; Tarzan find.'

'No,' repeated the ape-man. 'Tarzan does not like big village. It is full of bad smells and sickness and men and other evils. Tarzan no go.'

'Bwana d'Arnot say Tarzan come,' added Ogabi, as though by second thought.

'd'Arnot in Loango?' demanded the ape-man. 'Why didn't you say so in the first place? For Bwana d'Arnot, Tarzan come.'

And so, with a parting word to Tantor, Tarzan swung off along the trail in the direction of Loango, while Ogabi trotted peacefully at his heels.

It was hot in Loango; but that was nothing unusual, as it is always hot in Loango. However, heat in the tropics has its recompenses, one of which is a tall glass filled with shaved ice, rum, sugar, and lime juice. A group on the terrace of a small colonial hotel in Loango was enjoying several recompenses.

Captain Paul d'Arnot of the French Navy stretched his long legs comfortably beneath the table and permitted his eyes to enjoy the profile of Helen Gregory as he slowly sipped his drink. Helen's profile was well worth anyone's scrutiny, and not her profile alone. Blonde, nineteen, vivacious, with a carriage and a figure charming in chic sports clothes, she was as cool and inviting as the frosted glass before her.

'Do you think this Tarzan you have sent for can find Brian, Captain d'Arnot?' she asked, turning her face toward him after a brief reverie.

'Your full face is even more beautiful than your profile,' thought d'Arnot, 'but I like your profile better because I can stare at it without being noticed.' Aloud, he said, 'There is none knows Africa better than Tarzan, Ma'moiselle; but you must remember that your brother has been missing two years. Perhaps—'

'Yes, Captain,' interrupted the third member of the party, 'I realise that my son may be dead; but we shan't give up hope until we *know.*'

'Brian is *not* dead, Papa,' insisted Helen. 'I *know* it. Everyone else was accounted for. Four of the expedition were killed – the rest got out. Brian simply disappeared – vanished. The others brought back stories – weird, almost unbelievable stories. Anything might have happened to Brian, but *he is not dead!*'

'This delay is most disheartening,' said Gregory. 'Ogabi has been gone a week, and no Tarzan yet. He may never find him. I really think I should plan on getting started immediately. I have a good man in Wolff. He knows his Africa like a book.'

'Perhaps you are right,' agreed d'Arnot. 'I do not wish to influence you in any way against your better judgment. If it were possible to find Tarzan, and he would accompany you, you would be much better off; but of course there is no assurance that Tarzan would agree to go with you even were Ogabi to find him.'

'Oh, I think there would be no doubt on that score,' replied Gregory; 'I should pay him handsomely.'

d'Arnot lifted a deprecating palm. '*Non! Non! mon ami!*' he exclaimed. 'Never, never think of offering money to Tarzan. He would give you one look from those grey eyes of his – a look that would make you feel like an insect – and then he would fade away into the jungle, and you would never see him again. He is not as other men, Monsieur Gregory.'

'Well, what can I offer him? Why should he go otherwise than for recompense?'

'For me, perhaps,' said d'Arnot; 'for a whim – who knows? If he chanced to take a liking for you; if he sensed adventure – oh, there are many reasons why Tarzan might take you through his forests and his jungles; but none of them is money.'

At another table, at the far end of the terrace, a dark girl leaned toward her companion, a tall, thin East Indian with a short, black chin beard. 'In some way one of us must get acquainted with the Gregorys, Lal Taask,' she said. 'Atan Thome expects us to do something beside sit on the terrace and consume Planters' Punches.'

'It should be easy, Magra, for you to strike up an acquaintance with the girl,' suggested Lal Taask. Suddenly his eyes went wide as he looked out across the compound toward the entrance to the hotel grounds. 'Siva!' he exclaimed. 'See who comes!'

The girl gasped in astonishment. 'It cannot be!' she exclaimed. 'And yet it is. What luck! What wonderful luck!' Her eyes shone with something more than the light of excitement.

The Gregory party, immersed in conversation, were oblivious to the approach of Tarzan and Ogabi until the former stood beside their table. Then d'Arnot looked up and leaped to his feet. 'Greetings, *mon ami!*' he cried.

As Helen Gregory looked up into the ape-man's face, her eyes went wide in astonishment and incredulity. Gregory looked stunned.

'You sent for me, Paul?' asked Tarzan.

'Yes, but first let me introduce – why, Miss Gregory! What is wrong?'

'It is Brian,' said the girl in a tense whisper, 'and yet it is not Brian.'

'No,' d'Arnot assured her, 'it is not your brother. This is Tarzan of the Apes.'

'A most remarkable resemblance,' said Gregory, as he rose and offered his hand to the ape-man.

'Lal Taask,' said Magra, 'it *is* he. That is Brian Gregory.'

'You are right,' agreed Lal Taask. 'After all these months that we have been planning, he walks right into our arms. We must get him to Atan Thome at once – but how?'

'Leave it to me,' said the girl. 'I have a plan. Fortunately, he has not seen us yet. He would never come if he had, for he has no reason to trust us. Come! We'll go inside; then call a boy, and I'll send him a note.'

As Tarzan, d'Arnot, and the Gregorys conversed, a boy approached and handed a note to the ape-man. The latter glanced through it. 'There must be some mistake,' he said; 'this must be meant for someone else.'

'No, Bwana.' said the boy. 'She say give it Big Bwana in loincloth. No other Bwana in loincloth.'

'Says she wants to see me in little salon next to the entrance,' said Tarzan to d'Arnot. 'Says it's very urgent. It's signed, "An old friend"; but, of course, it must be a mistake. I'll go and explain.'

'Be careful, Tarzan,' laughed d'Arnot; 'you're used only to the wilds of Africa, not to the wiles of women.'

'Which are supposed to be far more dangerous,' said Helen, smiling.

A slow smile lighted the face of the Lord of the Jungle as he looked down into the beautiful eyes of the girl. 'That is easy to believe,' he said. 'I think I should warn d'Arnot.'

'Oh, what Frenchman needs schooling in the ways of women?' demanded Helen. 'It is the women who should be protected.'

'He is very nice,' she said to d'Arnot, after Tarzan had left; 'but I think that one might be always a little afraid of him. There is something quite grim about him, even when he smiles.'

'Which is not often,' said d'Arnot, 'and I have never heard him laugh. But no one who is honourable need ever be afraid of Tarzan.'

As Tarzan entered the small salon he saw a tall, svelte brunette standing by a table at one side of the room. What he did not see was the eye of Lal Taask at the crack of a door in the opposite wall.

'A boy brought me this note,' said Tarzan. 'There is some mistake. I don't know you, and you don't know me.'

'There is no mistake, Brian Gregory,' said Magra. 'You cannot fool such an old friend as I.'

Unsmiling, the ape-man's steady gaze took the girl in from head to foot;

then he turned to leave the room. Another might have paused to discuss the matter, for Magra was beautiful; but not Tarzan – he had said all that there was to say, as far as he was concerned.

'Wait, Brian Gregory!' snapped Magra. 'You are too impetuous. You are not going now.'

Tarzan turned back, sensing a threat in her tone. 'And why not?' he asked.

'Because it would be dangerous. Lal Taask is directly behind you. His pistol is almost touching your back. You are coming upstairs with me like an old friend, arm in arm; and Lal Taask will be at your back. A false move, and – poof! You are dead.'

Tarzan shrugged. 'Why not?' he thought. In some way these two were concerning themselves with the affairs of the Gregorys, and the Gregorys were d'Arnot's friends. Immediately the ape-man's sympathies were enlisted upon the side of the Gregorys. He took Magra's arm. 'Where are we going?' he asked.

'To see another old friend, Brian Gregory,' smiled Magra.

They had to cross the terrace to reach the stairway leading to the second floor of another wing of the hotel, Magra smiling and chatting gaily, Lal Taask walking close behind; but now his pistol was in his pocket.

d'Arnot looked up at them in surprise as they passed.

'Ah, so it *was* an old friend,' remarked Helen.

d'Arnot shook his head. 'I do not like the looks of it,' he said.

'You *have* changed, Brian Gregory,' said Magra, smiling up at him, as they ascended the stairway. 'And I think I like you better.'

'What is this all about?' demanded Tarzan.

'Your memory shall soon be refreshed, my friend,' replied the girl. 'Down this hall is a door, behind the door is a man.'

At the door they halted and Magra knocked.

'Who is it?' inquired a voice from the interior of the room.

'It is I, Magra, with Lal Taask and a friend,' replied the girl.

The voice bade them enter, and as the door swung open Tarzan saw a plump, greasy, suave-appearing Eurasian sitting at a table at one side of an ordinary hotel room. The man's eyes were mere slits, his lips thin. Tarzan's eyes took in the entire room with a single glance. There was a window at the opposite end; at the left, across the room from the man, was a dresser; beside it a closed door, which probably opened into an adjoining room to form a suite.

'I have found him at last, Atan Thome,' said Magra.

'Ah, Brian Gregory!' exclaimed Thome. 'I am glad to see you again – shall I say "my friend"?'

'I am not Brian Gregory,' said Tarzan, 'and of course you know it. Tell me what you want.'

'You are Brian Gregory, and I can understand that you would wish to deny it to me,' sneered Thome; 'and, being Brian Gregory, you know what I want. I want directions to the city of Ashair – The Forbidden City. You wrote those directions down; you made a map; I saw you. It is worth ten thousand pounds to me – that is my offer.'

'I have no map. I never heard of Ashair,' replied Tarzan.

Atan Thome's face registered an almost maniacal rage as he spoke rapidly to Lal Taask in a tongue that neither Tarzan nor Magra understood. The East Indian, standing behind Tarzan, whipped a long knife from beneath his coat.

'Not that, Atan Thome!' cried Magra.

'Why not?' demanded the man. 'The gun would make too much noise. Lal Taask's knife will do the work quietly. If Gregory will not help us, he must not live to hinder us. Strike, Lal Taask!'

II

'I cannot understand,' said d'Arnot, 'why Tarzan went with those two. It is not like him. If ever a man were wary of strangers, it is he.'

'Perhaps they were not strangers,' suggested Helen. 'He seemed on the best of terms with the woman. Didn't you notice how gay and friendly she appeared?'

'Yes,' replied d'Arnot, 'I did; but I also noticed Tarzan. Something strange is going on. I do not like it.'

Even as d'Arnot was speaking, Tarzan, swift as Ara, the lightning, wheeled upon Lal Taask before the knife hand struck; and, seizing the man, lifted him above his head, while Atan Thome and Magra shrank back against the wall in stark amazement. They gasped in horror, as Tarzan hurled Lal Taask heavily to the floor.

Tarzan fixed his level gaze upon Atan Thome. 'You next,' he said.

'Wait, Brian Gregory,' begged Thome, backing away from the ape-man and dragging Magra with him. 'Let us reason.'

'I do not reason with murderers,' replied Tarzan. 'I kill.'

'I only wished to frighten you, not to kill you,' explained Atan Thome, as he continued to edge his way along the wall around the room, holding tightly to Magra's hand.

'Why?' demanded Tarzan.

'Because you have something I want – a route map to Ashair,' replied Thome.

'I have no map,' said Tarzan, 'and once again I tell you that I never heard of Ashair. What is at Ashair that you want?'

'Why quibble, Brian Gregory?' snapped Atan Thome. 'You know as well as I do that what we both want in Ashair is The Father of Diamonds. Will you work with me, or shall you continue to lie?'

Tarzan shrugged. 'I don't know what you're talking about,' he said.

'All right, you fool,' growled Thome. 'If you won't work with me, you'll not live to work against me.' He whipped a pistol from a shoulder holster and levelled it at the ape-man. 'Take this!'

'You shan't!' cried Magra, striking the weapon up as Thome pressed the trigger; 'you shall not kill Brian Gregory!'

Tarzan could not conceive what impelled this strange woman to intercede in his behalf, nor could Atan Thome, as he cursed her bitterly and dragged her through the doorway into the adjoining room before Tarzan could prevent.

At the sound of the shot d'Arnot, on the terrace below, leaped to his feet. 'I knew it,' he cried. 'I knew there was something wrong.'

Gregory and Helen rose to follow him. 'Stay here, Helen,' Gregory commanded; 'we don't know what's going on up there.'

'Don't be silly, Dad,' replied the girl. 'I'm coming with you.'

Long experience had taught Gregory that the easiest way to control his daughter was to let her have her own way, inasmuch as he would have it anyway.

d'Arnot was in the upper hall calling Tarzan's name aloud by the time the Gregorys caught up with him. 'I can't tell which room,' he said.

'We'll have to try then all,' suggested Helen.

Again d'Arnot called out to Tarzan, and this time the ape-man replied. A moment later the three stepped into the room from which voice had come to see him trying to open a door in the left-hand wall.

'What happened?' demanded d'Arnot, excitedly.

'A fellow tried to shoot me,' explained Tarzan. 'The woman who sent me the note struck up his gun; then he dragged her into that room and locked the door.'

'What are you going to do?' asked Gregory.

'I am going to break down the door and go in after him,' replied the ape-man.

'Isn't that rather dangerous?' asked Gregory. 'You say the fellow is armed.'

For answer Tarzan hurled his weight against the door and sent it crashing into the next room. The ape-man leaped across the threshold. The room was vacant. 'They've gone,' he said.

'Stairs lead from that verandah to the service court in the rear of the hotel,' said d'Arnot. 'If we hurry, we might overtake them.'

'No,' said Tarzan. 'Let them go. We have Lal Taask. We can learn about the others from him.' They turned back to re-enter the room they had just quitted. 'We'll question him and and he'll answer.' There was a grimness about his tone that, for some reason, made Helen think of a lion.

'If you didn't kill him,' qualified d'Arnot.

'Evidently I didn't,' replied the ape-man; 'he's gone!'

'How terribly mysterious!' exclaimed Helen Gregory.

The four returned to their table on the terrace, all but Tarzan a little nervous and excited. Helen Gregory was thrilled. Here were mystery and adventure. She had hoped to find them in Africa, but not quite so far from the interior. Romance was there, too, at her elbow, sipping a cool drink; but she did not know it. Over the rim of his glass d'Arnot inspected her profile for the thousandth time.

'What did the woman look like?' Helen asked Tarzan.

'Taller than you, very black hair, slender, quite handsome,' replied the ape-man.

Helen nodded. 'She was sitting at that table at the end of the terrace before you came,' she said. 'A very foreign looking man was with her.'

'That must have been Lal Taask,' said Tarzan,

'She was a very striking looking girl,' continued Helen. 'Why in the world do you suppose she lured you to that room and then ended up by saving your life?'

Tarzan shrugged. 'I know why she lured me to the room, but I don't understand why she struck up Atan Thome's hand to save me.'

'What did they want of you?' asked d'Arnot.

'They think I am Brian Gregory, and they want a map of the route to Ashair – The Forbidden City. According to them, The Father of Diamonds is there. They say that your brother made such a map. Do you know anything about it? Is this safari of yours just for the purpose of finding The Father of Diamonds?' His last query was addressed to Gregory.

'I know nothing about any Father of Diamonds,' replied Gregory. 'My only interest is in finding my son.'

'And you have no map?'

'Yes,' said Helen, 'we have a very rough map that Brian drew and enclosed in the last letter we received from him. He never suspected that we'd have any use for it, and it was more by way of giving us an idea of where he was than anything else. It may not even be accurate, and it is certainly most sketchy. I kept it, however, and I still have it in my room.'

'When the boy brought you the note,' said d'Arnot, 'you had just asked me why I had sent for you.'

'Yes,' said Tarzan.

'I was here in Loango on a special mission and met Monsieur and

Ma'moiselle Gregory,' explained d'Arnot. 'I became very much interested in their problem, and when they asked me if I knew of anyone who might help them find Ashair, I thought immediately of you. I do not mean that I should venture to ask you to accompany them, but I know of no one in Africa better fitted to recommend a suitable man to take charge of their safari.'

That half smile that d'Arnot knew so well, and which was more of the eyes than of the lips, lighted Tarzan's face momentarily. 'I understand, Paul,' he said. 'I will take charge of their safari.'

'But that is such an imposition,' exclaimed Helen. 'We could never ask you to do that.'

'I think it will be interesting,' said Tarzan – 'since I have met Magra and Lal Taask and Atan Thome. I should like to meet them again. I think if I remain with you our paths shall cross.'

'I have no doubt of it,' said Gregory.

'Have you made any preparations?' asked Tarzan.

'Our safari is being gathered in Bonga,' replied Gregory, 'and I had tentatively employed a white hunter named Wolff to take charge of it, but of course, now—'

'If he will come along as a hunter we can use him,' said Tarzan.

'He is coming to the hotel in the morning. We can talk with him then. I know nothing about him, other than that he had some rather good references.'

Behind Wong Feng's shop is a heavily curtained room. A red lacquer Buddha rests in a little shrine. There are some excellent bronzes, a couple of priceless screens, a few good vases; the rest is a hodgepodge of papier mâché, cheap cloisonné, and soapstone. The furniture is of teak, falling apart after the manner of Chinese furniture. Heavy hangings cover the only window, and the air is thick with incense – sticky, cloying. Atan Thome is there and Magra. The man is coldly, quietly furious.

'Why did you do it?' he demanded. 'Why did you strike up my gun?'

'Because,' commenced Magra; then she stopped.

'"Because," "Because!"' he mimicked. 'The eternal feminine. But you know what I do to traitors!' He wheeled on her suddenly. 'Do you love Gregory?'

'Perhaps,' she replied, 'but that is my own affair. What concerns us now is getting to Ashair and getting The Father of Diamonds. The Gregorys are going there. That means they haven't the diamond, and that they do have a map. You know that Brian made a map. You saw him. We must get it, and I have a plan. Listen!' She came and leaned close to Thome and whispered rapidly.

The man listened intently, his face lighting with approval. 'Splendid, my dear,' he exclaimed. 'Lal Taask shall do it tomorrow, if he has recovered sufficiently. Wong Feng's working on him now. But if that fails, we still have Wolff.'

'If he lands the job,' said Magra. 'Let's have a look at Lal Taask.'

They stepped into a small bedroom adjoining the room in which they had been talking. A Chinese was brewing something in a kettle over an oil lamp. Lal Taask lay on a narrow cot. He looked up as the two entered.

'How are you feeling?' asked Atan Thome.

'Better, Master,' replied the man.

'Him all light mollow,' assured Wong Feng.

'How in the world did you escape?' asked Magra.

'I just pretended to be unconscious,' replied Lal Taask, 'and when they went into the next room I crawled into a closet and hid. After dark I managed to get down into the back court and come here. I thought I was going to die, though. I can almost believe that man when he says he's not Brian Gregory, unless he's developed an awful lot of strength since we saw him last.'

'He's Brian Gregory all right,' said Thome.

Wong poured a cupful of the concoction he had brewed and handed it to Lal Taask. 'Dlink!' he said.

Lal Taask took a sip, made a wry face, and spat it out. 'I can't drink that nasty stuff,' he said. 'What's in it? Dead cats?'

'Only li'l bit dead cat,' said Wong. 'You dlink!'

'No,' said Lal Taask. 'I'd just as soon die.'

'Drink it,' said Atan Thome.

Like a whipped cur, Lal Taask raised the cup to his lips and, gagging and choking, drained it.

III

The Gregorys, with Tarzan and d'Arnot, were breakfasting on the terrace the next morning when Wolff arrived. Gregory introduced him to Tarzan. 'One o' them wild men,' observed Wolff, noting Tarzan's loincloth and primitive weapons. 'I seen another one once, but *he* ran around on all fours and barked like a dog. You taking it with us, Mr Gregory?'

'Tarzan will be in full charge of the safari,' said Gregory.

'What?' exclaimed Wolff. 'That's my job.'

'It was,' said Tarzan. 'If you want to come along as a hunter there's a job open for you.'

Wolff thought for a moment. 'I'll come,' he said, 'Mr Gregory's goin' to need me plenty.'

'We're leaving for Bonga on the boat tomorrow,' said Tarzan. 'Be there. Until then we shan't need you.'

Wolff walked off grumbling to himself.

'I'm afraid you've made an enemy of him,' said Gregory.

Tarzan shrugged. 'I did nothing to him,' he said, 'but give him a job. He'll bear watching, though.'

'I do not care for that fellow's looks,' said d'Arnot

'He has good recommendations,' insisted Gregory.

'But he is, obviously, no gentleman,' said Helen.

Her father laughed good naturedly. 'But we are hiring a hunter,' he said. 'Whom did you expect me to sign on, the Duke of Windsor?'

'I could have stood it,' laughed Helen.

'Wolff has only to obey orders and shoot straight,' said Tarzan.

'He's coming back,' announced d'Arnot, and the other looked up to see Wolff approaching.

'I got to thinking,' he said to Gregory, 'that I ought to know just where we're goin', so I could help lay out the route. You see, we gotta be careful we don't get out o' good game country. You got a map?'

'Yes,' replied Gregory. 'Helen, you had it. Where is it?'

'In the top drawer of my dresser.'

'Come on up, Wolff; and we'll have a look at it,' said Gregory.

Gregory went directly to his daughter's room and Wolff accompanied him, while the others remained on the terrace chatting. The older man searched through the upper drawer of Helen's dresser for a moment, running through several papers, from among which he finally selected one.

'Here it is,' he said, and spread it on a table before Wolff.

The hunter studied it for several minutes; then he shook his head. 'I know the country part way,' he said, 'but I ain't never heard of none of these places up here – Tuen-Baka, Ashair.' He pointed them out with a stubby forefinger. 'Lemme take the map,' he said, 'and study it. I'll bring it back tomorrow.'

Gregory shook his head. 'You'll have plenty of time to study it, with Tarzan and the rest of us on the boat to Bonga,' he said; 'and it's too precious – it means too much to me – to let out of my hands. Something might happen to it.' He walked back to the dresser and replaced the map in the upper drawer.

'O.K.,' said Wolff. 'It don't make no difference, I guess. I just wanted to help all I could.'

'Thanks,' said Gregory; 'I appreciate it.'

'Well, then,' said Wolff, 'I'll be running along. See you at the boat tomorrow.'

Captain Paul d'Arnot, being of an inventive turn of mind, discovered various reasons why he should remain in the vicinity of Helen Gregory the remainder of the morning. Luncheon was easy – he simply invited the Gregorys and Tarzan to be his guests; but when the meal was over he lost her.

'If we're leaving for Bonga tomorrow,' she said, 'I'm going to do some shopping right now.'

'Not alone?' asked d'Arnot.

'Alone,' she replied, smiling.

'Do you think it quite safe – a white woman alone?' he asked, 'I'll be more than glad to go with you.'

Helen laughed. 'No man around while I'm shopping – unless he wants to pay the bills. Goodbye!'

Loango's bazaar lay along a narrow, winding street, crowded with negroes, Chinese, East Indians, and thick with dust. It was an unsavoury place of many odours – all strange to occidental nostrils and generally unpleasant. There were many jutting corners and dark doorways; and as Helen indulged the feminine predilection for shopping for something to shop for, Lal Taask, slithering from corner to doorway, followed relentlessly upon her trail.

As she neared the shop of Wong Feng, she stopped before another stall to examine some trinkets that had attracted her eye, and while she was thus engaged Lal Taask slipped past behind her and entered the shop of Wong Feng.

Helen dawdled a few moments before the stall, and then, unconscious of impending danger, approached the shop of Wong Feng, while, from the interior, Lal Taask watched her as a cat might watch a mouse. The girl was entirely off her guard, her mind occupied with thoughts of her shopping and anticipation of the adventurous expedition in search of her missing brother, so that she was stunned into momentary inaction and helplessness as Lal Taask seized her as she was passing the shop of Wong Feng and dragged her through the doorway into the dark interior – but only for a moment. When she realised her danger she struggled and struck at her assailant. She tried to scream for help, but the man clapped a palm roughly over her mouth, stifling her cries, even though they would have brought no help in this vicious neighbourhood.

Lal Taask was a wiry, powerful man, and Helen soon realised the futility of struggling against him as he dragged her toward the rear of the shop.

'Come quietly,' he said, 'and you will not be harmed.'

'What do you want of me?' she asked, as he removed his palm from across her mouth.

'There is one here who would question you,' replied Lal Taask. 'It is not for me to explain – the Master will do that. Whatever he advises will be for your own good – obey him in all things.'

At the far end of the shop Lal Taask opened a door and ushered Helen into the dimly lighted room that we have seen before. Magra was standing at one side, and Helen recognised her as the woman who had lured Tarzan to the hotel room where, but for her, he would have been killed. The plump Eurasian sitting at the desk and facing her she had never before seen, and now, for the first time, she saw the face of the man who had seized her, and recognised him as the hotel companion of the woman.

'You are Helen Gregory?' asked the man at the desk.

'Yes. Who are you, and what do you want of me?'

'In the first place,' said Atan Thome suavely, 'let me assure you that I deeply regret the necessity for this seeming discourtesy. Your brother has something that I want. He would not listen to reason, so there was no other alternative than force.'

'My brother? You have not talked with him. He is lost somewhere in the interior.'

'Don't lie to me,' snapped Thome. 'I know your brother well. I was with him on the first expedition. He reached Ashair and made a map of the vicinity, but he would not let me have a copy. He wanted The Father of Diamonds all for himself. It is the route map to Ashair that I want, and I shall hold you until I get it.'

Helen laughed in his face. 'Your intrigue and melodrama have been quite unnecessary,' she said. 'All that you would have had to do would have been to ask my father for the map. He would have let you make a copy of it. If this man will come back to the hotel with me he can copy the map now.' She indicated Lal Taask with a nod.

Atan Thome sneered. 'You think you can trap me as easily as that?' he demanded.

Helen made a gesture of resignation. 'Go on with your play acting if you must,' she said, 'but it will only waste time and get everyone in trouble. What do you wish me to do?'

'I wish you to write and sign the note I shall dictate to your father,' replied Thome. 'If that doesn't bring the map he'll never see you again. I'm leaving for the interior immediately, and I shall take you with me. There are black sultans there who will pay a good price for you.'

'You must be quite insane to think that you can frighten me with any such wild threats. Those things are not done today, you know, outside of story books. Hurry up and dictate your note, and I'll promise you'll have the map back as quickly as your messenger can bring it, but what assurance have I that you'll keep your end of the bargain and release me?'

'You have only my word,' replied Atan Thome, 'but I can assure you that I have no wish to harm you. The map is all I wish. Come and sit here while I dictate.'

As the sun sank into the west behind tall trees and the shadows lengthened to impart to Loango the semblance of a softened beauty, the which the squalid little village did not possess in its own right, the three men discussing the details of the forthcoming safari became suddenly aware of the lateness of the hour.

'I wonder what can be keeping Helen,' said Gregory; 'it's almost dark. I don't like to have her out so late in a place like this. She should have been back long ago.'

'She should never have gone alone,' said d'Arnot. 'It is not safe here for a woman.'

'It is not,' agreed Tarzan. 'It is never safe where there is civilisation.'

'I think we should go and look for her,' suggested d'Arnot.

'Yes,' said Tarzan, 'you and I. Mr Gregory should remain here in case she returns.'

'Don't worry, Monsieur Gregory,' said d'Arnot, as he and Tarzan left the room; 'I'm sure we'll find her safe and sound in some curio shop,' but his words were only to reassure Gregory. In his heart was only fear.

As he waited Gregory tried to convince himself that there was nothing to worry about. He tried to read, but could not fix his mind upon the book. After he had re-read one sentence half a dozen times without grasping its sense, he gave up; then he commenced to pace the floor, smoking one cigar after another. He was on the point of starting out himself to search when d'Arnot returned. Gregory looked at him eagerly.

d'Arnot shook his head. 'No luck,' he said. 'I found a number of shop keepers who recalled seeing her, but none who knew when she left the bazaar.'

'Where is Tarzan?' asked Gregory.

'He is investigating in the native village. If the blacks have any knowledge of her Tarzan will get it out of them. He speaks their language in every sense of the term.'

'Here he is now,' said Gregory as the ape-man entered the room.

Both men looked up at him questioningly. 'You didn't find any trace of her?' asked d'Arnot.

Tarzan shook his head. 'None. In the jungle I could have found her; but here – here, in civilisation, a man cannot even find himself.'

As he ceased speaking a windowpane crashed behind them and a missile fell to the floor.

'*Mon dieu!*' exclaimed d'Arnot. 'What is that?'

'Look out!' cried Gregory. 'It may be a bomb.'

'No,' said Tarzan; 'it is just a note tied to a stone. Here, let's have a look at it.'

'It must be about Helen,' said Gregory, taking the note from Tarzan's hand. 'Yes, it is. It's from her. Listen! "Dear Dad – The people who are holding me want Brian's route map to Ashair. They threaten to take me into the interior and sell me if they don't get it. I believe they mean it. Tie the map to a stone and throw it out window. Do not follow their messenger, or they will kill me. They promise to return me unharmed as soon as they get the map." Yes, it's from Helen all right – it's her handwriting. But the fools! They could have had the map for the asking. I only want to find Brian. I'll get the map.'

He rose and went into Helen's room, which adjoined his. They heard him strike a match to light a lamp, and then give vent to an exclamation of astonishment that brought the other two men into the room. Gregory was standing before the open upper drawer of the dresser, his face white.

'It's gone,' he said. 'Someone has stolen the map!'

IV

In a squalid room Wolff sat at a table laboriously wielding a pencil by the light of a kerosene lamp – evidently an unaccustomed task. Every time he made a mark he wet the tip of the pencil on his tongue, which, in the interims, he chewed. At last his work was completed, and as he eyed it, not without pride, he heaved a sigh and rose.

'I guess this ain't a pretty night's work or anything!' he soliloquized complacently. 'Now they'll both pay – and how!'

Atan Thome sat alone in the back room of Wong Feng's shop. If he were nervous, the only outward indication of it were the innumerable cigarettes that he smoked. Magra was guarding Helen in the little bedroom adjoining. All three were waiting for the return of Lal Taask with the route map to Ashair. Helen, alone, was positive that it would be forthcoming. The others only hoped.

'Will he let me go when the map comes?' asked Helen.

'He may have to keep you until he can get safely away,' replied Magra, 'but I'm sure he will let you go then.'

'Poor Dad,' said the girl. 'He'll be worrying terribly. If there's going to be any delay about my release I'd like to write him another note.'

'I'll try and arrange it,' said Magra. 'I'm very sorry about all this, Miss Gregory,' she added after a short silence. 'I am really quite as helpless in the matter as you, for reasons which I may not explain; but I may tell you that Atan Thome is obsessed by this desire to possess The Father of Diamonds. At heart he is not a bad man, but I know that he will stop at nothing to realise this one desire, so I hope your father sends the map.'

'You really think that he would sell me in the interior if he didn't get it?' demanded the American girl.

'Absolutely,' replied Magra. 'If he were pressed, he might kill you.'

Helen shuddered. 'I am glad that he is going to get the map,' she said.

Lal Taask opened the door to the back room of Wong Feng's shop and entered. Atan Thome looked up. 'Well?' he inquired.

'They threw it out all right,' said Taask; 'here it is.' He handed the paper to Thome. It was still wrapped around the stone. Thome opened it and read. His face turned dark.

'Is it the map?' asked Lal Taask.

'No,' growled Thome. 'They say the map has been stolen. They lie! They can't fool Atan Thome, though. They'll never see the girl again, and I'll find Ashair without their map. Listen! There is someone at the door. See who it is.'

Lal Taask opened the door a crack and looked out. 'It is Wolff,' he said.

'Bring him in.'

'Nice evening,' said Wolff, as he entered the room.

'You didn't come here to tell me that,' said Thome. 'What is it?'

'What would you give for the route map to Ashair?' asked Wolff.

'Five hundred pounds,' replied Thome.

'Not enough. Make it a thousand and a half interest in the diamond, and I'll get the map for you.'

'How?'

'I already have it. I stole it from the girl's room.'

'Have you got it here?' inquired Thome.

'Yes,' replied Wolff, 'but don't try any funny business. I left a note with the old woman I'm stopping with. If I'm not back in an hour she'll take it to the police.'

'Let's see the map,' said Thome.

Wolff took it from his pocket and held it up in front of the other man, but not near enough for him to snatch it. 'Fork over the money, and the map's yours,' he said.

Atan Thome drew a thick wallet from an inner pocket and counted out five hundred pounds in Bank of England notes.

'If I had that roll of yours I wouldn't be riskin' my neck lookin' for no Father of Diamonds,' said Wolff, as he took the notes and stuffed them in his pocket.

'Are you still going along with the Gregory safari?' asked Thome.

'Sure,' replied Wolff. 'A poor man's got to work; but I'm goin' to be right with you when you get that diamond. I'm goin' to have my half.'

'You can do something more to help me,' said Thome, 'that will also make the diamond safer for us.'

'What's that?' asked Wolff, suspiciously.

'I'm going to have Magra try to go along with the Gregorys. You may be able to help in that. I want her to make friends with them – and make love to Brian Gregory; then if anything goes wrong she'll have some influence with them. I don't want to hang, and neither do you.'

'Where do I come in?' asked Wolff.

'You go along and lead them off on to a wrong trail. When they're good and lost, bring Magra up toward Ashair. You've seen the map, so you'll know about where to go. You'll find one of my old camps, and wait there for me. Do you understand?'

'Yes.'

'And you'll do it?'

'Sure. Why not?'

'All right. Now go along. I'll be seeing you up around Ashair in a couple of months.'

After Wolff had left Thome turned to Lal Taask. 'We've got to get out of here tonight,' he said. 'Go down to the river and bribe the captain of that boat to get up steam and leave for Bonga tonight.'

'You are very clever, Master,' said Lal Taask. 'You will let the young lady go, now that you have the map?'

'No. They didn't give me the map. They may catch up with us; and if they do, it will be just as well to have a hostage.'

'Again, Master – you are clever.'

It was past midnight when Atan Thome went aboard the river steamer with Lal Taask and Helen. At the gangplank he bid Magra goodbye. 'Join the Gregory safari by any ruse,' he directed. 'They may reach Ashair, and I want someone with them I can trust. I must be prepared for any eventuality. If they should beat me to it and get the diamond you must find some way to communicate with me. You may even get an opportunity to steal the diamond. Watch Wolff. I don't trust him. He has agreed to lead them astray and then bring you of toward Ashair to meet me when I come out. It's a good thing you're in love with Brian Gregory. That will help. Work it for all its worth. I didn't like the idea at first; but when I got to thinking about it I saw where we could make use of it. Now, goodbye; and remember all I have told you.'

Taask and Helen had boarded the steamer, the man walking very close to the girl, his pistol pressed against her side, lest she make an outcry.

'I think you are very foolish not to set her free,' said Magra.

'I can't now,' replied Thome – 'not until after you have left the Gregory party. Can't you see?'

'Well, see that no harm comes to her – remember the arm of English law is long.' Then Magra turned and walked back into the village.

*

After a sleepless night of searching for Helen, Gregory, Tarzan and d'Arnot were gathered in Gregory's room to formulate their plans.

'I'm afraid there's nothing left to do but notify the authorities,' said d'Arnot.

'I suppose you're right,' agreed Gregory. 'I was so afraid they'd kill her if we notified the police, but now there seems to be nothing else to do.'

There was a knock at the door and the three men looked up. 'Come in!' said Gregory.

The door swung slowly open and Magra stepped into the room.

'You!' exclaimed d'Arnot.

She paid no attention to him, but looked straight at Tarzan. 'Brian Gregory,' she said, 'I have come to help you find your sister.'

'What do you know about her? Where is she?' demanded Gregory.

'Atan Thome is taking her into the interior. He left for Bonga the river boat last night.'

'But the boat doesn't sail until today,' interrupted d'Arnot.

'Atan Thome bribed the captain to sail last night,' Magra explained. 'I was to have gone, but – well, why I didn't is immaterial.'

'This woman is not to be trusted,' said Tarzan.

'You can trust me – always, Brian Gregory.' She turned to Gregory. 'If you doubt me, keep me with you – as a hostage, perhaps. It is possible that I may be able to help you.'

Gregory appeared not to hear her. He seemed stunned. 'Both my children,' he said. 'First Brian, now Helen, sacrificed – and for what?'

'Do not despair, Monsieur Gregory,' said d'Arnot, 'There must be a way.'

'But how?' demanded the older man. 'In four days Thome will be in Bonga. The boat will lie there at least one day. Coming back with the current she will make the return trip in two and a half days, perhaps. Even if we can persuade the captain to return to Bonga immediately Thome will have had six or seven days' start of us. He will be far into the interior. He probably has the map that was stolen from Helen's room. We have none. We will not know where to look for him.'

'Do not worry on that score,' urged d'Arnot. 'If Thome is in Africa, Tarzan of the Apes will find him.'

'Yes,' agreed Gregory dully. 'But what will have happened to my poor girl in the meantime?'

'Wait!' exclaimed d'Arnot. 'I have it! There is yet a way. We have a naval seaplane here. I'm sure the authorities will fly us to Bonga. We shall be there when Monsieur Thome lands. What a surprise for Mousieur Thome, eh?'

'Wonderful!' cried Gregory. 'How can I ever thank you, Captain?'

Whatever her reaction, Magra's face showed no emotion.

V

At d'Arnot's request, the authorities were glad to cooperate, and with a delay of only a couple of hours, the party was boarding a seaplane anchored in the river. Magra's expression suggested utmost self-satisfaction, as d'Arnot helped her aboard from the native canoe that had brought the party from shore. Wolff, who had never flown, swaggered a bit to hide his inward perturbation. Ogabi's eyes rolled fearfully.

'You see how easily everything was arranged?' exclaimed d'Arnot.

'Thanks to you,' replied Gregory.

'How long will it take you to fly to Bonga, Lieutenant?' Tarzan asked the pilot.

'Between two and three hours,' replied Lavac.

'It will take the steamer four days, against the current,' said d'Arnot. 'Atan Thome will find a reception committee waiting at the dock.'

As the plane raced up the river into the wind for the take-off Ogabi closed his eyes and clutched the seat with both hands. When he opened his eyes again he looked down upon the top of a forest. His face was no longer black – it was a sickly ashen colour.

'This is no place for man, Bwana, in belly of bird,' he said to Tarzan.

'But you *are* a man, Ogabi,' replied the ape-man; 'therefore you are not afraid. Remember that when the storm strikes us.'

'What storm?' asked Gregory.

'A storm is coming,' replied Tarzan.

'How do you know?' demanded Gregory. 'There is not a cloud in the sky.'

'Tarzan always knows,' said d'Arnot.

How Tarzan had known that a storm was approaching not even we could have explained. Perhaps he shared with the wild things, by which and among which he had been raised, a peculiar sensitivity beyond the appreciation of men. However that may be, a half hour after he had foretold it the ship raced into the heart of a tropical storm.

Lavac, who was accustomed to sudden tropical storms, assumed that it covered but a small area and would soon be astern of them. An experienced flier, with a ship equipped with all the instruments necessary for blind flying, he merely increased his elevation and flew into it. The ship rolled and tossed, and Ogabi became a few shades lighter. Wolff clenched his fists until his knuckles were white.

After an hour of it, Lavac turned and motioned d'Arnot to come forward. 'It's worse than I'd anticipated, Captain,' he said. 'Had I better turn back?'

'Got plenty of petrol?' asked d'Arnot.

Lavac nodded. 'Yes, Sir,' he replied.

'Everything else all right?'

'I'm not so sure about the compass.'

'Then we wouldn't be any better off flying back than going on,' said d'Arnot. 'Let's keep on. We're bound to be out of it sooner or later.'

For two long hours more Lavac bucked the storm; then the engine spluttered. D'Arnot went forward hurriedly, but before he reached Lavac's side the engine caught itself again and was purring sweetly. It had been a tense moment for these two. D'Arnot breathed a deep sigh of relief – and then the engine spluttered again and stopped. Lavac worked furiously with a hand pump. D'Arnot turned back toward the cabin.

'Fasten your life belts,' he said. 'We may have to come down.'

'The line's clogged,' said Lavac, 'and I can't clear it.'

d'Arnot glanced at the altimeter. 'You've got about three thousand metres,' he said. 'The average elevation in the vicinity of Bonga is around two hundred. Glide as far as you can, looking for a hole.'

'And if I don't find one?' asked Lavac.

d'Arnot shrugged and grimaced. 'You're the pilot,' he said, 'and I understand you're a very good one.'

'Thanks,' said Lavac. 'It will take a *very* good pilot to fly this ship through a forest. I am not that good. Are you going to them?'

'What's the use?' asked d'Arnot.

'They might wish to take up some matters with God – matters they have been neglecting to discuss with Him.'

'What's wrong?' demanded Wolff. 'The engine isn't running.'

'You have answered your own question,' said d'Arnot, walking back to his seat.

'We're coming down,' said Wolff. 'He can't see to land. We'll crash.'

'Be calm,' admonished d'Arnot; 'we have not crashed yet.'

The passengers sat in tense expectancy as the ship nosed down through storm-racked clouds.

'What altitude now, Lavac?' asked d'Arnot.

'Three hundred metres.'

'That means we can't be more than three hundred feet from the ground at the best,' said Gregory. 'I remember looking at a map the other day. Nearly all this country back here runs about six hundred feet elevation.'

Suddenly Wolff leaped to his feet. 'I can't stand it,' he cried. 'I'm going to jump!'

Tarzan seized him and threw him back into his seat. 'Sit still,' he said.

'Yes, sit still!' snapped d'Arnot. 'Is it not bad enough without that?'

Lavac voiced an exclamation of relief. 'We're out of it!' he cried, 'And there's water just below us.'

A moment later the ship glided to an easy landing on the bosom of a little lake. Only the forest and the jungle were there to welcome it. If there were eyes to see, they remained hidden; and the voices of the jungle were momentarily stilled. The rain beat upon the water and the wind moaned in the forest. Of these things and of their miraculous escape from death Ogabi was unconscious – he had fainted.

'Do you know where we are, Lieutenant?' asked d'Arnot.

'I haven't the least idea,' replied Lavac. 'Never saw this lake before.'

'Then we are lost?' asked Gregory.

Lavac nodded. 'I'm afraid so, Sir. My compass wasn't behaving very well; and then, naturally, we must have been blown way off our course.'

'How lonely and depressing it looks,' said Magra.

'It is the jungle,' breathed Tarzan, almost as one might say, 'It is home!'

'How discouraging,' said Gregory. 'Just when it seemed certain that we had overcome every obstacle and found a way to circumvent Thome and rescue Helen, this had to happen. Now we are absolutely helpless. We shall never reach her now, poor child.'

'*Non! Non!* my dear Monsieur Gregory, you must not give up,' said d'Arnot. 'This is only a temporary delay. Lieutenant Lavac will have that fuel line cleared in no time, and as soon as the weather lifts we'll take off again. We have plenty of time. Thome will not reach Bonga for three days yet. As soon as the weather clears the lieutenant can find Bonga even with no compass at all.'

Lavac worked on the fuel line for half an hour; then he called d'Arnot. 'The line was not clogged, Sir,' he said. He looked worried.

'Then what was the trouble?' demanded d'Arnot.

'We are out of fuel. The tank must have been leaking badly, as we had a full load when we left.'

'But the reserve tank – what of that?' demanded d'Arnot.

'It was the reserve tank that leaked, and we have emptied the other.'

D'Arnot shook his head. 'That poor little girl!' he said.

VI

Ogabi was singing as he grilled antelope steaks over a fire beside which lay the carcass of the animal. Ogabi's spirits had been rising for four days, for now he was four marches away from that horrible bird thing, in the belly of which he had almost ridden to his death. He had been very fearful that the white men would decide to return to it and fly again. If they had, however, he would have run away into the jungle and hidden. Five white men sat around the fire watching him.

'Pretty well convinced you know where we are now, Tarzan?' asked d'Arnot.

'Yes. I'm quite certain that we are east of Bonga and a little South. That buck I killed ranges in that district.'

'Thome probably left Bonga today,' said Gregory. 'By the time we reach Bonga he'll be many marches ahead of us. We'll never overtake him.'

'We don't have to go to Bonga,' said Tarzan. 'We can strike out directly North-east and cut his trail; then we can follow on faster than he can travel – boys with packs will slow him down. We're not handicapped by anything like that.'

'You mean we can travel without porters or provisions?' demanded Gregory.

'We have been for the last four days,' Tarzan reminded him. He looked quickly about the camp. 'Where's Magra?' he asked. 'I told her not to leave camp. This is lion country; and, if I'm right about the location, it's also cannibal country.'

Magra had not meant to go far from the camp, but the forest was intriguing, and it seemed so quiet and peaceful. She walked slowly, enjoying the blooms, watching the birds. She stopped before a lovely orchid, which, like some beautiful woman, sucked the life-blood from the giant that supported it. Presently she recalled Tarzan's injunction and turned to retrace her steps to camp. She did not see the great lion behind her which had caught her scent and was stalking her on silent, padded feet.

The men in the camp saw Tarzan rise to his feet, his head up, his nostrils quivering; then, to their amazement, they saw him run a few steps, swing into a tree and disappear. They did not know that Usha, the wind, had brought the acrid scent spoor of Numa, the lion, to the sensitive nostrils of the ape-man, and that mingled with it was the delicate scent of the perfume that Magra loved, revealing to him an impending tragedy and sending him into the trees in the hope that he would reach the scene in time.

As Magra walked toward camp an angry snarl from the King of beasts brought her suddenly about and to awareness of the danger that confronted her. Instantly she realised the hopelessness of her situation and the futility of calling for help that could not reach her in time to prevent the inevitable. With her accustomed courage, she resigned herself to death; but even with death staring her in the face, she could scarcely restrain an involuntary exclamation of admiration for the magnificence of the great beast facing her. His size, his majestic bearing, the sheer ferocity of his snarling mien thrilled every fibre of her being. She did not want to die, but she felt that there could be no more noble death than beneath the mighty fangs and talons of the King of beasts.

Now the lion was creeping toward her, belly to ground, the end of his tail twitching nervously. Just for a yard or so he came thus; then he rose, but still crouching a little as he advanced. Suddenly, with a mighty roar, he charged; and at the same instant a man leaped from a tree above full upon his back.

'Brian!' she cried with a gasp of astonishment.

The man clung to the back of the carnivore, his growls mingling with those of the great cat, as he drove his hunting knife again and again into the tawny side of the leaping, striking beast. Thrilled and horrified, Magra watched, fascinated, until the pierced heart ceased forever and the great beast died. Then Magra had reason to shudder in real horror, as the Lord of the Jungle placed a foot upon the carcass of his kill and voiced the victory cry of the bull ape. Every fibre of the girl's body vibrated to a new thrill as she watched the man she now knew was not Brian Gregory.

As the uncanny cry broke the stillness of the jungle, Wolff, Gregory and Lavac sprang to their feet. Wolff seized his rifle. 'My God!' he cried. 'What was that?'

'Tarzan has made a kill,' said d'Arnot.

'The Big Bwana has killed Simba,' said Ogabi. 'Are the white men deaf that they did not hear Simba roar?'

'Sure I heard it,' said Wolff, 'but that wild man never killed no lion – he had nothin' but a knife, I'd better go out there an' look after him.' Carrying his rifle, he started in the direction of the sound that had startled them, Gregory and Lavac following. 'That yell was when the lion got *him*,' said Wolff. 'He's deader'n a smelt right now.'

'He doesn't look very dead to me,' said Lavac, as Tarzan and Magra came into view.

'I'm afraid I was so out of breath that I didn't – well, thank is a most inadequate word under the circumstance; but I can't think of another – thank you for saving my life. How silly and banal that sounds, but you know what I'm trying to say. You were wonderful, and a little terrifying, too; but I know now that you are not Brian Gregory. He could not have killed the lion as you did. No other man in the world could have done it.' She paused. 'Until a few minutes ago I thought that I loved Brian.'

The implication of Magra's words and tone was quite apparent, yet Tarzan elected to ignore it. 'We shall do our best to find him,' he said, 'not only on Mr Gregory's account, but on yours.'

Magra shrugged. She was rebuffed, but she could bide her time. 'And the diamond?' she asked.

'I'm not interested in that,' said Tarzan.

*

A well-equipped safari moved toward the North-east ten marches out of Bonga. A girl and two men were the only whites, but the porters seemed to be carrying enough equipment and provisions for two or three times that number.

'Rather clever of me,' said one of the men to the girl, 'taking your father's safari. It will take him a week or longer to get another one together and equip it. By that time we'll be so far ahead that he'll never overtake us. I should like to see his face when he reaches Bonga and learns the truth.'

'You are about as clever as the late Mr Dillinger and Baby Face Nelson,' replied Helen, 'and you'll end up the same way.'

'Who are they?' demanded Thome.

'They were kidnappers and murderers who ware also addicted to grand larceny. If you were not a fool, you'd turn me loose and send me back to Bonga. You have the map. I can be of no further use to you. Until I am returned safely to him my father will never give up until he finds you. I can't see why you want to hold me any longer.'

'Perhaps I have taken a liking to you, my dear,' replied Thome.

The girl shuddered at the implication of the man's words. All the rest of the day she plodded on in silence, waiting always for a chance to escape, but either Atan Thome or Lal Taask was always at her side. She was spent and weary when they finally made camp, but much of her weariness was from nervous exhaustion – all day long the words of Atan Thome had preyed upon her mind.

After the evening meal she went to her tent, which had been pitched across the camp from that occupied by Thome, for the man knew that while she might attempt to escape by day, she would not dare to venture the dangers of the forest by night.

Thome and Taask stood talking before the former's tent, Thome's eyes upon the girl entering hers. The two men had been talking and Lal Taask was watching the other intently.

'You are my Master, Atan Thome,' he said, 'but out of loyalty, your servant must warn you. The girl is white, and the arm of the white man's power is long. Into the depth of the jungle or to the frozen wastes of the poles it would reach and drag you back to an accounting.'

'Mind your own affairs,' snapped Thome. 'I mean the girl no harm.'

'I am glad to hear you say that. I do not want the white man's anger upon me. If you are wise you will do as the girl suggested. Send her back to Bonga tomorrow.'

Atan Thome thought a moment; then he nodded. 'Perhaps you are right,' he said. 'She shall go back to Bonga tomorrow, if she wishes.'

The two men separated, each going to his own tent, and silence fell upon the sleeping camp, a single askari, nodding beside the beast fire, the only suggestion of life within the rude boma that had been thrown up against the intrusion of predatory beasts.

Presently Atan Thome emerged from his tent. His eyes swept the camp. Only the askari was in evidence. At sight of Thome he simulated an alertness which was, considering the hour and his inclinations, anachronistic; but he was sufficiently aroused to watch the white man creep silently across the camp, and when he understood Atan Thome's evident goal, he grinned. In the distance a lion roared. This and the love note of the cicada alone broke the silence of the night.

Sleepless from nervous apprehension, Helen's mind was filled with dread and misgiving. The altered attitude of Atan Thome worried her. Every slightest sound bore a menace to her expectant ears. Finally she arose from her couch and looked out through the flap of her tent. Her heart sank as she saw Atan Thome creeping toward her.

Again a lion roared out of the mysterious void of blackness that was the jungle night, but a far greater menace lay in the oily man who parted the flaps at the front of the girl's tent. An aura of repulsiveness surrounded Thome. The girl had always sensed it, feeling in his presence as one might in the presence of a cobra.

Atan Thome pushed the curtains aside and stepped into the tent. The ingratiating, oily smile upon his lips vanished as he discovered that it was vacant. He did not know that the girl had crawled beneath the back wall but a moment before he had entered. For all he knew she might have been gone an hour or more; but he was sure that she must be somewhere about the camp, for he could not imagine that she would have dared the dangers of the jungle night to escape him. Yet this was what she had done.

Frightened, she groped through the darkness which was only partly moderated by the newly risen moon. Again the roar of a hunting lion reverberated through the forest, nearer now; and her heart sank. Yes she steeled herself and stumbled on, more terrified by thoughts of the man behind her than of the lion ahead. She hoped the beast would continue to roar, for in this way she could always locate its position. If it stopped roaring that might mean that it had caught her scent and was stalking her.

By accident she had stumbled upon a game trail, and this she followed. She thought that it was the back trail toward Bonga, but it was not. It ran in a more southerly direction, which was, perhaps, just as well for her, as the lion was on the Bonga trail, and the sound of its roars receded as she stumbled on through the forest.

After a night of terror, the girl came to an open plain during the early morning. When she saw it she knew that she had missed the trail to Bonga, for the safari had crossed no plain like this on its trek from the river town. She realised that she was lost, and now she had no plan other than to escape from Thome. Her future, her life lay in the palm of a capricious Fate. How, in this savage land, it could be other than a cruel Fate, she could not imagine; yet she must carry on – and hope.

She was so glad to be out of the forest that she struck out across the plain toward a range of low hills, ignoring the fact that while the forest might be gloomy and depressing, it offered her concealment and escape from many dangers among the branches of its trees. Behind her lay Thome and the memory of the hunting lion. It was well for her peace of mind that she did not know what lay just ahead.

VII

Chemungo, son of Mpingu, Chief of the Buiroos, was hunting with three other warriors for a man-eater which had been terrorising the villages of his people. They had tracked him through the hills to the edge of a plain beyond which lay a forest; but when they reached a low elevation from which they could survey the plain they discovered other quarry than that for which they were hunting.

'A white woman,' said Chemungo. 'We shall take her to my father.'

'Wait,' counseled a companion; 'there will be white men with guns.'

'We can wait and see,' agreed Chemungo, 'for she comes this way. Perhaps there are no white men.'

'White women do not come here without white men,' insisted the other warrior.

'She may have wandered away from camp and become lost,' argued Chemungo; 'these white women are very helpless and very stupid. See, she has no weapons; so she is not hunting, therefore she must be lost.'

'Perhaps Chemungo is right,' admitted the other.

They waited until Helen was well out into the plain, then Chemungo, leaping to his feet, signalled the others to follow him, and the three ran toward the white girl, shouting and waving their spears.

So sudden and so unexpected was the appearance of this new menace that, for a moment, Helen stood paralyzed by terror, almost regretting that she had left either Thome or the lion; then she turned and fled back toward the forest.

Lithe, athletic, the girl seemed in a fair way to outdistance her pursuers. She felt that if she could reach the forest before they overtook her she might elude them entirely. Behind her the cries of Chemungo and his fellows were angry cries now, threatening cries, as they redoubled their efforts to overtake their quarry. Terror lent wings to the girl's flying feet, and the warriors, burdened by their spears and shields, were falling behind. Helen, glancing over her shoulder, felt that escape was almost assured, when her retreat was suddenly cut off by the appearance of a great lion which was emerging from the forest directly in front of her. It was the man-eater.

The pursuing warriors redoubled their shouting, and the lion, confused, paused momentarily. Now, indeed, was the girl faced by a major dilemma, either horn of which would prove fatal. In an attempt to escape both, she turned to the right – a brave but futile gesture of self-preservation. The moving quarry attracted the lion, which started in pursuit, while the warriors, apparently unafraid, raced to intercept him. They might have succeeded had not Helen tripped and fallen.

As the girl fell the lion charged and sprang upon her prostrate form; but the shouts of the warriors and their proximity attracted his snarling attention before he had mauled her, and as the four closed in upon him Chemungo cast his spear. It seemed an act of temerity rather than of courage, but these were warriors of a famous lion-hunting clan, well versed in the technique of their dangerous sport.

Chemungo's spear drove deep into the body of the lion, and, simultaneously, those of two of his companions; the fourth warrior held his weapon in reserve. Roaring horribly, the lion abandoned the girl and charged Chemungo, who threw himself backward upon the ground, his entire body covered by his great shield, while the other warriors danced around them, yelling at the top of their lungs, irritating and confusing the lion; and the fourth warrior awaited his opportunity to drive home the lethal thrust. It came presently, and the lion fell with the spear through his savage heart.

Then Chemungo leaped up and dragged the hapless girl to her feet. She was too stunned by the frightful ordeal through which she had passed to feel either fear or relief. She was alive! Later she was to wonder if it would not have been better had she died.

For hours they dragged her roughly across the plain and through hills to another valley and a village of thatched huts surrounded by a palisade; and as they dragged her through the village street angry women surrounded them, striking at the girl and spitting upon her. She showed no fear, but half smiled as she likened them to a room full of envious old women in some civilised city, who might have done likewise but for their inhibitions.

Chemungo took her before his father, Mpingu, the chief. 'She was alone,' said Chemungo. 'No white man can ever know what we do with her. The women wish her killed at once.'

'I am chief,' snapped Mpingu. 'We shall kill her tonight,' he added hastily, as he caught the eye of one of his wives. 'Tonight we shall dance – and feast.'

The Gregory safari debouched from a forest at the edge of a plain which stretched before them, tree dotted, to the foot of a cone-shaped hill. 'I know where we are now,' said Tarzan, pointing at the hill. 'We have to travel North and west to reach Bonga.'

'If we had grub and porters we wouldn't have to go back,' volunteered Wolff.

'We've got to go back to Bonga to get on Thome's trail and find Helen,' said Gregory. 'If we only had the map we'd be all right on that score.'

'We don't need no map,' said Wolff. 'I know the way to Ashair.'

'That's odd,' commented Tarzan. 'Back in Loango you said you didn't know the way.'

'Well, I know it now,' growled Wolff, 'and if Gregory wants to pay me a thousand pounds and cut me in on the diamond, fifty-fifty, I'll take him to Ashair.'

'I think you are a crook,' said the ape-man, 'but if Gregory wants to pay you, I'll take him through without porters.'

Catching Tarzan entirely off his guard, and without warning, Wolff knocked the ape-man down. 'There can't no damn monkey-man call me a crook,' he cried, whipping his pistol from its holster, but before he could fire Magra seized his arm.

'If I were you, Monsieur Wolff,' said d'Arnot, 'I should run. I should run very fast – before Tarzan gets up.'

But Tarzan was already up, and before Wolff could escape, he seized him by the throat and belt and lifted him high above his head, as though to hurl him to the ground.

'Don't kill him, Tarzan!' cried Gregory, stepping forward. 'He is the only man who can lead us to Ashair. I will pay him what he asks. He can have the diamond, if there is one. All I want is to find my daughter and my son. Thome is on his way to Ashair. If Helen is with him, Wolff offers our only hope of rescuing her.'

'As you wish,' said the ape-man, dropping Wolff upon the ground.

The safari crossed the plain and, skirting the foot of the cone-shaped hill, entered a forest, where camp was made beside a small stream. It was a most primitive camp, as they had no equipment – just rude shelters, a makeshift boma, and a fire. Magra, being the only woman, fared best. Hers was the largest and best-constructed shelter, the shelters of the men encircling it for protection. As she stood before it, Wolff passed and she stopped him. It was the first opportunity she had had to speak to him alone since his altercation with Tarzan.

'Wolff, you *are* a scoundrel,' she said. 'You promised Atan Thome you'd lead Gregory off the trail. Now you've sold out to him and promised to lead him to Ashair. When I tell Atan Thome that—' She shrugged. 'But you do not know Atan Thome as well as I.'

'Perhaps you will not tell Atan Thome anything,' replied Wolff, meaningly.

'Don't threaten me,' warned the girl. 'I'm not afraid of you. Either of two men would kill you if I said the word. Tarzan would wring your neck openly. Thome would have someone stick a knife in your back.'

'He might do the same to you if I told him you were in love with the monkey-man,' shot back Wolff, and Magra flushed.

'Don't be a fool,' she said. 'I have to keep on the good side of these people; and if you had even a semblance of good sense you'd do the same.'

'I don't want to have nothing to do with that monkey-man,' growled Wolff. 'Me and him ain't in the same class.'

'That's obvious,' said Magra.

'But with me and you it's different,' continued Wolff, ignoring the implication. 'We ought to be more friendly. Don't you know we could have a swell time if you'd loosen up a bit. I ain't such a bad fellow when you gets to know me.'

'I'm glad to hear that. I was afraid you were.'

Wolff knitted his brows. He was trying to digest this when his attention was attracted to Tarzan. 'There goes the monkey-man,' he said. 'Look at him, swingin' through the trees. You can't tell *me* he ain't half monkey.'

Magra, tiring of Wolff, walked toward d'Arnot just as Gregory came up. 'Where's Tarzan going?' asked the latter.

'To reconnoitre for a native village,' replied the Frenchman, 'on the chance we can get some supplies and a few "boys" – askaris and porters, and, perhaps, a cook. That would give Tarzan a chance to go on ahead and search for your daughter.'

As the Lord of the Jungle swung through the trees in search of some indication of the presence of native habitation his active mind reviewed the events of the past several weeks. He knew that three scoundrels were pitted against him – Thome, Taask, and Wolff. He could cope with them, but could he cope with Magra? He could not understand the girl. Twice she had saved him from the bullets of would-be assassins, yet he knew that she was an associate, perhaps an accomplice, of Thome. The first time it might have been because she had thought him to be Brian Gregory, but now she knew better. It was all quite beyond him. With a shrug, he dismissed the whole matter from his mind, content to know that he was forewarned and, consequently, on guard.

The day was coming to a close as Tarzan gave up the search for a native village and decided to return to camp. Suddenly he stood erect upon a branch of a great tree, head up, statuesque, alert, listening. A vagrant breeze had brought to his nostrils the scent of Wappi, the antelope, suggesting that he take meat back to camp; but as he prepared to stalk his prey, the booming of distant native drums came faintly to his ears.

VIII

As night fell, Helen, lying bound in a filthy hut, heard the booming of drums in the village street outside. Eerie and menacing they sounded, mysterious, threatening. She felt that they were beating for her – a savage, insistent dirge, foretelling death. She wondered what form it would take, when it would come to her. She felt that she might almost welcome it as an escape from the terror that engulfed her. Presently, warriors came and jerked her roughly to her feet after removing the bonds that confined her ankles; then they dragged her out into the village street before the hut of Mpingu, the chief, and tied her to a stake, while around her milled screaming women and shouting warriors. In the glare of the cooking fires the whole scene seemed to the doomed girl the horrible phantasmagoria of some hideous nightmare from which she must awaken. It was all too fantastic to be real, but when spear point pierced her flesh and warm blood flowed, she knew she did not dream.

A well-equipped safari lay in an ordered camp. Porters and askaris squatted around tiny cook fires; and before the central beast fire, two men who were not black talked with Mbuli, the headman, while faintly from afar came the sullen sound of native drums.

'They are at it,' said Atan Thome. 'Mbuli tells me this is cannibal country and that we had better get out quickly. Tomorrow we'll make a long trek toward Ashair. The girl is lost. The drums may be for her.'

'Her blood is on your head, Master,' said Lal Taask.

'Shut up!' snapped Thome. 'She is a fool. She might have lived happily and enjoyed the fruits of The Father of Diamonds.'

Lal Taask shook his head. 'The ways of women are beyond the comprehension of even thou, Master. She was very young and very beautiful; she loved life; and you took it from her. I warned you, but you would not heed. Her blood is on your head.'

Atan Thome turned irritably away, but the drums followed him to his tent and world give him no rest.

*

'The drums!' said d'Arnot. 'I do not like them, so often they spell death for some poor devil. The first time I heard them, I was tied to a stake; and a lot of painted devils were dancing around me pricking me with shears. They don't quite kill you at first, they just torture you and let you live as long as possible so that you may suffer more, for your suffering is their pleasure.'

'But how did you escape?' asked Lavac.

'Tarzan came' said d'Arnot.

'He has not returned,' said Magra. 'I am afraid for him. Perhaps the drums are for him.'

'Do you suppose they could have got him?' asked Gregory.

'No such luck,' snarled Wolff. 'The damn monkey has as many lives as a cat.'

D'Arnot turned angrily away; and Gregory, Lavac, and Magra followed him, leaving Wolff alone, listening to the beating of the distant drums.

The drums had carried their message to Tarzan. They told him of impending torture and sacrifice and death. The lives of strangers meant nothing to the ape-man, who, all his life, had lived with death. It was something that came to all creatures. He had no fear of it, he who feared nothing. To avoid it was a game that added zest to life. To pit his courage, his strength, his agility, his cunning against Death, and win – there was the satisfaction. Someday Death would win, but to that day Tarzan gave no thought. He could fight or he could run away; and in either event preserve his self-respect, for only a fool throws his life away uselessly; and Tarzan had no respect for fools; but if the stake warranted it, he could lightly accept the gravest risks.

As he heard the drums against the new night, he thought less of their sinister portent than of the fact that they would guide him to a native village where, perhaps, he might obtain porters later. First, however, he must reconnoitre and investigate to learn the temper of the natives. If they were fierce and warlike, he must avoid their country, leading his little party around it; and the message of the drums suggested that this would be the case.

As the radio beam guides the flier, the drums of the Buiroos guided Tarzan as he swung through the trees toward their village. He moved swiftly, anticipating a sport he had enjoyed many times in the course of his savage existence – that of frustrating the Gomangani in the exercise of weird rites of torture and death. The drums told him that a victim was to die, but that death had not as yet been meted out. Who the victim was, was of no importance to the ape-man. All that mattered was the sport of cheating the torturers of the final accomplishment of their aims. Perhaps he would arrive in time, perhaps not. Also, if he did arrive in time, he might fail to accomplish his design. It was these factors that lent interest to the savage game that Tarzan loved to play.

*

As Tarzan neared the village of Mpingu, the chief, Atan Thome and Lal Taask sat smoking beside the fire that burned brightly in their camp as a discourager of predatory felines.

'Curse those drums!' snapped Lal Taask. 'They give me the creeps; they have my nerves on edge.'

'Tomorrow night we shall not hear them,' said Atan Thome, 'for then we shall be a long way on the trail to Ashair – to Ashair and The Father of Diamonds.'

'Wolff will have difficulty catching up with us,' said Lal Taask, 'and if we come back from Ashair by another route, he will never catch up with us.'

'You forget Magra,' said Thome.

'No,' replied Taask. 'I do not forget Magra. She will find her way to Paris as the homing pigeon finds its cote. We shall see her there.'

'You underestimate Wolff's cupidity,' said Thome. 'He will come through for his half of the diamond. Never fear.'

'And get this!' Lal Taask touched his knife.

'You are psychic,' laughed Thome.

'Those drums!' growled Lal Taask.

'Those drums!' exclaimed Magra. 'Did you ever hear anything so horribly insistent?'

'A radio fan's nightmare,' said Gregory. 'A boring broadcast that one can't dial out.'

'I am so worried about Tarzan,' said Magra, 'out there all alone in that awful forest.'

'I wouldn't worry too much about him,' d'Arnot reassured her. 'He has spent his life in awful forests, and has a way of taking care of himself.'

Wolff grunted. 'We don't need him nohow. I can take you to Ashair. We'd be well rid of the monkey-man.'

'I've heard about all of that that I care to, Wolff,' said d'Arnot.

'Tarzan is our only hope either of reaching Ashair or getting out of this country alive. You stick to your hunting job. Even at that you haven't been doing so well. Tarzan has brought in all the meat we've had so far.'

'Listen!' exclaimed Lavac. 'The drums! They've stopped!'

The howling pack circled the helpless girl. Now and then a spear point touched her lightly, and involuntarily her flesh recoiled. Later the torture might be more excruciating, or some maddened black, driven to frenzy by the excitement of the dance, might plunge his spear through her heart and with unintentional mercy deliver her from further suffering.

As Tarzan reached the edge of the clearing where lay the village of Mpingu, the chief, he dropped to the ground and ran swiftly toward the palisade. This side of the village was in darkness, and he knew that all the tribesmen would be gathered around the great fire that lighted the foliage of the trees that grew within the village. He would not be seen, and what slight noise he might make would be drowned by the throbbing of the drums.

With the agility of Sheeta, the panther, he scaled the palisade and dropped down into the shadow of the huts beyond; then he crept silently toward a great tree which overhung the hut of the chief and commanded a view of the main street of the village, where the fire burned and the dancers leaped and howled. Swinging up among the branches, he crossed to the other side of the tree and looked down upon the scene of savagery below. It was almost with a sense of shock that he recognised the victim at the stake. He saw the horde of armed warriors incited to frenzy by the drums, the dancing, the lust for human flesh. He fitted an arrow to his bow.

As one of the dancing savages, carried away by the excitement of the moment, paused before the girl and raised his short spear above his head to drive it through her heart a sudden hush fell upon the expectant assemblage; and Helen closed her eyes. The end had come! She breathed a silent prayer. The ominous hush was broken only by the increased madness of the drums; then came a scream of mortal agony.

The assurance of the blacks vanished, as an arrow, mysteriously sped, pierced the heart of the executioner. It was then that the drums stopped.

At the scream of the stricken warrior, Helen opened her eyes. A man lay dead at her feet, and consternation was written on the faces of the savage Buiroos. She saw one, braver than the rest, creeping toward her with a long knife ready in his hand; then a weird and uncanny cry rang out from somewhere above her, as Tarzan of the Apes rose to his full height; and, raising his face to Goro, the moon, voiced the hideous victory cry of the bull ape that had made a kill. Louder than the drums had been, it carried far out into the night.

'Yes,' said d'Arnot, 'the drums have stopped – they have probably made the kill. Some poor thing has found relief from torture.'

'Oh, what if it were Tarzan!' cried Magra; and as she spoke an eerie scream was wafted faintly across the still, African night.

'*Mon Dieu!*' exclaimed Lavac.

'It is Tarzan who has made a kill,' said d'Arnot.

'By the beard of the prophet!' exclaimed Lal Taask. 'What a hideous sound!'

'It is Africa, Lal Taask,' said Atan Thome, 'and that was the victory cry of a bull ape. I have heard it before, on the Congo.'

'It was far away,' said Lal Taask.

'Still, it was too close for comfort,' replied Atan Thome. 'We shall break camp very early in the morning.'

'But why should we fear apes?' demanded Lal Taask.

'It is not the apes I fear,' explained Atan Thome. 'I said that that noise was the victory cry of a bull ape, but I am not so sure. I have been talking with Mbuli. Perhaps the man we thought was Brian Gregory was not Brian Gregory at all. I asked Mbuli if he had ever heard of a white man called Tarzan. He said that he had; that some thought that he was a demon, and that all who did wrong, feared him. When he kills, Mbuli says, he gives the kill cry of the bull ape. If what we heard was not a bull ape, it was Tarzan; and that means that he is looking for us and is far too close for comfort.'

'I do not wish to see that man again,' said Lal Taask.

As the blood-curdling cry crashed the silence of the night, the warrior who had been creeping up on Helen straightened up and stepped back, frightened. The others, terror-stricken, shrank from the menace of the fearsome sound; then Tarzan spoke.

'The demon of the forest comes for the white Memsahib,' he said. 'Beware!' And as he spoke he dropped to the ground near the stake, trusting, by the very boldness of his move, to overawe the blacks for the few moments it would take to free Helen and escape; but he had reckoned without knowing of the courage of Chemungo, son of Mpingu, standing ready with his knife.

'Chemungo, son of Mpingu, is not afraid of the demon of the forest,' shouted the black, as he sprang forward with upraised knife; and as the last of Helen's bonds fell away, Tarzan slipped his own knife back into its sheath, and turned to meet the chief's son, the challenging 'Kree-e-gah!' on his lips. With bare hands he faced the infuriated black.

As Chemungo closed with upraised knife hand ready to strike, Tarzan seized him by the right wrist and at the belly and swung him above his head as lightly as though he had been a child. The knife dropped from Chemungo's hand as the steel muscles of the ape-man closed with vice like grip upon his wrist.

Helen Gregory, almost unable to believe her own senses, looked with astonishment upon this amazing man who dared face a whole cannibal village alone and could see no hope but that two lives instead of one must now be sacrificed. It was a brave, a glorious gesture that Tarzan had made; but how pathetically futile!

'Open the gates!' he commanded the astounded blacks. 'Or Chemungo, son of Mpingu, dies.'

The villagers hesitated. Some of the warriors grumbled. Would they obey, or would they charge?

IX

'Come!' said Tarzan to Helen, and without waiting for any reply from the blacks, he started toward the gate, still carrying Chemungo above his head; and Helen walked at his side.

Some of the warriors started to close upon them. It was a tense moment, fraught with danger. Then Mpingu spoke. 'Wait!' he commanded his warriors; and then to Tarzan, 'If I open the gates, will you set Chemungo free, unharmed?'

'When I have gone a spear-throw beyond the gates, I will free him,' replied the ape-man.

'How do I know that you will do that?' demanded Mpingu. 'How do I know that you will not take him into the forest and kill him?'

'You know only what I tell you, Gomangani,' replied Tarzan. 'I tell you that if you open the gates and let us go out in safety, I shall free him. If you do not open the gates, I shall kill him now.'

'Open the gates!' commanded Mpingu.

And so Tarzan and Helen passed in safety out of the village of the cannibals and into the black, African night; and beyond the gates Tarzan liberated Chemungo.

'How did you happen to fall into the hands of those blacks?' Tarzan asked Helen, as they set their faces toward the Gregory camp.

'I escaped from Atan Thome's camp last night and tried to make my way back to Bonga; but I got lost, and then they got me. There was a lion, too. He had me down, but they killed him. I have had a horrible time. I couldn't believe my eyes when I saw you. How in the world did you happen to be there?'

He told her of the events that had led up to his discovery of her in the cannibal village.

'It will be good to see Dad again,' she said. 'I can scarcely believe it even now. And Captain d'Arnot came, too – how wonderful.'

'Yes,' he said, 'he is with us, and Lavac, the pilot who flew us out of Loango, and Wolff, and Magra.'

She shook her head. 'I don't know about Magra,' she said. 'I can't understand her. She seemed very sorry for me in Loango after I was kidnapped, but she couldn't do anything for me. I think she was afraid of Atan Thome. Yet she is linked with him in some way. She is a very mysterious woman.'

'She will bear watching,' said Tarzan; 'both she and Wolff.'

The sun was an hour high as Magra came from her shelter and joined the others around the fire where Ogabi was grilling the remainder of the antelope. Her eyes were heavy, and she appeared unrested. They bade her good morning, but their faces suggested that it seemed anything but a good morning. She looked quicky about, as though searching for someone.

'Tarzan did not return?' she asked.

'No,' said Gregory.

'This suspense is unbearable,' she said. 'I scarcely closed my eyes all night, worrying about him.'

'And think of Monsieur Gregory and me, ma'moiselle,' d'Arnot reminded her. 'Not only have we to worry about Tarzan, but Helen – Miss Gregory – as well.' Gregory shot a quick glance at the Frenchman.

A few minutes later, the others walked away, leaving Magra and d'Arnot alone.

'You are very fond of Miss Gregory, are you not?' asked Magra.

'*Oui.*' admitted d'Arnot. 'Who would not be?'

'She is very nice,' agreed Magra. 'I wish that I might have helped her.'

'Helped her? What do you mean?'

'I can't explain; but, believe me, no matter what appearances may be or what you may all think of me, I have been helpless. I am bound by the oath of another – an oath I must in honour respect. I am not a free agent. I cannot always do as I wish.'

'I shall try to believe,' said d'Arnot, 'even though I do not understand.'

'Look!' cried Magra, suddenly. 'Here they are now – both of them! How can it be possible?'

D'Arnot looked up to see Tarzan and Helen approaching the camp; and, with Gregory, ran forward to meet them. Gregory's eyes filled with tears as he took Helen in his arms, and d'Arnot could not speak. Lavac joined them and was introduced to Helen, after which his eyes never left her when he could look at her unobserved. Only Wolff held back. Sullen and scowling, he remained seated where he had been.

The greetings over, Tarzan and Helen finished what was left of the antelope; and while they ate, Helen recounted her adventures.

'Thome shall pay for this.' said Gregory.

'He should die for it,' exclaimed d'Arnot.

'I should like to be the one to kill him,' muttered Lavac.

Day after day the little party trudged on through forests, across plains, over hills; but never did they strike a sign of Atan Thome's trail. Either Lavac or d'Arnot was constantly at the side of Helen Gregory in a growing rivalry of which only Helen seemed to be unaware, but then one cannot always know of just how much a woman is unaware. She laughed and joked or talked seriously with either of them impartially. D'Arnot was always affable and in high spirits, but Lavac was often moody. Tarzan hunted for the party, as Wolff seemed never to be able to find game. The latter occasionally went off by himself and studied the route map to Ashair. He was the guide.

Early one morning Tarzan told Gregory that he might be away from the safari all that day and possibly the next.

'But why?' asked the latter.

'I'll tell you when I get back,' replied the ape-man.

'Shall we wait here for you?'

'As you wish. I'll find you in any event.' Then he was gone at the swinging, easy trot with which he covered so much distance on foot.

'Where's Tarzan gone?' asked d'Arnot as he joined Gregory.

The older man shrugged. 'I don't know. He wouldn't tell me. Said he might be away a couple of days. I can't imagine why he went.'

Wolff joined them then. 'Where's the monkey-man gone now?' he asked. 'We've got enough meat for two days – all we can carry.'

Gregory told him all he knew, and Wolff sneered. 'He's ditching you,' he said. 'Anyone could see that. There's no reason for him goin' except that. You won't never see him again.'

D'Arnot, usually slow to anger, struck Wolff heavily across the cheek. 'I've heard all of that from you I intend to,' he said.

Wolff reached for his gun, but d'Arnot had him covered before he could draw. Gregory stepped between them.

'We can't have anything like this,' he said. 'We've enough troubles without fighting among ourselves.'

'I'm sorry, Monsieur Gregory,' said d'Arnot, holstering his weapon.

Wolff turned and walked away, muttering to himself.

'What had we better do, Captain?' asked Gregory. 'Wait here for Tarzan, or go on?'

'We might just as well go on,' said d'Arnot. 'We might just lose a day or two by staying here.'

'But if we go on, Tarzan might not be able to find us,' objected Gregory.

D'Arnot laughed. 'Even yet, you do not know Tarzan,' he said. 'You might as well fear to lose yourself on the main street of your native city as think that Tarzan could lose us in two days, anywhere in Africa.'

'Very well,' said Gregory, 'let's go on.'

As they moved on behind Wolff, Lavac was walking beside Helen.

'What a deadly experience this would be,' he said, 'if it were not for—'
He hesitated.

'Not for what?' asked the girl.

'You,' he said.

'Me? I don't understand what you mean.'

'That is because you've never been in love,' lie replied, huskily.

Helen laughed. 'Oh,' she cried, 'are you trying to tell me you're in love with me? It must be the altitude.'

'You laugh at my love?' he demanded.

'No,' she said, 'at you. Magra and I are the only women you have seen for weeks. You were bound to have fallen in love with one of us, being a Frenchman; and Magra is so obviously in love with Tarzan that it would have been a waste of time to have fallen in love with her. Please forget it.'

'I shall never forget it,' said Lavac, 'and I shall never give up. I am mad about you, Helen. Please give me something to hope for. I tell you I'm desperate. I won't be responsible for what I may do, if you don't tell me that there may be a little hope for me.'

'I'm sorry,' she said, seriously, 'but I just don't love you. If you are going to act like this, you will make everything even more disagreeable than it already is.'

'You are cruel,' grumbled Lavac; and for the rest of the day walked moodily alone, nursing his jealousy of d'Arnot.

And there was another who was imbued with thoughts of love that clamoured for expression. It was Wolff, and just to be charitable let us call the sentiment that moved him love. He had been leading the safari, but the game trail he was following was too plain to be missed; so he dropped back beside Magra.

'Listen, beautiful,' he said. 'I'm sorry for what I said the other day. I wouldn't hurt you for nothin'. I know we ain't always hit it off so good, but I'm for you. There ain't nothin' I wouldn't do for you. Why can't we be friends? We could go a long way, if we worked together.'

'Meaning what?' asked Magra.

'Meaning I got what it takes to make a woman happy – two strings on that big diamond and two thousand pounds of real money. Think what me and you could do in God's country with all that!'

'With *you!*' she sneered.

'Yes, with me. Ain't I good enough for you?' he demanded.

Magra looked at him, and laughed.

Wolff flushed. 'Look here,' he said, angrily, 'if you think you can treat me like dirt and get away with it, you're all wrong. I just been offerin' to marry you, but I ain't good enough. Well, let me tell you this – I always get what I go after. I'll get you; and I won't have to marry you, neither. You're stuck on that monkey-man; but he can't even see you, and anyway he hasn't got tuppence to rub together.'

'A guide belongs at the head of the safari,' said Magra. 'Goodbye.'

Late in the afternoon, Tarzan dropped from the branches of a tree into the midst of the trekking safari, if the six whites and Ogabi could be called a safari. The seven stopped and gathered around him.

'I'm glad you're back,' said Gregory. 'I'm always worried when you are away.'

'I went to look for Thome's trail,' said Tarzan, 'and I found it.'

'Good!' exclaimed Gregory.

'He's a long way ahead of us,' continued the ape-man, 'thanks to you, Wolff.'

'Anyone can make a mistake,' growled Wolff.

'You made no mistake,' snapped Tarzan. 'You have tried, deliberately, to lead us off the trail. We'd be better off without this man, Gregory. You should dismiss him.'

'You can't turn me out alone in this country,' said Wolff.

'You'd be surprised what Tarzan can do,' remarked d'Arnot.

'I think it would be a little too drastic,' said Gregory.

Tarzan shrugged. 'Very well,' he said, 'as you will; but we'll dispense with his services as guide from now on.'

X

Atan Thome and Lal Taask stood at the head of their safari, which had just emerged from a dense forest. At their right ran a quiet river; and before them stretched rough, open country. In the distance, visible above low hills, rose the summit of what appeared to be a huge extinct volcano.

'Look, Lal Taask!' exclaimed Thome. 'It is Tuen-Baka. Inside its crater lies Ashair, The Forbidden City.'

'And The Father of Diamonds, Master,' added Lal Taask.

'Yes, The Father of Diamonds. I wish that Magra were here to see. I wonder where they are? Wolff must be on his way here with her by now. Perhaps we shall meet them when we come out; they could scarcely have overtaken us – we have moved too swiftly.'

'If we do not meet them, there will be fewer with whom to divide,' suggested Lal Taask.

'I promised her mother,' said Thome.

'That was a long time ago; and her mother is dead, and Magra never knew of the promise.'

'The memory of her mother never dies,' said Thome. 'You have been a faithful servitor, Lal Taask. Perhaps I should tell you the story; then you will understand.'

'Your servant listens.'

'Magra's mother was the only woman I ever loved. The inexorable laws of caste rendered her unobtainable by me. I am a mongrel. She was the daughter of a maharaja. I was trusted in the service of her father; and when the princess married an Englishman, I was sent to England with her in her entourage. While her husband was hunting big game in Africa, he stumbled upon Ashair. For three years he was a prisoner there, undergoing cruelties and torture. At last he managed to escape, and returned home only to die as a result of his experiences. But he brought the story of The Father of Diamonds, and exacted from his wife a promise that she would organise an expedition to return to Ashair and punish those who had treated him so cruelly. The Father of Diamonds was to be the incentive to obtain volunteers; but the map he made became lost, and nothing was ever done. Then the princess died, leaving Magra, who was then ten years old, in my care; for the old maharaja was dead, and his successor would have nothing to do with the daughter of the Englishman. I have always had it in my mind to look for Ashair, and two years ago I made the first attempt. It was then that I learned that Brian Gregory was on a similar quest. He reached Ashair and made a map, though he never actually entered the city. On his second venture, I followed him, but got lost. I met the remnants of his safari coming out. He had disappeared. They refused to give me the map; so I swore to obtain it, and here I am with the map.'

'How did you know he made a map?' asked Lal Taask.

'Our safaris met for one night, after his first trip in. I just happened to see him making the map. It is the one I have, or, rather, a copy of it that he sent home in a letter.

'Because Magra's father died because of The Father of Diamonds, a share of it belongs to her; and there is another reason. I am not yet an old man. I see in Magra the reincarnation of the woman I loved. Do you understand, Lal Taask?'

'Yes, Master.'

Atan Thome sighed. 'Perhaps I dream foolish dreams. We shall see, but now we must move on. Come, Mbuli, get the boys going!'

The blacks had been whispering among themselves while Thome and Taask talked, now Mbuli came to Atan Thome.

'My people will go no farther, Bwana,' he said.

'What!' exclaimed Thome. 'You must be crazy. I hired you to go to Ashair.'

'In Bonga, Ashair was a long way off; and the spirits of my people were brave. Now Bonga is a long way off and Ashair is near. Now they remember that Tuen-Baka is taboo, and they are afraid.'

'You are headman,' snapped Thome. 'You make them come.'

'No can do,' insisted Mbuli.

'We'll camp here by the river tonight,' said Thome. 'I'll talk with them. They may feel braver tomorrow. They certainly can't quit on me now.'

'Very well, Bwana; tomorrow they may feel braver. It would be well to camp here tonight.'

Atan Thome and Lal Taask slept well that night, lulled by the soothing murmuring of the river; and Atan Thome dreamed of The Father of Diamonds and Magra. Lal Taask thought that he dreamed when the silence of the night was broken by a sepulchral voice speaking in a strange tongue, but it was no dream.

The sun was high when Atan Thome awoke. He called his boy, but there was no response; then he called again, loudly, peremptorily. He listened. The camp was strangely silent. Rising, he went to the front of the tent and parted the flaps. Except for his tent and Lal Taask's, the camp was deserted. He crossed to Taask's tent and awakened him.

'What is the matter, Master?' asked Lal Taask.

'The dogs have deserted us,' exclaimed Thome.

Taask leaped to his feet and came out of his tent. 'By Allah! They have taken all our provisions and equipment with them. They have left us to die. We must hurry after them. They can't be very far away.'

'We shall do nothing of the sort,' said Thome. 'We're going on!' There was a strange light in his eyes that Lal Taask had never seen there before. 'Do you think I have gone through what I have gone through to turn back now because a few cowardly natives are afraid?'

'But, Master, we cannot go on alone, just we two,' begged Lal Taask.

'Silence!' commanded Thome. 'We go on to Ashair – to the Forbidden City and The Father of Diamonds. The Father of Diamonds!' He broke into wild laughter. 'Magra shall wear the finest diamonds in the world. We shall be rich, rich beyond the wildest dreams of avarice – she and I – the richest people in the world! I, Atan Thome, the mongrel, shall put the maharajas of India to shame. I shall strew the streets of Paris with gold. I—' He stopped suddenly and pressed a palm to his forehead. 'Come!' he said presently in his normal tone. 'We'll follow the river up to Ashair.'

In silence, Lal Taask followed his Master along a narrow trail that paralleled the river. The ground was rough and broken by gullies and ravines, the trail was faint across rocky, barren ground. Near noon they reached the mouth of a narrow gorge with precipitous cliffs on either side, cliffs that towered high above them, dwarfing the two men to Lilliputian proportions. Through the gorge flowed the river, placidly.

'Siva! What a place!' exclaimed Lal Taask. 'We can go no farther.'

'It is the trail to Ashair,' said Thome, pointing. 'See it winding along the face of the cliff?'

'That a trail!' exclaimed Taask. 'It is only a scratch that a mountain goat couldn't find footing on!'

'Nevertheless, it is the trail that we follow,' said Thome.

'Master, it is madness!' cried Lal Taask. 'Let us turn back. All the diamonds in the world are not worth the risk. Before we have gone a hundred yards we shall have fallen into the river and drowned.'

'Shut up,' snapped Thome, 'and follow me!'

Clinging precariously to a narrow footpath scratched in the face of the towering cliff, the two men inched their way along the rocky wall. Below them flowed the silent river that rose somewhere in the mystery that lay ahead. A single misstep would cast them into it. Lal Taask dared not look down. Facing the wall, with arms outspread, searching for handholds that were not there, trembling so that he feared his knees would give beneath him and hurl him to death, he followed his Master, sweat gushing from every pore.

'We'll never make it,' he panted.

'Shut up and come along!' snapped Thome. 'If I fall, you may turn back.'

'Oh, Master, I couldn't even do that. No one could turn around on this hideous trail.'

'Then keep coming and quit making such a fuss. You make me nervous.'

'And to think you take such risks for a diamond! If it were as big as a house and I had it now, I'd give it to be back in Lahore.'

'You are a coward, Lal Taask,' snapped Thome.

'I am, Master; but it is better to be a live coward than a dead fool.'

For two hours the men moved slowly along the narrow footpath until both were on the verge of exhaustion, and even Thome was beginning to regret his temerity; then, as he turned a jutting shoulder in the cliff, he saw a little wooded canyon that broke the face of the mighty escarpment and ran gently down to the river. Down into this canyon the trail led. When they reached it, they threw themselves upon the ground in total exhaustion; and lay there until almost dark.

Finally they aroused themselves and built a fire, for with the coming of night a chill settled upon the canyon. All day they had been without food; and they were famished, but there was nothing for them to eat, and they had to content themselves by filling their bellies with water at the river. For warmth, they huddled close to their little fire.

'Master, this is an evil place,' said Lal Taask. 'I have a feeling that we are being watched.'

'It is the evil within you speaking, fool,' growled Thome.

'Allah! Master, look!' faltered Taask. 'What is it?' He pointed into the blackness among the trees; and then a sepulchral voice spoke in a strange tongue, and Lal Taask fainted.

XI

Ungo, the King ape, was hunting with his tribe. They were nervous and irritable, for it was the period of the Dum-Dum; and as yet they had found no victim for the sacrificial dance. Suddenly, the shaggy King raised his head and sniffed the air. He growled his disapproval of the evidence that Usha, the wind, brought to his nostrils. The other apes looked at him questioningly.

'Gomangani, Tarmangani,' he said. 'They come.' Then he led his people into the underbrush and hid close to the trail.

The little band of men and women who formed the Gregory 'safari' followed the plain trail left by Atan Thome's safari, while Tarzan hunted for meat far afield.

'Tarzan must have had difficulty in locating game,' said d'Arnot.

'I haven't heard his kill-call yet.'

'He's marvellous,' said Magra. 'We'd have starved to death if it hadn't been for him – even with a *hunter* along.'

'Well, you can't shoot game where there ain't none,' growled Wolff.

'Tarzan never comes back empty-handed,' said Magra; 'and he hasn't any gun, either.'

'The other monkeys find food, too,' sneered Wolff; 'but who wants to be a monkey?'

Ungo was watching them now, as they came in sight along the trail. His close-set, bloodshot eyes blazed with anger; and then suddenly and without warning he charged, and his whole tribe followed him. The little band fell back in dismay. D'Arnot whipped out his pistol and fired, and an ape fell, screaming; then the others were among them, and he could not fire again without endangering his companions. Wolff ran. Lavac and Gregory were both knocked down and bitten. For a few moments all was confusion, so that afterwards no one could recall just what happened. The apes were among them and gone again; and when they went, Ungo carried Magra off under one great hairy arm.

Magra struggled to escape until she was exhausted, but the powerful beast that carried her paid little attention to her struggles. Once, annoyed, he cuffed her, almost knocking her insensible; then she ceased, waiting and hoping for some opportunity to escape. She wondered to what awful fate she was being dragged. So manlike was the huge creature, she shuddered as she contemplated what might befall her.

Half carrying her, half dragging her through the woods, with his huge fellows lumbering behind, Ungo, the King ape, bore the girl to a small, natural clearing, a primitive arena where, from time immemorial, the great apes had held their sacrificial dance. There he threw her roughly to the ground, and two shes squatted beside her to see that she did not escape.

Back on the trail, the little party of whites, overwhelmed by the tragedy of this misadventure, stood debating what they had best do.

'We could follow them,' said d'Arnot; 'but we haven't a chance of overtaking them, and if we did, what could we do against them, even though we are armed?'

'But we can't just stand here and do nothing,' cried Helen.

'I'll tell you,' said d'Arnot. 'I'll take Wolff's rifle and follow them. I may be able to pick off enough of them to frighten the others away if I come up with them after they halt; then, when Tarzan returns, send him after me.'

'Here's Tarzan now,' said Helen, as the ape-man came trotting along the trail with the carcass of his kill across his shoulder.

Tarzan found a very disorganised party as he joined them. They were all excited and trying to talk at the same time.

'We never saw them 'til they jumped us,' said Lavac.

'They were as big as gorillas,' added Helen.

'They were gorillas,' put in Wolff.

'They were not gorillas,' contradicted d'Arnot; 'and, anyway, you didn't wait to see what they were.'

'The biggest one carried off Magra under his arm,' said Gregory.

'They took Magra?' Tarzan looked concerned. 'Why didn't you say so in the first place? Which way did they go?'

D'Arnot pointed in the direction the apes had made off.

'Keep on this trail until you find a good place to camp,' said Tarzan, then he was gone.

As the moon rose slowly over the arena where Magra lay beside a primitive earthen drum upon which three old apes beat with sticks, several of the great shaggy bulls commenced to dance around her. Menacing her with heavy sticks, the bulls leaped and whirled as they circled the frightened girl. Magra had no knowledge of the significance of these rites. She only guessed that she was to die.

The Lord of the Jungle followed the trail of the great apes through the darkness of the forest as unerringly as though he were following a well-marked spoor by daylight, followed it by the scent of the anthropoids, that clung to the grasses and the foliage of the underbrush, tainting the air with the effluvia of the great bodies. He knew that he would come upon them eventually, but would he be in time?

As the moon rose, the throbbing of the earthen drum directed him toward the arena of the Dum-Dum; so that he could take to the trees and move more swiftly in a direct line. It told him, too, the nature of the danger that threatened Magra. He knew that she still lived, for the drum would be stilled only after her death, when the apes would be fighting over her body and tearing it to pieces. He knew, because he had leaped and danced in the moonlight at many a Dum-Dum when Sheeta, the panther, or Wappi, the antelope, was the sacrificial victim.

The moon was almost at zenith as he neared the arena. When it hung at zenith would be the moment of the kill; and in the arena, the shaggy bulls danced in simulation of the hunt. Magra lay as they had thrown her, exhausted, hopeless, resigned to death, knowing that nothing could save her now.

Goro, the moon, hung upon the verge of the fateful moment, when a Tarmangani, naked but for a G string, dropped from an overhanging tree into the arena. With growls and mutterings of rage, the bulls turned upon the intruder who dared thus sacrilegiously to invade the sanctity of their holy of holies. The King ape, crouching, led them.

'I am Ungo,' he said. 'I kill!'

Tarzan, too, crouched and growled as he advanced to meet the King ape. 'I am Tarzan of the Apes,' he said in the language of the first-men, the only language he had known for the first twenty years of his life. 'I am Tarzan of the Apes, mighty hunter, mighty fighter. I kill!'

One word of the ape-man's challenge Magra had understood – 'Tarzan.' Astounded, she opened her eyes to see the King ape and Tarzan circling one another, each looking for an opening. What a brave but what a futile gesture the man was making in her defence! He was giving his life for her, and uselessly. What chance had he against the huge, primordial beast?

Suddenly, Tarzan reached out and seized the ape's wrist; then, turning quickly, he hurled the great creature over his shoulder heavily to the ground; but instantly Ungo was on his feet again. Growling and roaring horribly, he charged. This time he would overwhelm the puny man-thing with his great weight, crush him in those mighty arms.

Magra trembled for the man, and she blanched as she saw him meet the charge with growls equally as bestial as those of the ape. Could this growling, snarling beast be the quiet, resourceful man she had come to love? Was he, after all, but a primitive Dr Jekyll and Mr Hyde? Spellbound and horrified, she watched.

Swift as Ara, the lightning, is Tarzan; as agile as Sheeta, the panther. Dodging, and ducking beneath Ungo's great flailing arms, he leaped upon the hairy back and locked a full nelson on the raging ape. As he applied the pressure of his mighty thews, the ape screamed in agony.

'Kreeg-ah!' shouted Tarzan, bearing down a little harder. 'Surrender!'

The members of the Gregory party sat around their campfire listening to the throbbing of the distant drum and waiting in nervous expectancy, for what, they did not know.

'It is the Dum-Dum of the great apes, I think,' said d'Arnot. 'Tarzan has told me about them. When the full moon hangs at zenith, the bull kills a victim. It is, perhaps, a rite older than the human race, the tiny germ from which all religious observances have sprung.'

'And Tarzan has seen this rite performed?' asked Helen.

'He was raised by the great apes,' explained d'Arnot, 'and he has danced the dance of death in many a Dum-Dum.'

'He has helped to kill men and women and tear them to pieces?' demanded Helen.

'No, no!' cried d'Arnot. 'The apes rarely secure a human victim. They did so only once while Tarzan ranged with them, and he saved that one. The victim they prefer is their greatest enemy, the panther.'

'And you think the drums are for Magra?' asked Lavac.

'Yes,' said d'Arnot, 'I fear so.'

'I wish I'd gone after her myself,' said Wolff. 'That guy didn't have no gun.'

'He may not have had a gun,' said d'Arnot, 'but at least he went in the right direction.' Wolff lapsed into moody silence. 'We all had a chance to do something when the ape first took her,' continued d'Arnot; 'but, frankly, I was too stunned to think.'

'It all happened so quickly,' said Gregory. 'It was over before I really knew what *had* happened.'

'Listen!' exclaimed d'Arnot. 'The drums have stopped!' He looked up at the moon. 'The moon is at zenith,' he said. 'Tarzan must have been too late.'

'Them gorillas would pull him apart,' said Wolff. 'If it wasn't for Magra, I'd say good riddance.'

'Shut up!' snapped Gregory. 'Without Tarzan, we're lost.'

As they talked, Tarzan and Ungo battled in the arena; and Magra watched in fearful astonishment. She could scarcely believe her eyes as she saw the great ape helpless in the hands of the man. Ungo was screaming in pain. Slowly, relentlessly, his neck was being broken. At last he could stand it no longer, and bellowed, 'Kreeg-ah!' which means 'I surrender'; and Tarzan released him and sprang to his feet.

'Tarzan is King!' he cried, facing the other bulls.

He stood there, waiting; but no young bull came forward to dispute the right of Kingship with him. They had seen what he had done to Ungo, and they were afraid. Thus, by grace of a custom ages old, Tarzan became King of the tribe.

Magra did not understand. She was still terrified. Springing to her feet, she ran to Tarzan and threw her arms about him, pressing close. 'I am afraid,' she said. 'Now they will kill us both.'

Tarzan shook his head. 'No,' he said, 'they will not kill us. They will do whatever I tell them to do, for now I am their King.'

XII

In the light of early morning, after a night of terror, Atan Thome and Lal Taask started to retrace their steps along the precarious pathway they had so laboriously risked the day before.

'I am glad, Master, that you decided to turn back,' said Lal Taask.

'Without porters and askaris, it would be madness to attempt to force our way into The Forbidden City,' growled Thome. 'We'll return to Bonga and enlist a strong force of men who fear no taboos.'

'If we live to get to Bonga,' said Lal Taask.

'Cowards invite death,' snapped Thome.

'After last night who would not be a coward in this damnable country?' demanded Taask. 'You saw it, didn't you? You heard that voice?'

'Yes,' admitted Thome.

'What was it?'

'I don't know.'

'It was evil,' said Taask. 'It breathed of the grave and of Hell. Men cannot prevail against the forces of another world.'

'Rot!' ejaculated Thome. 'It has some rational and mundane explanation, if we only knew.'

'But we don't know. I do not care to know. I shall never return here, if Allah permits me to escape alive.'

'Then you will get no share of the diamond,' threatened Atan Thome.

'I shall be content with my life,' replied Lal Taask.

At last the two men succeeded in negotiating the return trip in safety, and stood again upon level ground near the mouth of the gorge. Lal Taask breathed a sigh of relief, and his spirits rose; but Atan Thome was moody and irritable. He had built his hopes so high that to be turned back at what he believed to be the threshold of success plunged him into despondency. With bowed head, he led the way back over the rough terrain toward their last camp at the edge of the forest.

As they were passing through one of the numerous ravines, they were suddenly confronted by a dozen white warriors who leaped from behind great lava boulders and barred their way. They were stalwart men, wearing white plumes and short tunics on the breasts and backs of which were woven a conventionalised bird. They were armed with spears and knives which hung in scabbards at their hips.

The leader spoke to Thome in a strange tongue; but when he discovered that neither could understand the other, he gave an order to his men who herded Thome and Taask down the ravine to the river, where lay such a craft as may have floated on the Nile in the days of the Pharaohs. It was an open galley, manned by twenty slaves chained to the thwarts.

At the points of spears, Thome and Taask were herded aboard; and when the last of the warriors had stepped across the gunwale, the boat put off and started up stream.

Atan Thome broke into laughter; and Lal Taask looked at him in surprise, as did the warriors near him.

'Why do you laugh, Master?' asked Lal Taask, fearfully.

'I laugh,' cried Thome, 'because after all I shall reach The Forbidden City.'

As Helen came from her shelter early in the morning, she saw d'Arnot sitting beside the embers of the dying beast fire; and she joined him.

'Sentry duty?' she asked.

He nodded. 'Yes,' be said, 'I have been doing sentry duty and a lot of thinking.'

'About what, for instance?' she asked.

'About you – us; and what we are going to do,' he replied.

'I talked with father last night, just before I went to bed,' she said, 'and he has decided to return to Bonga and organise a safari. He doesn't dare go on without Tarzan.'

'He is wise,' said d'Arnot. 'Your life is too precious to risk further.' He hesitated, embarrassed. 'You don't know what it means to *me*, Helen. I knew that this is no time to speak of love; but you must have seen – haven't you?'

'*Et tu Brute!*' exclaimed the girl.

'What do you mean?' he demanded.

'Lieutenant Lavac also thinks that he is in love with me. Can't you see, Paul, that it is just because I am practically the only girl available – poor Magra was so much in love with Tarzan.'

'That is not true with me,' he said. 'I do not believe it is the explanation as far as Lavac is concerned. He is a fine fellow. I can't blame him for falling in love with you. No, Helen, I'm quite sure of myself. You see, I have taken to losing my appetite and looking at the moon.' He laughed. 'Those are certain symptoms, you know. Pretty soon I shall take to writing poetry.'

'You're a dear,' she said. 'I'm glad you have a sense of humour. I'm afraid the poor lieutenant hasn't, but then maybe he hasn't had as much experience as you.'

'There should be an S.P.C.L.,' he said.

'What's that?'

'Society for the Prevention of Cruelty to Lovers.'

'Idiot. Wait until you get back where there are lots of girls, then—' She stopped as she glanced across his shoulder. Her face went white, and her eyes were wide in terror.

'Helen! What is it?' he demanded.

'Oh, Paul – the apes have come back!'

D'Arnot turned to see the great beasts lumbering along the trail; then he shouted for Gregory and Lavac. 'Name of a name!' he cried an instant later. 'Tarzan and Magra are with them!'

'They are prisoners!' exclaimed Helen.

'Non,' said d'Arnot. 'Tarzan is leading the apes! Was there ever such a man?'

'I'm faint with relief,' said Helen. 'I never expected to see them again. I'd given them up for lost, especially Magra. It is like seeing a ghost. Why, we even knew the minute that she died last night – when the drumming stopped.'

Tarzan and Magra were greeted enthusiastically, and Magra had to tell her story of adventure and rescue. 'I know it seems incredible,' she added, 'but here we are, and here are the apes. If you don't believe me, ask them.'

'What are them beggars hangin' 'round for?' demanded Wolff. 'We ought to give 'em a few rounds for luck. They got it comin' to 'em for stealin' Magra.'

'They are my people,' said Tarzan. 'They are obeying orders. You shall not harm them.'

'They may be your people,' grumbled Wolff, 'but they ain't mine, me not bein' no monkey.'

'They are going along with us,' said Tarzan to Gregory. 'If you'll all keep away from them and not touch them, they won't harm you; and they may be helpful to us in many ways. You see, this species of anthropoid ape is highly intelligent. They have developed at least the rudiments of cooperation, the lack of which among the lower orders has permitted man to reign supreme over other animals which might easily have exterminated him. They are ferocious fighters when aroused; and, most important of all, they will obey me. They will be a protection against both beasts and men. I'll send them away now to hunt in the vicinity; but when I call, they'll come.'

'Why, he talks to them!' exclaimed Helen, as Tarzan walked over and spoke to Ungo.

'Of course he does,' said d'Arnot. 'Their language was the first he ever learned.'

'You should have seen him fight with that great bull,' said Magra. 'I was almost afraid of him afterwards.'

That night, after they had made camp, Lavac came and sat on a log beside Helen. 'There is a full moon,' he said.

'Yes,' she replied. 'I'd noticed it. I shall never see a full moon again without hearing the throbbing of that awful drum and thinking of what Magra went through.'

'It should bring happier thoughts to you,' he said, 'as it does to me – thoughts of love. The full moon is for love.'

'It is also for lunacy,' she suggested.

'I wish you could love me,' he said. 'Why don't you? Is it because of d'Arnot? Be careful with him. He is notorious for his conquests.'

The girl was disgusted. How different this from d'Arnot's praise of his rival. 'Please don't speak of it again,' she said. 'I don't love you, and that's that.' Then she got up and walked away, joining d'Arnot near the fire. Lavac remained where he was, brooding and furious.

Lavac was not the only member of the party to whom the full moon suggested love. It found Wolff receptive, also. His colossal egotism did not permit him to doubt that eventually he would break down Magra's resistance, and that she would fall into his arms. Being an egotist, he always seized upon the wrong thing to say to her, as he did when he caught her alone that evening.

'What do you see in that damn monkey-man?' was his opening sally in the game of love. 'He ain't got nothin' but a G string to his name. Look at me! I got two thousand pounds and a half interest in the biggest diamond in the world.'

'I am looking at you,' replied Magra. 'Perhaps that's one of the reasons I don't like you. You know, Wolff, there must be a lot of different words to describe a person like you; but I don't know any of them that are bad enough to fit you. I wouldn't have you if you owned the father and mother of diamonds, both, and were the last man on earth into the bargain. Now, don't ever mention this subject to me again, or I'll tell the "monkey-man" on you; and he'll probably break you in two and forget to put you back together again. You know, he isn't in love with you either.'

'You think you're too good for me, do you?' growled Wolff. 'Well, I'll show you. I'll get you; and I'll get your dirty monkey-man, too.'

'Don't let him see you doing it,' laughed Magra.

'I ain't afraid of him,' boasted Wolff.

'Say, you wouldn't even dare stab Tarzan in the back. You know, I saw you running away when that ape grabbed me. No, Wolff, you don't scare me worth a cent. Everybody in this camp has your number, and I know just what sort of a yellow double-crosser you are.'

XIII

As the barge in which Thome and Taask were prisoners was being rowed upriver, the former heard one of the warriors speak to a black galley-slave in Swahili.

'Why did you take us prisoners?' he asked the warrior in command, speaking in Swahili; 'And what are you going to do with us?'

'I took you prisoners because you were too near The Forbidden City,' replied the warrior. 'No one may approach Ashair and return to the outer world. I am taking you there now. What will become of you rests in the hands of Queen Atka, but you may rest assured that you will never leave Ashair.'

Just ahead of the galley, Thome saw the mighty wall of Tuen-Baka rising high into the blue African sky; and from a great, black opening in the wall the river flowed. Into this mighty, natural tunnel the galley was steered. A torch was lighted and held in the bow, as the craft was rowed into the Stygian darkness ahead; but at last it emerged into the sunlight and on to the bosom of a lake that lay at the bottom of the great crater of Tuen-Baka.

Ahead and to the left, Thome saw the domes of a small, walled city. To right and left, beyond the lake, were forest and plain; and in the far distance, at the upper end of the lake, another city was dimly visible.

'Which is Ashair?' he asked a warrior.

The man jerked a thumb in the direction of the nearer city at the left. 'There is Ashair,' he said. 'Take a good look at it, for unless Atka sentences you to the galleys, you'll never see the outside of it again.'

'And the other city?' asked Thome. 'What is that?'

'That's Thobos,' replied the man. 'If you happen to be sentenced to a war galley, you may see more of Thobos, when we go there to fight.'

As the galley approached Ashair, Atan Thome turned to Lal Taask, who sat beside him in the stern. Thome had been looking at the city, but Lal Taask had been gazing down into the clear depths of the lake.

'Look!' exclaimed Thome. 'My dream come true! There is The Forbidden City; there, somewhere, lies The Father of Diamonds. I am coming closer and closer to it. It is Fate! I know now that it is written that I shall possess it.'

Lal Taask shook his head. 'These warriors have sharp spears,' he said.

'There are probably more warriors in Ashair. I do not think they will let you take The Father of Diamonds away with you. I even heard one say that we should never leave, ourselves. Do not get your hopes too high. Look down into this lake instead. The water is so clear, you can see the bottom. I have seen many fish and strange creatures such as I have never seen before. It is far more interesting than the city, and it may be the only time we shall ever look at it. By the beard of the prophet, Atan Thome! Look! There is a marvel, indeed, Master.'

Thome looked over the side of the galley; and the sight that met his eyes wrung an exclamation of surprise and incredulity from him, for, clearly discernible it the bottom of the lake there was a splendid temple. He could see lights shining from its windows, and as he watched it, spellbound, he saw a grotesque, manlike figure emerge from it and walk on the bottom of the lake. The creature carried a trident, but what it was doing and where it was going Atan Thome was doomed not to discover, for the rapidly propelled barge passed over the creature and the temple; and they were lost to view, as the craft approached the quay of The Forbidden City.

'Come!' commanded the warrior in charge of the party, and Thome and Taask were herded off the galley on to the quay. They entered the city through a small gateway, and were led through narrow, winding streets to a large building near the centre of the city. Armed warriors stood before the gate of the walled building, who, after a brief parley, admitted the captives and their guard; then Atan Thome and Lal Taask were escorted into the building and into the presence of an official, who listened to the report of their captors and then spoke to them in Swahili.

The man listened to Thome's explanation of their presence near Ashair; then he shrugged. 'You may be telling the truth, or you may be lying,' he said. 'Probably you are lying, but it makes no difference. Ashair is a forbidden city. No stranger who enters Tuen-Baka may leave alive. What becomes of him here – whether he be destroyed immediately or permitted to live for whatever useful purpose he may serve – rests wholly with the discretion of the Queen. Your capture will be reported to her; when it suits her convenience, your fate will be decided.'

'If I might have audience with her,' said Thome, 'I am sure that I can convince her that my motives are honourable and that I can give Ashair valuable service. I have information of the greatest importance to her and to Ashair.'

'You may tell me,' said the official. 'I will communicate the information to her.'

'I must give it to the Queen in person,' replied Atan Thome.

'The Queen of Ashair is not in the habit of granting audiences to prisoners,' said the man, haughtily. 'It will be well for you if you give this information to me – if you have any.'

Atan Thome shrugged. 'I have it,' he said, 'but I shall give it to no one but the Queen. If disaster befalls Ashair, the responsibility will rest with you. Don't say that I didn't warn you.'

'Enough of this impudence!' exclaimed the official. 'Take them away and lock them up – and don't overfeed them.'

'Master, you should not have antagonised him,' said Lal Taask, as the two men lay on cold stone, chained to the wall of a gloomy dungeon. 'If you had information to impart to the Queen – and Allah alone knows what it might be – why did you not tell the man what it was? Thus it would have reached the Queen.'

'You are a good servant, Lal Taask,' said Thome, 'and you wield a knife with rare finesse. These are accomplishments worthy of highest encomiums, but you lack versatility. It is evident that Allah felt he had given you sufficient gifts when he gave you these powers; so he gave you nothing with which to think.'

'My Master is all-wise,' replied Lal Taask. 'I pray that he may think me out of this dungeon.'

'That's what I am trying to do. Don't you realise that it would be useless to appeal to underlings? This Queen is all-powerful. If we can reach her, personally, we place our case directly before the highest tribunal; and I can plead our case much better than it could be pleaded second-hand by one who had no interest in us.'

'Again I bow to your superior wisdom,' said Lal Taask, 'but I am still wondering what important information you have to give the Queen of Ashair.'

'Lal Taask, you are hopeless,' sighed Thome. 'The information I have to give to the Queen should be as obvious to you as a fly on the end of your nose.'

For days, Atan Thome and Lal Taask lay on the cold stone of their dungeon floor, receiving just enough food to keep them alive; and having all Atan Thome's pleas for an audience with the Queen ignored by the silent warrior who brought their food.

'They are starving us to death,' wailed Lal Taask.

'On the contrary,' observed Atan Thome, 'they appear to have an uncanny sense of the calorific properties of food. They know just how much will *keep* us from starving to death. And look at my waistline, Lal Taask! I have often had it in mind to embark upon a rigid diet for the purpose of reducing. The kind Ashairians have anticipated that ambition. Presently, I shall be almost sylph-like.'

'For you, perhaps, that may be excellent, Master; but for me, who never had an ounce of surplus fat beneath his hide, it spells disaster. Already, my backbone is chafing my navel.'

'Ah!' exclaimed Atan Thome, as footfalls announced the approach of someone along the corridor leading to their cell. 'Here comes Old Garrulity again!'

'I did not know that you knew his name, Master,' remarked Taask, 'but someone accompanies him this time – I hear voices.'

'Perhaps he brings an extra calory, and needs help,' suggested Thome. 'If he does, it is yours. I hope it is celery.'

'You like celery, Master?'

'No. It shall be all for you. Celery is reputed to be a brain food.'

The door to the cell was unlocked, and three warriors entered. One of them removed the chains from the prisoners' ankles.

'What now?' asked Atan Thome.

'The Queen has sent for you,' replied the warrior.

The two men were led through the palace to a great room, at the far end of which, upon a dais, a woman sat upon a throne hewn from a single block of lava. Warriors flanked her on either side, and slaves stood behind her throne ready to do her every bidding.

As the two men were led forward and halted before the dais, they saw a handsome woman, apparently in her early thirties. Her hair was so dressed that it stood out straight from her head in all directions to a length of eight or ten inches and had woven into it an ornate headdress of white plumes. Her mien was haughty and arrogant as she eyed the prisoners coldly, and Atan Thome read cruelty in the lines of her mouth and the latent fires of a quick temper in the glint of her eyes. Here was a woman to be feared, a ruthless killer, a human tigress. The equanimity of the smug Eurasian faltered before a woman for the first time.

'Why came you to Ashair?' demanded the Queen.

'By accident, majesty; we were lost. When we found our way blocked, we turned back. We were leaving the country when your warriors took us prisoners.'

'You have said that you have valuable information to give me. What is it? If you have imposed upon me and wasted my time, it shall not be well for you.'

'I have powerful enemies.' said Atan Thome. 'It was while trying to escape from them that I became lost. They are coming to Ashair to attempt to steal a great diamond which they believe you to possess. I only wished to befriend you and help you trap them.'

'Are they coming in force?' asked Atka.

'That I do not know,' replied Thome. 'But I presume they are. They have ample means.'

Queen Atka turned to one of her nobles. 'If this man has spoken the truth, he shall not fare ill at our hands. Akamen, I place the prisoners in your charge. Permit them reasonable liberties. Take them away.' Then she spoke to another. 'See that the approaches to Ashair are watched.'

Akamen, the noble, conducted Atan Thome and Lal Taask to peasant quarters in a far wing of the palace. 'You are free to go where you will inside the palace walls, except to the royal wing. Nor may you go beneath the palace. There lie the secrets of Ashair and death for strangers.'

'The Queen has been most magnanimous,' said Thome. 'We shall do nothing to forfeit her good will. Ashair is most interesting. I am only sorry that we may not go out into the city or upon the lake.'

'It would not be safe,' said Akamen. 'You might be captured by a galley from Thobos. They would not treat you as well as Atka has.'

'I should like to look down again at the beautiful building at the bottom of the lake,' said Thome. 'That was my reason for wishing to go upon the lake. What is the building? And what the strange creature I saw coming from it?'

'Curiosity is often a fatal poison,' said Akamen.

XIV

The trail of Atan Thome's safari was not difficult to follow, and the Gregory party made good time along it without encountering any obstacles to delay them. The general mistrust of Wolff, the doubts concerning Magra's position among them, and the moody jealousy of Lavac, added to the nervous strain of their dangerous existence, and the hardships they had undergone had told upon their nerves, so that it was not always a happy company that trudged the days' long trails. Only Tarzan remained serene and unruffled.

It was midday, and they had halted for a brief rest, when Tarzan suddenly became alert. 'Blacks are coming,' he said. 'There are a number of them, and they are very close. The wind just changed and brought their scent to me.'

'There they are now,' said Gregory. 'Why, it's another safari. There are porters with packs, but I see no white men.'

'It is your safari, Bwana,' said Ogabi. 'It is the safari that was to have met you at Bonga.'

'Then it must be the one that Thome stole,' said d'Arnot, 'but I don't see Thome.'

'Another mystery of darkest Africa, perhaps,' suggested Helen. Mbuli, leading his people back toward Bonga, halted in surprise as he saw the little party of whites; then, seeing that his men greatly outnumbered them, he came forward, swaggering a little.

'Who are you?' demanded Tarzan.

'I am Mbuli,' replied the black.

'Where are your bwanas? You have deserted them.'

'Who are you, white man, to question Mbuli?' demanded the black, arrogantly, the advantage of numbers giving him courage.

'I am Tarzan,' replied the ape-man.

Mbuli wilted. All the arrogance went out of him. 'Forgive, Bwana,' he begged. 'I did not know you, for I have never seen you before.'

'You know the law of the safari,' said Tarzan. 'Those who desert their white Masters are punished.'

'But my people would not go on,' explained Mbuli. 'When we came to Tuen-Baka they would go no farther. They were afraid, for Tuen-Baka is taboo.'

'You took all their equipment,' continued the ape-man, glancing over the loads that the porters had thrown to the ground. 'Why, you even took their food.'

'Yes, Bwana; but they needed no food – they were about to die – Tuen-Baka is taboo. Also, Bwana Thome lied to us. We had agreed to serve Bwana Gregory, but he told us Bwana Gregory wished us to accompany him instead.'

'Nevertheless, you did wrong to abandon him. To escape punishment, you will accompany us to Tuen-Baka – we need porters and askaris.'

'But my people are afraid,' remonstrated Mbuli.

'Where Tarzan goes, your people may go,' replied the ape-man. 'I shall not lead then into danger needlessly.'

'But, Bwana—'

'But nothing,' snapped Tarzan; then he turned to the porters.

'Up packs! You are going back to Tuen-Baka.'

The porters grumbled, but they picked up their packs and turned back along the trail they had just travelled, for the will of the white man was supreme; and, too, the word had spread among them that this was the fabulous Tarzan who was half man half demon.

For three days they trekked back along the trail toward Ashair, and at noon on the seventh day the safari broke from the forest beside a quiet river. The terrain ahead was open, but rocky and barren. Above low hills rose the truncated cone of an extinct volcano, a black, forbidding mass.

'So that is Tuen-Baka,' said d'Arnot. 'It is just an old volcano, after all.'

'Nevertheless, the boys are afraid,' said Tarzan. 'We shall have to watch them at night or they'll desert again. I'm going on now to see what lies ahead.'

'Be careful,' cautioned d'Arnot. 'The place has a bad reputation, you know.'

'I am always careful,' replied Tarzan.

D'Arnot grinned. 'Sometimes you are about as careful of yourself as a Paris taxi driver is of pedestrians.'

Tarzan followed a dim trail that roughly paralleled the river, the same trail that Lal Taask and Aton Thome had followed. As was his custom, he moved silently with every sense alert. He saw signs of strange animals and realised that he was in a country that might hold dangers beyond his experience. In a small patch of earth among the boulders and rough lava rocks he saw the imprint of a great foot and caught faintly the odour of a reptile that had passed that way recently. He knew, from the size of the footprint, that the creature was large; and when he heard ahead of him an ominous hissing and roaring he guessed that the maker of the footprint was not far off. Increasing his speed, but not lessening his caution, he moved forward in the direction of the sound; and coming to the edge of a gully, looked down to see a strangely garbed white warrior facing such a creature as Tarzan had never seen on earth. Perhaps he did not know it, but he was looking at a small edition of the terrible Tyrannosaurus Rex, that mighty King of carnivorous reptiles which ruled the earth eons ago. Perhaps the one below him was tiny compared with his gigantic progenitor, but he was still a formidable creature – as large as a full-grown bull.

Tarzan saw in the warrior either a hostage or a means of securing information concerning this strange country and its inhabitants. If the dinosaur killed the man he would be quite valueless; so, acting as quickly as he thought, he leaped from the cliff just as the brute charged. Only a man who did not know the meaning of fear would have taken such a risk.

The warrior facing the great reptile with his puny spear was stunned to momentary inaction as he saw an almost naked bronzed giant drop, apparently from the blue, on to the back of the monster he had been facing without hope. He saw the stranger's knife striking futilely at the armoured back, as the man clung with one arm about the creature's neck. He could have escaped, but he did not, and as Tarzan found a vulnerable spot in the dinosaur's throat and drove his knife home again and again, he rushed in to the ape-man's aid.

The huge reptile, seriously hurt, screamed and hissed as it threw itself about in vain effort to dislodge the man-thing from its back; but, hurt though it was, it was, like all the reptilia, tenacious of life and far from overcome.

As Tarzan's knife found and severed the creature's jugular vein, the warrior drove his spear through the savage heart, and, with a last convulsive shudder, it crashed to the ground, dead; then the two men faced one another across the great carcass.

Neither knew the temper or intentions of the other, and both were on guard as they sought to find a medium of communication more satisfactory than an improvised sign language. At last the warrior hit upon a tongue that both could speak and understand, a language he and his people had learned from the negroes they had captured and forced into slavery – -Swahili.

'I am Thetan of Thobos,' he said. 'I owe you my life, but why did you come to my aid? Are we to be friends or foes?'

'I am Tarzan,' said the ape-man. 'Let us be friends.'

'Let us be friends,' agreed Thetan. 'Now tell me how I may repay you for what you have done for me.'

'I wish to go to Ashair,' said Tarzan.

The warrior shook his head. 'You have asked me one thing that I cannot do for you,' he said. 'The Asharians are our enemies. If I took you there we'd both be imprisoned and destroyed; but perhaps I can persuade my King to let you come to Thobos; then, when the day comes that we conquer Ashair, you may enter the city with us. But why do you wish do go to Ashair?'

'I am not alone,' said Tarzan, 'and in my party are the father and sister of a man we believe to be a prisoner in Ashair. It is to obtain his release that we are here.'

'Perhaps my King will let you all come to Thobos,' said Thetan, rather dubiously. 'Such a thing would be without precedent; but because you have saved the life of his nephew and because you are enemies of Ashair, he may grant permission. At least it will do no harm to ask him.'

'How may I know his answer?' asked Tarzan.

'I can bring it to you, but it will be some time before I can do so,' replied Thetan. 'I am down here on a mission for the King. I came by way of the only land trail out of Tuen-Baka, a trail known only to my people. I shall sleep tonight in a cave I know of, and tomorrow start back for Thobos. In three days I shall return if Herat will permit you to enter Thobos. If I do not come back you will know that he has refused. Wait then no more than one day; then leave the country as quickly as you can. It is death for strangers to remain in the vicinity of Tuen-Baka.'

'Come back to my camp,' said Tarzan, 'and spend the night there. We can discuss the matter with my companions.'

Thetan hesitated. 'They are all strangers to me,' he said, 'and all strangers are enemies.'

'My friends will not be,' the ape-man assured him. 'I give you my word that they will have no desire to harm you. In the world from which they come no strangers are considered enemies until they prove themselves to be such.'

'What a strange world that must be,' remarked Thetan. 'But I'll accept your word and go with you.'

As the two men started back toward the Gregory camp a party of warriors embarked in a galley at the quay of Ashair, despatched by Queen Atka to intercept and harass the Gregory expedition, against which Atan Thome had warned her in order that he might win the favour of the Queen and prevent Tarzan and Gregory from reaching Ashair. The wily Eurasian had hopes of so ingratiating himself with the Queen that he might remain in Ashair until he could formulate a plan for stealing The Father of Diamonds and making his escape. So obsessed was he by his desire to possess the diamond that he was totally unable to appreciate the futility of his scheme.

The members of the Gregory party were astonished to see Tarzan walk into camp with this strangely apparalled warrior. Thetan wore the black plumes of Thobos, and upon the breast and back of his tunic there was embroidered the figure of a bull. Their friendly greetings put him at his ease, and though the Swahili of Gregory, Helen and Lavac was a little lame, they all managed fairly well in the conversation that ensued. He told them much of Tuen-Baka, of Thobos and Ashair; but when the subject of The Father of Diamonds was broached he was evasive, and, out of courtesy, they did not press him. But his reticence only served to whet their curiosity, as they sensed the mystery that surrounded the fabulous stone.

Late that night the silence of the sleeping camp was broken by sepulchral voices keening out of the mystery of the surrounding darkness. Instantly the camp was awake and in confusion, as the terrified blacks milled in panic. So terrified were they that they might have bolted for the forest had it not been that glowing death-heads suddenly appeared floating in the air around the camp, as the voices warned, 'Turn back! Turn back! Death awaits you in forbidden Ashair.'

'The Asharians!' cried Thetan.

Tarzan, seeking to solve the mystery of the weird apparitions, sprang into the night in the direction of the nearest death's head. D'Arnot sought to rally the askaris, but they were as terrified as the porters, many of whom crouched with their foreheads pressed to the ground, while others covered their ears or their eyes with trembling hands.

Into the midst of this confusion burst half a dozen Asharian warriors. The whites met them with drawn pistols. Wolff fired and missed; then the intruders were gone as suddenly as they had come. Above the turmoil of the camp rose a woman's terrified scream.

Pursuing the grinning skull into the darkness, the ape-man seized a flesh and blood man, as he had expected. The fellow put up a fight, but he was no match for the steel thewed man of the jungles, who quickly disarmed him and dragged him back into camp.

'Look!' said Tarzan to the blacks, pointing to the phosphorescent mask of hi s prisoner. 'It is only a trick; you need be afraid no more. He is a man, even as you and I.' Then he turned to his prisoner. 'You may go,' he said. 'Tell your people that we do not come as enemies, and that if they will send Brian Gregory out to us we will go away.'

'I will tell them,' said the warrior; but when he was safely out of the camp he called back, 'You will never see Brian Gregory, for no stranger who enters The Forbidden City ever come out alive.'

'We are well out of that,' said Gregory, with a sigh. 'I don't take much stock in what that fellow just said. He was just trying to frighten us. That was what the voices and the death heads and the raid were for, but for a while I thought that we were in for a lot of trouble.'

'Who screamed?' asked Tarzan.

'It sounded like one of the girls,' said Lavac, 'but it may have been a porter. They were scared nearly to death.'

It was then that Magra came running toward them. 'Helen is gone!' she cried. 'I think they got her,' and at that moment Asharian warriors were dragging Helen into a galley at the edge of the river only a short distance from the camp. During the confusion they had deliberately caused in the Gregory camp, a warrior had seized Helen, and then they had all made off for the river where the galley lay. A palm over her mouth had silenced the girl; and she was helpless against their strength, as they hurried her aboard the craft.

'Come!' cried Thetan. 'Their galley must be close by in the river. We may be able to overtake them before they can put off,' and, followed by the others, he ran from the camp; but when they reached the river they saw the galley already out of their reach and moving steadily up-stream beneath the steady strokes of its long oars.

'Mon Dieu!' exclaimed d'Arnot. 'We must do something. We cannot let them take her away without doing something.'

'What can we do?' asked Gregory in a broken voice.

'I am afraid you will never see her again,' said Thetan. 'She is beautiful, so they will probably take her to the temple of The Father of Diamonds to be handmaiden to the priests. No alien who enters there ever comes out alive. Tomorrow she will be as dead to the outer world as though she had never existed.'

'Is there no way to overtake them?' asked Tarzan.

'Wait!' exclaimed Thetan. 'There is a bare possibility. If they camp tonight this side of the tunnel that leads into Lake Horus we might be able to do so; but it is a hard trail, and only strong men could travel it.'

'Will you guide me?' asked Tarzan.

'Yes,' replied Thetan, 'but what can we two alone expect to accomplish against a galley load of Asharian warriors?'

For answer, Tarzan raised his face toward the heavens and voiced a weird cry, then he turned to d'Arnot. 'Come,' he said, 'you will go with us.'

'I'll go, too,' said Lavac. 'You'll need all the men you can get.'

'You'll stay here,' said Tarzan. 'We must have protection for the camp.'

Lavac grumbled, but he knew that when Tarzan gave an order it was to be obeyed, and, scowling at d'Arnot, he watched the three men disappear into the darkness.

As Thetan led them by the way he knew, his mind was occupied by thoughts of this strange, white giant who had come into his life. His great strength and his fearlessness impressed the Thobotian, but the man seemed eccentric. That strange cry he had given just as they were leaving camp! Now, what could have been his reason for that? He was still pondering it when he heard grumblings and growlings coming out of the night behind them and growing louder. Something was following them. He glanced back and saw a blur of great black forms on the trail behind the two men who followed him.

'Something is behind you!' he warned them.

'Yes,' replied Tarzan. 'My apes are coming with us. I called them before we left camp.'

'Your apes!' exclaimed Thetan.

'Yes; they will make good allies, and they can go where even strong men cannot. The Asharians will be surprised to see them.'

'Yes,' agreed Thetan, who was very much surprised himself, and his awe increased, not for the apes, but for the man who could control them.

The way grew steeper as Thetan led them up into the hills to reach the head of the ravine where the Asharians would camp if they camped at all.

'How much farther is it?' asked Tarzan.

'We should get there just about dawn,' replied Thetan. 'If they are camped there we should take them by surprise, for they could not imagine that anyone could reach them, and consequently they may not have anyone on watch.'

'Poor Helen!' said d'Arnot. 'What will become of her if they went on to Ashair without stopping?'

'You will never see her again,' replied Thetan. 'For generations my people have been trying to conquer Ashair and reach the temple and The Father of Diamonds, yet we have never succeeded. How can you hope to accomplish what we have never been able to?'

'She must be there,' said d'Arnot. 'She must!'

'There is a possibility,' exclaimed Thetan, 'but it is only a possibility.'

XV

Wolff was genuinely terrified. The weird occurrences, the raid on the camp, the show of force by the Asharians had all contributed to impress him with the grave dangers and the futility of the venture. His desire to live outweighed his avarice, and The Father of Diamonds was forgotten in his anxiety to escape what he believed to be the certain fate of the party if it sought to enter The Forbidden City of Ashair.

When, at last, the camp slept, he awoke Mbuli. 'Are you and your people going to stay here and be killed or forced into slavery?' he demanded.

'My people are afraid,' replied the headman, 'but what are we to do? We are afraid to stay here, and we are afraid to run away from the great Bwana Tarzan.'

'You will never see that monkey-man again,' Wolff assured the black. 'He and the frog-eater will be killed by the Asharians, who will then come back and either kill all of us or take us with them as slaves. How would you like to be chained to a galley all the rest of your life?'

'I would not like it, Bwana,' replied Mbuli.

'Then listen to me. The girl here is in danger. I got to save her; so I orders you and your boys to take us back to Bonga. How many do you think will come with you?'

'All, Bwana.'

'Good! Now get busy. Have 'em get their packs together, but see that they don't make no noise. When everything's ready, you take a couple of boys and get the girl. Don't let her make no noise.'

After a night of sleeplessness and terrified apprehension for the future, Helen's attention was attracted by a slight noise in the forest behind the camp where her captors had halted for the night. Dawn was breaking, its ghastly light relieving the darkness that had enveloped the little ravine and revealing to the girl's astonished eyes the figures of great apes and men stealing stealthily upon the camp.

At first she was terrified by this new menace; then she recognised Tarzan and almost simultaneously saw d'Arnot behind him; and hope, that she had thought dead, welled strong within her, so that she could scarcely restrain a cry of relief as she realised that rescue was at hand; then an Asharian awoke and saw the danger. With a shout that aroused the others, he leaped to his feet; and, guessing that an attempt was being made to rescue the captive, he seized her and dragged her, struggling, toward the galley.

With a shout of encouragement to her, d'Arnot sprang forward in pursuit while two warriors engaged Tarzan, and Thetan and the apes fell upon the others. The warrior who was carrying Helen off was almost at the galley. He shouted to the slaves to make ready to put off the moment he was aboard, but d'Arnot was pressing him so closely he was compelled to turn and defend himself. D'Arnot faced him with drawn pistol as the man raised his spear. Behind d'Arnot, another warrior, who had escaped the apes, was running to the aid of his fellow. The Frenchman could not fire at the warrior facing him without endangering Helen, and he did not know that another was approaching from behind.

What takes so long to tell occupied but a few seconds of time, for as the warrior was about to cast his spear, Helen, realising d'Arnot's predicament, threw herself to one side, exposing her captor; and d'Arnot's fired.

Tarzan, Thetan, and the apes had disposed of the remainder of the Asharians, with the exception of the one who was threatening d'Arnot from behind. The ape-man saw his friend's danger, but he was too far away to reach the warrior who was threatening him, before the man should drive his spear into d'Arnot's back. Helen realised the danger, and cried a warning to the Frenchman. D'Arnot swung about, his pistol ready; and pressed the trigger, but the hammer fell futilely upon an imperfect cap; then Tarzan launched his spear. His target was far beyond the range of any spear but that of the Lord of the Jungle. With all of his great strength, backed by the weight of his body, he cast the weapon; and. as the Asharian was lunging at d'Arnot, it passed through his body, piercing his heart. As the man fell dead at d'Arnot's feet, Helen went suddenly weak. She would have fallen had not d'Arnot taken her in his arms.

'Whew!' exclaimed Thetan. 'That was a close call, but what a cast! In all my life I have never seen one that could compare with it.'

'In all your life,' said d'Arnot, 'you have never seen such a man as Tarzan of the Apes.'

Tarzan had passed them and reached the galley, where the slaves sat bewildered, not knowing what to do; then he called the apes and ordered them into the galley among the terrified slaves.

'They won't harm you,' Tarzan assured the blacks, and when Helen, d'Arnot and Thetan were aboard, he directed the slaves to row them downriver to the Gregory camp.

D'Arnot sat in the stern with his arm around Helen, who evinced no inclination to resent the familiarity. On the contrary, she seemed quite content.

'I thought I had lost you, darling,' he whispered.

She made no reply, other than to snuggle closer and sigh happily, which, to d'Arnot, was at least an acceptance of his love, if not an avowal of her own. He was content to leave the matter as it stood.

Gregory, Lavac and Ogabi were standing by the river when the galley rounded a bend and came within sight.

'The Asharians are returning!' cried Gregory. 'We'd better get into the forest and hide. We three haven't a chance against them.'

'Wait!' said Lavac. 'That boat's full of apes.'

'By George! So it is!' exclaimed Gregory.

'And there is Bwana Tarzan,' exclaimed Ogabi.

A few moments later the boat touched shore; and as the apes poured out, Gregory took his daughter in his arms. 'Thank God, you've found her,' he said to Tarzan. 'But now we have some bad news for you.'

'What now?' demanded d'Arnot.

'Magra and Wolff deserted with all the men and equipment last light,' said Gregory.

'Oh, I can't believe that Magra would have done a thing like that,' exclaimed Helen.

Gregory shook his head. 'Don't forget,' he reminded her, 'that she was in cahoots with Thome.'

'Anyway,' said Lavac, 'she's gone.'

'What are we to do now?' demanded Gregory. 'It looks like the end of the trail to me.'

'On the way down,' said Tarzan, 'I questioned some of the galley slaves. They tell me that a white man is held prisoner in the temple of The Father of Diamonds at Ashair. It may be your son. I have talked with Thetan; and he believes it may be possible that the King of Thobos will receive us kindly and even help in the rescue of your son, if there is any possibility that it may be accomplished. Under the circumstances, it may be well to go to Thobos. We have a galley, and by entering the lake after dark we should be able to pass Ashair safely.'

'I should like to do that,' said Gregory, 'but I can't ask the rest of you to risk your lives further for me. Had I had any idea that we were to encounter such dangers, I should never have started out without a strong force of white men.'

'I'll go with you.' said d'Arnot.

'And I,' said Lavac.

'Where Bwana Tarzan goes, I go,' said Ogabi.

'Then we all go,' said the ape-man.

An exhausted warrior stumbled into the presence of Atka, Queen of Ashair. 'We were camped for the night in the ravine below the tunnel,' he reported. 'We had with us a girl whom we had captured in the camp of the strangers. At dawn we were attacked by three men and a band of apes. One of the men was a Thobotian. The leader was a naked white warrior. In the beginning of the fight, I was knocked senseless. I knew nothing more until I regained consciousness and found myself alone with the dead. The galley was gone. I think they must have thought me dead.'

'Which way did they go?' demanded Atka.

'That I do not know,' replied the warrior, 'but it is probable that they went back downstream to their camp.'

The Queen turned to a noble standing near the throne. 'Man six galleys,' she ordered, 'and bring me those people, dead or alive! They shall taste the anger of Brulor!'

XVI

Wolff had stumbled along the back trail all night, and his disposition had not been improved by the fact that he had had to drag a resisting Magra most of the way. He had stopped now for a brief rest. The boys had dropped their packs and thrown themselves to the ground. Wolff was wiping the sweat from his forehead and glaring at the girl.

'You might as well come along peaceable,' said the man. 'It'll be easier for both of us. I got you, and I'm goin' to keep you. You might as well make up your mind to that.'

'You're wasting your time,' replied Magra. 'You can lead a horse to water, you know—'

'And I can make it drink, too,' growled Wolff. 'Come here, you!' He seized her and drew her to him.

With her right hand, Magra attempted to push him away, while her left hand sought the pistol at his hip. 'Stop!' she cried. 'Or, before God, I'll kill you!' But Wolff only laughed at her and drew her closer.

He died with the ugly grin upon his face, as Magra wrested his weapon from its holster and shot him through the chest. As Wolff fell, Mbuli leaped to his feet, followed by his boys. The white girl was alone now in their power; and Mbuli knew where she would bring a good price. Also, there were two thousand English pounds on the dead man.

Magra swung around and faced Mbuli. 'Pick up your loads and get going back to camp!' she ordered. Mbuli hesitated and came toward her. His attitude was insubordinate and threatening. 'Do as I tell you, Mbuli,' snapped the girl, 'or you'll get what Wolff got.'

'We are tired,' said Mbuli, seeking time. 'Let us rest.'

'You can rest in camp. Get going!'

Urging the men on, Magra drove them back along the trail toward camp. They grumbled; but they obeyed, for they had seen her kill Wolff. She walked behind them, with Mbuli just in front of her; and she never let him forget that a pistol was aimed at the small of his back. She would have driven them faster had she known that her companions were about to abandon the camp along a route she could not follow, but she did not know.

As the others in the Gregory camp discussed their plans, Lavac stood aside moodily, eyeing d'Arnot and Helen who stood hand in hand; and as the others went to their tents to gather a few of the personal belongings the deserting porters had left behind, he accosted d'Arnot.

'You are very familiar with Ma'moiselle Helen,' he said, 'and I resent it, but I suppose she prefers you because you are a captain and have more money than I.'

D'Arnot, ordinarily slow to anger, flushed and then went white. 'And I resent *that*, you pig!' he snapped, slapping Lavac across the face.

'You can't do that to me!' growled Lavac, whipping his gun from its holster.

Fortunately, Tarzan chanced to be passing close to Lavac. He leaped between the two men and seized the lieutenant's gun hand. 'None of that!' he snapped. 'We've enough troubles without fighting among ourselves. I'll keep your gun until you cool off and get a little sense. Now, into the barge, all of you! We're leaving for Thobos at once.'

'We can't have any of this,' said Gregory. 'If Lieutenant Lavac feels as he does, I think he had better wait here for us.'

'How about it, Lavac?' asked Tarzan.

'It will not occur again,' said the man. 'I lost my head. If Captain d'Arnot will accept my apology, I offer it.'

'Certainly,' said d'Arnot. 'I regret the whole affair, and I am sorry that I struck you.' Then the two men shook hands quite perfunctorily, and separated coldly. It was obvious that from now on nothing but bad blood would exist between them.

'What about the apes?' asked Gregory, more to bridge the awkward silence than because he was interested.

'I have told them to stay around here for a moon and hunt,' replied Tarzan. 'If they don't forget it, they'll stay; unless the hunting is very poor.'

As Tarzan was about to board the galley, his keen ears caught the sound of approaching footsteps from the direction of the forest. 'Someone is coming,' he said. 'We'll wait and see who it is. Be ready to push off – they may not be friends.'

Presently the head of a safari came into view, debouching from the forest.

'Why, those are our men!' exclaimed Helen.

'Yes,' said Tarzan, 'and there's Magra bringing up the rear. You were quite right about her.'

'I was sure she'd never desert us like that,' said Helen. 'I wonder where Wolff is.'

'She's got a gun on Mbuli,' said d'Arnot. 'There is a woman!'

Magra herded the blacks down to the river, where she told briefly of how Wolff had persuaded the black to abduct her and desert, and of Wolff's death. 'I found these on him,' she said, 'the two thousand pounds of which he defrauded Mr Gregory and Thome and the map he stole from Helen's room.'

'We are well rid of him,' said Gregory.

Tarzan ordered the blacks to load all of the supplies and equipment on board the galley, and when they had done so he dismissed them.

'You may wait here for us if you wish,' he said, 'or you may go back to your own country. Eventually you will be punished for what you have done.'

Bending to their oars, the slaves drove the galley up-stream, as the members of the party momentarily relaxed from the nervous strain of the past hours. Lavac sat in the bow, looking forward, so that he would not see d'Arnot and Helen sitting close to one another. Magra sat beside Tarzan. All were quiet, grateful for the peace and restfulness of the river. For a time, at least, their way seemed assured as far as Thobos, for they would pass Ashair by night. What their reception in Thobos would be was uncertain. Even Thetan could assure them of nothing more than that he would intercede with his uncle, the King, in their behalf; but he thought that the fact that Tarzan had saved his life and that they were all enemies of the Asharians would go a long way toward ensuring them a friendly attitude on the part of King Herat.

Magra sighed and turned to Tarzan. 'You have all been so splendid to me,' she said, 'although you knew that I was an accomplice of Thome. I want you to know that I am loyal to you now.'

Tarzan made no reply. His attention was centred on another matter. The galley was too heavily laden. Its gunwales were almost awash as it moved slowly up the narrow gorge.

'We'll have to put some of this stuff ashore in that ravine where we found Helen,' he said, 'If we ran into swift water in the river or any sort of a blow on the lake, we'd founder.'

'Look!' cried Lavac. 'Here comes a galley.'

'An Asharian!' exclaimed Thetan. 'And there are others right behind it.'

'Six of 'em,' said Lavac.

'Good Lord!' exclaimed Gregory. 'We'd better turn back.'

'They'd overhaul us in no time,' said Thetan. 'We're in for it.' Tarzan smiled. 'There is nothing to do, then, but fight,' he said.

'We haven't a chance, have we?' asked Magra.

'It doesn't look like it,' replied d'Arnot.

'If there is such a thing as a jinx,' said Helen, 'we certainly have one camping on our trail.'

The narrow gorge echoed to the war cries of the Asharians, as their galleys bore down on their hapless victims. Gregory's party met them with gunfire and arrows, while the short Asharian spears hurtled about them. As the men had leaped to their feet to fire over the heads of the slaves, the galley tipped dangerously, shipping water and spoiling their aim. A spear struck one of the oarsmen; and as he lurched forward, dead, his oar fouled that of another slave; and a moment later the galley swung broadside across the river as the leading Asharian galley, sped downstream by forty oars, bore down upon it.

There was a crash of splintering wood as the prow of the enemy rammed the Gregory galley amidships. Already listing crazily, she careened to the impact, and as the water poured over her port gunwale, she began to sink, leaving her passengers floundering in the river and her slaves screaming in their chains; then the other galleys moved in to pick up the survivors.

D'Arnot and Helen were dragged into the galley farthest upstream, which immediately set out for Ashair. The other members of the party had drifted downstream before they were finally picked up by a second galley. Tarzan had swum beside Magra, encouraging and supporting her, while Gregory, Lavac and Ogabi remained nearby. Night was falling, and it would soon be dark in the narrow gorge. When they were in the craft, they saw that Thetan was already there, having been picked up before they were; but Helen and d'Arnot were not there; and the boat in which they were prisoners was out of sight around a bend in the river.

'Did you see anything of Helen?' asked Gregory, but no one had.

'I could almost wish that she drowned,' he added. 'God! Why did I ever undertake this stupid venture?'

'It would have been better had we all drowned,' said Thetan. 'There is no hope for those who fall into the hands of the Asharians.'

'All that has happened to us so far,' said Tarzan, 'is that we have got wet. Wait until something really bad happens before you give up hope.'

'But look at what lies ahead of us!' exclaimed Lavac.

'I do not know what lies ahead of us, and neither do you,' the ape-man reminded him. 'Therefore we might as well anticipate the best as the worst.'

'A most excellent philosophy,' commented Gregory, 'but a strain on one's credulity.'

'I think it is good,' said Magra.

In the leading galley, Helen and d'Arnot sat huddled together, shivering with cold.

'I wonder what became of the others?' said the girl.

'I don't know, dear,' replied d'Arnot, 'but thank God that you and I were not separated.'

'Yes,' she whispered, and then, 'I suppose this is the end; but we shall go together.'

'Keep a stiff upper lip, darling. Don't give up hope; they haven't harmed us yet.'

'Poor Dad,' said Helen. 'Do you suppose he and all the others drowned?'

'They may have been picked up, too,' encouraged d'Arnot.

'Little good it will do any of us,' continued the girl. 'No wonder poor Brian never returned from Ashair. What was that?'

An eerie scream shattered the silence of the night, reverberating weirdly in the narrow gorge.

XVII

Atan Thome and Lal Taask were taking their ease on the terrace of Atka's palace, overlooking the lake. They were treated like guests, but they knew that they were prisoners. Lal Taask would have given his soul to be well out of the country; but Atan Thome still harboured dreams of The Father of Diamonds, which he pictured as a stone as large as a football. He often amused himself by trying to compute its value; then he translated it into pounds sterling and bought yachts and castles and great country estates. He gave the most marvellous dinner that Paris had ever known, and was fawned upon by the world's most beautiful women, whom he covered with furs and jewels. But the walls of Ashair still rose about him; and, towering above those, the walls of Tuen-Baka.

As they sat there, the noble Akamen joined them. 'Your enemies have probably been captured by this time,' he said.

'What will happen to them?' asked Lal Taask. He was thinking of what might be going to happen to him sooner or later.

'They shall know the wrath of Brulor,' replied Akamen.

'Who is Brulor?' asked Thome.

'Brulor is our god, The Father of Diamonds,' explained the Asharian. 'His temple lies at the bottom of Lake Horus, guarded by the priests of Brulor and the waters of sacred Horus.'

'But I thought that The Father of Diamonds was a diamond,' exclaimed Atan Thome, terrified by the suggestion that it was a man.

'What do you know of The Father of Diamonds?' demanded Akamen.

'Nothing,' said Thome, hastily. 'I have just heard the term.'

'Well,' said Akamen, 'it's something we are not supposed to discuss with barbarians, but I don't mind telling you that The Father of Diamonds is the name given both to Brulor and The Father of Diamonds that reposes in the casket on the altar before his throne in the temple.'

Atan Thome breathed a sigh of relief. So there was a Father of Diamonds after all. Suddenly there came faintly to their ears a weird scream from far down the lake toward the tunnel that leads to the outside world and carries the waters of Horus down to the sea thousands of miles away.

'I wonder what that was?' said Akamen. 'It sounded almost human.'

'Are there any apes around here?' asked Thome.

'No,' replied Akamen. 'Why?'

'That sounded a little like an ape,' said Atan Thome.

*

'It will be very dark inside there,' said Tarzan, as the galley in which he and his fellow-prisoners were being taken to Ashair approached the mouth of the tunnel leading to Lake Horus. He spoke in English. 'Each of you pick a couple of men; and when I say "Kreeg-ah," throw them overboard. If we act very quickly, taking them off their guard, we can do it; and as soon as you have two overboard, go after more. I can't tell either Thetan or Ogabi now, as the Asharians understand Swahili; but as soon as I give you the signal, I shall tell them.'

'And then what?' asked Lavac.

'Why, we'll take the boat, of course,' said Gregory.

'We're likely to be killed,' said Lavac, 'but that's all right with me.'

As the galley neared the tunnel, a warrior in the bow lighted a torch, for within the tunnel there would not be even the sky to guide the helmsman. Tarzan regretted the torch, but he did not give up his plan. Perhaps it might be more difficult now, but he felt that it still had an excellent chance to succeed.

Suddenly the ape-man sprang to his feet, and as he hurled a warrior into the water his 'Kre-e-gah!' rang through the tunnel.

'Overboard with them!' he shouted, and Thetan and Ogabi grasped the intent of his plan instantly.

Chaos and confusion reigned aboard the galley, as the five desperate and determined men fell upon the Asharian warriors, throwing or pushing them overboard. The astonished Asharians were so taken by surprise that they at first fell easy victims to the plan, but later those who had escaped the first sudden rush of the prisoners, rallied and put up a defence that threatened the success of the ape-man's bold plan.

Magra, seated amidships, was in the centre of the mêlée. Crouched between two galley slaves, she watched the savage scene with fascinated, fearless eyes. The flaring torch in the bow of the galley painted the scene in dancing high lights and deep shadows against a background of Stygian gloom, a moving picture of embattled souls upon the brink of Hell; and through it moved, with the strength, the agility, and the majesty of a great lion, the godlike figure of the Lord of the Jungle. She saw, too, the threat of defeat that she was helpless to avert; and then she heard Thetan shout: 'Help us, slaves, and win your freedom!'

Almost as one man the slaves rose in their chains and lashed out at their former Masters with oars or fists. Screaming, cursing men were hurled into the black waters. A warrior lunged at Tarzan's back with his sword; but Magra caught his ankle and tripped him, and he fell between two slaves, who pitched him overboard.

As the yells and screams echoed through the tunnel, Helen pressed closer to d'Arnot. 'They are fighting back there,' she said.

'Yes,' replied the Frenchman. 'The first scream was Tarzan's warning "Kreeg-ah"; so you may rest assured that they are fighting.'

'At least we know that they were not all drowned,' said the girl. 'Perhaps Dad is still alive, but what chance have they against all those warriors?'

'There is always a chance for the side upon which Tarzan fights,' replied d'Arnot. 'I'd feel much better on your account if you were back there in the galley that he's in.'

'If you were there, too,' she said. 'Otherwise I'd rather be here.'

He pressed her closer to him. 'What an ironical fate that we could only have met and loved under circumstances such as these! For me, it is worth the price, no matter what that price may be. But for you – well, I wish you had never come to Africa.'

'Is that the gallant Frenchman?' she teased.

'You know what I mean.'

'Yes; but you are still glad that I came to Africa, and so am I – no matter what happens.'

Back in the rearmost galley, the last of their adversaries disposed of, the little company took stock of their losses. 'Where is Ogabi?' asked Tarzan.

'An Asharian dragged him overboard,' said Magra. 'Poor fellow.'

'He was well avenged,' said Lavac.

'Only Helen and d'Arnot are missing now,' said Gregory. 'If they weren't drowned, they must be in one of the galleys ahead of us. Is there no way in which we might rescue them?'

'There are five galleys ahead of us,' said Thetan. 'We are only four men. We would stand no chance against five galleys of Asharian warriors. The only possible hope that we may entertain of saving them is in enlisting my King's aid, but I have already told you that the Thobotians have never been able to enter Ashair. About the best we may hope to do is to save ourselves, and that may not be so easy if any of the galleys ahead of us are lying in wait for us. We'll have to put out our torch and take a chance in the darkness.'

When the galley finally reached the end of the tunnel and the lake spread before them, a seemingly vast expanse of water beneath the dim light of the stars, they saw the glimmering torches of five galleys far to their left and just beyond them the lights of Ashair. No galley had lain in wait for them, and the way to Thobos lay open to them.

It was shortly after dawn that they approached the quay at Thobos. A company of warriors stood ready to receive them, and even though Thetan stood in full view of them in the bow of the galley, their attitude was no less belligerent.

'They don't seem very friendly,' remarked Magra. 'Perhaps we are jumping from the frying pan into the fire.'

'Who comes?' demanded one of the warriors.

'Thetan, nephew of King Herat,' replied Thetan.

'We recognise Thetan, but the others are strangers,' said the warrior.

'They are friends,' explained Thetan.

'They are strangers, and strangers may only enter Thobos as prisoners,' insisted the warrior. 'If they would land without battle, let them throw down their arms.'

Under these conditions, the party was allowed to land; but they were immediately surrounded by scowling warriors. 'You know, Thetan,' said the leader, 'that it is against the law to bring strangers to Thobos; and therefore, even though you be nephew to him, I must arrest you with the others and take you all before King Herat.'

XVIII

Helen and d'Arnot were imprisoned briefly in a dungeon of the palace at Ashair, then they were summoned to appear before the Queen. As they were led into the throne room, Helen exclaimed in amazement.

'Why, there are Thome and Taask!' she whispered to d'Arnot. 'There, at the side of the dais.'

'So that is Thome,' said d'Arnot. 'I'd like to get my hands on him. They don't seem to be prisoners. I wonder what it means?'

'Silence!' ordered one of their guard.

As they were led to the foot of the dais, Atka eyed them sternly. 'Why came you to The Forbidden City?' she demanded.

'To find my brother, Brian Gregory,' replied Helen.

'You lie!' snapped Atka. 'You came to steal The Father of Diamonds.'

'The girl is innocent, O Queen,' said Thome. 'It was the man and his companions who sought The Father of Diamonds. If you will give the girl into my keeping, I will be responsible for her.'

'The girl speaks the truth,' cried d'Arnot. 'She came solely to find her brother, but that man lies. It was he who came to steal The Father of Diamonds. Why else should he have come? He has no brother here. There is no other reason why he should have undertaken the expensive and dangerous journey to Ashair.'

'You all lie,' snapped Atka, 'Send the girl to the temple as handmaiden to the priests. Imprison the men.'

Suddenly, before they could prevent, d'Arnot tore away from his guards and leaped upon Atan Thome, his strong fingers closing upon the Eurasian's throat to kill him.

'If it's the last thing in life I do!' he cried; but warriors leaped in and dragged him away before he could consummate his design.

'To the cages with him!' ordered Atka. 'He shall spend the rest of his life looking at The Father of Diamonds he would have profaned.'

'Goodbye, Helen!' he called back, as warriors dragged him from the throne room.

'Goodbye, Paul!' That was all; but tears welled in her eyes as they strained after the man she loved, whom she believed she was looking upon for the last time.

As warriors seized Atan Thome and Lal Taask, Akamen stepped close to the Queen and whispered a few words to her. She nodded, and ordered the warriors to release the two men.

'I give these men into the keeping of Akamen,' she said. 'He shall be responsible for them. Take the girl away. Let the women purify her before she is taken to the priests.'

Two warriors led d'Arnot down a long ramp to a crude elevator operated by slaves at a windlass on the floor above. They entered the cage with him, and the descent began down a dark shaft.

'I hope you took a good look at the world before you were brought into the palace,' remarked one of the warriors, 'for it's the last you'll ever see of it.'

'Why?' asked d'Arnot. 'Where are you taking me?'

'To the temple of Brulor,' replied the warrior. 'It lies at the bottom of Lake Horus, the sacred. You will spend the rest of your life there. It may be a short life, or it may be a long one. After you've spent a few weeks in the temple, you'll pray that it will be short.'

D'Arnot could not judge the depth of the long shaft down which he was being lowered to what fate he could not guess. He might have descended two hundred feet, or it might have been more. Whatever it was, he was convinced that there could be neither escape nor rescue. At the foot of the shaft, the warriors turned him over to two priests, who conducted him along a corridor that extended far out beneath the lake. At the end of the corridor, he was led into a large, oblong room, at the far end of which an old man sat upon an ornate throne. Surrounding him were priests and handmaidens, and before him an altar on which rested a large, jewelled casket.

Along both sides of the room were several cages, which reminded d'Arnot of the cages in the lion house of a zoo; but here there were no lions, only a few emaciated, almost naked men with unkempt hair and beards.

The priests led d'Arnot to the foot of the throne. 'Here is a would-be profaner of The Father of Diamonds that Queen Atka has sent as an offering to Brulor,' said one of the priests.

'We already have too many to feed,' grumbled the old man.

'Zytheb, put him in a cage.'

A tall priest, carrying a great ring of keys at his belt, came forward and led the way to one of the cages, which he unlocked and motioned d'Arnot to enter. As the door clanged behind him, a sudden chill ran through the Frenchman's body as though he were entering his own tomb.

A half-starved, bearded man in the next cage looked at d'Arnot curiously. 'Poor devil!' he said. 'Did you, too, come in search of The Father of Diamonds?'

'No,' said d'Arnot. 'I came looking for a man.'

'What man?' asked the other.

'A man named Gregory, who is supposed to be a prisoner here,' replied d'Arnot.

'Most interesting,' said the man. 'But I cannot but wonder what interest you would have had in looking for Brian Gregory, for, you see, I am he; and I do not recall having known you.'

'So you are Brian Gregory!' exclaimed d'Arnot. 'I have found you at last, but much good it will do either of us. But may I introduce myself? I am Captain d'Arnot, of the French Navy.'

'That makes it all the more puzzling,' said Gregory. 'Why should the French Navy be looking for me?'

'It is not,' replied d'Arnot. 'I just chanced to be in Loango when your father was arranging his expedition to come in search of you, and I joined it.'

'Oh, so Dad was coming after me? I hope he didn't.'

'He did; and your sister, also.'

'Helen? She didn't come here!'

D'Arnot nodded. 'I regret to say that she did.'

'Where is she? Where is Dad?'

'I don't know where your father is, but your sister was taken prisoner with me. She is here in Ashair.'

'God!' exclaimed Gregory. 'And I brought them to this! I and that damned thing out there in that casket.'

'It is The Father of Diamonds?' asked d'Arnot.

'Yes; and that is what Brulor is called, too – The Father of Diamonds. The big diamond is in the casket, and Brulor is the god who guards it; so they call him The Father of Diamonds, too.'

'The old man on the throne is Brulor?' asked d'Arnot.

Brian nodded. 'The old devil!'

D'Arnot's gaze wandered about the cages and the other prisoners. 'Are these all men from the outside world?' he asked.

'No,' replied Brian. 'Some are Asharians who have aroused the wrath of Atka, some are from Thobos, and the one in the next cage is Herkuf. He was a priest; but somehow he got in Dutch with the old man, and here he is.'

'And there is no escape?' asked the Frenchman.

'None,' said Brian.

As the two men talked, Asharian women had completed anointing the body of Helen with aromatic oils in a chamber in the palace; and were clothing her in the scant garments of a handmaiden.

'It is fortunate for you that you are beautiful,' said one of the women, 'for because of that you will go to the priests instead of to the warriors or the slaves. Of course you may be chosen for sacrifice; but if not, you will not go to the warriors or slaves until you are old and ugly.'

The toilet completed, Helen was taken down the long shaft and along the corridor to the throne room of Brulor; and as she entered, two men saw her and their hearts went cold. One of them called her by name as she was being led past his cage. She turned in astonishment.

'Brian!' she cried. 'Oh, Brian, what have they done to you?' Then she recognised the man in the next cage. 'Paul! You are both here!'

'Silence, woman!' commanded one of the priests escorting her; then she was led before Brulor.

As the old man examined her, Zytheb, the priest who carried the keys at his belt, whispered in Brulor's ear.

'What is your name, girl?' demanded Brulor.

'Helen,' she replied.

'From what country do you come?'

'America.'

Brulor scratched his head. 'There is no such country,' he said. 'There is a prisoner here who said he was from that country, but I knew he was lying. You must not lie. You will get along better here if you always tell the truth. Zytheb, you will take your place beside the girl. Helen,' he continued, 'you shall serve Zytheb, Keeper of the Keys; and see, girl, that you serve him well. Learn the holy rites of the temple and obey Zytheb.' He made some mystic passes above the jewelled casket and mumbled in a strange jargon. When he ceased, he looked up at the two standing before him. 'Zytheb and Helen are now man and wife!' he announced.

'What's happening?' demanded d'Arnot.

'The old devil's married Helen to that beast, Zytheb,' replied Brian with an oath; 'and here we are caged up like wild beasts, unable to help her. You can't know what it means to me, her brother!'

'And you don't know what it means to me, Brian,' said d'Arnot. 'I love her.'

XIX

Thetan, with Tarzan, Gregory, Magra and Lavac, was taken before Herat as a prisoner. Surrounding the throne of the King were black plumed warriors; and at his side sat his Queen, Mentheb. Herat was a large man with a black spade beard and a smooth upper lip. His face was hard, arrogant, and cruel. He scowled as he looked at Thetan.

'You know the laws of Thobos,' he said, 'and yet you dared bring strangers here. Even my nephew may not thus break the laws of Thobos with impunity. What have you to say for yourself?'

'I was being attacked by one of the great reptiles of the outer slopes of Tuen-Baka,' explain Thetan. 'I should have been killed, had not this man, Tarzan, at the risk of his own life, killed the beast and saved mine. When I found that he and his companions were enemies of the Asharians, I tried to help them, for I owed Tarzan a great debt. I thought, my King, that you would feel even as I. They may be strangers, but they are not enemies – they are my friends, and they should be accepted as friends by my people and my King.'

Herat's scowl relaxed a little, and he sat in thought for several minutes. 'What you tell me,' he said, 'lessens your guilt; and I forgive you, but the fact remains that they are strangers and should be destroyed. However, because of the extraordinary circumstances, I shall be lenient and give them a chance to live. Their lives shall depend upon the fulfilment of three conditions: that, in the arena, one of them kills an Asharian warrior. That is the first. The second is that one of them kills a wild lion in the arena, and the third that they bring me The Father of Diamonds from the temple at Ashair.'

Thetan turned to Tarzan. 'I am sorry, my friend,' he said, 'that I have brought you all here to die. You deserve a better fate.'

'We are not dead yet,' said the ape-man.

'Turn the girl over to the women. They will see that no harm befalls her,' said Herat. 'Imprison the men until I send for one of them to meet the Asharian. Take them away.'

Warriors conducted Tarzan, Gregory and Lavac to a cell in a dungeon and chained them to a wall. The place was damp and cold, and there was not even straw for them to lie upon.

'Hospitable country,' remarked Lavac.

'At least the King has a sense of humour,' said Tarzan.

'It is reflected in his benign countenance,' said Gregory.

'One of us might kill the Asharian,' reflected Lavac, 'but scarcely a wild lion. Well, there are three of us left. I wonder which will be the next to go?'

'And I wonder what will become of Magra?' said Gregory.

'Old Herat couldn't keep his eyes off her,' said Lavac. 'I'll bet he knows where she is.'

'They turned her over to the women,' said Tarzan. 'I hope Thetan will be able to help her.'

'She's going to need help,' remarked Lavac, 'and there will be none.'

In Ashair, Atan Thome and Lal Taask sat in a pleasant room with the noble Akamen. If the wages of sin are death, it must have been that the paymaster was napping, for Atan Thome and Lal Taask seemed launched upon a life of ease and luxury.

'It is fortunate for you,' said Akamen, 'that I have influence with the Queen; otherwise, you would both be languishing in the cages of the temple of Brulor; and I can assure you that that is not a pleasant place to be.'

'We owe you a great debt of gratitude, my friend,' replied Atan Thome.

'One which you may be able to repay, perhaps,' said Akamen. 'You will recall what I told you.'

Atan Thome nodded. 'Yes,' he said. 'That you are cousin of the Queen and that when she dies you will be King.'

'Quite right,' said Akamen. 'But the most important to you is that if I were King, your lives would no longer be in danger; and, if you so desired, it might be arranged that you leave Ashair and return to your own country.'

'With your guidance and advice, most noble Akamen,' Atan Thome assured him, 'I am sure that it can be accomplished most expeditiously.'

Gregory and Lavac were stiff and lame when they awoke the following morning after a night of fitful slumber. Tarzan, inured to hardships, had fared better.

'Lord, what a night!' groaned Gregory. 'If the builders of this place had searched every geological formation of the earth's crust they couldn't have found any stone harder than these lava slabs.'

'Nor colder,' added Lavac. 'Don't you suppose there is any way in which we could escape? I'd rather take any risk than stay here. Couldn't we overpower whomever brings our food?'

'Quiet!' cautioned Tarzan. 'Someone is coming.'

The others had heard nothing. It was the keen ears of the ape-man which had caught the faint sound of sandals on the stone floor of the corridor leading to the cell. A moment later a key was turned in the lock, and three warriors entered.

'One of you is to fight an Asharian,' said one. 'He is a giant, a famous killer of men. If he wins, and he will, he gets his freedom. Which one of you wishes to be killed first?'

'Let me go,' said Lavac. 'I would as soon be dead as here.'

'No,' said Gregory. 'Let me go. I am old.'

'I shall go,' said Tarzan, 'and I shall not be killed.'

The warriors laughed. 'Boast while you may,' said one.

They led Tarzan to a small arena, a courtyard enclosed by the palace buildings that surrounded it. At one end was a gallery for spectators, and here sat King Herat and Queen Mentheb with their court. Tarzan glanced up at them, and saw that Thetan was there, too. A guard of plumed warriors stood behind the King and Queen, and at either end of the gallery a trumpeter was posted. As Tarzan stood waiting in the centre of the arena, the trumpeters raised their instruments to their lips and sounded a fanfare; and through a small doorway beneath the royal box a huge man entered the arena.

'Good luck, Tarzan!' shouted Thetan.

'He'll need it,' said Herat. 'A thousand to one he dies.'

'Taken!' said Thetan.

The Asharian approached Tarzan and commenced to circle about him, looking for an opening. 'I have killed such men as Memet,' he boasted. 'I shall take great pleasure in killing you.'

Tarzan only growled, as early training and environment had taught him to do; but that growl brought a startled look to the face of the Asharian, for it was the growl of a lion. It shook his nerves a little, and he decided to get the thing over as quickly as possible; so he charged to close quarters with the intention of crushing his adversary in his mighty embrace. Thus he had crushed Memet, caving in his chest until his splintered ribs punctured his heart; and Tarzan let him get his hold. It was the hold he wished the other to have. The Asharian applied all the pressure of his great strength, but that mighty chest did not give an inch. He was amazed. It was unbelievable. Then Tarzan, growling, sought his foe's jugular with his teeth; and the Asharian was frankly terrified. Quickly he broke away and stepped back.

'What are you?' he cried. 'Man or beast?'

'I am Tarzan of the Apes. I kill!' growled the ape-man. Like a cornered rat fearing death but forced to fight for self-preservation, the Asharian charged with lowered head; and as Tarzan sought to sidestep, he slipped; and the other caught him full in the chest with his head, knocking him to the ground; then the Asharian turned and leaped high in the air to land upon his fallen foe and crush him.

A shout arose from the royal box. 'I win!' cried Herat.

'Perhaps.' admitted Thetan, 'But not yet – look!' While the Asharian was in mid-air, Tarzan rolled quickly to one side; and the other landed heavily on the flagging. Both men sprang to their feet instantly; and the Asharian, whipping a dagger from his sash, sprang at the ape-man. He had broken the rules of the contest, but he was too terrified to care about that. His only thought was to kill the beast-man.

As his foe charged with raised dagger, Tarzan leaped to one side, wheeled quickly and seized him from behind; then he swung him high above his head and hurled him to the flagging. He could have killed him then, but he preferred to play with him as a cat plays with a mouse. It was the Asharian's punishment for attempting to use a dagger; and, too, it was the humour of the jungle, which is grim and terrible.

The man scrambled to his feet; and as Tarzan slunk slowly toward him, he turned and fled, begging for mercy. The ape-man pursued him; and, though he could have caught him easily, he remained just a few paces behind him, voicing an occasional growl to add to the terror of his quarry.

'Did you invite us here to watch a foot race?' asked Thetan, laughing.

King Herat smiled. 'Something seems to have gone wrong with the famous killer of men,' he said.

Driven to desperation by terror, the Asharian turned at bay. Tarzan stopped and commenced to circle his adversary, low growls rumbling in his throat. Suddenly the terrified man raised his dagger and plunged it into his own heart.

'You lose, Herat,' laughed Thetan.

'But your Tarzan didn't kill him,' objected the King.

'He frightened him to death,' said Thetan.

Herat laughed. 'You win,' he admitted. 'Send for the man. I have something to say to him.'

'Never have I seen such a man,' said Queen Mentheb. 'Such a one should not be destroyed.'

Tarzan, brought to the royal box, stood before the King and Queen.

'You have won your freedom fairly,' said Herat, 'and I am going to change the conditions. You shall be free regardless of the fulfilment of the other two conditions. The others each may win his freedom in turn.'

'And the girl?' asked Tarzan. 'How about her?'

Herat looked a bit uncomfortable, shooting a quick glance at his Queen, as he answered. 'The girl shall not be harmed,' he said, 'and if all the conditions be fulfilled, she shall have her liberty. You shall remain as a guest of Thetan until your companions have either succeeded or failed; then you may leave the country. Decide among yourselves tonight which of the other two is to fight the lion tomorrow.'

'I shall kill the lion myself,' said Tarzan.

'But you have won your freedom!' exclaimed Queen Mentheb.

'You do not have to throw away your life.'

'I shall kill the lion,' reiterated Tarzan.

Herat looked questioningly at the Queen. 'If he wishes to be killed, he shall,' he snapped.

XX

The throne room of the temple of Brulor was vacant except for the poor prisoners in their cages. 'They have all gone, and taken Helen,' said d'Arnot. 'What will they do with her?'

'I don't know,' replied Brian, dejectedly. 'One knows nothing here. One just lives and suffers. If lucky, he may be chosen for sacrifice, and die. Sometimes they choose one of us prisoners, sometimes one of the handmaidens. It is a cruel and bloody spectacle.'

As he ceased speaking, a grotesque figure entered the throne room through a doorway on the opposite side. It appeared to be a man in a skin-tight suit with a strange helmet covering his entire head and an odd-looking contraption strapped to his back between his shoulders. He carried a trident on the end of which a large fish wriggled. Water dripped from his helmet and his suit.

'*Mon Dieu!*' exclaimed d'Arnot. 'What is that?'

'It is a ptome with our dinner,' replied Brian. 'The ptomes are lesser priests and greater fishermen. They go out on to the bottom of Lake Horus through watertight compartments and spear the fish with which we are fed. That affair on his back furnishes oxygen that it extracts from the water, which enters it in small quantities. They say that with one of those helmets a man could live underwater almost indefinitely, as far as his air supply was concerned. You will notice the heavy metal soles on his shoes, that prevent him from turning over and floating to the surface, feet up.'

'The whole thing is quite astonishing,' commented d'Arnot, 'and so is that fish, for that matter. I never saw one like it before.'

'You will see plenty of them from now on,' replied Brian, 'and I hope you like raw fish. If you don't, you'd better cultivate a taste for it – it's about all you'll get to eat here; but you'll be able to watch the priests and the handmaidens dine sumptuously. They throw a banquet in here every once in a while just to add to our misery.'

Zytheb led Helen to one of the upper floors of the temple where his apartments were situated. At the end of a corridor, he threw open a door. 'This is your new home,' he said. 'Is it not beautiful?'

The room was a jumble of strange-appearing furniture, with odd lamps and heavy vases. A frieze of skulls and bones encircled the walls just below the ceiling. Through a window at the far end of the room, the girl could see fishes swimming in the lake. She entered, like one in a trance, and passed

412

through the room to stand beside a table at the window. A heavy vase of strange workmanship stood on the table, and hazily she thought how interesting it might be were her mind not in such a turmoil of hopelessness and terror. Zytheb had followed her, and now laid a hand upon her shoulder.

'You are very beautiful,' he said.

She shrank away from him, backing against the table. 'Don't touch me!' she whispered.

'Come!' he said 'Remember what Brulor told you. You are my wife, and you must obey me.'

'I am not your wife. I shall never be. I should rather die. Keep away from me, I tell you, keep away!'

'You shall learn to obey and be a good wife – and like it,' snapped Zytheb. 'Come, now, and kiss me!'

He attempted to take her in his arms; and, as he did so, she seized the vase from the table and struck him heavily over the head. Without a sound, he slumped to the floor; and she knew that she had killed him. Her first reaction was solely of relief. She had no regrets, but what was she to do now? What possibility of escape was there from this frightful place beneath the waters of Horus?

For a time she stood looking down at the dead body of the man she had killed, fascinated by the very horror of it; then slowly came the realisation that she must do something. At least she could gain time by hiding the body. She looked about the room for some place where she might conceal it, shuddering at the thought of the gruesome ordeal; but she steeled herself, and dragged the body to a closet across the room. The body was heavy; but terror gave her strength, and at last she succeeded in getting it into the closet. Before she closed the door, she took the keys and his dagger. If there was any avenue of escape, she might need the keys; and she was sure that she would need the dagger.

Her first thought now was to find the throne room again and see d'Arnot and her brother. If escape were possible, she could take them with her. At least she might see them once more. Creeping along deserted corridors, she found her way down the winding stairways up which Zytheb had led her, as she searched for the throne room where the cages were. In constant fear of discovery, she came at last to a door she thought she recognised. But was this the room? If it were, would she find priests or guards within? For a moment she hesitated; then she opened the door. Yes, it was the throne room; and, except for the prisoners in their cages, it was vacant. So far fortune had favoured her; and she had achieved the impossible, but how much longer might she depend upon the fickle goddess? As she crossed the room to d'Arnot's cage she saw that the prisoners were all asleep. This fact and the quietness of the temple gave her new assurance, for if escape were possible it might be best accomplished while the temple slept. That the Asharians were confident that there could be no escape was suggested by the fact that no guards watched the prisoners, an inference that was not encouraging.

Helen leaned against the bars of d'Arnot's cage and whispered his name. The few seconds it took to awaken him seemed an eternity to the frightened girl, but at last he opened his eyes.

'Helen!' he exclaimed in astonishment. 'What has happened? How did you get here?'

'Quiet!' she cautioned. 'Let me get you and Brian out of those cages; then we can plan.' She was trying different keys in the lock of the cage door as she talked to him, and at last she found the one that fitted.

As the door swung open he sprang out and took her in his arms, 'Darling!' he whispered. 'You have risked your life for this; but you shouldn't have, for what good will it do? There is no escape from this place.'

'Perhaps not,' she agreed, 'but at least we can have these few minutes together – they can never take those away from us – and as far as risking my life is concerned will make no difference. I have already forfeited it.'

'What do you mean?'

'I have killed Zytheb,' she replied, 'and when they find his body, I imagine they'll make short work of me.' Then she told him what had happened in the apartment above.

'How brave you are,' he said. 'You deserve life and freedom for what you have undergone.'

D'Arnot took the keys from her and unlocked Brian's cage, and as the latter opened his eyes and saw Helen and d'Arnot standing outside, he thought that he was dreaming. He had to come out and touch them before he could believe his eyes. Briefly they explained what had happened.

'And now that we are out, what?' demanded d'Arnot. 'There can be no escape from this place.'

'I'm not so sure of that,' replied Brian. 'The priests have a secret passage that can be used if the windlass fails or if the temple should be in danger of flooding.'

'Little good that will do us,' said d'Arnot, 'unless you know where the entrance to this secret passage is.'

'I don't know, but there is one here who does. One of these prisoners, the one in the cage next to mine, is a former priest. If we liberate him, he might lead us out. I know he is anxious to escape. I'll wake him.'

'Let's liberate all the poor creatures,' suggested Helen.

'We certainly shall,' said Brian; then he awoke Herkuf, the former priest, and explained what he had in mind, while d'Arnot released the other prisoners, cautioning them to silence, as they gather around Brian and Herkuf.

'It will mean death by torture if we are caught,' explained the latter, 'and a life of danger if we escape, for we shall have no place to go in Tuen-Baka and must live in caves and hide for the remainder of our lives.'

'I shall have a place to go,' said a Thobotian. 'I can go back to Thobos, and I can show the rest of you a secret foot trail out of Tuen-Baka, that only we of Thobos know.'

'Anything, even death,' said Brian, 'would be better than these filthy cages and the treatment we receive here.'

'Well,' exclaimed the man from Thobos, 'why do we stand here talking? Will you lead us out, Herkuf?'

'Yes,' said the unfrocked priest. 'Come with me.'

He led them along the corridor that ran beneath the lake to the bottom of the elevator shaft. For a moment he fumbled at a great slab of lava that formed a part of one of the walls of the corridor beside the shaft. Presently it swung toward him, revealing the mouth of an opening as dark as Erebus.

'You'll have to feel your way along this corridor,' he said. 'There are many stairways, some of them winding; but there are no pitfalls and no side corridors. I shall go slowly.'

After all were inside the mouth of the corridor, Herkuf pulled the slab back in place; then he took the lead; and the long, slow climb commenced.

'It commences to look as though the impossible were about to be achieved,' said d'Arnot.

'And a few minutes ago it appeared so very impossible,' replied Helen. 'And we owe it all to you, darling.'

'We owe it to Zytheb,' she corrected, 'or to Brulor for selecting the Keeper of the Keys as my husband.'

'Well, whatever it was, we sure got a break at last,' said Brian, 'and the Lord knows we had one coming to us.'

It was still dark when the nine fugitives emerged into the open air at the end of the secret passage.

'Where are we?' asked Brian.

'We are on the hillside above Ashair,' replied Herkuf, 'and we shall breathe pure air and freedom for a few hours at least.'

'And which way do we go now?'

'We should head toward the upper end of the lake,' said the Thobotian. 'It is there that the trail begins that leads out of Tuen-Baka.'

'Very well,' said Herkuf, 'come on! I know a canyon we can hide in if we don't want to travel by day. We can just about reach it by sunrise. As soon as they find we have escaped, they will search for us; so the farther away we can get and the more secluded the hiding-place, the better off we shall be.'

XXI

In no dungeon had Magra been incarcerated, but in well-appointed apartments with black slave women to attend her. She wondered why she had been accorded these luxuries, until the door opened and King Herat entered; then she guessed the reason for her preferment. He wore an ingratiating smile and the self-satisfied look of a cat which has cornered a canary.

'You are being well treated and well served?' asked Herat.

'Yes, Your Majesty,' replied Magra.

'I am glad; I wish you to be happy. You are my guest, you know,' he explained.

'That is very kind of you. I hope you are treating my companions as generously.'

'Scarcely,' he replied, 'though I have been very fair and lenient with them. But do you know why I am treating you so well?'

'Because the Thobotians are a kindly people, I suppose,' she replied, 'and their King a kindly King.'

'Bosh!' exclaimed Herat. 'It is because you are beautiful, my dear; and because you please me. Those who please a King may fare very well indeed.' He came toward her. 'I shall see that you live like a Queen,' he said, suddenly taking her into his arms.

'I shall not please you for long,' she snapped, 'nor will you ever be pleased by anything again if you don't get out of here and leave me alone,' and as she spoke, she snatched his dagger from its sheath and pressed the point of it against his side.

'You she-devil!' he cried, as he jumped away. 'You'll pay for this.'

'I think not,' said Magra, 'but you shall, if you annoy me or try to punish me.'

'You dare threaten me, slave?'

'I certainly do.' Magra assured him, 'and it is no idle threat, either.'

'Huh!' sneered Herat. 'What can you do, other than threaten?'

'I can see that the Queen learns of this. My slaves have told me that she has a high temper.'

'You win,' said Herat, 'but let us be friends.'

While King Herat visited Magra, Queen Mentheb lay on a couch in one of her apartments while slave women enamelled her toenails and arranged her hair.

'That story is so old it smells,' said the Queen, peevishly.

'I am sorry, Majesty,' said the woman who had just sought to amuse Mentheb with story; 'but have you heard the one about the farmer's wife?'

'About a hundred times,' snapped the Queen. 'Every time Herat drinks too much wine he tells it. I am the only one who doesn't have to laugh at it every time he tells it. That is one of the advantages of being a Queen.'

'Oh, I know one, Your Majesty,' exclaimed another of the women. 'It seems there were two Romans—'

'Shut up!' commanded Mentheb. 'You all bore me.'

'Perhaps we could send for an entertainer to amuse Your Majesty,' suggested another.

Mentheb thought for a moment before she replied. 'Now, there is one whom it would amuse me to talk with,' she said. 'That man who killed the Asharian in the arena. He is a man, indeed. Mesnek, suppose you go fetch him!'

'But, Majesty, what of the King? Other men are not supposed to come to these apartments. Suppose the King should come while he was here?'

'Herat won't come here tonight,' said the Queen. 'He is gaming with his nobles. He told me so and that he would not be here tonight. Go, fetch this superman, Mesnek; and hurry!'

As Tarzan and Thetan talked in Thetan's apartments, a black slave entered. 'Most noble Thetan,' he said, 'Her Majesty, Queen Mentheb, commands the presence of him who slew the Asharian in the arena.'

'Where?' asked Thetan.

'In Her Majesty's apartments.'

'Wait outside the door to guide him to Her Majesty,' Thetan directed the slave; and when the fellow had gone, he turned to Tarzan. 'You'll have to go,' he said, 'but be very careful. Get away as quickly as you can, and while you are there be as discreet as you know how to be. Mentheb fancies that she is something of a siren, and Herat is insanely jealous. I think he is more fearful of being made a fool of than anything else.'

'Thanks,' said Tarzan. 'I shall be discreet.'

As Tarzan was ushered into the presence of Mentheb, she greeted him with a winning smile. 'So you are the man who killed the famous killer of men,' she said. 'That was very amusing. I do not know when I have seen anything so amusing or so entertaining.'

'Is it amusing to see men die?' asked the ape-man.

'Oh, well, he was only an Asharian,' said the Queen, with a shrug. 'What are you called?'

'Tarzan.'

'"Tarzan"! It is a nice name; I like it. Come and sit down beside me and tell me that you will not fight the lion. I wish you to live and remain here.'

'I shall fight the lion,' said Tarzan.

'But the lion will kill you; and I do not wish you to die, Tarzan.' Her tone was almost a caress.

'The lion will not kill me,' replied the ape-man. 'If I kill him, will you intercede with the King in behalf of my friends?'

'It would be useless,' she said. 'The law is the law, and Herat is just. They will die anyway, but you must live and remain in Thobos.' Suddenly she started up. 'Isis!' she cried. 'Here comes the King! Hide!'

Tarzan remained standing where he was with arms folded, making no move to hide; and there the King found him when he entered the apartment.

Herat's face clouded with an angry scowl as he saw the ape-man. 'What means this?' he demanded.

'I came in search of you, but found the Queen instead,' replied Tarzan, 'and I was just asking her to intercede in behalf of my friends.'

'I think you lie,' said Herat, 'for, while I don't know you, I know my Queen. I think I shall let you fight *two* lions.'

'Her Majesty is blameless,' said the ape-man. 'She was very angry because I came.'

'She looked more frightened at my sudden appearance than angry,' observed Herat.

'You are most unfair to me, Herat,' accused Mentheb. 'And you are also unfair to this man, who speaks the truth.'

'How am I unfair to him?' demanded the King.

'Because you have already promised that it should be one lion,' she explained.

'I can change my mind,' grumbled the King; 'and, anyway, I do not see why you should be so concerned in the matter. You but substantiate my suspicions, and cause me to recall the young warrior whom I had to send to the arena last year. I had hoped that you would permit me to forget him.'

Mentheb subsided into a pout, and Herat ordered Tarzan back to his quarters. 'The lions have been starved,' he said. 'They will be quite hungry tomorrow.'

'You should not starve your fighting lions, Herat,' said Tarzan. 'Starvation weakens them.'

'They will still be able to give a good account of themselves,' replied the King, 'for starvation will make them more ravenous and ferocious. Now, go!'

It was near noon the next day that two warriors came to conduct Tarzan to the arena. Thetan had already gone to join the King and Queen in the royal box, after having assured the condemned man of his chagrin at the unfortunate outcome of the whole adventure into Thobos.

As Tarzan walked to the centre of the arena and stopped, Herat turned to his Queen. 'Your taste is excellent, Mentheb,' he said. 'The man is indeed a magnificent specimen. It is too bad that he must die.'

'And I must compliment you on your good taste,' replied the Queen, 'for the woman also is a splendid specimen. It is too bad that she must die,' and thus Herat learned that Mentheb had heard about his visit to Magra. The King looked most uncomfortable, for Mentheb had taken no pains to lower her voice; and the nobles about them overheard; so he was very glad as he saw the two lions slink into the arena.

Tarzan saw them, too. They were big lions, and he realised that his visit to Mentheb might cost him his life. One lion he might have conquered, but how could any man withstand the attack of two such mighty beasts? He realised that this was not intended to be a contest, but an execution; yet, as the lions approached, he showed no fear. One lion came directly toward him, while the other stood for a few moments looking about the arena; and when the latter started to follow his companion he was quite some distance behind him. It was that suggested to Tarzan the only plan that he thought might prove successful against them. Had they charged simultaneously, he felt that would have been hope for him.

Suddenly, the leading lion made a rush and reared above the ape-man. Herat leaned forward, his lips parted, his eyes dilated. Above all things he loved a good kill; he liked to see blood spilled and bodies mauled. Mentheb stifled a scream.

Tarzan sprang to one side and leaped behind the lion; then he seized it and swung it above his head, wheeling about again as the second lion charged.

'What strength!' marvelled Thetan.

'I am almost sorry that I pitted him against two lions,' exclaimed Herat. 'He really deserved a better fate.'

'What?' sneered Mentheb. 'Three lions?'

'I don't mean that,' said Herat, irritably. 'I mean that such a man deserves better than death.'

'Name of Isis!' exclaimed Thetan. 'Look at him now!'

Tarzan had hurled the first lion into the face of the one that was charging, and both were down on the stone flagging of the arena.

'Incredible!' exclaimed Mentheb. 'If he survives, the girl may live.'

'And if he survives I swear that he shall have his freedom,' cried Herat, 'but I'm afraid there's no hope for him. They'll both be at him in a moment.'

In her excitement, Mentheb had risen and was leaning over the parapet. 'Look! They are fighting one another!'

It was as Tarzan had believed that it would be. One lion, thinking that the other had attacked him, tore into his fellow, and with hideous roars and growls, the two fell upon one another, rending with powerful talons and giant fangs.

'The man has not only marvellous strength, but great cunning,' said Herat.

'He is superb,' exclaimed the Queen.

As the two lions fought they moved nearer and nearer to the royal box, until its occupants had to lean far over the parapet to watch them. Tarzan, too, had moved back and was standing just below the box. In her excitement Mentheb lost her balance and toppled over the parapet. At her frightened scream the ape-man looked up just in time to catch her in his arms as she dropped toward him. Realising the woman's danger in the event that one of the lions dispatched the other or the two should cease fighting and turn their savage attention upon their natural enemies, Tarzan started toward the doorway through which he had entered the arena, shouting to Herat to order it opened.

All was confusion and chaos in the royal box. Herat was shouting commands and warriors were rushing down toward the entrance to the arena, but they were to be too late. With a final shake of the dead body of his weaker antagonist, the victorious lion turned with a savage roar and charged after Tarzan and the Queen. There was no time now in which to reach the doorway, and the ape-man, lowering Mentheb to her feet, turned with drawn knife to meet the oncoming carnivore. Growling, he crouched, and Mentheb felt her flesh turn cold in horror.

'That lion will kill them both!' cried Herat – 'He is a devil.'

'So is the man,' said Thetan.

Mentheb stood paralyzed by the bestial ferocity of the scene, and before the warriors had reached the doorway to rescue her the lion was upon Tarzan. Eluding the flailing talons, the ape-man seized the black mane and swung to the beast's back, driving his knife into the tawny side. Roaring horribly, the lion threw itself about in an endeavour to dislodge the man-thing from its back, and the growls of the ape-man mingled with those of the carnivore, until Mentheb scarcely knew which one to fear the most.

At last the knife found the savage heart, the beast rolled over upon its side, and, with a final convulsive shudder, died; then Tarzan placed a foot upon the body of his kill and, raising his face to the sky, voiced the weird victory cry of the bull ape, and Mentheb, the Queen, stood in helpless fascination as her warrior nobles rushed to her rescue.

'He is a demon,' exclaimed Herat, '—or a god!'

Mentheb commanded Tarzan to accompany her before Herat. She was still too shaken to do more than thank him feebly, and when she reached the box she sank into a chair.

'You have saved my Queen,' said the King, 'and thus won your freedom doubly. You may remain in Thobos or you may go, as you wish.'

'There is still another condition to be fulfilled,' Tarzan reminded the King.

'What is that?' asked Herat.

'I must go to Ashair and bring you Brulor and his casket,' replied Tarzan.

'You have done enough,' said Herat; 'let your friends do that.'

'No,' replied Tarzan. 'I shall have to go. Neither of the others could accomplish anything. Perhaps I cannot, but I shall have a better chance, and Gregory's daughter and my best friend are there.'

'Very well,' assented Herat, 'but we'll give you any assistance you wish. It's a task that one man cannot accomplish alone.'

'Nor a hundred,' said Mentheb. 'We should know, who have tried it so often.'

'I shall go alone,' said Tarzan. 'If I need help, I'll come back for it.'

XXII

Self-satisfied, contented, Atan Thome lounged at his ease in an apartment in the palace of Queen Atka at Ashair, while Lal Taask paced the floor nervously.

'I do not like it,' grumbled the latter. 'We shall all die for it.'

'It is perfectly safe,' Atan Thome assured him. 'Everything is arranged, and when it is over we shall be safe, favourites of the ruler of Ashair – and that much nearer The Father of Diamonds.'

'I have a presentiment,' said Lal Taask, 'that we shall not be safe.'

'Put your trust in Akamen,' urged Thome. 'He will lead you to the Queen's bedroom; then you will know what to do.'

'Why not you?' demanded Lai Taask. 'It is you who wants The Father of Diamonds so badly, not I.'

'I do not do it because you are more experienced with a dagger,' replied Thome, smiling. 'Come! Have you lost your nerve?'

'I do not wish to do it,' said Lal Taask emphatically.

'You will do as I command!' snapped Thome.

Lal Taask's eyes fell before those of his Master. 'Just this once,' he said. 'Promise that you will not ask such a thing of me again.'

'I promise that after tonight I shall ask nothing more of you,' agreed Thome. 'S-s-h! Someone is coming!'

As he ceased speaking the door opened and Akamen entered the room. He was pale and nervous. He looked at Atan Thome questioningly. The latter nodded.

'It is all understood,' he said. 'Lal Taask will do his duty.'

'Very well,' said Akamen. 'I have arranged everything. The Queen has retired. There are no guards before her door. It will be over in five minutes. Suspicion will be directed against the noble in command of the guard. The Queen disciplined him severely a short time ago, and it is known that he was very bitter. Come with me, Lal Taask.'

Akamen led the way through silent corridors to the Queen's bedroom. Without noise, he opened the door, and as the assassin, dagger in hand, slunk stealthily toward his victim, Akamen, flattened against the wall of the corridor, awaited the blow that would make him King of Ashair. Seconds seemed as hours to him as he waited for Lal Taask to reach the side of the Queen's bed and strike.

He was almost there! The dagger hand was rising! And then there was sudden commotion in the room as warriors leaped from behind hangings and fell upon the would-be assassin and his accomplice, and Queen Atka sat up in bed, a bitter smile of triumph on her lips.

'Summon my nobles to the throne room,' she directed, 'and take these two and the man Thome there, also, that justice may be done.'

When a warrior came to Atan Thome's apartments and summoned him to the throne room in the Queen's name, the Eurasian could scarcely restrain an expression of exultation, though he simulated surprise that Atka should wish to see him at so late an hour.

'Akamen,' said the Queen, as the three men were lined up before the throne, 'you conspired with these two strangers to assassinate me, that you might be King. One of your accomplices, hoping to curry favour with me, informed upon you. To my mind, he is even more vile than you, if that be possible; and his punishment shall be the same as yours. I sentence all three of you to the cages of the temple for life – a far greater punishment than a quick and merciful death. As added punishment, you shall all be half starved all of the time and tortured periodically, at each full moon. At the first, you shall each have one eye burned out; at the next, another; after that you shall lose first your right hands, then your left hands, your feet shall follow, one by one, and after that I am sure that I can devise other means whereby you may be reminded that treachery is a dangerous avocation.' She turned to one of her nobles. 'Take them away!'

Atan Thome, Lal Taask and Akamen in adjoining cages were the only prisoners now in the Temple of Brulor, Father of Diamonds. Lal Taask and Akamen glared at Atan Thome, cursing him; but he seemed oblivious to everything except the casket on the altar before the throne.

'Lowest of the low!' growled Akamen. 'You betrayed us. But for you I should be King of Ashair.'

'There is The Father of Diamonds!' whispered Atan Thome.

'Dog!' cried Taask. 'For years I have served you faithfully, and now you have sacrificed me!'

'There lies The Father of Diamonds,' droned Thome. 'For that I would betray my mother or my god.'

A ptome approached, bearing a wriggling fish upon a trident. 'Here is your dinner, damned ones!' he cried.

'It is not cooked!' exclaimed Atan Thome. 'Take it away!'

'Sure, I'll take it away,' said the ptome; 'but then you'll go hungry. We do not cook the fish for such as you.'

'Give me the fish!' screamed Lal Taask, 'and let him starve, but not too much – he must be saved for my dagger.'

'It is I who should have the right to kill him,' growled Akamen. 'He who kept me from being a King.'

'You are both fools,' cried Atan Thome. 'Nothing matters but The Father of Diamonds. Help me get that, and I shall make us all rich. Think, Taask, what it would buy in the capitals of Europe! I would give my soul for it.'

'You have no soul, you beast!' screamed Taask. 'Only let me get my dagger into you!'

Tarzan and Thetan came with a warrior to the cell where Gregory and Lavac were chained. 'Herat has reprieved you,' explained Tarzan, while the warrior removed their chains. 'You are to have freedom within the city until I return from Ashair.'

'Why are you going to Ashair?' asked Gregory.

'I want to find out if your daughter and d'Arnot are there, and ascertain if there is any way in which they may be rescued, if they are there; then there is the matter of Brulor and The Father of Diamonds. To win freedom for all of us they must be brought to Herat.'

'The other conditions have been fulfilled?' asked Lavac. 'You have killed the lions?'

'They are both dead,' replied Tarzan.

'I shall go to Ashair with you,' said Lavac.

'And I,' said Gregory.

'It is better that I go alone,' said Tarzan.

'But I must go,' insisted Lavac. 'I must do something to atone for my beastliness to d'Arnot. Please let me go with you.'

'I must go, too,' insisted Gregory.

'I can take one of you,' replied Tarzan. 'Herat insists that one of us remain here as a hostage. You may come, Lavac.'

The morning was still young as Thetan bid Tarzan and Lavac farewell as they were setting out for Ashair. 'I have told you all that I know of Ashair and the Temple of Brulor at the bottom of Lake Horus,' said the Thobotian. 'May the gods be with you!'

'I need no gods,' said Tarzan.

'Tarzan is enough,' added Lavac.

All night the nine fugitives had tramped from their last hiding place, and they were footsore and weary. There had been no indication of pursuit, but Herkuf knew his own people well enough to know that they would not be allowed to escape so easily.

'Now that it is light,' he said, 'it is time that we found a hiding place.'

'We are only a few hours from Thobos,' said the Thobotian, 'and before that I can show you the trail out of Tuen-Baka.'

'Nevertheless, I think it better that we hide through the day,' insisted Herkuf. 'I have no wish to be caught and taken back to the cages.'

'What is another day, if by hiding we can escape?' asked Brian.

'I think Herkuf is right,' said d'Arnot. 'We should not take a single risk, however small it may seem.'

'Listen!' whispered Helen. 'I hear voices. Someone is coming behind us.'

'It can be no one but the Asharians who are looking for us,' said Herkuf. 'Quick! We'll turn off the trail here and hide. Make no noise – just follow me. I know this place.'

They moved silently along a narrow trail for a quarter of a mile, coming at last to a little clearing. 'This is the place,' said Herkuf. 'I do not think they will look here for us. They will think that we kept on straight up the valley.'

'I don't hear them any more,' said Helen.

'The trouble with this,' said d'Arnot, 'is that now they'll be between us and where we want to go.'

'I don't think so,' replied Herkuf. 'They won't dare go too near Thobos; so, if they don't find us they'll have to turn around and come back. They'll pass us again later in the day, and tonight we can go on in safety.'

'I hope you're right,' said Brian.

Six Asharian warriors, following the trail of the fugitives, came to the place at which they had turned off. 'Their tracks are plain here,' said the leader. 'Here's where they turned off the main trail, and not so long ago. We should soon have them – remember to take the woman and the strange men alive.'

Half crouching, the six crept along the trail of their quarry – a trail as plain as a board walk. They did not speak now, for they felt that the fugitives were not far ahead, but moved with the utmost quiet and stealth. Each was thinking of what Atka would do to them if they failed.

As Tarzan and Lavac followed a forest trail toward Ashair the ape-man suddenly stopped and tested the air with his keen nostrils. 'There are men ahead,' he said. 'You stay here; I'll take to the trees and investigate.'

'They must be men from Ashair,' said Lavac, and Tarzan nodded and was off into the trees.

Lavac watched him until he disappeared among the foliage, marvelling at his strength and agility. Though he had seen him take to the trees many times, it never ceased to thrill him; but when Tarzan was gone he felt strangely alone and helpless.

As the ape-man swung through the trees the scent spoor became plainer, and among that of many men he detected the delicate aroma of a white woman. It was faintly familiar but still too tenuous to identify – just a suggestion of familiarity, but it spurred him to greater speed, and while he swung silently through the lower terrace of the forest the six Asharian warriors broke into the clearing upon the fugitives with shouts of triumph. Some of the nine started to run, bringing a shower of spears upon them, but d'Arnot, Helen, Brian and Herkuf stood still, knowing that there could be no escape now. A spear drove through one of the fleeing men, and as he fell, screaming, the others gave up hope and stopped.

Tarzan heard the shouts of the Asharians as they broke into the clearing and the scream of him who had received the spear. The sounds were close now. In another moment he would be on the scene.

The Asharians, having recovered their spears, rounded up the fugitives and commenced to belabour them with the hafts of their weapons. They struck indiscriminately, venting their hatred on all; but when one of them threatened Helen, d'Arnot knocked him down, and instantly another raised his spear to drive it through the Frenchman's back. It was this scene upon which Tarzan looked as he reached the edge of the clearing.

As Helen screamed in horror and warning, an arrow pierced the warrior's heart, and, shrieking, he fell dead. Instantly, the other Asharians looked about, but they saw no one who could have sped the missile. They knew that it could not have come from any of the unarmed prisoners, and they were frightened and mystified. Only d'Arnot could even hazard a guess as to the identity of the bowman.

'It seems incredible,' he whispered to Helen, 'but who in the world but Tarzan could have shot that arrow?'

'Oh, if it only were!' she exclaimed.

None knew better than Tarzan of the Apes how to harass and mystify an enemy. He had seen the surprise that the mysterious messenger of death had caused in the clearing below. A grim half-smile touched his lips as he drew his bow again and selected another victim – then he sped the arrow.

Once again the mysterious killer had struck, and as another Asharian screamed and fell the others looked about in consternation.

'Who is it?' cried one. 'I see nobody.'

'Where is he?' demanded another. 'Why doesn't he show himself?'

'It is the god of us outside people,' said d'Arnot. 'He will kill you all.'

'If he doesn't kill us, Atka will,' said a warrior, 'if we don't bring you back to Ashair.' then the four remaining warriors sought to herd their prisoners on to the back trail toward the city.

'Let's make a break for it,' suggested Brian. 'They're confused and frightened.'

'No,' counselled d'Arnot. 'They'd get some of us with their spears. We can't take the chance now.'

Suddenly there burst upon the surprised ears of the Asharians a deep voice that spoke the Swahili they all understood. 'I am Tarzan of the Apes,' it boomed. 'Go, and leave my friends!'

'We might as well die here as in Ashair,' a warrior shouted back 'for the Queen will have us killed if we come back empty handed, so we are going to take our prisoners with us. or kill them here.'

'Kill them now!' cried another, and turned upon Brian, who was closest to him; but as he raised his spear an arrow passed through his heart, and then, with the rapidity of machine gun fire, three more arrows brought down the remaining Asharians while the surviving fugitives looked on in amazement.

'There is only one man in the world who could have done that,' said d'Arnot, 'and we are very fortunate that he is our friend.'

As Tarzan dropped to the ground among them they surrounded him, voicing their thanks; but he silenced them with a gesture. 'What are your plans?' he asked.

'There is a Thobotian with us who is going to show us a secret trail out of Tuen-Baka,' explained d'Arnot. 'We didn't know that anyone but us was left alive.'

'Have you seen anything of Dad?' interrupted Helen. 'Was he drowned?'

'No,' replied Tarzan. 'He and Magra are in Thobos and safe for the moment. Lavac is back there on the trail waiting for me. He and I were on our way to Ashair to look for you.'

'Then we can all turn back to Thobos,' said Brian.

'It is not as simple as that,' replied Tarzan. 'I shall have to go to Ashair and bring back a god and a diamond to Herat before he will release your father and Magra.'

'It looks like a mansize job,' commented d'Arnot, with a rueful smile. 'I shall go with you.'

'And I,' said Helen.

Tarzan shrugged. 'You'd be little better off in Thobos,' he said, 'and I doubt very much that you could ever make it back to Bonga if you succeed in getting out of Tuen-Baka alive.'

'I think we should all stick together,' said Brian. 'I'm going along with you.'

'My duty lies near Ashair,' said Herkuf. 'I shall go with you. Perhaps, of all of us, I can be of the most help in getting what you want.'

'Very well,' agreed the ape-man. 'I'll go back and bring Lavac.'

A half hour later the little party was on its way back to Ashair, the Forbidden City of Tuen-Baka.

XXIII

As Magra sat in her apartment in the palace of Herat musing over the strange series of adventures that had brought her to this half civilised, half barbaric city, and dreaming of the godlike man she had come to love, the door opened and the King entered.

Magra rose and faced him. 'You should not come here,' she said. 'It will do you no good and only endanger my life. The Queen knew of the other time. She will know of this, and she will have me killed.'

'Have no fear,' said Herat, 'for I am King.'

'You only think you are,' snapped Magra contemptuously.

'I am Herat, the King!' cried the monarch. 'No one speaks to me like that, woman.'

'Oh, they don't, don't they?' demanded an angry voice behind him, and, turning, he saw the Queen standing in the doorway. 'So no one speaks to you like that, eh? You haven't heard anything yet; wait till I get you alone!' She turned her blazing eyes on Magra. 'And as for you, trollop; you die tomorrow!'

'But, my dear,' expostulated Herat.

'"But me", nothing!' snapped Mentheb. 'Get out of here!'

'I thought that you said you were King,' taunted Magra; then they were both gone and the girl was left alone. Never in her life had she felt so much alone, so helpless and so hopeless. She threw herself upon a couch, and, had she been another woman, she would have burst into tears; but Magra had never cried for herself. Self-pity was not for her. She had said once that it was like cheating at solitaire, for nobody else knew about it and nobody cared and no one was hurt but herself. How she wished that Tarzan were here! He would have helped her – not with useless commiseration; but with action. He would have found a way to save her. She wondered if would grieve for her, and then she smiled, for she knew that the philosophy of the wild beast had little place for grief. It was too accustomed to death, held life in such low esteem. But she must do something. She struck a gong that summoned a slave girl.

'Do you know where the prisoners, Gregory and Lavac, are quartered?' she asked.

'Yes, my mistress.'

'Take me to them!'

When she entered Gregory's apartment she found Thetan with him. At first she hesitated to talk before the Thobotian, but she recalled that he had befriended them, so she told them all that had just happened.

'I must escape tonight,' she said. 'Will you help me?'

'Mentheb is rather a decent sort,' said Thetan. 'She may come to realise that the fault is not yours, and of course she knows that it is not, and alter her decision to have you killed; but it would be dangerous to depend on that. I know you are guiltless, and I know that you are a friend of Tarzan; so I am going to help you to escape.'

'Will you help me to go with her?' asked Gregory.

'Yes,' said Thetan. 'I got you into this, and I should get you out of it. I shall help you because you are Tarzan's friends, and Tarzan saved my life. But never return to Thobos, for if you escape her now, Mentheb will never forget. Follow the trail on the west side of the lake South; it will bring you to Ashair and probably to death there – it is the law of Tuen-Baka.'

A half hour later Thetan led Magra and Gregory to a small gate in the city wall and wished them luck as they went out into the night and set their faces toward The Forbidden City.

'Well,' said d'Arnot, 'here we are right back where we started from,' as the party of six reached the entrance to the secret passage to the Temple of Brulor on the rocky hillside above Ashair.

'I spent two years trying to get out of that hole,' said Brian, 'and now here I am trying to get back in again. That Herat certainly gave you a tough job, Tarzan.'

'It was merely the old boy's way of condemning us all to death,' said Lavac, '—an example of Thobotian humour. At least, it was at first; but after Tarzan disposed of the bad man from Ashair and the two lions, I really believe that Herat came to the conclusion that might actually bring back Brulor and The Father of Diamonds.'

'Why does he want them so badly?' asked Helen.

'The Father of Diamonds belongs in Thobos,' explained Herkuf, 'where the temple of the true god, Chon, is located. It was stolen by Atka's warriors years ago when they attacked and sank Chon's galley in which it was being carried during a solemn religious rife. Brulor is a false god. Herat wishes to destroy him.'

'Do you think that there is any possibility that we may be able to recover The Father of Diamonds and kidnap Brulor?' asked d'Arnot.

'Yes,' replied Herkuf, 'I do. We have the temple keys that Helen took from Zytheb, and I know where Brulor sleeps and the hours of the day that are supposedly set apart for meditation; but which, in reality, Brulor devotes to sleeping off the effects of the strong drink to which he is addicted. During these periods the throne room is deserted, and all the inmates of the temple are compelled to remain in their own quarters. We can go directly to the throne room and get the casket, and then to Brulor's room. If we threaten him with death he will come with us without making any outcry.'

'It all sounds very easy,' said Brian. 'Almost too easy.'

'I shall keep my fingers crossed all the time,' said Helen.

'When can we make the attempt?' asked d'Arnot.

Herkuf looked up at the sun. 'Now,' he said, 'would be a good time.'

'Well, how about getting started, Tarzan?' asked Brian.

'Herkuf and I shall go in,' said the ape-man. 'The rest of you hide near here and wait for us. If we are not out within an hour you will know that we have failed; then you must try to save yourselves. Find the trail over the rim. It lies somewhere near Thobos. Get out of Tuen-Baka. It will be useless for you to try to do anything for Herkuf or me or to rescue Magra and Gregory.'

'Am I not to go in with you, Tarzan?' asked d'Arnot.

'No. Too many of us might result in confusion and discovery; and, anyway, your place is with Helen. Come, Herkuf, let's get started.'

As the two entered the secret passage a sentinel priest, who had been crouching behind a boulder watching the party, turned and ran as fast as he could toward the nearest city gate, while, miles away, the objects of all this now useless risk and sacrifice trudged doggedly along the trail to Ashair in an effort to avert it.

Ignorant of anything that had transpired in Ashair, not knowing that his son and daughter lived and were free, Gregory accompanied Magra rather hopelessly, his only inspiration loyalty to Tarzan and Lavac, whom he knew to be risking their lives in an effort to save his and Magra's. Magra was inspired by this same loyalty and by love – a love that had done much to change and ennoble her.

'It all seems so utterly hopeless,' said Gregory. 'Only four of us left, pitting our puny efforts against two cities filled with enemies. If one of them doesn't get us, the other will.'

'I suppose you are right,' agreed Magra. 'Even the forces of nature are against us. Look up at that towering escarpment of lava, always frowning down upon us, threatening, challenging; and yet how different it would all seem if Tarzan were with us.'

'Yes, I know,' said Gregory. 'He inspires confidence. Even the walls of

Tuen-Baka would seem less unsurmountable if he were here. I think he has spoiled us all. We have come to depend upon him to such an extent that we are really quite helpless without him.'

'And he is going to almost certain death for us,' said Magra. 'Thetan told me that it would be impossible for him to escape alive from Ashair, if he succeeded in getting in; and, knowing Tarzan, we know that he will get in. Oh, if we could only reach him before he does!'

'Look!' exclaimed Gregory. 'Here come some men!'

'They have seen us,' said Magra. 'We can't escape them.'

'They look very old and weak,' said Gregory.

'But they carry spears.'

The three surviving fugitives from the cages of the Temple of Brulor who had chosen to go on in search of freedom rather than return to Ashair with Tarzan's party halted in the trail.

'Who are you?' they demanded.

'Strangers looking for a way out of Tuen-Baka,' replied Gregory.

The three whispered among themselves for a moment, then one of them said, 'We, too, are looking for a way out of Tuen-Baka. Perhaps we should go together, for in numbers there is strength.'

'We can't go until we find our friends,' replied Magra. 'They were on their way to Ashair.'

'Perhaps we saw them. Was one of them called Tarzan?'

'Yes. Have you seen him?' demanded Gregory.

'We saw him yesterday. He and his friends went back to Ashair.'

'His friends? There was but one with him,' said Magra.

'There were five with him. Four men and a girl went back to Ashair with him.'

'Whom could they have been, do you suppose?' Gregory asked Magra.

'Do you know who they were?' she inquired of the fugitive who had been acting as spokesman.

'Yes. One was called Herkuf, and one Lavac, and there was d'Arnot, and Brian Gregory was with him and a girl called Helen.'

Gregory turned very pale. Magra caught his arm, for she thought he was going to fall. 'I'm stunned,' he said. 'I can't believe that they're all alive. It's just like having people come back from the grave – I was so sure that they were dead. Think of it, Magra! My son and my daughter both alive – and on their way back to that terrible city. We must hurry on. Maybe we can overtake them. Tell us,' he said to the fugitive, 'where we may find them if they have not already been captured by the Asharians.'

The man gave them explicit directions for locating the hidden entrance to the secret passage to the temple. 'That is where you will find them,' he said, 'if they have not already entered the city; but do not enter. As you value your lives, do not enter the passage. If they have done so, they are lost; you might as well give them up, for you will never see them again.'

'They weren't very encouraging,' said Magra, as she and Gregory continued on their way; 'but perhaps they overestimate the dangers – let's hope so.'

Gregory shook his head. 'I'm afraid they didn't,' he said. 'I doubt if the dangers that lurk in The Forbidden City of Ashair can be overestimated.'

'It is a strange place, this Tuen-Baka,' said Magra. 'No wonder that it is taboo.'

XXIV

Tarzan and Herkuf followed the dark passageway and the winding stairs down to the lava slab that closed the secret doorway leading to the corridor they must follow beneath the lake to reach the temple.

'Here we are,' said Herkuf. 'If the gods are with us we shall soon be in Brulor's room behind the throne. I'll attend to him, you get the casket. I have waited years for such an opportunity to avenge Chon, the true god, and make Brulor pay for the indignities and torture he imposed upon me. I see now how I have lived through all that I have lived through. It was for this hour. If we fail, it will mean death; but if we fail I shall welcome death.'

Beyond the lava slab a group of Asharian warriors, their short spears ready, awaited them, for the sentinel priest had done his duty well.

'They must be close,' said the leader of the warriors. 'Be ready! But do not forget that it is the Queen's command that we take them alive for torture before death.'

'I should hate to be Herkuf when Brulor gets him back in his cage,' said a warrior.

'And that wild man,' said another. 'It was he who killed so many of our warriors that night in the tunnel. I should hate to be the wild man when Atka gets him.'

The lava slab was thick, and it was skilfully fitted in the aperture, so the voices of the whispering warriors did not reach the ears of the two upon the other side of it. Ignorant of the trap into which they were walking, they paused for a moment while Herkuf groped for the knob which would open the door.

And while they paused upon the brink of disaster another detail of warriors crept up upon the unsuspecting four who were waiting at the entrance to the secret passageway, ignorant of the imminent peril that hovered just above them among the boulders of the hillside.

'At last, darling,' said d'Arnot, 'I can see a ray of hope. Herkuf knows the customs of the temple, and before the inmates leave their apartments again he and Tarzan will be back with Brulor and the accursed Father of Diamonds.'

'I have grown to hate the very name of the thing,' said the girl. 'There surely must be a curse upon it and everything connected with it. I feel that so strongly that I can't believe it possible that it is going to be the means of releasing Dad and Magra. Something will happen to turn success into failure.'

'I don't wonder you're pessimistic and sceptical, but this time I'm sure you're wrong.'

'I certainly hope so. I don't know when I've ever so wanted to be wrong.'

Lavac and Brian were sitting on the ground a few paces from Helen and d'Arnot, the former with his back toward them that he might not see the little intimacies that still hurt him so sorely, notwithstanding his honest intention to give up all hope of winning the girl. He was facing up the slope of the rocky hillside above which towered the stupendous rampart of Tuen-Baka, and so it was he who first saw the Asharian warriors as they broke cover and started down toward their quarry. As he leaped to his feet with a cry of warning, the others turned, and in the instant their hopes came tumbling about their heads like a house of matchwood. The Asharians were yelling triumphantly now, as they charged down the hill, brandishing their short spears. The three men might have put up a battle even against these terrific odds, futile as it would have been, had they not feared for the safety of the girl should they invite the Asharians to hurl their spears, so they stood in silence while the warriors surrounded them, and a moment later they were being herded down toward the nearest city gate.

'You were right, after all,' said d'Arnot.

'Yes,' she replied, dejectedly; 'the curse of the diamond is still on us. Oh, Paul, I'd rather die than go back to that awful place! This time there will be no hope for us, and what I dread most is that they will *not* kill me.'

As the four prisoners were being marched down to the city Herkuf pulled the lava slab toward him, and the two men stepped into the trap that had been laid for them. They hadn't a chance, not even the mighty ape-man, for the Asharians had planned well. As they stepped from the mouth of the passageway two warriors, crouching low, seized them around their ankles and tripped them, and as they fell a dozen others swarmed upon them, slipping nooses about their ankles and wrists.

'You knew we were coming?' Herkuf asked one of the warriors as they were being led along the corridor toward the temple.

'Certainly,' replied the man. 'A sentry has been watching above the city, for Atka thought that you might come back to Ashair to steal a galley. It was the only way that the strangers could escape from Tuen-Baka. It would have been better had you stayed in your cage, Herkuf, for now Brulor will have you tortured, and you know what that means.'

The throne room of the temple was silent and vacant, except for the three prisoners in the cages, as Tarzan and Herkuf were led in, for it was still the period of meditation, during which the inmates of the temple were compelled to remain in their quarters; and so there was a delay while a warrior sought permission from Brulor to summon the Keeper of the Keys that the cages might be unlocked to receive the new prisoners.

Presently, Herkuf touched Tarzan on the arm. 'Look!' he said. 'The others have been taken also.'

Tarzan turned to see Helen, d'Arnot, Brian and Lavac being herded into the chamber, and greeted them with one of his rare smiles. Even in the face of death he could see the humour of the situation, that they who had come so confidently to conquer should have been so ignominiously conquered themselves without the striking of a blow. d'Arnot saw the smile and returned it.

'We meet again, *mon ami*,' he said, 'but not where we expected to meet.'

'And for the last time,' added Lavac. 'There will be no more meetings after this one for any of us, at least not in this life. As for me, I shall be glad. I have nothing to live for.' He did not look at Helen, but they all knew what he meant.

'And you all die because of me,' said Brian, 'because of my stupid avarice; and I shall die without being able to atone.'

'Let's not talk about it,' urged Helen. 'It's bad enough as it is without constantly reminding ourselves of it.'

'When one is about to die by slow torture one does not have to be reminded of it,' said Herkuf. 'It occupies one's mind to the exclusion of all else. Sometimes it is a relief to talk of it.'

Atan Thome looked out between the bars of his cage at the six prisoners. 'So we are reunited at last!' he cackled. 'We who sought The Father of Diamonds. There it is, in that casket there; but do not touch it – it is mine. It is for me alone,' then he broke into loud, maniacal laughter.

'Silence, you crazy pig!' growled Lal Taask.

It was then that the Keeper of the Keys came and opened the cages. 'Into their dens with them,' snapped an officer, 'all but this fellow here.' He nodded at Tarzan. 'The Queen wants to see him.'

Atka sat upon her lava throne surrounded by her white plumed nobles as the Lord of the Jungle, his hands still bound behind him, was brought before her. For a long time she sat studying him with half-closed, appraising eyes; and with neither deference nor boldness Tarzan returned her scrutiny, much as a captive lion might regard a spectator outside his cage.

'So you are the man who killed so many of my warriors,' she said at last, 'and captured one of my galleys.'

Tarzan stood silent before her. Finally she tapped her toe upon the floor of the daïs. 'Why do you not reply?' she demanded.

'You asked me nothing,' he said. 'You simply told me something I already knew.'

'When Atka speaks the person who is thus honoured makes some reply.'

Tarzan shrugged. 'I do not like useless talk,' he said, 'but if you like to hear it, I admit that I killed some of your warriors. I should have killed more that night on the river had there been more in the galley. Yesterday I killed six in the forest.'

'So that is why they did not return!' exclaimed Atka.

'I think that must be the reason,' Tarzan admitted.

'Why did you come to Ashair?' the Queen demanded.

'To free my friends who were prisoners here.'

'Why are you my enemy?' asked Atka.

'I am not your enemy. I wish only the freedom of my friends,' the ape-man assured her.

'And The Father of Diamonds?' added Atka.

'I care nothing for that,' replied Tarzan.

'But you are an accomplice of Atan Thome,' she accused, 'and he came to steal The Father of Diamonds.'

'He is my enemy' said Tarzan.

She looked at him again for some time in silence, apparently playing with a new idea. At last she spoke.

'I think,' she said, 'that you are not the type that lies. I believe what you have told me, and so I would befriend you. They have told me how you fought with your ape allies at the camp below the tunnel and also of the fight in the galley, for all of the warriors did not drown, two of them swimming out of the tunnel to safety. Such a man as you would be valuable to me, if loyal. Swear loyalty to me and you shall be free.'

'And my friends?' asked Tarzan. 'They will be freed too?'

'Of course not. They are no good to me. Why should I free them? The man, Brian Gregory, came here solely for the purpose of stealing The Father of Diamonds. I think the others came to help him. No, they shall die in good time.'

'I told you that I came here to free them,' said Tarzan. 'The granting of their freedom is the only condition under which I will remain.'

'Slaves do not impose conditions upon Atka,' snapped the Queen imperiously. She turned to a noble. 'Take him away.'

They returned Tarzan to the throne room of the temple then, but they did not free his hands until they had him locked safely in a cage. It was evident that the fighting men of Ashair held him in deep respect.

'What luck?' asked d'Arnot.

'I am here in cage,' replied Tarzan. 'That is answer enough. The Queen wishes us all dead.'

'I imagine her wish will come true,' said d'Arnot ruefully.

'Queens have but to wish.'

It was a dejected and disheartened company that awaited the next eventuality of their disastrous adventure. There were only two of them who appeared to be not entirely without hope – the ape-man, whose countenance seldom revealed his inward feelings, and Atan Thome, who continually cackled and prated of The Father of Diamonds.

When life began to stir in the throne room with the ending of the period of meditation, priests and handmaidens appeared; and finally Brulor entered and took his place upon the throne, while all knelt and beat their heads upon the floor. After a brief religious ceremony, some of the handmaidens commenced to dance before Brulor, a suggestive, lascivious dance in which some of the priests soon joined, in the midst of which a plumed warrior entered from the long corridor and announced the coming of the Queen. Instantly, the music and the dancing stopped, and the dancers took their places in sanctimonious attitudes about the throne of Brulor. A loud fanfare of trumpets billowed from the mouth of the corridor, and a moment later the head of a procession appeared and marched down the centre of the room toward the dais where Brulor sat. Surrounded by warriors, the Queen moved majestically to the dais, where she took her place in a second throne chair that stood beside Brulor's.

A long and tedious ceremony ensued, after which the Queen pronounced sentence upon the new prisoners, a privilege she occasionally usurped to the chagrin of Brulor, who was a god only on sufferance of the Queen.

'Let all but the woman,' ordered Atka, 'be offered in sacrifice, each in his turn, and with slow torture, that their spirits may go out into the world of barbarians to warn others never to seek entry to The Forbidden City of Ashair.'

She spoke in a loud voice that could be heard throughout the chamber; and her words brought a ray of hope to d'Arnot, for Helen had not been sentenced to torture and death, but his hopes were dashed by the Queen's next words.

'The woman shall be taken to the little chamber to die slowly as a sacrifice to Holy Horus. This shall be her punishment for the killing of Zytheb, the priest. Let her be taken away at once. The sentences of the others shall be carried out at the discretion of Brulor.'

A priest scurried from the throne room to return presently with three ptomes, one of which carried an extra water suit and helmet. The Keeper of the Keys led them to Helen's cage, which he unlocked, after which the ptomes entered, removed the girl's outer clothing and dressed her in the water suit. Before they placed the helmet over her head she turned toward d'Arnot, who stood with ashen face pressed against the partition bars that separated their cages.

'Once more, goodbye,' she said. 'It will not be for long now.'

Emotion stifled the man's reply; and tears blinded him, as the ptomes fitted the helmet over Helen's head; then they led her away. He watched until she passed from sight through a doorway on the opposite side of the temple; then he sank to the floor of his cage and buried his head in his arms. Brian Gregory cursed aloud. He cursed Atka and Brulor and The Father of Diamonds, but most of all he cursed himself.

The Queen and her entourage left the temple, and presently Brulor and the priests and the handmaidens were gone, leaving the doomed men to their own unhappy company. Atan Thome jabbered incessantly about The Father of Diamonds, while Lal Taask and Akamen threatened and reviled him. Lavac sat on his haunches staring at the doorway through which Helen had disappeared to pass out of his life forever, but he knew that she was no more lost to him than she had been before. Brian paced the length of his cage, mumbling to himself. Tarzan and Herkuf spoke together in low tones. D'Arnot was almost ill from desperation and hopelessness. He heard Tarzan asking many questions of Herkuf, but they made no impression on him. Helen was gone now forever. What difference did anything else make? Why did Tarzan ask so many questions? It was not like him; and anyway, he too would soon be dead.

Silhouetted against the blue African sky, Ungo and his fellow-apes stood at the rim of the crater of Tuen-Baka and looked down into the valley. They saw the green of the plains and the forests; and they looked good to them after the barren outer slopes of the mountain.

'We go down,' grunted Ungo.

'Perhaps Tarzan there,' suggested another.

'Food there,' said Ungo. 'Tarzan not there, we go back old hunting grounds. This bad country for Mangani.'

XXV

Helen Gregory was, despite her flair for adventure and her not inconsiderable fortitude, essentially feminine. She was the type that stirred the deepest protective instincts of men; and, perhaps because of that very characteristic, she subconsciously craved protection, though she would have been the last to realise it. Fortified by the knowledge that masculine aid was within call, she might have dared anything; while the realisation that she was alone among enemies, hopelessly cut off from all natural protectors, left her a frightened little girl upon the verge of panic. That she did not break under the strain speaks well for her strength of character.

Her steps did not falter as the three ptomes led her from the throne room and down a short corridor, through a room where many ptomes were gathered lying upon narrow cots or playing at games, their water suits and helmets hung upon pegs against the wall, their tridents standing in racks, and along another corridor to a massive door secured by huge bolts and flanked by valve handwheels and levers. Here, one of the ptomes turned wheels and pulled on levers, and they all waited while he watched a gauge beside the door.

This, she thought, must be the door to the torture chamber; and she wondered what lay behind and how long death would be in coming to her rescue. Death! Man's last refuge when hope is gone, his last friend, his life's ultimate goal. She thought of her father and of Brian and of Paul d'Arnot. They would be following her soon. She wished that she and d'Arnot might have gone together. It would have been easier for both had it been that way.

At last the door swung open and the ptomes pushed her into a cylindrical chamber, following her in and closing and bolting the door. Here were other handwheels and levers and gauges; and there was an identical door on the opposite side of the chamber, flanked by similar gadgets. She saw no signs of instruments of torture, and she wondered how they were going to kill her and why they had brought her here to do it and why they all wore the strange helmets. She watched while a ptome turned a handwheel, and caught her breath as she saw water rushing into the chamber. They couldn't be going to drown her, for if she drowned, they would drown too. The chamber filled rapidly; and when it was full, one of them manipulated the wheels and levers beside the second door; and when it swung open, they led her out into the diffused light of the lake bottom.

Under other circumstances she would have been entranced by the beauty of the scene upon which the sun filtered down through the clear waters of

Horus. She found herself being led along a gravel path between neat gardens of marine plants which other ptomes were tending to serve as delicacies for the courts of Atka and Brulor. Strange and beautiful fishes swam about them, and great turtles paddled clumsily away as they approached, while crabs of many colours scurried from their path. Here and there were marine trees towering high, their foliage undulating gracefully to the movement of the water, while bright coloured fishes played among it like gay birds among the branches of terrestrial trees. All was beauty and movement and – silence. To the girl, the silence spoke more loudly than the beauty or the movement – it bespoke the silence of the tomb.

Inside the temple she had found walking arduous and slow, impeded by the heavy metal soles of the shoes they had put on her; but here she moved as though walking on air, lightly as a feather, effortless as the passing of a shadow. She felt that she might leap high above the trees if one of the ptomes were not holding her by the arm; but these were only flashes of thought breaking occasionally the dense gloom of the horror that engulfed her.

Presently she saw ahead of them a small circular building topped by a single dome, and realised that it was toward this the ptomes were leading her. When they reached the building, which seemed to have neither doors nor windows, two ptomes seized Helen's arms, one on either side, and leaped lightly upward, carrying her with them, the third ptome following. A few swimming strokes carried them to the top of the dome, where the girl saw a circular door, which she recognised now, from the gadgets flanking it, as the entrance to an air chamber such as that through which she had passed from the temple to the lake bottom.

The chamber below was filled with water when they entered it, and it was several minutes before it emptied; then the ptomes removed her helmet and suit, lifted a trap-door in the floor, pointed to a ladder, and motioned her to descend. As in the upper chamber, there was a window in the wall on the side opposite to that from which they had approached the come, which she had previously thought windowless; and through this window the diffused light of the lake bottom dimly illuminated the interior of the circular room in which she was imprisoned. It was entirely bare – the walls, the window, and the ladder constituted he world. The ptomes had closed the trap-door above her, and presently she heard water gushing into the chamber above; then it commenced to trickle down one wall of her prison, and presently the trickle became a little stream. As water covered the floor of her cell, she understood the nature of the torture and death that confronted her. The chamber would fill slowly. She might prolong life and agony by climbing the ladder, but the end was inevitably the same.

She realised what exquisite mental torture the minds of these people had conceived, that one should be condemned to die alone, drowned like a rat in a trap. She wondered if she would have the courage to end it quickly when the water was deep enough, or if she would drag out the torture to the topmost rung of the ladder.

And, as the water rose slowly in Helen's death cell, Herkuf whispered to Tarzan through the bars of his cage: 'It will soon be time. Do you think you can do it?'

'I can do my part,' the ape-man assured him. 'When the time comes, let me know.'

When night came and darkness settled above Horus, a faint light still filtered down through the waters to the death cell where Helen waited for the end. It was the light of heavenly stars, but it brought no hope to the doomed girl. The water was at her knees now; and she stood with one hand on the ladder, still wondering what she should do. She turned wearily; and, with both arms resting on a rung of the ladder, buried her face in them. She thought of d'Arnot and the happiness that might have been theirs had they met under different circumstances; and, even with hope gone, that thought made her want to cling to life as long as she could, for at least there was a certain sad happiness in envisioning the happiness she had been denied. She thought of Brian; and, without bitterness toward him, she execrated the avarice that had lured him to this awful place and cost the lives of so many people, people who loved him. And she prayed.

Again Herkuf whispered to Tarzan. 'It is time,' he said. 'They will all be asleep. But the bars are very strong.'

'Not so strong as Tarzan,' replied the ape-man. 'I have tried them – watch!'

As he spoke, he seized two bars. The muscles stood out upon his shoulders as he exerted his strength upon the insensate metal. Herkuf watched, breathless, and filled with doubt; then he saw the bars spreading apart, and a moment later saw Tarzan squeeze between them and push them back into place. Similarly the ape-man liberated Herkuf.

'You are as strong as a bull elephant,' gasped the priest.

'Come!' said Tarzan. 'We have no time to waste. Lead the way.'

'No,' replied Herkuf, 'we have no time to waste. Even if we get through without delay, we may still be too late.'

Silently, stealthily, Herkuf and Tarzan crossed the temple toward a closed door. The other prisoners slept. No one had seen Tarzan escape and release Herkuf. Even the bars, bent back almost to normal position, gave little evidence of the manner of their liberation; and few would have believed the truth, for many had been the prisoners who had sought to bend them; but never before had it been done.

Herkuf led Tarzan down a short corridor to the room of the ptomes; and as the priest opened the door, Tarzan saw the lesser priests sleeping on their hard benches. He saw their water suits hanging on their pegs and their tridents in the racks. The ptomes slept thus without sentries and the temple went unguarded because it was considered impregnable.

Cautiously the two men took three water suits and helmets from their pegs, gathered up three tridents, and crossed the room to the doorway on the opposite side without awakening a ptome. Once past the door, each donned a suit.

'The gods have been with us so far,' whispered Herkuf, 'and if we can pass through the air chamber without being discovered, we stand a good chance to succeed – if we are in time.'

As the water rose to Helen's shoulders she finally gave up all thought of suicide. She would cling to life to the last moment. They might rob her of that; but they could not rob her of her courage, and as the water rose still higher she stepped to the lowest rung of the ladder.

Reminiscences rioted through her mind as she waited for death, and pleasant thoughts and bitter. She pondered the futility of man's quest for sudden wealth and of the evil and suffering it entailed. Of what avail would success be now to either Brian or Thome if, by some chance, it should come to one of them? For one had lost his sister and, perhaps, his father; and the other had lost his mind. Now the water forced her up to a higher rung of the ladder. Step by step, she was climbing to her rendezvous with Death.

Herkuf and Tarzan passed safely through the air chamber out into the waters of the lake. Through the garden of the ptomes they made their way toward the watery cell where Death was creeping relentlessly upon Helen Gregory, and dark shapes glided sinuously about them in this mysterious world of silence.

At last they reached the air chamber above Helen's cell; and Herkuf started the pump that would eject the water, but it seemed to both men that it would never empty the chamber. They knew that the water had been rising for hours in the death cell beneath them and that death might come to the girl before they reached her, if she were not already dead.

Just below them, clinging to the last few precious moments of life, Helen had ascended the ladder as far as she could go; but the water pursued her relentlessly. Already her head was touching the ceiling. She could climb no farther. The cold hand of Death caressed her cheek. Suddenly she became alert, listening. She heard noises in the chamber above. What might they signify? Not rescue, certainly; perhaps some new torture.

At last the air chamber was emptied. Tarzan and Herkuf attempted to raise the trap-door leading into Helen's cell; but it defied their every effort, even the Herculean strength of the Lord of the Jungle. And what was happening, or had happened, in the cell below – cell or tomb?

And while Tarzan and Herkuf laboured with the trap-door, a ptome awoke and sat up upon his hard bench, rubbing his eyes. He had had a strange, disquieting dream in which enemies had passed through the room of the ptomes. He looked about to see if anyone was there who should not be. Mechanically, he looked for his water suit and helmet. They were gone, and two other pegs were empty. Instantly he awoke his fellows and disclosed his discovery, telling them of his dream. They were all much perturbed, for such things had never happened before in the memory of man. They started to investigate immediately, going first to the throne room, where they soon discovered that two of the prisoners were missing.

'Herkuf is gone and the man called Tarzan,' said one.

'But three suits and tridents were taken,' pointed out another.

By this time the prisoners were awake; and they questioned them, with many threats; but they learned nothing for the prisoners knew nothing, and were quite as surprised as the ptomes.

'I have it!' cried a ptome at last. 'It is quite plain that they have gone to the little chamber in the lake to release the girl; that is why they took the extra suit. Quick! Into your helmets! In the name of Atka, hurry!'

'We must not all go, or the rest of the prisoners may escape as the others did,' suggested one. So only six of them donned their suits and hurried into the waters of Horus in pursuit of the two missing prisoners. Armed as they were, with tridents and knives, they had no thought but that they could easily overcome and recapture their quarry.

For many precious minutes the trap-door refused to yield to the efforts of Tarzan and Herkuf; but at last it gave way, and they threw it open. Looking down into the darkness, they at first saw nothing; then Tarzan espied, dimly, a wan face apparently floating on the surface of the water. Were they, after all, too late? Was this the face of a dead girl?

Holding to the ladder and floating with her nose just above the water, Helen heard increasing sounds of activity just above her; then the trap-door was lifted, and she saw two ptomes looking down at her. As they dragged her into the air chamber, she guessed that they had come to inflict some new torture.

They helped her to don the extra water suit, and led her out of the air chamber into the lake. In their suits and helmets, she did not recognise them; and as there was no means of communication, she went on with them, ignorant of their identity, wondering what next Fate had in store for her.

As Herkuf led them away from the vicinity of the temple, the pursuing ptomes discovered them and hurried to overtake them. In the silence of the watery depths, no sound reached the ears of the fugitives; and they were ignorant of the danger approaching from behind; until, finally, Tarzan, always the wary jungle beast, looked back and saw the ptomes approaching. He touched Herkuf and Helen and pointed; then he gathered them together, so that they all stood back to back to await the assault of the enemy he well knew they could not outdistance in flight. What the outcome of such a battle would be, he could not even guess. He knew that they were all unused to fighting in such a medium and with such weapons. A single rent in a suit might mean death by drowning, and doubtless their antagonists were adepts in the use of tridents. What he did not know was that the ptomes were as unused to underwater fighting as was he. Sometimes they had to defend themselves from the more dangerous denizens of the deep, but never had they been called upon to face human antagonists and weapons identical to their own.

So it was that Tarzan and Herkuf drew first blood; and now, for the first time, Helen realised that she might be in the hands of friends; yet that seemed entirely implausible, for how could she have friends among the ptomes?

With two of their number dead in the first encounter with the enemy, the four remaining ptomes became more wary. They circled cautiously, waiting for an opening; but there seemed no opening in the impregnable defence of the three, who could not be lured from the compact formation that presented a trident on every front. Suddenly one of the ptomes leaped above the heads of the quarry to attack them from a new angle; and, as he did so, his fellows rushed in. But they rushed too close, and two of them went to their deaths on the tridents of Herkuf and Tarzan; then the one above them floated down and struck at the ape-man. As he did so, Helen jabbed suddenly upward with her trident, catching the fellow squarely in the chest. He wriggled horribly, like a speared fish, and then sank limply at her feet. The girl had to steel herself to keep from fainting.

With his fellows dead, the remaining ptome turned and fled toward the temple; but Tarzan dared not let him escape to bring reinforcements; so he pursued him, feeling like one in a bad dream, who makes strenuous efforts but accomplishes little or nothing. However, the ptome had the same watery medium to contend with; but not the giant muscles to overcome it that his pursuer possessed; so gradually Tarzan gained on him, while Herkuf and Helen followed in his wake.

When the ptome realised that he could not make good his escape, he turned at bay and prepared to fight; and Tarzan found him the most danger-ous antagonist or all, for he was fighting with the desperation of a cornered rat. It was the strangest duel the ape-man had ever fought. The weird, mys-terious silence of the depths; the grotesque figure facing him; the strange weapons; the watery medium that retarded his every movement; all baffled him. He was accustomed to fighting on one plane and not having antagonists leap above his head and thrust down at him, as the ptome suddenly did; but he fended the thrust, and seized his foe by the ankle. The ptome struggled to free himself, thrusting savagely with his trident; but at last Tarzan was sure of himself, as he dragged the lesser priest toward him.

At close quarters, the tridents were useless; and both men discarded them, each drawing his knife, the ptome slashing viciously but awkwardly at Tarzan, while the ape-man sought to seize the other's knife wrist; and while they fought, a large fish, swimming low, approached them; and Helen and Herkuf hurried up, like two hideous robots held back by an invisible hand.

Tarzan's fingers were touching the wrist of the ptome; he had almost succeeded a seizing the hand that held the dagger, when the great fish, frightened by the approach of Helen and Herkuf, darted past in an effort to escape, struck Tarzan's legs a heavy blow and upset him. As the ape-man fell backward, the ptome saw and seized his opportunity. He lunged forward upon the falling Tarzan, his knife ready to plunge into his foe's heart.

But once again Tarzan fended the weapon aside; and as he parried the blow, Helen and Herkuf reached him and plunged their tridents into the body of the ptome. As Tarzan floated to his feet, Helen wondered whose life it was she had helped to save and what his intentions toward her might be.

XXVI

In the temple of Brulor all was confusion and excitement. Priests and warriors filled the throne room, investigating the mysterious disappearance of two prisoners. The locks of their cages were intact, and only d'Arnot guessed the truth as he noted a slight bend in two of the bars of Tarzan's cage.

'Once again here is hope,' he whispered to Brian.

An excited ptome ran into the throne room; and, tearing off his helmet, hurried to the foot of Brulor's throne. 'O Father of Diamonds,' he cried, 'I went to the little chamber in the lake. The woman is gone!'

'Gone? Where?' demanded Brulor.

'Who knows?' replied the ptome. 'All that I know is that she is not there and that scattered over the bottom of Horus are the bodies of six ptomes, their water suits stripped from three. A demon is in our midst, O Father!'

Brulor leaped to his feet, trembling with rage. 'They are not demons,' he cried, 'but mortal men who may die. One is that renegade, Herkuf; the other is the man called Tarzan. Whoever brings them to me, dead or alive, may name his own reward; but bring them alive if you can. Whoever profanes the temple of Brulor must die. So it is written.'

And while Brulor raged, the objects of his wrath, led by Herkuf, were far out on the bottom of Horus. Having stripped the water suits from three of the dead ptomes, they had followed Herkuf, who was bent on leading them across the lake in accordance with the plan that he and Tarzan had decided upon before their escape from the temple. Good fortune had given them possession of three extra water suits, which would fit in nicely with the plan they had in mind, a mad plan; but the only one that seemed at all likely to succeed.

As they approached deeper water, they descended into a valley of huge marine plants; and here they encountered the larger denizens of the deep, so that they were constantly compelled to fight off attacks, as monstrous, shadowy shapes glided about them. Mighty, grotesque plants waved their fronds above them in the dim light of the fading stars.

Helen was frankly terrified. She had no idea who these men were, nor where they were taking her, nor what their intentions toward her; and in addition to these, she did not see how they could escape the terrifying dangers that surrounded them, made doubly terrifying by the darkness and the strangeness of the scene. She felt that she could endure no more, and then a huge sea serpent swam from among the giant trees and rushed to attack them.

The men faced its horrible jaws with their puny tridents, while its long, sinuous tail wreathed in spirals above them, like a sentient Damoclean sword that might destroy them at any moment. Its protruding eyes glaring, its forked tongue darting from its fanged jaws, the serpent suddenly wrapped its tail about Helen and swam off. Instantly Tarzan dropped the extra water suit and helmet he had been carrying and sprang up in an effort to reach them, as Herkuf stood helpless on the lake bottom below.

Just by chance, the ape-man succeeded in seizing one of Helen's ankles; but he could not wrest her from the grip of that powerful tail. Slowly he drew himself up over the body of the girl in an effort to reach the body of the serpent. At the same time he tried to wrest her free; but the coils only tightened about her; and as the angry saurian turned and twisted, he had difficulty in holding on at all. It was only his great strength and agility that, despite his encumbering water suit, permitted him, finally, to climb to the monster's back. Again and again he drove his knife into the cold body, while Helen marvelled at the courage and strength of her unknown paladin.

Painfully, but not seriously wounded, the saurian dropped the girl and turned upon the man-thing that dared thus to question its supremacy. Bleeding, hurt, infuriated, a creature of demoniacal fury, its one thought now was to destroy this rash thing that threatened its right to self-preservation. Fending the jaws with his sharp knife that inflicted hurts which caused the serpent to recoil, Tarzan climbed steadily toward the great throat. Numa, the lion;

Sheeta, the leopard; Wappi, the antelope; and man he had killed by severing the jugular. Why not this creature, too, in which blood flowed?

At last he reached his goal; and here, beneath the great throat, he found the tenderest skin his blade had yet pierced; and with a single stroke he severed the vein he had been seeking. There was a gush of blood, the creature writhed convulsively for a few moments; and then, as Tarzan slipped from its back, it turned belly up and floated away; while the ape-man sank gently toward the floor of the lake, where Helen stood, wide-eyed and wondering, looking up at him.

Dawn was breaking; and the increasing light made it possible for them to see to greater distances than before, and as Tarzan looked about for Herkuf, he saw him approaching. bringing along the water suit and helmet that Tarzan had discarded

From this point on, the lake bottom rose steeply, taxing Helen's energies to such an extent that Tarzan had to help her for the remainder of the way to shore. Herkuf was not much better off than Helen but he managed to stagger out of the water to fall exhausted on the bank. Only Tarzan seemed fresh and untired.

They lost no time in removing the uncomfortable helmets, and when Helen saw Tarzan's face she cried out in astonishment. 'Tarzan!' she exclaimed. 'But I might have known that it was you, for who else could have done for me what you have?'

'Paul,' he said, with a smile.

'You're sweet,' she said. 'Oh, what a relief to feel safe once more! How wonderful to be alive after all that we have gone through, after that terrible chamber where they would have drowned me. I can't believe yet that I have escaped.'

Close to shore, Herkuf had speared a fish; and now he led them to a cave he knew of; and while Helen and Tarzan lay on the ground, he built a fire and broiled his catch.

'What are your plans?' Helen asked Tarzan.

'Herkuf knows where a boat is hidden on this side of the lake. We thought it safer to come here rather than to attempt to steal one from the quay at Ashair, knowing that after our escape was discovered there would be sentries everywhere. Tonight, we shall row across the lake; and Herkuf and I will go down in water suits and try to get past the ptomes again and bring out d'Arnot, Brian and Lavac. That is why we took the three suits from the ptomes we killed. We were going to try to steal them from the ptomes' room. Now we won't have to go through that room as we did before to steal suits, as Herkuf says there is a way around it.'

'After we have eaten and rested,' said Herkuf, 'I'll go and see if the boat is still where I hid it. That was many years ago; but it was well hidden, and it is seldom that anyone comes to this part of the valley. I sank it in a tiny inlet beneath bushes that overhung the water.'

'It has probably rotted away by this time,' suggested Helen. 'No, I think not,' replied Herkuf. 'It would only rot if exposed to the air.'

As they ate the broiled fish, they discussed their plans and recalled the adventures through which they had passed; and Helen asked Herkuf how it had been possible to construct the temple at the bottom of the lake. 'That seems to me,' she said, 'an engineering feat far beyond the capabilities of the Asharians, for nothing else that they have accomplished, as far as I have seen, suggests more than a primitive knowledge of engineering. With the exception of these diving helmets, I have seen nothing that indicates great inventive genius, either.'

'It was the invention of the diving helmet, coupled with a natural phenomenon, that made it possible to build the temple,' explained Herkuf. 'We are a very ancient race. We have occupied the valley of Tuen-Baka for perhaps three thousand years. Our origin is legendary, but it is believed that our early ancestors came down from the North, bringing with them a well-developed civilisation and considerable engineering knowledge. There were two factions or tribes. One settled at what is now Thobos, the other at Ashair. It was an Asharian who invented the diving helmet. He was always pottering around with metals and chemicals, trying to make gold from common substances; and during his experiments he accidentally discovered a combination of chemicals that, when water was poured on them, generated air that could be breathed; but he had a sad end just as he was about to transmute a black powder he had compounded into gold. All that was necessary, he believed, was to apply great pressure suddenly; so he placed a little bit of it on a piece of lava and struck it with a hammer. There was a terrific noise and much smoke; and the roof blew off the inventor's house, and he went with it. One of his assistants, who miraculously escaped death, saw it all. But, though he did not succeed in making gold, he left behind him a great invention in the form of the diving helmet, which was thoroughly perfected and in common use, though more for sport than for any practical purpose.'

'But what had that to do with the building of the temple?' asked Helen.

'I am coming to that. Off shore from Ashair, at the point above where the temple now stands, the water was always in constant turmoil, a jet of it often flying into the air fifty or a hundred feet with a great hissing sound. The origin of this phenomenon was a mystery which the Asharians would have liked to solve; so, one day, a venturesome youth donned a water suit and helmet and set forth on the bottom of the lake to investigate. He was gone about half an hour, when watchers on the shore saw him shoot up, above the surface of the water at the spot where the phenomenon occurred. By a miracle, he was not killed; and when he finally came back to shore, he reported that a great geyser of air was shooting up from a hole in the bottom of the lake.

'It was many years later that someone conceived the idea of building a temple around the air geyser to house the priesthood and holy of holies. Thousands of slaves were captured and set to cutting the lava blocks that were to form the temple walls. Innumerable water suits and helmets were made. The most difficult part of the work was the capping of the air geyser, but this was finally accomplished; then the building of the temple commenced. It took a thousand years and cost twice that many lives. When it was completed and tightly sealed, it was, of course, entirely filled with water; but when the valve that had been installed in the geyser cap was opened, the water was forced out of the temple through a one-way valve. Today, the geyser furnishes pure air for the temple and actuates the doors of the air chambers.'

'How wonderful!' commented Helen. 'But where does this air supply come from?'

'It is, of course, mere conjecture,' replied Herkuf. 'But the theory is that during a great eruption, when Tuen-Baka was an active volcano, the entire top of the mountain was blown off and that when a great portion of it fell back into the crater it imprisoned a vast quantity of air, under great pressure, in a subterranean reservoir.'

'And when that supply is exhausted?' enquired the girl.

Herkuf shrugged. 'Horus will reclaim the temple. But there is yet a second theory. It is possible that there exists beneath the temple an immense deposit of the very chemicals that we use in our helmets, and that the trickling of water from the lake into this deposit is constantly generating fresh air.'

'What a world of thought and labour and lives must have gone into the building of that structure!' exclaimed Helen. 'And to what purpose? Why do men so waste their energies?'

'Does your race build no temples to its gods?' asked Herkuf.

XXVII

Magra and Gregory halted on a rocky hillside above Ashair. The hot sun beat down upon them from a cloudless sky, the frowning walls of Tuen-Baka towered above them, below them stretched the calm waters of sacred Horus; and in the distance the entrance to the tunnel leading to the outer world beckoned to them and mocked them.

'Well, here we are,' said Gregory. 'This must be the secret entrance to the tunnel.'

'Yes,' said Magra, 'we are here; but what now?'

'After what those poor devils told us,' replied Gregory, 'I think it would be foolish to throw our lives away uselessly by entering such a trap.'

'I quite agree with you,' said Magra. 'We could accomplish nothing if we succeeded in getting into the temple. We'd only be captured and upset all of Tarzan's plans if he is successful in what he is attempting.'

'What I can't understand,' said Gregory, 'is what has become Of Helen, Brian, d'Arnot, and Lavac. Do you suppose they all went into the temple to help Tarzan?'

'They may have, or they may all have been recaptured. About all we can do is wait.'

'Suppose we go on below Ashair and look for a hiding-place? If we are between Ashair and the entrance to the tunnel, they will have to pass us to get out of the valley, for there is no other way out, so far as I know.'

'I think you are right,' agreed Gregory, 'but I wonder if it will be safe to try to pass Ashair in the daytime?'

'Just as safe as it is to remain here at the mouth of this secret passage to their temple. Some of the Asharians may stumble upon us here at any time.'

'All right,' said Gregory, 'let's try it. There are quantities of enormous lava blocks farther up at the foot of the escarpment. We may be able to make our way past the city and be entirely screened from it by them.'

'Let's go,' said Magra.

They climbed the laborious ascent to the jumbled pile of lava that had fallen from above; and though the going was rough, they found that they were entirely hidden from the city; and eventually came down again close to the lake well beyond Ashair.

Between them and the lake a low, limestone ridge shut off their view of the water. It paralleled the shore line, and extended for about a quarter of a mile, falling gradually to the level of the surrounding land. Upon its summit shrubs grew sparsely and a few gnarled trees. A rise of land hid it from Ashair.

'Look!' said Magra, pointing. 'Isn't that a cave?'

'It looks like one,' replied Gregory. 'We'll have a look at it. If it's habitable, we're in luck, for we can hide there and keep a lookout for the others from the summit of the ridge.'

'How about food?' asked Magra.

'I imagine we can find fruit and nuts in some of those larger trees just below the ridge,' replied Gregory, 'and if I have any luck at all I should be able to get a fish now and then.'

As they talked, they approached the entrance to the cave, which, from the outside, appeared to be perfectly adapted to their needs; but they entered it cautiously. For a short distance only was the interior visible in the dim light that came through the entrance; beyond that they could see nothing.

'I think I'll explore a little before we settle down to light housekeeping,' said Gregory.

'I'll go with you.'

The cave narrowed into a dark corridor, which they followed, gropingly, in almost total darkness; but at a sharp turn it became lighter, and presently they came into a large cavern into which the sun poured through an opening in the roof. The cavern was large and grotesquely beautiful. Stalactites of various hues depended from ceiling and walls, while strangely-shaped stalagmites covered much of the floor. Erosion had wrought strange limestone figures which rose like the creations of some mad sculptor among the tinted stalagmites.

'What a gorgeous spectacle!' exclaimed Magra.

'It is marvellous, and the colouring is beautiful,' agreed Gregory, 'but I think we should explore a little farther to make certain that it is a safe place for us to hide.'

'Yes,' said Magra, 'you're quite right. There's an opening there at the far end of the cavern that may lead to something else. Let's have a look at it.'

They found that the opening led into another corridor, dark and tortuous; and as they felt their way along it, Magra shuddered.

'There is something uncanny about this place,' she whispered.

'Nonsense,' said Gregory. 'That's just because it's dark in here. Women don't like the dark.'

'Do you?' she asked.

'Well, no; but just because a place is dark doesn't mean that it's dangerous.'

'But,' she insisted, 'I have a feeling that we are being watched by unseen eyes.'

'Oh, that's just your imagination, my dear child,' laughed Gregory. 'Your nerves are unstrung; and I don't wonder, after all that you have gone through. It's surprising that we're not all nervous wrecks.'

'I don't believe that it's imagination,' replied Magra. 'I tell you I can feel that we are not alone. Something is near us. Something is watching us. Let's go back and get out of this terrible place. It's evil. I know it.'

'Try and calm yourself, my dear,' soothed Gregory. 'There's on one near us; and anyway, if the place is evil, we want to know it.'

'I hope you're right,' said Magra. 'But I'm still terrified; and, as you know, I'm not easily frightened. Here's an opening in the wall. It may be another corridor. Which one had we better take?'

'I think we'll keep right on in this one,' replied Gregory. 'It seems to be the main corridor. If we start turning off, we may become lost. I've heard of people being lost down in caves in Kentucky or Virginia or somewhere, and never being found again.'

Just then a hand seized Magra from behind and whisked her through the opening they had just passed. Gregory heard a single piercing scream behind him, and wheeled about. To his horror, he found that he was alone. Magra had disappeared. He called her name aloud, but there was no reply; then he turned to go back and search for her. As he did so, another hand reached out from an opening on the opposite side of the corridor and seized him. He struggled and fought; but all his efforts were futile, and he was dragged into the darkness of a side corridor.

Magra, too, had fought for her liberty; but uselessly. The powerful creature that had seized her, dragged her along the dark corridor in silence. She did not know whether she were in the clutches of a man or a beast. After her experience with Ungo, it was only natural that she might have been in doubt.

The corridor was not long, and presently it ended in a second large cavern. It was then that she saw that her captor was a white-robed figure with hooded face. She saw the bare hands; and knew that it was no ape that had seized her, but a man. There were a number of others like him in the cavern, in the centre of which was a pool of water.

At the far end of the cavern a throne stood upon a dais; and before the throne was an altar, while directly behind it was an opening, roughly arched, looking out upon the lake, which was almost on a level with the floor of the cavern. The cavern was beautiful; but the whole scene was given a weird aspect by the presence of the sinister, silent, white-robed figures that stood staring at her through dimly-seen eyes that showed through slits in their hoods.

Magra had scarcely more than taken in the scene before her when she saw Gregory being dragged in as she had been. They looked at one another resignedly, and Gregory shook his head. 'Guess we're in for it,' he said. 'Looks like the Ku Klux Klan. You were right. Some of them must have been watching us.'

'I wonder what they are,' she said, 'and what they want of us? God! Haven't we been through enough, without this?'

'I don't wonder Tuen-Baka is taboo and Ashair forbidden. If I ever get out of it, it will be taboo far as I am concerned.'

'If we ever get out,' she said rather wistfully.

'We got out of Thobos,' he reminded her.

'Yes, I know; but we have no Tarzan nor any Thetan here. Now we are on our own, and we are helpless.'

'Maybe they don't intend us any harm,' he suggested. 'If I only knew their language, I'd ask 'em. They have a language. They've been whispering together ever since they brought us in.'

'Try Swahili,' she suggested. 'Everyone else we've seen in this accursed country speaks it.'

'My Swahili is a little lame,' he said, 'but if they understand Swahili maybe they can make it out.' He turned toward the nearest white-robed figure, and cleared his throat. 'Why did you bring us here?' he asked. 'What are you going to do with us? We haven't done anything to you.'

'You dared enter the temple of the true god,' replied the man. 'Who are you to dare enter the sacred temple of Chon?'

'They are minions of Atka,' said another.

'Or spies of the false Brulor,' suggested a third.

'We are nothing of the kind,' said Magra. 'We are just strangers who became lost. All we want to do is find our way out of Tuen-Baka.'

'Then why did you come here?'

'We were looking for a place to hide until we could get out,' replied the girl.

'You are probably lying. We shall keep you here until the true god returns; then you shall learn your fate and the manner of your death.'

XXVIII

After they had rested, Herkuf, Helen, and Tarzan went to look for the boat that Herkuf had hidden, in which they were to return to the temple of Brulor in an attempt to rescue d'Arnot, Brian and Lavac. The inlet in which he had sunk it was not a great distance from the cave they had chosen and as almost the entire distance was through wooded country, they had no fear of being detected by the occupants of any of the Asharian galleys which occasionally passed within eyesight of the shore, as they patrolled the lower end of Horus in eternal quest of their hereditary enemies from Thobos.

When they reached the inlet, Herkuf parted the overhanging bushes and looked down into the shallow water. 'This is the place,' he muttered to himself. 'I know it is the place. I cannot be mistaken.'

'What's wrong?' asked Tarzan. 'Can't you find it?'

'This is the place,' repeated Herkuf, 'but the boat is not here. Though I hid it carefully, someone found it. Now all our plans are wrecked. What are we to do?'

'Can't we walk around the end of the lake and enter the water near the temple from the Asharian shore?' asked Helen.

'The escarpment at the lower end of the lake is unscalable,' replied Herkuf. 'If we went by way of Thobos, we should most certainly be captured; and although I was once a priest of Chon at Thobos, no one would know me now; and we should all be imprisoned.'

'Maybe we could build a raft,' suggested the girl.

Herkuf shook his head. 'We have no tools,' he said, 'and even if we had, we'd never dare attempt it, as the Asharians would be sure to discover us.'

'Must we give up, then?' demanded Helen. 'Oh, we can't do that and leave Paul and Brian and Lavac to die.'

'There is a way,' said Tarzan.

'What is it?' demanded Herkuf.

'When it is dark, I'll swim to Ashair and steal a boat from the quay there.'

'That is impossible,' said Herkuf. 'You saw with what we had to contend when we crossed last night. You wouldn't get halfway across, swimming at the surface. We'd better walk back.'

'It was only by the best of luck that we got across last night,' Tarzan reminded him. 'We might not be so lucky another time; and, if we did succeed, we should still be without a boat to return to Thobos or escape through the tunnel. You know that the success of our whole plan rested upon our having a boat. I shall swim the lake tonight.'

'Don't do it, Tarzan; please don't!,' begged Helen. 'You would just be throwing your life away uselessly.'

'I do not intend to throw my life away at all,' he replied. 'I have my knife.'

They returned to the cave to await darkness; and, finding it impossible to dissuade Tarzan from his plan, Herkuf and Helen finally gave up in despair; and, when darkness fell, they stood at the shore line and watched him wade into the dark waters of Horus. With straining eyes they watched his progress until he disappeared from their view in the darkness, and even then they remained where they were, staring out into the black void across the blacker waters.

Tarzan had completed about half the distance to the Asharian shore without encountering any dangers, when he saw a torch flare suddenly in the bow of a galley only a short distance from him. He watched it; and when it altered its course and came toward him, he realised that he had been discovered. To be taken now by an Asharian galley would doubtless mean death not only for him but for the men he was risking his life to save, and so he grasped at the only chance he had to elude them. Diving, he swam away, trying to escape the circle of their torch's light; and, glancing back, he felt that he might succeed, for the light appeared to be receding; but as he rose toward the surface for air before diving again, he saw a shadowy form approaching him; and knew that at last the thing that Helen and Herkuf had so feared had happened. He recalled his words of assurance to them, 'I have my knife,' and half smiled as he drew it.

On Ashair's distant wall, a sentry saw the flare of the torch out upon the lake and summoned an officer. 'A galley from Thobos,' he said, 'for there are no Asharian galleys out tonight.'

The officer nodded. 'I wonder why they risked a light,' he said. 'They always sneak by in the night without torches. Well, it is our good luck, and because of it we shall have a prize tonight and some more victims for Atka and Brulor.'

As the great shark turned on its back to seize Tarzan, he plunged his knife into its belly and ripped it open for a distance of several feet. Mortally hurt, the great fish thrashed about in its agony, dyeing the water crimson with its blood and creating a great commotion upon the surface of the lake, a commotion that attracted the attention of those in the galley.

The ape-man, avoiding the lashing tail and angry jaws of the shark, now saw other great forms converging upon them, silent, sinister tigers of the deep attracted at first, like their fellow, by the light of the torch in the bow of the galley; but now by the blood of the wounded shark. Terrible creatures, they were coming for the kill.

His lungs bursting, Tarzan swam toward the surface for air, confident that the wounded shark would occupy the attention of the others. He knew, from the radiance of the water, that he would come up close to the galley; but he had to choose between that and death from drowning; there was no other alternative.

As he broke the surface of the water, he was close beside the galley; and warriors seized him and drew him over the gunwale. Here now was an end to all the fine plans he and Herkuf had concocted, for to fall into the hands of the Asharians must be equivalent to the signing of his death warrant; but as he looked at his captors he saw the black plumes of Thobos and heard a familiar voice call him by name. It was Thetan's.

'We were sneaking past Ashair without lights,' he said, 'on our way downriver to capture a few slaves; but what in the world were you doing out here in the middle of Horus?'

'I was swimming to Ashair to steal a boat,' replied the ape-man.

'Are you crazy?' demanded Thetan. 'No man could hope to live in these waters. Why, they are alive with flesh-eaters.'

'So I discovered, but I think I should have got through. I must have been halfway across. It was not my life that was at stake, Thetan, but those of my friends who are prisoners in Ashair. I must reach Ashair and get a boat.'

Thetan thought for a moment; then he said, 'I'll take you. I can land you on the shore below the city, but I advise you to give up all thought of it. You cannot enter Ashair without being discovered, and that will be the end of you.'

'I don't want to go ashore,' replied Tarzan. 'I have two companions across the lake from the city. If you will take the three of us to a point above the temple of Brulor, I won't have to go ashore and steal a boat.'

'What good will that do you?' demanded Thetan.

'We have water suits and helmets. We are going into the temple to get our friends, and I've got to take Brulor and The Father of Diamonds to Herat to get him to release Magra and Gregory.'

'They've already escaped,' said Thetan, 'and Herat is furious.' He did not say that he had helped them, as other Thobotian warriors were listening.

'That really doesn't make much difference,' said Tarzan. 'We can't escape from Tuen-Baka without Herat's aid. We'll need a galley and provisions. If I bring Brulor and The Father of Diamonds to him, he'll give us what we need, I'm sure.'

'Yes,' agreed Thetan, 'but you won't ever bring Brulor and The Father of Diamonds to Herat. What chance have you, practically unaided, to do what we have been trying to do for years?'

Tarzan shrugged. 'I still must try,' he said. 'Will you help me?'

'If I can't dissuade you, I'll help you. Where are your friends?'

Tarzan pointed in the general direction of the cave where he had left Helen and Herkuf, the torch was extinguished, and the galley's nose turned toward the shore.

From the quay at Ashair, six galleys put out without lights into the darkness of the night to search for the quarry, which they could no longer see since the torch had been extinguished; and as they rowed from shore, they fanned out, some upriver, some down, to cover the most territory in their search.

The shore line ahead of the galley bearing Tarzan was a long, black silhouette against the night sky. No landmarks were visible; and the shore was a straight, black line without breaks or indentations. Only the merest chance might bring them to the spot where Helen and Herkuf waited. When they were quite close to shore, Tarzan called Herkuf's name in a low voice; and immediately there came an answering hail from their right A few minutes later the keel of the galley touched gravel a few yards from shore, and Tarzan leaped out and waded to where Helen and Herkuf stood. They were amazed that he had returned so soon, amazed that he had returned at all, for they had seen the torchlit galley and believed that he had been captured by Asharians.

Briefly he explained what had occurred; and, telling Herkuf to follow with the water suits and helmets and weapons, he tossed Helen to a shoulder and waded back to the galley, which turned its nose toward Ashair as soon as Herkuf was aboard. Tarzan, Helen and Herkuf immediately donned their water suits, leaving their helmets off, temporarily, so that they could talk.

Silently, the galley glided out into the lake, the oars dipping without noise as they were plied by thirty well-trained slaves, who had learned by long experience the necessity for stealth in passing through the lower waters of

Horus where Asharian galleys might be lying in wait for them – Asharian galleys and Asharian warriors who might send them to the bottom chained to their thwarts.

About mid-lake a torch suddenly burst into flame to the right of them, then another to the left, and in quick succession four more between them, forming a semi-circle toward the centre of which they were moving, With the lighting of the torches, a loud Asharian war cry broke the deathly stillness of the night; and the Asharian galleys moved to encircle that of Thetan.

Nothing but immediate flight might save the Thobotians; and as the prow of the galley turned quickly toward the lower end of the lake in an effort to elude the jaws of the closing circle of enemy galleys, Tarzan called to Helen and Herkuf to don their helmets as he adjusted his own; then, seizing Helen's hand and signalling Herkuf to follow, he leaped overboard with the girl, while Thetan urged his slaves to greater speed.

XXIX

Hand in hand, Tarzan and Helen sank gently down to the darkness of the lake's bottom. If Herkuf were near them, they could see nothing of him; and so Tarzan waited for the coming of the new day that would lift the black veil from the mysteries of Horus' depths, as to proceed without Herkuf might easily foredoom the entire venture to failure. That they might never find him, Tarzan was aware; but he could only wait and hope.

It was an eerie experience for Helen Gregory that was rendered doubly trying by the recollection of her previous experiences in this silent world of horrors. Dimly seen, great forms glided through the forest of grotesque tree-like plants that waved their dark foliage on every hand. Momentarily, the girl expected some hideous monster to attack; but the night passed and dawn broke without their having once been threatened. It seemed a miracle to her, but the explanation probably lay in the fact that they had remained quietly sitting on the gravelly bottom. Had they been moving, it might have been different.

As the light of the new day filtered down to them, Tarzan looked about for Herkuf; but he was nowhere to be seen. Reluctantly, the ape-man started off across the lake toward the temple of Brulor. What he could accomplish alone, he did not know, as part of the plan was to enter the temple during a period of meditation and release the prisoners; but of the three, only Herkuf was familiar with the mechanism that operated the doors to the air chamber and emptied and refilled it; only Herkuf knew the exact time of the periods of meditation.

Unable to communicate with Tarzan, Helen followed where he led, ignorant of his new plans but more secure in her faith in him than he was of himself in this particular venture, where every condition varied so from all that he had been accustomed to meet in the familiar jungles that he knew so well.

They had gone but a short distance in the direction in which Tarzan thought the temple lay, when they came upon Herkuf. He, too, had been waiting for daylight, feeling certain that Tarzan would have done the same and that, having leaped overboard almost simultaneously, they could not be far separated. It was with feelings of the greatest relief that they found themselves reunited.

Herkuf took the lead now, and with Tarzan and Helen following, commenced the tiresome and dangerous journey toward Ashair, all of them now greatly encouraged after the long hours of doubt and uncertainty.

They had not gone far when they came upon the wreck of a large galley partly embedded in the sand. That it had been there for years was attested by the size of the marine growth which had sprouted through its ribs, entwining the skeletons of its slaves still lying in their rusted chains.

Herkuf evinced considerable excitement; and, motioning them to wait, clambered into the interior of the craft, from which he presently emerged carrying a splendid jewelled casket. That he was overcome by excitement was obvious, but hampered by his helmet he could only express it by waving the casket before their faces and dancing jubilantly. What it was he had recovered, they could not guess, unless it were that the casket contained treasure of fabulous worth.

At last, and without further adventure, they approached the temple of Brulor; and here they went cautiously, seeking the shelter of the trees and plants that grew in the gardens of the ptomes, moving stealthily from one to another, each time assuring themselves that no ptome was in sight, knowing that at any moment one might emerge from the air chamber that they could now see. Approaching the temple, they found a place where they could hide concealed from the gardens and the air chamber door. Here they must wait until Herkuf signalled that the time had arrived when it might be safe to enter the temple. How long that would be only he could guess with any degree of accuracy. Near them was a window through which they could have looked into the temple had they dared; but as long as it was light outside they could not take the risk; and so they waited, tired, hungry, and thirsty; waited for night to fall.

Inside the temple the caged prisoners were gnawing on their evening meal of raw fish. Atan Thome enlarged in glowing terms upon his plans when he should come into possession of The Father of Diamonds and dazzle the world with his wealth. Lal Taask, scowling, cursed him. Akamen brooded in silence upon his lost liberty and his vanished dream of power. Brian and d'Arnot spoke together in low tones. Lavac paced his cage like a captive polar bear.

'I think your friend, Tarzan, has run off and left us,' remarked Brian.

'You think that because you don't know him as well as I do,' replied d'Arnot. 'As long as he and we live he will try to rescue us.'

'He will have to be a superman to do it,' said Brian.

'He is – that and all of that. He may fail, of course, but he will come nearer succeeding than any man who lives.'

'Well, anyway, he got Helen out of that torture chamber they'd put her in,' said Brian. 'Wasn't old Brulor sore, though! Of course, he really hasn't had time to get her to a place of safety and come back for us; but every minute is an hour in here, and so it seems like a very long time since he went away. Did you know he was going?'

'Yes, he told me; but I didn't know when he and Herkuf left. I was asleep. I am sure he must have got her out; otherwise he'd have been back after us.'

'Unless he was killed,' suggested Brian. 'Anyway, we know he took her out. That was what old Brulor was raving about.'

'I mean out of the lake – to some place of safety. Sometimes I think I'll go crazy if I don't know.'

'We've got one nut here now,' said Brian, nodding toward Atan Thome. 'We couldn't stand another. Anyway, wait until you've been here as long as I have; then you'll really have an excuse to go cuckoo.'

'They're all clearing out of the throne room now,' said d'Arnot. 'The period of meditation has come. I wonder what they meditate about.'

'Meditate, hell!' exclaimed Brian. 'Ask the handmaidens!' Outside the temple the weary trio waited. Since the evening before they had had neither food nor water, nor spoken a single word; but now Herkuf cautiously moved to a spot opposite the window but not too close to it. It was dark now, and there was little danger that he would be seen from the inside. The throne room was deserted except for the prisoners. He came back to Tarzan and Helen and nodded that all was right; then he left the casket at Helen's feet and motioned that she was to remain where she was. She was very lonely after Tarzan and Herkuf left her.

This was the moment for which the two men had been waiting. What did it hold for them? Carrying out the plan they had carefully laid out in every detail, the two men each speared a fish; then, with their quarry wriggling on their tridents, they went to the air chamber. It was only a matter of a few moments before they had passed through it and stood in the corridor leading to the ptomes' room.

Beside them was another door opening into a passageway that led to the throne room, avoiding the ptomes' room. Herkuf tried to open it, but could not. He shrugged. There was nothing to do now but make the attempt to pass through the room where the ptomes should be sleeping. They prayed that they were sleeping. Cautiously, Herkuf opened the door to that room and looked in; then he beckoned Tarzan to follow him.

The entire success of their venture depended upon their reaching the throne room unchallenged. They had almost succeeded, when a ptome, awakening, sat up and looked at them. With their fish upon their tridents, the two men continued on unconcernedly across the room. The sleepy ptome, scarce awake, thought them two of his kind, and lay down to sleep again. Thus they came in safety to the throne room, while outside, Helen waited in the loneliness of the black water. She was almost happy, so certain was she that Tarzan and Herkuf would succeed in liberating d'Arnot, Brian and Lavac; but then she was not aware of the figure in a white water suit that was swimming down toward her from above and behind. Whatever it was, it was evident that it had discovered her and was swimming directly toward her.

Tarzan and Herkuf hurried directly to the cages, tossing their fish to the floor. The excited prisoners watched them, for they had never seen ptomes behave like this. Only d'Arnot really guessed who they were. Seizing the bars in his powerful grasp, Tarzan released them one after the other, cautioning them to silence with a gesture; then he removed his helmet and told d'Arnot, Brian and Lavac to put on the three water suits that Herkuf carried.

'The rest of you,' he said, 'may be able to escape by the secret passage at the end of the long corridor. Does any of you know where to find it and open it?'

'I do,' replied Akamen.

'So do I,' said Atan Thome. 'I learned from Akamen.' As he spoke he darted toward the altar and seized the casket containing The Father of Diamonds, the accursed casket that had wrought such havoc.

As Helen felt a hand seize her from behind, she turned to see the strange figure in white confronting her; and her vision of a successful termination of their venture faded. Once again she was plunged into the depths of despair. She tried to wrench herself free from the restraining hand, but she was helpless to escape. She realised that she must not be taken now, for it might jeopardise the lives and liberty of all her companions; she knew that they would search for her and that delay might prove fatal to them. A sudden rage seized her; and, wheeling, she tried to drive her trident into the heart of her captor. But the creature that held her was alert and powerful. It wrenched the trident from her hands and cast it aside; then it seized her by a wrist and swam up with her toward the surface of the lake. The girl still struggled, but she was helpless. To what new and unpredictable fate was she being dragged? Who, now, might find or save her?

In the throne room of the temple, Tarzan and Herkuf saw all their efforts, their risks, and their plans being brought to nothing by the stupid avarice of three men, for as Atan Thome had seized the casket, Lal Taask and Brian Gregory had leaped upon him; and the three were fighting for the vast treasure for which they had risked their lives. At sight of the casket in the hands of another, Brian had forgotten all his fine resolutions; and cupidity dominated him to the exclusion of all else.

Tarzan ran forward to quiet them, but they thought that he too wanted the casket; so they fought down the throne room in an effort to evade him; and then that happened which Tarzan had feared – a door burst open and a horde of ptomes poured into the throne room. They wore no encumbering water suits or helmets, but they carried tridents and knives. Tarzan, Herkuf and the liberated prisoners waited to receive them. Brian and Lal Taask, realising that here was a matter of life and death, abandoned the casket temporarily to assist in the attempt to repulse the ptomes but Atan Thome clung desperately to his treasure, and sneaking stealthily behind the others he made for the corridor at the far end of when was the entrance to the secret passageway that led to the rocky hillside above Ashair.

It devolved upon Tarzan to bear the brunt of the battle with the ptomes. Beside him, only Herkuf was armed; and the others fought with their bare hands but with such desperation that the ptomes fell back, while Tarzan speared them on his trident and tossed them among their fellows.

It was upon this scene that Brulor burst, red of face and trembling with rage; then above the yells and curses of the battling men there rose his screaming voice as he stood behind the empty altar.

'Curses!' he cried. 'Curses upon the profaners of the temple! Death to them! Death to him who hath raped the casket of The Father of Diamonds! Summon the warriors of Ashair to avenge the sacrilege!'

Herkuf saw his nemesis standing defenceless before him, and he saw red with the pent-up hatred of many years. He leaped to the dais, and Brulor backed away, screaming for help: but the ptomes who remained alive were too busily engaged now, for all the prisoners who remained had armed themselves with the tridents and knives of the ptomes who had fallen.

'Die, impostor!' screamed Herkuf. 'For years I have lived in the hope of this moment. Let the warriors of Ashair come, for now I may die happy. The true god shall be avenged and the wrong you did me wiped out in your blood.'

Brulor dropped to his knees and begged for mercy; but there was no mercy in the heart of Herkuf, as he raised his trident and drove it with both hands deep into the heart of the terrified man grovelling before him. Thus died Brulor, the false god.

A breathless ptome had staggered into the presence of Atka, who sat among her nobles at a great banquet. 'What is the meaning of this?' demanded the Queen.

'Oh, Atka,' cried the lesser priest. 'The prisoners have been liberated and they are killing the ptomes. Send many warriors at once or they will all be slain.'

Atka could not conceive of such a thing transpiring in the throne room of the temple of Brulor, yet she realised that the man was in earnest, so she gave orders that warriors were to be sent at once to quell the disturbance.

'They will soon bring order,' she said, and returned to her feasting.

When the last ptome had fallen Tarzan saw that Akamen was dead and that Taask and Thome had disappeared with the casket. 'Let them go,' he said. 'The Father of Diamonds is bad luck.'

'Not I,' said Brian. 'I shan't let them go. Why do you suppose I have suffered in this hell-hole? Now I have a chance to reap my reward; and when another man steals it, you say, "Let him go."'

Tarzan shrugged. 'Do as you please,' he said, then he turned to the others. 'Come, we must get out of here before they get a chance to send a lot of warriors down on top of us.'

All four were now in their water suits and were adjusting their helmets as they made their way toward the corridor that led to the water chamber. Brian had reached the end of the throne room. He was the first to realise that the warriors of Ashair were already upon them. Throwing himself to the floor, he feigned death as the warriors rushed past him into the throne room.

When the others saw them they thought that they were lost, but Herkuf motioned them to follow him, as he hurried on toward the air chamber. Tarzan had no idea what Herkuf planned to do. He only knew that there would not be time to pass through the air chamber before the warriors reached it and reversed the valves, then they would be caught like rats in a trap. He had no intention of inviting any such situation. He would turn his back to the wall and fight. Maybe he could delay the warriors long enough for the others to escape. That was what he thought, so he turned at the doorway leading from the throne room and took his stand. The others, glancing back, saw what he was doing. D'Arnot took his place beside him, ignoring the ape-man's attempt to motion him on. Herkuf ran rapidly toward the air chamber. Lavac could have followed him safety, but instead he took his stand beside d'Arnot in the face of certain death.

While Herkuf fastened on toward the air chamber, the warriors hesitated in the throne room, appalled by the bloody shambles that met their astonished view and confused by the fact that the three who faced them appeared to be ptomes of the temple; but at last, seeing no other enemy, the officer in charge of Atka's warriors ordered them forward, while, out of sight, Herkuf worked feverishly with the controls of the air chamber, spinning valve handles and pulling levers.

Shouting now, the warriors came steadily down the length of the throne room toward the forlorn hope making a last stand before overwhelming odds, and the warriors looked for an easy victory. Nor were they alone in this belief, which was shared by the three who opposed them.

As the warriors closed upon the three, Tarzan met the leader in a duel between spear and trident, while d'Arnot and Lavac stood upon either side of him, determined, as was the ape-man, to sell their lives dearly; and as they fought thus there was a sudden rush of water through the doorway behind them.

Herkuf had thought and acted quickly in the emergency that had confronted them, taking advantage of the only means whereby he and his companions could be saved from the vengeance of the warriors. Throwing open both doors of the air chamber, he had let the waters of Horus pour in to fill the temple.

Safe in their water suits, Tarzan, d'Arnot and Lavac watched the gushing torrent drive back their foes, as, cursing and yelling, the warriors of Ashair sought to climb over one another in their mad panic to escape the watery death Herkuf had loosed upon them out of sacred Horus; but not one escaped as the water filled the throne room and rose through the upper chambers of the temple. It was a gruesome sight from which the three turned gladly at a signal from Tarzan and followed him toward the air chamber, beyond which he had left Helen waiting in the garden of the ptomes.

XXX

Up and up through the waters of Horus, Helen was dragged by the ghostly figure until, at last, they reached the precipitous cliff, the summit of which forms the coastline near Ashair. Here the creature dragged his captive into the mouth of a dark cavern, a den of horror to the frightened girl.

Magra and Gregory had been held captives in the cavern for a night and a day waiting for the return of the true god, Chon, who was to decide their fate. They had not been ill-treated, and they had been given food, but always there was the feeling of menace. It was in the air, in the strange vestments of their captors, in their whisperings and in their silences. It affected both Magra and Gregory similarly, leaving them blue and despondent.

They were sitting beside the pool in the centre of the cavern almost exactly twenty-four hours after their capture, the white robed figures crouching around them, when there was a sudden breaking of the still surface of the water and two grotesque diving helmets appeared, one white, the other dark.

'The true god has returned,' cried one of the priests. 'Now the strangers shall be judged, and punishment meted to them.'

As the two figures emerged from the pool and removed their helmets Magra and Gregory gasped in astonishment.

'Helen!' cried the latter. 'Thank God that you still live. I had given you up for dead.'

'Father!' exclaimed the girl. 'What are you doing here? Tarzan told us that you and Magra were prisoners in Thobos.'

'We escaped,' said Magra, 'but perhaps we would have been better off there. God only knows what we face here.'

The figure in white that had emerged with Helen proved, when he removed his helmet, to be an old man with a bushy white beard. He looked at Helen in astonishment.

'A girl!' he cried. 'Since when has false Brulor made ptomes of girls?'

'I am not a ptome,' replied Helen. 'I was a prisoner of Brulor, and adopted this method to escape.'

'Perhaps she lies,' said a priest.

'If these be enemies,' said the old man, 'I shall know when I consult the oracle in the entrails of the man. If they be not enemies, the girls shall become my handmaidens; but if they be, they shall die, as the man dies, on the altar of the true god Chon and lost Father of Diamonds.'

'And if you find that we are not enemies,' demanded Magra, 'what good will that do this man, whom you will have already killed? We tell you that we are friends, meaning you no harm. Who are you to say that we are not? Who are you to kill this good man?' Her voice was vibrant with just anger.

'Silence, woman!' commanded a priest. 'You are speaking to Chon, the true god.'

'If he were any sort of a god at all,' snapped Magra, 'he would know that we are not enemies. He would not have to cut up an innocent man and ask questions of his entrails.'

'You do not understand,' said Chon, indulgently. 'If the man is innocent and has told the truth, he will not die when I remove his entrails. If he dies that will prove his guilt.'

Magra stamped her foot. 'You are no god at all,' she cried. 'You are just a wicked old sadist.'

Several priests sprang forward threateningly, but Chon stopped them with a gesture. 'Do not harm her,' he said; 'she knows not what she says. When we have taught her to know the truth she will be contrite. I am sure that she will become a worthy handmaiden, for she has loyalty and great courage. Treat them all well while they are among us waiting for the hour of inquisition.'

Atan Thome fled upward along the secret passageway from the temple of Brulor, hugging the precious casket to his breast; and behind him came Lal Taask, his mind aflame with what was now the one obsession of his life – the killing of his erstwhile Master. Secondary to that was his desire to possess the great diamond which reposed in the jewelled casket. Ahead of him he could hear the screams and gibberings of the madman, which served to inflame his rage still further. And behind them both came Brian Gregory, all his fine resolutions forgotten now that The Father of Diamonds seemed almost within his grasp. He knew that he might have to commit murder to obtain it; but that did not deter him in the least, for his avarice, like that of many men, bordered almost upon madness.

Out into the open and along the rocky hillside fled Atan Thome. When Lal Taask reached the open, he saw his quarry scarce a hundred yards ahead of him. Other eyes saw them both, the eyes of Ungo the great bull ape, which, with his fellows, hunted for lizards among the great rocks farther up the hillside. The sight of the two men, the screaming Atan Thome, excited him. He recalled that Tarzan had told him that they must not attack men unless he were attacked; but there had been no interdiction against joining in their play, and this looked like play to Ungo. It was thus that playful apes chased one another. Of course, Ungo was a little old for play, being a sullen, surly old bull; but he was still imitative, and what the Tarmangani did, he desired to do. His fellows were imbued with the same urge toward emulation.

As Brian Gregory came out into the open from the mouth of the secret passageway, he saw the great apes, jabbering with excitement, bounding down the hillside toward Atan Thome and the pursuing Lal Taask. He saw the men stop and then turn and flee in terror from the mighty beast-men charging down upon them.

For the moment, Lal Taask discarded all thoughts of vengeance, as the first law of Nature dominated and directed him; but Atan Thome clung tenaciously to his precious casket. Ungo was delighted with this new game, as he came bounding after the fleeing, screaming Thome, whom he easily overtook. The man, thinking that death was upon him, tried to beat off the ape with one hand while he clung tightly to the casket with the other; that, he would not give up, even in death. Killing, however, was not in the mind of the anthropoid. It was the game in which he was interested; so he snatched the casket from the screaming man as easily as one takes another's wife in Hollywood, and went bounding off, hoping that someone would pursue him that the game might continue.

Lal Taask, running away, glanced back over his shoulder to see his dream of riches irremediably shattered, leaving nothing now in life for him but his hatred of Atan Thome and his desire for vengeance. Furious with hate and thwarted avarice, he ran back to Thome to wreak his final revenge, bare-handed, upon the screaming maniac.

Lal Taask was choking and beating Atan Thome when Brian Gregory reached them and dragged the infuriated Indian from his victim. 'What are you fools thinking of?' he demanded. 'You're making enough noise to attract every warrior in Ashair. I ought to kill both of you; but right now we've got to forget all of that and work together to escape, for we'll never see that casket again.'

Lal Taask knew that Gregory was right, but Atan Thome knew nothing. He could only think of The Father of Diamonds which he had lost, and impelled by a new maniacal impulse he suddenly broke away from Brian and ran screaming in the direction in which Ungo had disappeared with the casket. Lal Taask started after him, a curse upon his lips; but Brian laid a detaining hand on the man's arm.

'Let him go,' he said, 'he'll never get the casket from Ungo – he'll probably get himself killed instead. That accursed casket! So many have suffered and died because of it, and that poor fool has gone mad.'

'Perhaps he is the most fortunate of all,' said Lal Taask.

'I wish that I had never heard of it,' continued Brian. 'I have lost my father and sister and probably all of their friends are dead because of my greed. A moment ago I would still have risked my life for it, but the sight of that gibbering idiot has brought me to my senses.

'I wouldn't have the thing now; I am not superstitious, but I believe there is a curse on it.'

'Perhaps you are right,' said Lal Taask. 'I do not care so much about the casket as I did about killing that mad devil, but the gods have willed it otherwise. I shall have to be content.'

Apelike, Ungo soon tired of his new bauble, and tossed the casket carelessly to the ground, his thoughts reverting to the matter of lizards and other dainty articles of food. He was about to lead his tribe in search of sustenance when they were attracted by loud screams. Instantly on guard, they stood watching the approach of the mad Thome. Nervous, irritable beasts, it was a question whether they would run away or attack, as the man dashed among them and threw himself on the ground, clutching the casket to his breast. For a moment they stood there, apparently undecided, their little red-rimmed eyes blazing; then they moved slowly away, their menacing growls lost upon the poor maniac.

'It is mine! It is mine!' he shrieked. 'I am rich! In all the world there is none so rich as I!'

The great apes lumbered down the hillside, their short tempers upset by the screaming and jabbering of Thome, until Ungo was about to return and silence him forever. Just then he espied Brian and Lal Taask and transferred his anger to them. They were Tarmangani, and suddenly Ungo wanted to kill all Tarmangani.

Attracted by the growls of the anthropoids, the two men looked up and saw the herd charging down the hill toward them. 'Those beasts mean business,' cried Brian. 'It's time we got out of here.'

'There's a cave,' said Lal Taask, pointing toward the cliff. 'If we can reach it ahead of them, we may be able to hide from them. There's just a chance that they may be afraid to go into a dark hole like that.'

Running at top speed, the men reached the cave long before the apes could overtake them. The interior was not entirely dark, and they could see that the cave extended beyond the range of their vision.

'We'd better go as far in as we can,' said Brian. 'We'll be in a devil of a fix if they do come in and follow us; but perhaps if they can't see us at first, they may give up the chase.'

'It may be a cul-de-sac,' admitted Lal Taask, 'but it was the only chance we had; they'd have had us sure if we'd stayed in the open.'

They followed a dark corridor that ended suddenly in a magnificent grotto, the splendour of which fairly took their breath away.

'Great Scott!' exclaimed Brian. 'Did you ever see anything so gorgeous?'

'It's magnificent,' agreed Taask; 'but, right now, quite incidental – the apes are coming! I hear them growling.'

'There's another cave on the other side of this cavern,' said Brian. 'Let's try that.'

'There is nothing else to try,' returned Lal Taask.

As the two men disappeared into the dark opening in the rear of the cavern, Ungo and his fellows streamed into the chamber they had just quitted, unimpressed by its magnificence; and still holding to the idea that dominated them for the moment – the chase. A bug, a beetle, or a bat might distract their attention and launch them upon a new adventure, for they could not hold long to a single objective; but there were none of these, and so they searched the grotto for their quarry. They circled the place, looking behind stalagmites, sniffing here and there, wasting much time while the two men followed a new corridor deeper into the heart of the cliff.

XXXI

Tarzan, d'Arnot, Herkuf and Lavac hastened through the air chamber out on to the bottom of the lake to the spot where Helen had been left to await their return; but she was not there, though the casket lay undisturbed where Herkuf had hidden it. There was no clue to her whereabouts; and the men were at a loss as to the direction in which they should search. They dared not separate, and so they followed Tarzan as he wandered here and there about the garden of the ptomes looking for some trace of the missing girl. While they were thus engaged, the ape-man's attention was attracted by the approach of several large marine animals the upper portions of which closely resembled the head and neck or a horse. There were six of them, and it was soon evident that they meant to attack. That they were extremely dangerous, Herkuf knew and the others soon realised, for they were as large as a man; and each was armed with a long, sharp horn which grew upward from the lower end of their snouts.

Two of them attacked Tarzan, and one each the other three men, while the sixth circled about as though awaiting an opening through which it might take an antagonist unaware. Tarzan succeeded in despatching one of those attacking him; and d'Arnot seemed to be experiencing no great difficulty with his. Lavac was hard pressed, but when he saw the sixth seahorse gliding up behind d'Arnot to impale him on its horn he turned to the rescue of his companion; as he did so, exposing himself to the attack of the seahorse with which he had been engaged.

It was an act of heroism on the part of the man who had wronged d'Arnot, an act that made full amends but cost a brave life, for the seahorse he had abandoned to come to d'Arnot's rescue plunged its powerful horn between his shoulders. Thus died Lieutenant Jacques Lavac.

As Tarzan thrust his trident into the heart of a second antagonist, the remaining beasts swam away in defeat, d'Arnot dropped to one knee beside Lavac and examined him as best he could. Then he stood up and shook his head. The others understood, and sadly the three turned away and resumed their fruitless search, wondering, possibly, which would be the next to die in this land of danger and sudden death.

At last, by signs, they agreed to abandon the search, for even d'Arnot now felt certain that Helen must be dead; and, following Herkuf, who had brought the casket with him, they scaled the steep ascent to the lake shore, emerging at last a short distance below Ashair.

D'Arnot was heartbroken; Herkuf was filled with renewed hope, for he knew what the casket contained and what it meant to him; only Tarzan of the Apes was unmoved. 'Brulor is dead,' he said, 'and The Father of Diamonds stolen. I must return to Thobos as I promised Herat.'

'It will not be necessary, if you wish to remain here and search for your other friends,' said Herkuf. 'I shall explain everything to Herat, and for what you have done to restore this to him, he will grant you any favour.' He tapped the lid of the casket.

'What is it?' asked d'Arnot.

'In this is the true Father of Diamonds,' replied Herkuf. 'Many years ago, Chon, the true god, was making his annual tour of Holy Horus in a great galley. As was the custom, he carried The Father of Diamonds with him. Queen Atka, jealous of Herat, attacked and sank the galley; and Chon was drowned, while I was taken prisoner. As you, Tarzan, will recall, when we found the wrecked galley at the bottom of Horus, I recognised it and retrieved the casket that had lain there so many years. Now I am sure that if we restore The Father of Diamonds to Thobos, Herat will grant any request we may make, for without The Father of Diamonds, Thobos has been without a god all these years.'

'You and Herkuf take the casket to Herat,' said d'Arnot to Tarzan. 'I cannot leave here. Helen may live and may come ashore. Somehow, I can't believe that she is dead.'

'Take the casket to Herat, Herkuf,' directed Tarzan. 'I shall remain here with d'Arnot. Tell Herat I'll come back to Thobos if he wishes me to. I may come anyway. We'll have to have a galley to get out of Tuen-Baka.'

Herkuf made good time to Thobos, nor was there any delay on the part of Herat in granting him an audience when the King learned that he claimed to be the long-lost priest, Herkuf and that he had The Father of Diamonds in his possession; and it was not long after his arrival at the city gate before Herkuf stood before the King.

'Here, Herat, is the sacred casket with The Father of Diamonds. Had it not been for the man, Tarzan, it would never have been recovered. I know that he and his friends are in grave peril, for they are close to Ashair. Will you not send galleys and warriors to rescue them?'

'With this,' cried Herat, touching the casket, 'our forces cannot lose, for we shall again have god upon our side.' He turned to one of his aides. 'Let all the war galleys be prepared and manned. We shall attack Ashair at once; and at last the followers of the true god, Chon, shall prevail; and the traitors and the wicked shall be destroyed. All that is lacking to our complete triumph is the presence in the flesh of the holy Chon.'

'He will be with us in spirit,' Herkuf reminded him.

So King Herat put out from Thobos with many war galleys, to avenge the wrong that Atka had done his god and to succour the strangers who had been instrumental in recovering the true Father of Diamonds from the bottom of Holy Horus; and Queen Mentheb and her ladies waved to them from the quay and wished them godspeed.

The true god, Chon, and his priests were gathered in the cavern temple on the shore of Horus. The three prisoners stood below the altar before the throne. At a word from Chon, several priests seized Gregory, stripped his clothing from him, and threw him to his back across the altar. Chon rose from his throne and stood above him.

'From the entrails of this man let the oracle speak!' he cried. He paused, and the priests intoned a weird chant, while Helen and Magra looked on, horrified and helpless.

'No! No!' cried Helen. 'You must not! My father has done nothing to wrong you.'

'Then why is he here in forbidden Tuen-Baka?' demanded Chon.

'I have told you time and again that we came here only in search of my brother, who is lost.'

'Why was your brother here?'

'He came with a scientific expedition of exploration,' explained the girl.

Chon shook his head. 'It is death to all who enter forbidden Tuen-Baka from the outer world,' he replied. 'But we know why they really came. They came only for The Father of Diamonds. To us it is the emblem of godhood; to them it is a priceless object of incalculable value. There is nothing that they would not do to possess it. They would defile our temples; they would murder us. The fact that they could never succeed in obtaining it, does not lessen their guilt.'

'My father would not have done these things. He only wanted his son back. He cares nothing for your diamond.'

'There is no diamond where anyone can steal it,' said Chon, 'for The Father of Diamonds lies at the bottom of Horus, lost forever. If I am wrong in thinking that you came solely to steal it, you shall go free. I am a just god.'

'But you *are* wrong,' urged Helen. 'Won't you please take my word for it? If you kill my father – oh, what good will it do you to find out later that you are wrong?'

'You may speak the truth,' replied Chon, 'but you may lie. The oracle will not lie. From the entrails of this man the oracle shall speak. Priests of the true god, prepare the sacrifice!'

As the priests stretched Gregory across the altar and sprinkled a liquid over him, the others commenced a solemn chant; and Helen stretched her arms toward Chon.

'Oh, please!' she begged. 'If you must have a sacrifice, take me, not my father.'

'Silence!' commanded Chon. 'If you have lied, your time will come. Soon we shall know.'

After Herkuf left them, Tarzan and d'Arnot started back toward Ashair. They had no plan, nor much hope. If Helen lived, she might be in Ashair. If she were dead, d'Arnot did not care what fate befell him. As for Tarzan, he was seldom concerned beyond the present moment. Suddenly he was alert. He pointed toward a cliff ahead of them.

'One of Ungo's apes just went into that cave,' he said. 'Let's take a look. The Mangani are not ordinarily interested in caves. Something unusual may have impelled that one to enter; we'll see what.'

'Oh, why bother?' queried d'Arnot. 'We are not interested in apes.'

'I am interested in everything,' replied the ape-man.

Brian and Taask stumbled through the dark corridor to burst suddenly into the cavern temple upon the scene of Gregory's impending sacrifice. At sight of them, Chon, the true god, recoiled, dropping his knife hand at his side.

'In the name of Isis!' he shouted. 'Who dares interrupt?'

'Brian!' cried Helen.

'Helen!' The man started across the room toward his sister; but half a dozen priests sprang forward and seized him, and others intercepted Helen as she tried to run to meet him.

'Who are these men?' demanded Chon.

'One is my brother,' replied Helen. 'Oh, Brian, tell him we don't want their diamond.'

'Save your breath, man,' snapped Chon. 'Only the oracle speaks the truth! On with the sacrifice to truth!'

'Marvellous! Stupendous!' exclaimed d'Arnot, as he and Tarzan entered the outer cavern of Chon's temple.

'Yes,' admitted the ape-man, 'but where are the Mangani we saw coming in here? I smell many of them. They have just been in this cave. I wonder why?'

'Have you no soul?' demanded d'Arnot.

'I don't know about that,' smiled Tarzan, 'but I have a brain. Come on, let's go after those apes. I detect the scent spoor of men, too. The stink of the apes is so strong that it almost hides the other.'

'I smell nothing,' said d'Arnot, as he followed Tarzan toward the opening at the far end of the cavern.

Chon was furious. 'Let there be no more interruptions!' he cried. 'There are many questions to be asked of the oracle. Let there be silence, too; if the oracle is to be heard, the man must be opened in silence.' Three times he raised and lowered the sacrificial knife above the prostrate Gregory. 'Speak, oracle, that the truth may be known!'

As he placed the point of the knife at the lower extremity of the victim's abdomen, the great apes, led by Ungo, streamed into the cavern; and once again the rite of human sacrifice was interrupted, as Chon and his priests looked, probably for the first time, at these hairy beast-men.

The sight of so many Tarmangani and the strange garments of the priests confused and irritated the apes, with the result that they attacked without provocation, forgetting the injunction of Tarzan.

The surprised priests, who had been holding Gregory, released him; and he slipped from the altar to stand leaning against it in a state bordering on collapse. Chon raised his voice in impotent curses and commands, while all the others tried to fight off the attacking apes.

Zu-tho and Ga-un saw the two girls, and Zu-tho recalled that Ungo had run off with a she Tarmangani; so, impelled by imitative desire, he seized Magra; and Ga-un, following the lead of his fellow, gathered up Helen; then the two apes sought to escape from the cavern with their prizes. Being confused, they chanced upon a different corridor from that by which they had entered the cavern, a corridor that rose steeply to a higher level.

Before anyone had been seriously injured by the apes, a commanding voice rang out from the rear of the cavern. 'Dan-do, Mangani!' it ordered in a tongue no other human knew, and the great apes wheeled about to see Tarzan standing in the entrance to the Cavern. Even Chon ceased his cursing.

Tarzan surveyed the gathering in the temple. 'We are all here but Helen, Magra, and Lavac,' he said, 'and Lavac is dead.'

'The girls were here a minute ago,' said Gregory, as he hastily donned his clothes without interruption by Chon or the priests.

'They must have hidden somewhere when the apes came,' suggested Brian.

'Helen was here!' gasped d'Arnot. 'She is not dead?'

'She was here,' Gregory assured him.

Brian was calling the girls loudly by name, but there was no reply. Chon was trying to gather his wits together.

Zu-tho and Ga-un dragged their captives through a steep, short corridor that ended in a third cavern with an arched opening that looked out over Horus far below. Zu-tho held Magra by the hair, while Ga-un dragged Helen along by one ankle. The apes stopped in the middle of the cavern and looked about. They didn't know what to do with their prizes now that they had them. They released their holds upon the girls and jabbered at one another, and as they jabbered, Helen and Magra backed slowly away from them toward the opening overlooking the lake.

'These are Tarzan's shes,' said Zu-tho. 'Ungo and Tarzan will kill us.'

'Look at their hairless skins and little mouths,' said Ga-un. 'They are hideous and no good. If we kill them and throw them into the water, Tarzan and Ungo will never know that we took them.'

Zu-tho thought that this was a good idea; so he advanced toward the girls, and Ga-un followed him.

'I kill!' growled Zu-tho, in the language of the great apes.

'I kill!' snarled Ga-un.

'I believe the beasts are going to kill us,' said Magra.

'I can almost hope so,' replied Helen.

'We'll choose our own death,' cried Magra. 'Follow me!'

As Magra spoke, she turned and ran toward the opening overlooking the lake, and Helen followed her; Zu-tho and Ga-un charged to seize them, but they were too late, and the girls leaped out into space over the waters of sacred Horus, far below; while Asharian warriors in a passing galley watched.

XXXII

In the cavern temple, Chon had finally regained control of his shattered nerves. He could curse again, and he did. 'Curses on all who defile the temple of Chon, the true god!' he cried.

'Chon!' exclaimed Tarzan, 'But Chon is dead!'

'Chon is not dead,' replied the god. 'I am Chon!'

'Chon was drowned when his galley was sunk, many years ago,' insisted the ape-man.

'What do you know of all this?' demanded Chon.

'I know what Herkuf told me,' replied Tarzan, 'and he was a priest of Chon.'

'Herkuf!' exclaimed Chon. 'Does he live?'

'Yes, Chon; he is on his way now to Thobos with the casket of The Father of Diamonds which we found in the wreck of your galley at the bottom of Horus.'

'Thanks be to Isis!' exclaimed Chon. 'When Atka's galleys attacked us,' he went on to explain, 'I donned my water suit and helmet and leaped overboard. Thus I escaped, and eventually I found this cavern. Here I have lived for many years, watching my chance to capture ptomes from the temple of the false Brulor – ptomes who were still at heart faithful to the true god. If you have spoken the truth you shall all go free with my blessing.'

'First of all,' said Tarzan, 'we must find the girls. D'Arnot, you come with me. Ungo, bring the Mangani. The rest of you search the main corridor,' and so the survivors set out in search of the missing girls, while Chon and his priests chanted a prayer for the safe return of The Father of Diamonds.

As the Asharians saw the girls leap into the water, the officer in charge of the galley directed that its course be changed; and it was rowed rapidly in their direction. Helen and Magra saw it coming and tried to find a place where they could gain the shore and escape, for they knew that there would be only enemies in the galley; but the precipitous cliff that fronted the lake at this point made escape impossible. The galley overtook them, and they were soon dragged into the craft.

'By Brulor!' exclaimed one of the Asharians. 'This is the woman who murdered Zytheb, keeper of the keys of the temple. Atka will reward us well for this, for it was, doubtless, this woman who also contrived the flooding of the temple and the drowning of all within it.'

Magra looked at Helen. 'What more can happen to us?' she asked wearily.

'This must be the absolute end,' replied Helen, 'and I hope it is. I am very tired.'

When they finally reached the city and were taken into Atka's presence, the Queen scowled horribly at them and pointed at Helen. 'It was because of you,' she cried, 'that the temple was flooded and all the priests and handmaidens drowned. I cannot think of any punishment adequate to your crime, but I shall. Take them away!'

In the dungeon in which they were chained, they sat looking at another, rather hopelessly. 'I wonder how long it will take her to think up a punishment to fit the crime,' said Helen. 'Too bad she can't call in Gilbert and Sullivan.'

Magra smiled. 'I am glad you can joke,' she said. 'It makes it much easier to endure.'

'Why not joke while we can?' asked Helen. 'We shall soon be dead, and death is no joke.'

The mad Thome wandered aimlessly near the banks of Horus, jabbering constantly of the things his great wealth would purchase from the fleshpots of Europe. He had no idea where Europe was nor how to reach it. He only recalled that it was a place where one might satisfy the cravings of every appetite. He was so engrossed in his mad dreaming that he did not see Taask approaching.

The Indian had been searching for Helen, and had become separated from Gregory and Brian, when suddenly he came upon Atan Thome and saw the casket in his hands. Instantly he sloughed every thought but one – to get possession of the accursed thing that held the priceless diamond. Sneaking up on Thome, he leaped upon him. They rolled upon the ground, biting, kicking and clawing. Taask was a younger, stronger man, and he soon wrenched the casket from Atan Thome, and, leaping to his feet, started to run away with it.

Screaming at the top of his voice, the madman picked up a rock and pursued him. There was murder in the eyes and heart of Atan Thome as he chased his erstwhile servant across the rocky ground above Ashair. Seeing that he could not overtake Lal Taask, Atan Thome hurled the rock at him; and by chance it struck the fleeing man full on the head, knocking him to the ground; and his mad pursuer was soon upon him. Recovering the rock, Thome pounded with all his strength upon the skull of Lal Taask until it was but a mass of splintered bone and brains; then, clutching the casket to his breast and screaming a challenge to the world, he fled.

Following the scent spoor of the two girls, Tarzan and d'Arnot found themselves in a third cavern of the temple, facing two bull apes.

'Where are the shes?' demanded Tarzan.

Zu-tho pointed toward the lake. 'They jump,' he said, 'in water.'

Tarzan looked out to see the Asharian galley rowing in the direction of the city; then he and d'Arnot returned to the throne room and related what they had seen. 'I am going to take the apes to Ashair,' he said. 'With their help, I may be able to bring the girls out.'

'My priests shall go with you,' said Chon, and the party soon set out from the temple, the men armed with tridents and knives, the apes with their terrible fangs and their mighty muscles.

An excited warrior rushed into the throne room of Atka and knelt before her. 'O Queen!' he cried. 'A great fleet of war galleys is approaching from Thobos.'

Atka turned to one of her aides. 'Order out the entire fleet,' she directed. 'This day we shall destroy the power of Thobos forever!'

As the Asharian horde embarked at the quay, Tarzan of the Apes looked down from the hillside above the city and watched them; and, in the distance, approaching Ashair, he saw the war fleet of Herat approaching.

'Now is the time,' he said to his motley following, 'we shall have fewer warriors to oppose us.'

'We cannot fail,' said a priest, 'for Chon has blessed us.'

A few minutes later, the Lord of the Jungle led his little band over the wall into The Forbidden City. It was a bold, rash venture – at best a forlorn hope that thus they might succeed in saving Helen and Magra from death or an even more horrible fate. Success or failure – which would it be?

As the two fleets met amid the war cries of the opposing warriors, quarter was neither asked nor given, for each side felt that this was to be a battle to the death that would determine for all time which city was to rule the valley of Tuen-Baka. And while this bloody battle was being waged on sacred Horus, another battle was taking place before the gates of Atka's palace, as Tarzan sought to lead his little band into the presence of the Queen. It was

Atka he sought, for he knew that with Atka in his power he could force the Asharians to give up their prisoners – if they still lived.

Finally they overcame the resistance at the gates, and Tarzan forced his way at the head of his company into the throne room of the Queen.

'I have come for the two women,' he said. 'Release them to me, and we will go away; refuse, and we shall go away; but we shall take you with us.'

Atka sat in silence for a few minutes, her eyes fixed upon Tarzan. She was trembling slightly and appeared to be making an effort to gain control over her emotions. At last she spoke. 'You have won,' she said. 'The women shall be fetched at once.'

As Tarzan and his triumphant band led the girls from Ashair, Magra clung to his arm. 'Oh, Tarzan,' she whispered, 'I knew that you would come. My love told me that you would.'

The ape-man shook his head impatiently. 'I do not like such talk,' he said. 'It is not for us. Leave that to Helen and Paul.'

Herat, victorious, entered Ashair, the first King of Thobos to set foot within The Forbidden City. From the opening in the cavern of Chon that looked out over the lake, Chon had seen the Asharian fleet demolished and the victorious Thobotian fleet steer toward Ashair; and when Tarzan and his party returned and the ape-man learned of the successful outcome of Herat's expedition, he had Chon send a messenger to Ashair to summon Herat, in the true god's name, to the temple.

When the greetings between Herat and Chon were concluded, the true god blessed the entire party, giving credit to the strangers for their part in the restoration of The Father of Diamonds to the temple of Chon and the successful reuniting of the King and the true god; then Herat, to demonstrate his own appreciation, offered to outfit the Gregory party and furnish them with galleys to take them out of Tuen-Baka. At last, their troubles seemed over.

'We are reunited and safe,' said Gregory, 'and, above all others, we owe it to you, Tarzan. How can we ever repay you?'

Gregory was interrupted by maniacal screams, as two of Herat's warriors who had been among the guard left at the outer entrance to the caverns, entered the temple, dragging Atan Thome between them.

'This man has a casket,' reported one of the warriors, 'which he says contains The Father of Diamonds.'

'The true Father of Diamonds, which Herkuf just brought with him from Thobos,' said Chon, 'rests here in its casket on the altar before me. There cannot be two. Let us have a look at what the man has in his casket.'

'No!' shrieked Atan Thome. 'Don't open it! It is mine, and I have been waiting to open it in Paris. I shall buy all of Paris with it and be King of France!'

'Silence, mortal!' commanded Chon; then, very deliberately, he opened the casket, while the trembling Thome stared with mad eyes at the contents – a small lump of coal!

At sight of it, realising what it was, Atan Thome screamed, clutched his heart, and fell dead at the foot of the altar of the true god.

'For this false and accursed thing,' exclaimed Brian Gregory, 'we have all suffered, and many have died; yet the irony of it is that it is, in truth, The Father of Diamonds.'

'Men are strange beasts,' said Tarzan.

TARZAN AND THE FOREIGN LEGION

To Brigadier General Truman H. Landon

My knowledge of Sumatra at the time that I chose it as the scene of a Tarzan story was pathetically inadequate; and as there was not a book on Sumatra in the Honolulu Public Library, nor in any of the book stores, it bade fair to remain inadequate.

I wish therefore to acknowledge my indebtedness to those whose kindness furnished me with the information I sought. If this volume happens to fall into the hands of any of them, I hope they will not feel that I abused that kindness.

And so, my sincere thanks to Messrs. K. van der Eynden, S. J. Rikkers, and Willem Folkers of the Netherlands India Government; to Mr C. A. Mackintosh, Netherlands Consul in Honolulu; to Messrs. N. A. C. Slotemaker de Bruine, Director, B. Landheer, and Leonard de Greve of The Netherlands Information Bureau, New York, and to my good friend Capt. John Philip Bird, A.A.C. of S., G-2, USAFPOA, who arranged my first meeting with the Netherlanders.

Edgar Rice Burroughs
Honolulu,
11 Sep. 1944

1

Probably not all Dutchmen are stubborn, notwithstanding the fact that stubbornness is accounted one of their national characteristics along with many virtues. But if some Dutchmen lacked stubbornness, the general average of that intangible was maintained in the person of Hendrik van der Meer. As practiced by him, stubbornness became a fine art. It also became his chief avocation. His vocation was that of rubber planter in Sumatra. In that, he was successful; but it was his stubbornness that his friends boasted of to strangers.

So, even after the Philippines were invaded and Hong Kong and Singapore fell, he would not admit that the Japanese could take Netherland East India. And he would not evacuate his wife and daughter. He may be accused of stupidity, but in that he was not alone. There were millions in Great Britain and the United States who underestimated the strength and resources of Japan – some in high places.

Furthermore, Hendrik van der Meer hated the Japanese, if one can hate what one looks upon contemptuously as vermin. 'Wait,' he said. 'It will not be long before we chase them back up their trees.' His prophecy erred solely in the matter of chronology. Which was his undoing.

And the Japs came, and Hendrik van der Meer took to the hills. With him went his wife, who had been Elsje Verschoor, whom he had brought from Holland eighteen years before, and their daughter, Corrie. Two Chinese servants accompanied them – Lum Kam and Sing Tai. These were motivated by two very compelling urges. The first was fear of the Japanese, from whom they knew only too well what to expect. The other was their real affection for the van der Meer family. The Javanese plantation workers remained behind. They knew that the invaders would continue to work the plantation and that they would have jobs. Also, this Greater East Asia Co-Prosperity appealed to them. It would be nice to have the tables turned and be rich and have white men and women to wait on them.

So the Japs came, and Hendrik van der Meer took to the hills. But not soon enough. The Japs were always right behind him. They were methodically tracking down all Netherlanders. The natives of the kampongs where the van der Meers stopped to rest kept them informed. By what natural or uncanny powers the natives knew while the Japs were still miles away is beside the question. They knew, as primitive people always know such things as quickly as more civilized peoples might learn them by telegraph or radio. They even knew how many soldiers composed the patrol – a sergeant, a corporal, and nine privates.

'Very bad,' said Sing Tai, who had fought against the Japs in China. 'Maybe one time an officer is a little human, but enlisted men never. We must not let them catch,' he nodded toward the two women.

As they went higher into the hills, the going became bitter. It rained every day, and the trails were quagmires. Van der Meer was past his prime, but he was still strong and always stubborn. Even had his strength given out, his stubbornness would have carried him on.

Corrie was sixteen then, a slender blonde girl. But she had health, strength, and endurance. She could always have kept up with the men in the party. But with Elsje van der Meer it was different. She had the will but not the strength. And there was no rest. They would scarcely reach a kampong and throw themselves down on the floor of a hut, wet, muddy, exhausted, before the natives would warn them away. Sometimes it was because the Jap patrol was gaining on them. But often it was because the natives feared to let the enemy find them harboring whites.

Even the horses gave out at last, and they were compelled to walk. They were high in the mountains now. Kampongs were far apart. The natives were fearful and none too friendly. Only a few years ago they had been cannibals.

For three weeks they stumbled on, searching for a friendly kampong where they might hide. By now it was obvious that Elsje van der Meer could go but little farther. For two days they had come upon no kampong. Their food was only what the forest and the jungle offered. And they were always wet and cold.

Then late in the afternoon they came upon a wretched village. The natives were surly and unfriendly, but still they did not deny them such poor hospitality as they could offer. The chief listened to their story. Then he told them that while they could not remain in his village, he would have them guided to another far off the beaten track, where the Japs would never find them.

Where, a few weeks before, he might have commanded, van de Meer now swallowed his pride and begged the chief to permit them at least to remain overnight that his wife might gain strength for the journey that lay ahead. But Hoesin refused. 'Go now,' he said, 'and I will furnish guides. Remain, and I will make you prisoners and turn you over to the Japanese when they come.' Like the headmen of other villages through which they had passed, he feared the wrath of the invaders should they discover that he was harboring whites.

And so the nightmare journey was resumed through terrain cut by a frightful chasm, river eroded in tuff strata laid down through the ages by nearby volcanoes. And this river cut their trail, not once, but many times. Some times they could ford it. Again it could be crossed only on frail, swaying rope bridges. And this long after dark on a moonless night.

Elsje van der Meer, now too weak to walk, was carried by Lum Kam in an improvised sling strapped to his back. The guides, anxious to reach the safety of a kampong, urged them constantly to greater speed, for twice they had heard the coughing of tigers – that coughing grunt that chills the blood.

Van der Meer walked close to Lum Kam to steady him should he slip upon the muddy trail. Corrie followed behind her father, and Sing Tai brought up the rear. The two guides were at the head of the little column.

'You tired, missy?' asked Sing Tai. 'Maybe so better I carry you.'

'We all are tired,' replied the girl; 'but I can carry on as long as any of you. I wonder how much farther it is.'

They had started to ascend a trail steeply. 'Pretty soon there,' said Sing Tai, 'Guide say kampong top of cliff.'

But they were not pretty soon there, for this was the most arduous part of the journey. They had to stop often and rest. Lum Kam's heart was pounding. But it was this loyal heart and an iron will that kept him from sinking down exhausted.

At long last they reached the top, and presently the barking of dogs told them that they were approaching a kampong. The natives, aroused, challenged them. The guides explained their presence, and they were admitted. Taku Muda, the chief, greeted them with friendly words.

'You are safe here,' he said. 'You are among friends.'

'My wife is exhausted,' explained van der Meer. 'She must have rest before we can go on. But I do not wish to expose you to the anger of the Japanese should they discover that you had helped us. Let us rest here tonight; and tomorrow, if my wife can be moved, find us a hiding place deeper in the mountains. Perhaps there is a cave in some isolated gorge.'

'There are caves,' replied Taku Muda, 'but you will remain here. Here you are safe. No enemy will find my village.'

They were given food and a dry house in which to sleep. But Elsje van der Meer could eat nothing. She was burning with fever, but there was nothing they could do for her. Hendrik van der Meer and Corrie sat beside her the remainder of the night. What must have been the thoughts of this man whose stubbornness had brought this suffering upon the woman he loved? Before noon Elsje van der Meer died.

There is such a thing as a grief too poignant for tears. Father and daughter sat for hours, dry eyed, beside their dead, stunned by the catastrophe that had overwhelmed them. They were only dully conscious of sudden turmoil and shouting in the compound. Then Sing Tai burst in upon them.

'Quick!' he cried. 'Japs come. One man guide last night bring 'um. Hoesin bad man. He send 'um.'

Van der Meer rose. 'I will go and talk with them,' he said. 'We have done nothing. Maybe they will not harm us.'

'You no know monkey-men,' said Sing Tai.

Van der Meer shrugged. 'There is nothing else I can do. If I fail, Sing Tai, try to get missy away. Do not let her fall into their hands.'

He went to the door of the hut and descended the ladder to the ground. Lum Kam joined him. The Japs were on the far side of the compound. Van der Meer walked boldly toward them, Lum Kam at his side. Neither man was armed. Corrie and Sing Tai watched from the dark interior of the hut. They could see, but they could not be seen.

They saw the Japs surround the two men. They heard the voice of the white man and the monkey jabber of the Japs, but they could not make out what was said. Suddenly they saw a rifle butt rise above the heads of the men. It was thrust as suddenly downward. They knew that on the other end of the rifle was a bayonet. They heard a scream. Then more rifle butts were raised and lunged downward. The screams ceased. Only the laughter of the sub-men was to be heard.

Sing Tai seized the girl's arm. 'Come!' he said, and drew her to the rear of the hut. There was an opening there and, below, the hard ground. 'I drop,' said Sing Tai. 'Then missy drop. I catch 'um. Savvy?'

She nodded. After the Chinese had dropped safely, the girl leaned from the opening to reconnoiter. She saw that she could climb most of the way down. To drop into Sing Tai's arms might easily have injured him. So she came safely down to within a few feet of the ground, and Sing Tai lowered her the rest of the way. Then he led her into the jungle that grew close to the kampong.

Before dark they found a cave in a limestone cliff and hid there for two days. Then Sing Tai returned to the kampong to investigate and to get food if the Japs had left.

Late in the afternoon he returned to the cave empty handed. 'All gone,' he said. 'All dead. Houses burned.'

'Poor Taku Muda,' sighed Corrie. 'This was his reward for an act of humanity.'

Two years passed. Corrie and Sing Tai had found asylum in a remote mountain kampong with Chief Tiang Umar. Only occasionally did news from the outside world reach them. The only news that would be good news to them would have been that the Japs had been driven from the island. But that news did not come. Some times a villager, trading far afield, would return with stories of great Japanese victories, of the American Navy sunk, of German victories in Africa, Europe, or Russia. To Corrie the future seemed hopeless.

One day a native came who did not belong to the village of Tiang Umar. He looked long at Corrie and Sing Tai, but he said nothing. After he had gone away, the Chinese told the girl. 'That man bad news,' he said. 'Him from kampong Chief Hoesin. Now he go tell and monkey-men come. Maybeso you better be boy. Then we go away and hide some more.'

Sing Tai cut Corrie's golden hair to the proper length and dyed it black. He painted her eyebrows, too. She was already deeply tanned by the equatorial sun, and with the blue trousers and the loose blouse he fashioned for her, she could pass as a native boy anything but the closest scrutiny. Then they went away again, taking up their interminable flight. Tiang Umar sent men to guide them to a new sanctuary. It was not far from the village – a cave close to a tiny mountain stream. There were to be found many varieties of the edible things that grow in a Sumatran forest jungle, and in the stream there were fish. Occasionally, Tiang Umar sent some eggs and a chicken. Once in a while pork or dog meat. Corrie could not eat the latter, so Sing Tai got it all. A youth named Alam always brought the food. The three became fast friends.

Captain Tokujo Matsuo and Lieutenant Hideo Sokabe led a detachment of soldiers deep into the mountains to locate strategic positions for heavy coastal guns and survey practical roads leading to them.

They came to the kampong of Hoesin, the chief who had betrayed the van der Meers. They knew of him by report as one who would collaborate with the Japanese. Still it was necessary to impress him with their superiority; so, when he failed to bow from the waist when they approached him, they slapped his face. One of the enlisted men ran a bayonet through a native who refused to bow to him. Another dragged a screaming girl into the jungle. Captain Matsuo and Lieutenant Sokabe smiled toothy smiles. Then they demanded food.

Hoesin would rather have cut their throats, but he had food brought to them and to their men. The officers said that they would honor him by making his village their headquarters while they remained in the vicinity. Hoesin saw ruin staring him in the face. Frantically he searched his mind for some artifice by which he could rid himself of his unwelcome guests. Then he recalled the story that one of his people had brought him a few days before from another village. It did not seem to him very likely to be of value in ridding himself of these monkeys, but it would do no harm to try. He thought about it during a sleepless night.

The following morning he asked them if they were interested in finding enemies who had taken refuge in the mountains. They said that they were. 'Two years ago three whites and two Chinese came to my village. I sent them on to another village, because I would not harbor enemies of Greater East Asia. The white man's name was van der Meer.'

'We have heard of him,' said the Japs. 'He was killed.'

'Yes. I sent guides to show your soldiers where they were hiding. But the daughter and one of the Chinese escaped. The daughter is very beautiful.'

'So we have heard. But what of it?'

'I know where she is.'

'And you have not reported it?'

'I only just discovered her hiding place. I can give you a guide who will lead you to it.'

Captain Matsuo shrugged. 'Bring us food,' he ordered.

Hoesin was crushed. He had food sent them, and then he went to his hut and prayed to Allah or Buddha or whatever god he prayed to, asking him to strike the monkey-men dead, or at least cause them to depart.

Matsuo and Sokabe discussed the matter over their meal. 'Perhaps we should look into the matter,' said the former. 'It is not well to have enemies in our rear.'

'And they say that she is beautiful,' added Sokabe.

'But we cannot both go,' said Matsuo. Being both lazy and the commanding officer, he decided to send Lieutenant Sokabe with a detachment to find the girl and bring her back. 'You will kill the Chinese,' he ordered, 'and you will bring the girl back – unharmed. You understand? Unharmed.'

Lieutenant Hideo Sokabe came a few days later to the kampong of Tiang Umar the Chief. Being a very superior person, Lieutenant Sokabe slapped the old chief so hard that he fell down. Then Lieutenant Sokabe kicked him in the belly and face. 'Where are the white girl and the Chinese?' he demanded.

'There is no white girl here, nor any Chinese.'

'Where are they?'

'I do not know what you are talking about.'

'You lie. Soon you will tell the truth.' He ordered a sergeant to get him some bamboo splinters, and when they were brought, he drove one beneath one of Tiang Umar's fingernails. The old man screamed in agony.

'Where is the white girl?' demanded the Jap.

'I know of no white girl,' insisted Tiang Umar.

The Jap drove another splinter beneath another nail, but still the old man insisted that he knew nothing of any white girl.

As Sokabe was preparing to continue the torture, one of the chief's wives came and threw herself upon her knees before him. She was an old woman – Tiang Umar's oldest wife. 'If you will hurt him no more, I will tell you how you may find the white girl and the Chinese,' she said.

'This is better,' said Sokabe. 'How?'

'Alam knows where they hide,' said the old woman, pointing to a youth.

Corrie and Sing Tai sat at the mouth of their cave. It had been a week since Alam had brought them food, and they were expecting him soon with eggs perhaps, and pork or a piece of dog meat. Corrie hoped that it would be eggs and a chicken.

'Pretty soon someone come,' said Sing Tai, listening. 'Too many. Come back into the cave.'

Alam pointed out the cave to Lieutenant Hideo Sokabe. Tears welled from the youth's eyes. Had his life alone been forfeit, he would have died before he would have led these hated monkey-men to the hiding place of this girl whom he fairly worshipped. But the lieutenant had threatened to destroy everyone in the village if he failed to do so, and Alam knew that he would keep his word.

Hideo Sokabe and his men entered the cave, Sokabe with drawn sword, the men with fixed bayonets. In the dim light, Sokabe saw a Chinese and a young native boy. He had them dragged out. 'Where is the girl?' he demanded of Alam. 'You shall die for this, and all your people. Kill them,' he said to his men.

'No!' screamed Alam. 'That is the girl. She only wears the clothes of a boy.'

Sokabe tore open Corrie's blouse. Then he grinned. A soldier ran a bayonet through Sing Tai, and the detachment marched away with their prisoner.

2

S/sgt. Joe 'Datbum' Bubonovitch of Brooklyn, assistant engineer and waist gunner, stood in the shade of the wing of Lovely Lady with the other members of the combat crew of the big Liberator.

'I've found them pretty swell guys,' he said in evident disagreement with a remark made by ball turret gunner S/Sgt. Tony 'Shrimp' Rosetti of Chicago.

'Yeah? So I suppose dat Geo'ge Toid was a swell guy. Say, we got a mayor in Chicago oncet wot dared dat guy to come on over. He said he'd punch him in de snoot.'

'You got your dates mixed, Shrimp.'

'Yeah? Well, I don't like cartin' no bloody Britisher around in de Lovely Lady. An' I hear he's a dook, or sumpn.'

'I guess here comes your Duke now,' said Bubonovitch.

A jeep pulled up beneath the wing of the B-24, disgorging three officers – an RAF colonel, an AAF colonel, and an AAF major. Capt. Jerry Lucas of Oklahoma City, pilot of the Lovely Lady, stepped forward; and the AAF colonel introduced him to Col. Clayton.

'All set, Jerry?' asked the American colonel.

'All set, Sir.'

Electricians and armorers, having given the final, loving check-up to their gadgets and guns, dropped through the bomb bay doors; and the combat crew climbed aboard.

Col. John Clayton was flying as an observer on a reconnaissance and photographic mission over Jap held Sumatra in Netherland East Indies, from an air field in (censored). Going forward to the flight deck when he came aboard, he stood behind the pilots during the take-off. Later, on the long flight, he took the co-pilot's place, sometimes the pilot's. He talked with the navigator and the radio engineer. He edged his way aft along the catwalk through the bomb bay between auxiliary gas tanks necessitated by the long flight. The plane carried no bombs.

Shrimp and Bubonovitch and the tail gunner and the other waist gunner were sprawled on the deck against life rafts and parachutes. Shrimp was the first to see Clayton open the little door forward of the ball turret.

'Hst!' he warned. 'Here comes the dook.'

Clayton edged around the ball turret, stepped over Shrimp and Bubonovitch, and stopped beside the photographer, who was fiddling with his camera. None of the enlisted men stood up. When a fighting plane takes to the air, military formality is left grounded. The photographer, a Signal Corps sergeant, looked up and smiled. Clayton smiled back and sat down beside him.

Cold wind was swirling up around the ball turret and hurtling out the tail gunner's open window. The noise of the motors was deafening. By placing his mouth within an inch of the photographer's ear and shouting, Clayton asked some questions about the camera. The photographer screamed his replies. A B-24 in flight discourages conversation, but Clayton got the information he wished.

Then he sat down on the edge of a life raft between Shrimp and Bubonovitch. He passed around a package of cigarettes. Only Shrimp refused. Bubonovitch offered Clayton a light. Shrimp looked disgusted. He remembered George III, but he couldn't remember what he had done. All he knew what that he didn't like Britishers.

Shouting, Clayton asked Bubonovitch his name and where he came from. When Bubonovitch said Brooklyn, Clayton nodded. 'I've heard a lot about Brooklyn,' he said.

'Probably about dem bums,' said Bubonovitch.

Clayton smiled and nodded.

'They call me "Dat Bum,"' said Bubonovitch, grinning. Pretty soon he was showing the English colonel pictures of his wife and baby. Then they signed each other's Short Snorter bills. That brought the other waist gunner, the tail gunner, and the photographer into the picture. Shrimp remained aloof and superior.

After Clayton had gone forward, Shrimp allowed that he'd just as soon have Tojo or Hitler sign his Short Snorter bill as a 'dirty Britisher.' 'Look wot they done at the Alamo,' he challenged.

'You mean Thermopylae,' said Bubonovitch.

'Well, wot's the difference?'

'He's a good guy,' said the tail gunner.

'Like our officers,' said the other waist gunner. 'No side.'

It was dawn when they sighted the Northwesterly tip of Sumatra, and a perfect day for a photographic mission. There were clouds above the mountains that form the backbone of the eleven hundred miles long island that sprawls across the equator South and west of the Malay Peninsula; but the coastline, as far as they could see it, was cloudless. And it was the coastline they were primarily interested in.

The Japs must have been taken wholly by surprise, for they had been photographing for almost half an hour before they encountered any flak. And this was most ineffective. But as they flew down the coast, it increased in volume and accuracy. The plane got some shrapnel from near misses, but luck held with them for a long time.

Near Padang, three Zeros roared down on them out of the sun. Bubonovitch got the leader. They could see the plane burst into flame and plummet earthward. The other two peeled off, and kept at a respectful distance for a while. Then they turned back. But the ack-ack increased in volume and accuracy. The inboard starboard engine got a direct hit, and shrapnel sprayed the cockpit. Lucas' flak vest saved him, but the co-pilot got a direct hit in the face. The navigator slipped the co-pilot's safety belt and dragged him from the cockpit to administer first aid. He was already dead.

So thick and so close was the flak by now, that the great ship seemed to be bucking like a broncho. To attempt to avoid it, Lucas turned inshore away from the coast where he knew that most of the anti-aircraft batteries would be located. In shore, too, were clouds above the mountains in which they could hide as they turned back toward home.

Home! Liberators had made great flights in the past on three engines. The twenty-three year old captain had to think quickly. It was a snap judgment, but he knew it was sound. He ordered everything thrown overboard except their parachutes – guns, ammunition, life rafts, everything. It was the only chance they had of making their base. Zeros didn't worry Lucas. Zeros usually kept their distance from heavy bombers. Except for one stretch of water, the crossing of Malacca Strait, he could keep near land all the way, skirting the coast of Malaya Northwest. If they had to bail out over water, they would be near shore; and their Mae Wests would have to answer. That was why he felt that he could jettison the life rafts.

As they turned in toward the mountains and the clouds, the flak came thicker and thicker. The Japs must have guessed the pilot's plan. Lucas knew that some of the mountain peaks rose to twelve thousand feet. He was flying at twenty thousand now, but slowly losing altitude. But he was leaving the shore batteries behind.

They were well above the mountains when a mountain battery opened up on them. Lucas heard a terrific burst, and the plane careened like a wounded thing. He fought the controls. He spoke into the intercom, asking reports. There was no reply. The intercom was dead. He sent the radio man back to check the damage. Clayton, in the co-pilot's seat, helped with the controls. It required the combined strength of both men to keep the plane from nosing over.

Lucas called to the navigator. 'Check and see that everybody jumps,' he said. 'Then you jump.'

The navigator poked his head into the nose to tell the nose gunner to jump. The nose gunner was dead. The radio man came back to the flight deck. 'The whole goddam tail's shot off,' he said. 'Butch and that photographer went with it.'

'Okay,' said Lucas. 'Jump, and make it snappy.' Then he turned to Clayton. 'Better bail out, Sir.'

'I'll wait for you, if you don't mind, Captain,' said Clayton.

'Jump!' snapped Lucas.

Clayton smiled. 'Right-o!' he said.

'I've opened the bomb bay doors,' said Lucas. 'It's easier out that way. Make it snappy!'

Clayton reached the catwalk in the bomb bay. The ship was falling off on one wing. It was evidently going into a spin. One man could not hold it. He wanted to hang on until Lucas jumped – until the last minute. It was the last minute. The ship careened, throwing Clayton from the catwalk. His body struck the side of the bomb bay and then rolled out into thin air.

Unconscious, he hurtled toward death. Through heavy, enveloping clouds his body fell. Lovely Lady, her three motors still roaring, raced past him. Now, when she crashed she was sure to burn, leaving nothing for the enemy to learn or salvage.

But momentarily stunned, Clayton soon regained consciousness. But it took several seconds before he realized his situation. It was like awakening in a strange room. He had passed through the cloud bank, and was now in a torrential tropical rain below it. Perhaps it was to the cold rain that he owed his salvation. It may have revived him just in time to pull the rip cord while there was still a margin of seconds.

His chute billowed above him, and his body snapped grotesquely at the sudden retardation of his fall. Directly beneath him a sea of foliage billowed to the pounding of hurtling masses of rain. In a matter of seconds his body crashed through leaves and branches until his chute caught and held him suspended a couple of hundred feet above the ground. This close had he come to death.

Simultaneously, he heard a rending and crashing a few hundred yards away – a dull explosion followed by a burst of flame. Lovely Lady's funeral pyre lit up the dismal, dripping forest.

Clayton seized a small branch and pulled himself to a larger one that would support him. Then he slipped off the chute harness and his Mae West. His uniform and his underclothes, to the skin, were soaked and soggy. He had lost his cap during his fall. Now he removed his shoes and threw them away. His pistol and ammunition belt followed. Then his socks, tunic, trousers, and underclothes. He retained only a web belt and his knife in its scabbard.

He next climbed upward until he could release the snagged chute. He cut away all the lines, wrapped the silk in a small bundle; and, together with the lines, tied it to his back. Then he commenced the descent toward the ground. He swung down easily from branch to branch. From the lowest branches, giant creepers depended to the ground undergrowth below. Down these he clambered with the agility of a monkey.

From the silk of his chute, he fashioned a loincloth. A sense of wellbeing, of happiness surged through him. Now, that which he had lost he had regained. That which he loved most. Freedom. The habiliments of civilization, even the uniform of his country's armed forces, were to him but emblems of bondage. They had held him as his chains hold the galley slave, though he had worn his uniform with pride. But to be honorably free of it was better. And something told him that Fate may have ordained that he was to serve his country quite as well naked as uniformed. Else why had Fate plunged him thus into an enemy stronghold?

The pouring rain sluiced down his bronzed body. It tousled his black hair. He raised his face to it. A cry of exaltation trembled on his lips but was not voiced. He was in the country of the enemy.

His first thought now was of his companions. Those who had alighted within sound of the crashing plane would naturally attempt to reach it. He made his way toward it. As he went, he searched the ground. He was looking for a certain plant. He did not entertain much hope of finding it in this strange, far away land. But he did. He found it growing luxuriantly. He gathered some and macerated the great leaves between his palms. Then he spread the juice over his entire body, face, limbs, and head.

After that he took to the trees where travelling was easier than through the lush and tangled undergrowth. Presently he overtook a man stumbling toward the wrecked plane. It was Jerry Lucas. He stopped above him and called him by name. The pilot looked in all directions, except up, and saw no one. But he had recognized the voice.

'Where the heck are you, Colonel?'

'If I jumped, I'd land on your head.'

Lucas looked up, and his mouth dropped open. An almost naked giant was perched above him. He thought quickly: The guy's gone off his bean. Maybe he hit his head when he landed. Maybe it was just shock. He decided to pay no attention to the nudity. 'Are you all right?' he asked.

'Yes,' replied Clayton. 'And you?'

'Fit as a fiddle.'

They were but a short distance from the Lovely Lady. The flames were ris-ing high above her, and some of the trees were blazing. When they got as close to her as the heat would permit they saw Bubonovitch. Bubonovitch saw Lucas and greeted him happily. But he did not see Clayton until the latter dropped from a tree and alighted in front of him. Bubonovitch reached for his .45. Then he recognized the Englishman.

'Migawd!' he exclaimed. 'What happened to your clothes?'

'I threw them away.'

'Threw them away!'

Clayton nodded. 'They were wet and uncomfortable. They weighed too much.'

Bubonovitch shook his head. His eyes wandered over the Englishman. He saw the knife. 'Where's your gun?' he asked.

'I threw that away, too.'

'You must be crazy,' said Staff Sergeant Bubonovitch.

Lucas, standing behind Clayton, shook his head vigorously at his crew-man. But the remark didn't seem to excite Clayton, as the pilot had feared it might. He just said, 'No, not so crazy. You'll be throwing yours away pretty soon. Inside of twenty-four hours it will be rusty and useless. But don't throw your knife away. And keep it clean and sharp. It will kill and not make as much noise as a .45.'

Lucas was watching the flames licking through the openings in his beloved plane. 'Did they all get out?' he asked Bubonovitch.

'Yes. Lieut. Burnham and I jumped together. He should be close around here somewhere. All those who were alive got out.'

Lucas raised his head and shouted: 'Lucas calling! Lucas calling!'

Faintly an answer came: 'Rosetti to Lucas! Rosetti to Lucas! For Pete's sake come an' get me down outta dis.'

'Roger!' shouted Lucas, and the three men started in the direction from which Shrimp's voice had come.

They found him – dangling in the harness of his chute a good hundred feet above the ground. Lucas and Bubonovitch looked up and scratched their heads – at least figuratively.

'How you goin' to get me down?' demanded Shrimp.

'Damifino,' said Lucas.

'After a while you'll ripen and drop,' said Bubonovitch.

'Funny, ain'tcha, wise guy? Where'd you pick up dat dope wid out no clothes?'

'This is Colonel Clayton, half-wit,' replied Bubonovitch.

'Oh.' It is amazing how much contempt can be crowded into a two letter word. And S/Sgt. Tony Rosetti got it all in. It couldn't be missed. Lucas flushed.

Clayton smiled. 'Is the young man allergic to Englishmen?'

'Excuse him, colonel; he doesn't know any better. He's from a suburb of Chicago known as Cicero.'

'How you goin' to get me down?' demanded Shrimp again.

'That's just what I don't know,' said Lucas.

'Maybe we'll think of some way by tomorrow,' said Bubonovitch.

'You ain't a-goin' to leaf me up here all night!' wailed the ball turret gunner.

'I'll get him down,' said Clayton.

There were no vines depending from the tree in which Shrimp hung that came close enough to the ground to be within reach of Clayton. He went to another tree and swarmed up the vines like a monkey. Then he found a loose liana some fifty feet above the ground. Testing it and finding it secure, he swung out on it, pushing himself away from the bole of the tree with his feet. Twice he tried to reach a liana that hung from the tree in which Shrimp was isolated. His outstretched fingers only touched it. But the third time they closed around it.

The strength of this liana he tested as he had the other; then, keeping the first one looped around an arm, he climbed toward Shrimp. When he came opposite him, he still could not quite reach him. The gunner was hanging just a little too far from the bole of the tree.

Clayton tossed him the free end of the liana he had brought over with him from an adjoining tree. 'Grab this,' he said, 'and hang on.'

Rosetti grabbed, and Clayton pulled him toward him until he could seize one of the chute's shrouds. Clayton was seated on a stout limb. He drew Rosetti up beside him.

'Get out of your chute harness and Mae West,' he directed.

When Shrimp had done so, Clayton threw him across a shoulder, seized the liana he had brought from the nearby tree, and slipped from the limb.

'Geeze!' screamed Rosetti as they swung through space.

Holding by one hand, Clayton seized a waving branch and brought them to a stop. Then he clambered down the liana to the ground. When he swung Rosetti from his shoulder, the boy collapsed. He could not stand. And he was shaking like a leaf.

Lucas and Bubonovitch were speechless for a moment. 'If I hadn't seen it with my own eyes, I never would have believed it,' said the pilot.

'I still don't believe it,' said Bubonovitch.

'Shall we look for the others?' asked Clayton. 'I think we should try to find them and then get away from the plane. That smoke can be seen for miles, and the Japs will know exactly what it is.'

They searched and called for several hours without success. And just before dark they came upon the body of Lieut. Burnham, the navigator. His chute had failed to open. With their knives they dug a shallow grave. Then they wrapped him in his chute and buried him. Jerry Lucas said a short prayer. Then they went away.

In silence they followed Clayton. His eyes were scanning the trees as they passed them, and it was evident that he was searching for something. Quite spontaneously, they all seemed to have acquired unlimited confidence in the big Englishman. Shrimp's eyes seldom left him. Who may say what the little Cicero mucker was thinking? He had not spoken since his rescue from the tree. He had not even thanked Clayton.

It had stopped raining and the mosquitoes swarmed about them. 'I don't see how you stand it, colonel,' said Lucas, slapping at mosquitoes on his face and hands.

'Sorry!' exclaimed Clayton. 'I meant to show you.' He searched about and found some of the plants he had discovered earlier in the afternoon. 'Mash these leaves,' he said, 'and rub the juice on all the exposed parts of your body. The mosquitoes won't bother you after that.'

Presently, Clayton found that for which he had been looking – trees with interlacing branches some twenty feet above the ground. He swung up easily and commenced to build a platform. 'If any of you men can get up here, you can help me. We ought to get this thing done before dark.'

'What is it?' asked Bubonovitch.

'It's where we're going to sleep tonight. Maybe for many nights.'

The three men climbed slowly and awkwardly up. They cut branches and laid them across the limbs that Clayton had selected, forming a solid plat-form about ten by seven feet.

'Wouldn't it have been easier to have built a shelter on the ground?' asked Lucas.

'Very much,' agreed Clayton, 'but if we had, one of us might be dead before morning.'

'Why?' demanded Bubonovitch.

'Because this is tiger country.'

'What makes you think so?'

'I have smelled them off and on all afternoon.'

S/Sgt. Rosetti shot a quick glance at Clayton from the corners of his eyes and then looked as quickly away.

3

The Englishman knotted several lengths of chute shrouds together until he had a rope that would reach the ground. He handed the end of the rope to Bubonovitch. 'Haul in when I give you the word, Sergeant,' he said. Then he dropped quickly to the ground.

'Smelled 'em!' said S/Sgt. Rosetti, exuding skepticism.

Clayton gathered a great bundle of giant elephant ears, made the end of the rope fast to it, and told Bubonovitch to haul away. Three such bundles he sent up before he returned to the platform. With the help of the others, he spread some on the floor of the platform and with the remainder built an overhead shelter.

'We'll get meat tomorrow,' said Clayton. 'I'm not familiar with the fruits and vegetables here except a few. We'll have to watch what the monkeys eat.'

There were plenty of monkeys around them. There had been all afternoon – chattering, scolding, criticizing the newcomers.

'I recognize one edible fruit,' said Bubonvitch. 'See? In that next tree, *Durio zibethinus*, called durian. That siamang is eating one now – *Symphalangus syndactylus* – the black gibbon of Sumatra, largest of the gibbons.'

'He's off again,' said Shrimp. 'He can't even call a ant a ant.'

Lucas and Clayton smiled. 'I'll get some of the fruit of the *Durio zibeth-*whatever-you-call-it,' said the latter. He swung agilely into the adjoining tree and gathered four of the large, prickly skinned durians, tossing them one by one to his companions. Then he swung back.

Rosetti was the first to cut his open. 'It stinks,' he said. 'I ain't that hungry.' He started to toss it away. 'It's spoiled.'

'Wait,' cautioned Bubonovitch. 'I've read about the durian. It does stink, but it tastes good. The natives roast the seeds like chestnuts.'

Clayton had listened to Bubonvitch attentively. As they ate the fruit, he thought; What a country! What an army! A sergeant who talks like a college professor – and comes from Brooklyn at that! He thought, too, how little the rest of the world really knew America – the Nazis least of all. Jitterbugs, play-boys, a decadent race! He thought of how gallantly these boys had fought their guns, of how Lucas had made sure that his crew and his passenger were out before he jumped. Of how the boy had fought hopelessly to save his ship.

Night had fallen. The jungle sounds and the jungle voices were different now. There was movement everywhere around them – unseen, stealthy. A hollow, grunting cough rose from the foot of their tree.

'Wot was dat?' asked Shrimp.

'Stripes,' said Clayton.

Shrimp wanted to ask what stripes was, but so far he had addressed no word to the Britisher. However, curiosity at last got the best of pride. 'Stripes?' he asked.

'Tiger.'

'Geeze! You mean they's a tiger loose down there?'

'Yes. Two of them.'

'Geeze! I seen 'em once at the zoo in Chicago. I guess it wouldn't be so healthy down there. I heard they ate people.'

'We've got to thank you, Colonel, that we're not down there,' said Jerry Lucas.

'I guess we'd be a lot of babes in the woods without him,' said Bubonovitch.

'I learned a hell of a lot in Colonel Saffarrans' jungle training outfit,' said Shrimp, 'but nothin' about wot to do about tigers.'

'They hunt mostly at night,' Clayton explained. 'That's when you have to be on your guard.' After a while he said to Bubonovitch, 'From what little I have read about Brooklyn I was lead to believe that Brooklynites had a special pronunciation of English all their own. You talk like anyone else.'

'So do you,' said Bubonovitch.

Clayton laughed. 'I was not educated at Oxford.'

'Bum had a higher Brooklyn education,' explained Lucas. 'He went through sixth grade.'

Bubonovitch and Rosetti dropped off to sleep. Clayton and Lucas sat at the edge of the platform, their legs dangling, planning for the future. They agreed that their best chance lay in getting a boat from friendly natives (if they could find any) on the southwest coast of the island and then trying to make Australia. They spoke of this and many other things. Lucas talked about his crew. He spoke of them with pride. Those who were unaccounted for, he worried about. Those who were dead were dead. There was nothing to be done about that now. But Clayton could tell by the tenseness in his voice when he spoke of them how he felt about them.

He spoke of Rosetti. 'He's really a good kid,' he said, 'and a top ball turret gunner. Nature molded him for the job. There isn't much room in a ball turret. Bum says the War Department should breed 'em, crossing midgets with pygmies. Shrimp has the DFC and Air Medal with three clusters. He's a good kid all right.'

'He certainly hasn't much use for Britishers,' laughed Clayton.

'What with all the Irish and Italians in Chicago, it's not surprising. And then Shrimp never had much of a chance to learn anything. His father was killed in Cicero in a gang war when he was a kid, and I guess his mother was just a gangland moll. She never had any use for Shrimp, nor he for her. But with a background like that, you've got to hand it to the kid. He didn't get much schooling, but he kept straight.'

'Bubonovitch interests me,' said the Englishman. 'He's an unusually intelligent man.'

'Yes. He's not only intelligent, but he's extremely well educated. The former is not necessarily a corollary of the latter. Bubonovitch is a graduate of Columbia. His father, a school teacher, saw to that. Bum got interested in the exhibits in The American Museum of Natural History in New York when he was in high school. So he specialized in zoology, botany, anthropology, and all the other ologies that a fellow has to know to be valuable to the museum. And when he graduated, he landed a job there. He likes to pull scientific names of things on Shrimp just to annoy him.'

'Then it's probably a good thing for Sgt. Rosetti's blood pressure that I haven't an Oxford accent,' said Clayton.

As Corrie van der Meer trudged along with her captors her mind was occupied with but two problems: how to escape and how to destroy herself if she could not escape. Alam, walking beside her, spoke to her in his own language, which she understood but which the Japs did not.

'Forgive me,' he begged, 'for leading them to you. They tortured Tiang Umar, but he would not tell. Then his old wife could stand it no longer, and she told them that I knew where you were hiding. They said that they would kill everyone in the village if I did not lead them to your hiding place. What could I do?'

'You did right, Alam. Sing Tai and I were only two. It is better that two die than all the people of a village.'

'I do not want you to die,' said Alam. 'I would rather die myself.'

The girl shook her head. 'What I fear,' she said, 'is that I may not find the means to die – in time.'

Lieut. Sokabe spent the night in the kampong of Tiang Umar. The villagers were sullen and glowering; so Sokabe posted two sentries before the door of the house where he and his captive slept. To further preclude the possibility that she might escape, he bound her wrists and her ankles. Otherwise, he did not molest her. He had a healthy fear of Capt. Tokujo Matsuo, whose temper was notoriously vile; and he had a plan.

When he set out the next morning, he took Alam along to act as interpreter should he require one. Corrie was glad of the company of this friendly youth. They talked together as they had the previous day. Corrie asked Alam if he had seen any of the guerrilla bands that she had heard rumors of from time to time, bands made up of Dutchmen who had escaped to the hills – planters, clerks, soldiers.

'No, I have not seen them; but I have heard of them. I have heard that they have killed many Japanese. They are desperate men. The Japanese are always searching for them. They offer the native people rich rewards for pointing out their hiding places; so these men are suspicious of all natives they do not know, thinking they may be spies. It is said that a native who falls into their hands never returns to his village unless they know that they can trust him. And who can blame them? I have also heard that many natives have joined them. Now that we have learned that Greater East Asia Co-Prosperity is for the Japanese alone, we hate them.'

They passed the spot where the village of Taku Muda had stood. There was no evidence that man had ever set foot there, so completely had the jungle reclaimed it.

'This is the prosperity that the Japanese bring us,' said Alam.

The morning wore on. They marched beneath sullen clouds in a tropical downpour. The gloomy forest stunk of rotting vegetation. It exhaled the vapors of death. Death! The girl knew that every step she took was bringing her closer to it. Unless – hope does not die easily in the breast of youth. But unless what?

She heard the roar of motors overhead. But she was used to that sound. The Japs were always flying over the island. Then, from a distance, there came to her ears a crashing and rending followed by a dull explosion. She did not hear the motors again. She thought, of course, that it was an enemy plane; and it filled her with satisfaction. The Japs jabbered about it excitedly. Lt Sokabe considered investigating. He talked with a sergeant. At last they decided that they could never find the plane in this tangle of jungle and forest. It was too far away.

It was almost dark when they reached the kampong that Capt. Tokujo Matsuo had commandeered for the use of his detachment. Standing in the doorway of the house that two officers had taken for their quarters, Matsuo watched the party approach.

He called to Sokabe. 'Where are the prisoners?'

The lieutenant seized Corrie roughly by the arm and pulled her out of line and toward the captain. 'Here,' he said.

'I sent you for a Chinaman and a yellow haired Dutch girl, and you bring back a black haired native boy. Explain.'

'We killed the Chinaman,' said Sokabe. 'This is the Dutch girl.'

'I do not feel like joking, you fool,' snarled Matsuo.

Sokabe prodded the girl up the ladder that led to the doorway. 'I do not joke,' he said. 'This is the girl. She has disguised herself by dyeing her hair black and wearing the clothing of a native boy. Look!' Roughly he parted Corrie's hair with his dirty fingers, revealing the blonde color close to the scalp.

Matsuo scrutinized the girl's features closely. Then he nodded. 'She suits me,' he said. 'I shall keep her.'

'She belongs to me,' said Sokabe. 'I found her and brought her here. She is mine.'

Matsuo spat. His face turned red. But he managed to restrain himself. 'You forget yourself, Lieutenant Sokabe,' he said. 'And take your orders from me. I am commanding officer here. You will find yourself other quarters at once and leave the girl here.'

'You may be a captain,' said Sokabe; 'but now, because of the great size of the imperial army and the many casualties, many officers are low born. My honorable ancestors were samurai. My honorable uncle is General Hideki Tojo. Your father and all your uncles are peasants. If I write a letter to my honorable uncle, you will not be a captain any more. Do I get the girl?'

There was murder in Matsuo's heart. But he chose to dissemble his wrath until such time as Sokabe might meet an accidental death. 'I thought you were my friend,' he said, 'and now you turn against me. Let us do nothing rash. The girl is nothing. Descendants of the gods should not quarrel over such a low born creature. Let us leave the matter to the decision of our colonel. He will be here to inspect us soon.' And before he gets here, thought Matsuo, an accident will befall you.

'That is fair enough,' agreed Sokabe. It will be most unfortunate, he thought, should my captain die before the colonel arrives.

The girl understood nothing that they said. She did not know that for the time being she was safe.

Early the next morning Alam left the kampong to return to his village.

4

Jerry Lucas was awakened by the violent shaking of the platform. It awakened Bubonovitch and Rosetti, also. 'Wot t'ell!' exclaimed the latter.

Bubonovitch looked around. 'I don't see anything.' Jerry leaned far out and looked up. He saw a huge black form a few feet above him, violently shaking the tree. 'Cripes!' he exclaimed. 'Do you guys see what I see?'

The other two looked up. 'Geeze!' said Rosetti. 'Wot a mug! I never knew monkeys came dat big.'

'That is not a monkey, you dope,' said Bubonovitch. 'It is known as *Pongo pygmaeus*, but why the *pygmaeus* I have not pursued my studies far enough to ascertain. It should be *Pongo giganteum*.'

'Talk United States,' growled Shrimp.

'It's an orangutan, Shrimp,' said Lucas.

'From the Malay *oran utan*, meaning wild man,' added Bubonovitch.

'What does it want?' inquired Shrimp. 'Wot in 'ell 's it shakin' the tree like dat for? Tryin' to shake us out? Geeze! Wot a mug. Is he a man-eater, Perfesser Bubonovitch?'

'He is chiefly herbivorous,' replied Bubonovitch.

Rosetti turned to Lucas. 'Do monks eat people, Cap?'

'No,' replied Lucas. 'Just leave 'em alone, and they'll leave you alone. But don't get fresh with that baby. He could take you apart like nobody's business.'

Shrimp was examining his .45. 'He ain't a-goin' to take me apart, not while I got Big Bertha here.'

The orangutan, having satisfied his curiosity, moved slowly off. Shrimp started stripping his .45. 'Geeze! It's started to rust already, just like—' He looked around. 'Say! Where's the dook?'

'Cripes! He's gone,' said Lucas. 'I never noticed.'

'Maybe he fell off,' suggested Rosetti, peering over the edge. 'He wasn't a bad guy fer a Britisher.'

'That's sure some concession, coming from you,' said Bubonovitch. 'Do you know, Cap'n, Shrimp wouldn't play billiards even for fear he might have to put English on the cue ball.'

Shrimp sat up suddenly and looked at the others. 'I just happened to think,' he said. 'Did either of youse hear dat scream last night?'

'I did,' said Lucas. 'What of it?'

'It sounded like someone bein' kilt. Didn't it?'

'Well, it did sound sort of human.'

'Sure. Dat's it. The dook fell off an' a tiger got 'im. That was him screamin'.'

Bubonovitch pointed. 'Here comes his ghost.'

The others looked. 'Fer Pete's sake!' said Rosetti. 'Wot a guy!'

Swinging through the trees toward them, the carcass of a deer slung over one shoulder, was the Englishman. He swung onto the platform. 'Here's breakfast,' he said. 'Go to it.'

Dropping the carcass, he drew his knife and hacked out a generous portion. Tearing the skin from the flesh with powerful fingers, he squatted in a far corner of the platform and sank his strong teeth into the raw flesh. Shrimp's jaw dropped and his eyes went wide. 'Ain't you goin' to cook it?' he asked.

'What with?' inquired Clayton. 'There's nothing around here dry enough to burn. If you want meat, you'll have to learn to eat it raw until we can find a permanent camp and get something that will burn.'

'Well,' said Shrimp, 'I guess I'm hungry enough.'

'I'll try anything once,' said Bubonovitch.

Jerry Lucas hacked off a small piece and started to chew it. Clayton watched the three men chewing on bits of the warm raw meat. 'That's not the way to eat it,' he said. 'Tear off pieces you can swallow, and then swallow them whole. Don't chew.'

'How did youse learn all dis?' inquired Rosetti.

'From the lions.'

Rosetti glanced at the others, shook his head, and then tried to swallow too large a piece of venison. He gagged and choked. 'Geeze!' he said, after he had disgorged the morsel, 'I never went to school to no lions.' But after that he did better.

'It's not so bad when you swallow it whole,' admitted Lucas.

'And it fills your belly and gives you strength,' said Clayton.

He swung into the next tree and got more durian fruit. They ate it now with relish. 'After dis,' said Shrimp, 'there ain't nuthin' I can't eat.'

'I passed a stream near here,' said Clayton. 'We can drink there. I think we'd better get started. We've got to do some reconnoitering before we can make any definite plans. You might take some of this meat along in your pockets if you think you'll be hungry again soon. But there's plenty of game everywhere. We won't go hungry.'

No one wanted to take any of the meat; so Clayton tossed the carcass to the ground. 'For Stripes,' he said.

The sun was shining, and the forest teemed with life. Bubonovitch was in his element. Here were animals and birds he had studied about in books, or whose dead and mounted frames he had seen in museums. And there were many that he had neither seen nor heard of. 'A regular museum of natural history on the hoof,' he said.

Clayton had led them to the stream, and after they had quenched their thirsts he guided them to a well marked game trail he had discovered while hunting for their breakfast. It wound downward in the direction he and Lucas had decided they would take – toward the west coast, many, many long marches away.

'There have been no men along this trail recently,' said Clayton, 'but there have been many other animals – elephant, rhinos, tigers, deer. It was on this trail that I found our breakfast.'

Shrimp wanted to ask how he had caught the deer, but realized that he had recently been altogether too familiar with a Britisher. Probably a friend of George Thoid, he thought, and winced. It curled his hair to think what the mob would say could they know of it. Still, he had to admit that the guy wasn't a bad guy, even though he hated to admit it.

They were moving upwind, and Clayton paused and and raised a warning hand. 'There is a man ahead of us,' he said in a low tone.

'I don't see no one,' said Rosetti.

'Neither do I,' said Clayton, 'but he's there.' He stood still for a few minutes.

'He's going the same way we are,' he said. 'I'll go ahead and have a look at him. The rest of you come along slowly.' He swung into a tree and disappeared ahead.

'You can't see no one, you can't hear no one; and this guy tells us there's a guy ahead of us – and w'ich way he's goin'!' Rosetti looked appealingly at Lucas.

'He hasn't been wrong yet,' said Jerry.

Sing Tai did not die. The Jap bayonet inflicted a cruel wound, but pierced no vital organ. For two days Sing Tai lay in a welter of blood, deep hidden in his cave. Then he crawled out. Suffering from shock, weak from loss of blood and lack of food and water, often on the verge of fainting from pain, he staggered slowly along the trail toward the village of Tiang Umar. Orientals are more easily resigned to death than are occidentals, so greatly do their philosophies differ. But Sing Tai would not die. While there was hope that his beloved mistress might live and need him, he, too, must live.

In the village of Tiang Umar he might get word of her. Then he might be able to determine whether to live or die. So Sing Tai's loyal heart beat on, however weakly. Yet there were moments when he wondered if he would have the strength to carry on to the village. Such thoughts were depressing him when he was startled to see an almost naked giant appear suddenly in the trail before him – a bronzed giant with black hair and gray eyes. This, perhaps, is the end, thought Sing Tai.

Clayton had dropped into the trail from an overhanging tree. He spoke to Sing Tai in English, and Sing Tai replied in English which had just a trace of pidgin. In Hong Kong, Sing Tai had lived for years in the homes of Englishmen.

Clayton saw the blood soaked garments and noted the outward signs of weakness that seemed to verge on collapse. 'How you get hurt?' he asked.

'Jap monkey-man run bayonet through me – here.' He indicated the spot in his side.

'Why?' asked Clayton, and Sing Tai told his story.

'Are there Japs near here?'

'Me no think so.'

'How far is this village you are trying to reach?'

'Not very far now – maybe so one kilometer.'

'Are the people of that village friendly to the Japanese?'

'No. Very much hate Japs.'

Clayton's companions appeared now from around a curve in the trail. 'You see,' said Lucas. 'Right again.'

'That guy is always right,' muttered Shrimp, 'but I don't see how he done it – not with no glass ball nor nuthin'.'

'Not even with the aid of mirrors,' said Bubonovitch.

Sing Tai looked at them apprehensively as they approached. 'They are my friends,' said Clayton – 'American aviators.'

'Melicans!' breathed Sing Tai with a sigh of relief. 'Now I know we save missie.'

Clayton repeated Sing Tai's story to the others, and it was decided that they should go on to Tiang Umar's village. Clayton gathered the Chinese gently into his arms and carried him along the trail. When Sing Tai said that they were near the village, the Englishman put him down, and told them all to wait while he went ahead to investigate. The Jap detachment might still be there. It was not, and he soon returned.

Tiang Umar received them well when Sing Tai had explained who they were. With Sing Tai acting as interpreter, Tiang Umar told them that the Japs had left the previous morning, taking the Dutch girl and one of his young men with them. What was their destination, he did not know. He knew that there was a Jap camp one day's march to the southwest. Perhaps they had gone to that camp. If they would wait in his kampong, he was sure that the youth, Alam, would return, as the Japs had taken him along only to act as interpreter in the villages they might pass through.

They decided to wait. Clayton was especially anxious to; and when it was decided, he went off into the forest alone. 'He'll probably come back wit one of them there water buffalo under his arm,' predicted Shrimp. But when he came back he had only some tough and slender branches and some bamboo. With these and some chicken feathers and fiber cord given him by Tiang Umar, he fashioned a bow, some arrows and a spear. The tips of his weapons he fire hardened. With parachute silk, he made a quiver.

His companions watched with interest. Rosetti was not greatly impressed when Clayton explained that his armament would serve not only to insure them plenty of game but as weapons of defense and offense against men. 'Do we hold de game w'ile he shoots at it?' he asked Bubonovitch. 'Say, an' if any guy ever pricked me wid one of dem t'ings, an' I found it out—'

'Don't be corny,' said Bubonovitch. But weapons, to Rosetti, meant .45s, tommy guns, machine guns, not slivers of bamboo with chicken feathers at one end.

Late in the afternoon, Alam returned. He was immediately surrounded by a crowd of jabbering natives. Sing Tai finally got his story and retold it to Clayton. Alam knew that the two Jap officers had quarrelled over the girl and that she was still safe at the time he had left the village that morning.

Sing Tai, with tears in his eyes, begged Clayton to rescue Corrie from the Japs. Clayton and the Americans discussed the matter. All were in favor of the attempt, but not all for the same reasons. Clayton and Bubonovitch wished to save the girl. Lucas and Rosetti wished to discomfit the Japs. They were little interested in the girl, both being misogynists. Lucas was a woman hater because the girl he had left behind in Oklahoma City had married a 4-F two months after Jerry had gone overseas. Rosetti's hatred of them stemmed from his lifelong hatred of his mother.

Early the following morning they set out, guided by Alam.

5

They moved slowly and cautiously, Clayton reconnoitering ahead of the others. Shrimp didn't see why they had brought Alam, and was sure that they would become lost. In a weird sign language of his own invention, he was constantly asking Alam if they were on the right trail. The native, not having the slightest idea what Shrimp's wild gesticulating meant, nodded and smiled as soon as Rosetti started to point and grimace.

Lucas and Bubonovitch were not as much concerned as Shrimp. They had more confidence in the Englishman than he. However, they could not know that Clayton needed no guide to show him the trail of a detachment of soldiers accompanied by a white girl and a native youth. Everywhere along the trail the signs of their recent passage were obvious to his trained senses.

It was dark when they approached the village. Clayton had the others wait while he went ahead to investigate. He found the village poorly guarded and entered it with ease. The night was moonless and clouds hid the stars. There were dim lights in a few of the houses. Conditions were ideal for the furtherance of the plan Clayton had worked out.

Close to the point at which he had entered his keen sense of smell located the white girl. He heard the angry jabbering of two Japs in the house with her. They would be the two officers still quarrelling over her.

He left the village at the same point at which he had entered it and passed around it to its lower end. There was a sentry here. Clayton did not wish any sentry at this point. The fellow patrolled back and forth. Clayton crouched behind a tree, waiting. The sentry approached. Something leaped upon him from behind; and before he could voice a cry of warning, a keen blade bit deep into his throat.

Clayton dragged the corpse out of the village, and returned to his companions. He whispered instructions; then he led them to the lower end of the village. 'Your .45s,' he had said, 'will probably fire the cartridges that are in the chambers. The chances are that the mechanisms are so rusted by this time that they will not eject the shell nor reload, but fire as long as they will fire. When they jam, throw rocks into the village to keep attention attracted in this direction. And all the while, yell like hell. Start this in three minutes. In four minutes, get out of there and get out quick. We'll rendezvous on the back trail above the village. Keep your watch dial hidden from the village, Captain.' Then he was gone.

He returned to the upper end of the village and hid beneath the house in which were the two officers and the girl. A minute later, shots rang out at the lower end of the village and loud yells shattered the silence of the night. Clayton grinned. It sounded as though a strong force were attacking the village.

A second later the two officers ran from the house, screaming orders, demanding explanations. Soldiers swarmed from other houses and all ran in the direction of the disturbance. Then Clayton ran up the ladder that led to the doorway of the house and entered. The girl lay on sleeping mats at the rear of the single room. Her wrists and ankles were bound.

She saw this almost naked man cross the floor toward her at a run. He stooped down and gathered her in his arms, carried her from the house and out into the jungle. She was terrified. What new horror awaited her?

In the dim light within the room, she had only seen that the man was tall and that his skin was brown. Out along a jungle trail he bore her for a short distance. Then he halted and put her down. She felt something cold press against her wrists – and her hands were free. Then the cords around her ankles were cut.

'Who are you?' she demanded in Dutch.

'Quiet!' he cautioned.

Presently, four others joined them; and they all moved in silence with her along the dark trail. Who were they? What did they want of her? The one word, quiet, spoken in English had partially reassured her. At least they were not Japs.

For an hour they moved on in unbroken silence, Clayton constantly alert for sounds of pursuit. But none developed. At last he spoke. 'I think we confused them,' he said. 'If they are searching, it is probably in the other direction.'

'Who are you?' asked Corrie, this time in English.

'Friends,' replied Clayton. 'Sing Tai told us about you. So we came and got you.'

'Sing Tai is not dead?'

'No, but badly wounded.'

Alam spoke to her then and reassured her. 'You are safe now,' he said. 'I have heard that Americans can do anything. Now I believe it.'

'These are Americans?' she asked incredulously. 'Have they landed at last?'

'Only these few. Their plane was shot down.'

'That was a pretty cute trick, Colonel,' said Bubonovitch. 'It certainly fooled them.'

'It came near doing worse than that to me, because I forgot to caution you as to the direction of your fire. Two bullets came rather too close to me for comfort.' He turned to the girl. 'Do you feel strong enough to walk the rest of the night?' he asked.

'Yes, quite,' she replied. 'You see I am used to walking. I have been doing a lot of it for the past two years, keeping out of the way of the Japs.'

'For two years?'

'Yes, ever since the invasion. I have been hiding in the mountains all this time, Sing Tai and I.' Clayton drew her out, and she told her story – the flight from the plantation, the death of her mother, the murder of her father and Lum Kam, the treachery of some natives, the loyalty of others.

They reached the village of Tiang Umar at dawn, but they remained there only long enough to get food; then they moved on, all but Alam. A plan had been worked out during the night. It was based on the belief that the Japs would eventually return to this village to look for the girl. Furthermore Corrie wished to have nothing done that would jeopardize the safety of these people who had befriended her.

Corrie and Sing Tai knew of many hiding places in the remote fastnesses of the mountains. They had been forced to move closer to Tiang Umar's village because of their inability to get proper or sufficient food for themselves in these safer locations. But now it would be different. The Americans could do anything.

They had been forced to leave Sing Tai behind, as he was in no condition to travel. Tiang Umar assured them that he could hide the Chinese where the Japs could not find him if they should return to the village.

'If I can, I shall let you know where I am, Tiang Umar,' said Corrie; 'then, perhaps, you will send Sing Tai to me when he is strong enough to travel.'

Corrie led the party deep into the wilds of the mountain hinterland. Here there were rugged gorges and leaping streams, forests of teak, huge stands of bamboo, open mountain meadows man deep with tough grasses.

Lucas and Clayton had decided to go thus deeper into the mountains and then cut to the southeast before turning toward the coast. In this way they would avoid the area in which the plane had crashed, where the Japs had probably already instituted a thorough search. They would also encounter few if any villages whose inhabitants might put Japs upon their trail.

Clayton often foraged ahead for food, always returning with something. It might be partridge or pheasant, sometimes deer. And now at their camps he made fire, so that the Americans could cook their food.

On the trail, Clayton and Corrie always led the way, then came Bubonovitch, with Lucas and Shrimp bringing up the rear, keeping as far away from the Dutch girl as possible. They were unreconciled to the presence of a woman. It was not so much that Corrie might jeopardize their chances to escape. It was just that they objected to women on general principles.

'But I suppose we gotta put up wit de dame,' said Rosetti. 'We can't leaf the Japs get her.'

Jerry Lucas agreed. 'If she were a man, or even a monkey, it wouldn't be so bad. But I just plain don't have any time for women.'

'Some dame double-cross you?' asked Shrimp.

'I could have forgiven her throwing me over for a 4-F as soon as I was out of sight,' said Jerry, 'but the so-and-so was a Republican into the bargain.'

'She ain't hard to look at,' conceded Shrimp, grudgingly.

'They're the worst,' said Jerry. 'Utterly selfish and greedy. Always gouging someone. Gimme! Gimme! Gimme! That's all they think of. If you ever decide to marry, Shrimp,' advised Jerry, pedantically, 'marry an old bag who'd be grateful to anyone for marrying her.'

'Who wants to marry an old bag?' demanded Shrimp.

'You wouldn't have to worry about wolves.'

'Whoever marries dis little Dutch number'll have plenty to worry about. All de wolves in de woods'll be howlin' round his back door. Ever notice dem lamps w'en she smiles?'

'You falling for her, Shrimp?'

'Hell, no; but I got eyes, ain't I?'

'I never look at her,' lied Jerry.

Just then a covey of partridges broke cover. Clayton already had an arrow fitted to his bow. Instantly the string twanged and a partridge fell. The man's movements were as swift and sure and smooth as the passage of light.

'Geez!' exclaimed Rosetti. 'I give. The guy's not human. Howinell did he know them boids was goin' to bust out? How could he hit 'em with dat t'ing?'

Jerry shook his head. 'Search me. He probably smelled 'em, or heard 'em. Lots of the things he does are just plain uncanny.'

'I'm goin' to learn to shoot one of dem t'ings,' said Shrimp.

Presently, Rosetti overcame his Anglophobia sufficiently to permit him to ask Clayton to show him how to make a bow and arrows. Lucas and Bubonovitch expressed a similar desire. The next day Clayton gathered the necessary materials, and they all set to work under his guidance to fashion weapons, even Corrie.

The Dutch girl braided the bow strings from fibers from the long tough grasses they found in open spaces in the mountains. Clayton shot birds for the feathers, and taught the others how properly to fletch their arrows. The fashioning of the weapons was a pleasant interlude to long days of scaling cliffs, battling through jungle undergrowth, marching down one declivity only to climb up once more to descend another. It was the first time that the five had had any protracted social intercourse, for after each hard day's march their greatest need had been sleep.

The Dutch girl sat near Jerry Lucas. He watched her nimble fingers braiding the fibers, and thought that she had pretty hands – small and well shaped. He noticed, too, that notwithstanding two years of bitter hardships she still gave attention to her nails. He glanced at his own, ruefully. Somehow, she always looked trim and neat. How she accomplished it was beyond him.

'It will be fun to hunt with these,' she said to him in her precise, almost Oxford English.

'If we can hit anything,' he replied. She speaks better English than I, he thought.

'We must practice a great deal,' she said. 'It is not right that we four grown-up people should be dependent upon Colonel Clayton for everything, as though we were little children.'

'No,' he said.

'Is he not wonderful?'

Jerry mumbled a 'Yes,' and went on with his work. With awkward, unaccustomed fingers he was trying to fletch an arrow. He wished the girl would keep still. He wished she were in Halifax. Why did there have to be girls around to spoil a man's world?

Corrie glanced up at him, puzzled. Her eyes reflected it. Then she noticed his awkward attempts to hold a feather in place and fasten it there with a bit of fiber. 'Here,' she said. 'Let me help you. You hold the feather and I'll bind the fiber around the shaft. Hold it close in the groove. There, that's right.' Her hands, passing the fiber around the arrow, often touched his. He found the contact pleasant; and because he found it so, it made him angry.

'Here,' he said, almost rudely, 'I can do this myself. You need not bother.'

She looked up at him, surprised. Then she went back to braiding the bow strings. She did not say anything, but in that brief glance when their eyes had met he had seen surprise and hurt in hers. He had seen the same once in a deer he had shot, and he had never again shot a deer.

You're a damned heel, he thought of himself. Then, with a great effort of willpower, he said, 'I am sorry. I did not mean to be rude.'

'You do not like me,' she said. 'Why? Have I done something to offend you?'

'Of course not. And what makes you think I don't like you?'

'It has been quite obvious. The little sergeant does not like me, either. Sometimes I catch him looking at me as though he would like to bite off my head.'

'Some men are shy around women,' he said.

The girl smiled. 'Not you,' she said.

They were silent for a moment. Then he said, 'Would you mind helping me again? I am terribly awkward at this.'

Corrie thought, *He is a gentleman, after all.*

Again she bound the feathers fast while he held them in place. And their hands touched. Chagrined, Jerry found himself moving his so that they would touch oftener.

6

Much time was devoted to archery even on the march. Corrie shamed the men. She was very quick and very accurate, and she drew a strong bow – the full length of a two foot, eight inch arrow until the feathers touched her right ear.

Clayton complimented her. Shrimp told Bubonovitch that it was a sissy sport anyway. Jerry secretly admired her prowess and was ashamed of himself for admiring it. He tried to concentrate on the girl in Oklahoma City and the Republican 4-F.

Corrie explained that she had belonged to an archery club for two years in Holland while there at school, and that she had kept up the practice after she returned to her father's plantation. 'If I were not good at it by this time, I should think myself very stupid.'

Eventually, even Shrimp commenced to brag about his marksmanship. They were all pretty good, and woe betide any game bird or animal that crossed their path. They had found a couple of dry caves in a limestone cliff, and Clayton had decided that they should remain there until some new clothing and footwear could be fashioned, for their shoes were practically gone and their clothing in shreds.

The Englishman had roughly cured a deer skin, and had fashioned an awl and needles from bamboo. With the same tough fiber used for their bows and arrows, Corrie was making crude sandals for them with these materials and tools.

She worked alone one morning while the men went out to hunt. Her thoughts ranged over the two years that had passed – years of sorrow, hardship, and danger. Years of pain and unshed tears and hate. She thought of her present situation – alone in the vastness of a mountain wilderness with four strange men, four foreigners. And she realized that she had never felt safer and that for the first time in two years she was happy.

She smiled when she thought of how terrified she had been when that almost naked brown man had carried her off into the forest. And how surprised she had been when she learned that he was a Royal Air Force colonel.

She had liked him and Sergeant Bubonovitch from the very beginning. Her heart had warmed to the sergeant from the moment that he had shown her the pictures of his wife and baby. She had not liked 'the little sergeant' nor Captain Lucas. They are both boors, she had thought; but the captain is the worse because he is an educated man and should know better than to behave toward me as he has.

That was what she had thought until lately, but since the day that she had helped him fletch his arrows he had been different. He still did not seek her company, but he did not avoid her as he had in the past. Bubonovitch had told her what a fine pilot he was and how his crew worshiped him. He cited several examples of Lucas' courage, and they lost nothing in the telling. Crew members are that way if they like an officer.

So Corrie concluded that Lucas was a man's man and possibly a woman hater. And she found the latter idea intriguing. It was also amusing. She smiled as she thought of how a woman hater must feel in such a situation – forced into close companionship with a woman day after day. And a young and pretty woman, she added mentally. For Corrie was eighteen, and she knew that she was even more than pretty – even in rags and with that horrid head of hair, mostly a rusty black, but blonde at the roots. She had no mirror, but she had seen her reflection in still pools of water. That always made her laugh. She laughed easily and often these days, for she was strangely happy.

She wondered if Captain Lucas would have disliked her if they had met under normal conditions – she with lovely gowns and her beautiful, golden hair becomingly arranged. Had she been given to self analysis, she would probably have wondered also why he was so much in her thoughts. Of course he was good looking in an extremely masculine way. She thought of him as old, and would have been surprised to have learned that he was only twenty-three. Responsibility and many hours of intense nervous strain had matured him rapidly. To hurl thirty tons of aluminum and steel and high explosives into the air and into battle, to feel that upon you alone depends the safety of a beautiful, half million dollars worth of plane and the lives of nine of your best friends is sufficient responsibility to bring lines of maturity to any face. They had left their mark on Jerry Lucas'.

Her thoughts were interrupted by the sound of voices. At first she assumed that the hunters were returning. Then, as the sounds came nearer, she recognized the intonation of native speech; and a moment later several Sumatrans appeared in the mouth of the cave. They were dirty, vicious looking men. There were ten of them. They took her away with them. From their conversation she soon learned why: the Japs had offered a reward for the capture of her and Sing Tai.

*

The sun was setting when the hunters returned to the cave. The brief equatorial twilight would soon be followed by darkness. The men missed the girl immediately and commenced to speculate on the explanation.

'She probably run out on us,' said Shrimp. 'You can't trust no dame.'

'Don't be a damn fool,' snapped Lucas. Shrimp's jaw dropped in surprise. He had been sure that the captain would agree with him. 'Why should she run out on us?' demanded Lucas. 'We offer her the only chance she has to escape the Japs. She probably went hunting.'

'What makes you think she has run away from us, Rosetti?' asked Clayton, who was examining the ground just outside of the cave entrance.

'I know skoits,' said Shrimp.

'I'd want better evidence than that,' said the Englishman.

'Well, she didn't go hunting,' said Bubonovitch from the back of the cave.

'How do you know?' asked Lucas.

'Her bow and arrows are here.'

'No, she didn't go hunting and she didn't run away,' said Clayton. 'She was taken away by force by a band of natives. There were about ten men in the band. They went that way.' He pointed.

'You got a crystal ball, Colonel?' asked Bubonovitch skeptically.

'I have something more dependable – two eyes and a nose. So have you men, but yours are no good. They have been dulled by generations of soft living, of having laws and police and soldiers to surround you with safeguards.'

'And how about you, Colonel?' asked Lucas banteringly.

'I have survived simply because my senses are as acute as those of my enemies – usually far more acute – and are combined with experience and intelligence to safeguard me where there are no laws, no police, no soldiers.'

'Like in London,' observed Bubonovitch. Clayton only smiled.

'What makes you sure she didn't go with the natives willingly?' asked Jerry Lucas. 'She might have had some good reason that we, of course, can't know anything about. But I certainly don't believe that she deserted us.'

'She was taken by force after a very brief struggle. The signs are plain on the ground. You can see here where she held back and was dragged along a few feet. Then her tracks disappear. They picked her up and carried her. The stink of natives clings to the grasses.'

'Well, what are we waiting for then?' demanded Lucas. 'Let's get going.'

'Sure,' said Shrimp. 'Let's get after the dirty so-and-sos. They can't take—' He stopped suddenly, surprised by the strange reaction the abduction of the hated 'dame' had wrought.

It had started to rain – a sudden tropical deluge. Clayton stepped into the shelter of the cave. 'There is no use in starting now,' he said. 'This rain will obliterate the scent spoor, and we couldn't follow the visible spoor in the dark. They will have to lie up somewhere for the night. Natives don't like to travel after dark on account of the big cats. So they won't gain on us. We can leave immediately it is light enough in the morning for me to see the trail.'

'The poor kid,' said Jerry Lucas.

The moment that it was light enough to see, they were off to track down Corrie's abductors. The Americans saw no sign of any spoor, but to the habituated eyes of the Englishman it ran clear and true. He saw where they had put Corrie down a short distance from the cave and made her walk.

It was mid-morning when Clayton stopped and sniffed the breeze that blew gently from the direction from which they had come. 'You'd better take to the trees,' he said to the others. 'There's a tiger coming down the trail behind us. He's not very far away.'

Corrie's abductors had camped at the edge of a mountain meadow as darkness approached. They built a fire to keep the great cats away, and huddled close to it, leaving one man on guard to tend it.

Tired, the girl slept for several hours. When she awoke, she saw that the fire was out and knew that the guard must have fallen asleep. She realized that now she might escape. She looked toward the dark, forbidding forest – just a solid blank of blackness. But in it lurked possible death. In the other direction, the direction in which these men were taking her, lay something worse than death. She balanced the certainty against the possibility and reached her decision quickly.

Silently she arose. The guard lay stretched beside the ashes of the dead fire. She passed around him and the others. A moment later she entered the forest. Though the trail was worn deep it was difficult to follow it in the darkness; and she made slow progress, often stumbling. But she went on, that she might put as much distance between herself and her captors as possible before daylight, being certain that they would follow her.

She was frightened. The forest was full of sound – stealthy, menacing sound. And any one of them might be the footsteps or the wings of Death. Yet she felt her way on, deeper and deeper into the impenetrable gloom until she heard a sound that turned her blood cold – the cough of a tiger. And then she heard it crashing through the undergrowth as though it had caught her scent or heard her.

She groped to the side of the trail, her hands outstretched. She prayed that she might find a tree she could scale. A hanging vine struck her in the face as she blundered into it. She seized it and started to climb. The crashing of the beast's body through the tangle of shrubbery sounded closer. Corrie clawed her way upward. From below came a series of hideous growls as the tiger sprang. The impact of his body nearly tore the vine from her grasp, but terror and desperation lent her strength.

Once more the vine swayed violently as the beast sprang again, but now the girl knew that it could not reach her if the vine held. There lay the danger. Twice more the tiger sprang, but at last Corrie reached one of the lower branches – a leafy sanctuary at least from the great cats. But there were other menaces in the jungle that could range far above the ground. The most fearsome of these was the python.

The carnivore remained beneath the tree for some time. Occasionally it growled. At last the girl heard it move away. She considered descending and continuing her flight. She was sure that Clayton at least would search for her, but he could do nothing until daylight. She thought of Jerry Lucas. Even if he did not like her, he would probably help in the search for her – not because she was Corrie van der Meer, but because she was a woman. And of course Bubonovitch would come, and the little sergeant might be shamed into it.

She decided to wait until daylight. Sometimes Stripes hunted in the day-time, but most usually at night. And this was what the Malays called tiger weather – a dark, starless, misty night.

Eventually the long night ended, and Corrie clambered down into the trail and continued her interrupted flight. She moved swiftly now.

7

From the branches of a tree that overhung the trail, the survivors of Lovely Lady waited for the tiger to pass and permit them to descend. They had no intention of interfering with his passage. The Americans assured one another that they had not lost a tiger, and grinned as though the remark was original.

They had accompanied Clayton into trees so many times that Shrimp said he expected to sprout a tail most any time. 'That's all you need,' Bubonovitch assured him.

Around them were the ordinary daylight sounds of the forest, to which they were now so accustomed – the raucous cries of birds, the terrific booming of siamang gibbons, the chattering of the lesser simians – but no sound came from the tiger. Shrimp decided that it was a false alarm.

Below them, not more than a hundred feet of the trail was visible between two turnings – about fifty feet in each direction. Suddenly the tiger appeared, slouching along loose-jointed and slab-sided, noiseless on his cushioned pads. Simultaneously a slender figure came into view around the opposite turning. It was Corrie. Both the tiger and the girl stopped, facing one another less than a hundred feet apart. The tiger voiced a low growl and started forward at a trot. Corrie seemed frozen with horror. For an instant she did not move. And in that instant she saw an almost naked man drop from above onto the back of the carnivore. And following him instantly, three other men dropped to the trail, jerking knives from their sheaths as they ran toward the man battling with the great cat. And first among them was S/Sgt. Rosetti, the British hater.

A steel thewed arm encircled the tiger's neck, mightily muscled legs were locked around its groin, and the man's free arm was driving a keen blade deep into the beast's left side. Growls of fury rumbled from the savage throat of the great cat as it threw itself about in agony and rage. And, to Corrie's horror, mingled with them were equally savage growls that rumbled from the throat of the man. Incredulous, the three Americans watched the brief battle between the two – two jungle beasts – powerless to strike a blow for the man because of the wild leapings and turnings of the stricken tiger.

But what seemed a long time to them was a matter of seconds only. The tiger's great frame went limp and sank to the ground. And the man rose and put a foot upon it and, raising his face to the heavens, voiced a horrid cry – the victory cry of the bull ape. Corrie was suddenly terrified of this man who had always seemed so civilized and cultured. Even the men were shocked.

Suddenly recognition lighted the eyes of Jerry Lucas. 'John Clayton,' he said, 'Lord Greystoke – Tarzan of the Apes!'

Shrimp's jaw dropped. 'Is dat Johnny Weismuller?' he demanded.

Tarzan shook his head as though to clear his brain of an obsession. His thin veneer of civilization had been consumed by the fires of battle. For the moment he had reverted to the savage primordial beast that he had been raised. But he was almost instantly his second self again.

He welcomed Corrie with a smile. 'So you got away from them,' he said.

Corrie nodded. She was still shaken and trembling, and almost on the verge of tears – tears of relief and thanksgiving. 'Yes, I got away from them last night; but if it hadn't been for you, it wouldn't have done me much good, would it?'

'It is fortunate that we happened to be at the right place at the right time. You had better sit down for a while. You look all in.'

'I am.' She sat down at the edge of the trail, and the four men gathered around her. Jerry Lucas beamed with pleasure and relief. Even Shrimp was happy about it all.

'I'm sure glad you're back, Miss,' he said. Then, when he realized what he had said, he turned red. Shrimp's psyche had recently received terrific jolts. A couple of lifelong phobias were being knocked into a cocked hat. He had come to admire an Englishman and to like a dame.

Corrie told them of her capture and escape, and she and the Americans discussed the killing of the tiger. 'Weren't you afraid?' she asked Tarzan.

Tarzan, who had never been afraid in his life, only cautious, was always at a loss to answer this question, which had been put to him many times before. He simply did not know what fear was.

'I knew I could kill the beast,' he said.

'I thought you were crazy when I saw you drop on it,' said Bubonovitch. 'I was sure scared.'

'But you came down just the same to help me, all of you. If you thought you might be killed doing it, that was true bravery.'

'Why haven't you told us you were Tarzan?' asked Jerry.

'What difference could it have made?'

'We were sure dumb not to have recognized you long ago,' said Bubonovitch.

Corrie said that she could go on. The men gathered the bows they had flung aside when they dropped to the ground, and they started back toward their camp. 'Funny none of us thought to shoot it wit arrows,' said Shrimp.

'They would only have infuriated it,' said Tarzan. 'Of course, if you got one through his heart that would kill a tiger; but he would live long enough to do a terrible lot of damage. Many a hunter has been mauled by lions after sending a large caliber bullet through its heart. These great cats are amazingly tenacious of life.'

'To be mauled by a lion or tiger must be a terrible way to die,' said Corrie, shuddering.

'On the contrary, it would seem to be a rather nice way to die – if one had to die,' said Tarzan. 'A number of men who had been mauled by lions and lived have recorded their sensations. They were unanimous in declaring that they felt neither pain nor fear.'

'Dey can have it,' said Shrimp. 'I'll take a tommy gun for mine.'

Tarzan brought up the rear of the little column on the way back to camp, that Usha the wind might bring to his nostrils warning of the approach of the Sumatrans, if they were pursuing Corrie, before they came too close.

Shrimp walked beside him, watching his every move with admiring eyes. To think, he said to himself, that I'd ever be runnin' around in a jungle wit Tarzan of de Apes. Bubonovitch had convinced him that it was not Johnny Weismuller. Jerry and Corrie led the way. He walked just behind one of her shoulders. He could watch her profile from that position. He found it a very nice profile to watch. So nice that, though he tried, he couldn't conjure up the likeness of the girl in Oklahoma City for any length of time. His thoughts kept coming back to the profile.

'You must be very tired,' he said. He was thinking that she had walked this trail all the day before and all this day, with practically no sleep.

'A little,' she replied. 'But I am used to walking. I am very tough.'

'We were frightened when we found you gone and Tarzan discovered that you had been abducted.'

She threw him a quick, quizzical glance. 'And you a misogynist!' she chided.

'Who said I was a misogynist?'

'Both you and the little sergeant.'

'I didn't tell you that, and Shrimp doesn't know what a misogynist is.'

'I didn't mean that. I meant that you are both misogynists. No one told me. It was quite obvious.'

'Maybe I thought I was,' he said. Then he told her about the girl in Oklahoma City.

'And you love her so much?'

'I do not. I guess my pride was hurt. A man hates to be brushed off.'

'Brushed off? What is that?'

'Jilted – and for a Republican 4-F.'

'Is that such a terrible person? I never heard of one before.'

Jerry laughed. 'Really, no. But when you're mad you like to call names, and I couldn't think of anything else. The fellow is really all right. As a matter of fact I am commencing to love him.'

'You mean that it is better to discover, before marriage, that she is fickle rather than after?'

'We'll settle for that – for the time being. I just know that I would not want her to be in love with me now.'

Corrie thought that over. Whatever she deduced from it, she kept to herself. When they reached camp a few minutes later, she was humming a gay little tune.

After she had gone into the cave, Bubonovitch said to Jerry, 'How's the misogynist this afternoon?'

'Shut your trap,' said Jerry.

Tarzan, in questioning Corrie about her abductors, had ascertained that there had been ten of them and that they were armed with kris and parang. They carried no firearms, the Japs having confiscated all such weapons as they could find.

The five were gathered at the mouth of the cave discussing plans for the future, which included tactics in the event the tribesmen returned and proved belligerent. Those who wished always had an equal voice in these discussions; but since they had left the ship, where Jerry's authority had been supreme, there had been a tacit acknowledgement of Tarzan's position as leader. Jerry realized the fitness of this. There had never been any question in his mind, nor in the minds of the others, that the Englishman was better equipped by knowledge and experience of the jungle, acute sense perceptivity, and physical prowess to guide and protect them than were any of the others. Even Shrimp had had to acknowledge this, and at first that had been hard. Now he would have been one of the Britisher's most ardent supporters had there been any dissidents.

'Corrie tells me,' said Tarzan, 'that there are ten men in the party that took her. Most of them, she says, are armed with a long straight kris, not the wavy bladed type with which most of us are familiar. They all carry parangs, a heavy knife designed more for use as a tool than a weapon. They have no firearms.

'If they come, we shall have to stop them before they get to close quarters. Corrie will act as interpreter. While they outnumber us more than two to one, we should have no difficulty in holding our own. We are four bows—'

'Five,' corrected Corrie.

Tarzan smiled. 'We are five bows, and we are all good shots. We shall try to convince them that they had better go away and leave us alone. We shall not shoot until it is absolutely necessary.'

'Nuts,' said Shrimp. 'We'd ought to let 'em have it for stealin' de kid.' Corrie gave him a look of surprise and incredulity. Jerry and Bubonovitch grinned. Shrimp turned red.

'There goes another misogynist,' Bubonovitch whispered to Jerry.

'I know how you feel, Rosetti,' said Tarzan. 'I think we all feel the same way. But years ago I learned to kill only for food and defense. I learned it from what you call the beasts. I think it is a good rule. Those who kill for any other reason, such as for pleasure or revenge, debase themselves. They make savages of themselves. I will tell you when to fire.'

'Perhaps they won't come after all,' said Corrie.

Tarzan shook his head. 'They will come. They are almost here.'

8

When Iskandar awoke the sun was shining full in his face. He raised himself on an elbow. His eyes took in the scene before him. His nine companions slept. The sentry slept beside a dead fire. The captive was not there.

His cruel face distorted in rage, Iskandar seized his kris and leaped to his feet. The shrieks of the sentry awakened the other sleepers. 'Pig!' screamed Iskandar, hacking at the head and body of his victim as the man tried to crawl away from him on hands and knees. 'The tigers could have come and killed us all. And because of you, the woman has escaped.'

A final blow at the base of the brain, which severed the spinal column, ended the torture. Iskandar wiped his bloody kris on the garments of the dead man and turned his scowling face upon his men. 'Come!' he ordered. 'She cannot have gotten far. Hurry!'

They soon picked up Corrie's footprints in the trail and hurried in pursuit. Half way along the trail to the cave where they had captured her, they came upon the body of a tiger. Iskandar examined it closely. He saw the knife wounds behind its left shoulder. He saw many footprints in the muddy trail. There were those of the girl and others made by the same crude type of sandal that she had worn, but larger – the footprints of men. And there were prints of the bare feet of a man. Iskandar was puzzled. There seemed ample evidence that someone had stabbed the tiger to death. But that was impossible. No one could have come within reach of those terrible talons and jaws and lived.

They pushed on, and in the afternoon they came within sight of the cave.

'Here they come,' said Jerry Lucas.

'There are but four men,' said Iskandar. 'Kill the men, but do not harm the woman.' The nine tribesmen advanced confidently with bared kris.

Tarzan permitted them to approach within a hundred feet; then he had Corrie address them. 'Stop!' she said. 'Do not come any closer.'

Each of the five had fitted an arrow to his bow. The left hand of each held additional arrows. Iskandar laughed and gave the word to charge. 'Let them have it,' said Tarzan, sending an arrow through Iskandar's leg, dropping him. Four others were hit by that first flight of arrows. Two of the others stopped, but two came on yelling like demons. Tarzan drove an arrow through the heart of each. They were too close to be spared as he had spared Iskandar. So close that one of them fell almost touching Tarzan's feet.

He turned to Corrie. 'Tell them that if they throw down their weapons and put their hands up, we will not kill them.'

After the girl had translated the instructions, the Sumatrans grumbled sullenly; but they did not throw down their weapons nor raise their hands.

'Fit arrows to your bows and advance slowly,' ordered Tarzan. 'At the first threatening move, shoot to kill.'

'You wait here, Corrie,' said Jerry. 'There may be a fight.'

She smiled at him but ignored his directions; so he put himself in front of her as they advanced. It was a long arrow that Tarzan had fitted to his bow, a heavy bow that only Tarzan could draw. He aimed the arrow at Iskandar's heart, and whispered to Corrie.

'He will count to ten,' the girl explained to the Sumatran. 'If you have not all thrown down your weapons and raised your hands before he finishes counting he will kill you. Then we will kill the others.'

Tarzan commenced to count, Corrie translating. At five, Iskandar gave in. He had looked into the gray eyes of the giant standing above him and he was afraid. The others followed the example of their leader.

'Rosetti,' said Tarzan, 'gather up their weapons and retrieve our arrows. We will keep them covered.'

Rosetti gathered the weapons first; then he yanked the arrows from the limbs and bodies of the five who had been hit but not killed. With the dead he was more gentle.

'Tell them to take their dead and get out of here, Corrie. And that if they ever annoy us again we will kill them all.'

Corrie translated, adding a punch line of her own devising: 'This man who speaks to you through me is no ordinary man. Armed only with a knife, he leaped upon the back of a tiger and killed it. If you are wise, you will obey him.'

'Just a minute, Corrie,' said Jerry. 'Ask them if they have seen any American fliers recently who had bailed out of a damaged plane, or heard of any.'

Corrie put the question to Iskandar and received a sullen negative. The chief got to his feet and gave orders to his men, none of whom was seriously wounded. They picked up their dead and started away, but Iskandar stopped them. Then he turned to Tarzan. 'You will let us take our weapons?' he asked. Corrie translated.

'No.' This seemed to need no translation or admit of argument. The chief had looked again into the gray eyes of the giant who had killed the tiger he had seen upon the trail, and what he had seen there had frightened him. They are not the eyes of a man, he thought. They are the eyes of a tiger.

Snarling a Malayan oath beneath his breath, he ordered his men to march, and followed them.

'We'd orter have killed 'em all,' said Shrimp. 'They'll tell the foist yellow-bellies they see where to find us.'

'If we followed that plan to its logical conclusion,' said Tarzan, 'we'd have to kill every human being we meet. Any of them might tell the Japs.'

'You don't believe much in killin' people.'

Tarzan shook his head in negation.

'Not even Japs?'

'That is different. We are at war with them. Neither in hatred nor revenge and with no particular pleasure I shall kill every Jap I can until the war is over. That is my duty.'

'Don't you even hate 'em?'

'What good would it do if I did? If all the many millions of people of the allied nations devoted an entire year exclusively to hating the Japs it wouldn't kill one Jap nor shorten the war one day.'

Bubonovitch laughed. 'And it might give 'em all stomach ulcers.'

Tarzan smiled. 'I can recall having felt hatred but once in my life or killing for revenge but once – Kulonga, the son of Mbonga. He killed Kala, my foster mother. Not only was I very young then, but Kala was the only creature in the world that loved me or that I loved. And I thought then that she was my own mother. I have never regretted the killing.'

While they talked, Corrie was cooking their supper. Jerry was helping her – not that she needed any help. They were grilling pheasants and venison over a fire just inside the mouth of the cave. Bubonovitch was examining the weapons left by the Sumatrans. He selected a kris for himself. Jerry and Shrimp followed his example, and Jerry brought Corrie a parang.

'Why did you ask that bandit if he had heard of any American fliers who had bailed out recently?' Corrie asked Lucas.

'Two of my crew, who are known to have bailed out, are unaccounted for – Douglas, my radioman, and Davis, a waist gunner. We hunted for them, but could find no trace of them. We found the body of Lieutenant Burnham whose chute had failed to open. So we figured that if either of the other chutes had failed to open we should have found the body nearby. We all jumped within a matter of a few seconds.'

'How many were you?'

'Eleven – nine in the crew, Colonel Clayton, and a photographer. My bombardier was left behind because he was sick. Anyway, we weren't carrying any bombs. It was just a reconnaissance and photographic mission.'

'Let's see,' said Corrie. 'There are four of you here, Lieutenant Burnham makes five, and the two unaccounted for make seven. What became of the other four?'

'Killed in action.'

'Poor boys,' said Corrie.

'It is not those who are killed who suffer,' said Jerry. 'It is those who are left behind – their buddies and their folks back home. Maybe they're better off. After all, this is a hell of a world,' he added bitterly, 'and those who get out of it are the lucky ones.'

She laid her hand on his. 'You mustn't feel that way. There may be a lot of happiness in the world for you yet – for all of us.'

'They were my friends,' he said, 'and they were very young. They hadn't had a chance to get much out of life. It just doesn't seem right. Tarzan says that it does no good to hate, and I know he's right. But I do hate – not the poor dumb things who shoot at us and whom we shoot at, but those who are responsible for making wars.'

'I know,' she said. 'I hate them, too. But I hate all Japs. I hate the "poor dumb things who shoot at us and whom we shoot at." I am not as philosophical as you and Tarzan. I want to hate them. I often reproach myself because I think I am not hating bitterly enough.' Jerry could see that hate reflected in her eyes, and he thought what a horrible thing it was that such an emotion could have been aroused in the breast of one so innately sweet and kind. He said to her what she had said to him: 'You mustn't feel that way,' and he added, 'You were never made for hate.'

'You never saw your mother hounded to death and your father bayoneted by those yellow beasts. If you had and didn't hate them you wouldn't be fit to call yourself a man.'

'I suppose you are right,' he said. He pressed her hand. 'Poor little girl.'

'Don't sympathize with me,' she said almost angrily. 'I didn't cry then. I haven't cried since. But if you sympathize with me, I shall.'

Had she emphasized *you?* He thought that she had – just a little. Why, he asked himself, should that send a little thrill through him? I must be going ga-ga, he thought.

Now the little band gathered around the cooking fire for supper. They had broad leaves for plates, sharpened bamboo splinters for forks, and of course they had their knives. They drank from gourds.

Besides pheasant and venison, they had fruit and the roasted seeds of the durian. They lived well in this land of plenty. 'T'ink of de poor dogfaces back at base,' said Shrimp, 'eatin' canned hash an' spam.'

'And drinking that goddam GI coffee,' said Bubonovitch. 'It always made me think of one of Alexander Woolcott's first lines in *The Man Who Came to Dinner.*'

'I'll trade places with any dogface right now,' said Jerry.

'What's a dogface?' asked Corrie.

'Well, I guess originally it was supposed to mean a doughboy; but now it sort of means any enlisted man, more specifically a private.'

'Any GI Joe,' said Shrimp.

'What a strange language!' said Corrie. 'And I thought I understood English.'

'It isn't English,' said Tarzan. 'It's American. It's a young and virile language. I like it.'

'But what is a doughboy? And a GI Joe?'

'A doughboy is an infantryman. A GI Joe is an American soldier – Government Issue. Stick with us, Corrie, and we'll improve your American and ruin your English,' concluded Jerry.

'If you will pay special attention to Sergeant Rosetti's conversation they will both be ruined,' said Bubonovitch.

'Wot's wrong wit my American, wise guy?' demanded Shrimp.

'I think Sergeant Shrimp is cute,' said Corrie.

Rosetti flushed violently. 'Take a bow, cutie,' said Bubonovitch.

Shrimp grinned. He was used to being ribbed, and he never got mad, although sometimes he pretended to be. 'I ain't heard no one callin' you cute, you big cow,' he said, and he felt that with that comeback his honor had been satisfied.

9

Before supper, Tarzan had cut two large slabs of bark from a huge tree in the forest. The slabs were fully an inch thick, tough and strong. From them he cut two disks, as nearly sixteen and a half inches in diameter as he could calculate. In about one half of the periphery of each disk he cut six deep notches, leaving five protuberances between them.

After supper, Jerry and the others, sitting around the fire, watched him. 'Now what the heck are those for?' asked the pilot 'They looked like round, flat feet with five toes.'

'Thank you,' said Tarzan. 'I didn't realize that I was such a good sculptor. These are to deceive the enemy. I have no doubt but that that old villain will return with Japs just as quickly as he can. Now those natives must be good trackers, and they must be very familiar with our spoor, for they followed it here. Our homemade sandals would identify our spoor to even the stupidest tracker. So we must obliterate it.

'First we will go into the forest in a direction different from the one we intend taking, and we will leave spoor that will immediately identify our party. Then we will cut back to camp through the undergrowth where we can walk without leaving footprints, and start out on the trail we intend taking. Three of us will walk in single file, each stepping exactly in the footprints of the man ahead of him. I will carry Corrie. It would tire her to take a man's stride. Bubonovitch will bring up the rear, wearing one of these strapped to each foot. With one of them he will step on each and every footprint that we have made. He will have to do a considerable split to walk with these on, but he is a big man with long legs. These will make the footprints of an elephant and obliterate ours.'

'Geeze!' exclaimed Rosetti. 'A elephant's feet ain't that big!'

'I'm not so sure myself about these Indian elephants,' admitted Tarzan. 'But the circumference of an African elephant's front foot is half the animal's height at the shoulder. So these will indicate an elephant approximately nine feet in height. Unfortunately, Bubonovitch doesn't weigh as much as an elephant; so the spoor won't be as lifelike as I'd like. But I'm banking on the likelihood that they won't pay much attention to elephant spoor while they are looking for ours. If they do, they are going to be terribly surprised to discover the trail of a two-legged elephant.

'Had we been in Africa the problem would have been complicated by the fact that the African elephant has five toes in front and three behind. That would have necessitated another set of these, and Jerry would have had to be the hind legs.'

'De sout' end of a elephant goin' nort', Cap,' said Shrimp.

'I'm not selfish,' said Jerry. 'Bubonovitch can be the whole elephant.'

'You'd better put Shrimp at the head of the column,' said Bubonovitch, 'I might step on him.'

'I think we'd better turn in now,' said Tarzan. 'What time have you, Jerry?'

'Eight o'clock.'

'You have the first watch tonight – two and a half hours on. That will bring it just right. Shrimp draws the last – 3:30 to 6:00. Goodnight!'

They started early the following morning after a cold breakfast. First they made the false trail. Then they started off in the direction they intended taking, Bubonovitch bringing up the rear, stamping down hard on the footprints of those who preceded him. At the end of a mile, which was as far as Tarzan thought necessary to camouflage their trail, he was a pretty tired elephant. He sat down beside the trail and took off his cumbersome feet. 'Migawd!' he said. 'I'm just about split to the chin. Whoever wants to play *elephas maximus* of the order Proboscidea can have these goddam things.' He tossed them into the trail.

Tarzan picked them up and threw them out into the underbrush. 'It was a tough assignment, Sergeant; but you were the best man for it.'

'I could have carried Corrie.'

'An' you wit a wife an' kid!' chided Shrimp.

'I think the colonel pulled rank on you,' said Jerry.

'Oh, no,' said Tarzan; 'it was just that I couldn't think of throwing Corrie to the wolves.'

'I guess dat will hold you,' observed Shrimp.

Corrie was laughing, her eyes shining. She liked these Americans with their strange humor, their disregard for conventions. And the Englishman, though a little more restrained, was much like them. Jerry had told her that he was a viscount, but his personality impressed her more than his title.

Suddenly Tarzan raised his head and tested the air with his nostrils. 'Take to the trees,' he said.

'Is something coming?' asked Corrie.

'Yes. One of the sergeant's relatives – with both ends. It is a lone bull, and sometimes they are mean.'

He swung Corrie to an overhanging branch, as the others scrambled up the nearest trees. Tarzan smiled. They were becoming proficient. He remained standing in the trail.

'You're not going to stay there?' demanded Jerry.

'For a while. I like elephants. They are my friends. Most of them like me. I shall know in plenty of time if he is going to charge.'

'But this is not an African elephant,' insisted Jerry.

'Maybe he never heard of Tarzan,' suggested Shrimp.

'The Indian elephant is not so savage as the African, and I want to try an experiment. I have a theory. If it proves incorrect, I shall take to the trees. He will warn me, for if he is going to charge, he will raise his ears, curl up his trunk, and trumpet. Now, please don't talk or make any noise. He is getting close.'

The four in the trees waited expectantly. Corrie was frightened – frightened for Tarzan. Jerry thought it foolish for the man to take such chances. Shrimp wished that he had a tommy gun – just in case. Every eye was glued on the turn in the trail, at the point where the elephant would first appear.

Suddenly the great bulk of the beast came into view. It dwarfed Tarzan. When the little eyes saw Tarzan, the animal stopped. Instantly the ears were spread and the trunk curled up. It is going to charge was the thought of those in the trees.

Corrie's lips moved. Silently they formed the plea, 'Quick, Tarzan! Quick!'

And then Tarzan spoke. He spoke to the elephant in the language that he believed was common to most beasts – the mother tongue of the great apes. Few could speak it, but he knew that many understood it. 'Yo, Tantor, yo!' he said.

The elephant was weaving from side to side. It did not trumpet. Slowly the ears dropped and the trunk uncurled. 'Yud!' said Tarzan.

The great beast hesitated a moment, and then came slowly toward the man. It stopped in front of him and the trunk reached out and moved over his body. Corrie clutched the tree branch to keep from falling. She could understand how, involuntarily, some women scream or faint in moments of high excitement.

Tarzan stroked the trunk for a moment, whispering quietly to the huge mass towering above him. 'Abu tand-nala!' he said presently. Slowly, the elephant knelt. Tarzan wrapped the trunk about his body and said, 'Nala b'yat!' and Tantor lifted him and placed him upon his head.

'Unk!' commanded Tarzan. The elephant moved off down the trail, passing beneath the trees where the astonished four sat, scarcely breathing.

Shrimp was the first to break the long silence. 'I've saw everyt'ing now. Geeze! wot a guy!'

'Are you forgetting Goige de Toid?' demanded Bubonovitch.

Shrimp muttered something under his breath that was not fit for Corrie's ears.

Presently Tarzan returned on foot and alone. 'We'd better be moving along,' he said, and the others dropped down from the trees.

Jerry was not a little irritated by what he thought had been an egotistical display of courage and prowess, and his voice revealed his irritation when he asked, 'What was the use of taking such a risk, Colonel?'

'In the haunts of wild beasts one must know many things if one is to survive,' Tarzan explained. 'This is strange country to me. In my country the elephants are my friends. On more than one occasion they have saved my life. I wanted to know the temper of the elephants here and if I could impose my will on them as I do at home. It is possible that someday you may be glad that I did so. The chances are that I shall never see that bull again; but if we should meet, he will know me and I shall know him. Tantor and I have long memories both for friends and enemies.'

'Sorry I spoke as I did,' said Jerry; 'but we were all frightened to see you take such a risk.'

'I took no risk,' said Tarzan; 'but don't you do it.'

'What would he have done to one of us?' asked Bubonovitch.

'Gored you probably, knelt on you, and then tossed the pulp that had been you high into the forest.'

Corrie shuddered. Shrimp shook his head. 'An' I uset to feed 'em peanuts at de coicus.'

'The wild beasts I've seen here in the open look larger and more menacing than those I used to see in menageries and zoos,' said Bubonovitch.

'Or in a museum, stuffed,' said Jerry.

'Mounted,' corrected Bubonovitch.

'Purist,' said Jerry.

Presently they entered a forest of enormous straight trunked trees, enveloped by giant creepers, vines, and huge air plants that formed a thick canopy overhead. The dim light, the cathedral vistas, the sounds of unseen things depressed the spirits of all but Tarzan. They plodded on in silence, longing for the light of the sun. And then, at a turning in the trail, they came suddenly into its full glare as the forest ended abruptly at the edge of a gorge.

Below them lay a narrow valley cut through the ages into the tuff and limestone formation of the terrain by the little river that raced riotously along its bottom. It was a pleasant valley, green and tree dotted.

Tarzan scrutinized its face carefully. There was no sign of human life; but some deer fed there, and his keen eyes recognized a black blob, almost indistinguishable in the dense shade of a tree. He pointed it out to the others. 'Beware of him,' he cautioned. 'He is infinitely more dangerous than Tantor, and sometimes even than Stripes.'

'What is it, a water buffalo?' asked Jerry.

'No. It is Buto the rhinoceros. His sight is very poor, but his hearing and scent are extremely acute. He has an ugly and unpredictable disposition. Ordinarily, he will run away from you. But you can never tell. Without any provocation he may come thundering down on you as fast as a good horse; and if he gets you, he'll gore and toss you.'

'Not ours,' said Corrie. 'They have lower tusks, and they use those instead of their horns.'

'I remember now,' said Tarzan, 'hearing that. I was thinking of the African rhino.'

The trail turned abruptly to the right at the edge of the escarpment and hurled itself over the rim, angling steeply downward, narrow and precarious. They were all glad when they reached the bottom.

'Stay here,' said Tarzan, 'and don't make any noise. I am going to try to get one of those deer. Buto won't get your scent from here; and if you don't make any noise, he won't hear you. I'll circle around to the left. Those bushes there will hide me until I get within range of the deer. If I get one, I'll go right on down to the river where the trail crosses it. You can come on then and meet me there. The trail passes Buto at about a hundred yards. If he gets your scent, or hears you, and stands up, don't move unless he starts toward you; then find a tree.'

Tarzan crouched and moved silently among the tall grasses. The wind, blowing from the direction of the deer toward the rhinoceros, carried no scent of the intruders to either. It would to the latter when Tarzan reached the deer and when the others crossed the wind to reach the river.

Tarzan disappeared from the sight of those who waited at the foot of the cliff. They wondered how he could find cover where there seemed to be none. Everything seemed to be moving according to plan when there was a sudden interruption. They saw a deer suddenly raise its head and look back; then it and the little herd of which it was a part were off like a flash, coming almost directly toward them.

They saw Tarzan rise from the grasses and leap upon a young buck. His knife flashed in the sun, and both fell, disappearing in the grass. The four watchers were engrossed by this primitive drama – the primordial hunter stalking and killing his quarry. Thus it must have been ages and ages ago.

Finally Jerry said, 'Well, let's get going.'

'Geeze!' Shrimp exclaimed, pointing. 'Lookut!'

They looked. Buto had arisen and was peering this way and that with his dull little eyes. But he was listening and scenting the wind, too.

'Don't move,' whispered Jerry.

'An' they ain't no trees,' breathed Shrimp. He was right. In their immediate vicinity there were no trees.

'Don't move,' cautioned Jerry again. 'If he's going to charge, he'll charge anything that moves.'

'Here he comes,' said Bubonovitch. The rhino was walking toward them. He seemed more puzzled than angry. His dim vision had, perhaps, discovered something foreign to the scene. Something he could neither hear nor smell. And curiosity prompted him to investigate.

The three men, by one accord, moved cautiously between Corrie and the slowly oncoming beast. It was a tense moment. If Buto charged, someone would be hurt, probably killed. They watched the creature with straining eyes. They saw the little tail go up and the head down as the rhino broke into a trot. He had seen them and was coming straight for them. Suddenly he was galloping. 'This is it,' said Jerry.

At the same instant, Shrimp leaped away from them and ran diagonally across the path of the charging brute. And the rhino swerved and went for him. Shrimp ran as he had never run before; but he couldn't run as fast as a horse, and the rhino could.

Horror-stricken, the others watched. Horror-stricken and helpless. Then they saw Tarzan. He was running to meet the man and the beast, who were headed directly toward him. But what could he do? the watchers asked themselves. What could two relatively puny men do against those tons of savage flesh and bone?

The beast was close behind Shrimp now and Tarzan was only a few yards away. Then Shrimp stumbled and fell. Corrie covered her eyes with her hands. Jerry and Bubonovitch, released as though from a momentary paralysis, started running toward the scene of certain tragedy.

Corrie, impelled against her will, removed her hands from her eyes. She saw the rhino's head go down as though to gore the prostrate man now practically beneath its front feet.

Then Tarzan leaped, turning in air, and alighted astride the beast's shoulders. The diversion was enough to distract the animal's attention from Shrimp. It galloped over him, bucking to dislodge the man-thing on its back.

Tarzan held his seat long enough to plunge his knife through the thick hide directly behind the head and sever the brute's spinal cord. Paralyzed, it stumbled to the ground. A moment later it was dead.

Soon the entire party was gathered around the kill. A relieved and, perhaps, a slightly trembling party. Tarzan turned to Shrimp. 'That was one of the bravest things I ever saw done, sergeant,' he said.

'Shrimp didn't rate medals for nothing, Colonel,' said Bubonovitch.

10

They were now well supplied with meat – too well. A deer and a rhinoceros for five people seemed more than ample. Tarzan had taken some choice cuts from the young buck and cut the hump from the rhino. Now, beside the river, he had built a fire in a hole that he had dug. Over another fire, the others were grilling bits of venison.

'You ain't goin' to eat that are you?' asked Shrimp, pointing at the big hunk of rhino meat with the skin still attached.

'In a couple of hours you'll eat it,' said Tarzan. 'You'll like it.'

When he had a bed of hot coals in the bottom of the hole he had dug, he laid the hump in with the skin side down, covered it with leaves and then with the dirt he had excavated.

Taking a piece of venison, he withdrew a little from the others, squatted down on his haunches and tore off pieces of the raw flesh with his strong teeth. The others had long since ceased to pay attention to this seeming idiosyncrasy. They had, on occasion, eaten their meat raw; but they still preferred it cooked – usually charred on the outside, raw on the inside, and covered with dirt. They were no longer fastidious.

'What was on your mind, Shrimp, while you were legging it in front of *Rhinoceros Dicerorhinus sumatrensis?*' asked Bubonovitch. 'You sure hit nothing but the high spots. I'll bet you did the hundred yards in under eight seconds.'

'I'll tell you wot I was thinkin'. I'd started on Ave Maria w'en I seen it was nothin' less 'n Whirlaway on my tail. I was thinkin' if I could just finish that one Ave Maria before it caught up with me, I might have a chance. Then I stumbled. But the Blessed Mary heard me and saved me.'

'I thought it was Tarzan,' said Bubonovitch.

'Of course it was Tarzan; but whoinell do you suppose got him there in time, you dope?'

'There are no atheists at the business end of a rhinoceros,' said Jerry.

'I prayed, too,' said Corrie. 'I prayed that God would not let anything happen to you who were risking you life to save ours. You are a very brave man, sergeant, for you must have known that you didn't have one chance in a million.'

Rosetti was very unhappy. He wished that they would talk about something else. 'You got me all wrong,' he said. 'I just ain't got no sense. If I had, I'd a run the other way; but I didn't think of it in time. The guy who had the guts was the colonel. Think of killin' a deer an' dat rhino wit nothin' but a knife.' This gave him an idea for changing the subject. 'An' think of all dat meat lyin' out there an' the poor suckers back home got to have ration coupons an' then they can't get enough.'

'Think of the starving Armenians,' said Bubonovitch.

'All the Armenians I ever seen could starve as far as I'm concerned,' said Shrimp. He took another piece of venison and lapsed into silence.

Jerry had been watching Corrie when he could snatch a quick look without actually staring at her. He saw her tearing at the meat with her fine, white teeth. He recalled what she had said about hating the Japs: 'I want to hate them. I often reproach myself because I think I am not hating bitterly enough.'

He thought, *what kind of a woman will she be after the war – after all that she has gone through?*

He looked at Tarzan tearing at raw meat. He looked at the others, their hands and faces smeared with the juices of the venison, dirty with the char of the burned portions.

'I wonder what sort of a world this will be after peace comes,' he said. 'What kind of people will we be? Most of us are so young that we will be able to remember little else than war – killing, hate, blood. I wonder if we can ever settle down to the humdrum existence of civilian life.'

'Say! If I ever get my feet under a desk again,' said Bubonovitch, 'I hope God strikes me dead if I ever take them out again.'

'That's what you think now, Bum. And I hope you're right. For myself, I don't know. Sometimes I hate flying, but it's in my blood by now. Maybe it isn't just the flying – it's the thrill and excitement, possibly. And if that is true, then it's the fighting and the killing that I like. I don't know. I hope not. It will be a hell of a world if a great many young fellows feel that way.

'And take Corrie. She has learned to hate. She was never made for that. That is what war and the Japs have done to her. I wonder if hate twists a person's soul out of shape, so that he's never the same as he was before – if, like an incipient cancer, it eats at the roots of character without one's being aware that one has a cancer.'

'I think you need not worry,' said Tarzan. 'Man readily adapts himself to changed conditions. The young, especially, react quickly to changes of environment and circumstance. You will take your proper places in life when peace comes. Only the weak and the warped will be changed for the worse.'

'Wit all de different ways of killin' and maimin' wot we've learnt, like sneakin' up behind a guy an' cuttin' his throat or garrotin' him an' a lot of worse t'ings than dat even, they's goin' to be a lot of bozos startin' Murder Incorporateds all over de U. S., take it from me,' said Shrimp. 'I knows dem guys. I didn't live all my life in Chi fer nuttin'.'

'I think it will change us very much,' said Corrie. 'We will not be the same people we would have been had we not gone through this. It has matured us rapidly, and that means that we have lost a great deal of our youth. Jerry told me the other day that he is only twenty-three. I thought that he was well along in his thirties. He has lost ten years of his youth. Can he be the same man he would have been had he lived those ten years in peace and security? No. I believe he will be a better man.

'I believe that I shall be a better woman for the very emotion which he and Tarzan deplore – hate. I do not mean petty hatreds. I mean a just hate – a grand hate that exalts. And for the compensations it entails, such as loyalty to one's country and one's comrades, the strong friendships and affections which are engendered by a common, holy hatred for a common enemy.'

For a while no one spoke. They seemed to be considering this unique eulogy of hate. It was Jerry who broke the silence. 'That is a new angle,' he said. 'I never thought of hate in that way before. As a matter of fact, fighting men don't do a lot of hating. That seems to be the prerogative of non-combatants.'

'Bosh,' said Corrie. 'That is just a heroic pose on the part of fighting men. When a Jap atrocity hits close to home, I'll bet they hate – when a buddy is tortured, when they learn that Allied prisoners of war have been beheaded. That has happened here, and I'll warrant that our Dutch fighting men learned then to hate, if they had not hated before. And furthermore,' said Corrie acidly, 'I do not consider myself a non-combatant.'

Jerry smiled. 'Forgive me. I didn't mean that remark derogatorily. And anyway it wasn't aimed at you. You are one of us, and we are all combatants.'

Corrie, mollified, smiled back at him. She may have been a good two-fisted hater, but that was not hate that shone from her eyes at the moment.

Shrimp interrupted the discussion. 'Geeze!' he exclaimed. 'Get a load of dis. It smells like heaven.'

They looked, to see Tarzan removing the roast from the improvised oven. 'Come an' get it!' called Shrimp.

To their surprise, they found the rhino hump juicy, tender, and delicious. And as they ate, a pair of eyes watched them from the concealment of bushes that grew at the edge of the cliff beyond the river – watched them for a few minutes; then the owner of the eyes turned back into the forest.

That night, the wild dogs fought over the carcasses of Tarzan's kills until, near dawn, a tiger came and drove them from their feast to stand in a dismal, growling circle until the Lord of the jungle should depart.

Wars make words. World War II is no exception. Probably the most notorious word for which it is responsible is quisling. Wars also unmake words. Collaborationist formerly had a fair and honorable connotation, but I doubt that it ever will live down World War II. No one will ever again wish to be known as a collaborationist.

They are to be found in every country where the enemy is to be found. There are collaborationists in Sumatra. Such was Amat. He was a miserable creature who bowed low to every Jap soldier and sought to curry favor with them. He was a human jackal that fed off the leavings of the arrogant invaders who slapped his face when he got underfoot.

So, when he saw the five white people camped by the river in the little valley, he licked his full lips as though in anticipation of a feast, and hurried back along the trail toward the village of his people where a detachment of Jap soldiers was temporarily billeted.

He had two reasons for hurrying. He was anxious to impart his information to the enemy. That was one reason. The other was terror. He had not realized how late it was. Darkness would fall before he could reach the village. It is then that my Lord the tiger walks abroad in the forest.

He was still a couple of kilometers from home, and dusk was heralding the short equatorial twilight when Amat's worst fear was realized. The hideous face of the Lord of the jungle loomed directly in his path. The terrifying eyes, the wrinkled, snarling face of a tiger, between which and its intended victim there are no iron bars and only a few yards of lonely jungle trail, are probably as horrifying a sight as the eyes of man have ever envisaged.

The tiger did not for long leave Amat in any doubt as to its intentions. It charged. Amat shrieked, and leaped for a tree. Still shrieking, he clawed his way upward. The tiger sprang for him; and, unfortunately, missed. Amat scrambled higher, sweating and panting. He clung there, trembling; and there we may leave him until morning.

11

'Geeze! Wot a country,' growled Shrimp, as they toiled up the steep trail out of the valley in the light of a new day. 'If you ain't crawlin' down into a hole, you're crawlin' up outta one. God must a-been practicin' when He made this.'

'And when He got through practicing, I suppose, He made Chicago,' suggested Bubonovitch.

'Now you're shoutin', wise guy. God sure made Chi. W'en He wasn't lookin', somebody else made Brooklyn. Geeze! I wisht I was in dear ol' Chi right now. Why, de steepest hill dere is de approach to de Madison Street bridge.'

'Look at the view, man. Have you no eye for beauty?'

'Sure, I got an eye for beauty; but my feet ain't. They joined up for de air force, an' now they ain't nuttin' but goddam doughboys.'

But all things must end, and eventually they reached the top of the escarpment. Tarzan examined the trail. 'There was a native here recently,' he said. 'Probably late yesterday afternoon. He may have seen us. He stood right here for several minutes, where he could look down on our camp.'

As the little party continued along the trail into the forest, Amat rushed breathlessly into his village, bursting with the information that had been seething within him during a night of terror. So excited was he that he failed to bow to a Jap private and got slapped and almost bayoneted. But at last he stood before Lt Kumajiro Tada, this time not forgetting to bow very low.

Excitedly he rattled off an account of what he had seen. Tada, not understanding a word of the native dialect and being particularly godlike thus early in the morning, kicked Amat in the groin. Amat screamed, grabbed his hurt, and sank to the ground. Tada drew his sword. It had been a long time since he had lopped off a head, and he felt like lopping off a head before breakfast.

A sergeant who had overheard Amat's report and who understood the dialect saluted and bowed. Sucking wind through his teeth, he informed the honorable lieutenant that Amat had seen a party of whites and that that was what he had been trying to tell the honorable lieutenant. Reluctantly, Tada scabbarded his sword and listened as the sergeant interpreted.

A couple of miles from the point at which they had entered the forest, Tarzan stopped and examined the trail minutely. 'Here,' he said, 'our native friend was treed by a tiger. He remained in this tree all night, coming down only a short time ago, probably as soon as it was light. You can see where the pugs of the beast obliterated the spoor the fellow made last night. Here is where he jumped down this morning and continued on his way.'

They continued on and presently came to a fork in the trail. Again Tarzan stopped. He showed them which way the native had gone. In the other fork he pointed out evidence that a number of men had gone that way perhaps several days before. 'These were not natives,' he said, 'nor do I think they were Japs. These are the footprints of very large men. Jerry, suppose you folks follow along the trail the native took, while I investigate the other one. These chaps may be Dutch guerrillas. If they are, they might prove mighty helpful to us. Don't travel too fast, and I may catch up with you.'

'We'll probably come to a native village,' said Jerry. 'If we do, perhaps we'd better hole up in the jungle until you come along; so that we can all approach it together. In the meantime, I'll look the place over.'

Tarzan nodded assent and swung into the trees, following the left hand fork of the trail. They watched him until he was out of sight. 'That guy likes to travel de hard way?' said Shrimp.

'It doesn't look so hard when you watch him,' said Bubonovitch. 'It's only when you try to do it yourself.'

'It's an ideal way to travel, under the circumstances,' Jerry said. 'It leaves no trail, and it gives him every advantage over any enemy he might meet.'

'It is beautiful,' said Corrie. 'He is so graceful, and he moves so quietly.' She sighed. 'If we could all do it, how much safer we should be!'

'I t'ink I'll practice up,' said Shrimp. 'An' wen I gets In home I goes out to Garfield Park and swings t'rough de trees some Sunday wen dey's a gang dere.'

'And get pinched,' said Bubonovitch.

'Sure I'd get pinched, but I'd make de front pages wit pitchurs. Maybe I'd get a job wit Sol Lesser out in Hollywood.'

'Where'd you get the reefers, Shrimp?' inquired Bubonovitch.

Shrimp grinned. 'Me? I don't use 'em. I don't work fer Petrillo. I just get dat way from associatin' wit you.'

They were moving leisurely along the trail toward Amat's village, Bubonovitch in the lead, Rosetti behind him. Jerry and Corrie followed several yards in the rear. Then Corrie stopped to retie the laces of one of her moccasins, and Jerry waited for her. The others passed out of sight beyond a turn in the winding trail.

'Don't you feel a little lost without Tarzan?' Corrie asked as she straightened up. Then she voiced a little exclamation of dismay. 'Oh, I don't mean that I haven't every confidence in you and Bubonovitch and Rosetti, but—'

Jerry smiled. 'Don't apologize. I feel the same way you do. We're all out of our natural environment. He's not. He's right at home here. I don't know what we should have done without him.'

'We should have been just a lot of babes in the—'

'Listen!' cautioned Jerry, suddenly alert. He heard voices ahead. Hoarse shouts in a strange tongue. 'Japs!' he exclaimed. He started to run toward the sounds. Then he stopped and turned back. His was a cruel decision any way he looked at it. He must desert either his two sergeants or the girl. But he was accustomed to making hair trigger decisions.

He seized Corrie by an arm and dragged her into the tangle of undergrowth beside the trail. They wormed their way in farther and farther as long as the sound of the voices came no nearer. When they did, indicating that the Japs were investigating the trail in their direction, they lay flat on the ground beneath a riot of equatorial verdure. A searcher might have passed within a foot of them without seeing them.

A dozen soldiers surprised and captured Bubonovitch and Rosetti. They didn't have a chance. The Japs slapped them around and threatened them with bayonets until Lt Tada called them off. Tada spoke English. He had worked as a dishwasher in a hotel in Eugene while attending the University of Oregon, and he had sized up the prisoners immediately as Americans. He questioned them, and each gave his name, rank, and serial number.

'You were from that bomber that was shot down?' demanded Tada.

'We have given you all the information we are required or permitted to give.'

Tada spoke to a soldier in Japanese. The man advanced and pushed the point of his bayonet against Bubonovitch's belly. 'Now will you answer my question?' growled Tada.

'You know the rules governing the treatment of prisoners of war,' said Bubonovitch, 'but I don't suppose that makes any difference to you. It does to me, though. I won't answer any more questions.'

'You are a damn fool,' said Tada. He turned to Rosetti. 'How about you?' he demanded. 'Will you answer?'

'Nuttin' doin',' said Rosetti.

'There were five in your party – four men and a girl. Where are the other three? – Where is the girl?' the Jap persisted.

'You seen how many was in our party. Do we look like five? Or can't you count? Does eider of us look like a dame? Somebody's been stringin' you, Tojo.'

'O.K., wise guy,' snapped Tada. 'I'm goin' to give you until tomorrow morning to think it over. You answer all my questions tomorrow morning, or you both get beheaded.' He tapped the long officer's sword at his side.

'Anday I-ay essgay e-hay ain'tay oolin-fay,' said Rosetti to Bubonovitch.

'You bet your sweet life I ain't foolin', Yank,' said Tada.

Shrimp was crestfallen. 'Geeze! Who'd a-thought a Nip would savvy hog latin!' he moaned to Bubonovitch.

Tada sent two of his men along the trail to search for the other members of the party. He and the remainder turned back toward Amat's village with the two prisoners.

Jerry and Corrie had overheard all that had been said. They heard the main party move off in the direction from which they had come, but they did not know of the two who had been sent in search of them. Believing that they were now safe from detection, they crawled from their concealment and returned to the trail.

Tarzan, swinging easily through the middle terrace of the forest, had covered perhaps two miles when his attention was arrested by a commotion ahead. He heard the familiar grunts and growls and chattering of the great apes, and guessed that they were attacking or being attacked by an enemy. As the sounds lay directly in his path, he continued on.

Presently he came within sight of four adult orangutans swinging excitedly among the branches of a great tree. They darted in and out, striking and screaming. And then he saw the object of their anger – a python holding in its coils a young orangutan.

Tarzan took in the whole scene at a glance. The python had not as yet constricted. It merely held the struggling victim while it sought to fight off the attacking apes. The screams of the young one were definite proof that it was still very much alive.

Tarzan thrilled to the savage call to battle, to the challenge of his ancient enemy, Histah the snake, to the peril of his friends, the Mangani – the great apes. If he wondered if they would recognize him as friend, or attack him as foe, the thought did not deter him. He swung quickly into the tree in which the tragedy was being enacted, but to a branch above the python and its victim.

So intent were the actors in this primitive drama upon the main issue that none were aware of his presence until he spoke, wondering if, like Tantor, the great apes would understand him.

'Kreeg-ah!' he shouted. 'Tarzan bundolo Histah!'

The apes froze and looked up. They saw an almost naked man-thing poised above the python, in the man-thing's hand a gleaming blade.

'Bundolo! Bundolo!' they shouted – *Kill! Kill!* And Tarzan knew that they understood. Then he dropped full upon the python and its victim. Steel thewed fingers gripped the snake behind its head, as Tarzan clung to the coils and the young ape with powerful legs. His keen blade cut deep into the writhing body just back of the hand that held its neck in a viselike grasp. The whipping coils, convulsed in agony, released the young orangutan and sought to enmesh the body of the creature clinging to them. Its frantic struggles released the python's hold upon the branches of the tree, and it fell to earth, carrying Tarzan with it. Other branches broke their fall, and the man was not injured. But the snake was far from dead. Its maddened writhings had made it impossible for Tarzan to wield his blade effectively. The snake was badly wounded, but still a most formidable foe. Should it succeed in enmeshing Tarzan in its mighty coils, his body would be crushed long before he could kill it.

And now the apes dropped to the ground beside the contestants in this grim battle of life and death. Growling, chattering, screaming, the four mighty adults leaped upon the beating coils of the python, tearing them from the body of the man-thing. And Tarzan's knife found its mark again.

As the severed head rolled to the ground, Tarzan leaped aside. So did the apes, for the death struggles of the giant snake might prove as lethal as though guided by the tiny brain.

Tarzan turned and faced the apes; then he placed a foot on the dead head and, raising his face to the heavens, voiced the victory cry of the bull ape. It rang wild and weird and terrifying through the primeval forest, and for a moment the voices of the jungle were stilled.

The apes looked at the man-thing. All their lives his kind had been their natural enemies. Was he friend or foe?

Tarzan struck his breast, and said, 'Tarzan.'

The apes nodded, and said, 'Tarzan,' for tarzan means white-skin in the language of the great apes.

'Tarzan yo,' said the man. 'Mangani yo?'

'Mangani yo,' said the oldest and largest of the apes – *great apes friend.*

There was a noise in the trees, like the coming of a big wind – the violent rustling and swishing of leaves and branches. Apes and man looked expectantly in the direction from which the sound came. All of them knew what created the sound. The man alone did not know what it portended.

Presently he saw ten or twelve huge black forms swinging toward them through the trees. The apes dropped to the ground around them. They had heard Tarzan's piercing call, and had hastened to investigate. It might be the victory cry of an enemy that had overcome one of the tribe. It might have been a challenge to battle.

They eyed Tarzan suspiciously, some of them with bared fangs. He was a man-thing, a natural enemy. They looked from Tarzan to Uglo, the oldest and largest of the apes. Uglo pointed at the man and said, 'Tarzan. Yo.' Then, in the simple language of the first-men and with signs and gestures, he told what Tarzan had done. The newcomers nodded their understanding – all but one. Oju, a full grown, powerful young orangutan, bared his fangs menacingly.

'Oju bundolo!' he growled – *Oju kill!*

Vanda, mother of the little ape rescued from the python, pressed close to Tarzan, stroking him with a rough and horny palm. She placed herself between Tarzan and Oju, but the former pushed her gently aside.

Oju had issued a challenge which Tarzan could not ignore and retain the respect of the tribe. This he knew, and though he did not want to fight, he drew his knife and advanced toward the growling Oju.

Standing nearly six feet in height and weighing fully three hundred pounds, Oju was indeed a formidable opponent. His enormously long arms, his Herculean muscles, his mighty fangs and powerful jaws dwarfed the offensive equipment of even the mighty Tarzan.

Oju lumbered forward, his calloused knuckles resting on the ground. Uglo would have interfered. He made a halfhearted gesture of stepping between them. But Uglo was really afraid. He was King, but he was getting old. He knew that Oju was minded to challenge his Kingship. Should he antagonize him now, he might only hasten the moment of his dethronement. He did not interfere. But Vanda scolded, and so did the other apes which had witnessed Tarzan's rescue of Vanda's balu.

Oju was not deterred. He waddled confidently to close quarters, contemptuous of this puny man-thing. Could he lay one powerful hand upon him, the fight would be as good as over. He extended a long arm toward his intended victim. It was a tactical error.

Tarzan noted the slow, stupid advance, the outstretched hand; and altered his own plan of battle. Carrying the knife to his mouth and seizing the blade between his teeth, he freed both hands. Then he sprang forward, grasped Oju's extended wrist with ten powerful fingers, wheeled quickly, bent forward, and threw the ape over his head – threw him so that he would fall heavily upon his back.

Badly shaken, roaring with rage, Oju scrambled awkwardly to his feet. Tarzan leaped quickly behind him while he was still off balance, leaped upon his back, locked powerful legs about his middle, and wrapped his left arm about his neck. Then he pressed the point of his knife against the beast's side – pressed it in until it brought a scream of pain from Oju.

'Kagoda!' demanded Tarzan. That is ape for surrender. It is also ape for I surrender. The difference is merely a matter of inflection.

Oju reached a long arm back to seize his opponent. The knife dug in again. This time deeper. Again Tarzan demanded, 'Kagoda!' The more Oju sought to dislodge the man-thing from his back, the deeper the knife was pressed. Tarzan could have killed the ape, but he did not wish to. Strong young bulls are the strength of a tribe, and this tribe was mostly friendly to him.

Oju was standing still now. Blood was streaming down his side. Tarzan moved the point of the knife to the base of Oju's brain and jabbed it in just enough to draw blood and inflict pain.

'Kagoda!' screamed Oju.

Tarzan released his hold and stepped aside. Oju lumbered off and squatted down to nurse his wounds. Tarzan knew that he had made an enemy, but an enemy that would always be afraid of him. He also knew that he had established himself as an equal in the tribe. He would always have friends among them.

He called Uglo's attention to the spoor of men in the trail. 'Tarmangani?' he asked. Tar is white, Mangani means great apes; so Tarmangani, white great apes, means white men.

'Sord Tarmangani,' said Uglo – *bad white men.*

Tarzan knew that to the great apes, all white men were bad. He knew that he could not judge these men by the opinion of an ape. He would have to investigate them himself. These men might prove valuable allies.

He asked Uglo if the white men were travelling or camped. Uglo said that they were camped. Tarzan asked how far away. Uglo extended his arms at full length toward the sun and held his palms facing one another and about a foot apart. That is as far as the sun would appear to travel in an hour. That, Tarzan interpreted as meaning that the camp of the white men was about three miles distant – as far as the apes would ordinarily move through the trees in an hour.

He swung into a tree and was gone in the direction of the camp of the Tarmangani. There are no 'Goodbyes' nor 'Au revoirs' in the language of the apes. The members of the tribe had returned to their normal activities. Oju nursed his wounds and his rage. He bared his fangs at any who came near him.

12

Jerry was smarting under self-censure. 'I feel like a heel,' he said, 'letting those two fellows take it while I hid. But I couldn't leave you here alone, Corrie, or risk your capture.'

'Even if I hadn't been here,' said Corrie, 'the thing for you to do was just what you did. If you had been captured with them, you could not have done anything more for them than they can do for themselves. Now, perhaps, you and Tarzan and I can do something for them.'

'Thanks for putting it that way. Nevertheless, I—' He stopped, listening. 'Someone is coming,' he said, and drew the girl back into the concealment of the underbrush.

From where they were hidden, they had a clear view back along the trail for a good fifty yards before it curved away from their line of sight. Presently they heard voices more distinctly. 'Japs,' whispered Corrie. She took a handful of arrows from the quiver at her back and fitted one to her bow. Jerry grinned and followed her example.

A moment later, two Jap soldiers strolled carelessly into view. Their rifles were slung across their backs. They had nothing to fear in this direction – they thought. They had made a token gesture of obeying their officer's instructions to search back along the trail for the three missing whites, whom they had been none too anxious to discover waiting in ambush for them. They would loaf slowly back to camp and report that they had made a thorough search.

Corrie leaned closer to Jerry and whispered, 'You take the one on the left. I'll take the other.' Jerry nodded and raised his bow.

'Let 'em come to within twenty feet,' he said. 'When I say now, we'll fire together.'

They waited. The Japs were approaching very slowly, jabbering as though they had something worthwhile to say.

'Monkey talk,' said Jerry.

'S-sh!' cautioned the girl. She stood with her bow drawn, the feathers of the arrow at her right ear. Jerry glanced at her from the corners of his eyes. Joan of Sumatra, he thought. The Japs were approaching the dead line.

'Now!' said Jerry. Two bow strings twanged simultaneously. Corrie's target pitched forward with an arrow through the heart. Jerry's aim had not been so true. His victim clutched at the shaft sunk deep in his throat.

Jerry jumped into the trail, and the wounded Jap tried to unsling his rifle. He had almost succeeded when Jerry struck him a terrific blow on the chin. He went down, and the pilot leaped upon him with drawn knife. Twice he drove the blade into the man's heart. The fellow twitched convulsively and lay still.

Jerry looked up to see Corrie disentangling the slung rifle from the body of the other Jap. He saw her stand above her victim like an avenging goddess. Three times she drove the bayonet into the breast of the soldier. The American watched the girl's face. It was not distorted by rage or hate or vengeance. It was illumined by a divine light of exaltation.

She turned toward Jerry. 'That is what I saw them do to my father. I feel happier now. I only wish that he had been alive.'

'You are magnificent,' said Jerry.

They took possession of the other rifle and the belts and ammunition of the dead men. Then Jerry dragged the bodies into the underbrush. Corrie helped him.

'You can cut a notch in your shootin' iron, woman,' said Jerry, grinning. 'You have killed your man.'

'I have not killed a man,' contradicted the girl. 'I have killed a Jap.'

' "Haughty Juno's unrelenting hate," ' quoted Jerry.

'You think a woman should not hate,' said Corrie. 'You could never like a woman who hated.'

'I like you,' said Jerry gently, solemnly.

'And I like *you*, Jerry. You have been so very fine, all of you. You haven't made me feel like a girl, but like a man among men.'

'God forbid!' exclaimed Jerry, and they both laughed.

'For you, Jerry, I shall stop hating – as soon as I have killed all the Japs in the world.'

Jerry smiled back at her. 'A regular Avenging Angel,' he said. 'Let's see – who were The Avenging Angels?'

'I don't know,' said Corrie. 'I've never met any angels.'

'Now I remember,' said Jerry. 'A long while ago there was an association of Mormons, the Danite Band. They were known as The Avenging Angels.'

'The Mormons are the people who have a lot of wives, aren't they? Are you a Mormon?'

'Perish the thought. I'm not that courageous. Neither are the present day Mormons. Just imagine being married to a WAC sergeant, a welder, and a steamfitter!'

'And an Avenging Angel?' laughed Corrie.

He didn't answer. He just looked at her, and Corrie wished that she had not said it. Or did she wish that she had not said it?

Tarzan, swinging through the trees overlooking the trail, stopped suddenly and froze into immobility. Ahead of him he saw a man squatting on a platform built in a tree that gave a view of the trail for some distance in the direction from which Tarzan had come. The man was heavily bearded and heavily armed. He was a white man. Evidently he was a sentry watching a trail along which an enemy might approach.

Tarzan moved cautiously away from the trail. Had he not been fully aware of the insensibility of civilized man he would have marvelled that the fellow had not noted his approach. The stupidest of the beasts would have heard him or smelled him or seen him.

Making a detour, he circled the sentry; and a minute or two later came to the edge of a small mountain meadow and looked down upon a rude and untidy camp. A score or so of men were lying around in the shade of trees. A bottle passed from hand to hand among them, or from mouth to mouth. Drinking with them were a number of women. Most of these appeared to be Eurasians. With a single exception, the men were heavily bearded. This was a young man who sat with them, taking an occasional pull at the bottle. The men carried pistols and knives, and each had a rifle close at hand. It was not a nice looking company.

Tarzan decided that the less he had to do with these people the better. And then the branch on which he sat snapped suddenly, and he fell to the ground within a hundred feet of them. His head struck something hard, and he lost consciousness.

When he came to he was lying beneath a tree, his wrists and ankles bound. Men and women were squatting or standing around him. When they saw that he had regained consciousness, one of the men spoke to him in Dutch. Tarzan understood him, but he shook his head as though he did not.

The fellow had asked him who he was and what he had been doing spying on them. Another tried French, which was the first spoken language of civilized man that he had learned; but he still shook his head. The young man tried English. Tarzan pretended that he did not understand; and addressed them in Swahili, the language of a Mohammedan Bantu people of Zanzibar and the East coast of Africa, knowing that they would not understand it.

'Sounds like Japanese,' said one of the men.

'It ain't though,' said one who understood that language.

'Maybe it's Chinese,' suggested another.

'He looks about as much like a Chink as you do,' said the first speaker.

'Maybe he's a wild man. No clothes, bow and arrows. Fell out of a tree like a monkey.'

'He's a damned spy.'

'What good's a spy who can't talk any civilized language?'

They thought this over, and it seemed to remove their suspicion that their prisoner might be a spy, at least for the moment. They had more important business to attend to, as was soon demonstrated.

'Oh, to hell with him,' said a bleary-eyed giant. 'I'm getting dry.'

He walked back in the direction of the trees beneath which they had been lolling – in the direction of the trees and the bottle – and the others followed. All but the young man with the smooth face. He still squatted near Tarzan, his back toward his retreating companions. When they were at a safer distance and their attention held by the bottle, he spoke. He spoke in a low whisper and in English.

'I am sure that you are either an American or an Englishman,' he said. 'Possibly one of the Americans from the bomber that was shot down some time ago. If you are, you can trust me. I am practically a prisoner here myself. But don't let them see you talking to me. If you decide that you can trust me, you can make some sign that you understand me.

'You have fallen into the hands of a band of cutthroats. With few exceptions they are criminals who were released from jail and armed when the Japs invaded the island. Most of the women are also criminals who were serving jail sentences. The others are also from the bottom of the social barrel – the ultimate dregs.

'These people escaped to the hills as the Japs took over. They made no attempt to aid our armed forces. They thought only of their own skins. After my regiment surrendered, I managed to escape. I ran across this outfit; and supposing it to be a loyal guerrilla band, I joined it. Learning my background, they would have killed me had it not been that a couple of them are men I had befriended in times past. But they don't trust me.

'You see, there are loyal guerrillas hiding in the hills who would kill these traitors as gladly as they'd kill Japs. And these fellows are afraid I'd get in touch with them and reveal the location of this camp.

'About the worst these people have done so far is to trade with the enemy, but they are going to turn you over to the Japs. They decided on that before you regained consciousness. They also thought that you were one of the American fliers. The Japs would pay a good price for you.

'These fellows distill a vile spirit which they call schnapps. What they don't drink themselves they use to barter with the Japs and natives. They get juniper berries, ammunition, and rice, among other things, from the Japs. That the Japs let them have ammunition indicates that they consider them friendly. However, it is little more than an armed truce; as neither trusts the other to any great extent. Natives are the go-betweens who deliver the schnapps and bring the payment.'

Tarzan, knowing now that his fate had already been decided, realized that nothing would be gained by further attempts to deceive the young man. Also, he had gained a good impression of the man; and was inclined to believe that he was trustworthy. He glanced in the direction of the others. They were all intent upon a loudmouthed quarrel between two of their fellows, and were paying no attention to him and his companion.

'I am English,' he said.

The young man grinned. 'Thanks for trusting me,' he said. 'My name is Tak van der Bos. I am a reserve officer.'

'My name is Clayton. Would you like to get away from these people?'

'Yes. But what good would it do? Where could I go? I'd certainly fall into the hands of the Japs eventually, if a tiger didn't get me instead. If I knew where one of our guerrilla outfits was located, I'd sure take the chance. But I don't.'

'There are five in my party,' said Tarzan. 'We are trying to reach the southern end of the island. If we are lucky, we hope to commandeer a boat and try to reach Australia.'

'A rather ambitious plan,' said van der Bos. 'It's more than twelve hundred miles to the nearest point on the Australian continent. And it's five hundred miles to the southern end of this island.'

'Yes,' said Tarzan. 'We know, but we are going to take the chances. We all feel that it would be better to die trying it than to hide in the woods like a lot of hunted rabbits for the duration.'

Van der Bos was silent for a few moments, thinking. Presently he looked up. 'It is the right thing to do,' he said. 'I'd like to come with you. I think I can help you. I can find a boat much nearer than you plan on travelling. I know where there are friendly natives who will help us. But first we've got to get away from these fellows, and that will not be easy. There is only one trail into this little valley, and that is guarded day and night.'

'Yes, I saw him. In fact I passed close to him. I can pass him again as easily. But you are different. I do not think that you could though. If you can get me a knife tonight, I will get you past the sentry.'

'I'll try. If they get drunk enough, it should be easy. Then I'll cut your bonds, and we can have a go at it.'

'I can break these bonds whenever I wish,' said Tarzan.

Van der Bos did not comment on this statement. This fellow, he thought, is very sure of himself. Maybe a little too sure. And the Dutchman began to wonder if he had been wise in saying that he would go with him. He knew, of course, that no man could break those bonds. Maybe the fellow couldn't make good on his boast that he could pass the sentry, either.

'Do they watch you very carefully at night?' asked Tarzan.

'They don't watch me at all. This is tiger country. Had you thought of that yourself?'

'Oh, yes. But we shall have to take that chance.'

13

Slapped around, prodded in the backsides with bayonets, spit on, Rosetti and Bubonovitch were two rage filled and unhappy men long before they reached the native village. Here they were taken into a native house, trussed up, and thrown to the floor in a corner of the room. There they were left to their own devices, which consisted almost wholly of profanity. After describing the progenitors of all Japs from Horohito down, and especially those of Lt Kumajiro Tada, in the picturesque and unprintable patois of Cicero, Brooklyn, and the Army, they worked back up to Hirohito again.

'What's the use?' demanded Bubonovitch. 'We're just working up blood pressure.'

'I'm workin' up my hate,' said Rosetti. 'I know just how dat Corrie dame feels, now. I sure love to hate 'em.'

'Make the most of it while you can,' advised Bubonovitch. 'That ocher looie's going to lop your hater off in the morning.'

'Geeze,' said Rosetti. 'I don't wanna die, Bum.'

'Neither do I, Shrimp.'

'Geeze! I'm scairt.'

'So am I.'

'Let's pray, Bum.'

'Okay. The last time you prayed to Her, She sent Tarzan.'

'I'm just leavin' it to Her. I don't care how She works it.'

There was not much sleep for them that night. Their bonds cut into wrists and ankles. Their throats were dry and parched. They were given neither food nor water. The night was an eternity. But at last it ended.

'Geeze! I wisht they'd come an' get it over wit. Thinkin' about it is the worst part.'

'Thinking about my wife and baby is the hardest part for me. My wife and I had such great plans. She'll never know what happened to me, and I'm glad for that. All she'll ever know is that my plane took off from somewhere for somewhere and never came back. Did you pray a lot, Shrimp?'

'Most all night.'

'So did I.'

'Who did you pray to, Bum?'

'To God.'

'One of 'em must have heard us.'

The sound of scuffing feet ascending the ladder to the house reached their ears.

'I guess this is it,' said Bubonovitch. 'Can you take it, Shrimp?'

'Sure.'

'Well, so long, fellow.'

'So long, Bum.'

A couple of soldiers entered the room. They cut away the bonds, and dragged the two men to their feet. But they couldn't stand. Both of them staggered and fell to the floor. The soldiers kicked them in head and stomach, laughing and jabbering. Finally they dragged them to the doorway and slid them down the ladder one by one, letting them fall most of the way to the ground.

Tada came over and examined them. 'Are you ready to answer my questions?' he demanded.

'No,' said Bubonovitch.

'Get up!' snapped the Jap.

Circulation was returning to their numbed feet. They tried to rise, and finally succeeded. But they staggered like drunken men when they walked. They were taken to the center of the village. The soldiers and the natives formed a circle around them. Tada stood beside them with drawn sword. He made them kneel and bend their heads forward. Bubonovitch was to be first.

'I guess They didn't hear us, Shrimp,' he said.

'Who didn't hear you?' demanded Tada.

'None of your goddam business, Jap,' snapped Bubonovitch.

Tada swung his sword.

When the camp quieted down and most of the men and women slept in a drunken stupor, van der Bos crept to Tarzan's side. 'I've got a knife,' he said. 'I'll cut your bonds.'

'They've been off a long while,' said Tarzan.

'You broke them?' demanded the Dutchman in amazement.

'Yes. Now come along and come quietly. Give me the knife.'

A short distance inside the forest, Tarzan halted. 'Wait here,' he whispered. Then he was gone. He swung quietly into the trees, advancing slowly, stopping often to listen and to search the air with his nostrils. Finally he located the sentry and climbed into the same tree in which had been built the platform on which the man was squatting. He was poised directly over the fellow's head. His eyes bored down through the darkness. They picked out the form and position of the doomed man. Then Tarzan dove for him headfirst, the knife in his hand. The only sound was the thud of the two bodies on the platform. The sentry died in silence, his throat cut from ear to ear.

Tarzan pitched the body to the trail and followed it down with the man's rifle. He walked back until he came to van der Bos. 'Come on,' he said. 'You can get past the sentry now.'

When they came to the body, van der Bos stumbled over it. 'You certainly made a neat job of it,' he said.

'Not so neat,' said Tarzan. 'He spurted blood all over me. I'll be walking bait for stripes until we reach some water. Take his pistol belt and ammunition. Here's his rifle. Now let's get going.'

They moved rapidly along the trail, Tarzan in the lead. Presently they came to a small stream, and both washed the blood from them, for the Dutchman had acquired some while removing the belt from the corpse.

No tiger delayed them, and they soon came to the fork at which Tarzan had last seen his companions. There was no scent of them, and the two men followed along the trail the others were to have taken. It was daylight when they heard a shot close and in front of them.

Jerry and Corrie decided to remain where they were, waiting for Tarzan. They thought that he would soon return. It was well for their peace of mind that they did not know the misadventure that had befallen him. For greater safety they had climbed into a tree where they perched precariously and uncomfortably some twenty feet above the ground. Jerry worried about the fate of Bubonovitch and Rosetti, and finally decided to do something about it. The night had dragged on interminably, and still Tarzan had not returned.

'I don't think he's coming,' said Jerry. 'Something must have happened to him. Anyway, I'm not going to wait any longer. I'm going on to see if I can locate Bubonovitch and Rosetti. Then if Tarzan does come, we'll at least know where they are; and maybe together we can work out a plan to free them. You stay here until I come back. You're safer here than you would be down on the ground.'

'And suppose you don't come back?'

'I don't know, Corrie. This is the toughest decision I've ever had to make – to decide between you and those two boys. But I have made the decision, and I hope you'll understand. They are prisoners of the Japs, and we all know how Japs treat their prisoners. You are free and well armed.'

'There was only one decision you could make. I knew that you would go after them, and I am going with you.'

'Nothing doing,' said Jerry. 'You stay right where you are.'

'Is that an order?'

'Yes.'

He heard a faint suggestion of a laugh. 'When you give an order on your ship, Captain, even a general would have to obey you. But you are not captain of this tree. Here we go!' and Corrie slipped from the branch on which she had been sitting and climbed to the ground.

Jerry followed her. 'You win,' he said. 'I might have known better than to try to boss a woman.'

'Two guns are better than one,' said Corrie, 'and I'm a good shot. Anyway, I'd sat on that darned limb until I was about ready to scream.'

They trudged along the trail side by side. Often their arms touched; and once Corrie slipped on a muddy stretch, and Jerry put an arm around her to keep her from falling. He thought, I used to paw that girl back in Oklahoma City, but it never gave me a thrill like this. I think you have fallen for this little rascal, Jerry. I think you have it bad.

It was very dark, and sometimes they bumped into trees where the trail curved; so their progress was slow. They could only grope their way along, praying that dawn would soon break.

'What a day we've had,' said Jerry. 'All we need now, to make it perfect, is to run into a tiger.'

'I don't think we need worry about that,' said Corrie. 'I've never heard of a tiger attacking a white man with a rifle. They seem to know. If we leave them alone, they'll leave us alone.'

'I guess that's right. They probably know when a man is armed. When I was riding after cattle back home, I'd see plenty of coyotes when I didn't have a gun. But if I was packing a gun, I'd never see one.'

'"Back home,"' repeated Corrie. 'You poor boys are so very, very far from back home. It makes me very sad to think of it. Bubonovitch with that pretty wife and baby way on the other side of the world. Missing the best years of their life.'

'War is rotten,' said Jerry. 'If we ever get home, I'll bet we'll do something about the damned Nips and Krauts that'll keep 'em from starting wars for a heck of a long time. There'll be ten or twelve millions of us who are good and fed up on war. We're going to elect an artillery captain friend of mine governor of Oklahoma and then send him to the senate. He hates war. I don't know a soldier who doesn't, and if all America will send enough soldiers to Congress we'll get some place.'

'Is Oklahoma nice?' asked Corrie.

'It's the finest state in the Union,' admitted Jerry.

The new day was kicking off the covers and crawling out of bed. It would soon be wide awake, for close to the equator the transition from night to day takes place quickly. There is no long drawn out dawning.

'What a relief,' said Corrie. 'I was very tired of night.'

'Cripes!' exclaimed Jerry. 'Look!' He cocked his rifle and stood still. Standing in the trail directly in front of them was a tiger.

'Don't shoot!' warned Corrie.

'I don't intend to if he'll just mind his own business. This dinky little .25 caliber Jap rifle wouldn't do anything more than irritate him, and I never did like to irritate tigers so early in the morning.'

'I wish he'd go away,' said Corrie. 'He looks hungry.'

'Maybe he hasn't heard of that theory of yours.'

The tiger, a large male, stood perfectly still for several seconds, watching them; then it turned and leaped into the underbrush.

'Whee-oo!' exclaimed Jerry with a long sigh of relief. 'My heart and my stomach were both trying to get into my mouth at the same time. Was I scared!'

'My knees feel weak,' said Corrie. 'I think I'll sit down.'

'Wait!' cautioned Jerry. 'Listen! Aren't those voices?'

'Yes. Just a little way ahead.'

They moved forward very cautiously. The forest ended at the edge of a shallow valley, and the two looked down upon a little kampong scarcely a hundred yards from them. They saw natives and Jap soldiers.

'This must be where the boys are,' said Jerry.

'There they are!' whispered Corrie. 'Oh, God! He's going to kill them!'

Tada swung his sword. Jerry's rifle spit, and Lt Kumajiro Tada lunged forward, sprawling in front of the men he had been about to kill. Then Corrie fired, and a Jap soldier who was rushing toward the two prisoners died. The two kept up a fusillade that knocked over soldier after soldier and put the village into panic.

Tarzan, hurrying forward at the first shot, was soon at their side; and van der Bos joined them a moment later, adding another rifle and a pistol. Tarzan took the latter.

Bubonovitch and Rosetti, taking advantage of the confusion in the kampong, seized rifles and ammunition from two of the dead soldiers and backed toward the forest, firing as they went. Rosetti had also acquired a couple of hand grenades, which he stuffed into his pockets.

A Jap sergeant was trying to collect his men, forming them up behind a house. Suddenly they charged, screaming. Rosetti threw his grenades in quick succession among them; then he and Bubonovitch turned and ran for the forest.

The firing had ceased before the two sergeants reached the little group just within the forest. Rosetti's grenades had put an end to this part of World War II, at least temporarily. The Japs were definitely demoralized or dead.

'Geeze!' said Rosetti. 'They did hear us.'

'They sure did,' agreed Bubonovitch.

'Who heard you?' asked Jerry.

'God and the Blessed Mary,' explained Rosetti.

The little party had been so intent upon the battle that they had scarcely looked at one another while it was progressing. Now they relaxed a little and looked around. When Corrie and Tak van der Bos faced one another they were speechless for a moment. Then they both exclaimed simultaneously: 'Corrie!' 'Tak!'

'Darling!' cried Corrie, throwing her arms around the young Dutchman. Jerry was not amused.

Then followed introductions and brief resumes of their various adventures. While the others talked, Tarzan watched the kampong. The Japs seemed utterly confused. They had lost their officer and their ranking non-commissioned officers. Without them, the ordinary private soldier was too stupid to think or plan for himself.

Tarzan turned to Jerry. 'I think we can take that village and wipe out the rest of the Japs if we rush them now while they are demoralized and without a leader. We have five rifles, and there aren't more than a dozen Japs left who are in any shape to fight.'

Jerry turned to the others. 'How about it?' he asked.

'Come, on!' said Bubonovitch. 'What are we waiting for?'

14

The fight was short and sweet, and some of the Japs were helpful – they blew themselves up with their own grenades. Corrie had been left behind in the forest. But she hadn't stayed there. Jerry had no more than reached the center of the kampong when he saw her fighting at his side.

Bubonovitch and Rosetti went berserk, and their bayonets were dripping Jap blood when the fight was over. They had learned to hate.

The natives cowered in their houses. They had collobarated with the Japs and they expected the worst, but they were not molested. They were, however, required to furnish food and prepare it.

Tarzan and Jerry questioned several of them, Corrie and Tak acting as interpreters. They learned that this had been an advance post of a much larger force that was stationed about twenty-five kilometers down in the direction of the southwest coast. It had expected to be relieved in a day or two.

They also learned that there was a group of guerrillas farther along in the mountains toward the southeast. But none of the natives knew just where or how far. They seemed terribly afraid of the guerrillas.

Amat tried to curry favor with the newcomers. He was a confirmed opportunist, a natural born politician. He was wondering if it would advantage him to hurry to the main camp of the Japs and report the presence of these men and the havoc they had wreaked. But he abandoned the idea, as he would have had to travel through bad tiger country. It was well for Amat that neither Bubonovitch nor Rosetti knew the part he had played leading up to their capture.

But perhaps the two sergeants would have been inclined toward leniency, for they were very happy. Their prayers had wrought a miracle and they had been saved by the little margin of a split second. That was something to be happy about. In addition to this, they had indulged in a very successful orgy of revenge. In the blood of their enemies they had washed away the blows and insults and humiliation that had been heaped upon them.

'Geeze! Bum, we sure had a close shave.'

'I couldn't see; because I was looking at the ground,' said Bubonovitch, 'but Corrie said that Jap looie was swinging his sword when Jerry nicked him. It was that close. But we sure evened things up, eh, Shrimp?'

'How many did you get?'

'I don't know. Maybe three or four. I was just shooting at everything in sight. But you certainly hit the jackpot with those two grenades. Boy! Was that something?'

'Say, did you see dat dame get right into the fightin'? She's keen.'

'Migawd! Shrimp, are you falling for a skirt?'

'I ain't fallin' for no skoit, but she's all to the good. I ain't never see a dame like her before. I didn't know they come like dat. I'll go to bat for her any old time.'

'The last of the misogynists,' said Bubonovitch. 'Jerry took the count a long while ago, and has he fallen hard!'

'But did you see her fall on dat Dutchman's neck? You should have saw Jerry's face. Dat's de trouble wit dames – even dis one. Dey just can't help causin' wot dem Hawaiians back on De Rock calls pilikia. We was just one happy family until her old boy friend blew into the pitcher.'

'Maybe he is just an old friend,' suggested Bubonovitch. 'I noticed that when the fight was on, she fought right at Jerry's side.'

Rosetti shook his head. He had already made a great concession, but his prejudice was too deep rooted to permit him to go all out for the ladies. He was for Corrie, but with mental reservations. 'Do you throw your arms around an old friend's neck and yell, "Darling!"? I ask.'

'That all depends. You are an old friend of mine, Shrimp; but I can't imagine throwing my arms around your neck and calling you darling.'

'You'd get a poke in de snoot.'

'But if you were Ginger Rogers!'

'Geeze! What gams! I never seen gams before until I see *Lady in de Dark*. Boy!'

Tarzan and Jerry were holding a consultation of war. Corrie and Tak were recounting to each other their adventures of the past two years.

'I'd like to do a little reconnoitering before we move on,' said Tarzan. 'I'd like to do it alone, because I can move so much faster than the rest of you. But if you remain here, that Jap relief may show up before I come back. There will probably be about twenty of them, as there were in this detail. That's pretty heavy odds against you.'

'I'll chance it,' said Jerry, 'if the others are willing. We're five guns. We've got enough Jap ammunition to fight a war – lots of grenades. We know the trail they'll come in on. All we have to do is keep a sentry far enough out on it to give us plenty of warning. Then we can plaster them with grenades from ambush. Let's see what the others think.' He called them over and explained the situation.

'Geeze!' said Shrimp. 'On'y four to one? It's a cinch. We done it before. We can do it again!'

''Atta boy!' said Jerry.

'The main camp is fifteen or sixteen miles from here,' said Bubonovitch. 'They'll probably take most of the day to make the march, for they won't be in any hurry. But we'd better start being on the lookout for them this afternoon. They might come today.'

'You're right,' said Jerry. 'Suppose you go on out along the trail for about a mile. You'll hear them coming before they get in sight of you; then you can beat it back here, and we'll be ready for them.'

'Here's an idea,' said Corrie. 'Suppose we load up with hand grenades and all go out and take positions in trees along both sides of the trail. If we're spread out enough, we can get the whole detachment in range before we open up. We should be able to get them all that way.'

'Great!' said Jerry.

'What a bloodthirsty person you've become, Corrie!' exclaimed Tak, grinning.

'You don't know the half of it,' said Jerry.

'It's a good idea,' said Tarzan. 'We know the enemy is coming. We don't know just when; so we should always be prepared for him. You can come in as soon as it is dark, as I'm sure they won't march at night. There is no reason why they should. But I think you should post a guard all night.'

'Definitely,' agreed Jerry.

Tarzan, the matter settled, walked away and disappeared into the forest.

Hooft awoke bleary eyed and with a terrific headache. His mouth tasted like the bottom of a mouse cage. He was never in a very good humor at best. Now his disposition was vile to murderous. He bellowed to awaken the others, and soon the camp was astir. The slovenly, slatternly women began to prepare breakfast for the men.

Hooft stood up and stretched. Then he looked over the camp. 'Where's the prisoner?' he shouted.

Everyone else looked around. There was no prisoner. 'The other one's gone, too,' said a man.

Hooft roared out lurid profanities and horrid obscenities. 'Who's on guard?' he demanded.

'Hugo was to wake me up at midnight to relieve him,' said another. 'He didn't.'

'Go out and see what's become of him,' ordered Hooft. 'I'll skin him alive for this. I'll cut his heart out – falling asleep and letting both those men escape!'

The man was gone but a few minutes. When he returned, he was grinning. 'Somebody beat you to it, Chief,' he said to Hooft. 'Hugo's a mess. His throat's been cut from ear to ear.'

'It must have been that wild man,' said Sarina.

'Van der Bos must have cut his bonds,' said Hooft. 'Wait 'til I get hold of him.'

'If you ever do,' said Sarina. 'He'll go right to the nearest guerrillas, and pretty soon we'll have them down on us.'

One of the men had walked over to the spot where Tarzan had lain. He returned with the bonds and handed them to Hooft. 'These weren't cut,' he said. 'They were broken.'

'No man could have broken them,' said Hooft.

'The wild man did,' said Sarina.

'I'll wild man him,' growled Hooft. 'Let's eat and get going. We're going after them. You women stay here.' No one demurred. No one ever argued with Hooft when he was in a bad humor, with the exception of Sarina. She was the only one of the murderous crew whom Hooft feared, but Sarina did not argue now. She had no desire to go tramping through the forest.

The outlaws were good trackers, and Tarzan and van der Bos had made no effort to obliterate their spoor. It was plain going for Hooft and his gang of cutthroats.

Jerry and his little company gathered all the grenades they could carry and went out into the forest in the direction from which the Jap relief would have to come. Through van der Bos, Jerry warned the natives not to remove any of the rifles and ammunition which they left behind. 'Tell 'em we'll burn the village if we find anything gone when we return.'

Van der Bos embellished this threat by assuring the chief that in addition to burning the village they would cut off the heads of all the villagers. The chief was impressed.

So was Amat. He had intended following the strangers out into the forest to spy on them. When he discovered how bloodthirsty they were, he changed his mind. They might catch him at his spying. Instead, he went out on another trail to gather durian fruit.

And so it was that while he was thus engaged among the branches of a durian tree, and negligent, Hooft discovered him. Hooft ordered him down. Amat was terrified. Hooft and his party were as villainous looking a gang as ever Amat had laid eyes on.

Hooft questioned him, asking if he had seen the two fugitives and describing them. Amat was relieved. He could give these men a great deal of information and thus win safety. They would reward him at least with his life.

'I have seen them,' he said. 'They came to our village with two others this morning. One was a woman. They rescued two men that the Japanese had taken prisoners; then the six killed all the Japanese.'

'Where are they now?'

'They went out into the forest on another trail. I do not know why. But they are returning this evening. They said so. Now may I go?'

'And warn those people? I'll say not.'

'Better kill him,' said one of the men. He spoke Amat's dialect, and Amat trembled so that he nearly fell down. He did drop to his knees and beg for his life.

'You do what we say, and we won't kill you,' said Hooft.

'Amat will do anything you want,' said the frightened man. 'I can tell you something more. The Japanese would pay well for the girl that was in our village today. The Japanese who were stationed there talked about her. The Japanese have been hunting for her for two years. Maybe I can help you get her. I will do anything for you.'

Amat did not know how he could help them get Corrie, but he was willing to promise anything. If he couldn't get her, maybe he could run off into the forest until these terrible men had gone away. They were more terrifying even than the Japanese who had cuffed and kicked him.

Further discussion was interrupted by the sound of explosions beyond the village, somewhere off in the forest; but not far. 'Hand grenades,' said one of the men.

'Sounds like a regular battle,' said Hooft.

The louder detonations were punctuated by the ping of rifle shots. 'Those are Jap .25's,' said Grotius.

Rising above the detonations were the piercing screams of men in agony. The whole thing lasted but a few minutes. There were a few scattered rifle shots at the end; then silence. One could almost reconstruct the scene from the sounds. There had been a sharp engagement. Between whom? wondered the outlaws. One side had been annihilated. Which one? The final rifle shots had liquidated the wounded.

The victors would certainly come to the village. Hooft and his followers approached the edge of the forest and lay in concealment. The little valley and the kampong were in plain sight below them.

They had not long to wait. Four white men and a white girl emerged from the forest trail. They were heavily laden with all the weapons and ammunition they could carry. They were talking excitedly. The men went to one of the native houses, the girl to another.

Hooft thought quickly. He must find a way to get the girl without risking a brush with her companions. Hooft, like all bullies, was yellow. He could stab or shoot a man in the back, but he couldn't face an armed opponent. He preferred to accomplish his ends by intrigue and cunning.

He turned to Amat. 'Take this message to the girl. Tell her an old friend of hers is waiting at the edge of the forest. He doesn't want to come into the village until he is sure her companions are loyal to the Dutch. Tell her to come alone to the edge of the forest and talk with him. He is an old friend of her father. And, Amat, don't tell anyone else we are here. If anyone but the girls comes, we won't be here; but we'll come back someday and kill you. You can tell the girl, too, that if she does not come alone, I won't be here. Repeat the message to me.'

Amat repeated it, and Hooft motioned him on his way. Amat felt like a condemned man who has just received a pardon, or at least a reprieve. He slipped quietly into the village, and went to the foot of the ladder leading to the door of the house where Corrie was quartered. He called to her, and a native girl came to the doorway. When she saw Amat, her lip curled in contempt. 'Go away pig!' she said.

'I have a message for the white woman,' said Amat.

Corrie overheard and came to the doorway. 'What message have you for me?' she asked.

'It is a very private message,' said Amat. 'I cannot shout it.'

'Come up here, then.'

Lara, the native girl, turned up her nose as Amat passed into the house. She knew him for a liar and a sneak, but she did not warn Corrie. What business was it of hers?

Amat delivered his message. Corrie pondered. 'What was the man like?' she asked.

'He is a white man with a beard,' said Amat. 'That is all I know.'

'Is he alone?'

Amat thought quickly, if she knows there are twenty of them, she will not go; then someday the man will come and kill me. 'He is alone,' said Amat.

Corrie picked up her rifle and descended the ladder to the ground. The men of her party were still in the house they had taken over. They were cleaning and oiling the rifles they had acquired. There were no natives about. Only Amat and Lara saw the white girl leave the kampong and enter the forest.

15

Tarzan had not been able to gather much information about the guerrillas from the natives. They had heard it rumored that there was one band near a certain volcano about sixty-five kilometers to the southeast. They were able to describe the appearance of this volcano and various landmarks that might help to guide Tarzan to it, and with this meager information he had set out.

He travelled until night fell, and then lay up until morning in a tree. His only weapons were his bow and arrows and his knife. He had not wished to be burdened with the Jap rifle and ammunition. In the morning he gathered some fruit and shot a hare for his breakfast.

The country through which he passed was extremely wild and destitute of any signs of man. Nothing could have suited Tarzan better. He liked the companions whom he had left behind; but notwithstanding all his contacts with men, he had never become wholly gregarious. His people were the wild things of the forest and jungle and plain. With them, he was always at home. He liked to watch them and study them. He often knew them better than they knew themselves.

He passed many monkeys. They scolded him until he spoke to them in their own language. They knew their world, and through them he kept upon the right route to the volcano. They told him in what direction to go to reach the next landmark of which the natives had spoken – a little lake, a mountain meadow, the crater of an extinct volcano.

When he thought that he should be approaching his destination, he asked some monkeys if there were white men near a volcano. He called it argo ved – *fire mountain*. They said there were, and told him how to reach their camp. One old monkey said, 'Kreeg-ah! Tarmangani sord. Tarmangani bundolo,' and he mimicked the aiming of a rifle, and said, 'Boo! Boo!' *Beware! White men bad. White men kill.*

He found the camp in a little gorge, but before he came to it he saw a sentry guarding the only approach. Tarzan came out into the open and walked toward the man, a bearded Dutchman. The fellow cocked his rifle and waited until Tarzan came to within twenty-five or thirty yards of him; then he halted him.

'Who are you and what are you doing here?' he demanded.

'I am an Englishman. I should like to talk with your chief.'

The man had been appraising Tarzan with some show of astonishment. 'Stay where you are,' he ordered. 'Don't come any closer;' then he called down into the gorge: 'de Lettenhove! There's a wild man up here wants to talk to you.'

Tarzan repressed a smile. He had heard this description of himself many times before, but never with quite such blatant disregard of his feelings. Then he recalled that he had spoken to the man in English and said that he was an Englishman, while the fellow had called to de Lettenhove in Dutch, doubtless believing that the 'wild man' did not understand that language. He would continue to let them believe so.

Presently, three men came up out of the valley. All were heavily armed. They were bearded, tough looking men. They wore patched, tattered, nondescript clothing, partly civilian, partly military, partly crudely fashioned from the skins of animals. One of them wore a disreputable tunic with the two stars of a first lieutenant on the shoulder tabs. This was de Lettenhove. He spoke to the sentry in Dutch.

'What was this man doing?'

'He just walked up to me. He made no effort to avoid me or hide from me. He is probably a harmless half-wit, but what the devil he's doing here gets me. He says he is English. He spoke to me in that language.'

De Lettenhove turned to Tarzan. 'Who are you? What are you doing here?' he asked in English.

'My name is Clayton. I am a colonel in the RAF. I understood that a company of Dutch guerrillas was camped here. I wanted to talk with their commanding officer. Are you he? I know that there are also bands of outlaws in the mountains, but the only way I could find out which you are was to come and talk with you. I had to take that chance.'

'I am not the commanding officer,' said de Lettenhove. 'Capt. van Prins is in command, but he is not here today. We expect him back tomorrow. Just what do you want to see him about? I can assure you,' he added with a smile, 'that we are outlaws only in the eyes of the Japs and the native collaborationists.'

'I came because I wanted to make contact with people I could trust, who could give me information as to the location of Jap outposts and native villages whose people are friendly to the Dutch. I wish to avoid the former and, perhaps, obtain help from the latter. I am trying to reach the coast, where I shall try to obtain a boat and escape from the island.'

De Lettenhove turned to one of the men who had accompanied him from the camp in the valley. 'I was commencing to believe him,' he said in Dutch, 'until he sprung that one about getting a boat and escaping from the island. He must think we're damn fools to fall from any such silly explanation of his presence here. He's probably a damn German spy. We'll just hang onto him until van Prins gets back.' Then, to Tarzan, in English: 'You say you are an English officer. Of course you have some means of identification?'

'None,' replied Tarzan.

'May I ask why an English officer is running around in the mountains of Sumatra naked and armed with bow and arrows and a knife?' His tone was ironical. 'My friend, you certainly can't expect us to believe you. You will remain here until Capt. van Prins returns.'

'As a prisoner?' asked Tarzan.

'As a prisoner. Come, we will take you down to camp.'

The camp was neat and well policed. There were no women. There was a row of thatched huts laid out with military precision. The red, white, and blue flag of the Netherlands flew from a staff in front of one of the huts. Twenty or thirty men were variously occupied about the camp, most of them cleaning rifles or pistols. Tattered and torn and shabby were their clothes, but their weapons were immaculate. That this was a well disciplined military camp Tarzan was now convinced. These were no outlaws. He knew that he could trust these men.

His entrance into the camp caused a mild sensation. The men stopped their work to stare at him. Some came and questioned those who accompanied him.

'What you got there?' asked one. 'The Wild Man of Borneo?'

'He says he's an RAF colonel, but I've got two guesses. He's either a harmless half-wit or a German spy. I'm inclined to believe the latter. He doesn't talk like a half-wit.'

'Does he speak German?'

'Don't know.'

'I'll try him.' He spoke to Tarzan in German; and the latter, impelled by the ridiculousness of the situation, rattled off a reply in impeccable German.

'I told you so,' said the two-guesser.

Then Tarzan turned to de Lettenhove. 'I told you that I had no means of identification,' he said. 'I haven't any with me, but I have friends who can identify me – three Americans and two Dutch. You may know the latter.'

'Who are they?'

'Corrie van der Meer and Tak van der Bos. Do you know them?'

'I knew them very well, but they have both been reported dead.'

'They were not dead yesterday,' said Tarzan.

'Tell me,' said de Lettenhove. 'How do you happen to be in Sumatra anyway? How could an English colonel get to Sumatra in wartime? And what are Americans doing here?'

'An American bomber was supposed to have crashed here some time ago,' one of the men reminded de Lettenhove in Dutch. 'This fellow, if he is working with the Japs, would have known this. He would also have been able to get the names of Miss van der Meer and Tak. Let the damn fool go on. He's digging his own grave.'

'Ask him how he knew our camp was here,' suggested another.

'How did you know where to find us?' demanded de Lettenhove.

'I'll answer all your questions,' said Tarzan. 'I was aboard the bomber that was shot down. That's how I happen to be here. The three Americans I have mentioned were also survivors from that plane. I learned in a native village yesterday about the general location of your camp. These villagers have been collaborating with the Japs. There was a Jap outpost garrisoned there. We had an engagement with them yesterday, and wiped out the entire garrison.'

'You speak excellent German,' said one of the men accusingly.

'I speak several languages,' said Tarzan, 'including Dutch.' He smiled.

De Lettenhove flushed. 'Why didn't you tell me all these things in the first place?' he demanded.

'I wished first to assure myself that I was among potential friends. You might have been collaborationists. I just had an experience with a band of armed Dutchmen who work with the Japs.'

'What decided you that we were all right?'

'The appearance of this camp. It is not the camp of a band of undisciplined outlaws. Then, too, I understood all that you said in Dutch. You would not have feared that I might be a spy had you been on friendly terms with the Japs. I am convinced that I can trust you. I am sorry that you do not trust me. You probably could have been of great assistance to me and my friends.'

'I should like to believe you,' said de Lettenhove. 'We'll let the matter rest until Capt. van Prins returns.'

'If he can describe Corrie van der Meer and Tak van der Bos, I'll believe him,' said one of the men. 'If they're dead, as we've heard, he can't ever have seen them, for Corrie was killed with her father and mother over two years ago way up in the mountains, and Tak was captured and killed by the Japs after he escaped from the concentration camp. They couldn't possibly have been seen by this man unless they are still alive and together.'

Tarzan described them both minutely, and told much of what had befallen them during the past two years.

De Lettenhove offered Tarzan his hand. 'I believe you now,' he said, 'but you must understand that we have to be suspicious of everyone.'

'So am I,' replied the Englishman.

'Forgive me if I appear to be rude,' said the Dutchman, 'but I'd really like to know why you go about nearly naked like a regular Tarzan.'

'Because I am Tarzan.' He saw incredulity and returning suspicion in de Lettenhove's face. 'Possibly some of you may recall that Tarzan is an English- man and that his name is Clayton. That is the name I gave you, you will recall.'

'That's right,' exclaimed one of the men. 'John Clayton, Lord Greystoke.'

'And there's the scar on his forehead that he got in his fight with the gorilla when he was a boy,' exclaimed another.

'I guess that settles it,' said de Lettenhove.

The men crowded around, asking Tarzan innumerable questions. They were more than friendly now, trying to make amends for their former suspicions.

'Am I still a prisoner?' he asked de Lettenhove.

'No, but I wish you would remain until the captain gets back. I know that he'll be more than anxious to be of assistance to you.'

16

As Corrie entered the forest she saw a man standing in the trail about a hundred feet from her. It was Hooft. He removed his hat and bowed, smiling. 'Thank you for coming,' he said. 'I was afraid to go down into the village until I was sure the people there were friendly.'

Corrie advanced toward him. She did not recognize him. Even though smiling, his appearance was most unprepossessing; so she kept her rifle at ready. 'If you are a loyal Dutchman,' she said, 'you will find the white men in this village friendly. What do you want of them?'

She had advanced about fifty feet when suddenly men leaped from the underbrush on both sides of the trail. The muzzle of her rifle was struck up and the weapon seized and wrenched from her grasp.

'Don't make no noise and you won't be hurt,' said one of the men.

Pistols were levelled at her as a warning of what would happen to her if she cried out for help. She saw that the men surrounding her were Dutchmen, and realized that they were probably of the same band of outlaws from which Tak and Tarzan had escaped. She reproached herself for having stupidly put herself in their power.

'What do you want of me?' she demanded.

'We ain't goin' to hurt you,' said Hooft. 'Just come along quietly, and we won't keep you long.' They were already moving along the trail, men in front of her and behind her. She realized that escape now was impossible.

'But what are you going to do with me?' she insisted.

'You'll find that out in a couple of days.'

'My friends will follow, and when they catch up with you you'll wish that you never had seen me.'

'They won't never catch up,' said Hooft. 'Even if they should, there are only four of them. We'd wipe 'em out in no time.'

'You don't know them,' said Corrie. 'They have killed forty Japs today, and they'll find you no matter where you hide. You had better let me go back; because you will certainly pay if you don't.'

'Shut up,' said Hooft.

They hurried on. Night fell, but they did not stop. Corrie thought of Jerry and the others. Most of all, she thought of Jerry. She wondered if they had missed her yet. She didn't wonder what they would do when they did miss her. She knew. She knew that the search for her would start immediately. Probably it already had started. She lagged, pretending to be tired. She wanted to delay her captors; but they pushed her roughly on, swearing at her.

Back in the village, Jerry was the first to wonder why Corrie hadn't joined them as the natives prepared their evening meal. He saw Amat, and asked van der Bos to send him after Corrie. The native went to the house Corrie had occupied and pretended to look for her. Presently he returned to say that she was not there. 'I saw her go into the forest a little while ago,' he said. 'I supposed that she had returned, but she is not in her house.'

'Where into the forest?' asked van der Bos. Amat pointed to a different trail from that which Corrie had taken.

When van der Bos had interpreted what Amat had said, Jerry picked up his rifle and started for the forest. The others followed him.

'What in the world could have possessed her to go wandering off into the forest alone?' demanded Jerry.

'Maybe she didn't,' said Rosetti. 'Maybe dat little stinker was lyin'. I don't like dat puss o' his. He looks like a rat.'

'I don't believe the little so-and-so, either,' said Bubonovitch. 'It just isn't like Corrie to do a thing like that.'

'I know,' said Jerry, 'but we'll have to make a search anyway. We can't pass up any chance of finding her, however slim.'

'If that little yellow runt was lyin', if he knows wot become of Corrie, I'm goin' to poke a bayonet clean through his gizzard,' growled Rosetti.

They went into the forest, calling Corrie aloud by name. Presently they realized the futility of it. In the pitch darkness of the forest night they could have seen no spoor, had there been one to see.

'If only Tarzan were here,' said Jerry. 'God! But I feel helpless.'

'Somethin' dirty's been pulled,' said Rosetti. 'I t'ink we should orter go back an' give de whole village de toid degree.'

'You're right, Shrimp,' said Jerry. 'Let's go back.'

They routed the natives out and herded them into the center of the village. Then van der Bos questioned them. Those first questioned denied any knowledge even of Corrie's departure. They disclaimed having any idea of where she might be. As Lara's turn came, Amat started to sneak away. Shrimp saw him, for he had been keeping an eye on him, grabbed him by the scruff of the neck, wheeled him around, and pushed him into the center of the stage, at the same time giving him a swift kick in the pants.

'This louse was tryin' to beat it,' he announced. 'I told you he was a wrong guy.' He held the business end of his bayonet in the small of Amat's back.

Van der Bos questioned Lara at length and then interpreted her replies to the others. 'This girl says that Amat came and told Corrie that a friend of her father was waiting at the edge of the forest and wanted to see her, but for her to come alone, as he didn't know whether or not the rest of us were friendly to the Dutch. She went into the forest on that trail there.' He pointed. It was not the trail which Amat said she had taken.

'I told you so!' shouted Rosetti. 'Tell this skunk to say his prayers, for I'm goin' to kill him.'

'No, Rosetti,' said Jerry. 'He's the only one who knows the truth. We can't get it out of him if he's dead.'

'I can wait,' said Rosetti.

Tak van der Bos questioned Amat at length, while Rosetti kept the point of a bayonet pressed against the frightened native's left kidney.

'According to this man's story,' said Tak, 'he went into the forest to gather durians. He was almost immediately captured by a band of white men. He says there were about twenty of them. One of them forced him to take that message to Corrie, threatening to come back and kill him if Corrie didn't come out alone. He says he was very much frightened. Also, he thought the man merely wished to talk with Corrie. Says he didn't know that they would keep her.'

'Is dat all?' demanded Shrimp.

'That's his whole story.'

'May I kill him now, Cap?'

'No,' said Jerry.

'Aw, hell! Why not? You know de bum's lyin'.'

'We're not Japs, Rosetti. And we've got other things to do right now.' He turned to van der Bos. 'Isn't it likely that those fellows were the same ones that you and Tarzan got away from?'

'I think there's no doubt of it.'

'Then you can lead us to their camp?'

'Yes.'

'At night?'

'We can start now,' said van der Bos.

'Good!' exclaimed Jerry. 'Let's get going.'

Rosetti gave Amat a quick poke with his bayonet that brought a frightened scream from the Sumatran. Jerry wheeled toward the sergeant.

'I didn't kill him, Cap. You didn't tell me not to jab him once for luck.'

'I'd like to kill him myself, Shrimp,' said Jerry. 'But we can't do things that way.'

'I can,' said Rosetti, 'if you'll just look de udder way a second.' But Jerry shook his head and started off toward the mouth of the trail. The others followed, Shrimp shaking his head and grumbling. 'T'ink of dat poor kid out dere wit dem bums!' he said. 'An' if dis little stinker had a-told us, we'd a-had her back before now. Just for a couple seconds I wish we was Japs.'

Bubonovitch made no wisecrack about misogynists. He was in no wisecracking mood, but he couldn't but recall how violently upset Shrimp had been when they had had to add a 'dame' to their company.

Finding that her delaying tactics won her nothing but abuse, Corrie swung along at an easy stride with her captors. Presently, she heard three sharp knocks ahead, as though someone had struck the bole of a tree three times with a heavy implement. The men halted, and Hooft struck the bole of a tree three times with the butt of his rifle – two knocks close together and then a third at a slightly longer interval.

A woman's voice demanded, 'Who is it?' and the outlaw chief replied, 'Hooft.'

'Come on in,' said the woman. 'I'd know that schnapps bass if I heard it in Hell.'

The party advanced, and presently the woman spoke again from directly above them. 'I'm coming down,' she said. 'Post one of your men up here, Hooft. This is no job for a lady.'

'What give you the idea you was a lady?' demanded Hooft, as the woman descended from the platform from which she had been guarding the trail to the camp. She was Hooft's woman, Sarina.

'Not you, sweetheart,' said the woman.

'We won't need no guard here no more,' said Hooft. 'We're pullin' out quick.'

'Why? Some cripple with a slingshot chasin' you?'

'Shut up!' snapped Hooft. 'You're goin' to shoot off your gab just once too often one of these days.'

'Don't make me laugh,' said Sarina.

'I'm gettin' damn sick of you,' said Hooft.

'I've been damn sick of you for a long while, sweetheart. I'd trade you for an orangutan any day.'

'Oh, shut up,' grumbled one of the men. 'We're all gettin' good an' goddam sick of hearin' you two bellyache.'

'Who said that?' demanded Hooft. No one replied.

Presently they entered the camp and aroused the women, whereupon considerable acrimonious haggling ensued when the women learned that they were to break camp and take the trail thus late at night.

Some torches were lighted, and in their dim and flickering illumination the band gathered up its meager belongings. The light also served to reveal Corrie to the women.

'Who's the kid?' demanded one of them. 'This ain't no place for a nice boy.'
'That ain't no boy,' said a man. 'She's a girl.'

'What you want of her?' asked a woman suspiciously.

'The Japs want her,' explained Grotius, the second in command.

'Maybe they won't get her?' said Hooft.

'Why not?' demanded Grotius.

'Because maybe I've taken a fancy to her myself. I'm goin' to give Sarina to an ape.' Everybody laughed, Sarina louder than the others.

'You ain't much to look at, you ain't much to listen to, and you ain't much to live with,' she announced; 'but until I find me another man, you don't go foolin' around with any other woman. And see that you don't forget it,' she added.

Sarina was a well built woman of thirty-five, lithe and muscular. An automatic pistol always swung at her hip and her carbine was always within reach. Nor did she consider herself fully clothed if her parang were not dangling in its sheath from her belt. But these were only outward symbols of Sarina's formidableness. It was her innate ferocity when aroused that made her feared by the cutthroats and degenerates of Hooft's precious band. And she had come by this ferocity quite as a matter of course. Her maternal grandfather had been a Borneo head hunter and her maternal grandmother a Batak and a cannibal. Her father was a Dutchman who had lived adventurously in and about the South Seas, indulging in barratry and piracy, and dying at last on the gibbet for murder. Sarina, herself, carrying on the traditions of her family, though not expiating them so irrevocably as had her sire, had been serving a life sentence for murder when released from jail at the time of the Japanese invasion.

It is true that the man she had murdered should have been murdered long before; so one should not judge Sarina too harshly. It is also true that, as is often the case with characters like Sarina, she possessed many commendable characteristics. She was generous and loyal and honest. At the drop of a hat she would fight for what she knew to be right. In fact, it was not necessary even to drop a hat. Hooft feared her.

Corrie had listened with increasing perturbation to the exchange of pleasantries between Hooft and Sarina. She did not know which to fear more. She might be given over to the Japs, taken by Hooft, or killed by Sarina. It was not a pleasant outlook. She could but pray that Jerry and the others would come in time.

The outlaws had left the camp by a trail other than that along which Corrie had been brought. Hooft had issued orders for the march that would insure that their spoor would completely deceive anyone attempting to track them, and when Corrie heard them the last ray of hope seemed to have been extinguished. Only prayer was left.

On the march, Sarina walked always close to her. Corrie hoped that this would keep Hooft away. Of the two, she feared him more than she did the woman.

17

Tak Van der Bos led Jerry, Bubonovitch, and Rosetti through the Cimmerian darkness of the equatorial forest toward the camp of the outlaws. The night noises of the jungle were all about them; but they saw nothing, not even one another. They were guided solely by the slight sounds given off by the accounterments of the man directly ahead. If van der Bos slowed down or stopped as he felt for the trail they bumped into one another. Often they collided with trees or stumbled over obstacles, cursing softly. Otherwise they moved in silence. They did not talk.

Strange sounds came out of the jungle – unaccountable crashings, occasionally a scream of terror or agony. Life and death were all about them. And sometimes there were strange silences, more ominous than the noises. Then, Bubonovitch would think: *Death is abroad. The jungle is waiting to see where he will strike, each creature fearing to call attention to itself.*

Rosetti felt as a man walking in a dream. He walked and walked and walked, and never got anywhere. It was as though he had walked forever and would keep on walking in darkness throughout eternity.

Jerry thought only of what might be happening to Corrie, and chafed at the slowness of their progress. He was wondering for the thousandth time how much longer it would be before they would reach the camp, when he bumped into van der Bos. Then Rosetti and Bubonovitch bumped into him.

Van der Bos got them into a huddle, and whispered: 'Get your guns ready. We are approaching their sentry. We may be able to sneak by in the darkness. If he challenges, Jerry and I will let him have it; then we'll charge the camp, yelling like hell. But we can't shoot there until we have located Corrie. When we do, we can commence shooting; then keep right on through the camp. There is a trail on the other side. And keep together.'

'I think we should go in shooting, but in the air,' suggested Jerry.

'That's better,' agreed van der Bos. 'Come on!'

There was no sentry, and so they crept silently into the deserted camp to reconnoiter. It was not so dark here in the open, and they soon discovered that their quarry had flown. Their reactions to this disappointment were expressed variously and profanely.

'Where do we go from here?' demanded Rosetti.

'We'll have to wait for daylight before we can pick up their trail,' said Jerry. 'The rest of you get some sleep. I'll stand guard for an hour. Then one of you can relieve me for an hour. By that time it should be light.'

'Lemme stand guard, Cap,' said Rosetti. 'I can take it better'n you.'

'What makes you think that?' demanded Jerry.

'Well – well, you see you're pretty old. You'd orter get your rest.'

Jerry grinned. 'Ever hear of a general named Stilwell?' he asked. 'Thanks just the same, Shrimp; but I'll take the first trick, then I'll call you.'

As soon as it was light, they searched for the tracks of the outlaws; but they found none leading out of the camp. It seemed baffling until Bubonovitch suggested that they had gone out by the same trail along which they themselves had come in, and thus the spoor of the outlaws had been obliterated by their own.

'They must have kept right ahead at the fork,' said van der Bos. 'I guess we'll have to go back there and start all over again.' But when they reached the forks, there was no sign of fresh spoor continuing on the main trail.

'Wotinell become of 'em?' demanded Rosetti. 'They's somethin' phoney about it – people vanishin' like dat.'

'They probably used vanishing cream,' said Bubonovitch.

'We must have got some of it on our brains,' said Jerry, disgustedly.

'Or up our noses and in our eyes and ears,' said Bubonovitch. 'Tarzan was right. Civilization has robbed us of most of our physical sensibilities. I suppose that he would have found that spoor just like that.' He snapped his fingers.

'He's pretty slick,' said Rosetti, 'but even Tarzan can't find no trail when they ain't none.'

'About all we can do,' said Jerry, 'is go back to the village and wait for him. A bunch of dummies like us couldn't ever find her, and if we try it we might miss Tarzan entirely when he gets back.'

It was a dejected party that returned to the village. When Amat saw Rosetti entering the village he disappeared into the forest and climbed a tree. There he remained until after dark, a terrified and unhappy collaborator.

Tarzan waited in the camp of the guerrillas until Capt. Kervyn van Prins returned. Van Prins, de Lettenhove, and Tarzan conferred at length. Tarzan told them of the destruction of the Jap detachment in the village and of the extra rifles and ammunition, which he thought the guerrillas might use to advantage.

'When I left yesterday,' he said, 'my friends were going out to ambush the Jap relief party that was expected at almost any time. If it has arrived I haven't much doubt as to the outcome of that engagement; so there should be quite a little additional equipment for you if you care to come and get it. I think that village needs a lesson, too. Those people are undoubtedly working with the Japs.'

'You say you believe the Jap relief party would consist of some twenty men,' said van Prins, 'and your party had only five people, and one of them a girl. Aren't you rather overconfident in thinking that an engagement would result in a victory for your people?'

Tarzan smiled. 'You don't know my people,' he said. 'Too, they had a tremendous advantage over the Japs. They knew that the Japs were coming; but the Japs didn't know we were there and waiting for them in trees on both sides of the trail, armed with rifles and hand grenades. And don't discount the fighting ability of the girl, Captain. She is a crack shot, and she already has several Japs to her credit. She is imbued with a hatred of Japs that amounts almost to religious exaltation.'

'Little Corrie van der Meer!' exclaimed van Prins. 'It is almost unbelievable.'

'And two of our Americans,' continued Tarzan. 'They were captured and abused by the Japs, and were about to be beheaded when the American captain and Corrie arrived in time to save them. I think they are good for at least five Japs apiece, if not more. They have become two fisted haters. No, I don't think we need worry about the outcome of the fight, if there was one. As the Americans would say, "we did it before; we can do it again."'

'Very well,' said van Prins; 'we'll go with you. We can certainly use more rifles and ammunition. Possibly we should join forces. We can discuss that when we all get together. When do you want to start back?'

'I am going now,' replied Tarzan. 'We'll wait in the village for you.'

'We can go along with you,' said van Prins.

Tarzan shook his head. 'Not the way I travel, I'm afraid. By forced marches, you may make it by sometime tomorrow. I'll be back there tonight.'

The Dutchman gave a skeptical shrug; but he smiled and said, 'Very good. We'll see you some time tomorrow.'

Day was breaking as the outlaws emerged from the forest into a narrow valley. They had brought their supply of schnapps along with them, and most of them were drunk. More than anything else, they wanted to lie down and sleep. They made camp under some trees beside the little river that wound down the valley toward the sea.

Hooft said that the women could stand guard, as they had had some sleep the night before. As Sarina was the only woman who had not drunk during the night, she volunteered to stand the first trick. Soon the others were sprawled out and snoring. But Corrie could not sleep. Plans for escape raced through her mind, banishing thoughts of slumber. She saw that all but Sarina were dead to the world. Perhaps Sarina might succumb to fatigue, too. Then she could get away. She knew exactly where she was and where to find the trail that led back to the village. Farther down the valley she would probably find the bones of the rhinoceros and the deer that Tarzan had killed. Just beyond, she would come to the trail that led up out of the valley and into the forest.

She eyed the weapons of the sleeping men and women. If she could but steal a parang without Sarina seeing her. She would only have to get close to the woman then. In time, her attention would be distracted. She would turn her head away. Then one terrific blow with the heavy knife, and Corrie, armed with rifle, pistol, and parang, would be far on her way to the village before these drunken sots awakened.

Corrie did not even wonder that she entertained such thoughts. Her once sheltered life had become a battle for mere existence. If enemies could not be eluded, they must be destroyed. And this woman was an enemy. Corrie feared her fully as much as she feared the men. She thought of her as a terrible creature, steeped in vice.

Sarina was still a comparatively young woman. She had the sultry beauty that so many Eurasian women have and the erect, graceful carriage that marks the women of Java and Sumatra, and the slimness and physical perfection. But Corrie saw her through eyes of hate and loathing.

Sarina was staring at Corrie, her brows puckered in concentration. Would the woman never look away. 'What is your name?' asked Sarina.

'Van der Meer,' replied the girl.

'Corrie van der Meer?' Sarina smiled. 'I thought so. You look like your mother.'

'You knew my mother?' demanded Corrie. 'You couldn't have.' Her tone suggested that the woman had insulted her mother's memory just by claiming to have known her.

'But I did,' said Sarina. 'I knew your father, too. I worked for them while you were in school in Holland. They were very good to me. I loved them both. When I got in trouble, your father hired a fine attorney to defend me. But it did no good. Justice is not for Eurasians, or perhaps I should say mercy is not for Eurasians. I was guilty, but there were circumstances that would have counted in my favor had I been white. That is all past. Because your father and mother were kind to me and helped me, I shall help you.'

'What is your name?' asked Corrie.

'Sarina.'

'I have heard both my father and mother speak of you. They were very fond of you. But how can you help me?'

Sarina walked over to one of the sleeping men and took his rifle and some ammunition from him. She brought them back to Corrie. 'Do you know how to get back to the village where they found you?'

'Yes.'

'Then get started. These drunken beasts will sleep a long time.'

'How can I thank you, Sarina?' she said. She thought, and I was going to kill her!

'Don't thank me. Thank your father and mother for being kind to an Eurasian. Do you know how to use a rifle?'

'Yes.'

'Then, goodbye and good luck!'

Impulsively, Corrie threw her arms about the woman she would have killed, and kissed her. 'God bless you, Sarina,' she said. Then she swung off down the valley. Sarina watched her go, and there were tears in her eyes. She touched the spot on her cheek where Corrie had kissed her, touched it almost reverently.

Corrie took advantage of the cover afforded by the trees that grew along the left bank of the river. It was much farther to the trail leading up out of the valley than she had imagined, and it was late afternoon before she saw it winding across the valley from the opposite side. She saw something else, too. Something that made her heart sink. Some natives were making camp for the night directly in her path, and there were two Jap soldiers with them. Now she would have to wait for darkness, and then try to sneak past them.

She climbed into a tree, and tried to make herself comfortable. She was very tired and very sleepy. But she did not dare sleep for fear she would fall out of the tree. At last she found a combination of branches into which she could wedge her body and from which she could not fall. She was very uncomfortable; but nevertheless she fell asleep, utterly exhausted.

When she awoke, she knew that she had slept for some time, as the moon was high in the heavens. She could see the fire burning in the camp of the natives. Now she could slip past them and reach the trail to the village. She was preparing to descend when she heard the coughing grunt of a tiger. It sounded very close. From a little distance there arose the barking and growling of wild dogs. Corrie decided to remain where she was.

18

It was late when Tarzan reached the village. Bubonovitch, who was on guard, challenged him. 'Colonel Clayton,' responded Tarzan.

'Advance to be recognized, Colonel; but I know your voice anyway. And thank the Lord you're back.'

Tarzan approached. 'Something wrong, Sergeant?' he asked.

'I'll say there's something wrong. Corrie's been abducted,' then he told Tarzan all that he knew about the matter.

'And you couldn't find their trail?'

'There wasn't any.'

'There has to be,' said Tarzan.

'I sure hope you're right, Sir.'

'We can't do anything until morning. We'll start as soon as it's light.'

Jerry was on guard when Tarzan awoke at daylight. The American, anxious to get the search under way, had already routed out the others. They called Lara from her house. She was the only one of the natives they felt they could trust. Van der Bos talked to her. He told her that a band of guerrillas would arrive in the village sometime during the day, and instructed her to tell them what had happened and ask them to remain until the searchers returned.

When Corrie was safely out of sight of the camp of the outlaws, Sarina awoke the woman whom she thought had been most overcome by drink and told her to relieve her as guard. She said nothing about the escape of the prisoner, assuming that the woman's brain would be so befuddled that she would not notice. Sarina was right.

The guard was changed twice more before Hooft awoke. When he discovered that Corrie was missing, he was furious. He questioned all the women who had been on guard. Sarina insisted that Corrie had been there when she relinquished the post to another. The others insisted that the prisoner had not left while they were on duty. Hooft got nowhere.

He had slept all day. It was now getting dark and too late to start a search. All he could do about it was to curse the women roundly and try to find solace in a schnapps bottle.

At about the same time that Tarzan and the others were starting out from the village to search for her the following morning, Corrie was impatiently watching the camp of the natives and the two Japs. She dared not descend until they had left. She watched them prepare and eat their breakfast leisurely, thinking that they would never finish. But at long last they did.

They came in her direction, and Corrie hid in the tree where the foliage was densest. At last they filed by, quite close; and Corrie recognized Iskandar, the leader of the natives who had once abducted her, and several of his band. When they were at a safe distance, Corrie descended to the ground and followed the trail up the cliff and into the forest. At last she was safe, for all her known enemies were behind her and she was on a familiar trail that led directly back to her friends.

Iskandar continued on with his party until they came within sight of the outlaws; then the two Japs hid, and the natives approached Hooft and his people. There was a brief parley between Iskandar and Hooft; then the native sent one of his men back to tell the Japs that the white men were friendly.

After the two Japs joined them, the schnapps bottles were passed around as the men discussed plans. The Japs were non-commissioned officers from the detachment of Capt. Tokujo Matsuo, and so were naturally anxious to recapture Corrie. So were Iskandar and Hooft, each of whom visualized some form of reward if they returned the girl to the Japanese officer.

Unfortunately for their plans they drank too much schnapps; and though they started out in the right direction, they never picked up Corrie's spoor. When they reached the trail leading up into the forest, the trail that Corrie had taken, Sarina claimed to have discovered the spoor and led them on down the valley. Thus again the kindness of her dead father and mother intervened to save the girl.

Tarzan, Jerry, and the others marched rapidly to the abandoned camp of the outlaws. Tarzan examined the spoor that had confused and deceived his companions; then he led them out along the trail that the outlaws had taken. The others were dubious, but they followed.

'Them tracks is all pointin' toward the camp,' said Rosetti. 'We're goin' the wrong way, an' just wastin' time.'

'They tell me you're a great ball turret gunner, Shrimp,' said Tarzan; 'but you're a mighty poor tracker. The people we're after passed along this trail last night in the same direction that we're going.'

'Then they must o' came back again, Colonel. All these footprints is pointin' the other way.'

'The majority of them went in advance,' explained Tarzan; 'then three men and a woman walked backward behind them, obliterating the spoor of those who had gone ahead. About every hundred yards, three other men and a woman relieved the spoor obliterators; because it is tiresome walking backward.'

'I don't see how you tell that,' persisted Rosetti.

'When you walk forward your heels strike the ground first; then you push yourself forward with the balls of your feet, at the same time pushing the dirt back in the opposite direction. When you walk backward, the balls of your feet strike the ground first and you push yourself forward with your heels, still pushing the dirt in the direction opposite from that in which you are going. Examine the ground carefully, and you will see for yourself. If you follow the trail long enough, and are sufficiently observant, you will see that about every hundred yards there is a change in the sizes of the footprints, showing that new people took up the job.'

Not only Rosetti, but the others, fell to examining the spoor. 'Cripes, but we're dumb,' said Jerry.

'I should have knowed enough to keep my fool trap shut,' said Rosetti. 'The colonel ain't never wrong.'

'Don't get that idea,' said Tarzan. 'I don't want to try to live up to anything like that. But remember, about this tracking, that I've been doing it all my life, ever since I was a child, and that innumerable times my life has depended upon my knowing what I was doing. Now I am going on ahead. We don't want to run into that outfit without warning.'

An hour later the rest of the party emerged from the forest into the open valley and found Tarzan waiting for them. 'Your outlaws passed down the valley a short time ago,' he told them. 'I have also found Corrie's trail. She was hours ahead of them and alone. Evidently she managed to escape from them. I am pretty sure that they did not discover her spoor, as theirs is often yards to the right of hers and never touches it.

'There were a number of men and women in the party, several natives, and two Jap soldiers. At least two of the men were short legged and wore working tabi; so I assume they were Japs. I am going on ahead, following Corrie's trail. If she took the trail leading up into the forest, I'll cut a single blaze on a tree near the trail. If she kept on down the valley, I'll cut two blazes. If there are three, you will know that the outlaws took the same trail that Corrie took; otherwise, they took a different trail.' Tarzan turned then, and was off at the even trot that he could maintain for hours when he chose to keep to the ground, the gait for which Apache Indians are famous.

'I don't know what good we are,' said Bubonovitch. 'That guy doesn't need us.'

'He lets us come along for the ride,' said Jerry.

'I think we are just in his way,' remarked van der Bos; 'but he's mighty patient about it.'

'I'm goin' to practice swingin' t'rough de trees,' said Shrimp.

'And jumping down on tigers?' asked Bubonovitch.

As Corrie followed what was to her now the homeward trail, she was happy and lighthearted. She was returning to Tak and Jerry and Tarzan and Bubonovitch and The Little Sergeant, of whom she had finally become very fond. In fact, she was very fond of all of them. Of course, she had known Tak all her life; but it was as though she had known the others always, also. She decided that she loved them all. She could scarcely wait to see them all again and tell them of her adventures. She had a little score to settle, too – a little score to settle with Amat. But she quickly put that out of her mind. She wished to think only of pleasant things.

So she was thinking of pleasant things, one of which was Jerry, when she suddenly became conscious of something moving through the underbrush parallel with the trail. It was something large. Corrie had her rifle ready, her finger on the trigger, as she peered into the tangle of foliage. What she saw drove every pleasant thought from her mind – just a little glimpse of black and yellow stripes. A tiger was stalking her.

How utterly inadequate was the .25 caliber Jap rifle she was carrying! When she stopped, the tiger stopped. Now she could see his eyes – terrifying eyes – as he stood with lowered head returning her gaze. Would he attack? Why else would he be stalking her?

Corrie glanced about. Close beside her was a durian tree from which a stout liana depended. If the tiger charged, he would reach her before she could clamber out of danger. If she moved too quickly, he would charge. Any sudden movement on her part would doubtless mean as sudden death.

Very carefully, she leaned her rifle against the bole of the tree; then she grasped the liana. She watched the tiger. He had not moved. He still stood there watching her. Corrie drew herself up very slowly. Always she watched the tiger. The beast seemed fascinated. As she climbed, she saw his eyes following her. Suddenly he moved forward toward her.

Then Corrie scrambled upward as fast as she could go, and the tiger charged. But he was in an awkward position. He had to run half way around the tree and out into the trail before he could gather himself to spring up to seize her. He did spring, but he missed. And Corrie clawed her way upward to safety.

She sat there astride a limb, trembling, her heart pounding. And the tiger lay down in the trail at the foot of the tree. He was old and mangy. Because he was old, he had probably been unable to overhaul a meal for so long that he was reduced to hunting by day for anything that he might find. And having found something, he had evidently determined to wait right where he was until his prey either came down or fell out of the tree. Every once in a while he looked up at Corrie, bared his yellow fangs, and growled.

Corrie, though not given to any but the mildest of epithets, nevertheless swore at him. The creature had shattered her dream of getting back to her boys quickly. He just lay there, growling at her occasionally. An hour passed. Corrie was becoming frantic. Another hour, and still the stupid beast held tenaciously to his post. Corrie wondered which one of them would starve to death first.

Presently she was joined by some monkeys. They, too, scolded the tiger and probably swore at him in monkey language. Then Corrie had an idea. She knew that monkeys were imitative. She picked a durian fruit and threw it at the tiger. It struck him, much to Corrie's surprise, and elicited a savage growl. She threw another, and missed. Then the monkeys got the idea. Here was sport. They and Corrie bombarded the great cat with durian fruit. It rose, growling, and tried to leap into the tree; but it only fell back, lost its balance, and rolled over on its back. A durian struck it full on the nose. Durians rained upon it. Finally it gave up and went crashing off into the jungle. But for a long while Corrie did not dare leave her sanctuary. And she was a wary and frightened girl when she finally slipped down and retrieved her rifle.

Every little sound startled her now as she hurried along the trail toward the village, but finally she became convinced that she had seen the last of Stripes.

A huge creature bulked large and black in a tree beneath which Corrie passed. She did not see it. It moved silently above and behind her, watching her. It was Oju, the young orangutan which Tarzan had fought. Corrie's rifle kept him at a distance. Oju was afraid of the black sticks that made a loud noise. But he was patient. He could wait.

Presently other monstrous shapes appeared in the trees and in the trail in front of Corrie. She stopped. She had never seen so many orangutans together before. Corrie did not believe that they would harm her, but she was not certain. They grimaced at her, and some of them made threatening gestures, stamping on the ground and making little short rushes toward her. She kept her finger on the trigger of her rifle and backed away. She backed directly beneath Oju, who was now perched on a limb but a few feet above her head.

Ordinarily, the great apes avoid humans, going away when one appears. Corrie wondered why these did not go away. She thought that they would presently; so she waited, not daring to advance along the trail which some of them occupied. She thought that probably their numbers gave them courage to remain in the presence of a human being. It was not that, however. It was curiosity. They wanted to see what Oju was going to do. They did not have long to wait.

Oju looked down with bloodshot eyes, weighing the situation. He saw that this she Tarmangani's whole attention was held by the other apes. He dropped upon Corrie, hurling her to the ground; and at the same time he wrenched the rifle from her grasp. The girl's finger being on the trigger at the time, the weapon was discharged. That terrified Oju, and he swung into a tree and off into the forest. But, having a one track mind, he neglected to loosen his grasp about Corrie's body; so he took her with him.

The shot also frightened the other apes; and they, too, swung off into the forest, but not in the same direction that Oju had taken. Now, the trail was quiet and deserted; but Corrie was not there to take advantage of it. She was beating futilely with clenched fists on the monstrous, hairy body of her abductor. Eventually, this annoyed Oju; and he cuffed her on the side of the head. It was fortunate for Corrie that this was merely a gentle reminder that Oju objected to being beaten, even though the beating did not hurt him in the least; for it only rendered her unconscious, whereas, had Oju really exerted himself, she would doubtless have been killed.

When Corrie regained consciousness, which she did very quickly, she thought at first that she was experiencing a horrible nightmare; but that was only for a moment before the complete return of reason. Now she was indeed horrified. The great, hairy beast was hurrying through the trees, constantly looking back over its shoulder as though something were pursuing it.

Corrie was armed with both a pistol and a parang, but the orangutan held her so that one of his great arms was clamped over both of the weapons in such a way that she could withdraw neither of them. And the creature was carrying her deeper and deeper into the forest, and toward what horrible fate?

19

Jerry, Bubonovitch, Rosetti, and van der Bos followed the river down the valley until they came to the trail leading to the left out of the valley and into the forest at the summit of the cliff. Here they found a single blaze upon the bole of a tree and knew that Corrie had taken the trail back toward the village and that her erstwhile captors had not followed her.

When they reached the top of the cliff they heard, very faintly, a shot far ahead of them. Tarzan had carried no firearm, and they could not know that Corrie had been armed. The natural assumption was that she had not. The outlaws had not come this way, so none of them could have fired the shot. The natives had been warned not to touch the Jap weapons that the whites had hidden in their village, nor would they have dared so to arm themselves against the proscription of the Japs, of whom they stood in mortal terror.

The four men discussed these various conclusions as they pushed on along the trail. 'A Jap must have fired that shot,' said van der Bos. 'And where there is one Jap there are doubtless others.'

'Bring 'em on,' said Rosetti. 'I ain't killed no Jap for two days.'

'We'll have to be careful,' said Jerry. 'I'll go on ahead about a hundred yards. I'll fire at the first Jap I see, and then fall back. You fellows get into the underbrush on one side of the trail when you hear my shot and let 'em have it when you can't miss. Let 'em get close.'

'Geeze, Cap, you hadn't orter do that. Lemme do it,' said Rosetti.

'Or me,' said Bubonovitch. 'That's not your job, Captain.'

'Okay,' said Jerry. 'You go ahead, Shrimp, and keep your ears unbuttoned.'

'Why don't you swing through the trees?' inquired Bubonovitch. Shrimp grinned and ran ahead.

Tarzan had followed Corrie's trail for no great distance when he came to the spot at which she had been treed by the tiger. He read the whole story as clearly as he might have from a printed page. Even the scattered durians told him how the tiger had finally been driven off. He smiled and followed the now fresh trail that indicated that the girl had resumed her journey but a short time before. Then he heard a shot ahead.

He took to the trees now, and moved swiftly above the trail. Like the men following behind him, he thought that a Jap had fired the shot. He also thought that Corrie had doubtless fallen into the hands of a detail of Jap soldiers. And then he saw a rifle lying in the trail.

Tarzan was puzzled. The Japs would not have gone away and left a rifle behind them. Too, there was no odor of Japs; but the scent spoor of great apes was strong. He dropped into the trail. He saw that Corrie's spoor ended where the rifle lay. He saw what appeared to indicate that the girl had fallen or been thrown to the ground. He also saw the manlike imprints of the feet of a large orangutan superimposed upon those made by Corrie, but these imprints were only directly beneath the tree where Tarzan stood.

The implication was clear: an orangutan had dropped from the tree, seized Corrie, and carried her off. Tarzan swung into the tree and was off on the trail of Oju. The arboreal spoor was plain to his trained senses. A crushed beetle or caterpillar, the bark on a limb scuffed by a horny hand or foot, a bit of reddish brown hair caught by a twig, the scent spoor of both the ape and the girl which still hung, even though faintly, in the quiet air of the forest.

In a little natural clearing in the forest Tarzan overtook his quarry. Oju had been aware that he was being followed, and now he elected to stand and fight, if fighting were to be necessary, in this open space. He still clung to his prize, and it happened that he was holding Corrie in such a position that she could not see Tarzan.

She knew that Oju was facing an enemy, for he was growling savagely. And she heard his opponent growl in reply, but this sounded more like the growl of a lion. Of course there were no lions in Sumatra, but the voice was not the voice of a tiger. She wondered what manner of beast it might be.

The voice was coming closer. Suddenly the orangutan dropped her and lumbered forward. Corrie raised herself on her hands and looked back. And at that instant Tarzan closed with Oju. Corrie leaped to her feet and drew her pistol. But she dared not fire for fear of hitting Tarzan. The two were locked in an embrace of death. Oju was attempting to close his powerful jaws on the man's throat, and the man held the yellow fangs away with one mighty arm. Both were growling, but lower now. Corrie was suddenly conscious of the feeling that she was watching two beasts fighting to the death – and for her.

Tarzan was holding Oju's jaws from his throat with his right arm. His left was pinned to his side by one of the ape's. Tarzan was straining to release himself from this hold. Inch by inch he was dragging his left arm free. Inch by inch Oju was forcing his fangs closer and closer to the man's throat.

Corrie was horrified. She circled the struggling combatants, trying to get a shot at the orangutan; but they were moving too rapidly. She might as easily have hit Tarzan as his opponent.

The two were still on their feet, pulling and straining. Suddenly Tarzan locked one leg around those of the ape and surged heavily against him. Oju fell backward, Tarzan on top of him. In trying to save himself, the ape had released his hold on the man's left arm. Then Corrie saw a knife flash, saw it driven into the ape's breast, heard his screams of pain and rage. Again and again the knife was driven home. The screaming waned, the great body quivered and lay still. Oju was dead.

Tarzan rose and placed a foot upon the body of his foe. He raised his face toward the heavens – and then, suddenly, he smiled. The victory cry of the bull ape died in his throat. Why he did not voice it, he himself did not know.

Corrie felt very limp. Her legs refused to hold her, and she sat down. She just looked at Tarzan and shook her head. 'All in?' he asked. Corrie nodded. 'Well, your troubles are over for today at least, I hope. Jerry, van der Bos, and the sergeants are coming along the trail. We'd better get over there and meet them.' He swung her across his shoulder and swung back along the leafy way that the ape had brought her, but how different were her feelings now!

When they reached the trail, Tarzan examined it and found that the others had not yet passed; so they sat down beside it and waited. They did not talk. The man realized that the girl had undergone terrific shock, and so he left her alone and did not question her. He wanted her to rest.

But finally Corrie broke the silence herself. 'I am an awful fool,' she said. 'I have had to exert all the willpower I possess to keep from crying. I thought death was so near, and then you came. It was just as though you had materialized out of thin air. I suppose that it was the reaction that nearly broke me down. But how in the world did you know where I was? How could you have known what had happened to me?'

'Stories are not written in books alone,' he said. 'It was not difficult.' Then he told her just how he had trailed her. 'I had an encounter with that same ape a few days ago. I got the better of him then, but I refrained from killing him. I wish now that I had not. His name was Oju.'

'You never said anything about that,' she said.

'It was of no importance.'

'You are a very strange man.'

'I am more beast than man, Corrie.'

She knitted her brows and shook her head. 'You are very far from being a beast.'

'You mean that for a compliment. That is because you don't know the beasts very well. They have many fine qualities that men would do well to emulate. They have no vices. It was left for man to have those as well as many disagreeable and criminal characteristics that the beasts do not have. When I said that I was more beast than man, I didn't mean that I possessed all their noble qualities. I simply meant that I thought and reacted more like a beast than a man. I have the psychology of a wild beast.'

'Well, you may be right; but if I were going out to dinner, I'd rather go with a man than a tiger.'

Tarzan smiled. 'That is one of the nice things about being a beast. You don't have to go to dinners and listen to speeches and be bored to death.'

Corrie laughed. 'But one of your fellow beasts may leap on you and take you for his dinner.'

'Or a nice man may come along and shoot you, just for fun.'

'You win,' said Corrie.

'The others are coming,' said Tarzan.

'How do you know?'

'Usha tells me.'

'Usha? Who is Usha?'

'The wind. It carries to both my ears and my nostrils evidence that men are coming along the trail. Each race has its distinctive body odor; so I know these are white men.'

A moment later, Rosetti came into view around a curve in the trail. When he saw Tarzan and Corrie he voiced a whoop of pleasure and shouted the word back to those behind him. Soon the others joined them. It was a happy reunion.

'Just like old home week,' observed Bubonovitch.

'It seems as though you had been gone for weeks, Corrie,' said Jerry.

'I went a long way into the Valley of the Shadow,' said Corrie. 'I thought that I should never see any of you again in this world. Then Tarzan came.'

Tak van der Bos came and kissed her. 'If my hair hasn't turned white since you disappeared, then worry doesn't turn hair white. Don't you ever get out of our sight again, darling.'

Jerry wished that he didn't like van der Bos. He would greatly have enjoyed hating him. Then he thought: *You are an idiot, Lucas. You haven't a ghost of a show anyway, and those two were made for each other. They are both swell.* So Jerry lagged along behind and left them together as they resumed the march toward the village.

Tarzan had gone ahead to act as point. The others listened as Corrie recounted her adventures, telling of Amat's treachery, of Sarina's unexpected help, of her horrifying experience with Oju, and of her rescue by Tarzan.

'He is magnificent,' she said. 'In battle he is terrifying. He seems to become a wild beast, with the strength and agility of a tiger guided by the intelligence of a man. He growls like a beast. I was almost afraid of him. But when the fight was over and he smiled he was all human again.'

'He has added one more debt which we owe him and can never repay,' said Jerry.

'Dat guy's sure some guy,' said Rosetti, 'even if he is a Britisher. I bet he didn't have nuttin' to do wit dat Geo'ge Toid.'

'That's a safe bet, Shrimp,' said Bubonovitch. 'You can also lay 100 to 1 that he didn't run around with Caligula either.'

Tak van der Bos found these Americans amusing. He liked them, but often he could not make head nor tail of what they were talking about.

'Who was Geo'ge Toid?' he asked.

'He is dat King of England wot Mayor Thompson said he would poke in de snoot if he ever came to Chicago,' explained Rosetti.

'You mean George Third?'

'Dat's who I said – Geo'ge Toid.'

'Oh,' said van der Bos. Bubonovitch was watching him, and noticed that he did not smile. He liked him for that. Bubonovitch could rib Shrimp, but he wouldn't stand for any foreigner ribbing him.

'This lame brain,' he said, jerking a thumb in Rosetti's direction, 'doesn't know that the War of the Revolution is over.'

'You disliked Englishmen because of what George Third did?' Tak asked Shrimp.

'You said it.'

'Maybe you won't think so badly of Englishmen if you'll just remember that George Third was not an Englishman.'

'Wot?'

'He was a German.'

'No kiddin'?'

'No kidding. Many of the Englishmen of his day didn't like him any more than you do.'

'So de guy was a Heinie! Dat explains everyt'ing.' Shrimp was satisfied now. He could like Tarzan and not be ashamed of it.

Presently they caught up with Tarzan. He was talking to two bearded white men. They were sentries posted by the guerrillas who had occupied the village. The two other trails were similarly guarded.

Within a few minutes the returning party had entered the kampong; and as they did so, Amat departed into the forest on the opposite side of the village. He had caught a glimpse of Rosetti.

20

Capt. van Prins and Lieut. de Lettenhove, as well as several others of the guerrilla force, knew both Corrie and Tak, whom they had believed to be dead. They gathered around them, laughing and talking, congratulating them and exchanging snatches of their various experiences during the more than two years since they had seen one another. Corrie and Tak asked of news of old friends. Some were known to be dead, others had been prisoners of the Japs when last heard of. They spoke in their own tongue.

Jerry, feeling very much an outsider, sought Bubonovitch and Rosetti. They sat together beneath a tree and cleaned their rifles and pistols, for since they had captured the equipment of the Japs they had all that was necessary to keep their weapons cleaned and oiled, an endless procedure in the humid equatorial atmosphere of the Sumatran mountains.

Presently van Prins and de Lettenhove joined them to discuss plans for the future. Corrie and Tak were sitting together in the shade of another tree at a little distance. Corrie had noticed that Jerry had been avoiding her of late; so she did not suggest joining the conference. She wondered if she had done anything to offend him, or if he were just tired of her company. She was piqued, and so she redoubled her attentions to Tak van der Bos. Jerry was keenly aware of this and was miserable. He took no part in the discussion that was going on. Both Bubonovitch and Rosetti noticed this and wondered at the change that had come over him.

The conference resulted in a decision that the two parties would join forces for the time being at least, but it was not thought wise to remain where they were. When the detail that was to have been relieved did not return to the base, there would be an investigation, unquestionably in force; and the Dutchmen did not wish to risk a major engagement. They had other plans for harassing the enemy.

It was therefore decided to move to an easily defended position of which they knew. This would mean back-tracking for Tarzan and the Americans, but van Prins assured them that in the end it would improve their chances of reaching the southwest coast.

'From where I plan on making camp,' he explained, 'there is a comparatively easy route over the summit. You can then move down the east side of the mountains where, I am informed, there are comparatively few Japs in the higher reaches, while on this side there are many. I will furnish you with a map and mark out a route that will bring you back to the west side at a point where I think you will find it much easier to reach the coast, if you decide to persist in what I believe a very foolhardy venture.'

'What do you think about it, Jerry?' asked Tarzan.

Jerry, awakened from a daydream, looked up blankly. 'Think about what?' he demanded.

Tarzan looked at him in surprise. Then he repeated the plan. 'Whatever suits the rest of you suits me,' said Jerry indifferently.

Bubonovitch and Rosetti looked at one another. 'Wot the hell's happened to the "old man"?' whispered the latter.

Bubonovitch shrugged and looked in the direction of Corrie and van der Bos. 'Cherchez la femme,' he said.

'Talk American,' said Rosetti.

'I think the captain is going to be a misogynist again pretty soon,' said Bubonovitch.

'I getcha. I guess maybe as how I'll be one of dem t'ings again myself. Trouble is a dame's middle name – trouble, trouble, nuttin' but trouble.'

'When do you plan on leaving?' Tarzan asked van Prins.

'I think we can remain here safely today and tomorrow. The Japs won't really commence to worry about that detail for several days, and then it will take them another day to reach this village. We can leave here day after tomorrow, early in the morning. That will give my men time to fix up their foot gear. I can't call the things we are wearing shoes. The chief here has plenty of material, and some of the women are helping us make sandals. We were just about barefoot when we got here. Even if the Japs do come, we shall be ready for them. Some of my men are cutting a trail from the village paralleling the main trail toward the Jap base. I'm having them run it out about five hundred yards. If the Japs come, we'll have a surprise for them.'

The conference broke up. Van Prins went out into the forest to see how his men were getting ahead with the trail. The other Dutchmen went to work on their sandals or cleaned their weapons. Corrie had been surreptitiously watching Jerry. She noticed how glum he looked and that he only spoke when directly addressed, and then curtly. Suddenly she thought that he might be ill. She had been angry with him, but that thought destroyed her anger and filled her with compassion. She walked over to where he was now sitting alone, reassembling the Jap pistol that he had stripped and cleaned. She sat down beside him.

'What's the matter, Jerry?' she asked. 'You're not ill, are you?'

'No,' he said. He had worked himself into such a state of utter misery that he couldn't even be civil.

Corrie looked at him in surprise and hurt. He did not see the expression on her face; because he pretended to be engrossed with the pistol. He knew that he was being sophomoric and he hated himself. *What the hell is the matter with me?* he thought. Corrie arose slowly and walked away. Jerry thought about committing suicide. He was being an ass, and he knew it. But Jerry was very young and very much in love. He slammed the last piece of the pistol into place viciously and stood up.

Corrie was walking toward the little house she occupied with the native girl, Lara. Jerry walked quickly after her. He wanted to tell her how sorry he was. As she reached the foot of the ladder leading up into the house, he called to her: 'Corrie!' She did not pause nor look back. She climbed the ladder and disappeared through the doorway.

He knew that she had heard him. He also knew that Tarzan and Bubonovitch and Rosetti had witnessed the whole thing. But worst of all, so had Tak van der Bos. Jerry could feel his face burning. He stood there for a moment, not knowing what to do. *The hell with all women*, he thought. He had faced death many times, but to face his friends now was worse. It required all his willpower to turn around and walk back to them.

No one said anything as he sat down among them. They appeared wholly occupied by whatever they were doing. Tarzan broke the silence. 'I am going out to see if I can bring in some fresh meat,' he said. 'Anyone want to come with me?' It was the first time he had ever asked anyone to hunt with him. They all knew that he meant Jerry; so no one spoke, waiting for Jerry.

'Yes, I'd like to, if no one else wants to,' he said.

'Come along,' said Tarzan.

They picked up rifles and went out into the forest.

Bubonovitch and Rosetti were sitting a little apart from the Dutchmen. 'That was swell of Tarzan,' said the former. 'I sure felt sorry for Jerry. I wonder what's got into Corrie.'

'Oh, hell; they're all alike,' said Rosetti.

Bubonovitch shook his head. 'It wasn't like Corrie – she's different. Jerry must have said something. He's been as grouchy as a bear with a sore head.'

'It's dat Dutchman,' said Rosetti. 'He and Corrie are just like dat.' He crossed a middle finger over an index finger. 'An' I tought all de time she was fallin' for de Cap'n. I told you w'en we foist picked up dat dame dat it meant trouble.'

'You sort of fell for her yourself, Shrimp.'

'I liked her all right. Maybe she ain't done nuttin'. Maybe de Cap'n's de wrong guy. Dey don't have to do nuttin'. Just bein' a dame spells trouble. Geeze! I t'ink w'en I gets back to Chi I'll join a convent.'

Bubonovitch grinned. 'That would be just the place for you, Shrimp – a nice convent without any women. If you can't find one in Chicago, you might try Hollywood. Anything that's screwy, Hollywood's got.'

Shrimp knew that Bubonovitch was ribbing him, but he didn't know just how. 'Yes, Sir! I fink I'll be a monk.'

'The correlative wisecrack is too obvious.'

'Talk American, Perfessor.'

Tarzan and Jerry were gone a little more than an hour. They returned to the village with the carcass of a deer. Tarzan had shot it. Jerry was glad that he had not had to. Of course it was all right to kill for food, but still he didn't like to kill deer. He didn't mind killing Japs. That was different. The way he felt this afternoon, he would have enjoyed killing almost anything. But he was still glad that he hadn't killed the deer.

That evening, Corrie ate apart with the Dutchmen. She shouldn't have done it, and she knew that she shouldn't. She should have carried on just as though nothing had happened. Afterward she wished that she had, for she realized that now she had definitely acknowledged the rift. It would be difficult to close it again. It would probably widen. She was most unhappy; because she loved those men with whom she had been through so much – to whom she owed so much. She was sorry now that she hadn't waited when Jerry had called to her.

She made up her mind to swallow her pride and go over to them; but when she did so, Jerry got up and walked away. So she passed them and went to her house. There she threw herself down on her sleeping mats and cried. For the first time in years, she cried.

The day was drawing to a close and Amat was very tired when he reached the Jap base. He bowed low to the sentry who halted him, and in the few Japanese words he had learned he tried to explain that he had important news for the commanding officer.

The sentry called a non-commissioned officer of the guard who happened to have learned a smattering of the native dialect; and to him Amat repeated what he had told the sentry, almost forgetting to bow. So he bowed twice.

The sergeant took him to the adjutant, to whom Amat bowed three times. When the sergeant had reported, the adjutant questioned Amat, and what Amat told him excited him greatly. He lost no time in conducting Amat to the commanding officer, a Col. Kanji Tajiri, to whom Amat bowed four times.

When the colonel learned that some forty of his men had been killed, he was furious. Amat also told him just how many white men there were in the party in his village. He told about the sentries out on the trails. He told about the white girl. He told everything.

Tajiri gave orders that Amat should be fed and given a place to sleep. He also directed that two full companies should march at dawn to attack the village and destroy the white men. He himself would go in command, and they would take Amat along. If Amat had known this, he would not have slept so easily as he did.

21

At breakfast the following morning, the cleavage was again definitely apparent. The Dutch prepared and ate their breakfast a little apart from the Americans and Tarzan. The Englishman knew that it was all very wrong and very stupid and that if the condition persisted it would affect the morale of the entire company. At the same time, however, he could not but be amused; for it was so obvious that the two principals who were responsible were very much in love with each other. They were probably the only ones who did not realize this. He knew that they must be in love; because it is only people who are very much in love who treat each other so damnably.

After they had eaten, Tarzan and the Americans went into the forest to inspect the trail the Dutchmen had cut. They found that it gave excellent concealment from the main trail, but Tarzan thought that the sentry post was not far enough in advance of the trail's outer end.

Capt. van Prins had posted four men on this post with orders to hold up the Japs as long as possible should they come, falling back slowly to give the main force of the guerrillas time to come from the village and prepare the ambush.

'I think he should have had one man very much farther in advance,' Tarzan said to Jerry, 'and at least half his force posted constantly in this paralleling trail. He is not prepared for a surprise, and he is not giving the Japs credit for the cunning they possess.'

'They'll have a man way out in front,' said Jerry. 'He'll be well camouflaged, and he'll sneak through the jungle like a snake. He'll see the guys on this post and then go back and report. Pretty soon some more will sneak up and toss a few grenades. That'll be the end of the sentries, and the Japs will rush the village before van Prins can get his men out here to ambush them.'

'Let's go back and talk with him,' suggested Tarzan.

Shortly after breakfast, Lara had sought out Corrie. 'I have just discovered,' she said, 'that Amat did not return to the village last night. He left yesterday. I know him. He is a bad man. I am sure that he went to the big Japanese camp and reported everything that has happened here.'

Corrie was repeating this to van Prins when Tarzan and Jerry returned. The Dutchman called them over; and as they came, Corrie walked away. Van Prins told them of Lara's warning, and Tarzan suggested the plan that he and Jerry had discussed.

'I think I'll put most of my force out there,' said van Prins. 'I'll just leave a welcoming committee here in case some of them break through to the village.'

'It might be a good idea to withdraw your sentries entirely,' suggested Jerry. 'Then the Japs will walk right into the ambush without any warning.'

'I don't know about that,' said van Prins. 'I'd like a little advance information myself, or we might be the ones who would be surprised.'

Tarzan didn't agree with him, but he said, 'I'll get advance information to you much sooner than your sentries could. I'll go out four or five miles, and when the Japs show up I'll be back with the word long before they reach your ambush.'

'But suppose they see you?'

'They won't.'

'You seem pretty sure of yourself, Sir,' said the Dutchman, smiling.

'I am.'

'I'll tell you what we'll do,' said van Prins. 'Just to make assurance doubly sure, I'll leave my sentries out. I'll tell them that when you come back, you'll order them in. How's that?'

'Fine,' said Tarzan. 'I'll go along out now, and you can get your men camouflaged and posted for the ambush. O.K.?'

'O.K.,' said van Prins.

Tarzan swung into a tree and was gone. The Dutchman shook his head. 'If I had a battalion like him, I could pretty near chase the Japs off this island.'

Jerry, Bubonovitch, and Rosetti, loaded down with ammunition and hand grenades, preceded the guerrillas into the ambush. They went to the far end of the paralleling trail and prepared to make themselves comfortable and also inconspicuous. With leaves and vines they camouflaged their heads and shoulders until they became a part of the surrounding jungle. Even had there not been several feet of shrubbery intervening between them and the main trail, an enemy would have had to be right on top of them before he could have discovered them.

The guerrillas were soon stationed and busy camouflaging themselves. Capt. van Prins walked back and forth along the main trail checking on the effectiveness of each man's camouflage. Finally he gave his orders.

'Don't fire until I fire, unless you are discovered; then start firing. A couple of men at the head of the line can use grenades if they can throw them far enough so as not to endanger our own people. The same goes for a couple at the opposite end, in case some of the Japs get past us. Try to get the Japs directly in front of you. If everything works out as I hope, each one of you will have Japs in front of him when I give the signal to commence firing. Any questions?'

'If they retreat, shall we follow them?' asked one of the men.

'No. We might run into an ambush ourselves. All I want to do is give them a little punishment and put the fear of God in them for Dutchmen.' He came and took up a position about the center of the line.

Jerry presently discovered that van der Bos was next to him in line. Tak had had a little talk with Corrie shortly before. 'What's the matter between you and Jerry?' he had asked.

'I didn't know there was anything the matter.'

'Oh, yes you do. What's wrong with him?'

'I'm not interested in what's wrong with him. I'm not interested in him at all. He's a boor, and I'm not interested in boors.'

But Tak knew that she was interested, and he suddenly conceived an idea of what the trouble was. It came to him in a flash and made him voice a little whistle of amazement.

'What are you whistling about?' Corrie had asked.

'I whistle in amazement that there are so many damn fools in the world.'

'Meaning me?'

'Meaning you and Jerry and myself.'

'Whistle if you like, but mind your own business.'

Tak chucked her under the chin and grinned; then he went out with van Prins into the forest.

Jerry was not particularly pleased to have van der Bos next to him. Of all the people he could think of van der Bos was the one he was least desirous of being chummy with. He hoped the fellow wouldn't try to start a conversation.

'Well, I guess we're in for a long wait,' said van der Bos.

Jerry grunted.

'And no smoking,' added van der Bos.

Jerry grunted again.

As Jerry was not looking at him, van der Bos allowed himself the luxury of a grin. 'Corrie wanted to come out and get into the fight,' he said; 'but van Prins and I turned thumbs down on that idea.'

'Quite right,' said Jerry.

'Corrie's a great little girl,' continued van der Bos. 'We've known each other all our lives. She and my wife have been chums ever since either of them can remember. Corrie's exactly like a sister to us.'

There was a silence. Van der Bos was enjoying himself greatly. Jerry was not. Finally he said, 'I didn't know you were married.'

'That only just occurred to me a few minutes ago,' said van der Bos.

Jerry held out his hand. 'Thanks,' he said. 'I am a goddam fool.'

'Quite right,' said van der Bos.

'Did your wife get away?'

'Yes. We tried to get old van der Meer to send Corrie and her mother out, too; but the stubborn old fool wouldn't. God! And what a price he paid. That man's stubbornness was notorious all over the island. He gloried in it. Aside from that, he was a very fine person.'

'Do you suppose that Corrie has inherited any of her father's stubbornness?' asked Jerry, fearfully.

'I shouldn't be surprised.' Van der Bos was having the time of his life. He liked this American, but he felt that he had a little punishment coming to him.

Bubonovitch and Rosetti noticed with growing wonder the cordiality that existed between Jerry and van der Bos. As the day wore on, they also noticed that 'the old man' was becoming more and more like his former self.

They commented on this. 'He's gettin' almost human again,' whispered Rosetti. 'Whatever was eatin' him must o' quit.'

'Probably died of indigestion,' said Bubonovitch. 'We've known "the old man" a long while, but we've never seen him like he's been the last day or so.'

'We never seen him wit a dame around. I'm tellin' you—'

'You needn't tell me. I know it all by heart. Dames are bad medicine. They spell nothing but trouble. You give me a pain in the neck. The trouble with you is that you never knew a decent girl. At least not till you met Corrie. And you haven't met my wife. You'd sing a different tune if you fell in love with some girl. And when you do, I'll bet you fall heavy. Your kind always does.'

'Not a chance. I wouldn't have Dorothy Lamour if she got down on her knees and asked me.'

'She won't,' said Bubonovitch.

This edifying conversation was interrupted by the return of Tarzan. He sought out van Prins. 'Your little brown cousins are coming,' he said. 'They are about two miles away. There are two full companies, I should judge. They have light machine guns and those dinky little mortars they use. A colonel is in command. They have a point of three men out only about a hundred yards. Your sentries are coming in.'

'You have certainly done a swell job, Sir,' said van Prins. 'I can't thank you enough.' He turned to the men nearest him. 'Pass the word along that there is to be no more talking. The enemy will be along in thirty-five or forty minutes.' He turned back to Tarzan. 'Pardon me, Sir,' he said; 'but they are not brown. The bastards are yellow.'

Groen de Lettenhove had been left in command of the guerrillas who had been ordered to remain in the village. He was trying to persuade Corrie to find a place of safety against the possibility that some of the enemy might break through into the village.

'You may need every rifle you can get,' she countered; 'and furthermore, I haven't settled my account with the Japs.'

'But you might get killed or wounded, Corrie.'

'So might you and your men. Maybe we'd all better go and hide.'

'You're hopeless,' he said. 'I might have known better than argue with a woman.'

'Don't think of me as a woman. I'm another rifle, and I'm a veteran. I'm also a darned good shot.'

Their conversation was interrupted by a burst of rifle fire from the forest.

22

Jerry was the first to see the approaching Japs, as he happened to be in a position that gave him a view of about a hundred feet of the trail just where it curved to the right toward the village directly in front of him. It was the three man point. They were advancing cautiously, watching the trail ahead of them. They were evidently so sure that their attack would be a surprise that they did not even consider the possibility of an ambush. They paid no attention to the jungle on either side of the trail. They passed the men lying in wait for the main body and stopped at the edge of the forest. The village lay below them. It appeared deserted. The guerrillas, concealed in and behind houses, saw them and waited.

Presently, Jerry saw the main body approaching. The colonel marched at the head of the column with drawn samurai sword. Behind him slogged Amat, and behind Amat a soldier walked with the tip of his bayonet aimed at a Sumatran kidney. Evidently, Amat had attempted to desert somewhere along the route. He did not appear happy. Shrimp saw him pass, and mentally cautioned his trigger finger to behave.

The trail was crowded with the men of the first company. They had closed up into a compact mass when the head of the column was halted behind the point at the edge of the forest. Then van Prins fired, and instantly a withering volley was poured into the ranks of the surprised enemy. Jerry hurled three grenades in quick succession down the back trail into the second company.

The Japs fired wildly into the jungle; then some who had not been hit turned and broke in retreat. A few leaped into the undergrowth with fixed bayonets in an effort to get into close quarters with the white men. Shrimp was enjoying a field day. He picked off Japs as fast as he could fire, until his rifle got so hot that it jammed.

Among those in the mad rush to escape were the colonel and Amat. Miraculously they had so far escaped unscathed. The colonel was shrieking in Japanese, which Amat could not understand; but he had glanced behind him, and was aware that the colonel had lethal designs upon him. As he fled, Amat screamed. He would have been deeply hurt had he known that the colonel was accusing him of having traitorously led them into ambush, and that it was for this reason that he wished to kill Amat.

Rosetti saw them just before they came abreast of him. 'Nothing doing, yellow belly,' he yelled. 'That guy is my meat. They don't nobody else kill him if I can help it.' Then he shot the colonel with his pistol. He took another shot at Amat and missed. 'Doggone!' said Rosetti, as the terrified native dove into the underbrush farther along the trail.

Wholly disorganized, the remainder of the Jap force fled back into the forest, leaving their dead and wounded. Van Prins detailed a number of men to act as rear guard, others to collect the enemy's weapons and ammunition, and the remainder to carry the Jap wounded and their own into the village.

A moment later, a wounded Jap shot the Dutchman who was trying to help him. Shortly thereafter there were no wounded Japs.

Bubonovitch and Rosetti, who had jumped out into the trail to fire on the fleeing enemy, were helping gather up the abandoned Jap weapons and ammunition. Suddenly, Rosetti stopped and looked around. 'Where's the Cap'n?' he asked.

Jerry was nowhere in sight. The two men forced their way back into the underbrush where they had last seen him. They found him there, lying on his back, his shirt, over his left breast, blood soaked. Both men dropped to their knees beside him.

'He ain't dead,' said Rosetti. 'He's breathing.'

'He mustn't die,' said Bubonovitch.

'You said a mouthful, soldier,' said Rosetti.

Very tenderly, they picked him up and started back toward the village. The Dutchmen were carrying in three of their own dead and five wounded.

Tarzan saw the two sergeants carrying Jerry. He came and looked at the unconscious man. 'Bad?' he asked.

'I'm afraid so, Sir,' said Bubonovitch. They passed on, leaving Tarzan behind.

As the men entered the village with their pathetic burdens, those who had been left behind came to meet them. The dead were laid in a row and covered with sleeping mats. The wounded were placed in the shade of trees. Among the guerrillas was a doctor. He had no medicines, no sulfanilamide, no anaesthetics. He just did the best he could, and Corrie helped him. At the edge of the jungle, men were already digging the graves for the three dead. Native women were boiling water in which to sterilize bandages.

Bubonovitch and Rosetti were sitting beside Jerry when the doctor and Corrie finally reached him. When Corrie saw who it was, she went white and caught her breath in a sudden gasp. Both Bubonovitch and Rosetti were watching her. Her reaction told them more than any words could have; because words are sometimes spoken to deceive.

With the help of the two sergeants and Corrie, each trying to do something for the man they all loved, the doctor removed Jerry's shirt and examined the wound carefully.

'Is it very bad?' asked Corrie.

'I don't think so,' replied the doctor. 'It certainly missed his heart, and I'm sure it missed his lungs, also. He hasn't brought up any blood, has he, sergeant?'

'No,' said Bubonovitch.

'He's suffering mostly from shock and partly from loss of blood. I think he's going to be all right. Help me turn him over – very gently, now.'

There was a small round hole in Jerry's back just to the right of his left shoulder blade. It had not bled much.

'He must have been born under a lucky star,' said the doctor. 'We won't have to probe, and that's a good thing; because I have no instruments. The bullet bored straight through, clean as a whistle.' He washed the wounds with sterile water, and bandaged them loosely. 'That's all I can do,' he said. 'One of you stay with him. When he comes to, keep him quiet.'

'I'll stay,' said Corrie.

'You men can help me over here, if you will,' said the doctor.

'If you need us, Miss, just holler,' said Rosetti.

Corrie sat beside the wounded man and bathed his face with cool water. She didn't know what else to do, but she knew she wanted to do something for him. Whatever mild rancor she had thought that she felt toward him had been expunged by the sight of his blood and his helplessness.

Presently he sighed and opened his eyes. He blinked them a few times, an expression of incredulity in them, as he saw the girl's face close above his. Then he smiled; and reaching up, he pressed her hand.

'You're going to be all right, Jerry,' she said.

'I am all right – now,' he said.

He had held her hand for but a second. Now she took his and stroked it. They just smiled at each other. All was right with the world.

Capt. van Prins was having litters built for the wounded. He came over to see Jerry. 'How you feeling?' he asked.

'Fine.'

'Good. I've decided to move out of here just as soon as possible. The Japs are almost sure to sneak back on us tonight, and this is no place to defend successfully. I know a place that is. We can make it in two marches. As soon as the litters are finished and our dead buried, we'll move out of here. I'm going to burn the village as a lesson to the natives. These people have been collaborating with the enemy. They must be punished.'

'Oh, no!' cried Corrie. 'That would be most unfair. You would be punishing the innocent with the guilty. Take Lara, for instance. She has helped us twice. She has told me that there are only two people here who wanted to help the Japs – the chief and Amat. It would be cruel to burn down the homes of those who are loyal. Remember – if it had not been for Lara, the Japs might have taken us by surprise.'

'I guess that you are right, Corrie,' said van Prins. 'Anyway, you've given me a better idea.'

He walked away, and ten minutes later the chief was taken to one side of the village and shot by a firing squad.

The guerrillas gathered around the graves of their dead. The doctor said a short prayer, three volleys were fired, and the graves were filled. The wounded were lifted onto the litters, the rear guard marched into the village, the little company was ready to move.

Jerry objected to being carried, insisting that he could walk. Bubonovitch, Rosetti, and Corrie were trying to dissuade him when the doctor walked up. 'What's going on here?' he asked. They told him. 'You stay on that litter young man,' he said to Jerry, and to Bubonovitch and Rosetti, 'If he tries to get off of it, tie him down.'

Jerry grinned. 'I'll be good, Doc,' he said, 'but I hate to have four men carrying me when I can walk just as well as not.'

Following the shooting of the chief, the natives were afraid. They did not know how many more might be shot. Lara came to Corrie just as van Prins came along. He recognized the girl.

'You can tell your people,' he said, 'that largely because of you and the help you gave us we did not burn the village as we intended. We punished only the chief. He had been helping our enemies. When we come back, if Amat is here we will punish him also. The rest of you need never fear us if you do not help the enemy. We know that you have to treat them well, or be mistreated. We understand that, but do not help them any more than is absolutely necessary.' He took a quick look around the kampong. 'Where is Tarzan?' he asked.

'That's right,' said Bubonovitch. 'Where is he?'

'Geeze,' said Rosetti. 'He never come back to the village after the scrap. But he wasn't wounded. He was all right when we seen him last, just before we brung the Cap'n out.'

'Don't worry about him,' said Bubonovitch. 'He can take care of himself and all the rest of us into the bargain.'

'I can leave some men here to tell him where we are going to camp,' said van Prins.

'You don't even have to do that,' said Bubonovitch. 'He'll find us. Lara can tell him which way we went out. He'll track us better than a bloodhound.'

'All right,' said van Prins, 'let's get going.'

When Tarzan had looked at the wounded American, the latter had seemed in a very bad way. Tarzan was sure the wound was fatal. His anger against the Japs flared, for he liked this young flier. Unnoticed by the others, he swung into the trees and was off on the trail of the enemy.

He caught up with them at a point where a captain and two lieutenants had rallied them – the only surviving officers of the two companies. High in the trees above them, a grim figure looked down upon them. It fitted an arrow to its bow. The twang of the bow string was drowned by the jabbering of the monkey-men, the shouted commands of their officers. The captain lurched forward upon his face, a bamboo shaft through his heart. As he fell upon it, the arrow was driven through his body, so that it protruded from his back.

For a moment the Japs were stunned to silence; then the shouting commenced again, as they fired into the jungle in all directions with rifles and machine guns. Seventy-five feet above their bullets, Tarzan watched them, another bolt already to be shot.

This time he picked out one of the lieutenants. As he loosed the missile, he moved quietly to another position several hundred feet away. As their second officer fell, struck down mysteriously, the Japs commenced to show signs of panic. Now they fired wildly into the underbrush and into the trees.

When the last officer went down the Japs began to run along the trail in the direction of their main camp. They had had enough. But Tarzan had not. He followed them until all his arrows were gone, each one imbedded in the body of a Jap. The screaming wounded were tearing arrows from backs and bellies. The silent dead were left behind for the tigers and the wild dogs.

Tarzan unslung the rifle from across his back and emptied a clip into the broken ranks of the fleeing enemy; then he turned and swung back in the direction of the village. His American friend had been avenged.

He did not follow the trail. He did not even travel in the direction of the village for long. He ranged deep into the primeval forest, viewing ancient things that perhaps no other human eye had ever looked upon – patriarchs of the forest, moss covered and hoary with age, clothed in giant creepers, vines, and huge air plants, garlanded with orchids.

As the wind changed and a vagrant breeze blew into his face, he caught the scent of man. And presently he saw a little trail, such as men make. Dropping lower, he saw a snare, such as primitive hunters set for small game. He had come into the forest to be alone and get away from men. He was not anti-social; but occasionally he longed for solitude, or the restful companionship of beasts. Even the jabbering, scolding monkeys were often a welcome relief, for they were amusing. Few men were.

There were many monkeys here. They ran away from him at first, but when he spoke to them in their own language, they took courage and came closer. He even coaxed one little fellow to come and perch on his hand. It reminded him of little Nkima, boastful, belligerent, diminutive, arrant little coward, which loved Tarzan and which Tarzan loved. Africa! How far, far away it seemed.

He talked to the little monkey as he had talked to Nkima, and presently the little fellow's courage increased, and he leaped to Tarzan's shoulder. Like Nkima, he seemed to sense safety there; and there he rode as Tarzan swung through the trees.

The man's curiosity had been aroused by the strange scent spoor, and so he followed it. It led him to a small lake in the waters of which, along the shore, were a number of rude shelters built of branches and leaves upon platforms that were supported a few feet above the water by crude piling that had been driven into the mud of the lake's bottom.

The shelters were open on all sides. Their occupants were a people below average height, their skins a rich olive brown, their hair jet black. They were naked savages whom civilization had never touched. Fortunate people, thought Tarzan. Several men and women were in the water fishing with nets. The men carried bows and arrows.

The little monkey said that they were bad Gomangani. 'So manu,' he said – *eat monkey*. Then he commenced to scream at them and scold, feeling secure in doing so by virtue of distance and the presence of his big new friend. Tarzan smiled, it reminded him so much of Nkima.

The monkey made so much noise that some of the natives looked up. Tarzan made the universal sign of peace that has been debauched and befouled by a schizophrenic in a greasy raincoat, but the natives threatened him with their arrows. They jabbered and gesticulated at him, doubtless warning him away. The Lord of the Jungle was in full sympathy with them and admired their good judgment. Were they always successful in keeping white men at a distance they would continue to enjoy the peace and security of their idyllic existence.

He watched them for a few minutes, and then turned back into the forest to wander aimlessly, enjoying this brief interlude in the grim business of war. Keta, the little monkey, rode sometimes on the man's shoulder. Sometimes he swung through the trees with him. He seemed to have attached himself permanently to the big Tarmangani.

23

S/Sgt. Tony Rosetti squatted on the sentry platform on the trail outside the former camp of the outlaws where the guerrillas were now bivouacked for a day to let their wounded rest.

His tour of duty was about completed, and he was waiting for his relief when he saw a figure approaching him along the trail. It was a slender, boyish figure; but even in the dim, cathedral light of the forest afternoon the sergeant realized that, notwithstanding the trousers, the rifle, the pistol, the parang, and the ammunition belt, it was no boy.

When the woman caught sight of Rosetti, she stopped. 'Halt!' commanded Rosetti, bringing his rifle to the ready.

'I am already halted,' said the woman in good English.

'Who are you and where do you think you're goin' wit all dat armor?'

'You must be the cute little sergeant Corrie van der Meer told me about – the one who hates women and speaks funny English.'

'I don't speak English. I speak American. And wot's funny about it? And who are you?'

'I am Sarina. I am looking for Corrie van der Meer.'

'Advance,' said Rosetti. Then he dropped down off the platform into the trail. He stood there with a finger on the trigger of his rifle and the point of his bayonet belly high. The woman came and stopped a few feet from him.

'I wish that you would aim that thing some other way,' she said.

'Nuttin' doin', sister. You belong to dat outlaw gang. How do I know you ain't just a front an' de rest of dem is trailin' behind you? If dey are, youse is goin' to get shot, sister.'

'I'm alone,' said Sarina.

'Maybe you are, an' maybe you ain't. Drop dat gun an' stick up your mitts. I'm goin' to frisk you.'

'Speak English, if you can,' said Sarina. 'I don't understand American. What are mitts, and what is frisk?'

'Put up your hands, an' I'll show you what friskin' is. An' make it snappy, sister.' Sarina hesitated. 'I ain't goin' to bite you,' said Rosetti; 'but I ain't goin' to take no chances, neither. W'en you've sloughed dat arsenal, I'll take you into camp as soon as my relief shows up.'

Sarina laid her rifle down and raised her hands. Shrimp made her face the other way; then, from behind, he took her pistol and parang. 'Okay,' he said. 'You can put 'em down now.' He put her weapons in a pile behind him. 'Now you know wot frisk means,' he said.

Sarina sat down beside the trail. 'You are a good soldier,' she said. 'I like good soldiers. And you *are* cute.'

Rosetti grinned. 'You ain't so bad yourself, sister.' Even a misogynist may have an eye for beauty. 'How come you're wanderin' around in de woods alone? – If you are alone.'

'I *am* alone. I quit those people. I want to be with Corrie van der Meer. She should have a woman with her. A woman gets very tired of seeing only men all the time. I shall look after her. She *is* here, isn't she?'

'Yep, she's in camp; but she don't need no dame to look after her. She's got four men dat have made a pretty good job of it so far.'

'I know,' said Sarina. 'She has told me, but she will be glad to have a woman with her.' After a silence, she said, 'Do you suppose that they will let me stay?'

'If Corrie says so, dey will. If you are really de dame dat broke her outta dat camp, we'll all be strong for you.'

'American is a strange language, but I think I know what you were trying to say: If I am really the woman who helped Corrie escape from Hooft, you will like me. Is that it?'

'Ain't dat wot I said?'

A man coming along the trail from the direction of the camp interrupted their conversation. He was a Dutchman coming to relieve Rosetti. He did not speak English. His expression showed his surprise when he saw Sarina, and he questioned Rosetti in Dutch.

'No soap, Dutchie,' said the American.

'He did not ask for soap,' explained Sarina. 'He asked about me.'

'You savvy his lingo?' asked Shrimp.

Sarina shook her head. 'Please try to speak English,' she said. 'I cannot understand you. What is "savvy his lingo"?'

'Do you talk Dutch?'

'Oh, yes.'

'Den wot did he say?'

'He asked about me.'

'Well tell him, and also tell him to bring in your armor w'en he comes off. I can't pack dat mess an' guard a prisoner all at de same time.'

Sarina smiled and translated. The man answered her in Dutch and nodded to Rosetti. 'Get goin',' said the sergeant to Sarina. He followed her along the trail into camp, and took her to Jerry, who was lying on a litter beneath a tree.

'Sergeant Rosetti reportin' wit a prisoner, Sir,' he said.

Corrie, who was sitting beside Jerry, looked up; and when she recognized Sarina, she sprang to her feet. 'Sarina!' she cried. 'What in the world are you doing here?'

'I came to be with you. Tell them to let me stay.' She spoke in Dutch, and Corrie translated to Jerry.

'As far as I am concerned she can stay if you want her to,' said Jerry; 'but I suppose that Capt. van Prins will have to decide. Take your prisoner and report to Capt. van Prins, sergeant.'

Rosetti, who recognized no higher authority than that of Jerry, showed his disgust; but he obeyed. 'Come along, sister,' he said to Sarina.

'All right, brother,' she replied; 'but you don't have to keep that bayonet in my back all the time. I know you are a good soldier, but you don't have to overdo it.' Corrie looked at her in surprise. This was the first intimation she had had that Sarina spoke English. And good English, too, she thought. She wondered where Sarina had learned it.

'Okay, sweetheart,' said Rosetti. 'I guess you won't try to make no break now.'

'I'll come along,' said Corrie. 'If I vouch for you, I am sure Capt. van Prins will let you remain with us.'

They found the captain, and he listened intently to all that Sarina and Corrie had to say. Then he asked, 'Why did you choose to join that outlaw band and stay with it?'

'It was either them or the Japs,' said Sarina. 'I have always intended to leave them and join a guerrilla company when I could find one. This is the first opportunity I have had.'

'If Miss van der Meer vouches for you and Capt. Lucas has no objection, you may remain.'

'Then that settles it,' said Corrie. 'Thanks, Kervyn.'

Rosetti no longer had a prisoner, but he walked back with Corrie and Sarina to where Jerry lay. He pretended that he came to inquire about Jerry's wound, but he sat down and remained after Jerry had assured him that he was all right.

At a little distance from them, Bubonovitch was cleaning his rifle. He thought that Rosetti would soon join him, and then he could ask about the woman Shrimp had brought in. But Shrimp did not join him. He remained with Jerry and the two women. It was most unlike Shrimp, to choose the society of ladies when he could avoid it. Bubonovitch was puzzled; so he went over and joined the party.

Sarina was telling about her encounter with Rosetti. 'He told me to stick up my mitts, and said he was going to frisk me. American is a very funny language.'

Jerry was laughing. 'Rosetti doesn't speak American – just Chicagoese.'

'Where in the world did you learn to speak English, Sarina?' asked Corrie.

'In a Catholic missionary school in the Gilberts. My father always took my mother and me on all his cruises. Except for the two years I spent at the mission at Tarawa, I lived my entire life on board his schooner until I was twenty-nine. My mother died when I was still a little girl, but my father kept me with him. He was a very wicked man, but he was always kind to us. We cruised all over the South Seas, and about every two years we made the Gilberts, trading at different islands along the way, with piracy and murder as a side line.

'Father wanted me to have an education; so, when I was twelve, he left me at that mission school until his next trip two years later. I learned a great deal there. From my father, I learned Dutch. I think he was a well educated man. He had a library of very good books on his ship. He never told me anything about his past – not even his true name. Everybody called him Big Jon. He taught me navigation. From the time I was fourteen I was his first mate. It was not a nice job for a girl, as father's crews were usually made up of the lowest types of criminals. No one else would sail with him. I got a smattering of Japanese and Chinese from various crew members. We shipped all nationalities. Oftentimes father Shanghaied them. When father was drunk, I captained the ship. It was a tough job, and I had to be tough. I carried on with the help of a couple of pistols. I was never without them.'

Rosetti never took his eyes from Sarina. He seemed hypnotized by her. Bubonovitch watched him with something akin to amazement. However, he had to admit that Sarina was not hard on the eyes.

'Where is your father now?' asked Jerry.

'Probably in Hell. One of his murders finally caught up with him, and he was hanged. It was after he was arrested that Mr and Mrs van der Meer were so kind to me.'

The gathering broke up a moment later, when the doctor came to check on Jerry. Corrie and Sarina went to the shelter occupied by the former, and Bubonovitch and Rosetti went and sat down in front of theirs.

'Wot a dame!' exclaimed Rosetti.

'Who? Corrie?'

Shrimp shot a quick glance at Bubonovitch and caught the tail end of a fleeting smile. He guessed he was being ribbed.

'No,' he said. 'I was referrin' to Eleanor.'

'Did you by any chance notice that pistol packin' mamma with Corrie?' asked Bubonovitch. 'Now there is a cute little piece of femininity after my own heart. I sure fell for her.'

'You got a wife an' a kid,' Shrimp reminded him.

'My affection is merely platonic. I shouldn't care to have a lady pirate take me too seriously. I suppose that if any of her gentlemen friends annoyed her, she made them walk the plank.'

'Just think of dat little kid alone on a ship wit a lot of pirates an' her ol' man drunk!'

'I sort of got the impression that the little lady can take care of herself. Just take a slant at her background. You remember Corrie told us one of her grandfathers was a head hunter and the other was a cannibal, and now it develops that her father was a pirate and a murderer. And just to make the whole picture perfect Sarina was doing life in the clink for a little murder of her own.'

'Just the same she's awful pretty,' said Rosetti.

'Migawd!' exclaimed Bubonovitch. '*Et tu, Brute!*'

'I don't know wot you're talkin' about; but if you're crackin' wise about dat little dame – don't.'

'I was not cracking wise. I wouldn't think of offending your sensibilities for the world, Shrimp. I was merely recalling a statement you made quite recently. Let's see – how did it go? "I wouldn't have Dorothy Lamour if she got down on her knees and asked me!"'

'Well, I wouldn't. I wouldn't have none of 'em. But can't a guy say a dame's pretty widout you soundin' off?'

'Shrimpy, I saw you looking at her – goggle-eyed. I know the symptoms. You've gone plain ga-ga.'

'You're nuts.'

24

They broke camp the following morning and moved slowly, the wounded men still litter borne. Where the trail was wide enough, Corrie walked beside Jerry's litter. Sarina was behind her, and Rosetti walked with Sarina. Bubonovitch and several Dutchmen formed a rear guard. As none of the latter spoke English and Bubonovitch spoke no Dutch, the American had opportunity for meditation. Among other things, he meditated on the remarkable effect that some women had on some men. Reefers or snow made men goofy. Corrie and Sarina seemed to have a similar effect on Jerry and Rosetti. In Jerry's case it was not so remarkable. But Shrimp! Shrimp was a confirmed woman hater, yet all of a sudden he had gone overboard for a brown skinned Eurasian murderess old enough to be his mother.

Bubonovitch had to admit that Sarina was plenty good-looking. That was the hell of it. He was mighty fond of Rosetti, and so he hoped that the little sergeant didn't go too far. He didn't know much about women, and Sarina didn't seem exactly the safe type to learn from. Bubonovitch recalled a verse from Kipling;

She knifed me one night 'cause I wished she was white, An' I learned about women from 'er.

Bubonovitch sighed. After all, he thought, maybe Shrimp wasn't altogether wrong when he said, 'Dey don't have to do nuttin'. Just bein' a dame spells trouble.'

He abandoned this line of thought as unprofitable, and commenced to wonder about Tarzan. Jerry was wondering about him, too; and he voiced his misgivings to Corrie. 'I'm commencing to worry about Tarzan,' he said. 'He's been gone two days now, and shortly after he disappeared some of the men thought they heard firing far off in the forest from the direction in which the Japs retreated.'

'But what in he world would he be doing back there?' objected Corrie.

'He is not like other men; so it would be useless for one of us to try to imagine what might impel him to the commission of any act. At times, as you well know, he acts like a wild beast. So there must be stimuli which cause him to think and react like a wild beast. You know how he feels about taking life, yet you heard him say that it was his duty to kill Japs.'

'And you think he may have followed them in order to kill some more of them?' suggested Corrie.

'Yes, and maybe got killed himself.'

'Oh, no! That is too terrible, even to think.'

'I know, but it is possible. And if he doesn't show up, we'll have to carry on without him. Cripes! I haven't half realized how dependent we have been on him. We'd certainly have been on short rations most of the time if he hadn't been along to hunt for us.'

'I should long since have quit needing rations but for him,' said Corrie. 'I still see that tiger sometimes in my dreams. And Oju – ugh!'

They were silent for a while. Jerry lay with his eyes half closed. He was rolling his head slightly from side to side. 'Feeling all right?' Corrie asked.

'Yes – fine. I wonder how much farther it is to camp.'

'I think Kervyn plans on camping for the night about where the outlaws were camping when I escaped,' said Corrie. 'That is not far.' She noticed that Jerry's face was very red, and placed a hand on his forehead. She dropped back and whispered to Sarina, and word was passed down the line for the doctor. Then she returned to the side of Jerry's litter.

The American was muttering incoherently. She spoke to him, but he did not reply. He was turning restlessly, and she had to restrain him to prevent his rolling off the litter. She was terribly frightened.

She did not speak when Dr Reyd came up to the other side of the litter. Jerry's condition was too obvious to require explanation. Practically the only tool of his profession that Dr Reyd had salvaged was a clinical thermometer. When he read it two minutes later, he shook his head.

'Bad?' asked Corrie.

'Not too good. But I don't understand it. I expected him to run a little fever the night he was wounded, but he didn't. I thought he was pretty safe by now.'

'Will he—? Will he—?'

The doctor looked across the litter at her and smiled. 'Let's not worry until we have to,' he said. 'Millions of people have survived much worse wounds and higher temperatures.'

'But can't you *do* something for him?'

Reyd shrugged. 'I have nothing with which to do. Perhaps it is just as well. He is young, strong, in good condition, and physically as near perfect as a man can be. Nature is a damn good doctor, Corrie.'

'But you'll stay here with him, won't you, Doctor?'

'Certainly. And don't you worry.'

Jerry mumbled, 'Three Zeros at two o'clock,' and sat up.

Corrie and the doctor forced him back gently. Jerry opened his eyes and looked at Corrie. He smiled and said, 'Mabel.' After that he lay quietly for a while. Rosetti had come up and was walking beside the litter. He had seen that perhaps Corrie and the doctor might need help. His eyes reflected worry and fear.

Jerry said, 'Lucas to Melrose! Lucas to Melrose!'

Rosetti choked back a sob. Melrose had been the tail gunner who had been killed – and Jerry was talking to him! The implication terrified Rosetti, but he kept his head. 'Melrose to Lucas,' he said. 'All quiet on de western front, Cap'n.'

Jerry relaxed, and said, 'Roger.'

Corrie patted Rosetti's shoulder. 'You're sweet,' she said. Shrimp flushed. 'Who is Melrose?' Corrie asked.

'Our tail gunner. He was killed before the Lovely Lady crashed. An' he was talkin' to him! Geeze!'

Jerry turned and twisted. It was all that three of them could do to keep him on the litter. 'I guess we'll have to tie him down,' said the doctor.

Rosetti shook his head. 'Get Bubonovitch up here, an' me and him'll take care of him. The Cap'n wouldn't want to be tied down.'

Word was passed back down the column for Bubonovitch. Jerry was trying to get off the litter when he arrived. It took the combined strength of four to force him back. Bubonovitch was swearing softly under his breath. 'The goddam Japs. The yellow bastards.' He turned on Rosetti. 'Why in hell didn't you send for me before?' he demanded. 'Why didn't somebody tell me he was like this?'

'Keep your shirt on, Bum,' said Rosetti. 'I sends for you as soon as he needs you.'

'He hasn't been this way long,' Corrie told Bubonovitch.

'I'm sorry,' said the latter. 'I was frightened when I saw him this way. You see, we're sort of fond of the guy.'

Tears almost came to Corrie's eyes. 'I guess we all are,' she said.

'Is he very bad, Doctor?' asked Bubonovitch.

'He is running quite a fever,' replied Reyd; 'but it isn't high enough to be dangerous – yet.'

They had come out of the forest into the valley where they were to camp. Now, out of the narrow trail, Sarina had come up beside the litter. When Jerry yelled, 'Cripes! I can't get her nose up. You fellows jump! Make it snappy!' and tried to jump off the litter, she helped hold him down.

Corrie stroked his forehead and said, soothingly, 'Everything's all right, Jerry. Just lie still and try to rest.'

He reached up and took her hand. 'Mabel,' he said and sighed. Then he fell asleep. Rosetti and Bubonovitch tried not to look at Corrie.

Reyd sighed, too. 'That's the best medicine he could have,' he said.

A half hour later, van Prins called a halt; and they made camp beneath some trees beside the little stream that ran through the valley.

Jerry slept through the remainder of the afternoon and all the following night. Corrie and Sarina slept on one side of the litter, Bubonovitch and Rosetti on the other. They took turns remaining awake to watch over their patient.

When it was Corrie's turn to remain awake, she kept thinking of Mabel. She had never heard the name of that girl in Oklahoma City who had married the 4-F, but she knew now that her name was Mabel. So he still loved her! Corrie tried not to care. Wasn't Mabel lost to him? She was married. Then she thought that maybe it was some other girl named Mabel, and maybe this other girl wasn't married. She wanted to ask Bubonovitch what the name of the girl in Oklahoma City was, but her pride wouldn't let her.

When Jerry awoke he lay for several seconds looking up at the leafy canopy above him, trying to coax his memory to reveal its secrets. Slowly he recalled that the last thing he had been conscious of was being very uncomfortable on a litter that was being borne along a narrow forest trail. Now the litter had come to rest and he was very comfortable. Quite near him he heard the purling laughter of the little river rippling among the boulders as it hurried gaily on to keep its assignation with the sea.

Jerry looked toward it and saw Bubonovitch and Rosetti kneeling on its grassy bank washing their hands and faces. He smiled happily as he thought how fortunate he had been in the comrades the war had given him. He fought away the sadness for those he would never see again. A fellow mustn't brood about things like that, those inescapable concomitants of war.

Turning his head away from the river, he looked for Corrie. She was sitting close beside his litter, cross-legged, elbows on knees, her face buried in her opened palms. Her hair was gold again; but she still wore it bobbed, being, as she was, a very practical little person. That, too, was why she continued to wear pants.

Jerry looked at her fondly, thinking what a cute boy she looked. And also thinking, thank God she's not. He knew she wasn't; because he wouldn't have wanted to take a boy in his arms and kiss him. And that was exactly what he wanted to do with Corrie that very moment, but he didn't have the nerve. Coward! he thought.

'Corrie,' he said, very softly.

She opened her eyes and raised her head. 'Oh, Jerry!'

He reached over and took one of her hands. She placed her other hand on his forehead. 'Oh, Jerry! Jerry! Your fever is all gone. How do you feel?'

'As though I could eat a cow, hoofs, horns, and hide.'

Corrie choked back a sob. This sudden relief from fear and strain broke down the barriers of emotional restraint that had been her spiritual shield and buckler for so long. Corrie scrambled to her feet and ran away. She took refuge behind a tree and leaned against it and cried. She couldn't recall when she had been so happy.

'Wot,' Rosetti asked Bubonovitch, 'was de name of dat dame in Oklahoma City wot gave de Cap'n de brush-off?'

'I don't know,' said Bubonovitch.

'I wonder was it Mabel,' wondered Rosetti.

'Could be.'

Jerry looked after Corrie, with knitted brows. Now what the hell? he thought. Sarina, having attached herself to Corrie and the Americans, was preparing their breakfast nearby. Dr Reyd, making the round of his patients, came to Jerry. 'How goes it this morning?'

'Feeling great,' Jerry told him. 'Won't have to be carried any longer.'

'Maybe that's what you think,' said Reyd, grinning. 'But you're wrong.'

Captain van Prins and Tak van der Bos came over. 'Think you can stand another day of it?' the former asked Jerry.

'Sure I can.'

'Good! I want to start as soon as possible. This place is too exposed.'

'You had us worrying yesterday, Jerry,' said van der Bos.

'I had a good doctor,' said Jerry.

'If I'd had you back in civilian life,' said Reyd, 'I'd have given you a pill yesterday; and this morning I'd have told you how near death's door you were yesterday.'

Corrie came out from behind her tree and joined them. Jerry saw that her eyes were red, and knew why she had run away. 'Just getting up, lazy?' Tak asked her.

'I've been out looking for a cow,' said Corrie.

'A cow! Why?'

'Jerry wanted one for breakfast.'

'So he'll eat rice,' said van Prins, grinning.

'When I get off your lovely island,' said Jerry, 'and anyone says rice to me, he'd better smile.'

The others went on about their duties, leaving Corrie alone with Jerry. 'I must have passed out cold yesterday,' he said. 'Can't remember a thing after about a couple of hours on the trail.'

'You were a very sick man – just burning up with fever. You kept trying to jump off the litter. It took four of us to hold you down. The doctor wanted to tie you to the litter, but that sweet little sergeant wouldn't hear of it. He said, "De Cap'n wouldn't want to be tied down"; so he and Bubonovitch and the doctor and Sarina and I walked beside the litter.'

'Shrimp's a good little guy,' said Jerry.

'Those boys are very fond of you, Jerry.'

'That works both ways,' said Jerry. 'Members of a combat crew have to like one another. You don't trust a guy you don't like, and we got enough worries when we're flying a mission without having to worry about some fellow we can't trust. I'm sorry I was such a nuisance yesterday.'

'You weren't a nuisance. We were just frightened; because we thought you were so terribly sick. And your being delirious made it seem much worse than it really was.' She paused a moment, and then she said, 'Who is Mabel?'

'Mabel? What do you know about Mabel?'

'Nothing. But you kept asking for her.'

Jerry laughed. 'That's what Dad called Mother. It isn't her name, but he started calling her Mabel even before they were married. He got the name from a series of "Dere Mabel" letters that were popular during World War I; and we kids thought it was funny to call her Mabel, too.'

'We were all wondering who Mabel was,' said Corrie, lamely.

'I suppose it had Shrimp and Bubonovitch and Sarina and the doctor terribly worried,' said Jerry.

'That is not funny, and you are not nice,' said Corrie.

25

At the head of the valley, where the stream was born in a little spring that gurgled from beneath a limestone cliff, there were many caves, easily defendable. Here van Prins decided to make a more or less premanent camp and await the coming of Allied forces under MacArthur, for since the Americans had come he had learned for the first time that MacArthur was really drawing nearer week by week. When the Allies established a beachhead, he and other guerrilla leaders would come down out of the mountains and harass the enemy's rear and communications. In the meantime about all that they could accomplish was an occasional sally against a Jap outpost.

From this camp the Americans planned to cross over to the other side of the mountains, as soon as Jerry was fully recovered, and follow a trail along the eastern side of the range to the point where they would recross to the west and try to make their way to the coast. Tak van der Bos was going with them; because it was thought that his knowledge of Sumatra and the location of Jap positions might prove of value to the Allied forces. 'In the very doubtful eventuality that you ever reach them,' said van Prins.

He had little hope for the success of what he considered a mad venture, and he tried to persuade Corrie not to take the risk. 'We can hide you here in the mountains indefinitely,' he told her, 'and you will be safe among your own people.'

Jerry wasn't so sure that she would be safe. If the Japs ever made a serious effort to liquidate the guerrillas, using both infantry and planes, Corrie would be anything but safe. Yet he did not urge her to come with him. He would have felt much more assured of the chances for the success of their venture if Tarzan had not been lost to them.

Tak van der Bos agreed with van Prins. 'I really think you'd be safer here, Corrie,' he told her. 'And I think that we four men would stand a better chance of getting away if – if—'

'If you weren't burdened with a couple of women. Why don't you say it, Tak?'

'I didn't know just how to say it inoffensively, Corrie; but that's what I meant.'

'Sarina and I will not be a burden. We'll be two more rifles. We have proved that we can hold our own on the trail with any of you men. I think you will admit that Sarina would prove an even more ferocious fighter than any of you, and I have already shown that I won't scream and faint when the shooting starts. Besides all that, Sarina believes that she knows exactly where she can locate a boat for us and get it provisioned by friendly natives. And another thing to consider: Sarina has sailed these seas all her life. She not only knows them, but she is an experienced navigator. I think that we can be a lot of help to you. As far as the danger is concerned, it's six of one and half a dozen of the other. The Japs may get us if we try to get away, or they may get us if we stay. Sarina and I want to go with you men; but if Jerry says no, that will settle it.'

Bubonovitch and Rosetti were interested listeners to the discussion. Jerry turned to them. 'What do you fellows think?' he asked. 'Would you want Corrie and Sarina to come with us, or would you rather they didn't?'

'Well, it's like this,' said Bubonovitch. 'If we had two men who were as good soldiers as they are, there wouldn't be any question. It's just that a man hesitates to place a woman in danger if he can avoid it.'

'That's the hell of it,' said Jerry. He looked at Rosetti, questioningly, Rosetti the confirmed woman hater.

'I say let's all go, or all stay. Let's stick togedder.'

'Corrie and Sarina know what dangers and hardships may be involved,' said Bubonovitch. 'Let them decide. I can't see that any of us has any right to do their thinking for them.'

'Good for you, sergeant,' said Corrie. 'Sarina and I have already decided.'

Captain van Prins shrugged. 'I think you are crazy,' he said; 'but I admire your courage, and I wish you luck.'

'Look!' exclaimed Rosetti, pointing. 'Everyt'ing's goin' to be hotsy-totsy now.'

Everyone looked in the direction that Rosetti was pointing. Coming toward them was the familiar, bronzed figure that the Americans and Corrie had so grown to lean upon; and upon one of its shoulders squatted a little monkey; across the other was the carcass of a deer.

Tarzan dropped the deer at the edge of camp and walked toward the group gathered around Jerry's litter. Keta encircled Tarzan's neck with both arms, screaming at the strange Tarmangani, hurling jungle invective at them. Little Keta was terrified.

'They are friends, Keta,' said Tarzan in their common language. 'Do not be afraid.'

'Keta not afraid,' shrilled the monkey. 'Keta bite Tarmangani.'

Tarzan was welcomed with enthusiasm. He went at once to Jerry and stood looking down at him, smiling. 'So they didn't get you,' he said.

'Just nicked me,' said Jerry.

'The last time I saw you, I thought you were dead.'

'We have been afraid that you were dead. Did you get into some trouble?'

'Yes,' replied Tarzan, 'but it wasn't my trouble; it was the Japs'. I followed them. No matter what they may do to you in the future, you are already avenged.'

Jerry grinned. 'I wish I had been there to see.'

'It was not pretty,' said Tarzan. 'Soulless creatures in a panic of terror – living robots helpless without their Masters. I was careful to pick those off first.' He smiled at the recollection.

'You must have followed them a long way,' suggested van Prins.

'No; but after I finished with them I wandered deep into the forest. I am always curious about a country with which I am not familiar. However, I did not learn much of value. Late yesterday afternoon I located an enemy battery of big guns; and this morning, another. If you have a map, I can mark their positions fairly closely.

'The first day, I found an isolated village of natives. It was built in the shallow waters near the shore of a lake in a great primeval forest which appeared to me impenetrable. The people were fishing with nets. They threatened me with bows and arrows after I gave them the peace sign.'

'I think I know the village,' said van Prins. 'Fliers have seen it; but as far as is known, no other civilized men have seen it and lived. One or two have tried to reach it. Maybe they did, but they never came back. The inhabitants of that village are thought to be the remnants of an aboriginal people from whom the Bataks descended – true savages and cannibals. Until recently the modern Bataks were cannibals – what one might call beneficent cannibals. They ate their old people in the belief that thus they would confer immortality upon them, for they would continue to live in the persons of those who devoured them. Also, the devourer would acquire the strengths and virtues of the devoured. For this latter reason, they also ate their enemies – partly cooked and with a dash of lemon.'

'These lake dwellers,' said van der Bos, 'are also supposed to have discovered the secret of perpetual youth.'

'That, of course, is all tommyrot,' said Dr Reyd.

'Perhaps not,' said Tarzan.

Reyd looked at him in surprise. 'You don't mean to tell me that you believe any such silly nonsense as that, do you?' he demanded.

Tarzan smiled and nodded. 'Naturally, I believe in those things which I have myself seen or experienced; and I have twice seen absolute proof that perpetual youth can be achieved. Also, I learned long ago not to deny the possibility of anything emanating from the superstitions of religions of primitive peoples. I have seen strange things in the depths of Darkest Africa.' He ceased speaking, evidently having no intention to elaborate. His eyes, wandering over the faces of his listeners, fixed on Sarina. 'What is that woman doing here?' he asked. 'She belongs to Hooft and his gang of outlaws.'

Corrie and Rosetti both tried to explain simultaneously, the latter fairly leaping to Sarina's defense. When he had heard the story, Tarzan was satisfied. 'If Sergeant Rosetti is satisfied to have *any* woman around, she must be beyond criticism.'

Rosetti flushed uncomfortably, but he said, 'Sarina's okay, Colonel.'

Dr Reyd cleared his throat. 'What you said about the verity of the superstitions and religions of primitive peoples and that perpetual youth might be achieved, interests me. Would you mind being more explicit?'

Tarzan sat down cross-legged beside Jerry. 'On numerous occasions, I have known witch-doctors to kill people at great distances from them; and some times after a lapse of years. I do not know how they do it. I merely know that they do do it. Perhaps they plant the idea in the mind of their victim and he induces death by autosuggestion. Most of their mumbo jumbo is pure charlatanism. Occasionally it appears as an exact science.'

'We are easily fooled, though,' said Jerry. 'Take some of these fellows who have made a hobby of so-called parlor magic. They admit that they are tricking you; but if you were an ignorant savage and they told you it was true magic, you'd believe them. I had a friend in Honolulu when I was stationed at Hickam, who was as good as any professional I have ever seen. Paint Colonel Kendall J. Fielder black, dress him up in a breechclout and a feather headdress, give him some odds and ends of bones and pieces of wood and a zebra's tail, and turn him loose in Africa; and he'd have all the other witch-doctors green with envy.

'And what he could do with cards! I used to play bridge against him, and he always won. Of course his game was on the level, but he had two strikes on you before you started – just like Tarzan's witch-doctors had on *their* victims. You just autosuggested yourself to defeat. It was humiliating, too,' added Jerry, 'because I am a very much better bridge player than he.'

'Of course anyone can learn that kind of magic,' said Reyd, 'but how about perpetual youth? You have really seen instances of this, Colonel?'

'When I was a young man,' said Tarzan, 'I saved a black from a man-eating lion. He was very grateful, and wished to repay me in some way. He offered me perpetual youth. I told him that I didn't think such a thing was possible. He asked me how old I thought he was, and I said that he appeared to be in his twenties. He told me that he was a witch-doctor. All the witch-doctors I had ever seen were much older men than he; so I rather discounted that statement as well as his claim to being able to confer perpetual youth on me.

'He took me to his village, where I met his chief. He asked the chief how long he had known him. "All my life," replied the chief, who was a very old man. The chief told me that no one knew how old the witch-doctor was; but that he must be very old, as he had known Tippoo Tib's grandfather. Tippoo Tib was born, probably, in the 1840's, or, possibly, the 1830's; so his grandfather may have been born as long ago as the eighteenth century.

'I was quite young and, like most young men, adventurous. I would try anything; so I let the witch-doctor go to work on me. Before he was through with me, I understood why he was not conferring perpetual youth wholesale. It required a full month of concocting vile brews, observing solemn rituals, and the transfusion of a couple of quarts of the witch-doctor's blood into my veins. Long before it was over, I regretted that I had let myself in for it; because I didn't take any stock in his claims.' Tarzan ceased speaking as though he had finished his story.

'And you were quite right,' said Dr Reyd.

'You think I will age, then?'

'Most certainly,' said the doctor.

'How old do you think I am now?' asked Tarzan.

'In your twenties.'

Tarzan smiled. 'That which I have told you of occurred many years ago.'

Dr Reyd shook his head. 'It is very strange,' he said. It was evident that he was not convinced.

'I never gave a thought to your age, Colonel,' said Jerry; 'but I remember now that my father said that he read about you when he was a boy. And I was brought up on you. You influenced my life more than anyone else.'

'I give up,' said Dr Reyd. 'But you said that you had known of two instances in which perpetual youth was achieved. What was the other one? You've certainly aroused my interest.'

'A tribe of white fanatics in a remote part of Africa compounded a hellish thing that achieved perpetual youth. I mean the way that they obtained one of the principal ingredients was hellish. They kidnaped young girls, killed them, and removed certain glands.

'In the course of tracing a couple of girls they had stolen, I found their village. To make a long story short, my companions and I succeeded in rescuing the girls and obtaining a supply of their compound.* Those who have taken it, including a little monkey, have shown no signs of aging since.'

'Amazing!' said Dr Reyd. 'Do you expect to live forever?'

'I don't know what to expect.'

'Maybe,' suggested Bubonovitch, 'you'll just fall to pieces all at once, like the One Hoss Shay.'

'Would you want to live forever?' asked van der Bos.

'Of course – if I never had to suffer the infirmities of old age.'

'But all your friends would be gone.'

'One misses the old friends, but one constantly makes new ones. But really my chances of living forever are very slight. Any day, I may stop a bullet; or a tiger may get me, or a python. If I live to get back to my Africa, I may find a lion waiting for me, or a buffalo. Death has many tricks up his sleeve beside old age. One may outplay him for a while, but he always wins in the end.'

* See *Tarzan's Quest*.

26

The little band that was to make the attempt to reach Australia, comprising, as it did, Americans, Dutch, an Englishman, and a Eurasian, had been dubbed The Foreign Legion by the guerrillas. Jerry amplified the basis for this designation by calling attention to the fact that Bubonovitch was Russian, Rosetti Italian, and he himself part Cherokee Indian.

'If poor old Sing Tai were with us,' said Corrie, 'the four principal Allied Nations would be represented.'

'If Italy hadn't surrendered,' said Bubonovitch, 'we'd have had to liquidate Shrimp. He's the only Axis partner in our midst.'

'I ain't a Eyetalian,' said Rosetti, 'but I'd rather be a Eyetalian than a lousy Russian communist.' Bubonovitch grinned, and winked at Corrie.

Captain van Prins, who was sitting a little apart with Tarzan, said in a low tone, 'It's too bad that there's hard feelings between those two. It may cause a lot of trouble before you're through.'

Tarzan looked at him in surprise. 'I guess you don't know Americans very well, Captain. Either one of those boys would willingly risk his life for the other.'

'Then why do they try to insult each other?' demanded van Prins. 'This is not the first time I have heard them.'

Tarzan shrugged. 'If I were an American, perhaps I could tell you.'

Where the guerrillas had made their camp, the valley narrowed and ended in a box canyon the limestone walls of which were pitted with several large caves on each side. Rifles and machine guns firing from the mouths of these caves could develop a deadly crossfire that might render the position impregnable. Another advantage lay in the ability to conceal all evidence of the presence of men which the caves offered. Occasionally, a Jap plane flew over. At the first sound of its motors, the company vanished into the caves.

A sentry, posted on a cliff above the camp, had a full view down the valley as far as binoculars would reach. Should he discover even a single human being approaching, his signal would similarly empty the floor of the canyon.

In this camp, for the first time, The Foreign Legion felt reasonably secure. It was a relief from the constant nervous strain they had been undergoing, and they relaxed and rested while waiting for Jerry's wound to heal and for him to regain his strength.

Tarzan was often away on reconnaissance missions or hunting. It was he who kept the camp supplied with fresh meat, as he could kill quietly, which was most desirable. A rifle shot might attract the attention of an enemy patrol.

Occasionally, Tarzan was away for several days at a time. On one such mission he found the camp of the outlaws far down the valley. It was located not far from the kampong where Captain Tokujo Matsuo and Lieutenant Hideo Sokabe still held forth, and it was evident that the outlaws were openly collaborating with the Japs.

The outlaws had set up a still and were making schnapps, with which they carried on a brisk trade with the enemy. Tarzan saw much drunkenness in both camps. One observable result of this was a relaxation of discipline and alertness in the enemy camp. There were no sentries out on the trails leading to the village. A single soldier was on guard beside a small barbed wire enclosure. Inside this, beneath a flimsy shelter, Tarzan could see two figures, but he could not make out who nor what they were. They were evidently prisoners, but whether natives or Japs he could not tell. They did not interest him.

As Tarzan turned to leave the village and return to the camp of the guerrillas, a radio blared from one of the houses. He paused a moment to listen; but the voice spoke in Japanese, which he could not understand, and he continued on his way.

However, Lieutenant Hideo Sokabe understood it, and he did not like what he heard. Captain Tokujo Matsuo understood it and was pleased. He was not a little drunk on schnapps, as was Sokabe also. The schnapps heightened the acclaim with which Matsuo received the broadcast from Tokyo. He was quite noisy about it.

'So your honorable uncle has been kicked out,' he exulted. 'You may now write to your honorable uncle, General Hideki Tojo, every day; but I shall remain a captain – until I am promoted. Now the situation is reversed. The "Singing Frog" is now Premier. He is not my uncle, but he is my friend. I served under him in the Kwantung army in Manchuria.'

'So did a million other peasants,' said Sokabe.

Thus was the bad blood between the two officers made worse, which was not well for the morale and discipline of their command.

Corrie had often expressed concern over the fate of Sing Tai whom they had left in hiding in the village of Tiang Umar; so Tarzan decided to visit this village before returning to the camp of the guerrillas. This necessitated a considerable detour, but only rarely did either time or distance cause the Lord of the Jungle any concern. One of the features of civilization to which he could never accustom himself was the slavish subservience of civilized man to the demands of time. Sometimes his lack of conformity with established custom proved embarrassing to others, but never to Tarzan. He ate when he was hungry, slept when he was sleepy. He started on journeys when the spirit or necessity moved him, without concerning himself about the time which might be involved.

He moved leisurely now. He made a kill, and after eating, laid up for the night. It was mid-morning when he approached the kampong of Tiang Umar. Motivated by the inherent caution and suspicion of the wild beast, Tarzan moved silently through the trees which encircled the kampong, to assure himself that no enemy lurked there. He saw the natives carrying on their normal, peaceful activities. Presently he recognized Alam, and a moment later he dropped to the ground and walked into the village.

As soon as the natives recognized him, they greeted him cordially and gathered around him, asking questions in a language he could not understand. He asked if anyone in the village spoke Dutch; and an old man replied in that language, saying that he did.

Through the interpreter Alam inquired about Corrie, and showed his pleasure when told that she was safe. Then Tarzan asked what had become of Sing Tai, and was told that he was still in the village but never ventured out in the daytime, which was well, as twice Jap scouting parties had come to the kampong without warning.

Tarzan was taken to the Chinese. He found him entirely recovered from his wound and in good physical condition. His first question was of Corrie, and when he was assured that she was all right and among friends he beamed with pleasure.

'Do you want to stay here, Sing Tai,' Tarzan asked, 'or do you want to come with us? We are going to try to escape from the island.'

'I come with you,' replied Sing Tai.

'Very well,' said Tarzan. 'We'll start now.'

The Foreign Legion was becoming restless. Jerry had entirely recovered, had regained his strength, and was anxious to move on. He only awaited the return of Tarzan, who had been away for several days.

'Wish he would show up,' he said to Corrie. 'I know he can take care of himself, but something *could* happen to him.' Several of the party were gathered beneath the concealing branches of a tree. They had been stripping, oiling, and reassembling their weapons. The stripping and reassembling they did with their eyes closed. It was a game that relieved the monotony of this ceaseless attention to weapons in the humid atmosphere of these equatorial mountains. Occasionally they timed one another; and, much to the chagrin of the men, it was discovered that Corrie and Sarina were the most adept.

Sarina replaced the bolt in her rifle, aimed at the sky, and squeezed the trigger. She leaned the piece against the tree, and looked long and searchingly down the valley. 'Tony has been gone a long time,' she said. 'If he does not come soon, I shall go and look for him.'

'Where did he go?' asked Jerry.

'Hunting.'

'The orders are no hunting,' said Jerry. 'Rosetti knows that. We can't take the chance of attracting the attention of the Japs with rifle fire.'

'Tony took his bow and arrows for hunting,' Sarina explained. 'He will not fire his rifle except in self defense.'

'He couldn't hit anything smaller than an elephant with that archery set of his,' said Bubonovitch.

'How long has he been gone?' asked Jerry.

'Too long,' said Sarina; 'three or four hours at least.'

'I'll go look for him,' said Bubonovitch. He picked up his rifle and stood up.

Just then the sentry on the cliff called down: 'A man coming. Looks like Sergeant Rosetti. Yes, it is Sergeant Rosetti.'

'Is he carrying an elephant?' Bubonovitch shouted.

The sentry laughed. 'He is carrying something, but I do not think it is an elephant.'

They all looked down the valley, and presently they could see a man approaching. He was still a long way off. Only the sentry with binoculars could have recognized him. After a while Rosetti walked into camp. He was carrying a hare.

'Here's your supper,' he said, tossing the hare to the ground. 'I missed three deer, and then I gets this little squirt.'

'Was he asleep at the time, or did somebody hold him for you?' asked Bubonovitch.

'He was runnin' like a bat outta hell,' said Rosetti, grinning. 'He runs into a tree an' knocks hisself cold.'

'Nice work, Hiawatha,' said Bubonovitch.

'Anyway, I tried,' said Rosetti. 'I didn't sit around on my big, fat fanny waitin' for some udder guy to bring home de bacon.'

'That is right, Sergeant Bum,' said Sarina.

'Always the perfect little gentleman, I will not contradict a lady,' said Bubonovitch. 'Now the question is, who is going to prepare the feast? There are only fifty of us to eat it. What is left, we can send to the starving Armenians.'

'De starvin' Armenians don't get none of dis rabbit. Neither do you. It's all for Sarina and Corrie.'

'Two people coming up the valley!' called down the sentry. 'Can't make them out yet. Something peculiar about them.' Every eye was strained down the valley, every ear waiting to hear the next report from the sentry. After a few moments it came: 'Each of them is carrying some sort of load. One of them is naked.'

'Must be Tarzan,' said Jerry.

It was Tarzan. With him was Sing Tai. When they reached camp, each of them dropped the carcass of a deer to the ground. Corrie was delighted to see Sing Tai and to learn that he had completely recovered from his wound. And Jerry was relieved and delighted to see Tarzan.

'I'm sure glad you're back,' he said. 'We're all ready to shove off, and have only been waiting for you.'

'I think we have another job to do before we can start,' said Tarzan. 'I located Hooft's gang far down the valley, not far from the village where we got Corrie away from the Japs. The Japs are still there, and while I was scouting the place I saw two prisoners behind barbed wire. I couldn't make out what they were, but on the way back here from Tiang Umar's kampong Sing Tai told me that some Japs had passed through the kampong a few days ago with two American prisoners. The Japs told the natives that they were fliers whose plane had been shot down some time ago.'

'Douglas and Davis!' exclaimed Bubonovitch.

'Must be,' agreed Jerry. 'They are the only two unaccounted for.'

Bubonovitch buckled on his ammunition belt and picked up his rifle. 'Let's go, Captain,' he said.

Tarzan glanced at the sun. 'If we travel fast,' he said, 'we can make it while it is still dark; but we should take only men who can travel fast.'

'How many?' asked van Prins.

'Twenty should be enough. If everything goes all right, I can do it alone. If everything doesn't go all right, twenty men plus the element of surprise should make everything all right.'

'I'll come along with enough of my men to make the twenty,' said van Prins.

All the members of The Foreign Legion were preparing to go, but Tarzan said no to Corrie and Sarina. They started to argue the matter, but Tarzan was adamant. 'You'd be an added responsibility for us,' he said. 'We'd have to be thinking of your safety when our minds should be on nothing but our mission.'

'The Colonel is right,' said Jerry.

'I suppose he is,' admitted Corrie.

'That's the good soldier,' said Tak.

'There is another who should not go,' said Doctor Reyd. Everybody looked at Jerry. 'Captain Lucas has been a very ill man. If he goes on a long forced march now, he'll be in no condition to undertake the trying marches to the South which you are contemplating.'

Jerry glanced questioningly at Tarzan. 'I wish you wouldn't insist, Jerry,' said the Englishman.

Jerry unbuckled his ammunition belt and laid it at the foot of the tree. He grinned ruefully. 'If Corrie and Sarina can be good soldiers, I guess I can, too; but I sure hate to miss out on this.'

Ten minutes later twenty men started down the valley at a brisk pace that was almost a dogtrot. Tarzan, at the head of the column with van Prins, explained his plan to the Dutchman.

Captain Tokujo Matsuo and Lieutenant Hideo Sokabe had been drinking all night – drinking and quarreling. There had been much drinking among their men, too. The native men of the kampong had taken their women into the forest to escape the brutal advances of the drunken soldiers. But now, shortly before dawn, the camp had quieted, except for the quarreling of the two officers; for the others lay for the most part in a drunken stupor.

The single guard before the prison pen had just come on duty. He had slept off some of the effects of the schnapps he had drunk, but he was still far from sober. He resented having been awakened; so he vented some of his anger on the two prisoners, awakening them to revile and threaten them. Having been born and educated in Honolulu, he spoke English. He was an adept in invective in two languages. He loosed a flow of profanity and obscenity upon the two men within the barbed wire enclosure.

Staff Sergeant Carter Douglas of Van Nuys, California, stirred on his filthy sleeping mat, and raised himself on one elbow. 'Aroha, sweetheart!' he called to the guard. This plunged the Jap into inarticulate rage.

'What's eatin' the guy?' demanded Staff Sergeant Bill Davis of Waco, Texas.

'I think he doesn't like us,' said Douglas. 'Before you woke up he said he would kill us right now except that his honorable captain wanted to lop our beans off himself in the morning.'

'Maybe he's just handin' us a line to scare us,' suggested Davis.

'Could be,' said Douglas. 'The guy's spiflicated. That stuff they drink must be potent as hell. It sounded like everybody in camp was drunk.'

'Remember that butterfly brandy they tried to sell us in Noumea at eighty-five smackers a bottle? Three drinks, and a private would spit in a captain's face. Maybe that's what they're drinking.'

'If this guy had got a little drunker,' said Douglas, 'we could have made our get away tonight.'

'If we could get out of here, we could rush him.'

'But we can't get out of here.'

'Hell's bells! I don't want to have my head lopped off. What a hell of a birthday present.'

'What do you mean, birthday present?'

'If I haven't lost track, tomorrow should be my birthday,' said Davis. 'I'll be twenty-five tomorrow.'

'You didn't expect to live forever, did you? I don't know what you old guys expect.'

'How old are you, Doug?'

'Twenty.'

'Gawd! They dragged you right out of the cradle. Oh, hell!' he said after a moment's pause. 'We're just tryin' to kid ourselves that we ain't scared. I'm good and goddam scared.'

'I'm scairt as hell,' admitted Davis.

'What you talk about in there?' demanded the guard. 'Shut up!'

'Shut up yourself, Tojo,' said Douglas; 'you're drunk.'

'Now, for that, I kill you,' yelled the Jap. 'I tell the captain you try to escape.' He raised his rifle and aimed into the darkness of the shelter that housed the two prisoners.

Silently, in the shadows of the native houses, a figure moved toward him. It approached from behind him.

Matsuo and Sokabe were screaming insults at one another in their quarters at the far end of the kampong. Suddenly, the former drew his pistol and fired at Sokabe. He missed, and the lieutenant returned the fire. They were too drunk to hit one another except by accident, but they kept blazing away.

Almost simultaneously with Matsuo's first shot, the guard fired into the shelter that housed the two Americans. Before he could fire a second shot, an arm encircled his head and drew it back, and a knife almost severed it from his body.

'Were you hit, Bill?' ask Douglas.

'No. He missed us a mile. What's going on out there? Somebody jumped him.'

Aroused by the firing in their officers' quarters, dopey, drunken soldiers were staggering toward the far end of the village, thinking the camp had been attacked. Some of them ran so close past Tarzan that he could almost have reached out and touched them. He crouched beside the dead guard, waiting. He was as ignorant of the cause of the fusillade as the Japs. Van Prins and his party were at the opposite end of the kampong; so he knew that it could not be they firing.

When he thought the last Jap had passed him, he called to the prisoners in a low tone. 'Are you Douglas and Davis?'

'We sure are.'

'Where's the gate?'

'Right in front of you, but it's padlocked.' Van Prins, hearing the firing, thought that it was directed at Tarzan; so he brought his men into the village at a run. They spread out, dodging from house to house.

Tarzan stepped to the gate. Its posts were the trunks of small saplings.

Douglas and Davis had come from the shelter and were standing close inside the gate.

Tarzan took hold of the posts, one with each hand. 'Each of you fellows push on a post,' he said, 'and I'll pull.' As he spoke, he surged back with all his weight and strength; and the posts snapped off before the prisoners could lend a hand. The wire was pulled down to the ground with the posts, and Douglas and Davis walked out to freedom over it.

Tarzan had heard the men coming in from van Prins' position, and guessed it was they. He called to van Prins, and the latter answered. 'The prisoners are with me,' said Tarzan. 'You'd better assemble your men so that we can get out of here.' Then he took the rifle and ammunition from the dead Jap and handed them to Davis.

As the party moved out of the village, they could hear the Japs jabbering and shouting at the far end. They did not know the cause of the diversion that had aided them so materially in the rescue of the two men without having suffered any casualties, and many of them regretted leaving without having fired a shot.

Bubonovitch and Rosetti fairly swarmed over their two buddies, asking and answering innumerable questions. One of Davis' first questions was about Tarzan. 'Who was that naked guy that got us out?' he asked.

'Don't you remember the English dook that come aboard just before we shoved off?' asked Rosetti. 'Well, that's him; and he's one swell guy. An' who do you t'ink he is?'

'You just told us – the RAF colonel.'

'He's Tarzan of the Apes.'

'Who you think you're kiddin'?'

'On the level,' said Bubonovitch. 'He's Tarzan all right.'

'The old man ain't here,' said Douglas. 'He wasn't—?'

'No. He's O.K. He got wounded, and they wouldn't let him come along; but he's all right.'

The four talked almost constantly all the way back to the guerrilla camp. They had fought together on many missions. They were linked by ties more binding than blood. There existed between them something that cannot be expressed in words, nor would they have thought of trying to. Perhaps Rosetti came nearest it when he slapped Davis on the back and said, 'You old sonofabitch!'

27

Two days later, The Foreign Legion, now numbering ten, said goodbye to the guerrillas and started on their long march toward a hazy destination. Douglas and Davis took their places in the little company with the easy adaptability of the American soldier. Douglas called it the League of Nations.

At first the two newcomers had been skeptical of the ability of the two women to endure the hardships and the dangers of the almost trackless mountain wilderness that the necessity of avoiding contact with the enemy forced them to traverse. But they soon discovered that they were doing pretty well themselves if they kept up with Corrie and Sarina. There were other surprises, too.

'What's happened to Shrimp?' Davis asked Bubonovitch. 'I thought he didn't have time for any fem, but he's always hangin' around that brown gal. Not that I blame him any. She could park her shoes in my locker any time.'

'I fear,' said Bubonovitch, 'that Staff Sergeant Rosetti has fallen with a dull and sickening thud. At first he was coy about it, but now he is absolutely without shame. He drools.'

'And the old man,' said Davis. 'He used to be what you called a misnogomist.'

'That isn't exactly what I called it,' said Bubonovitch, 'but you have the general idea. Maybe he used to be, but he isn't any more.'

'Sort of silly,' remarked Carter Douglas. 'What do old men know about love?'

'You'd be surprised, little one,' said Bubonovitch.

The going was cruel. With parangs, they hacked their way through virgin jungle. Deep gorges and mountain torrents blocked their advance with discouraging frequency. Often, the walls of the former dropped sheer for hundreds of feet, offering no hand nor toe hold, necessitating long detours. Scarcely a day passed without rain, blinding, torrential downpours. They marched and slept in wet, soggy clothing. Their shoes and sandals rotted.

Tarzan hunted for them, and those who had not already done so learned to eat their meat raw. He scouted ahead, picking the best routes, alert for enemy outposts or patrols. By night, they slept very close together, a guard constantly posted against the sudden, stealthy attack of tigers. Sometimes muscles flagged, but morale never.

Little Keta did all the scolding and complaining. When Tarzan had gone to the rescue of Davis and Douglas, Keta had been left behind tied to a tree. He had been very indignant about this and had bitten three Dutchmen who had tried to make friends with him. Since then he had usually been left severely alone, consorting only with Tarzan. The only exception was Rosetti. He voluntarily made friends with the little sergeant, often curling up in his arms when the company was not on the march.

'He probably recognizes Shrimp as a kindred spirit,' said Bubonovitch, 'if not a near relative.'

'He t'inks you're one of dem big apes we seen dat he's a-scairt of.'

'You refer, I presume, to *Pongo pygmaeus*,' said Bubonovitch.

Shrimp registered disgust. 'I wisht I was a poet. I'd write a pome.'

'About me, darling?'

'You said a mouthful. I got a word wot you rhyme with.'

They had stopped for the night earlier than usual because Tarzan had found a large dry cave that would accommodate them all. It had probably been occupied many times before, as there were charred pieces of wood near the entrance and a supply of dry wood stored within it. They had a fire, and they were sitting close to it, absorbing its welcome warmth and drying as much of their clothing as the presence of mixed company permitted them to remove. Which was considerable, as the silly interdictions of false modesty had largely been scrapped long since. They were a company of 'fighting men.'

Jerry, Bubonovitch, and Rosetti were looking at the rough map that van Prins had drawn for them. 'Here's where we crossed over to the east side of the range,' said Jerry, pointing, '– just below Alahanpandjang.'

'Geeze, wot a moniker fer a burg! Or is it a burg?'

'It's just a dot on a map to me,' admitted Jerry.

'Lookit,' continued Rosetti. 'Here it says dat to where we cross back again to de udder side it is kilometers. Wot's dat in United States?'

'Oh-h, about one hundred and five or six miles. That's in an air line.'

'What do you think we're averaging, Jerry?' asked Bubonovitch.

'I doubt if we're making five miles a day in an air line.'

'Today,' said Bubonovitch, 'I doubt that we made five miles on any kind of a line – unless it was up and down.'

'Geeze!' said Rosetti. 'De Lovely Lady would have got us dere in maybe twenty-twenty-five minutes. Sloggin' along like dogfaces it probably take us a mont'.'

'Maybe more,' said Jerry.

'Wot t'ell!' said Rosetti. 'We're lucky to be alive.'

'And the scenery is magnificent,' said Bubonovitch. 'When we can see it through this soup, it looks mighty nice and peaceful down there.'

'It sure does,' agreed Rosetti. 'It doesn't seem like dere could be a war in pretty country like dat. I don't suppose dey ever had no wars here before.'

'That's about all they ever did have until within the last hundred years,' said Tak van der Bos. 'During all historic times, and probably during all pre-historic times back to the days of *Pithecanthropus erectus* and *Homo Modjokertensis*, all the islands of the East Indies have been almost constantly overrun by warring men – the tribal chiefs, the petty princes, the little Kings, the sultans. The Hindus came from India, the Chinese came, the Portuguese, the Spaniards from the Philippines, the English, the Dutch, and now the Japs. They all brought fleets and soldiers and war. In the thirteenth century, Kubla Khan sent a fleet of a thousand ships bearing 200,000 soldiers to punish a King of Java who had arrested the ambassadors of the Great Khan and sent them back to China with mutilated faces.

'We Dutch were often guilty of perpetrating cruelties and atrocities upon the Indonesians; but neither we, nor all the others who came before us, devasted the land and enslaved and massacred its people with the cruel ruthlessness of their own sultans. These drunken, rapacious, licentious creatures massacred their own subjects if it satisfied some capricious whim. They took to themselves the loveliest women, the fairest virgins. One of them had fourteen thousand women in his harem.'

'Geeze!' exclaimed Rosetti.

Tak grinned and continued. 'And if they were still in power, they would still be doing the same things. Under us Dutch, the Indonesians have known the first freedom from slavery, the first peace, the first prosperity that they have ever known. Give them independence after the Japs are thrown out and in another generation they'll be back where we found them.'

'Haven't all peoples a right to independence?' asked Bubonovitch.

'Get a soap box, communist,' jeered Rosetti.

'Only those people who have won the right to independence deserve it,' said van der Bos. 'The first recorded contact with Sumatra was during the reign of Wang Mang, a Chinese emperor of the Han dynasty, just prior to A.D. 23. Indonesian civilization was ancient then. If, with all that background of ancient culture plus the nearly two thousand years before the Dutch completed the conquest of the islands, the people were still held in slavery by tyrant rulers; then they do not deserve what you call independence. Under the Dutch they have every liberty. What more can they ask?'

'Just to keep the record straight,' said Bubonovitch, with a grin, 'I'd like to state that I am not a communist. I am a good anti-New Deal Republican. But here is my point: I thought that freedom was one of the things we were fighting for.'

'Hell,' said Jerry. 'I don't think any of us know what we are fighting for except to kill Japs, get the war over, and get home. After we have done that, the goddam politicians will mess things all up again.'

'And the saber rattlers will start preparing for World War III,' said van der Bos.

'I don't think they will rattle their sabers very loudly for a while,' said Corrie.

'Just about in time to catch our children in the next war,' said Jerry.

There was an embarrassed silence. Jerry suddenly realized the interpretation that might be placed on his innocent remark, and flushed. So did Corrie. Everybody was looking at them, which made it worse.

Finally, van der Bos could no longer restrain his laughter; and they all joined him – even Corrie and Jerry. Sing Tai, who had been busy over a cooking fire, further relieved the tension by repeating a time honored phrase that he had been taught by Rosetti: 'Come and get it!'

Wild pig, grouse, fruits, and nuts formed the menu for the meal.

'We sure live high,' said Davis.

'De Drake Hotel ain't got nuttin' on us,' agreed Rosetti.

'We have the choice of an enormous market, and without ration coupons,' said Tarzan.

'And no coin on de line,' said Rosetti. 'Geeze! Dis is de life.'

'You gone batty?' inquired Bubonovitch.

'Come back here after the war, sergeant,' said van der Bos, 'and I'll show you a very different Sumatra.'

Bubonovitch shook his head. 'If I ever get back to Brooklyn,' he said, 'I'm going to stay there.'

'And me for Texas,' said Davis.

'Is Texas a nice state?' asked Corrie.

'Finest state in the Union,' Davis assured her.

'But Jerry told me that Oklahoma was the finest state.'

'That little Indian reservation?' demanded Davis. 'Say! Texas is almost four times as big. She grows more cotton then any other state in the Union. She's first in cattle, sheep, mules. She's got the biggest ranch in the world.'

'And the biggest liars,' said Douglas. 'Now if you really want to know which is the finest state in the Union, I'll tell you. It's California. You just come to the good old San Fernando Valley after the war and you'll never want to live anywhere else.'

'We haven't heard from New York State,' said Jerry, grinning.

'New Yorkers don't have to boast,' said Bubonovitch. 'They are not plagued by any inferiority feeling.'

'That's going to be a hard one to top,' said van der Bos.

'How about your state, Tony?' asked Sarina.

Rosetti thought for a moment. 'Well,' he said, 'Illinois had Public Enemy Number One.'

'Every American,' said Tarzan, 'lives in the finest town in the finest county in the finest state in the finest country in the world – and each one of them believes it. And that is what makes America a great country and is going to keep her so.'

'You can say that again,' said Davis.

'I have noticed the same thing in your Army,' continued the Englishman. 'Every soldier is serving in "the best damned outfit in this man's Army," and he's willing to fight you about it. That feeling makes for a great Army.'

'Well,' said Jerry, 'we haven't done so bad for a nation of jitterbugging playboys. I guess we surprised the world.'

'You certainly have surprised Hitler and Tojo. If you hadn't come in, first with materiel and then with men, the war would be over by now, and Hitler and Tojo would have won it. The world owes you an enormous debt.'

'I wonder if it will pay it,' said Jerry.

'Probably not,' said Tarzan.

28

Corrie was sitting with her back against the wall of the cave. Jerry came and sat down beside her. Sarina and Rosetti had wandered out of the cave together, arm in arm.

'Shrimp has become absolutely shameless,' said Jerry. 'Do you know, he really hated women. I think you are the first one he ever tolerated. He is very fond of you now.'

'You weren't particularly keen about us yourself,' Corrie reminded him.

'Well, you see, I'd never known a Dutch girl.'

'That was nice. You're improving. But don't tell me that the finest State in the Union hasn't the finest girls in the world.'

'There is only one "finest girl in the world," and she is not from Oklahoma.'

Corrie laughed. 'I know what you're doing!'

'What?'

'You're handing me a line. Isn't that what you Americans call it?'

'I'm not handing you a line, Corrie. You know how I feel about you.'

'I'm not a mind reader.'

'You're the most wonderful thing that has ever come into my life.'

'Now don't tell me that you're making love to me!'

'That is the general idea that I have in mind,' said Jerry, 'but I guess I'm not so hot at it.' He was looking into her eyes. Their misty depths reflected the firelight, but deep below the surface there burned another light, such a light as he had never seen in a woman's eyes before. 'God! But you're wonderful,' he said.

Corrie smiled. 'That's what you said before, but that time you called me a thing. They tell me you're a great pilot, Captain.'

He knew she was making fun of him; but he didn't care – he could still see that light in her eyes. 'I'm not a great pilot. I'm a great coward. I'm so scared of you that I can't say three little words.' Corrie laughed, and she didn't try to help him. 'Listen!' he blurted. 'How do you think you'll like living in Oklahoma?'

'I shall like it very much,' she said.

'Darling!' said Jerry. 'I've got to kiss you. I've got to kiss you right now – if it weren't for all these people in here.'

'We could go outside,' said Corrie.

Sergeant Rosetti held Sarina in his arms. His mouth covered hers. Her arms about his neck pressed him to her fiercely. Corrie and Jerry, coming from the firelight into the night, nearly bumped into them. Then they walked on to a distance.

'I suppose sergeants aren't supposed to be able to teach their captains anything,' said Corrie; 'but then Sergeant Rosetti is a most unusual sergeant.' She was panting a little a moment later when she gently pushed him away. 'You misogynists!' she gasped.

Sergeant Bubonovitch was sitting by the fire just inside the mouth of the cave. He had seen Shrimp and Sarina go out arm in arm; then Corrie and Jerry had gone out into the darkness. 'I gotta have love,' said Bubonovitch, trying to make friends with little Keta. Little Keta bit him. 'Nobody loves me,' said the sergeant, sorrowfully.

Day after day The Foreign Legion fought with nature for every hard won mile. Often some of them were so exhausted by the time they made camp at the end of a day that they fell asleep without eating. They were too tired even to talk much. But there was no complaining. Corrie and Sarina held their own with the men, who were very proud of them.

'They're lucky they haven't much to carry,' remarked Bubonovitch. 'Add them together and they wouldn't weigh any more than I do. Maybe they could throw in Shrimp, too. After the war I think I'll hire the three of them and start a flea circus.'

'Yeah? Wot you ought to have did,' said Shrimp, 'is went in de Navy. Den you'd a had a battlewagon to haul you around, you big cow.'

'What you should have done; not "Wot you ought to have did," ' corrected Sarina, who had been laboring to bring Shrimp's English more into line with that which the Catholic sisters had taught her, to the secret amusement of the rest of the company.

Bubonovitch had once said to Jerry: 'The granddaughter of a Borneo head hunter teaching an American English! I have seen everything now.'

Sarina made no effort to spare Shrimp's feelings. She corrected him in front of everybody, and often in the middle of a sentence. And Shrimp never objected. He just grinned and started over. And he was improving. He had almost stopped saying dis and dat, but did and done still troubled him. Douglas said: 'Ain't love wonderful!'

They were nearing Mt Masoerai, slightly short of which they were to recross the range and start down toward the sea. It had already been a month since they had left the camp of the guerrillas, and they had had only hardships with which to contend. Never had any of them been in great danger, nor had they seen a human being other than themselves. And then, out of a clear sky, disaster struck. Tarzan was captured by the Japs.

They were following a well marked game trail, Tarzan moving through the trees a short distance ahead of them, as usual. Suddenly he came upon a patrol of Japs. They had stopped in the trail to rest. Tarzan moved closer to determine the strength of the detachment. He still had ample time to return and warn his companions and dispose them for whatever might eventuate. Little Keta rode upon his shoulder. Tarzan cautioned him to silence.

The man's attention was riveted upon the Japs. He was unaware of the menace hanging just above him. But Keta saw it and commenced to scream. The Japs looked up. The coils of a huge python encircled the body of the man, galvanizing him to action. His knife flashed. The wounded snake writhed frantically in pain and rage, loosing its hold upon the branch that had supported it, and the two fell into the trail at the feet of the Japs. Keta fled.

The Japs fell upon the snake with bayonets and swords, killing it quickly. And Tarzan was at their mercy. There were too many of them. A dozen bayonets were hovering but inches above his body as he lay in the trail upon his back, helpless.

They took his bow and arrows and knife from him. An officer stepped close and kicked him in the side. 'Get up!' he said, in English. He had been a truck gardener in Culver City. He was short and bandy legged. He had buck teeth, and he wore horn rimmed glasses. He might have stepped out of a Lichty cartoon. His men had nicknamed him 'Whale' on account of his size. He stood a full five feet six in his sandals.

'Who are you?' demanded the officer.

'Col. John Clayton, Royal Air Force.'

'You're an American,' said the Jap. Tarzan did not reply. 'What are you doing here?' was the next question.

'I have told you all that I am required to tell you, and all that I intend telling you.'

'We'll see about that.' He turned to a sergeant and gave instructions in

Japanese. The sergeant formed the detachment, half in front of and half behind the prisoner, then they started along the trail in the same direction that the Foreign Legion was travelling. Tarzan saw from indications along the trail that they were retracing their steps from the point at which they had halted. He assumed that whatever their mission had been, they had completed it and were returning to camp.

Little Keta fled through the trees until he sighted the Foreign Legion; then he dropped down and leaped to Shrimp's shoulder. He threw both arms about the man's neck and screamed and jabbered in his ear.

'Something must have happened to Tarzan,' said Jerry. 'Keta is trying to tell us. He wouldn't leave Tarzan if things were all right with him.'

'May I go along the trail and take a look, Cap?' asked Rosetti. 'I can travel faster'n the rest of you.'

'Yes. Get going. We'll follow.'

Shrimp moved at an easy trot. Keta seemed satisfied now; so the man was sure that Jerry had been right. Tarzan was in trouble. Soon Shrimp heard voices ahead and the clank of accouterments. The Japs, apprehending no danger, marched carelessly. Shrimp came closer; and presently, towering above the little pseudo men, he saw the head and shoulders of Tarzan. Tarzan a prisoner of the Japs! It was incredible. Shrimp's heart sank – the heart which, not so long ago, had been filled with hatred of Englishmen.

The news that Rosetti brought back to the others appalled them all. The loss of the Lord of the Jungle would be a sore blow to the little company, but they thought first of Tarzan's safety rather than their own. He had inspired within the breasts of all not only respect and admiration, but real affection as well. That was because, as Shrimp had once confided to Bubonovitch, 'De guy's regular.'

'How many Japs were there, Rosetti?' asked Jerry.

'About twenty. They's nine of us, Cap'n, which is more than enough.'

'You can say that again,' said Bubonovitch. 'Let's go get him.'

'We can't attack them from the rear on this narrow trail without endangering Tarzan. We'll have to trail them until we find a better place to attack,' said Jerry.

The trail broke from the forest at the rim of a narrow canyon. Below him, Tarzan saw what was evidently a temporary camp. Half a dozen Jap soldiers guarded some equipment and a few pack animals. The equipment was scattered about in a disorderly manner. Some of it, probably perishable provisions, was covered with tarpaulin. There were no shelters. From the appearance of the camp, Tarzan concluded that the officer was inefficient. The less efficient, the easier he would be to escape from.

2nd Lieut. Kenzo Kaneko snapped instructions at a sergeant, and the sergeant bound the prisoner's wrists behind his back. Though the lieutenant may have been inefficient, the sergeant was not. He bound Tarzan's wrists so securely and with so many strands that not even the muscles of the Lord of the Jungle could have freed him.

The sergeant similarly bound the captive's ankles. This done, he pushed and tripped him, so that Tarzan fell to the ground heavily. A horse was brought and the packsaddle adjusted. A line was made fast to the saddle, the other end was then attached to Tarzan's feet. Lieut. Kaneko came and stood over him. He smiled benignly.

'I should hate to have the horse whipped into a run,' he said. 'It would hurt me, but it would hurt you more.'

The horse had been bridled, and a soldier carrying a whip had mounted it. The other soldiers stood about, grinning. They were about to witness an exhibition that would appeal to their sadistic natures.

'If you will answer my questions,' continued Kaneko, 'the horse will not be whipped, the line will be detached. How many are in your party and where are they?'

Tarzan remained silent. Kaneko no longer smiled. His features became convulsed with rage, or maybe he was only simulating rage in order to frighten his victim. He stepped closer and kicked Tarzan in the side.

'You refuse to answer?' he demanded.

Tarzan returned the Jap's stare. His face registered no emotion, not even the contempt he felt for this grotesque caricature of man. Kaneko's eyes fell beneath those of his prisoner. Something in those eyes frightened him, and that really filled him with genuine rage.

He snapped a command at the man on the horse. The fellow leaned forward and raised his whip. A rifle cracked. The horse reared and toppled backward. Another shot. 2nd Lieut. Kenzo Kaneko screamed and sprawled upon his face. Then came a fusillade of shots. Soldiers fell in rapid succession. Those who could, fled down the valley in utter demoralization as nine riflemen leaped down the steep trail into the camp.

A wounded Jap rose on an elbow and fired at them. Corrie shot him. Then Rosetti and Sarina were among them with bayonet and parang, and there were no more wounded Japs.

Jerry cut Tarzan's bonds. 'You arrived just about on time,' said Tarzan.

'Just like the cavalry in a horse opera,' said Bubonovitch.

'What do you think we'd better do now?' Jerry asked Tarzan.

'We must try to finish off the rest of them. This is evidently just a detachment from a larger force. If any of these fellows get back to that force, we'll be hunted down.'

'Have you any idea how many there were?'

'About twenty-five or twenty-six. How many have we killed?'

'Sixteen,' said Rosetti. 'I just counted 'em.'

Tarzan picked up a rifle and took a belt of ammunition from one of the dead Japs. 'We'll go back up to the rim of the valley. I'll go ahead through the trees and try to head them off. The rest of you work down along the rim until you can fire down on them.'

A half mile below the camp Tarzan overhauled the survivors. There were ten of them. A sergeant had gathered them together, and was evidently exhorting them to return to the fight. As they turned back, none too enthusiastically, Tarzan fired and brought down the sergeant. A private started to run down the valley. Tarzan fired again, and the man dropped. Now, the others realized that the shots had come from farther down the valley. They sought cover from that direction. Tarzan held his fire so as not to reveal his position.

The Foreign Legion, hearing the two shots, knew that Tarzan had contacted the enemy. They pushed forward through the trees at the rim of the valley. Jerry was in the lead. Presently he saw a Jap who had taken cover behind a fallen tree. Then he saw another and another. He pointed them out, and the firing commenced. Tarzan also started firing again.

The Japs, cut off in both directions in the narrow valley, without a leader, lacking sufficient intelligence or initiative to act otherwise, blew themselves up with their own grenades.

'They're damned accommodating,' said Douglas.

'Nice little guys,' said Davis; 'trying to save us ammunition.'

'I'm goin' down to help 'em out,' said Rosetti, 'if any of 'em are left alive.' He slid and rolled down the steep cliff-side, and Sarina was right behind him.

'There,' said Bubonovitch, 'is the ideal helpmeet.'

29

Six weeks later the Foreign Legion came down to the coast below Moekemoeko. It had been a strenuous six weeks beset by many hazards. Jap positions in increasing numbers had necessitated many long detours. Only the keen sensibility of the Lord of the Jungle, ranging well ahead of the little company, had saved them from disaster on numerous occasions.

There was a Jap anti-aircraft battery about a kilometer up the coast from where they lay concealed. Between them and the battery was a native village. It was in this village that Sarina expected to find friends who could furnish them a boat and provisions.

'If I had a sarong,' she said, 'I could walk right into the village in daytime, even if Japs were there; but this outfit might arouse suspicion. I'll have to take a chance, and sneak in after dark.'

'Perhaps I can get you a sarong,' said Tarzan.

'You will go into the village?' asked Sarina.

'Tonight,' replied Tarzan.

'You will probably find sarongs that were washed today and hung out to dry.'

After dark Tarzan left them. He moved silently through the stagnant air of the humid, equatorial night. In the camp that he had left that was not a camp but a hiding place, the others spoke in whispers. They were oppressed by the heat and the humidity and the constant sense of lurking danger. When they had been in the mountains they had thought their lot rather miserable. Now they recalled with regret the relative coolness of the higher altitudes.

'I have been in the hills for so long,' said Corrie, 'that I had almost forgotten how frightful the coast climate can be.'

'It is rather rotten,' agreed van der Bos.

'Dutchmen must be gluttons for punishment,' said Bubonovitch, 'to colonize a Turkish bath.'

'No,' said van der Bos; 'we are gluttons for profit. This is a very rich part of the world.'

'You can have it,' said Rosetti. 'I don't want no part of it.'

'We wish that the rest of the world felt the same way,' said van der Bos.

Tarzan swung into a tree that overlooked the village. A full moon lighted the open spaces. The ornate, native houses cast dense shadows. Natives squatted in the moonlight, smoking and gossiping. Three sarongs hung limp in the dead air from a pole across which they had been thrown to dry. Tarzan settled himself to wait until the people had gone into their houses for the night.

After a while a man entered the kampong from the west. In the bright moonlight, Tarzan could see him plainly. He was a Jap officer, the commanding officer of the anti-aircraft battery a short distance away. When the natives saw him they arose and bowed. He approached them with an arrogant swagger, speaking a few words to a young woman. She arose meekly and followed him into the house that he had commandeered for his own use.

When his back was turned the natives made faces at him, and obscene gestures. Tarzan was content. What he had seen assured him that the natives would be friendly to any enemy of the Japs. After a while the natives went into their houses and silence descended upon the kampong.

Tarzan dropped to the ground and moved into the shadow of a building. He stole silently to a point as near to the sarongs as he could get without coming out into the moonlight. He stood there for a moment listening; then he stepped quickly across the moon drenched space and seized a sarong.

Returning, he had almost reached the shadow when a woman stepped from behind the corner of a building. They met face to face in the moonlight. The woman, startled, opened her mouth to scream. Tarzan seized her and clapped a hand over her parted lips. Then he dragged her into the shadow.

'Quiet!' he commanded in Dutch, 'and I will not harm you.' He hoped that she understood Dutch. She did.

'Who are you?' she asked.

'A friend,' he replied.

'Friends do not steal from us,' she said.

'I am only borrowing this sarong. It will be returned. You will not tell the Jap about this? He is my enemy, too.'

'I will not tell him. We tell them nothing.'

'Good,' said Tarzan. 'The sarong will be returned tomorrow.'

He wheeled and was lost in the shadows. The woman shook her head, and climbed the ladder that gave entrance to her house. She told her family of the adventure that had befallen her.

'You will never see the sarong again,' said one.

'For the sarong, I do not care,' she replied. 'It did not belong to me. But I should like to see the wild man again. He was very beautiful.'

The following morning, Sarina entered the village. The first woman she met recognized her, and soon she was surrounded by old friends. She warned them away for fear that there might be Japs in the village who would recognize from their greetings that she must be a newcomer and therefore someone to be investigated. Sarina did not wish to be investigated by any Japs. The villagers understood, and returned to their normal activities. Then Sarina sought out Alauddin Shah, the village chief. He seemed glad to see her, and asked her many questions, most of which she avoided answering until she could determine what his relations were with the Japs.

She soon learned that he hated them. Alauddin Shah was a proud old man, a hereditary chief. The Japs had slapped and kicked him and forced him to bow low even to their enlisted men. Satisfied, Sarina told her story, explained what she and her companions needed, and solicited his aid.

'It will be a hazardous journey,' he said. 'There are many enemy ships in these waters, and it is a long way to Australia. But if you and your friends wish to risk it, I will help you. There is a large proa hidden in the river a few kilometers down the coast from the village. We will provision it for you, but it will take time. We are not regularly watched; because we have given the Japs no trouble, but they are in and out of the kampong almost every day. One officer sleeps here every night. Everything that we do must be done with the utmost caution.'

'If you will leave provisions every day in a house near the edge of the kampong, we will come at night and take them to the proa,' Sarina told him. 'Thus you can escape blame if we are discovered. You can be very much surprised when you discover that someone has come into the village at night and stolen food.'

Alauddin Shah smiled. 'You are a true daughter of Big Jon,' he said.

A month passed, a month of narrow escapes from detection, a month of harrowed nerves; but at last the proa was provisioned. And now they waited for a moonless night and a favorable wind. Barbed wire and obstructions at the mouth of the stream had been left in place until the proa was ready. Now they had to be removed – a dangerous job in waters infested with crocodiles. But at last even that was accomplished.

At last it came – N-Night they called it. The tide was right. There was no moon. There was a brisk off-shore wind. Slowly they poled the proa down to the sea. The great lateen sail was hoisted. Close in the lee of the shore it caught little wind, but farther out it bellied to a strong breeze, and the proa gained speed.

While moonless, the night was clear. They set a course due South, the Southern Cross their lodestar. They had fashioned a crude log and log line, and while the knots were running they tried to estimate their speed. Sarina guessed twelve knots. She was not far off.

'If this wind holds,' she said, 'we'll be well off the southern tip of Nassau Island before 2:00 o'clock tomorrow morning. Then we'll take a southwesterly course. I want to get out of the coastal waters of Sumatra and Java before we swing to the southeast toward Australia. This way we'll give Engano a wide berth. Then there'll be only the Cocos Islands to worry about, as far as land is concerned. I don't know if the Japs have anything on Cocos.'

'Are they the same as the Keeling Islands?' asked Jerry.

'Yes, but my father always called them the Cocos Islands because he said Keeling was "a damned Englishman."' She laughed, and so did Tarzan.

'Nobody loves an Englishman,' he said. 'But I'm not so sure that Keeling was an Englishman.'

'There's a light at 2:00 o'clock,' said Davis.

'Probably on Nassau,' said Sarina. 'Let's hope so, for if it isn't, it's a ship's light; and we don't want any business with ships.'

'I don't think their ships would be showing any lights,' said Jerry. 'There are too many Allied subs in these waters.'

Morning found them in an empty ocean – just a vast, round cauldron of tumbling gray water. The wind had freshened, and great seas were running. S/Sgt. Rosetti was sick. Between spasms he remarked, 'I got a half-wit cousin. He joined the Navy.' After a while he said, 'It won't be long now. This crate won't stand much more, and it can't come too soon to suit me. This is the first time in my life I ever wanted to die.' Then he leaned over the rail and heaved again.

'Cheer up, Shrimp,' said Bubonovitch. 'It won't be long now before we go ashore on Australia – maybe only a month or so.'

'Geeze!' groaned Rosetti.

'You will get over being sick pretty soon, Tony,' said Sarina.

'Some admirals always get sick when they first go to sea after shore duty,' said Tarzan.

'I don't want to be an admiral. I joins up for air, and what do I get? For couple or three months I been a doughboy; now I'm a gob. Geeze!' He leaned over the rail again.

'Poor Tony,' said Sarina.

The long days passed. The wind veered into the southeast. The southeast trade wind that would blow for ten months had started. Sarina took long tacks, first to starboard and then to port. It was slow going, but their luck had held. They were well past the Keeling Islands now, and no sign of enemy shipping.

Douglas, who had been standing his trick as lookout, had come aft. 'It's an awful lot of water,' he said. 'Flying it, it seems terrible big – the Pacific, I mean; but down here on the surface it seems like there isn't anything in the world but water; and this is only the Indian Ocean, which ain't a drop in the bucket alongside the Pacific. It makes you feel pretty small and insignificant.'

'There's sure a lot of water in the world,' agreed van der Bos.

'Three quarters of the whole surface of the Earth is water,' said Corrie.

'And the Pacific has a greater area than all the land surfaces of the Earth combined,' said Jerry.

'If I owned it,' said Rosetti, 'I'd trade the whole damn works for any old street corner in Chi.'

'What I don't like about it,' said Douglas, 'is the total absence of scenery. Now, in California—'

'He's off again,' said Bubonovitch.

'But he's got something just the same,' said Davis. 'Gawd! How I'd like to see a cow – just one measly little cow deep in the heart of Texas.'

'I'll settle for land, any old land, right now,' said Rosetti. 'Even Brooklyn would look good. I might even settle down there. I'm fed up on travellin'.'

'Travel is broadening, Shrimp,' said Bubonovitch. 'Just look what it's done for you. You like a Britisher, you love a dame, and you have learned to speak fairly intelligible English, thanks to Sarina.'

'I ain't getting broadened much lately,' objected Rosetti. 'We ain't seen nothing but water for weeks. I'd like to see something else.'

'Smoke at eleven o'clock!' called Jerry, who had gone forward as lookout.

Sarina smiled. The airmen's method of indicating direction always amused her, but she had to admit that it was practical.

Everybody looked in the direction indicated where a black smudge was showing just above the horizon.

'Maybe you're going to see something beside water now, Shrimp,' said Davis. 'Your wish was granted in a hurry.'

'That must be a ship,' called Jerry, 'and I think we'd better hightail it out of here.'

'Toward five o'clock?' asked Sarina.

'Keerect,' said Jerry, 'and pronto.'

They came about and sailed before the wind in a Northwesterly direction, every eye on that ominous black smudge. 'It might be British,' said Corrie, hopefully.

'It might be,' agreed Tak, 'but we can't take any chances. It might just as well be Jap.'

For what seemed a long time there was no noticeable change in the appearance of the thing they watched so fearfully; then Tarzan's keen eyes discerned the superstructure of a ship rising above the horizon. He watched closely for a few minutes. 'It is going to cut right across our course,' he said. 'It will pass astern, but they're bound to sight us.'

'If it's Jap,' said Sarina, 'it's bound for Sumatra or Java. Our only chance is to hold this course and pray – pray for wind and more wind. If it's one of those little Jap merchant ships, we can outrun it if the wind picks up. Or if we can just hold our lead until after dark, we can get away.'

The proa seemed never to have moved more slowly. Straining eyes watched the menace grow larger, as the hull of a ship climbed over the rim of the world. 'It's like a bad dream,' said Corrie, 'where something horrible is chasing you, and you can't move. And the wind is dying.'

'You guys ain't prayin' hard enough,' said Rosetti.

'All I can remember,' said Davis, 'is "now I lay me down to sleep," and I can't remember all of that.'

A sudden gust of wind bellied the great sail, and the speed of the proa increased noticeably. 'Somebody hit the jackpot,' said Douglas.

But the strange ship continued to gain on them. 'She's changed course,' said Tarzan. 'She's heading for us.' A moment later he said, 'I can see her colors now. She's a Jap all right.'

'I should have gone to church like Mom always wanted me to,' said Davis. 'I might have learned some good prayers. But if I can't pray so good,' he said a moment later, 'I sure can shoot good.' He picked up his rifle and slipped a clip into the magazine.

'We can all shoot good,' said Jerry, 'but we can't sink a ship with what we got to shoot with.'

'That's a small, armed merchantman,' said Tarzan. 'She probably carries 20 mm anti-aircraft guns and .30 caliber machine guns.'

'I guess we're out-gunned,' said Bubonovitch, with a wry grin.

'The effective range of the 20s is only about 1200 yards,' said Jerry. 'These pop guns will do better than that. We ought to be able to get a few Nips before they finish us off – that is if you folks want to fight.' He looked around at them. 'We can surrender, or we can fight. What do you say?'

'I say fight,' said Rosetti.

'Think it over carefully,' admonished Jerry. 'If we put up a fight, we shall all be killed.'

'I don't intend to let those yellow sonsabitches knock me around again,' said Bubonovitch. 'If the rest of you don't want to fight, I won't either; but I won't be taken alive.'

'Neither shall I,' said Corrie. 'How do you feel about it, Jerry?'

'Fight, of course.' He looked at Tarzan. 'And you, Colonel?'

Tarzan smiled at him. 'What do you think, Captain?'

'Does anyone object to fighting rather than surrendering?' No one did. 'Then we'd better check our rifles and load 'em. And may I say in conclusion, it's been nice knowing you.'

'That sounds terribly final,' said Corrie, 'even if you did mean it for a joke.'

'I'm afraid it is – final and no joke.'

The merchantman was closing up on them rapidly now, for after that one fitful gust the wind had slackened to a breeze that didn't even fill the great triangular sail of the proa.

'We've been mighty lucky for a long time,' said Tak. 'According to the law of chance, it should be about time for our luck to run out.'

There was a red flash aboard the Jap, followed by a puff of smoke. A moment later a shell burst far short of them.

'Lady Luck is getting ready to hit the breeze,' said Rosetti.

30

'Beautiful gunnery!' said Bubonovitch. 'The poor sap doesn't even know the range of his gun.'

'Itchy fingers probably,' said Douglas.

'I doubt that the little admirals put their top gunnery officers aboard little merchantmen,' said Jerry; 'so maybe our luck is holding.'

The proa was barely making headway now, as it rose and fell on long swells.

The forefoot of the oncoming ship plowed through the deep blue of the ocean, turning up white water, as the moldboard of a plow turns up the rich loam of a field.

Again the Jap fired. This shell fell wide, but not so short. Jerry and Corrie were sitting close together, one of his hands covering one of hers. 'I guess van Prins was right,' said Jerry. 'He said we were crazy. I shouldn't have brought you along, darling.'

'I wouldn't have it otherwise,' said Corrie. 'We've had this much time together, that we wouldn't have had if I hadn't come with you. I've never had a chance to say "for better or for worse," but it has been in my heart always.'

He leaned closer to her. 'Do you, Corrie, take this man to be your wedded husband?'

'I do,' said Corrie, very softly. 'Do you, Jerry, take this woman to be your wedded wife, to cherish and protect until death do you part?'

'I do,' said Jerry, a little huskily. He slipped the class ring from his finger and on to Corrie's ring finger. 'With this ring I do thee wed, and with all my worldly goods endow.' Then he kissed her.

'I think,' said Corrie, 'that as far as the service is concerned our memories were a little lame; but we had the general idea at least. And I feel very much married, sweetheart.'

A near miss deluged them with water. They did not seem to notice it.

'My wife,' said Jerry. 'So young, so beautiful.'

' "Wife!", repeated Corrie.

'The guy's gettin' closer,' said Rosetti.

The fin of a shark cut the water between the proa and the Jap. Little Keta watched it, fortunately unaware of what it might portend. Tarzan raised the sights on his rifle and fired at the figures lining the rail of the Jap. The others followed his example, and presently ten rifles were blazing away. If they accomplished nothing else, they emptied the rail of sightseers and caused much confusion aboard the merchantman. Yes, they accomplished one more thing: they spurred the anti-aircraft gunners into frenzied activity. Shell bursts dotted the ocean.

'If their ammo holds out,' said Rosetti, 'they got to hit us just accidentally. Geeze! What lousy shootin'!'

At last it came, as they knew it must – a direct hit. Jerry saw half of Sing Tai's body hurled fifty feet into the air. Tak van der Bos' right leg was torn off. The entire company was thrown into the ocean; then the Jap moved in and commenced to machine gun them as they swam about or clung to pieces of the wreckage. The aim of the gunners was execrable, but again they knew that this was the end of the Foreign Legion – that eventually some of those hundreds of whining bullets would find them all.

Bubonovitch and Douglas were holding up van der Bos, who had fainted.

Jerry was trying to keep between Corrie and the machine guns. Suddenly something commenced to drag van der Bos down. One of Bubonovitch's feet struck a solid body moving beneath. 'Migawd!' he yelled. 'A shark's got Tak.' Bullets were ricocheting off the water all around them.

Tarzan, who had been thrown some distance by the shell burst, was swimming toward Bubonovitch and Douglas when he heard the former's warning. Diving quickly beneath the surface, he drew his knife. A few swift, strong strokes brought him close to the shark. A mighty surge of his knife arm ripped open the belly of the huge fish, disemboweling it. It released its hold on van der Bos and turned on Tarzan, but the man eluded its jaws and struck again and again with his knife.

The water was red with blood as another shark darted in and attacked its fellow. The first shark swam sluggishly away while the other bit and tore at it. For the moment the survivors were freed from one menace, but the bullets still pinged close.

With Tarzan's help, Bubonovitch and Douglas got van der Bos to a large piece of wreckage – one of the outrigger floats. Tarzan tore a strip from what remained of van der Bos' trousers, and while he and Douglas held the man on the float, Bubonovitch applied a tourniquet. Tak still breathed, but fortunately he was unconscious.

Bubonovitch shook his head. 'He ain't got a chance,' he said. 'But then, neither have we.'

'The sharks are going to have plenty good feeding today,' said Douglas.

They were all looking at the Jap ship. Again the rail was lined with bandy legged little men. Some of them were firing pistols at the people in the water. Keta, perched on a piece of wreckage, scolded and threatened.

There was a terriffic detonation. A great fan shaped burst of flame shot hundreds of feet into the air from amidships of the merchantman, and a pillar of smoke rose hundreds of feet higher. A second explosion followed and the ship broke in two, the bow hurled almost clear of the water. The two halves sunk almost immediately, leaving a few scorched and screaming creatures struggling in burning oil.

For a few moments the survivors of the proa looked on in stunned silence, which was broken by Rosetti. 'I knew She'd hear me,' he said. 'She ain't ever failed me yet.'

'She'll have to pull a real miracle yet to get us out of the middle of the Indian Ocean before we drown or the sharks get us,' said Jerry.

'Pray like hell, Shrimp,' said Bubonovitch.

'Don't think I ain't, brother,' said Rosetti.

'Look! Look!' shouted Corrie, pointing.

Three hundred yards beyond the burning oil a submarine was surfacing. The Union Jack was painted on the side of its conning tower.

'There's your miracle, Cap'n,' said Rosetti. 'She ain't ever failed me yet. I mean in a real pinch.'

'What do you think of the British now, sergeant?' asked Tarzan, smiling.

'I love 'em,' said Rosetti.

The sub circled to windward of the burning oil and drew alongside the wreckage of the proa. The hatch spewed men to haul the castaways aboard. Tarzan and Bubonovitch passed van der Bos up first. He died as they laid him gently on the deck.

Corrie and Sarina followed, and then the men. Lt Cmdr Bolton, skipper of the sub, was full of amazement and questions. Corrie knelt beside van der Bos' body, trying to hold back the teers. Jerry joined her.

'Poor Tak,' she said.

They did not take him below. He was buried at sea, Bolton reading the burial service. Then they all went below for dry clothing and hot coffee, and presently the sorrow and depression seemed less, for they were all young and they had all seen much of death.

When Bolton heard their story, he said, 'Well, you have certainly played in luck from the start; but my happening to be right where I was when you needed me is little short of a miracle.'

'It hasn't been luck, Sir,' said Rosetti. 'It's been Holy Mary, Mother of Jesus from start to finish, including the miracle.'

'I can well believe it,' said Bolton, 'for none of you has any business being alive now, by all the laws of chance. Nothing but divine intervention could have preserved you. It even arranged that I saved my last two fish for that Jap. You really should all be dead.'

'Mary certainly helped in a pinch,' said Jerry, 'but if Tarzan hadn't been on the job all the time, pinch-hitting for her, we'd have been sunk months ago.'

'Well,' said Bolton, 'I think you won't have to call on either Mary or Tarzan from now on. I'm ordered to Sydney, and it won't be so long now before you can sit down in Ushers Hotel with a steak and kidney pie in front of you.'

'And drink warm beer,' said Bubonovitch.

Later that evening Jerry and Rosetti approached Bolton. 'Captain,' said the former, 'are you authorized to perform marriage ceremonies at sea?'

'I certainly am.'

'Then you got two jobs right now, skipper,' said Rosetti.

TARZAN AND THE MADMAN

ONE

Friends or Enemies

Man has five senses, some of which are more or less well developed, some more or less atrophied. The beasts have these same senses, and always one and sometimes two of them are developed to a point beyond the conception of civilized man. These two are the sense of smell and the sense of hearing. The eyesight of birds is phenomenal, but that of many beasts is poor. Your dog invariably verifies the testimony of his eyes by coming close and smelling of you. He knows that his eyes might deceive him, but his nose never.

And the beasts appear to have another sense, unknown to man. No one knows what it is, but many of us have seen demonstrations of it at one time or another during our lives – a dog suddenly bristling and growling at night and glaring intently and half-fearfully at something you cannot see. There are those who maintain that dogs can see disembodied spirits, or at least sense their presence.

Tarzan of the Apes had the five senses that men and beasts share in common, and he had them all developed far beyond those of an ordinary man. In addition, he possessed that strange other sense of which I have spoken. It was nothing he could have defined. It is even possible he was not aware that he possessed it.

But now as he moved cautiously along a jungle trail, he felt a presentiment that he was being stalked – the hunter was being hunted. None of his objective senses verified the conclusion, but the ape-man could not shake off the conviction.

So now he moved even more warily, for the instinct of the wild beast for caution warned him not to ignore the portent. It was not fear that prompted him, for he did not know fear as you and I. He had no fear of death, who had faced it so often. He was merely activated more or less unconsciously by Nature's first law – self-preservation. Like the dog that senses the presence of a ghost at night, he felt that whatever had impinged upon his consciousness was malign rather than beneficent.

Tarzan had many enemies. There were his natural enemies, such as Numa the lion and Sheeta the panther. These he had had always, ever since the day he had been born in the lonely cabin on the far West Coast. He had learned of them even as he suckled at the hairy breast of his foster-mother – Kala the great she-ape. He had learned to avoid them, but never to fear them; and he had learned how to bait and annoy them.

But his worst enemies were men – men whom he had to punish for their transgressions – African natives and white men, to him, Gomangani and Tarmangani in the language of his fierce, shaggy people.

Numa and Sheeta he admired – his world would have been desolate without them; but the men who his enemies he held only in contempt. He did not hate them. Hate was for them to feel in their small, warped brains. It was not for the Lord of the Jungle.

Nothing out of the ordinary may go unchallenged or uninvestigated by the wild beast which would survive; and so Tarzan took to the trees and doubled back upon his trail, directed by a natural assumption that if he were being stalked the stalker had been following behind him.

As he swung downwind through the trees, following the middle terrace where the lower branches would better conceal him from the eyes of the enemy on the ground, he realized that the direction of the wind would carry the scent spoor of him he sought away from him and that he must depend wholly upon his ears for the first information of the presence of a foe. He commenced to feel a little foolish as the ordinary noises of the jungle were unbroken by any that might suggest a menace to him. He commenced to compare himself with Wappi the antelope, which is suspicious and fearful of everything. And at last he was upon the point of turning back when his keen ears detected a sound that was not of the primitive jungle. It was the clink of metal upon metal, and it came faintly from afar.

Now there was a point to his progress and a destination, and he moved more swiftly but nonetheless silently in the direction from which the sound had come. The sound that he had heard connoted men, for the wild denizens of the jungle do not clink metal against metal. Presently he heard other sounds, the muffled tramp of booted feet, a cough, and then, very faintly, voices.

Now he swung to the left and made a wide detour that he might circle his quarry and come upon it from behind and upwind, that thus he might determine its strength and composition before risking being seen himself. He skirted a clearing which lay beside a river and presently reached a position to which Usha the wind bore the scent of a party of blacks and whites. Tarzan judged there to be some twenty or thirty men, with not more than two or three whites among them.

When he came within sight of them, they had already reached the clearing beside the river and were preparing to make camp. There were two white men and a score or more of blacks. It might have been a harmless hunting party, but Tarzan's premonition kept him aloof. Concealed by the foliage of a tree, he watched. Later, when it was dark, he would come closer and listen, for he might not wholly ignore the warning his strange sense had given him.

Presently another noise came to his ears, came from up the river – the splash of paddles in the water. Tarzan settled down to wait. Perhaps friendly natives were coming, perhaps hostile; for there were still savage tribes in this part of the forest.

The men below him gave no signs that they were aware of the approach of the canoes, the noise of which was all too plain to the ape-man. Even when four canoes came into sight on the river, the men in the camp failed to discover them. Tarzan wondered how such stupid creatures managed to survive. He never expected anything better from white men, but he felt that the natives should long since have been aware of the approach of the strangers.

Tarzan saw that there were two white men in the leading canoe, and even at a distance he sensed something familiar in one of them. Now one of the blacks in the camp discovered the newcomers and shouted a warning to attract his fellows. At the same time the occupants of the leading canoe saw the party on the shore and, changing their direction, led the others towards the camp. The two white men, accompanied by some askaris, went down to meet them; and presently, after a conversation which Tarzan could not over-hear, the four canoes were dragged up on the bank and the newcomers prepared to make camp beside the other party.

TWO

The Two Safaris

As the two white men stepped from their canoe, Pelham Dutton was not greatly impressed by their appearance. They were hard and sinister looking, but he greeted them cordially.

Bill Gantry, Dutton's guide and hunter, stepped forward towards one of the men with outstretched hand. 'Hello, Tom. Long time no see.' Then he turned towards Dutton: 'This is Tom Crump, Mr Dutton, an old timer around here.'

Crump nodded crustily. 'This here's Minsky,' he said, indicating his companion.

From a tree at the edge of the clearing, Tarzan recognized Crump as a notorious ivory poacher whom he had run out of the country a couple of years before. He knew him for an all round rotter and a dangerous man, wanted by the authorities of at least two countries. The other three men,

Dutton, Gantry and Minsky, he had never seen before. Dutton made a good impression upon the ape-man. Gantry made no impression at all; but he mentally catalogued Ivan Minsky as the same type as Crump.

Crump and Minsky were occupied for a while, directing the unloading of the canoes and the setting up of their camp. Dutton had walked back to his own camp, but Gantry remained with the newcomers.

When Crump was free he turned to Gantry. 'What you doin' here, Bill?' he asked; then he nodded towards Dutton, who was standing outside his tent. 'Who's that guy, the law?' It was evident that he was nervous and suspicious.

'You don't have to worry none about him,' said Gantry, reassuringly. 'He ain't even a Britisher. He's an American.'

'Hunting?' asked Crump.

'We was,' replied Gantry. 'I was guide and hunter for this Dutton and a rich old bloke named Timothy Pickerall – you know, Pickerall's Ale. Comes from Edinburgh, I think. Well, the old bloke has his daughter, Sandra, with him. Well, one day, a great big guy comes into camp wearing nothing but a G string. He's a big guy and not bad-lookin'. He said his name was Tarzan of the Apes. Ever hear of him?'

Crump grimaced. 'I sure have,' he said. 'He's a bad 'un. He run me out of good elephant country two years ago.'

'Well, it seems that the Pickerall gal and her old man had heard of this here Tarzan. They said he was some sort of a Lord or Duke or something, and they treated him like a long-lost brother. So one day they goes hunting, and the girl goes out alone with this here Tarzan, and they never come back; so we thought they got killed or something, and we hunt for them for about a week until we meets up with a native what had seen them. He said this here Tarzan had the girl's hands tied behind her and was leading her along with a rope around her neck; so then we knew she'd been abducted. So old man Pickerall gets a heart attack and nearly croaks, and this here Dutton says he'll find her if it's the last thing he does on earth, because the guy's soft on this Pickerall gal. So the old man says he'll give a £1000 for the safe return of his daughter, and £500 for Tarzan dead or alive. The old man wanted to come along, but on account of his heart he didn't dare. So that's why we're here; and you don't have to worry none about nothin'.'

'So you'd like to find this here Tarzan, would you?' demanded Crump.

'I sure would.'

'Well, so would I. I got somethin' to settle with him, and with £500 on his head it's gonna be worth my while to give a little time to this here matter; and I'm the guy that can find him.'

'How's that?' demanded Gantry.

'Well, I just been up in the wild Waruturi country, aimin' to do a little tradin'. They're a bad lot, those Waruturi – cannibals and all that, but I gets along swell with old Mutimbwa, their chief. I done him a good turn once, and I always take him a lot of presents. And while I was there, they told me about a naked white man who had stolen a lot of their women and children. They say he lives up beyond the great thorn forest that grows along the foot-hills of the Ruturi Mountains. That's bad country in there. I don't guess no white man's ever been in it; but the natives give it a bad name.

'Some of the Waruturi followed this guy once, and they know pretty much where he holes up; but when they got beyond the thorn forest, they got scared and turned back, for all that country in there is taboo.' Crump was silent for a moment; then he said, 'Yes, I guess I'll join up with you fellows and help find the girl and that Tarzan guy.'

'You'd like a shot at your old friend Tarzan, wouldn't you?' said Gantry.

'And at the £1500,' added Crump.

'Nothin' doin',' said Gantry. 'That's mine.'

Crump grinned. 'Same old Gantry, ain't you?' he demanded. 'But this time I got you over a barrel. I can go in alone, for I know the way; and if you try to follow, you'll end up in the Waruturi cooking pots. All I got to do is tell 'em you're comin' and they'll be waitin' for you with poisoned bamboo splinters in every trail. The only reason I'd take you along at all is because the more guns we have, the better the chance we got.'

'O.K.,' said Gantry. 'You win. I was only kiddin' anyhow.'

'Does Dutton get a cut?' asked Crump.

'No, he's doin' it because he's soft on the girl. Anyway, he's got skads of boodle.'

'We'll have to cut Minsky in.'

'The hell we will!' exclaimed Gantry.

'Now wait a second, Bill,' said Crump. 'Me and him split everything fifty-fifty. He's a good guy to have for a friend, too; but look out for him if he don't like you. He's got an awful nervous trigger finger. You'd better see that he likes you.'

'You're the same old chiseler, aren't you?' said Gantry, disgustedly.

'I'd rather have a chisel used on me than a gun,' replied Crump, meaningly.

The brief equatorial twilight had passed on and darkness had fallen upon the camp as the white men finished their evening meal. The black boys squat-ted around their small cooking fires while a larger beast fire was being prepared to discourage the approach of the great cats. The nocturnal noises of the forest lent a mystery to the jungle that Pelham Dutton sensed keenly. To the other whites, long accustomed to it, and to the natives to whom it was a lifelong experience, this distance-muted diapason of the wilderness brought no reaction – the crash of a falling tree in the distance, the crickets, the shrill piping call of the cicadae, the perpetual chorus of the frogs, and the doleful cry of the lemur to his mate, and, far away, the roar of a lion.

Dutton shuddered – he was thinking that out there somewhere in that hideous world of darkness and savagery and mystery was the girl he loved in the clutches of a fiend. He wished that she knew that he loved her. He had never told her, and he knew now that he had not realized it himself until she had been taken from him.

During the evening meal, had told him what he had in the Warturi country, and that no woman that the ape-man, as Crump called him, had stolen had ever been returned. Dutton's waning hope had been slightly renewed by Crump's assurance that he could lead them to the haunts of the abductor, and Dutton tried to console himself with the thought that if he could not effect a rescue he might at least have vengeance.

The beast fire had been lighted, and now the flames were leaping high illuminating the entire camp. Suddenly a black cried out in astonishment and alarm, and as the whites looked up they saw a bronzed giant, naked but for a G string, slowly approaching.

Crump leaped to his feet. 'It's the damned ape-man himself,' he cried; and, drawing his pistol, fired point-blank at Tarzan.

THREE

Hunted

Crump's shot went wild and, so instantaneous are the reactions of Tarzan, it seemed that almost simultaneously an arrow drove through Crump's right shoulder, and his pistol arm was useless.

The incident had occurred so suddenly and ended so quickly that momentarily the entire camp was in confusion; and in that moment, Tarzan melted into the blackness of the forest.

'You fool!' cried Dutton to Crump. 'He was coming into camp. We might have questioned him.' And then he raised his voice and cried, 'Tarzan, Tarzan, come back. I give you my word that you will not be harmed. Where is Miss Pickerall? Come back and tell us.'

Tarzan heard the question, but it was meaningless to him; and he did not return. He had no desire to be shot at again by Crump, whom he believed had fired at him for purely personal reasons of revenge.

That night he lay up in a tree wondering before he fell asleep who Miss Pickerall might be and why anyone should think that he knew her whereabouts.

Early the next morning he stalked a small buck and made a kill. Squatting

beside it, he filled his belly while Dango the hyena and Ungo the jackal circled him enviously, waiting for his leavings.

Later in the day he became aware that there were a number of natives
ahead of him, but this was still a friendly country in which there were no
natives hostile to the ape-man. He had ranged it for years and knew that the
natives looked upon him as a friend and protector; and so he was less cautious than usual, having no thought of danger until a spear flashed past him
from ambush so close that he felt the wind of its passing.

If you would kill or cripple a wild beast it is well to see that your first missile does not miss him. Almost before his assailant could determine whether
or not his cast had been true, Tarzan had swung into the lower terraces of the
forest and disappeared.

Making a wide detour, Tarzan circled about and came back, cautiously,
along the middle terrace, to learn the identity of his assailant; and presently
he came upon some twenty warriors huddled together and evidently suffering from an excess of terror.

'You missed him,' one of them was saying, 'and he will come and take vengeance upon us.'

'We were fools,' said another. 'We should have waited until he came to our
village. There we would have treated him like a friend; and then, when he
was off his guard, fallen upon him and bound him.'

'I do not like any of it,' said a third. 'I am afraid of Tarzan of the Apes.'

'But the reward was very large,' insisted another. 'They say that it is so great
that it would buy a hundred wives for every man in the village, and cows and
goats and chickens the number of which has never been seen.'

This was all very puzzling to the ape-man, and he determined to solve the
mystery before he went farther.

He knew where lay the village of these black men, and after dark he
approached it and lay up in a tree nearby. Tarzan knew the habits of these
people, and he knew that because it was a quiet evening without dancing or
drinking they would soon all be wrapped in slumber on their sleeping mats
within their huts and that only a single sentry would be on guard before the
King's hut; so he waited with the infinite patience of the beast watching the
lair of its quarry, and when utter quiet had fallen upon the village he
approached the palisade from the rear. He ran the last few steps and, like a
cat, scrambled to the top; then he dropped quietly into the shadows beyond.

Swiftly and with every sense alert he planned his retreat. He noted a large
tree, one branch of which overhung the palisade. This would answer his purpose, though he would have to pass several huts to reach it. The guard before
the chief's hut had built a little fire to keep him warm, for the night was chill;
but it was burning low – an indication to Tarzan that the man might be
dozing.

Keeping in the denser shadows of the huts, the ape-man moved silently towards his quarry. He could hear the heavy breathing of the sleepers within the huts, and he had no fear of detection by them; but there was always the danger that some yapping cur might discover him.

The light of the stars moving across the face of a planet makes no noise. As noiseless was the progress of the ape-man; and so he came to the chief's hut, undiscovered, and there he found what he had expected – a dozing sentry. Tarzan crept up behind the man. Simultaneously, steel-thewed fingers seized the man's throat and a strong hand was clapped over his mouth. A voice spoke in his ear: 'Silence, and I will not kill.'

The man struggled as Tarzan threw him across his shoulder. For a moment the fellow was paralyzed with terror, but presently he jerked his mouth momentarily from Tarzan's palm and voiced a terrified scream; then the ape-man closed upon the fellow's windpipe and commenced to run towards the tree that overhung the palisade; but already the village was aroused. Curs came yapping from the huts, followed by warriors sleepy-eyed and confused. A huge warrior for buck blocked his way; but the Lord of the Jungle threw himself against him before the fellow could use his weapon, hurling him to the ground, and then, leaping over him, ran for the tree with curs and warriors now in hot pursuit.

Wind-driven as a sapling, the tree leaned towards the palisade at an angle of some forty-five degrees; and before the foremost warrior could overtake him, Tarzan, running up the inclined bole, had disappeared in the foliage. A moment later he dropped to the ground outside the palisade, quite confident that the natives would not pursue him there, at least not until they had wasted much time and talk, which is a characteristic of the African savage, and by that time he would be far away in the forest with his captive. Now he loosened his grip on the black's throat and set him on his feet. 'Come with me quietly,' he said, 'and you will not be harmed.'

The black trembled. 'Who are you?' he asked. It was too dark for him to see his captor's features, and previously he had been in no position to see them.

'I am Tarzan,' replied the ape-man.

Now the black trembled violently. 'Do not harm me, Bwana Tarzan,' he begged, 'and I will do anything that you wish.'

Tarzan did not reply, but led the man on into the forest in silence.

He stopped just beyond the edge of the clearing and took his captive into a tree from which point of vantage he could see if any pursuit developed.

'Now,' he said, when he had settled himself comfortably upon a limb, 'I shall ask you some questions. When you answer, speak true words if you would live.'

'Yes, Bwana Tarzan,' replied the black, 'I will speak only true words.'

'Why did the warriors of your village attack me today and try to kill me?'

'The drums told us to kill you because you were coming to steal our women and our children.'

'Your people have known Tarzan for a long time,' said the ape-man. 'They know that he does not steal women or children.'

'But they say that Tarzan's heart has gone bad and that now he does steal women and children. The Waruturi have seen him taking women to his village, which lies beyond the thorn forest that grows along the little hills at the foot of the Ruturi Mountains.'

'You take the word of the Waruturi?' demanded Tarzan. 'They are bad people. They are cannibals and liars, as all men know.'

'Yes, Bwana, all men know that the Waruturi are cannibals and liars; but three men of my own village saw you, Bwana, less than a moon ago when you went through our country leading a white girl with a rope about her neck.'

'You are not speaking true words, now,' said Tarzan. 'I have not been in your country for many moons.'

'I am not saying that I saw you, Bwana,' replied the black. 'I am only repeating what the three men said they saw.'

'Go back to your village,' said the ape-man, 'and tell your people that it was not Tarzan whom the three warriors saw, but some man with a bad heart whom Tarzan is going to find and kill so that your women and children need fear no longer.'

Now Tarzan had a definite goal, and the following morning he set out in the direction of the Ruturi Mountains, still mystified by the origin of these reports of his atrocities but determined to solve the enigma and bring the guilty one to justice.

Shortly after noon, Tarzan caught the scent spoor of a native approaching him along the trail. He knew that there was only one man, and so he made no effort to conceal himself. Presently he came face to face with a sleek, ebony warrior. The fellow's eyes dilated in consternation as he recognized the ape-man, and simultaneously he hurled his spear at Tarzan and turned and ran as fast as his legs would carry him.

Tarzan had recognized the black as the son of a friendly chief; and the incident, coupled with the recent experiences, seemed to indicate that every man's hand was against him, even those of his friends.

He was quite certain now that someone was impersonating him; and, as he must find this man, he might not overlook a single clue; therefore he pursued the warrior and presently dropped upon his shoulders from the foliage above the trail.

The warrior struggled, but quite hopelessly, in the grip of the ape-man. 'Why would you have killed me?' demanded Tarzan. 'I, who have been your friend!'

'The drums,' said the warrior; and then he told much the same story that the black sentry had told Tarzan the previous night.

'And what else did the drums tell you?' demanded the ape-man.

'They told us that four white men with a great safari are searching for you and the white girl that you stole.'

So that was why Crump had shot at him. It explained also the other man's question: 'Where is Miss Pickerall?'

'Tell your people,' said Tarzan to the black warrior, 'that it was not Tarzan who stole their women and children, that it was not Tarzan who stole the white girl. It is someone with a bad heart who has stolen Tarzan's name.'

'A demon, perhaps,' suggested the warrior.

'Man or demon, Tarzan will find him,' said the ape-man. 'If the whites come this way, tell them what I have said.'

FOUR
Captured

The gloom of the forest lay heavy upon Sandra Pickerall, blinding her to the beauties of the orchids, the delicate tracery of the ferns, the graceful loops of the giant lianas festooned from tree to tree. She was aware only that it was sinister, mysterious, horrible.

At first she had been afraid of the man leading her like a dumb beast to slaughter with a rope about her neck; but as the days passed and he had offered her no harm her fear of him lessened. He was an enigma to her. For all the weary days that they had tramped through the interminable forest, he had scarcely spoken a word. Upon his countenance she often noticed an expression of puzzlement and doubt. He was a large, well built man, possibly in his late twenties, she thought, with a rather nice, open face. He did not look at all like a scoundrel or a villain, she concluded; but what did he want of her? Where was he taking her? Now as they sat down to rest and to eat, she demanded for the hundredth time, 'Who are you? Where are you taking me? Why don't you answer me?'

The man shook his head as though trying to shake the cobwebs from his mind. He looked at her intently.

'Who am I? Why, I am Tarzan. I know I am Tarzan; but they call me God – but,' – he leaned closer towards her – 'sh-h-h, I am not God; but don't tell them that I told you.'

'Who are "they"?' she demanded.

'The Alemtejos,' he replied. 'Da Gama says that I am God, but old Ruiz says that I am a devil who has been sent to bring bad luck to the Alemtejos.'

'Who are da Gama and Ruiz?' asked the girl, wondering at this sudden break in the man's silence and hoping to stimulate it by her questions.

'Da Gama is King,' replied the man, 'and Ruiz is high priest. He wants to get rid of me because he doesn't want a god around. You see, a god is more powerful than a high priest. At first he tried to get da Gama to kill me; but da Gama wouldn't do that; so finally Ruiz said that a god was no good without a goddess. Well, after a while, da Gama agreed to that and told me to go and find a goddess; otherwise I should be killed. You are the goddess. I am taking you back, and now they won't kill me.'

'Why do you go back?' she demanded. 'This high priest will only find some other excuse to kill you.'

'Where would I go, if I didn't go back to Alemtejo?' he demanded.

'Go back to where you came from,' said the girl.

Again that puzzled expression crossed his face. 'I can't do that,' he said. 'I came from heaven. Da Gama said so; and I don't know how to get back. He said I floated down from heaven. In fact, they all say so. They say that they saw me; but I do not know how to float up again, and if I did I would not know where to find heaven. However, I do not think that I am God at all. I am Tarzan.'

'I tell you what you do,' said Sandra. 'You come back with me to my people. They will be kind, if you bring me back. I will see that they do not harm you.'

He shook his head. 'No, I must do as da Gama says, or he will be very angry.'

She tried to argue the question with him, but he was adamant. The girl came to the conclusion that the man must be simple-minded, and that, having been given an idea by da Gama, it had become fixed in his mind to such an extent that he was unable to act on any other suggestion; yet he did not look like a half-wit. He had a well shaped head and an intelligent face. His speech was that of an educated man, his attitude towards her that of a gentleman.

Sandra had heard stories of Tarzan of the Apes, but all that she had heard had convinced her that he was far too intelligent to permit him even to entertain the idea that he might be a god, and as for running at the beck and call of this da Gama or anyone else she was quite sure that would be out of the question; yet this man insisted that he was Tarzan. With a shrug, Sandra gave up in despair.

As they took up their journey again after their rest, the man continued talking. It was as though there had been a dam across his reservoir of speech, and now that it was broken he felt relieved that the words would flow.

'You are very beautiful,' he said, suddenly. 'You will make a beautiful goddess. I am sure that da Gama will be pleased. It took me a long time to find you. I brought them black women and children, but they did not want these for goddesses; so many of them were fed to the guardians of Alemtejo. One has to offer sacrifices to them occasionally, even a god; so now I always try to take a woman or a child with me. The guardians of Alemtejo do not care so much for the flesh of men.'

'Who are the guardians of Alemtejo, who eat human beings?' demanded Sandra; but her question was not answered, for at the instant that she voiced it a score of painted warriors rose up about them.

'The Waruturi,' whispered the false Tarzan.

'It is Tarzan,' cried Mutimbwa the chief.

Two warriors leaped forward with levelled spears, but Mutimbwa the chief stepped between them and the white man. 'Do not kill him,' he said. 'We will take them to the village and summon the tribe to a feast.'

'But he stole our women and children,' objected one of the warriors.

'So much the better, then, that he die slowly; so that he will remember,' said Mutimbwa.

'You understand what they are saying?' Sandra asked the man.

He nodded. 'Yes, do you?'

'Enough,' she said.

'Do not worry,' said the man. 'I shall escape; and then I shall come and get you.'

'How can you escape?' she demanded.

'I can try,' he said; 'and if I am God, as da Gama has said I am, it should be easy for me to escape; and if I am Tarzan, as I know I am, it should be very easy.'

They were moving along the forest trail now with blacks in front of them and behind them. It did not seem to Sandra that it would be an easy thing for even a god to escape. Suddenly he who said that he was Tarzan raised his head and voiced a piercing scream, strange and weird. A black struck him with the haft of his spear, and told him to be quiet; but that cry had made the Waruturi nervous, and they kept casting apprehensive glances about them.

From far away came an answering cry. The blacks jabbered excitedly among themselves, and often Sandra caught the word for demon. Mutimbwa the chief urged the party into a trot. Apparently the entire company was seized with nervous apprehension.

'Something answered your cry,' said the girl to the man. 'What was it?'

He smiled at her. 'One of God's servants,' he said. 'Presently they will come and take me away.'

The girl was mystified. The thing was uncanny, for the sound that had come to them could not have come from a human throat.

Presently they came to a more open part of the forest and, to Sandra's relief, the gait was reduced to a walk. She had eaten neither regularly nor much since her capture, and the long and exhausting marches had sapped her strength. Suddenly she was startled by a loud cry of alarm behind her and, turning, she saw what was to her as fearsome a sight as it must have been to the genuinely terrified blacks – a band of huge, manlike apes, snarling and growling, had charged among the Waruturi. Their mighty fangs, their huge muscular arms and hands were wreaking havoc with the terrified blacks. With one accord, they bolted, carrying Sandra Pickerall along with them. The great apes pursued them for a short distance and then turned back. When Mutimbwa had succeeded in quieting and rallying his warriors, it was discovered that the white prisoner, whom they thought was Tarzan, had disappeared.

So God had escaped! Sandra was more than half-glad that she had not escaped with him, for those great, hairy apes seemed to be more terrifying than the blacks. The blacks were men. She might persuade them, in view of the ransom that she knew she could offer, to take her back to her people; but then Sandra did not know the Waruturi or their customs. There was, however, just one little doubt in her mind. She had noticed, from the first moment that she had been able to note these warriors carefully, that there was not one of them but wore golden ornaments. Armlets, anklets, of solid gold were common; and nearly all of them wore golden rings in their ears. What temptation would her father's money be to a people possessing so much wealth as these?

When they reached the palisaded village of the Waruturi chief, she saw even greater evidence of gold and wealth.

Once inside the village, she was turned over to the women, who struck her and spit upon her and tore most of her clothes from her. They would have killed her had not Mutimbwa the chief intervened.

'You have done enough,' said the chief. 'Leave her alone; and the night after this night we shall feast.'

'You are the chief?' asked Sandra.

Mutimbwa nodded. 'I am Mutimbwa the chief,' he said.

'Take me back to my people,' said the girl, 'and you can name your own ransom.' She spoke in broken Swahili.

Mutimbwa laughed at her. 'If the white man has anything we want, we will go and take it away from him,' he said.

'What are you going to do with me?' demanded Sandra.

Mutimbwa pointed at a cooking pot and rubbed his belly.

FIVE

Cannibal Feast

The ape-man was in new and unfamiliar country now, as he aproached the illy-defined borders of the Waruturis' domain. He knew these people by reputation only. He knew that they were fierce, uncivilized savages and cannibals; but his only concern as far as they were concerned was to be constantly on guard against them.

His business was to trail the white man who was impersonating him, and destroy him. The rescue of the white girl was incidental. If he could find her and take her back to her people, well and good; but first he must destroy the impostor who was stealing the women and children of those who had been his friends.

The second night since he had entered the Waruturi country had fallen. He had seen no Waruturi nor had he come upon the trail of the impostor and the girl. His immediate plan was to enter the Ruturi Mountains and search there.

Late in the afternoon he had made a kill and had eaten. Now he was lying up for the night in the fork of a great tree. The night sounds of the jungle were lulling him to sleep when there came to his ears above these the sounds of drums. The ape-man listened intently. The drums were calling the tribe to a feast that would be held the following night. He guessed that they were Waruturi drums.

He put together the things that he knew. The white girl and her captor would have had to pass through the Waruturi country. The Waruturi were cannibals. They were summoning their people from other villages to a feast. It was unlikely that this would be true unless it were to be a cannibal feast. Tarzan decided to investigate. The direction from which the sounds came and their volume gave him some idea of the location of the village and its distance. He settled himself comfortably in the crotch of the tree, and slept. Tomorrow he would go to the village.

The second night of Sandra Pickerall's captivity was approaching. The village of Mutimbwa the chief was crowded. All day, warriors and women and children had been straggling in from other villages. Sandra could see them through the doorway of the hut where she was imprisoned. As she estimated their number, she was grimly aware that there would not be enough of her to go around. Even in the face of so horrible an end, the girl smiled. That was the stuff of which she was made. At last they came for her. The cooking pots were simmering. Five bleating goats were trussed up and lying beneath the great tree in front of the chief's hut. Sandra was dragged to a place beside the goats. The witch-doctor and a few bucks commenced to dance around them. They were chanting, and the drums were keeping melancholy time.

Suddenly, with a loud scream, the witch-doctor darted in and fell upon a goat, severing its jugular with his knife; then the chanting rose to a wail, and all the villagers joined in.

Sandra sensed that this was in the nature of a religious rite. She saw that it was a priest who cut up the body of the goat. He mumbled gibberish over each piece as he handed it to a warrior, who in turn took it to a woman who transferred it to one of the cooking pots.

One by one the goats were slaughtered and butchered thus. The witch-doctor was dismembering the fifth goat. Sandra knew that it would be her turn next. She tried to be brave. She must not show fear before these bestial savages. The goats had bleated, but not she. She thought of her father and her friends. She thought of Pelham Dutton. She prayed that in searching for her they might not fall into the hands of the Waruturi.

The last morsel of the fifth goat had been disposed of in a cooking pot. The witch-doctor was coming toward her. The warriors were dancing about her. The chant rose in volume and savagery.

The final moment had come. The witch-doctor darted toward her, his blood-smeared hands grasping his bloody knife, the knife which was to sever her jugular. Suddenly the witch-doctor stopped, voiced a single scream of agony and collapsed upon the ground, the haft of an arrow protruding from his heart. Simultaneously, a white man, naked but for a G-string, dropped from the tree above to the ground beside her. Into the very midst of the dancing cannibals he dropped just as the dancing ceased and every eye was upon the body of the witch-doctor.

It was all done so quickly that afterwards no one, probably, could have told how it was accomplished. One moment the victim was there and the witch-doctor's knife was almost at her jugular. The next instant the witch-doctor was dead and the captive was gone.

Even Sandra could not have told how it was done. She had stood there waiting for imminent death when suddenly she was seized about the waist and lifted from the ground. The next instant she was in the tree above the chief's hut and was being borne away through the foliage in the darkness of the night. How they surmounted the palisade, she never knew. She was half unconscious from surprise and fright as they crossed the clearing. The first thing that she could ever recall was sitting high in the branches of a tree in the forest with a man's strong arm about her to keep her from falling.

'Who are you?' she gasped.

'I am Tarzan of the Apes,' replied a deep voice.

'Da Gama must have been right,' she said. 'You must be God, for nobody else could have rescued me.' The voice had seemed different, but this could not be other than her strange captor who had promised to come and rescue her.

'I don't know what you are talking about,' said Tarzan.

'Only what you told me yesterday,' she said, 'that you thought you were Tarzan but da Gama insisted you were God.'

'I did not see you yesterday,' said the ape-man. 'I have never seen you before. I am Tarzan of the Apes.'

'You mean to tell me that you did not steal me from my father's camp and bring me here to this country?'

'That was another man who is impersonating me. I am searching for him to kill him. Do you know where he is? Was he also a captive of the Waruturi?'

'No, he escaped; but he promised to come back and rescue me.'

'Tell me something about him,' said the ape-man.

'He was a strange creature,' replied the girl. 'I think he had been a gentlemen. He did not harm me, and he was always considerate and respectful.'

'Why did he steal you, then?'

'He said that da Gama insisted that he was a god, and had sent him out to find a white woman to be his goddess. I think –' she hesitated – 'I think he was not quite right in the head; but he was so certain that he was Tarzan of the Apes. Are you sure that you are?'

'Quite,' said the ape-man.

'Why did you rescue me?' she asked. 'How did you know that I was in the village of the Waruturi?'

'I did not know. The drums told me that the Waruturi were feasting tonight; and knowing them to be cannibals and knowing that you were in this part of the forest, I came to their village to investigate.'

'And now you will take me back to my father?'

'Yes,' said the ape-man.

'You know where his safari is?'

'There is a safari with four white men looking for me to kill me,' said Tarzan with a grim smile. 'That is doubtless the safari of your father.'

'There were only three white men with our safari,' said Sandra, 'my father, Pelham Dutton, and our guide and hunter, a man by the name of Gantry.'

'There was a man by the name of Crump with this safari. He shot at me but missed.'

'There was no man by the name of Crump with our safari.'

'What did your father look like?'

After the girl had described her father to him, Tarzan shook his head. 'Your father is not with that safari.' But when she described Dutton and Gantry he recognised them.

'Crump and the fourth man joined Dutton and Gantry some time ago. Crump is a bad man. I don't know the other one; but if he is ranging with Crump he is no good either,' Tarzan told her.

Sandra Pickerall slept that night on a rude platform that Tarzan built for her high among the branches of a patriarch of the jungle, and she slept well for she was exhausted; and she slept without fear for there was something about the man with her which imbued her with confidence.

When she awoke in the morning she was alone, and when she realized her situation she was afraid. She was totally unprepared to cope with the dangers of the forest, nor had she the remotest idea in which direction to search for the safari that was looking for her.

She wondered why the man had deserted her. It seemed so inconsistent with the thing he had done the night before in risking his life to save her from the Waruturi. She came to the conclusion that all the wild men of the jungle were irresponsible and, perhaps, a little bit insane. It didn't seem credible that a white man in his right sense would run around almost naked in the jungle in preference to living in a civilized environment.

She was very hungry, but she hadn't the remotest idea how to obtain food. Some of the fruits of the forest trees she knew to be safe; but she saw none around her which she recognized, and she did not dare eat the others. It all seemed very hopeless, so hopeless that she commenced to wonder how long it would take before she died of starvation, if some beast of the jungle did not kill her in the meantime.

And then at the very depths of despondency, she heard a noise in the tree behind her and, turning, saw her rescuer of the night before swing lightly to the branch at her side, one arm laden with fruits.

'You are hungry?' he asked.

'Very.'

'Then eat; and when you have eaten, we will start out in search of the safari of your friends.'

'I thought you had deserted me,' she said.

'I will not leave you,' he replied, 'until I have returned you safely to your people.'

Tarzan could only guess at the general direction in which to hunt for the safari of the girl's friends; but he knew that eventually he could find it, though the great forests of Central Africa cover over three hundred thousand square miles of territory.

The men of Dutton's safari were hungry for fresh meat; and so the white men decided to remain in camp for a day and do some hunting. Early in the morning they set out, each in a different direction, with their gun-bearers. At perhaps a mile from camp, Crump stumbled upon a water hole evidently much used by the jungle beasts; and finding concealment among some bushes, he lay down to wait for his quarry to come to him.

He had been lying in concealment for about an hour without seeing any signs of game when he heard someone approaching. He could hear their voices before he saw them and thought that he recognized one as being that of a woman; so he was not surprised when Tarzan and Sandra Pickerall came into view.

Crump's lips curled in a nasty grin as he cautiously raised his rifle and took careful aim at the ape-man. When he squeezed the trigger, Tarzan pitched forward upon his face, blood gushing from a head wound.

SIX

In Cold Blood

As Tarzan fell, Crump leaped to his feet and called the girl by name as he strode towards her.

'Who are you?' she demanded.

'I am one of the guys that's looking for you,' he said. 'My name is Tom Crump.'

'Why did you shoot him?' she demanded. 'You've killed him.'

'I hope so,' said Crump. 'He had it comin' to him for goin' and stealin' you.'

'He didn't steal me. He saved my life, and he was bringing me to Pelham Dutton's safari.'

'Well, he's dead,' said Crump, pushing Tarzan's limp body with his boot. 'Come along with me. I'll take you to Dutton. Our camp's only about a mile from here.'

'Aren't you going to do anything for him?' she demanded.

'I've done everything I wanted to with him already,' said Crump with a laugh. 'Come along now.'

'Aren't you going to bury him?'

'I ain't no gravedigger. The hyenas and jackals'll bury him. Come along now. I can't waste no more time here. If there were any game around, that shot has scared it away by this time.' He took her by the arm and started off towards camp.

'He said you were a bad man,' said Sandra.

'Who said I was a bad man?'

'Tarzan.'

'Well, I was too good for him.'

As they departed, a pair of close-set, bloodshot eyes watched them from a concealing thicket, and then turned back to rest upon the body of Tarzan of the Apes.

Sandra and Crump reached camp before the others returned; and it was not until late in the afternoon that Dutton, the last of the three, came in with a small buck and a couple of hares.

When he saw the girl, he dropped his game and came running towards her. 'Sandra!' he exclaimed, grasping both her hands. 'Is it really you? I had about given up hope.' His voice shook with emotion, and the girl saw tears in his eyes, tears of relief and happiness. 'Who found you?' he asked.

'I found her,' said Crump; 'and I got that damned Tarzan guy, too. He won't never steal no more girls.'

'He did not steal me,' said Sandra. 'I've told this man so a dozen times. He rescued me from a Waruturi village last night just as they were going to kill me; and this man shot him in cold blood and left him out there in the forest. Oh, Pelham, won't you come back with me, and bring some of the boys, and at least give him a decent burial?'

'I certainly will,' said Dutton; 'and I'll do it right away, if we can make it before dark.'

'It's not far,' said Sandra.

'Do you think you can find the place?' he asked.

'I don't know,' she said.

'If it'll make you feel any better to bury him,' said Crump, 'I'll show you where he is; but I think it's damned foolishness. He's probably bein' et right now. It don't take hyenas long to locate a feed, or the vultures either.'

'Horrible!' exclaimed Sandra. 'Let's start at once, Pelham.'

Dutton gathered a half dozen of the black boys and, with Gantry leading the way, he and Sandra started out in search of Tarzan's body. Gantry and Minsky, curious to see the ape-man close up, accompanied them.

A half hour later they came to the water hole. Crump, who was in the lead, halted in his tracks with an oath and an exclamation of surprise.

'What's the matter?' demanded Dutton.

'The son-of-a-gun ain't here,' said Crump.

'You must have just wounded him,' said Dutton.

'Wounded nothing! I shot him in the head. He was as dead as a doornail. It's sure damned funny, what's become of him.'

'Dead men don't walk away,' said Gantry.

'Then something took him away,' said Crump.

'He may be close by,' said Sandra; and she called Tarzan's name aloud several times, but there was no reply.

'This is all very mystifying,' said Dutton. 'First you are captured by one Tarzan, Sandra, and then you are rescued by another Tarzan. I wonder which one was Tarzan, or if either of them were.'

'The one I killed was Tarzan,' said Crump. 'I never seen the other one; but I knew this bloke all right.'

'We might as well go back to camp,' said Gantry. 'There's no use hangin' around here.'

'If only I knew,' said Sandra.

'Knew what?' asked Dutton.

'Whether or not he's lying around somewhere near here only wounded, perhaps unconscious again and prey for the first prowling beast that comes upon him. He was so brave. He risked his life to save me.'

'Well, he ain't lying around wounded nowhere,' said Crump. 'He's dead. Some lion or somethin' drug him off; and, anyway I don't see no sense in makin' such a fuss about a damn monkey-man.'

'At least he was a man and not a brute,' said Sandra bitterly.

'If I'd knowed you had a crush on him, I wouldn't have shot him,' said Crump.

'Shut up!' snapped Dutton. 'We've taken all we're going to from you.'

'So what?' demanded Crump.

'Don't,' begged Sandra. 'Don't quarrel. We've been in enough trouble without that. Take me back to camp, please, Pelham; and tomorrow we'll take our own safari and start back to father's.'

'Yeah?' sneered Crump; 'and Minsky and I'll come with you.'

'We won't need you,' said Dutton.

'Maybe you don't need us; but we're comin' with you anyway. I'm comin' to collect that reward.'

'What reward?' demanded Sandra.

'Your father offered a reward of a £1000 for your return,' explained Dutton, 'and £500 for the capture, dead or alive, of the man who stole you.'

'Then no one can collect either reward,' said the girl. 'You killed the man who rescued me; and the man who stole me is still at large.'

'We'll see about that,' growled Crump.

As the party made its way back to camp, savage eyes watched them. Among them was one pair of eyes that were neither savage nor unfriendly. They were the eyes of the man who thought he was Tarzan. The other eyes belonged to the great, shaggy, man-like apes which he called the servants of God.

After the party they were watching had disappeared towards their camp, the man and his companions came out into the open. The man was leading a black woman, a rope about her neck. He had been surprised to see Sandra Pickerall, for he had supposed that by this time she had been killed by the Waruturi. At sight of her his spirits had risen, for now again there was a chance that he might take back a white goddess with him to Alemtejo. He had been a little bit afraid to return again without one; so he had captured the Waruturi woman to take back as a slight peace-offering to da Gama.

After darkness had fallen on the jungle, the false Tarzan and his fierce band crept close to the camp of the whites where the man might watch and plan.

Sandra and Dutton sat before her tent discussing past events and planning for the future, while, out of earshot, Crump, Minsky, and Gantry spoke in whispers.

'I ain't goin' to be done out of my share of that reward,' Crump was saying, 'and I gotta plan that ought to bring us twice as much.'

'What is it?' asked Gantry.

'This guy, Dutton, gets killed accidental-like; then Minsky and I take the girl. You go back to the old man and tell him you put up a fight but we were too many for you. You tell him we let you go, so you could go back and report to him that we're holding the girl for £3000 ransom. There's three of us. We'll split it three ways. We each get a £1000, and you don't take no risk.'

'I won't have nothin' to do with murder,' said Gantry. 'I gotta pretty clean record in Africa, and I ain't gonna spoil it.'

'That's because you ain't never been caught,' said Crump.

'And I don't intend to get caught now,' retorted Gantry, 'and, anyway, this Dutton is a pretty good guy.'

'There ain't no use killin' him nohow,' said Minsky. 'Listen to me.'

'Shoot,' said Crump.

'After Dutton and the girl turn in tonight,' continued Minsky, 'Crump and I'll get our safari loaded up; then we'll bind and gag you in your tent and steal the girl. When Dutton finds you in the mornin' you can tell him that we got the drop on you, but before we left with the girl we told you that her old man could have her if he would send £3000.'

'Where to?' asked Gantry.

'I'm coming to that,' said Minsky. 'You know where old Chief Pwonja's village is on the Upindi River, don't you?'

'Yes,' said Gantry.

'Well, that's where we'll take the girl. We'll wait there two months. If you haven't come with the ransom money by that time, we'll know what to do with her.'

'But if I know where you are, that makes me a party to the whole business,' said Gantry.

'No it don't,' said Minsky. 'Just tell 'em you had to take your choice between doin' what we tell you to do or gettin' killed and gettin' killed if you double-cross us. Knowin' Tom's reputation, they'll believe you.'

'Your reputation doesn't smell so sweet,' growled Crump.

'Well, between the two of us, our reputation ought to be worth £3000,' said Minsky with a grin, 'and them's pretty valuable reputations to have.'

'But suppose you double-cross me?' demanded Gantry.

'Not a chance, Bill,' said Crump. 'You know I wouldn't never double-cross a pal.'

But Gantry didn't know anything of the kind, nor did he know what was passing in the minds of these men, nor did they know what was passing in his mind. Neither Crump nor Minsky had the slightest intention of turning any of the £3000 over to Gantry; and, after it was once safely in their hands, Crump planned to kill Minsky and keep the entire amount; while Gantry hadn't the slightest intention of going to the village of Chief Pwonja on the Upindi River once he got his hands on the money. He had heard a lot about Hollywood, and he thought he could have a good time there with £3000. He could live there under an assumed name, and no one would be the wiser. And so these three precious characters laid their plans; and the moon crept behind a cloud; and Sandra and Dutton went to their respective tents.

The man who thought he was Tarzan watched and waited patiently. He noted the tent into which the girl had gone, and now he waited for the others to go to theirs. Finally, Gantry repaired to his tent; but Crump and Minsky were busy among the porters. The false Tarzan watched the blacks loading up their packs, and wondered; then he saw one of the whites go to the tent occupied by Gantry. In a few minutes he came out again and joined his companion. Presently the porters shouldered their packs and started off towards the west.

This was all very interesting. The man who thought he was Tarzan crept closer. He wished the two white men would go away with their porters; then he could easily go and get the girl; but they did not leave, and the man grew slightly impatient.

Sandra found it difficult to sleep. She was physically tired, but her mind and her nerves were dancing like dervishes. She could not drive from her thoughts the recollection of the murder of Tarzan. She still saw that magnificent figure crumpling in death, one instant so vital and alert, the next an inert lump of clay.

She loathed Crump for the thing that he had done; and now for weeks she would have to see him every day as they made the slow and laborious return trip to her father's camp; but she thanked God for Pelham Dutton. Without him, that return trip would be unthinkable. She tried to drive the death of Tarzan from her mind by thinking of Pelham. Her intuition told her that the man was very fond of her. He had never spoken a word of love; but there had been that in his eyes when he had greeted her this day that spoke far more eloquently than his words. She tried to evaluate her own feelings. Like any normal girl, she had her infatuations and her little flirtations. Sometimes she had felt that they were love, but they had never lasted long enough for her to find out. She knew that she felt differently towards Pelham Dutton than she ever had towards any other man. It was a more solid, substantial, and satisfying feeling; and it was exhilarating, too. When he had grasped her hand at their meeting this day, she had had to deny a sudden impulse to creep into his arms and snuggle close to him for protection and sympathy; but that, she told herself, might have been a natural reaction after all that she had passed through. She might have felt the same way about any friend whom she liked and trusted.

She was still intent upon her problem when the flap of her tent was lifted and Crump and Minsky entered.

SEVEN

Abducted

A great bull-ape had come alone to the water hole to drink; but, like all wild beasts who are natural prey of Numa the lion or Sheeta the panther, he had reconnoitred first before coming out into the open. From the concealment of a dense thicket, he had surveyed the scene; and presently he had seen the top of a bush near the water hole move. There was no wind to move it; and immediately the anthropoid became suspicious. He waited, watching; and presently he saw a Tarmangani with a rifle raise himself just above the bush, take aim and fire. It was not until Tarzan pitched forward to the ground that the ape saw him and the girl with him. He waited until the girl and the man who had shot Tarzan had gone away; then he came out into the open and approached the body of the ape-man. He turned it over on its back and sniffed at it, making a little moaning noise in his throat; then he picked it up in his great, hairy arms and carried it off into the jungle.

Sandra Pickerall sat up on her cot. 'Who are you?' she demanded. 'What do you want?'

'Shut up,' growled Crump. 'We ain't gonna hurt you, if you keep your trap shut. We're gettin' out of here, and you're comin' with us.'

'Where's Mr Dutton?' she demanded.

'If he's lucky, he's asleep. If you make any noise and wake him up, he's gonna get killed.'

'But what do you want of me? Where are you going to take me?' she demanded.

'We're gonna take you some place where you'll be safe,' said Crump.

'Why not tell her?' said Minsky. 'Listen, lady, we're taking you where nobody won't find you until your old man comes across with £3000; and if you know what's good for you and this Dutton guy, you won't make us no trouble.'

Sandra thought quickly. She knew that if she called for help, Dutton would come and he would be killed; for these were dangerous, desperate men whose situation would be affected little by any additional crime.

'Let me dress and get some of my things together,' she said, 'and I'll come quietly.'

'Now you're talkin' sense,' said Crump; 'but just to be on the safe side, we'll wait for you while you dress.'

The false Tarzan, followed closely by the servants of God, had crept close to the camp which lay unguarded, Crump having sent the askaris along with the porters.

As Crump, Sandra, and Minsky came from the girl's tent, the man who thought that he was Tarzan ran forward, closely followed by the great apes. Growling, striking, rending, the hairy beasts fell upon the two men, while their human leader seized the girl and dragged her quickly from the camp.

It was all over in a few seconds; but the noise had aroused Dutton, who came running from his tent, rifle in hand. In the flickering light of the camp-fire, he saw Crump and Minsky rising slowly to their feet, dazed and groggy, with blood streaming from several superficial wounds.

'What's the matter?' demanded Dutton. 'What has happened?'

Minsky was the first to grasp the situation. 'I seen something prowling around Miss Pickerall's tent,' he said, 'and I woke Crump and we come up here; then about a dozen gorillas jumped on us, but I seen a white man grab the girl and run off with her. It was that Tarzan again.'

'Come on,' said Dutton. 'We've got to find her. We've got to follow them and take her away from them.'

'It ain't no use,' said Crump. 'In the first place, there's too many of them. In the second place, it's too dark. We couldn't never find their trail. Even if we did come up with them, we couldn't shoot for fear of hitting the girl.'

'But there must be something we can do,' insisted Dutton.

'Wait 'til morning,' said Crump.

While the two were talking, Minsky had crept into Gantry's tent and unbound him, at the same time telling him what had happened. 'He wants to go out lookin' for the girl,' he concluded. 'You go a little way with him and then make him come back, or let him go on alone for all I care; and in the meantime, we'll get the boys back into camp. If they come in while he's here, he'll sure be suspicious.'

'O.K.,' said Gantry, and led the way out of his tent.

Dutton saw them coming, but Minsky forestalled his suspicions. 'This guy is sure some sleeper,' he said. 'He slept through it all. I had to go in and wake him up.'

'I'm going out to search for Miss Pickerall,' said Dutton. 'Are you men coming with me?'

'I'm not,' said Crump, 'because it wouldn't do no good.'

'I'll go along with you, Mr Dutton,' said Gantry.

'All right then, come along,' said the American, and started off in the direction that Crump had said the girl's abductors had taken her.

For a quarter of an hour they stumbled through the forest. Occasionally, Dutton called Sandra's name aloud; but there was no reply.

'It ain't no use, Mr Dutton,' said Gantry, presently. 'We can't find them at night, and even if we did stumble on 'em by accident, what could we do? Crump said there were ten or fifteen of 'em. We wouldn't stand a chance with 'em; and we wouldn't dare shoot for fear of hitting Miss Pickerall.'

'I guess you're right,' said Dutton despondently. 'We'll have to wait until morning; then we'll take every man that we have a gun for, and follow them until we catch up with them.'

'I think that's more sensible-like,' said Gantry; and the two turned back towards camp. By the time they reached it, the porters and askaris were back; and there was no indication that they had been away.

When morning came it found the false Tarzan leading two women with ropes around their necks. One was a black Waruturi, the other was Sandra Pickerall. Trailing them were the shaggy, savage servants of God.

The two women were very tired, but the man forced them on. He knew that until they reached the thorn forest which lies at the base of the Ruturi foothills, he would not be safe either from the Waruturi or the white men whom he was sure would follow them; and he must not lose the white goddess again or da Gama would be very angry with him. It was a gruelling grind, with only occasional brief stops for rest. They had no food, for the man did not dare leave them alone long enough to search for it; but by nightfall, even the man who thought he was Tarzan was upon the verge of exhaustion; and so they lay down where they were and slept until morning.

Ravenously hungry, but rested, they took up the march again at break of day; and, by noon, they came to the edge of the thorn forest.

There didn't seem to be a break in that interminable stretch of armed trees; but finally the man located a place where, by creeping upon all fours, they could avoid the thorns. They proceeded this way for a few yards, and then a trail opened up before them upon which they could walk erect.

After he had first captured her, the man had scarcely spoken for a long time, and he had been equally taciturn upon this occasion, speaking only when it was necessary to give orders; but when they had passed through the thorn forest and come out into the open, his attitude changed.

He breathed a sigh of relief. 'Now we are safe,' he said. 'This time I shall bring da Gama the white goddess.'

'Oh, why did you do it?' she said. 'I have never harmed you.'

'And I have never harmed you,' he retorted; 'nor do I intend to. I am doing you a great favour. I am taking you to be a goddess. You will have the best of everything that Alemtejo can give, and you will be worshipped.'

'I am only an English girl,' she said. 'I am not a goddess, and I do not wish to be.'

'You are very ungrateful,' said the man.

Their trail wound up into the foothills; and ahead of them, Sandra could see a lofty escarpment, a formidable barrier, the Maginot Line, perhaps, of the Ruturi Range. Before they reached the escarpment they came to the narrow mouth of a gorge across which had been built a strong palisade. Sandra thought that this was the village to which she was being taken. A stream of clear water, sparkling in the sunlight, ran beneath the palisade and down through the foothills towards the great forest.

'Is that Alemtejo?' Sandra asked.

The man shook his head. 'No,' he replied. 'It is the home of the guardians of Alemtejo. Alemtejo lies beyond.'

Suddenly there burst upon the girl's ears a savage roar, which was followed by others in such tremendous volume that the ground shook.

Sandra looked around fearfully. 'Lions!' she exclaimed. 'Where can we go if they attack us?'

'They will not attack us,' said the man, with a smile, 'for they cannot get at us.'

As they came closer to the palisade, the uprights of which were some six inches apart, Sandra could see beyond it into the widening gorge. Lions! Lions! She had never seen so many together before. They had caught the scent of man and they were coming towards the palisade growling and roaring.

At one end of the palisade a narrow trail ran up the side of the gorge. It was very steep; and it was only because rude steps had been hacked out of it that it could be scaled at all. Here the man took the rope from about Sandra's neck and turned her over to two of the apes, each of which seized one of her hands; then the man took the rope from about the neck of the black woman and urged her up the trail ahead of him. After the trail had topped the palisade it levelled off and ran along the side of the gorge. Below them, roaring lions leaped in an effort to reach them. The trail was narrow. A single misstep and one would be hurled down to the ravening lions below. The great apes edged along the trail, one in front of Sandra, one behind, clinging to her hands. The man and the black woman were just ahead.

Sandra could scarcely tear her eyes from the lions, some of them leaped so high and came so near to reaching them. The ape in front of her stopped; and as it did so she looked up to see why, just in time to see the white man push the black woman from the narrow trail.

There was a piercing scream as the woman hurtled to the lions below. There was a rush of padded feet and savage roars and growls below.

Sandra could not look. 'You beast!' she cried. 'Why did you do that?'

The man turned, a look of surprise upon his face. 'I am no beast,' he said. 'The guardians of Alemtejo must eat.'

'And I am next?' she asked.

'Of course not,' he said. 'You are a goddess.'

They went on now in silence, the trail rising steeply to the far end of the canyon above which towered tremendous cliffs two or three thousand feet in height – sheer, almost vertical cliffs, over the summit of which fell a beautiful waterfall to form the stream which Sandra had seen running beneath the palisade.

Sandra wondered what they would do now. The mighty cliff blocked their progress forward. To their right was the unscalable, vertical wall of the canyon; to their left, the gorge and the lions.

Where the trail ended at the foot of the cliff, it widened considerably for a short distance. Here the ape directly behind her dropped her hand and passed her and the man who had halted at the trail's end. The creature took the man's hand and commenced to ascend, helping the man from one precarious hold to the next. Sandra blenched from the implication, but the ape pulled her forward; and then he, too, commenced to ascend, dragging her after him.

There were crevices and tiny ledges and little handholds and footholds, and here and there a sturdy shrub wedged in some tiny crack. The girl was terrified, almost numb from fright. It seemed fantastic to believe that any creature other than a lizard or a fly could scale this terrific height; and below, the lions were waiting.

They came at last to a chimney, a narrow chute up which the apes wormed their way. Here they moved a little less slowly for the sides of the chimney were rough and there were occasional transverse cracks affording excellent foot and handholds.

Sandra glanced up. She saw the leading ape and the man above her. They had gained a little distance, for the man required less help than she. She did not dare look down. The very thought of it palsied her.

Up and up they climbed, stopping occasionally to rest and breathe. An hour passed, an hour of horror, and then a second hour. Would they never reach the top? The girl was suddenly seized with a horrid premonition that she would fall, that she must fall, that nothing could avert the final tragedy; yet up and up they made their slow, laborious way. Sandra's nerves were on edge. She wanted to scream. She almost wanted to jerk herself from the ape and jump, anything to end this unspeakable horror.

And then it happened! The ape placed his foot upon a jutting fragment; and, as he bore his weight upon it to lift himself to a new hand-hold, it broke away and he slipped back, falling full upon the girl. Frantically, blindly, she clawed for some support. Her fingers clutched a crevice. The ape struck her shoulder and bounded outward; but the impact of his body broke her hold and she toppled backward.

EIGHT

Alemtejo

The light of the sun slanted through the foliage of ancient trees to mottle the sward of a small, natural clearing in the heart of the forest. It was quiet and peaceful there. The leaves of the trees whispered softly, purring to the caresses of a gentle breeze, here in the heart of an ancient forest as yet uncontaminated by the ruthless foot of man.

A dozen great apes squatted about something that lay in the shade at one side of the clearing. It was the lifeless body of a white man.

'Dead,' said Ga-un.

Ungo, the King ape, shook his head. 'No,' he growled.

A she-ape came with water in her mouth and let it run upon the forehead of the man. Zu-tho shook the giant body gently.

'Dead,' said Ga-un.

'No,' insisted Ungo; and once again Zu-tho shook the ape-man gently.

Tarzan's lids fluttered and then opened. He looked dazedly up into the faces of the great apes. He looked about the clearing. His head ached terribly. Weakly, he raised a hand to a temple, feeling the caked blood of an ugly wound. He tried to raise himself on an elbow, and Ungo put an arm beneath him and helped him. He saw then that his body was splotched with dried blood.

'What happened, Ungo?' he asked.

'Tarmangani came with thunderstick. Bang! Tarzan fall. Tarzan bleed. Ungo bring Tarzan away.'

'The she-Tarmangani?' asked Tarzan. 'What became of her?'

'She go away with Tarmangani.'

Tarzan nodded. She was safe then. She was with her own people. He wondered who had shot him, and why. He had not seen Crump. Well, every man's hand seemed to be against him. All the more reason why he should mend quickly and search out the impostor who was the cause of it all.

Tarzan recovered quickly from the effects of the wound which had creased his skull but had not fractured it.

One day when he felt quite himself again, he questioned Ungo. He asked him if he had ever seen another white man who went naked as Tarzan did. Ungo nodded and held up two fingers.

Tarzan knew that Ungo had seen such a man twice.

'With strange Mangani,' added Ungo.

That was interesting – a man who said he was Tarzan, and who consorted with great apes.

'Where?' asked Tarzan.

Ungo made a comprehensive gesture that might have taken in half the great forest.

'Ungo take Tarzan?' asked the ape-man.

Ungo discussed the matter with the other apes. Some of them wished to return to their own hunting ground. They had been gone a long time, and they were restless; but at last they agreed to go with Tarzan, and the following day Tarzan of the Apes with his great anthropoid friends started off towards the Ruturi Mountains.

When the body of the ape above her struck Sandra's shoulder, its course was sufficiently deflected so that it missed the other apes below it; but Sandra fell full upon the ape beneath her. Clinging precariously to scant holds, the beast grasped one of the girl's ankles; and though he could not retain his hold, his action retarded her fall, so that the ape below him was able to catch and hold her.

Hanging with her head down, the girl saw the body of the ape which had fallen hurtling downward to the gorge far below. Fascinated, she watched the grotesquely flailing arms and legs; but just before the body struck the ground she closed her eyes; then to her ears came the roars and growls of the great carnivores fighting over the body.

Looking down from above, the man, who had reached a ledge which afforded comparatively substantial footing, saw the predicament of the girl and the ape which held her. He saw that the great anthropoid could neither advance nor retreat, nor could the ape above him or the ape below him assist their fellow; while the girl, hanging with her head down, was absolutely helpless.

The horrified girl realized her plight, too. The only way that the ape could save himself was to relinquish his hold upon her. How long would it be before the great brute would surrender to the law of self-preservation?

Presently she heard the voice of the man above her. 'I'm throwing a rope down to you. Tie it securely around your body. Sancho and I can pull you up then.' As he spoke, he fastened together the ropes with which he had been leading the two women, and dropped one end down to the girl. With great difficulty, but as quickly as she could, Sandra fastened it securely about her body beneath her arms.

'I am ready,' she said; and closed her eyes again.

The great ape, Sancho, and the man drew her slowly upward, inch by inch, in what seemed to her a protracted eternity of horror; but at last she stood on the tiny ledge beside her rescuer. She had been very brave through the hideous ordeal, but now the reaction came and she commenced to tremble violently.

The man placed a hand upon her arm. 'You have been very courageous,' he said. 'You must not go to pieces now. The worst is over and we shall soon be at the summit.'

'That poor ape,' she said, shuddering. 'I saw him fall all the way – all the way down to the lions.'

'Yes,' he said, 'that was too bad. Fernando was a good servant; but those things sometimes happen. They are not without their compensations, however. The guardians of Alemtejo are none too well fed. Sometimes they kill one another for flesh. They are always ravenous.'

Presently Sandra regained control of herself, and the ascent was resumed; but this time Sancho and the man retained hold of the rope.

Soon they came to a point where the chimney had been eroded far back into the cliff from the summit, so that it slanted upward at an angle of about forty-five degrees. By comparison with what had gone before, this was, to the girl, almost like walking on level ground; and in half an hour, during which they rested several times, they reached the summit.

Spreading before her eyes the girl saw a vast level mesa. In the near distance was a forest, and in the foreground a little stream wound down to leap over the edge of the cliff and form the waterfall to whose beauty she had been blinded by the terrors of the ascent.

The man who was called God let the girl lie down on the green turf and rest. 'I know what you have endured,' he said sympathetically; 'but it is over, and now you are safe. I am very happy to have brought you here safely.' He hesitated, and the bewilderment that she had noted before was reflected in his eyes. 'I am always happy when I am with you. Why is it? I do not understand.'

'Nor I,' said the girl.

'I did not want a goddess,' he continued. 'I did not want to go and look for one. When I found you, I did not want to bring you here. I know that you hate me, and that makes me sad; yet I am quite happy when you are with me. I do not think that I was ever happy before. I do not recall ever having been happy.'

'But you did not have to bring me here,' she said. 'You could have stayed with my father's safari.'

'But I did have to bring you here. Da Gama told me to bring you, and he would have been very angry had I not done so.'

'You didn't have to come back here. I don't believe that you belong here. You are a very strange man.'

'Yes. I am strange,' he admitted. 'I do not understand myself. You know,' he leaned close to her, 'I think that I am a little mad – in fact, I am sure of it.'

Sandra was more than sure of it; but she didn't know what to say, and so she said nothing.

'You think I'm mad, don't you?' he demanded.

'You have done some very strange things,' she admitted, 'some very inconsistent things.'

'Inconsistent?' he asked. 'In what way have I been inconsistent?'

'Notwithstanding the fact that you stole me from my father, and later from my friends, you have been very kind and considerate of me; yet in cold blood and without provocation, you pushed that poor black woman to the lions.'

'I see nothing wrong in that,' he said. 'All of God's creatures must eat. The Waruturi eat their own kind. Why should not the lions, who must live, too, eat Waruturi? You eat many of God's creatures that people have gone out and killed for you. Why is it wrong for the lions to eat one of God's creatures, but perfectly right for you to do so?'

'But there is a difference,' she said. 'That woman was a human being.'

'She was a cruel and savage cannibal,' said the man. 'The little antelopes you eat are harmless and kindly; so if either is wrong, it must be you.'

'I am afraid neither one of us can ever convince the other,' said Sandra, 'and what difference can it make anyway?'

'It makes a lot of difference to me,' he said.

'And why does it?' she asked.

'Because I like you,' he said, 'and I wish you to like me.'

'Don't you think you are a little optimistic in believing I might like the man who stole me from my father and brought me to this awful place from which I may never hope to escape?'

'Alemtejo is not an awful place,' he said. 'It is a nice place to live.'

'No matter how awful or how nice it is,' she replied, 'I shall have to stay here, for I never could go down over that awful cliff.'

'I hoped you would learn to like Alemtejo and me, too,' he said hopefully.

'Never,' replied the girl.

The man shook his head sadly. 'I have no friends,' he said. 'I thought perhaps at last I had found one.'

'You have your people here,' she said. 'You must have friends among them.'

'They are not my people,' he said. 'I am God, and God has no friends.'

He lapsed into silence and presently they started on again in the direction of the forest that lay across the mesa. They followed the stream beside which was a well-worn trail that finally led into the forest, which they had penetrated for about half a mile when there suddenly burst before the astonished eyes of the girl a great castle set in a clearing. It was such a castle as she had seen in Abyssinia upon one of her father's former hunting expeditions, such a castle as the Portuguese, Father Pedro Diaz, built there at the beginning of the 17th Century.

Sandra had at that time read a great deal about Portugal's attempted colonization of Abyssinia, and was quite familiar with the details of that ill-fated plan. Many times she had heard her captor speak of da Gama; but the name held no particular significance for her until she saw this castle. Now the derivation of the other names he had used was explicable, such as Ruiz the high priest, and Fernando and Sancho, the apes – all Portuguese.

Now a new mystery confronted her.

NINE

When the Lion Charged

Dutton was up before dawn the morning after Sandra's abduction by the false Tarzan and his servants of God. He searched for his boy, but was unable to find him. Mystified, he aroused the headman, telling him to arouse the other boys, get breakfast started, and prepare the packs for he had determined to take the entire safari along to search for Sandra; then he aroused Gantry and the other two whites.

When dawn came, it was apparent that a number of the boys were missing, and Dutton sent for the headman. 'What has happened?' he demanded 'What has become of the porters and askaris who are not in camp?'

'Bwana,' said the headman, 'they were afraid, and they must have deserted during the night.'

'What were they afraid of?' demanded Dutton.

'They know that Tarzan and his apes came into camp last night and took the girl. They are afraid of Tarzan. They do not wish to make him angry. They are also afraid of the Waruturi, who are cannibals; and they are a long way from home. They wish to return to their own country.'

'They have taken some of our provisions,' said Dutton. 'When we get back, they will be punished.'

'Yes, Bwana,' replied the headman; 'but they would rather be punished at home than be killed here. If I were you, Bwana, I would turn back. You can do nothing in this country against Tarzan and the Waruturi.'

'Tarzan's dead,' said Crump. 'I ought to know. I killed him myself. And as far the Waruturi, we can keep away from their villages. Anyway, we've got enough guns to keep them off.'

'I will tell my people,' said the headman; 'but if I were you, I would turn back.'

'I think he's got somethin' there,' said Gantry. 'I don't like the looks of it at all.'

'Go back if you want to,' said Crump; 'but I ain't gonna give up that reward as easy as all that.'

'Nor I,' agreed Minsky.

'And I shall not give up,' said Dutton, 'until I have found Miss Pickerall.'

It was not a very enthusiastic band of porters and askaris who started out with the four white men that morning. Dutton and Gantry headed the column, following the plain trail the apes had made, while Crump and Minsky brought up the rear to prevent desertion. The natives were sullen. The headman, ordinarily loquacious, walked in silence. There was no singing. The atmosphere was tense and strained. They marched all day with only one rest at noon; but they did not overhaul the girl and her captor.

Late in the afternoon, they surprised a lone warrior. He tried to escape, but Crump raised his rifle and shot him.

'A Waruturi,' he said, as he examined the corpse. 'See them filed teeth?'

'Holy smoke!' exclaimed Gantry. 'Look at them gold ornaments. Why, the bloke's fairly loaded down with gold.'

The blacks of the safari gathered around the corpse. They noted the filed teeth. 'Waruturi,' they murmured.

'Mtu mla watu,' said one, in a frightened voice.

'Yes,' said the headman, 'cannibals.' It was evident that even he was impressed and fearful, notwithstanding the fact that once in his own country he had been a noted warrior.

It was a glum camp they had that night; and in the morning when the white men awoke, they were alone.

Crump was furious. He went cursing about the camp like a madman. 'The black devils have taken all of our provisions and most of our ammunition,' he raved.

'That cannibal you killed finished them,' said Gantry, 'and I don't know that I blame them much. Them cannibals ain't so nice. I think the boys had a hell of a lot more sense than we've got.'

'You scared?' demanded Crump.

'I ain't sayin' I'm scared, and I ain't sayin' I ain't,' replied Gantry evasively. 'I been in this country longer than you, Tom, and I've seen some of the things these cannibals do; and I've heard stories from old-timers all the way back to Stanley's time. There ain't nothin' these cannibals won't do for human flesh. Why, they even followed Stanley's safari when his men were dying of small-pox and dug up the corpses and et 'em. I think we ought to turn back, men.'

'And pass up that reward?' demanded Minsky.

'And abandon Miss Pickerall to her fate without even trying to find her?'

'We have tried to find her,' said Gantry. 'There ain't one chance in a million that the four of us can get through this country alive. There ain't one chance in ten million that we can rescue her, if we caught up with that Tarzan guy and his apes.'

'Well, I'm going on,' said Dutton. 'The rest of you can do whatever you please.'

'And I'm going with you,' said Crump.

'You'd do anything for a few measly pounds,' said Gantry.

'There's more than a few measly pounds in this,' replied Crump. 'You seen the gold on that warrior I killed yesterday, didn't you? Well, that reminded me about somethin' I heard a couple of years ago. That gold came from the Ruturi Mountains. It come out of there in lumps as big as your two fists. There's the mother lode of all mother lodes somewhere in them hills. If the Waruturi can find it, we can.'

'I guess you'll have to go back alone, Gantry,' said Minsky.

'You know damned well I could never get through alone,' replied Gantry. 'I'll go with you, but I get my share of the reward and any gold we find.'

'There's a lot of funny stories about that gold,' said Crump, reminiscently. 'They say its guarded by a thousand lions and two tribes that live way back in the Ruturi Mountains.'

'Well, how do the Waruturi get it then?' asked Minsky.

'Well, those people back there in the mountains have no salt nor no iron. They send down gold to purchase them from the Waruturi, not very often but once in a while. The Waruturi buys salt and iron from other tribes, with ivory, for they know that sooner or later them guys will come down out of the mountains and bring gold.'

'What makes you think you can find this here gold mine?' demanded Gantry.

'Well, it's up in the Ruturi Mountains and there must be trails leadin' to it.'

'How about you, Dutton?' asked Gantry. 'Are you in on it?'

'We have reason to believe that Miss Pickerall is being taken into the Ruturi Mountains. You are going there in search of your gold mine. As long as our routes lie in the same direction, we might as well stick together. I will agree to help you in your search, if you will agree to help me in mine. As long as we stick together, we have a better chance of getting through. Four guns are better than one, or two, or three.'

'That makes sense,' said Minsky. 'We'll stick together.'

'One thing we've got to do, no matter which way we go,' said Gantry, 'is eat! And we ain't got nothin' to eat. We'll have to do some huntin' tomorrow.'

Early the next morning the four set out in different directions to hunt. Dutton went towards the west. The forest was open, and the going good. He hoped one of them would make a kill, so they could go on in search of Sandra Pickerall. He believed they were definitely on the trail of her abductors, and his hopes of finding her were high. He hated delay, even to hunt for food; but he had had to defer to the wishes of the others. After all, a man could not travel forever on an empty stomach.

He kept constantly alert for signs of game, but he was a civilized man with a background of hundreds of years of civilization behind him. His senses of smell and hearing were not keen. He could have passed within ten feet of the finest buck in the world, if the animal had been hidden from his sight; but there were other hunters in the forest with keen noses and ears.

Numa the lion had made no kill the night before. He was getting old. He did not spring as swiftly or as surely as in former days. He was missing the target all too often, sometimes only by a grazing talon. Today he was hungry. He had been stalking Dutton for some time; but the unfamiliar scent of the white man had made him unusually wary. He slunk along behind the American, keeping out of sight as much as possible, lying suddenly flat and motionless when Dutton stopped, as he had occasionally, to listen and look for game.

There was another hunter in the forest with keener senses and a finer brain than either Dutton or Numa. Usha the wind had carried the scent spoor of both the man and the lion to his sensitive nostrils; and now, prompted more by curiosity than humanitarianism, he was swinging silently and gracefully through the trees upwind towards the two.

Dutton was commencing to believe there was no game in the forest. He thought perhaps he was going in the wrong direction, and decided to strike off to the left to see if he could not find a game trail in which was the spoor of some animal he might follow.

The lion was now fully in the open; and the instant Dutton stopped the great cat flattened itself on the ground; but there was no concealment, and as Dutton turned to the left his eye caught the tawny coat of the King of beasts. He looked to see what it was, and his heart sank. He had never killed a lion, but he had heard enough stories about them to know that even if your bullet pierced their heart they still might live long enough to maul and kill you. In addition to this was the fact that he knew he was not a very good shot. He started to back away towards a tree, with the thought in his mind that he might gain sanctuary among its branches before the lion reached him.

Numa rose very slowly and majestically and came towards him, baring his great yellow fangs and growling deep in his belly. Dutton tried to recall all he had heard about lion killing. He knew that the brain was very small and lay far in the back of the skull well protected by heavy bone. The left breast was the point to hit, just between the shoulder and the neck. That would pierce the heart, but the target looked very small; and even though the lion was only walking it moved from side to side and up and down. Suddenly, backing up, Dutton bumped into a tree. He breathed a sigh of relief and glanced up. His heart sank, for the nearest branch was ten feet above the ground. He did not know it, but if the branch had been only four feet the lion could have reached him, had it charged, long before he could have climbed out of harm's way; for there are few things on earth swifter than a charging lion.

The great lion was coming closer. He seemed to grow larger as he came; and now he was growling horribly, his yellow-green eyes glaring balefully at his victim.

Dutton breathed a little silent prayer as he raised his rifle and took aim. There was a sharp report as he squeezed the trigger. The lion was thrown back upon its haunches, stopped momentarily by the impact of the bullet; then, with a hideous roar, it charged.

TEN

Human Sacrifice

As Sandra Pickerall stood before the imposing castle of Alemtejo her hopes rose; for she felt that such an imposing edifice must be the abode of civilized men and women – people who would sympathize with her situation and perhaps eventually might be persuaded to return her to her own people.

She had expected to be taken to some squalid, native village, ruled over probably by a black sultan, where she would be reviled and mistreated by perhaps a score of wives and concubines. Her captor's insistence that she would be a goddess had never impressed her, for she was definitely convinced that the man was insane and thought his stories were but a figment of a deranged mentality.

'So this is the castle of Alemtejo!' she said, half aloud.

'Yes,' said the man. 'It is the castle of Christoforo da Gama, the King of Alemtejo.'

There was no sign of life outside the castle; but when her companion stepped forward and pounded upon the great gate with the hilt of his knife, a man leaned from the barbican and hailed him.

'Who comes?' he challenged; and then, 'Oh, it is God who has returned.'

'Yes,' replied the girl's captor, 'it is he whom the King calls God. Admit us, and send word to Christoforo da Gama, the King, that I have returned and brought a goddess.'

The man left the opening, and Sandra heard him calling to someone upon the inside of the gate, which presently swung slowly open; and a moment later Sandra and her captor filed into the ballium, while the servants of God turned back into the forest.

Inside the gate stood a number of chocolate-coloured soldiers wearing helmets of gold and cuirasses of golden chainmail. Their brown legs were bare, and their feet were shod in crude sandals. All wore swords and some carried battle-axes, and others ancient muskets, the latter looking very impressive notwithstanding the fact that there had been no ammunition for them in Alemtejo for nearly four hundred years.

The ballium, which was wide and which evidently extended all around the castle, was laid out with rows of growing garden truck, among which both men and women were working. These, too, like the soldiers at the gate, were mostly chocolate-coloured. The men wore leather jerkins and broad-brimmed hats, and the women a garment which resembled a sarong wound around their hips. The women were naked from the waist up. All showed considerable excitement as they recognized the man; and when, later, he and Sandra were being conducted across the ballium towards the main entrance to the castle, they knelt and crossed themselves as he passed.

Sandra was dumbfounded at this evidence that these people, at least, thought that her companion was a god. Maybe they were all insane. The thought caused her considerable perturbation. It was bad enough to feel that one might be associating with a single maniac, but to be a prisoner in the land of maniacs was quite too awful to contemplate.

Inside the castle they were met by half a dozen men with long gowns and cowls. Each wore a chain of beads from which a cross depended. They were evidently priests. These conducted them down a long corridor to a great apartment which Sandra immediately recognized as a throne room.

People were entering this apartment through other doorways, as though they had recently been summoned, and congregating before a dais on which stood three throne chairs.

The priests conducted Sandra and her companion to the dais, and as they crossed the room the people fell back to either side and knelt and crossed themselves.

'They really take him seriously,' thought Sandra.

After mounting the dais, three of the priests conducted the man, who thought he was Tarzan and who was called God, to the right-hand throne chair as one stood facing the audience chamber, while the other three seated Sandra in the left-hand chair, leaving the centre chair vacant.

Presently there was a blaring of trumpets at the far end of the apartment. Doors were thrown wide, and a procession entered led by two trumpeters. Behind them was a fat man with a golden crown on his head, and behind him a double file of men with golden helmets and cuirasses and great, double-edged swords which hung at their sides. All these filed up onto the dais, all but the fat man with the crown passing behind the three thone chairs and taking their stations there.

The man with the crown paused a moment before Sandra, half knelt and crossed himself; then he crossed over in front of the man whom they called God and repeated his genuflexion before him, after which he seated himself in the centre throne-chair.

The trumpets sounded again, and another procession entered the throne room. It was led by a man in a long black robe and a cowl. From a string of beads around his neck depended a cross. He was much darker that most of the others in the apartment, but his features were not negroid. They were more Semitic and definitely hawk-like. He was Ruiz the high priest. Behind him walked the seven wives of the King. The women came and sat on buffalo robes and lion skins spread on the dais at the foot of the centre chair. The high priest stood just below the dais, facing the audience.

When he spoke, Sandra recognized the language as a mixture of Portuguese and Bantu and was able to understand enough to get the sense of what the man was saying. He was telling them that now they had both a god and a goddess and that nothing but good fortune could attend them hereafter.

Ruiz stood behind a low, stone altar which appeared to have been painted a rusty-brown red.

For a long time, Ruiz the high priest held the centre of the stage. The rites, which were evidently of a religious nature, went on interminably. Three times Ruiz burned powder upon the altar. From the awful stench, Sandra judged the powder must have consisted mostly of hair. The assemblage intoned a chant to the weird accompaniment of heathenish tom-toms. The high priest occasionally made the sign of the cross, but it seemed obvious to Sandra that she had become the goddess of a bastard religion which bore no relationship to Christianity beyond the symbolism of the cross, which was evidently quite meaningless to the high priest and his followers.

She heard mentioned several times Kibuka, the war-god; and Walumbe, the god of death, was often supplicated; while Mizimo, departed spirits, held a prominent place in the chant and the prayers. It was evidently a very primitive form of heathenish worship from which voodooism is derived.

All during the long ceremony the eyes of the audience were often upon Sandra, especially those of Christoforo da Gama, King of Alemtejo.

At first, the rites had interested the new goddess; but as time wore on, she found them monotonous and boring. At first, the people interested her. They evidently represented a crossing of Portuguese with blacks and were slightly Moorish in appearance. The vast quantities of gold in the room aroused her curiosity, for, with the exception of herself and the man who was called God and Ruiz the high priest, everyone was loaded down with ornaments or equipment of gold. The wives of the King bore such burdens of gold that she wondered they could walk.

Sandra was very tired. They had given her no opportunity to rest; and she still wore the tattered garments that had been through so much, and the dirt and grime of her long trek. Her eyes were heavy with sleep. She felt her lids drooping, and she caught herself nodding when suddenly she was startled into wakefulness by loud screams.

Looking up, she saw a dozen naked dancing girls enter the apartment, and behind them two soldiers dragging a screaming negro girl of about twelve. Now the audience was alert, necks craned and every eye centred upon the child. The tom-toms beat out a wild cadence. The dancers, leaping, bending, whirling, approached the altar; and while they danced the soldiers lifted the still screaming girl and held her face up, upon its stained, brown surface.

The high priest made passes with his hands above the victim, the while he intoned some senseless gibberish. The child's screams had been reduced to moaning sobs, as Ruiz drew a knife from beneath his robe. Sandra leaned forward in her throne-chair, clutching its arms, her wide eyes straining at the horrid sight below her.

A deathly stillness fell upon the room, broken only by the choking sobs of the girl. Ruiz's knife flashed for an instant above his victim; and then the point was plunged into her heart. Quickly he cut the throat, and dabbing his hands in the spurting blood sprinkled it upon the audience, which surged forward to receive it; but Sandra Pickerall saw no more. She had fainted.

ELEVEN

The Voice in the Night

As the lion charged, Dutton fired again and missed; then, to his amazement, he saw an almost naked man drop from the tree beneath which he stood full upon the back of the lion, momentarily crushing the great beast to the ground.

His attention now diverted from his intended prey, the great cat turned it upon the man-thing clinging to his back. A steel-thewed arm encircled his neck and powerful legs were locked beneath his belly. He reared upon his hind feet and sought to shake the creature from his back.

Dutton looked on, stunned and aghast. He saw the gleaming blade in the man's left hand plunge time and again into the beast's side, and he heard the former's growls mingle with those of the carnivore; and the flesh on his scalp crept. He wanted to help the man; but there was nothing he could do, for the swiftly moving, thrashing bodies rendered it impossible to use his rifle without endangering his would-be rescuer.

Soon it was over. The lion, mortally wounded by both rifle and knife, stood still for a moment on trembling legs and then fell heavily to the ground to lie quietly in death.

What happened next, Dutton knew would remain indelibly impressed upon his memory throughout his life. The victor rose from the body of his vanquished foe, and placing one foot upon the carcass raised his face towards the sky and voiced a hideous long-drawn-out scream. It was the victory cry of the bull ape; though that, Dutton did not know. Then the man turned to him, the savage light of battle already dying in his eyes. 'You are Pelham Dutton?' he asked.

'Yes,' replied Dutton, 'but how did you know?'

'I have seen you before; and the girl you are searching for told me your name and described you to me.'

'And who are you?'

'I am Tarzan of the Apes.'

'Which one?' demanded Dutton.

'There is only one Tarzan.'

Dutton noticed the half-healed wound on Tarzan's temple. 'Oh,' he said, 'you are not the one who stole Miss Pickerall. You are the one who rescued her, the one whom Crump shot.'

'So it was Crump who shot me,' said Tarzan.

'Yes, it was Crump. He thought it was you who had stolen Miss Pickerall.'

'Mostly, however, he was thinking of the reward and his revenge. He is a bad man. He should be destroyed.'

'Well, the law will probably get him eventually,' said Dutton.

'I will get him eventually,' replied Tarzan. He said it very simply, but Dutton was glad he was not Crump.

'What were you doing here in the forest alone?' demanded Tarzan.

'Hunting,' replied the American. 'The boys of our safari deserted us, taking all our provisions and equipment. We had no food; and so we started out in different directions this morning to hunt.'

'Who are the others?' asked Tarzan, 'Crump, Minsky, and Gantry?'

'Yes,' said Dutton; 'but how did you know their names?'

'The girl told me. She also told me that you are the only one of the four she trusted.'

'I certainly wouldn't trust either Crump or Minsky,' agreed Dutton, 'and

I'm not so sure about Gantry. He's been whispering with them too much lately, and his mind is more on the reward than it is on saving Miss Pickerall. You see, her father offered £1000 reward for her return.'

'And £500 for me dead or alive,' added Tarzan with a grim smile.

'Well, he offered that for the man who stole his daughter – a man who had told us he was Tarzan of the Apes.'

'What have you done with Miss Pickerall while you are hunting?' Tarzan asked.

'She is not with us,' said Dutton. 'She was stolen again by a band of apes led by a white man. It must have been the same one who said he was Tarzan of the Apes.'

'And are you looking for her?' asked the ape-man.

'Yes,' replied Dutton.

'Then our paths lie in the same direction, for I am searching for the man who stole her. He has caused too much trouble already. I shall destroy him.'

'You will come with us?' asked Dutton.

'No,' replied the ape-man, 'I do not like your companions. I am surprised that three such men, familiar with Africa, would take the chance they are taking for little more than £300 apiece, at the most £500 – if they kill me, too – for I should say that without a safari, and only four guns, you haven't a chance on earth.'

'They have another incentive,' said Dutton.

'What is it?' asked the ape-man.

'A fabulous gold mine, which is supposed to lie in the Ruturi Mountains.'

'Yes,' replied Tarzan, 'I have heard of it. I think there is no doubt that it exists, but they will never reach it.'

'But you are planning on going into the Ruturi Mountains alone,' said Dutton. 'How do you expect to do it, if you think that four of us would fail?'

'I am Tarzan,' replied the ape-man.

Dutton thought about that. The man's simple assurance that he could do what four men could not do impressed him. He was also impressed by the man's prowess as evidenced by his victory over the King of beasts in hand-to-hand combat.

'I should like to go with you,' he said. 'You are going to find the man who stole Miss Pickerall; so if you find him I shall find her; and as you have rescued her once, I am sure you will help me to rescue her again. As for the other three, they are motivated solely by avarice. If there were no reward they would not turn a hand to save Miss Pickerall. If they find the gold mine, they will abandon their search for her.'

'You are probably right,' said Tarzan.

'Then I may come with you?' asked Dutton.

'How about the other three?' demanded the ape-man.

'They'll think something happened to me; but they won't even look for me. They really haven't much use for me.'

'Very well,' said the ape-man, 'you may come with me if you can take it.'

'What do you mean?' asked Dutton.

'I mean that you will be consorting with wild beasts. You will have to learn to think and act like a wild beast, which may be difficult for a civilized man. Wild beasts are not motivated by avarice, and but seldom by thoughts of vengeance. They have more dignity than man. They kill only in self-defence or for food. They do not lie or cheat, and they are loyal to their friends.'

'You think a great deal of the wild beasts, don't you?' commented Dutton.

'Why shouldn't I?' asked the ape-man. 'I was born and reared among them. I was almost a grown man before I saw another human being or realized that there were others of my kind. I was a grown man before I saw a white person.'

'But your parents?' asked Dutton.

'I do not remember them,' said Tarzan. 'I was an infant when they died.'

'I think I understand how you feel about men,' said Dutton. 'I sometimes feel the same way. I will come with you.'

'Do you wish to go back to your camp first?' asked Tarzan.

'No. I have everything with me that I possess.'

'Then come with me.' Tarzan turned and started off towards the North.

Dutton followed along, wondering what lay in store for him with this strange creature. He felt a certain confidence in him; perhaps that was because he had felt no confidence at all in his three companions. Presently they came to an open glade through which ran a stream. Dutton involuntarily stopped and fingered his rifle, for squatting around the glade were a dozen huge anthropoid apes, great, shaggy, savage looking fellows. He saw them rise, growling, as Tarzan approached them; then he heard the man speak in a strange tongue, and he saw the apes relax as they answered him.

Tarzan turned and saw that Dutton had stopped. 'Come on,' he said. 'Let them smell of you and get acquainted with you. I have told them that you are my friend. They will not harm you; but they will not be friendly. Just leave them alone, especially the shes and the balus.'

'What are balus?' asked Dutton.

'The babies, the young ones,' explained Tarzan.

Dutton approached, and the great apes came and sniffed him and touched him with their horny hands. Suddenly one of them grasped his rifle and tore it from his hand. Tarzan spoke to the ape, which then relinquished the rifle to him. 'They don't like firearms,' he said. 'I have told them that you would only use it to obtain food or to defend the tribe. See that that is all you use it for.'

'Speaking of food,' said Dutton, 'do you suppose I could get a shot at something around here? I am nearly famished. I have had nothing but a little fruit in the last couple of days.'

Tarzan raised his head and sniffed the air. 'Wait here,' he said. 'I'll bring you food.' And with that he swung into a tree and disappeared in the foliage.

Dutton looked about at the great savage beasts around him, and he did not feel any too happy. It was true that they ignored him, but he recalled stories he had heard about the bulls going berserk for no apparent reason. He fell to thinking, and suddenly a doubt assailed him. Here was a white man who consorted with apes. A white man, accompanied by a band of apes, had stolen Sandra. Could there be two such creatures in the jungle? Could there be such a coincidence? He commenced to doubt Tarzan's sincerity, and he looked about him for some sign of Sandra. He got up and walked about, peering behind bushes. There could be some clue. There was always a clue in story books – a handkerchief, a bit of cloth torn from a garment, a dainty footprint. He found none of these; but still he was not satisfied, and he was still wandering about in the vicinity of the clearing when Tarzan returned, a small antelope across one shoulder.

Tarzan cut the hind quarter from his kill and tossed it to Dutton. 'You can build a fire?' he asked.

'Yes,' said the American.

'Cut off what you want to eat now,' said the ape-man; 'and save the rest for tomorrow.'

'I'll cook enough for you too,' said Dutton. 'How much can you eat?'

'Cook your own,' said Tarzan, 'I will take care of myself.' He butchered the carcass, cutting off several pieces; then he carried the viscera downwind and tossed it among the bushes. When he came back he handed pieces to each of the apes, which, while generally herbivorous, occasionally eat flesh. They squatted down where they were, Tarzan among them, and tore at the raw meat with their fangs, growling a little as they did so.

Dutton was horrified, for the man was eating his meat raw as the beasts did and growling as they growled. It was horrible. He grew more and more apprehensive. He wouldn't have given a lead nickel for his chances now.

Night had fallen as they completed their meal. 'I shall be back presently,' Tarzan said to Dutton. 'You may lie down anywhere and sleep. The apes will warn you if any danger threatens.' Then he told Ungo to see that no harm befell the man. Ungo grunted.

It had been late when the last of the three men returned to camp. None of them had had any luck. Each had gathered and eaten some fruits and nuts; but it was flesh they craved, good red meat to give them strength.

'I wonder where the toff is,' said Gantry. 'I thought we'd find him here when we got back.'

'I don't give a damn where he is,' said Crump. 'The sooner I don't never see him again, the better I like it. I ain't got no use for them blighters.'

'He weren't such a bad lot,' said Gantry.

'He was like the rest of 'em,' said Minsky. 'You know what they all think of us; think we're a lot of scum and treat us like it. I hate all the damn bourgeoisie. They're part and parcel of the capitalistic system, takin' the bread out of workers' mouths, grindin' down the proletariat under the iron heel of imperialism.'

'Rot!' said Crump. 'I ain't got no use for 'em myself, but I got less for a damned fool bolshie.'

'That's because you're a creature of capitalism,' said Minsky. 'You probably even belong to a church and believe in God.'

'Shut up,' said Crump.

'Say,' commenced Gantry, more to change the subject than anything else, 'did you guys hear a scream this afternoon?'

'Yes,' said Minsky. 'What was it, do you suppose?'

'I heard it, too,' said Crump. 'It sounded sort of like – well – I don't know what.'

'Sounded like a banshee to me,' said Gantry. 'The natives have told me though that bull-apes sometimes scream like that when they have made a kill.'

'I'm turnin' in,' said Gantry.

'O.K.,' said Crump. 'I'll stand guard for four hours; then I'll wake you. Minsky will follow you. Keep up the fire and see that you don't go to sleep while you're on watch, either of you.'

Minsky and Gantry lay down upon the ground, while Crump threw some more wood on the fire and squatted beside it. It was very quiet. Beyond the limits of the firelight there was a black void. Their whole universe was encompassed in that little circle of firelight.

Crump was thinking of what he could do with the ransom money and the riches he hoped to bring back from the fabulous Ruturi gold mine, when the quiet was suddenly broken by a voice coming out of the darkness.

'Go back,' it cried. 'Go back to your own country. Go back before you die.'

Gantry and Minsky sat up suddenly. 'What the hell was that?' whispered the latter in a frightened voice.

TWELVE
The King Comes

When Sandra regained consciousness, she was lying on a couch covered with buffalo skins, Ruiz the high priest was leaning over her mumbling a lot of incomprehensible mumbo-jumbo; while looking on were four native women and a lad of about nineteen. The natives were staring at her, wide-eyed and frightened; and when they saw that her eyes were open, they dropped upon their knees and crossed themselves.

Ruiz nodded. 'I have brought her back from heaven, my children,' he said. 'Attend her well. It is the command of Christoforo da Gama, King of Alemtejo, and of Ruiz the high priest;' then he crossed himself and left the room.

The natives were still kneeling. 'Get up,' she said; but they did not move. She tried again in Swahili and they stood up. 'Who are you?' she asked in the same tongue.

'Your slaves,' replied the lad.

'Why do you look so frightened?' she demanded.

'We are afraid,' he said, 'to be so near a goddess. Do not kill us. We will serve you faithfully.'

'Of course I won't kill you. What made you think I would?'

'The high priest kills many natives and throws them to the guardians of Alemtejo. A goddess would want to kill more than a high priest, would she not?'

'I do not want to kill anyone. You need not be afraid of me. What is your name?'

'Kyomya,' said the lad. 'How may we serve you, goddess?'

Sandra sat up on the edge of the cot and looked around.

The room was large and rather bare. It was simply furnished with a table and several benches. The floor was covered with skins of buffalo and lion. The windows were two narrow, unglazed embrasures. At one side of the room was a large fireplace. As long at she was a goddess, she thought, she might as well make the most of it.

'Kyomya,' she said.

'Yes, goddess.'

'I want a bath, and some clean clothes, and food. I am famished.'

The natives looked surprised, and it occurred to Sandra that perhaps they felt that a goddess should not be famished – that she shouldn't need food at all.

Kyomya turned to one of the girls. 'Prepare a bath,' he said; and to another, 'Go, and fetch food. I will bring raiment for the goddess.'

After a while the three girls took her to an adjoining apartment where water was being heated over a charcoal brazier. They undressed her, and two of them bathed her while a third combed her hair. Sandra was commencing to feel very much like a goddess.

Presently Kyomya came with raiment; and it was raiment, not just ordinary clothing or even apparel. Evidently Kyomya had never heard of Emily Post, for he walked into the room without knocking and seemed perfectly oblivious of the fact that Sandra was naked. He laid the raiment on a bench, and walked out; and then the three girls clothed her. Her undergarment was a softly tanned doeskin, over which they fitted a skirt of fine gold mesh that was split down one side. Two highly ornamented golden discs supported her breasts. The straps of her sandals were studded with gold, and there was a golden ornament for her hair, as well as anklets, armlets, and rings of the same metal.

She felt that her garment was just a little more than decollete; but inasmuch as none of the women she had seen in Alemtejo had worn anything at all above the waist, she realized that she was quite modestly gowned; and anyway who was she to say how a goddess should dress? Even Schaparelli might not know that.

The bath had refreshed and rejuvenated her, and now, richly clothed, she could almost feel that she was a goddess; but try as she would, she could not erase the memory of the frightful scene she had been forced to witness in the throne room. As long as she lived she would see that pitiful figure on the altar and hear the screams and the racking sobs.

In the next room, food was laid out for her on the table; and while she ate, the five slaves hovered about, handing her first this and then that.

There were fresh fruits and vegetables, and a stew she later learned was buffalo meat. It was highly seasoned and entirely palatable, and there was a heavy wine which reminded her of port, and strong black coffee. Evidently the King of Alemtejo lived well. It was no wonder he was fat.

Just as she was finishing her meal, the door was thrown open to the blaring of trumpets; and the King entered.

Sandra Pickerall was quick-witted; otherwise she might have arisen and curtsied; but in the same instant that she knew it was the King, she remembered she was a goddess; and so she remained seated.

The King advanced, half bent a knee and crossed himself.

'You may be seated,' said Sandra. She spoke in Swahili, hoping the King might understand; and she spoke quickly before he could sit down without permission. It was just as well to put a King in his place from the start.

Da Gama looked a little surprised, but he sat down on a bench opposite her; then he ordered her slaves to leave the apartment.

'Kyomya will remain,' she said.

'But I sent him away,' said the King.

'He will remain,' said Sandra the goddess, imperiously.

Da Gama shrugged. Evidently he had found a real goddess. 'As you will,' he said.

Poor Kyomya looked most uncomfortable. Beads of sweat stood on his forehead, and the whites of his eyes showed all around the irises. It was bad enough to be constantly risking the displeasure of a goddess without actually displeasing a King.

'You have been well attended?' asked da Gama. She felt naked beneath his gaze.

'Quite,' she said. 'My slaves are very attentive. I have been bathed and clothed, and I have eaten. Now all I desire is rest,' she concluded, pointedly.

'Where did God find you?' he asked.

'Where does one find a goddess?' she retorted.

'Perhaps he spoke the truth, then,' said the King.

'What did he say?' she asked.

'He said you were sent directly to him from heaven.'

'God knows,' she said.

'You are very beautiful,' said the King. 'What is your name?'

'My name is Sandra,' she replied; 'but you may call me either Holy One or Goddess. Only the gods may call me Sandra.'

'Come, come,' he said. 'Let's be friends. Let's not stand on ceremony. After all, I am a King. You may call me Chris, if you wish to.'

'I do not wish to,' she said. 'I shall call you da Gama; and by the way, da Gama, how did you get that name?'

'I am Christoforo da Gama, brother of Vasco da Gama.'

'What makes you think so?' said Sandra.

'What makes me think so!' exclaimed the King. 'It is recorded in the history of Alemtejo. It has been handed down from father to son for four hundred years.'

'Unless my memory has failed me or history lies, Christoforo da Gama, the brother of Vasco da Gama, was defeated by the Moslems and killed with all his four hundred and fifty musketeers. At least, da Gama was put to death.'

'Then your history lies,' said the King. 'Christoforo da Gama escaped with half his musketeers. A horde of Moslems chased them South, until finally they found sanctuary here. They made slaves, and prospered; and during the first hundred years they built this castle, they, and their descendants; but the Moslems camped on the other side of the valley and constantly made war upon Alemtejo. Their descendants are still there and still making war upon us, except during those times when we are making war upon them.'

'Alemtejo,' said the girl. 'The name is very familiar, yet I cannot place it.'

'It is the name of the country from which the da Gamas originally came,' said the King; and then she recalled.

'Oh, yes,' she said, 'it is a province in Portugal.'

'Portugal,' he said. 'Yes, that is mentioned in our history. I used to think I would go out and conquer the world and find Portugal; but it is very pleasant here in Alemtejo; so why should I go out among naked barbarians whose food is probably atrocious?'

'I think you are quite wise,' said Sandra. 'I am sure it would not be worth your while to conquer the world. Oh, by the way, have you conquered the Moslems across the valley yet?'

'Why, of course not,' he said quickly. 'If I conquered them, we would have no one to fight; and life would be very dull.'

'That seems to be the general feeling all over the world,' she admitted; 'and now, da Gama, you may go. I wish to retire.'

He looked at her through half-closed eyes. 'I'll go this time,' he said, 'but we are going to be friends. We are going to be very good friends. You may be a goddess, but you are also a woman.'

As the King left Sandra's apartment he met Ruiz in the corridor. 'What are you doing here, Chris?' demanded the high priest.

'There you go again,' whined da Gama. 'Anybody'd think you were King here. Isn't this my castle? Can't I go where I please in it?'

'I know you, Chris. You keep away from the goddess. I saw the way you looked at her today.'

'Well, what of it?' demanded da Gama. 'I am King. Do I not sit on a level with God and his goddess? I am as holy as they. I am a god, as well as a King; and the gods can do no wrong.'

'Rubbish!' exclaimed the high priest. 'You know as well as I do that the man is no god and the woman no goddess. Fate sent the man down from the skies – I don't know how; but I'm sure he's as mortal as you or I; then you got the idea that by controlling him you could control the church, for you know that who controls the church controls the country. You were jealous of me, that was all; then you conceived the idea of having a goddess, too, which you thought might double your power. Well, you have them; but they're going to be just as useful to me as they are to you. Already, the people believe in them; and if I should go to them and say that you had harmed the girl, they would tear you to pieces. You know, you don't stand any too well with the people, Chris, anyway; and there are plenty of nobles who think that da Serra would make a better King.'

'Sh-h-h,' cautioned da Gama. 'Don't talk so loud. Somebody may overhear you. But let's not quarrel, Pedro. Our interests are identical. If Osorio da Serra becomes King of Alemtejo, Pedro Ruiz will die mysteriously; and

Quesada the priest will become high priest. He might even become high priest while I am King.'

Ruiz scowled, but he paled a little; then he smiled and slapped the King on the shoulder. 'Let us not quarrel, Chris,' he said. 'I was only thinking of your own welfare; but then, of course, you are King, and the King can do no wrong.'

THIRTEEN

Captured by Cannibals

Gantry had not slept well the night the voice had come to them out of the darkness. It had spoken but the once; yet all through an almost sleepless night, Gantry had heard it again and again. It was the first thing he thought of as he awoke. Crump and Minsky were already on their feet.

'We'd better be movin',' said the former. 'We got to kill us some meat today.'

'What do you suppose it was?' said Gantry.

'What do I suppose what was?' demanded Crump.

'That voice last night.'

'How should I know?'

'It spoke Swahili, but it didn't sound like no native voice,' continued Gantry. 'It told us to turn back or we'd be killed.'

'How's a voice gonna kill you?' demanded Minsky.

'There was somethin' back of that voice,' said Gantry, 'and I don't think it was human.'

'Bunk!' exclaimed Crump. 'Come along. We got to be movin'.'

'Which way you goin'?' demanded Gantry.

'Where do you suppose I'm goin'? To the Ruturi Mountains, of course.'

'Then I ain't goin' with you,' said Gantry. 'I know when I've had enough, and I'm going back.'

'I always thought you were yellow,' said Crump.

'Think whatever you damn please,' said Gantry. 'I'm goin' back.'

'That's O.K. by me,' said Crump. 'One less to divide the reward with.'

'Dead men can't spend no reward,' said Gantry.

'Shut up!' said Minsky.

'And get the hell out of here,' added Crump.

'You bet I will,' said Gantry, swinging his rifle to the hollow of his arm and starting off towards the South.

Just before he passed out of sight, he turned and looked back at his two former companions. Did he have a premonition that he was looking for the last time on the faces of white men?

Two days later the drums of the Waruturi bid the tribesmen to a feast.

When Tarzan went away, leaving Dutton alone with the apes, the American had tried to sleep; but his mind had been so active in reviewing his recent experiences and in an attempt to solve some of the baffling enigmas that had presented themselves, that he had been unable to do so.

The more he thought about Tarzan and the apes, the more convinced he became that Tarzan was the man who had abducted Sandra; but why had Tarzan befriended him? Perhaps he was only pretending, so he could hold him for ransom, also, as Dutton was commencing to believe was the real reason for the abduction of Sandra, unless the man were, in fact, an irresponsible madman.

In either event, he could gain nothing by remaining with Tarzan, and his only hope of rescuing Sandra would depend upon his reaching her before Tarzan did.

Finally, he decided that his only recourse was to escape from the madman and make his way alone to the Ruturi Mountains; and inasmuch as Tarzan was away, he might not find a better time.

Dutton rose and walked slowly away from the apes. Those which were not already asleep paid no attention to him; and a moment later he had plunged into the forest.

Occasional glimpses of the stars aided him in maintaining his direction. A small pocket-compass which he carried would serve the same purpose during the day; so he groped his way through the dark night, a helpless thing only half appreciating his helplessness; and while he moved slowly on towards the North, Tarzan of the Apes swung back to the camp of the great apes where he quickly discovered the absence of the American. Assuring himself that he was not in the immediate vicinity, he called Dutton's name aloud, but there was no response; then he awakened the apes and questioned them. Two of them had seen the Tarmangani walk out of the camp. Further than that, they knew nothing. Another might have thought they had disposed of the man and were lying to Tarzan, for it had been obvious that they had not liked him and had not wished him around; but Tarzan knew that beasts do not lie.

Tarzan is seldom in a hurry. Time means nothing to the denizens of the jungle. Eventually, he knew, he would catch up with the impostor and destroy him; but it was immaterial whether it was today, tomorrow, or next month; and so it was that Tarzan and his great shaggy companions moved in a leisurely fashion towards the Ruturi Mountains, the apes foraging for food while the man lay in dreamy indolence during the heat of the day.

Very different, however, it was with the young American straining to the limit of his physical ability to reach his goal before he was overtaken by the man whom he now believed to be mad and a menace to both him and Sandra Pickerall.

During his brief experience in Africa, Dutton had always had someone with him with far greater experience upon whom to depend, with the result that he had not profited greatly by his weeks in the jungle; and so was pathetically vulnerable to surprise and attack, blundering on seemingly oblivious to the dangers which surrounded him.

Elephants, rhinoceroses, buffaloes, leopards, and lions do not hide behind every bush in Africa. Men have crossed the whole continent without seeing a single lion; yet there is always a chance that one of these dangerous beasts may be encountered, and he who would survive must always be on the alert.

To move quietly is to move with greatest safety, for noise apprises a keen-eared enemy of your approach, at the same time preventing you from hearing any noise that he may make.

His mind occupied with his problems, it is possible he was unaware of the fact that he often whistled little tunes or sometimes sang; but if he was not aware of it, there came a time when a dozen dusky warriors were. They stopped to listen, whispering among themselves; and then they melted into the undergrowth on either side of the trail; and when Dutton came abreast of them they rose up, encircling him and menacing him with threatening spears. He saw the golden ornaments and the filed teeth, and he knew, from what he had heard, that he was confronted by Waruturi cannibals. His first thought was of recourse to his rifle; but almost simultaneously he realized the futility of offering resistance, and a moment later the temptation was entirely removed by a villainous-looking warrior who snatched the weapon from him.

They handled him pretty roughly then, striking him and poking him with their spears; and then they bound his hands behind his back and put a rope about his neck and led him back along the way he had just come in the direction of the trail which turned east towards the Waruturi village.

Tarzan was coming North along the trail the Waruturi were following South with their captive; but he was moving very slowly, so slowly that there was little doubt but that the savages would turn from this trail onto the one leading to the east before he reached the intersection; this close was Dutton to possible succour.

Dutton realized the seriousness of his situation. He knew he had been captured by cannibals. How could he persuade them to release him? He could think only of a reward; but when he saw the golden ornaments with which they were adorned he realized the futility of that. Threats would be of no avail, for they were too far back in the hinterland to have knowledge of the white man's law or of his might; and even if there were some argument by which he could persuade or coerce them into releasing him, how was he to transmit it to them in the few words of Swahili with which he was familiar?

There was, however, one hope to which to cling. He knew that the mad Tarzan was coming North towards the Ruturi Mountains. He had saved Sandra Pickerall from these same cannibals. Might he not, then, find the means to rescue him, also; or had he sacrificed any right to expect this because of his desertion of Tarzan?

With these troubling thoughts was Dutton's mind occupied, when presently the Waruturi turned to the left upon a new trail; then the American's heart sank, for now there was no hope at all.

The warrior who took Dutton's rifle from him was very proud of his acquisition and was constantly fingering it and playing with it until, inadvertently, he cocked it and squeezed the trigger. As the muzzle happened to be pointing at the back of the man in front of him at the time, the result was most disastrous to the man in front; but, fortunately for him, he was never aware of his misfortune, since the projectile passed cleanly through his heart.

This accident necessitated a halt and a long palaver, during which Dutton was struck several times with the haft of a spear by the brother of the man who had been killed, and would have been killed himself had not the leader of the party intervened in his behalf, wisely realizing that it was much easier to get beef home on the hoof than to carry it.

More time was occupied in the construction of a rude litter on which to carry the body of the dead buck back to the village, for, from being a boon companion, he had now suddenly been transformed into a prospective feast; thus considerably assuaging their grief. I think you can probably see how that would be yourself, if you were very hungry and your rich uncle died, and you could not only inherit his wealth but also eat him into the bargain; but of course that is neither here nor there, as you probably haven't a rich uncle, and if you have, the chances are that he will leave his money to a foreign mission in the nature of a bribe to Saint Peter to let him in.

Before resuming the march, the Waruturi unbound Dutton's hands and made him carry one end of the litter upon which lay the corpse.

FOURTEEN
'Then the Door Opened'

After the King left her apartment, Sandra's slaves prepared her for bed. Thesy snuffed out the cresset which had lighted the room; and Kyomya lay down across the threshhold of the doorway which opened onto the corridor. Faintly and from far away came the roars of the guardians of Alemtejo, as the exhausted girl sank into slumber.

The following day passed without incident. She saw neither the King nor Ruiz. In the afternoon, she walked out, attended by Kyomya and guarded by two warriors. She left the castle upon the opposite side from which she had entered, and there she saw a village of thatched huts extending from the castle wall out onto the plain. Here lived the common people, the tillers of the soil, the herdsmen, the artisans, and the common soldiers. There were many of them; and all whom she passed, knelt and crossed themselves. Kyomya was very proud.

At one side of the village were large corrals in which were many buffalo. At sight of them, Sandra expressed surprise, for she had always understood that the African buffalo was a savage, untamable beast, perhaps the most dangerous of all the wild animals of the Dark Continent.

'But what can they be used for?' she asked Kyomya.

'These are the war buffalo,' he told her. 'We have many more, but the herders have them out on pasture now. These, the warriors of Alemtejo use when they go to war with the Moslems.'

'The Moslems! Who are they?' demanded Sandra.

'They are my people,' said Kyomya. 'We live in a village in the mountains across the plain. Sometimes we come down to raid and kill, or steal the buffalo of Alemtejo. We are Gallas, but they call us Moslems. I do not know why. We also use buffalo when we make war. I was with a raiding party of Gallas three rains ago. It was then that I was captured by the Alemtejos and made a slave.'

'They keep all these buffalo just for war?' asked Sandra.

'For their meat, too; for their milk and their hides. They are very valuable to the Alemtejos and to us. My father owned many buffaloes. He was a rich man. When the Alemtejos kill a buffalo, they waste nothing; for what they do not use themselves, they throw over the great cliff to the lions.'

Kyomya told her many things that day. He told her of the rich gold mine in the mountains beyond the valley. 'Why, the gold is so plentiful that it is taken out in great pieces sometimes as large as your head, and all pure gold.

Often, a buffalo cannot carry the load that is collected in a single day; but it is not easy for the Alemtejos to get the gold, because the mine is in the mountains not far from our village; and almost always when they come to work the mine, we attack them.'

That evening after dinner there was a knock upon Sandra's door. It surprised her. because no one had ever knocked before. Those who wished to do so had merely entered without any formality.

To her invitation to come in the door opened; and the man who was called God entered the apartment.

When she saw him she thought immediately of the King's visit, and jumped to the conclusion that this man had come for the same purpose.

He looked around the room. 'They seem to have made you comfortable,' he remarked.

'Yes,' she replied. 'Now, if they will only leave me alone.'

'What do you mean?' he asked.

She told him about the visit of the King and his advances, more to warn him than for any other purpose.

'The beast!' he said. He laid a hand gently upon hers. 'Can you ever forgive me for bringing you here?' he said. 'I am so sorry; but I always seem to be confused. I don't know just why I do things, except that they tell me to, and I have to do what they say; but why should I? Am I not God? Yes, I am God; and yet I have wronged you, the one person in the world whom I would not have wished to wrong; but perhaps I can make it up to you,' he said suddenly.

'How?' she asked.

'By trying to take you away from here,' he replied.

'Would you do that?' she asked.

'I would do anything for you, Sandra. There is nothing in all the world I would not do for you.'

There was that in his tone of voice and in his eyes that warned her; and yet, suddenly and for the first time, she was not afraid of him.

They talked for a half hour, perhaps; and then he bade her goodnight and left; and now she wondered about him more than before. His remorse for having abducted her was, she felt, quite genuine; and it was quite obvious that he really believed he had been compelled to do it, that he could not at that time have refused to obey the King. Now she knew it was different. He was no longer obsessed by any false sense of loyalty.

She sat thinking of him after he had left, and wondering about him, for he unquestionably presented an enigma for which she could find no solution. Sandra discovered that her interest in the man was growing. At first, she had actively hated him for what he had done; and then it had become only resentment for his act; and then, as she saw more of him, her attitude towards him had changed, until now she found herself trying to make excuses for him. It angered her a little, because she could not understand this attitude of hers; nor could she find any sane explanation of his attitude towards her. She tried to analyse some of the things he had said to her, and she always came back to the same assumption; yet it was so ridiculous she could not harbour it. But was it ridiculous that this man should love her? They had been together much. She knew she was an attractive girl; and she was the only white woman he had seen during all these weeks. She was sure that whatever his sentiments towards her might be, they were not dictated by purely brute passion. He had had her absolutely in his power for a long time, and he had never offered her even the slightest incivility.

The girl wondered – wondered if this strange man loved her, and of a sudden she wondered what she thought about it.

After the man who was called God left her apartment, he walked towards his own, which was at the far end of the same corridor. As he was entering the doorway of his apartment, he happened to glance back along the corridor just as Ruiz entered it from another, transverse corridor.

The man watched the priest. He saw that he was going in the direction of Sandra's room; then he entered his own apartment and closed the door.

Sandra's slaves were disrobing her for the night, when the door of the apartment opened and Ruiz the high priest entered.

'What do you mean,' the girl demanded, 'by entering my apartment without permission?'

A sneering smile curled Ruiz's lips. 'Don't put on airs with me,' he said. 'If you can entertain God in your apartment at night, you can certainly entertain his high priest. For your information, I will tell you that I have my spies everywhere in the castle; and one of them told me that God was here and that he had been here a long time. He must just have left before I came.'

'Get out of here,' she commanded.

'Come, come, let us be friends,' he coaxed. 'If you are good to me, you can have just about anything you want in Alemtejo; and you and I can rule the country.'

'Get out,' she repeated.

He came towards her, leering. 'Don't touch me,' she cried, shrinking away.

He seized her arm and drew her towards him, while Kyomya and the four slave-girls cowered, terrified, in a corner.

'Help me, Kyomya,' cried the girl.

Kyomya hesitated a moment, and then leaped to his feet and ran towards the couch. Ruiz heard him coming and turned to meet him, still clinging to Sandra. With his free hand he struck the boy heavily in the face and knocked him to the floor.

Kyomya leaped to his feet. 'Leave my goddess alone,' he cried. 'Leave her alone, or I'll kill you;' and then he leaped full upon the priest.

Ruiz had to relinquish his hold upon Sandra then, and grapple with the Galla slave; but the advantage was all upon the side of the high priest, for almost instantly he whipped a knife from beneath his robe and plunged it deep into the heart of Kyomya. One of the slave-girls in the corner shrieked, for she was in love with Kyomya.

Sandra tried to elude Ruiz and reach the door; but he seized her again and dragged her back to the couch. She struck at him and kicked him, but he forced her slowly back; and then the door opened.

FIFTEEN
'Set the White Man Free!'

The great apes searched for food: plantain, banana, tender shoots, and occasionally a juicy caterpillar. Tarzan arose and stretched. 'Come,' he said to them. 'Now we go.'

He started slowly along the trail towards the North, when there came distinctly to his ears the report of a rifle. That would be Dutton, he thought. Was he hunting? Or was he in trouble? The shot came from the direction in which Tarzan was going; and he decided to investigate. Scaling a nearby tree, he swung away in a direct line towards the point from which the report of the rifle shot had come.

The Waruturi moved on in the direction of their village, urging Dutton on with blows and prodding him occasionally with the point of a spear.

The white man had had no sleep the night before, and practically no food all day; and he staggered beneath the burden and the blows. Several times he was on the point of throwing down his load and attacking his tormentors, feeling that it was better to die at once than to suffer further maltreatment only to be tortured and killed in the end. He wished now that he had put up a fight while he still had his rifle; but at that time he had felt there might be some hope; now he knew there was none.

Two natives carried the front end of the litter, while he carried the rear alone. Suddenly, one of the blacks screamed and pitched forward upon his face, an arrow protruding from between his shoulders. The other blacks stopped in consternation and gathered around, looking in all directions for the author of the attack.

'The white man,' cried the brother of the man who had been shot. 'He has done this.' And he raised his spear to thrust it through Dutton's heart; and then he, too, collapsed, an arrow in his own.

The blacks were thoroughly mystified and frightened now; and then a voice came to them, saying, 'Set the white man free.'

The blacks conferred for a moment; and then decided to push on with their prisoner, abandoning their three dead, for three were too many for them to carry while a mysterious enemy lurked somewhere near them.

Again came the voice. 'Set the white man free.' But now the blacks pushed on almost at a run.

A third man fell, pierced by an arrow; and once again the voice demanded that they liberate their prisoner.

This was too much for the blacks; and a moment later Dutton stood alone in the trail, while the Waruturi fled towards home.

A moment later, Tarzan of the Apes dropped into the trail near Dutton. 'You should never wander away from camp,' he said. 'It is always dangerous. The apes will protect you.' He thought that Dutton had walked away from the camp the previous night and been captured by the Waruturi.

'You certainly came just in time,' said Dutton. 'I don't know how I can ever repay you.' He realized that Tarzan did not guess he had run away from camp, and he decided that the safest procedure was to remain the captive of the madman until he found Sandra; then wait for a reasonably good opportunity to present itself.

Early the next morning they reached the thorn forest, where Tarzan found little difficulty in locating the secret entrance, and a little later they reached the gorge and saw the guardians of Alemtejo.

The apes had not been over-enthusiastic about negotiating the narrow trail above the lions; but at Tarzan's insistence they had done so; and at last they all reached the foot of the towering precipice.

Tarzan looked up towards the summit, and his keen eye quickly detected indications that the cliff had been scaled recently. He turned to Dutton. 'It looks rather formidable, doesn't it?' he said.

'Yes,' replied the American; 'but it's not impossible. I have done a lot of mountain climbing in North-west Canada, the United States, and Switzerland; but I wouldn't advise you to attempt it.'

'Oh, I think I'll try it,' said the ape-man.

'But do you think you can make it?' demanded Dutton.

'I think so. The man I am looking for and the girl must have come this way; and if they could do it, I think I can.'

'You mean Miss Pickerall went up that awful place?' demanded Dutton.

'Well, she's not here; and unless she fell to the lions, she went up, because I have followed her spoor all the way – she, and the man who calls himself Tarzan, and the apes that were with them.'

'The apes must have gone back,' said Dutton, 'just as yours will have to.'

'Why will they have to go back?' asked Tarzan.

'Why, they're too big and heavy and clumsy to scale this cliff.'

For answer, Tarzan spoke to Ungo. The ape grunted something to the other apes; then he started the ascent, followed by his fellows.

Dutton was amazed at their agility and the speed with which they ran up the vertical cliff; and a moment later he was still more amazed when Tarzan followed them, equally as agile, he thought, as the anthropoids; and then, a moment later, he realized that the ape-man was more agile and far swifter.

With a shake of his head, Dutton followed; but he could not keep up with them. They not only climbed more rapidly than he, but they did not have to stop and rest, with the result that they reached the summit a full hour before he. Dutton threw himself on the sward, panting. Tarzan looked at him, the suggestion of a smile touching his lips.

'Well, the apes and I managed to make it, didn't we?' he said.

'Don't rub it in,' said Dutton, smiling ruefully. 'I already feel foolish enough.'

After Dutton had rested, they started on again. The trail, lying clear to the eyes of the ape-man, stretched across the plain towards the forest. Presently they heard shouts and screams in the distance ahead of them.

'I wonder what that is?' said Dutton.

The ape-man shook his head. 'It sounds like a battle,' he said.

'But I don't hear any shots,' said Dutton.

'There are still people in the world who kill one another with primitive weapons,' explained the ape-man. 'They are using bows-and-arrows and, of course, probably spears.'

'How do you know they are using bows-and-arrows?' asked Dutton.

'I can hear the twang of the bow strings,' replied the ape-man.

Dutton made no reply, but he was all the more convinced that the man was crazy. How could anyone identify the twang of a bow string through all that tumult and at such a distance?

'What had we better do?' asked Dutton.

'We'll have to go and see what is happening. Maybe your girl friend is in trouble; and somewhere ahead the man I am looking for is waiting to die.'

'You are going to kill him?' demanded Dutton.

'Certainly. He is a bad man who should be destroyed.'

'But the law!' exclaimed Dutton.

'Here, I am the law,' replied Tarzan.

As they entered the woods the sounds grew in volume, and there was no doubt in the mind of either but that a battle was raging a short distance ahead of them. They advanced cautiously; and the sight that met their eyes when they reached the far edge of the strip of forest filled even the phlegmatic ape-man with wonder, for there stood a huge medieval castle, its barbican and its walls manned by brown warriors in golden helmets and golden cuirasses hurling darts and javelins and boulders down upon a horde of screaming, cursing, black warriors armed with bows-and-arrows and lances.

'Amazing!' exclaimed Dutton. 'Look at them on that scaling ladder. They are certainly heroic, but they haven't a chance. And look what's coming now!' He pointed.

Tarzan looked and saw a tower the height of the wall surrounding the castle. It was filled with black warriors, and it was being dragged towards the wall by a team of twenty buffaloes, urged on by screaming blacks wielding heavy whips.

So engrossed were the two men with watching the thrilling incident occurring before their eyes that neither of them, not even the keen-sensed Tarzan of the Apes or his shaggy fellows, were aware that a detachment of black warriors had discovered them and was creeping upon them from the rear. A moment later they charged with savage yells.

Momentarily, they overwhelmed the two men and the apes; but presently the great anthropoids and the Lord of the Jungle commenced to take toll of their attackers; but in the melee two of the apes were killed and Dutton captured.

Against such odds, Tarzan was helpless; and as the blacks, reinforced by another detachment, charged him, he swung into the trees and disappeared.

SIXTEEN

The Plan That Failed

The night preceding the capture of Dutton by the black Galla warriors, the man whom da Gama called God had entered his room and closed the door. For a moment he stood there in indecision. He had seen Ruiz the high priest turn down the corridor in the direction of Sandra's apartment. He recalled what the girl had told him about the King's visit; and he was troubled. Presently he reopened the door and stepped back into the corridor. It would do no harm to investigate. As he walked slowly along the corridor, he heard a woman scream; and then he broke into a run.

As he opened the door of Sandra's apartment he saw Ruiz choking the girl and forcing her back upon the couch. He saw the body of Kyomya lying on the floor and the four terrified slave-girls huddled in a corner.

An instant later a heavy hand fell upon the shoulder of the high priest. It jerked him from his victim and whirled him about to stand face to face with the man he called God. As Ruiz recognized his assailant, his features became contorted with rage.

'You fool!' he cried, and losing all control whipped a knife from beneath his robe. A futile gesture.

The man who thought he was Tarzan grasped the other's wrist and, wrenching the knife from his grasp, hurled it across the room. He spoke no word, but whirling Ruiz around again he seized him by the scruff of the neck and propelled him towards the door which still stood open. There he gave him a push and planted a kick that sent the man sprawling out into the corridor; then he closed the door.

He turned to the girl. 'I am glad I came in time,' he said.

'I can never repay you,' she said; 'but what will they do to you now?'

The man shrugged. 'What can they do to God?' he demanded.

Sandra shook her head. 'But you are not God – try to realize that. Ruiz and da Gama don't think you are a god or that I am a goddess. They are just using that to fool the people for political reasons.'

'What makes you think so?' he asked.

'Poor Kyomya overheard them talking in the corridor last night.'

'I am not surprised,' he said. 'I never did think I was God; but I didn't know who or what I was; and when they insisted that I was God, it seemed easier to agree. I am glad I'm not. I'm glad you are not a goddess.'

'But who *are* you?' she asked.

'I don't know.' She saw the strange, puzzled expression return to his face. Suddenly he brightened. 'I am Tarzan of the Apes. I had almost forgotten that.'

'But you are not Tarzan of the Apes,' she said. 'I have seen him; and you do not even look alike except that you are about the same size, and neither of you wears enough clothes.'

'Then who am I?' he asked, hopelessly.

'But can't you recall anything of your past life?' she asked.

'Only that I was here and that they told me I had come out of the sky, and that I was God, even when I insisted I was Tarzan.'

'But how were you dressed when you came? Your clothing should certainly give you some clue as to your origin and, perhaps, to your identity.'

'I was dressed just as you see me now – just a loincloth – and I carried my knife and my bow and arrows.'

'It is absolutely inexplicable,' said the girl. 'People just don't happen like that, fully grown; and how in the world did you get to my father's camp? It must have been over a hundred miles from here.'

'When da Gama sent me out to look for a goddess, the servants of God went with me to help me and protect me; and we kept on going until we found you.'

'You went through all that dangerous country without a safari, without provisions, and still without a mishap?'

696

'We met lions and leopards, but they never attacked us. Perhaps they were afraid of the apes; and the few natives we saw certainly were. As for food, the apes took care of themselves and I had no trouble getting game. I am an excellent shot with bow and arrow as Tarzan of the Apes should be.'

'I wish I knew,' she said; and he seemed to sense what she meant.

'I wish I did,' he said.

Presently he dragged Kyomya's body into the corridor, and closed the door; then he gathered up some of the skins from the floor and laid them across the doorway.

'What are you doing?' asked Sandra.

'I am going to sleep here,' he said. 'I would not dare leave you alone again.'

'Thank you,' she said. 'I am sure that I shall sleep better, knowing you are here.' It did not even occur to her to wonder at the change that had come over her feelings in respect to this man whom she had so recently feared and hated and thought mad.

While Alemtejo slept, black warriors came down from the mountains beyond the plain and gathered in the forest behind the castle; and they were still there the next morning when the four slaves served breakfast for two in the apartment of Sandra Pickerall.

While she and the man ate, they discussed their plans for the future. 'I think we should try to get out of here,' said the man. 'You will never be safe in the castle of da Gama.'

'But how can we leave?' she asked.

'To everyone but da Gama and Ruiz, we are still a god and a goddess. I have left the castle whenever I pleased and no one has attempted to stop me.'

'But where can we go?'

'We can go back the way we came, back to the camp of your father,' he said.

'But that cliff,' she exclaimed. 'I never could go down that awful place. I know that I should fall.'

'Don't worry about that,' he said. 'I'll see that you get down, and we'll take the servants of God along to help and to protect us on the way.'

The girl shuddered. 'I don't believe I can do it,' she said.

'You are going to do it, Sandra,' he stated emphatically. 'I brought you here, and I am going to take you away.'

'But if you and I go out of the castle with all those apes, someone will suspect something.'

'They are probably already out in the forest,' he told her. 'There is where they spend most of their time. When we are safely in the woods, I will call them and they will come.'

'Very well,' she said. 'Let's get it over.'

'We'll go out the front gate,' he said, 'and then circle the castle to the woods. If they look for us they will think we are in the village.'

They made their way down the stairway, across the ballium, and to the front gate without difficulty. It was there that Sandra was sure they would be halted; but as they approached the gate, the soldiers knelt and crossed themselves, and the two passed out into the village.

In a leisurely manner, so as not to arouse suspicion, they circled the castle and entered the forest.

'That was miraculously easy,' said the girl. 'It is something to be a goddess.'

'It will all be as easy as that,' he assured her. 'You are practically safe now;' but even as he spoke, a horde of black warriors surrounded them.

Resistance was useless. They were outnumbered fifty to one. The man thought quickly. He knew these were ignorant savages and thought that if the slightly more civilized inhabitants of Alemtejo believed that he was god, perhaps these Gallas might believe it, too.

'What do you want of us?' he demanded, imperiously. 'Do you not know that I am God and that this is my goddess?'

It was evident the blacks were impressed, for the leader drew aside with several of his lieutenants and they whispered together for a few minutes. At last, the leader came back and stood before them.

'We have heard of you,' he said.

'Then stand aside and let us go,' commanded the man.

The black only shook his head. 'We will take you to the Sultan,' he said. As he ceased speaking, a great shouting and tumult came from the opposite side of the castle. 'They have come!' he exclaimed. 'Now we must attack from this side;' then he turned to one of his lieutenants.

'Take ten warriors and conduct these two to the Sultan.'

SEVENTEEN
The White Slave

Minsky was hungry for good red meat; but when he saw a buck and would have shot it, Crump stopped him. 'Don't you know we're in the Waruturi country, you fool?' he said. 'Do you want to tell 'em where they'll find some good meat for their cooking pots, and have a whole pack of the devils down on us in no time?'

'I thought you was such a friend of old Chief Mutimbwa,' said Minsky. 'You was tellin' us how chummy you and him was, and how we couldn't get through the Waruturi country without you. You was always goin' to his village and takin' him presents.'

'That was so they wouldn't beef about our goin' along with 'em,' said Crump. 'I didn't want to have no trouble if I didn't have to. I never been to the Waruturi village and I never seen old Mutimbwa but once; and then I was on a safari with twenty guns. I give him some trade goods for some goats and chickens, and he give us permission to pass through his country; but the real reason was he was afraid of them twenty guns. If he caught us two alone, we could just kiss ourselves goodbye; so I guess you'll have to go on eatin' bananas and plantain for a while – unless you like grasshoppers and white ants.'

Minsky thought this over very carefully, and the more he thought of it the more bitterly he resented what Crump had done to him. He would not have entered the Waruturi country for any amount of gold, had he not believed that Crump was on friendly terms with Mutimbwa. Now he was in a trap from which he might never escape; but if he ever did, the first thing that he would do would be to kill Crump. He brooded on this constantly as they slunk stealthily through the dark forest.

At last, they came to open country; and across a rolling tree-dotted plain they saw the Ruturi range looming purple in the distance.

'Well,' said Crump, 'that was not so bad.'

'What was not so bad?' demanded Minsky.

'We are out of the Waruturi country. They're forest people. There isn't one chance in a thousand we'll run into any of 'em out here; and there's the mountains where the gold is, and there's the thorn forest.'

'And there's some men,' said Minsky, pointing towards the right.

The two men drew back into the concealment of the forest, and watched a file of men coming from their right up near the edge of the thorn forest. They counted fifteen walking in single file.

'Them's not Waruturi,' said Crump.

'What they wearin'?' demanded Minsky. 'They got on shiny coats and hats.'

'Five of 'em is carryin' packs on their heads,' commented Crump. 'It looks like a safari all right, but it's the doggonest lookin' safari I ever seen.'

'Well, they're probably white men; and as long as they ain't Waruturi, they'll probably be friendly. Let's go out and see.'

Shortly after Crump and Minsky came out into the open, they were discovered by the other party, which halted; and the two men could see that every face was turned towards them. They were still too far separated to distinguish details. They could not tell whether the men were white or black; but they naturally assumed there were white men in the safari, which did not continue the march but stood waiting for their approach.

'They ain't white,' said Minsky presently.

'And they ain't blacks, either,' replied Crump, 'only four of the porters – they're blacks all right. The fifth one looks like a white man. Say, those guys have got on golden shirts and hats.'

'Their skins are light brown like they was tanned,' said Minsky. 'Maybe they are white men, after all.'

'I don't care what colour they are,' said Crump. 'They sure know where that gold mine it, and wherever they go we're goin' with 'em.'

Presently a voice hailed them. 'I say,' it called out. 'Do you understand English?'

Crump and Minsky saw that it was the white porter who was speaking. 'Sure, we understand English,' replied Crump. 'Why?'

'Because then you can understand me when I tell you to get the hell out of here before these people get hold of you. Get word to the nearest English official that Francis Bolton-Chilton is a prisoner in the Ruturi Mountains.'

'You mean they'll kill us if they get hold of us?' asked Crump.

'No,' replied the man, 'they'll make a slave of you as they have of me.'

'We could rescue that guy,' said Minsky. 'Those other guys ain't got no guns. We could pick 'em off one by one.' He started to raise his rifle.

'Hold on,' said Crump. 'We're lookin' for that gold mine, ain't we? Well, here's a way to find where it is. Let 'em make slaves of us. After we've located the mine and got what we want, we can always escape.'

'That's takin' a hell of a chance,' said Minsky.

'I've taken worse chances that this for a few hundred pounds of ivory,' replied Crump. 'Are you with me, or are you goin' back through the Waruturi country alone?'

'I'll stick,' said Minsky. 'As long as they don't kill us, we always got a chance. I wouldn't have none down there in the Waruturi country alone.' He was thinking what a fool he was to have come with Crump in the first place. He was more than ever determined now to kill his partner when he no longer needed him. Crump was already moving forward again towards the strangers, and Minsky fell in at his side.

'Go back,' shouted Bolton-Chilton. 'Didn't you understand what I told you?'

'We're comin' along, buddy,' replied Crump. 'We know what we're doin'.'

As they reached the safari they were surrounded by six or eight brown warriors wearing golden cuirasses and helmets. One of the warriors addressed them in a language they did not understand but which was faintly familiar.

Bolton-Chilton sat down on his pack. 'You're a couple of blooming asses,' he said.

'What they sayin'?' asked Crump. 'I can't understand their lingo.'

'They're telling you that you're prisoners and to throw down your guns. If you want to talk to them, try Swahili. They understand it, even way up here.'

'Those guys from Zanzibar covered a lot of ground in their day,' said

Crump. 'I ain't never been nowhere in Africa yet that someone didn't understand Swahili.' He turned then and spoke to the warrior who had addressed him. 'We're friends,' he said. 'We want to come along with you to your village and talk with your chief.' He spoke in Swahili.

The warriors closed in upon them. 'You will come to Alemtejo with us,' said the leader; then their guns were snatched from their hands. 'You will come as slaves. Pick up two of those loads. The other slaves need a rest.'

'Didn't I tell you you were blooming asses?' said Bolton-Chilton.

'He's got your number all right, Crump,' said Minsky, disgustedly.

'Hold on here,' said Crump to the leader of the party. 'You ain't got no right to do that. I tell you we're friends. We ain't no slaves.'

'Pick up those two loads,' said the warrior, pointing, and at the same time he prodded Crump with his spear.

Grumbling profanely, Crump hoisted one of the packs to his head; and then Minsky picked up the other one.

'They ain't no use beefin',' said Crump. 'Ain't we gettin' nearer to that gold mine all the time? And, anyway, these packs ain't so heavy.'

'It's not the weight,' said Bolton-Chilton. 'It's the bally humiliation – carrying packs for half-breeds!' he concluded, disgustedly.

'Where are they headin' for?' asked Minsky. 'Where are they takin' us?'

'To Alemtejo,' replied the Englishman.

'What sort of place is that?' asked Crump.

'I've never been there,' explained Bolton-Chilton. 'About two years ago I was captured by Gallas, who live in a village overlooking the plain where Alemtejo is. I have seen the castle of Alemtejo from a distance, but I have never been there. A couple of weeks ago I was coming down from a mine with a bunch of other slaves and an escort of Galla warriors, when we ran into these bounders. There was a bit of a scrimmage and I was captured. The Gallas didn't treat me so bad. They're pretty good primitives; but I've heard some beastly stories about these Alemtejos. They've some sort of heathenish religion with human sacrifices and that kind of stuff, and the Gallas say they feed people to a bunch of captive lions.'

'You been here two years,' asked Minsky, 'and never had no chance to escape?'

'Not a chance,' said Bolton-Chilton.

'You mean we got to stay here all the rest of our lives?' demanded Minsky.

'I've been here two years,' said the Englishman, 'and there hasn't been a waking minute of that time that I haven't been looking for a chance to escape. Of course, I wouldn't have known in what direction to go; and I probably would not have lived to get through the Waruturi country; but a man had better be dead than to spend a long life in slavery, only eventually to die of starvation or to be fed to lions. When a slave of the Gallas becomes unable to work through sickness or old age, they quit feeding him; so he just naturally dies of starvation; and the Alemtejos, I am told, throw their old slaves to the lions. If you two had done as I asked you, you would not have been captured and I might have been rescued.'

'That was this wise guy,' said Minsky, tossing an angry look at Crump. 'We could have rescued you ourselves, with our two guns; but no, this fellow has to find a gold mine.'

Bolton-Chilton laughed a little bitterly. 'He'll find his gold mine all right,' he said; 'but he'll work it under the hot sun like a galley slave. Before he's through with it, he'll hate the sight of gold.'

'I'll take the chance,' said Crump, 'and I won't stay here no two years neither.'

They walked on in silence for some time; and presently the leader of the detachment deployed his men and the slaves with intervals of a few feet between the men.

'What's the idea?' asked Minsky of the Englishman. 'We ain't goin' into battle, are we?'

'They spread out like this,' replied Bolton-Chilton, 'so they won't leave a well defined path to a secret entrance they have through that thorn forest there.'

Again silence for some time; and again it was broken by Minsky. 'What's in these here packs?' he asked.

'Salt and iron,' replied the Englishmen. 'We brought down gold to the Waruturis to trade for salt and iron. Both the Gallas and the Alemtejos do it several times a year.'

When they had passed through the thorn forest, they saw a well defined trail leading straight in the direction of a towering escarpment; but the Alemtejo warriors did not follow this path. Instead, they turned to the left, deployed once again, and moved off almost at right angles to the path.

'The Gallas say that trail there is mostly to fool people,' said Bolton-Chilton. 'Sometimes the Alemtejos do scale that cliff, but it's difficult and dangerous. The other way onto the plateau is much easier; but they try never to take the same way twice and never march in single file, except in one place where there is but one way to ascend. If you ever expect to escape, watch very carefully where we go and take note of every landmark. I did it coming down and I am going to do it again going up.'

'Then there is a chance to escape?' asked Minsky.

'There is always hope,' replied Francis Bolton-Chilton.

EIGHTEEN
King of All the Apes

The battle of Alemtejo, little more than a swift raid, was soon over. The defenders repulsed the blacks who would have scaled the wall on the forest side of the castle; and when the enemy bore down upon the village on the opposite side, the great gates of the castle swung open and Osorio da Serra led a sortie of twenty chariots drawn by charging buffaloes and filled with warriors. In a solid line they bore down at a mad gallop upon the Galla warriors, who turned and fled after setting fire to a few grass-thatched huts and making off with the several peasants they had captured to take into slavery.

Osorio da Serra did not pursue the fleeing blacks, for such was not according to the rules of warfare that long years of custom had evolved.

These sudden raids were in the nature of a game that was played between the 'Moslems' and 'Christians' and they had their rules, which were more or less strictly observed. They served to give a little spice to life and an outlet to the natural exhibitionism of man. The Alemtejos liked to wear cuirass and helmet and carry obsolete muskets for which there was no ammunition. The Gallas loved their war paint and their feathers and their spears. The prototype of each is to be found in the sabre-clanking Prussians and the loud-mouthed, boastful, European dictator.

So the victorious Osorio da Serra rode back triumphantly through the gates of Alemtejo, and the fat King writhed with jealousy that was fuel to his hate.

Tarzan of the Apes watched the battle on the forest side of the castle, an interested spectator, only to see it end as quickly and as unexpectedly as it had begun. He saw the black warriors gather up their dead and wounded and take them away, together with their scaling ladders and a great tower drawn by twenty buffaloes which had served no purpose whatever.

Tarzan wondered at the futility of it all and the useless waste of men and material – the silly expenditure of time and effort to no appreciable end; and his low estimate of man became still lower. Tarzan had already made his plans, and this silly encounter had interfered with them. He intended to present himself boldly at the gate of the castle and expect that hospitality which he knew to be common among civilized people; but he must wait now until the following day, because he knew that the attack on their fortress would leave the defenders nervous and suspicious.

Tarzan's reveries were presently rudely interrupted by a medley of growls and savage grunts, among which he recognized an occasional 'kreeg-ah!' and 'bundolo!' Thinking that the apes of Ungo were preparing to fight among themselves, he aroused himself and swung through the trees in the direction from which the disturbance had come. 'Kreeg-ah' is a warning cry, and 'bundolo' means to kill or fight to kill – either one may be a challenge. When he came above the spot where the apes were congregated, he found Ungo and his fellows facing a band of strange apes. Each side was endeavouring to work itself up to a pitch of excitement that must eventually lead to battle.

Tarzan, poised above them, saw the seriousness of the situation at a glance. 'I kill,' growled Ungo; and a great bull ape facing him bared his fangs and repeated the challenge.

'I am King of the apes of Ungo,' screamed Ungo.

'I am Mal-gash, King of the apes,' cried the other.

The ape-man dropped from the tree between the two great brutes and faced Mal-gash. 'I am Tarzan, King of all the apes,' he said.

For a moment, Mal-gash and his fellows, the servants of God, were perplexed, for the man went naked except for a G-string just as the other, whom they knew as Tarzan, had gone; and he gave the same name – Tarzan, which means white-skin in the language of all the apes and the monkeys.

Mal-gash lumbered back to his fellows and they jabbered together for a few moments; then he turned and came back towards the ape-man. 'Tarmangani not Tarzan,' he said. 'Mal-gash kill.'

'Tarzan kill,' growled the ape-man.

'Kreeg-ah!' screamed Mal-gash, and leaped for the man with huge, flailing arms.

The other apes watched, making no move to take part in the combat, for when King ape meets King ape they must decide the issue between themselves, and upon its result depends the sovereignty of one or the other. If Mal-gash defeated Tarzan, either by killing him or causing him to surrender, then Mal-gash might truly proclaim himself King of all the apes. Of course, he had no doubt but that he was already all of that; but it would be good to feel his fangs sink into the throat of this puny and presumptuous man-thing. As he rushed forward he sought to seize Tarzan; but as his great arms closed, Tarzan was not between them, and Mal-gash felt a blow on the side of his head that sent him reeling momentarily. With a savage roar he turned upon the ape-man again; and again he missed a hold as his agile opponent ducked beneath his outstretched arms and, turning, leaped upon his back. A steel forearm passed around his short neck and closed tightly beneath his chin. He tore at the arm with both hands, but repeated blows behind one of his ears dazed and weakened him.

The watching apes were restless, and those of Mal-gash suddenly apprehensive, for they had expected a quick victory for their King. As they watched, they saw the ape-man turn suddenly and bend forward; and then they saw the huge body of Mal-gash thrown completely over his antagonist's head and hurled heavily to the ground. At he fell, Tarzan leaped forward and seized one of the hairy arms; and once more the body of Mal-gash flew over the head of the ape-man to crash heavily to the hard ground.

This time Mal-gash lay still; and Tarzan leaped upon him, his great hunting knife flashing in the air. 'Kagoda?' he demanded.

Mal-gash, surprised and dazed, saw the knife flashing above him, felt the fingers at his throat. 'Kagoda,' he said, which means either 'Do you surrender?' or 'I do surrender,' depending upon inflection.

Tarzan rose to his feet and beat his chest, for he knew these anthropoids and he knew that a King must not only prove his right to rule but constantly impress the simple minds of his followers by chest-beating and boasting, much as a simple fascist mind is impressed. 'I am Tarzan, King of all the apes,' he cried; and then he looked about the congregated apes to see if there was any who dared to question his right to rule; but they had seen what he had done to the mighty Mal-gash, and the servants of God started to drift slowly away with self-conscious nonchalance; but Tarzan called them back.

'Mal-gash is still your King,' he said, 'and Ungo the King of his tribe; but you will live together in peace while Ungo remains in your country. Together you will fight your common enemies; and when I, Tarzan of the Apes, call, you will come.'

Mal-gash, a little shaky, clambered to his feet. 'I am Mal-gash,' he said, beating his breast; 'I am Mal-gash, King of the apes of Ho-den.'

So Mal-gash remained King of the apes of the forest; but a couple of young and powerful bulls cast speculative eyes upon him. If the puny Tarmangani could make Mal-gash say 'kagoda,' each of these thought he might do the same and become King; but when they appraised the great muscles and the powerful yellow fangs of Mal-gash, each decided to wait a bit.

Tarzan ranged with the apes the remainder of the day, but when night came he left them and lay up in a tree near the wall of the castle of Alemtejo.

NINETEEN

The Mad Buffalo

As dawn broke, Tarzan arose and stretched; then he sought the little stream that ran close to the wall at one end of the castle on the way to its terrific plunge over the cliff at the end of the plateau. After drinking and bathing, he sought what food the forest afforded. His plans were made, but he was in no hurry; and it was mid-morning before he approached the gates of Alemtejo.

The sentry in the barbican saw him and thought that God was returning; and the warriors who swung the gate open thought he was God, too, until after he had passed them; and then their suspicions were aroused; but before they could stop him or question him, their attention was diverted by screams and shouts from the far end of the ballium. All eyes turned in the direction of the disturbance to see frightened peasants scampering panic-stricken from the path of a snorting bull buffalo.

In the centre of the ballium, directly in the path of the beast, stood a magnificent figure helmeted and cuirassed in solid gold. It was Osorio da Serra, the great noble of Alemtejo. For a moment the man hesitated, half drawing his great sword; but evidently realizing the futility of such a defence he turned and fled; and now the red-eyed beast, foam flecking his neck and sides, centred its charge upon the fleeing man, the natural reaction of any maddened animal.

As da Serra passed close to Tarzan, the ape-man saw that in another few yards the bull would overhaul its quarry. It would toss him and then it would gore and trample him.

Tarzan knew that if he stood still the animal would pass him by, its whole attention being riveted upon the man who ran, the moving figure beckoning it to pursuit.

As the bull came abreast him, the ape-man took a few running steps close to its shoulder; then he launched himself at its head, grasping one horn and its nose, twisting the head downward and to one side. The bull stumbled and went down, almost tearing loose from the ape-man's grasp; but that grip of steel still held, and though the great brute struggled, snorting and bellowing, the man twisted its head and held it so that it could not arise.

Da Serra, realizing that he could not outdistance the charging bull, had turned with drawn sword to face the oncoming beast; and so he had witnessed the act of the stranger, marveling at his courage and his superhuman strength. Now he ran towards the struggling man and beast, summoning warriors to his assistance; but before they reached the two the mighty bull wrenched his head free and staggered to his feet.

Tarzan had retained his hold upon one horn, and now he seized the other as man and beast stood facing one another. The bull shook its lowered head as, snorting and bellowing, it pawed the earth; then it surged forward to gore and trample the ape-man. The muscles of the Lord of the Jungle tensed beneath his bronzed skin, as, exerting his mighty strength, he held the bull and slowly twisted its head.

The awe-struck Alemtejos watched in wide-eyed wonder as once again the giant white man brought the great bull to its knees and then, with a final twist, rolled it over on its side.

This time Tarzan held the struggling brute until, finally, it lay still, panting and subdued; then herders came, twenty of them, and put ropes round its horns; and when Tarzan released his hold, and the buffalo scrambled to its feet, they led it away, ten men on either side.

Osorio da Serra came close to the ape-man. 'I owe you my life,' he said. 'Who are you and how may I repay you?'

'I am Tarzan of the Apes,' replied the Lord of the Jungle.

Da Serra looked his surprise. 'But that cannot be,' he said. 'I know Tarzan of the Apes well; for two years he has been God in Alemtejo.'

'I am Tarzan of the Apes,' repeated the ape-man. 'The other is an impostor.'

The eyes of Osorio da Serra narrowed fleetingly in thought. 'Come with me,' he said. 'You are my guest in Alemtejo.'

'And who are you?' demanded Tarzan.

'I am Osorio da Serra, Captain-General of the warriors of Alemtejo.'

Da Serra turned to the soldiers who were crowding close in admiration of the white giant who could throw and subdue a bull buffalo. 'This, my children, is the real God,' he said. 'The other was an impostor,' and all within earshot dropped to their knees and crossed themselves.

By no slightest change in expression did Tarzan reveal his surprise. He would wait until he should have discovered just what this silly assumption meant to him. Perhaps it would improve his position among a strange people. He wondered what motive the man da Serra had in proclaiming him a God. He would wait and see.

'Come,' said da Serra, 'we will go to my apartment,' and led the way into the castle.

Within the gloomy corridors, where it was not easy to distinguish features, all whom Tarzan passed knelt and crossed themselves; and the word spread quickly through the castle that God had returned. It came to the ears of da Gama, who immediately summoned Ruiz the high priest.

'What is this I hear?' demanded the King – 'that God has returned.'

'I just heard it myself,' replied Ruiz. 'They say that he subdued a mad buffalo in the ballium, and that da Serra has taken him to his apartment.'

'Summon them both,' commanded da Gama.

In the quarters of the Captain-General of Alemtejo, da Serra was speaking earnestly to Tarzan. 'You saved my life. Now let me save you from slavery or death.'

'What do you mean?' asked the ape-man.

'All strangers who fall into the hands of da Gama, the King, are doomed to slavery for the remainder of their lives, or are sacrificed upon the altar of Ruiz the high priest. I mean that if we can convince the people that you are the true God, neither da Gama nor Ruiz will dare enslave or kill you. Do as I say, and you need not be afraid.'

'I am not afraid,' said the ape-man. 'Had I been afraid, I should not have come here.'

'Why did you come?' inquired da Serra.

'To kill the man who calls himself Tarzan of the Apes, and who stole women and children, bringing the hatred of my friends upon me.'

'So you came here to kill God?' said da Serra. 'You are a brave man to tell me that. Suppose I had believed in the man whom da Gama calls God?'

'You didn't believe in him?' asked Tarzan.

'No, neither did da Gama nor Ruiz; but the people believed that he was God. Da Gama and Ruiz will know you are not God; but that will make no difference, if the people believe; and when they hear the story of the buffalo, they will know that no mortal man could have done the thing you did.'

'But why should I deceive the people?' asked Tarzan.

'You will not be deceiving them. They will deceive themselves.'

'To what purpose?' demanded the ape-man.

'Because it is easy to control the common people through their superstitions,' exclaimed da Serra. 'It is for their own good; and, furthermore, it pleases them to have a god. He tells him what to do, and they believe him.'

'I do not like it. I shall not say that I am God; and after I have killed the man who calls himself Tarzan, I shall go away again. Where is he? And where is the girl he brought here with him?'

'They were stolen yesterday by the Moslems during a great battle.'

'You mean the negroes who attacked the castle yesterday?' asked Tarzan.

'Yes.'

'They looked like Gallas to me,' said the ape-man.

'They are Gallas; but they are also Moslems. Their village lies in the foothills above the plain.'

'I shall go there and find him,' said Tarzan.

'You would be killed,' said da Serra. 'The Moslems are very fierce people.'

'Nevertheless, I shall go.'

'There is no hurry,' said da Serra. 'If they have not already killed him, he will remain there as a slave as long as he lives. Therefore, you can stay in Alemtejo for a while and help me.'

'How can I help you?'

'Da Gama is a bad King, and Ruiz the high priest is another scoundrel. We want to get rid of them and choose a new King and a new high priest. After we find that the people have sufficient faith in you, it will only be necessary for you to command them to rise against da Gama.'

'And then you will be King,' suggested Tarzan.

Da Serra flushed. 'Whomever the nobles and the warriors choose will be King,' he said.

As da Serra ceased speaking, a messenger appeared and summoned them to the throne room by order of the King.

TWENTY
The Sultan

Howling blacks greeted the prisoners as their escort marched them into the village of Ali, the sultan.

'Escape!' said Sandra Pickerall, bitterly. 'We were infinitely better off in Alemtejo.'

The man walked with bowed head. 'All that I do is wrong,' he said. 'I have brought all this misery upon you – I who would die for you.'

She touched his arm gently. 'Do not reproach yourself,' she said. 'I know now that you did not know what you were doing; but perhaps, after all, it was fate,' she added, enigmatically.

The village was a hodgepodge of grass huts, houses of sod or clay, and several constructed of native rocks. The largest of these stood in the centre of the village at one side of a large plaza. To this building they were conducted, surrounded by a horde of screaming blacks. They were halted there; and presently a huge Negro emerged from the interior with warriors marching on either side and before and behind him, a slave carrying an umbrella above his head, while another brushed flies from him with a bunch of feathers fastened to the end of a stick. The fat man was the sultan, Ali. He seated himself upon a stool, and his court gathered about and behind him.

The leader of the escort guarding the prisoners advanced and knelt before the sultan. 'We have been victorious in our battle with the Alemtejos,' he reported, 'and we bring these two prisoners to our sultan.'

'You dare to disturb me,' cried Ali, 'to bring me two of the Alemtejo's white slaves? Take them to the prison compound; and as for you—'

'Patience, O Sultan,' cried the warrior. 'These are no slaves. They are the god and goddess of Alemtejo.'

The sultan Ali scowled. 'They are not gods,' he bellowed. 'There is no god but Allah. Take the man to the compound. The woman pleases me. Perhaps I shall keep her; or if the Alemtejos wish their gods returned to them, I will send them back when they send me two hundred buffaloes. Take that word to King Christoforo – two hundred buffaloes before the full moon.'

'Yes, O Sultan,' cried the warrior, prostrating himself. 'I go at once to Alemtejo, carrying a flag of truce.'

Sandra took a step towards the black sultan. 'Why would you keep us here as prisoners?' she asked in faltering Swahili. 'We are not enemies. We have not harmed you. We were prisoners of the Alemtejos. Now that you have rescued us from them, let us go. We are no good to you.'

'The man is strong,' said Ali. 'He will work in the mines. You are beautiful; but if Christoforo sends two hundred buffaloes, I shall send you back to him.'

'My father will give you more than the value of two hundred buffaloes, if you will let me go,' said Sandra.

'What will he give me?' demanded Ali.

'He will give you gold,' she said.

The sultan laughed. 'Gold!' he exclaimed. 'I have more gold than I know what to do with.'

'My people are rich and powerful,' insisted the girl. 'There are many of them. Someday they will come and punish you, if you do not let us go.'

The sultan sneered. 'We do not fear the white man. They fear us. When they come, we make slaves of them. Have they ever sent soldiers against us? No; they are afraid; but enough of this. Take the man to the compound and turn the girl over to the women. Tell them to see that she is not harmed, or they will feel the wrath of Ali.'

Sandra turned to the man who thought that he was Tarzan. 'I guess it is quite useless,' she said hopelessly.

'I am afraid so,' he said; 'but don't give up hope. We may find a way to escape. I shall think of nothing else.'

Some women came then and took Sandra away, and a couple of warriors pushed her fellow prisoner in the opposite direction; and as he was being taken away towards the compound he kept looking back, feasting his eyes for perhaps the last time upon this girl whom he had learned to love.

The compound, a filthy place surrounded by a high palisade, was deserted. There was a single entrance closed by a heavy gate, secured upon the outside by huge bars. Inside, the man saw a shed at one end of the enclosure. Its floor was littered with dried grasses and filthy sleeping mats, while scattered about were a number of equally filthy cooking pots.

With his eyes the man gauged the height of the palisade, and as he did so he saw a human head hanging near the top. It was covered with buzzing flies, which crawled in and out of the ears, the nostrils, and the open mouth. The man turned away with a shudder of disgust.

The late afternoon sun cast a shadow of one wall halfway across the compound. The man went and sat down in the shade, leaning against the wall. Physically he was not tired, but mentally he was exhausted. He continually reproached himself for the hideous wrongs he had done the girl. Through his mind ran a procession of mad schemes for her deliverance. He kept repeating to himself, 'I am Tarzan. I am Tarzan. There is nothing that I cannot do.' But always he must return and face the fact that he was utterly helpless.

Late in the afternoon, the compound gates swung open and fifteen or twenty slaves filed in. All but one were emaciated and filthy blacks or Alemtejos. That one was a white man. It was Pelham Dutton.

The man leaped to his feet and hurried forward. 'Dutton!' he exclaimed. 'How in the world did you get here?'

The American's eyes flashed angrily. 'I wish to God I had something with which to kill you,' he said.

The man shook his head. 'I don't blame you any,' he said. 'I deserve to die for what I have done; but I want to live so I can help to save her.'

The American sneered. 'What kind of a line is that you're handing me?' he demanded. 'You stole her not once but twice. You dragged her to this infernal country. God knows what you have done to her; and now you try to tell me you want to live to save her. Do you expect me to believe that?'

The other shook his head. 'No,' he admitted, 'I suppose not; but the fact remains that I regret what I have done and would like to help her.'

'Why this sudden change of heart?' demanded Dutton, sceptically.

'You see, I never knew why I did these things.' Dutton noted a pained, bewildered expression in the man's eyes. 'I just did everything that da Gama told me to do. I thought I had to. I can't explain why. I don't understand it. He told me to go and get a white woman to be a goddess; and it just happened that Sandra Pickerall was the first white woman I found; but after we got back to Alemtejo, I discovered that neither the King nor the high priest believed me to be a god. They were just using me to fool the common people. She taught me that. She taught me a lot of things that I evidently didn't have brains enough to discover for myself. You see, I had always thought I was really doing her a favour by bringing her to Alemtejo to be a goddess; but when I found that even the man who had sent me for her did not believe she was a goddess, when I found out how I had been deceived and made a fool of, and made to commit this wrong, I determined then to find some way to rescue her and take her back to her father. We succeeded in escaping from the castle this morning and were on our way out of the country when we were captured by these Moslems.'

'Sandra was captured with you?' demanded Dutton. 'She is in the hands of these black devils?'

'Yes.'

'You were really trying to take her out?' asked Dutton.

'I give you my word,' said the other.

'I don't know why I should,' said Dutton, 'but somehow I believe you.'

'Then we can work together to get her out of here,' said the man, extending his hand as though to seal the bargain.

Dutton hesitated; then he grasped the proffered hand.

'I hope you're on the level,' he said, 'and somehow I feel you are, notwithstanding your phony name and all the rest of it.'

'I thought that was my name until she told me it was not.'

'Well, what is your name?' asked Dutton.

'That is the only name I know.'

'Batty,' thought Dutton.

'Where did you just come from?' asked the man who called himself Tarzan.

'From the gold mine,' replied Dutton. 'They take us there to work nearly every day.'

'Then if they take us out of the compound, we may get a chance to escape.'

'Not on your life! They send too many warriors with us.'

'We must make an opportunity then,' said the man, 'if we are going to get her away from here before it is too late. Ali has already sent a messenger to da Gama, offering to release us on payment of two hundred buffaloes; and if da Gama doesn't send the buffaloes, Ali says he will keep Sandra for himself; and you know what that means.'

'Do you know where she is?' asked Dutton.

'Yes. I saw some woman take her into a hut near the sultan's – palace, I suppose he calls it.'

Until they sank into exhausted sleep that night, the two men schemed futilely to escape.

TWENTY-ONE
The New God

When the King's messenger entered the apartment of da Serra and his eyes fell upon Tarzan his demeanour expressed his amazement; and, for an instant, he half knelt. He had been sent to summon da Serra and 'the stranger', and at the first glance he had thought the man was God.

In the instant that he hesitated before delivering his message, da Serra spoke sharply to him. 'Kneel!' he commanded. 'How dare you stand in the presence of God?'

Bewildered, the fellow dropped to one knee and crossed himself; and in that position he delivered the message from da Gama.

'Tell the King,' said da Serra, 'to summon the nobles and the warriors to the throne room to receive fittingly the true God who has come at last to Alemtejo,' so another convert went out through the castle to spread the word that the true God has come to Alemtejo, and the word spread like wildfire through the castle and out into the village where the common people live.

By the time the message reached the King everyone in the castle had heard it, so that the nobles and warriors commenced arriving in the throne room almost upon the heels of the messenger. There they repeated to one another with embellishments the story of the superhuman strength of this true God who could overcome a bull buffalo with his bare hands.

Da Gama was furious. 'This is a trick of da Serra's,' he complained to Ruiz. 'He wants a God whom he can control. Listen to the fools – they have not even seen the stranger; yet already they are speaking of him as the true God. They will believe anything.'

'Then why not tell them that the fellow is an impostor,' counselled the high priest.

'You should tell them,' countered the King. 'You are high priest; so you should know God when you see him, better than any other.'

Ruiz thought this over. If he denied this God and the people accepted him, he would be discredited. On the other hand, if the people accepted him, da Serra would be all-powerful, and that, Ruiz feared, might be the end of both him and da Gama. Reasoning thus, he quickly reached a decision, and stepping down from the dais he took his place behind the altar and commanded silence.

'You all know that the true God was stolen by the Moslems,' he said. 'If this, perchance, is the true God returned, we should all be thankful; but if it is not he, then the fellow is an impostor and should go either into slavery or to the guardians of Alemtejo.'

There were murmurings in the crowded throne room; but whether in acquiescence or dissent, one could not tell.

Presently a voice rang out from the rear of the chamber. It was Osorio da Serra's. 'The true God is here!' cried the Captain-General.

Every eye turned in the direction of the two men standing in the doorway, and as they advanced slowly towards the dais many knelt and crossed themselves, but many did not. 'The true God,' cried some. 'Impostor!' cried others.

Da Serra halted in the centre of the room. 'Many of you have heard of how this true God stopped the charge of a maddened bull buffalo in the ballium and held him and threw him to the ground. Could the other have done this? Could any mortal man have done it? If you are still in doubt, let me ask you if you think a true God could have been captured by the Moslems. He would have struck them dead.'

At this, there were many cries of assent, and more warriors and nobles dropped to their knees. Some of the nobles turned to Ruiz. 'Is this man the true God?' they demanded.

'No,' shouted the high priest. 'He is an impostor.'

'This is a trick of da Serra's,' cried da Gama. 'Seize them both, the impostor and the traitor. To the lions with them!'

A few nobles and warriors rushed towards Tarzan and da Serra.

'Down with da Gama and Ruiz,' shouted the latter, drawing his sword.

A warrior struck at Tarzan with his heavy broadsword, but the ape-man leaped to one side and, closing with his antagonist, lifted him high above his head and hurled him heavily in the faces of his fellows. After that there was a lull, and a voice cried out, 'Down with da Gama. Long live King Osorio,' and, like magic, nobles and warriors clustered around da Serra and Tarzan, offering a ring of steel blades to the handful who had remained loyal to da Gama.

Ruiz the high priest cursed and reviled, exhorting the warriors to remain faithful to their King and to the true God, who, he promised, would soon return to them; but he who had been so feared was equally hated. Hands reached for him, and he fled screaming through the small doorway at the back of the dais; and with him went King Christoforo. Thus did Osorio da Serra become King of Alemtejo, and Tarzan of the Apes the true God.

As da Serra and Tarzan took their places on the thrones upon the dais, the priest Quesada emerged from the crowd and knelt before the ape-man.

Da Serra leaned towards Tarzan. 'This is your new high priest,' he whispered. 'Announce him to the people.'

Now Tarzan did not like the part he was playing, nor did he know how a god should act; so he said nothing, and it was finally da Serra who ordained Quesada high priest of Alemtejo.

The new King ordered a feast for all; and while it was being prepared, word was brought him that a detachment of warriors had returned with three white slaves and five loads of salt and iron.

Da Serra ordered them brought to the throne room. 'It is a good omen,' he said, 'at the beginning of my reign. We seldom capture white slaves; and not in the memory of the oldest man have we captured three at the same time.'

Tarzan was becoming bored and restless. Everything these men did seemed silly to him. Their credulity was amazing. He compared them with the apes, and the apes lost nothing by comparison. Whatever the apes did had some purposeful and practical meaning. These men changed Gods and rulers without knowing whether or not they were bettering themselves. When the apes changed Kings they knew they had a more powerful leader to direct and protect them.

Tarzan rose and stretched. He had decided that he had had enough and that he was going away, and when he arose everyone fell to his knees and crossed himself. The ape-man looked at them in surprise and at that moment saw warriors entering the throne room with three white men and recognized two of them as Crump and Minsky. Here was something of interest. Tarzan sat down again and the nobles and warriors rose to their feet.

As the three men were pushed forward towards the dais, Crump voiced a profane exclamation of surprise. He nudged Minsky. 'Look,' he said, 'the damned ape-man.'

'And he's sittin' on a throne,' said Minsky. 'I'd hate to be in your boots. You won't never live to see no gold mine.'

As the three sat at the foot of the dais, Tarzan accorded Crump and Minsky scarcely a glance; but his gaze rested on Bolton-Chilton.

'You are an Englishman?' asked Tarzan.

'Yes.'

'How do you come to be in the company of these two men?'

'The men who captured me happened to capture them later,' replied Bolton-Chilton.

'Then they are not your friends?' asked the ape-man.

'I never saw them before.'

'How did you happen to get captured?' asked Tarzan.

'I was captured two years ago by the Gallas of old Sultan Ali, and the other day these blighters got me.'

'You lived in the Galla village for two years?'

'Yes. Why?'

'Perhaps I can use you and get you out of here into the bargain.'

'Are you the chief?' asked the Englishman.

The shadow of a smile touched the ape-man's lips. 'No,' he said, jerking his head towards da Serra; 'he is King. I am God.'

Bolton-Chilton whistled. 'That's rather top-hole, anyway, I should say, if a fellow doesn't take it too seriously.' He had noted the smile.

'I don't,' said Tarzan.

'What is he saying?' demanded da Serra. 'Do you know him?'

'I know them all,' said Tarzan. 'This man is my friend. I will take him. The others you may do with as you please.'

'Hold on now,' said da Serra. 'After all, I shall decide. I am King, you know.'

'But I am God,' said the ape-man, 'or at least all those people out there think so. Do I get my man without trouble?'

Da Serra was not a bad sort, but his Kingship was new to him and he was jealous of his authority. 'After all,' he said, 'I owe you a great deal. You may have that man as your slave.'

When Crump and Minsky were taken away to the slave quarters, Chilton was left behind; and at the conclusion of the feast he accompanied Tarzan and da Serra back to the latter's apartment.

Tarzan crossed to a window and looked out across the thatched village towards the distant mountains. Finally he turned to Bolton-Chilton. 'You know the Galla village well?' he asked. 'You know their customs and their fighting strength?'

'Yes,' replied Chilton.

'There is a man there I have come a long way to kill,' said the ape-man; 'and a prisoner with him is an English girl whom I should like to rescue. It will be easier if I have someone with me who knows the ground thoroughly; and at the same time, if I am successful, you will be able to escape.'

The other shook his head. 'There is no escape,' he said. 'You will only be captured yourself, God or no God,' he added, with a grin.

The same half-smile curved the ape-man's lips. 'I know that I am not God,' he said; 'but I do know I am Tarzan of the Apes.'

Bolton-Chilton looked at him in surprise; then he laughed. 'First God, and now Tarzan of the Apes!' he exclaimed. 'What next? The Archbishop of Canterbury? I have never seen any of them, but any one of them is famous and powerful enough.'

It was evident to Tarzan that the man did not believe him; but that was immaterial. He turned to da Serra. 'The man I am going to kill, and an English girl, are prisoners in the Galla village.'

'Yes,' said da Serra, 'I know. A messenger came this morning from the Sultan Ali, offering to release the man and the woman if da Gama would send two hundred buffaloes as a ransom. da Gama refused.'

'Let us go there and get them,' said Tarzan.

'What do you mean?' asked da Serra.

'Let us take all your warriors and attack the village.'

'Why should I do that?' demanded da Serra.

'You have just become King, and I notice that they didn't all accept you enthusiastically. If you immediately win a great victory over your enemies, you will command the loyalty of all your warriors. Men like Kings who win battles.'

'Perhaps you are right,' said da Serra. 'At least, it is worth thinking about.'

TWENTY-TWO

The Battle

Clothed in the gorgeous habiliments that da Gama had thought befitting a goddess, Sandra Pickerall lay in the squalor and filth of a Galla hut waiting almost apathetically for whatever blow fate might next deliver her. If da

Gama sent the two hundred buffaloes to ransom her and her fellow prisoner, they would at least be together again, though she felt that she would be no safer one place than the other.

Her mind dwelt much upon this man who had come into her life to alter it so completely. She no longer reproached him, because she felt he was not responsible. At first, she had thought he might be demented; but the better she had come to know him the more convinced she had become that this was not true. While she had never encountered any cases of amnesia, she knew enough about it from hearsay and from reading to convince her that the man was a victim of this strange affliction. The mystery surrounding him piqued her curiosity. Who was he? What had he been? She thought about him so continually that she began to be a little frightened as she questioned herself; but she was honest and she had to admit that from hate had grown friendship that was verging upon an attachment even stronger.

She caught her breath at the realization. How terrible it would be to permit herself to fall in love with a man concerning whom she knew absolutely nothing – a man who knew absolutely nothing about himself. He might be a criminal, or, even worse, he might be married.

No, she must not think such thoughts. She must put him out of her mind entirely; but that was easier thought than done. Regardless of her good intentions, he kept obtruding himself upon her every reverie; and, labouring in the gold mine beneath the hot, African sun, the man, on the contrary, strove to conjure memories of the girl and revel in the knowledge that he loved her; notwithstanding the fact that he realized the hopelessness of his infatuation; and Dutton, working beside him, fell upon similar memories and was gladdened by his love of the same girl. It was well for the peace of mind of each that he could not read the thoughts of the other.

While the Galla overseers were hard taskmasters, they were not unnecessarily cruel. Though several of them carried whips, they seldom used them, and then only to spur on an obvious shirker; but if the men were not cruel to their charges, the older women would have treated Sandra with every indignity and cruelty had they not feared Ali, who had given orders that she was not to be harmed.

There was a young girl who brought her food who was kind to her, and from her she learned that the messenger had returned from da Gama and that the King of Alemtejo had refused to ransom her and the man who thought he was Tarzan.

She asked the girl what was to become of her; and the answer was not long in coming, as an old hag entered the hut snarling through yellow fangs, cursing and raging as she spread what was now common gossip in the village. Ali had proclaimed the white prisoner his new wife and had set the day for the marriage rites.

The old hag was furious, because as the oldest wife of the sultan it was her duty to supervise the preparation of the bride.

Sandra was frantic. She pleaded with the young girl who had been kind to her to bring her a knife that she might destroy herself; but the girl was afraid. The marriage was to be celebrated with a feast and orgy of drinking the following day and consummated at night; in the meantime she must find some way to escape or kill herself, but she was being so closely watched now that the accomplishment of either seemed impossible.

After the slaves returned from the mine the gossip filtered into the prisoners' compound. The two white men heard it and were appalled.

'We must get out of here,' said the man who thought he was Tarzan.

Dutton pointed to the grisly head swinging from the top of the palisade. 'That is what happens to slaves who try to escape,' he said.

'Nevertheless, we must try,' insisted the other. 'Perhaps tomorrow, marching to or from the mine, we may find an opportunity,' but the next day brought no opportunity as they trod the familiar path to the mine.

In the village, preparations for the celebration were under way. Food and beer were being prepared; and the terrified bride was being instructed as to her part in the rites.

In mid-afternoon a warrior, breathless from exertion, entered the village and ran to the sultan's palace, where he reported to Ali that he had seen an army of Alemtejos encamped in the hills behind the village.

This was a new technique, and it bewildered Ali. Always before, the Alemtejos had come charging across the plain with blaring trumpets and hoarse war cries. To have them sneak upon him thus from the rear was something new. He wondered why they had gone into camp. That seemed a strange thing to do if they had come to make war. One of his headmen suggested they might be waiting to attack after dark, and Ali was scandalized. Such a thing had never been done before.

The sultan gave orders to recall the soldiers and slaves from the mine and to arm all the slaves, for the report he had received led him to believe that the Alemtejos might far outnumber his own fighting men.

Notwithstanding the preparations for battle, the preparations for the wedding went on as contemplated.

In all that went on, Sandra had no part, being kept under close guard in her hut; but the bridegroom ate and drank much beer, as did his warriors; and what with the dancing and feasting and drinking, the enemy at their gate was almost forgotten.

Scarcely a mile away, hidden in the hills, a thousand buffaloes were being herded slowly towards the village as night was falling. The chariots of war had been left behind in Alemtejo, for this was to the Alemtejos a new style of war and they accepted it because it had been ordered by their God.

On one flank of the slowly marching buffaloes marched Tarzan and Chilton; and behind the Lord of the Jungle came Ungo and Mal-gash with all their apes. Tarzan knew that herding these half-domesticated buffaloes at night was fraught with danger. As darkness fell, they had become more and more nervous and irritable; but they were still moving slowly towards the village, and they were, much to his relief, remarkably quiet. What little lowing and bellowing there was was drowned out in the village by the shouts and yells of the dancers and the screams of the women.

Sultan Ali, half drunk and reeling, entered the hut where Sandra Pickerall was confined. Pushing the women aside, he seized the girl by the arm and dragged her out of the hut and towards his palace, just as a sentry rushed into the village shouting a warning.

'The Alemtejos come!' he screamed. 'The Alemtejos are here!'

The shock seemed to sober Ali. He dropped Sandra's arm and commenced to shout orders rapidly to his headmen and his warriors. The armed slaves were released from the compound and were herded into line at the edge of the village facing the oncoming Alemtejos.

'Now is our chance,' the man who thought he was Tarzan whispered to Dutton. 'Work your way slowly over this way with me, towards Sandra's hut. During the confusion of the fighting, we'll get her out of here.'

Out in the night beyond the village, Tarzan issued the command for which the warriors of Alemtejo had been waiting; and at that signal, trumpets blared as war cries rang out behind the startled buffaloes. Warriors rushed at the rear guard of the shaggy beasts, belabouring them with the hafts of spears. Bellowing and snorting, the frightened beasts broke into a run; and presently the whole great herd was charging towards the village of Ali the Sultan; and with them raced Tarzan and Chilton and the band of great apes.

Confusion and chaos reigned in the village, as the thundering beasts came charging through. The false Tarzan ran to Sandra's hut and called her, but there was no response. The girl was standing where Ali had left her in the shadow of the palace.

Some of the Gallas stood their ground, hurling spears and firebrands at the charging buffaloes. Others turned and fled with the women and children from the path of the now maddened beasts, only to be set upon by the apes of Ungo and Mal-gash.

Sandra Pickerall heard the Alemtejo warriors shouting behind the herd of buffalo and realized that in a few minutes they would enter the village and she would be recaptured. She saw an opening in the herd as it scattered out; and she darted through it, hoping to escape from the village. The false Tarzan saw her and ran towards her, followed by Dutton. He called her by name and, seizing her hand, ran dodging among the buffaloes, until presently they were clear of the herd and out of the village. Shielded by the darkness, they hurried on, with the bellowing of the buffaloes, the roaring of the apes, and the shouts of warriors still ringing in their ears but in diminishing volume as they increased their distance from the village.

Once Sandra glanced back. 'Someone is following us,' she said.

'That's Dutton,' said the man.

Sandra stopped and turned about. 'Pelham!' she cried. 'It is really you?'

The happiness in her voice fell like cold lead in the heart of the man who thought he was Tarzan, for he guessed that Dutton loved the girl and realized there was every reason why Sandra should return his love; whereas, as far as he was concerned, he deserved nothing but her loathing and contempt.

Dutton ran forward with outstretched hands. 'Oh, Sandra,' he cried, 'what you have gone through! But maybe it is over now. Maybe we can get out of this accursed country, after all.'

As they moved on through the night, Sandra and Dutton recounted to each other the adventures they had passed through since they had been separated. They seemed very happy, but the man walking a little behind them was sad.

TWENTY-THREE
In Hiding

The rout of the Gallas was complete; and as the buffaloes finally passed on out of the village, Osorio da Serra and his warriors entered it. They found Tarzan searching for the girl and for the man he had come to kill, but the search was futile; and Tarzan surmised that they had escaped from the village with the fugitive blacks. It was useless to look for them tonight. Tomorrow he would find them. But they did find Sultan Ali hiding in his palace; and Osorio da Serra took him prisoner to carry back to Alemtejo in triumph.

The victorious Alemtejos made themselves at home in the village, finishing the feast and the beer that the Gallas had left behind.

Tarzan called the apes; and as they gathered about him, he told them to go back to their own countries, for he realized that not even he could hold them much longer; and presently they wandered out of the village, much to the relief of the Alemtejo warriors.

'And now what?' asked Chilton. 'It looks to me like a good time for me to make my getaway.'

Tarzan nodded. 'We'll both go presently,' he said. 'I want to take one more look around the village to make sure that the man I came to kill is not here.'

'Do you really mean that you came into this country just to find this man and kill him?' asked Chilton. 'Why, you can't do that, you know. That would be murder.'

'If you crushed a poisonous spider with your boot, you wouldn't call that murder,' replied the ape-man. 'To me, this man is no better than a spider.'

'He must have done something pretty awful to you,' ventured Bolton-Chilton.

'He did. He stole my name, and then took the women and children of my friends and carried them away to slavery or death.'

'What did he call himself?' asked the Englishman.

'Tarzan of the Apes.'

Bolton-Chilton scratched his head. 'It must be contagious,' he said.

Tarzan went through the village again, searching the huts and questioning the Alemtejo warriors and their prisoners; but he found no trace either of Sandra or the man he sought; and presently he came back to Chilton, and the two left the village without attracting attention.

'Do you know,' said Chilton, 'I always thought all those native villages were surrounded by a palisade.'

'The situation here is unique,' replied Tarzan. 'Da Serra explained it to me. The Gallas have only one enemy – the Alemtejos; and for four hundred years the latter's method of attack has always been the same. They come across the plain with blaring trumpets and war cries. The Gallas rush out to meet them. There is a very brief conflict in which some men are killed and some taken prisoners; then each side returns to its village. The Alemtejos have never before attempted to enter the village of the Gallas. The idea this time was mine, because, otherwise, I could not have found the girl nor the man for whom I sought.'

'The Gallas had better start building a palisade,' said Chilton.

They walked on in silence for a time, and then the Englishman asked Tarzan what his plans were.

'I shall find my man; and after I have killed him, I'll take you down to some settlement on the Congo where you can get transportation out of the country.'

'I understand there are only two trails out of here,' said Bolton-Chilton.

'I know of only one,' replied Tarzan, 'and it's a rather nasty descent over a cliff.'

'I have heard of that,' said the other; 'but I have twice been over an easy trail, which I think I can find again, and we won't have to go anywhere near Alemtejo and risk recapture.'

'All right,' replied the ape-man, 'we will find the other trail.'

'But how about the girl?'

'He probably has her with him,' said Tarzan.

*

While da Serra had been preparing to march out of Alemtejo with his army, all of the slaves had been detailed to round up the buffaloes that were to be driven ahead of the advancing force; and in the confusion, Crump and Minsky had succeeded in escaping into the woods behind the castle, where they hid until night fell; then, after night had fallen, they started out across the plain towards the mountains.

'In the morning,' said Crump, 'we'll look around for that gold mine.'

'In the morning,' retorted Minsky, 'we'll look for the trail out of this damned country! I don't want no part of it, gold mine or no gold mine.'

'If I'd knowed you was yellow,' said Crump, 'I wouldn't have brought you along.'

'If I'd knowed you didn't have no more sense than a jackass, I wouldn't have come,' retorted Minsky. 'What with havin' no weapons to kill game with or nothin', I should be wastin' my time lookin' for a gold mine. Outside of lookin' for the trail that'll take me out of here, the only other thing I got time to look for is food.'

Crump grumbled as he plodded along. He didn't like the idea of being alone, even though his companion were as helpless as he; but the lure of the gold was stronger than any other force that played within him.

Because they had taken a circuitous route in order to avoid meeting any of the Alemtejo warriors who might be returning from the Galla village, it was almost morning when, hungry, dirty, and exhausted, the two men reached the hills and lay down to rest. In the same hills Sandra, Dutton, and the man who thought he was Tarzan also were hiding.

Sandra was the first to awaken in the morning. She saw the men stretched on either side of her protectively. She had slept but fitfully and was far from rested; so she did not disturb them, being content to lie there quietly. Through her mind ran the strange sequence of events that had been crowded into the past long weeks of danger and hopelessness which made it seem an eternity since she had been snatched from the protection of her father. She was free. She tried to think only of that as she dared not look into the future that offered little more of hope than had the past.

She was free, but for how long? If she were not recaptured by the Gallas or the Alemtejos, she still had the horrid Waruturi country to pass through; and there was always the menace of predatory beasts as well as predatory men, her only protection these two men armed with the bows, arrows and spears which had been given them at the order of Ali the Sultan when he had commanded that the slaves be placed in the front rank to meet the attacking Alemtejos. What protection could these pitiful weapons offer against Waruturi, lion, or leopard? She knew these two to be brave men, but they were not supermen; and then she thought of Tarzan of the Apes whom she believed Crump had killed. How safe she had felt with him!

Her head turned and her eyes rested upon the man who had stolen Tarzan's name, and at once her mind was filled with speculation as to who and what he really was. She watched his chest rise and fall to his regular breathing. She saw a lock of tousled hair falling across his forehead, and she wanted to reach out and brush it back. It was an urge to caress, and she realized it and was puzzled and ashamed. She turned her head then and looked at Dutton. Here was a man of her own caste, a man whom she was confident loved her; yet she felt no urge to brush his forehead with her palm. The girl sighed and closed her eyes. Here was something more to plague and harass her, as though the other trials which confronted her were not enough. She wished she had never seen the man who called himself Tarzan; but when next she opened her eyes they looked straight into his. He smiled, and the world took on a new effulgence and she was glad that she was alive and here, for he was here. A realization of her reaction brought a sudden flush to her face, but she smiled back and said 'Good morning.'

Dutton awoke then and sat up. 'We ought to be making our plans,' he said. 'We had no opportunity last night. Personally, I think we ought to hide here in the hills for several days; and then, at night, make our way past Alemtejo to the cliff.'

Sandra shuddered. 'I know I can never go down there,' she said.

'There is another way out,' said the man who thought he was Tarzan. 'They say it is a very much easier way, but I do not know where it is. I think it is somewhere in this direction, and he pointed towards the North-west.

'While we are waiting here in the hills then,' suggested Sandra, 'let's look for it. If there is another way out, there should be a trail leading to it.'

'We've got to find food,' said Dutton; 'so let's look for it in that direction.' And so the three set forth towards the North-west.

TWENTY-FOUR

Captured By The Great Apes

The apes of Ungo and the apes of Mal-gash had wandered off into the hills after the battle, the two bands separating almost immediately; and in the morning each band started out in search of food.

Naturally nervous, suspicious, and short-tempered, the great beasts were doubly dangerous now, for they were not only hungry but were still emotionally unstrung as a result of the battle of the previous night.

They were constantly quarrelling among themselves; and had the two bands remained together there would have been a pitched battle eventually, for between different tribes of apes there is no more feeling of brotherhood than there is between different tribes of men. They do not search each other out solely for the purpose of killing one another, as men do; but an accidental meeting may easily result in bloodshed.

Sandra Pickerall and her two companions were also searching for food, but so far without any success. The girl was very tired. She wondered how much longer she could go on, marvelling at the punishment that human flesh could endure; but she made no complaint. Dutton was the weaker of the two men, for he had been longer on the poor fare of a Galla slave, nor had he the splendid physique of the man who said he was Tarzan; but neither did he by sign or word give evidence that he felt he was nearing exhaustion.

However, the other man noted the occasional faltering steps of his companions. 'You are both very tired,' he said. 'Perhaps it would be better if you stopped here and rested while I hunt for food. There is a patch of bamboo ahead of us and to the left a forest. In one or the other, I may find game.'

'I do not think we should separate,' said Sandra. 'There is always strength in numbers, even though they are few; and at least there is a feeling of greater security.'

'I quite agree,' said Dutton. 'Let's stick together until one of us can go no farther; then we can decide what to do. In the meantime, we may bag game; and a good meal will certainly give us renewed strength.'

The other man nodded his assent. 'Just as you say,' he agreed. 'At least, we should find a safer and more concealed spot than this.'

As they talked, close-set angry eyes watched them from the concealment of the bamboo thicket towards which they were moving; and when the three had come very close to it, the owner of the eyes turned to move away. 'There's something in there,' said the man who called himself Tarzan, 'some big animal. I am going to take a chance.' And with that, he swiftly fitted an arrow to his bow and shot the missile into the thicket at the form he could dimly see moving there.

Instantly there was a scream of pain and rage, a crashing of bamboo, and a huge bull ape burst into view; then the whole thicket seemed to burst into life. It swayed and groaned and crashed to the great bodies of a dozen more apes responding to the cry of their fellow.

Sandra was appalled as the great beasts lumbered forward towards them, growling and beating their mighty chests. 'The servants of God!' exclaimed the man who called himself Tarzan; and then he spoke to them in the language the Alemtejos had taught them. He commanded them to stop; and for a moment they hesitated, but only for a moment; and then, led by the wounded bull, they charged.

The two men had time to discharge a single arrow each; but these only served to infuriate the apes the more. Perhaps they recognized the man who had been God, the man who called himself Tarzan; but if they did, their former allegiance to him was dissipated by the rage engendered by his attack upon them.

The two men dropped their bows and picked up their spears, standing ready to defend themselves and Sandra with their lives. The girl might have run then and possibly made her escape; but instead, she stood behind her men, waiting and watching. How puny and helpless they looked beside these hairy monsters and how superlatively courageous.

She saw the man who called himself Tarzan lunge at an ape with his spear, and she saw the beast seize it and tear it from the man's grasp as easily as though he had been a little child; and then she saw the ape swing the spear and crash it against the side of the man's head. Down went one of her defenders, dead, she thought; and then another huge bull seized Dutton. The man struggled, striking futilely with his fists; but the great beast dragged him close and sank his yellow fangs in his jugular; and then it was that Sandra turned to run. There was nothing she could do to aid her companions, both of whom were quite evidently dead. Now she must think of herself; but she had taken only a few steps when a great hairy paw fell upon her shoulder and she was dragged back with such violence that she fell to the ground.

A mighty ape stood over her, growling and roaring, and presently she was surrounded by the others. Another bull came and attempted to seize her. Her captor, roaring, leaped upon him; and as the two locked in deadly combat, a young bull picked her from the ground and, carrying her under one huge arm, lumbered away as fast as his short legs and the burden he was carrying permitted.

But he was not to get off with his prize so easily. Another bull pursued him, and presently he was obliged to drop his captive and turn upon his fellow.

Bruised, terrified, almost exhausted, Sandra with difficulty staggered to her feet. She saw the forest a short distance ahead. If she could only reach it she might find sanctuary among the trees. She glanced back. The two bulls were still fighting, and the other apes were not following her. There was a chance and she seized upon it. Momentarily endowed with new power by the emergency confronting her, she managed to run, where a few minutes before she had felt she could not for much longer even walk.

But her flight was short-lived. The bull which had run off with her had bested his antagonist, and while the latter backed away, growling, the other turned and pursued Sandra. It was only a matter of seconds before he had overhauled her. Again he picked her from the ground and waddled off toward the forest. Glancing back, Sandra saw that the other apes were now following. They were not pursuing, they were merely following, but the ape which carried her evidently did not dare stop for fear the others would overhaul him and take his prize away; and so he lumbered on into the forest followed by the entire band, while back beside the bamboo thicket lay the bodies of Pelham Dutton and the man who called himself Tarzan.

TWENTY-FIVE

Alone

All day, Crump and Minsky had searched unavailingly for food. They had found water, and that was all that had permitted them to carry on at all. They were close to exhaustion when they lay down at dusk. The night grew cold, and they huddled together shivering. They heard a lion roar as it came down out of the hills to hunt; and they were terrified. Later, they heard him growl again, and he sounded very close. The lion had growled as he came upon the bodies of two men. At first he was startled by the scent of man, and a little fearful; but presently he came closer and sniffed at one of the bodies. He was not a man-eater and he did not like the odour of this meat; but he was ravenously hungry and presently he seized the body by one shoulder and, lifting it, carried it deep into the bamboo thicket.

Perhaps the dead man had saved the life of Crump or Minsky, for the lion would hunt no more that night.

With the coming of dawn, the lion, his belly filled, pushed his way deeper into the thicket and lay down to sleep. Crump and Minsky, numb and stiff, staggered to their feet. 'We got to keep movin',' said the latter. 'We can't just lie here and either starve to death or freeze to death.'

'Maybe we could find some birds' eggs or somethin' in that bamboo,' suggested Crump.

'There's a forest the other side of it,' said his companion. 'We ought to find somethin' in one of 'em.'

They moved on then in the direction of the bamboo thicket; and presently Minsky, who was ahead, stopped. 'What's that?' he demanded pointing.

'It's a man,' said Crump. 'He's been sleepin' there. He's just gettin' up. Why, it's that ape, Tarzan!'

'No,' said Minsky, 'it's the other one, the guy that kept swipin' the girl.'

'The girl!' said Crump. 'I wonder where she is? She's still good for £3000, if we can find her.'

'And get her through the Waruturi country,' added Minsky.

The man who thought he was Tarzan was sitting up and looking around.

He had just regained consciousness. He was cold and numb and stiff. He looked about him for Sandra and Dutton, but he saw neither of them; then he saw the two men approaching, and recognized them. What were they doing here? He knew they were bad men. He wondered if they had had anything to do with the disappearance of Sandra; then he suddenly recalled the attack of the apes. He had been badly stunned by the blow of the spear and his wits were slow in returning. He stood up and faced the two men.

'I ought to kill the guy,' said Crump to Minsky in a low tone that did not reach the ears of the man awaiting their coming.

'What'd you kill him with?' demanded Minsky. 'Maybe you'd scare him to death, eh? You ain't got nothin' but your mouth to kill him with.'

They were coming closer to the man now. 'Hello,' called Crump.

The man nodded. 'How did you get here?' he demanded. 'Have you seen anything of Miss Pickerall?'

'No,' replied Crump, 'not since you stole her from my camp. What have you done with her? Where is she?'

'She and Dutton were with me until late yesterday afternoon; then we were set upon by a band of great apes, and that is the last that I remember until just now. One of them cracked me over the head with my spear. Dutton and Miss Pickerall must have been carried off by the apes.'

'Maybe they weren't,' suggested Minsky. 'Maybe they just run out on you. You know, he was pretty soft on the girl and they didn't neither of 'em have much use for you after you stole her a couple of times.'

'I don't believe they would do that,' said the man. 'We are good friends now, and I was trying to take her back to her father.'

'Look at that blood there,' said Crump. 'There must have been a gallon of it. Was you wounded?'

'No,' replied the man who called himself Tarzan. 'It must have been one of the others.' He knelt and examined the great pool of blood which was still only partly coagulated.

'Which one?' asked Minsky.

'I wish to God I knew,' said the man. 'It might have been either of them.'

'If they killed one and took the other,' said Crump, 'it would have been the girl they took, not the man.'

'I've got to follow them and find out,' said the man who called himself Tarzan.

'We'll go with you,' said Crump; 'but we ain't had nothin' to eat for so long that our bellies are wrapped around our backbones. You got a bow and arrow. You can do some huntin' while we're lookin'.'

'Yes,' said the man, 'come;' and he started in the direction of the forest, following the plain spoor of the great apes.

*

When Sandra had been carried off by the bull-ape the afternoon before, the creature had been kept constantly on the move by his fellows who dogged his trail. He had dragged Sandra through brush – he had scraped her against trees and bushes. Her flesh was scratched and torn, and her golden breast-plate and skirt of gold mesh had almost been scraped from her body on numerous occasions. However, they had held and had formed some protection from the hazards of this hideous journey.

The girl had thought that other situations in which she had found herself during the past weeks had been hopeless, but now they faded into insignificance when compared with this – alone and unarmed, a captive of great apes with the only two men who might have saved her lying dead where they had tried to defend her.

The apes of Ungo fed in the forest. It was a poor hunting ground, and they were hungry and irritable. Often they quarrelled among themselves; and Ungo, the King ape, had often to chastise one of his subjects in order to keep the peace. He had just separated Zu-tho and another ape, both of whom wanted the same caterpillar, when Ga-un voiced a warning kreeg-ah!

Instantly, every member of the band became alert to danger. Listening, they heard something approaching; and presently they saw the cause of Ga-un's alarm. It was Sancho, one of the servants of God, coming towards them with a she Tarmangani beneath one hairy arm. When he first came in sight, he was looking back at the apes which were following him; and so did not immediately see the apes of Ungo. When he did he stopped and bared his great fangs in warning. Ungo voiced a challenge and approached, followed by his great bulls. Sancho fell back, screaming his own challenges and summoning his fellows.

Ungo rushed forward and seized the girl by an arm, trying to wrest her from the grasp of Sancho. They pulled and tugged while they struck at each other with their free paws, and would have torn her apart had not the other servants of God come upon the scene, precipitating a battle that caused both Sancho and Ungo to relinquish their hold upon the girl, so they might defend themselves.

Sandra fell to the ground while the great apes fought above and around her. She saw them rend one another with their powerful fangs and strike terrific blows with their great paws, screaming and roaring in pain and rage.

It was a battle of the primordials, such as the ancestors of the first men might have waged for possession of a prize. It was bestial and primitive, lacking the civilizing refinements of machine guns and poison gas and far less effective, for the wounds were, for the most part, superficial, and the noise far more a *sine qua non* than destruction.

As they pushed and pulled, and shoved and hauled, snarling, biting, screaming, the apes of Ungo slowly pushed the servants of God back. Sandra

Pickerall saw her chance then and crawled away, unnoticed. Glancing back, she saw that the apes were paying no attention to her; and so she came laboriously to her feet and staggered away into the forest.

For some time, she could hear the sound of battle diminishing in the distance; and Sandra Pickerall found herself again free, but alone in a strange forest with nothing to look forward to but death by starvation or beneath the fangs and talons of some wild beast. These things she feared, but she feared them less than she feared man.

TWENTY-SIX
Gold

Crump, Minsky, and 'Tarzan' searching for signs of the girl, searching for food, found neither one nor the other. They were tired and discouraged, Crump and Minsky practically exhausted. 'Tarzan' was hungry, but his mind was not on food. It was occupied with thoughts of Sandra Pickerall and conjecture as to her fate. Had it been her blood or Dutton's that they had seen on the turf near the bamboo thicket? That it was the blood of one of them, he was positive; and if one of them had been killed, how could the other have escaped? He did not concur in Crump's theory that she had been carried off by apes, for though he had often heard stories of great apes stealing women and carrying them off he had never believed them. It seemed to him more probable that some wild beast had made off with the bodies of both Dutton and Sandra; yet his love for the girl would not permit him to abandon the search for her while there remained the slightest vestige of a doubt as to her fate. The result was that his hunting was perfunctory and, consequently, most unsuccessful.

Although he thought he was Tarzan, his woodcraft was little better than that of an ordinary civilized man; and so it was that he lost the trail of the great apes and followed a false trail which led farther up into the hills. That little digression was to have tragic consequences.

'This is a hell of a country,' said Minsky. 'I ain't even seen nothin' as big as a grasshopper; and believe you me, if I seen one, I'd eat it. God, how I'd like a bowl of bouillabaisse.'

'Shut up!' snapped Crump. 'Another crack like that and I'll—'

'You'll do nothin',' interrupted Minsky. 'And after the bouillabaisse, I'll have ham and eggs.'

Crump lunged at him but missed and fell down. Minsky laughed at him. 'Or maybe a great big thick steak smothered in onions!'

'Cut it out,' said Tarzan. 'Things are bad enough as they are, without start-ing a fight.'

'Who do you think you are to tell me what I can do and what I can't?' demanded Minsky. 'If I want oysters on the half-shell, or apple pie, or crepes suzette, I'm gonna have 'em and nobody ain't gonna stop me.'

'I'll stop you talking about them,' said 'Tarzan', slapping him with his open palm across the cheek. It was not a very hard blow, but Minsky stumbled backwards and sat down heavily. 'Now listen,' continued the man who said he was Tarzan, ' you'll cut all this scrapping out, both of you, or I'll leave you; and without my bow and arrows, you'll never get any food.'

'I ain't seen you kill nothin' yet,' said Crump.

'You heard me,' said Tarzan.' 'Take it or leave it.' Then he turned and moved on up a little ravine through which the trail ran. Crump and Minsky scram-bled to their feet and followed, sullen and morose, full of hatred for the man, full of hatred for one another.

Presently they came to an excavation in the side of the ravine. 'Tarzan' stopped at the edge of this and looked down. The excavation was perhaps twenty-five feet deep and covered about half an acre. The path led down into it.

Crump and Minsky came and stood beside him; and at the first glance into the hole, Crump voiced a cry of elation. 'The mine!' he exclaimed. 'Gold! Gold! Look at it!' And then he staggered down the trail with Minsky close at his heels.

It was indeed the fabulous mine of the Alemtejos and the Gallas, tempo-rarily abandoned because of the battle and the capture of Ali. Great lumps of pure gold that had been mined, but had not yet been removed, lay scattered over the workings.

Crump fell on them, greedily gathering together the largest he could find. 'These are mine,' he cried.

'What are you going to do with it?' asked 'Tarzan.'

'What am I going to do with it, you dope? I'm goin' to take it back to Eng-land. I'll be rich, that's what I'll be.' He slipped off his coat and, laying it on the ground, commenced to pile gold into it.

Minsky was similarly engaged. 'I'm gonna get me a yacht,' he said, 'and a French chef.'

'How far do you think you can carry that stuff?' demanded 'Tarzan.' 'You can hardly carry yourselves as it is.'

'You could help us, if you had a coat,' said Crump. 'Wait,' he added,' I'll take off my pants – they'll hold a lot.'

'You can leave your pants on,' said 'Tarzan.' 'I don't intend to carry any of the stuff.'

'What!' demanded Crump. 'You mean you ain't gonna help us? You mean you're gonna let all this stuff lie around here for a bunch of savages that don't know what to do with it? This is gold, man, gold! It will buy anything in the world – women, wine, horses. With enough of this, I could buy me a title – Sir Thomas Crump. It don't sound so bad neither.'

'You're balmy,' said Minsky. 'They don't make Lords out of the likes o' you. You gotta be a toff.'

Crump ignored him and turned back on 'Tarzan.' 'No wonder you ain't got no sense enough to wear pants,' he said. 'Help us carry some of this out and we'll split with you. You're stronger than we are, and you could carry twice as much.'

The man shook his head. 'I am not interested,' he said. 'I am going on to hunt and look for Miss Pickerall. If you want to get out of this country alive, you'd better forget this foolishness and come along with me.'

'Not on your life,' said Crump. 'Go on and hunt. I'll get out of this country and I'll take this gold with me.'

'Tarzan' shrugged and turned back down the ravine, for seeing that the trail ended at the mine he knew he had come in the wrong direction and must go back and try to pick up the ape spoor where he had lost it.

'How much of this here stuff do you suppose we can carry?' asked Minsky. He gathered up the corners of his coat and tested the weight of his load. 'Golly, but that's heavy,' he said.

Crump kept piling more gold on to his stack. 'I'm afraid that's about all I can lug,' he said finally; then he fastened the coat together as best he could and tried to lift the load to his shoulder; but he could not even raise it from the ground.

'I guess you'll have to leave the knighthood behind,' said Minsky sneeringly.

'I ought to kill you,' said Crump.

Minsky laughed at him, a taunting, sneering laugh; then he fastened his own coat around his hoard of gold and struggled to raise it from the ground. Finally he got it up on one knee; and then slowly, exerting all his waning strength, he managed to raise it to his shoulder.

Crump discarded a few pieces of gold and tried again, but with no better success. He cursed the gold, he cursed 'Tarzan,' he cursed Minsky; and then he took off some more gold and at last succeeded in lifting the heavy burden to his shoulder. He stood there, panting and trembling beneath the hot African sun, the sweat streaming down his forehead into his eyes, into his mouth. He wiped it away and cursed some more.

Minsky started up the trail out of the mine. Every few steps he had to stop and rest. About half way up, he fell. He lay where he had fallen, gasping for breath.

Crump was approaching him, cursing and sputtering. 'Get out of my way!' he said.

'You ain't got here yet,' said Minsky, 'and I'll lay you a couple of thousand pounds that you don't get here with that load,' The words were scarcely out of his mouth when Crump stumbled and fell. He lay there cursing horribly and almost foaming at the mouth.

'You better throw out a couple of racehorses and two or three girls,' suggested Minsky. 'You ain't strong enough to carry a racing stable and a whole harem all at the same time.'

'If I ever catch up with you, I'm gonna kill you,' said Crump.

'Oh, shut up!' said Minsky. 'If you'd thought of it, you could have carried your knighthood in that big yap of yours.'

Slowly Minsky got to one knee and tried to raise the sack again to get it to his shoulder. It was very heavy, and he knew that even if he succeeded in getting it to his shoulder he could not climb to the top of the excavation with it. Presently he thought of another plan. Still sitting down, he edged up the trail about a foot and then, very laboriously dragged the coat full of gold after him inch by inch; thus he hitched towards the top, and Crump, seeing that he was succeeding, followed his example.

It took them a long time, and when their great burdens finally lay at the top of the excavation they sprawled beside them to rest.

'I wonder how much we got?' said Crump.

'Maybe a million pounds,' said Minsky.

'Maybe two million,' suggested Crump.

TWENTY-SEVEN

Rateng The Hunter

How many of us, farm or city-bound to a humdrum existence, have longed for adventure, have dreamed of a life close to nature far from the noise and confusion and problems of civilization, and thrilled to imaginary encounters with wild beasts and savage men whom, by our superior cunning and prowess, we have invariably overcome. Before the radio, or comfortable in a big chair with a good book, we have lived dangerously, albeit vicariously.

Perhaps, after all, this is the best, and it is certainly the safest way to adventure, as Sandra Pickerall doubtless would have assured you as she wandered, lost and hopeless, in the hills of Alemtejo, for it was this longing for adventure which had brought her to Africa with her father. Now, as she searched for a trail from the tableland, she would have given all of the considerable inheritance that would someday have been hers, could she have been safe in Scotland once more.

Rateng, a Galla warrior from the village of Ali the Sultan, was hunting, so far without much success, in fact without any success. It seemed to Rateng that all the game had left the country. He had long ago become disheartened and had turned his steps back towards his village.

Many thoughts passed through the mind of Rateng the hunter as he made his silent way homeward. He wondered what the Alemtejos would do with Ali the Sultan now that they had captured him. Doubtless they would kill him, and then Ali's oldest son would become sultan. Ali was bad enough, thought Rateng, but his son was much worse. Rateng did not like him for many reasons, but the principal one was that he had taken to wife the girl Rateng had desired; then, too, he was haughty and arrogant and a hard task-master. When he became sultan he would be a tyrant.

Rateng had been among those who had captured the god and goddess of the Alemtejos in the woods behind the castle; and he had been with the detachment which escorted them to the village of Ali the Sultan. Of these things, he thought, too. He wondered what had become of the white god and goddess, whom he knew had escaped when the buffaloes and the great apes and the Alemtejos had attacked the village.

He let his mind dwell upon the white goddess. She had been very beautiful in her golden dress and breastplates and with the crown of gold upon her head. If the Alemtejos had not attacked, she would have been Ali's wife by this time. Rateng sighed. How nice it must be to be a sultan and have as many wives as one wished, even including a white goddess; but then he was not a sultan and he would never have a white wife. He would be lucky if he had more than one native one.

Though these and many other thoughts ran through the mind of Rateng the hunter, they did not dim his alertness. His ears and his eyes were keenly sentient constantly, and so it was that he heard something approaching from the direction in which he was going.

Rateng grasped his spear more firmly and found concealment behind a low bush. Crouching there he waited, watching, listening.

Whatever was coming came slowly. Perhaps it was game. Rateng laid his spear on the ground and fitted an arrow to his bow, and a moment later there walked into view the white goddess of whom he had been dreaming.

Rateng caught his breath. What a vision of loveliness she seemed to him. He noticed how weak she appeared, how faltering her steps; but there was no compassion in the heart of the Galla. He saw only a woman, and thought only of himself.

As she neared him, he rose up from behind the bush and confronted her.

Sandra stopped, aghast, and shrank back; and then, motivated solely by terror and without reasoning the futility of her act, she turned and ran.

Weakened by hunger and exhaustion she took only a few steps before Rateng overtook her and seized her roughly by an arm. He whirled her about and held her, looking into her face.

Rateng's countenance was savage, even by the standards of savagery. The girl closed her eyes to shut out that cruel, bestial face.

Rateng had captured the goddess, and he considered the matter from all angles. The windfall might prove a blessing or it might prove the reverse. Everything depended upon what advantage he took of his good fortune.

If he took her back to the village, he would not be able to keep her for himself. The sultan's son would take her away from him; and he would get nothing for his pains. Doubtless the Alemtejos would pay a reward for her, if they could get her back in no other way; but if he were to take her to Alemtejo, he was quite sure that his only reward would be slavery for life, unless they chose to sacrifice him to their heathenish god or throw him to the lion devils which they kept at the foot of the great cliff.

There was an alternative, however, a very pleasant-appearing alternative. He knew a place farther back in the hills where there was good water and pleasant fruits, and a snug cave beneath an overhanging rock. There, for a few days, he could make believe that he was a sultan; and when he was ready to go back to the village he could cut the girl's throat and leave her there; and nobody would be any the wiser. This was what Rateng decided to do.

'Are you alone?' he asked in Galla.

'I do not understand,' she replied in faltering Swahili.

He repeated the question in that language.

Sandra thought quickly. 'I am not alone,' she said. 'My friends are right behind me. They will be here soon.'

Rateng did not believe her, for his keen ears gave him no warning of others nearby; but it was as well to be on the safe side. He had no wish to be robbed of his prize.

'Come,' he said, and dragged her off towards the higher hills.

'What do you want of me?' she asked. 'What are you going to do with me?'

'You should know,' he said. 'You are a woman.'

'I am not a mortal woman. I am a goddess.' She grasped at a straw.

Rateng laughed at her. 'There is no God but Allah.'

'If you harm me, you will die,' she threatened.

'You are an infidel,' said Rateng; 'and for every infidel I kill, I shall have greater honour in heaven.'

'You are going to kill me?' she asked.

'Later,' said Rateng.

Until now, Sandra Pickerall thought the worst had befallen her. She had not conceived that there could be anything more. She tried to conjure some plan of escape. If she had her normal strength and vitality she believed she could have outdistanced him in flight; but in her weakened condition, even the thought of it was futile. Self-destruction seemed her only hope; but how was she to destroy herself without the means of destruction? She had no weapon – nothing. Suddenly her eyes fixed themselves upon the quiver of arrows hanging behind the man's naked shoulder. There lay the means, but how was she to take advantage of it?

Rateng grasped her right wrist firmly in his left hand as he dragged her along. She could not reach behind him with her left hand to filch an arrow from the quiver.

Finally, she evolved a plan. She hoped the native would be stupid enough to be taken in. 'You do not have to drag me along,' she said. 'You are hurting my wrist. I will come along with you, for I am too weak to run away.'

Rateng grunted and relinquished his hold upon her. 'You would not get far,' he said; 'and if you tried it, I would beat you.'

They walked on in silence. Little by little, inch by inch, the girl dropped back until her shoulder was behind the shoulder of the man; then she reached up and took hold of an arrow. She had to be very careful not to warn him by shaking the quiver unnecessarily.

Gently, gradually, she succeeded in withdrawing the arrow from the quiver. Now she held it firmly in her right hand. To thrust the point into her heart would require but an instant of supreme courage. In that instant there raced through her mind a thousand memories of her past life. She thought of her father. He would never know. Doubtless he had long since given her up for dead. No man in all the world, except this native savage, would know of her end or where her bones lay bleaching in the African sun after the hyenas and the jackals and the vultures had torn the flesh away. But she would have to drop farther back before she could accomplish her design, and that might arouse the suspicions of her captor. However, there was no other way. She must take the chance.

She dropped back a little farther. She saw the muscles of the man's shoulder rolling beneath his skin to the swinging of his arm – his left arm. That glossy back, those rolling muscles, fascinated her. Her eyes gleamed to a sudden inspiration. Her mouth went dry to the horror of the thought that filled her mind, but she did not hesitate. She drew back the hand that held the arrow and then, with all her strength, she plunged the missile deep into the body of Rateng the hunter.

With a scream of pain and rage, the savage turned upon her, his face contorted in a horrible grimace of hate and agony. With a wolfish snarl, he leaped upon her, his hands encircling her throat. She stumbled backward and fell, and the man, still clutching her throat, fell upon her.

TWENTY-EIGHT

Reunited

The man who thought he was Tarzan hunted for food. His heart was heavy with sadness, for he believed that the girl he loved was dead. Dutton was dead, too. He had liked Dutton, even though he had been jealous of him. He felt very much alone, for he did not consider Crump and Minsky as companions. He thought of them only with contempt, as he recalled them cursing and quarrelling over their gold. What a contemptible creature man could be, he thought.

He tried to plan, but now there seemed nothing to plan for. He and Sandra and Dutton had been going to escape together. They would have known where to go. He did not. This was the only world he knew. There seemed nothing now for him but to return to Alemtejo. He did not know that Osorio da Serra had seized the Kingship from da Gama; and even had he, it would have made no difference, for he knew his hold upon the common people who believed him to be God. In Alemtejo there would be a certain amount of peace and security, with many comforts and good food; but he knew there never could be peace of mind for him, for within him was a restlessness and a questioning that he could not understand. There was always within him the urge to search for something, without knowing what it was for which he searched. It was maddening, this constant groping for this unknowable, unattainable thing.

Of a sudden his melancholy reverie was interrupted by a hoarse and horrible scream. It was the scream of a human being in mortal agony. The man who thought he was Tarzan, motivated by the high humanitarian ideals which he attributed to the ape-man, sprang forward in the direction of the sound, jumping to the conclusion that a human being was being attacked by a wild beast, his heavy Galla spear ready in his hand.

He had covered little more than a hundred yards before he came upon a sight that filled him with apprehension. He saw the body of Sandra Pickerall lying motionless upon the ground, and, across it, the body of a black Galla warrior from whose back protruded the haft of an arrow. He shot a quick glance in every direction for the enemy that had attacked them, but there was no sign of any enemy; then he ran forward and dragged the body of the Galla from that of the girl. The man was quite dead.

He knelt beside Sandra and raised her in his arms. At first, he detected no sign of life; but as he pressed his ear against her bosom he heard the faint beating of her heart. He chafed her hands and wrists. He held her close to him as though to warm her, oblivious of the fact that the sun was beating down fiercely upon them.

Presently the girl opened her eyes, and they went wide as she looked up into his face. 'God!' she said weakly; then she closed her eyes and shuddered and snuggled closer to him. 'So this is death!' It was just a breath, almost inaudible, but he caught the words.

'It is not death,' he said. 'It means life now.'

'But you are dead,' she said. 'I saw the apes kill you, and if we are together again, it must be because I am dead also.'

He pressed her closer. 'No, my darling,' he said, 'neither one of us is dead.' It was the first time he had ever voiced an expression of endearment to her, but she did not take offence. Instead, she raised her arms and put them about his neck and strained still closer to him.

For a long minute, neither of them spoke. There was no need of speech. There was perfect understanding without it.

It was the man who broke the silence. 'What happened?' he asked. 'Who killed him?'

The girl shuddered; then she told him.

'How brave!' he said.

'It was desperation. I was so terribly afraid.'

'He must have died almost instantly,' said the man.

'Yes. He had his fingers at my throat, but he died before he could close them. The arrow must have pierced his heart.' Again she shuddered. 'I have killed a man.'

'You have killed a beast who would otherwise have killed you. Now we must think about ourselves and try to find a way out of this country.'

'Where is Pelham?' she asked. 'Did the apes kill him?'

He nodded. 'I am afraid so. We found no trace of him. We thought they had killed both him and you. How did you escape?'

She told him briefly of the horrible ordeal she had been through since he had last seen her. 'And now,' she said, 'I suppose we are the only ones left.'

'No; Crump and Minsky are still alive. I just left them at the Galla gold mine, loading themselves up with gold they will be unable to carry. I came away to hunt. None of us has eaten much lately, and they are weak from hunger and exhaustion.'

'You will have to hunt until you kill something then,' she said, 'and take it back to them.'

'No,' he said emphatically. 'They are not worth saving, though if I were alone I should have found food for them; but I'll never expose you to these two. They are the worst blackguards I have ever seen.'

'You will leave them to die?' she asked.

'They have their gold,' he said. 'That is what they wished more than anything else in the world. They should die happy.'

'What are we going to do?' she asked.

'We could go back to Alemtejo and be God and Goddess again,' he said, 'or I can take you down over the cliff and try to return you to your father.'

'Oh, I don't know,' she said. 'I want so to live, now that there is so much to live for.'

'We shall live,' he said, 'and we shall be happy. I know it.'

'Well, what must we do?' she asked. 'You decide, and I'll do anything you say.'

'We'll tackle the cliff,' he said.

With the man at her side, Sandra seemed to have acquired new strength. Much of her fatigue and exhaustion dropped from her, and she walked along at his side as they started down out of the hills towards the plain across which lay Alemtejo and the mighty barrier cliff.

Later in the afternoon he brought down a small buck with a lucky shot.

The animal had been drinking at a tiny stream, so now they had both food and water; and after a short search, the man found a little glade hidden away in a ravine where they might camp in comparative safety.

'We'll stay here,' he said, 'until you have regained your strength. You couldn't travel far in the condition you're in now. We've water and meat, and there's edible fruit in some of those trees.'

He busied himself butchering the buck; and when that was done, he gathered firewood, and after many futile attempts finally succeeded in coaxing a blaze by the primitive method of twirling a pointed stick in a tinder-filled hole in another piece of wood. As the first thin wisp of smoke arose, the girl clapped her hands.

'Marvellous!' she exclaimed. 'I thought you'd never be able to do it; and as hungry as I am, I don't believe I could have eaten raw meat.'

He grilled some of the meat on sharpened sticks. It was partly raw and partly charred; but when it was cool enough to eat without burning them, they ate it ravenously; and when they had eaten they went to the stream and, lying on their bellies, drank as the beasts drink.

The girl rolled over on her back in the deep grass, cupping her hands beneath her head. 'I never expected to feel so happy and contented and safe again,' she said. 'It's perfect here.'

'It would be perfect for me anywhere with you,' he replied.

'Maybe that's what makes it perfect for both of us,' she said, 'just being together; and to think that just a little while ago, I feared and hated you.'

He nodded. 'You had reason,' he said.

'And that even now I don't know your name, nor who you are, nor where you come from.'

'You know as much as I do,' he said.

'Do you suppose someday we'll know?' she asked.

He shrugged. 'What difference does it make? We know we love each other. Is that not enough?'

The sun set; and, in the distance, a lion roared.

TWENTY-NINE

Gold And Death

Crump and Minsky lay where they had fallen at the edge of the workings, too weak and exhausted to rise. Each clutched his bundle of gold, as though fearful someone might try to steal it from him. For some time they lay gasping beneath the pitiless sun; then Minsky raised himself on one elbow and looked around. He saw a tree nearby that cast a little shade, and laboriously he dragged himself and his horde of golden wealth towards it.

'What you doin'?' demanded Crump.

'Huntin' shade,' replied Minsky. 'I can't lie out in that sun no longer.'

Crump raised himself and hitched along in the direction of the tree, dragging his load with him; and at last they were both in the shade.

'If we rest a few minutes,' said Crump, 'we ought to be able to get goin'.'

'I ain't goin' no place 'til that guy comes back with food,' said Minsky. 'If we get a little grub under our belts, it'll put some pep in us.'

The afternoon wore on. The two men were suffering from thirst; but now they were afraid to leave for fear the hunter would return with food and they would miss him.

Night fell. 'What do you suppose has become of that damned ape-man?' asked Crump. 'He oughta been back a long while ago.'

'Maybe he ain't comin' back,' said Minsky.

'Why shouldn't he?' demanded Crump.

'Why should he?' asked Minsky. 'We don't mean nothing to him. What can we do for him? And he ain't got no reason to be in love with us.'

'If I ever lay my hands on him, I'll kill him,' said Crump.

'Oh, nuts!' growled Minsky. 'You're always gonna kill somebody. You won't never kill anybody now, 'cause you ain't got no gun to shoot 'em in the back with.'

Crump mumbled beneath his breath; and for a long time there was silence, which was broken finally by Minsky's stertorous breathing. He slept.

Crump half raised himself on an elbow and looked in the direction of his companion. He cursed himself because he was not strong enough to carry both loads of gold, for he was thinking how easy it would be to kill Minsky while he slept; but what was the use? He couldn't even carry his own load. Maybe later, when they had had food and water and regained strength, he would have another opportunity.

'Two million pounds,' he murmured before he fell into the sleep of exhaustion.

When morning came, the two men felt somewhat refreshed and much stronger than they had the afternoon before. They had given up any hope that the hunter would return, and Crump wasted a great deal of breath cursing him.

Minsky said nothing. He was the more intelligent of the two, and by far the more dangerous. Someday he would meet the ape-man, he thought, someday when Minsky carried his favourite weapon, the trigger of which he could almost feel beneath his finger.

Presently he cast these thoughts from his mind, and spoke. 'We better be movin',' he said. 'We gotta find water. We can get along for a while without food, but we gotta have water.'

The two men rose and laboriously raised their packs to their shoulders; and then, Minsky in the lead, they staggered back down the trail that led away from the Galla mine.

At first, in the cool of the morning, they got along fairly well, though they often staggered and sometimes almost fell; but when the sun rose higher and beat down upon them, they suffered the agonies of thirst; yet they kept doggedly on.

'There's gotta be water! There's gotta be water!' mumbled Crump, and he kept on repeating it over and over again.

'Shut up!' growled Minsky.

'There's gotta be water! There's gotta be water!' croaked Crump.

The interminable day dragged slowly on to the tempo of their shuffling, heavy feet; and there was no water. A gloating Nemesis, the implacable sun burned through their helmets, through their skulls, through their brains, conjuring weird visions and hallucinations. Repeatedly, Crump tried to swallow, but there was no saliva in his mouth, and the muscles of his throat refused to respond to his will. They no longer perspired. They were dried-out husks, animated only by a desire to live and by greed. It was difficult to say which of these two motivating forces was the stronger, which they would fight for longer – their gold or their lives.

Through cracked and swollen lips, Crump babbled of his past life, of his 'old woman', of food and of drink, of the men he had killed, and the girls he had had. Presently he commenced to laugh, a dry, cackling laugh.

Minsky looked at him. 'Shut up!' he snarled. 'You're goin' nuts.'

'Sir Thomas Crump,' mumbled Crump. 'That's what I am – Sir Thomas Crump; and you're my man. Hi, Minsky, fetch me monocle and me slippers. I'm going to call on the King, and have steak-and-kidney pie and four gallons of water – water – water!'

'Plumb daffy,' muttered Minsky.

For a time they plodded on in silence, always straining their eyes ahead for some sign of water. Minsky felt his mind wandering. At various times he saw streams, and pools, and once a lake where boats sailed; but he knew they were hallucinations, and each time with an effort of will he snapped back to normal.

They were weakening rapidly. Every few minutes they were forced to stop and rest; but they did not dare lay down their burdens, for they knew they would not have the strength to raise them again. They just stood for a minute or two, swaying and panting, and then once more took up the agonizing struggle.

Minsky, the stronger and more determined, was some hundred feet ahead of Crump when he stumbled against a rock hidden in the grass, and fell. He did not try to rise immediately, for, being down, he decided to lie there for a few minutes and rest.

Crump staggered forward a few steps towards Minsky. 'Don't drink it all,' he cried. 'Leave some for me, you swine!' He thought Minsky, lying on his stomach with his face against the ground, had found water. He had to stop and rest again. Each time he planted a foot, he could scarcely raise it from the ground without falling. He weaved from side to side, and forward and back, trying to maintain his balance; then he lurched forward a few more steps. At last he reached Minsky, and, dropping to his knees, fell forward on his face searching for the water. He began to curse horribly, applying every opprobrious epithet to Minsky to which he could lay his tongue. 'You drunk it all up,' he croaked, 'You drunk it all up. You didn't leave me a drop.'

'There wasn't no water,' said Minsky. 'I just fell down. I stubbed my toe. I'm gonna lie here and rest a few minutes.'

Crump made no reply; but presently he commenced to sob. 'I thought there was water,' he blubbered.

For half an hour they lay where they had fallen, the sun taking its toll of what little strength remained to them; then Minsky started to rise. 'We'd better be movin',' he said. 'I think I've been hearin' somethin'.'

'What?' asked Crump.

'Water,' said Minsky. 'I can hear it runnin'. It's in the bottom of this here ravine right in front of us.'

Crump listened intently. 'Yes,' he said, 'I hear it, too. We couldn't both be wrong.' Nor were they, for just a few yards ahead of them, at the bottom of a shallow ravine, a little stream ran down towards the plain, splashing over the rocks and gravel of its bed.

Minsky started to rise. 'We can leave the gold here,' he said, 'and come back for it.' Laboriously he sought to raise his body from the ground, but his arms gave beneath him and he sank back upon his face; then Crump tried to rise. He got to his knees, but he could get no farther. 'Get up, my man,' he said to Minsky, 'and fetch me water.'

'Go to hell,' said Minsky. 'Get up yourself;' but, nevertheless, he tried again to rise, and again he sank back, defeated.

Crump struck him. 'Get up, you fool,' he cried, 'and get water, or we'll both die.'

Again Minsky made the effort. Crump tried to help him, pulling on the back of his shirt; and at last Minsky came to his knees. He tried to get one of his feet beneath him; but the effort caused him to lose his balance, and he fell over upon his side.

'Get up! Get up, you swine!' shrieked Crump.

'I can't,' said Minsky.

'Yes, you can.' Crump's voice was a rasping scream. 'Yes, you can. You're just lyin' there waitin' for me to die, so you can get my gold; but I'll show you, I'll show you, you'll never have it.' He turned and rummaged in his coat until he had located a large piece of virgin gold. He leaned over Minsky, the great shining lump of metal in his hand.

Minsky lay upon his side as he had fallen. 'You won't never get mine,' said Crump; 'but I'll get yours.' He raised the lump of gold and brought it down heavily upon Minsky's temple. The man quivered convulsively and lay still.

'That'll learn you,' growled Crump, and struck again; then, in a sudden frenzy of maniacal fury, he crashed the metal again and again upon the other's skull, reducing it to a bloody pulp of bone and brain.

He sat back on his haunches and surveyed his handiwork. He commenced to laugh. 'I told you I'd kill you,' he said. 'The next time I tell you, you'll believe me.' He had gone completely mad.

'Now I'll have it all, yours and mine.'

Somehow he got to his knees and, seizing Minsky's horde of gold, he tried to raise it to his shoulder, but he could not even lift it from the ground. Again and again he tried, but each time he was weaker, and at last he turned and threw himself upon his own gold. Clutching at it with greedy fingers, he commenced to sob.

In the ravine, the little stream, cold and clear, shimmered and played in the sunlight.

THIRTY
Our First Home

Tarzan had been in no hurry to find the easier trail that led down from the plateau of Alemtejo. There was another matter of greater importance, the finding of the man who had stolen his name and brought it into disrepute; also, there was the matter of food. Observation had assured him that there was little or no game to be found in the foothills or on the plain; and so he had determined to go farther back into the hills, for he and Chilton must eat.

More than anything else, Chilton was interested in getting out of the country; but he soon discovered that he had no voice in the matter, unless he chose to go alone. It was Tarzan who made all the decisions; and whatever he did, he did without haste. Chilton thought he was lazy, but Chilton had never seen him act in an emergency.

In many ways, he reminded Chilton of a wild beast, particularly of a lion. Lions move slowly with a certain lazy majesty. They are unconscious of the passage of time; but Chilton knew that when a lion was aroused, he was a very different creature, and he wondered if the analogue would hold good if Tarzan were aroused.

The hunting carried them some distance back into the hills, but it proved successful, and they had flesh to eat along with the fruits and vegetables which Tarzan gathered.

The ape-man had divided his kill, giving half of it to Chilton and the latter was more than a little horrified when he saw his companion carry off his share to a little distance, and, squatting upon his haunches, tear the raw meat with his teeth like a wild beast; but he was still more horrified when he heard the low growls rumbling from the ape-man's chest, the while he fed.

Chilton eyed the great hunk of raw meat in his own hands. Finally he ventured a remark. 'I say, you know, I don't think I can stomach this raw.'

'Cook it,' said Tarzan.

'But we have no matches,' demurred Chilton.

'Gather some wood,' directed the ape-man. 'I'll make fire for you.'

The next day they wandered about, quite aimlessly, Chilton thought; but it was not aimless wandering insofar as Tarzan was concerned. Whenever he went into a new country he studied it, for he might have to return. He noted every landmark and he never forgot one. He discovered where the water lay and which way the wind blew, and the nature of the game and where it might be found. Tarzan might seem lazy and indifferent to Chilton, but that was because the man was not familiar with the ways of Tarzan or other wild beasts.

They were working down through the foothills towards the plain, when Tarzan suddenly stopped, instantly alert.

Chilton stopped, too, and looked around. 'Do you see something?' he asked.

'There is a white man over there,' said Tarzan, 'and he is dead.'

'I don't see anything,' said Chilton.

'Neither do I,' said. Tarzan, as he started off in the direction he had indicated.

Chilton was puzzled. It meant nothing to him that a gentle breeze was blowing directly into his face. He wondered if his companion were not a little balmy, and he would like to have wagered a few pounds that there was no dead man there. If it were Rand, now, he could get a bet. Rand was always keen to bet on anything.

Presently they topped a little rise, and below them, near the edge of the ravine, they saw the bodies of two men. Chilton's eyes went wide. 'I say,' he said, 'how did you know?'

'By training that is not included in the curriculum of either Oxford or Cambridge,' replied the ape-man, with a faint smile.

'Wherever you learned it, it's most extraordinary,' said Chilton.

They stopped beside the two men, and Tarzan stood looking down upon them. 'Both dead,' he said. 'They died of thirst and exhaustion.' He stopped and examined their packs.

'Gold!' exclaimed Chilton. 'My word, what a lot of it; and look at the size of those nuggets. They're not nuggets, they're chunks, chunks of pure gold.'

'The price of two worthless lives,' said the ape-man; 'but quite typical of civilized man that they should have died within a few yards of water rather than abandon their gold.'

'They would have been better off in Alemtejo,' said Chilton.

'It is better that two such scoundrels are dead,' replied Tarzan.

'You knew them before?' asked Chilton.

'I knew them. This one tried to kill me.' He touched Crump's body with his foot.

Chilton stooped and hefted the two bundles of gold. 'Quite a neat little fortune, what?' he said.

Tarzan shrugged. 'Would you like to carry it out with you?' he asked.

'And end up like this?' Chilton pointed to the two men. 'Thanks; but I have all I need, if I can ever get out to it.'

'Then let's be going,' said the ape-man.

*

The sun shining on her face half awakened Sandra, but she did not open her eyes. She had been dreaming of home, and she thought she was in her bed in her father's house. Presently it occurred to her that her bed was very hard, and she opened her eyes to look up into a blue sky. She was still not fully awake as she looked to her left and saw hills, and trees, and a little stream. For a moment she thought she was dreaming; and then she turned her head in the other direction and saw a sleeping man lying a short distance away; then she remembered, and momentarily her heart sank. It was as though she had suddenly been snatched away from home into a strange world, a savage, dangerous world; but as her eyes lingered upon the man, she became content; and she thought, better here with him than anywhere else in the world without him.

She rose silently and went to the little brook and drank; then she washed her hands and face in the clear, cold water. She recalled she had heard a lion roar the night before and that she had been afraid; but she had been so exhausted she had fallen asleep in the face of the menace the roar had connoted.

She would have been surprised and terrified, too, now, could she have known that the lion had come to the opposite side of the brook during the night and stood there looking at them as they lay in the moonlight. He had stood there a long time watching them; and then he had turned and moved majestically away, for the scent of a white was unfamiliar to his nostrils, and wild beasts are wary of things with which they are not familiar; then, too, he had not been ravenously hungry.

When she turned around again, the man was sitting up looking at her; and they exchanged good mornings.

'You slept well?' he asked.

'Yes; and I am so very much rested.'

'That is good, but we'll stay here today and give you a chance to recuperate your strength.'

She looked around. 'It's heavenly here,' she said. 'I almost wish we could stay forever. It is the first time in weeks and weeks that I have felt secure and have been happy.'

They spent the day resting and talking, they had so much to talk about. She told him of her home, of the mother she had lost when she was a little girl, and of the father whose pal she had been ever since.

He could go back only two years to the day he had found himself in the castle of Alemtejo; beyond that, he knew nothing. Of the future, there was little to say other than to compare hopes.

'One of the first things we'll do,' she told him, 'is to find out who you are. I know one thing about you for sure, and of another I am almost equally certain.'

'What, for instance?' he asked.

'Well, I know you are a gentleman.'

'Do gentlemen steal girls and carry them off into captivity?' he asked.

'That was not you, not the real you,' she defended him.

'I hope not,' he said. 'Now, what was the other thing you think you know about me?'

'I am certain that you are an American. I have known many of them from all parts of America; and you have a soft drawl that is typical of people who live in the Southern states.'

He shook his head. 'I have given up trying to remember. Sometimes I thought I should go crazy trying to force myself to recall something of my past life. Maybe, if I do recall it, I shall wish I hadn't. Suppose that I were a criminal, a fugitive from justice? For all you know, I may be a murderer or thief, or for all I know either.'

'It will make no difference to me,' she said.

He took her in his arms and kissed her.

'I shall hate to leave this spot,' she said; 'but always I shall carry the picture of it in my mind.'

'And I, too,' he replied. 'Our first home! But tomorrow we must leave it and go down out of the hills.'

THIRTY-ONE

'I Am Going To Kill You'

The next morning when Chilton awoke, he found himself alone. He looked around but found no sign of his erstwhile companion. 'I wonder if the blighter has deserted me,' he soliloquized. 'He didn't seem that sort; but then there's never any telling. These wild men are all a bit balmy, I'm told. Anyway, why shouldn't he go on his own? I'm not much use to him. He has to feed me and find water for me; and I rather imagine he'd have to protect me, if we got in trouble. Of course, I might find the trail out for him; but after being with him as long as I have, I rather imagine he can find it himself if he wants to. There doesn't seem to be anything about this blooming country that chap doesn't know.'

He looked around again rather anxiously. 'I say, Tarzan, or whatever your name is, where the devil are you?' he shouted. 'It's going to be beastly embarrassing to be left here alone,' he thought.

Presently he heard a noise behind him, and turning suddenly he recognized the ape-man who was carrying a young wild pig and some fruit. Chilton breathed a sigh of relief, but he said nothing to Tarzan of his fears.

'You had good luck,' said Chilton, nodding towards the pig.

'I had better luck than this, I think,' said Tarzan. 'I got to thinking last night about those two men we found yesterday, and it occurred to me that possibly they might prove a clue to the whereabouts of the man I am looking for; so I went back there to back-track their trail.'

'You don't mean to say you've been way back there this morning?' demanded Chilton.

'I've been considerably farther; but I left here a couple of hours before dawn. It was light shortly after I reached them, and I followed their trail back until I found the trail of a white man leading off towards the west. He was barefooted, the man who made that trail. There are very few white men in this part of the country and none, I think, other than myself and this impostor, who goes without boots. The trail was a couple of days old, but it is all I need. Now I know I shall soon find him and kill him. As soon as we have eaten, we'll go back and pick up that trail.'

'You don't really have to kill him, do you?' demanded Chilton. 'That seems beastly cold-blooded.'

'Why shouldn't I kill him?' asked Tarzan.

'Perhaps he had a good reason. Perhaps he can explain.'

'How can he explain stealing my name and the women and children of my friends?' demanded the ape-man. 'If I find him, he'll have to talk very fast. He'll have to say all he is ever going to say in the time it will take my arrow to reach him from the moment I lay my eyes upon him.'

'Oh, after all, my dear fellow, you can't do that, you know. It isn't done. It isn't human. Civilized men don't do things like that.'

'You are not talking to a civilized man,' replied Tarzan.

'Yes,' said Chilton, 'I was afraid of that.'

Hyenas were tearing at the bodies of Crump and Minsky when the two men reached them. The sight shocked and sickened Chilton; but Tarzan of the Apes strode by with scarcely a glance.

Presently they came to the spoor Tarzan was to follow, and turned to the left. Chilton saw no evidence that anyone had ever passed that way before; but Tarzan followed the spoor at a long, swinging stride, never losing it.

They had continued for almost an hour when Tarzan suddenly stopped, and Chilton could see that he was listening intently. 'Someone is coming,' he said presently. 'I'll go ahead. You can follow on, slowly.' Then he was off with a swinging trot that covered the ground rapidly.

'Most amazing person,' sighed Chilton. 'Can't see anyone, can't hear anyone. How in the devil does he know there is anyone? But at that I'll bet he's right. Most extraordinary, though, most extraordinary.'

Tarzan moved rapidly and silently towards the sound he had heard. At first it had been but a faint suggestion of a sound which overrode the rustling of the leaves and the humming of insects. It came to Tarzan's ears, though, as the sound of human voices. It puzzled him, however, because the spoor he was following was the spoor of a single person; and, as yet, he was too far away to in any way identify the voices, which might have been those of black men or of white. All that he was positive of was that they were voices.

Sandra and the man who thought he was Tarzan walked hand-in-hand down towards the floor of the valley. They were happy. It seemed to Sandra that such happiness never could be blasted. She was ebullient with optimism and hope. Perhaps it was the natural reaction after so many weeks of hopelessness, or perhaps she chose to ignore the possibilities of the future. It was enough that she was with the man she loved. It was well she could not know that coming silently through the jungle was a man endowed with all the savageness of a wild beast, coming nearer and nearer with murder in his heart, to kill this man.

And then, of a sudden, he stood before them. 'Tarzan!' she exclaimed. 'Oh, Tarzan, I thought you were dead.'

The ape-man made no reply. His cold grey eyes were fixed upon the man who said he was Tarzan. He had never seen him before; but he did not need to ask if he were the man he sought. His garb told him that, as well as the fact he was with the girl he had stolen.

Tarzan came quite close and stopped. He tossed his weapons to the ground. 'Throw down your bow and your spear,' he said.

The other looked puzzled. 'Why?' he asked.

'Because I am going to kill you; but I will give you your chance.'

The other threw down his weapons. 'I don't know why you want to kill me,' he said; 'but you are at liberty to try.' He showed no fear.

'I am going to kill you because you stole my name, and stole the women and children of my friends. You either killed them or carried them into slavery. My friends think it was I; and they have turned against me. Now I kill!'

Suddenly Sandra stepped between the two men, facing Tarzan. 'You must listen to me,' she said. 'You must not kill this man.'

Tarzan looked at her in surprise. 'Why not?' he demanded. 'Besides what he did to me, he stole you and took you into captivity. For that alone, he should be killed.'

'You don't understand,' said Sandra. 'Please listen. This man is not a bad man. Something has happened to him. He has lost his memory. He does not know who he is; but I have convinced him that he is not Tarzan. He was forced to do the things he did by Christoforo da Gama, King of Alemtejo. You must believe me. This man is a gentleman and a good man.'

'Is that all?' demanded Tarzan.

'No,' said the girl.

'What else, then?'

'I love him.'

Tarzan turned to the man. 'What have you to say?' he demanded.

'Miss Pickerall speaks the truth. I do not know who I am. Until she told me differently, I really thought I was Tarzan of the Apes. I did not know that the things I did were wrong. Now, I am trying to make amends. I am trying to take Miss Pickerall back to her father. I cannot bring back to life those whose death I caused, nor can I free those whom I took into slavery. I wish that I could.'

Tarzan had been watching the man intently and now he stood in silence for a moment regarding him; then he stooped and picked up his weapons. He was an excellent judge of character and he believed the man.

'Very well,' he said. 'I will help you to take Miss Pickerall back to her father. He will decide what is to be done to you.'

The other inclined his head. 'That is satisfactory to me,' he said. 'All I care about is getting her back safely.'

'Now I know we are going to be all right,' said Sandra to the ape-man, 'now that you are with us.'

'Where are the rest of your party?' asked Tarzan.

'Pelham Dutton was killed by the great apes a couple of days ago,' replied the girl. 'The others I have not seen for a long time.'

'Crump and Minsky are dead,' said Tarzan. 'I found their bodies yesterday. They died of thirst and exhaustion.'

'We are the only ones left,' said the man who had called himself Tarzan.

'Look!' exclaimed Sandra, pointing. 'Someone is coming. Who is that?'

THIRTY-TWO

Rand

Francis Bolton-Chilton plodded along in the direction Tarzan had taken, but none too sure that it was the right direction. He had no woodcraft. Tarzan's spoor would have been plain to Tarzan and to any other denizen of the jungle. There were no trails here. It was an open wood with practically no underbrush.

'How does the bally wild man expect me to follow him?' muttered Chilton. 'He just says, "Follow me," and ups and disappears. Most extraordinary fellow I ever saw, but a good sort even if he is a little balmy, running around in a bloomin' G-string, eating his meat raw, and growling like a lion in a zoo while he eats it. Sometimes he gives me the creeps; but, by gad, he inspires confidence. Somehow I feel safe when he's around, even though I never know what minute he may jump on me and bite a steak out of me. Most absurd, what?'

By accident, he stumbled upon the two men and the girl. 'My word,' he exclaimed, 'two of them!' as he saw another man garbed exactly as Tarzan was.

When Sandra exclaimed and pointed, Tarzan turned and saw Bolton-Chilton approaching. 'My friend,' he said simply.

When Bolton-Chilton came closer and got a better look at the man who had called himself Tarzan, he hurried towards him with extended hand. 'My word! Rand!' he exclaimed. 'This is wonderful, old fellow. I thought you dead for the last two years.'

The man he had called Rand knitted his brows in puzzlement and shook his head. 'You must be mistaken,' he said. 'I never saw you before.'

Chilton dropped his hand to his side. 'What!' he exclaimed. 'You mean to say that you don't remember me? I'm Francis – Francis Bolton-Chilton.'

The other shook his head. 'I never heard the name before,' he said.

Sandra turned to Bolton-Chilton. 'Do you know him?' she asked eagerly.

'Of course I know him,' said Chilton. 'What the devil does he mean by saying he doesn't know me? I can't understand it.'

'Something has happened to him,' said Sandra. 'He recalls nothing except what has happened during the last two years. Tell him who he is.'

'He is Colin T. Randolph, Jr, an American from West Virginia.'

'There, you see I was right,' said Sandra to Rand. 'I told you you were an American from the South.'

'Where have you been all this time?' demanded Chilton.

'In Alemtejo,' replied Rand. 'You are sure you know who I am? There can be no mistake?'

'Absolutely none, my boy.'

A look of relief came into Rand's eyes. 'It is something to know that somebody knows who I am, even if I can't remember,' he said. 'Maybe it will come back to me some time.'

'You know all about him?' asked Sandra.

'Pretty much everything there is to know. We flew together in Spain for a year. Men get pretty close under circumstances like that, you know, and talk a lot about home and their past lives. Say, I even know the names of the servants in his father's home, although I have never been there; and Rand knew as much about me before – before this happened.'

'Then you know –' she hesitated 'You'd know if – if –' she stopped short.

'If what?' asked Bolton-Chilton.

'Is he married?' she asked in a very faint voice.

Bolton-Chilton smiled and shook his head. 'No, my dear young lady,' he said, 'not unless he has married within the last two years.'

'I just thought he ought to know,' said Sandra lamely.

'Yes, it's quite customary for one to know if he's married,' agreed Chilton.

Tarzan had been an interested auditor. He was glad that the girl's belief had been substantiated and he was still more glad he had not killed the man; but now that the mystery was on the way to being cleared up, there was a more important thing to consider. He was faced with the responsibility of getting three people out of one hostile country and through another before any of them could be even remotely considered safe, and he wanted to get it over with. 'Come on,' he said, 'let's be moving.'

'Where to?' asked Rand.

'There is supposed to be an easy trail leading out of this valley. I am looking for it.'

'So were we,' said Rand.

Tarzan moved at a brisk pace and there was little opportunity for conversation until they made camp that night. It was cool, and they built a fire and gathered around it to roast bits of the meat that Chilton and Tarzan had brought with them from the kill Tarzan had made the previous day.

Sandra had been fairly consumed with curiosity all during the march to hear more about Colin T. Randolph, Jr, from the lips of Bolton-Chilton. So she sat very close to the man who had thought he was Tarzan. 'Rand,' she said. 'You don't know how wonderful it is to have a name for you. Do you know that during all the time I have known you I have never called you anything?'

'Well, you were sure I wasn't Tarzan, and maybe you were equally sure I was not God.'

'Quite,' she agreed; 'but now that I know who you are, I want to know what you are and all about you.' She turned to Bolton-Chilton. 'Won't you tell me,' she asked, 'all that you know – how he got here and all of that?'

'Gladly,' said the Englishman. 'You see, as I told you, Rand and I flew together in Spain. Finally, we got fed up with the slaughter and quit; and Rand stopped in England with me on his way back to America.

'There's one thing you ought to know about Rand. He's an inveterate gambler. I don't mean with cards, or dice, or anything like that. I mean he is always betting on something. He'd bet £20 that one raindrop would reach the bottom of a pane of glass before another raindrop. Before he'd take off for a raid, he'd bet he would return or he'd bet he wouldn't return. You could take your choice. He would bet on anything either way, just so he could get a bet. That's why he's here; that's why I'm here; and evidently that's why you are here.'

'And why I'm here,' said Tarzan.

'But I can't see what that's got to do with it,' said Sandra. 'He certainly didn't bet that he would come to Africa and abduct me. He'd never even heard of me.'

'I'll try to explain,' said Bolton-Chilton; 'but I'll have to go back a little. You see, Rand used to talk a lot about Tarzan of the Apes. It was a regular obsession with him. He said he had read so much about him for years and had admired him so much that he decided to emulate him; so he learned to do as many of the things Tarzan did as he was able. He developed his physique until he was as strong as a young bull and as agile as a cat. He practised at archery until he was pretty good with a bow and arrow. He told me that he used to win all the tournaments he entered.

'It was his ambition to come to Africa and try living like Tarzan; and I used to kid him a lot about it and tell him he'd starve to death in a week if he were set down in central Africa alone, that is, if some lion didn't get him before he starved; but he'd never admit there was a chance of either one or the other. Of course, it was all kidding, and neither one of us ever thought he would really try it. It helped to pass the time away when we weren't in the air.'

Rand was as interested a listener as Sandra or Tarzan, for to him the story was as new. His brows were knit in an effort to recall. Sandra noticed the strained expression in his eyes and placed her hand on his. 'Relax,' she said. 'It will all come back to you someday. Don't try to force it.'

'It makes a good story about somebody else,' he said with a wry smile; 'but if it is I he is talking about, it makes me appear something of a silly ass.'

'Not at all,' said Chilton. 'You were anything but that; and since I have met the real Tarzan, I think you were pretty bright in trying to emulate him.'

'Go on with the story.' said Sandra. 'How did it all lead up to this?'

'Well, after we got back to England,' continued Bolton-Chilton, 'we were sitting around my club one day, reading the papers, when Rand ran across a story from South Africa about a native boy who had been captured with a band of baboons. He acted just like them and ran around on all fours most of the time; and he didn't know a word of any language, unless it were baboon talk, if there is such a thing. "There," said Rand, showing me the article, "that proves my point. If that kid could do it, I could do it."

'"But he was a native, and he didn't know any other kind of life. If the baboons took him in at all, they would have fed him and protected him. You'd be on your own. No, you never could do it. You wouldn't last a week," I told him.

'"A thousand pounds says that I can," said Rand.

'So I took him up. We argued the thing for an hour, and the bet finally simmered down to this: I was to fly him to Central Africa; and after we had found a place in good game country where we could land, I was to leave him and pick him up in a month. He was to dress as Tarzan dressed and carry only the same weapons that Tarzan carried. Every few days, however, I was to fly over the district where he was; and if he were alive, he'd signal me with smoke from a fire – one smoke column, he was O.K. – two smoke columns, he needed help. If he stuck it out a month, he collected £1000. If he didn't, I collected the same amount.

'We took off in Rand's ship, and everything went lovely at first. As we neared the point where we wanted to commence looking for a landing place, Rand changed into his Tarzan outfit – loincloth, knife, rope, bow and arrow, and the rest of it.

'We ran into some pretty rough country with mountains and low clouds. It didn't look so good, for there was no place to land and the clouds seemed to be settling lower; so we decided to get above them. It was awful thick and we were flying blind, with every once in a while a mountain peak sticking its nose up too close for comfort; then, all of a sudden, our motor quit.

'Rand told me to jump. There wasn't anything else for it. It would have been suicide to try to make a dead-stick landing under the circumstances; so I jumped, and that's the last I saw of Rand until today. That was two years ago.

'I came down on an open tableland not far from a native village. I stayed where I was for a while watching for Rand to come down; but he didn't come; and then I made my way to the village. It was the village of Ali the Sultan; and I have been there ever since, a slave, working part of the time in the most fabulous goldmine I have ever seen or heard of. Well, that's about all there is to my story.'

'And what about you, Rand?' asked Sandra. 'Does this recall anything to your mind?'

'It only explains how I got to Alemtejo,' replied Rand. 'They said I came down out of the sky; so I must have bailed out and landed near da Gama's castle; but I don't remember anything about it. I've got to take Bolton-Chilton's word for it; but it is all very puzzling. I don't know the first thing about flying a ship.'

Bolton-Chilton shook his head. 'Perhaps you don't now,' he said; 'but you were one of the best pilots I ever saw.'

'I wonder what became of the ship?' said Sandra.

'It must have crashed somewhere near Alemtejo,' suggested Bolton-Chilton.

'If it had, I should have heard of it,' said Rand, 'and none of the Alemtejos ever reported anything like that.'

'Just another mystery,' said Sandra.

THIRTY-THREE
A Ship

The following morning they started down towards the plain in search of the trail to the low country. On the way, they passed the scattered bones of Crump and Minsky now picked almost clean by hyenas, jackals and vultures. They paused a moment to contemplate the two packs of gold which had contributed so greatly to the deaths of these men. Chilton hefted first one horde and then the other. 'Must be between £25,000 and £50,000,' he said. 'Quite a neat little fortune.'

'Well, I guess it'll have to stay here for the Gallas or the Alemtejos,' said Rand.

They continued on then, without regret, down towards the plain. They never found the trail that the Gallas and the Alemtejos knew; and they were miles from it when they came to a long, level shelf several hundred feet below the level of the main plateau. It was a treeless stretch perhaps a mile in length and half that in width, covered deeply with lush grasses. It lay far off the beaten track of either Galla or Alemtejo and had, perhaps, never been trod by the foot of man before.

Tarzan, who was in the lead when they came in sight of it, stopped and pointed. 'Look!' he said, 'a ship.'

The others clustered about him excitedly. 'What luck!' exclaimed Sandra. 'Perhaps he can take us all out.'

'By jove!' exclaimed Bolton-Chilton. 'It can't be – it can't be possible; but if that isn't Rand's plane, I'll eat it. I'd know it as far as I could see it.'

'It doesn't seem possible,' said Sandra, 'for that ship certainly never crashed.'

'Let's get down there and have a look at it,' said Bolton-Chilton. 'Be most extraordinary if we could fly it out, wouldn't it?'

'Not much chance of that,' said Sandra, 'after it has stood out in all sorts of weathers for two years. The fabric would be pretty well shot.'

'Wouldn't have hurt it a bit,' Bolton-Chilton assured her. 'It's an all-metal plane.'

It took them nearly an hour to clamber down to the shelf and make their way to the ship. 'It's Rand's all right,' said Bolton-Chilton; 'and from here it looks as airworthy as ever. It doesn't look as though even the landing gear were damaged.' And when they reached it, they found he was right. The tyres were flat, but otherwise it seemed to be in perfect condition.

'Rand must have landed it,' said Sandra; 'but of course he's forgotten.'

'I don't think I landed it,' said Rand, 'because the Alemtejos all insisted that I came down out of the sky, that is, that I floated down all by myself.'

'The ship landed itself,' said Bolton-Chilton. 'Of course, it's most unusual, but not without precedent. I remember reading of a couple of army fliers bailing out somewhere in California, a number of years ago. Their plane made a perfect landing by itself; and the pilot was court-martialled.'

Colin T. Randolph, Jr, walked all around his plane, examining it from every angle, an eager light in his eyes; then he clambered to the wing and entered the cabin, followed by the others. He entered the pilot's compartment and sat down in the pilot's seat. He examined the instrument board, running his hands over it caressingly. He grasped the wheel, gripping it so hard that his knuckles showed white. Suddenly he relaxed and turned towards them, tears in his eyes. 'Oh, Sandra! Sandra! It's all right now. I remember everything.' She came and stood beside him, but emotion choked whatever words were on her lips.

'I say,' said Bolton-Chilton, 'isn't this great? It just needed something like this to jar your memory loose, something you had loved a lot in your other life; and you certainly loved this ship.'

'I remember now,' said Rand slowly. 'I stayed with the ship about five minutes after you bailed out; then I jumped. I came down in the ballium of the castle of Alemtejo. I can see it all plainly now – that amazing castle here in the wilderness, and the strange little brown men with golden cuirasses standing gaping up at me. I was swinging badly; and just before I landed, I crashed against the castle wall. It must have been that that knocked me cuckoo.'

'Do you suppose she'll fly?' asked Sandra.

'If she won't, we'll make her,' said Rand.

While the others pumped up the tyres, praying fervently that they would hold, Rand disassembled the carburetter, found the trouble, and corrected it.

There followed inspection and lubrication; and two hours later, they sat tensely in the cabin, each holding his breath, as Rand prepared to start the engine.

Almost instantly they were rewarded with the roar of propeller and exhaust.

'Now if these tyres will hold,' said Rand. 'Perhaps you'd all better get out and let me try it alone.'

'No,' said Sandra, 'not I.' Nor would Tarzan nor Bolton-Chilton desert him.

Rand taxied along the shelf and turned back into the wind. 'If you want to take that gold out,' said Tarzan, 'now you have the means. There's a place to land not far from where Crump and Minsky died.'

'Not I,' said Bolton-Chilton. 'I have all I need; so has Rand; and I'm quite sure that the daughter of Timothy Pickerall doesn't need any more; but how about you, Tarzan?'

Tarzan smiled. 'What would I do with gold?' he asked.

Rand brought the ship around into the wind and started down the shelf, constantly accelerating. The tail lifted from the ground. The motor was running wide open now. The tyres held.

'Thank God,' murmured Sandra, as the ship rose gracefully into the air. 'Thank God for everything.'

TARZAN AND THE CASTAWAYS

TARZAN AND THE CASTAWAYS

I

It is sometimes difficult to know just where to begin a story. I recall an acquaintance of mine who, in telling of an accident wherein a neighbor had fallen down the cellar stairs and broken her leg, would recount all the marriages and deaths in the family for a generation or two back before getting to the point of the story.

In the present instance, I might go back to Ah Cuitok Tutul Xiu, the Mayan, who founded Uxmal in Yucatan in 1004 A.D.; and from him on to Chab Xib Chac, the Red Man, who destroyed Mayapan in 1451 and murdered the entire Cocom family of tyrants; but I shall not. I shall simply mention that Chac Tutul Xiu, a descendant of Ah Cuitok Tutul Xiu, motivated by that strange migratory urge of the Maya and by the advice of the Ah Kin Mai, or chief priest, left Uxmal with many of his followers, nobles, warriors, women, and slaves, and went to the coast where he constructed several large double dugout canoes and embarked therein upon the broad Pacific, never again to be heard of in his homeland.

That was in 1452 or 1453. From there I might make a broad calendric jump of some four hundred eighty-five or six years to modern times and to the island of Uxmal in the South Pacific, where Cit Coh Xiu is King; but I shall not do that either, since it would be anticipating my story.

Instead, I take you to the deck of the Saigon, a battered old tramp steamer awaiting at Mombasa to load wild animals for shipment to the United States. From below and from cages on deck come the plaints and threats of captured beasts; the deep-throated rumblings of lions, the trumpeting of elephants, the obscene 'laugh' of hyenas, the chattering of monkeys.

At the rail two men are deep in argument: 'But I tell you, Abdullah,' one was saying, 'we are practically ready to sail; the last consignment should be here within the week, and every day my expenses are mounting. It might take you a month to bring him in; you might not get him at all.'

'I cannot fail, Sahib Krause,' replied Abdullah Abu Néjm; 'he has received an injury; that I know from Ndalo, in whose country he now is; and so he may be taken easily. Think of it, Sahib! A real wild man, raised by apes from infancy, the play fellow of elephants, the killer of lions. Wellah? He would be

759

worth more than all your shipload of wild beasts in the land of the Nasara; he would make you a rich man, Sahib Krause.'

'As I understand it, the fellow speaks English as well as the damned British themselves; I have heard of him for years. How long do you suppose I could exhibit in a cage in the United States a white man who can speak English? Abdullah, you are always saying that we Nasara are mad; I think it is you who are mad.'

'You do not understand,' replied the Arab. 'This injury which he has suffered had deprived him of speech and the knowledge of speech; in that respect, he would be as your other beasts. They cannot complain, so that anyone can understand them; neither could he.'

'Aphasia,' muttered Krause.

'What did you say, Sahib?'

'That is the name of the affliction which has resulted in your man's loss of speech,' explained Krause; 'It is caused by a brain lesion. It puts a different aspect on the matter; the thing might be done – and very profitably; but yet—' He hesitated.

'You do not like the English, Sahib?' inquired Abdullah.

'I do not,' snapped Krause. 'Why do you ask?'

'This man is an Englishman,' replied the Arab in his oiliest tones.

'What would you want for bringing him in?'

'The expenses of my safari, which would be very little, and the price of one lion.'

'You do not ask much for so great a catch,' commented Krause; 'why is that? I expected you to rob me – as usual.'

The Arab's eyes narrowed, and his sinister face seemed a mask of hate. 'He is my enemy,' he said.

'How long will it take?'

'Less than a month,' replied Abdullah.

'I shall wait thirty days,' said Krause; 'then I shall sail, whether you are back or not.'

'I am bored,' said the girl. 'Mombasa! I hate it.'

'You are always complaining,' growled Krause; 'I don't know why the devil I brought you along; anyway, we sail in three days, whether that Arab dog is back or not; then I suppose you'll find something else to grouse about.'

'It must be a very valuable specimen Abdullah is bringing you,' said the girl. 'It is.'

'What is it, Fritz – a pink elephant or a crimson lion?'

'It is a wild man, but keep it to yourself – the English pigs would never let me take him aboard, if they knew.'

'A wild man! One of those whose heads come up to a little point on top, like a cone? He should have a little tuft of hair right on the tip top of the cone, and his nose should spread all across his face, and he shouldn't have any chin. Is he like that, Fritz?'

'I have never seen him, but I suppose he is just like that – that has been orthodox ever since Barnum's What-is-it.'

'Look, Fritz! Here comes Abdullah now.'

The swart Arab came over the side and approached them; his face betokened nothing of either the success or failure of his mission.

'Marhaba!' Krause greeted him. 'Ey khabar?'

'The best of tidings, Sahib,' replied Abdullah. 'I have him, just outside of town, in a wooden cage covered with matting, so that none may see what is within; but billah! What a time we had in capturing him! We took him in a net, but he killed three of Ndalo's warriors before they could tie his hands behind him. He is strong as el-fil. We have had to keep his hands tied ever since we got him: he would have torn that wooden cage to pieces in an instant, had we not.'

'I have an iron cage that he cannot tear to pieces,' said Krause.

'I would not be too sure of that,' cautioned the Arab. 'If your cage could not withstand the strength of el-fil, you had still better keep his hands tied.'

'My cage would not hold an elephant,' said Krause, 'but if it could, it would be strong enough.'

'I would still keep his hands tied,' persisted Abdullah.

'Has he spoken?' asked Krause.

'No; not a word – he just sits and looks. There is neither hate nor fear in his eyes – he reminds me of el adrea; I am always expecting to hear him roar. We have to feed him by hand, and when he eats his meat, he growls like el adrea.'

'Wonderful!' exclaimed Krause. 'He will be a sensation. I can just see those fool Americans begging to pay good money to see him. Now listen – I shall clear this afternoon and stand up the coast, returning after dark. Load the cage on a dhow below the town and stand straight out until you pick up my signal – I'll blink my running light three times in rapid succession at intervals; then you show a light. Do you understand?'

'It is already done,' said Abdullah Abu Néjm.

The wind had risen and a sea was running when Abdullah picked up the Saigon's signal. Maneuvering the dhow into position along the lee side of the steamer was finally accomplished. Tackle was lowered and made fast to the cage containing the wild man. Abdullah was guiding the cage as it was hoisted from the dhow, when suddenly the Saigon rolled over away from the smaller craft; the cage was jerked suddenly upward; and Abdullah, fearing that he would be hurled into the sea, clung to it. The cage crashed against the side of the steamer; the men above continued to hoist; then the Saigon rolled back and crashed down upon the dhow, swamping it.

All of the crew of the dhow were lost, and Abdullah was aboard the steamer bound for America. He filled the air with 'billahs!' and 'Wullah-bullahs!' and called upon Allah to preserve him.

'You're damn lucky to be alive,' Krause told him. 'You'll make a lot of money in America. I'll exhibit you, too, as the sheik who captured the wild man; they'll pay plenty to see a real sheik straight from the desert. I'll buy a camel for you, and you can ride through the streets with a banner advertising the show.'

'I, Abdullah Abu Néjm, exhibited like a wild beast!' screamed the Arab. 'Never!'

Krause shrugged. 'Have it your own way,' he said; 'but don't forget, you got to eat, and you won't find many free date trees in America. I'll feed you until we get there, but after that you're on your own.'

'Dog of a Nasrany!' muttered the Arab.

II

The following morning was fair, with a brisk wind, as the Saigon steamed Northeastward across the Indian Ocean. The animals on deck were quiet. A wooden cage, entirely covered with matting, was lashed down amidships. No sound came from it, either.

Janette Laon followed Krause on deck; her black hair was blowing in the wind, which pressed her light dress against her, revealing a figure of exceptional allure. Wilhelm Schmidt, the 2nd mate of the Saigon, leaning with his back against the rail, watched her through half-closed eyes.

'Now may I see your wild man, Fritz?' asked the girl.

'I hope he's still alive,' said the man; 'he must have got an awful beating when we hauled him aboard last night.'

'Haven't you tried to find out?' she demanded.

'Couldn't have done anything for him, anyway,' replied Krause. 'From what Abdullah told me, he'd be a mean customer to handle. Come on; we'll have a look at him. Hey, you!' he called to a Lascar sailor; 'Take the matting off that cage.'

As they watched the man at work, Schmidt came over and joined them. 'What you got in there, Mr Krause?' he asked.

'A wild man; ever see one?'

'I saw a Frenchie once, whose wife had run off with the chauffeur,' said Schmidt; 'he sure was a wild man.'

The sailor had removed the lashings, and now he dragged away the matting. Inside the cage, a giant figure squatted on his haunches, appraising them with level gaze.

'Why, he's a white man!' exclaimed the girl.

'So he is,' said Krause.

'You goin' to keep a man penned up in a cage like a beast?' asked Schmidt.

'He's only white on the outside,' said Krause – 'he's an Englishman.'

Schmidt spat into the cage. The girl stamped her foot angrily. 'Don't ever do that again,' she said.

'What's he to you?' demanded Krause. 'Didn't you hear me say he's nothing but a dirty English pig.'

'He's a human being and a white man,' replied the girl.

'He's a dummy,' retorted Krause; 'can't speak a word nor understand one. It's an honor for him to be spit on by a German.'

'Nevertheless, don't let Schmidt do it again.'

The ship's bell sounded, and Schmidt went to relieve the 1st mate on the bridge.

'He's the pig,' said the girl, looking after Schmidt.

The two stood looking at the wild man as Hans de Groote came down from the bridge and joined them. The Dutchman was a good-looking young fellow in his early twenties; he had been signed on as 1st mate at Batavia on the trip out, after his predecessor had mysteriously 'fallen overboard.' Schmidt, who thought that he should have had the assignment, hated him and made no effort to conceal the fact. That there was bad blood between them was nothing to cause comment aboard the Saigon, for bad blood was the rule rather than the exception.

Larsen, the captain, who was now confined to his cabin with a bad attack of fever, was not on speaking terms with Krause, who had chartered the ship; while the crew, made up principally of Lascars and Chinese, were always on the verge of knifing one another. On the whole, the captive beasts were the most admirable creatures aboard.

De Groote stood looking at the man in the cage for several seconds before he spoke. His reaction was almost identical with that of the girl and Schmidt. 'He's a white man!' he exclaimed. 'You're certainly not going to keep him in a cage like a wild beast!'

'That's exactly what I'm going to do,' snapped Krause, 'and it's none of your damned business, nor anyone else's,' and he shot a scowling glance at the girl.

'He's your wild man,' said de Groote, 'but at least free his hands; it's unnecessary cruelty to keep him tied up like that.'

'I'm going to free his hands,' said Krause, grudgingly, 'as soon as I can get an iron cage up from below; it would be too much of a job feeding him this way.'

'He's had nothing to eat or drink since yesterday,' said the girl. 'I don't care what he is, Fritz; I wouldn't treat a dog the way you're treating this poor man.'

'Neither would I,' retorted Krause.

'He is less than a dog,' said a voice behind them. It was the voice of Abdullah Abu Néjm. He came close to the cage and spat on the man within, and the girl slapped Abdullah Abu Néjm across the face with all her strength. The Arab's hand flew to his dagger, but de Groote stepped between the two and seized the man's wrist.

'You shouldn't have done that, Janette,' said Krause.

The girl's eyes were flashing fire, and the blood had left her face. 'I'll not stand by and see him insult that man,' she said; 'and that goes for the rest of you, too,' and she looked straight into Krause's eyes.

'And I'll back her up,' said de Groote. 'Maybe it's none of my business if you keep him in a cage, but I'll make it some of my business if you don't treat him decently. Have you ordered the iron cage up yet?'

'I'll treat him as I please,' said Krause; 'and what are you going to do about it?'

'I'll beat hell out of you,' replied de Groote, 'and then turn you in to the authorities at the first port of call.'

'Here comes the iron cage now,' said Janette. 'Get him into it and take those cords off his wrists.'

Krause was frightened at de Groote's threat to notify the authorities; that made him squirm. 'Oh, come,' he said in mollifying tones, 'I'm going to treat him all right. I got a lot of money tied up in him and I expect to make a lot out of him; I'd be a fool not to treat him well.'

'See that you do,' said de Groote.

A big iron cage was swung up from below and placed close to the wooden cage, the two doors close together. Krause drew a revolver; then both doors were raised. The man in the wooden cage did not move.

'Get in there, you dumb idiot!' yelled Krause, pointing the revolver at the man. He did not even look at Krause. 'Get a capstan bar, one of you men,' directed Krause, 'and poke him from behind.'

'Wait,' said the girl; 'let me try.' She walked to the opposite side of the iron cage and beckoned to the captive. He just looked at her. 'Come here a minute,' she said to de Groote; 'let me take your knife; now place your wrists together, as though they were bound; yes, that's it.' She took the knife and pretended to sever imaginary cords about de Groote's wrists; then she beckoned again to the man in the wooden cage. He arose, but still stooped, as he could not stand erect in the small wooden cage, and walked into the larger cage.

The girl was standing close to the bars, the knife in her hand; a sailor dropped the door of the iron cage; the captive approached the girl and, turning his back toward her, pressed his wrists against the bars.

'You said he was stupid,' Janette said to Krause; 'he's not stupid; I could tell that by just looking at him.' She cut the bonds from his wrists, which were discolored and swollen. The man turned and looked at her. He said nothing, but his eyes seemed to thank her.

De Groote was standing beside Janette. 'He's a fine-looking specimen, isn't he?' he said.

'And handsome,' said the girl. She turned to Krause. 'Have some water and food brought,' she directed.

'You going to be his nursemaid?' inquired Krause with a sneer.

'I'm going to see that he's treated decently,' she replied. 'What does he eat?'

'I don't know,' replied Krause. 'What *does* he eat, Abdullah?'

'The dog has not eaten for two days,' replied the Arab; 'so I guess he will eat almost anything. In the jungle he eats raw meat from his kills, like a beast.'

'We'll try him on some,' said Krause; 'it will be a good way of getting rid of any of the animals that die.' He sent a sailor to the galley for meat and water.

The man in the iron cage looked long at Abdullah Abu Néjm; so long that the Arab spat on the deck and turned away.

'I wouldn't want to be in your shoes if he ever got out of that cage,' said Krause.

'You should not have freed his hands,' said Abdullah; 'he is more danger-ous than the lion.'

When the sailor returned with the meat and water, Janette took them from him and passed them in to the wild man. He took a small swallow of water; then he went into a far corner of his cage, squatted on his haunches, and tore at the meat with his strong, white teeth; and as he ate, he growled.

The girl shuddered, and the men moved about uneasily. 'El adrea of the broad head eats thus,' said Abdullah.

'He sounds like a lion,' said Krause. 'By what name do the natives know him, Abdullah?'

'He is called Tarzan of the Apes,' replied the Arab.

III

The Saigon crossed the Indian Ocean to Sumatra, where Krause took on two elephants, a rhinoceros, three orangutans, two tigers, a panther, and a tapir. Fearing that de Groote would make good his threat to report the human cap-tive to the authorities at Batavia, Krause did not put in there as he had intended; but continued on to Singapore for monkeys, another tiger, and several boa constrictors; then the Saigon steamed across the South China Sea toward Manila, its last port of call on the long drag to the Panama Canal.

Krause was delighted; so far all his plans had worked out splendidly; and if he got his cargo to New York, he stood to clean up an excellent profit. Perhaps he would not have been so delighted had he known of all that went on aboard the Saigon. Larsen was still confined to his cabin, and while de Groote was a good officer, he was young, and new aboard the ship. Like Krause, he did not know all that was talked of in the forecastle and on deck at night when it was Schmidt's watch. At such times, the 2nd mate spoke long and earnestly with Jabu Singh, the Lascar; and he spoke in whispers. Afterward, Jabu Singh spoke long and earnestly with the other Lascars in the forecastle.

'But the wild beasts?' asked Chand of his fellow Lascar, Jabu Singh; 'what of them?'

'Schmidt says we throw them overboard along with de Groote, Krause, and the others.'

'They are worth much money,' objected Chand; 'we should keep them and sell them.'

'We should be caught and hanged,' said another Lascar.

'No,' Jabu Singh contradicted. 'While we were in Singapore, Schmidt learned that Germany and England have gone to war. This is an English ship; Schmidt says that a German has a right to capture it. He says we would get prize money; but he thinks the animals would be valueless, and they are a nuisance.'

'I know a man on the island of Illili who would buy them,' said Chand. 'We will not let Schmidt throw them overboard.'

The men spoke in their native dialect, confident that the Chinese sailors would not understand them; but in that they were wrong; Lum Kip had once sailed the China Sea aboard a felucca that had been captained and manned by Lascars, and he had learned their language. He had also learned to hate Lascars, as he had been treated very badly aboard the felucca and had been given no share of the spoils of their nefarious operations. But Lum Kip's face gave no indication that he understood what he overheard; it wore its usual expression of profound detachment, as he puffed on his long pipe with its little brass bowl.

The man in the large iron cage on deck often paced back and forth for hours at a time. Often he leaped and seized the bars at the top of the cage and swung to and fro from one end of the cage to the other, hand over hand. When anyone approached his cage, he would stop; for he was not doing these things for his amusement, nor for the amusement of others, but to keep his magnificent physique from deteriorating during his confinement.

Janette Laon came often to his cage; she saw that he was fed regularly and that he always had water; and she tried to teach him her native language,

French; but in this she made no headway. Tarzan knew what was the matter with him; and while he could neither speak nor understand speech, his thoughts were as coherent and intelligent as ever. He wondered if he would ever recover; but he was not greatly troubled because he could not converse with human beings; the thing that annoyed him most was that he could no longer communicate with manu, the monkey, or the Mangani, the great apes, with which he classed the orangutans that were aboard and confined in cages near his. Seeing the cargo that the Saigon carried, he knew the life that lay in store for him; but he also knew that sooner or later he would escape. He thought of that most often when he saw Abdullah Abu Néjm on deck.

He had tested the bars of his cage at night when nobody was near; and he was confident that he could spread them sufficiently to allow his body to pass between them; but he guessed that were he to do so, while at sea, he would only be shot down; for he knew that they feared him. With the patience of a wild beast he bided his time.

When Abdullah Abu Néjm or Schmidt were on deck, his eyes followed them; for these two had spat at him. Abdullah Abu Néjm had reason to hate him, for Tarzan had ended his lucrative career as a slave trader and ivory poacher; but the 2nd mate had been motivated only by the natural reactions of a bully and a coward who discovers one whom he considers his racial enemy powerless to retaliate.

Abdullah Abu Néjm, hating Krause and the girl and ignored by de Groote, consorted much with Schmidt, until the two men, finding much in common, became boon companions. Abdullah, glad of any opportunity to wreak vengeance on Krause, willingly agreed to aid Schmidt in the venture the 2nd mate was planning.

'The Lascars are with me to a man,' Schmidt told Abdullah, 'but we haven't approached the chinks; there's bad blood between them and the Lascars on this ship, and Jabu Singh says his men won't play if the chinks are to be in on it and get a cut.'

'There are not many,' said Abdullah, 'If they make trouble, they, too, can go overboard.'

'The trouble is, we need 'em to man the ship,' explained Schmidt; 'and about throwing 'em overboard; I've changed my mind; there ain't anybody going overboard. They're all going to be prisoners of war; then, if anything goes wrong, there's no murder charge against us.'

'You can run the ship without Larsen and de Groote?' asked the Arab.

'Sure I can,' replied Schmidt. 'I've got Oubanovitch on my side. Being a Red Russian, he hates Krause; he hates everybody who has a pfennig more than he. I'm making him 1st mate, but he'll have to keep on running the engine room too. Jabu Singh will be 2nd mate. Oh, I've got everything worked out.'

'And you are to be captain?' inquired the Arab.

'Certainly.'

'And what am I to be?'

'You? Oh, hell, you can be admiral.'

That afternoon Lum Kip approached de Groote. 'Maybe-so you make dead tonight,' said Lum Kip in a low whisper.

'What you driving at, Lum?' demanded de Groote.

'You savvy Schmidt?'

'Of course; what about him?'

'Tonight he takee ship; Lascars, they takee ship; 'banovitchee, he takee ship; man in long, white dless, he takee ship. They killee Larsen; killee you; killee Klause; killee evlybody. Chinee boy no takee ship; no killee. You savvy?'

'You having a pipe dream, Lum?' demanded de Groote.

'No pipe dleam; you waitee see.'

'How about Chinee boys?' asked de Groote, who was now thoroughly worried.

'They no killee you.'

'Will they fight Lascar boys?'

'You betee; you give 'em gun.'

'No have gun,' said de Groote; 'tell 'em get capstan bars, belaying pins; knives. You savvy?'

'Me savvy.'

'And when the trouble starts, you boys light into the Lascars.'

'You betee.'

'And thank you, Lum; I'll not forget this.'

De Groote went at once to Larsen; but found him rolling on his bunk, delirious with fever; then he went to Krause's cabin, where he found Krause and Janette Laon and explained the situation to them.

'Do you believe the Chink?' asked Krause.

'There's no reason for him to have made up such a cock-and-bull story,' replied de Groote; 'yes, I believe him; he's one of the best hands on the ship – a quiet little fellow who always does his work and minds his own business.'

'What had we better do?' asked Krause.

'I'll put Schmidt under arrest immediately,' said de Groote.

The cabin door swung open; and Schmidt stood in the doorway, an automatic in his hand. 'Like hell, you'll put me under arrest, you damned Dutchman,' he said. 'We saw that dirty little Chink talking to you, and we had a pretty good idea what he saying.'

Half a dozen Lascars pressed behind Schmidt, outside the doorway. 'Tie 'em up,' he said to them.

The sailors brushed past Schmidt into the cabin; de Groote stepped in front of the girl. 'Keep your dirty hands off her,' he said to the Lascars. One of them tried to push him aside and reach Janette, and de Groote knocked him down. Instantly there was a free-for-all; but only de Groote and Janette took part in it on their side; Krause cowered in a corner and submitted fearfully to having his hands tied behind his back. Janette picked up a pair of heavy binoculars and felled one of the Lascars while de Groote sent two more to the floor, but the odds were against them. When the fight was over, they were both trussed up and de Groote was unconscious from a blow on the head.

'This is mutiny, Schmidt,' said Krause; 'you'll hang for this if you don't let me go.'

'This is not mutiny,' replied Schmidt. 'This is an English ship, and I'm taking it in the name of our Fuhrer.'

'But I'm a German,' Krause objected; 'I chartered this ship – it is a German ship.'

'Oh, no,' said Schmidt; 'it is registered in England, and you sail it under English colors. If you're a German, then you're a traitor, and in Germany we know what to do with traitors.'

IV

Tarzan knew that something had happened aboard the ship, but he did not know what. He saw a Chinese sailor strung up by the thumbs and lashed. For two days he saw nothing of the girl or the young 1st mate, and now he was not fed regularly or kept supplied with water. He saw that the 2nd mate, who had spit on him, was in command of the ship; and so, while he did not know, he surmised what had happened. Abdullah Abu Néjm occasionally passed his cage, but without molesting him; and Tarzan knew why – the Arab was afraid of him, even though he were penned up in an iron cage. He would not always be in a cage: Tarzan knew this and Abdullah Abu Néjm feared it.

Now, Lascars swaggered about the ship and the Chinese did most of the work. These, Schmidt cuffed and kicked on the slightest provocation or on none at all. Tarzan had seen the man who had been strung up by his thumbs and lashed cut down after an hour and carried to the forecastle. The cruelty of the punishment disgusted him, but of course he did not know but that the man deserved it.

The 2nd mate never passed Tarzan's cage without stopping to curse him. The very sight of Tarzan seemed to throw him into a fit of uncontrollable rage, as did anything that stimulated his inferiority complex. Tarzan could not understand why the man hated him so; he did not know that Schmidt, being a psychopath, did not have to have a reason for anything that he did.

Once he came to the cage with a harpoon in his hands and jabbed it through the bars at the ape-man while Abdullah Abu Néjm looked on approvingly. Tarzan seized the haft and jerked the thing from Schmidt's hands as effortlessly as he might have taken it from a baby. Now that the wild man was armed, Schmidt no longer came close to the cage.

On the third day from that on which he had last seen the girl, Tarzan saw his wooden cage and a larger iron cage hoisted to the deck and lashed down near his; and a little later he saw the girl led on deck by a couple of Lascar sailors and put into the wooden cage; then de Groote and Krause were brought up and locked in the iron cage, and presently Schmidt came from the bridge and stopped in front of them.

'What is the meaning of this, Schmidt?' demanded de Groote.

'You complained about being locked up below, didn't you? You should thank me for having you brought on deck instead of finding fault. You'll get plenty of fresh air up here and a good tan; I want you all to look your best when I exhibit you with the other specimens of the lower orders in Berlin,' and Schmidt laughed.

'If you want to amuse yourself by keeping Krause and me penned up here like wild beasts, go ahead; but you can't mean that you're going to keep Miss Laon here, a white woman exhibited before a lot of Lascar sailors.' It had been with difficulty that de Groote had kept his anger and contempt from being reflected in his voice, but he had long since come to the conclusion that they were in the hands of a madman and that to antagonize him further would be but to add to the indignities he had already heaped upon them.

'If Miss Laon wishes to, she may share the captain's cabin with me,' replied Schmidt; 'I have had Larsen taken elsewhere.'

'Miss Laon prefers the cage of a wild animal,' said the girl.

Schmidt shrugged. 'That is a good idea,' he said; 'I shall see about putting you into the cage of one of Herr Krause's lions, or perhaps you would prefer a tiger.'

'Either one, to you,' replied the girl.

'Or maybe into the cage with the wild man you have been so fond of,' suggested Schmidt; 'that might afford a spectacle all would enjoy. From what Abdullah tells me, the man is probably a cannibal. I shall not feed him after I put you in with him.'

Schmidt was laughing to himself as he walked away.

'The man is absolutely crazy,' said de Groote. 'I have known right along that he was a little bit off, but I never suspected that he was an out-and-out madman.'

'Do you suppose that he will do what he has threatened?' asked Janette.

Neither de Groote nor Krause replied, and their silence answered her questions and confirmed her own fears. It had been all right to feed the wild man and see that he had water, but she had always been ready to spring away from his cage if he attempted to seize her. She had really been very much afraid of him, but her natural kindness had prompted her to befriend him. Furthermore, she had known that it annoyed Krause, whom she secretly detested.

Stranded in Batavia, Janette had seized upon Krause's offer so that she might get away, anywhere; and the prospect of New York had also greatly intrigued her. She had heard much of the great American metropolis and fabulous stories of the ease with which a beautiful girl might acquire minks and sables and jewels there, and Janette Laon knew that she would be beautiful in any country.

Although neither de Groote nor Krause had answered Janette's question, it was soon answered. Schmidt returned with several sailors; he and two of the Lascars were armed with pistols, and the others carried prod poles such as were used in handling the wild animals.

The sailors unlashed Janette's cage and pushed it against that in which Tarzan was confined, the two doors in contact; then they raised both doors.

'Get in there with your wild man,' ordered Schmidt.

'You can't do that, Schmidt,' cried de Groote. 'For God's sake man, don't do a thing like that!'

'Shut up!' snapped Schmidt. 'Get in there wench! Poke her up with those prods, you!'

One of the Lascars prodded Janette, and Tarzan growled and started forward. Three pistols instantly covered him, and sharp pointed prods barred his way. The growl terrified the girl; but, realizing that they could force her into the cage, she suddenly walked in boldly, her chin up. The iron gate of the cage dropped behind her, the final seal upon her doom.

De Groote, Krause, Schmidt, and the Lascars awaited in breathless silence for the tragedy they anticipated with varying emotions: Schmidt pleasurably, the Lascars indifferently, Krause nervously, and de Groote with such emotions as his phlegmatic Dutch psyche had never before experienced. Had he been a Frenchman or an Italian, he would probably have screamed and torn his hair; but, being a Dutchman, he held his emotions in leash within him.

Janette Laon stood just within the doorway of the cage, waiting; she looked at Tarzan and Tarzan looked at her. He knew that she was afraid, and he wished that he might speak to her and reassure her; then he did the only thing that he could; he smiled at her. It was the first time that she had seen him smile. She wanted to believe that it was a reassuring smile, a friendly smile; but she had been told such terrible stories of his ferocity that she was uncertain; it might be a smile of anticipation. To be on the safe side, she forced an answering smile.

Tarzan picked up the harpoon he had taken from Schmidt and crossed the cage toward her. 'Shoot him, Schmidt!' shouted de Groote; 'He is going to kill her.'

'You think I am crazy? – to kill a valuable exhibit like that!' replied Schmidt. 'Now we see some fun.'

Tarzan handed the harpoon to the girl, and went back and sat down at the far end of the cage. The implication of the gesture was unmistakable. Janette felt her knees giving from beneath her; and sat down quickly, lest she fall. Sudden relief from terrific nervous strain often induces such a reaction. De Groote broke into a violent sweat.

Schmidt fairly jumped up and down in rage and disappointment. 'Wild man!' he shrieked. 'I thought you said that thing was a wild man, Abdullah. You are a cheat! You are a liar!'

'If you don't think he's a wild man, Nasrany,' replied the Arab, 'go yourself into his cage.'

Tarzan sat with his eyes fixed on Schmidt. He had understood nothing that the man had said; but from his facial expressions, his gestures, his actions, and by all that had occurred, he had judged the man; another score was chalked up against Herr Schmidt; another nail had been driven into his coffin.

V

The next morning the two captives in the big iron cage were very happy. Janette was happy because she found herself safe and unharmed after a night spent with a creature who ate his meat raw and growled while he ate, a wild man who had killed three African warriors with his bare hands before they could overpower him, and whom Abdullah accused of being a cannibal. She was so happy that she sang a snatch of a French song that had been popular when she left Paris. And Tarzan was happy because he understood the words; while he had slept his affliction had left him as suddenly as it had struck.

'Good morning, he said in French, the first human language he had ever learned, taught to him by the French lieutenant he had saved from death on a far gone day.

The girl looked at him in surprise. 'I – good morning!' she stammered. 'I – I – they told me you could not speak.'

'I suffered an accident,' he explained; 'I am all right now.'

'I am glad,' she said; 'I –' she hesitated.

'I know,' interrupted Tarzan; 'you were afraid of me. You need not be.'

'They said terrible things about you; but you must have heard them.'

'I not only could not speak,' Tarzan explained, 'but I could not understand. What did they say?'

'They said that you were very ferocious and that you – you – ate people.'

Again one of Tarzan's rare smiles. 'And so they put you in here hoping that I would eat you? Who did that?'

'Schmidt, the man who led the mutiny and took over the ship.'

'The man who spit on me,' said Tarzan, and the girl thought that she detected the shadow of a growl in his voice. Abdullah had been right; the man did remind one of a lion. But now she was not afraid.

'You disappointed Schmidt,' she said. 'He was furious when you handed me the harpoon and went to the other end of the cage and sat down. In no spoken language could one have assured him of my safety more definitely.'

'Why does he hate you?'

'I don't know that he does hate me; he is a sadistic maniac. You must have seen what he did to poor Lum Kip and how he kicks and strikes others of the Chinese sailors.'

'I wish you would tell me what has gone on aboard the ship that I have not been able to understand and just what they intend doing with me, if you know.'

'Krause was taking you to America to exhibit as a wild man along with his other – I mean along with his wild animals.'

Again Tarzan smiled. 'Krause is the man in the cage with the 1st mate?'

'Yes.'

'Now tell me about the mutiny and what you know of Schmidt's plans.'

When she had finished, Tarzan had every principal in the drama of the Saigon definitely placed; and it seemed to him that only the girl, de Groote, and the Chinese sailors were worthy of any consideration – they and the caged beasts.

De Groote awoke, and the first thing that he did was to call to Janette from his cage. 'You are all right?' he asked. 'He didn't offer to harm you?'

'Not in any way,' she assured him.

'I'm going to have a talk with Schmidt today and see if I can't persuade him to take you out of that cage. I think that if Krause and I agree never to prefer charges against him, if he lets you out, he may do it.'

'This is the safest place on the ship for me; I don't want to get out as long as Schmidt is in control.'

De Groote looked at her in astonishment. 'But that fellow is half beast,' he exclaimed. 'He may not have harmed you yet; but you never can tell what he might do, especially if Schmidt starves him as he has threatened.'

Janette laughed. 'You'd better be careful what you say about him if you think he is such a ferocious wild man; he might get out of this cage some time.'

'Oh, he can't understand me,' said de Groote; 'and he can't get out of the cage.'

Krause had been awakened by the conversation, and now he came and stood beside de Groote. 'I'll say he can't get out of that cage,' he said, 'and Schmidt will see that he never gets the chance; Schmidt knows what he would get, and you needn't worry about his understanding anything we say; he's as dumb as they make 'em.'

Janette turned to look at Tarzan to note the effect of de Groote's and Krause's words, wondering if he would let them know that he did understand and was thoroughly enjoying the situation. To her surprise she saw that the man had lain down close to the bars and was apparently asleep; then she saw Schmidt approaching and curbed her desire to acquaint de Groote and Krause with the fact that their wild man could have understood everything they said, if he had heard them.

Schmidt came up to the cage. 'So you are still alive,' he said. 'I hope you enjoyed your night with the monkey man. If you will teach him some tricks, I'll exhibit you as his trainer.' He moved close to the cage and looked down at Tarzan. 'Is he asleep, or did you have to kill him?'

Suddenly Tarzan's hand shot between the bars and seized one of Schmidt's ankles; then the ape-man jerked the leg into the cage its full length, throwing Schmidt upon his back. Schmidt screamed, and Tarzan's other hand shot and plucked the man's pistol from its holster.

'Help!' screamed Schmidt. 'Abdullah! Jabu Singh! Chand! Help!'

Tarzan twisted the leg until the man screamed again from pain. Abdullah, Jabu Singh, and Chand came running in answer to Schmidt's cries; but when they saw that the wild man was pointing a pistol in their direction, they stopped.

'Have food and water brought, or I'll twist your leg off,' said Tarzan.

'The dog of an Engleys speaks!' muttered Abdullah. De Groote and Krause looked in amazement.

'If he speaks, he must have understood us,' said Krause. 'Maybe he has understood all along,' Krause tried to recall what he might have said that someday he might regret, for he knew that the man could not be kept in a cage forever – unless. But the fellow had a gun now; it would not be so easy to kill him. He would speak to Schmidt about it; it was as much to Schmidt's interests as his now to have the man put out of the way.

Schmidt was screaming for food and water. Suddenly de Groote cried, 'Look out, man! Look out! Behind you!' But it was too late; a pistol spoke, and Tarzan collapsed upon the floor of the cage. Jabu Singh had crept up behind the cage, unnoticed until the thing had been done.

Schmidt scrambled out of the way, but Janette recovered the pistol; and, turning, shot Jabu Singh as he was about to fire another shot into the prostrate man. Her shot struck the Lascar in the right arm, causing him to drop his weapon; then, keeping him covered, the girl crossed the cage, reached through the bars, and retrieved Jabu Singh's pistol. Now, she crossed back to Tarzan, knelt above him, and placed her ear over his heart.

As Schmidt stood trembling and cursing in impotent fury, a ship was sighted from the bridge; and he limped away to have a look at it. The Saigon was running without colors, ready to assume any nationality that Schmidt might choose when an emergency arose.

The stranger proved to be an English yacht; so Schmidt ran up the English flag; then he radioed, asking if they had a doctor on board, as he had two men suffering from injuries, which was quite true; at least Jabu Singh was suffering, with vocal accompaniment; Tarzan still lay where he had fallen.

The yacht had a doctor aboard, and Schmidt said that he would send a boat for him. He, himself, went with the boat, which was filled with Lascars armed with whatever they could find, a weird assortment of pistols, rifles, boat hooks, knives, and animal prods, all well hidden from sight.

Coming alongside the yacht, they swarmed up the Jacob's ladder and onto the deck before the astonished yachtsmen realized that they were being boarded with sinister intent. At the same time, the Saigon struck the English flag and ran up the German.

Twenty-five or thirty men and a girl on the deck of the yacht looked with amazement on the savage, piratical-appearing company confronting them with armed force.

'What is the meaning of this?' demanded the yacht's captain.

Schmidt pointed at the German flag flying above the Saigon. 'It means that I am seizing you in the name of the German Government,' replied Schmidt; 'I am taking you over as a prize, and shall put a prize crew aboard. Your engineer and navigating officer will remain aboard. My first mate, Jabu Singh, will be in command. He has suffered a slight accident; your doctor will dress the wound, and the rest of you will return to my ship with me. You are to consider yourselves prisoners of war, and conduct yourselves accordingly.'

'But, man,' expostulated the Captain, 'this vessel is not armed, it is not a warship, it is not even a merchant vessel; it is a private yacht on a scientific expedition. You, a merchantman, can't possibly contemplate taking us over.'

'But I say, old thing!' said a tall young man in flannels; 'you can't—'

'Shut up!' snapped Schmidt. 'You are English, and that is enough reason for taking you over. Come now! Where's that doctor? Get busy.'

While the doctor was dressing Jabu Singh's wound, Schmidt had his men search the ship for arms and ammunition. They found several pistols and sporting rifles; and, the doctor having finished with Jabu Singh, Schmidt detailed some of his men and left a few of the yacht's sailors to man the craft;

then he herded the remainder into the Saigon's boat and returned with them to the steamer.

'I say,' exclaimed the young man in white flannels, 'this is a beastly outrage.'

'It might have been worse, Algy,' said the girl; 'maybe you won't have to marry me now.'

'Oh, I say, old thing,' expostulated the young man; 'this might even be worse.'

VI

The bullet that had dropped Tarzan had merely grazed his head, inflicting a superficial flesh wound and stunning him for a few minutes; but he had soon recovered and now he and Janette Laon watched the prisoners as they came over the side of the Saigon. 'Schmidt has turned pirate,' remarked the girl. 'I wonder what he is going to do with all those people! There must be fifteen of them.'

She did not have long to wait for an answer to her inquiry. Schmidt sent the eight crew members forward when they agreed to help man the Saigon; then he had two more iron cages hoisted to the deck and lined up with the two already there. 'Now,' he said, 'I know I shouldn't do it, but I am going to let you choose your own cage mates.'

'I say!' cried Algernon Wright-Smith; 'You're not going to put the ladies in one of those things!'

'What's good enough for an English pig is good enough for an English sow,' growled Schmidt; 'hurry up and decide what you want to do.'

An elderly man with a white walrus mustache, harrumphed angrily, his red face becoming purple. 'You damned bounder!' he snorted; 'you can't do a thing like that to English women.'

'Don't excite yourself, Uncle,' said the girl; 'We'll have to do as the fellow says.'

'I shall not step a foot into one of those things, William,' said the second woman in the party, a lady who carried her fifty odd years rather heavily around her waist. 'Nor shall Patricia,' she added.

'Come come,' expostulated the girl; 'we're absolutely helpless, you know,' and with that she entered the smaller of the two cages; and presently her uncle and her aunt, finally realizing the futility of resistance, joined her. Captain Bolton, Tibbet, the second mate of the yacht, Dr Crouch, and Algy, were herded into the second cage.

Schmidt walked up and down in front of the cages, gloating. 'A fine menagerie I am getting,' he said; 'A French girl, a German traitor, a Dutch dog, and seven English pigs; with my apes, monkeys, lions, tigers, and elephants we shall be a sensation in Berlin.'

The cage in which the Leighs and their niece were confined was next to that occupied by Tarzan and Janette Laon; and beyond the Leigh's cage was that in which the other four Englishmen were imprisoned.

Penelope Leigh eyed Tarzan askance and with aversion. 'Shocking!' she whispered to her niece, Patricia; 'The fellow is practically naked.'

'He's rather nice looking, Aunty,' suggested Patricia Leigh-Burdon.

'Don't look at him,' snapped Penelope Leigh; 'and that woman – do you suppose that is his wife?'

'She doesn't look like a wild woman,' said Patricia.

'Then what is she doing alone in that cage with that man?' demanded Mrs Leigh.

'Perhaps she was put there just the way we were put here.'

'Well!' snorted Penelope Leigh; 'She looks like a loose woman to me.'

'Now,' shouted Schmidt, 'we are about the feed the animals; everyone who is not on duty may come and watch.'

Lascars, and Chinese, and several of the yacht's crew, gathered in front of the cages as food and water were brought; the former an unpalatable, nondescript mess, the contents of which it would have been difficult to determine, either by sight or taste. Tarzan was given a hunk of raw meat.

'Disgusting,' snorted Penelope Leigh, as she pushed the unsavory mess from her. A moment later her attention was attracted by growls coming from the adjoining cage; and when she looked, she gasped, horror-stricken. 'Look!' she whispered in a trembling voice; 'That creature is growling, and he is eating his meat raw; how horrible!'

'I find him fascinating,' said Patricia.

'Hurrumph!' growled Colonel William Cecil Hugh Percival Leigh; 'Filthy blighter.'

'Canaille!' snapped Mrs Leigh.

Tarzan looked up at Janette Laon, that shadowy smile just touching his lips, and winked.

'You understand English too?' she asked. Tarzan nodded. 'Do you mind if I have some fun with them?' she continued.

'No,' replied Tarzan; 'go as far as you wish.' They had both spoken in French and in whispers.

'Do you find the captain palatable,' she asked in English loudly enough to be heard in the adjoining cage.

'He is not as good as the Swede they gave me last week,' replied Tarzan.

Mrs Leigh paled and became violently nauseated; she sat down suddenly and heavily. The colonel, inclined to be a little pop-eyed, was even more so as he gazed incredulously into the adjoining cage. His niece came close to him and whispered, 'I think they are spoofing us, Uncle; I saw him wink at that girl.'

'My smelling salts!' gasped Mrs Leigh.

'What's the matter, colonel?' asked Algernon Wright-Smith, from the adjoining cage.

'That devil is eating the captain,' replied the colonel in a whisper that could have been heard half a block away. De Groote grinned.

'My word!' exclaimed Algy. Janette Laon turned her head away to hide her laughter, and Tarzan continued to tear at the meat with his strong, white teeth.

'I tell you they are making fools of us,' said Patricia Leigh-Burden. 'You can't make me believe that civilized human beings would permit that man to eat human flesh, even if he wished to, which I doubt. When that girl turned away, I could see her shoulders shaking – she was laughing.'

'What's that, William?' cried Mrs Leigh, as the roar of a lion rose from the hold.

The animals had been unnaturally quiet for some time; but now they were getting hungry, and the complaint of the lion started them off, with the result that in a few moments a blood-curdling diapason of savagery billowed up from below: the rumbling roars of lions, the coughing growls of tigers, the hideous laughter of hyenas, the trumpeting of elephants mingled with the medley of sounds from the lesser beasts.

'Oh-h-h!' screamed Mrs Leigh. 'How hideous! Make them stop that noise at once, William.'

'Harrumph!' said the colonel, but without his usual vigor. Presently, however, as the Chinese and Indian keepers fed the animals, the noise subsided and quiet was again restored.

As night approached, the sky became overcast and the wind increased, and with the rolling of the ship the animals again became restless. A Lascar came and passed buckets of water into all of the cages except that in which Tarzan was confined. To do this, he had to unlock the cage doors and raise them sufficiently to pass the pails through; then he passed in a broom, with which the inmates were supposed to clean their cages. Although he was accompanied by two other sailors armed with rifles, he did not unlock the door of Tarzan's cage, for Schmidt was afraid to take a chance on the wild man's escaping.

Tarzan had watched this procedure which had occurred daily ever since he had been brought aboard the Saigon. He knew that the same Lascar always brought the water and that he came again at about four bells of the first night watch to make a final inspection of the captives. On this tour of duty he came alone, as he did not have to unlock the cages; but Schmidt, in order to be on the safe side, had armed him with a pistol.

This afternoon, as he was passing the water into the cage occupied by the

Leighs, the colonel questioned him. 'Steward,' he said, 'fetch us four steamer chairs and rugs,' and he handed the Lascar a five pound note.

The sailor took the note, looked at it, and stuffed it into his dirty loincloth. 'No chairs; no rugs,' he said and started on toward the next cage.

'Hi, fellow!' shouted the colonel; 'Come back here! Who is captain of this ship? I want to see the captain.'

'Sahib Schmidt captain now,' replied the Lascar. 'Captain Larsen sick; no see three, four days; maybe dead;' then he moved on and the colonel made no effort to detain him.

Mrs Leigh shuddered. 'It *was* the captain,' she breathed in a horrified whisper, her terrified gaze rivetted on a bone in Tarzan's cage.

VII

Rain fell in torrents and the wind whistled through the cages, driving it in myriad needle points against the unprotected inmates. The sea rose and the Saigon rolled and pitched heavily; lightning flashes illuminated the ship momentarily and heralded the deep booming of the following thunder which momentarily drowned out the roars and growls and trumpeting of terrified beasts.

Tarzan stood erect in his cage enjoying the lashing of the rain, the thunder, and the lightning. Each vivid flash revealed the occupants of adjoining cages, and during one of them he saw that the Englishman had placed his coat around the shoulders of his wife and was trying to shield her body from the storm with his own. The English girl stood erect, as did Tarzan, seeming to enjoy this battle with the elements. It was then that the ape-man decided that he liked these two.

Tarzan was waiting; he was waiting for the Lascar to make his nightly inspection; but that night the Lascar did not come. The Lord of the Jungle could wait with that patience he had learned from the wild creatures among whom he had been reared; some night the Lascar would return.

The storm increased in fury; the Saigon was running before it now with great following seas always threatening to break over her stern. The wind howled in throaty anguish and hurled spume to join with the rain in deluging the miserable prisoners in their cages. Janette Laon lay down and tried to sleep. The English girl paced back and forth in the narrow confines of her cage. Tarzan watched her; he knew her type, an outdoor girl; the free swing of her walk proclaimed it. She would be efficient in anything she undertook, and she could endure hardship without complaining. Tarzan was sure of that, for he had watched her ever since she had been brought aboard the Saigon, had heard her speak, and had noticed her acceptance of the inevitable in a spirit similar to his own. He imagined that she would wait patiently until her opportunity came and that then she would act with courage and intelligence.

As he watched her now, taking the rain and the wind and the pitching of the ship as though they were quite the usual thing, she stopped at the side of her cage that adjoined his and looked at him.

'Did you enjoy the captain?' she asked with a quick smile.

'He was a little too salty,' replied Tarzan.

'Perhaps the Swede was better,' she suggested.

'Much; especially the dark meat.'

'Why did you try to frighten us?' she asked.

'Your uncle and aunt were not very complimentary in their remarks about us.'

'I know,' she said. 'I'm sorry, but they were very much upset. This has been a shocking experience for them. I am very much worried about them; they are old and cannot put up with much more of this. What do you think this man Schmidt intends doing with us?'

'There is no telling; the man is mad. His plan to exhibit us in Berlin is, of course, ridiculous. If he gets us to Berlin, we English will, of course, be interned.'

'You are an Englishman?'

'My father and mother were English.'

'My name is Burden – Patricia Leigh-Burden,' said the girl; 'may I ask yours?'

'Tarzan,' replied the ape-man.

'Just Tarzan?'

'That is all.'

'Do you mind telling me how you happen to be in that cage, Mr Tarzan?'

'Just Tarzan,' he corrected her; 'no mister. I happen to be in this cage because Abdullah Abu Néjm wished to be revenged; so he had me captured by an African chief who also had reason to wish to get rid of me. Abdullah sold me to a man by the name of Krause who was collecting animals to sell in America. Krause is in the cage next to mine on the other side. Schmidt, who was 2nd mate, has Krause's ship, his wild man, and all his animals. He also has Krause.'

'He won't have any of us long if this storm gets much worse,' said the girl. She was clinging to the bars of the cage now, as the ship dove into the trough of a sea, rolling and wallowing as it was lifted to the crest of the next.

'The Saigon doesn't look like much,' said Janette Laon, who had come to stand beside Tarzan, 'but I think she will weather this storm all right. We ran into a worse one coming out. Of course we had Captain Larsen in command then, and Mr de Groote was 1st mate; it may be a different story with Schmidt in command.'

The ship swung suddenly, quartering to the sea, and slithered down into the trough, heeling over on her beam-ends. There was a frightened scream as a flash of lightning revealed the colonel and his wife being thrown heavily against the bars of their cage.

'Poor Aunt Penelope!' cried the English girl; 'She can't stand much more of this.' She worked her way around the side of the cage to her aunt. 'Are you hurt, Auntie?' she asked.

'Every bone in my body is broken,' said Mrs Leigh. 'I never did approve of that silly expedition. Who cares what lives at the bottom of the ocean, anyway – you'd never meet any of them in London. Now we have lost the Naiad and are about to lose our lives in the bargain. I hope your uncle is satisfied.' Patricia breathed a sigh of relief, for she knew now that her aunt was all right. The Colonel maintained a discreet silence; twenty-five years experience had taught him when to keep still.

The long night passed, but the storm did not abate in fury. The Saigon still ran before it, slowed down to about five knots and taking it on her quarter. An occasional wave broke over the stern, flooding the decks, and almost submerging the inmates of the cages, who could only cling to the bars and hope for the best.

By her own testimony, Mrs Leigh was drowned three times. 'Hereafter, William,' she said, 'you should stick to *The Times*, Napoleon's campaigns, and Gibbon's Rome; the moment you read anything else you go quite off your head. If you hadn't read that Arcturus Adventure by that Beebe person, we would undoubtedly be safe at home in England this minute. Just because he fished up a lot of hideous creatures equipped with electric lights, you had to come out and try it; I simply cannot understand it, William.'

'Don't be too hard on Uncle,' said Patricia; 'he might have found some with hot and cold running water and become famous.'

'Humph!' snorted Mrs Leigh.

That day no one approached the cages, and neither food nor water was brought to the captives. The animals below deck fared similarly, and their plaints rose above the howling of the storm. It was not until late in the afternoon of the third day that two of the Chinese sailors brought food, and by this time the captives were so famished that they wolfed it ravenously, notwithstanding the fact that it was only a cold and soggy mess of ship's biscuit.

Mrs Leigh had lapsed into total silence; and both her niece and her husband were worried, for they knew that when Penelope Leigh failed to complain there must be something radically wrong with her.

At about nine o'clock that night, the wind suddenly died down; the calm that ensued was ominous. 'We have reached the center of it,' said Janette Laon.

'Soon it will be bad again,' said Tarzan.

'The fool should have run out of it, not into it,' said Janette.

Tarzan was waiting patiently, like a lion at a water hole – waiting for his prey to come. 'It is better thus,' he said to the girl.

'I do not understand,' she replied, 'I do not see how it could be worse.'

'Wait,' he said, 'and I think you will see presently.'

While the seas were still high, the Saigon seemed to be taking them better now, and presently Schmidt appeared on deck and came down to the cages. 'How's the livestock?' he demanded.

'These women will die if you keep them in here, Schmidt,' said de Groote. 'Why can't you take them out and give them a cabin, or at least put them below decks where they will be protected from the storm?'

'If I hear any more complaints,' said Schmidt, 'I'll dump the whole lot of you overboard, cages and all. What do you want anyway? You're getting free transportation, free food, and private rooms. You've been getting free shower baths, too, for the last three days.'

'But, man, my wife will die if she is exposed much longer,' said Colonel Leigh.

'Let her die,' said Schmidt, 'I need some fresh meat for the wild man and the other animals,' with which parting pleasantry, Schmidt returned to the bridge.

Mrs Leigh was sobbing, and the Colonel was cursing luridly. Tarzan was waiting, and presently that for which he was waiting came to pass; Asoka, the Lascar, was coming to make his belated inspection. He swaggered a little, feeling the importance of being keeper of English sahibs and their ladies.

The ship's lights relieved the darkness sufficiently so that objects were discernible at some distance, and Tarzan, whose eyes were trained by habit to see at night, had recognized Asoka immediately he came on deck.

The ape-man stood grasping two adjacent bars of his cage as Asoka passed, keeping well out of arm's reach of the wild man. Janette Laon stood beside Tarzan; she intuitively sensed that something important was impending.

Her eyes were on her cage mate; she saw the muscles of his shoulders and his arms tense as he exerted all their tremendous power upon the bars of his cage. And then she saw those bars slowly spread and Tarzan of the Apes step through to freedom.

VIII

Asoka, the Lascar, swaggered on past the cage of the Leigh's, and when he was opposite that in which the four Englishmen were confined, steel-thewed fingers closed upon his throat from behind, and his gun was snatched from its holster.

Janette Laon had watched with amazement the seeming ease with which those Herculean muscles had separated the bars. She had seen Tarzan over-take the Lascar and disarm him; and now she stepped through the opening after him, carrying the pistols they had taken from Schmidt and Jabu Singh.

Asoka struggled and tried to cry out until a grim voice whispered in his ear, 'Quiet, or I kill,' then he subsided.

Tarzan glanced back and saw Janette Laon behind him. Then he took the key to the cages which hung about Asoka's neck on a piece of cord and handed it to the girl. 'Come with me and unlock them,' he said, and passed around the end of the last cage to the doors, which were on the opposite side.

'You men will come with me,' said Tarzan in a whisper; 'the Colonel and the women will remain here.'

As Tarzan came opposite the cage of the Leigh's, Mrs Leigh, who had been dozing during the lull in the storm, awoke and saw him. She voiced a little scream and cried, 'The wild man has escaped!'

'Shut up, Penelope,' growled the Colonel; 'he is going to let us out of this damn cage.'

'Don't you dare curse me, William Cecil Hugh Percival Leigh,' cried Penelope.

'Quiet,' growled Tarzan, and Penelope Leigh subsided into terrified silence.

'You may come out,' said Tarzan, 'but remain close to the cages until we return.' Then he followed Janette to the cage in which de Groote and Krause were imprisoned and waited until she had removed the padlock.

'De Groote may come out,' he said; 'Krause will remain. Asoka, you get in there.' He turned to Janette. 'Lock them in,' he said. 'Give me one of the pistols and keep the other yourself; if either of these two tries to raise an alarm, shoot him. Do you think you could do that?'

'I shot Jabu Singh,' she reminded him.

Tarzan nodded and then turned to the men behind him; he handed Aso-ka's pistol to de Groote. He had appraised the other men since they had come aboard, and now he told Janette to give her second pistol to Tibbet, the second mate of the Naiad.

'What is your name?' he asked.

'Tibbet,' replied the mate.

'You will come with me. We will take over on the bridge. De Groote knows the ship. He and the others will look for arms. In the meantime, pick up anything you can to fight with, for there may be fighting.'

The ship had passed beyond the center of the storm, and the wind was howling with renewed violence. The Saigon was pitching and rolling violently as Tarzan and Tibbet ascended the ladder to the bridge, where the Lascar, Chand, was at the wheel and Schmidt on watch. By chance, Schmidt, happened to turn just as Tarzan entered, and seeing him, reached for his gun, at the same time shouting a warning to Chand. Tarzan sprang forward, swift as Ara, the lightning, and struck up Schmidt's hand just as he squeezed the trigger. The bullet lodged in the ceiling, and an instant later, Schmidt was disarmed. In the meantime, Tibbet had covered Chand and disarmed him.

'Take the wheel,' said Tarzan, 'and give me the other gun. Keep a lookout behind you and shoot anyone who tries to take over. You two get down to the cages,' he said to Schmidt and Chand. He followed them down the ladder to the deck and herded them to the cage where Krause and Asoka were confined.

'Open that up, Janette,' he said; 'I have two more animals for our menagerie.'

'This is mutiny,' blustered Schmidt, 'and when I get you to Berlin, you'll be beheaded for it.'

'Get in there,' said Tarzan, and pushed Schmidt so violently, that when he collided with Krause, both men went down.

Above the din of the storm they heard a shot from below, and Tarzan hurried in the direction from which the sound had come. As he descended the ladder, he heard two more shots and the voices of men cursing and screams of pain.

As he came upon the scene of the fight, he saw that his men had been taken from the rear by armed Lascars, but there seemed to have been more noise than damage. One of the Lascars had been wounded. It was he who was screaming. But aside from the single casualty, no damage seemed to have been done on either side. Three of the four Lascars remained on their feet, and they were firing wildly and indiscriminately, as Tarzan came up behind them carrying a gun in each hand.

'Drop your pistols,' he said, 'or I kill.'

The three men swung around then, almost simultaneously. Looking into the muzzles of Tarzan's two pistols, two of the Lascars dropped theirs, but the third took deliberate aim and fired. Tarzan fired at the same instant, and the Lascar clutched at his chest and lurched forward upon his face.

The rest was easy. De Groote found the pistols, rifles, and ammunition taken from the Naiad in Schmidt's cabin, and with all the rest of the party disarmed, Oubanovitch and the remaining Lascars put up no resistance. The Chinese and the impressed members of the Naiad's crew had never offered any, being more than glad to be relieved of service under a madman.

The ship safely in his hands, Tarzan gathered his party into the ship's little saloon. Penelope Leigh still regarded him with disgust not unmixed with terror; to her he was still a wild man, a cannibal who had eaten the Captain and the Swede and would doubtless, sooner or later, eat all of them. The others, however, were appreciative of the strength and courage and intelligence which had released them from a dangerous situation.

'Bolton,' said Tarzan to the captain of the Naiad, 'you will take command of the ship; de Groote will be your first mate, Tibbet your second. De Groote tells me there are only two cabins on the Saigon. Colonel and Mrs Leigh will take the Captain's cabin, the two girls will take that which was occupied by the mates.'

'He is actually giving orders to us,' Penelope Leigh whispered to her husband; 'you should do something about it, William; you should be in command.'

'Don't be silly, Auntie,' snapped Patricia Leigh-Burden, in a whisper; 'we owe everything to this man. He was magnificent. If you had seen him spread those bars as though they were made of lead!'

'I can't help it,' said Mrs Leigh; 'I am not accustomed to being ordered about by naked wild men; why doesn't somebody loan him some trousers?'

'Come, come, Penelope,' said the Colonel, 'if you feel that way about it I'll loan him mine – haw!! – then I won't have any – haw! haw!'

'Don't be vulgar, William,' snapped Mrs Leigh.

Tarzan went to the bridge and explained to de Groote the arrangements that he had made. 'I'm glad you didn't put me in command,' said the Dutchman; 'I haven't had enough experience. Bolton should be a good man. He used to be in the Royal Navy. How about Oubanovitch?'

'I have sent for him,' replied Tarzan, 'he should be here in a moment.'

'He's against everybody,' said de Groote, 'a died-in-the-wool communist. Here he comes now.'

Oubanovitch slouched in, sullen and suspicious. 'What are you two doing up here?' he demanded; 'Where's Schmidt?'

'He is where you are going if you don't want to carry on with us,' replied Tarzan.

'Where's that?' asked Oubanovitch.

'In a cage with Krause and a couple of Lascars,' replied the ape-man. 'I don't know whether you had anything to do with the mutiny or not, Oubanovitch, but if you care to continue on as engineer, nobody is going to ask any questions.'

The scowling Russian nodded. 'All right,' he said; 'you can't be no worse than that crazy Schmidt.'

'Captain Bolton is in command. Report to him and tell him that you are the engineer. Do you know what has become of the Arab? I haven't seen him for several days.'

'He's always in the engine room keeping warm.'

'Tell him to report to me here on the bridge and ask Captain Bolton to send us a couple of men.'

The two men strained their eyes out into the darkness ahead. They saw the ship's nose plow into a great sea from which she staggered sluggishly. 'It's getting worse,' remarked de Groote.

'Can she weather much more?' asked Tarzan.

'I think so,' said de Groote, 'as long as I can keep it on her quarter, we can keep enough speed to give her steerageway.'

A shot sounded from behind them, and the glass in the window in front of them shattered. Both men wheeled about to see Abdullah Abu Néjm standing at the top of the ladder with a smoking pistol in his hand.

IX

The Arab fired again, but the plunging and the pitching of the Saigon spoiled his aim and he missed just as Tarzan sprang for him.

The impact of the ape-man's body carried Abdullah backward from the ladder, and both men crashed heavily to the deck below, the Arab beneath – a stunned, inert mass.

The two sailors, whom Captain Bolton was sending to the bridge, came on deck just in time to see what had happened; and they both ran forward, thinking to find a couple of broken, unconscious men, but there was only one in that condition.

Tarzan sprang to his feet, but Abdullah Abu Néjm lay where he had fallen. 'One of you men go below and ask Miss Laon for the keys to the cages,' Tarzan directed; then he seized the Arab by the arms and dragged him back to the cage in which Krause and Schmidt were confined, and when the key was brought, he opened the door and tossed the Arab in. Whether the man were alive or dead, Tarzan did not know or care.

The storm increased in fury, and shortly before daylight the steamer fell into the trough of the sea, rolling on its beam-ends and hanging there for an instant, as though about to capsize; then it would roll back the other way and for another harrowing moment the end seemed inevitable. The change in the motion of the ship awakened Tarzan instantly, and he made his way to the bridge – a feat that was not too difficult for a man who had been raised in a forest by apes and swung through the trees for the greater part of his life, for he climbed to the bridge more often than he walked. He found the two sailors clinging to the wheel, and the Captain to a stanchion.

'What's happened?' he asked.

'The rudder's carried away,' said Bolton. 'If we could rig a sea anchor, we might have a chance of riding it out; but that is impossible in this sea. How the devil did you get up here, with the ship standing on her beam-ends as fast as she can roll from one side to the other?'

'I climbed,' said Tarzan.

Bolton grumbled something that sounded like, 'most extraordinary;' then he said, 'I think it's letting up; if she can take this, we ought to be able to pull through, though even then we're going to be in a pretty bad fix, as I understand from one of these men, that that fellow, Schmidt, destroyed the radio.'

As though to prove what she could do or couldn't do, the Saigon rolled over until her decks were vertical – and hung there. 'My God!' cried one of the sailors; 'She's going over!'

But she didn't go over; she rolled back, but not so far this time. The wind was coming in fitful gusts now; the storm was very definitely dying out.

Just before dawn, the Captain said, 'Listen, do you hear that?'

'Yes,' said Tarzan, 'I have been hearing it for some time.'

'Do you know what it is?' asked Bolton.

'I do,' replied the ape-man.

'Breakers,' said Bolton; 'that's all we need to finish us up completely.'

Slowly and grudgingly dawn came, as though held back by the same malign genie that had directed the entire cruise of the ill-fated Saigon. And, to leeward, the men on the bridge saw a volcanic island, its mountains clothed in tropical foliage, their summits hidden in low-hanging clouds. The seas were breaking on a coral reef a quarter-mile off shore, and toward this reef the Saigon was drifting.

'There is an opening in that reef to the right there,' said Bolton. 'I think we could lower boats now and get most of the people ashore.'

'You're the Captain,' said Tarzan.

Bolton ordered all hands on deck, and the men to their boat stations, but a number of Lascars seized the first boat and started lowering it away. De Groote rushed forward with drawn pistol in an effort to stop them; but he was too late, as they had already lowered away. His first inclination was to fire into them as an example to the others, but instead he turned and held off the remaining Lascars, who were about to seize a second boat. Bolton and Tibbet joined him with drawn pistols, and the Lascars fell back.

'Shoot the first man who disobeys an order,' directed Bolton. 'Now,' he continued, 'we'll wait to see how that boat fares before we lower another.'

The Saigon was drifting helplessly toward the reef, as passengers and crew lined the rail watching the crew of the lifeboat battling the great seas in an effort to make the opening in the reef.

'If they make it at all, it's going to be close,' said Dr Crouch.

'And the closer in the Saigon drifts, the more difficult it is going to be for following boats,' said Colonel Leigh.

'The bounders will never make it,' said Algy, 'and serves them jolly well right.'

'I believe they are going to make it,' said Patricia. 'What do you think, Tarzan?'

'I doubt it,' replied the ape-man, 'and if they can't make it with every oar manned and no passengers, the other boats wouldn't have a ghost of a show.'

'But isn't it worth trying?' asked the girl. 'If the Saigon goes on that reef, we are all lost; in the boat we would, at least, have a fighting chance.'

'The wind and the sea are both going down,' said Tarzan; 'there is quiet water just beyond the reef, and as the Saigon wouldn't break up immediately, I think we would have a better chance that way than in the boats, which would be stove in and sunk the moment they struck the reef.'

'I think you are right there,' said Bolton; 'but in an emergency like this, were all our lives are at stake, I can speak only for myself; I shall remain with the ship, but if there are enough who wish to take to a boat to man it properly, I will have number four boat lowered.' He looked around at the ship's company, but every eye was upon the boat driving toward the reef and no one seemed inclined to take the risk.

'They're not going to make it,' said Tibbet.

'Not by a long way,' agreed Dr Crouch.

'Look!' exclaimed Janette Laon, 'They're running straight for it now.'

'The bounders have got more sense than I thought they had,' growled Colonel Leigh; 'they see they can't make the opening and now they are going to try to ride a wave over the reef.'

'With luck they may make it,' said Bolton.

'They'll need the luck of the Irish,' said Crouch.

'There they go!' cried Algy. 'Look at the bloody blighters row.'

'They took that wave just right,' said Tibbet; 'they're riding it fast.'

'There they go!' cried Janette.

The lifeboat was rushing toward the reef just below the crest of a great sea, the Lascars pulling furiously to hold their position. 'They're over!' cried Patricia. But they were not; the prow struck a projecting piece of coral, and the onrushing breaker upended the boat, hurling the Lascars into the lagoon.

'Well, the men got across if the boat didn't,' remarked Crouch.

'I hope they can swim,' said Janette.

'I hope they can't,' growled the Colonel.

They watched the men floundering in the water for a minute or two as they started to swim toward shore, and then Janette exclaimed, 'Why, they're standing up; they're walking!'

'That not surprising,' said Bolton; 'many of these coral lagoons are shallow.'

Both the wind and the sea were dying down rapidly, and the Saigon was drifting, but slowly, toward the reef; however, it would not be long before she struck. The Saigon, ill equipped, afforded only a few life belts. Three of these were given to the women, and the others to members of the crew who said they could not swim.

'What do you think our chances are, Captain?' asked Colonel Leigh.

'If we are lifted on the reef, we may have a chance, if she hangs there for even a few minutes,' replied Bolton, 'but if she's stove in before she lodges, she'll sink in deep water on this side of the reef, and – well – you're guess is as good as mine, Sir; I'm going to have the rafts unshipped, the boats lowered on deck and out loose – get as much stuff loose as will float and carry people,' and he gave orders to the crew to carry out this work.

While the men were engaged in this work, there came a shout from amidships: 'Hi there, de Groote!' called Krause; 'Are you going to leave us here to drown like rats in a trap?'

De Groote looked at Tarzan questioningly, and the ape-man turned to Janette. 'Let me have the key to the cages,' he said, and when she had handed it to him, he went to the cage in which Krause and the others were confined. 'I'm going to let you out,' he said, 'but see that you behave yourselves; I have plenty of reason to kill all of you white men, and I won't need much more of an excuse.'

Abdullah was a sick-looking Arab, and all three of the white men were sullen and scowling as they came out of the cage.

As they approached the rail, Bolton shouted, 'Stand by the boats and rafts; she's going to strike!'

X

The ship's company stood in tense expectancy as a wave lifted the Saigon above a maelstrom of water surging over the reef.

As the sea dropped them with terrific impact upon the jagged coral rocks, the grinding and splintering of wood sounded her death knell. She reeled drunkenly toward the deep water outside the reef. More than one heart stood still in that tense moment; if she slipped back into the sea many would be lost, and there was no doubt now but that she was slipping.

'Percy,' said Mrs Leigh to the Colonel – she always called him Percy in her softer moods – 'Percy, if I have been trying at times, I hope that you will forgive me now that we face our Maker.'

'Harrumph!' grunted the Colonel. 'It is all my fault; I should never have read that Beebe yarn.'

As the Saigon slipped back into deep water, a following wave, larger than that which had preceded it, lifted the ship again and dropped her heavily upon the reef. This time she lodged firmly, and as the wave receded, she was left resting with her decks almost level.

'I say,' said Algy, 'this is a little bit of all right, what? Just like Noah's Ark – a bally old tub full of wild animals sitting high and dry on top of Mount Ararat.'

A succession of smaller waves beat against the Saigon while the men worked to get the boats and the rafts over into the lagoon; and then another large wave broke entirely over the ship, but she did not budge from her position.

Lines leading to the ship held the boats and the rafts from drifting away, but now the question arose as to how to get the women down to them. The reef was narrow, and the Saigon rested only a few feet from its shoreward side. An athletic man might leap from the rail, clear the reef, and land in the lagoon; but Mrs Leigh was not an athletic man, and she was the real problem.

She looked down over the rail of the ship at the waters still surging across the reef. 'I can never get down there, William,' she said; 'you go on. Pay no attention to me; perhaps we shall meet in a happier world.'

'Bosh and nonsense!' exclaimed the Colonel. 'We'll get you down someway.'

'I'll go down there,' said Tarzan, 'and you lower her from one of the ship's davits; I'll see that she's gotten on one of the rafts safely.'

'Never,' said Mrs Leigh emphatically.

Tarzan turned to Captain Bolton. 'I shall expect you to lower her immediately,' he said, 'and there will be no nonsense about it. I'm going down now to see how deep the water is inside the reef. Those who can't swim can jump in, and I will help them into one of the boats or onto a raft.' He climbed to the top of the rail, poised there a moment, and then leaped far out, and dove towards the lagoon.

All hands started towards the rail to watch him. They saw him make a shallow dive and then turn over and disappear beneath the surface. Presently his head broke the water, and he looked up. 'It is plenty deep right here,' he said.

Patricia Leigh-Burden stripped off her life belt, climbed to the rail, and dove. When she came up, Tarzan was beside her. 'I don't need to ask if you can swim,' he said.

She smiled. 'I'll stay here and help you with the others,' she said.

Janette Laon was the next to jump. She did not dive, and she just cleared the reef.

Tarzan had hold of her before she reached the surface. He still supported her when their heads were above water.

'Can you swim?' he asked.

'No,' she replied.

'You are a very brave girl,' he said, as he swam towards one of the boats with her and helped her aboard.

By this time, they had rigged a boatswain's chair and were lowering a highly irate and protesting Mrs Leigh over the ship's side. As she reached the surface of the lagoon, Tarzan was awaiting her.

'Young man,' she snapped, 'If anything happens to me, it will be your fault.'

'Be quiet,' said Tarzan, 'and get out of that chair.'

Probably in all her life, Penelope Leigh had never before been spoken to in the voice of real authority; it not only took her breath away, but it cowed her; and she slipped meekly out of the boatswain's chair and into Tarzan's arms. He swam with her to one of the rafts and helped her on, for they were easier to board than the lifeboats.

Tarzan swam back to the ship. The boatswain's chair was still swinging close above the water. He seized it and climbed hand over hand to the deck. One by one, men were jumping or diving from the rail when he stopped them.

'I want ten or fifteen volunteers for some very dangerous work,' he said; 'they have got to have what the Americans call "guts".'

'What do you intend doing,' asked Bolton.

'Now that everybody else is safely on shore, I am going to set the animals free,' said the ape-man, 'and make them take to the water.'

'But, man,' cried Colonel Leigh, 'many of them are dangerous beasts of prey.'

'Their lives are as important to them as ours are to us,' replied Tarzan, 'and I am not going to leave them here to die of starvation.'

'Quite right, quite right,' said the Colonel, 'but why not destroy them. That would be the humane way.'

'I did not suggest destroying your wife or your friends,' said Tarzan, 'and nobody is going to destroy my friends.'

'Your friends?' ejaculated the Colonel.

'Yes, my friends,' replied the Lord of the Jungle, 'or perhaps it would be better to say, my people. I was born and raised among them; I never saw a human being until I was almost grown, nor did I see a white man 'til I was fully twenty years old. Will anyone volunteer to help me save them?'

'By Jove!' exclaimed the Colonel; 'That is certainly a sporting proposition; I'm with you, young man.'

De Groote, Bolton, Tibbet, Crouch, a number of the Naiad crew and several Chinese volunteered to help him, as well as the three Indian keepers, who had been signed on by Krause to look after the animals.

While those who had not volunteered to remain with him were leaving the ship, Tarzan released the orangutans. He spoke to them in their own language, and they clung to him like frightened children; then he led his men below to the animal deck and opened the great double doors in the side of the ship, through which all of the larger animals had been loaded.

There were three Indian elephants, and these he liberated first, as they were docile and well trained. He had one of the Indian mahouts mount the best of these and told him to ride this one into the lagoon the moment that a wave covered the reef. There was a brief battle with the animal before it could be forced to take the plunge; but once he was swimming, it was comparatively easy to get the other two elephants to follow him, and then the African elephants were released. These were wild beasts and far more dangerous and difficult, but once their leader saw the Indian elephants swimming away he lumbered into the lagoon and followed, and his fellows trailed after him.

The cages of the lions and tigers were dragged one by one to the door, the doors of the cages opened, and the cages tilted until the beasts were spilled out. The lesser animals were disembarked in the same way.

It was a long and arduous job, but at last it was over, and only the snakes remained.

'What are you going to do about them?' asked Bolton.

'Histah, the snake, has always been my enemy,' replied Tarzan; 'him, we shall destroy.'

They stood in the doorway of the ship watching the beasts making their way toward shore, from which the empty boats and rafts were already being returned to the ship in accordance with Bolton's orders.

Along the shore line was a narrow beach, and beyond that dense jungle broke gradually upward to the foot of the green-clad, volcanic mountains which formed a fitting backdrop for the wild and desolate scene.

The landing party huddled on the beach as the wild creatures swam or waded to shore. But the animals bolted into the jungle as fast as they came out of the water. A single elephant turned and trumpeted, and a lion roared, whether in challenge or thanksgiving, who may know? And then the jungle closed about them, and they took up their new lives in a strange world.

Most of the sailors had returned to the ship with the rafts and boats, and the remainder of the day was spent in transporting the ship's stores to the beach.

For two days they worked, stripping the ship of everything that might add to their comfort or convenience, and while half of the men worked at this, the other half cut a clearing in the jungle for a permanent camp. They had chosen this site because a little stream of fresh water ran through it.

In the afternoon of the third day when the work was almost completed, a little party of a dozen men looked down upon the camp from the summit of the cliff that hemmed the beach upon the South. Concealed by the verdure there, they watched the first strangers who had come to their island for many a long year.

XI

The men who watched the castaways of the Saigon were warriors. They wore waist girdles which passed between their legs; the ends which hung down from the back, were elaborately embroidered with colored threads or feather mosaic work; over their shoulders was draped a square mantle, and they wore sandals made of hide. Their heads were adorned with feather head-dresses, and one among them wore one of feather mosaic; his dress ornaments were of jade, and his belt and sandals were studded with jade and gold, as were his armlets and leglets; in his nose was a carved ornament, which passed through a hole in the septum; his lip and earplugs were likewise of jade. All the trappings of this man were more gorgeous than those of his companions, for Xatl Din was a noble.

The brown faces of all were tattooed, but the tattooing on Xatl Din was by far the most elaborate. They were armed with bows and arrows, and each carried two quivers; each also carried a spear, and a sling to hurl stones. In addition to these weapons, each of the warriors carried a long sword made of hard wood, into the sides of which were set at intervals blades of obsidian. For protection, they carried wooden shields covered with the skins of animals. They watched the strangers for some time and then melted away into the jungle behind them.

The ship's charts and instruments had been brought ashore, and that noon Captain Bolton had sought to establish their position; but when he had done so and had consulted the chart, he discovered that there was no land within hundreds of miles in any direction.

'There must have been something wrong with my calculations,' he said to de Groote; so they checked and double-checked, but the result was always the same – they were somewhere in the middle of the South Pacific, hundreds of miles from land.

'It can't be possible,' said Bolton, 'that there is an undiscovered and uncharted island anywhere in the world.'

'I should have said as much,' agreed de Groote, 'until now; your figures are absolutely correct, Sir, and we are on an uncharted island.'

'With about as much chance of ever being picked up,' said Bolton, 'as we would be if we were on the moon. If no ship has touched here since the days of da Gama, it is safe to assume that no ship will touch here during the rest of our lifetime.'

'If no ship has touched here in four hundred years,' said de Groote, 'our chances are really excellent, for there has got to be a first time you know; and the law of chance, that this island will remain undiscovered, is just about run out.'

'You mean the statutes of limitations will operate in our favor,' laughed Bolton. 'Well, I hope you're right.'

Tarzan had worked with the others. Comfortable shelters had been erected for the Colonel and his wife and for the two girls.

Now Tarzan summoned the entire company. 'I have called you together,' he said, 'to say that we will form two camps. I will not have Abdullah, Krause, Schmidt, Oubanovitch, or the Lascars in this camp. They have caused all the trouble. Because of them we are castaways on an uncharted island, where, according to Captain Bolton, we may have to spend the rest of our lives. If we permit them to remain in our camp, they will again make trouble; I know the kind of men they are,' then he turned to Krause. 'You will take your party North, at least two long marches, and don't any of you come within ten miles of this camp. If you do, I kill. That is all. Go.'

'We'll go, all right,' said Oubanovitch, 'but we'll take our share of the provisions, firearms, and ammunition.'

'You will take your lives, and that is all,' said Tarzan.

'You don't mean that you're going to send them away into this strange jungle without food or weapons,' demanded the Colonel.

'That is exactly what I mean,' said Tarzan, 'and they are lucky that it is no worse.'

'You can't do that to us,' shouted Oubanovitch, 'you can't keep a lot of dirty Capitalists in affluence and grind down the poor working man. I know your type, a fawning sycophant, hoping to curry favor with the rich and powerful.'

'My word!' exclaimed Algy, 'the blighter's making a speech.'

'Just like Hyde Park,' said Patricia.

'That's right,' screamed Oubanovitch; 'the smart bourgeoisie ridiculing the honest laboring man.'

'Get out,' growled Tarzan.

Abdullah pulled at Oubanovitch's sleeve. 'You'd better come,' he whispered; 'I know that fellow; he is a devil; he would rather kill us than not.'

The others started moving away towards the North, and they dragged Oubanovitch along with them; but he turned and shouted back, 'I'll go, but I'll be back, when the poor slaves that are working for you now realize that they should be the Masters, not you.'

'Well!' exclaimed Penelope Leigh, 'I'm glad that they are gone; that is something, at least,' and she cast a meaningful glance at Tarzan.

Coconut palms and bananas grew in profusion in the jungle around the camp, and there were breadfruit and edible tubers and a few papaya trees, while the lagoon abounded in fish; so there was little likelihood of their starving, but Tarzan craved flesh.

After the camp was completed, he set to work to make the weapons of the chase which he liked best to use. His bow, arrows, and quiver, he had to make himself; but among the ships stores, he found a suitable knife and a rope and, from a gaff, he fashioned a spear. This last was a tacit acknowledgment of the presence of the great carnivores he had turned loose upon the island. And then, one morning, Tarzan disappeared from camp before the others had awakened. He followed the course of the little stream that ran down from the verdure-clad hills, but, to avoid the tangle of underbrush, he swung through the trees.

I said that he had left camp before the others were awake; and this was what Tarzan thought, but presently he sensed that he was being followed and looking back, saw the two orangutans swinging through the trees in his wake.

'Tarzan hunts,' he said in the language of the great apes, when they had come up to him; 'make no noise.'

'Tarzan hunts, Mangani make no noise,' one of them assured him. And so the three of them swung silently through the trees of the silent forest.

On the lower slopes of the mountains, Tarzan came upon the elephants eating on tender shoots. He spoke to them, and they rumbled a greeting in their throats. They were not afraid, and they did not move away. Tarzan thought he would learn how friendly they might be, and so he dropped down close beside a great African bull and spoke to him in the language that he had used all his life when conversing with his beloved Tantor.

It is not really a language, and I do not know what name to call it by, but through it Tarzan could convey his feelings more than his wishes to the great beasts that had been his playfellows since his childhood.

'Tantor,' he said, and laid his hand upon the great beast's shoulder. The huge bull swayed to and fro and reached back and touched the ape-man with his trunk, an inquisitive, questioning touch; and, as Tarzan spoke soothingly, the touch became a caress. And then the ape-man moved around in front of the great beast and laid his hand upon his trunk and said, 'Nala!' The trunk moved smoothly over his body, and Tarzan repeated, 'Nala! Tantor, Nala!'; and then the trunk wound around him and lifted him in air.

'B'yat, Tantor,' commanded Tarzan, 'tand b'yat!' and the bull lowered Tarzan to his head.

'Vando!' said Tarzan, and scratched the great beast behind his ears.

The other elephants went on with their feeding, paying no further attention to the ape-man, but the orangutans sat in a nearby tree and scolded, for they were afraid of Tantor.

Now, Tarzan thought that he would try an experiment, and he swung from the bull's back into a nearby tree and went off a little distance into the jungle; then he called back, 'Yud, Tantor, yud b'yat.'

Through the forest and the undergrowth came an answering rumble from the throat of the bull. Tarzan listened; he heard the cracking of twigs and the crashing of underbrush, and presently the great bulk of Tantor loomed above him.

'Vando, Tantor,' he said, and swung away through the trees, much to the relief of the orangutans, who had looked with disfavor upon this whole procedure.

The mountain rose steeply before them now, and there were often places where only Tarzan or his simian friends might go. At last the three came to a ledge that ran towards the South. It led away from the stream, however, from which Tarzan had departed at the foot of a waterfall which tumbled over a cliff the precipitous and slippery sides of which might have been negotiated by a fly or a lizard but by little else.

They followed the ledge around a shoulder of the mountain and came out upon a large level mesa dense with forest. It looked to Tarzan like a good hunting ground, and here he again took to the trees.

Presently, Usha, the wind, brought to his nostrils a familiar scent – the scent of Horta, the boar. Here was meat, and instantly Tarzan was the wild beast stalking its prey.

He had not gone far, however, before two other scents impinged upon his sensitive nostrils – the scent spoor of Numa, the lion, and mingled with it, that of man.

These two scent spoors could be mingled for but one of two reasons; either the man was hunting the lion, or the lion was hunting the man. And as Tarzan detected the scent of only a single man, he assumed that the lion was the hunter, and so he swung off through the trees, in the direction from which the scent came.

XII

Thak Chan was hunting no lion. It was impossible that he could have been hunting a lion, for he had never seen or heard of one in all his life; neither had any of his progenitors through all recorded time. A long time ago, before Chac Tutul Xiu had migrated from Yucatan, Thak Chan's people had known the jaguar, and the memory of it had been carried across the great water to this distant island and preserved in enduring stone in the temples and upon the stelae that had been built here. Thak Chan was a hunter from the city of Chichen Itza, that Chac Tutul Xiu had founded upon this island which he had found and had named Uxal for the city of his birth.

Thak Chan was hunting the wild boar, which, if aroused, may be quite as formidable as Numa, the lion; but, up to now, Thak Chan had had no luck.

Thak Chan entered a small natural clearing in the forest, and as he did so, his startled attention was attracted to the opposite side by an ominous growl. Confronting him was the snarling face of the most terrifying beast he had ever seen.

The great lion slunk slowly out into the clearing, and Thak Chan turned and fled. The thunderous roar that followed him almost paralyzed him with terror as he raced for his life through the familiar mazes of the forest, while close behind the hungry lion loped after its prey. There could have been no hope for Thak Chan in that unequal race even if he had remained upon his feet; but when he tripped and fell, he knew that it was the end. He turned to face this fearsome, unknown creature; but he did not arise, and, still sitting on the ground, he awaited the attack with poised spear.

The lion appeared then from around a curve in the jungle trail. His yellow-green eyes were round and staring. To Thak Chan, they seemed burning with fires of fury. The beast's great yellow fangs were bared in a snarl so malignant that Thak Chan quailed anew. The lion did not charge; he merely trotted towards his prey, for here was only a puny man-thing – no worthy antagonist for the King of Beasts.

Thak Chan prayed to strange gods as he saw death approaching; and then, as though in answer to his prayers, an amazing thing happened; a naked man, a giant to Thak Chan, dove from a tree above the trail full upon the back of that savage beast for which Thak Chan did not even have a name. A mighty arm went around the beast's neck, and powerful legs wrapped around the small of its body. It rose upon its hind legs, roaring hideously, and sought to reach the thing upon its back with fang or talon. It leaped into the air, twisting and turning; it threw itself upon the ground and rolled over in a frantic effort to free itself; but the silent creature clung to it tenaciously, and with its free hand, drove a long knife again and again into its tawny side, until, with a final thunderous roar, the beast rolled over upon its side, quivered convulsively for a moment and lay still.

Thak Chan had watched this amazing battle with feelings of mixed terror and hope, half convinced that this was indeed a god come to save him, but almost as fearful of the god as of the beast.

As the great beast died, Thak Chan saw the man, or god, or whatever it was, rise to his feet and place one of them upon the body of his kill and then raise his face to the heavens and voice a long drawn out scream so terrifying that Thak Chan shuddered and covered his ears with his palms.

For the first time since it had risen from the floor of the ocean the island of Uxmal heard the victory cry of a bull ape that had made its kill.

XIII

Thak Chan knew of many gods, and he tried to place this one. He knew them as the mighty ones, the captains that go before, and the old ones. There was Huitz-Hok, Lord Hills and Valleys; Che, Lord Forest; and innumerable earth gods; then of course there was Itzamna, ruler of the sky, son of Hunab Kuh, the first god and Hun Ahau, god of the underworld, Metnal, a cold, dank, gloomy place beneath the earth, where the rank and file and those who led evil lives went after death; and there was also Aychuykak, god of war, who was always carried into battle by four captains on a special litter.

Perhaps this one was Che, Lord Forest; and so Thak Chan addressed him thus, and being polite, thanked him for saving him from the strange beast. However, when Che replied, it was in a language that Thak Chan had never heard before, and which he thought perhaps was the language of the gods.

Tarzan looked at the strange little brown man who spoke this amazing language which he could not understand; then he said, 'Dako-zan,' which in the language of the great apes means 'meat;' but Thak Chan only shook his head and apologized for being so stupid.

Seeing that he was getting nowhere this way, Tarzan took an arrow from his quiver and with its point drew a picture of Horta, the boar, in the well-packed earth of the trail; then he fitted the arrow to his bow and drove the shaft into the picture behind the left shoulder.

Thak Chan grinned and nodded excitedly; then he motioned Tarzan to follow him. As he started away along the trail, he chanced to look up and see the two orangutans perched above him and looking down at him. This was too much for the simple mind of Thak Chan; first the strange and horrible beast, then a god, and now these two hideous creatures. Trembling, Thak Chan fitted an arrow to his bow; but when he aimed it at the apes, Tarzan snatched the weapon from him, and called to the orangutans, which came down and stood beside him.

Thak Chan was now convinced that these also were gods, and he was quite overcome by the thought that he was consorting with three of them. He wanted to hurry right back to Chichen Itza and tell everybody he knew of the miraculous happenings of this day, but then it occurred to him that nobody would believe him and that the priests might become angry. He recalled, too, that men had been chosen as victims of the sacrificial rites at the temple for much less than this.

There must be some way. Thak Chan thought and thought as he led Tarzan of the Apes through the forest in search of wild boar; and at last he hit upon a magnificent scheme; he would lead the three gods back to Chichen Itza that all men might see for themselves that Thak Chan spoke the truth.

Tarzan thought that he was being led in search of Horta, the boar; and when a turn in the trail brought them to the edge of the jungle, and he saw an amazing city, he was quite as surprised as Thak Chan had been when he had come to the realization that his three companions were gods. Tarzan could see that the central part of the city was built upon a knoll on the summit of which rose a pyramid surmounted by what appeared to be a temple. The pyramid was built of blocks of lava which formed steep steps leading to the summit. Around the pyramid were other buildings which hid its base from Tarzan's view; and around all this central portion of the city was a wall, pierced occasionally by gates. Outside the wall were flimsy dwellings of thatch, doubtless the quarters of the poorer inhabitants of the city.

'Chichen Itza,' said Thak Chan, pointing and beckoning Tarzan to follow him.

With the natural suspicion of the wild beast which was almost inherent with him, the ape-man hesitated. He did not like cities, and he was always suspicious of strangers, but presently curiosity got the better of his judgment, and he followed Thak Chan toward the city. They passed men and women working in fields where maize, and beans, and tubers were being cultivated – a monument to the perspicacity of Chac Tutul Xiu, who over four hundred years before, had had the foresight to bring seeds and bulbs with him from Yucatan.

The men and women in the fields looked up in amazement as they saw Thak Chan's companions, but they were still more amazed when Thak Chan announced proudly that they were Che, Lord Forest, and two of the earth gods.

By this time, however, the nerves of the two earth gods had endured all that they could; and these deities turned and scampered off toward the jungle, lumbering along in the half stooping posture of the great apes. Thak Chan called after them pleadingly, but to no avail, and a moment later he watched them swing into the trees and disappear.

By this time, the warriors guarding the gates they were approaching had become very much interested and not a little excited. They had summoned an officer, and he was awaiting Thak Chan and his companion when they arrived before the gate. The officer was Xatl Din, who had commanded the party of warriors that had discovered the castaways upon the beach.

'Who are you,' he demanded, 'and whom do you bring to Chichen Itza?'

'I am Thak Chan, the hunter,' replied Tarzan's companion, 'and this is Che, Lord Forest, who saved me from a terrible beast that was about to devour me. The two who ran away were earth gods. The people of Chichen Itza must have offended them or they would have come into the city.'

Xatl Din had never seen a god, but he realized that there was something impressive about this almost naked stranger who towered high above him and his fellows, for Tarzan's height was accentuated by the fact that the Maya are a small people; and compared with them, he looked every inch a god. However, Xatl Din was not wholly convinced, for he had seen strangers on the beach, and he guessed that this might be one of them.

'Who are you who comes to Chichen Itza?' he demanded of Tarzan. 'If you are indeed Che, Lord Forest, give me some proof of it, that Cit Coh Xiu, the King, and Chal Yip Xiu, the ah kin mai, may prepare to welcome you befittingly.'

'Che, Lord Forest, does not understand our language, most noble one,' interposed Thak Chan; 'he understands only the language of the gods.'

'The gods can understand all languages,' said Xatl Din.

'I should have said that he would not debase himself by speaking it,' Thak Chan corrected himself. 'Undoubtedly he understands all that we say, but it would not be meet for a god to speak the language of mortals.'

'You know a great deal for a simple hunter,' said Xatl Din superciliously.

'Those whom the gods make friends with must be very wise,' said Thak Chan loftily.

Thak Chan had been feeling more and more important all along. Never before had he had such a protracted conversation with a noble, in fact he had seldom ever said more than, 'Yes, most noble one,' or 'No, most noble one.' Thak Chan's assurance and the impressive appearance of the stranger were, at last, too much for Xatl Din, and he admitted them into the city, accompanying them himself toward the temple which was a part of the King's palace.

Here were warriors and priests and nobles resplendent in feathers and jade; and to one of the nobles who was also a priest, Xatl Din repeated the story that Thak Chan had told him.

Tarzan, finding himself surrounded by armed men, again became suspicious, questioning the wisdom of his entry into this city which might prove a trap from which he might find it difficult to escape.

A noble had gone to inform Chal Yip Xiu, the high priest, that one who claimed to be Che, Lord Forest, had come to visit him in his temple.

Like most high priests, Chal Yip Xiu was a trifle skeptical about the existence of gods: they were all right for the common people, but a high priest had no need for them. As a matter of fact, he considered himself as a personification of all the gods, and his power in Chichen Itza lent color to this belief.

'Go fetch the hunter and his companion,' he said to the noble who had brought the message.

Shortly thereafter, Tarzan of the Apes strode into the presence of Chal Yip Xiu, the high priest of Chichen Itza, and with him were Thak Chan, the hunter, and Xatl Din, the noble, with several of his fellows, and a score of warriors and lesser priests.

When Chal Yip Xiu saw the stranger, he was impressed; and, to be on the safe side, he addressed him respectfully; but when Xatl Din told him that the god refused to speak the language of mortals, the high priest became suspicious.

'You reported the presence of strangers on the beach,' he said to Xatl Din; 'could not this be one of them?'

'It could, holy one,' replied the noble.

'If this one is a god,' said Chal Yip Xiu, 'then the others must all be gods. But you told me that their ship was wrecked and that they were cast ashore.'

'That is right, holy one,' replied Xatl Din.

'Then they are only mortals,' said the high priest, 'for gods would have controlled the winds and the waves, and their ship would not have been wrecked.'

'That, too, is true, most wise one,' agreed Xatl Din.

'Then this man is no god,' stated Chal Yip Xiu, 'but he will make an excellent sacrifice to the true gods. Take him away.'

XIV

At this unlooked for turn of affairs, Thak Chan was so shocked and astounded that, although he was only a poor hunter, he dared raise his voice in protest to Chal Yip Xiu, the ah kin mai. 'But, most holy one,' he cried, 'you should have seen the things that he did. You should have seen the great beast which was about to devour me, and how he leaped upon its back and killed it; none but a god could have done such a thing. Had you seen all this and the two earth gods that accompanied him, you would know that he must indeed be Che, Lord Forest.'

'Who are you?' demanded Chal Yip Xiu in a terrible voice.

'I am Thak Chan, the hunter,' replied the now frightened man meekly.

'Then stick to your hunting, Thak Chan,' warned Chal Yip Xiu, 'or you will end upon the sacrificial block or in the waters of the sacred well. Get you gone.' Thak Chan went; he sneaked out like a dog with its tail between its legs.

But when warriors laid hands upon Tarzan, that was a different story. Although he had not understood Chal Yip Xiu's words, he had known by the man's tone and demeanor that all was not well, and when he had seen Thak Chan sneak away, he was doubly convinced of it; and then warriors closed in and laid hands upon him.

The high priest had received him in a colonnade upon one side of a peristyle, and Tarzan's keen eyes had quickly taken in the entire scene immediately after he was ushered into the presence of the high priest. He had seen the garden behind the row of columns and the low buildings beyond the peristyle. What lay immediately beyond these buildings he did not know, but he did know that the city wall was not far away, and beyond the wall and the fields there was the forest.

He shook off the detaining hands of the warriors and leaped to the low platform where Chal Yip Xiu sat; and, hurling the high priest aside, he leaped into the garden, crossed the peristyle at a run and swarmed up the wall of the building beyond.

Warriors pursued him across the peristyle with imprecations and arrows and stones from the slings they carried; but only the imprecations reached him, and they were harmless.

He crossed the roof of the building and dropped into a street beyond. There were people in the street, but they fell back in terror as this bronze giant brushed them aside and trotted on toward the city wall. At the end of this street was a gate, but it was not the gate through which he had entered the city, and the warriors stationed here knew nothing of him; to them he was only an almost naked stranger, evidently a man of an alien race, and thus an enemy who had no business within the walls of Chichen Itza; so they tried to bar his way and arrest him, but Tarzan seized one of them and, holding him by the ankles, used him as a club to force his way through the other warriors and out of the gate.

He was free at last, but then he had never had any doubt but what he would be free, for he looked with contempt upon these little men, primitively armed. How could they hope to hold Tarzan, Lord of the Jungle? Just then a stone from one of their slings struck him on the back of the head; and he fell forward upon his face, unconscious.

When Tarzan regained consciousness, he found himself in a wooden cage in a room dimly lit by a single window. The walls of the room were of beautifully dressed and fitted blocks of lava. The window was about two feet square and was near the ceiling; there was also a doorway in the room, closed by a heavy wooden door, which Tarzan guessed was bolted upon the outside. He did not know what fate lay in store for him, but he imagined that it would be most unpleasant, for the face of Chal Yip Xiu had been cruel indeed, as had the faces of many of the priests and nobles.

Tarzan tested the bars of his wooden cage and smiled. He knew that he could walk out of that whenever he pleased, but getting out of the room might be another question; the window would have been large enough had there not been two stone bars set in the opening; the door looked very substantial.

The back wall of the cage was about two feet from the back wall of the room. Upon this side, Tarzan ripped off two of the bars and stepped out of the cage. He went at once to the door but could neither open it nor force it; however, he waited patiently before it with one of the broken bars of his cage in his hand – he knew that someone would open that door eventually.

He did not know that he had been unconscious a long time and that night had passed and that it was day again. Presently he heard voices outside his cell; they grew in numbers and volume until he knew that there was a great concourse of people there, and now he heard the booming of drums and the throaty blasts of trumpets and the sound of chanting.

As he was wondering what was going on outside in the city, he heard the scraping of the bolt outside his door. He waited, the broken bar held firmly in one hand; and then the door opened and a warrior entered – a warrior to whom death came quickly and painlessly.

Tarzan stepped into the doorway and looked out. Almost directly in front of him, a priest stood in front of an altar across which a girl was stretched upon her back; four men in long embroidered robes and feather headdresses held her there, one at each leg and one at each arm. The priest stood above her with knife of obsidian raised above her breast.

Tarzan took in the whole picture at a glance. The girl meant nothing to him; the death of a human being did not mean much to him, he who had seen so many creatures die, and knew that death was the natural consequence of life; but the cruelty and heartlessness of the ceremony angered him, and he was imbued with a sudden desire to thwart the authors of it, rather than with any humanitarian urge to rescue the girl. The priest's back was toward him as he leaped from his cell and snatched the knife from the upraised hand; then he lifted the priest and hurled him against two of the lesser priests who held the girl, breaking their holds and sending them crashing to the temple floor.

The other two priests he struck down with his wooden club. The astounding performance left the onlookers stunned and breathless, and no hand was raised to stop him as he lifted the girl from the altar, slung her across one shoulder, and leaped through the temple doorway.

Tarzan recalled the route by which he had been brought to the palace temple, and he followed it back now out into the city, past two astounded guards at the palace gate. They saw him disappear into a side street; but they dared not desert their posts to follow him, but almost immediately a howling mob surged past them in pursuit of the stranger who had defiled their temple and snatched a sacrifice from the altar of their god.

The city was practically deserted, for all the inhabitants had gathered in the temple square to witness the sacrifice, and so Tarzan ran unmolested and unobserved through the narrow, winding side street of Chichen Itza. He ran swiftly, for he could hear the howls of the pursuing mob, and he had no wish to be overtaken by it.

The girl across his shoulder did not struggle to escape; she was far too terrified. Snatched from death by this strange almost naked giant, she could only apprehend what a terrible fate awaited her. She had heard the story that Thak Chan had told, for it had spread throughout the city; and she thought that perhaps this was indeed Che, Lord Forest. The vaguest hint of such a possibility would have so terrified little Itzl Cha that she could not have moved had she wished to, for gods are very terrifying creatures and not to be antagonized. If Che, Lord Forest, wished to carry her away, it would be certain death to oppose him; that she knew, and so Itzl Cha lay very quietly on the broad shoulder of her rescuer.

Tarzan could tell by the diminishing volume of the sounds of pursuit that he had thrown the mob off his trail. He soon reached the city wall at some distance from any gate. Alone he could have gained the top; but burdened with the girl, he could not; so he looked about him quickly for some means of scaling it.

Just inside the wall was a narrow street, about fifteen feet wide, which was lined with buildings and sheds of different heights, and here Tarzan saw his way. To reach the roof of a low shed with the girl was no feat for the ape-man, and from this shed he went to the roof of a higher structure, and then to another which was on a level with the top of the city wall.

Itzl Cha, who had kept her eyes tightly closed most of the time, now opened them again. She saw that Che, Lord Forest, had carried her to the roof of a building. Now he was running swiftly across the roof toward the narrow street which lay just within the wall. He did not slacken his speed as he approached the edge of the roof; and that made Itzl Cha close her eyes again very tightly, for she knew that they both were going to be dashed to death on the pavement in the street below.

At the edge of the roof, Tarzan leaped up and outward, alighting on the top of the wall on the opposite side of the street. Below him was the thatched roof of a laborer's hut, and to this he leaped, and from there to the ground. A moment later, with Itzl Cha gasping for breath, he was trotting across the cultivated fields toward the forest.

XV

Life in the camp of the castaways was well ordered and run along military lines, for Colonel Leigh had taken full command. Lacking bugles, he had set up the ship's bell, which rang at six o'clock each morning, a clanging imitation of reveille; it summoned the company to mess three times a day, and announced tattoo at nine, and taps at ten each night. Sentries guarded the camp twenty-four hours each day, and working parties policed it, or chopped wood, or gathered such natural foods as the jungle afforded. It was indeed a model camp, from which fishing parties rowed out upon the lagoon daily, and hunting parties went into the forest in search of game, wherewith to vary the monotony of their fruit and vegetable diet. It was the duty of the women to keep their own quarters in order and do such mending as might be required.

Tarzan's mysterious disappearance and protracted absence was the subject of considerable conversation. 'It is good riddance,' said Penelope Leigh. 'Never, since I first saw that terrible creature, have I felt safe until now.'

'I don't see how you can say such a thing,' said her niece; 'I should feel very much safer were he here.'

'One never knew when he might take it into his head to eat one,' insisted Mrs Leigh.

'I was shut up with him for days in that cage,' said Janette Laon; 'and he never showed me even the slightest incivility, let alone threatening to harm me.'

'Hmph!' snorted Penelope, who had never as yet condescended to recognize the existence of Janette, let alone speak to her. She had made up her mind on first sight that Janette was a loose woman; and when Penelope Leigh made up her mind, not even an act of Parliament might change it ordinarily.

'Before he went away, he had been making weapons,' recalled Patricia, 'and I suppose he went into the forest to hunt; perhaps a lion or a tiger got him.'

'Serve him right,' snapped Mrs Leigh. 'The very idea of turning all those wild beasts loose on this island with us. It will be a miracle if we are not all devoured.'

'He went out into the jungle without any firearms,' mused Janette Laon, half to herself; 'I heard Colonel Leigh say that not even a pistol was missing. Just think of going into that jungle where he knew all those ferocious beasts were, and with only a gaff and some homemade arrows and a bow.'

Mrs Leigh hated to acknowledge any interest in Janette Laon's conversation, but she couldn't resist the temptation of saying, 'He's probably a half-wit; most of these wild men are.'

'I wouldn't know,' said Janette Laon sweetly, 'never having had an occasion to associate with any.'

Mrs Leigh sniffed, and Patricia turned her back to hide a smile.

Algernon Wright-Smith, Captain Bolton, and Dr Crouch were hunting. They had gone Northward into the jungle hoping to bring fresh meat back to the camp. They were following a dim trail in the damp earth of which the footprints of pig could occasionally be identified, and these gave them hope and lured them on.

'Nasty place to meet a tusker,' remarked Crouch.

'Rather,' agreed Algy.

'Look here!' exclaimed Bolton, who was in advance.

'What is it?' asked Crouch.

'The pug of a tiger or a lion,' replied Bolton; 'fresh too – the blighter must just have crossed the trail.'

Crouch and Algy examined the imprint of the beast's pug in the soft earth. 'Tiger,' said Crouch; 'no doubt about it – I've seen too many of them to be mistaken.'

'Rotten place to meet old stripes,' said Algy; 'I –' a coughing grunt interrupted him. 'I say!' he exclaimed, 'There's the beggar now.'

'Where?' demanded Bolton.

'Off there to the left,' said Crouch.

'Can't see a bloody thing,' said Algy.

'I think we should go back,' said Bolton; 'we wouldn't have a chance if that fellow charged; one of us would be sure to be killed – maybe more.'

'I think you're right,' said Crouch; 'I don't like the idea of having that fellow between us and camp.' There was a sudden crashing in the underbrush a short distance from them.

'My God!' exclaimed Algy, 'Here he comes!' as he threw down his gun and clambered into a tree.

The other men followed Algy's example and none too soon, for they were scarcely out of harm's way when a great Bengal tiger broke from cover and leaped into the trail. He stood looking around for a moment, and then he caught sight of the treed men and growled. His terrible yellow-green eyes and his snarling face were turned up toward them.

Crouch commenced to laugh, and the other two men looked at him in surprise. 'I'm glad there was no one here to see that,' he said; 'it would have been a terrible blow to British prestige.'

'What the devil else could we do?' demanded Bolton. 'You know as well as I do that we didn't have a ghost of a show against him, even with three guns.'

'Of course not,' said Algy; 'couldn't have got a sight of him to fire at until he was upon us. Certainly was lucky for us there were some trees we could climb in a hurry; good old trees; I always did like trees.'

The tiger came forward growling, and when he was beneath the tree in which Algy was perched, he crouched and sprang.

'By jove!' exclaimed Algy, climbing higher; 'the beggar almost got me.'

Twice more the tiger sprang for one of them, and then he walked back along the trail a short distance and lay down patiently.

'The beggar's got us to rights,' said Bolton.

'He won't stay there forever,' said Crouch.

Bolton shook his head. 'I hope not,' he said, 'but they have an amazing amount of patience; I know a chap who was treed by one all night in Bengal.'

'Oh, I say, he couldn't do that, you know,' objected Algy. 'What does he take us for – a lot of bally asses? Does he think we're coming down there to be eaten up?'

'He probably thinks that when we are ripe, we'll fall off, like apples and things.'

'This is deucedly uncomfortable,' said Algy after a while; 'I'm pretty well fed up with it. I wish I had my gun.'

'It's right down there at the foot of your tree,' said Crouch; 'why don't you go down and get it?'

'I say, old thing!' exclaimed Algy; 'I just had a brainstorm. Watch.' He took off his shirt, commenced tearing it into strips which he tied together, and when he had a long string of this he made a slip noose at one end; then he came down to a lower branch and dropped the noose down close to the muzzle of his gun, which, because of the way in which the weapon had fallen, was raised a couple of inches from the ground.

'Clever?' demanded Algy.

'Very,' said Bolton. 'The tiger is admiring your ingenuity; see him watching you?'

'If that noose catches behind the sight, I can draw the bally thing up here, and then I'll let old stripes have what for.'

'You should have been an engineer, Algy,' said Crouch.

'My mother wanted me to study for the Church,' said Algy, 'and my father wanted me to go into the diplomatic corps – both make me bored; so I just played tennis instead.'

'And you're rotten at that,' said Crouch, laughing.

'Righto, old thing!' agreed Algy. 'Look! I have it.'

After much fishing, the noose had slipped over the muzzle of the gun, and as Algy pulled gently, it tightened below the sight; then he started drawing the weapon up towards him.

He had it within a foot of his hand when the tiger leaped to his feet with a roar and charged. As the beast sprang into the air towards Algy, the man dropped everything and scrambled towards safety, as the raking talons swept within an inch of his foot.

'Whe-e-ew!' exclaimed Algy, as he reached a higher branch.

'Now you've even lost your shirt,' said Crouch.

The tiger stood looking up for a moment, growling and lashing his tail, and then he went back and lay down again.

'I believe the beggar is going to keep us here all night,' said Algy.

XVI

Krause and his fellows had not gone two days march from the camp of the castaways, as Tarzan had ordered them to do. They had gone only about four miles up the coast, where they had camped by another stream where it emptied into the ocean. They were a bitter and angry company as they squatted disconsolately upon the beach and ate the fruit that they had made the Lascars gather. They sweated and fumed for a couple of days and made plans and quarrelled. Both Krause and Schmidt wished to command, and Schmidt won out because Krause was the bigger coward and was afraid of the madman. Abdullah Abu Néjm sat apart and hated them all. Oubanovitch talked a great deal in a loud tone of voice and argued that they should all be comrades and that nobody should command. By a single thread of common interest were they held together – their hatred of Tarzan, because he had sent them away without arms or ammunition.

'We could go back at night and steal what we need,' suggested Oubanovitch.

'I have been thinking that same thing myself,' said Schmidt. 'You go back now, Oubanovitch, and reconnoiter. You can hide in the jungle just outside their camp and get a good lay of the land, so that we shall know just where the rifles are kept.'

'You go yourself,' said Oubanovitch, 'you can't order me around.'

'I'm in command,' screamed Schmidt, springing to his feet.

Oubanovitch stood up too. He was a big hulking brute, much larger than Schmidt. 'So what!' he demanded.

'There's no sense in fighting among ourselves,' said Krause. 'Why don't you send a Lascar?'

'If I had a gun this dirty communist would obey me,' Schmidt grumbled, and then he called to one of the Lascar sailors. 'Come here, Chuldrup,' he ordered.

The Lascar slouched forward, sullen and scowling. He hated Schmidt; but all his life he had taken orders from white men, and the habit was strong upon him.

'You go other camp,' Schmidt directed; 'hide in jungle; see where guns, bullets kept.'

'No go,' said Chuldrup; 'tiger in jungle.'

'The hell you won't go!' exclaimed Schmidt, and knocked the sailor down. 'I'll teach you.' The sailor came to his feet, a boiling caldron of hate. He wanted to kill the white man, but he was still afraid. 'Now get out of here, you heathen dog,' Schmidt yelled at him; 'and see that you don't come back until you find out what you want to know.' Chuldrup turned and walked away, and a moment later the jungle closed behind him.

'I say!' exclaimed Algy. 'What's the blighter doing now?' The tiger had arisen and was standing, ears forward, looking back along the trail. He cocked his head on one side, listening.

'He hears something coming,' said Bolton.

'There he goes,' said Crouch, as the tiger slunk into the underbrush beside the trail.

'Now's our chance,' said Algy.

'He didn't go far,' said Bolton; 'he's right there; I can see him.'

'Trying to fool us,' said Crouch.

Chuldrup was very much afraid; he was afraid of the jungle, but he was more afraid to return to Schmidt without the information the man wanted. He stopped for a moment to think the matter over; should he go back and hide in the jungle for a while close to Schmidt's camp and then when there had been time for him to fulfill his mission go to Schmidt and make up a story about the location of the guns and bullets?

Chuldrup scratched his head, and then the light of a great idea broke upon him; he would go to the camp of the Englishmen, tell them what Schmidt was planning, and ask them to let him remain with them. That, he knew, was one of the best ideas that he had ever had in his life; and so he turned and trotted happily along the trail.

'Something is coming,' whispered Crouch; 'I can hear it,' and a moment later Chuldrup came trotting into view.

All three men shouted warnings simultaneously, but too late. As the Lascar stopped, amazed, and looked up at them, momentarily uncomprehending, a great tiger leaped from the underbrush and, rearing up above the terrified man, seized him by the shoulder.

Chuldrup screamed; the great beast shook him and then turned and dragged him off into the underbrush, while the three Englishmen, horrified, looked on helplessly.

For a few moments they could hear the screams of the man mingling with the growls of the tiger and then the screams ceased.

'My God!' exclaimed Algy, 'That was awful.'

'Yes,' said Bolton, 'but it's our chance; he won't bother anything now that doesn't go near his kill.'

Gingerly and quietly they descended to the ground, picked up their rifles, and started back toward camp; but all three were shaken by the tragedy they had witnessed.

In the camp the day's work was done; even Colonel Leigh could find nothing more to keep the men busy.

'I must be getting old,' he said to his wife.

'Getting?' she asked. 'Are you just discovering it?'

The Colonel smiled indulgently; he was always glad when Penelope was herself. Whenever she said anything pleasant or kindly he was worried. 'Yes,' he continued, 'I must be slipping; I can't think of a damn thing for these men to do.'

'It seems to me there should be plenty to do around here,' said Penelope; 'I am always busy.'

'I think the men deserve a little leisure,' said Patricia; 'they've been working steadily ever since we've gotten here.'

'There's nothing that breeds discontent more surely than idleness,' said the Colonel; 'but I'm going to let them knock off for the rest of the day.'

Hans de Groote and Janette Laon were sitting together on the beach talking.

'Life is funny,' said the man. 'Just a few weeks ago, I was looking forward to seeing New York City for the first time – young, fancy-free, and with three months pay in my pocket; what a time I was planning there! And now here I am somewhere in the Pacific Ocean on an island that no one ever heard of – and that's not the worst of it.'

'And what is the worst of it?' asked Janette.

'That I like it,' replied de Groote.

'Like it!' she exclaimed. 'But why do you like it?'

'Because you are here,' he said.

The girl looked at him in surprise. 'I don't understand,' she said; 'you certainly can't mean that the way it sounds.'

'But I do, Janette,' he said; 'I –' his tanned face flushed. 'Why is it that those three words are so hard to say when you mean them?'

She reached out and placed her hand on his. 'You mustn't say them,' she said; 'you mustn't ever say them – to me.'

'Why?' he demanded.

'You know what I have been – kicking around Singapore, Saigon, Batavia.'

'I love you,' said Hans de Groote, and then Janette Laon burst into tears; it had been long since she had cried except in anger or disappointment.

'I won't let you,' she said; 'I won't let you.'

'Don't you – love me a little, Janette?' he asked.

'I won't tell you,' she said; 'I won't ever tell you.'

De Groote pressed her hand and smiled. 'You have told me,' he said.

And then they were interrupted by Patricia's voice crying, 'Why, Algy, where is your shirt?'

The hunters had returned, and the Europeans gathered around to hear their story. When they had finished the Colonel harrumphed. 'That settles it,' he said; 'there will be no more hunting in the jungle; no one would have a chance against a tiger or a lion in that tangle of undergrowth.'

'It's all your fault, William,' snapped Mrs Leigh; 'you should have taken complete command; you should not have permitted that wild man to turn those beasts loose on us.'

'I still think that it was quite the sporting thing to do,' said the Colonel, 'and don't forget that it was quite as dangerous for him as for us. As far as we know the poor devil may have been killed by one of them already.'

'And serve him quite right,' said Mrs Leigh; 'anyone who will run around the way he does in the presence of ladies has no business to live – at least not among decent people.'

'I think the fellow was just a little bit of all right,' said the Colonel, 'and don't forget, Penelope, if it had not been for him, we would probably be a great deal worse off than we are now.'

'Don't forget, Aunt Penelope, that he rescued you from the Saigon.'

'I am doing my best to forget it,' said Mrs Leigh.

XVII

When Itzl Cha realized that she was being carried off toward the forest, she was not quite sure what her feelings were. Back in Chichen Itza was certain death, for the gods could not be lightly robbed of their victims; and, were she ever to return, she knew that she would be again offered up in sacrifice. What lay ahead she could not even guess; but Itzl Cha was young and life was sweet; and perhaps Che, Lord Forest, would not kill her.

When they reached the forest Che did an amazing thing: he leaped to the low branch of a tree and then swung upward, carrying her swiftly high above the ground. Now indeed was Itzl Cha terrified.

Presently Che stopped and voiced a long drawn-out call – an eerie cry that echoed through the forest; then he went on.

The girl had summoned sufficient courage to keep her eyes open, but presently she saw something that made her wish to close them again; however, fascinated, she continued to look at two grotesque creatures swinging through the trees to meet them, jabbering as they came.

Che replied in the same strange jargon, and Itzl Cha knew that she was listening to the language of the gods, for these two must indeed be the two earth gods of whom Thak Chan had spoken. When these two reached Che, all three stopped and spoke to each other in that language she could not understand. It was then that Itzl Cha chanced to glance down at the ground into a little clearing upon the edge of which they were, and there she saw the body of a terrible beast; and she knew that it was the same one from which Che had rescued Thak Chan, the hunter.

She wished that the skeptics in Chichen Itza could see all that she had seen, for then they would know that these were indeed gods; and they would be sorry and frightened because they had treated Lord Forest as they had.

Her divine rescuer carried her to a mountain trail, and there he set her down upon the ground and let her walk. Now she had a good look at him; how beautiful he was! Indeed a god. The two earth gods waddled along with them, and from being afraid Itzl Cha commenced to be very proud when she thought of the company in which she was. What other girl in Chichen Itza had ever walked abroad with three gods?

Presently they came to a place where the trail seemed to end, disappearing over the brink of a terrifying precipice; but Che, Lord Forest, did not hesitate; he merely took Itzl Cha across that broad shoulder again and clambered down the declivity with as great ease as did the two earth gods.

However, Itzl Cha could not help but be terrified when she looked down;

and so she closed her eyes tightly and held her breath and pressed her little body very close to that of Che, Lord Forest, who had become to her something akin to a haven of refuge.

But at last they reached the bottom and once again Lord Forest raised his voice. What he said sounded to Itzl Cha like 'Yud, Tantor, yud!' And that was exactly what it was: 'Come, Tantor, Come!'

Very shortly, Itzl Cha heard a sound such as she had never heard before – a sound that no other Mayan had ever heard; the trumpeting of an elephant.

By this time, Itzl Cha thought that she had seen all the miracles that there were to be seen in the world, but when a great bull elephant broke through the forest, toppling the trees that were in his path, little Itzl Cha screamed and fainted.

When Itzl Cha regained consciousness, she did not immediately open her eyes. She was conscious of an arm about her, and that her back was resting against a human body; but what caused that strange motion, and what was that rough surface that she straddled with her bare legs?

Fearfully, Itzl Cha opened her eyes; but she immediately screamed and closed them again. She was sitting on the head of that terrible beast she had seen!

Lord Forest was sitting behind her, and it was his arm that was around her, preventing her from falling to the ground. The earth gods were swinging along in the trees beside them; they seemed to be scolding. It was all too much for little Itzl Cha; in a brief hour or two, she had experienced a lifetime of thrills and adventure.

The afternoon was drawing to a close. Lum Kip was preparing dinner for the Europeans. This was not a difficult procedure; there was fish to fry, and some tubers to boil. Fruit made up the balance of the menu. Lum Kip was cheerful and happy; he liked to work for the foreign devils; they treated him well, and the work was not nearly as arduous as chopping wood.

The two girls in the party and most of the men were sitting on the ground, talking over the events of the day, especially the hunting trip which had ended in tragedy. Patricia wondered if they would ever see Tarzan again, and that started them talking about the wild man and his probable fate. The Colonel was in his hut shaving, and his wife was sitting out in front of it with her mending, when something attracted her attention, and, looking toward the forest she voiced a single ear-piercing shriek and fainted. Instantly everyone was on his feet; the Colonel, his face half lathered, rushed from the hut.

Patricia Leigh-Burden cried, 'Oh, my God, look!'

Coming out of the forest was a great bull elephant, and on its neck sat Tarzan holding an almost naked girl in front of him; two orangutans waddled along at a safe distance on one side. No wonder Penelope Leigh had fainted.

The elephant stopped a few paces outside the forest; the sight of all these people was too much for him, and he would come no farther. Tarzan, with the girl in his arms, slipped to the ground, and, holding her by the hand, led her toward the camp.

Itzl Cha felt that these must all be gods, but much of her fear was gone now, for Lord Forest had offered her no harm, nor had the earth gods, nor had that strange enormous beast on which she had ridden through the forest.

Patricia Leigh-Burden looked questioningly and a little suspiciously at the girl walking at Tarzan's side. One of the sailors working nearby said to another, 'That fellow is a fast worker.' Patricia heard it, and her lips tightened.

Tarzan was greeted by silence, but it was the silence of surprise. The Colonel was working over his wife, and presently she opened her eyes. 'Where is he?' she whispered. 'That creature! You must get him out of camp immediately, William, he and that wanton girl with him. Both of them together didn't have on enough clothes to cover a baby decently. I suppose he went off somewhere and stole a woman, an Indian woman at that.'

'Oh, quiet, Penelope,' said the Colonel, a little irritably; 'you don't know anything about it and neither do I.'

'Well, you'd better make it your business to find out,' snapped Mrs Leigh. 'I don't intend to permit Patricia to remain in the same camp with such people, nor shall I remain.'

Tarzan walked directly to Patricia Leigh-Burden. 'I want you to look after this girl,' he said.

'I?' demanded Patricia haughtily.

'Yes, you,' he replied.

'Come, come,' said the Colonel, still half lathered, 'what is the meaning of all this, Sir?'

'There's a city to the South of us,' said Tarzan, 'a good-sized city, and they have some heathen rites in which they sacrifice human beings; this girl was about to be sacrificed, when I was lucky enough to be able to take her away. She can't go back there because of course they would kill her; so we'll have to look after her. If your niece won't do it, I'm sure that Janette will.'

'Of course I'll look after her,' said Patricia; 'who said that I wouldn't?'

'Put some clothes on the thing,' said Mrs Leigh; 'this is absolutely disgraceful.'

Tarzan looked at her with disgust. 'It is your evil mind that needs clothes,' he said.

Penelope Leigh's jaws dropped. She stood there open-mouthed and speechless for a moment; then she wheeled about and stamped into her hut.

'I say, old thing,' said Algy, 'how the deuce did you get that elephant to let you ride on his head; that was one of the wild African bulls?'

'How do you get your friends to do you favors?' asked Tarzan.

'But, I say, you know, old thing, I haven't any friends like that.'

'That is too bad,' said the ape-man. Then he turned to the Colonel, 'We must take every precaution against attack,' he said; 'there were many warriors in that city, and I have no doubts but that a search will be made for this girl; eventually they will find our camp. Of course they are not accustomed to firearms, and if we are always on the alert, we have little to fear; but I suggest that only very strong parties be allowed to go into the jungle.'

'I have just issued orders that no one is to go into the jungle,' replied the Colonel. 'Captain Bolton, Dr Crouch, and Mr Wright-Smith were attacked by one of your tigers today.'

XVIII

For six weeks the life in the camp dragged on monotonously and without incident; and during that time, Patricia Leigh-Burden taught Itzl Cha to speak and understand enough English so that the little Mayan girl could carry on at least a sketchy conversation with the others, while Tarzan devoted much of his time to learning the Maya tongue from her. Tarzan, alone of the company, ventured occasionally into the jungle; and, from these excursions, he often returned with a wild pig.

His absence from camp always aroused Penelope Leigh's ire. 'He is impudent and insubordinate,' she complained to her husband. 'You gave strict orders that no one was to go into the jungle, and he deliberately disobeys you. You should make an example of him.'

'What do you suggest that I do with him, my dear?' asked the Colonel. 'Should he be drawn and quartered, or merely shot at sunrise?'

'Don't try to be facetious, William; it does not become you. You should simply insist that he obey the regulations that you have laid down.'

'And go without fresh pork?' asked the Colonel.

'I do not like pork,' snapped Mrs Leigh. 'Furthermore, I do not like the goings-on around this camp; Mr de Groote is far too intimate with that French woman, and the wild man is always around that Indian girl. Look at them now – always talking together; I can imagine what he is saying to her.'

'He is trying to learn her language,' explained the Colonel; 'something that may prove very valuable to us later on, if we ever have any dealings with her people.'

'Hmph!' snorted Mrs Leigh; 'A fine excuse. And the way they dress! If I can find some goods in the ship's stores, I shall make her a Mother Hubbard; and as for him – you should do something about that. And now look; there goes Patricia over to talk to them. William, you must put a stop to all this nonsense – it is indecent.'

Colonel William Cecil Hugh Percival Leigh sighed; his was not an entirely happy existence. Many of the men were becoming restless, and there were some who had commenced to question his right to command them. He rather questioned it himself, but he knew that conditions would become unbearable if there were no one in authority. Of course Algy, Bolton, Tibbet, and Crouch backed him up, as did de Groote and Tarzan. It was upon Tarzan that he depended most, for he realized that here was a man who would brook no foolishness in the event of mutiny. And now his wife wanted him to insist that this half-savage man wear trousers. The Colonel sighed again.

Patricia sat down beside Tarzan and Itzl Cha. 'How goes the class in Mayan?' she asked.

'Itzl Cha says that I am doing splendidly,' replied Tarzan.

'And Itzl Cha is mastering English, after a fashion,' said Patricia; 'she and I can almost carry on an intelligent conversation. She has told me some very interesting things. Do you know why they were going to sacrifice her?'

'To some god, I suppose,' replied Tarzan.

'Yes, to a god called Che, Lord Forest, to appease him for the affront done him by a man that claimed you were Che, Lord Forest.

'Itzl Cha is, of course, positive that she was rescued by no one less than Che, Lord Forest; and she says that many of her people will believe that too. She says that it is the first time in the history of her people that a god has come and taken alive the sacrifice being offered to him. It has made a deep impression on her and no one can ever convince her that you are not Che.

'Her own father offered her as a sacrifice in order to win favor with the gods,' continued Patricia. 'It is simply horrible, but it is their way; Itzl Cha says that parents often do this; although slaves and prisoners of war are usually the victims.'

'She has told me a number of interesting things about her people and about the island,' said Tarzan. 'The island is called Uxmal, after a city in Yucatan from which her people migrated hundreds of years ago.'

'They must be Mayas then,' said Patricia.

'That is very interesting,' said Dr Crouch, who had joined them. 'From what you have told us of your experiences in their city, and from what Itzl Cha has told us, it is evident that they have preserved their religion and their culture almost intact throughout the centuries since the migration. What a field this would be for the anthropologist and the archaeologist. If you could establish friendly relations with them, we might be able to solve the riddles of the hieroglyphs and their stelae and temples in Central America and South America.'

'As the chances are that we shall be here all the rest of our lives,' Patricia reminded him, 'our knowledge would do the world very little good.'

'I cannot believe that we shall never be rescued,' said Dr Crouch. 'By the way, Tarzan, is this village that you visited the only one on the island?'

'I don't know as to that,' replied the ape-man, 'but these Mayans are not the only people here. At the Northern end of the island, there is a settlement of what Itzl Cha calls "very bad people." The history of the island, handed down largely by word of mouth, indicates that survivors of a shipwreck intermarried with the aborigines of the island, and it is their descendants who live in this settlement; but they do not fraternize with the aborigines who live in the central part of the island.'

'You mean that there is a native population here?' asked Dr Crouch.

'Yes, and we are camped right on the south-western edge of their domain. I have never gone far enough into their country to see any of them, but Itzl Cha says that they are very savage cannibals.'

'What a lovely place fate selected for us to be marooned,' remarked Patricia, 'and then to make it all the cozier, you had to turn a lot of lions and tigers loose in it.' Tarzan smiled.

'At least we shall not perish from ennui,' remarked Janette Laon.

Colonel Leigh, Algy, and Bolton sauntered up, and then de Groote joined the party. 'Some of the men just came to me,' said the Dutchman, 'and wanted me to ask you, Colonel, if they could try to break up the Saigon and build a boat to get away from here. They said they would rather take a chance of dying at sea than spending the rest of their lives here.'

'I don't know that I can blame them,' said the Colonel. 'What do you think of it, Bolton?'

'It might be done,' replied the Captain.

'Anyway, it will keep them busy,' said the Colonel; 'and if they were doing something they wanted to do, they wouldn't be complaining all the time.'

'I don't know where they would build it,' said Bolton. 'They certainly can't build it on the reef; and it wouldn't do any good to build it on shore, for the water in the lagoon would be too shallow to float it.'

'There is deep water in a cove about a mile North of here,' said Tarzan, 'and no reef.'

'By the time the blighters have taken the Saigon apart,' said Algy, 'and carried it a mile along the coast, they'll be too exhausted to build a boat.'

'Or too old,' suggested Patricia.

'Who's going to design the boat?' asked the Colonel.

'The men have asked me to,' replied de Groote; 'my father is a shipbuilder, and I worked in his yard before I went to sea.'

'It's not a bad idea,' said Crouch; 'do you think you can build a boat large enough to take us all?'

'It depends upon how much of the Saigon we can salvage,' replied de Groote. 'If we should have another bad storm soon, the whole ship might break up.'

Algernon Wright-Smith made a sweeping gesture toward the forest. 'We have plenty of lumber there,' he said, 'if the Saigon fails us.'

'That would be some job,' said Bolton.

'Well, we've got all our lives to do it in, old thing,' Algy reminded him.

XIX

When two days had passed and Chuldrup had not returned, Schmidt drove another Lascar into the forest with orders to go to Tarzan's camp and get information about the guns and ammunition.

The Lascars had made a separate camp, a short distance from that occupied by Schmidt, Krause, Oubanovitch, and the Arab. They had been very busy, but none of the four men in the smaller camp had paid any attention to them, merely summoning one of them when they wanted to give any orders.

The second man whom Schmidt had sent in the forest never returned. Schmidt was furious, and on the third day he ordered two men to go. They stood sullenly before him, listening. When he had finished they turned and walked back to their own camp. Schmidt watched them; he saw them sit down with their fellows. He waited a moment to see if they would start, but they did not. Then he started toward their camp, white with rage.

'I'll teach them,' he muttered; 'I'll show them who's boss here – the brown devils;' but when he approached them, fifteen Lascars stood up to face him, and he saw that they were armed with bows and arrows and wooden spears. This was the work that had kept them so busy for several days.

Schmidt and the Lascars stood facing one another for several moments; then one of the latter said, 'What do you want here?'

There were fifteen of them, fifteen sullen, scowling men, all well armed.

'Aren't you two men going to find out about the guns and ammunition so that we can get them?' he asked.

'No,' said one of the two. 'You want to know, you go. We no take orders any more. Get out. Go back to your own camp.'

'This is mutiny,' blustered Schmidt.

'Get out,' said a big Lascar, and fitted an arrow to his bow.

Schmidt turned and slunk away.

'What's the matter?' asked Krause, when Schmidt reached his own camp.

'The devils have mutinied,' replied Schmidt, 'and they are all armed – made bows and arrows and spears for themselves.'

'The uprising of the proletariat!' exclaimed Oubanovitch. 'I shall join them and lead them. It is glorious, glorious; the world revolution has reached even here!'

'Shut up!' said Schmidt; 'You give me a pain.'

'Wait until I organize my glorious revolutionaries,' cried Oubanovitch; 'then you will sing a different song; then it will be "Comrade Oubanovitch, this," and "Comrade Oubanovitch, that." Now I go to my comrades who have risen in their might and cast the yoke of Capitalism from their necks.'

He crossed jubilantly to the camp of the Lascars. 'Comrades!' he cried. 'Congratulations on your glorious achievement. I have come to lead you on to greater victories. We will march on the camp of the Capitalists who threw us out. We will liquidate them, and we will take all their guns and ammunition and all their supplies.'

Fifteen scowling men looked at him in silence for a moment; then one of them said, 'Get out.'

'But!' exclaimed Oubanovitch, 'I have come to join you; together we will go on to glorious—'

'Get out,' repeated the Lascar.

Oubanovitch hesitated until several of them started toward him; then he turned and went back to the other camp. 'Well, Comrade,' said Schmidt, with a sneer, 'is the revolution over?'

'They are stupid fools,' said Oubanovitch.

That night the four men had to attend to their own fire, which the Lascars had kept burning for them in the past as a safeguard against wild beasts; and they had had to gather the wood for it, too. Now it devolved upon them to take turns standing guard.

'Well, Comrade,' said Schmidt to Oubanovitch, 'how do you like revolutions now that you are on the other side of one?'

The Lascars, having no white man to command them, all went to sleep and let their fire die out. Abdullah Abu Néjm was on guard in the smaller camp when he heard a series of ferocious growls from the direction of the Lascar's camp, and then a scream of pain and terror. The other three men awoke and sprang to their feet.

'What is it?' demanded Schmidt

'El adrea, Lord of the Broad Head,' replied the Arab.

'What's that?' asked Oubanovitch.

'A lion,' said Krause; 'he got one of them.'

The screams of the unfortunate victim was still blasting the silence of the night, but they were farther from the camp of the Lascars now, as the lion dragged his prey farther away from the presence of the other men. Presently the screams ceased, and then came an even more grisly and horrifying sound – the tearing and rending of flesh and bones mingled with the growls of the carnivore.

Krause piled more wood upon the fire. 'That damn wild man,' he said – 'turning those beasts loose here.'

'Serves you right,' said Schmidt; 'you had no business catching a white man and putting him in a cage.'

'It was Abdullah's idea,' whined Krause; 'I never would have thought of it if he hadn't put it into my head.'

There was no more sleep in the camp that night. They could hear the lion feeding until daylight, and then in the lesser darkness of dawn, they saw him rise from his kill and go to the river to drink; then he disappeared into the jungle.

'He will lie up for the day,' said Abdullah, 'but he will come out again and feed.'

As Abdullah ceased speaking, a foul sound came from the edge of the jungle, and two forms slunk out; the hyenas had scented the lion's kill, and presently they were tearing at what was left of the Lascar.

The next night, the Lascars built no fire at all; and another was taken. 'The fools!' exclaimed Krause; 'That lion has got the habit by now, and none of us will ever be safe again here.'

'They are fatalists,' said Schmidt; 'they believe that whatever is foreordained to happen must happen, and that nothing they can do about it can prevent it.'

'Well, I'm no fatalist,' said Krause. 'I'm going to sleep in a tree after this,' and he spent the next day building a platform in a tree at the edge of the forest, setting an example which the other three men were quick to follow. Even the Lascars were impressed, and that night the lion came and roared through empty camps.

'I've stood all of this that I can,' said Krause; 'I'm going back and see that fellow, Tarzan. I'll promise anything if he'll let us stay in his camp.'

'How are you going to get there?' asked Schmidt. 'I wouldn't walk through that jungle again for twenty million marks.'

'I don't intend to walk through the jungle,' said Krause. 'I'm going to follow the beach. I could always run out into the ocean if I met anything.'

'I think El adrea would be kinder to us than Tarzan of the Apes,' said the Arab.

'I never did anything to him,' said Oubanovitch; 'he ought to let me come back.'

'He's probably afraid you'd start a revolution,' said Schmidt. But they finally decided to try it; and early the next morning, they set out along the beach toward the other camp.

XX

Chand, the Lascar, watched Krause and his three companions start along the beach in the direction of Camp Saigon. 'They are going to the other camp,' he said to his fellows. 'Come, we will go too;' and a moment later they were trailing along the beach in the wake of the others.

In Camp Saigon, Tarzan was eating his breakfast alone. He had arisen early, for he had planned a full day's work. Only Lum Kip was astir, going about his work quietly preparing breakfast. Presently Patricia Leigh-Burden came from her hut and joined Tarzan, sitting down beside him.

'You are up early this morning,' she said.

'I am always earlier than the others,' he replied, 'but today I had a special reason; I want to get an early start.'

'Where are you going?' she asked.

'I'm going exploring,' he replied, 'I want to see what is on the other side of the island.'

Patricia leaned forward eagerly, placing a hand upon his knee. 'Oh, may I go with you?' she asked. 'I'd love it.'

From the little shelter that had been built especially for her, Itzl Cha watched them. Her black eyes narrowed and snapped, and she clenched her little hands tightly.

'You couldn't make it, Patricia,' said Tarzan, 'not the way I travel.'

'I've hiked through jungles in India,' she said.

'No,' he said, quite definitely; 'traveling on the ground in there is too dangerous. I suppose you've heard it mentioned that there are wild animals there.'

'Then if it's dangerous you shouldn't go,' she said, 'carrying nothing but a silly bow and some arrows. Let me go along with a rifle; I'm a good shot, and I've hunted tigers in India.'

Tarzan rose, and Patricia jumped to her feet, placing her hands on his shoulders. 'Please don't go,' she begged, 'I'm afraid for you,' but he only laughed and turned and trotted off toward the jungle.

Patricia watched him until he swung into a tree and disappeared; then she swished around angrily and went to her hut. 'I'll show him,' she muttered under her breath.

Presently she emerged with a rifle and ammunition. Itzl Cha watched her as she entered the jungle at the same place that Tarzan had, right at the edge of the little stream. The little Mayan girl bit her lips, and the tears came to her eyes – tears of frustration and anger. Lum Kip, working around the cook fire, commenced to hum to himself.

Chal Yip Xiu, the high priest, was still furious about the theft of Itzl Cha from beneath the sacred sacrificial knife. 'The temple has been defiled,' he growled, 'and the gods will be furious.'

'Perhaps not,' said Cit Coh Xiu, the King; 'perhaps after all that was indeed Che, Lord Forest.'

Chal Yip Xiu looked at the King, disgustedly. 'He was only one of the strangers that Xatl Din saw on the beach. If you would not arouse the anger of the gods, you should send a force of warriors to the camp of the strangers, to bring Itzl Cha back, for that is where she will be found.'

'Perhaps you are right,' said the King; 'at least it will do no harm,' and he sent for Xatl Din and ordered him to take a hundred warriors and go to the camp of the strangers and get Itzl Cha. 'With a hundred warriors, you should be able to kill many of them and bring back prisoners to Chichen Itza.'

Tibbet, with a boatload of sailors, was rowing out to the reef to continue the work of salvaging lumber from the Saigon, as the other members of the party came out for their breakfast. Itzl Cha sat silent and sullen, eating very little, for she had lost her appetite. Janette Laon came and sat beside de Groote, and Penelope Leigh looked at them down her nose.

'Is Patricia up yet, Janette?' asked the Colonel.

Janette looked around the company. 'Why, yes,' she said, 'isn't she here? She was gone when I woke up.'

'Where in the world can that girl be?' demanded Penelope Leigh.

'Oh, she must be nearby,' said the Colonel, but, as he called her name aloud, it was evident that he was perturbed.

'And that creature is gone too!' exclaimed Mrs Leigh. 'I knew that something terrible like this was going to happen sooner or later, William, if you permitted that man to remain in camp.'

'Now, just what has happened, Penelope?' asked the Colonel.

'Why he's abducted her, that's what's happened.'

Lum Kip, who was putting a platter of rice on the table, overheard the conversation and volunteered, 'Tarzan, she, go that way,' pointing toward the Northeast; 'Plateecie, him go that way,' and pointed in the same direction.

'Maybe Pat abducted him,' suggested Algy.

'Don't be ridiculous, Algernon,' snapped Mrs Leigh. 'It is quite obvious what happened – the creature enticed her into the jungle.'

'They talked long,' said Itzl Cha, sullenly. 'They go different times; they meet in jungle.'

'How can you sit there, William, and permit that Indian girl to intimate that your niece arranged an assignation in the jungle with that impossible creature.'

'Well,' said the Colonel, 'if Pat's in the jungle, I pray to high heaven that Tarzan is with her.'

Pat followed a stream that ran for a short distance in a Northeasterly direction, and when it turned southeast, she continued to follow it, not knowing that Tarzan had taken to the trees and was swinging rapidly through them almost due east toward the other side of the island. The ground rose rapidly now, and the little stream tumbled excitedly down toward the ocean. Pat realized that she was being a stubborn fool, but, being stubborn, she decided to climb the mountain a short distance to get a view of the island. It was a hard climb, and the trees constantly shut out any view, but the girl kept on until she came to a level ledge which ran around a shoulder of the mountain. As she was pretty well winded by this time, she sat down to rest.

'I should think some of you men would go out and look for Patricia,' said Mrs Leigh.

'I'll go,' said Algy, 'but I don't know where to look for the old girl.'

'Who's that coming along the beach?' said Dr Crouch.

'Why it's Krause and Schmidt,' said Bolton. 'Yes, and Oubanovitch and the Arab are with him.' Almost automatically the men loosened their pistols in their holsters and waited in silence as the four approached.

The men about the breakfast table had all risen and were waiting expectantly. Krause came to the point immediately. 'We've come to ask you to let us come back and camp near you,' he said. 'We have no firearms and no protection where we are. Two of our men have gone into the jungle and never returned, and two have been taken right out of camp by lions at night. You certainly must have a heart, Colonel; you certainly won't subject fellow men to such dangers needlessly. If you will take us back, we promise to obey you and not cause any trouble.'

'I'm afraid it will cause a lot of trouble when Tarzan returns and finds you here,' said the Colonel.

'You should let them remain, William,' said Mrs Leigh. 'You are in command here, not that Tarzan creature.'

'I really think it would be inhuman to send them away,' said Dr Crouch.

'They were inhuman to us,' said Janette Laon bitterly.

'Young woman,' exploded Penelope, 'you should be taught your place; you have nothing to say about this. The Colonel will decide.'

Janette Laon shook her head hopelessly and winked at de Groote. Penelope saw the wink and exploded again. 'You are an insolent baggage,' she said; 'you and the Indian girl and that Tarzan creature should never have been permitted in the same camp with gentlefolk.'

'If you will permit me, Penelope,' said the Colonel stiffly, 'I think that I can handle this matter without assistance or at least without recrimination.'

'Well, all that I have to say,' said Penelope, 'is that you must let them remain.'

'Suppose,' suggested Crouch, 'that we let them remain anyway until Tarzan returns; then we can discuss the matter with him – they are more his enemies than ours.'

'They are enemies to all of us,' said Janette.

'You may remain, Krause,' said the Colonel, 'at least, until Tarzan returns; and see that you behave yourselves.'

'We certainly shall, Colonel,' replied Krause, 'and thank you for letting us stay.'

Patricia got a view of the ocean from the ledge where she was sitting, but she could see nothing of the island; and so, after resting, she went on a little farther. It was far more open here and very beautiful, orchids clung in gorgeous sprays to many a tree, and ginger and hibiscus grew in profusion; birds with yellow plumage and birds with scarlet winged from tree to tree. It was an idyllic, peaceful scene which soothed her nerves and obliterated the last vestige of her anger.

She was glad that she had found this quiet spot and was congratulating herself, and planning that she would come to it often, when a great tiger walked out of the underbrush and faced her. The tip of his tail was twitching nervously, and his snarling muscles had drawn his lips back from his great yellow fangs.

Patricia Leigh-Burden breathed a silent prayer as she threw her rifle to her shoulder and fired twice in rapid succession.

XXI

'I certainly do not like the idea of having those men around here all the time,' said Janette; 'I am afraid of them, especially Krause.'

'I'll look after him,' said de Groote. 'Let me know if he ever makes any advances.'

'And now look!' exclaimed Janette, pointing along the beach. 'Here come all those Lascars back, too. Those fellows give me the creeps.'

As she ceased speaking, the report of two rifle shots came faintly but distinctly to their ears. 'That must be Patricia!' exclaimed the Colonel. 'She must be in trouble.'

'She has probably had to shoot that creature,' said Penelope hopefully.

The Colonel had run to his hut and gotten his rifle; and when he started in the direction from which the sound of the shot had come, he was followed by de Groote, Algy, Crouch, and Bolton.

As the foliage of the jungle closed about Bolton's back, Schmidt turned to Krause and grinned. 'What's funny?' demanded the latter.

'Let's see what we can find in the way of rifles and ammunition,' said Schmidt to the other three men. 'This looks like our day.'

'What are you men doing?' demanded Penelope Leigh. 'Don't you dare go into those huts.'

Janette started to run toward her hut to get her rifle, but Schmidt overtook her and hurled her aside. 'No funny business,' he warned.

The four men collected all the remaining firearms in the camp and then, at pistol points forced the Lascars to load up with such stores as Schmidt desired.

'Pretty good haul,' he said to Krause. 'I think we've got about everything we want now.'

'Maybe you have, but I haven't,' replied the animal collector; then he walked over to Janette. 'Come along, sweetheart,' he said; 'we're going to start all over again right where we left off.'

'Not I,' said Janette, backing away.

Krause seized one of her arms. 'Yes, you; and if you know what's good for you, you'd better not make any trouble.'

The girl tried to pull away, and Krause struck her. 'For heaven's sake, go along with him,' cried Penelope Leigh. 'Don't make a scene; I hate scenes. Anyway, you belong with him; you certainly have never belonged in my camp.'

Half-stunned by the blow, Janette was dragged away; and the Colonel's wife watched them start back along the beach in the direction from which they had come.

'The Colonel shall hear about your stealing our stores, you scoundrels,' she called after them.

Xatl Din and his hundred warriors came through the forest spread out in open order, that they might leave no well-marked trail; and as they came, they heard two sharp, loud sounds which seemed to come from but a short distance ahead of them. None of these men had ever heard the report of a firearm before, and so they had no idea of what it was. They crept cautiously forward, their eyes and ears constantly alert. Xatl Din was in the lead, and as he came to a more open place in the forest, he stopped suddenly, for a strange and unaccustomed sight met his eye. On the ground lay a huge, striped beast, such as he had never seen before. It was evidently dead, and above it stood a figure strangely garbed, who held a long black shiny thing that was neither bow, arrow, nor spear.

Presently Xatl Din realized that the creature was a woman; and, being an intelligent man, he surmised that the noise he had heard had come from that strange thing she held, and that with it, she had doubtless killed the huge beast which lay at her feet. Xatl Din further reasoned that if she could have killed so large and evidently ferocious an animal, she could even more easily kill men; and, therefore, he did not come out into the open, but withdrew and gave whispered instructions to his men.

Now the Mayans slipped silently around through the jungle until they had encircled Patricia, and then while Xatl Din beat on a tree with his sword to make a noise that would attract the girl's attention in his direction, two of his men slipped out of the jungle behind her, and crept noiselessly toward her.

As Patricia stood looking in the direction from which the sound had come, listening intently, arms were thrown around her from behind and her rifle was snatched from her hands; then a hundred strangely garbed warriors, resplendent in feathered headdresses and embroidered loincloths came running from the jungle to surround her.

Patricia recognized these men immediately, not only from the descriptions she had had from Itzl Cha and Tarzan, but also because she had read a great deal concerning the civilization of the ancient Mayans. She was as familiar with their civilization, their religion, and their culture as the extensive research of many archaeological expeditions had been able to bring to light. It seemed to her that she had been suddenly carried back centuries to a long dead past, to which these little brown men belonged. She knew what her capture meant to her, for she knew the fate of Mayan prisoners. Her only hope lay in the possibility that the men of her party might be able to rescue her, and that hope was strong because of her faith in Tarzan.

'What are you going to do with me?' she said in the broken Mayan she had learned from Itzl Cha.

'That is for Cit Coh Xiu to decide,' he said. 'I shall send you back to Chichen Itza, back to the palace of the King.' Then he instructed four of his warriors to take the prisoner to Cit Coh Xiu.

As Patricia was led away, Xatl Din and his remaining warriors continued on in the direction of Camp Saigon. The noble was quite pleased with himself. Even if he were not successful in bringing Itzl Cha back to Chichen Itza, he had at least furnished another sacrifice in her stead, and he would doubtless be praised by both the King and the high priest.

*

Colonel Leigh and his companions followed, quite by accident, the same trail by which Patricia had come. They climbed the ledge which ran around the shoulder of the mountain; and, although badly winded, kept on almost at a run. Their advance was noisy and without caution, for their one thought was to find Patricia as quickly as possible; and when they were suddenly met by a band of plumed warriors, they were taken wholly by surprise. With savage war cries, the Mayans charged, hurling stones from their slings.

'Fire over their heads!' commanded the Colonel.

The terrifying noise momentarily stopped the Mayans, but when Xatl Din realized that it was only noise and that it had not injured any of his men, he ordered them to charge again; and once more their hideous war cries sounded in the ears of the whites.

'Shoot to kill!' snapped the Colonel; 'We've got to stop those beggars before they reach us with their swords.'

The rifles barked again, and four warriors fell. The others wavered, but Xatl Din urged them on.

These things that killed with a loud noise at a distance terrified the Mayans; and although some of them almost came to grips with the whites, they finally turned and fled, taking their wounded with them. Following their strategy, they scattered through the jungle so as to leave no well-marked trail to their city; and the whites, going in the wrong direction, became lost, for it is diffi-cult to orient one's self in a dense jungle; and when they came to a steep declivity down a mountain side, they thought that they had crossed the mountain and were descending the opposite slope.

After stumbling about in dense shrubbery for an hour, they came sud-denly to the end of the jungle, only to stand looking at one another in amazement, for before them lay the beach and their own camp.

'Well, I'll be damned!' ejaculated the Colonel.

As they approached the camp, Tibbet came to meet them, a troubled look on his face.

'Something wrong, Tibbet?' demanded the Colonel.

'I'll say there's something wrong, Sir. I just came back from the Saigon with a load of planks to find that Schmidt and his outfit have stolen all the fire-arms and ammunition that were left in camp, as well as a considerable part of our stores.'

'The scoundrels!' ejaculated the Colonel.

'But that's not the worst of it,' continued Tibbet; 'they took Miss Laon away with them.'

De Groote went white. 'Which way did they go, Tibbet?' he asked.

'Back up the beach,' replied the second mate; 'probably to their old camp.'

De Groote, heartbroken and furious, started away. 'Wait,' said the Colonel; 'where are you going?'

'I'm going after them,' he said.

'They are all heavily armed,' said the Colonel; 'you couldn't do anything alone, and we can't spare men to go with you now – that is, we couldn't all go and leave Mrs Leigh alone here again, with the chance that those painted devils may attack the camp at any time.'

'I'm going anyway,' said de Groote doggedly.

'I'll go with you,' said Tibbet, and then two of the sailors from the Naiad also volunteered.

'I wish you luck,' said the Colonel, 'but for heaven's sake be careful. You'd better sneak up on the camp from the jungle side and snipe them from the concealment of the underbrush.'

'Yes, Sir,' replied de Groote, as he and the three who had volunteered to accompany him started up the beach at a dogtrot.

XXII

From a distance, Tarzan heard the firing during the encounter between the whites and the Mayans, and immediately turned and started back in the direction from which he thought the sounds came; but because of the echoes and reverberations caused by the mountains, he failed to locate it correctly, and went in the wrong direction. Also, he was misled by his assumption that any fighting there might be would naturally be around Camp Saigon or Schmidt's camp.

Knowing that he was nearer Schmidt's camp then Camp Saigon, he decided to go there first and follow along the beach to Camp Saigon, if the fight were not at the former place.

As he approached the end of the forest opposite Schmidt's camp, he went more slowly and carefully, and it was well that he did for as he came in view of the camp, he saw the men returning and that the four whites were heavily armed. He saw Janette Laon being dragged along by Krause, and the Lascars bearing loads. He knew what had happened: but how it had happened, he could not guess. He naturally assumed that the shooting he had heard had marked an engagement between these men and those at Camp Saigon, and the inference was that Schmidt's party had been victorious. Perhaps all the other whites had been killed, but where was Patricia? Where was little Itzl Cha? He was not concerned over the fate of Penelope Leigh.

The Colonel was on the horns of a dilemma. The camp could boast of only four armed men now, scarcely enough to defend it; and he couldn't go out to search for Patricia and leave Penelope unguarded, nor could he divide his little force, for even four men would scarcely be enough to repel another attack by Schmidt or by the Mayans if they came in force, nor could four men hope successfully to storm the city of Chichen Itza to which he was convinced Patricia had been taken. And as the Colonel sought in vain for a solution of his problem, Patricia Leigh-Burden was led into the throne room of Cit Coh Xiu, King of Uxmal Island, and the leader of her escort addressed the King.

'The noble Xatl Din ordered us to bring this prisoner to his King and Master, as Xatl Din and his warriors continued on to attack the camp of the strangers. There was a battle, for we heard the strange noises with which these white men kill, but how the battle went we do not know.'

The King nodded. 'Xatl Din has done well,' he said.

'He has done excellently,' said Chal Yip Xiu, the high priest; 'this woman will make a fitting offering to our gods.'

Cit Coh Xiu's eyes appraised the white girl and found her beautiful. She was the first white woman that he had ever seen, and it suddenly occurred to him that it would be a shame to give her to some god that might not want her. He didn't dare say so aloud, but he thought that the girl was far too beautiful for any god; and, as a matter of fact, by the standards of any race, Patricia Leigh-Burden was beautiful.

'I think,' said the King, 'that I shall keep her as one of my handmaidens for a while.'

Chal Yip Xiu, the high priest, looked at the King in well-simulated surprise. As a matter of fact, he was not surprised at all, for he knew his King, who had already robbed the gods of several pulchritudinous offerings. 'If she is chosen for the gods,' he said, 'the gods will be angry with Cit Coh Xiu if he keeps her for himself.'

'Perhaps it would be well,' said the King, 'if you were to see that she is not chosen – at least immediately. I don't think the gods want her anyway,' he added.

Patricia, listening intently, had been able to understand at least the gist of this conversation. 'A god has already chosen me,' she said, 'and he will be angry if you harm me.'

Cit Coh Xiu looked at her in surprise. 'She speaks the language of the Maya,' he said to the high priest.

'But not very well,' commented Chal Yip Xiu.

'The gods speak their own language,' said Patricia; 'they have little use for the language of mortals.'

'Can it be that she is a goddess?' demanded the King.

'I am the mate of Che, Lord Forest,' said Patricia. 'He is already very angry with you for the way you treated him when he came to Chichen Itza. If you are wise, you will send me back to him. If you don't, he will certainly destroy you.'

The King scratched his head and looked at his high priest questioningly. 'Well,' he said, 'you should know all about gods, Chal Yip Xiu; was it indeed Che, Lord Forest, who came to Chichen Itza? Was it a god that you put in a wooden cage? Was it a god who stole the offering from the sacrificial altar?'

'It was not,' snapped the high priest; 'he was only a mortal.'

'Nevertheless, we must not act hastily,' said the King. 'You may keep the girl temporarily; have her taken to the Temple of the Virgins, and see that she is well treated;' so Chal Yip Xiu summoned two lesser priests and told them to conduct the prisoner to the Temple of the Virgins.

Patricia felt that while she had not made much of an impression on the high priest, she had upon the King, and that at least she had won a reprieve which might give Tarzan and the others time in which to rescue her; and as she was lead from the Palace, her mind was sufficiently at ease to permit her to note the wonders of Chichen Itza.

Before her loomed a mighty pyramid of lava blocks, and up the steep stairs on one side of this, she was led to an ornately carved temple at the summit – the Temple of the Virgins. Here she was turned over to the high priestess who was in charge of the temple, in which were housed some fifty girls, mostly of noble families; for it was considered an honor to volunteer for this service. They kept the sacred fires alight and swept the temple floors. When they wished to, they might resign and marry; and they were always sought after by warriors and nobles.

Patricia stood in the temple colonnade and looked out over the city of Chichen Itza. She could see its palaces and temples clustered about the foot of the pyramid and the thatched huts of the common people beyond the wall, and beyond these the fields which extended to the edge of the jungle; and she fancied that she had been carried back many centuries to ancient Yucatan.

As Tarzan watched through the concealing verdure of the forest, he realized the futility of attempting to come out in the open and face four heavily armed men, while he was armed with only a bow. But Tarzan had ways of his own, and he was quite secure in the belief that he could take Janette away from these men without unnecessarily risking his own life.

He waited until they had come closer and the Lascars had thrown down their loads; then he fitted an arrow to his bow, and bending the latter until the point of the arrow rested against his left thumb, he took careful aim. The bow string twanged; and, an instant later, Krause screamed and pitched forward upon his face, an arrow through his heart.

The others looked about in consternation. 'What happened?' demanded Oubanovitch; 'What's the matter with Krause?'

'He's dead,' said Schmidt; 'someone shot him with an arrow.'

'The ape-man,' said Abdullah Abu Néjm; 'who else could have done it?'

'Where is he?' demanded Schmidt.

'Here I am,' said Tarzan, 'and I have plenty more arrows. Come straight toward my voice, Janette, and into the forest; and if anyone tries to stop you, he'll get what Krause got.'

Janette walked quickly toward the forest, and no hand was raised to detain her.

'That damn wild man!' ejaculated Schmidt, and then he broke into a volley of lurid profanity. 'I'll get him! I'll get him!' he screamed, and, raising his rifle, fired into the forest in the direction from which Tarzan's voice had come.

Again the bow string twanged; and Schmidt, clutching at an arrow in his chest, dropped to his knees and then rolled over on his side, just as Janette entered the forest, and Tarzan dropped to the ground beside her.

'What happened at the camp?' he asked, and she told him briefly.

'So they let Schmidt and his gang come back,' said Tarzan. 'I am surprised at the Colonel.'

'It was mostly the fault of that horrid old woman,' said Janette.

'Come,' said Tarzan, 'we'll get back there as quickly as we can,' and swinging Janette to his shoulder, he took to the trees. As he and Janette approached Camp Saigon, de Groote, Tibbet, and the two sailors came into sight of Schmidt's camp.

A quick glance around the camp did not reveal Janette, but de Groote saw two men lying on the ground, and the Lascars huddled to one side, apparently terrified.

Abdullah was the first to see de Groote and his party, and knowing that they had come for revenge and would show no quarter, he swung his rifle to his shoulder and fired. He missed, and de Groote and Tibbet ran forward, firing, the two sailors, armed only with gaffs, at their heels.

Several shots were exchanged without any casualties, and then de Groote dropped to one knee and took careful aim, and Tibbet followed his example. 'Take Oubanovitch,' said de Groote; 'I'll get the Arab.'

The two rifles spoke almost simultaneously, and Oubanovitch and Abdullah Abu Néjm dropped in their tracks.

De Groote and Tibbet ran forward, followed by the sailors, ready to finish off any of the men who still showed fight; but the Russian, the Arab, and Krause were dead, and Schmidt was writhing and screaming in agony, helpless to harm them.

De Groote bent over him. 'Where is Miss Laon?' he demanded.

Screaming and cursing, his words almost unintelligible, Schmidt mumbled, 'The wild man, damn him, he took her;' and then he died.

'Thank God!' ejaculated de Groote; 'She's safe now.'

The four took the arms and ammunition from the bodies of the dead men, and with the authority which they gave them, forced the Lascars to pick up their packs and start back toward Camp Saigon.

XXIII

As Tarzan and Janette stepped from the jungle and approached the camp, they were greeted by a disheartened and hopeless company, only one of whom found anything to be thankful for. It was Penelope Leigh. When she saw them, she said to Algy, 'At least Patricia was not with that creature.'

'Oh, come now, Aunt Pen,' said Algy impatiently; 'I suppose you will say now that Tarzan and Janette arranged all this so that they could meet in the jungle.'

'I should not have been at all surprised,' replied Mrs Leigh. 'A man who would carry on with an Indian girl might do anything.'

Tarzan was disgusted with all that had been happening during his absence, largely because his orders had been disobeyed, but he only said, 'They should never have been permitted within pistol shot of this camp.'

'It was my fault,' said Colonel Leigh; 'I did it against my better judgment, because it did seem inhuman to send them back there unarmed, with a man-eater hanging around their camp.'

'It was not the Colonel's fault,' said Janette, furiously; 'he was nagged into it. That hateful old woman is most to blame. She insisted; and now, because of her, Hans may be killed.' Even as she ceased speaking, they heard the distant reports of firearms, coming faintly from the direction of Schmidt's camp. 'There!' cried Janette; then she turned on Mrs Leigh: 'If anything happens to Hans, his blood is on your head!' she cried.

'What has been done has been done,' said Tarzan; 'the important thing now is to find Patricia. Are you positive that she was captured by the Maya?'

'We heard two shots,' explained the Colonel, 'and when we went to investigate, we were met by fully a hundred Maya warriors. We dispersed them, but were unable to follow their trail; and although we saw nothing of Patricia, it seems most probable that she had been captured by them before we met them.'

'And now, William, I hope you are satisfied,' said Mrs Leigh; 'it is all your fault, for coming on that silly expedition in the first place.'

'Yes, Penelope,' said the Colonel resignedly, 'I suppose that it is all my fault, but telling me that over and over again doesn't help matters any.'

Tarzan took Itzl Cha aside to talk to her away from the interruptions of the others. 'Tell me, Itzl Cha,' he said, 'what your people would probably do with Patricia.'

'Nothing, two, three days, maybe month,' replied the girl; 'then they offer her to a god.'

'Look at that creature now,' said Penelope Leigh, 'taking that little Indian girl off and whispering to her. I can well imagine what he is saying.'

'Would they put Patricia in the cage where they had me?' Tarzan asked.

'I think in the Temple of the Virgins at the top of the sacred pyramid; Temple of the Virgins very sacred place and well guarded.'

'I can reach it,' said Tarzan.

'You are not going there?' demanded Itzl Cha.

'Tonight,' said Tarzan.

The girl threw her arms about him. 'Please don't go,' she begged; 'you cannot save her, and they will kill you.'

'Look!' exclaimed Penelope Leigh; 'Of all the brazen things I've ever seen in my life! William, you must put a stop to it. I cannot stand it; I have never before had to associate with loose people,' and she cast a venomous glance at Janette.

Tarzan disengaged the girl's arms. 'Come, come, Itzl Cha,' he said; 'I shall not be killed.'

'Don't go,' she pleaded. 'Oh, Che, Lord Forest, I love you. Take me away into the forest with you. I do not like these people.'

'They have been very kind to you,' Tarzan reminded her.

'I know,' said Itzl Cha sullenly, 'but I do not want their kindness; I want only you, and you must not go to Chichen Itza tonight nor ever.'

Tarzan smiled and patted her shoulder. 'I go tonight,' he said.

'You love her,' cried Itzl Cha; 'that is the reason you are going. You are leaving me for her.'

'That will be all,' said Tarzan firmly. 'Say no more.' Then he left her and joined the others, and Cha, furious with jealously, went into her hut and threw herself upon the ground, kicking it with her sandaled feet and beating it with her little fists. Presently she arose and looked out through the doorway, just in time to see de Groote and his party returning, and while the attention of all the others was centered upon them, little Itzl Cha crept from her hut and ran into the jungle.

Janette ran forward and threw her arms about de Groote, tears of joy running down her cheeks. 'I thought that you had been killed, Hans,' she sobbed; 'I thought that you had been killed.'

'I am very much alive,' he said, 'and you have nothing more to fear from Schmidt and his gang; they are all dead.'

'I am glad,' said Tarzan; 'they were bad men.'

Little Itzl Cha ran through the jungle. She was terrified, for it was growing dark, and there are demons and the spirits of the dead in the forest at night; but she ran on, spurred by jealousy and hate and desire for revenge.

She reached Chichen Itza after dark, and the guard at the gate was not going to admit her until she told him who she was, and that she had important word for Chal Yip Xiu, the high priest. She was taken to him then, and she fell on her knees before him.

'Who are you?' he demanded, and then he recognized her. 'So you have come back,' he said. 'Why?'

'I came to tell you that the man who stole me from the sacrificial altar is coming tonight to take the white girl from the temple.'

'For this you deserve much from the gods,' said Chal Yip Xiu, 'and again you shall be honored by being offered to them,' and little Itzl Cha was placed in a wooden cage to await sacrifice.

Tarzan came slowly through the forest on his way to Chichen Itza. He did not wish to arrive before midnight, when he thought that the city would have quieted down and most of its inmates would be asleep. A gentle wind was blowing in his face, and it brought to his nostrils a familiar scent spoor – Tantor, the elephant, was abroad. He had found an easier trail to the plateau than the shorter one which Tarzan used, and he had also found on the plateau a plenteous supply of the tender shoots he loved best.

Tarzan did not call him until he had come quite close, and then he spoke in a low voice; and Tantor, recognizing his voice, came and verified his judgment by passing his trunk over the ape-man's body.

At a word of command, he lifted Tarzan to his withers, and the Lord of the Jungle rode to the edge of the forest just outside of the city of Chichen Itza.

Slipping from Tantor's head, Tarzan crossed the fields to the city wall. Before he reached it, he broke into a run, and when it loomed before him, he scaled it much as a cat would have done. The city was quiet and the streets were deserted; so that Tarzan reached the foot of the pyramid without encountering anyone.

Just inside the entrance to the Temple of the Virgins, a dozen warriors hid in the shadows as Tarzan climbed the steps to the summit. Outside the temple he stopped and listened; then he walked around to the lee side, so that the breeze that was blowing would carry to his sensitive nostrils the information that he wished.

He stood there for a moment; and then, satisfied, he crept stealthily around to the entrance. At the threshold he stopped again and listened; then he stepped inside, and as he did so a net was thrown over him and drawn tight, and a dozen warriors fell upon him and so entangled him in the meshes that he was helpless.

A priest stepped from the temple and, raising a trumpet to his lips, blew three long blasts. As by magic, the city awoke, lights appeared, and people came streaming towards the temple pyramid.

Tarzan was carried down the long flight of steps, and at the bottom, he was surrounded by priests in long embroidered cloaks and gorgeous headdresses. Then they brought Patricia. With trumpets and drums preceding them, Cit Coh Xiu, the King, and Chal Yip Xiu, the high priest, headed a procession that wound through the city and out of the east gate.

Tarzan had been placed on a litter that was carried by four priests; behind him walked Patricia, under guard; and behind her little Itzl Cha was carried in her wooden cage. A full moon cast its soft light on the barbaric procession, which was further illuminated by hundreds of torches carried by the marchers.

The procession wound through the forest to the foot of a mountain, up which it zig-zagged back and forth until it reached the rim of the crater of an extinct volcano at the summit. It was almost dawn as the procession made its way down a narrow trail to the bottom of the crater and stopped there at the edge of a yawning hole. Priests intoned a chant to the accompaniment of flutes, drums, and trumpets; and, just at dawn, the bag was cut away from Tarzan and he was hurled into the chasm, notwithstanding the pleas of Itzl Cha, who had repented and warned the priests that the man was really Che, Lord Forest. She had begged them not to kill him, but Chal Yip Xiu had silenced her and spoken the word that sent Tarzan to his doom.

XXIV

Patricia Leigh-Burden was not the type of girl easily moved to tears, but she stood now on the brink of that terrible abyss, her body racked by sobs; and then as the sun topped the rim and shed its light down into the crater, she saw Tarzan swimming slowly about in a pond some seventy feet below her. Instantly her mind leaped to the stories she had read of the sacred dzonot of ancient Chichen Itza in Yucatan, and hope burned again in her breast.

'Tarzan,' she called, and the man turned over on his back and looked up at her. 'Listen,' she continued. 'I know this form of sacrifice well; it was practiced by the Maya in Central America hundreds and hundreds of years ago.

The victim was thrown into the sacred well at Chichen Itza at dawn, and if he still lived at noon, he was taken out and raised to highest rank; he became practically a living god on earth. You must keep afloat until noon, Tarzan; you must! You must!'

Tarzan smiled up at her and waved. The priests eyed her suspiciously, though they had no idea what she had said to their victim.

'Do you think that you can, Tarzan?' she said. 'You must, because I love you.'

Tarzan did not reply, as he turned over and commenced to swim slowly around the pool, which was about a hundred feet in diameter with perpendicular sides of smooth volcanic glass.

The water was chilly but not cold, and Tarzan swam just strongly enough to keep from becoming chilled.

The people had brought food and drink; and as they watched through the long dragging hours, they made a fiesta of the occasion.

As the sun climbed toward zenith, Chal Yip Xiu commenced to show signs of strain and nervousness, for if the victim lived until noon, he might prove indeed to be Che, Lord Forest, which would be most embarrassing for the ah kin mai. Every eye that could see it was upon a crude sundial that stood beside the rim of the dzonot; and when it marked noon, a great shout arose, for the victim was still alive.

The high priest was furious as the people acclaimed Tarzan as Che, Lord Forest, and demanded that he be taken from the water. A long rope was thrown down to him, with a noose in the end of it by means of which he could be drawn out of the dzonot; but Tarzan ignored the noose and clambered up the rope, hand over hand. When he stepped out upon the rim, the people fell to their knees before him and supplicated him for forgiveness and for favors.

The King and the high priest looked most uncomfortable as Tarzan faced them. 'I came to earth in the form of a mortal,' he said, 'to see how you ruled my people of Chichen Itza. I am not pleased. I shall come again someday to see if you have improved. Now I go, and I take this woman with me,' and he placed a hand upon Patricia's arm. 'I command you to release Itzl Cha, and to see that neither she nor any others are sacrificed before I return.'

He took Patricia by the hand, and together they climbed the steep trail to the rim of the crater and then down the side of the volcano, the people following them, in a long procession, singing as they marched. As they reached the city, Tarzan turned and held up a hand. 'Come no farther,' he said to the people, and then to Patricia, 'Now I'll give them something to tell their grandchildren about.'

She looked up at him questioningly and smiled. 'What are you going to do?' she asked.

For answer, he voiced a long weird cry, and then, in the language of the great apes, shouted, 'Come, Tantor, come!' and as he and Patricia crossed the field and approached the forest, a great bull elephant came out of it to meet them, and a cry of astonishment and fear rose from the people behind them.

'Won't he gore us or something?' asked Patricia, as they approached the bull.

'He is my friend,' said Tarzan, laying his hand upon the trunk of the great beast. 'Don't be frightened,' he said to Patricia; 'he is going to lift you to his withers,' and at a word of command, Tantor swung the girl up and then lifted Tarzan.

As he wheeled to go into the forest, Tarzan and Patricia looked back to see the people of Chichen Itza all kneeling, their faces pressed against the ground.

'Their great-great-grandchildren will hear of this,' said Patricia.

In Camp Saigon, the discouraged company waited hopelessly for Tarzan's return. There had been little sleep the previous night for many of them, and the long hours of the morning had dragged heavily. Teatime came and Tarzan had not returned; but, as a matter of habit, they had tea served; and as they sat around the table, sipping it listlessly, the same thought must have been in the minds of all; they would never see Patricia or Tarzan again.

'You should never have let that creature go out after Patricia alone,' said Mrs Leigh; 'he probably found her all right, and there is no telling what has happened to her by this time.'

'Oh, Penelope!' cried the Colonel hopelessly. 'Why are you so bitter against that man? He has done nothing but befriend us.'

'Hmph!' exclaimed Penelope. 'You are very dense, William; I could see through him from the first – he is a climber; he wants to get into our good graces and then he will probably try to marry Patricia for the money she will inherit.'

'Madam,' said de Groote very icily, '"that creature," as you call him, is John Clayton, Lord Greystoke, an English viscount.'

'Bosh!' exclaimed Mrs Leigh.

'It is not bosh,' said de Groote; 'Krause told me who he was while we were locked up together in that cage. He got it from the Arab, who has known the man for years.'

Mrs Leigh's chin dropped, and she seemed to suddenly deflate, but she rallied quickly. 'I rather expected it,' she said after a moment. 'All that I ever criticized in him was his predilection for nudity. Why didn't you ever tell us this before, young man?'

'I don't know why I told you now,' replied de Groote; 'it is none of my business; if he had wanted us to know, he would have told us.'

'Here he comes now!' exclaimed Janette, 'And Patricia is with him!'

'How wonderful!' exclaimed Penelope. 'What a fine looking couple my niece and Lord Greystoke make.'

From the withers of the elephant, Patricia could see far out beyond the reef; and when she and Tarzan slipped to the ground, she ran toward the group awaiting them, pointing and crying, 'Look! A ship! A ship!'

It was a ship far out; and the men hastened to build a fire on the beach, and when it was burning, to throw on green leaves and kerosene until a great black smoke rose high into the sky.

De Groote and some of the sailors put out in one of the boats in a frantic, if potentially futile, effort to further attract the ship's attention.

'They don't see us,' said Janette.

'And there may not be another ship in a hundred years,' remarked Dr Crouch.

'Jolly long time to wait for anything, what?' said Algy.

'They've changed their course,' said Bolton; 'they're heading in.'

The Colonel had gone to his hut and now he came out with binoculars in his hand. He took a long look through them; and when he took the glasses down, there were tears in his eyes; and it was a moment before he could speak.

'It's the Naiad,' he said, 'and she *is* heading inshore.'

That night, under a full tropic moon, two couples lounged in comfortable chairs on the deck of the Naiad. Tarzan laid a hand on one of Patricia's. 'In your nervous excitement today at the dzonot, you said something, Patricia, that we must both forget.'

'I know what you mean,' she replied. 'You see, I didn't know then that it was impossible – but I meant it then, and I shall always mean it.'

'Tarzan!' called de Groote from the other side of the yacht. 'Janette is trying to convince me that the Captain can't marry us. She's wrong, isn't she?'

'I am quite sure that she is wrong,' replied the ape-man.

TARZAN AND THE CHAMPION

'Six – seven – eight – nine – *ten!*' The referee stepped to a neutral corner and hoisted Mullargan's right hand. 'The winnah and new champion!' he shouted.

For a moment the audience, which only partially filled Madison Square Garden, sat in stunned and stupefied silence; then there was a burst of applause, intermingled with which was an almost equal volume of boos. It wasn't that the booers questioned the correctness of the decision – they just didn't like Mullargan, a notoriously dirty fighter. Doubtless, too, many of them had had their dough on the champion.

Joey Marks, Mullargan's manager, and the other man who had been in his corner crawled through the ropes and slapped Mullargan on the back; photographers, sportswriters, police, and a part of the audience converged on the ring; jittery news-commentators bawled the epochal tidings to a waiting world.

The former champion, revived but a bit wobbly, crossed the ring and proffered a congratulatory hand to Mullargan. The new champion did not take the hand. 'Gwan, you bum,' he said, and turned his back …

'One-Punch' Mullargan had come a long way in a little more than a year – from amateur to preliminary fighter, to Heavyweight Champion of the World; and he had earned his sobriquet. He had, in truth, but one punch; and he needed but that one – a lethal right to the button. Sometimes he had had to wait several rounds before he found an opening, but eventually he had always found it. The former champion, a ten-to-one favorite at ringside, had gone down in the third round. Since then, One-Punch Mullargan had fought but nine rounds; yet he had successfully defended his championship six times, leaving three men with broken jaws and one with a fractured skull. After all, who wishes his skull fractured?

So One-Punch Mullargan decided to take a vacation and do something he always had wanted to do but which fate had always heretofore intervened to prevent. Several years before, he had seen a poster which read, 'JOIN THE NAVY AND SEE THE WORLD;' he had always remembered that poster; and now, with a vacation on his hands, Mullargan decided to go and see the world for himself, without any assistance from Navy or Marines.

'I ain't never seen Niag'ra Falls,' said his manager. 'That would be a nice place to go for a vacation. If we was to go there, that would give Niag'ra Falls a lot of publicity too.'

'Niag'ra Falls, my foot!' said Mullargan. 'We're goin' to Africa.'

'Africa,' mused Mr Marks. 'That's a hell of a long ways off – down in South America somewheres. Wot you wanna go there for?'

'Huntin'. You see them heads in that guy's house what we were at after the fight the other night, didn't you? Lions, buffaloes, elephants. Gee! That must be some sport.'

'We ain't lost no lions, kid,' said Marks. There was a note of pleading in his voice. 'Listen, kid: stick around here for a couple more fights; then you'll have enough potatoes to retire on, and you can go to Africa or any place you want to – but not me.'

'I'm goin' to Africa, and you're goin' with me. If you want to get some publicity out of it, you better call up them newspaper bums.'

Sports-writers and camera-men milled about the champion on the deck of the ship ten days later. Bulbs flashed; shutters clicked; reporters shot questions; passengers crowded closer with craning necks; a girl elbowed her way through the throng with an autograph album.

'When did *he* learn to write?' demanded a Daily *News* man.

'Wise guy,' growled Mullargan.

'Give my love to Tarzan when you get to Africa,' said another.

'And don't get fresh with him, or he'll take you apart,' interjected the Daily *News* man.

'I seen that bum in pitchers,' said Mullargan. 'He couldn't take nobody apart.'

'I'll lay you ten to one he could K.O. you in the first round,' taunted the Daily *News* man.

'You ain't got ten, you bum,' retorted the champion.

A heavily laden truck lumbered along the edge of a vast plain under the guns of the forest which had halted here, sending out a scattering of pickets to reconnoiter the terrain held by the enemy. Why the tree army never advanced, why the plain always held its own – these are mysteries.

And the lorry was a mystery to the man far out on the plain, who watched its slow advance. He knew that there were no tracks there, that perhaps since creation this was the first wheeled vehicle that had ever passed this way.

A white man in a disreputable sun-helmet drove the truck; beside him sat a black man; sprawled on top of the load were several other blacks. The lengthening shadow of the forest stretched far beyond the crawling anachronism, marking the approach of the brief equatorial twilight.

The man out upon the plain set his course so that he might meet the truck. He moved with an easy, sinuous stride that was almost catlike in its smoothness. He wore no clothes other than a loincloth; his weapons were primitive: a quiver of arrows and a bow at his back, a hunting-knife in a rude scabbard at his hip, a short, stout spear that he carried in his hand. Looped across one shoulder and beneath the opposite arm was a coil of grass rope. The man was very dark, but he was not a Negro. A lifetime beneath the African sun accounted for his bronzed skin.

Upon his shoulder squatted a little monkey, one arm around the bronzed neck. '*Tarmangani*, Nkima,' said the man, looking in the direction of the truck.

'*Tarmangani*,' chattered the monkey. 'Nkima and Tarzan will kill the *Tarmangani*.' He stood up and blew out his cheeks and looked very ferocious. At a great distance from an enemy, or when upon the shoulder of his Master, little Nkima was a lion at heart. His courage was in inverse ratio to the distance that separated him from Tarzan, and in direct ratio to that which lay between himself and danger. If little Nkima had been a man, he would probably have been a gangster and certainly a bully; but he still would have been a coward. Being just a little monkey, he was only amusing. He did, however, possess one characteristic which, upon occasion, elevated him almost to heights of sublimity. That was his self-sacrificing loyalty to his Master, Tarzan.

At last the man on the truck saw the man on foot, saw that they were going to meet a little farther on. He shifted his pistol to a more accessible position and loosened it in its holster. He glanced at the rifle that the boy beside him was holding between his knees, and saw that it was within easy reach. He had never been in this locality before, and did not know the temper of the natives. It was well to take precautions. As the distance between them lessened, he sought to identify the stranger.

'*Mtu mweusi?*' he inquired of the boy beside him, who was also watching the approaching stranger.

'*Mzungu, Bwana*,' replied the boy

'I guess you're right,' agreed the man. 'I guess he's a white man, all right, but he's sure dressed up like a native.'

'*Menyi wazimo*,' laughed the boy.

'I got two crazy men on my hands now,' said the man. 'I don't want another.' He brought the truck to a stop as Tarzan approached.

Little Nkima was chattering and scolding fiercely, baring his teeth in what he undoubtedly thought was a terrifying snarl. Nobody paid any attention to him, but he held his ground until Tarzan was within fifty feet of the truck; then he leaped to the ground and sought the safety of a tree nearby. After all, what was the use of tempting fate?

Tarzan stopped beside the truck and looked up into the white man's face. 'What are you doing here?' he asked.

Melton, looking down upon an almost naked man, felt his own superiority; and resented the impertinence of the query. Incidentally, he had noted that the stranger carried no firearms.

'I'm drivin' a lorry, buddy,' he said.

'Answer my question.' This time Tarzan's tone had an edge to it.

Melton had had a hard day. As a matter of fact, he had had a number of hard days. He was worried, and his nerves were on edge. His hand moved to the butt of his pistol as he formulated a caustic rejoinder, but he never voiced it. Tarzan's arm shot out; his hand seized Melton's wrist and dragged the man from the cab of the truck. An instant later he was disarmed.

Nkima danced up and down upon the branch of his tree and hurled jungle billingsgate at the enemy, intermittently screaming at Tarzan to kill the *Tarmangani*. No one paid any attention to him. That was a cross that Nkima always had to bear. He was so little and insignificant that no one ever paid any attention to him.

The blacks on the truck sat in wide-eyed confusion. The thing had happened so suddenly that it had caught their wits off guard. They saw the stranger dragging Melton away from the truck, shaking him as a dog shakes a rat. Tarzan had learned from experience that there is no surer way of reducing a man to subservience than by shaking him. Perhaps he knew nothing of the psychology of the truth, but he knew the truth.

The latter was a powerful man, but he was helpless in the grip of the stranger; and he was frightened, too. There was something more terrifying about this creature than his superhuman strength. There was the quite definite sensation of being in the clutches of a wild beast, so that his reactions were much the same as they had been many years before when he had been mauled by a lion – something of a fatalistic resignation to the inevitable.

Tarzan stopped shaking Melton and turned his eyes on the boy with the rifle, who had jumped down from the truck. 'Throw down the rifle,' he said in Swahili.

The boy hesitated. 'Throw it down,' ordered Melton; and then, to Tarzan: 'What do you want of me?'

'I asked you what you were doing here. I want an answer.'

'I'm guidin' a couple of bloomin' Yanks.'

'Where are they?'

Melton shrugged. 'Gawd only knows. They started out early this morning in a light car, and told me to keep along the edge of the forest. Said they'd come back an' meet me later in the day. They're probably lost. They're both balmy.'

'What are they doing here?' asked Tarzan.

'Hunting.'

'Why did you bring them here? This is closed territory.'

'I didn't bring 'em here; they brought me. You can't tell Mullargan nothing. He's one of those birds that knows it all. He don't need a guide; what he needs is a keeper. He's Heavyweight Champion of the World, and it's gone to his head. Try to tell him anything, and he's just as likely as not to slap you down. He's knocked the boys around something awful. I never saw such a rotten bounder in my life. The other one ain't so bad. He's Mullargan's manager. That's a laugh. Manager, my eye! All he says is, 'Yes, kid!' 'Okay, kid!' and all he wants to do is get back to New York. He's scared to death all the time. I wish to hell they was both back in New York. I wish I was rid of 'em.'

'Are they out alone?' asked Tarzan.

'Yes.'

'Then you may be rid of them. This is lion country. I have never seen them so bad.'

Melton whistled. 'Then I got to push on and try to find 'em. I don't like 'em, but I'm responsible for 'em. You' – he hesitated – 'you ain't goin' to try to stop me, are you?'

'No,' said Tarzan. 'Go and find them, and tell them to get out of this country and stay out.' Then he started on toward the forest.

When he had gone a short distance, Melton called to him. 'Who are you, anyway?' he demanded.

The ape-man paused and turned around. 'I am Tarzan,' he said.

Again Melton whistled. He climbed back into the cab of the truck and started the motor; and as the heavy vehicle got slowly under way, Tarzan disappeared into the forest.

The sun swung low into the west, and the lengthening shadow of the forest stretched far out into the plain. A light car bounced and jumped over the uneven ground. There were two men in the car. One of them drove, and the other braced himself and held on. His eyes were red-rimmed; he sneezed almost continuously.

'Fer cripe's sake, kid, can't you slow down?' wailed Marks. 'Ain't this hayfever bad enough without you tryin' to jounce the liver out of me?'

For answer Mullargan pressed the accelerator down a little farther.

'You won't have no springs or no tires or no manager, if you don't slow down.'

'I don't need no manager no more.' That struck Mullargan as being so funny that he repeated it. 'I don't need no manager no more; so I bounces him out in Africa. Gee, wouldn't dat give the guys a laugh!'

'Don't get no foolish ideas in your head, kid. You need a smart fella like me, all right. All you got is below them big cauliflower ears of yours.'

'Is zat so?'

'Yes, zat's so.'

Mullargan slowed down a little, for it had suddenly grown dark. He switched on the lights. 'It sure gets dark in a hurry here,' he commented. 'I wonder why.'

'It's the altitude, you dope,' explained Marks.

They rode on in silence for a while. Marks glanced nervously to right and left, for with the coming of night, the entire aspect of the scene had changed as though they had been suddenly tossed into a strange world. The plain was dimly lined in the ghostly light of pale stars; the forest was solid, impenetrable blackness.

'Forty-Second Street would look pretty swell right now,' observed Marks.

'So would some grub,' said Mullargan; 'my belly's wrapped around my backbone. I wonder what became of that so-an'-so. I told him to keep right on till he met us. Them English is too damn cocky – think they know it all, tellin' me not to do this an' not to do that. I guess the Champeen of the World can take care of himself, all right.'

'You said it, kid.'

The silence of the plain was broken by the grunting of a hunting lion. It was still some distance away, but the sound came plainly to the ears of the two men.

'What was that?' queried Mullargan.

'A pig,' said Marks.

'If it was daylight, we might get a shot at it,' observed Mullargan. 'A bunch of pork chops wouldn't go so bad right now. You know, Joey, I been thinkin' me and you could get along all right without that English so-an'-so.'

'Who'd drive the truck?'

'That's so,' admitted Mullargan; 'but he's got to stop treatin' us like we was a couple o' kids and he was our nurse-girl. Pretty soon I'm goin' to get sore and hand him one.'

'Look!' exclaimed Marks. 'There's a light – it must be the truck.'

When the two cars met, the tired men dropped to the ground and stretched stiffened limbs and cramped muscles.

'Where you been?' demanded Mullargan.

'Coming right along ever since we broke camp,' replied Melton. 'You know this bus can't cover the ground like that light car of yours, and you must have covered a lot of it today. Any luck?'

'No. I don't believe there's any game around here.'

'There's plenty. If you'll make a permanent camp somewhere, as I've been telling you, we'll get something.'

'We seen some buffaloes today,' said Marks, 'but they got away.'

'They went into some woods,' explained Mullargan. 'I followed 'em in on foot, but they got away.'

'Lucky for you they did,' observed Melton.

'What you mean – lucky for me?'

'If you'd shot one of 'em, you'd probably have been killed. I'd rather face a lion any day than a wounded buffalo.'

'Maybe you would,' said Mullargan, 'but I ain't afraid of no cow.'

Melton shrugged, turned and set the boys to making camp. 'We've got to camp where we are,' he said to the other two whites. 'We couldn't find water now; and we've got enough anyway, such as it is. Anyway, tomorrow we must turn back.'

'Turn back?' exclaimed Mullargan. 'Who says we gotta turn back? I come here to hunt, an' I'm goin' to hunt.'

'I met a man back there a way who says this is closed territory. He told me we'd have to get out.'

'Oh, he did, did he? Who the hell does he think he is, tellin' me to get out? Did you tell him who I was?'

'Yes, but he didn't seem to be much impressed.'

'Well, I'll impress him if I see him. Who was he?'

'His name is Tarzan.'

'Dat bum? Does he think he can run me out of Africa?'

'If he tells you to leave this part of Africa, you'd better,' Melton advised.

'I'll leave when I get good an' damn' ready,' said Mullargan.

'I'm ready to go right now,' said Marks, between sneezes. 'This here Africa ain't no place for a guy with hay fever.'

The boys were unloading the truck, hurrying to make camp. One was building a fire preparatory to cooking supper. There was much laughter, and now and then a snatch of native song. One of the boys, carrying a heavy load from the truck, accidentally bumped into Mullargan and threw him off balance. The fighter swung a vicious blow at the black with his open palm, striking him across the side of his head and knocking him to the ground.

'You'll look where you're goin' next time,' he growled.

Melton came up to him. 'That'll be all of that,' he said. 'I've stood it as long as I'm goin' to. Don't ever hit another of these boys.'

'So you're lookin' for it too, are you?' shouted Mullargan. 'All right, you're goin' to get it.'

Before he could strike, Melton drew his pistol and covered him. 'Come on,' he invited. 'I'm just waitin' for the chance to plead guilty to killin' you in self-defense.'

Mullargan stood staring at the gun for several seconds; then he turned away. Later he confided to Marks: 'Them English ain't got no sense of humor. He might of seen I was just kiddin'.'

The evening meal was a subdued affair. Conversation could not accurately have been said to lag, since it did not even exist until the meal was nearly over; then the grunting of a lion was heard close to the camp.

'There's that pig again,' said Mullargan. 'Maybe we can get him now.'

'What pig?' asked Melton.

'You must be deaf,' said Mullargan. 'Can't you hear him?'

'Cripes!' exclaimed Marks. 'Look at his eyes shine out there.'

Melton rose and stepping to the side of the truck switched on the spotlight and swung it around upon the eyes. In the circle of bright light stood a full-grown lion. Just for a moment he stood there; then he turned and slunk off into the darkness.

'Pig!' said Mullargan, disgustedly.

A chocolate-colored people are the Babangos, with good features and well-shaped heads. Their teeth are not filed; yet they are inveterate man-eaters. There are no religious implications in their cannibalism, no superstitions. They eat human flesh because they like it, because they prefer it to any other food; and like true gourmets, they know how to prepare it. They hunt man as other men hunt game animals, and they are hated and feared throughout the territory that they raid.

Recently, word had been brought to Tarzan that the Babangos had invaded a remote portion of that vast domain which, from boyhood, he had considered his own; and Tarzan had come, making many marches, to investigate. Behind him, moving more slowly, came a band of his own white-plumed Waziri warriors, led by Muviro, their famous chief ...

It was the morning following Tarzan's encounter with Melton. The ape-man was swinging along just inside the forest at the edge of the plain, his every sense alert. There was no slightest suggestion of caution in his free stride and confident demeanor; yet he moved as silently as a shadow. He saw the puff adder in the grass and the python waiting in the tree to seize its prey from above, and he avoided them. He made a little detour, lest he pass beneath a trumpet tree from which black ants might drop upon and sting him.

Presently he halted and turned, looking back along the edge of the forest and the plain. Neither you nor I could have heard what he heard, because our lives have not depended to a great extent upon the keenness of our hearing. There are wild beasts which have notoriously poor eyesight, but none with poor hearing or a deficient sense of smell. Tarzan, being a man and therefore poorly equipped by nature to survive in his savage world, had developed all his senses to an extraordinary degree; and so it was that now he heard pounding hoofs in the far distance long before you or I could have. And he heard another sound – a sound as strange to that locale as would be the after-kill roar of a lion on Park Avenue: the exhaust of a motor.

They were coming closer now; and they were coming fast. And now there came another sound, drowning out the first – the staccato of a machine gun. Presently they tore past him – a herd of zebra; and clinging to their flank was a light car. One man drove, and the other pumped lead from a submachine gun into the fleeing herd. Zebra fell, some killed, some only maimed; but the car sped on, its occupants ignoring the suffering beasts in its wake.

Tarzan, helpless to prevent it, viewed the slaughter in cold anger. He had witnessed the brutality of game-hogs before, but never anything like this. His estimate of man, never any too high, reached nadir. He went out into the plain and mercifully put out of their misery those of the animals which were hopelessly wounded, following the trail of destruction in the direction that the car had taken. Eventually he would come upon the two men again, and there would be an accounting.

Far ahead of him, the survivors of the terrified herd plunged into a rock gully; and clambering up the opposite side, disappeared over the ridge as Mullargan brought the car to a stop near the bottom.

'Gee!' he exclaimed. 'Was dat sport! When I gets all my heads up on a wall, I'll make that Park Avenue guy look like a piker.'

'You sure cleaned 'em up, kid,' said Marks. 'That was some shootin'.'

'I wasn't an expert rifleman in the Marine Corps for nothin', Joey. Now if I could just run into a flock of lions – boy!'

The forest came down into the head of the gorge, and the trees grew thickly to within a hundred yards of the car. There was a movement among the trees there, but neither of the dull-witted men were conscious of it. They had lighted cigars and were enjoying a few moments of relaxation.

'I guess we better start back an' mop up,' said Mullargan. 'I don't want to lose none of 'em. Say, at this rate I ought to take back about a thousand heads if we put in a full month. I'll sure give them newspaper bums somep'n to write about when I get home. I'll have one of them photographer bums take my pitcher settin' on top of a thousand heads – all kinds. That'll get in every newspaper in the U.S.'

'It sure will, kid,' agreed Marks. 'We'll sure give Africa a lot of publicity.' As he spoke, his eyes were on the forest up the gorge. Suddenly his brows knitted. 'Say, kid, lookit! What's that?'

Mullargan looked, and then cautiously picked up the machine gun. 'S-s-sh!' he cautioned. 'That's an elephant. What luck!' He raised the muzzle of the weapon and squeezed the trigger. An elephant trumpeted and lurched out into the open. It was followed by another and another, until seven of the great beasts were coming toward them; then the gun jammed.

'Hell!' exclaimed Mullargan. 'They'll get away before I can clear this.'

'They ain't goin' away,' said Marks. 'They're comin' for us.'

The elephants, poor of eyesight, finally located the car. Their trunks and their great ears went up, as, trumpeting, they charged; but by that time Mullargan had cleared the gun and was pouring lead into them again. One elephant went down. Others wavered and turned aside. It was too much for them – too much for all but one, a great bull, which, maddened by the pain of many wounds, carried the charge home.

The sound of the machine gun ceased. Mullargan threw the weapon down in disgust. 'Beat it, Joey!' he yelled; 'The drum's empty.'

The two men tumbled over the opposite side of the car as the bull struck it. The weight of the great body, the terrific impact, rolled the car over, wheels up. The bull staggered and lurched forward, falling across the chassis, dead.

The two men came slowly back. 'Gee!' said Mullargan. 'Look wot he went an' done to that jalopy! Henry wouldn't never recognize it now.' He got down on his hands and knees and tried to peer underneath the wreck.

Marks was shaking like an aspen. 'Suppose he hadn't of croaked,' he said; 'where would we of been? Wot we goin' to do now?'

'We gotta wait here until the truck comes. Our guns is all underneath that mess. Maybe the truck can drag the big bum off. We gotta have our guns.'

'I wish to Gawd I was back on Broadway,' said Marks, sneezing, 'where there ain't no elephants or no hay.'

Little Nkima was greatly annoyed. In the first place, the blast of the machine gun had upset him. It had frightened him so badly that he had abandoned the sanctuary of his Lord and Master's shoulder and scampered to the uttermost pinnacle of a nearby tree. When Tarzan had gone out on the plain, he had followed; and he didn't like it at all out on the plain, because the fierce African sun beat down, and there was no protection. And he was further annoyed because he had continued to hear the nerve-shattering sound intermittently for quite some time, and it came from the direction in which they were going. As he scampered along behind, he scolded his Master; for little Nkima saw no sense in looking for trouble in a world in which there was already more than enough looking for you.

Tarzan had heard the sound of the gunning, the squeals of hurt elephants and the trumpeting of angry elephants; and he visualized the brutal tragedy as clearly as though he saw it with his eyes; and his anger rose so that he forgot the law of the white man, for Tantor the elephant was his best friend. It was a wild beast, a killer, that set out at a brisk trot in the direction from which the sounds had come.

The sounds that had come to the ears of Tarzan and the ears of Nkima had come also to other ears in the dense forest beyond the gorge. Their owners were slinking through the shaded gloom on silent, stealthy feet to reconnoiter. They came warily, for they knew the sounds meant white men; and many white men with guns were bad medicine. They hoped that there were not too many.

As Tarzan reached the edge of the gorge and looked down upon the scene below, other eyes looked down from the opposite side.

These other eyes saw Tarzan; but the trees and the underbrush hid them from him, and the wind being at his back, their scent was not carried to his nostrils.

Of the two men in the gorge, Marks was the first to see Tarzan. He called Mullargan's attention to him, and the two men watched the ape-man descending slowly toward them. Nkima, sensing trouble, remained at the summit, chattering and scolding. Tarzan approached the two men in silence.

'Wot you want?' demanded Mullargan, reaching for the gun at his hip.

'You kill?' asked Tarzan, pointing at the dead elephant, and in his anger, reverting to the monosyllabic grunts which were reminiscent of his introduction to English many years before.

'Yes – so what?' Mullargan's tone was nasty.

'Tarzan kill,' said the ape-man, and stepped closer. He was five feet from Mullargan when the latter whipped his pistol from its holster and fired. But quick as Mullargan had been, Tarzan had been quicker. He struck the weapon up, and the bullet whistled harmlessly into the air; then he tore the gun from the other's hand and hurled it aside.

Mullargan grinned, a twisted, sneering grin. The poor boob was pretty fresh, he thought, getting funny like that with the Heavyweight Champion of the World. 'So you're dat Tarzan bum,' he said; then he swung that lethal right of his straight for Tarzan's chin.

He was much surprised when he missed. He was more surprised when the ape-man dealt him a terrific blow on the side of the head with his open palm, a blow that felled him, half-stunned.

Marks danced about in consternation and terror. 'Get up, you bum,' he yelled at Mullargan; 'get up and kill him.'

Nkima jumped up and down at the edge of the gorge, hurling defiance and insults at the *Tarmangani*. Mullargan came slowly to his feet. Instinctively, he had taken a count of nine. Now there was murder in his heart. He rushed Tarzan, and once again the ape-man made him miss; then Mullargan fell into a clinch, pinning Tarzan's right arm and striking terrific blows above one of the ape-man's kidneys, to hurt and weaken him.

With his free hand Tarzan lifted Mullargan from his feet and threw him heavily to the ground, falling on top of him. Steel-thewed fingers sought Mullargan's throat. He struggled to free himself, but he was helpless. A low growl came from the throat of the man upon him. It was the growl of a beast, and it filled the champion with a terror that was new to him.

'Help, Joey! Help!' he cried. 'The so-an'-so's killin' me.'

Marks was the personification of futility. He could only hop about, scream-ing: 'Get up, you bum; get up and kill him!'

Nkima hopped about too, and screamed; but he hopped and screamed for a very different reason from that which animated Marks, for he saw some-thing that the three men, their whole attention centered on the fight, did not see. He saw a horde of savages coming down out of the forest on the opposite side of the gorge.

The Babangos, realizing that the three men below them were thoroughly engrossed and entirely unaware of their presence, advanced silently, for they wished to take them alive and unharmed. They came swiftly, a hundred sleek warriors, muscled and hard, a hundred splendid refutations of the theory that the eating of human flesh makes men mangy, hairless and toothless.

Marks saw them first, and screamed a warning; but it was too late, for they were already upon him. By the weight of their numbers, they overwhelmed the three men, burying Tarzan and Mullargan beneath a dozen sleek dark bodies; but the ape-man rose, shaking them from him for a moment. Mul-largan saw him raise a warrior above his head and hurl him into the faces of his fellows, and the champion was awed by this display of physical strength so much greater than his own.

This momentary reversal was brief – there were too many Babangos even for Tarzan. Two of them seized him around the ankles, and three more bore him backward to the ground; but before they succeeded in binding him, he had killed one with his bare hands.

Mullargan was taken with less difficulty; Marks with none. The Babangos bound their hands tightly behind their backs; and prodding them from behind with their spears, drove them up the steep gorge side into the forest.

Little Nkima watched for a moment; then he fled back across the plain.

The gloom of the forest was on them, depressing further the spirits of the two Americans. The myriad close-packed trees, whose interlaced crowns of foli-age shut out the sky and the sun, awed them. Trees, trees, trees! Trees of all sizes and heights, some raising their loftiest branches nearly two hundred feet above the carpet of close-packed phyrnia, amoma, and dwarf bush that covered the ground. Loops and festoons of lianas ran from tree to tree, or wound like huge serpents around their boles from base to loftiest pinnacle. From the highest branches others hung almost to the ground, their frayed extremities scarcely moving in the dead air; and other, slenderer cords hung down in tassels with open thread work at their ends, the air roots of the epiphytes.

'Wot you suppose they goin' to do with us?' asked Marks. 'Hold us for ransom?'

'Mabbe. I don' know. How'd they collect ransom?'

Marks shook his head. 'Then what are they goin' to do with us?'

'Why don't you ask that big bum?' suggested Mullargan, jerking his head in the general direction of Tarzan.

'Bum!' Marks spat the word out disgustedly. 'He made a bum outta you, big boy. I wisht I had a bum like that back in Noo York. I'd have a real champeen then. He nearly kayoed you with the flat of his hand. What a hay-maker he packs!'

'Just a lucky punch,' said Mullargan. 'Might happen to anyone.'

'He picks you up like you was a flyweight; but when he turns you down you land like a heavyweight, all right. I suppose 'at was just luck.'

'He ain't human. Did you hear him growl? Just like a lion or somep'n.'

'I wisht I knew what they was goin' to do with us,' said Marks.

'Well, they ain't agoin' to kill us. If they was, they would of done it back there when they got us. There woudn't be no sense in luggin' us somewheres else to kill us.'

'I guess you're right, at that.'

The footpath that the Babangos followed with their captives wound errati-cally through the forest. It was scarcely more than eighteen inches wide, a narrow trough worn deep by the feet of countless men and beasts through countless years. It led at last to a rude encampment on the banks of a small stream near its confluence with a larger river. It was the site of an abandoned village in a clearing not yet entirely reclaimed by the jungle.

As the three men were led into the encampment, they were surrounded by yelling women and children. The women spat upon them, and the children threw sticks at them until the warriors drove them off; then, with ropes about their necks, they were tied to a small tree.

Marks, exhausted, threw himself upon the ground; Mullargan sat with his back against the tree; Tarzan remained standing, his eyes examining every detail of his surroundings, his mind centered upon a single subject – escape.

'Cripes,' said Marks. 'I'm all in.'

'You ain't never used your dogs enough,' said Mullargan, unsympatheti-cally. 'You was always keen on me doin' six miles of road work every day while you loafed in an automobile.'

'What was that?' suddenly demanded Marks.

'What's what?'

'Don't you hear it – them groans?' The sound was coming from the direc-tion of the stream, which they could not see because of intervening growth.

'Some guy's got a bellyache,' said Mullargan.

'It sounds awful,' said Marks. 'I wisht I was back in Gawd's country. You sure had a hell of a bright idea – comin' to this Africa. I wisht I knew what they was goin' to do with us.'

Mullargan glanced up at Tarzan. 'He ain't worryin' none,' he said, 'and he ought to know what they're goin' to do with us. He's a wild man himself.'

They had been speaking in whispers, but Tarzan had heard what they said. 'You want to know what they're going to do to you?' he asked.

'We sure do,' said Marks.

'They're going to eat you.'

Marks sat up suddenly. He felt his throat go dry, and he licked his lips. 'Eat us?' he croaked. 'You're kiddin', Mister; they ain't no cannibals no more, only in movin' pitchers an' story-books.'

'No? You hear that moaning coming from the river?'

'Uh-huh.'

'That part of it's worse than being eaten.'

'They're preparing the meat – making it tender. Those are men or women or little children that you hear – there are several of them. Two or three days ago, perhaps, they broke their arms and legs in three or four places with clubs; then they sank them in the river, tying their heads up to sticks; so they can't drown by accident or commit suicide. They'll leave them there three or four days; then they'll cut them up and cook them.'

Mullargan turned a sickly yellowish white. Marks rolled over on his side and was sick. Tarzan looked down on them without pity.

'You are afraid,' said Tarzan. 'You don't want to suffer. Out on the plain and in the forest are the zebra and elephant that you left to suffer, perhaps for many days.'

'But they're only animals,' said Mullargan. 'We're human bein's.'

'You are animals,' said the ape-man. 'You suffer no more than other animals, when you are hurt. I am glad that the Babangos are going to make you suffer before they eat you. You are worse than the Babangos. You had no reason for hunting the zebra and the elephant. You could not possibly have eaten all that you killed. The Babangos kill only for food, and they kill only as much as they can eat. They are better people than you, who will find pleasure in killing.'

For a long time the three were silent, each wrapped in his own thoughts. Above the noises of the encampment rose the moans from the river. Marks commenced to sob. He was breaking. Mullargan was breaking too, but with a different reaction.

He looked up at Tarzan, who still stood, impassive, above them. 'I been thinkin', Mister,' he said, 'about what you was sayin' about us hurtin' the animals an' killin' for pleasure. I ain't never thought about it that way before. I wisht I hadn't done it.'

A little monkey fled across the hot plain. He made a detour to avoid the lumbering truck following in the wake of the hunters. Shortly thereafter he took to the trees and swung through them close to the edge of the plain. He was a terrified little monkey, constantly on the alert for the many creatures to which monkey meat is an especial delicacy. It was sad that such an ardent nemophilist should be afraid in the forest, but that was because Histah the snake and Sheeta the panther were also arboreal. There were also large monkeys with very bad dispositions, which it were wise to avoid; so little Nkima traveled as quietly and unobtrusively as possible. It was seldom that he traveled, or did anything else, with such singleness of purpose; but today not even the most luscious caterpillar, the most enticing fruits, or even a nest of eggs could tempt him to loiter. Little Nkima was going places, fast …

Melton saw the carcasses of zebra pointing the way the hunters had gone. He was filled with anger and disgust, and he cursed under his breath. When he came to the edge of the gorge, he saw the wreck of the automobile lying beneath the body of a bull elephant; but he saw no sign of the two men. He got out and went down into the gorge.

Melton was an experienced tracker. He could read a story in a crushed blade of grass or a broken twig. A swift survey of the ground surrounding the wrecked automobile told him a story that filled him with concern – for himself. With his rifle cocked, he climbed back up the side of the gorge toward the truck, turning his eyes often back toward the forest on the opposite side. It was with a sigh of relief that he turned the truck about and started back across the plain.

'The bounders had it coming to them,' he thought. 'There's nothing I can do about it but report it, and by that time it will be too late.'

That night the Babangos feasted, and Tarzan learned from snatches of their conversation that they were planning to commence the preparation of him and the two Americans the following night; but Tarzan was of no mind to have his arms and legs broken. He lay down close to Mullargan.

'Turn on your side,' he whispered. 'I am going to lie with my back to yours. I'll try to untie the thongs on your wrists; then you can untie mine.'

'Oke,' said Mullargan.

Out in the forest toward the plain a lion roared, and the instant reaction of the Babangos evidenced their fear of the King of beasts. They replenished their beast fires and beat their drums to frighten away the marauder. They were not lion men, these hunters of humans; but after a while, hearing no more from the lion, the savages, once again feasting, dancing, drinking, relaxed their surveillance; and Tarzan was able to labor uninterruptedly for hours. It was slow work, for his hands were so bound that he could use the fingers of but one of them at a time; but at least one knot gave to his perseverance. After that it was easier, and in another half-hour Mullargan's hands were free. With two hands, he could work more rapidly; but time was flying. It was long past midnight. There were signs that the orgy would soon be terminated; then, Tarzan knew, guards would be placed over them. At last he was free. Marks' bonds responded more easily.

'Crawl on your bellies after me,' Tarzan whispered. 'Make no noise.' Mullargan's admission of his regret for the slaughter of the zebra had determined Tarzan to give the two men a chance to escape – that, and the fact that Mullargan had helped to release him. He felt neither liking nor responsibility for them. He did not consider them as fellow-beings, but as creatures further removed from him than the wild beasts with which he had consorted since childhood: those were his kin and his fellows.

Tarzan inched across the clearing toward the forest. Had he been alone, he would have depended upon his speed to reach the sanctuary of the trees where no Babangos could have followed him along the high-flung pathways that the apes of Kerchak had taught him to traverse; but the only chance the two behind him had was that of reaching the forest unobserved.

They had covered scarcely more than a hundred feet when Marks sneezed. Asthmatic, he had reacted to some dust or pollen that their movement had raised from the ground. He sneezed, not once but continuously; and his sneezing was answered by shouts from the encampment.

'Get up and run!' directed Tarzan, leaping to his feet; and the three raced for the forest, followed by a horde of yelling savages.

The Babangos overtook Marks first, the result of neglecting his road work; but they caught Mullargan too, just before he reached the forest. They caught him because he had hesitated momentarily, motivated by what was possibly the first heroic urge of his life, to attempt to rescue Marks. When they were upon him, and both rescue and escape were no longer possible, One-Punch Mullargan went berserk.

'Come on, you bums!' he yelled, and planted his famous right on a black chin. Others closed in on him and went down in rapid succession to a series of vicious rights and lefts. 'I'll learn you,' growled Mullargan, 'to monkey with the Heavyweight Champeen of the World!' Then a warrior crept up behind him and struck him a heavy blow across his head with the haft of a spear, and One-Punch Mullargan went down and out for the first time in his life.

Tarzan, perched upon the limb of a tree at the edge of the clearing, had been an interested spectator, correctly interpreting Mullargan's act of heroism. It was the second admirable trait that he had seen in either of these *Tarmangani*, and it moved him to a more active contemplation of their impending fate. Death meant nothing to him, unless it was the death of a friend, for death is a commonplace of the jungle; and his, the psychology of the wild beast, which, walking always with death, is not greatly impressed by it.

But self-sacrificing heroism is not a common characteristic of wild beasts. It belongs almost exclusively to man, marking the more courageous among them. It was an attribute that Tarzan could understand and admire. It formed a bond between these two most dissimilar men, raising Mullargan in Tarzan's estimation above the position held by the Babangos, whom he looked upon as natural enemies. Formerly, Mullargan had ranked below the Babangos, below Ungo the jackal, below Dango the hyena.

Tarzan still felt no responsibility for these men, whom he had been about to abandon to their fate; but he considered the idea of aiding them, perhaps as much to confound and annoy the Babangos as to succour Mullargan and Marks.

Once again Nkima crossed the plain, this time upon the broad, brown shoulder of Muviro, chief of the white-plumed Waziri. Once again he chattered and scolded, and his heart was as the heart of Numa the lion. From the shoulder of Muviro, as from the shoulder of Tarzan, Nkima could tell the world to go to hell; and did.

From his slow-moving lorry, Melton saw, in the distance, what appeared to be a large party of men approaching. He stopped the lorry and reached for his binoculars.

When he had focused them on the object of his interest, he whistled.

'I hope they're friendly,' he thought. One of his boys had told him that the Babangos were raiding somewhere in this territory, and the evidence he had seen around the wrecked automobile seemed to substantiate the rumor. He saw that the boy beside him had his rifle in readiness, and drove on again.

When they were closer, he saw that the party consisted of some hundred white-plumed warriors. They had altered their course so as to intercept him. He thought of speeding up the truck and running through them. The situation looked bad to him, for this was evidently a war party. He called to the boys on top of the load to get out the extra rifles and to commence firing if he gave the word.

'Do not fire at them, Bwana,' said one of the boys; 'they would kill us all if you did. They are very great warriors.'

'Who are they?' asked Melton.

'The Waziris. They will not harm us.'

It was Muviro who stepped into the path of the truck and held up his hand.

Melton stopped.

'Where have you come from?' asked the Waziri chief.

Melton told him of the gorge and what he had found in its bottom.

'You saw no other white men than your two friends?' asked Murivo.

'Yesterday, I saw a white man who called himself Tarzan.'

'Was he with the others when they were captured?'

'I do not know.'

'Follow us,' said Muviro, 'and camp at the edge of the forest. If your friends are alive, we will bring them back.'

Nkima's actions had told Muviro that Tarzan was in trouble, and this new evidence suggested that he might have been killed or captured by the same tribe that had surprised the other men.

Melton watched the Waziri swing away at a rapid trot that would eat up the miles rapidly; then he started his motor and followed ...

At the cannibal encampment, the Babangos, sleeping off the effects of their orgy, were not astir until nearly noon. They were in an ugly mood. They had lost one victim, and many of them were nursing sore jaws and broken noses as a result of their encounter with One-Punch Mullargan.

The white men were not in much better shape: Mullargan's head ached, while Marks ached all over; and every time he thought of what lay in store for him before they would kill him, he felt faint.

'They breaks our arms and legs in four places,' he mumbled, 'and then they soaks us in the drink for three days to make us tender. The dirty bums!'

'Shut up!' snapped Mullargan. 'I been tryin' to forget it.'

Tarzan, knowing that the Waziri were not far behind him, returned to the edge of the plain to look for them. Alone, and in broad daylight, he knew that not even he could hope to rescue the Americans from the camp of the Babangos. All day he loitered at the edge of the plain; and then, there being no sign of the Waziri, he swung back through the trees toward the cannibal encampment as the brief equatorial twilight ushered in the impenetrable darkness of the forest night.

He approached the camp from a new direction, coming down the little stream in which the remaining victims were still submerged. Above the camp, his nostrils caught the scent of Numa the lion and Sabor the lioness; and presently he made out their dim forms belows him. They were slinking silently toward the scent of human flesh, and they were ravenously hungry. The ape-man knew this, for the scent of an empty lion is quite different from that of one with a full belly. Every wild beast knows this; so it is far from unusual to see lions that have recently fed pass through a herd of grazing herbivores without eliciting more than casual attention.

The silence and hunger of these two stalking lions boded ill for their intended prey.

A dozen warriors approached Mullargan and Marks. They cut their bonds and jerked the two men roughly to their feet; then they dragged them to the center of the camp, where the chief and the witch-doctor sat beneath a large tree. Warriors stood in a semi-circle facing the chief, and behind them were the women and children.

The two Americans were tripped and thrown to the ground upon their backs; and there they were spread-eagled, two warriors pinioning each arm and leg. From the foliage of the tree above, an almost naked white man looked down upon the scene. He was weighing in his mind the chances of effecting a rescue, but he had no intention of sacrificing himself uselessly for these two. Beyond the beast fires two pairs of yellowish-green unblinking eyes watched. The tips of two sinuous tails weaved to and fro. A pitiful moan came from the stream nearby; and the lioness turned her eyes in that direction, but the great black-maned male continued to glare at the throng within the encampment.

The witch-doctor rose and approached the two victims. In one hand he carried a zebra's tail, to which feathers were attached; in the other a heavy club. Marks saw him and commenced to whimper. He struggled and cried out:

'Save me, kid! Save me! Don't let 'em do this to me!'

Mullargan muttered a half-remembered prayer. The witch-doctor began to dance around them, waving the zebra's tail over them and mumbling his ritualistic mumbo-jumbo. Suddenly he leaped in close to Mullargan and swung his heavy club above the pinioned man; then Mullargan, Heavyweight Champion of the World, tore loose from the grasp of the warriors and leaped to his feet. With all the power of his muscles and the weight of his body, he drove such a blow to the chin of the witch-doctor as he had never delivered in any ring; and the witch-doctor went down and out with a broken jaw. A shout of savage rage went up from the assembled warriors, and a moment later Mullargan was submerged by numbers.

The lioness approached the edge of the stream and stretched a taloned paw toward the head of one of the Babangos' pitiful victims, a woman. The poor creature screamed in terror, and the lioness growled horribly and struck. The Babangos, terrified, turned their eyes in the direction of the sounds; and then the lion charged straight for them, his thunderous roar shaking the ground. The savages turned and fled, leaving their two victims and the witch-doctor in the path of the carnivore.

It all happened so quickly that the lion was above Mullargan before he could gain his feet. For a moment the great beast stood glaring down at the prostrate man, who lay paralyzed with fright, staring back into those terrifying eyes. He smelled the fetid breath and saw the yellow fangs and the drooling jowls, and he saw something else – something that filled him with wonder and amazement – as Tarzan launched himself from the tree full upon the back of the great cat.

Mullargan leaped to his feet then and backed away, but was held by fascinated horror as he waited for the lion to kill the man. Marks scrambled up and tried to climb the tree, clawing at the great bole in a frenzy of terror. The lioness had dragged the woman from the stream and was carrying her off into the forest, her agonized screams rising above all other sounds.

Mullargan wished to run away, but he could not. He stood fixed to the ground, watching the incredible. Tarzan's legs were locked around the small of the lion's body, his steel-thewed arms encircling the black-maned neck. The lion reared upon his hind feet, striking futilely at the man-thing upon his back; and mingled with his roaring and his growling were the growls of the man. It was the latter which froze Mullargan's blood.

He saw the lion throw himself to the ground and roll over upon the man in a frantic effort to dislodge him, but when he came to his feet again the man was still there. One-Punch Mullargan had witnessed many a battle that had brought howls of approval for the strength or courage of the contestants, but never had he seen such strength and courage as were being displayed by this almost naked man in hand-to-hand battle with a lion.

The endurance of a lion is in no measure proportional to its strength, and presently the great cat commenced to tire. For a moment it stood squarely upon all four feet, panting; and in that first moment of opportunity Tarzan released his hold with one hand and drew his hunting-knife from its scabbard. At the movement, the lion wheeled and sought to seize his antagonist. The knife flashed in the firelight and the long blade sank deep behind the tawny shoulder. Voicing a hideous roar, the beast reared and leaped; and again the blade was driven home. In a paroxysm of pain and rage, the great cat leaped high into the air. Again the blade was buried in its side. Three times the point had reached the lion's heart; and at last it rolled over on its side, quivered convulsively and lay still.

Tarzan sprang erect and placed a foot upon the carcass of his kill, and raising his face to the heavens voiced the hideous victory cry of the bull ape. Marks' knees gave beneath him, and he sat down suddenly. Mullargan felt the hairs on his scalp rise. The Babangos, who had run into the forest to escape the lion, kept on running to escape the nameless horror of the weird cry.

'Come!' commanded Tarzan; and led the two men toward the plain – away from captivity and death and the cannibal Babangos.

Next day, Marks and Mullargan were in camp with Melton. Tarzan and the Waziri were preparing to leave in pursuit of the Babangos, to punish them and drive them from the country.

Before the ape-man left, he confronted the two Americans.

'Get out of Africa,' he commanded, 'and never come back.'

'Never's too damn soon for me,' said Mullargan.

'Listen, Mister,' said Marks 'I'll guarantee you one hundred G. if you'll come back to Noo York an' fight for me.'

Tarzan turned and walked away, joining the Waziri, who were already on the march. Nkima sat upon his shoulder and called the *Tarmangani* vile names.

Marks spread his hands, palms up. 'Can you beat it, kid?' he demanded. 'He turns down one hundred G. cold! But it's a good thing for you he did – he'd have taken that champeenship away from you in one round.'

'Who?' demanded One-Punch Mullargan. 'Dat bum?'

TARZAN AND THE JUNGLE MURDERS

I

The Hyeńa's Voice

A bronzed giant of a man, naked save for a breechclout, stalked silently along a forest trail. It was Tarzan, moving through his vast jungle domain in the crisp freshness of the early morning.

The forest was more or less open in this section, with occasional natural clearings in which only a few scattered trees grew. Consequently Tarzan's progress was rapid – rapid, that is, for ground movement.

If the jungle had been thick he would have taken to the trees, and gone hurtling through them with the strength of an ape and the speed of a monkey. For he was Tarzan of the Apes, who, despite his many contacts with civilization since the early days of his young manhood, had retained the fullness of all his jungle ways and powers.

He seemed indifferent to his surroundings, yet this indifference was deceptive, the result of his familiarity with the sights and sounds of the jungle. In reality, every sense in him was on the alert.

Tarzan knew, for example, that a lion was lying in a patch of brush a hundred feet to his left and that the King of beasts lay beside the partially eaten carcass of a slain zebra. He saw neither the lion nor the zebra, but he knew they were there. Usha, the wind, carried that information to his sensitive nostrils.

Long experience had taught this man of the jungle the characteristic odors of both lion and zebra. The spoor of a lion with a full belly is different from that of a hungry, stalking lion. So Tarzan passed on, unconcerned, knowing that the lion would not attack.

Tarzan preferred the evidence of his nostrils to any other way of finding things out. The eyes of a man could deceive him in the twilight and the night, the ears could be wrongly influenced by imagination. But the sense of smell never failed. It was always right; it always told a man what was what.

It was unfortunate, therefore, that a man could not always be traveling upwind – either the man himself changed his direction, or the wind itself shifted.

The former case applied to Tarzan now, as he moved across wind to avoid a stream which he was not in the mood to swim. Consequently his preternatural sense of smell, temporarily less useful, yielded place to his other information-bringing senses.

And so, something was borne in upon his hearing that would have escaped all ears but his – the far off cry of Dango, the hyena.

Tarzan's scalp tingled, as it always did when he heard that unpleasant sound. Toward all other animals, the crocodile alone excepted, Tarzan could have respect – but for Dango, the hyena, he could have only contempt. He despised the creature's filthy habits and loathed its odor. Chiefly because of this last, he usually avoided the vicinity of Dango whenever he could, lest he be moved to kill a living creature out of pure hate, which he did not consider good cause.

So long as Dango did not commit evil, Tarzan spared him – after all, he couldn't kill a beast just because he didn't like that animal's smell, could he? Besides, it was Dango's nature to smell the way he did.

Tarzan was about to change his direction once more, this time to avoid getting close to Dango, when suddenly a new note in Dango's voice caused him to change his mind completely. It was a strange note; it told of something unusual. Tarzan's curiosity was aroused, so he decided to investigate.

He increased his speed. When the forest closed in on him he took to the trees, hurtling through them in great leaps that ate up the distance. The monkeys chattered to him as he went past, and he replied to them with the same rapid sounds, telling them that he had not time to stop. At any other time he might have paused to cavort with the baby monkeys, while the mothers looked on in approval or the fathers tried to inveigle him into playing coconut-catch with them; but now he was in a hurry to find out what had put that strange note into Dango's voice.

Nevertheless, one particularly mischievous simian let fly with a coconut without giving warning. He did not do it viciously, because he knew the quickness of Tarzan's eye. And he was totally unprepared for Tarzan's swift return shot. Tarzan caught the missile and flung it back in almost one and the same motion, and the jungle baseball went through the monkey's grasp to bounce with a hollow thump against the hairy chest.

A chorus of monkey-laughter rose, and the mischievous monkey rubbed his chest ruefully with one hand while he scratched his head sheepishly with the other.

'Play with your brothers,' Tarzan sang out. 'Tarzan has no time for games today.'

And he increased his speed still more. The voices of Dango and his fellows came louder and louder to his ears, their smell grew still more offensive. In mid-air he spat his distaste, but he did not swerve from his course. And at last, at the edge of a clearing, he looked down on a sight that was strange indeed in this African wilderness.

There on the ground lay an aeroplane, partially wrecked. And there, prowling round and round the wreckage, was the source of the smell Tarzan hated – a half dozen slaver-dripping, tongue-lolling hyenas. On soft feet they padded, round and round in restless motion, occasionally jumping high against the plane's side in an obvious effort to get at something within.

Conquering his revulsion, Tarzan dropped lightly to the ground. Soft as the impact was, though, the hyenas heard and turned sharply. They snarled, then retreated a little. It is always the hyena's first impulse to retreat except from things already dead. Then, seeing that Tarzan was alone, some of the bolder among them inched forward with bared fangs. There was an old and mutual enmity between this man and the seed of Dango.

Tarzan seemed to pay the hyenas no heed. The bow and quiver of arrows at his back remained unslung. His hunting knife remained in its sheath. He did not even raise his spear in menace. He showed his contempt. But he was watchful. He knew the hyena of old. Cowardly, yes – but when goaded by hunger, capable of sudden daring attack with claw and fang. He smelled their hunger now, and while outwardly he remained contemptuous, inwardly he was vigilant.

Emboldened by Tarzan's outward indifference, the hyenas, moved closer to him. Then, with a sudden rush, the biggest of them leaped for his throat!

Before the wicked fangs could clamp together around his throat, Tarzan shot out a bronzed hand, grabbed the beast's neck. He swung the body once above his head, sent it hurtling with terrific force against the other hyenas, knocking three to the ground. The three were up almost at once but the one remained, and all the hyenas straightway fell upon the broken body of their leader and commenced devouring it. Aye, Tarzan of the Apes knew the best way of handling hyenas.

While they were busy at their loathsome feeding, Tarzan examined the plane and found it was not totally damaged. One wing was crumpled and the landing gear was shattered. But what was true of this thing of wire and metal was not true of the flesh and blood that had guided it – the flesh and blood which the hyenas had been unable to reach. The pilot, encased in his part of the cockpit, still sat at his controls, but his body was bent forward in death, his head resting against the instrument board.

The plane was an Italian army ship. Tarzan made a mental note of the number and insignia. Then clambering onto the wing to reach the cockpit, he drew away the wreckage from the pilot's accidental tomb and examined the man more closely.

'Dead – one, two days,' he muttered. 'Bullet hole in throat, a little to the left of larynx. Now, that's strange. I'd say this man was wounded while in the air. He lived long enough to land his ship. He had company with him, too. But they didn't shoot him.'

It took no special figuring on Tarzan's part to infer that the dead man had not been alone. The ground around the ship showed human footprints, not native ones, either, for the feet had been shod with civilized footgear. Also there were a number of cigarette butts and a piece of a cellophane wrapping.

But the deduction that the pilot had not been shot by his companions required much closer reasoning. On the face of it, it was incredible that it could have happened any other way – if they didn't shoot him, who did? Yet, a shot from his companions would have had to come either from the right side or from the rear. The bullet, however, had penetrated the throat at the left of the larynx.

A low, jungle oath escaped Tarzan.

'Impossible as it may seem,' he muttered, 'this man was shot while in the air – and not by his companions either. Who did it then?'

Once again he examined the wound. He shook his head, his brow furrowed.

'The bullet came down from above … Now how could that be … unless … unless it came from another plane. That's it. That must be it! It couldn't have happened in any other way.'

A strange mystery, indeed, in the heart of Africa, far from all traveled air-lanes. Tarzan interpreted its sign, as he would have read spoor along jungle trails, and the conclusions he reached were as certain, so certain that he now asked himself:

'Where did the other plane go?'

The sounds the hyenas were making – the tearing of flesh, the snufflings and champings and slaverings, the grinding of their teeth as they devoured one of their own kind – came to Tarzan and he spat his disgust. Almost he was minded to spring out with spear and knife and make an end of them – make food out of the feeders, food for vultures. But he muttered to himself:

'There are things here that are more important. Things that have to do with human beings. They come first.'

So he went on with his investigation. He found a single glove, a right-hand glove. He picked it up, opened it, smelled of the inside. His nostrils quivered. Then he dropped the glove – but he would not soon forget what he had learned from it.

He leaped to the ground. Now the sight of the hyenas at their gruesome work was coupled with the sounds they made and augmented by their smell. It was too much for Tarzan. A booming roar broke from his great chest and he hurtled toward the hyenas, spear brandished threateningly. They scattered. He knew they would be back to finish the carcass, but in the meantime, while he finished his survey, he would at least be free of their offensiveness.

Minutely he examined the ground.

'Two men,' he said softly. 'They started out' – he pointed downward, although he was talking to no one but himself – 'from here. And they went' – again he pointed – 'this way. The trail is about two days old, but not too cold to follow. I'll follow it.'

Several motives animated Tarzan's decision. If still alive, the men who had dropped down from the skies and were now in the jungle, were fellow human beings who might need help. In addition, those men were strangers, and it was Tarzan's business to find out who they were and what they were doing in his domain.

Accordingly he started out with no further deliberation.

Tantor, the elephant, trumpeted across his path and stood waiting with ready trunk to swing Tarzan onto his back, but Tarzan had no time for such luxuries. He could follow the trail better if close to the ground, so he shouted:

'Go back to your herd, Tantor!'

But lest the elephant should feel hurt, Tarzan vaulted upon his back, gave Tantor a quick rub behind the ears, jumped down and was off and away on the trail again. Tantor, content, lumbered off to rejoin his herd, his trunk lifted high.

It was Usha, the wind, which brought Tarzan his next interruption. Usha, shifting slightly, transmitted to Tarzan's nostrils an altogether new scent – a scent completely at variance with what anyone would have expected in the fastnesses of the African jungle. Straightway Tarzan swerved off the trail to follow up this new sign.

Swiftly the odor grew more pronounced until at last he recognized beyond further doubt the odor of gasoline.

Here again was mystery. Gasoline implied the presence of man, but he detected no man-odor on the breeze. Still, the gasoline scent was a kind of advance-evidence that he had been right in his assumption of the presence of another aeroplane.

The assumption was soon verified by actual sight. There it lay, the mass of crumpled wreckage that had once been a man-made bird, a ship winging through the air above Africa. Now it was broken and twisted – grim evidence of tragedy.

Here, Tarzan knew, was the second half of the puzzle. This was the other plane, which had held the man, who had fired the bullet, which had entered the throat of that other man and killed him. The tail of his plane showed the ravaging effect of machine gun fire. Yes, quite evidently there had been a fight in the air, an unequal fight, for apparently the man in this second plane had been armed only with a revolver.

Unequal or not however, Man Number Two had managed to escape the fate of Number One. See there, the trampled grass. Number Two had come back to the plane, then gone away.

Tarzan followed the spoor a short way, came to a tangled mass of rope and silk.

'Parachute,' he said. 'Number Two bailed out.'

Tarzan's brain was busy. His eyes held a faraway look as he was reconstructing what must have happened.

'Plane Number One attacked Plane Number Two. That's obvious, since Number One had a machine gun and Number Two did not. Pilot Number Two had a revolver. With it, he shot pilot Number One, who made a forced landing, then died, and was deserted by two companions. The machine gun bullets forced down Plane Number Two. Its pilot bailed out and landed here, several miles from Number One. All told, then, three men walked away from two planes.'

Were they still alive?

'And why has all this happened?' Tarzan wondered. But for that question he could give no answer. He could figure out *what* had happened; but he could not figure out *why*.

And this jungle, he knew, would probably lock the answer away in death. The jungle was harsh to those who did not know her ways. The three men who had been cast away in it had little chance, if they were not dead already.

Tarzan shook his head. He was not satisfied that this should be the answer. Humanitarian impulses stirred his breast. Plane Number Two was English – its pilot was probably English too, just as the other two men were probably Italian. In Tarzan's veins ran English blood.

To Tarzan, the life of a man was no better than the life of an antelope. Tarzan would help an antelope in trouble, and he would help a man in trouble if that man deserved it. The only difference was that an antelope in trouble always deserved help whereas man sometimes did not. But Tarzan could not say one way or another what these men, and in particular the Englishman, deserved.

'Englishman,' he said to himself, 'you first. Let's hope I can get to you before the lions or the Buiroos do.'

So Tarzan set out on the trail of a man whom he did not know. Tarzan set out on the trail of Lieutenant Cecil Giles-Burton.

II

The Thread of Fate

Fate is a thread that connects one event with another and one human being with another. The thread that was to lead to Tarzan in the African jungle began in the laboratory of Horace Brown in Chicago. From Tarzan it led back to Lieutenant Burton, from Burton it led back to a man named Zubanev in London, from Zubanev to Joseph Campbell, otherwise known as 'Joe the Pooch,' from Campbell to Mary Graham who talked too much, and finally from Mary Graham to Horace Brown, whose secretary she was.

It is a long thread, all the way from Chicago to Africa, and there is blood on it and the promise of more blood to come.

Horace Brown was an American inventor. He had a secretary, Mary Graham, who was in his confidence and who talked too much. Horace Brown invented something – something of extreme military importance. Mary knew about it, and Mary went to a party. It was at this party that Mary did her excessive talking.

She meant well, but alas, Mary was not pretty, and usually attempted to make up for this lack of beauty by sparkling conversation. This time, very unfortunately, she sparkled to the wrong man – Joseph Campbell, alias Joe the Pooch.

To Mary a man was a man, and although Campbell was not particularly attractive, his interest flattered her. And she mistook his interest in her conversation for interest in herself.

Horace Brown's invention was an electrical device designed to disrupt the ignition system of any internal combustion engine at any distance up to three thousand feet.

'You can readily see what that would mean in wartime,' Mary said brightly, gesturing with her left hand not so much for emphasis as to show that her efficient typist's fingers were naked of either wedding or engagement ring. 'No tanks or other motorized equipment of the enemy could approach within a thousand yards. Strafing planes could be brought down before they could inflict any serious damage on airdromes. Bombers, equipped with these machines, would be invulnerable to attack by pursuit planes—'

Mary rambled on, unaware of Lieutenant Cecil Giles-Burton, unaware of Zubanev, unaware of Tarzan of the Apes, unaware of all those people in far off places whose lives she was unconsciously influencing. She was aware only that here was a man who was showing interest in her.

Joseph Campbell, eyes reflecting admiration – admiration for the information he was getting which she mistook for admiration for herself – listened with both ears, a hard head and a flinty heart. He saw possibilities for profit – tremendous possibilities, but he was not yet quite sure how he could go about getting those profits.

'I'd like to see that gadget,' he said casually.

'You can't,' Mary said. 'No one can, at present. It's been dismantled as a precautionary measure against theft. Mr Brown has retained only the drawings, one set of them.'

'Well, I'd like to talk to him anyway,' said Campbell, and added with a meaning glance: 'It would give us a chance to see more of each other. Perhaps I might even finance Mr Brown.'

Mary shook her head regretfully.

'I'm afraid that's impossible, too. Mr Brown is on his way to London to negotiate with the British Government. You see, he means for only the two countries to have the invention …'

Thus did Mary Graham innocently weave the first length of fate's bloody thread.

When Joseph Campbell took leave of Mary Graham that night, he promised to call her the following evening. That was the last she heard of him. Joseph Campbell faded out of her life, just as Mary Graham, at this point, fades out of this narrative …

On the other side of the Atlantic a week later, Horace Brown, having arrived at a satisfactory arrangement with the British Government, was assembling his machine in a small machine shop in London. Since it was assumed that no one but himself and the authorities knew what he was doing, no unusual precautions were taken to safeguard him. Two reliable mechanics assisted him during the day. At night he took the plans home with him to the small boarding-house where he had found a room because it was close to his work.

Nikolai Zubanev, a Russian exile, was also a boarder there. He was a mysterious little man, but apparently harmless. Quite evidently the government did not consider him to be harmless, for it was having him watched as a matter of routine, only Zubanev did not know that. Neither did another boarder, a recent arrival from America who had become friendly with Zubanev. Yet, despite the government's watchfulness, Horace Brown one morning was found murdered and his plans missing. Missing, too, were Mr Zubanev and his newfound acquaintance, Campbell.

The government tapped its many and varied sources of information. A week later Messrs. Campbell and Zubanev were located in Rome, Italy. The meaning of this was plain – they had gone there to sell the stolen plans to the Italian Government. British agents in Rome got busy. Simultaneously, Lieut. Cecil Giles-Burton took off from Croydon in a fast plane for the Italian capital. The newspapers said that he was making a flight to Capetown, Africa.

There was only one man in Italy before whom Campbell and Zubanev wished to lay their proposition, and it wasn't easy to obtain an interview with him. Zubanev, trusting no one, conceived a plan to safeguard the drawings should the Italian authorities decide to take them from him by force. He hid them in the false bottom of a handbag, and left them in his hotel room.

At the interview, the Great Man became intensely interested. A price was agreed upon – such a price as would make both men independent for life, provided, of course, that the experimental machine to be built from the drawings could do what it was designed to accomplish.

Campbell and Zubanev exuded elation as they returned to their apartment.

Their elation, however, died on the threshold as they opened the door to Zubanev's room. Someone had been there during their absence and taken the place apart, forgetting to put it together again. Zubanev rushed to the bag with the false bottom. The bag was there, and so was the false bottom – but the plans were gone!

Frantic, they telephoned the Great Man, and things immediately commenced to happen. Orders were issued to search everyone leaving Rome and to repeat the search at every border. But a certain airport reported than an Englishman, Lieut. Cecil Giles-Burton, had taken off twenty-five minutes before the search order had been received, presumably for Capetown.

A hasty investigation revealed the further fact that the said aviator had been stopping at the same hotel as Campbell and Zubanev, and that he had checked out only about a half hour before their return and discovery of their loss.

Within the hour, Campbell and Zubanev took off in a fast military pursuit plane piloted by a Lieut. Torlini.

III

Broken Wings

The blue waters of the Mediterranean rolled below Lieut. Cecil Giles-Burton as he winged South toward the African shore. So far, the undertaking had progressed with extraordinary success and it would have been quite simple to circle to the west now, and swing back to London. But there were reasons for his not doing so.

His orders were to continue South to Bangali, where his father was Resident Commissioner. He was to leave the purloined plans with his father and continue on to Capetown, just as if this was really a sporting flight, as the newspapers had announced.

For the British Government thought it unwise to permit a friendly power to suspect that its agents had stolen the plans from under the nose of the Great Man, even though they had originally been stolen from them. And because Lieutenant Burton's father was Resident Commissioner at Bangali, the lieutenant had been selected for the mission. What could be more natural than that the son should stop to visit his father on his flight to Capetown? In fact, the government records would show that he had asked permission to do so.

Although Bangali had an emergency airport, it was off the main traveled air route, and there was a question as to whether or not a plane could be refueled there, so Burton decided to land at Tunis and fill his tanks.

While he was refueling at the Tunis airport, a little crowd of the curious surrounded his ship. The formalities of the French airport were quickly and pleasantly attended to, and while he was chatting with a couple of the officials, a native approached him.

'The Italians,' he said in excellent English, 'may beat you to Capetown, if you remain here too long.'

'Oh,' said one of the Frenchmen, 'a race. I did not know that.'

Burton thought swiftly. He was being pursued! And the Italian Government was seeking to give the impression that it was just a sportsman's race.

'It really isn't an official contest,' said Burton, laughing. 'Just a private wager with some Italian friends. If I don't want to lose, I'd better be hopping off.'

Five minutes later he was in the air again and winging South with wide-open throttle, grateful for the ingenuity and thoughtfulness of his confederates in Rome and the cleverness of their agent, the 'native' in Tunis.

Burton had lost half an hour at Tunis, but it would soon be dark, and if his pursuers did not come within sight of him soon, he hoped to lose them during the night. He was flying a straight course for Bangali, which would take him east of an airline course for Capetown and west of the regular airlane from Cairo to the Cape, the route that they might reasonably expect him to fly because of its far greater safety.

Occasionally he glanced back, and finally, in the last rays of the setting sun, he saw the shimmering silver reflected from the lower surface of the wings of an airplane far behind.

All night that plane followed him, guided by the flames from his exhaust. It was a faster ship and hung doggedly on his trail.

He wondered what the enemy's plans were. He knew they didn't want him; it was the papers he carried that they wanted. If he could reach Bangali, the plans would be safe, for he would find ample protection there.

But it was not to be. When dawn broke, the pursuing plane had drawn up beside him. Its wing tip almost touched his. He saw that it was an Italian military pursuit plane, piloted by an Italian officer. The two passengers he did not recognize, although he assumed that they were Campbell and Zubanev, whom he had never seen.

Open country lay beneath them, and the Italian officer was motioning him down. He believed that Bangali was not more than fifty miles away. When he shook his head at them, they turned the machine gun on him. He banked and dove, and banked again, coming up under their tail.

His only weapon was a service pistol. He drew it and fired up at the belly of the ship, hoping that he might be lucky enough to sever one of the controls. As the other ship banked and turned, he zoomed up.

They were coming from behind now, and coming fast. He turned and fired four more shots into them, and then a burst of machine gun fire tore away his rudder and stabilizer. Out of control, his ship went into a spin. He had done his best, but he had failed. Cutting the engine, he bailed out with his parachute and floated gently down to earth.

As he was floating downward, he watched the other ship. It was behaving erratically, and he wondered if he had hit the pilot or damaged the controls. The last he saw of it, it disappeared low over a forest a few miles to the South.

Thus the two ships went down to land at the separate spots where Tarzan of the Apes was afterward to find and wonder over them.

Burton quickly came to his feet and unbuckled the harness of his parachute. He looked about him. No living creature was in sight. He was in the midst of an African wilderness, with only a hazy notion of the distance to Bangali, which lay, he believed, a little east of South.

His plane lay, a crumpled mass of wreckage, a few hundred yards away. He was glad he had cut the engine and that his ship had not burned, for it contained a little food and some extra cartridges. He figured that he was in a hell of a fix, and he was – much worse than he realized.

But the plans for which he had risked his life were buttoned securely inside his shirt. He felt of them to make sure that they were still there. Satisfied, he walked over to the wrecked plane and got ammunition and food.

He set off immediately in the direction in which he thought Bangali lay, for he knew that if his pursuers had made a safe landing they would be looking for him. If Bangali were only fifty miles away, as he hoped, and lay in the direction he believed it did, he felt that he might reasonably expect to reach it on the third day. He prayed that he was not in lion country, and, if there were natives, that they were friendly.

But he was in lion country, and what natives there were were not friendly – and Bangali was three hundred miles away.

IV
Jungle Call

Two days were to pass before the thread which began with Horace Brown in Chicago, and was already soaked in one spot with Horace Brown's blood, was to reach out and wind itself about the hyena-hating Tarzan in Africa. The third day found Tarzan of the Apes following the cold trail of the Englishman, Cecil Giles-Burton. Then fate played a queer trick.

Cecil Giles-Burton, who had never set foot in Africa before, passed unharmed through the country of the savage Buiroos – but Tarzan of the Apes, born and bred in this land and the Master of its lore, was ambushed, wounded and captured!

It happened in this way: Tarzan was approaching a forest growth downwind, hence the scent spoor of any life ahead of him could not come to his sensitive nostrils. Thus he could not know that a score of Buiroo warriors were advancing through the forest in his direction. They were hunting, therefore moved silently, so Tarzan neither heard nor smelled them as they came on.

It was at this moment that a lion broke suddenly from the forest a little to his left. Blood was running from a wound in the lion's side, and it was in an ugly mood. The beast bounded past him a few yards, then abruptly turned and charged directly at him.

Tarzan, in perfect calm, raised his short, heavy spear above his right shoulder and waited. And now … his back was toward the forest …

It was then that the Buiroos came upon him from behind …

Their surprise was great, but it did not deter their action. Chemungo, son of Mpingu the chief, recognized the white man, recognized him as Tarzan – Tarzan who had once robbed the village of a captive who was to be tortured and sacrificed – Tarzan who had made a fool of Chemungo into the bargain.

Chemungo wasted no time. He hurled his spear, and the white man went down with the weapon quivering in his back. But the other warriors did not forget the lion. With loud shouts they rushed upon him, holding their enormous shields in front of them.

The beast leaped for the foremost warrior, striking the shield and throwing the man to the ground where the shield protected him while his fellows surrounded the lion and drove home their weapons.

Once more the lion charged, and once again a warrior went down beneath his shield, but now a spear found the savage heart and the battle was over.

There was great rejoicing in the village of Mpingu the chief when the warriors returned with a white prisoner and the carcass of a lion. Their rejoicing, however, was tempered with some misgivings when they discovered that their prisoner was the redoubtable Tarzan.

Some, incited by the village witch-doctor, advocated killing the prisoner at once, lest he invoke his powers of magic to do them injury. Others, however, counseled setting him free, arguing that the spirit of the murdered Tarzan might do them infinitely more harm than Tarzan alive.

Torn between two opposing ideas, Mpingu compromised. He ordered the prisoner to be securely bound and guarded, and his wounds treated. If, by the time he got well, nothing untoward had happened, they would treat him as they treated other prisoners; and then there would be dancing – and eating!

Tarzan had stopped bleeding. The wound would have killed an ordinary man, but Tarzan was no ordinary man. Already he was planning his escape.

His bonds were tight, and his captors took great pains to keep them that way. Each night they tightened them anew, wondering at the great strength that enabled the man to loosen them at least enough to cause the blood in his arms and legs to flow less sluggishly.

This nightly tightening of his bonds became a serious problem to Tarzan. It was more than that – it was an insult to his natural dignity.

'A man without the use of his arms,' he thought, 'is only half a man. A man without the use of his arms and legs is not a man at all. He is a child, who must be fed like a child, as the Buiroos are feeding me.'

And Tarzan's heart swelled with the indignity of it, an indignity thrice multiplied at being fed by a degenerate people like the Buiroos. Yet what availed the swelling of Tarzan's heart, if his wrists and ankles could not swell, too – swell and burst his bonds?

Tarzan's great heart burned within his breast, but his brain remained cool. 'They feed me to fatten me,' his brain told him. 'A man of muscle would make too tough eating for them. So they seek to put over me a layer of succulent fat. Is this a fit end for Tarzan – to wind up in the bellies of Buiroos? No, it is not a fit end for Tarzan – nor will it be the end! Tarzan will surely think of something.'

So Tarzan thought of this and that, and dismissed each thought in turn as useless. But his five senses, more highly developed than those of any other men, remained in tune.

Three of those senses did not matter much in his present condition. He could see, but of what use was sight when a man had only the walls of a mean hut to look at? What mattered touch when a man's hands and feet were bound? What good was taste when it meant tasting food not acquired by his own strong hands but fed to him by Buiroos, so that his muscles should take on a layer of fat to melt on their tongues and delight their palates?

No, two senses alone – hearing and smell – still meant something. And over and above them the mysterious sixth sense that Tarzan possessed to a degree unknown to other men.

So the days and nights passed, with Tarzan thinking in his waking hours and thinking even in his dreams. He was more alive than ever to all sounds and all smells; but more important than that, his sixth sense was alive to the jungle and any message it might bring him.

Messages there were many, but he waited for the one that would bring him hope. He heard Sheetah, the leopard. There was no hope there. He heard Dango again, and smelled the beast with his old disgust. Numa, the lion, voiced his hunger grunt from far away. Tarzan's keen ears heard it, but the sound was meaningless except to introduce the passing thought that it was nobler to be eaten by a lion than by Buiroos.

Then Tarzan – or rather Tarzan's sixth sense – received another message. A faint glow of surprise appeared in his eyes, his nostrils quivered.

Soon after that, Tarzan began to sway his torso backward and forward, gently, and a low chanting sound began to issue from his lips. The guard at the hut's opening peered in, saw Tarzan's gentle swaying, and asked:

'What are you doing?'

Tarzan interrupted his motion and chant only long enough to say, 'Praying.' Then he resumed.

The guard reported what he had seen to Mpingu. Mpingu grunted and said that the gods of the Buiroos were more powerful than Tarzan's.

'Let him pray,' Mpingu said. 'It will not save him. Soon our teeth and tongues will know him.'

The guard returned to the hut, resumed his post. Tarzan was still swaying and chanting, only a little louder now. He waited for the guard to tell him not to, but the guard said nothing, wherefore Tarzan knew that his plan was working.

The message still came to him, but now it was more than a message received by his sixth sense. The message was coming to his nostrils now, unmistakable!

But Tarzan was careful. He was sending out a call, but he increased its volume only gradually, so that the illusion of prayer could be kept in the minds of the Buiroos. And so gradually did the sounds he made increase in volume, that from one minute to the next the change was scarcely noticeable.

It was all at once that the Buiroos realized that Tarzan's voice was very loud, and for still another minute they explained it by the supposition that Tarzan could not make his gods listen to him. Then they heard, bursting upon their ear-drums, like thunder when the skies are black and angry, Tarzan's great bellow.

There was sudden quiet ...

Deep in the jungle, Tantor, the elephant, lifted his head to the night breeze, and the forepart of his trunk curled up spasmodically. His ears flapped. He turned partway around to face the breeze fully. Once more he sniffed – and then he trumpeted.

He trumpeted, calling his herd together. They came, stood upwind with him, listened, heard what he heard. They had wandered far, out of their usual stamping grounds, following their leader submissively, for their leader had been very restless the last few days, as though seeking something, and they had feared to cross his will.

Now they knew what had made him restless and what had drawn him, and now they, too, shook the air with their own trumpetings, trampled the ground with impatience, waiting only the signal from their leader to set out.

Tantor gave the awaited signal – and the herd marched!

It marched quickly, steadily, remorselessly – straight for its goal. It marched without swerving, except for the great trees. The saplings it juggernauted down as if they were matchwood. Straight and true, the great herd marched on the Buiroo village …

Tarzan, in his captive's lair, was the first to hear the thunder of the oncoming herd. His eyes lit up and his lips twisted in a smile. His 'prayers' had been heard! His deliverance came on apace – faster, faster – nearer, nearer!

Panicky cries rose in the outer air. Tarzan heard the ripping and rending of wood as the elephants pushed against the village stockade. Crash! A whole section of the stockade came shattering down. The elephants were in!

'Tantor! Tantor!' Tarzan's great voice called. 'Tantor! Tantor!' his voice yelled out. 'Come to me!'

But Tantor needed no vocal invitation to come to Tarzan. The scent of his man-friend alone was enough, and Tarzan's voice merely confirmed Tantor's knowledge of his presence there.

Tarzan heard the swoop of Tantor's trunk above him. The entire thatched roof of the hut he was in was swept away. Looking up, Tarzan beheld the tremendous bulk of Tantor, and beyond that the stars of heaven. The next instant Tantor's trunk dipped down, encircled Tarzan, lifted him and hung him up on his back.

Tantor lifted his trunk, waited. Now Tarzan and not Tantor was in command of the herd.

And it was Tarzan, with his great voice, who signaled that it was time to depart. The village was a shambles now, not a hut left standing, and the Buiroos had retreated in terror into the bush. Triumphantly, the herd left the village behind.

Dawn was breaking. Tantor and the herd had done its job. It was the monkeys and not the elephants who loosened Tarzan's bonds, and hopped about him, chattering with delight at seeing him again. Tarzan rubbed Tantor behind the ears, and Tantor knew he was being thanked.

Then, taking leave of his jungle friends, Tarzan swung off into the trees and disappeared from their sight.

There was no use any more, he knew, in following the spoor of the English aviator. Very likely the poor fellow had already died, either of starvation or beneath the fangs and talons of one of the great carnivorous beasts. No, Tarzan's destination now lay elsewhere – specifically in Bangali.

Nights before, while lying captive, he had heard native African drums relaying a message from the Resident Commissioner in Bangali to his friend Tarzan of the Apes – a message for Tarzan to come to Bangali.

V

The Safari

How Lieutenant Cecil Giles-Burton survived his aimless wanderings in the jungle was one of those miracles that sometimes happen in Africa. The Dark Continent, cruel to those who did not know her, spared this man. And the section of Fate's thread which bound him indirectly to a talkative maiden in far-off Chicago was not yet moistened with his own blood.

On two occasions Burton met lions. In each case, fortunately, a tree was handy, and he climbed it. One of those lions had been ravenously hungry and was on the hunt. Burton was treed by it for a whole day. He thought he would die of thirst.

But at last the lion's patience was snapped by its own hunger, and it went off after less difficult game.

The other lion Burton need not have worried about. Its belly was full and it would have paid no attention even to a fat zebra, its favorite food. But Burton, unlike Tarzan, could not tell the difference between a hungry lion and a sated one. Also, like most people ignorant of jungle ways, he held the notion that all lions were man-eaters and went about killing every living creature they could reach.

The getting of food was Burton's chief problem. He lost weight rapidly. He ate many strange things, such as locusts, and came to understand that a hungry man will eat anything.

The days passed swiftly, and he was still searching for Bangali; but he was searching in the wrong direction.

His clothes hung in rags. His hair and beard grew long. But his courage remained. Thin as a rail, he was still full of hope as one morning he sat upon a hillside looking down into a little valley.

His hearing had sharpened since his sojourn in the jungle, and now, suddenly, he heard sounds coming from the upper end of the valley. He looked – and saw men.

Men! Human beings! The first he had seen in days and days! His heart pounded, swelled in his now bony chest. His first impulse was to jump up and run down to them, crying aloud his joy. Then he restrained himself. Africa had taught him caution. Instead of rushing down, he concealed himself behind a bush and watched. He would look before he leaped.

It was a long file of men. As they came closer, he saw that some of them wore sun-helmets. But the majority of them wore not much of anything. He noted that those who wore the least clothing carried the heaviest burdens.

He knew what he was seeing now. It was a safari – a safari of white men and blacks.

Now he no longer hesitated. He rushed down to meet it.

The column was headed by a native guide and a group of whites. There were two women among the whites. Behind them trooped the long file of porters and *askaris*.

'Hello! Hello!' Burton shouted in a cracked voice. Tears came to his eyes and he choked, stumbling toward them with arms outstretched.

The safari halted and awaited his coming. No answering shouts of greeting came to him. He slowed his pace. Something of his habitual English reserve returned to him. He wondered at their lack of enthusiasm.

'How awful,' one of the women – no more than a girl – exclaimed at the soiled sight of him. But the exclamation was less in pity than in impolite shock at his scarecrow appearance.

Lieutenant Burton stiffened and his cracked lips twisted in a crooked smile that held a little bitterness. Was this the way a castaway was received by his own kind? Lieutenant Burton, looking at the girl, said quietly:

'I am sorry, Lady Barbara, that in your shock at my dirty rags, you fail to see that a human being is wearing them.'

The girl stared at him, aghast. Over her face spread a flush.

'You know me?' she said unbelievingly.

'Quite well. You are Lady Barbara Ramsgate. That gentleman – or am I wrong in using the word? – is your brother, Lord John. The others I do not know.'

'He must have heard rumors about our safari,' one of the other men interposed. 'That's how he knows the names. Well, man, what's your story? I suppose your safari deserted you, and you're lost and hungry, and want to join up with our safari. You're not the first derelict we picked up—'

'Stop it, Gault,' John Ramsgate snapped in an angry voice. 'Let the man tell his story.'

Lieutenant Burton shook his head. He sent a burning glance at each of them in turn.

'As snobbish in Africa as in London,' he said softly. 'One of your porters, meeting me like this, would not have asked questions, would have given me food and water even if it meant going without it himself.'

Gault opened his mouth to make a hot retort, but the girl stopped him. She looked ashamed.

'I'm sorry,' she said. 'We've all been under a strain and I'm afraid our veneer has cracked a bit to reveal that we're not as nice as we think we are underneath. I'll order food and water for you immediately.'

'No hurry now,' Burton said. 'I'll answer your unspoken questions first. I was flying from London to Capetown, and was forced down. I have been wandering around ever since, trying to find Bangali. You are the first human beings I've seen. Permit me to introduce myself. My name is Burton – Lieutenant Cecil Giles-Burton, of the Royal Air Force.'

'Impossible!' Lady Barbara exclaimed. 'You can't be.'

'We know Burton,' said Lord John. 'You don't look anything like him.'

'Blame Africa for that. I think if you look closely enough, you'll recognize your weekend guest at Ramsgate Castle.'

And Lord John, looking closer, finally murmured, 'Gad, yes,' and stretched out his hand. 'My apologies, old fellow.'

Burton did not take the hand. His shoulders sagged. He was ashamed of these people.

'That hand which you now offer to Lieutenant Burton should have been offered to the derelict stranger,' he said quietly. 'I'm afraid I can't shake it sincerely.'

'He's right,' Lord John said to his sister, and she nodded meekly. 'We're terribly sorry, Burton. I'd be honored very much if you took my hand, Lieutenant.'

So Burton shook his hand, and they all felt better. Lady Barbara introduced him to the man who stood at her side – Duncan Trent.

After eating, Burton met the other members of the safari. There was a tall, broad-shouldered man who was called Mr Romanoff, and it was Romanoff who gave Burton the astounding information that Bangali was fully two hundred miles away. Romanoff imparted this information while being shaved by his valet, Pierre. Evidently this Russian expatriate traveled in style.

Burton learned further that this safari was really two safaris.

'We ran into the Romanoff safari two weeks ago, and since we were both headed in the same direction, for Bangali, we joined forces. The difference is that the Romanoff safari hunts with guns while we hunt only with cameras.'

'Silly idea,' said Trent, who was evidently interested in Lady Barbara emotionally. 'John could have gone to the zoo and taken his silly pictures without all this walking and insect bites.'

Burton further learned that Gerald Gault, the man who had spoken so sneeringly to him at first, was Romanoff's guide. There was another Russian in the safari, Sergei Godensky, a professional photographer.

The interest of Burton was drawn to two other white men. These were the other derelicts that had been mentioned. Their names were Smith and Peterson. They had told a story of their native boys deserting them.

'They don't look very gay,' Burton said.

'They don't like to do their share of the work, either,' John Ramsgate snapped. 'Burton, you won't blame us so much for our conduct when you learn more about this rather mixed safari. Romanoff's man, Gault, is domineering and sarcastic. Everybody hates him. Pierre and my valet, Tomlin, are both in love with Violet, Barbara's maid. And I think there's no love lost between Godensky and Romanoff. All told, I wouldn't call it a very happy family.'

Coffee and cigarettes followed the dinner. Burton stretched and inhaled deeply.

'To think,' he said, 'that only this morning I was expecting to starve to death. One never knows what Fate has in store for one.'

Unconsciously he patted his shirt over his heart, where the plans for Horace Brown's invention reposed.

'Perhaps it's just as well that we can't look into the future,' said Lady Barbara.

It was just as well, so far as Burton's peace of mind was concerned.

Days passed. Burton grew very fond of John Ramsgate and especially fond of Barbara. Duncan Trent began to wear a scowl. In Burton he detected a rival.

Then trouble broke out in the safari over the maid, Violet, when Godensky made advances to her which she made clear she did not want. Burton, accidentally coming upon them, knocked Godensky down. Godensky, in a raging fury, drew his knife. Then Lady Barbara came suddenly upon the scene. Godensky put back his knife and walked away sullenly.

'You've made an enemy,' cautioned Barbara.

Burton shrugged his shoulders. He had been through so much already that one more enemy didn't matter.

But he had made more than one enemy. Trent came to him and told him in no uncertain terms to keep away from Lady Barbara.

'I think we can leave it to Lady Barbara to select what company she wants to keep,' Burton said quietly.

Tomlin, attracted by the conversation, came out of his tent. He saw Trent strike at Burton, saw Burton smash Trent down.

'Get into your tent and cool off,' Burton snapped to Trent, and entered his own tent.

The next morning, Ramsgate notified Godensky that he would not need his services after they reached Bangali. Everyone else ignored Godensky, even the two derelicts, Smith and Peterson, and he marched alone all day, nursing his anger. Duncan Trent brought up the rear of the column, glum and brooding.

Everyone seemed out of sorts, and the long trek under the hot, merciless sun did nothing to soothe jangled nerves. The carriers lagged, and Gault spent most of his time running up and down the line cursing and abusing them. Finally he lost his temper and knocked one of them down. When the man got up, Gault knocked him down again. Burton, who was nearby, interfered.

'Cut it out,' he ordered.

'You mind your own damned business. I'm running this safari,' retorted Gault.

'I don't care whose safari you're running. You're not going to abuse the men.'

Gault swung. Burton blocked the blow, and the next instant Gault was sent sprawling with a smashing left to the jaw. It was Burton's third fight since he had joined the safari. Three knockdowns – three enemies.

'I'm sorry, Ramsgate,' Burton said, later. 'I seem to be getting into trouble with everyone.'

'You did just right,' said Ramsgate approvingly.

'I'm afraid you've made a real enemy there, Cecil,' said Lady Barbara. 'I understand Gault has a pretty bad reputation.'

'One enemy more makes no difference any longer. We'll be in Bangali tomorrow.'

They talked for a few minutes longer and then, bidding each other good-night, went to their tents. Burton was happy. He knew that he had never been so happy before in his life. Tomorrow he would see his father. Tomorrow he would fulfill his mission; and he was in love. A serene quiet lay upon the camp, over which a drowsy *askari* kept watch. From far away came the roar of a hunting lion, and the man threw more wood upon the fire.

VI

The Coming of Tarzan

It was just before dawn, and it was very cold. The *askari* on guard was even more sleepy than the man he had relieved. Because it was cold, he sat very near the fire with his back against a log, and sitting there, he fell asleep.

When he awoke, he was so astounded and startled by the sight that met his eyes that he was for the moment incapable of any action. He just sat there, wide-eyed, looking at an almost-naked white man who squatted near him, warming his hands at the fire. Where had this apparition come from? It had not been there a moment before. The *askari* thought that perhaps he was dreaming. But, no. The visitor was too real, of such an immense physique.

The lips of the stranger parted.

'Whose safari is this?' he asked in the Swahili dialect.

The *askari* found his voice.

'Who are you? Where did you come from?' Suddenly his eyes went even wider and his jaw dropped. 'If you are a demon,' he said, 'I will bring you food, if you will not harm me.'

'I am Tarzan,' said the stranger. 'Whose safari is this?'

'There are two,' replied the *askari*, his eyes filled with awe. 'One is the safari of *Bwana* Romanoff, and the other is the safari of *Bwana* Ramsgate.'

'They are going to Bangali?' asked Tarzan.

'Yes. Tomorrow we shall be in Bangali.'

'They are hunting?'

'*Bwana* Romanoff hunts. *Bwana* Ramsgate takes pictures.'

Tarzan looked at him for a long time before he spoke again, and then he said:

'You should be whipped for falling asleep while on guard.'

'But I was not asleep, Tarzan,' said the *askari*. 'I only closed my eyes because the light of the fire hurt them.'

'The fire was nearly out when I came,' said Tarzan. 'I put more wood upon it. I have been here a long time and you were asleep. *Simba* could have come into camp and carried someone away. He is out there now, watching you.'

The *askari* leaped to his feet and cocked his rifle.

'Where? Where is *Simba?*' he demanded.

'Can't you see his eyes blazing out there?'

'Yes, Tarzan, I see them now.' He raised his rifle to his shoulder.

'Do not shoot. You might accidentally hit him only to wound him, and then he would charge. Wait.'

Tarzan picked up a stick, one end of which was blazing, and hurled it out into the darkness. The eyes disappeared.

'If he comes back, shoot over his head. That may frighten him away.'

The *askari* became very alert, but he was watching the stranger quite as much as he was watching for the lion. Tarzan warmed himself by the fire.

After a while the wind freshened and swung into a new quarter. Tarzan raised his head and sniffed the air.

'Who is the dead man?' he asked.

The *askari* looked around him quickly, but saw no one. His voice trembled a little as he answered.

'There is no dead man, *Bwana*,' the *askari* protested.

'There is a dead man over there in that part of camp,' said Tarzan, nodding toward the tents of the whites.

'There is no dead man, and I wish that you would go away with your talk of death.'

The other did not answer. He just squatted there, warming his hands.

'I must go and awaken the cooks,' the *askari* said, presently. 'It is time.'

Tarzan said nothing, and the *askari* went to awaken the cooks. He told them there was a demon in the camp, and when they looked and saw the white man squatting there by the fire, they, too became intensely frightened. They were still more frightened when the *askari* told them that the demon had said there was a dead man in the camp. They woke up all the other boys, for in numbers there is a greater sense of security.

Ramsgate's headman went to his Master's tent and awakened him.

'There is a demon in camp, *Bwana*,' he said, 'and he says there is a dead man here. There is no dead man in camp, is there, *Bwana?*'

'Of course not – and there are no demons either. I'll be out in a moment.'

Ramsgate dressed hurriedly and came out a few moments later to see the men huddled together fearfully, looking toward the fire, where the almost naked gigantic white man squatted. Ramsgate walked toward him, and as he approached the other arose, courteously.

'May I inquire,' said Ramsgate, 'who you are and to what we owe the pleasure of this visit?' Ramsgate had learned a lesson from Burton on how to treat strangers.

The other motioned toward the fire.

'That is the reason for my visit,' he said. 'It is unusually cold in the forest tonight.'

'Who are you, anyway, man, and what are you doing running around naked in the forest at night?'

'I am Tarzan,' replied the stranger. 'What is your name?'

'Ramsgate. What is the story you have been telling our boys about there being a dead man in the camp?'

'It is true. There is a dead man in one of those tents. He has not been dead very long.'

'But how do you know that? What gives you that queer idea?'

'I can smell him,' said Tarzan.

Ramsgate shivered, looked around the camp. The boys were still huddled together at a little distance, watching them; but otherwise everything appeared in order.

He looked again at the stranger, a little more closely this time, and saw that he was fine-looking and intelligent-appearing. Yet he was certain that the man was crazy, probably one of those human derelicts who are found occasionally even in civilized surroundings, wandering naked in the woods. They are usually called wild men, but most of them are only harmless half-wits. However, Ramsgate thought, remembering Burton's lesson, the best thing to do would be to humor this man and give him food.

He turned and called to the boys.

'Hurry up with that chuck. We want to get an early start today.'

Several of the whites had been aroused by the noise in the camp and were straggling from their tents. Gault was among them. He came over toward the fire, followed by the others.

'What have we here, m'Lord?'

'This poor devil got cold and came in to the fire,' said Ramsgate. 'It's perfectly all right, he's welcome. Will you see that he gets breakfast, Gault?'

'Yes, Sir.' Gault's meekness surprised Ramsgate.

'And say, Gault, will you have the boys awaken the others? I'd like to get an early start this morning.'

Gault turned toward the boys and called out some instructions in Swahili. Several of the boys detached themselves and went to the tents of their Masters to awaken them. Tarzan had resumed his place by the fire, and Ramsgate had gone to talk with the *askari* who had been on guard.

He had just started to question the man, when he was interrupted by a shout from the direction of the tents of the whites and saw Burton's boy running excitedly toward him.

'Come quick, *Bwana*,' shouted the boy. 'Come quick!'

'What is it? What's the matter?' demanded Ramsgate.

'I go in tent. I find *Bwana* Burton lie on floor, dead!'

Ramsgate dashed for Burton's tent, with Tarzan close at his elbow. Gault was directly behind them.

Burton's body, clad only in pajamas, lay face down upon the floor. A chair had been upset and there were other evidences of a fierce struggle.

While the three men were busily examining the body, Romanoff and Trent entered the tent.

'This is terrible,' Romanoff exclaimed, shuddering. 'Who could have done it?'

Trent said nothing. He just stood there, staring down at the body.

Burton had been stabbed in the back, the knife entering under the left shoulder blade from below and piercing the heart. There were black and blue marks on his throat, showing that the murderer had choked him to prevent him from making any outcry.

'Whoever did this must have been a very strong man,' said Romanoff. 'Lieutenant Burton was himself very powerful.'

Amazed, then, they saw the white stranger take command of the situation.

Tarzan lifted the body to the cot and covered it with a blanket. Then he bent low and examined the marks on Burton's throat. He went out and they followed him, mystified and frightened.

As they left the tent, before which practically the entire safari had congregated, Ramsgate saw his sister coming toward them from her tent.

'What's the matter?' she asked, 'What has happened?'

Ramsgate stepped to her side. 'Something pretty terrible has happened, Babs,' he said, avoiding her questioning glance. Then he led her back to her tent and told her.

Gault gruffly ordered the men back to their duties, summoned all the *askaris* who had been on guard during the night and questioned them. The other whites were gathered around them, but only Tarzan understood the questions and the answers, which were in Swahili.

There had been four *askaris* on duty during the night, and all insisted that they had seen or heard nothing unusual, with the exception of the last one, who reported that the strange white man had entered the camp just before dawn to warm himself at the fire.

'Did you see him all the time he was in camp?' demanded Gault.

The man hesitated.

'The fire hurt my eyes, *Bwana*, and I closed them. But only for a moment. All the rest of the time I saw him squatting by the fire, warming himself.'

'You are lying,' said Gault. 'You were asleep.'

'Perhaps I slept a little, *Bwana*.'

'Then this man might have had time to go to the tent and murder *Bwana* Burton?'

Gault spoke plainly because he did not know that Tarzan understood Swahili.

'Yes, *Bwana*,' replied the black. 'He might have. I do not know. But he knew there was a dead man there before anyone else knew it.'

'How do you know that?'

'He told me so, *Bwana*.'

'The man was dead before I came into camp,' said Tarzan calmly.

Gault was startled.

'You understand Swahili?' he asked.

'Yes.'

'Nobody knows how long you were in camp. You—'

'What's all this about?' interrupted Romanoff. 'I can't understand a word. Wait, here comes Lord John. He should carry on this investigation. Lieutenant Burton was his countryman.'

Ramsgate and Romanoff listened intently while Gault repeated what the *askari* had told him. Tarzan stood leaning upon his spear, his face impassive. When Gault had finished, Ramsgate shook his head.

'I see no reason to suspect this man,' he said. 'What motive could he have had? It certainly wasn't robbery, for Burton had nothing of value. And it couldn't have been revenge, for they didn't even know each other.'

'Perhaps he's batty,' suggested Smith. 'Nobody but a nut would run around naked in the woods. And you can't never tell what nuts will do.'

Trent nodded. 'Dementia praecox,' he said, 'with homicidal mania.'

Lady Barbara, dry-eyed and composed, came and stood beside her brother. Violet was with her, red-eyed and sniffling.

'Have you learned anything new?' Lady Barbara asked her brother.

Ramsgate shook his head.

'Gault thinks this man might have done it.'

Lady Barbara looked up. 'Who is he?' she asked.

'He says his name is Tarzan. He came into camp some time during the night. Nobody seems to know when. But I don't see any reason to suspect him. He could not possibly have had any motive.'

'There are several here who might have had a motive,' said Lady Barbara bitterly. She looked straight at Trent.

'Barbara!' Trent exclaimed. 'You don't think for a moment that I did this?'

'He was ready to kill him once, m'Lord,' said Tomlin to Ramsgate. 'I was there, Sir. I saw Burton knock him down. They were quarreling about her Ladyship.'

Trent looked uncomfortable. 'It's preposterous,' he protested. 'I'll admit I lost my temper, but after I cooled off I was sorry.'

Violet pointed an accusing finger at Godensky.

'He tried to kill him, too! He said he'd kill him. I heard him.'

'As far as that goes, Gault, here, threatened to get him, too,' said Romanoff. 'They didn't *all* kill him. I think the thing for us to do is present ourselves to the authorities at Bangali, and let them thrash the matter out.'

'That's all right with me,' said Gault. 'I didn't kill him, and I don't know that this fellow did. But it's certainly mighty funny that he was the only one in camp to know that Lieutenant Burton was dead.'

'There was another who knew,' said Tarzan.

'Who was that?' demanded Gault.

'The man who killed him.'

'I'd still like to know how you knew he was dead,' said Gault.

'So should I,' said Ramsgate. 'I must say that that looks a little suspicious.'

'It's quite simple,' said Tarzan, 'but I'm afraid none of you would understand. I am Tarzan of the Apes. I have lived here nearly all my life under precisely the same conditions as the other animals. Animals are dependent upon certain senses much more than are civilized man. The hearing of some of them is exceptionally keen. The eyesight of others is remarkable. But the best developed of all is the sense of smell.

'Without at least one of these senses highly developed, one couldn't survive for long. Man, being naturally among the most helpless of animals, I was compelled to develop them all. Death has its own peculiar odor. It is noticeable almost immediately after life has ceased. While I was warming myself at the fire and talking to the *askari*, the wind freshened and changed. It brought to my nostrils the evidence that a dead man lay a short distance away, probably in one of the tents.'

'Nuts,' said Smith disgustedly.

Godensky laughed nervously.

'He must think we're crazy, too, to believe a story like that.'

'I think we've got our man all right,' said Trent. 'A maniac doesn't have to have a motive for killing.'

'Mr Trent's right,' agreed Gault. 'We'd better tie him up and take him along to Bangali with us.'

None of these men knew Tarzan. None of them could interpret the strange look that came suddenly into his gray eyes. As Gault moved toward him, Tarzan backed away. Then Trent drew his pistol and covered him.

'Make a false move and I'll kill you,' Trent said.

Trent's intentions may have been of the best, but his technique was faulty. He was guilty, among others, of two cardinal errors. He was too close to Tarzan, and he did not shoot the instant that he drew his gun.

Tarzan's hand shot out and seized his wrist. Trent pulled the trigger, but the bullet plowed harmlessly into the ground. Then he cried out in anguish and dropped the weapon when the ape-man applied more pressure. It was all done very quickly, and then Tarzan was backing away from them holding Trent as a shield in front of him.

They dared not shoot for fear of hitting Trent. Gault and Ramsgate started forward. Tarzan, holding the man with one hand, drew his hunting knife.

'Stay where you are,' he said, 'or I kill.'

His tone was quiet and level, but it had the cutting edge of a keen knife. The two men stopped, and then Tarzan backed away toward the forest that came down to the edge of the camp.

'Aren't you going to do something?' shouted Trent. 'Are you going to let this maniac carry me off into the woods and butcher me?'

'What shall we do?' cried Romanoff to no one in particular.

'We can't do anything,' said Ramsgate. 'If we go after him, he'll surely kill Trent. If we don't, he may let him go.'

'I think we ought to go after them,' said Gault, but no one volunteered, and a moment later Tarzan disappeared into the forest dragging Trent with him ...

The safari did not get an early start that morning, and long before they got under way Trent came out of the forest and rejoined them. He was still trembling from fear.

'Give me a spot of brandy, John,' he said to Ramsgate. 'I think that demon broke my wrist. God, I'm about done up. That fellow's not human. He handled me as though I were a baby. When he was sure no one was following us, he let me go. And then he took to the trees just like a monkey. I tell you, it's uncanny.'

'Did he harm you in any way after he took you out of camp?' Ramsgate wanted to know.

'No. He just dragged me along. He never spoke once, never said a word. It was like – why, it was like being dragged off by a lion.'

'I hope we've seen the last of him,' said Ramsgate hopefully.

'Well, there's not much doubt about that,' replied Trent. 'He killed poor Burton, all right, and he's made a clean getaway.'

The safari moved slowly, four carriers bearing the body of Burton on an improvised stretcher. It brought up the rear of the column, and Barbara walked ahead with her brother so she would not have to see it.

They did not reach Bangali that day, and had to make another camp. Everyone was depressed. There was no laughing or singing among the native boys, and very shortly after the evening meal everyone turned in for the night.

About midnight the camp was aroused by wild shouting and a shot. Then Smith came running from the tent he shared with Peterson. Ramsgate leaped from his cot and ran out into the open in his pajamas, almost colliding with Smith.

'What's the matter, man? For God's sake, what's happened?'

'That crazy giant,' cried Smith. 'He was here again. He killed poor Peterson this time. I shot at him. I think I hit him, but I don't know. I couldn't be sure.'

'Where did he go?' snapped Ramsgate.

'Off there, into the jungle,' panted Smith, pointing.

Ramsgate shook his head.

'There's no use following,' he said. 'We could never find him.'

They went into Peterson's tent and found him lying on his cot, stabbed through the heart while he slept. There was no more sleep in camp that night and the whites as well as the *askaris* stood guard.

VII

Murder Will Out

In Bangali, Tarzan sat in the bungalow of Col. Gerald Giles-Burton.

'The shock of your news was not as great as it might have been,' said Colonel Burton. 'I'd given my boy up for dead a long while ago. Yet, to know that he was alive all the time, and almost here – that's what is hard to bear. Did they have any idea who killed him?'

'They're all pretty sure I did it.'

'Nonsense,' said Burton.

'There are three men in the safari he had trouble with. They all threatened to get him. But from what I heard, the threats were all made in the heat of anger, and probably didn't mean anything. Only one of them might have thought he had reason to kill.'

'Who was that?' asked Burton.

'A chap by the name of Trent, who was in love with Lady Barbara. That was the only real motive, so far as I could learn.'

'Sometimes a very strong motive,' said Burton.

'However,' continued Tarzan, 'Trent didn't kill your son. He couldn't have. If the murderer was in camp, I could have found him if they hadn't run me out.'

'Will you remain here and help me find him when the safari gets in?'

'Of course. You didn't need to ask.'

'There is something else I think you ought to know. At the time that he was lost, my son was carrying some very important papers for the Government. He was ostensibly flying from London to Capetown, but his instructions were to stop here and leave the papers with me.'

'And he was being pursued by three men in an Italian military plane,' said Tarzan.

'Gad, man! How did you know that?' demanded Burton.

'I ran across both planes. Your son's plane was shot down, but he had bailed out safely. I found his parachute near the plane. But before he bailed out, he shot the pilot of the other plane. The fellow brought his plane down safely before he died. I found him still sitting at the controls. The two men with him got out all right. One of them may have been hurt a little, for I noticed that he limped, but he might have been lame before. That, of course, I do not know.'

'Did you see them?' asked Burton.

'No. I followed their tracks for a little way until I came across your son's ship. Then, knowing he was an Englishman, or believing so because he was piloting an English plane, I started off after him. You see, he had landed in lion country. You know, the Buiroo country.'

'Yes; and the Buiroos are worse than the lions.'

'Yes,' said Tarzan, reminiscing, 'I've had business with them before. They nearly put an end to me this time. After I got away from them I started for Bangali again, and early this morning I stumbled onto this safari.'

'Do you think those two men had a chance to get the papers away from my son?'

'No. They were following different trails. They are probably both dead by this time. It's bad country where they came down. They were a couple of Italians, I suppose.'

Colonel Burton shook his head.

'No. One was an American and the other was a Russian. Their names were Campbell and Zubanev. I got a full report on them from London. They were wanted for espionage and murder back there.'

'Well, I don't think they'll bother anyone again,' said Tarzan. 'And in the morning you'll have the papers.'

'Yes, I'll have the papers,' said Burton sadly. 'It is strange, Tarzan, how little we appreciate happiness until we lose it. I'm not vindictive, but I'd like to know who killed my son.'

'Africa is a large place, Burton,' said the ape-man, 'but if the man who murdered your boy is still alive, I'll get him before he gets out of Africa. I promise you that.'

'If you can't find him, no one can,' said Burton. 'Thanks, Tarzan.'

Tarzan shook Burton's hand warmly.

Eight stretcher bearers, carrying the bodies of Cecil Burton and Peterson, brought up the rear of the safari as it halted just on the outskirts of Bangali and prepared to go into camp.

Ramsgate and Romanoff went immediately to report to Colonel Burton. They found him sitting in his office, a screened veranda along one side of his bungalow. He stood up as they entered and held out his hand to the young Englishman.

'Lord John Ramsgate, I presume,' he said, then turning to the Russian, 'and Mr Romanoff. I have been expecting you gentlemen.'

'We come on a very sad mission, Colonel Burton,' said Ramsgate, a catch in his voice.

'Yes, I know,' said Burton.

Ramsgate and Romanoff looked astonished.

'You know!' exclaimed Romanoff.

'Yes. Word was brought to me last night.'

'But that is impossible,' said Ramsgate. 'We must be referring to different things.'

'No. We are both referring to the murder of my son.'

'Extraordinary!' exclaimed Ramsgate. 'I don't understand. But Colonel, we are pretty sure now that we know who the murderer is. Last night there was another similar murder committed in our camp, and one of the members of our safari saw the murderer in the act of committing the crime. He fired at him, and thinks that he hit him.'

At this moment the door of the bungalow opened and Tarzan stepped suddenly out onto the veranda!

Ramsgate and Romanoff both leaped to their feet.

'There's the man! There's the murderer!' cried Ramsgate.

Colonel Burton shook his head.

'No, gentlemen,' he said quietly. 'Tarzan of the Apes would not have murdered my son, and he could not have murdered the other man because he was here in my bungalow all last night!'

'But,' said Romanoff, 'Smith said that he saw this man and recognized him when Peterson was murdered last night.'

'Well, in a moment of excitement like that,' said Burton, 'and in the darkness, a man might easily make a mistake. Suppose we go to your camp and question some of the people involved. I understand that three of them had either attacked or threatened my son.'

'Yes,' said Ramsgate. 'Both my sister and I wish a most thorough investigation be made, and I am sure that Mr Romanoff feels as we do about it.'

Romanoff inclined his head in assent.

'You will come with us, of course, Tarzan?' asked Burton.

'If you wish,' Tarzan replied.

It was with mixed emotions that the members of the safari saw Tarzan enter the camp with Ramsgate, Romanoff and Colonel Burton, and a detail of native constabulary.

'They got him,' said Gault to Trent. 'That was quick work.'

'They ought to handcuff him,' said Trent, 'or he'll get away just as he did before. They haven't even taken his weapons away from him.'

At Colonel Burton's suggestion all the whites in the party were gathered together for questioning. While they were being summoned Tarzan carefully examined the body of Peterson. He looked particularly at the man's hands and feet. Then he scrutinized the wound over the heart. Just for a moment he bent low over the body, his face close to the sleeve of the man's tunic. Then he returned to where the company was gathered in front of Colonel Burton.

One by one, the English official questioned them. He listened intently to the evidence of Violet, Tomlin and Lady Barbara. He questioned Godensky, Gault and Trent. He questioned Smith about the murderer of Peterson.

'I understand that you said you saw this man kill Peterson.' He indicated Tarzan.

'I thought it was him,' said Smith, 'but I might have been mistaken. It was very dark.'

'Well, now, as to my son,' said Burton. 'Is there anyone here who cares to make a direct charge of murder against any individual?'

Lady Barbara Ramsgate stiffened.

'Yes, Colonel,' she said. 'I charge Duncan Trent with the murder of Cecil Giles-Burton.'

Trent paled considerably, but did not speak. All eyes were turned upon him. Tarzan bent close and whispered something in Burton's ear. The latter nodded.

'Tarzan wishes to ask a few questions,' said Burton. 'You will please answer them as you would if I asked them.'

'May I see your knife?' asked Tarzan, pointing at Pierre.

'I do not carry one, Sir.'

'And yours?' He indicated Gault.

Gault withdrew his knife from its scabbard and handed it to the ape-man, who examined it for a moment and then returned it. Then he asked for Tomlin's knife; but Tomlin did not carry one. In rapid succession he asked for and examined the knives of Smith, Godensky, and Trent. Then he turned to Smith.

'Smith,' he said, 'you were in the tent after Peterson was murdered. Can you tell me how he was lying on his cot?'

'He was lying flat on his back,' Smith said.

'Which side of his cot was against the side of the tent?'

'The left side.'

Tarzan turned to Ramsgate.

'How long have you known this man Smith?' he asked.

'A few weeks only,' replied Ramsgate. 'We found him and Peterson wandering around lost. They said their boys had deserted them.'

'He was limping when you found him, wasn't he?'

John Ramsgate looked his astonishment.

'Yes,' he said. 'He told us he had sprained his ankle.'

'What's that got to do with it?' demanded Smith. 'Didn't I tell you the guy's a nut?'

Tarzan stepped close to Smith.

'Let me have your gun,' he said.

'I ain't got no gun,' growled Smith.

'What is that bulge underneath the left side of your shirt?' As he spoke, Tarzan placed his hand quickly over the spot.

Smith grinned. 'You ain't as smart as you think you are,' he said.

Tarzan turned to Lady Barbara.

'Mr Trent did not kill Burton,' he said with great conviction. '*Smith killed him. Smith killed Peterson, too.*'

'It's a damn lie!' cried Smith. 'You killed 'em yourself! I'm being framed! Can't you all see it?'

'What makes you think Smith is the murderer?' asked Colonel Burton.

'Well, I'll make one change in my statement,' said Tarzan. 'It was *Campbell* who killed them. This man's name is not Smith. It is Campbell. The real name of the man he killed last night was not Peterson, but Zubanev!'

'I tell you it's a damned lie!' shouted Smith. 'You ain't got nothin' on me! You can't prove nothin'!'

Tarzan towered over the rest of the company. A hush fell over the group. Even Smith was silent.

'A very powerful, left-handed man with the second finger of his right hand missing killed Lieutenant Burton,' Tarzan said. 'The wound which killed Burton could only have been inflicted if the knife were held in the left hand. On his throat were the imprints of a thumb, a first, third, and little finger.

'You will notice that the second finger of Smith's, or rather Campbell's, right hand is missing. Also I noticed that when I asked the men to hand me their knives, Campbell was the only man who passed the weapon to me with his left hand. The knife wound in Zubanev's chest was made by a knife held in a left hand.'

'But the motive for these murders,' exclaimed Romanoff.

'Colonel Burton will find them inside of Campbell's shirt! They are the papers that Lieutenant Burton was carrying when he was shot down by the pursuing plane that carried Campbell and Zubanev. I know that Peterson, or rather Zubanev, was on that plane. The other man with him limped when he walked away from the plane. That man was Campbell, who calls himself Smith.'

'But why did Smith or Campbell, or whatever his name is, want to kill Burton and Peterson?' asked John Ramsgate.

'He and Zubanev wanted the papers that Burton carried,' Tarzan explained. 'No one else knew about the papers. Campbell knew that if he stole the papers and let Burton live, the latter would immediately launch an intensive search through the safari for them. He had to kill Burton. He killed Zubanev so that he would not have to share with him the money that he expected to get for the papers, which they had already tentatively sold to the Italian Government. Here' – Tarzan ripped open Campbell's shirt – 'are the papers!'

The native constabulary dragged Joseph Campbell, alias Joe the Pooch, away.

'How did you know that Zubanev was on that Italian plane?' Ramsgate asked curiously.

'I found his glove in the rear cockpit,' replied the ape-man.

Ramsgate shook his head in bewilderment.

'I still don't understand,' he said.

Tarzan smiled.

'That is because you are a civilized man,' he said. 'Numa, the lion, or Sheeta, the leopard, would understand. When I found that glove I took its scent. Therefore I carried in my memory the smell of Zubanev. Then when I smelled Peterson, I knew he was Zubanev. Hence, Smith must be Campbell. And now—'

Tarzan paused, swept them with his glance.

'I am going home,' he said. 'Goodbye, my friends. It was good to see some of my own people again, but the call of the jungle is stronger. Goodbye ...'

And Tarzan of the Apes returned to the jungle.

If you've enjoyed these books and would
like to read more, you'll find literally thousands
of classic Science Fiction & Fantasy titles
through the **SF Gateway**

✱

*For the new home of
Science Fiction & Fantasy . . .*

✱

*For the most comprehensive collection
of classic SF on the internet . . .*

✱

Visit the SF Gateway

www.sfgateway.com

Edgar Rice Burroughs (1875–1950)

Edgar Rice Burroughs was a prolific American author of the 'pulp' era. The son of a Civil War veteran, he saw brief military service with the 7th U.S. Cavalry before he was diagnosed with a heart problem and discharged. After working for five years in his father's business, Burroughs left for a string of disparate and short-lived jobs, and was working as a pencil sharpener wholesaler when he decided to try his hand at writing. He found almost instant success when his story 'Under the Moons of Mars' was serialised in *All-Story Magazine* in 1912, earning him the then-princely sum of $400.

Burroughs went on to have tremendous success as a writer, his wide-ranging imagination taking in other planets (John Carter of Mars and Carson of Venus), a hollow earth (Pellucidar), a lost world, westerns, historicals and adventure stories. Although he wrote in many genres, Burroughs is best known for his creation of the archetypal jungle hero, Tarzan. Edgar Rice Burroughs died in 1950.